D0475540

The

LITERATURE
of
AUSTRALIA

Deputy General Editor
David McCooey

Contributing Editors
Kerryn Goldsworthy
Anita Heiss
Peter Minter
Nicole Moore
Elizabeth Webby

Advisory Publishing Editor
Mary Cunnane

Director for the Centre for the
Macquarie PEN Anthology of Australian Literature
Jill Roe

Project Coordinator
Chris Cunneen

Contributors

AH	Anita Heiss	KG	Kerryn Goldsworthy
AV	Anne Vickery	MC	Max Coltheart
CC	Chris Cunneen	MCR	Margaret Clunies Ross
DM	David McCooey	MD	Maryanne Dever
EL	Elaine Lindsay	MM	Michele Madigan
EW	Elizabeth Webby	NJ	Nicholas Jose
HH	Helen Hewson	NM	Nicole Moore
IB	Ian Britain	PM	Peter Minter
JR	Jill Roe	PS	Paul Salzman

FOREWORD

'They call her a young country but they lie,' runs the opening line of a not entirely complimentary but classic poem by A.D. Hope, 'Australia'. They do lie, in fact. As an immigrant society Australia is relatively young, dense though it may be in literary aspiration. But as a crucible for the world's oldest culture it is the most antique of the earth's continents—the first of lands, a milieu which predates the landscapes and the inhabiting deities which sparked European sensibility from the Greeks onwards. This tension between antiquity and the recent is often palpable in Australian writing—it can be seen in the great modernist novels of Patrick White, and in the poet Judith Wright's wonder at her particular inheritance in the magnificent 'South of My Days'.

But that is not the only creative contradiction which will become apparent in these pages. As is well known, Australia as a modern community had its origins in a penal experiment. Though other colonial societies might have had an admixture of convicts, this is the only major society in the world to derive from a purpose-designed convict netherworld. Our book of Genesis featured a pre-fallen Adam and Eve, and that pattern remained long after the end of the convict era—Australia was imagined as a place where all was reversed and the damned became the rescued. If literature has a measurable purpose, as well as the immeasurable and imponderable function it performs for the species, one of the purposes of Australian writing has been to define this netherworld, this anti-Europe.

The associated irony is that Australia was always a strange place to find people of Northern European descent, separated from the wellsprings of their blood and culture by the mass and archipelagos of Asia. And so a further tension arose, which began with mistrust, arguments and sundry legislated and induced hysterias, but which involved an increasing embrace of Asia—both by receiving Asian immigration and by Australia's increasing engagement in the region. Though cultural comprehension of Asia has lagged behind trade and diplomacy, the presence of Asia is reflected in these pages.

And a few more things that might aid in enjoyment of this collection: There was a time when Australia—perhaps to distinguish itself from the republican United States—defined itself as ruggedly and monolithically British. The reality is otherwise—a most ethnically diverse community inhabits the country; many claim, the most ethnically diverse on earth.

So within this book one encounters a literary community unexpectedly diverse, one influenced internally by the nature of the continent, and externally by the reality of its position on the globe; an English-language literature arising as far as you could get from European wellsprings of language and sensibility, and at the terminus of Asia to the north, and with the breath of Antarctica on it from the south. It was always a place designed to produce a voice like no other.

The editors have defined this voice in the broadest terms possible. They begin with the first diarists of the colonial experiment, they encompass the letters of Aborigines, the poetry of convicts, the journals of explorers and enquirers, the stories of settlers. They introduce us to the earliest self-appointed Sons of the Southern Cross, poets of national consciousness, men such as Charles Harpur, child of convicts. They trace the near-normalisation of a literary culture in the second half of the nineteenth century, and the ongoing and tragic discourse between displaced natives and immigrant society: two cultures plagued by mutual incomprehension but one possessing the arms to express their chagrin more fatally.

In the nineteenth century, the great voices which would flower in the twentieth century were born either in soon-to-be emigrant households in Europe or in one of the states or colonies of an as yet unfederated Australia. There was the most popularly nationalist Henry Lawson, born in a gold camp in New South Wales, and a poet of such sublime Blakean sophistication as Shaw Neilson, born in 1872 in South Australia. The splendid novelist Henry Handel Richardson was born in Melbourne in 1870, and in the same year in Sydney was born the fine symbolist poet Christopher Brennan.

Given that Australia acquired in the world—and cultivated for itself—a reputation for hard-handed taciturnity, the lusciousness of twentieth-century Australian verse found here will break on the reader as a revelation, involving unexpected lightnings. It is a poetry the reverse of laconic—it is sensual, mystical and richly colloquial. Nor does Australian fiction tend towards minimalism. It is more urgent than that, with its sense that there is so much to reveal.

The apogee of Australian fiction may well have been the stylistic spaciousness and the piercing gaze of Nobel-Prize-winner Patrick White, and of other writers of his generation such as Christina Stead. There was a lot of what people might call *business* to be done in fiction, non-fiction, verse in the mid-twentieth century. Almost as much as in 1788, Australia was still seen by the world as an antipodes into which immigrants vanished to live unexplained and unexamined lives. Australian writing sought to define that condition, to examine those unexamined lives, and—in the ambiguous way of literature—to celebrate them.

From the 1970s, however, when Australian writing and publishing came to flourish in new ways, until, like Australian art and film, it was almost as visible to the community as the game of cricket, the tone changed. Australians started to engage with the Aboriginal cosmos, as the Aboriginal poet Oodgeroo Noonuccal wrote her *Aboriginal Charter of Rights*—'give us Christ, not crucifixion'. Australia's geographic Dead Heart became a central enlivening inheritance. The country became more and more racially diverse and more and more urbanised; and the American connection and the realities of Asia increasingly engaged our attention. Post-colonial straining eased. The voice became more relaxed in its location, more secure and above all more urban, less dependent on the Australian picturesque. The brilliant and assured stories of David Malouf are characteristic of a newer writing, not disconnected from the Australian tradition but without any intrusion of national questions which occupied much previous literature. It is always the preserve of writing to deal with alienation. But the issues that arise in the work of Malouf and other modern Australian writers are not to do with whether we should feel alienated in what was once a European Hades. Such questions have all been rendered irrelevant not only by the certain instincts of writers such as Malouf but by the arrival of new populations whose experience raises other and probably richer questions.

I was fortunate enough to witness the origins of this remarkable collection, unprecedented in the breadth of what it offers from both the ancient and the recent literature of my country.

The idea was proposed at a meeting of the Sydney PEN Centre at the University of Technology, Sydney, by Mary Cunnane, an American-born Australian literary agent and former senior editor at W.W. Norton & Company, whose comprehensive anthologies are in wide use in the United States. It was time Australian writing was gathered in such a collection, she argued. Earlier, over lunch with the writer Nicholas Jose, then president of Sydney PEN, Mary had asked about the Australian equivalent of the Norton. When Nick said there wasn't one, Mary said: 'Let's do it.' So the proposition was hatched, to be taken up enthusiastically by the Sydney PEN committee, and by others. As a result of considerable effort, the patronage of good friends and much public support, here is that envisioned volume of treasures.

The editors deserve praise for having so skilfully found a balance between disparate presences and for generously including so many voices. These include our significant expatriate writers, from Germaine Greer to the dazzling poet Peter Porter. And they manage to provide readers with a sense, too, that one of the benefits of a literature such as Australia's is that, despite a massive accomplishment, the room for expansion, or more accurately for freshness, seems unlimited. The definitive word has not yet been fully spoken, the canon is not set in place but open-ended. Wrongly interpreted, this could seem an excuse for what has gone before. It is not that. It is a celebration of what has happened and an excitement for what is still possible.

I am sure this volume is so rich in quality as to instigate in you an enduring interest in what we write here, in what we tell you of ourselves and of yourselves, of the fascination of lives lived, and lives still to be lived, on 'this fifth part of the earth'.

And now, just start reading.

Thomas Keneally

ABOUT THE EDITORS

Kerryn Goldsworthy is an independent scholar and a freelance writer, reviewer, critic and essayist. She lectured in literature at the University of Melbourne from 1981 to 1997, specialising in Australian literature and creative writing. A former editor of *Australian Book Review*, she has also edited four anthologies of Australian short fiction. Her books include a collection of short stories, *North of the Moonlight Sonata*, and a critical study of the work of Helen Garner. She lives in Adelaide.

Anita Heiss is a member of the Wiradjuri nation of central NSW and a writer, poet, activist, social commentator and academic. She is author of *Dhuuluu-Yala: Publishing Aboriginal literature, Not Meeting Mr Right* and *Who Am I?: The diary of Mary Talence, Sydney 1937*. She won the 2004 NSW Premier's History Award (audio/visual) for *Barani: The Aboriginal history of Sydney*. She is National Coordinator of AustLit's Black Words subset and co-editor of the *Macquarie PEN Anthology of Aboriginal Literature*.

Nicholas Jose has published short stories, essays, several acclaimed novels, including *Paper Nautilus* (1987), *The Custodians* (1997), *The Red Thread* (2000) and *Original Face* (2005), and a memoir, *Black Sheep: Journey to Borroloola* (2002). He has written widely on contemporary Asian and Australian culture. He was president of Sydney PEN (2002–05) and held the Chair of Creative Writing at the University of Adelaide from 2005 to 2008. He has a Chair in Writing with the Writing and Society Research Group, University of Western Sydney and holds a Harvard Chair of Australian Studies for 2009–10.

David McCooey is the author of *Artful Histories: Modern Australian autobiography* (1996) and *Blister Pack* (2005), a collection of poems. *Artful*

Histories won a NSW Premier's Literary Award. *Blister Pack* was awarded the Mary Gilmore Award. He has written numerous book chapters, essays, poems and reviews for many national and international publications. He is Associate Professor in Literary Studies at Deakin University, Geelong.

Peter Minter is an award-winning poet, editor and scholar. He is the author of several collections of poetry, including *blue grass*, *Empty Texas* and *Rhythm in a Dorsal Fin*, was the editor of the *Varuna New Poetry* series, a founding editor of *Cordite Poetry and Poetics Review* and co-editor of *Calyx: 30 Contemporary Australian Poets*. From 2000 to 2005 he was poetry editor of *Meanjin*, and guest editor of two special issues. He is co-editor of the *Macquarie PEN Anthology of Aboriginal Literature*. He lectures in Indigenous Studies and Poetics at the Koori Centre, University of Sydney.

Nicole Moore has published widely, both nationally and internationally, on twentieth-century Australian literature. She is editor of a scholarly edition of Jean Devanny's novel *Sugar Heaven*. With Marita Bullock, she is the author of *Banned in Australia* (2008), the first comprehensive bibliography of federal literary censorship in Australia. Her history of Australian literary censorship is forthcoming. She teaches Australian literature and Australian Studies at Macquarie University, where she is a senior lecturer.

Elizabeth Webby has been carrying out research into the literary and cultural history of Australia for over 45 years. Her publications include *Early Australian Poetry* (1982), *Colonial Voices* (1989), *Modern Australian Plays* (1990), *The Cambridge Companion to Australian Literature* (2000), as well as jointly edited anthologies, literary histories and scholarly editions. From 1988 to 1999 she was editor of *Southerly*, Australia's oldest literary quarterly. She was a judge of the Miles Franklin Literary Award from 1999 to 2004. In 2004 she received an AM in recognition of her contributions to teaching and research in Australian Literature. She is now Emeritus Professor of Australian Literature at the University of Sydney.

ABBREVIATIONS

ABC: Australian Broadcasting Corporation
ADB: Australian Dictionary of Biography
AIATSIS: Australian Institute of Aboriginal and Torres Strait Islander Studies
AIF: Australian Imperial Force
ALS: Australian Literary Studies
ANU: Australian National University, Canberra
ANZAC: Australia and New Zealand Army Corps
APA: Aborigines Progressive Association
ASIO: Australian Security Intelligence Organisation
ATSIC: Aboriginal and Torres Strait Islander Commission
DLB: Dictionary of Literary Biography
FCAATSI: Federal Council for the Advancement of Aborigines and Torres Strait Islanders
HREOC: Human Rights and Equal Opportunity Commission
NAIDOC: National Aborigines and Islanders Day Observance Committee
NIDA: National Institute of Dramatic Art
NSW: New South Wales
NT: Northern Territory
NZ: New Zealand
RAF: Royal Air Force
RAAF: Royal Australian Air Force
RMIT: Royal Melbourne Institute of Technology
RSL: The Returned Services League of Australia
SA: South Australia
SBS: Special Broadcasting Service
WA: Western Australia
WRANS: Women's Royal Australian Navy Service

ACKNOWLEDGEMENTS

As work began on *The Literature of Australia: An anthology*, a team of expert editors was invited to make the initial selection. Indigenous author and activist Dr Anita Heiss and poet and scholar Peter Minter were asked to compile the Aboriginal Literature component, a different configuration of which has appeared separately as the *Macquarie PEN Anthology of Aboriginal Literature*. Emeritus Professor Elizabeth Webby, Professor of Australian Literature at Sydney University until her retirement in 2007, took responsibility for the literature of the period to 1900. Dr Nicole Moore, Senior Lecturer in English at Macquarie University and key researcher into early and mid-twentieth century Australian writing, especially radical women's voices, covered the period from 1900 to 1950. Dr Kerryn Goldsworthy, essayist, reviewer and research fellow at the University of Adelaide, was responsible for the fiction and drama from 1950 to the near present. Poet and scholar Dr David McCooey, Associate Professor in Literary Studies at Deakin University, selected the poetry and non-fiction from 1950 on and assisted in the role of deputy general editor. These six gifted writers and scholars are the primary makers of this anthology. They have stayed with the project for five years and are to be thanked for their dedication, inspiration, judgement and good humour. They have contributed the introductory essays that variously contextualise the literature represented in the selections they have made. They have also written or coordinated the introductions that precede each author's work and compiled lists of selected reading and provided all kinds of other editorial help. The selection consists of authors who were established by 2000, and includes some works after that date by the authors chosen.

The editorial team has been closely and indispensably supported throughout by the Centre for the Macquarie PEN Anthology of Australian Literature established at Macquarie University by the then Dean of

Humanities Professor Christina Slade. The Centre has operated under the directorship of Professor Emerita Jill Roe. Dr Chris Cunneen, the Centre's expert coordinator, and his able research assistant, Dr Geoff Payne, have brought scholarly passion and camaraderie to every aspect of the project. Thanks, too, to Terry Mangan, Jan Zwar, Jenny O'Brien, Dr Teresa Petersen, Dr Trevor Evans, Dr Bert Peeters, Dr Karin Speedy at the Warawara Department of Indigenous Studies, and the research work of Dr Marita Bullock, all at Macquarie, Dr Mary-Anne Gale at Adelaide and Dr Maria Takolander and Alistair Welsh at Deakin.

No less integral to the team has been the publisher, Allen & Unwin, especially Elizabeth Weiss, Angela Handley, Pedro de Almeida, Ali Lavau, Jo Lyons, and Renée Senogles, with their professionalism, enthusiasm and good counsel. Our advisory publishing editor Mary Cunnane, vice-president of Sydney PEN when the idea for the project arose, has also played a continuing and crucial role and must take a good deal of any credit.

Seed funding for the project came from the Australian Academy of the Humanities and Macquarie University. We are grateful to Professor Iain McCalman, past president of the Academy, and Dr John Byron, its executive director, for their early encouragement and support. We also thank the Academy for generously providing funding to enable us to print the anthology on library-grade, acid-free paper for archival purposes. After preliminary consultation with a further group of advisers that included Dr Debra Adelaide, Professor Virginia Blain, James Bradley, Professor Ian Donaldson, Professor Ivor Indyk, Miri Jassy, Professor Susan Lever, Professor Stephen Muecke, Dr Vivian Smith and Dr Annette Stewart, we held a series of workshops as we worked towards a table of contents. Essential to this process was the involvement of Associate Professor Donna Gibbs and Dr Kerry-Ann O'Sullivan, experienced curriculum advisers from the School of Education at Macquarie University, whose work supplemented our market research and user surveys with information and guidance about the needs and interests of secondary school students.

It took many hours of debate and exchange among the editorial group before the contents could be agreed upon in draft form. All of us benefited from the vigorous discussion and close consultation that marked this phase of the project—and so did the anthology. We were now ready for feedback from an expanded group of national and international scholarly and educational advisers. In naming them, we not only thank them for their constructive commentary, but also acknowledge that the book in final form takes its shape in part from their input, as it is shaped by the contribution of all those mentioned here and many others besides. This anthology has always been conceived as a collaborative project, significantly owned by those for whom it is intended. Sincere thanks to our distinguished advisers, beginning with those overseas: Associate Professor Chadwick Allen, Ohio State University; Dr Susan Ballyn, Universitat de Barcelona, Spain; Professor Nicholas Birns, New School University, New York; Associate Professor Chen Hong, East China Normal University, Shanghai; Associate Professor Donna Coates, University of Calgary, Alberta, Canada; Professor Witi Ihimaera Smiler, University of Auckland, New Zealand; Professor Paul Kane, Vassar College, New York; Professor Santosh Sareen, Jawaharlal Nehru University, New Delhi; Professor Angela Smith, University of Stirling, United Kingdom; Dr Irene Vernon, University of California at Berkeley; Professor Albert Wendt, University of Hawaii; Professor Lydia Wevers, Victoria University of Wellington, New Zealand; and Professor Adi Wimmer, University of Klagenfurt, Austria. In Australia: Adrian Atkins, University of Sydney; Associate Professor Catherine Beavis, Deakin University; Professor Larissa Behrendt, University of Technology, Sydney; Professor Bruce Bennett, University of New South Wales and Australian Defence Force Academy; Associate Professor Delys Bird, University of Western Australia; Associate Professor Tracey Bunda, Flinders University; Dr Kate Fagan, University of Sydney; Dr Delia Falconer, University of Technology, Sydney; Professor Marcia Langton, University of Melbourne; Dr Wendy Morgan, Queensland University of Technology; Phillip Morrissey, University of Melbourne; Associate Professor Marnie O'Neill, University of Western Australia; Dr Selina Samuels, Head of English, Ascham School, Sydney; Sandra Smith, Museum Victoria; Dr Penny van Toorn, University of Sydney; Emeritus Professor Chris Wallace-Crabbe, University of Melbourne; and Sam Watson, University of Queensland. This is also the place to thank those scholars who contributed author introductions and all those who made suggestions for texts to be included or provided other, often hard to come by, information.

The project began with Sydney PEN in accord with PEN's charter to nurture literary heritage and make it available to contemporary audiences. We are grateful to PEN, and especially those members, notably John Durack SC and Angela Bowne SC, who assisted the project with legal advice. Nor would a major initiative of this kind have been possible without generous support from partner institutions and philanthropic bodies for research infrastructure and, especially, copyright permissions costs: the Australian Research Council; the Australia Council for the Arts, especially the Aboriginal and Torres Strait Islander Arts Board and the Literature Board; the Myer Foundation; the Nelson Meers Foundation; the University of Adelaide; the University of Sydney, especially its Koori Centre; Deakin University; and AIATSIS. There are individuals to thank too: Louise Walsh of the Australia Council's Artsupport Australia, Imre Saluszinsky as Chair of the

Literature Board, director Josie Emery and her successor Susan Hayes and their staff all contributed in important ways. The editorial and research work required for a project such as this also draws extensively on the scholarship and productivity of our predecessors and peers. We gratefully acknowledge the earlier publications, compilations, reference works and resources (see Selected Reading), as well as the many library and other institutional collections that have been made available to us, particularly the National Library of Australia and the State Library of New South Wales. Special mention must be made of the *Australian Dictionary of Biography*, the *Dictionary of Literary Biography* Australian volumes edited by Dr Selina Samuels, and the AustLit database and its executive manager Dr Kerry Kilner. Let me express, on behalf of all involved, our appreciation for a remarkable set of partnerships with which we are proud to be associated. Finally we wish to thank those authors who are living and the representatives of the estates of those authors who are not, and the publishers, agents and family members who have cooperated with us so magnanimously to produce this anthology. The continuing development of the project, including resources and links for teachers and students, can be followed on our website: www.macquariepenanthology.com.au

Nicholas Jose, General Editor

A Note on the Dates

The anthology is arranged chronologically by year of birth of author and then by date of first publication in book form of work or extract, as indicated at the end of each item. The date of first journal publication or year of writing is used if book publication did not occur until much later; in this case, both dates are given. Anonymous works are ordered by year of production or first publication following the author of the work of closest date. The date of a play's first performance is given in italics in the introductions and author biographies.

Texts derive from authoritative editions or manuscripts as indicated in the list of Sources and Permissions and generally follow original spelling and punctuation.

GENERAL INTRODUCTION

Looking from my window seat as the plane crosses Australia, I can't help reading stories into the country that unfolds below. From the leafy street grid of suburbs hugging the blue coast to the channels that run like arteries through interior red earth, from the brown geometry of farm roads and fenced paddocks, spotted with salinity, to flash new settlements staked in the verdant tropics, the patterns revealed in the landscape and in the marks of human habitation modulate like some great epic. Like many an Australian traveller before me, I reflect on the intimate relationship between this extreme, subtle land and the human experiences it has shaped and been shaped by. My contemplation starts with the long custodianship of the land by Aboriginal Australians, and continues on to later visitors from across the seas, including those who became settlers—none more decisively than the small band of mainly British Europeans who landed at Sydney Cove in 1788. Their arrival made what would be called Australia a predominantly English-speaking country and bequeathed English literature and its related modes and rhetoric as the primary framework for giving expression to what would happen, be felt or imagined here for succeeding years. Human experience and creativity would be shared among those who lived in this new and often difficult society largely through speech and writing in English, and would likewise be recorded, reported abroad and passed on to posterity. Australian writing, then, is inseparable from the environment and circumstances of its origins. As Judith Wright wrote in *Preoccupations in Australian Poetry* (1965), 'Australia has from the beginning … been the outer equivalent of an inner reality … of exile … and of newness and freedom … a condition of life [that] loomed large in the consciousness of her white invaders'. Just as the landscape unfolds its meaning in patterns formed through time across marvellous and changing terrain, so Australian literature, as a mosaic of individual utterances, reveals a larger picture: a variegated, lively and quite distinctive version of the world and its possibilities. In the preface to his landmark *History of Australian Literature* (1961), H.M. Green called it 'the long range, with its unusual shape and colouring, and its … strange fascination'. That's what we explore and honour in this new anthology.

The first and foremost aim of this book is to make available to readers and students a sampling of the range of Australian writing, putting striking works from recent times together with works from the past that have become less familiar. By ordering the material chronologically, in a historical sweep from the first writing in English done in Australia to innovative work from the early years of the twenty-first century, and by encompassing a jostling variety of genres and styles, including letters, journals, speeches and songs, we intend that the anthology show the phases of change and development in Australian literature, and in Australian society and culture more generally. Our criteria for selection include that the work, written by someone born or living in, or writing about, Australia, should be compelling for a contemporary reader: significant or representative or exciting in its literary qualities. Given the vast body of material at our disposal, and the severe pressure of space in even such a substantial volume as this, the works that qualify as impressive and important pieces of writing often refer directly to life in Australia, making them recognisably about Australia, although that was not a requirement for inclusion. The anthology then implies different ways of being Australian as well as displaying different kinds of literary creativity.

The advocacy of a home-grown literature began in colonial times and has continued since then without losing much of its insistence. Looking back on the 1890s, for example, my forebear Arthur Wilberforce Jose, editor of Banjo Paterson and Henry Lawson and an early historian of Australian literature, enthusiastically recalled 'a naissance rather than a renaissance' when 'everything Australian was worth writing about' (*The Romantic Nineties*, 1933). By the 1980s it seemed that the battle for Australian literature had been won, with the subject firmly entrenched in school and university curricula and proudly supported by national institutions such as the Australia Council for the Arts. Survey anthologies that are precursors of this one, and to which we acknowledge our debt, appeared: *The Oxford Anthology of Australian Literature* in 1985 and *The Macmillan Anthology of Australian Literature* in 1990. But by 2003, when author members of the Australian Centres of International PEN, the world association of writers, joined the chorus of concern that Australian literature was losing its place—in bookshops, on publishers' lists, in classrooms—those two anthologies, and many works by major writers, were out of print. The reasons for this state of affairs can be summed up as a combination of changing intellectual approaches in the academy, including resistance to nationalist constructions of literature; shorter-term, market-driven publishing arrangements in an increasingly competitive and globalised media environment; reduced responsibility for cultural heritage, especially literature, in public policy; and the changing habits of new generations of consumers. Thus, our work has taken place against the background of a sense of crisis, real or imagined, in the standing of Australian literature.

The crisis can also appear exaggerated, however, in view of the expanding number of books being bought and read by Australians; the crowds attending literary festivals and participating in other community literary activities, especially the growing cohort who, as practising writers, read and react to Australian books; and the regular presence of Australian authors on international award lists. Things have changed since 1973 when the Nobel Prize for Literature was awarded to Patrick White for an art that 'introduced a new continent into literature'. If there is a problem now, perhaps it is the lack of perceived connection between a more vibrant contemporary situation and its literary antecedents. The literature of the past lives in the reading and writing of the present, but not always visibly. It requires a 'bonafide, continuous, affined readership', in author Frank Moorhouse's words, to make possible a literary culture and hold it together. As an initiative to bring Australian literature to new readers around the world, the present anthology, produced by a leading trade and academic publisher, has received generous support from public and private funding bodies, and from scholars, teachers, reviewers and members of the public—all of which indicates a high level of concern and interest. The moment seems right to look again at the Australian literary archive with a view to framing Australian literature afresh for contemporary needs. As Australian literature enters the wider stream of Anglophone or world literature, now may be the time to engage understanding and appreciation of its continuing traditions, larger contexts and distinctive energies. Hence the editorial motto: Texts for Our Times.

In considering how such an anthology might be compiled so as to present Australian literature in the best way for the broadest range of readers, the editorial team acknowledged from the start the complexities of the undertaking. The anthologiser's agony is that for every inclusion there is also an exclusion, given limitations of time, space and resources. By working with a broad definition of 'literature' and an inclusive definition of 'Australian'— from George Worgan's and Bennelong's letters in the first decade after 1788 to J.M. Coetzee's fiction (set in Australia) and Chi Vu's text for performance set in Vietnam in the 2000s—we have only made our task more difficult. Our aim has been to represent the main currents of Australian writing and to indicate its diversity, including the work of less familiar writers alongside iconic works while also giving an adequate sampling of major authors. Where necessary we have relied on extracts from novels, plays and other longer texts, choosing passages that are self-contained and offer a good introduction to an author's work. The selection is made in the knowledge that work by many of the authors mentioned is available online or in good libraries for readers who wish to follow up, and this initiative is complemented by a number of other current undertakings designed to promote Australian literature. We're also aware that there are alternative ways of doing what we've attempted. As Ken Goodwin and Alan Lawson wrote in the introduction to their admirable *Macmillan Anthology of Australian Literature*, 'We may still cherish the delusion of comprehensiveness … but such efforts are fated to be imperfect and incomplete … What is printed is, in both its selection and ordering, only one of a multitude of possibilities.'

In public discussion of the project, the question of content quickly arises, followed inevitably by the question of how we have defined Australian. Those issues have been vigorously debated by the editorial team, too, and not only in theoretical terms, as we have carried out the task of piecing together the jigsaw that is this book. As well as the merits of individual pieces, we have borne in mind the connections—affinities, oppositions, echoes and contrasts—that readers may find between texts. The multifarious story of Australian literature involves changing literary styles and approaches, and changing relationships between writers and readers. In the public domain literature has questioned and enlarged understandings of what Australia is or might be. Some authors have actively sought to contribute to the development of a national literature, or have been seen as doing so: the metaphor of a culture that is growing from youth to maturity persists. Other authors are identified as Australian in the international arena by dint of overtly Australian subject matter. Others resist such identification, perhaps strategically, and assert their freedom to engage imaginatively with worlds elsewhere. Among the great Australian novels are *Voss* by Patrick White and *True History of the Kelly Gang* by Peter Carey, works that recreate national historical figures of legendary status. But they are joined on any list by *The Man Who Loved Children* by Christina Stead, set in Washington, DC, *An Imaginary Life* by David Malouf, set on the margins of imperial Rome, *Schindler's Ark* by Thomas Keneally (also published as *Schindler's List*), which deals with Nazi Germany and the Holocaust, and Helen Garner's *The Children's Bach*, set in ordinary, urban Melbourne. Other authors question the category of Australian as a limiting construction and might even prefer the oppositional description 'un-Australian'. Successive waves of literary expression have challenged convention and the status quo: the social realist fiction of the 1930s, the best produced by women such as Katharine Susannah Prichard (a communist) writing against a male-dominated literary establishment; the modernists who broke with formalist conservatism in the 1940s, and were hoaxed in turn by the mythical poet Ern Malley; the Generation of '68, when poets looked experimentally to American countercultural models, and the work of second-wave feminists in the 1970s; and the long succession of writers of migrant and minority background who have brought their experience and creativity into Australian life, often through translation, from Taam Sze Pui and Judah Waten to Elizabeth Jolley and Yahia Al-Samawy. And most importantly for this anthology, and not without irony, there is the cry against Australian society at its most oppressive and most indifferent in the body of work by Aboriginal Australian writers.

Australian literature is thus cosmopolitan on one hand while having the strengths of locality on the other. A.A. Phillips, who diagnosed the 'cultural cringe' by which Australians showed their insecurity about their own cultural achievements, observed that we all live 'at the centre of a series of concentric circles of felt membership', from the familial to the universal—suggesting that in each overlapping community, art is 'fertilised by the … sense of a common identity and pride' ('Cultural Nationalism in the 1940s and 1950s: A personal account', 1988). In the search for a layering of words to express that complex and sometimes divided condition, Australian literature comes into being. It comes with anxiety about what would happen if the records and stories, the poetry and drama that give us ourselves—as individuals and communities—were not carried on.

Features of Australian writing include the contending identifications of class (convict or settler?), race, gender, region (the city or the bush, Brisbane or Perth, the suburb or the overseas trip?), background, belonging, politics—and sheer good fortune or the lack of it. It can be a literature of impersonation and reinvention, whether comic or tragic, of plainness or exaggeration, of fate and the roll of the dice; a literature of struggle, survival and making it (up). It can be brooding or sparkling, frequently irreverent, occasionally solemn, cheeky, gentle, outlandish or impassioned. Sometimes, combining terms that are unsettled and open to redefinition, Australian literature has a do-it-yourself quality—creating new from old, folding in the non-literary, turning the literary outward to social agency. This may explain the open-endedness and formal indeterminacy of many of the most intriguing works. Australian literature can even seem to be a fugitive phenomenon, which gives it a certain charm. The image comes from the fabled library at Borroloola on the Gulf of Carpentaria where books were borrowed and never returned, eaten by termites, dispersed by cyclones, shelved in the police lock-up to inspire inmates, sold off and forgotten. But in another way the contents of that library were recycled, lingering in readers' minds in a tall tale or a fine phrase, a half-remembered understanding or an exchange of ideas that passed across plains and oceans of separation to feed a people's imaginary.

Writing in Australia begins with the impulse to document and chronicle the experience of a place or a situation that has not been written before. That spirit extends through explorers' journals and early settlers' letters home to petitions for land rights and, later, memoirs of displacement. It moves through fiction such as Marcus Clarke's convict classic *His Natural Life* and autobiographies such as A.B. Facey's *A Fortunate Life* a century later, as well as the work of historians and environmental writers. Yet the documentary responsibility to life, such as it is—*Such is Life* being the title of Joseph Furphy's great Australian novel—so often tips over into something more unruly, fantastic or subversive as other writerly energies of craft and invention intensify. Irony, speculation and passion come into play in the conjuring of language and form for what is unprecedented and unmade. Partly that comes in the will to create literature that can argue with its own origins, as Judith Wright put it in a poem for an English colleague:

> I battle that heritage
> For room in another country, want to speak
> Some quite new dialect, never can …
> Any time I flower, it's in the English language.

But in the flowering of a poet such as Wright the language is renewed and changed. As readers, we share in the capacity, and the responsibility, for that renewal.

The transforming struggle with existing realities and existing forms of expression is characteristic of Australian literature as it reaches beyond normative bounds for new kinds of utterance. It's felt in the sardonic minimalism of Henry Lawson's prose sketches and the contrasting 'Quality of Sprawl' lauded and exemplified by Les Murray in so many poems. It's there in the defiant zest of Miles Franklin's *My Brilliant Career* and the grand dystopic projections of M. Barnard Eldershaw's *Tomorrow and Tomorrow and Tomorrow*. It's heard in the unanswerable eloquence of Oodgeroo Noonuccal's 'We Are Going'. This is disruptive writing that finds its power and grace in being so. The quality calls to mind the phrase from Ern Malley that historian Humphrey McQueen borrowed for his study of emergent Australian modernism: *The Black Swan of Trespass* (1979). Australian literature has been formed through the apparition and intervention of many such black swans of trespass, making their arresting and beautiful appeal.

Let me say that no one is more mindful of the inevitable limitations of this book than myself as general editor. There are always more voices to be heard and other stories to be told. Yet gathered here are some of the best, most distinctive, most significant examples of writing to come from Australia. As I look out from that plane window, I am aware of looking through a small lens at the virtually boundless and quite extraordinary country below. In the same way we hope that *The Literature of Australia: An anthology* will give readers an opening to the enduring literature of Australians.

Nicholas Jose

ABORIGINAL LITERATURE

The works by Aboriginal writers in this anthology represent the range and depth of Aboriginal writing in English from the late eighteenth century to the present day. Our selection begins with Bennelong's letter of 1796, the first known text in the English language by an Aboriginal author. At the time of the letter's composition, Bennelong had recently returned home from three years in England, where he had met King George III and only just survived as a racial curiosity. Bennelong's short, disarming enquiry after the wellbeing of his sponsor, Lord Sydney, and his slightly melancholic petition for shipments of fine clothes and shoes, speaks of one man's experience at the cusp of a sudden transformation in the human condition of all Aboriginal peoples. The Aboriginal-authored contributions to this anthology therefore record the history of that transformation as it was witnessed in writing ranging from the journalism, petitions and political letters of the nineteenth and early twentieth centuries, to the works of poetry and prose that are recognised widely today as significant contributions to the literature of the world.

In selecting works in English by Aboriginal authors, we also aim to introduce readers to the power, eloquence and beauty of a remarkable tradition within Australian writing; a set of stories, poems, plays and political works that, with all their grief and suffering, demand attention and celebration. Such a project necessarily begins with the fact of colonisation and the sudden arrival of the English language amidst Aboriginal societies and their modes of exchange. On 22 August 1770, Lieutenant James Cook raised the flag at Possession Island and declared Britain's acquisition of the east coast of Australia. This grandiose assertion was upheld eighteen years later by the tentative but nevertheless permanent British settlement of the continent at Sydney Cove, where on 26 January 1788 a crew of convicts and naval officers disembarked from the ships of the First Fleet, establishing under

Governor Arthur Phillip the colony of New South Wales. With them came not only the hopes and fears of a remote and tenuous European settlement; this moment also marks the arrival of English among Aboriginal people as an unexpected, perhaps unwanted, but eventually prevailing language.

With this in mind, we can address the development of Aboriginal literature not only from the perspective of history, but also with an awareness of the sudden appearance among Aboriginal people of a new set of linguistic and rhetorical conditions. At its inception, Aboriginal literary writing grew directly from a complex and ancient wellspring of oral and visual communication and exchange. It is generally agreed that at the end of the eighteenth century there were many hundreds of distinct Aboriginal societies in Australia, each of which possessed rich cultural, mercantile and day-to-day languages and forms of expression that had been intact for tens of thousands of years. But just as the Crown's acquisition of 1770 had made sovereign Aboriginal land *terra nullius*, it also made Aboriginal people *vox nullius*. It took only a few generations for almost two-thirds of the pre-contact Aboriginal languages to be made extinct. During the nineteenth century, Aboriginal people were dispossessed of their lands and many were interned on reserves and missions, institutions in which common human rights were rigorously limited by legislative machinery and ideological imperatives to 'smooth the pillow of a dying race'. Particularly in the eastern and southern parts of the continent, Aboriginal people were unable to live traditionally and were prevented from speaking their native languages.

For Aboriginal people, the use of English became a necessity within the broader struggle to survive colonisation. From the early days, writing became a tool of negotiation in which Aboriginal voices could be heard in a form recognisable to British authority. Aboriginal men and women were highly motivated by the duress under which they and their communities lived, and it is in their transactions with colonial administrations that the principal characteristics of the early literature were forged. Aboriginal authorship, as a practice and a literary category, first appears in genres that are common to political discourse: letters by individuals to local authorities and newspapers, petitions by communities in fear of further forms of dispossession or incarceration, and the chronicles of those dispossessed. The Aboriginal works included here demonstrate a range of moving and persuasive voices which are all the more valuable for their scarcity. These works reveal modes of performativity that are central to literary writing. They also demonstrate one of the persistent and now characteristic elements of Aboriginal literature— the nexus between the literary and the political.

The federation of the Commonwealth of Australia in 1901 did little to advance the social and political conditions of Aboriginal people. The new constitution specifically restricted the capacity of the Commonwealth to legislate in Aboriginal affairs, responsibility for which remained with each of the states and territories. From the late nineteenth century so-called 'Protection Acts', such as the 1869 *Act for the Protection and Management of the Natives of Victoria*, had evolved in each colony, and during the first decade of the twentieth century state and territory bureaucracies consolidated their authority over nearly every aspect of Aboriginal life. While the federal constitution had determined that Aboriginal people were effectively non-citizens, the Protection and later Aboriginal Welfare Acts saw lower tiers of government intensify control over what are generally considered to be fundamental human rights. For instance, Aboriginal people were forced to seek permission from authorities to exercise freedoms of movement and association, to enter into employment, or to marry. Governments and Protection boards acquired authority over the welfare of Aboriginal children, removing thousands from their families. Many of these children were placed in institutions and trained to work in menial, labour-intensive occupations. Aboriginal people were systematically disenfranchised from their traditional lands, their cultural practices and their languages.

The Aboriginal literature of the first decades of the twentieth century is characterised by a concerted and unmistakably public struggle against the overtly assimilationist legislative regimes endured by Aboriginal people. Between Federation and the 1960s, as had occurred in the nineteenth century, Aboriginal authorship appeared in letters and petitions to authorities—but now also in the political manifestos and pronouncements of Aboriginal activist organisations that had begun to coordinate resistance to government control. Organisations such as the Australian Aboriginal Progressive Association, the Australian Aborigines League and the Aborigines Progressive Association united Aboriginal men and women from across the south-eastern states between 1925 and 1938, focusing their shared confrontation with mainstream Australia. William Cooper's 'Petition to the King' and the APA's manifesto 'Aborigines Claim Citizen Rights!' are representative of writing at this time. In such texts we see responses to the extreme disadvantages suffered by Aboriginal communities denied access to land, property, education and health care, and a strong clarification of arguments against the various regimes of Protection. Demonstrations such as the 'Aboriginal Day of Mourning & Protest', held in Sydney on 26 January 1938 as the Commonwealth celebrated 150 years of British settlement, deepened the bond between political protest and Aboriginal writing.

The 1929 publication of *Native Legends*, David Unaipon's collection of his people's traditional stories, was a similarly significant development in Aboriginal writing. Unaipon was born and educated at the Point McLeay mission in South Australia during the early years of the assimilationist era, but as a gifted scholar, inventor, public speaker and writer he was able to successfully negotiate the complexities of life inside and outside the mission. His slim volume, produced by a metropolitan publisher for a white, middle-class readership in Australia and England, marks the arrival of a new genre of Aboriginal literature in English. Unaipon's *Native Legends* draws directly from the living wellspring of his traditional culture, but is also literary in its adaptation of his cultural imagination to particular modes of authorship and narration. Unaipon's achievement in publication, like that of his peers, was of course also political in nature. In writing *Native Legends*, Unaipon preserved in the English language something of his traditional Aboriginal culture, which he feared was already disappearing under the weight of colonisation. His legacy is fortunately twofold: Unaipon also gave subsequent Aboriginal writers a significant precedent by which to imagine their authorship of a culturally grounded future literature.

It would be another generation, however, before the next authored volume of Aboriginal writing appeared. Following the Second World War, the attention of Aboriginal activists returned to the domestic struggle for Aboriginal citizenship and the removal of state-based Protection and Welfare boards. During the 1950s and '60s organisations such as FCAATSI coordinated the first nationwide movements agitating for Aboriginal rights and constitutional transformation. Included in the anthology are a number of letters and petitions from a period in which the winds of change helped give Aboriginal political writing greater impetus and focus. Inspired by the worldwide radicalisation of Black politics and writing during the 1960s, particularly the American civil rights and the South African anti-apartheid movements, Aboriginal writing was at the forefront of a renewed and partially successful resistance to state authority. Aboriginal writer-activists such as Kath Walker helped lead the fight for full citizenship while producing the early poetry and political pieces that became major contributions to Aboriginal literature. Walker's first book of poetry, *We Are Going*, was—in 1964—only the second volume of Aboriginal literature published following Unaipon's work of 1929, and the first by an Aboriginal woman. Like Unaipon, Walker drew deeply from the traditional sources of her cultural imagination; however, her literature's political aspirations were far more explicit. Directed to both her own community and to an enthusiastic mainstream audience, *We Are Going* marks the arrival of Aboriginal poetry as one of the most important genres in contemporary Aboriginal political and creative literature.

Key political texts were also produced during the escalating struggle for land rights. Having been on the Aboriginal rights agenda for many decades, demands for land rights took shape in the mid-1960s when tribal councils in the Northern Territory began taking on governments in their fight for the recognition of traditional land rights. Aboriginal stockmen and their entire communities walked off cattle stations and went on strike for equal pay and the return of their traditional lands. The 'Yirrkala Petition to the House of Representatives, August 1963' (Yirrkala Bark Petition) and the Gurindji Petition led by Vincent Lingiari in 1967 are both representative. The Yirrkala Bark Petition remains especially significant. Authored by tribal elders at a pivotal moment in the expression of Aboriginal autonomy, it is written in Yolngu with an English translation, and is bordered by traditional Yolngu designs that express Yolngu law and rights to land. It was the first traditional document prepared by Aboriginal authority that was recognised by the Commonwealth Parliament, and is thus the first recognition of Aboriginal people and language in Australian law.

Aboriginal literature as we know it today had its origins in the late 1960s, as the intensification of Aboriginal political activity posed an increasing range of aesthetic questions and possibilities for Aboriginal authors. Momentum for change took a significant turn with the success of the 1967 constitutional referendum. However, practical changes were slow to come, and the period between 1967 and the election of the reformist Whitlam government in 1972 saw a new radicalisation in Aboriginal politics. With the political agenda focused on land rights and cultural self-determination, Aboriginal literature began to play a leading role in the expression of Aboriginal cultural and political life. New and challenging works of modern poetry and prose combined the traditions of protest established during the nineteenth and early twentieth centuries with the energy of the 'Black Power' movement. The period between 1967 and the mid-1970s is particularly significant for the sudden growth in Aboriginal authorship across a broad range of genres. Aboriginal writers began publishing volumes of poetry and fiction with both mainstream and grassroots presses, works for the theatre were successfully produced, published and widely read, and around the country Aboriginal journalists were contributing to the pamphlets, newsletters, newspapers and magazines from which an independent Aboriginal print media has since grown and flourished. The growing confidence of Aboriginal people throughout Australia, most of whom still lived in poor and ideologically isolated communities, was frequently demonstrated on the streets in marches and protests, the most prominent of which was the Aboriginal Tent Embassy built in 1972 on the lawn outside the capital's Parliament House. The literature of the 1970s, inspired by the broad push for political and territorial self-determination, demonstrates a fusion of political and creative energies. As new forms of agency were articulated in Aboriginal social and political life, new categories of authorship were explored and invented. Included are works by writers such as Kath Walker, Jack Davis, Kevin Gilbert, Monica Clare, Gerry Bostock and Lionel Fogarty, all of whom were active in the political sphere while simultaneously catalysing a nascent Aboriginal publishing industry and writing their own vanguard pieces of creative literature.

Following the uncertain political gains of the 1970s, many Aboriginal communities continued to suffer severe social and economic hardship, and political fights for social equity, land rights and cultural expression were intensified. During the 1980s, Aboriginal people around Australia sought to consolidate gains made in Commonwealth land rights legislation and the promise of self-determination. Aboriginal writers also maintained the rage, as was seen during the lead-up to the Commonwealth Bicentenary celebrations of 1988 when Aboriginal people and their supporters held nationwide demonstrations drawing attention to the Aboriginal rights agenda. They were often led by Aboriginal authors and activists such as Kath Walker, who, in protest against the Bicentenary, returned her MBE and readopted her traditional name, Oodgeroo Noonuccal. Noonuccal's defiant recovery of her true name is a defining moment in the evolution of contemporary Aboriginal literature, reflecting both an individual and a collective resurgence in the confidence of Aboriginal culture. In the final two decades of the twentieth century, the reach and impact of Aboriginal literature grew exponentially, attracting large mainstream audiences that were increasingly sympathetic to Aboriginal cultural and political demands. Behind the scenes, a new generation of Aboriginal authors, editors and publishers were working alongside elders to consolidate a vigorous and commercially independent network of Aboriginal literary presses. Mainstream publishers also took a strong interest in Aboriginal authors, and by the end of the 1980s Aboriginal writing was firmly established as a major force in Australian letters.

The recognition in Australian law of Aboriginal rights to land was significantly advanced in the High Court of Australia's 1992 Mabo decision, in which Eddie Koiki Mabo's claim of uninterrupted ownership of his people's traditional land at Mer Island was accepted by the court's full bench, thus finally admitting the falsehood of the assumption that Australia was *terra nullius* in 1788. This event foreshadowed a period of great potential during which government policy and public sentiment were broadly supportive of the recognition of the impacts of colonisation and the need for reconciliation between Aboriginal and mainstream Australia. Aboriginal voices gained widespread public attention as their stories were heard in national inquiries and reports, such as the Royal Commission into Aboriginal Deaths in Custody and the *Bringing Them Home* report on the separation of Aboriginal children from their families (the stolen generation). While the worst years of the assimilation period were over, the expression of its legacies in the stories of communities, families and individuals was at the forefront of the recovery of Aboriginal cultural memory and the articulation of contemporary Aboriginal life and aspirations. Autobiographical narratives and testimonial fiction became the key storytelling genres of the late 1980s and '90s, particularly for the growing number of Aboriginal women who found in literary writing a vehicle for both authorial independence and cultural responsibility. The growth in Aboriginal media also saw Aboriginal voices in film, television and music gain increased popularity, their political messages more frequently heard in everyday Australian life. The confidence and reach of recent Aboriginal literature has also been reflected in the work of a vigorous community of Aboriginal scholarly and critical writers, and in the essays, lectures and speeches by political voices who remind us that Aboriginal literature remains grounded in the shared experiences of contemporary Aboriginal men and women.

The survey of Aboriginal writing in this anthology ends in the middle of the first decade of a new century, perhaps a fortuitous moment at which to observe a body of literature that is now just over two centuries in the making. As is always the case with compiling anthologies, however, it has not been possible to include everything. The sheer range of available material made our editorial tasks both rewarding and difficult. Our guiding principle has been to seek out work that is not only eminently representative of a significant event, author or genre, but that is also clear and strong writing of the highest quality. We also sought texts in a variety of forms, such as the early letters, petitions and political manifestos, and contemporary works such as the song lyrics of Kev Carmody, Archie Roach and Bob Randall. Due to considerations of space, we have been unable to collect more than just a few excerpts from the rich number of available plays, and scripts for film and television have not been represented at all. At the time of writing, new texts of outstanding quality in poetry and prose have already made their marks but were published too late for us to include. Decisions were also made regarding the eligibility of some texts and authors.

The resurgence of Aboriginal writing in recent years has taken place during a widespread and vigorous renewal in Aboriginal culture. In the visual arts, performance, film, photography and music, Aboriginal practitioners and their critical communities produce highly significant works that speak to audiences around the world. The selection of Aboriginal writing in this anthology attempts to make a central contribution to the appreciation and study of a literature that over 200 years has borne witness to lives that were articulate, resolute and sensitive to their cultural and political milieus. Their voices are a challenge and an invitation.

Anita Heiss and Peter Minter

LITERATURE TO 1900

Books arrived in Australia in January 1788 with Governor Phillip's First Fleet, along with paper, ink, type and a printing press, though it was to be a few more years before the new British colony could boast a printer. Even before 1788 much had been written about different parts of Australia, under the various names by which they were known: Terra Australis Incognita, New Holland, New South Wales, Botany Bay. The accounts of earlier explorers such as William Dampier, who visited the west coast, were supplemented by those of James Cook and Joseph Banks relating their discoveries along the eastern seaboard in 1770. In the next couple of decades much ink was devoted to debating the wisdom of establishing a convict colony in this new southern land to replace the ones lost following the American War of Independence.

After the arrival of the First Fleet, paper and ink were in regular use. Governor Phillip was required to send regular reports back to London. Many of his officers were busy writing their accounts of the new land and its Aboriginal inhabitants, with Watkin Tench and David Collins competing to see who would be first to get his to the London publishers. Tench won the race, and his has remained one of the best-known accounts of first settlement. Those involved in exploring and charting the new land also needed to make notes, drawings and maps of what they had seen so that others could benefit from their experiences. Such works also served to stimulate the imagination of readers. Publication of Matthew Flinders's *A Voyage to Terra Australis* (1814) provided the first detailed charting of the whole of Australia's coast. Others were busy exploring and writing about inland regions, often meeting resistance from Aboriginal occupiers, as we learn from the extract by Charles Sturt.

Whether visitors or settlers, people also wrote at length about their experiences in Australia in a private capacity, sending long letters back to relatives and friends in England or keeping personal diaries. Many such letters and diaries have survived, been acquired by libraries and frequently printed. As naval surgeon George Worgan's 1788 letter to his brother demonstrates, writers would often have expected their letters to be quite widely read, given the intense interest in the new land. Elizabeth Macarthur's letter to her old friend has a more personal tone, describing the progress of the colony but also speaking of family matters. Eliza Brown, writing to her father from the new colony of Western Australia, similarly combines the personal—though the actual birth of her baby occurs between the lines—with more general information about a settler's life. Such letters are a reminder that, for many, the Australian colonies were always perceived as a place of refuge rather than a place of exile.

Such was not, of course, the experience of many convicts, though a number did do very well in Australia after their emancipation. The origins of the ballads 'Jim Jones at Botany Bay' and 'Moreton Bay' remain obscure but their passionate language demonstrates a strong sense of grievance and the resentment of authority often seen as part of the Australian character. This echoes down the decades to be seen again in Ned Kelly's 'Jerilderie Letter' as he denounces the colonial establishment, especially its police force. But not all literature written by convicts was violent and illiterate. In 'A Convict's Tour of Hell' Frank the Poet gets his revenge by imagining his enemies tormented in hell while Frank and his cronies are welcomed into heaven. In *The Hermit in Van Diemen's Land*, Henry Savery uses the persona of a rather naive visitor to present satirical insights into life in early Hobart.

While there was a continued demand in Britain during the nineteenth century for non-fictional and, later, fictional works about the Australian colonies, there was little interest in Australian poetry. Poems were regularly published in local newspapers and magazines from 1804 onwards but collected in volumes only at the expense of the author. Few nineteenth-century Australian authors were able to make a living from writing and these few depended heavily on journalism. Much of the early fiction and poetry therefore was written by people who came to Australia as settlers or in some official capacity. Barron Field's *First Fruits of Australian Poetry* (1819) has the distinction of being the first book of poetry to be published in Australia. Self-funded, it is something of a literary joke, since the idea of poetry being produced in a penal colony was to European eyes as anomalous as the kangaroo. Other poets published prolifically in local papers and magazines but could not afford to pay for collections of their work. Eliza Dunlop prepared a manuscript collection of her poems, entitled 'The Vase', presumably in the hope of publication. It is now in Sydney's Mitchell Library, along with the much more voluminous manuscripts of Charles Harpur, whose poems were carefully copied for a never-realised English edition.

After his death, Harpur's widow, the 'Rosa' of his love sonnets, managed to fund a collection but unfortunately Harpur's poems were edited to conform to late nineteenth-century taste. Hence a true measure of his achievement only became possible once scholars, including the poet Judith Wright, went back to his manuscripts. Harpur's work was distinguished not only by his belief in himself as Australia's first 'native-born' poet but by the range of verse forms he employed. As well as being adept at political satire, which flourished in local newspapers, he attempted the more ambitious poetic forms of epic and tragedy.

Many of Harpur's successors also wrote the long poems then seen as the true mark of poetic achievement, but those who established lasting reputations did so with their shorter works: Henry Kendall through his lyrical descriptions of bush scenery, especially 'Bell-birds', once recited by generations of Australian schoolchildren, and Adam Lindsay Gordon for his 'horsy' ballads, especially 'The Sick Stockrider'. Kendall's poem in memory of Gordon—he also wrote one for Harpur—is included here as an example of a popular contemporary genre as well as a reminder that many nineteenth-century Australian poets died early and in financial difficulties. And they were not the only ones. Despite his intelligence, wit, and rhetorical and literary skills, D.H. Deniehy did not reach his fortieth birthday; as with Harpur, Kendall, Gordon, Marcus Clarke and, later, Henry Lawson, the struggle to provide for his family, plus heavy drinking, contributed to his early death. His speech opposing W.C. Wentworth's proposal to introduce a colonial equivalent of Britain's House of Lords contributed the wonderful phrase 'bunyip aristocracy' to the store of great Australian expressions.

The discovery of gold in New South Wales in 1851, soon followed by even richer finds in Victoria, altered perceptions of Australia from a dumping ground for criminals and other undesirables to a potential El Dorado. Writers were among those attracted to the colonies and, if none of them found much gold, several were able to profit through their accounts of life on the goldfields. Ellen Clacy's is unusual in providing a vivid account from a woman's perspective of the ceaseless pursuit of a golden fortune which she encountered. Like Clacy, Mary Fortune arrived in Victoria during the gold fever; she, however, stayed to become one of the rare women who managed to scrape a living in nineteenth-century Australia through her pen. 'The Spider and the Fly' recounts the not uncommon fate of many other women who had to rely on their bodies rather than their minds to support themselves. The eponymous heroine of Catherine Helen Spence's *Clara Morison*, when finding herself alone in Adelaide without a job, escapes this fate by determining to become a servant, even though this involves her in many difficulties.

The vast increase in population and prosperity brought by the gold discoveries, especially to Victoria, also increased the production of local newspapers and magazines. Spence later found that she could make much more money from her journalism than from fiction. Thanks to a rate of production that is hard to conceive of today, Fortune was able to support herself mainly by writing fiction, especially detective stories, for the monthly *Australian Journal* (1865–1956), which published local as well as British and American fiction. One of its early editors was Marcus Clarke and it was in the pages of the *Australian Journal* in 1870–72 that his classic novel of the convict system, *His Natural Life*, first appeared. Like Fortune, Clarke was amazingly prolific, turning out vast amounts of copy that, although variable in quality, at its best provides highly entertaining glimpses of life in 'Marvellous Melbourne'. Like all who write for money, he was also good at recycling; much of his preface to Adam Lindsay Gordon's poems was originally written as an accompaniment to photographs of pictures in Melbourne's National Gallery. Notwithstanding its origins, Clarke's description of the bush as a place imbued with 'weird melancholy' resonated with many later readers, and is quoted in Henry Lawson's 'In a Wet Season'.

Given the size of Australia, and the range of climates and geographies encountered as one moves from east to west and north to south, no single image could ever be expected to sum up the landscape. In 1874, William Ranken, following in the footsteps of earlier natural history writers such as Louisa Atkinson, succeeded in capturing some of the diversity and spectacle of Australia in *The Dominion of Australia*. As settlement spread further inland in the second half of the century, driven by the need to open up more land for the steadily increasing population, images of the dry interior, the 'never never', began to appear. Explorer Ernest Giles recounted his life-and-death struggles across the deserts of central and northern Australia, and novelists and poets were not far behind. While the gloomy note of Barcroft Boake's 'Where the Dead Men Lie' may have been produced by his temperament as much as the landscape—he committed suicide soon afterwards—it also hints at the increasing conflict between labour and capital that was to be another theme in literature of the 1890s. Mary Hannay Foott's 'Where the Pelican Builds' provides a more lyrical description of the outback but death and loss are still a feature of her representation.

If death was never far away in the desert, it was also a fairly certain fate for those young men who became bushrangers. Many, from the Wild Colonial Boy onwards, were remembered in popular ballads, and the self-perpetuation of the myth of the heroic bushranger can be seen in Ned Kelly's reference to such ballads in his 'Jerilderie Letter'. Rolf Boldrewood's classic tale of bushranging, *Robbery Under Arms*, was inspired in part by the notoriety of Kelly and his gang, captured just a couple of years before the novel was begun. Boldrewood's use of a distinctive local vernacular, one which clearly influenced the work of Henry Lawson and others, was not, however, itself influenced by Kelly's vernacular writing, since the 'Jerilderie Letter' was not published until much later. The Australian idiom can be found in earlier work, such as A.J. Boyd's 'The Shepherd', one of a series of brief sketches of bush types published in the *Queenslander* (1875–76). But Boldrewood was the first to make an Australian working-class man the narrator of a novel, even if his decision to use Captain Starlight, an aristocratic Englishman, as that novel's main hero was not approved by later nationalist critics.

Like Boldrewood's novels, many of Ada Cambridge's were serialised in Australian newspapers before being taken up by British publishers—in the absence of a viable local industry, this was about the only way writers could make money. As 'The Wind of Destiny' demonstrates, Cambridge specialised in witty and ironic depictions of contemporary life, mainly set in Melbourne, though her best-known novel, *A Marked Man* (1890), is set in Sydney. She was also Australia's most notable nineteenth-century woman poet; *Unspoken Thoughts* (1887) includes many poems that radically question women's role in marriage, the sexual double standard and conventional religious belief. Cambridge was one of a number of women novelists who began writing about Australia in the 1880s and '90s, including the prolific expatriate Rosa Praed and the Adelaide-based Catherine Martin, whose *An Australian Girl* (1890) also deals with many of the central social and religious issues of the day. Regrettably, Praed's and Martin's fine novels cannot be adequately represented by brief extracts. While Tasma's novels also had mainly city settings, her story 'Monsieur Caloche' uses both bush and city to explore such current questions as relations between capital and labour, and gendered assumptions about women's roles, questions to be taken up later by Joseph Furphy in *Such is Life*.

In the last decades of the nineteenth century, as writers began to speculate on the possibilities of a national literature and debate its distinctive features, there was general agreement that it should be, in the words of one critic, 'racy of the soil'. This meant set in the bush, even though Australia's population was already starting to concentrate in the cities. Hence the failure to recognise writing by women, and the enthusiasm for the work of writers associated with the Sydney magazine the *Bulletin*, hailed by later critics as marking the beginnings of a truly Australian literature. In fact the *Bulletin*, when it began publication in 1880, was aimed more at readers in the city than the bush, with its shorter paragraphs and snappy features, strongly influenced by developments in American journalism, designed to appeal to commuters. In the 1890s, under the proprietorship of J.F. Archibald, and with A.G. Stephens as literary editor, it took a distinct turn inland. Many of Banjo Paterson's most famous poems first appeared in the *Bulletin*; when later collected for publication by the new firm of Angus & Robertson, *The Man from Snowy River and Other Poems* became a bestseller. The scenario of 'Clancy of the Overflow', where the narrator, stuck in the dingy city, longs to be riding in the bush with Clancy, suggests one of the reasons why Paterson's works had such wide appeal. Henry Lawson's view of life in the bush was much grimmer than Paterson's and in 1892 they conducted a poetic debate in the pages of the *Bulletin* as to whose representations were the truest. Although Paterson painted Lawson as someone who should stick to city life, Lawson also saw plenty to criticise there as 'Faces in the Street' shows. His early radicalism derived not only from his own struggles but from the influence of his mother Louisa, one of the leaders of the 1890s fight for women's rights, including the right to vote. Through her journal *The Dawn* (1888–1905) she carried on her campaigns as well as providing much practical advice and entertainment for her readers. Louisa Lawson's character, and her determination to make a mark in a male-dominated society, are well captured in A.G. Stephens's interview, even if his title, 'A Poet's Mother', like that of 'The Drover's Wife', gives top billing to the male.

A similar emphasis on the male rather than the female protagonist can be seen in A.G. Stephens's change of title for Barbara Baynton's 'The Chosen Vessel': it was published in the *Bulletin* as 'The Tramp'. Furthermore, the third section of the story, dealing with Peter Hennessey's supposed vision of the Virgin Mary, was omitted, making the narrative much more direct but removing Baynton's daring equation of the mother who is raped with the Holy Mother. When Baynton's *Bush Studies* (1902) was eventually published in London, Stephens acknowledged in a review that her work was too shocking for local publishers. Much more to their taste—and the public's taste—were the stories of Steele Rudd, which began appearing in the *Bulletin* in 1895. Although initially they echoed the black humour of Lawson's accounts of life on a poor selection, the immense popularity of Rudd's stories led them to become more broadly comic as time went on. A succession of adaptations for stage, screen, radio and television during the twentieth century led to Rudd's Dad and Dave becoming Australian folk heroes, who even figured in dirty jokes.

The *Bulletin* did not give space only to tales of the bush; the stories collected in Price Warung's *Tales of the Convict System* (1892) and its sequels had originally appeared in its columns. In depicting the cruelty of the British convict system, Warung was furthering another aspect of the *Bulletin*'s political program: republicanism and a total separation of Australia from what it saw as the hated British yoke. Victor Daley's sometimes comic, sometimes serious verses also often appeared in the *Bulletin*, including 'Correggio Jones', his satire on what was to become known as the 'cultural cringe'—the feeling that Europe was the only place for Australian artists. A.G. Stephens's 'Red Page', so called because it was printed on the inside of the magazine's reddish-coloured paper covers, even featured articles by Christopher Brennan on the French symbolist poets as well as some of Brennan's own symbolist-inspired poems. On 23 November 1894 the young Ethel Turner, whose classic children's story *Seven Little Australians* had been published two months earlier, went to a party held by fellow writer Louise Mack. There, as she noted in her diary, she met Chris Brennan, 'said to be a genius but slightly mad. Splendid to talk to though.' A few weeks later, she recorded the appearance of her story 'The Little Duchess' in the Christmas number of the *Bulletin*, which always featured additional literary works by leading writers: she and Mack were the only women included. By 1894 women had won the vote in South Australia, well in advance of their British sisters, but literary equality was still a long way off.

Today nineteenth-century Australian authors are read for their vivid, individual responses to the challenge and fascination of their often new and strange circumstances, and their remarkable achievements in the face of many obstacles. Through their work the foundations of Australian literature were established.

Elizabeth Webby

LITERATURE 1900–1950

'My heart is a pomegranate full of sweet fancies,' wrote Lesbia Harford in 1917. 'See, it has opened for you!' Her direct voice is unnervingly modern. The poetry's playfulness and lively imagery speak to us, in intimate and yet calculated ways, of what we might feel are twenty-first-century emotions. Yet it is removed from us by the passage of 90 years and was almost unknown for much of the twentieth century.

Lesbia Harford is a good example of an author whose work received little recognition during her lifetime but has been reclaimed by subsequent generations. Writing as a radical university student opposed to wartime conscription, Harford identified with the struggles of industrial workers, especially women factory workers, and was in love with both the women and men who were her intellectual and political colleagues. She kept her writing under wraps during her short life; it was left to feminist scholars of the 1980s to seek out her work and to publish a full collection of her distinctive, and affecting yet intellectual poetry. Now Harford's witty, feeling voice speaks more expressively to us than many other writers who were then, perhaps, more of their time.

The Australia evoked in writing from the first half of the twentieth century is close enough to our own time to be familiar, yet is different in ways that can be unexpected. The flare of 'flurite' gas in Kenneth Slessor's image of a tram with lit windows flashing past like a strip of celluloid is difficult to imagine now. It is from a lexicon of imagery few of us can easily conjure. At the same time, so much writing from 1900 to 1950 in Australia is consciously modern, determinedly written for the future, whether stylistically modernist or not. This is the period when Australia claimed for itself a 'national literature' and the legacy for contemporary readers is complex. We encounter an attempt at a national voice yet a literature so diverse as to be conflicted with itself: writing with which we can feel at home and writing that enacts a history we weren't part of, or would even wish away.

These complexities are just a few of those presented by literature of and from times different from but close to our own. Literature does not merely tell us of the past, nor is it simply a part of that past: it is the past's imaginary. This is the case even as its time is always the moment of reading, since it means nothing—or does not mean—without our contemporary eye.

Frank Wilmot, for example, produced substantial collections of poetry under the pseudonym Furnley Maurice through the early decades of the twentieth century. He delivered the first of the Commonwealth Literary Fund's lectures on Australian literature at the University of Melbourne and his *Melbourne Odes* (1934), designed to educate an isolated Australian readership, were thought to exemplify the principles of modernism brought to verse. Yet his work can seem stale to contemporary readers. Hugh McCrae likewise had a strong reputation at his death in 1958. His poetry features fauns, nymphs and satyrs—reflecting Norman Lindsay's bowdlerised classicist aesthetic, a particular note for Sydney bohemia through the 1920s—that now seem almost laughably florid.

By contrast, Western Australian writer J.M. Harcourt's 1934 novel *Upsurge* was banned as obscene by the Commonwealth Book Censorship Board and not released from censorship until 1958. This extraordinary novel, a nuanced and forthright portrait of a Perth divided by economic extremes during the Depression of the early 1930s, culminates with an uprising of unemployed workers who hijack a train from their camps south of Perth in an attempt to take over the Western Australian treasury. Its banning caused a storm in the 1930s but Australian readers were only reintroduced to the novel in 1986, after it had been rediscovered by literary historians. It is now appreciated as the first example of the international genre of socialist realism in Australia, and its frank treatment of commercial sex is recognised as a lively part of its critique of alienated human relations.

Contemporary readers can follow the drama of *Upsurge* but may find McCrae's poetry of merely historical interest, as evidence of the complexity and difference of the past. Even a poet like the socialist Marie Pitt, writing in the years before the First World War about rights for Aborigines and reproductive rights for women—both very 'modern' subjects—employed an elaborately formal and allegorical Edwardian style that makes her verses hard work today.

Bernard O'Dowd's poem 'Australia' from 1900 is another example, and can be compared with two other poems titled 'Australia' from the period, all setting out to represent the new nation. Marie Pitt's long-term companion, O'Dowd was a prominent and voluble figure in turn-of-the-century Melbourne. His poetry was in the radical nationalist tradition with an emphasis on the democratic values of rural and bush life. In a famous address, 'Poetry Militant', he argued for a socially engaged literature, able to change its world. Written during the debates leading up to Federation, 'Australia' asks what the new entity may be. 'Last sea-thing dredged by sailor Time from Space' posits the first line, echoing a trope from early colonial poet Barron Field's satirical musing on 'The Kangaroo', in which Australia is seen as the 'afterbirth' of Europe's age of exploration. Is Australia 'a drift Sargasso' (a net of drifting weed in which marine life thrives) where the West may rebuild itself from the waste of the old world? Perhaps fatally? But fatally for whom? Loaded with classical and rhetorical allusion, working ponderously to prove the country's European heritage, the poem holds the new nation up as a mysterious paradox. What is its uncertain destiny? Both promise and doom say the 'omens' and 'auguries' of the landscape: perhaps Australia is a land for liberty, perhaps for death.

O'Dowd's poem is markedly of its time, an exercise in nationalist fabulism in which Australian settler writing could be intently curious about its own developing imaginary. O'Dowd's hints of scepticism about that project are still merely hints. By comparison, Mary Gilmore's 'Australia', from 1932, engages with the profound challenge that Indigenous Australia presents to the legitimacy of settler culture. The poem's exploration of the onomatopoeia of Aboriginal languages acknowledges their vision for an Australian landscape as 'great beauty' lost. Even in the poem's reductive primitivism and fatalism there remains a bald protest at the suffering of Indigenous Australians and the loss of traditional languages.

A.D. Hope's 'Australia' from 1939 has perhaps the most intently modern nationalism of these three poems, rendered via its decisive split with the nation of 'second hand Europeans' pullulating 'on the edge of alien shores'. This occurs even though Hope's work in general opts for a traditionalist aesthetic, full of classical allusions and a formalism rendered almost brutal by his use of gendered metaphor. The final lines of 'Australia' call for a local version of modernity, sourced in the 'savage and scarlet' spirit of the desert. Read through contemporary eyes, Hope's poem marks a claim for a particular antipodean modernism that was in many measures unfulfilled. It resonates with the Ern Malley hoax in unanticipated ways, and also projects an assertively white and masculine modern, in which Australia itself is cast as not only again 'the last of lands' but a 'woman beyond her change of life'—empty and dry.

One of the most striking characteristics of Australian writing from the first half of the twentieth century is the strong representation, even dominance, of women writers, particularly in the decades between the wars and particularly in the genre of the novel. Henry Handel Richardson, Katharine Susannah Prichard, Christina Stead, Eleanor Dark, Jean Devanny,

Kylie Tennant, Eve Langley, Dymphna Cusack and Ruth Park were among the leading writers of their day and their novels remain appealing to readers. Their dominance raises interesting questions about the nature of an Australian modern, since the literary culture of the 1920s to the '40s was distinguished from international currents not only by a prevailing realism but by the high profile of work created by women, some of it experimental and modernist to varying degrees.

Susan Lever argues in *Real Relations: The feminist politics of form in Australian fiction* (2000) that the dominance of women can be accounted for by the absence of men at war and, during the Depression, in itinerant work. The collaborative writing duo of Marjorie Barnard and Flora Eldershaw, writing together as M. Barnard Eldershaw through the 1930s and '40s, would have disagreed. They argued that novel writing had become the preserve of women 'like nursing', and that this was because a 'tardiness in recognising the novel as a form of art' had allowed women to develop their own tradition: 'Women had won their spurs before anyone thought of telling them they were incapable of doing so.'

M. Barnard Eldershaw looked forward, in the declamatory, predictive mode of the 1930s, to the development of a national literary tradition as the natural expression of a 'mature' and modern nation. Humphrey McQueen claims in *The Black Swan of Trespass* (1979) that the writing duo's *Essays in Australian Fiction* was the 'most thoughtful' of a crop of books about Australian literature from the late 1930s. Much of the crop was polemical and determinedly partisan, engaged in the fiery culture wars of the turbulent 1930s, such as P.R. 'Inky' Stephensen's long, idiosyncratic essay 'The Foundations of Culture in Australia' from 1936. Radically nationalist in its refusal of imperialist ties to Britain, in line with Stephensen's endeavours to foster a domestic publishing industry, it was also radically wrong in its valorising of Australia as 'the only continent on the earth inhabited by one race, under one government, speaking one language'.

Stephensen's vision of a uniquely homogeneous nation was contradicted not only by other writing of the period, but by his own work. He supported the publication of the Indigenous newspaper the *Abo Call* in 1936, and edited and published Xavier Herbert's complexly populated 1938 novel about the Northern Territory—*Capricornia*—which features a vocal and philosophical hero of mixed Aboriginal and British heritage. Modern Indigenous theatrical performances of *Capricornia* which foreground the charged identity questions of the stolen generation have given this momentous novel a purposeful new resonance. Stephensen's vision was also countered more broadly by the sporadic publication of memoirs, histories, recollections and journalism that have kept alive the history of diverse Australian heritages, predating the White Australia policy, for contemporary readers.

The autobiography of Taam Sze Pui, *My Life and Work*, recalls experiences from the 1870s, while in *Tom Petrie's Reminiscences of Early Queensland*, Constance Campbell Petrie records memories that date back to 1837. Both works came into print many decades after the events described. The Petrie memoir was published in 1904, before Tom Petrie's death in 1910, and Taam's book was published in pamphlet form in Innisfail in 1925, in English with facing Chinese text. These accounts show us two very different Queenslands—Tom Petrie's memories of the games played by Turrbal children in their country, the rivers and mountains just north of Brisbane, evoke a sophisticated and playful culture of learning and belonging, even then being encroached on by European settlement. Taam's moving account of the arduous journey undertaken from China to work on the North Queensland goldfields is an extraordinary document of colonial Chinese experience. Its bitterness resonates in this anthology with Mary Gilmore's short, imagistic poem commemorating the Lambing Flat goldfields riots of 1860–61, in one of which fourteen Chinese men were murdered.

E.J. Banfield's journalism about life on Dunk Island was collected as *The Confessions of a Beachcomber* in 1908. Removed from colonial Australia's civilisation, life on this beautiful tropical island is inscribed as an idyll of the first order. Banfield's accounts were strongly influential in establishing the world's image of the Great Barrier Reef as a natural paradise. The extract included here highlights his luscious nature writing, a combination of precise observation and lyrical exuberance through which detail spills into a gorgeous excess of foliage, flowers and fruits, in a landscape awash with luxuriance and plenty. 'At no season of the year is the island fragrantless,' Banfield notes.

The ecstatic description needs replacing in its context, however. *The Confessions of a Beachcomber* begins with a description of the Indigenous inhabitants of the island, set in a past whose distance is not properly measured:

> In years gone by, Dunk Island, 'Coonanglebah' of the blacks, had an evil repute. Fertile and fruitful . . . it carried dusky denizens who were fat, proud, high-spirited, resentful, treacherous, and far from friendly or polite to strangers . . . [But] why invoke those long-silent spectres, white as well as black, when all active boorishness is of the past? Civilisation has almost fulfilled its inexorable law; only four out of a considerable population remain, and they remember naught of the bad old time when the humanising processes, or rather the results of them, began to be felt.

Banfield's 'years gone by' invokes a removed past, but it is clear that the 'bad old time' he wished readers to forget was not then past. The impact of the 'humanising processes', as he only somewhat ironically describes the imposition of white rule, was an ongoing reality for the surviving members of decimated families, despite his denial.

What we witness, in fact, is the conquest of paradise, and the displacement and 'dispersal' of the North Queensland groups to make way for Banfield's untainted isolation. His prose confronts us with the colonising force of rhetoric—the work done by the uninhabited tropical island imagined by Defoe for Robinson Crusoe, for example—to effect the dispossession of local people of country held for thousands of years. While, in fact, the Wangamaygan still live on the island, Banfield reinscribes its ravishing beauty with his vivid, exultant prose, as '[w]holly uninhabited, entirely free from the mauling paws of humanity, lovely in its mantle of varied foliage'.

White racist discourses of decline, and even of extirpation, were still active in some writing from the early to mid-twentieth century and entail difficult decisions now about how and whether to represent colonial racism. It was an ideology fully at play in some literature of the period, even as, at Federation, Australia removed the imperial overseer and appeared to come into modern democracy, to no longer be colonial. If we treat Australia as only modern—filtered through our contemporary 'feelings', as we might do for Lesbia Harford—rather than as also still colonial, the impulse is to remove the racist representations completely.

This would have two effects. One is to offer the illusion of a past less exclusionary and oppressive than it was—to whitewash and ignore the complex past that still impacts on contemporary understanding and experience. The other is to paper over the degree to which international and domestic writers and readers were interested in, and even preoccupied with, the question of Australia's 'settlement'; the character of its colonised populations (even as their 'inferiority' was actively constructed by those discourses); and exactly what the continuing presence of Indigenous Australian populations and communities other than 'white Australian' meant for a 'modern' Australian nation, and vice versa. Randolph Bedford's *White Australia: The empty north*, billed as a 'patriotic drama' in 1909, amplified the race panics of the early century by staging a Japanese invasion of Queensland. It doesn't make it into this anthology but the racist epithets of Herbert's *Capricornia* do, while Prichard's 1940s short story 'Marlene' carries something of the protest that some white writers needed to voice.

What do we want from writing? 'The anthologist must needs play the critic from beginning to end of his work of selection and rejection: what need, then, of any further airing of his likes and dislikes?' asks Walter Murdoch in his preface to *The Oxford Book of Australasian Verse* (1918). Some explanation, nevertheless, is needed for what may seem to be the neglect of some forms of Australian writing from the period—especially theatre, but also the popular publications of a period in which modern appetites for commercial genres were answered by printing technology that could feed mass markets.

Louis Esson's witty, Wildean theatrical satire from 1912 is represented because it works so well on the page. The more modern and psychological dramas of the 1930s and '40s, including some of the poignant and political plays written by women, often for radio, are more like scripts and harder to extract. As a result, reading them is a less satisfactory experience. It is important to emphasise, nevertheless, that Australians could see and appreciate theatre with Australian plots, settings and vernacular dialogue well before the supposed breakthrough of Ray Lawler's *Summer of the Seventeenth Doll* in 1955.

In the 1920s, under the colonial book-trade agreements of the British empire, Australians imported 3.5 million books annually. The most popular authors were British, in a broadly Anglophilic reading culture, while the best-selling Australian title of 1935 was the perennially popular detective fiction, Fergus Hume's *The Mystery of a Hansom Cab*, from 1886. Angus & Robertson, then Australia's only really successful publishing house, sustained itself through the 1930s and '40s by publishing the books of Ion Idriess and Frank Clune, whose dashing personas and prolific outback yarns crystallised for many readers the popular myth of a laconic yet adventurous, pioneering rural Australia.

C.J. Dennis's long comic poem *The Sentimental Bloke*, first published in book form in 1915, won a large audience for its citified charm instead. Popular at the same time that Harford was writing her intensely personal poetry in Melbourne, Dennis's talkative 'Bloke' spoke with a spectacular vernacular. His voice is edged with both satire and deep affection for an Australian working-class urban experience, as the larrikin Bloke meets and woos Doreen and then moves to a berry farm on the city fringe. A distraction from the ferocity of Australian debates over conscription and the carnage of the Western Front, Dennis's popular poem can be set against literary responses to the First World War of a quite different kind.

Much of it grief-ridden, all of it sombre, some significant examples of Australian writing of the First World War were published up to a decade later, when anti-war protests were less subject to censorship. John Le Gay Brereton's 'ANZAC' has often been anthologised, thanks to its title, but Mary E. Fullerton's pithy poem, about women's experiences waiting for the postman to bring the tragic telegram, has a strong story to tell, too. Expatriate Frederic Manning's *The Middle Parts of Fortune*, published in London in 1929, reminds us of the heavy losses sustained by Australians, even as his hero is deliberately given no nationality within the imperial forces—an everyman soldier whose flat desperation and exhausted bitterness confront directly the inhuman irrationality of war.

From war to the Depression to war again, from intense class struggle to Menzies' exclusive vision of a middle-class country, from Federation to Americanisation, from the roaring twenties to the atom bomb, the first half of the twentieth century in Australia witnessed great turbulence and transformation. Literature was at once a witness to this history and an agent in its making; the diversity and complexity of writing from 1900 to 1950 evince the period's difference from the present, as well as rendering the past more fully present to us now. But it is not possible to trace a single national story from that complexity.

Despite the retrospective impulse to organise it that way, literature from the first half of the twentieth century was never merely about the nation. From Banfield's paradise to Douglas Stewart's stony desert, from patriotic love of a 'sunburnt country' to lament for an eroded, over-grazed land, writing from the period was divided even about how to encode an Australian landscape. When the cities were so full of experience, how was the bush a national place? 'We'll all be rooned,' sang Hanrahan for those on the land, and Judith Wright knew enough to mourn the loss of natural habitat. The Jindyworobak group looked to Indigenous Australia for a national identity in the 1930s and '40s, while Aboriginal writers struggled to assert control over their own work. From realism to modernism and back again, a realist nationalist tradition became radical while modernism found itself first hoaxed, then in court.

M. Barnard Eldershaw and others saw the beginnings of a national literary tradition developing in the 1930s and '40s. Contemporary understandings instead question the limits of all three of those terms—nation, literature, tradition—emphasising the diverse threads by which meaning comes to us through time and may be valued and ordered into a heritage. Our contemporary ideas corral, reorder and select that literary heritage, but also reveal new understandings and new ways to read what is otherwise the profound otherness of the past. Writing from the first half of the twentieth century in Australia shows contemporary readers that debate, dissent and diversity mark literature from earlier eras, not only our own. And in many illuminating ways, this debate, dissent and diversity characterised the years from 1900 to 1950 even more than our own.

Nicole Moore

FICTION AND DRAMA FROM 1950

The last half-century has seen Australian literature emerge from constraints of various kinds, proliferating in many directions, especially in fiction, supported by a growing publishing industry and the changing enthusiasms of readers. Alongside more literary writing, genre fiction, including crime, fantasy and romance, has flourished. At its best, contemporary Australian fiction can be read against the most original and distinctive elements of earlier Australian writing in ways that surprise and appeal.

By the early 1950s, Australian writing and writers were beginning to recover from the effects of the Second World War, only for many literary figures on the left—Vance Palmer, Judah Waten, Frank Hardy, Dorothy Hewett, Eleanor Dark and Kylie Tennant, among others—to be affected and to some extent silenced a few years later by the climate and events of the Cold War. The year 1950, however, saw the publication or stage production of new works by several established writers who had been flourishing in the 1930s and '40s; among these were John Morrison's short-story collection *Port of Call*, Dymphna Cusack's play *Comets Soon Pass*, and Katharine Susannah Prichard's *Winged Seeds*, the third volume in her goldfields trilogy. In the same year Frank Hardy published the controversial and influential *Power Without Glory*, which resulted in a nine-month criminal trial for libel.

In 1952, two important but very different books of autobiographical fiction were published: Martin Boyd's *The Cardboard Crown* and Judah Waten's *Alien Son* both deal, albeit from different social and ideological perspectives, with the experiential contrasts and conflicts between life in Australia and life elsewhere, and document changing patterns in Australian society and culture.

While literary nationalism had flourished in fiction before and during the Second World War and continued to do so after the war, drama had remained more tightly tied to British and European models, which is one of the reasons why Ray Lawler's play *Summer of the Seventeenth Doll* (*1955*/1957), in which the characters talk, think and act like 'ordinary Australians', was regarded as a major breakthrough. Patrick White's fourth novel, *The Tree of Man*, was published the same year; it, too, celebrates 'ordinary Australians', by exploring what White refers to in his highly influential essay 'The Prodigal Son' (1958) as 'the extraordinary within the ordinary'. The first-ever stage appearance of Barry Humphries' character Edna Everage also took place in 1955, her surname an unsubtle indication that Humphries, too, deplored what White had in the same essay called the 'exaltation of the average' in the cautious, conservative monoculture of 1950s Australian life. While Humphries was satirising his own time and place, the projects of White and Lawler were more positive and surprisingly similar: both works address and redeem Australian 'ordinariness', White's by leavening it with intimations of the metaphysical and the mystical, and Lawler's by amplifying the mythic dimensions of his characters' emotional lives.

Implicit in the title of Leslie Rees's *Towards an Australian Drama* (1953) is the assumption that Australia had not yet, at that date, arrived at the destination. In the sense of the word that Rees's title suggests, 'Australian' fiction and poetry were already flourishing and had been doing so for many years, but the history of drama in Australia is usually represented as turning on the fulcrum that was *Summer of the Seventeenth Doll*, an idea that has remained a truism in Australian literary history. But drama was, before that date, steadily moving 'towards' a national identity of its own.

Although it has not proved practicable to include more than a few short extracts from some representative examples of Australian drama in this anthology, drama has been an important form of entertainment and self-expression since early colonial days, and has continued to feed the imaginations of Australians through film and television in recent years. Some background remarks about this lively form may direct readers to some of the key works. The earliest Australian plays were based on known facts about real-life bushrangers and began to be staged from the 1830s. Theatrical life in colonial Australia was plentiful and colourful, but while much of it used specifically Australian subject matter, the writing and performance were still closely tied to British and European conventions and standards, and were also firmly under the control of authorities both formal and informal: 'It was not until the 1970s that theatre broke free of the direct censorship of the state and . . . from the more powerful control of respectable, politically conservative and fashionable audiences' (Richard Fotheringham, 'Theatre from 1788 to the 1960s', in *The Cambridge Companion to Australian Literature*, 2000).

Louis Esson is the most prominent Australian playwright of the early twentieth century, writing fourteen plays between 1910 and 1930, of which the best known is the political comedy *The Time is Not Yet Ripe* (*1912*/1912). While his name stands out as an exception, the history of Australian drama up to mid-century otherwise tends to be dominated by the titles of particular plays rather than the names of particular playwrights. Resembling her novel *Coonardoo* (1929) in its frank and controversial treatment of sex and race, Katharine Susannah Prichard's play *Brumby Innes* won a prize in 1927 but was not staged till the 1970s—unlike Betty Roland's *The Touch of Silk* (1928), which has been repeatedly revived, as has Dymphna Cusack's *Morning Sacrifice* (1942). Poet Douglas Stewart is also known for his verse drama, especially the radio play *Fire on the Snow* (1941) and the stage play *Ned Kelly* (1942), while Sumner Locke Elliot's anti-war play *Rusty Bugles* (1948) is the one most often cited as a precursor to *Summer of the Seventeenth Doll* in its 'Australianness', as is Dick Diamond and Miles Maxwell's *Reedy River* (1953).

Summer of the Seventeenth Doll was the joint winner of the 1955 Play-wrights Advisory Board competition with the feminist play *The Torrents* by Oriel Gray, but the former was chosen for stage production while *The Torrents* was not published until it appeared in *The Penguin Anthology of Australian Women's Writing* (1988). But other Australian women writers, telling stories of women's lives, fared better. Dymphna Cusack and Florence James's novel *Come in Spinner* (1951) is a tale of the exploitation of women in wartime. The later 1950s saw the emergence of two of this period's most sophisticated literary novelists, both women: Elizabeth Harrower published her first novel, *Down in the City* (1956), while Thea Astley, whose first novel, *Girl With A Monkey*, was published in 1958, was to become a landmark in the Australian literary landscape for the next four decades. Poet and playwright Dorothy Hewett's first novel, *Bobbin Up* (1959), explores a topic that few Australian novels apart from *Come in Spinner* had ever tackled before: women at work.

Australia's most prestigious and coveted literary prize, the Miles Franklin Literary Award, was won in the year of its inauguration, 1957, by Patrick White for his fifth novel, *Voss* (1957). The prize was won the following year by one of two new young writers who were to become major figures in Australian fiction over the next few decades: Randolph Stow, who won it for his first novel, *To the Islands* (1958). Christopher Koch's first novel, *The Boys in the Island*, was published the same year.

Alan Seymour's play *The One Day of the Year* (*1960*/1962) encapsulates not just one but several different phenomena that were beginning to make themselves felt in Australian society by the beginning of the 1960s. While the play is mainly about the problematic celebration of Anzac Day, a tragic day in Australian history, it also goes further to explore what seemed to be a growing gap between the generations, and to dramatise class tensions in Australian society. Seymour's play is within the tradition of the three-act play with naturalistic dialogue and action, and follows *Summer of the Seventeenth Doll* in this as in its extensive use of Australian speech patterns and idioms.

But the 1960s saw further departures, in both fiction and theatre, from the norms of realism and naturalism. 'Two important playwrights working in the 1960s and '70s, Patrick White and Dorothy Hewett,' says Helen Thomson in *The Oxford Literary History of Australia* (1998), 'had . . . broken with stage naturalism and written non-naturalistic plays which owed much to the world-wide movements of expressionism and surrealism.' As a fiction writer White was already known, if not notorious, for having departed from and railed against the preponderant 'dun-coloured realism' of Australian fiction, as he put it in 'The Prodigal Son', and although it is the emergent 'fabulists' of the 1970s—Peter Carey, Murray Bail, David Ireland and others—who are more usually credited with a decisive departure from realist norms in Australian writing, White, along with Dal Stivens and Hal Porter, was already well advanced along that path.

White's play *The Ham Funeral*, which had been written some years before, had its world premiere in Adelaide in 1961, the same year he published his sixth novel, *Riders in the Chariot*. While less deliberately anti-realist than some of his earlier work, this novel further explores the vein that Carole Ferrier has described in *The Oxford Literary History of Australia* as 'White's simultaneous engagement with the "dun-coloured" and the metaphysical', which is, she argues, what gives his novels 'their peculiar force'. The same year saw the publication of Colin Thiele's *The Sun on the Stubble*, which might now be described as young adult or 'crossover' fiction and which, with George Johnston's *My Brother Jack* (1964) and Randolph Stow's *The Merry-Go-Round in the Sea* (1965), formed a trio of autobiographical fictions of Australian life that were widely studied in schools in the 1960s and left their mark on a generation of Australians.

Thomas Keneally's *Bring Larks and Heroes* (1967), like Hal Porter's earlier novel *The Tilted Cross* (1961), explores the moral and metaphorical complications of Australia's convict history. Peter Mathers's *Trap* (1965) also looks to the country's origins, and was described by Ken Gelder and Paul Salzman in *The New Diversity* (1989) as a precursor to later novels by David Foster and Peter Carey. *Trap* is a disquieting picaresque fantasy about the search for Australia's historical origins 'showing with elaborate and unsettling care', as poet and critic Vincent Buckley wrote in 1974, 'the hypocrisy inherent in current notions of how and why to conduct such a search'.

The 1960s drew to their end with an event that was to catapult the young playwright David Williamson into early fame a couple of years later with the success of his play *Don's Party* (1971). Set on the night of 1969's cliffhanger federal election, in which the Australian Labor Party was narrowly defeated, *Don's Party* shows the effects of the social and sexual revolutions that took place in many parts of the world in the 1960s. But although those effects did not really start to become apparent in Australian literature until the early 1970s, the publication in 1966 of Elizabeth Harrower's *The Watch Tower*, with its savage critique of patriarchal power, and in 1969 of Frank Moorhouse's first book *Futility and Other Animals*, with its explicit treatment of sexual matters, were early indications of what was to come. So were the opening of Sydney's Jane Street Theatre in 1966 and of Melbourne's La Mama the following year, two theatres associated with the 'New Wave' in Australian drama that was gathering force as the decade ended.

In the first half of the 1970s a number of major events took place that transformed Australian literary life. The New Wave dramatists, particularly the Australian Performing Group in Melbourne, were committed to new forms of drama in new venues, produced in accordance with a collaborative ethos that valued rawness and immediacy. The young Sydney short-story writers Frank Moorhouse and Michael Wilding, with Carmel Kelly, established a form of nomadic short-story magazine called *Tabloid Story* in 1972, its successive issues hosted by different existing magazines and journals as an outlet for the more explicit and more experimental writing for which it was otherwise difficult to find a publisher. There was abruptly increased infrastructural and financial support from various sources for theatre in particular and for literature in general, especially after the establishment of the Australia Council for the Arts. During this period Australian censorship restrictions were challenged and eased, having been tested by the violence of Alex Buzo's play *Norm and Ahmed* in 1968. Jack Hibberd's iconic one-man play *A Stretch of the Imagination* (1972/1973) is a brilliant, surreal, obscenity-laced monologue that could not have been staged and probably would not have been written five years earlier.

The publication of Frank Moorhouse's 'discontinuous narrative' *The Americans, Baby* (1972) consolidated his reputation as a major Australian writer, which he has sustained ever since. The mid-1970s saw the publication of three debut collections of short fiction by writers who would go on to became equally significant novelists in the following decades: David Foster's *North South West: Three novellas* (1973), Peter Carey's *The Fat Man in History* (1974) and Murray Bail's *Contemporary Portraits* (1975). Moorhouse, Bail and Carey, with Morris Lurie and Michael Wilding, made up the five writers who featured in Brian Kiernan's influential 1977 short-story anthology *The Most Beautiful Lies*; the five writers have in common, argues Kiernan in his introduction, 'a tendency for their stories to present themselves self-consciously as "fictions", to be less mimetic, less concerned with character and social situation and more with style and form . . . and a tendency to employ less realistic forms, such as the fable and the science-fiction tale'. Other important fiction writers of the 1970s include short-story writer

Peter Cowan and novelists Barbara Hanrahan, Thea Astley and David Ireland, the last-named sharing the 'fabulist' label with Carey and Bail. Ireland's highly politicised novels won him three Miles Franklin Awards in eight years, for *The Unknown Industrial Prisoner* (1971), *The Glass Canoe* (1976) and *A Woman of the Future* (1979).

While literary-historical fiction questioning the long-held assumptions of traditional, triumphalist Australian history was to dominate Australian writing through the late 1980s and '90s, there was in the mid-1970s an early anticipation of this trend by three novelists in particular: Thomas Keneally in *The Chant of Jimmie Blacksmith* (1972) and Thea Astley in *A Kindness Cup* (1974) both revisit historical events revolving around racial tension and violence, while Jessica Anderson's *The Commandant* (1975) is a small but powerful fictional treatment of the Moreton Bay penal settlement's notoriously harsh Captain Patrick Logan and his mysterious, violent death in 1830.

The contents of *The Most Beautiful Lies* appeared to suggest that all the most significant fiction writers in Australia were men. But in the same year that anthology was published, Helen Garner's *Monkey Grip* (1977) became a cult novel—particularly in Garner's home city of Melbourne—with its frankness about the countercultural life, its fearless and stylistically precise treatment of emotional conditions and states, and perhaps most of all in the way it unselfconsciously placed female subjectivity at the centre of its world view. Jessica Anderson's equally successful *Tirra Lirra by the River*, published the following year, is likewise a novel about female emancipation and the difficulties of achieving and maintaining an independent life. And as the influence of second wave feminism began to make itself felt in Australian writing, the two main women dramatists of the 1970s, Alma de Groen and Dorothy Hewett, were both writing complex, allusive and non-naturalistic plays along increasingly feminist lines—though Hewett, in her poetry and fiction as well as in her plays, had been focusing on women's experience and consciousness from the beginning of her writing career.

Along with *Monkey Grip* and *Tirra Lirra by the River*, four more notable novels from the end of the decade were Christopher Koch's *The Year of Living Dangerously* (1978), Patrick White's last full-length novel, *The Twyborn Affair* (1979), David Ireland's controversial *A Woman of the Future* (1979) and Murray Bail's first novel, the sophisticated and ambitious *Homesickness* (1980). These six major achievements ushered in a decade of unprecedented productivity and achievement in Australian fiction, much of it written by women; writers and publishers alike had begun to realise by the late 1970s that there was a vast market for literary fiction by women writers. Those who emerged in the course of the 1980s as major figures included Elizabeth Jolley, Beverley Farmer, Kate Grenville and Olga Masters, in addition to

Anderson, Hanrahan and Garner, who all continued to publish fiction. Thea Astley had been publishing fiction steadily since the late 1950s, but her contemporaries Jolley and Masters had late-blooming careers.

After Peter Carey's first novel, *Bliss* (1981), he produced a novel at the steady rate of one every three years for the next 25 years, many of them winning national and international prizes; despite his relocation to New York, Carey has continued to write fiction about Australia. David Malouf, who began his literary career as a poet before diversifying into fiction in the mid-1970s, published *Harland's Half Acre* in 1984, while Tim Winton gained notice in his early twenties with his first novel, *An Open Swimmer* (1982); like Carey, both Malouf and Winton have continued to dominate Australian fiction into the twenty-first century. Others who began to publish fiction in this period—often collections of short stories, which seemed to go abruptly out of fashion some time in the early 1990s—and who have remained productive over the subsequent two decades include Robert Drewe, Marion Halligan, Barry Hill, Nicholas Jose, Gerald Murnane and Gerard Windsor. Peter Cowan also reappeared in the second half of the 1980s, publishing three novels in four years, and Peter Goldsworthy, better known up to this point as a poet and short-story writer, published his first novel, *Maestro*, in 1989.

What Helen Thomson in *The Oxford Literary History of Australia* has identified as the 'second wave' emerging in contemporary Australian drama in the late 1970s was dominated through to the following decade by Stephen Sewell, Michael Gow and the particularly prolific Louis Nowra. Gow's popular and accessible *Away* (*1986*/1986) has been repeatedly revived. Sewell is known for passionate, overtly political drama with an international focus. Nowra, too, has given many of his plays international and often exotic settings; another distinguishing characteristic of his work is the frequent inclusion of Aboriginal characters and issues. Thomson adds Dorothy Hewett's, Patrick White's and Alma de Groen's later plays to this 'second wave' group, partly to distinguish them from the different goals and techniques of the early 1970s 'first wave'.

The 1980s saw unprecedented infrastructural support for literature, as the Literature Board of the Australia Council expanded its programs, more and more literary prizes were established, publishers including the influential Brian Johns at Penguin expanded their Australian operations, and writers' centres and writers' festivals were established in almost every capital city. The 1988 Australian Bicentenary saw a large number of historical novels, stories and plays that coincided with the Bicentennial by accident or design: Peter Carey's *Oscar and Lucinda*, Kate Grenville's fantasy-feminist-revisionist *Joan Makes History* and Rodney Hall's *Captivity Captive* were all published, and Michael Gow's *1841* first produced, in 1988. Negative literary reactions to the Bicentenary, apart from Grenville's feminist critique, included

Sam Watson's novel of Aboriginal revenge and violence *The Kadaitcha Sung* (1990), Andrew McGahan's anti-triumphalist novel *1988* (1995), and Patrick White's deliberate delaying of the publication of *Patrick White Speaks* (1989) in order to avoid, as a form of protest against the triumphalist celebrations, publishing anything that year at all.

The early 1990s saw the emergence of three important new women playwrights, each with one particularly successful play: Hannie Rayson's *Hotel Sorrento* (1990) and Joanna Murray-Smith's *Honour* (1995) both deal with the same kinds of middle-class dilemmas directly reflecting theatre audiences' lives that David Williamson had been mining for material since 1970, while *Diving for Pearls* (1991) by Katherine Thomson, who has also won awards for screenwriting, has a more politicised focus on working-class Australians and their struggles in an economic-rationalist climate. Other significant plays of the 1990s included Louis Nowra's *Cosi* (1992) and *Radiance* (1993), Michael Gow's *Furious* (1991), Nick Enright's *Daylight Saving* (1991) and *Blackrock* (1995), *All Souls* (1993) by Daniel Keene, and David Williamson's *Dead White Males* (1995). Some of these plays, and other works of fiction and drama, from classic to contemporary, have been adapted for the screen according to the fluctuating fortunes of the Australian film and television industry.

During the same period several major novels were published by established fiction writers, including David Malouf's *The Great World* (1990) and *Remembering Babylon* (1993), Tim Winton's *Cloudstreet* (1991), Frank Moorhouse's *Grand Days* (1993) and Kate Grenville's *Dark Places* (1994), the bleakly powerful sequel to her first novel *Lilian's Story* (1985). From the so-called grunge school of the early 1990s emerged novelists Andrew McGahan and Christos Tsiolkas, now both established literary figures with a broadened set of approaches and techniques and a substantial body of work.

In 1995, a productive but strange year for the Australian novel, Christos Tsiolkas's *Loaded* and Helen Demidenko's *The Hand that Signed the Paper* both sparked extended controversy for quite different reasons. The former was sexually graphic and explicit, while the latter was an award-winning hoax that raised troubling questions about the ethical responsibilities of fiction writers. Christopher Koch continued his long-standing engagement with Asian–Australian relations in *Highways to a War* and Amanda Lohrey moved from the more overtly politicised fiction of her earlier books to the more personal politics of cohabitation and food in *Camille's Bread*. The following year saw the publication of David Foster's large, complex and brilliant novel *The Glade Within the Grove*, which demonstrates all of Foster's best gifts as a satirist and storyteller and brings together the various broad-ranging concerns that have characterised his fiction over the last twenty years.

Brian Castro and Gail Jones, two writers whose work engages substantially and self-referentially with issues of literary and psychoanalytic theory and sometimes even uses them as subject matter, became increasingly visible figures in the literary landscape during the 1990s and have emerged as major novelists in the twenty-first century, as have two younger writers whose first novels appeared a year apart: Delia Falconer (*The Service of Clouds*, 1997) and Elliot Perlman (*Three Dollars*, 1998).

The interest in historical fictions continued through the 1990s with a number of novels. Robert Drewe's *Our Sunshine* (1991) is a brief but poetic and evocative treatment of the seemingly inexhaustible Ned Kelly story, while Rodney Hall's *Yandilli Trilogy* (1988–93) spans over a century. Malouf's *Remembering Babylon* deals with early contact between Aboriginal people and white settlers, and Peter Carey's *Jack Maggs* (1997) is a postcolonial revisiting of the convict character Magwitch from *Great Expectations*, as well as a fictional version of Dickens himself. Along with Elizabeth Jolley's semi-autobiographical trilogy—*My Father's Moon* (1989), *Cabin Fever* (1990) and *The Georges' Wife* (1993)—Malouf's *The Great World*, Moorhouse's *Grand Days* and Kim Scott's *Benang* (1999) all revisit earlier eras of the twentieth century.

Historical fiction of the 'literary' kind was certainly nothing new in Australian writing, but such had been its dominance in the late 1980s and through the 1990s that writers Drusilla Modjeska (in *Timepieces*, 2002) and David Marr (in 'The Role of the Writer in John Howard's Australia', 2003) were both moved to make public pleas that fiction writers should focus more on contemporary life. But since 2000 it has been the playwrights who have engaged most directly with the immediate concerns of Australian public and political life, the Australian stage dominated by such plays as Rayson's *Life After George* (2000), Sewell's *Myth, Propaganda and Disaster in Nazi Germany and Contemporary America* (2003) and Williamson's *Influence* (2005).

In fiction, however, many writers continued to examine the past and use it to shed light on the present. Moorhouse's *Dark Palace* (2000), a 'companion novel' to *Grand Days*, furthers his exploration of the League of Nations and its ideals, while Carey's *True History of the Kelly Gang* (2000) retells yet again one of Australian history's most enduring stories. Richard Flanagan's wildly imaginative *Gould's Book of Fish* (2001) is set mainly in 1828 and tells the appalling story of the massacre of the Tasmanian Aborigines; Roger McDonald's *The Ballad of Desmond Kale* (2005) is also set in the early nineteenth century, exploring the origins of the sheep and wool trade that formed a central plank of Australia's prosperity for so long. Kate Grenville's *The Secret River* (2005) is again set during the same period, based on the true story of a convict ancestor and addressing the history of first contact between Aboriginal Australians and settlers in NSW.

But Tim Winton's *Dirt Music* (2001), Peter Goldsworthy's *Three Dog Night* (2003), Alex Miller's *Journey to the Stone Country* (2002) and Robert Drewe's *Grace* (2005) are all set in contemporary Australia; some of these engage with Aboriginal issues past and present, as Gail Jones's *Sorry* (2007) does more directly and dramatically. Brian Castro's 'autobiographical fiction' *Shanghai Dancing* (2003) is itself a meditation on race, origins and identity, while Venero Armanno's *The Volcano* (2001) is about the postwar wave of European immigration to Australia and the lives of the migrants thereafter. Elliot Perlman's *Seven Types of Ambiguity* (2003) engages directly and passionately with contemporary social issues in Australian life, while the prolific Thomas Keneally's *The Tyrant's Novel* (2003), like Eva Sallis's *The Marsh Birds* (2005) and Drewe's *Grace*, critically addresses Australia's treatment of asylum seekers from the Middle East.

The field of Australian fiction has been enriched by the presence of Nobel laureate J.M. Coetzee, who migrated to Australia in 2002 and whose most recent novels' Australian characters and settings have not obscured his internationalist concerns. Several of the younger fiction writers who were making their names in the 1990s—including Delia Falconer, Elliot Perlman, Michelle de Kretser, Christos Tsiolkas, Sonya Hartnett, James Bradley, Hsu-Ming Teo, and Malcolm Knox—have also had national and international successes since 2000 with new books.

But perhaps the most important development in Australian fiction since the turn of the century has been the emergence of Aboriginal writer Alexis Wright, whose multi-award-winning novel *Carpentaria* (2006) recalls a handful of other large, complex and wholly original Australian novels over the preceding century—Joseph Furphy's *Such is Life* (1903), Xavier Herbert's *Capricornia* (1938), David Foster's *The Glade Within the Grove* (1996)—and seems set to become, like them, a giant in the Australian literary landscape. *Carpentaria* breaks new ground not only in its subject matter and technique, but also in furthering white Australia's understanding of Aboriginal thought and ways of being.

Kerryn Goldsworthy

POETRY AND NON-FICTION
FROM 1950

Central to Australian literature since 1950 are the ideological conflicts that became part of an emergent 'Australian modernity', seen through economic, technological and social developments, as well as in renewed forms of cultural nationalism. While the British empire (transformed into the Commonwealth) and that mythical place 'the bush' continued to be important to notions of Australian identity, such concepts operated in a new context in which writers and artists began to imagine Australia as urban, coastal, modern and, more anxiously, multicultural and Indigenous. This change in self-representation was a response to material changes in Australian society and a signal of a new self-consciousness that is a distinguishing feature of the period.

One response to this burgeoning cultural nationalism was a potentially paradoxical one: expatriation. Germaine Greer, Clive James, Robert Hughes and Barry Humphries are the most famous literary figures of a large group of postwar expatriate Australian artists. In the light of expatriation (both a remnant of Australia's colonial status, and a new form of cultural independence) it is notable that issues of identity have informed the writing of all four, who have written autobiographies, and have periodically concerned themselves with anatomising Australian 'identity' in polemical, satirical, iconoclastic and comic ways.

These writers illustrate a clear link between literature and public-sphere issues such as 'national identity'. But it is also important, in any representation of Australian writing since 1950, to be open to alternative and competing versions of 'the literary' and 'Australia'. The poems of Michael Leunig are paradigmatic in this respect. Leunig's poems usually occur within apparently non-literary contexts: his cartoons. Appearing in the metropolitan press, they may not seem to be 'literature' at all, or else they are examples of literature in its most public and politically engaged state. And yet even his most 'political' work gestures towards a realm beyond politics, where the poetic, the comic and the existential coexist as a way of making life in the political realm more bearable.

The question of what constitutes literature, then, has become more complex in recent decades. And while literature in the 1950s was understood in its most constricted sense—as fiction, prose and drama—fifty years on, two of that era's defining literary documents are essays: A.A. Phillips's 'The Cultural Cringe' and Patrick White's 'The Prodigal Son'. Concerned with Australian cultural independence, both essays present an anxious, if ultimately optimistic, approach to literary production and its role in defining Australian identity.

Poetry Since 1950

The 1970s are generally remembered as an especially fertile time for poetry. However, the 'poetry explosion' of the 1970s should not obscure for us the extraordinary developments in Australian poetry between 1950 and 1970—developments noted by Francis Webb in 1964 when he wrote to Gwen Harwood that 'surely nowhere save perhaps in the Middle Ages has there been such an efflorescence of poetry as this here in Australia'. But the period after the Second World War has also been characterised as one of reaction, a rejection of the radicalism of the 1940s seen in the work of the Jindyworobaks, the Angry Penguins and, most disruptively, the fictitious poet Ern Malley. The Ern Malley affair was often blamed for impeding the development of poetic modernism in Australia. Certainly, and despite their differing positions regarding modernism, most of the major poets of the mid-twentieth century—Douglas Stewart, A.D. Hope, James McAuley, Judith Wright, Francis Webb, David Campbell and Rosemary Dobson—favoured clarity of expression and a formalist style.

Despite the political conservatism of the Menzies years (1949–66) and the apparent stylistic conservatism of the poetry of the period, one shouldn't too quickly make assumptions about the closeness of fit between formalist and rationalist—or reactionary—impulses in that poetry. The powers of the irrational and primitive are seen in the poetry of Hope, McAuley and Harwood. Webb's poetry is especially attracted to the frightening limits of the imagination. His most important works present disquieting landscapes of the self through the trope of exploration, presenting the inner states of Australian explorers caught within expressionistic landscapes. The importance of such poems is seen in Douglas Stewart's anthology, *Voyager Poems* (1960). The opening poem, Kenneth Slessor's 'Five Visions of Captain Cook' (1931), formed the template for such works, being a highly lyrical, historically self-conscious sequence.

The 1960s saw a continuation of many of the concerns and modes of the 1950s. In addition to its formalist and traditionalist tendencies, poetry in the period was concerned with history (political and cultural) and a wide-ranging intertextuality in a revisionist project that reassessed both past and present in the light of Australian modernity and cultural nationalism. Such 'intellectual' poetry—to quote Rodney Hall and Thomas Shapcott in their 1968 anthology, *New Impulses in Australian Poetry*—suggests the self-conscious (even 'political') nature of the mid-century poets, perhaps best exemplified in the work of Judith Wright. Modernist in outlook, if not style, Wright approaches modernity as a series of crises—concerning the human subject, the environment and politics—that can be responded to through metaphysical and ethical frameworks.

The period's historical self-consciousness is also seen in the revitalisation of the pastoral mode. Wright's pastoral poems prefigure David Campbell's revisions of the ballad form in works like *The Miracle of Mullion Hill* (1956) and, more radically, the later 'Kelly Country' (1974). Such works showed the new complexity of the pastoral mode, which allowed (albeit ambivalently) a place for women and Indigenous Australians. It is also worth noting the attention poets gave to the suburbs, those ambiguous sites of modern Australian identity. The early poetry of Chris Wallace-Crabbe, Bruce Dawe and Gwen Harwood often represent the suburbs as sources of both authenticity and alienation.

However much the 'New Australian Poetry' of the 1970s (or the Generation of '68) wished to appear entirely new, it was nevertheless furthering developments begun in the 1950s and '60s, especially that period's cultural self-consciousness and revisionist nationalism. Part of the difference of post-1970 poetry can be ascribed to changes in cultural production and politics: new and cheaper printing and copying technologies; changing attitudes towards the war in Vietnam; and the dissolution of censorship (after a last-gasp resurgence in the 1960s). Such changes helped produce an explosion of poetry (in magazines, collections and readings), and a rejection by many younger poets of 'establishment' values (mainstream journals, sponsorship by the academy and the reification of the 'well-made' poem).

The New Australian Poetry sought modernisation through free verse, open forms, concrete poetry, prose poetry, poetry readings and so on. Its progressivist poetics were mixed (not always coherently) with a social-revolutionary project in which notions of quality were sometimes presented as reactionary. Early examples tended towards late-modernist neo-Romanticism, as exemplified by Michael Dransfield—dead in his twenties—but the term neo-Romantic is less stable when considering Robert Adamson, who ranges widely across concerns and styles. Poets associated with the Generation of '68, such as Alan Wearne, John A. Scott, John Tranter, Laurie Duggan, John Forbes and Martin Johnston, were all notably anti-Romantic in their poetics. Despite these poets' differences, they are all recognisably postmodern in their elaborate engagements with textuality, which include an attraction to irony, intertextuality and parody.

Two radical poetry anthologies of the 1970s and '80s show that the Generation of '68, while sensitive to progressivist poetics, was not a movement especially attuned to the politics of gender and race. *Mother I'm Rooted: An anthology of Australian women poets* (1975), edited by Kate Jennings, was a response to the patriarchal nature of the literary establishment, while *Inside Black Australia: An anthology of Aboriginal poetry* (1988), edited by Kevin Gilbert, was a response to 200 years of dispossession. In both, usual notions of 'good' or 'bad' poetry are seen as products of hegemonic, white, patriarchal discourse. Given the long-standing suppression of women's political speech it is notable how much political poetry since the 1970s has come from women poets, such as Gig Ryan, J.S. Harry, Pam Brown and Jennifer Maiden, whose work is also often marked by an attendant obliquity. The work of older poets such as Fay Zwicky and Jennifer Strauss thematically links the political and the personal through wide-ranging essays into the relationship between identity and responsibility.

Other approaches were being taken throughout the 1970s and '80s, as seen in the poetry of Kevin Hart, Geoff Page, Alan Gould, Robert Gray and Geoffrey Lehmann, all of whom wrote poetry that is recognisably different in style and temperament from that of the Generation of '68. Often less openly 'experimental', such poets were nevertheless all internationalist and strongly contemporary in approach. Hart's pared-back lyrics, for instance, show an affinity with non-Anglophone poetic traditions and postmodern literary theory.

Poets born between 1925 and 1940—including Vincent Buckley, Bruce Beaver, Peter Porter, Vivian Smith, Andrew Taylor, R.A. Simpson, David Malouf, Wallace-Crabbe, Strauss, Zwicky, Shapcott and Hall—all wrote (or write) poetry deeply informed by a variety of contemporary poetics. Beaver's *Letters to Live Poets* (1969), with its use of confession, American models and freed-up prosody, was influential on the younger poets of the 1970s. In turn, poets such as Buckley (and the older Campbell) changed their own poetics in response to developments in the 1970s. The poet-critic Martin Harrison is surely right, then, to argue in *Who Wants to Create Australia?* (2004) that Australian literary histories have been overly reliant on 'an underlying genetic mode' dependent on notions of inheritance, derivation and generationalism.

Harrison's additional argument that two key thematic continuities in contemporary Australian poetry are self and place becomes especially important in light of the social changes brought about by postwar migration. Despite associations with nationalist ideology and nostalgia, place has remained a central poetic trope for diverse poets, especially those of ethnic minority backgrounds who have emerged since the 1980s. By emphasising the complexity of cultural identity (especially identity as performative, hybrid and ambiguous), poets such as Ania Walwicz, Peter Skrzynecki, Adam Aitken, Yahia Al-Samawy and Ouyang Yu show in diverse ways how profoundly (and problematically) related are the concepts of self and place.

Even an approach to self and place as apparently nationalist as Les Murray's illustrates complexity and diversity. Murray—the most internationally successful and most locally recognised of Australia's modern poets—is a complex figure. His career has been marked by polemic and controversy, and his poetry—despite its populist ambitions—is linguistically complex, formally sophisticated and encyclopaedic in interest. It is also the most significant instance of the renewal of the pastoral mode in this period, figuring the bush as a source of revitalisation and social cohesion.

Despite (or because of) Murray's success, the pastoral mode has increasingly provoked anti-pastoral expression among other poets, such as Philip Hodgins and John Kinsella, who powerfully de-romanticise rural life. Kinsella's anti-pastoral works, such as *The New Arcadia* (2005), reveal the hidden violence of the pastoral scene: the violent dispossession of Indigenous people, eroded and poisoned landscapes, and brutal farming practices. Kinsella is also one of a number of writers from this period who illustrate the importance of 'regionalism' in modern literary culture (though he is Australia's most 'international regionalist', as a poem like 'The Vital Waters' shows).

An important feature of poetry since the 1990s has been the move away from the lyric mode, something evident in Kinsella's experimental works, collected as *Doppler Effect* (2004). Poets such as Harry, Maiden, Duggan, Pam Brown and Ken Bolton habitually use the essayistic mode, in part as a critique of the lyric mode and its representational claims. The development of the lyric mode is also seen in the number of ambitious and eccentric works published in recent times, including Luke Davies's ecstatic love poetry in *Totem* (2004) and Harry's 'Peter Henry Lepus' poems collected in *Not Finding Wittgenstein* (2007). To this list we might add John Clarke's parodies, *The Complete Book of Australian Verse* (1989).

A turn to narrative, something prefigured by the Voyager poems, occurred in the 1970s and is still observable today. The most popular narrative poems have been Dorothy Porter's verse novels, especially *The Monkey's Mask* (1994). Other notable verse novels include Murray's *The Boys Who Stole the Funeral* (1980) and *Fredy Neptune* (1998), Hodgins's *Dispossessed* (1994), Philip Salom's *The Well Mouth* (2005) and those by Geoff Page. The period has also seen the rise of 'documentary' poetry, such as Duggan's *The Ash Range* (1987) and Jordie Albiston's *Botany Bay Document* (1996).

Nevertheless, lyric poetry as traditionally conceived remains the default mode for most poets. The work of Peter Steele, Judith Beveridge and Sarah Day shows the returns that continued investment in the well-made lyric can offer. Other poets, such as Kevin Brophy, Jennifer Harrison, Craig Sherborne and Tracy Ryan, have a more hybrid style, accessing the unsettling energies of the subconscious through surrealism and literary revisionism. And poets such as Stephen Edgar illustrate a return to formalism, less weighted by the humanist politics of the postwar generation. In the lyric poetry of Peter Rose, Peter Goldsworthy, David Malouf and Peter Porter, wit attempts to exert a hold over the brute conditions of reality.

The lyric mode remains viable in part because it is so often placed under pressure. Poets such as Kinsella, Emma Lew, Anthony Lawrence and Jill Jones routinely offer uncanny versions of the world that are both lyrical and suspicious of the lyric impulse. We could term this a 'new lyricism', in which a toughness and pronounced theoretical sophistication can be found within lyrical expression. The common factor between these younger poets, their older contemporaries and the postwar poets is their self-conscious attitude to modernity, national identity and the project of poetry itself.

Non-fiction From 1950

While the essay was integral to literary culture in the 1950s, it was the rise of autobiography in the 1960s, and the associated, later rise of 'life writing' in the 1990s, that confirmed the heightened literary status of non-fiction in Australia. Hal Porter's *The Watcher on the Cast-Iron Balcony* (1963) has become the definitive Australian literary autobiography of the period, no doubt in part because of its conspicuous, and self-conscious, *literary* condition. Its highly stylised account of childhood relies on an almost-hypnotic listing of detail, a rich evocation of place, complex narrative techniques and a mythopoeic attitude towards childhood.

Autobiography of childhood has been the most successful form of literary autobiography since the 1960s. By choosing to understand the relationship between the self and society through the trope of childhood, modern Australian autobiographers such as Porter and Jill Ker Conway (in *The Road from Coorain*, 1989) engaged in profoundly political discussions to do with nationhood and personal identity in terms that were (or appeared to be) relatively ideologically neutral. The political dimension can be seen, however, in the emphasis in such works on beginnings. Autobiographies of childhood are narratives of beginnings, and beginnings are important and volatile things for a settler nation, since they are inherently related to issues of identity and legitimacy. The emphasis on personal beginnings in modern Australian autobiography usually relates to wider social or historical beginnings, which often raise non-Indigenous anxieties concerning Australian identity. The relationship between place and anxiety concerning beginnings is found, for instance, in the emphasis in modern Australian autobiography on childhood houses. Malouf's *12 Edmondstone Street*—and his related essay, 'A First Place'— deals with the anxieties (personal, familial, national) engendered by a culture (symbolised by the family home) that is deemed 'too close to beginnings'.

A more pointed emphasis on place and displacement can be seen in the autobiographies of migrant writers through the period. Mary Rose Liverani's

The Winter Sparrows (1975) charts the author's migration from Scotland to Australia in a relatively early example of modern migration-autobiography. Since the 1990s, ethnic minority writing has become increasingly central to the literature. Works such as Andrew Riemer's *Inside Outside* (1992) and Alice Pung's *Unpolished Gem* (2006) have figured the complex interaction between memory and forgetting, as well as the relationship between identity and parody in the migrant experience. The works of Chi Vu and William Yang show not only the rise of Asian-Australian voices, but also the move of autobiographical writing into multi-modal representation (such as theatre and photography).

Since the early 1990s, autobiography has been both formally diverse and politically charged. Eric Michaels's *Unbecoming: An AIDS diary* (1990) and Sasha Soldatow and Christos Tsiolkas's dialogic autobiography *Jump Cuts* (1996) are self-reflexive works that deal explicitly with the relationship between sexual identity and politics. These join a long list of formally divergent works—such as Drusilla Modjeska's ficto-auto/biographical *Poppy* (1990)—that have been part of a shift in thinking away from 'autobiography' to 'life writing'. The hybridity of the latter term can be seen in Helen Garner's *The First Stone* (1995) and *Joe Cinque's Consolation* (2004), which are by turns reportage, biography and autobiography. Garner's emphasis on justice and social and personal responsibility is indicative of a change in literary culture, in which auto/biographical life writing has become associated with the figure of the public intellectual as a mode for discussing the self in terms of larger historical and social issues. Related to this interest in larger issues has been the rising importance of crisis in auto/biographical writing. Crises—of identity, nation, history and faith—are central to works as diverse as Inga Clendinnen's *Tiger's Eye* (2000), Robert Dessaix's *A Mother's Disgrace* (1994), Robert Drewe's *The Shark Net* (2000) and Jacob G. Rosenberg's *East of Time* (2005).

While biography has tended to retain its status as 'factual' writing, the form in this period has also become more 'literary'. Works such as Brian Matthews' ground-breaking (and un-extractable) biography of Louisa Lawson, *Louisa* (1987), have self-reflexively undermined the authority of the univocal, objective biographer. In her double biography of the Australian artists Stella Bowen and Grace Cossington Smith, *Stravinsky's Lunch* (1999), Modjeska highlights the imaginative component of biographical thinking. David Marr's biography of Patrick White (1990) is an account of being gay as much as being a writer, and shows the growing importance of identity politics to the genre.

Like auto/biography, the essay has linked issues of public importance with personal reflection. While the essays by Phillips and White show the importance of the essay to public literary culture (especially in the 1950s and '60s), a work such as Helen Garner's 'At the Morgue' shows the form's potential range, covering the personal and the public, the practical and the metaphysical, the humorous and the profound. The essay form can also accommodate the utterly individual voice of a writer like Gerald Murnane, as well as the literary advocacy of Rosie Scott's 'The Value of Writers'.

Even more than the essay, historical writing has an ambiguous status as a form of literary discourse. The best-known history of the period is the most literary: Manning Clark's *A History of Australia* (six volumes, 1962–87). The use of large-scale themes, leitmotifs and a language that borrows heavily from the Bible, the Book of Common Prayer and the canonical works of literature give Clark's narrative an epic quality not often found in scholarly history.

The other significant historian of the period, Geoffrey Blainey, was also an iconoclast, as seen in his anti-radical interpretation of the Eureka Stockade in *The Rush that Never Ended* (1963). The title of Blainey's *The Tyranny of Distance* (1966) gave an idiomatic phrase to Australian self-definition. More contentiously, Blainey also coined the term 'black-armband history' to describe what he saw as a version of Australian history that focused unduly on Indigenous dispossession, environmental damage and a culture of sexism and racism. The contestatory nature of contemporary history can be seen in the revisionism of feminist historians in the 1970s. Anne Summers's *Damned Whores and God's Police: The colonisation of women in Australia* (1975) was a landmark feminist critique of Australian history and society. Other historians have helped revise notions of nationhood in less overtly ideological ways, such as Ken Inglis in *Sacred Places: War memorials in the Australian landscape* (1998).

More ephemeral forms of non-fiction, such as the speech, the letter and the diary, also have a place in Australian literary culture. As a public marking of events, speeches seek to be both of the moment and enduring, and they require a diction that is both literary and demotic. Paul Keating's 'Redfern' speech recognised that 'complex as our contemporary identity is, it cannot be separated from Aboriginal Australia'. His speech on 'Waltzing Matilda' illustrates the connections that Australians continue to make with their colonial, and literary, past.

Letters, unlike speeches, are generally private documents between individuals, coming to light only after the death of their authors. Significant editions of letters by modern literary figures have appeared in recent years, including those of Mary Gilmore, Patrick White, Xavier Herbert, Christina Stead, Judith Wright and Gwen Harwood. The private element of letters and diaries can allow for new perspectives on the past. The diary of the artist Donald Friend shows a cosmopolitan and erotic element not always associated with 'Australianness'.

David McCooey

The

LITERATURE

of

AUSTRALIA

GEORGE WORGAN
1757–1838

Letter writer George Worgan was born in London. He trained as a naval surgeon and in this capacity served on board the *Sirius*, the flagship of Governor Phillip's First Fleet, which arrived in Sydney in January 1788 to establish a British penal settlement. He made several expeditions to the Hawkesbury River and Broken Bay areas north of Sydney and spent a year on Norfolk Island after the *Sirius* was wrecked there. In 1791 he returned to England, leaving the navy in about 1800 to settle on a farm. His letter to his brother, which includes a journal kept between January and July 1788, provides many insights into the early days of the settlement, including the first encounters with Aboriginal people. The manuscript was donated to the Mitchell Library in 1955 and published as *Journal of a First Fleet Surgeon* in 1978. EW

From *Journal of a First Fleet Surgeon*
Letter to His Brother

Sirius, Sydney Cove, Port Jackson
June 12th 1788

Dear Richard,

I think I hear You saying, 'Where the D–ce is Sydney Cove Port Jackson?' and see You whirling the Letter about to find out the Name of the Scribe: Perhaps You have taken up Salmons Gazetteer, if so, pray spare your Labour, and attend to Me for half an Hour—We sailed from the *Cape of Good Hope* on the 12th of November 1787—As that was the last civilised Country We should touch at, in our Passage to *Botany Bay* We provided ourselves with every Article, necessary for the forming a civilised Colony, Live Stock, consisting of Bulls, Cows, Horses Mares, Colts, Sheep, Hogs, Goats Fowls and other living Creatures by Pairs. We likewise, procured a vast Number of Plants, Seeds & other Garden articles, such as Orange, Lime, Lemon, Quince Apple, Pear Trees, in a Word, every Vegetable Production that the Cape afforded. Thus Equipped, each Ship like another Noah's Ark, away we steered for *Botany Bay*, and after a tolerably pleasant Voyage of 10 Weeks & 2 Days *Governour Phillip*, had the Satisfaction to see the whole of his little Fleet safe at Anchor in the said *Bay*.

As we were sailing in We saw 8 or 10 of the Natives, sitting on the Rocks on the South Shore, and as the Ships bordered pretty near thereto, we could hear them hollow, and observe them talking to one another very earnestly, at the same time pointing towards the Ships; they were of a black reddish sooty Colour, entirely naked, walked very upright, and each of them had long Spears and a short Stick in their hands, soon after the Ships had anchored, the Indians went up into the Wood, lit a Fire, and sat Around about it, as unconcerned (apparently,) as tho' nothing had occurred to them. Two Boats from the *Sirius*, were now Manned and armed, and the *Governor*, accompanied by Captn. Hunter, and several other Officers, went towards the Shore, where they had seen the Natives, who perceiving the Boats making towards the Beach, came out of the Wood, and walked along, some distance from the Water-side, but immediately on the Boats landing, they scampered up into the Woods again, with great Precipitation. On this, the Governor, advised, that we should seem quite indifferent about them, and this apparent Indifference had a good Effect, for they very soon appeared in sight of Us, When, the Governor held up some Beads, Red Cloth & other Bawbles and made signs for them to advance, but they still were exceedingly shy & timid, and would not be enticed by our allurements; which the Governor perceiving, He shewed them his Musket, then laid it on the Ground, advancing singly towards them, they now seeing that He had nothing in his Hands like a Weapon, one of the oldest of the Natives gave his Spears to a younger, and approached to meet the Governor, but not without discovering manifest tokens of Fear, and distrust, making signs for the things to be laid on the Ground which, the *Governor* complying with, He advanced, tooke them up, and went back to his Companions; Another, came forth and wanted some of the same kind of Presents, which, were given to Him by the same Method, at length, after various Methods to impress them with the Belief that We meant them no harm, they suffered Us to come up to them, and after making them all presents, which they received with much the same kind of Pleasure, which Children shew at such Bawbles, just looking at them, then holding out their Hands for more, some laughing heartily, and jumping extravagantly; they began to shew a Confidence, and became very familiar, and curious about our Cloaths, feeling the Coat, Waistcoat, and even the Shirt and on seeing one of the Gentlemen pull off his Hat, they all set up a loud Hoop, one was curious enough to take hold of a Gentlemans Hair that was cued, and called to his Companions to look at it, this was the occasion of another loud Hoop, accompanied with other Emotions of Astonishment. In a Word, they seemed pretty well divested of their Fears, and became very funny Fellows.

They suffered the Sailors to dress them with different coloured Papers, and Fools-Caps, which pleased them mightily, the strange contrast these Decorations made with their black Complexion brought strongly to my Mind, the Chimney-Sweepers in London on a May-Day.—They were all Men & Boys in this Tribe.

I should have told You, that the Governor, left the *Sirius* soon after we sailed from the *Cape of Good Hope*; and Embarked on Board the *Supply Brig* & Gave up the Command of the Convoy to Captn. Hunter, in order that he might proceed on before the main Body of the Fleet, but he arrived in Botany Bay, only two Days before Us. In this Time, He had obtained an Intercourse or two, with some Natives on the *North Shore*, but, as the Means which he took to gain their Confidence, and effect a Parley, were much the same as those, I have given you an account of, I shall only mention a few singular Circumstances that occurred in these Intercourses. The *Supply Brig*, arrived in the *Bay* about 2 °Clk in the Afternoon, of the 18th January and at 4 °Clock, The Governor, attended by several Officers, went in two armed Boats towards a part of the Shore where, 6 of the Natives, were, and had been sitting the whole time the *Supply* was entering the Bay, looking and pointing at Her with great Earnestness; When the Boats had approached pretty near this Spot, two of the Natives got up, and came close to the Waters-Edge, making Motions, pointing to another part of the Shore and talking very fast & loud, seemingly, as if the Part to which they pointed, was better landing for the Boats, they could not however, discern any thing unfriendly, or threatening in the Signs and Motions which the Natives made.—Accordingly the Boats coasted along the Shore in a Direction for the Place, to which, they had been directed, the Natives following on the Beach. In the mean Time, the Governor, or somebody in his Boat, made Signs that they wanted Water, this they signified by putting a Hat over the Side of the Boat and seeming to take up some of the salt Water put it to his Mouth, the Natives, immediately, understood this Sign and with great Willingness to Oblige, pointed to the Westward, and walked that Way, apparently with an Intention to show their Visitors the very Spot. The Boats steered towards the Place, and soon discovered the Run of fresh Water, opposite to which, they landed, and tasting it found it to be very good. The Natives had stopped about 30 Yards from the Place where the Boat landed, to whom, the Gentlemen made signs of thanks for their friendly Information, at the same time offering Presents, and doing every thing they could think of, to make them lay aside their Fears and advance towards them, but this point was gained only, by the Methods that I have mentioned: and when they did venture to come and take the things out of the Governor's & the other Gentlemen's Hands, it was with evident Signs of Fear, the Gentlemen now having distributed all their Presents among them, returned on Board.

Thus, was our first Intercourse obtained, with these *Children of Nature*.— About 12 of the Natives appeared the next Morning, on the Shore opposite to the *Supply*, they had a Dog with them, (something of the Fox Species); The Governor and the same Gentlemen that were of his Party Yesterday went on Shore, and very soon came to a Parley with them, there were some of their Acquaintances among the Number, and these advanced first (leaving their Spears with their Companions who remained behind at a little Distance) as they had done Yesterday; They all of them in a short time became Confident, Familiar & *vastly funny* took anything that was offered them, holding out their Hands and making Signs for many things that they saw, laughed when we laughed, jumped extravagantly, and grunted by way of Music, & Repeated many Words & Phrases after Us. The Gentlemen having passed about an hour with them, returned on Board, but could not induce any of the Natives to accompany them there. A Party of Us made an Excursion up an Arm in the North part of the *Bay*, where we had not been long landed before we discovered among the Bushes a Tribe of the Natives, who at first did not discover such an inoffensive & friendly Disposition, as those I have spoke of, above; for these rude, unsociable Fellows, immediately threw a Lance, which fell very near one of the Sailors, and stuck several Inches in the Ground, we returned the Compliment by firing a Musket over their Heads, on which I thought they would have broken their Necks with running away from Us. about an hour after, we, in our Ramble, fell in with them again, they stood still, but seemed ready for another Start. One of Us, now laid down the Musket and advanced towards them singly, holding out some Bawbles, and making Signs of Peace; In a little time they began to gain Confidence, and two of them approached to meet the Gentlemen who held out the Presents, the Introduction being amicably settled, they all joined Us, and took the Trinkets we offered them; The same Emotions of Pleasure, Astonishment, Curiosity & Timidity, appeared in these poor Creatures, as had been observed in our first Acquaintances—There were some Old and young Women in this Tribe, whom the Men seemed very jealous & careful of, keeping them at Distance behind some young Men, who were armed with Spears, Clubs & Shields, apparently as a Guard to them. We could see these curious *Evites* peeping through the Bushes at Us, and we made signs to the Men, who were still with Us, that We wished to give some Trinkets to the Women, on which, One of their Husbands, or Relations (as we supposed) hollowed to them in an authoritative Tone, and one of these Wood-Nymphs (as naked as Eve before she knew Shame) obeyed and came up to Us; when; we presented her with a Bracelet of blue Beads for her obliging Acquiescence; She was extremely shy & timid, suffering Us, very reluctantly, even to touch Her; Indeed, it must be merely from the Curiosity, to see how they would behave, on an Attempt to be familiar with them, that one would be induced to touch one of Them, for they are Ugly to Disgust, in their Countenances and stink of Fish-Oil & Smoke, *most sweetly*.—I must not omit mentioning a very singular Curiosity among the Men here, arising from a Doubt of what Sex we are, for from our not having, like themselves, long Beards, and not seeing when they open our Shirt-Bosoms (which they do very roughly and without any Ceremony) the usual distinguishing Characteristics of Women, they start Back with Amazement, and give a Hum! with a significant look, implying. What kind of Creatures are these?!—As it was not possible for Us to satisfy their Inquisitiveness in this Particular, by the simple Words. *Yes* or *No*. We had Recourse to the Evidence of *Ocular Demonstration*, which made them laugh, jump & Skip in an extravagant Manner.—In a Tribe of these funny, curious Fellows, One of them, after having had His Curiosity gratified by this mode of Conviction, went into the Wood, and presently came forth again, jumping & laughing with a Bunch of broad Leaves tied before Him, by Way of a Fig-leaf Veil.—Before we took our leave of the Tribe that threw the Lance; they endeavoured to convince Us, that it was not thrown by general Consent, and one of them severely reprimanded the Man who threw it, and several of them struck him, but more to shew Us their Disapprobation of what he had done, than as a Punishment for it.

During our stay at *Botany Bay*, the *Governor* had made himself well acquainted with the Situation of the Land Nature of the Soil &c. &c. which he not finding so Eligible, as he could Wish, for the Purpose of forming a Settlement, He determined, before he fixed on it, to visit an Inlet on the Coast, about 12 Miles to the Northward of this *Bay* which, our great Circumnavigator, *Captn. Cook*, discovered, and named, (in honour of one of the then Commissioners of the Navy) *Port Jackson* accordingly, the Governor, attended by a Number of Officers went in 3 boats, on this Expedition, and the third day, they returned, gave it as their Opinion, that *Port Jackson* was one of the most spacious and safe Harbours in the known World, and said they had already fixed on a Spot, on which the Settlement was to be formed. In Consequence of this Success, the Idea was entirely given up, of establishing a Colony at *Botany Bay*, and three days after, the Wind favouring our Designs, the Fleet sailed for *Port Jackson* and in the Evening of the Day of our Departure, We arrived, and anchored in one of the many beautiful Coves which it Contains, which *Cove* Sir, the *Governor* has, (in honour of *Lord Sydney*), named *Sydney Cove*.

Though the Description given by the Gentlemen who first, visited this *Port* was truly luxuriant, and wore the air of Exaggeration, Yet they had by no means done its Beauties and Conveniences Justice, for as an Harbour, None, that has hitherto been described, equals it in Spaciousness and Safety. the Land forms a Number of pleasant Coves in most of which 6 or 7 Ships may lie secured to the Trees on Shore. It contains likewise a Number of small Islands, which are covered with Trees and a variety of Herbage, all which appears to be Evergreens. The Whole, (in a Word) exhibits a Variety of Romantic Views, all thrown together into sweet Confusion by the careless hand of Nature. Well, Dear Dick, now I have brought you all the way to *Sydney Cove*, I must tell you what we have done, since our arrival in these Seas, & in this Port—what we are doing, what has happened &c. &c.

On the Evening of our Arrival (26th January 1788) The Governor & a Number of the Officers assembled on Shore where, they Displayed the British Flag and each Officer with a Heart, glowing with Loyalty drank his Majesty's Health and Success to the Colony. The next Day, all the Artificers & an 100 of the Convicts were landed, carrying with them the necessary Utensils for clearing the Ground and felling the Trees. By the Evening, they were able to pitch a Number of Tents and some Officers and private Soldiers slept on shore that Evening. In the Interval of that time and the Date of this Letter, the principal Business has been the clearing of Land, cutting, Grubbing and burning down Trees, sawing up Timber & Plank for Building, making Bricks, hewing Stone, Erecting temporary Store-houses, a Building for an Hospital, another for an Observatory, Enclosing Farms & Gardens, making temporary Huts, and many other Conveniences towards the establishing of a Colony. [. . .]

1788/1978

WATKIN TENCH
1758–1833

Watkin Tench might justly be called the author of the first Australian international bestseller as *A Narrative of the Expedition to Botany Bay; with an Account of New South Wales, Its Productions, Inhabitants, &c* (1789) had in its year of publication alone three editions in London, two in Paris and one in each of Dublin, New York, Amsterdam and Frankfurt. Tench was born in England and in 1776 joined the Marine Corps as a second lieutenant. In 1786 he volunteered for a three-year tour of duty to the new British penal colony at Botany Bay. While in Sydney, Tench took part in several expeditions as well as recording all the day-to-day activities of the settlement in his journal. After nearly four years in Australia, he returned to London in 1792 and married shortly afterwards. *A Complete Account of the Settlement at Port Jackson in New South Wales, Including an Accurate Description of the Situation of the Colony, of the Natives, and of Its Natural Productions* was published in 1793. His personable narrative style, humour, wit and Enlightenment views, combined with a strong interest in everything he saw, make Tench's accounts the most perceptive and literary of those written about the first years of settlement. *EW*

From *A Complete Account of the Settlement at Port Jackson*
Chapter III: Transactions of the Colony, from the
Commencement of the Year 1789, until the End of March

Pursuant to his resolution, the governor on the 31st of December sent two boats, under the command of Lieutenant Ball of the *Supply*, and Lieutenant George Johnston of the marines, down the harbour, with directions to those officers to seize and carry off some of the natives. The boats proceeded to Manly Cove, where several Indians were seen standing on the beach, who were enticed by courteous behaviour and a few presents to enter into conversation. A proper opportunity being presented, our people rushed in among them, and seized two men: the rest fled; but the cries of the captives soon brought them back, with many others, to their rescue: and so desperate were their struggles, that, in spite of every effort on our side, only one of them was secured; the other effected his escape. The boats put off without delay; and an attack from the shore instantly commenced: they threw spears, stones, firebrands, and whatever else presented itself, at the boats; nor did they retreat, agreeable to their former custom, until many musquets were fired over them.

The prisoner was now fastened by ropes to the thwarts of the boat; and when he saw himself irretrievably disparted from his countrymen, set up the most piercing and lamentable cries of distress. His grief, however, soon diminished: he accepted and eat of some broiled fish which was given to him, and sullenly submitted to his destiny.

1789. When the news of his arrival at Sydney was announced, I went with every other person to see him: he appeared to be about thirty years old, not tall, but robustly made; and of a countenance which, under happier circumstances, I thought would display manliness and sensibility; his agitation was excessive, and the clamourous crowds who flocked around him did not contribute to lessen it. Curiosity and observation seemed, nevertheless, not to have wholly deserted him; he shewed the effect of novelty upon ignorance; he wondered at all he saw: though broken and interrupted with dismay, his voice was soft and musical, when its natural tone could be heard; and he readily pronounced with tolerable accuracy the names of things which were taught him. To our ladies he quickly became extraordinarily courteous, a sure sign that his terror was wearing off.

Every blandishment was used to soothe him, and it had its effect. As he was entering the governor's house, some one touched a small bell which hung over the door: he started with horror and astonishment; but in a moment after was reconciled to the noise, and laughed at the cause of his perturbation. When pictures were shewn to him, he knew directly those which represented the human figure: among others, a very large handsome print of her royal highness the Dutchess of Cumberland being produced, he called out, woman, a name by which we had just before taught him to call the female convicts. Plates of birds and beasts were also laid before him; and many people were led to believe, that such as he spoke about and pointed to were known to him. But this must have been an erroneous conjecture, for the elephant, rhinoceros, and several others, which we must have discovered did they exist in the country, were of the number. Again, on the other hand, those he did not point out, were equally unknown to him.

1789. His curiosity here being satiated, we took him to a large brick house, which was building for the governor's residence: being about to enter, he cast up his eyes, and seeing some people leaning out of a window on the first storey, he exclaimed aloud, and testified the most extravagant surprise. Nothing here was observed to fix his attention so strongly as some tame fowls, who were feeding near him: our dogs also he particularly noticed; but seemed more fearful than fond of them.

He dined at a side-table at the governor's; and eat heartily of fish and ducks, which he first cooled. Bread and salt meat he smelled at, but would not taste: all our liquors he treated in the same manner, and could drink nothing but water. On being shewn that he was not to wipe his hands on the chair which he sat upon, he used a towel which was gave to him, with great cleanliness and decency.

In the afternoon his hair was closely cut, his head combed, and his beard shaved; but he would not submit to these operations until he had seen them performed on another person, when he readily acquiesced. His hair, as might be supposed, was filled with vermin, whose destruction seemed to afford him great triumph; nay, either revenge, or pleasure, prompted him to eat them! but on our expressing disgust and abhorrence he left it off.

To this succeeded his immersion in a tub of water and soap, where he was completely washed and scrubbed from head to foot; after which a shirt, a jacket, and a pair of trowsers, were put upon him. Some part of this ablution I had the honour to perform, in order that I might ascertain the real colour of the skin of these people. My observation then was (and it has since been confirmed in a thousand other instances) that they are as black as the lighter cast of the African negroes.

Many unsuccessful attempts were made to learn his name; the governor therefore called him Manly, from the cove in which he was captured: this cove had received its name from the manly undaunted behaviour of a party of natives seen there, on our taking possession of the country.

To prevent his escape, a handcuff with a rope attached to it, was fastened around his left wrist, which at first highly delighted him; he called it 'Ben-gàd-ee' (or ornament), but his delight changed to rage and hatred when he discovered its use. His supper he cooked himself: some fish were given to him for this purpose, which, without any previous preparation whatever, he threw carelessly on the fire, and when they became warm took them up, and first rubbed off the scales, peeled the outside with his teeth, and eat it; afterwards he gutted them, and laying them again on the fire, completed the dressing, and ate them.

A convict was selected to sleep with him, and to attend him wherever he might go. When he went with his keeper into his apartment he appeared very restless and uneasy while a light was kept in; but on its extinction, he immediately lay down and composed himself.

Sullenness and dejection strongly marked his countenance on the following morning; to amuse him, he was taken around the camp, and to the observatory: casting his eyes to the opposite shore from the point where he stood, and seeing the smoke of fire lighted by his countrymen, he looked earnestly at it, and sighing deeply two or three times, uttered the word 'gweè-un' (fire).

His loss of spirits had not, however, the effect of impairing his appetite; eight fish, each weighing about a pound, constituted his breakfast, which he dressed as before. When he had finished his repast, he turned his back to the fire in a musing posture, and crept so close to it, that his shirt was caught by the flame; luckily his keeper soon extinguished it; but he was so terrified at the accident, that he was with difficulty persuaded to put on a second.

1st. January, 1789. Today being new-year's-day, most of the officers were invited to the governor's table: Manly dined heartily on fish and roasted pork; he was seated on a chest near a window, out of which, when he had done eating, he would have thrown his plate, had he not been prevented: during dinner-time a band of music played in an adjoining apartment; and after the cloth was removed, one of the company sang in a very soft and superior style; but the powers of melody were lost on Manly, which disappointed our expectations, as he had before shown pleasure and readiness in imitating our tunes. Stretched out on his chest, and putting his hat under his head, he fell asleep.

To convince his countrymen that he had received no injury from us, the governor took him in a boat down the harbour, that they might see and converse with him: when the boat arrived, and lay at a little distance from the beach, several Indians who had retired at her approach, on seeing Manly, returned: he was greatly affected, and shed tears. At length they began to converse. Our ignorance of the language prevented us from knowing much of what passed; it was, however, easily understood that his friends asked him why he did not jump overboard, and rejoin them. He only sighed, and pointed to the fetter on his leg, by which he was bound.

In going down the harbour he had described the names by which they distinguish its numerous creeks and headlands: he was now often heard to repeat that of *Weè-rong* (Sydney), which was doubtless to inform his countrymen of the place of his captivity; and perhaps invite them to rescue him. By this time his gloom was chased away, and he parted from his friends without testifying reluctance. His vivacity and good humour continued all the evening, and produced so good an effect on his appetite, that he eat for supper two Kangaroo rats, each of the size of a moderate rabbit, and in addition not less than three pounds of fish.

Two days after he was taken on a similar excursion; but to our surprise the natives kept aloof, and would neither approach the shore, or discourse with their countryman: we could get no explanation of this difficulty, which seemed to affect us more than it did him. Uncourteous as they were, he performed to them an act of attentive benevolence; seeing a basket made of bark, used by them to carry water, he conveyed into it two hawks and another bird, which the people in the boat had shot, and carefully covering them over, left them as a present to his old friends. But indeed the gentleness and humanity of his disposition frequently displayed themselves: when our children, stimulated by wanton curiosity, used to flock around him, he never failed to fondle them, and, if he were eating at the time, constantly offered them the choicest part of his fare.

February, 1789. His reserve, from want of confidence in us, continued gradually to wear away: he told us his name, and Manly gave place to Ar-ab-a-noo. Bread he began to relish; and tea he drank with avidity: strong liquors he would never taste, turning from them with disgust and abhorrence. Our dogs and cats had ceased to be objects of fear, and were become his greatest pets, and constant companions at table. One of our chief amusements, after the cloth was removed, was to make him repeat the names of things in his language, which he never hesitated to do with the utmost alacrity, correcting our pronunciation when erroneous. [. . .]

1793

BENNELONG
c. 1764–1813

A senior man of the Wangal people, captured near Sydney in November 1789, Bennelong became one of the first Aboriginal people to be introduced to English culture—learning English, adopting European ways and dress, and helping Governor Arthur Phillip learn the local language and traditions. He gave Phillip an Aboriginal name, which located him in a kinship relationship and thus enabled the communication of customs and relationships to the land. Bennelong travelled to England in 1792, and in 1795 returned home in poor health, unable to rebuild relations with his people and out of favour in the colony. *AH/PM*

Letter to Mr Philips, Lord Sydney's Steward

Sidney Cove
New S. Wales Augst 29
1796

Sir

I am very well. I hope you are very well. I live at the Governor's. I have every day dinner there. I have not my wife: another black man took her away: we have had murry doings: he spear'd me in the back, but I better now: his name is now Carroway. all my friends alive & well. Not me go to England no more. I am at home now. I hope Sir you send me anything you please Sir. hope all are well in England. I hope Mrs Phillip very well. You nurse me Madam when I sick. You very good Madam: thank you Madam, & hope you remember me Madam, not forget. I know you very well Madam. Madam I want stockings. thank you Madam; send me two Pair stockings. You very good Madam. Thank you Madam. Sir, you give my duty to Ld Sydney. Thank you very good my Lord. very good: hope very well all family. very well. Sir, send me you please some Handkerchiefs for Pocket. you please Sir send me some shoes: two pair you please Sir.

Bannalong

1796

ELIZABETH MACARTHUR
1766–1850

Letter writer and pioneer settler Elizabeth Macarthur was born in England and grew up in the Devon countryside, where she obviously received a good education. In 1788 she married John Macarthur and soon afterwards accompanied him to Sydney with his regiment, the NSW Corps. From Elizabeth Farm, near Parramatta, established in 1794, and later Camden Park, she managed their merino sheep empire, fostering the now-famous fine wool industry of the colony during the often prolonged absences of her irascible husband in England. Her letters to relatives and friends in England provide many insights into the circumstances of life in early Australia as well as the thoughts and feelings of this remarkable woman. They were first published in 1984 as *The Journal and Letters of Elizabeth Macarthur. EW*

Letter to Brigid Kingdon

To Brigid Kingdon

Elizabeth Farm,
Parramatta 1st Septr 1798

Once again, my much loved friend, it is permitted me to sit down under a conviction that the letter I am about to write will be received by you with pleasure. By the Capture of a Ship off the Coast of Brazil we were left without any direct intelligence from Europe for twelve months. We firmly believed that a revolution or some national calamity had befallen Great Britain, & that we should be left altogether to ourselves, until things at home had resumed some degree of order, & the tempest a little subsided. These fears however have by a late arrival proved without foundation.

This Country possesses numerous advantages to persons holding appointments under Government; It seems the only part of the Globe where quiet is to be expected—We enjoy here one of the finest Climates in the world—The necessaries of life are abundant, & a fruitful soil affords us many luxuries. Nothing induces me to wish for a change but the difficulty of educating our children, & were it otherwise it would be unjust towards them to confine them to so narrow a society. My desire is that they may see a little more of the world, & better learn to appreciate this retirement.

Such as it is the little creatures all speak of going home to England with rapture—My dear Edward almost quitted me without a tear. They have early imbibed an idea that England is the seat of happiness & delight, that it contains all that can be gratifying to their senses, & that of course they are there to possess all they desire. It would be difficult to undeceive young people bred up in so secluded a situation, if they had not an opportunity given them of convincing themselves. But hereafter I shall much wonder if some of them make not this place the object of their choice.—By the date of this letter you will see that we still reside on our Farm at Parramatta—a native name signifying the head of a river, which it is.

The town extends one mile in length from the landing place, & is terminated by the Government House which is built on an Eminence named Rose Hill. Our Farm, which contains from four to five hundred acres, is bounded on three sides by Water. This is particularly convenient. We have at this time, about one hundred & twenty acres in wheat, all in a promising state. Our Gardens with fruit & vegetables are extensive & produce abundantly. It is now Spring, & the Eye is delighted with a most beautiful variegated landscape—Almonds—Apricots, Pear and Apple Trees are in full bloom. The native shrubs are also in flower, & the whole Country gives a grateful perfume. There is a very good Carriage road new made from hence to Sydney, which by land is distant about fourteen miles; & another from this to the river Hawkesbury, which is about twenty miles from hence in a direct line across the Country—Parramatta is a central position between both—I have once visited the Hawkesbury & made the journey on horse back. The road is through an uninterrupted wood, with the exception of the village of Toongabie, a farm of Government, & one or two others which we distinguish by the name of Greenlands, on account of the fine grass, & there being few trees compared with the other parts of the Country, which is occasionally brushy & more or less covered with underwood. The greater part of the country is like an English Park, & the trees give to it the appearance of a Wilderness or shrubbery, commonly attached to the habitations of people of fortune, filled with a variety of native plants placed in a wild irregular manner. I was at the Hawkesbury three days. It is a noble fresh water river, taking its rise in a precipitous range of mountains, that it has hitherto been impossible to pass. Many attempts have been made altho' in vain. I spent an entire day on this river, going in a boat to a beautiful spot, named by the late Governor Richmond Hill, high & overlooking a great extent of Country. On one side are those stupendous barriers to which I have alluded, rising as it were, immediately above your head; below, the river itself, still & unruffled—out of sight is heard a Waterfall whose distant murmurs add awfulness to the scene . . .

I have had the misfortune to lose a sweet Boy of eleven months old who died very suddenly by an illness occasioned by teething. The other three Elizabeth John & Mary are well. I have lately been made very happy by learning the safe arrival of Edward in England.

We often remember & talk over in the evening the hospitalities which we have both received in Bridgerule Vicarage & happy shall I be if it is ever permitted me to mark my remembrance more strongly than is expressed in these lines.

If you are in the habit of visiting the Whitstone family I pray that you will kindly remember me to them. The benevolence of the Major's heart will dispose him to rejoice at the success which has attended us, & that the activity which was very early discernable in the mind of Mr Macarthur has had a field for advantageous exertion.

How is it my dearest friend that you are still single—Are you difficult to please—or has the War left you so few Bachelors from amongst whom to choose. But suffer me to offer you a piece of advice—abate a few of your scruples & marry—I offer in myself an instance that it is not always with all our wise foreseeings, those marriages which promise most or least happiness, prove in their result such as our friends may predict. Few of mine I am certain when I married thought that either of us had taken a prudent step. I was considered indolent & inactive; Mr Macarthur too proud & haughty for our humble fortune or expectations, & yet you see how bountifully Providence has dealt with us.

At this time I can truly say no two people on earth can be happier than we are. In Mr Macarthur's society I experience the tenderest affection of a Husband who is instructive & cheerful as a companion. He is an indulgent Father—beloved as a Master, & universally respected for the integrity of his Character. Judge then my friend if I ought not to consider myself a happy woman.

I have hitherto in all my letters to my friends forborne to mention Mr Macarthur's name lest it might appear to me too ostentatious. Whenever you marry, look out for good sense in a husband. You would never be happy with a person inferior to yourself in point of understanding—So much my early recollection of you & of your character bids me say.

E.M.
1798/1984

MATTHEW FLINDERS
1774–1814

Navigator Matthew Flinders developed a desire to go to sea partly from reading Defoe's *Robinson Crusoe* and joined the navy when he was fifteen. After serving as a midshipman under William Bligh on a voyage to Tahiti, in 1795 he sailed for Sydney where, with George Bass, he explored parts of the NSW coast in a small boat. From 1798 to 1799, again with Bass, he circumnavigated Van Diemen's Land (Tasmania), demonstrating that it was an island. Flinders then returned to England, where he published *Observations on the Coasts of Van Diemen's Land, on Bass's Strait and its Islands, and on part of the Coasts of New South Wales* (1801). In 1801 he returned to Australia as commander of the *Investigator*, with instructions to chart the parts of the southern Australian coastline that were still unknown. While thus engaged, he met French captain Nicolas Baudin at Encounter Bay. After repairing his ship in Sydney, Flinders sailed north to make a detailed survey of the Queensland coast. In the Torres Strait, the *Investigator* began leaking so badly that Flinders had to give up his survey, though he still managed to circumnavigate the continent, returning to Sydney in 1803. On his way back to England to secure another ship, he called in at Mauritius where he was detained as a prisoner, since England and France were once more at war, and was not able to return to England until 1810. In poor health, he prepared *A Voyage to Terra Australis* (1814) for the press; it appeared the day before his death. Its publication demonstrated that Flinders was not only a brilliant navigator but a man of considerable literary ability, as well as intelligence and perception. *EW*

From *A Voyage to Terra Australis*
Volume I, Chapter VIII

[…] *8 April*—Before two in the afternoon we stretched eastward again; and at four, a white rock was reported from aloft to be seen ahead. On approaching nearer, it proved to be a ship standing towards us; and we cleared for action, in case of being attacked. The stranger was a heavy-looking ship, without any top-gallant masts up; and our colours being hoisted, she showed a French ensign, and afterwards an English Jack forward, as we did a white flag. At half past five, the land being then five miles distant to the north-eastward, I hove to; and learned, as the stranger passed to leeward with a free wind, that it was the French national ship *Le Géographe*, under the command of Captain Nicolas Baudin. We veered round as *Le Géographe* was passing, so as to keep our broadside to her, lest the flag of truce should be a deception; and having come to the wind on the other tack, a boat was hoisted out, and I went on board the French ship, which had also hove to.

As I did not understand French, Mr Brown, the naturalist, went with me in the boat. We were received by an officer who pointed out the commander, and by him were conducted into the cabin. I requested Captain Baudin to show me his passport from the Admiralty; and when it was found and I had perused it, offered mine from the French marine minister, but he put it back without inspection. He then informed me that he had spent some time in examining the south and east parts of Van Diemen's Land, where his geographical engineer, with the largest boat and a boat's crew, had been left, and probably lost. In Bass' Strait Captain Baudin had encountered a heavy gale, the same we had experienced in a less degree on 21 March, in the Investigator's Strait. He was then separated from his consort, *Le Naturaliste*; but having since had fair winds and fine weather, he had explored the south coast from Western Port to the place of our meeting, without finding any river, inlet, or other shelter which afforded anchorage. I inquired concerning a large island, said to lie in the western entrance of Bass' Strait; but he had not seen it, and seemed to doubt much of its existence.

Captain Baudin was communicative of his discoveries about Van Diemen's Land; as also of his criticisms upon an English chart of Bass' Strait, published in 1800. He found great fault with the north side of the strait, but commended the form given to the south side and to the islands near it. On my pointing out a note upon the chart, explaining that the north side of the strait was seen only in an open boat by Mr Bass, who had no good means of fixing either latitude or longitude, he appeared surprised, not having before paid attention to it. I told him that some other, and more particular charts of the strait and its neighbourhood had been since published; and that if he would keep company until next morning, I would bring him a copy, with a small memoir belonging to them. This was agreed to, and I returned with Mr Brown to the *Investigator*.

It somewhat surprised me, that Captain Baudin made no inquiries concerning my business upon this unknown coast, but as he seemed more desirous of communicating information, I was happy to receive it; next morning, however, he had become inquisitive, some of his officers having learned from my boat's crew that our object was also discovery. I then told him, generally, what our operations had been, particularly in the two gulfs, and the latitude to which I had ascended in the largest; explained the situation of Port Lincoln, where fresh water might be procured; showed him Cape Jervis, which was still in sight; and as a proof of the refreshments to be obtained at the large island opposite to it, pointed out the kangaroo-skin caps worn by my boat's crew; and told him the name I had affixed to the island in consequence. At parting, the captain requested me to take care of his boat and people, in case of meeting with them; and to say to *Le Naturaliste*, that he should go to Port Jackson so soon as the bad weather set in. On my asking the name of the captain of *Le Naturaliste*, he bethought himself to ask mine; and finding it to be the same as the author of the chart which he had been criticising, expressed not a little surprise; but had the politeness to congratulate himself on meeting me. [. . .]

1802/1814

BARRON FIELD
1786—1846

Poet and judge Barron Field was born in England, educated at Christ's Hospital and called to the Bar in 1814. In 1816 he was appointed judge of the Supreme Court of Civil Judicature in NSW. Before leaving England he had moved in literary and theatrical circles, contributing poems and essays to Leigh Hunt's *Examiner* and *Reflector* as well as other journals. He was also a close friend and correspondent of Charles Lamb. In 1819 Field published the first collection of poems to appear in Australia, a slim volume entitled rather grandiosely *First Fruits of Australian Poetry*. Lamb claimed that Wordsworth and Coleridge were 'hugely taken' with 'The Kangaroo'. Field was an active member of the Philosophical Society of Australasia and in 1825 edited *Geographical Memoirs on New South Wales by Various Hands*, to which he also contributed. He returned to England in 1824 and later became the first chief justice of Gibraltar. *EW*

The Kangaroo

'*Mixtumque genus, prolesque biformis.*'[1]
—Virgil; *Aeneid VI*

KANGAROO, Kangaroo!
Thou Spirit of Australia,
That redeems from utter failure,
From perfect desolation,
And warrants the creation   5
Of this fifth part of the Earth,
Which would seem an after-birth,
Not conceiv'd in the Beginning
(For GOD bless'd His work at first,
And saw that it was good),   10
But emerg'd at the first sinning,
When the ground was therefore curst;—
And hence this barren wood!

Kangaroo, Kangaroo!
Tho' at first sight we should say,   15
In thy nature that there may
Contradiction be involv'd,
Yet, like discord well resolv'd,
It is quickly harmoniz'd.
Sphynx or mermaid realiz'd,   20
Or centaur unfabulous,
Would scarce be more prodigious,
Or Labyrinthine Minotaur,
With which great Theseus did war,
Or Pegasus poetical,   25
Or hippogriff[2]—chimeras all!
But, what Nature would compile,
Nature knows to reconcile;

---

1   'The mixed offspring of two species': Virgil's description of the Minotaur.
2   A mythical beast, part griffin, part horse.

And Wisdom, ever at her side,
Of all her children's justified.   30

She had made the squirrel fragile;
She had made the bounding hart;
But a third so strong and agile
Was beyond ev'n Nature's art;
So she join'd the former two   35
    In thee, Kangaroo!

To describe thee, it is hard:
Converse of the camélopard,[1]
Which beginneth camel-wise,
But endeth of the panther size,   40
Thy fore half, it would appear,
Had belong'd to some 'small deer',
Such as liveth in a tree;
By thy hinder, thou should'st be
A large animal of chace,   45
Bounding o'er the forest's space;—
Join'd by some divine mistake,
None but Nature's hand can make—
Nature, in her wisdom's play,
On Creation's holiday.   50

For howsoe'er anomalous,
Thou yet art not incongruous,
Repugnant or preposterous.
Better-proportion'd animal,
More graceful or ethereal,   55
Was never follow'd by the hound,
With fifty steps to thy one bound.
Thou can'st not be amended: no;
Be as thou art; thou best art so.

When sooty swans are once more rare,   60
And duck-moles[2] the Museum's care,
Be still the glory of this land,
Happiest Work of finest Hand!

                                                            1819

1   Giraffe.
2   Platypuses.

ANONYMOUS

'The Native's Lament' is one of a number of early newspaper poems that adopted the point of view of an Aboriginal person to lament the impact of the arrival of white settlers. It was published in Hobart's *Colonial Times* on 5 May 1826. *EW*

The Native's Lament

Oh! where are the wilds I once sported among,
When free as my clime through its forests I sprung;
When no track but the few which our fires had made,
Had tarnished the carpet that nature had laid;
When the lone waters dashed down the darksome ravine;   5
O'erhung by the shade of the Huon's dark green;
When the broad morning sun o'er our mountains could roam,
And not see a slave in our bright Island home.

When our trees were unscath'd, nor our echoes awoke,
To the hum of the stranger, or woodman's wild stroke;   10
When our rocks proudly rose 'gainst the dash of the main,
And saw not a bark on the wide, azure plain;
When the moon through the heavens roll'd onward and smil'd,
As she lighted the home of the free and the wild.

Oh! my country, the stranger has found thy free clime,   15
And he comes with the sons of misfortune and crime;
He brings the rude refuse of countries laid waste,
To tread thy fair wilds and thy waters to taste;
He usurps the best lands of thy native domains,
And thy children must fly, or submit to his chains.   20

He builds his dark home, and he tricks it about,
With trinkets and trifles within and without;
When the bright sun of nature sinks into the main,
He lights little suns to make day-light again;
And he calls a crowd round him, to see him preside,   25
And our tyrant himself is the slave of his pride!

Oh! dearer to us, is our rude hollow tree,
Where heart joins to heart with a pulse warm and free,
Or our dew-covered sod, with no canopy o'er it,
But the star-spangl'd sky,—we can lay and adore it!   30
Or if worn with fatigue, when the bright sun forsakes us,
We lay down and sleep, till he rises and wakes us!

Our wants are but few, and our feelings are warm,
We fear not the sun, and we fear not the storm;
We are fierce to our foes, to our loves we are fond,   35
Let us live and be free—life has nothing beyond.
Oh! I would not exchange the wild nature I bear,
For life with the tame sons of culture and care,
Not give one free moment as proudly I stand,
For all that their arts and their toils can command.   40
Away to the mountains, and leave them the plains,
To pursue their dull toils, and to forge their dark chains.

1826/1993

HENRY SAVERY
1791–1842

Novelist and essayist Henry Savery was born in England. While working in Bristol as a sugar refiner, he forged bank bills when trying to avoid a second bankruptcy and was sentenced to transportation for life. After arriving in Hobart in 1825, as an educated convict he worked as a clerk in various government departments. When imprisoned for debt in 1829, Savery wrote satirical sketches of local scenes and characters for the *Colonial Times*, modelled on Felix McDonough's popular *The Hermit in London* (1821). These were later collected as *The Hermit in Van Diemen's Land* (1829), the first book of essays to be published in Australia. Savery went on to write the first novel to be published in Australia, *Quintus Servinton* (1830–31); it was partly autobiographical but had a happy ending denied to Savery in real life. In 1838 he received a conditional pardon and became a farmer. Once more getting into debt, however, he again forged bills and was sent to Port Arthur, where he died. *EW*

From *The Hermit in Van Diemen's Land*
No. 2. Hobart Town, June 12, 1829

It was a remarkably fine clear day when I landed from the ship on the Wharf. What was my surprise, to observe the large handsome stone buildings, into which, porters were busily engaged rolling casks and other packages, and at several civil looking well dressed young men, who were standing with pens behind their ears, and memorandum books in their hands, paying the most diligent attention to what was going on. A number of other persons formed little knots or circles; and the hallooing of ferrymen, the cracking of whips, and the vociferation of carters, struck me as creating altogether, a scene of bustle and activity, which indeed I had little expected. For the moment it occurred to me, that our Captain, in the hurry and confusion which the quarrels on board had occasioned, has missed his reckoning, and had made a wrong port; and accordingly seeing a fat, portly, sleek-looking, apparently good-humoured Gentleman approaching, I enquired of him, with an apology, in what place I was?—Judging from my manner and appearance that I must be a stranger, he very civilly replied, that I was in Hobart Town, the capital of Van Diemen's Land, adding, 'Perhaps, Sir, you would like to walk into our Commercial Room, to which I can introduce you.' I then accompanied my new acquaintance up a flight of stone steps into a rather elegantly fitted-up room, in which were three or four plainly dressed Gentlemen reading Newspapers. One of them, who appeared bordering upon sixty, wore spectacles, and had a considerable degree of eagerness in his manner,[1] rose upon my entrance, and addressed me, 'Just from England, eh, Sir? What news, Sir, when you left? The Colony is much talked of at home, Sir. Suppose you heard of our Association, but things are not now as they used to be.' Before I could make a reply, he offered me a Newspaper, farther acquainting me, that the town maintained three such publications; one of which, said he, is so dull and prosy, that nobody reads it; another has lately been at death's door, owing to some Government regulations, but has now, Phoenix-like, risen with redoubled splendour; and the other is made up of short paragraphs and country letters written in town, but commands an extensive circulation. I expressed my thanks for the information, and for my courteous reception, and mentally wondering at a commodious Wharf, fine Stone-buildings, a Chamber of Commerce, and three Newspapers, felt that so many other things, to be in character, must still await my attention, that I made my bow to the company, and proceeded on my tour through the town. The fat portly Gentleman was my companion to the end of the Wharf, and then, with a true John Bull air and manner, left me, and turned into one of the stone warehouses.

How great was my astonishment, at the magnificent straight line of street, extending apparently for more than a mile, by which my sight was greeted upon leaving the Quay. I could scarcely credit my senses, that I was in a town, which is only as it were of yesterday. As I proceeded along, my surprise was increased by seeing other fine streets, meeting at right angles, the one by which I was walking towards a handsome brick church, with a steeple like the extinguisher upon a flat candlestick, my left being flanked by well laid out gardens and shrubberies, in the centre of which stood the Governor's residence; and every here and there, the right being ornamented by large two story brick or stone houses. The church door happening to be open, I took the opportunity of judging of its interior, and I could almost have fancied myself in one of the modern churches of the metropolis of the world. Such regular well-arranged pews, so beautifully finished a pulpit and reading desk, made of wood, which I at first thought was Spanish mahogany, quite astonished me; upon a nearer examination,

---

1   Anthony Fenn Kemp (1773–1868), a leading Hobart merchant.

however, and upon enquiry of a man who was dusting the aisles, I learnt that it was the produce of a tree, indigenous to the Colony, known by the name of Myrtle. While I was thus employing myself, a Gentleman wearing a Clerical hat,[1] approached, and with much affability of manner, addressed me as a stranger, and gave me some general information respecting the religious institutions of the place. He had a lisp in his speech, which was by no means disagreeable, and his well cased ribs bore evident marks that, whatever other doctrines he might preach, that of fasting was not one upon which he laid much stress, at least in its practice. He acquainted me, that independent of the congregations belonging to this large Church, a Presbyterian Chapel, a Roman Catholic Chapel, and a Wesleyan Meeting House, were each well attended every Sunday, and it gave me great pleasure afterwards to be told of this Gentleman, as he himself had beautifully expressed of his brother labourers in the vineyard, that in their lives and conduct the religion they all professed received its brightest ornament— that they each made a well formed cornerstone of the superstructure they supported. Oh! thought I, this must be the effect of a virtuous and industrious population. Arts, architecture, literature, religion, and commerce must here thrive so well, because so many excellent people, for whom Old England was not good enough, have congregated, and because so many others have been cleansed of their sins, and are now restored to innocence. Happy people, and thrice happy Simon Stukeley, to have left your retirement, to come among them!—Everything seemed indeed greatly superior to my expectations. Well dressed and elegant Ladies were promenading one street, well mounted Equestrians were galloping along another, respectably attired Pedestrians helped to add to the scene, which was still more enlivened by the relief-guard of the Military as it approached the Main-guard House from the Barracks, and by the rapid passing and re-passing of gigs, carts, and other wheel vehicles. I was completely in a reverie, scarcely knowing through which street I would perambulate, or which object best claimed my attention. The entire absence of all beggars, or indigent persons, added to my wonder, but after a little reflection, I accounted for it in my own mind, by considering that as all the inhabitants were either pure or purified, it was quite of a piece with their religion and virtue to be charitable, this being the brightest of the cardinal gems. I continued my walk for a long time, each moment more astonished than before at the progress which had been made in laying out and building the town—at the excellent shops in the different streets—at the wide well macadamised thoroughfares, and their convenient causeways, and at a hundred other matters which excited my admiration, until I found myself in a quarter of the town situated on

---

1   Rev. William Bedford (1781–1852), senior military chaplain and rector of St David's Church, Hobart.

an eminence at some distance from the Church, and where the houses and inhabitants seemed rather of an inferior description to those I had before seen. In their manners and style of conversation, upon the different subjects, respecting which I interrogated them, they exhibited however all the easy confidence of virtue. The calls of my appetite now warned me that the day was fast waning, and I applied my hand to my fob to ascertain the hour, when to my utter dismay I found that one of Hawley's best gold watches, with which I had provided myself previous to my departure from England, was missing. To have lost it in any other manner than by accident, did not cross my mind for an instant, and I pictured to myself what delight would be the portion of him who had found it, when he should know to whom it was to be restored, and therefore pursued my journey to the Macquarie Hotel, with the view of taking up my quarters there, and obtaining some refreshment.

Having knocked at the door, it was opened by a smart dapper waiter, who ushered me into a large and well-furnished room, which I had scarcely entered before the Landlord, an obliging well-behaved man, paid his respects and enquired what I pleased to order. Upon my telling him that I was exceedingly hungry, he said that if I should not object to dine in a public room, dinner was now serving up, and that the company who were there, were all very respectable. I used to like table d'hote dinners before my seclusion from the world, and the idea now pleased me. Accordingly, I followed my host into the opposite room, in which were the Landlady, whose appearance and manners were greatly in her favour, and four visitors. They were all men well informed, and of lively conversation, and as I am ever a good listener, I brought this quality into full play on the occasion, carefully noting all that passed. It would be tedious to repeat what I then learned; one thing, however, I discovered to my sorrow, that my ideas of purity and virtue were like snow before the sun—beautiful, but easily dispelled, and that most probably my chronometer and I had parted company for ever. I determined however to make my loss the subject of a visit next morning to the Police-office. Ruminating upon the events of the day, and full of reflections at what I had heard and seen, I retired to my pillow, and being weary both in body and mind, was soon in the arms of Morpheus.

Amongst my plans for the succeeding day, I had purposed paying my respects at Government-house. Perhaps the result of my visit, as well there as at the Police-office, and the manner in which I spent the remainder of the day, may be communicated to my readers, when they next hear from me, till when, I am their obedient servant,

SIMON STUKELEY.
1829

ANONYMOUS

Eclogues usually celebrate the joys of rural life; this anonymous parody records the disastrous beginnings of the Swan River settlement in Western Australia in 1829 under the command of Governor James Stirling (1791–1865). There were problems in allocating land, and delays in establishing suitable crops led to food shortages. Many migrants left for elsewhere in Australia—including, one assumes, the author of this poem, since it appeared in a Hobart newspaper, the *Tasmanian*, on 26 March 1830. *EW*

A Swan River Eclogue

'Compare her face with some that I shall shew,
And I will make thee think thy Swan a Crow.'
　　　　　　　　　　　　　　Shakespeare

Though the classical bards, to cajole us,
　　Miraculous stories have told,
Of the glittering river Pactolus,
　　Whose margins were sanded with gold;
Of the Styx, whose ferruginous water,　　　　　　　5
　　Encrusting Achilles with steel,
Insured him for ever from slaughter,
　　Unless he were shot in the heel;—

Tho' Europe has many a river
　　To fame and to poetry known,　　　　　　　　10
The Tagus, the Po, Guadalquiver,
　　The Tiber, the Rhine, and the Rhone;
Tho' Nile throughout Africa ranges,
　　From Nubia down to the coast,
Tho' Hindoos are proud of the Ganges,　　　　　　15
　　And Yankees their Potomac boast;—

They must all hide their heads, and knock under,
　　(Old Nilus already has gone,)
To this mystical, magical wonder,
　　The river that's christened the Swan.　　　　　20
Oh! this is the river of rivers,
　　For curing all ills of the Fates,
Spleen, bad reputations and livers,
　　Empty pockets, and emptier plates!

The Captain who found it was STERLING!   25
 So no one should stare when he's told,
That its waves are for ever unfurling
 Supplies of Pactolian gold.
I cannot suppose they deride us,
 Or give us a shadow to clutch,   30
For all who have ears such as Midas,
 May safely make sure of his touch!

That the country is Paradisaic,
 To a certain extent I believe,
For the natives, both cleric and laic,   35
 Are naked as Adam and Eve,
With spear, some facetious mad sinner,
 Your short ribs may tickle and poke,
Dispatch you, and eat you for dinner—
 But lord, 'twill be only in joke!   40

Of the swans, whence it took its cognomen,
 The river may soon be bereft!
But none need repine at the omen,
 For *black-legs* enough will be left.
Failing these, there are *geese*—not the Roman, 45
 For *they* could their *capital* save;
With *jail-birds* acknowledged by no man,
 And *lame-ducks* for each passing wave.

How pleasant for civilized creatures,
 With a savage's life to be curst!   50
Not knowing whose morals or features,
 The white, brown or black man's are worst!
How cheering, instead of a cottage,
 In rain-dripping tents to reside;
To eat an opossum in pottage,   55
 Or feast on a kangaroo's hide!

How charming, with thousands of acres,
 A failure and famine to dread;
To have plenty of butchers and bakers,
 But wanting both cattle and bread!   60
How delightful to find your next neighbour,
 A thief, or a clown, or a sot;

Like a negro to drudge and to labour,
    And yet have a pennyless lot!

To the new Eldorado then hasten   65
    All ye who leave nothing behind,
And quickly, your fancies to chasten,
    You'll learn you have nothing to find.
Would you picture Swan River before a
    Full view to your eyes is unroll'd,   70
Imagine the box of Pandora,
    Without any Hope in its hold!

                             1830

ANONYMOUS

Unlike most other convict ballads, such as 'Moreton Bay', which lament the sufferings endured by the protagonist, 'Jim Jones at Botany Bay' is a defiant rejection of authority, with Jim threatening revenge on those responsible for his imprisonment. Although not collected until 1907, it has been dated to c. 1830 because of the reference to bushranger Jack Donohoe who was active in the late 1820s. *EW*

Jim Jones at Botany Bay

O, listen for a moment lads, and hear me tell my tale—
How, o'er the sea from England's shore I was compelled to sail.
The jury says 'he's guilty, sir,' and says the judge, says he—
'For life, Jim Jones, I'm sending you across the stormy sea;
And take my tip before you ship to join the Iron-gang,   5
Don't be too gay at Botany Bay, or else you'll surely hang—
Or else you'll hang,' he says, says he, 'and after that, Jim Jones,
High up upon the gallows-tree th' crows will pick your bones—
You'll have no time for mischief then; remember what I say,
They'll flog th' poachin' out of you, out there at Botany Bay.'   10

The winds blew high upon th' sea, and th' pirates came along,
But the soldiers on our convict ship were full five hundred strong.
They opened fire and somehow drove that pirate ship away.
I'd rather have joined that pirate ship than come to Botany Bay:
For night and day the irons clang, and like poor galley slaves,   15
We toil, and toil, and when we die must fill dishonoured graves.
But bye-and-bye I'll break my chains: into the bush I'll go,

And join th' brave bushrangers there—Jack Donohoo and Co.
And some dark night when everything is silent in the town
I'll kill the tyrants, one and all; and shoot th' floggers down: 20
I'll give th' Law a little shock: remember what I say,
They'll yet regret they sent Jim Jones in chains to Botany Bay.

c. 1830/1907

CHARLES STURT
1795–1869

Explorer Charles Sturt was born in India, where his father was a judge in Bengal, and educated in England. He joined the army in 1813 and after serving in Canada, France and Ireland was promoted to captain in 1825. In 1826 he embarked with his regiment for NSW, where he became military secretary to Governor Darling. From 1828 to 1831 he led expeditions into the interior of NSW, in which he traced the courses of the Macquarie, Murrumbidgee, Murray and Darling rivers. His account of his discoveries was published in London as *Two Expeditions into the Interior of Southern Australia, During the years 1828, 1829, 1830, and 1831: With observations on the soil, climate and general resources of the Colony of New South Wales* (1833). After retiring from the army, he settled on a farm near Sydney, but financial problems caused him to move to Adelaide in 1839. When denied his promised appointment as surveyor-general of South Australia, Sturt determined to make another expedition into the interior of Australia, in search of a presumed inland sea. Over eighteen months from 1844 to 1846, his party suffered extreme privations but were able to demonstrate that the interior consisted of desert rather than water. His *Narrative of an Expedition into Central Australia* appeared in 1849 and he returned to England in 1853. *EW*

From *Two Expeditions into the Interior of Southern Australia*
Volume II, Chapter IV

[...] After breakfast, we proceeded onwards as usual. The river[1] had increased so much in width that, the wind being fair, I hoisted sail for the first time, to save the strength of my men as much as possible. Our progress was consequently rapid. We passed through a country that, from the nature of its soil and other circumstances, appeared to be intersected by creeks and lagoons. Vast flights of wild fowl passed over us, but always at a considerable elevation, while, on the other hand, the paucity of ducks on the river excited our surprise. Latterly, the trees upon the river, and in its neighbourhood, had been a tortuous kind of box. The flooded-gum grew in groups on the spaces subject to inundation, but not on the levels above the influence of any ordinary rise of the stream. Still they were much smaller than they were observed to be in the higher branches of the river. We had proceeded about nine miles, when we were surprised by the appearance in view, at the termination of a

---

1   The Murrumbidgee River, NSW.

reach, of a long line of magnificent trees of green and dense foliage. As we sailed down the reach, we observed a vast concourse of natives under them, and, on a nearer approach, we not only heard their war-song, if it might so be called, but remarked that they were painted and armed, as they generally are, prior to their engaging in deadly conflict. Notwithstanding these outward signs of hostility, fancying that our four friends were with them, I continued to steer directly in for the bank on which they were collected. I found, however, when it was almost too late to turn into the succeeding reach to our left, that an attempt to land would only be attended with loss of life. The natives seemed determined to resist it. We approached so near that they held their spears quivering in their grasp ready to hurl. They were painted in various ways. Some who had marked their ribs, and thighs, and faces with a white pigment, looked like skeletons, others were daubed over with red and yellow ochre, and their bodies shone with the grease with which they had besmeared themselves. A dead silence prevailed among the front ranks, but those in the back ground, as well as the women, who carried supplies of darts, and who appeared to have had a bucket of whitewash capsized over their heads, were extremely clamorous. As I did not wish a conflict with these people, I lowered my sail, and putting the helm to starboard, we passed quietly down the stream in mid channel. Disappointed in their anticipations, the natives ran along the bank of the river, endeavouring to secure an aim at us; but, unable to throw with certainty, in consequence of the onward motion of the boat, they flung themselves into the most extravagant attitudes, and worked themselves into a state of frenzy by loud and vehement shouting.

It was with considerable apprehension that I observed the river to be shoaling fast, more especially as a huge sand-bank, a little below us, and on the same side on which the natives had gathered, projected nearly a third-way across the channel. To this sand-bank they ran with tumultuous uproar, and covered it over in a dense mass. Some of the chiefs advanced to the water to be nearer their victims, and turned from time to time to direct their followers. With every pacific disposition, and an extreme reluctance to take away life, I foresaw that it would be impossible any longer to avoid an engagement, yet with such fearful numbers against us, I was doubtful of the result. The spectacle we had witnessed had been one of the most appalling kind, and sufficient to shake the firmness of most men; but at that trying moment my little band preserved their temper coolness, and if any thing could be gleaned from their countenances, it was that they had determined on an obstinate resistance. I now explained to them that their only chance of escape depended, or would depend, on their firmness. I desired that after the first volley had been fired, M'Leay and three of the men, would attend to the defence of the boat with bayonets only, while I, Hopkinson, and Harris, would keep up the fire as being more used to it. I ordered, however, that no shot was to be fired until after I had discharged both my barrels. I then delivered their arms to the men, which had as yet been kept in the place appropriated for them, and at the same time some rounds of loose cartridge. The men assured me they would follow my instructions, and thus prepared, having already lowered the sail, we drifted onwards with the current. As we neared the sand-bank, I stood up and made signs to the natives to desist; but without success. I took up my gun, therefore, and cocking it, had already brought it down to a level. A few seconds more would have closed the life of the nearest of the savages. The distance was too trifling for me to doubt the fatal effects of the discharge; for I was determined to take deadly aim, in hopes that the fall of one man might save the lives of many. But at the very moment, when my hand was on the trigger, and my eye was along the barrel, my purpose was checked by M'Leay, who called to me that another party of blacks had made their appearance upon the left bank of the river. Turning round, I observed four men at the top of their speed. The foremost of them as soon as he got a-head of the boat, threw himself from a considerable height into the water. He struggled across the channel to the sand-bank, and in an incredibly short space of time stood in front of the savage, against whom my aim had been directed. Seizing him by the throat, he pushed him backwards, and forcing all who were in the water upon the bank, he trod its margin with a vehemence and an agitation that were exceedingly striking. At one moment pointing to the boat, at another shaking his clenched hand in the faces of the most forward, and stamping with passion on the sand; his voice, that was at first distinct and clear, was lost in hoarse murmurs. Two of the four natives remained on the left bank of the river, but the third followed his leader, (who proved to be the remarkable savage I have previously noticed) to the scene of action. The reader will imagine our feelings on this occasion: it is impossible to describe them. We were so wholly lost in interest at the scene that was passing, that the boat was allowed to drift at pleasure. For my own part I was overwhelmed with astonishment, and in truth stunned and confused; so singular, so unexpected, and so strikingly providential, had been our escape.

We were again roused to action by the boat suddenly striking upon a shoal, which reached from one side of the river to the other. To jump out and push her into deeper water was but the work of a moment with the men, and it was just as she floated again that our attention was withdrawn to a new and beautiful stream, coming apparently from the north. The great body of the natives having posted themselves on the narrow tongue of land formed by the two rivers, the bold savage who had so unhesitatingly interfered on our account, was still in hot dispute with them, and I really feared his generous warmth would have brought down upon him the vengeance of the tribes. I hesitated, therefore, whether or not to go to his assistance. It appeared, however, both to M'Leay and myself, that the tone of the natives had moderated, and the old and young men having listened to the remonstrances of our friend, the middle-aged warriors were alone holding out against him. A party of about seventy blacks were upon the right bank of the newly discovered river, and I thought that by landing among them, we should make a diversion in favour of our late guest; and in this I succeeded. If even they had still meditated violence, they would have to swim a good broad junction, and that, probably, would cool them, or we at least should have the advantage of position. I therefore, ran the boat ashore, and landed with M'Leay amidst the smaller party of natives, wholly unarmed, and having directed the men to keep at a little distance from the bank. Fortunately, what I anticipated was brought about by the stratagem to which I had had recourse. The blacks no sooner observed that we had landed, than curiosity took place of anger. All wrangling ceased, and they came swimming over to us like a parcel of seals. Thus, in less than a quarter of an hour from the moment when it appeared that all human intervention was at an end, and we were on the point of commencing a bloody fray, which, independently of its own disastrous consequences, would have blasted the success of the expedition, we were peacefully surrounded by the hundreds who had so lately threatened us with destruction; nor was it until after we had returned to the boat, and had surveyed the multitude upon the sloping bank above us, that we became fully aware of the extent of our danger, and of the almost miraculous intervention of Providence in our favour. There could not have been less than six hundred natives upon that blackened sward. But this was not the only occasion upon which the merciful superintendance of that Providence to which we had humbly committed ourselves, was strikingly manifested. If these pages fail to convey entertainment or information, sufficient may at least be gleaned from them to furnish matter for serious reflection; but to those who have been placed in situations of danger where human ingenuity availed them not, and where human foresight was baffled, I feel persuaded that these remarks are unnecessary.

It was my first care to call for our friend, and to express to him, as well as I could, how much we stood indebted to him, at the same time that I made him a suitable present; but to the chiefs of the tribes, I positively refused all gifts, notwithstanding their earnest solicitations. We next prepared to examine the new river, and turning the boat's head towards it, endeavoured to pull up the stream. Our larboard oars touched the right bank, and the current was too strong for us to conquer it with a pair only; we were, therefore, obliged to put a second upon her, a movement that excited the astonishment and admiration of the natives. One old woman seemed in absolute ecstasy, to whom M'Leay threw an old tin kettle, in recompense for the amusement she afforded us.

As soon as we got above the entrance of the new river,[1] we found easier pulling, and proceeded up it for some miles, accompanied by the once more noisy multitude. The river preserved a breadth of one hundred yards, and a depth of rather more than twelve feet. Its banks were sloping and grassy, and were overhung by trees of magnificent size. Indeed, its appearance was so different from the water-worn banks of the sister stream, that the men exclaimed, on entering it, that we had got into an English river. Its appearance certainly almost justified the expression; for the greenness of its banks was as new to us as the size of its timber. Its waters, though sweet, were turbid, and had a taste of vegetable decay, as well as a slight tinge of green. Our progress was watched by the natives with evident anxiety. They kept abreast of us, and talked incessantly. At length, however, our course was checked by a net that stretched right across the stream. I say *checked*, because it would have been unfair to have passed over it with the chance of disappointing the numbers who apparently depended on it for subsistence that day. The moment was one of intense interest to me. As the men rested upon their oars, awaiting my further orders, a crowd of thoughts rushed upon me. The various conjectures I had formed of the course and importance of the Darling passed across my mind. Were they indeed realised? An irresistible conviction impressed me that we were now sailing on the bosom of that very stream from whose banks I had been twice forced to retire. I directed the Union Jack to be hoisted, and giving way to our satisfaction, we all stood up in the boat, and gave three distinct cheers. It was an English feeling, an ebullition, an overflow, which I am ready to admit that our circumstances and situation will alone excuse. The eye of every native had been fixed upon that noble flag, at all times a beautiful object, and to them a novel one, as it waved over us in the heart of a desert. They had, until that moment been particularly loquacious, but the sight of that flag and the sound of our voices hushed the tumult, and while they were still lost in astonishment, the boat's head was speedily turned, the sail was sheeted home, both wind and current were in our favour, and we vanished from them with a rapidity that surprised even ourselves, and which precluded every hope of the most adventurous among them to keep up with us.

1833

ELIZA DUNLOP
1796–1880

Poet Eliza Dunlop was born in Ireland where she began contributing verse to magazines such as the *Dublin Penny Journal*. With her second husband, David Dunlop, she arrived in Sydney in 1838. 'The Aboriginal Mother (from Myall's Creek)' was written as a protest against the Myall Creek Massacre and published at a time of intense debate as

---

1   The Murray River.

to whether the white stockmen responsible for this brutal murder of Aboriginal people should be hanged as punishment. After her husband was appointed police magistrate and Protector of Aborigines at Wollombi, north of Sydney, in 1839, they built a stone house, Mulla Villa, which is still standing. Eliza Dunlop continued to publish her poems in local newspapers and magazines with some being set to music by composer Isaac Nathan. She was one of the first Europeans to value Aboriginal culture and appreciate the poetic quality of Indigenous songs, translating some into English and also helping to record local vocabularies. A manuscript volume of her poems, 'The Vase', is in the Mitchell Library, and a small selection of them was published as *The Aboriginal Mother and Other Poems* (1981). *EW*

The Aboriginal Mother (from Myall's Creek)

Oh! hush thee—hush my baby,
    I may not tend thee yet.
Our forest-home is distant far,
    And midnight's star is set.
Now, hush thee—or the pale-faced men   5
    Will hear thy piercing wail,
And what would then thy mother's tears
    Or feeble strength avail!

Oh, could'st thy little bosom,
    That mother's torture feel,   10
Or could'st thou know thy father lies
    Struck down by English steel;
Thy tender form would wither,
    Like the *kniven* in the sand,
And the spirit of my perished tribe   15
    Would vanish from our land.

For thy young life, my precious,
    I fly the field of blood,
Else had I, for my chieftain's sake,
    Defied them where they stood;   20
But basely bound my woman's arm,
    No weapon might it wield:
I could but cling round him I loved,
    To make my heart a shield.

I saw my firstborn treasure   25
    Lie headless at my feet,
The *goro* on this hapless breast,
    In his life-stream is wet!

And thou! I snatched thee from their sword,
    It harmless pass'd by thee!   30
But clave the binding cords—and gave,
    Haply, the power to flee.

To flee! my babe—but wither?
    Without my friend—my guide?
The blood that was our strength is shed!   35
    He is not by my side!
Thy sire! oh! never, never
    Shall *Toon Bakra* hear our cry:
My bold and stately mountain-bird!
    I thought not he could die.   40

Now who will teach thee, dearest,
    To poise the shield, and spear,
To wield the *koopin*, or to throw
    The *boommerring*, void of fear;
To breast the river in its might;   45
    The mountain tracks to tread?
The echoes of my homeless heart
    Reply—the dead, the dead!

And ever must the murmur
    Like an ocean torrent flow: 50
The parted voice comes never back,
    To cheer our lonely woe:
Even in the region of our tribe,
    Beside our summer streams,
'Tis but a hollow symphony—   55
    In the shadow-land of dreams.

Oh hush thee, dear—for weary
    And faint I bear thee on—
His name is on thy gentle lips,
    My child, my child, *he's gone!*   60
Gone o'er the golden fields that lie
    Beyond the rolling clouds,
To bring thy people's murder cry
    Before the Christian's God.

Yes! o'er the stars that guide us,   65
    He brings my slaughter'd boy:

To shew their God how treacherously
    The stranger men destroy;
To tell how hands in friendship pledged
    Piled high the fatal pire;   70
To tell, to tell of the gloomy ridge!
    And the *stockmen's human fire.*

1838/1981

FRANK THE POET
c. 1810—c. 1861

Francis MacNamara, better known as Frank the Poet, was born in Ireland and from his writing appears to have received a good education. In 1832 he was convicted of larceny and sentenced to seven years' transportation to NSW. It is possible that he was also involved in political agitation while in Ireland. Certainly, he rebelled against the convict system, absconding and receiving repeated floggings and other punishments, including an extended sentence. As a repeat offender, he was sent to Port Arthur in Van Diemen's Land (Tasmania) in 1842, where he finally received a ticket of leave in 1847 and his freedom in 1849. His cheeky, often improvised verse, which included epigrams and ballads as well as the more polished and longer 'A Convict's Tour to Hell', would not have won him any favours from the authorities though relished by his fellow prisoners and many others. While only one poem was published in his lifetime, a number of others have survived in manuscript form in the Mitchell Library. The ballad 'Moreton Bay' has also been attributed to MacNamara. *EW*

A Convict's Tour to Hell

> '*Nor can the foremost of the sons of men*
> *Escape my ribald and licentious pen.'*
>   Swift

You prisoners all of New South Wales
Who frequent watchhouses and gaols
A story to you I will tell
'Tis of a Convict's Tour to Hell
Whose valour had for years been tried   5
On the highway before he died.
At length he fell to death a prey
To him it proved an happy day
Downwards he bent his course I'm told
Like one destined for Satan's fold   10
And no refreshment would he take
'Till he approached the Stygian lake.
A tent he then began to fix
Contiguous to the River Styx
Thinking that no one could molest him   15

He leaped when Charon thus addressed him
Stranger I say from whence art thou
And thy own name pray tell me now.
Kind sir I came from Sydney gaol
My name I don't mean to conceal   20
And since you seem anxious to know it
On earth I was called Frank the Poet.
[Are you that person? Charon cried]
I'll carry you to the other side
So Stranger do not troubled be   25
For you shall have a passage free
Five or sixpence I mostly charge
For the like passage in my barge.
Frank seeing no other succour nigh
With the invitation did comply   30
And having a fair wind and tide
They soon arrived at the other side
And leaving Charon at the ferry
Frank went in haste to Purgatory
And rapping loudly at the gate   35
Of Limbo or the Middle State
Pope Pius the 7th soon appeared
With gown, beads, crucifix and beard
And gazing at the Poet the while
Accosts him in the following style   40
Stranger art thou a friend or foe
Your business here I fain would know.
Quoth the Poet for Heaven I'm not fitted
And here I hope to be admitted.
Pius rejoined vain are your hopes   45
This place was made for Priests and Popes
'Tis a world of our own invention
But friend I've not the least intention
To admit such a foolish elf
Who scarce knows how to bless himself.   50
Quoth Frank were you mad or insane
When first you made this world of pain
For I can see nothing but brimstone and fire
A share of which I can't desire
Here I see weeping wailing gnashing   55
And torments of the newest fashion
Therefore I call you silly elf

Who made a rod to whip yourself
And may you like all honest neighbours
Enjoy the fruit of all your labours. 60
Frank then bade the Pope farewell
And hurried to that place called Hell
And having found the gloomy gate
Frank rapped aloud to know his fate
He louder knocked and louder still 65
When the Devil came, pray what's you will?
Alas cried the Poet I've come to dwell
With you and share your fate in Hell.
Says Satan such can't be, I'm sure
For I detest and hate the poor 70
And none shall in my kingdom stand
Except the grandees of the land
But Frank I think you're going astray
For convicts never come this way
But soar to Heaven in droves and legions 75
A place so called in the upper regions
So Frank I think with an empty purse
You shall go farther and fare worse.
Well cried the Poet since 'tis so
One thing of you I'd like to know 80
As I'm at present in no hurry
Have you one here called Captain Murray?[1]
Yes Murray is within this place
Will you said Satan see his face?
May God forbid that I should view him 85
For on board the Phoenix Hulk I knew him.
Who is that Sir in yonder blaze
Who on fire and brimstone seems to graze?
'Tis Captain Logan of Moreton Bay
And Williams who was killed the other day 90
He was overseer at Grosse Farm
And done poor prisoners no little harm
Cook who discovered New South Wales
And he that first invented gaols
Are both tied to a fiery stake 95
Which stands in yonder boiling lake.
Hark do you hear this dreadful yelling

1   Superintendent of the Phoenix Hulk and Governor of Carter's Barracks.

It issues from Doctor Wardell's[1] dwelling
And all those fiery seats and chairs
Are fitted up for Dukes and Mayors   100
And nobles of Judicial orders
Barristers, Lawyers and Recorders.
Here I beheld legions of traitors
Hangmen, Gaolers and Flagellators
Commandants, Constables and Spies   105
Informers and Overseers likewise
In flames of brimstone they were toiling
And lakes of sulphur round them boiling
Hell did resound with their fierce yelling
Alas how dismal was their dwelling   110
Then Major Morriset[2] I espied
And Captain Cluney[3] by his side
With a fiery belt they were lashed together
As tight as soles to upper leather
Their situation was most horrid   115
For they were tyrants down at the Norrid
Prostrate I beheld a petitioner
It was the Company's Commissioner.
Satan said he my days are ended
For many years I've superintended   120
The Australian Company's affairs
And I punctually paid all arrears
Sir should you doubt the hopping Colonel[4]
At Carrington you'll find my journal
Legibly penned in black and white   125
To prove that my accounts were right
And since I've done your will on earth
I hope you'll put me in a berth.
Then I saw old Serjeant Flood[5]
In Vulcan's hottest forge he stood   130
He gazed at me his eyes with ire
Appeared like burned coals of fire
In fiery garments he was arrayed
And like an Arabian horse he brayed

---

1   Robert Wardell (1793–1834), barrister and newspaper proprietor, shot by escaped convict John Jenkins.
2   James Thomas Morisset (1780?–1852), commandant at Newcastle, 1818–23, and later at Norfolk Island.
3   James Oliphant Clunie (1795–1851), commandant at Moreton Bay, 1830–35.
4   Henry Dumaresq (1792–1838), severely wounded at Waterloo.
5   Member of the 28th Regiment, stationed at Newcastle in 1836–37.

He on a bloody cutlass leaned 135
And to a lamp-post he was chained
He loudly called out for assistance
Or begged me to end his existence.
Cheer up said I be not afraid
Remember No. Three Stockade 140
In the course of time you may do well
If you behave yourself in Hell
Your heart on earth was fraught with malice
Which oft drove convicts to the gallows
But you'll now atone for all the blood 145
Of prisoners shed by Serjeant Flood.
Then I beheld that well known Trapman
The Police Runner called Izzy Chapman[1]
Here he was standing on his head
In a river of melted boiling lead. 150
Alas he cried behold me stranger
I've captured many a bold bushranger
And for the same I'm suffering here
But lo, now yonder snakes draw near
On turning round I saw slow worms 155
And snakes of various kinds and forms
All entering at his mouth and nose
To devour his entrails as I suppose.
Then turning round to go away
Bold Lucifer bade me to stay 160
Saying Frank by no means go man
Till you see your old friend Dr Bowman[2]
Yonder he tumbles groans and gnashes
He gave you many a thousand lashes
And for the same he does bewail 165
For Osker with an iron flail
Thrashes him well you may depend
And will till the world comes to an end.
Just as I spoke a coach and four
Came in full poste haste to the door 170
And about six feet of mortal sin
Without leave or licence trudged in

---

1   Israel Chapman (1794?–1868), convict who received an absolute pardon in 1827 for his services to the
    police, especially in capturing bushrangers.
2   James Bowman (1784–1846), principal surgeon, Sydney Hospital, 1819–28.

At his arrival 3 cheers were given
Which rent I'm sure the highest Heaven
And all the inhabitants of Hell 175
With one consent rang the great bell
Which never was heard to sound or ring
Since Judas sold our Heavenly King
Drums were beating flags were hoisting
There never before was such rejoicing 180
Dancing, singing, joy or mirth
In Heaven above nor on the earth
Straightway to Lucifer I went
To know what these rejoicings meant.
Of sense cried Lucifer I'm deprived 185
Since Governor Darling[1] has arrived
With fire and brimstone I've ordained him
And Vulcan has already chained him
And I'm going to fix an abode
For Captain Rossi[2] he's on the road. 190
Frank don't go till you see the novice
The magistrate from the Police Office.
Oh said the Poet I'm satisfied
To hear that he is to be tied
And burned in this World of Fire 195
I think 'tis high time to retire
And having travelled many days
O'er fiery hills and boiling seas
At length I found that happy place
Where all the woes of mortals cease 200
And rapping boldly at the wicket
Cried Peter, where's your certificate
Or if you have not one to shew
Pray who in Heaven do you know?
Well I know Brave Donohue 205
Young Troy and Jenkins too
And many others whom floggers mangled.
And lastly were by Jack Ketch[3] strangled.
Peter, says Jesus, let Frank in
For he is thoroughly purged from sin 210

1   Sir Ralph Darling (1772–1858), governor of NSW, 1824–31.
2   Francis Nicholas Rossi (1776–1851), superintendent of police in NSW, 1825–34.
3   Hangman at the assizes of Judge Jeffreys in 1685, his name became synonymous with the profession.

And although in convict's habit dressed
Here he shall be a welcome guest.

    Isiah go with him to Job
    And put on him a scarlet robe
    St Paul go to the flock straightway   215
    And kill the fatted calf today
    And go tell Abraham and Abel
    In haste now to prepare the table
    For we shall have a grand repast
    Since Frank the Poet has come at last   220
    Then came Moses and Elias
    John the Baptist and Mathias
    With many saints from foreign lands
    And with the Poet they all join hands.

Thro' Heaven's Concave their rejoicings rang   225
And hymns of praise to God they sang
And as they praised his glorious name
I awoke and found 'twas but a dream.

                1839/1979

ANONYMOUS

Also known as 'The Convict's Lament', this ballad is set in the penal colony of Moreton Bay, near Brisbane, established in 1824 and notorious for its harsh commandant, Captain Patrick Logan (1791–1830). It has been attributed to Frank the Poet (qv), though there is no evidence that he was ever at Moreton Bay. Many versions exist; this one was published in Jack Bradshaw, *The Quirindi Bank Robbery* (c. 1899). *EW*

Moreton Bay

    I am a native of the land of Erin,
    And lately banished from that lovely shore,
    I left behind me my aged parents,
    And the girl I adore.

    In transit storms as I set sailing,   5
    Like a bold mariner my coast did steer,
    Sydney harbour was my destination—
    That cursed harbour at length drew near;
    I then joined banquet in congratulation
    On my safe arrival from the briny sea;   10

But alas! alas! I was mistaken—
Twelve years transported to Moreton Bay.

Early one morning as I carelessly wandered,
By the Brisbane waters I chanced to stray,
I saw a prisoner sadly bewailing,   15
While on the sunbeaming banks he lay.
He said, I have been a prisoner at Port Macquarie,
At Norfolk Island, and Emu Plain,
At Castle Hill, and cursed Towngabbie—
And at all those places I've worked in chains;   20

But of all the places of condemnation
In each penal station of New South Wales
Moreton Bay I found no equal,
For excessive tyranny each day prevails.
Early in the morning, as the day is dawning,   25
To trace from heaven the morning dew,
Up we are started at a moment's warning,
Our daily labour for to renew;

Our overseers and superintendents,
All these cursed tyrants' language we must obey,   30
Or else at the triangles our flesh is mangled—
That is our wages at Moreton Bay.
For three long years I've been beastly treated;
Heavy irons each day I wore,
My poor back from flogging has been lacerated,   35
And oftimes painted with crimson gore.

Like the Egyptians or ancient Hebrews,
We were sorely oppressed by Logan's yoke,
Till kind Providence came to our assistance,
And gave this tyrant his fatal stroke.   40
Yes, he was hurried from that place of bondage,
Where he thought he would gain renown;
But a native black, who lay in ambush,
Gave this monster his fatal wound.

Now that I've got once more to cross the ocean,   45
And leave this place called Moreton Bay,
Where many a man from downright starvation

Lies mouldering to-day beneath the clay.
Fellow prisoners be exhilarated,
And your former sufferings don't bear in mind,   50
For its when from bondage you are extricated,
We will leave those tyrants far, behind.

c. 1840/c. 1899

ELIZA BROWN
1810–1896

Letter writer Eliza Brown was born in England and migrated to WA with her husband to settle in the York district near Perth. Her letters home, mostly written to her father, William Bussey, began in 1840 while in London waiting to board ship. They continued until 1852, when the family moved to Perth, and give rare insights into a settler's life from a female perspective. They were edited by her great-great-grandson, the writer Peter Cowan, and published as *A Faithful Picture: The letters of Eliza and Thomas Brown at York in the Swan River Colony 1841–1852* (1977). *EW*

Letter to Her Father

My dearest Papa,

I am in the joyful possession of your letters to Mr Brown and myself of the dates Feby 26th from Cuddesdon and July 16th from the Isle of Wight. My husband was from home with his teams taking sandalwood down to Guildford, think what a delight it was to me to read your letters to him on his return which happened on the day I received them, Decr. 11th. I thought it so problematical whether you would find it convenient to help us or be willing to trust us further while we are still in your debt to so large an amount that the surprise was very great and you may judge that we are both of us very much elated and more thankful than we can express ourselves. Everything now looks up, sandalwood is increased in value since I last wrote, Mr Bland gives my husband twelve pounds per ton for it *delivered at Fremantle*. This was agreed upon and a large quantity contracted for on Mr Bland's part while reports were good with respect to its value in China. A trial cargo has been shipped which Luke Leake (son of Mrs Luke Leake our fellow passenger on the *Sterling*) went with in the *Bandicoot* to Hong Kong. He has very lately returned saying it was three weeks before he could dispose of his cargo and then only at sixteen pounds per ton. He was at first in high spirits as the merchants told him he would get forty but when they came to examine the wood they declared it to be of an inferior sort. Now Luke Leake has but a very young head on his shoulders, albeit a very steady trustworthy lad, and he may have been taken in. It looks well that he is going with another cargo and that the speculators have not ceased to buy. It is in the interest of these parties to keep prices in the Colony as low as possible and they would not be likely to sound a trumpet as to its great value in China. In general only seven or eight pounds per ton is given for it here now. I must drive Mr Brown to the pen to tell you of prices current, horses, cattle, sheep, and more particulars about Mr Bland and sandalwood, though under the rose let me tell you I have not lived with him these twelve years without becoming aware that he is a very awkward subject either to lead or drive, though if I do put the pen in his hand perhaps he will be telling you something just as pretty of me.

I have so much to tell you I hardly know what to begin with first, but as I know you are gallant enough to take a great interest in the fair sex I will introduce a young Lady to your notice, Matilda Brown, who opened her eyes upon this world on Thursday the 25th November. We call her a Kenneth child she is like him but has smaller features than he had when a baby. I write at the present moment with her in my arms, she is just a fortnight and four days old, at least will be before midnight. The Doctor was not here when I was taken poorly and when we sent for the Nurse she was prevented from coming by the obstinacy of her husband who declared she should not leave him and her children to wait on any lady. In the dilemma we applied to Mr Bland who very promptly sent his Housekeeper, a very experienced nurse who was with dear Mrs Bland in her fatal illness. I had such comfort from the kind attentions of this good creature, Mrs Heffron.

It is with a view of giving some insight into the social characteristics of this place that I mention the circumstance of having administered myself the necessary attentions to two women of the labouring class who were without Nurse, Doctor, or neighbour or any female but myself within several miles at the time of their illness. In both instances before their husbands returned who had been despatched for the Doctor the women were partaking of their gruel very snugly in bed with the Infant beside them in best bib and tucker.

And now my dear Papa I should make you tremble with what I have to relate did I not first tell you all is safe now, but Kenneth has been within a hair's breadth of having his life taken. He has been speared in the side, but not by a Native, the Natives when they saw he was wounded ran to his assistance intending to knock the barb off the spear but it was a blunt pointed spear without a barb, and Kenneth had pushed it out of his side before they reached it. It penetrated the flesh in his side the length of my forefinger, when I saw the wound which was four days from the time he received it, it was festering where the spear went in and where it came out. He concealed the injury from me all that time fearing it would make me ill to know of it. I had been but a few days confined and he saw that I was in delicate health. His Papa was on one of his weekly trips with the sandalwood. Our shepherd boy who did it was in agony of apprehension fearing for the child and wished it to be told but Kenneth made him be silent and went quietly over to Mr Hardey's to have it dressed. The evening before his Papa came home it all transpired for the servant girl told me, she had become alarmed because it was festering. My nerves are better than people think, I saw at once that the danger was over and was not agitated. I believe if there had been danger I should very calmly have endeavoured to mitigate it and sent in the mean time for a medical adviser. Kenneth is very fond of throwing the spear at a mark or at a bird and prides himself upon being able to jump a spear, that is jump out of the way of one after it is thrown. This he was attempting to do when he got wounded and I hope it will be a good lesson to him not to run such a risk again. Dr de Lille the military surgeon asked to see the wound (he happened to come up with Mr Brown) and he said that the spear very narrowly escaped fixing itself in the liver. How curious that we should receive a warning from you not to trust him in the way of the Natives just about the time that danger has threatened to happen to him from one of their missile weapons.

About the middle of October I went down to Perth, took little Aubrey this time. I had not visited the Capital for nearly two years, the old saying 'out of sight out of mind' came into my head along with the wish to see and be seen. I met with no opposition from the quarter where I rather expected it, found my partner very complying, quite agreeable to my proposal, so he drove us down with great good humour.

We called at the Colonial Chaplain's (J.B. Wittenoom), he opened the door himself, his first exclamation was 'A Star shot from its hemisphere'. 'Yes (I replied in a very dignified manner) to come jolting down in a spring cart.' I had before been told there would be an eclipse of the sun upon my leaving York by the grave Mr Bland, which was literally true, but I gave him to understand that other spheres would not be brightened by that circumstance. [. . .]

There is one more subject to discuss with you my dear Papa and that the most important of any that has yet been touched upon except your bounty in clearing us of our difficulties which will go far towards establishing my husband in worldly respect and honor. I cannot read your affectionate mention of my boys without emotion, your hint that one would be welcome were we to send him to England is not lost upon me. Were we at any time to act upon it it would be Kenneth I should send. I am in great hopes that your valuable life will be prolonged for many years and if when you write in reply to this the wish still continues to see my boy and you feel after all your acts of generosity that your income will bear the additional burden of getting him efficiently instructed I think I should be acting against his most important interests to keep him back from such a privilege. He has no idea of being a settler in this country, his thoughts revert to England from whence we brought him and where for the little time he dwelt he lived the life of an angel for happiness, health and advantages. The son of a settler becoming a settler in this Colony leads but a very obscure life, much more so than the parent who comes from England, I am aware of the fact but cannot now give the reasons. Before I am quite exhausted with writing I hope to give you my wishes of what he should be brought up to that his education may be conducted with a view to his after career. My hopes perhaps may be too ambitious. I wish him to jostle it with other boys at a public school for about four years, Eton, Westminster, Harrow, or the High School of Edinburgh, then if we are prosperous we might send him to College, then the Inner Temple and Lincolns Inn after which he would be eligible to go the circuit with the judges and make an excellent Sergeant Bother'em I fancy, he has a judicial turn and the boy seems to keep constant to the idea that he will be a Barrister.

Now my dearest Papa

> Farewell
> Yours gratefully and affectionately
> Eliza Brown

(the midnight oil has fallen upon my paper)

Received May 2 1848

1847/1977

LOUISA ANNE MEREDITH
1812–1895

Writer, artist and naturalist Louisa Anne Meredith was born in England and educated mostly by her mother. Her first book, a collection of poems illustrated by herself, mainly dealing with natural objects, especially flowers, appeared in 1835. It was followed by five others in a similar style, illustrated either by herself or others. After marrying her cousin Charles Meredith in 1839, she travelled with him to NSW where he had pastoral interests. In 1840 he purchased land in Van Diemen's Land (Tasmania), where his family lived, but the 1842 drought and depression saw him in financial difficulties. Louisa Meredith's lively account of her first years in Australia, *Notes and Sketches of New South Wales, During a Residence in that Colony from 1839 to 1844* (1844) sold well in England, going through several editions, but her criticisms of local customs and manners were not well received in Sydney. She later produced two further travel books: *My Home in Tasmania, During a Residence of Nine Years* (1852) and *Over the Straits: A visit to Victoria* (1861) as well as novels, plays, poems and illustrated volumes. In 1884 she received a pension from the Tasmanian government in recognition of her 'services to the Cause of Science, Literature and Art'. *EW*

From *Notes and Sketches of New South Wales*
Chapter VI

The market in Sydney is well supplied, and is held in a large commodious building, superior to most provincial market-houses at home. The display of fruit in the grape season is very beautiful. Peaches also are most abundant, and very cheap; apples very dear, being chiefly imported from Van Diemen's Land, and frequently selling at sixpence each. The smaller English fruits, such as strawberries, &c. only succeed in a few situations in the colony, and are far from plentiful. Cucumbers and all descriptions of melon abound. The large green water-melon, rose-coloured within, is a very favourite fruit, but I thought it insipid. One approved method of eating it is, after cutting a sufficiently large hole, to pour in a bottle of Madeira or sherry, and mix it with the cold watery pulp. These melons grow to an enormous size (an ordinary one is from twelve to eighteen inches in diameter), and may be seen piled up like huge cannonballs at all the fruit-shop doors, being universally admired in this hot, thirsty climate.

There are some excellent fish to be procured here, but I know them only by the common Colonial names, which are frequently misnomers. The snapper, or schnapper, is the largest with which I am acquainted, and is very nice, though not esteemed a proper dish for a dinner-party—why, I am at a loss to guess; but I never saw any native fish at a Sydney dinner-table—the preserved or cured cod and salmon from England being served instead, at a considerable expense, and, to my taste, it is not comparable with the cheap fresh fish, but being expensive, it has become 'fashionable', and that circumstance reconciles all things. The guardfish is long and narrow, about the size of a herring, with a very singular head, the mouth opening at the top, as it were, and the lower jaw, or nose, projecting two-thirds of an inch beyond it. I imagine it must live chiefly at the bottom, and this formation enables it more readily to seize the food above it. They are most delicate little fish. The bream, a handsome fish, not unlike a perch in shape (but much larger, often weighing four or five pounds), and the mullet, but especially the latter, are excellent. The whiting, much larger than its English namesake, is perhaps the best of all; but I pretend to no great judgment as a gastronome. I thought the rock-oysters particularly nice, and they are plentiful and cheap; so are the crayfish, which are very similar to lobsters, when small, but the large ones rather coarse. I must not end my list of fish that we eat without mentioning one that is always ready to return the compliment when an opportunity offers, namely, the shark, many of whom are habitants of the bright tempting waters of Port Jackson. Provisions vary much in price from many circumstances. Everything was very dear when we landed in New South Wales, and at the present time prices are much too low to pay the producers.

The dust is one main source of annoyance in Sydney. Unless after very heavy rain, it is *always* dusty; and sometimes, when the wind is in one particular point, the whirlwinds of thick fine powder that fill every street and house are positive miseries. These dust-winds are locally named 'brick-fielders', from the direction in which they come; and no sooner is the approach of one perceived than the streets are instantly deserted, windows and doors closely shut, and everyone who can remains within till the plague has passed over, when you ring for the servant with a duster, and collect enough fine earth for a small garden off your chairs and tables.

Flies are another nuisance; they swarm in every room in tens of thousands, and blacken the breakfast or dinner table as soon as the viands appear, tumbling into the cream, tea, wine, and gravy with the most disgusting familiarity. But worse than these are the mosquitoes, nearly as numerous, and infinitely more detestable to those for whose luckless bodies they form an attachment, as they do to most new comers; a kind of initiatory compliment which I would gladly dispense with, for most intolerable is the torment they cause in the violent irritation of their mountainous bites. All houses are furnished with a due attention to these indefatigable gentry, and the beds have consequently a curious aspect to an English eye accustomed to solid four-posters, with voluminous hangings of chintz or damask, and a pile of feather-beds which would annihilate a sleeper in this climate. Here you have usually a neat thin skeleton-looking frame of brass or iron, over which is thrown a gauze garment, consisting of curtains, head, and tester, all sewn together; the former full, and resting on the floor when let down, but during the day tied up in festoons. Some of these materials are very pretty, being silk, with satin stripes of white or other delicate tints on the green gauze ground. At night, after the curtains are lowered, a grand hunt takes place, to kill or drive out the mosquitoes from within; having effected which somewhat wearisome task, you tuck the net in all round, leaving one small bit which you carefully raise, and nimbly pop through the aperture into bed, closing the curtain after you. This certainly postpones the ingress of the enemy, but no precaution that my often-tasked ingenuity could invent will prevent it effectually. They are terrible pests, and very frequently aided in their nocturnal invasions of one's rest by the still worse and thrice-disgusting creatures familiar to most dwellers in London lodgings or seaport inns, to say nothing of fleas, which seem to pervade this colony in one universal swarm. The thickest part of a town, or the most secluded spot in the wild bush, is alike replete with these small but active annoyances.

One day we drove out to the lighthouse on the South Head, about eight miles from Sydney. Soon after leaving the town the road passes the new court-house and gaol, and its handsome front, in the Doric or Ionic style (I forget which), is the only architectural building the 'city' could boast when I was there, though I suppose that ere this the new Government House, a mansion in the Elizabethan-Gothic style, is completed. We began shortly to ascend a hill, the road being all sea-sand apparently, and nothing but sand was visible all around. Great green mat-like plats of the pretty

Mesembryanthemum aequilaterale, or fig-marigold, adorned the hot sandy banks by the roadside. It bears a bright purple flower, and a five-sided fruit, called by children 'pig-faces'. A very prickly species of solanum also grew here, with large green spiky leaves, more difficult to gather even than holly, and pretty bluish potato-like blossoms. The universal tea-tree, and numberless shrubs which I knew not, adorned the sandy wastes in all directions. As we continued to ascend, the road became very rough, huge masses of rock protruding like gigantic steps, over which the wheels scraped and grated and jumped in a way that made me draw rather strong comparisons between the character of roads at home and abroad. As we approached the summit, the hollow formed by the road was suddenly filled by a background (forgive the paradox) of deep blue water; it was the open sea that gradually rose before us, seen over the rocks, and spreading out bright and blue, with small waves sparkling in the fervid sunshine, and the white diamond-crested spray dashing high against the iron-bound coast, here broken into a low craggy amphitheatre, into which the rolling waves came surging on, breaking over the groups of rocks, and forming bright little basins among them. On either side the rocks rose again in large masses, presenting a precipitous face to the sea, being part of the dark formidable cliffs we had seen in approaching the Heads by sea. The road, after descending the hill, turned to the left, through some sandy scrub, crowded with such exquisite flowers that to me it appeared one continued garden, and I walked for some distance, gathering handfuls of them—of the same plants that I had cherished in pots at home, or begged small sprays of in conservatories or greenhouses! I had whole boughs of the splendid metrosideros, a tall handsome shrub, bearing flowers of the richest crimson, like a large bottle-brush; several varieties of the delicate epacris; different species of acacia, tea-tree, and corraea, the brilliant 'Botany-Bay lily', and very many yet more lovely denizens of this interesting country, of which I know not even the name. One, most beautiful, was something like a small iris, of a pure ultra-marine blue, with smaller petals in the centre, most delicately pencilled; but ere I had gathered it five minutes, it had withered away, and I never could bring one home to make a drawing from. Surely it must have been some sensitive little fay, who, charmed into the form of a flower, might not bear the touch of a mortal hand!

Numbers of parrots, those

> Strange bright birds, that on starry wings
> Bear the rich hues of all glorious things,[1]

---

1   Felicia Hemans (1793–1835), 'The Better Land'.

were flying from tree to tree, or crossing the road in chattering, screaming parties, all as gay and happy as splendid colours and glad freedom could make them. Often they rose close before us from the road, like living gems and gold, so vividly bright they shone in the sun; and then a party of them would assemble in a tree, with such fluttering, and flying in and out, and under and over; such genteel-looking flirtations going on, as they sidled up and down the branches, with their droll sly-looking faces peering about, and inspecting us first with one eye, then with the other, that they seemed quite the monkeys of the feathered tribes.

On nearing the lighthouse, after ascending one or two slight hills, we passed several small houses, and others were building; the views from thence are doubtlessly very grand, but it must be a most exposed situation, with nothing to break the force of the strong sea-breezes, and but little vegetation to moderate the glare of the sun.

The view from the cliffs is indeed grand,

> O'er the glad waters of the dark-blue sea;[1]

and looking down over the dizzy height, the eye glances from crag to crag, till it catches the snowy puffs of foam flung up from the breakers that roar and dash in the cavernous chasms below, booming among them like subterranean thunder. As I fearfully gazed down, something leaped between me and the dark water—it was a goat, and there were some half-dozen of the agile creatures far down the slippery precipitous crags, leaping, jumping, and frolicking about, with scarcely an inch of foot-room, and only the boiling surf below.

Opposite to us rose the corresponding cliff, called the North Head, bluff and bare, and wearing on its hoary front the hues with which thousands of storms have dyed it. Myriads of sea-fowl were soaring and screaming around, and several vessels in the offing, and nearer shore, were apparently shaping their course to the port, but too distant for us to wait their entrance through these most grand and stupendous gates. The lighthouse itself is not in any way remarkable; close by is the signal-staff, by means of which the intelligence of vessels arriving is speedily transmitted to Sydney and Paramatta.

We drove back by a different road, nearer to the port, and less hilly, but equally beautiful with that by which we came. It led us through a moister-looking region, with more large trees, greener shrubs, and more luxuriant herbage, and commanding most lovely views, that appeared in succession like pictures seen through a natural framework of high white-stemmed gum-trees and tall acacias. Here and there peeped forth a prettily situated

---

1   Lord Byron (1788–1824), 'The Corsair'.

residence, with its shady garden and cool piazza, looking down into one of the small bays I have before mentioned, and beyond that to the estuary.

On one large dead gum-tree a whole council of black cockatoos was assembled in animated debate, sidling up and down the branches, erecting and lowering their handsome gold-tipped top-knots, as if bowing to each other with the politest gestures imaginable; and accompanying the dumb show with such varied intonations of voice as made it impossible to doubt that a most interesting discussion was going on, all conducted in the most courteous manner: perhaps a reform of the grub laws was in agitation, for the business was evidently one of grave importance, and we respectfully remained attentive spectators of the ceremony until 'the House' adjourned, and the honourable members flew away. These birds are by no means common in the neighbourhood of Sydney, nor did I see any more during my stay in the colony. [. . .]

1844

CHARLES HARPUR
1813–1868

Although his work long remained little known, Charles Harpur has come to be regarded as Australia's most important nineteenth-century poet. He was born in Windsor, NSW; both his parents were convicts but Joseph Harpur ensured that his children received a good basic education. During the 1830s, when Harpur's early poems began to appear in Sydney newspapers, he worked as a postal clerk and, briefly and unsuccessfully, as an actor. In 1835 extracts from his blank verse drama, 'The Tragedy of Donohoe', were published in the *Sydney Monitor*, whose editor commended Harpur's youthful ambition but regretted his choice of bushranger hero. Harpur later reworked the play as *The Bushrangers* (1853), removing the specific reference to Jack Donohoe, but it was never performed.

In the 1840s Harpur published much satirical and other verse in the radical newspaper the *Weekly Register* and, like its editor W.A. Duncan, Henry Parkes and others, attempted to break the power of the large landowners and squatters, led by William Charles Wentworth. 'The Beautiful Squatter' was the first of a series of 'Squatter Songs' written for the *Register* in reply to a series of the same name praising the squatters then being published in the *Atlas*. During this period Harpur was mainly living in the Hunter Valley region, working at various times as a postal officer, school teacher and farmer. His long courtship of Mary Doyle, daughter of a prosperous local farmer, whom he met in 1843, is recorded in his 'Rosa' love sonnets. 'The Consummation', in which he is finally able to replace 'Rosa' with Mary, marks the end of his suit; they married in 1850. Harpur remained farming in the Hunter Valley until 1859 when he was appointed assistant commissioner on the southern goldfields. After this post was terminated in 1866, his financial problems, together with the accidental death of one of his sons, contributed to his early death.

Unlike earlier poets such as Barron Field (qv), Harpur saw the land of his birth not as weird or melancholy but as a place filled with natural beauty and sublimity. 'A Mid-Summer Noon in the Australian Forest' captures the silence of the bush during the heat of the day, with particular attention to the few insects that are still active. Longer poems like 'The Creek of the Four Graves', 'A Bush Fire', 'The Storm in the Mountains' and 'The Kangaroo Hunt' show Harpur's determination to prove that Australian subjects were suitable for the higher forms of poetry, something then doubted. During his lifetime, Harpur could only afford to publish one substantial collection of his work and continued to revise his poems for a never-realised English edition. These manuscripts are now held in the Mitchell Library. After Harpur's death, his wife managed to raise funds for a memorial edition but unfortunately the poems included were heavily and unsympathetically edited. A *Complete Poems*, edited by the late Elizabeth Perkins, was published in 1984 but Harpur still awaits a full scholarly edition. *EW*

The Beautiful Squatter

Where the wandering Barwin delighteth the eye,
Befringed with the myall and golden-bloomed gorse,
Oh a beautiful Squatter came galloping by,
With a beard on his chin like the tail of his horse!
And his locks trained all round to so equal a pitch,   5
That his mother herself, it may truly be said,
Had been puzzled in no small degree to find which
Was the front, or the back, or the sides of his head.

Beside a small fire 'neath a fair-spreading tree,
(A cedar I think—but perhaps 'twas a gum)   10
What vision of Love did that Squatter now see,
In the midst of a catch so to render him dumb?
Why, all on the delicate herbage asquat,
And smiling to see him so flustered and mute,
'Twas the charming Miss Possumskin having a chat   15
With the elegant Lady of Lord Bandycoot.

The Squatter dismounted—what else could he do?
And meaning her tender affections to win,
'Gan talking of dampers and blankets quite new
With a warmth that soon ruined poor Miss Possumskin!   20
And Lord Bandycoot also, while dining that day
On a baked kangaroo of the kind that is red,
At the very third bite to King Dingo did say—
O, how heavy I feel all at once in the head!

But alas for the Belles of the Barwin! the Youth   25
Galloped home, to forget all his promises fair!
Whereupon Lady Bandycoot told the whole truth
To her Lord, and Miss Possumskin raved in despair!

And mark the result! royal Dingo straightway,
And his Warriors, swore to avenge them in arms: 30
And that Beautiful Squatter one beautiful day,
Was waddied to death in the bloom of his charms.

1845/1984

A Mid-Summer Noon in the Australian Forest

Not a bird disturbs the air,
There is quiet everywhere;
Over plains and over woods
What a mighty stillness broods.

Even the grasshoppers keep   5
Where the coolest shadows sleep;
Even the busy ants are found
Resting in their pebbled mound;
Even the locust clingeth now
In silence to the barky bough: 10
And over hills and over plains
Quiet, vast and slumbrous, reigns.

Only there's a drowsy humming
From yon warm lagoon slow coming:
'Tis the dragon-hornet—see!   15
All bedaubed resplendently
With yellow on a tawny ground—
Each rich spot nor square nor round,
But rudely heart-shaped, as it were
The blurred and hasty impress there,   20
Of a vermeil-crusted seal
Dusted o'er with golden meal:
Only there's a droning where
Yon bright beetle gleams the air—
Gleams it in its droning flight   25
With a slanting track of light,
Till rising in the sunshine higher,
Its shards flame out like gems on fire.

Every other thing is still,
Save the ever wakeful rill,   30
Whose cool murmur only throws
A cooler comfort round Repose;

Or some ripple in the sea
Of leafy boughs, where, lazily,
Tired Summer, in her forest bower   35
Turning with the noontide hour,
Heaves a slumbrous breath, ere she
Once more slumbers peacefully.

O 'tis easeful here to lie
Hidden from Noon's scorching eye,   40
In this grassy cool recess
Musing thus of Quietness.

                                            1851/1883

A Confession

She loves me! From her own bliss-breathing lips
    The live confession came, like rich perfume
    From crimson petals bursting into bloom!
And still my heart with the remembrance skips
Like a young lion, and my tongue, too, trips   5
    Drunken with joy! whilst every object seen
    In life's diurnal round wears in its mien
Smiles that all recollected smiles eclipse!
    And if all common things of nature now
Are like old faces flushed with new delight,   10
    Much more the consciousness of that rich vow
Deepens the beautiful and refines the bright,
    While throned I seem on Love's divinest height,
    With clouds of visioned bliss purpling around my brow!
                                            1853/1883

The Consummation

Mine after all—my Mary! Why should I
    That most loved, sweet name any more disguise,
    Now that beneath the conscious-seeming skies
My joy may spread itself as openly?
I weep—and fondly ask the reason why: 5
    Thinking my happy heart in no such wise
    Should keep effusing through my happy eyes,
Now that She's mine by an enduring tie!
Mine after all—my Mary! Lo, the Past
    With all its doubt and dread and passionate sorrow 10

But travailed with Content! since thus at last,
Love's whole light full into my lot is cast:
    Even as the sun ariseth on the morrow
Out of the broken storm—cloudless and vast!

1853/1984

MARY ANN ARTHUR
c. 1819–1871

Mary Ann Cochrane was born in Van Diemen's Land (Tasmania), the daughter of Tarenootairer (Sarah Cochrane). One of the Palawa people removed from their homelands to Flinders Island by George A. Robinson, in March 1838 she married Walter George Arthur (qv). The couple accompanied Robinson to Port Phillip in 1839, and returned to Flinders Island in 1842 but soon fell out with the superintendent Henry Jeanneret. Both were literate and as unofficial leaders of their community were involved in writing a petition to the Queen of England. Later they lived at Oyster Cove where, after Walter's death, Mary Ann married Adam Booker. *AH/PM*

Letter to Colonial Secretary, Van Diemen's Land

I thank my Father the Govr that he has told us black people that we might write him & tell him if we had any complaint to make about ourselves. I want now to tell the Govr that Dr. Jeanneret wants to make out my husband & myself very bad wicked people & talks plenty about putting us into jail & that he will hang us for helping to write the petition to the Queen from our country people. I send the Gov. two papers one from Dr. Milligan & one from Mr. Robinson of Port Philip to tell the Govr that they know us a long time & had nothing to say bad of us but Dr. Jeanneret does not like us for we do not like to be his slaves nor wish our poor Country to be treated badly or made slaves of. I hope the Govr will not let Dr. Jeanneret put us into Jail as he likes for nothing at all as he used he says he will do it & frightens us much with his big talk about our writing to the Queen he calls us all liars but we told him & the Coxswain who Dr. Jeanneret made ask us that it was all true what we write about him. I remain, Sir, Your humble Aborigine Child, Mary Ann Arthur.

1846

WALTER GEORGE ARTHUR
c. 1820–1861

The son of Rolepa, who was known to Europeans as 'King George', Walter was born in north-eastern Van Diemen's Land (Tasmania). Separated from his people as a child, he became a petty thief in Launceston, and was known as 'Friday'. In 1832, George A. Robinson took him to Flinders Island and then to the Orphan School near Hobart, where he was educated. He returned to Flinders Island in 1835, and in January 1836 Friday was renamed in honour of the Governor (Sir) George Arthur. He became a teacher, worked as a carpenter and shoemaker and co-edited with Thomas Brune (qv) the settlement's newspaper, the *Flinders Island Chronicle*. After their marriage in 1838, Arthur and his wife Mary Ann (qv) worked as shepherds. From 1839 to 1842 they were with Robinson at Port Phillip (Melbourne).

Back on Flinders Island, Walter was briefly imprisoned for his outspokenness. In 1847 the few survivors of Robinson's experiment were moved to Oyster Cove, and again the Arthurs demanded improved conditions for their people. It is thought that in May 1861 Walter fell overboard while rowing home to Oyster Cove from Hobart; his body was never found. *AH/PM*

Letter to Colonial Secretary, Van Diemen's Land

I send you with this letter a Statement which I have written of my Imprison-ment here in Flinders Jail by Doctor Jeanneret for 14 days and nights will you please to give this letter and my statement to my good Father His Excellency the Governor please tell him His Excellency that I hope he will do for me as if I was a Free white man to send to Flinders two Magistrates to take my informations against Doctor Jeanneret and other People for falsely putting me into Jail—for refusing to take my Bail—for wanting to get £50 from me to let me out—for keeping in Jail without a Committal wanting me to sign a Petition to him to Call myself a bad wicked man—and allso for not sending to the Governor our original Letter about our Petition being true, which we gave him open to read first and ask him to send it to the Governor for us We sent the Duplicate of it among our other letters to the Colonial Sec^{ty} in June last—Neigther myself or my Wife can live here under Doctor Jeanneret he treats us so badly and wants to make such Slaves of us all and is always revenging what took place when he was here before. I pray his Excellency the Governor will take Care of us poor Black people and send us the Magistrates to whom we will tell our Pitiful Story of what we poor Creatures are suffering different from what Col. Arthur and Mr. Robinson told us when we gave them our own Countrys of Van Diemens Land—the People are now all so frightened from Doctor Jeanneret constant growl and threatenings to put them in Jail and telling them he has full power this time to do as he likes with us all and that his Excellency has no power either over him or the black people that they do not know what to do and they are so watched that they are afraid to write to his Excellency any more as their letters wont be sent by Doctor Jeanneret. they Black People had to send their letters to the Governor in another way than by the Mail. Doctor Jeanneret says we will all be hung for high treason for writing against him he is worst on me for he knows I can speak English and that I do not like to see my poor Ignorant Country people badly treated or made Slaves of. I send you Sir a Certificate for his Excellency to read that I got from Mr. Clark our Catechist for he knows my wife and myself from we were young; and he knows how badly we are all treated here and that I did nothing to make Doctor Jeanneret put me into Jail but because I was one of the people who signed the Letter for to be sent to the Governor and because my wife put her name down in it both Doctor Jeanneret and Mrs Jeanneret Called her a Villain and is making out plenty of bad things about my wife and myself which I can very soon prove are not true. All I now request of his Excellency is that he will have full Justice done to me the same as he would have done to a white man and a freeman and according to the agreement between both Col. Arthur the old Governor and us black people when we were free people and when we gave up our Country and came to live at Flinders Island. 6th June Since I wrote this much the Fortitude has arrived I am too much frighted for Doctor Jeanneret to send my statements which I have write out for to tell the Governor of how I have been treated I must keep it until the Governor writes me leave to send it. I must inclose this letter to a friend in Hobart town to put into the Post Office for me for Doctor Jeanneret says he will send no letters for us. I want to tell the Governor that plenty bad salt beef has Issued out for us all for the last month and some of the fresh beef was of the worst kind on Saturday the 1st August we all got for our Ration of meat Stinking Salt Mutton. But these we had to throw out for we must not refuse anything he gives us. I am sure the Governor will be sorry to hear that my poor Country-people cry out plenty that they are very hungry from the bad meat Doctor Jeanneret gives them. I again pray the Governor will do some thing for us and not let us be badly treated in the way we are if Governor would send down some person they would very soon find that all I have wrote is true I know Doctor Jeanneret write plenty about us black people to the Governor but I hope Governor will ask ourselves first for we know that he says plenty of things that is not true of us.

I remain, Sir, Your humble Aborigine Servant, Walter G. Arthur Chief of Ben Lomond Tribes.

Please will the Governor give me and my Wife Mary Ann Arthur leave to go up to Hobarttown with Mr. Clark our Catechist when he gose to Town.

1846

ELLEN CLACY
c. 1820—?

Travel writer Ellen Clacy was born in England and apparently travelled to the Victorian goldfields with her brother in 1852, although no record has been found of her arrival. She married and returned to England with her husband the following year. *A Lady's Visit to the Gold Diggings of Australia in 1852–53: Written on the spot* (1853) gives a lively account of goldfields' scenes and characters from a female perspective and was reprinted in 1963. Clacy also published a collection of short stories, *Lights and Shadows of Australian Life* (1854), as well as children's books under the pseudonym Cycla. *EW*

From *A Lady's Visit to the Gold Diggings*
of Australia in 1852–1853
Chapter VI: The Diggings

[…] Let us take a stroll round Forest Creek—what a novel scene!—thousands of human beings engaged in digging, wheeling, carrying, and washing, intermingled with no little grumbling, scolding and swearing. We approach first the old Post-office Square; next our eye glances down Adelaide Gully, and over the Montgomery and White Hills, all pretty well dug up; now we pass the Private Escort Station, and Little Bendigo. At the junction of Forest, Barker, and Campbell Creeks we find the Commissioners' quarters—this is nearly five miles from our starting point. We must now return to Adelaide Gully, and keep alongside Adelaide Creek, till we come to a high range of rocks, which we cross, and then find ourselves near the head-waters of Fryer's Creek. Following that stream towards the Loddon, we pass the interesting neighbourhood of Golden Gully, Moonlight Flat, Windlass and Red Hill; this latter which covers about two acres of ground is so called from the colour of the soil, it was the first found, and is still considered as the richest auriferous spot near Mount Alexander. In the wet season, it was reckoned that on Moonlight Flat one man was daily buried alive from the earth falling into his hole. Proceeding north-east in the direction of Campbell's Creek, we again reach the Commissioners' tent.

The principal gullies about Bendigo are Sailor's, Napoleon, Pennyweight, Peg Leg, Growler's, White Horse, Eagle Hawk, Californian, American, Derwent, Long, Piccaninny, Iron Bark, Black Man's, Poor Man's, Dusty, Jim Crow, Spring, and Golden—also Sydney Flat, and Specimen Hill—Haverton Gully, and the Sheep-wash. Most of these places are well-ransacked and tunnelled, but thorough good wages may always be procured by tin dish washing in deserted holes, or surface washing.

It is not only the diggers, however, who make money at the Gold Fields. Carters, carpenters, storemen, wheelwrights, butchers, shoemakers, &c., usually in the long run make a fortune quicker than the diggers themselves, and certainly with less hard work or risk of life. They can always get from £1 to £2 a day without rations, whereas they may dig for weeks and get nothing. Living is not more expensive than in Melbourne: meat is generally from 4d. to 6d. a pound, flour about 1s. 6d. a pound, (this is the most expensive article in housekeeping there,) butter must be dispensed with, as that is seldom less than 4s. a pound, and only successful diggers can indulge in such articles as cheese, pickles, ham, sardines, pickled salmon, or spirits, as all these things, though easily procured if you have gold to throw away, are expensive, the last-named article (diluted with water or something less innoxious) is only to be obtained for 30s. a bottle.

The stores, which are distinguished by a flag, are numerous and well stocked. A new style of lodging and boarding house is in great vogue. It is a tent fitted up with stringy bark couches, ranged down each side the tent, leaving a narrow passage up the middle. The lodgers are supplied with mutton, damper, and tea, three times a day, for the charge of 5s. a meal, and 5s. for the bed; this is by the week, a casual guest must pay double, and as 18 inches is on an average considered ample width to sleep in, a tent 24 feet long will bring in a good return to the owner.

The stores at the diggings are large tents generally square or oblong, and everything required by a digger can be obtained for money, from sugar-candy to potted anchovies; from East India pickles to Bass's pale ale; from ankle jack boots to a pair of stays; from a baby's cap to a cradle; and every apparatus for mining, from a pick to a needle. But the confusion—the din—the medley—what a scene for a shop walker! Here lies a pair of herrings dripping into a bag of sugar, or a box of raisins; there a gay-looking bundle of ribbons beneath two tumblers, and a half-finished bottle of ale. Cheese and butter, bread and yellow soap, pork and currants, saddles and frocks, wide-awakes[1] and blue serge shirts, green veils and shovels, baby linen and tallow candles, are all heaped indiscriminately together; added to which, there are children bawling, men swearing, store-keeper sulky, and last, not *least*, women's tongues going nineteen to the dozen. [. . .]

Sly grog selling is the bane of the diggings. Many—perhaps nine-tenths—of the diggers are honest industrious men, desirous of getting a little there as a stepping-stone to independence elsewhere; but the other tenth is composed of outcasts and transports—the refuse of Van Diemen's Land—men of the most depraved and abandoned characters, who have sought and gained the lowest abyss of crime, and who would a short time ago have expiated their crimes on a scaffold. They generally work or rob for a space, and when well stocked with gold, retire to Melbourne for a month or so, living in drunkenness and debauchery. If, however, their holiday is spent at the diggings, the sly grog-shop is the last scene of their boisterous career. Spirit selling is strictly prohibited; and although Government will license a respectable public-house on the *road*, it is resolutely refused *on* the diggings. The result has been the opposite of that which it was intended to produce. There is more drinking and rioting at the diggings than elsewhere, the privacy and risk give the obtaining it an excitement which the diggers enjoy as much as the spirit itself; and wherever grog is sold on the sly, it will sooner or later be the scene of a riot, or perhaps murder. Intemperance is succeeded by quarrelling and fighting, the neighbouring tents report to the police, and the offenders are lodged in the lock-up; whilst the grog-tent,

1   Wide-brimmed felt hats.

spirits, wine, &c., are seized and taken to the Commissioners. Some of the stores, however, manage to evade the law rather cleverly—as spirits are not *sold*, 'my friend' pays a shilling more for his fig of tobacco, and his wife an extra sixpence for her suet; and they smile at the store-man, who in return smiles knowingly at them, and then glasses are brought out, and a bottle produced, which sends forth *not* a fragrant perfume on the sultry air.

It is no joke to get ill at the diggings; doctors make you pay for it. Their fees are—for a consultation, at their own tent, ten shillings; for a visit out, from one to ten pounds, according to time and distance. Many are regular quacks, and these seem to flourish best. The principal illnesses are weakness of sight, from the hot winds and sandy soil, and dysentry, which is often caused by the badly-cooked food, bad water, and want of vegetables.

The interior of the canvas habitation of the digger is desolate enough; a box on a block of wood forms a table, and this is the only furniture; many dispense with that. The bedding, which is laid on the ground, serves to sit upon. Diogenes in his tub would not have looked more comfortless than anyone else. Tin plates and pannicans, the same as are used for camping up, compose the breakfast, dinner, and tea service, which meals usually consist of the same dishes—mutton, damper, and tea.

In some tents the soft influence of our sex is pleasingly apparent: the tins are as bright as silver, there are sheets as well as blankets on the beds, and perhaps a clean counterpane, with the addition of a dry sack or piece of carpet on the ground; whilst a pet cockatoo, chained to a perch, makes noise enough to keep the 'missus' from feeling lonely when the good man is at work. Sometimes a wife is at first rather a nuisance; women get scared and frightened, then cross, and commence a 'blow up' with their husbands; but all their railing generally ends in their quietly settling down to this rough and primitive style of living, if not without a murmur, at least to all appearance with the determination to laugh and bear it. And although rough in their manners, and not over select in their address, the digger seldom wilfully injures a woman; in fact, a regular Vandemonian will, in his way, play the gallant with as great a zest as a fashionable about town—at any rate, with more sincerity of heart.

Sunday is kept at the diggings in a very orderly manner: and among the actual diggers themselves, the day of rest is taken in *verbatim* sense. It is not unusual to have an established clergyman holding forth near the Commissioners' tent, and almost within hearing will be a tub orator expounding the origin of evil, whilst a 'mill' (a fight with fisticuffs) or a dog fight fills up the background.

But night at the diggings is the characteristic time: murder here—murder there—revolvers cracking—blunderbusses bombing—rifles going off— balls whistling—one man groaning with a broken leg—another shouting because he couldn't find the way to his hole, and a third equally vociferous because he has tumbled into one—this man swearing—another praying—a party of bacchanals chanting various ditties to different time and tune, or rather minus both. Here is one man grumbling because he has brought his wife with him, another ditto because he has left his behind, or sold her for an ounce of gold or a bottle of rum. Donnybrook Fair is not to be compared to an evening at Bendigo. [. . .]

1853

CAROLINE CARLETON
c. 1820–1874

Poet Caroline Carleton was born and educated in England, where she became skilled in music and languages. In 1836 she married medical student Charles Carleton and they arrived in South Australia in 1839. He worked in various professions, including medical officer and pharmacist, but died from tuberculosis in 1861. Caroline then supported her five children by running private schools. When the Gawler Institute offered a prize in 1858 for the best patriotic song, her 'Song of Australia' was chosen from 96 entries and set to music by Carl Linger. Her *South Australian Lyrics* (1860) was the first book of verse by a woman to be published in South Australia. *EW*

The Song of Australia

There is a land where summer skies
Are gleaming with a thousand dyes,
Blending in witching harmonies;
And grassy knoll and forest height
Are flushing in the rosy light,   5
And all above is azure bright—
     Australia!

There is a land where honey flows,
Where laughing corn luxuriant grows,
Land of the myrtle and the rose;   10
On hill and plain the clust'ring vine
Is gushing out with purple wine,
And cups are quaffed to thee and thine—
     Australia!

There is a land where treasures shine   15
Deep in the dark unfathom'd mine
For worshippers at Mammon's shrine;
Where gold lies hid, and rubies gleam,
And fabled wealth no more doth seem

The idle fancy of a dream—   20
         Australia!

There is a land where homesteads peep
From sunny plain and woodland steep,
And love and joy bright vigils keep;
Where the glad voice of childish glee   25
Is mingling with the melody
Of nature's hidden minstrelsy—
        Australia!

There is a land where floating free
From mountain top to girdling sea   30
A proud flag waves exultingly!
And Freedom's sons the banner bear,
No shackl'd slave can breathe the air,
Fairest of Britain's daughters fair—
        Australia!   35
                  1860

THOMAS BRUNE
c. 1823–1841

Born probably on Bruny Island, Van Diemen's Land (Tasmania), and educated at the Orphan School near Hobart, Brune was with George A. Robinson (1791–1866) on Flinders Island from 1836. Robinson, who had arrived from England in 1824, was commissioned in the 1930s to repatriate Indigenous Tasmanians to this camp on Bass Strait. Brune taught at the school and was apprenticed to the shoemaker. Among the few who could read and write English with any fluency, he and Walter George Arthur (qv) (who signs himself as Walter Juba Martin at the end of the following extract) produced and wrote the *Flinders Island Chronicle*. In 1839, Brune accompanied Robinson to Port Phillip (Melbourne). He died there after a fall from a tree. *AH/PM*

The Aboriginal or Flinders Island Chronicle
UNDER THE SANCTION OF THE COMMANDANT

The object of this journal is to promote christianity civilization and Learning amongst the Aboriginal Inhabitants at Flinders Island. The chronicle professes to be a brief but accuate register of events of the colony Moral and religious. This journal will be published weekly on Saturday the copies to be in Manuscript and written exclusively by the Aboriginals the Size half foolcap and the price two pence.

The Profit arising from the Sale of the journal to be equally divided among the writers which it is hoped may induce Emmulation in writing excite a desire for useful knowledge and promote Learning generally.

Proof Sheets are to be Submitted to the commandant for correction before publishing. Persons out of the colony may Subscribe.

[Signed] Thomas Brune
[Signed] Walter Juba Martin

Prospectus
I Certify that this Copy was written by one of the Aboriginals at Flinders Island whose Signature is herewith attached.

[Signed] G.A. Robinson
Commandant
Aboriginal Settlement
Flinders Island
10th September 1836

1836

The Flinders Island Weekly Chronicle

17TH NOVEMBER 1837

Now my friends you see that the commandant is so kind to you he gives you every thing that you want when you were in the bush the commandant had to leave his friends and go into the bush and he brought you out of the bush because he felt for you and because he knowed the white men was shooting you and now he has brought you to Flinders Island where you get every thing and when you are ill tell the Doctor immediately and you get relief you have now fine houses. I expect that you will not vex one another.

To morrow there will be a Market my friends will you thank the Commandant for all that he done for you in bringing you out of the bush when you knew not God and knew not who made the trees that where before you when you were living in the woods yes my friends you should thank the Commandant yes you should thank the Commandant. There is many of you dying my friends we must all die and we ought to pray to God before we get to heaven yes my friends if we dont we must have eternal punishment.

The brig Tamar arrived this morning at green Island. I cannot tell perhaps we might hear about it by and by when the ship boat comes to the Settlement we will hear news from Hobarton. Let us hope it will be good news and that something may be done for us poor people they are dying away the Bible says some of all shall be saved but I am much afraid none of us will be alive by and by as then as nothing but sickness among us. Why dont the black fellows pray to the king to get us away from this place.

[Signed] Thomas Brune Editor and Writer Commandant office.

1837

Weekly Chronicle

21ST DECEMBER 1837

The people of Van Diemen's land is gone in the bush with Commandant the other side of the Island and Richard had a swan and [Uptra ?] took it away from him and Uptra put it on the fire and roast it and he give Richard only bone of the swan, and why did not you give the Commandant any thing to eat. No because you was so greedy.

Why Commandant give you every thing and why dident you give the Commandant a pice of a kangaroo. No you would not because you was so greedy you was like hogs eating away as fast as you can could you threwed it on the fire as quick as you can in case that the Commandant should want a pice of it he did not want your kangaroos and he did not want your ducks and he did not want your downs and you did not make his breackwind you was to laze and you did not make his bread and he had making it for his own self and his bread also.

You ought my freinds you must behaved yourselves better than you do or else the Commandant be so angry with you and he wont give you any thing no more. And the Commandant his very soon go away from you Natives and he will leave you alway and he will be so glad you must get another Commandant …

And now my freinds do Let us come to the Commandant with kindess and he now give you every thing what you want and obey him and look out what he says to you and not to be going on in the foolish ways that always carrying on …

And now my freinds let us love the Commandant and let him not be growling at us for our greed and let us love him …

[Signed] Thomas Brune
Aboriginal youth
Editor and writter.

1837

WILLIAM BARAK
c. 1824—1903

An artist and elder of the Wurundjeri people, also known as 'the King of the Yarra Tribe', Barak was moved from his country when Melbourne was settled. He was educated at a mission school (1837–39) and was later a member of the Native Police Force. From 1863 he lived at Coranderrk, an Aboriginal reserve, where he undertook religious studies and was baptised and confirmed a Presbyterian.

Barak became a respected spokesman for his people in the late 1870s. Until his death he was the acknowledged leader at Coranderrk, and his petitions, public appearances and contact with leaders such as Alfred Deakin were important spurs to action between colonial authority and Aboriginal people. *AH/PM*

Letter to the Editor by the Coranderrk Aborigines

Sir,—We beg of you to put our little column in you valuable paper please. We have seen and heard that the managers of all the stations and the Central Board to have had a meeting about what to be done, so we have heard that there is going to be very strict rules on the station and more rules will be to much for us, it seems we are all going to be treated like slaves, far as we heard of it,—we wish to ask those Managor of the station Did we steal anything out of the colony or murdered anyone or are we prisoners or convict. We should think we are all free any white men of the colony. When we all heard of it, it made us very vex it enough to make us all go mad the way they are going to treat us it seems very hard. We all working in peace and quiteness and happy, pleasing Mr. Goodall, and also showing Mr Goodall that we could work if we had a good manager expecting our wishes to be carried out, what we have ask for, but it seem it was the very opposite way. So we don't know what to do since we heard those strict rules planned out. It has made us downhearted. We must all try again and go to the head of the Colony.—We are all your

Most Obedient Servants, Wm Barak (X), Thos. Avoca, Dick Richard (X), Thos. Mickey (X), Lankey (X), Lankey Manto, Thos Dunolly, Robert Wandon, Alfred Morgan, Wm Parker. Coranderrk, August 29th, 1882.

1882

CATHERINE HELEN SPENCE
1825–1910

Novelist and political reformer Catherine Spence was born and educated in Scotland, migrating to Adelaide with her family in 1839 after her father got into financial difficulties. This put an end to her hope of further education; initially, she worked as a governess, while reading widely as she was to do all her life. Her first and best-known novel, *Clara Morison: A tale of South Australia during the gold fever* (1854), was published anonymously in London. It was followed by *Tender and True: A colonial tale* (1856), *Mr Hogarth's Will* (1865) and *The Author's Daughter* (1868). All reflect Spence's own determination to work and become self-supporting rather than, as a middle-class woman, relying on the usual profession of marriage. So, in *Clara Morison*, when Clara fails to find work as a governess after arriving in Adelaide, she takes the very radical step of becoming a servant, though completely inexperienced at housework.

As well as writing fiction, Spence had also been contributing to local newspapers for many years, initially under her brother's name. By the 1870s, as she noted in her *Autobiography* (1910), she found that journalism paid better than novels and concentrated more of her energy there, becoming a regular, paid correspondent for the *South Australian Register*, as well as writing literary criticism and social commentary for journals such as the *Melbourne Review*. From the 1870s she also wrote and spoke to promote causes she believed in, especially women's and children's welfare and education and, from the 1890s, reform of the electoral system. At first, this involved advocating proportional representation but she later became involved in the fight for female suffrage, achieved in South Australia in 1894. In 1905, during celebrations of her 80th birthday, Catherine Spence was described as Australia's most distinguished woman because of her wide and varied contributions to public life at a time when most women were still excluded from the public sphere. Two novels written in the 1880s, *Handfasted* and *Gathered In*, dealt with then controversial issues of trial marriage and illegitimacy and were not published as books until 1984 and 1977 respectively. *Ever Yours, C.H. Spence*, an annotated reprinting of Spence's *Autobiography*, together with her previously unknown 1894 diary and selected letters, was published in 2006. *EW*

From *Clara Morison*
Chapter VIII: At Service

When young ladies in novels are set to any work to which they are unaccustomed, it is surprising how instantaneously they always get over all the difficulties before them. They row boats without feeling fatigued, they scale walls, they rein in restive horses, they can lift the most ponderous articles, though they are of the most delicate and fragile constitutions, and have never had such things to do in their lives.

It was not so with Clara, however. She found the work dreadfully hard, and by no means fascinating; and though she was willing and anxious even to painfulness, the memory that had tenaciously kept hold of hard names and dates, which her father had trusted to as to an encyclopaedia, seemed utterly to fail her in recollecting when saucepans were to be put on and taken off, and every day brought the same puzzling uncertainty as to how plates and dishes were to be arranged at the breakfast and dinner-table, which Mrs. Bantam had more than once shown her, with a particular desire that she should do it exactly in the same way.

Then she was very awkward at lighting a fire, and would often let it go out black just when it was most wanted. The camp-oven was a perfect heart-break to her, for she could never hit upon any medium between scorching heat and lukewarmness. Mrs. Bantam said that every new comer from England was awkward with the wood-fires and the camp-oven at first, so she excused her; but Clara knew that she should have been no better if the fires had been of coal, and the oven the newest invented patent cooking apparatus, but this opinion she prudently kept to herself.

She made a considerable smashing of crockery the first week; next week she scalded her arm pretty severely, and felt almost unable to move it for two days; the third week she was becoming more fit to be trusted, but yet she was conscious that if Mrs. Bantam had not been a paragon of good nature she would not have patience with her even for the month that she got no wages. And as for her work ever being done, she never could see over the top of it. Mrs. Bantam came into the kitchen every day to bring up arrears, and Clara with hopeless admiration saw her quietly put one thing after another out of her hands finished.

'I am afraid I shall never learn,' said Clara to her mistress one day. 'I am sorry I am so dreadfully stupid.'

'I dare say you will learn in time, though you seem determined to take your time to it, Clara; but where in all the world can you have been brought up to be so helpless. I do not know a young *lady* in the colony so ignorant of all household matters. The people next door, whom you see sometimes in the back yard, keep no servant, and do all their own work, but yet everybody knows the Miss Elliots are ladies, though I do not visit them myself.'

'I am heartily ashamed of my ignorance,' said Clara, 'but I was a spoilt child at home, and am suffering for it now. I fear you do not think me anxious to do right from the many failures I make.'

'You are too anxious, I think, and get nervous. Keep yourself cooler in future, and you will do better.'

Clara endeavoured to keep herself cooler during the last week of her month's probation, for she was very anxious to remain with Mrs. Bantam. It seemed to be a quiet place, and neither her master nor mistress was unreasonable. She was too busy to feel her solitary kitchen dull, and though she ached all over every morning from the exertions of the preceding day, that was preferable to the headache which Mrs. Handy's young gentlemen had inflicted upon her every evening. She was subjected to no impertinence; the butcher and baker called her 'Miss' when they came with their commodities; Mrs. Bantam did not send her out on many errands, and though waiting at table was a humiliating piece of work, there had been no strangers as yet to make her feel it deeply.

The month having expired, Mrs. Bantam was of opinion that though a very great deal was yet to be learned, some progress had been made; and offered Clara four shillings a week to stay. 'You are nothing of a servant,' said she, 'but you are civil and honest, so I will try you a little longer. If you would only learn to be methodical you would suit me.'

Clara was grateful and happy, and sat down forthwith to write to her uncle, in order to give him a clear statement of the new position in which she was placed. She had not considered it advisable to write on the subject till the month of trial had expired. To Susan she would have written on the same day, but could not find time, and was forced to delay it till the next Sunday evening, when she entered into detail, describing her mode of life at

Mrs. Handy's, her two unsuccessful attempts at getting a situation as governess, and her final settlement as maid of all work, with a very kind lady.

'Do not fancy that it is so very dreadful, my dear sister, or that I am completely miserable. I am determined to be happy if it is possible, and though now I feel the toil fatiguing, because I am new to bodily labour, in time I shall feel it nothing, and have leisure in the long winter evenings which are coming on to read and to write to you.

'The house I am living in is situated in a little garden; it is a real cottage of one story, which almost all the houses in Adelaide are, with only a trap ladder leading up to the little attic where I sleep. I have a fine view of the hills from my bed-room window, and now that the great heat has moderated I think the climate delightful. I still sleep with my window open that I may have enough of fresh air, and it is no uncommon thing in summer for people to leave all their doors and windows open through the night. I think that shows that the colony must be an honest place; but you must always bear in mind that this never has been a penal settlement.

'I do not think you would fancy the trees here, at least taken separately. They are evergreens, and looked fresh when everything else was burnt up, but now the newly sprung grass makes them look rather lugubrious. They are somewhat scraggy, and the bark is white on the greater proportion of the trees around the town, which gives them quite a ghostly appearance by moonlight. There are a few near the river Torrens which look really pretty, and I have been told that in the bush there are much finer trees than in the neighbourhood of town. They say that South Australian wood, being of slow growth, and consequently very hard, makes the best fuel possible, but I find it no easy matter to kindle it, and am always getting splinters of it in my hands; but of course I shall learn to do better soon.

'I suppose that when you receive this you will be in London with my uncle and aunt to see the world, and to wonder at the Great Exhibition. But, Susan, I am seeing life, and learning lessons which I hope I shall never forget; it is not merely the things I am learning to do, useful as they undoubtedly are, but the new thoughts and feelings which my present employments awaken, which will benefit me much. I have hitherto lived too much in books, and thought them all-important; now I see what things fill the minds of nine-tenths of my sex—daily duties, daily cares, daily sacrifices. I see now the line of demarcation which separates the employers from the employed; and if I ever, by any chance, should again have a servant under me, I shall surely understand her feelings, and be considerate and kind. How I reproach myself now for the unnecessary trouble I used to give our good faithful Peggy and Helen, and all through want of thought.

'So again I say, do not pity me much; feel for me a little, but rest assured that these little trials I meet with will do a great deal of good to

'Your most affectionate sister,

'CLARA.'

1854

ROLF BOLDREWOOD
1826–1915

Thomas Alexander Browne, who wrote under the pseudonym Rolf Boldrewood, was born in England, arriving in Sydney with his parents in 1831. He attended Sydney College but after his father's financial collapse in 1842 left school to become a pioneer squatter in the Western District of Victoria. In the 1860s he himself got into financial difficulties, lost his properties and spent time working as a drover. He began his writing career during this time, contributing articles about bush life to English and Australian periodicals. In 1871 he was appointed police magistrate and mining warden at the Gulgong goldfields in NSW. From 1874 he began writing longer works for the *Australian Town and Country Journal*, mostly drawing on his own experiences in the bush and elsewhere.

In 1881, after being posted to Dubbo, he began his best-known novel, *Robbery Under Arms* (1888). While no doubt partly inspired by the recent notoriety of Ned Kelly (qv) and his gang, Boldrewood deliberately set his bushranging tale back at mid-century and drew on the exploits of an earlier gang associated with Ben Hall and Frank Gardiner. In a radical move, he chose to tell his story from the point of view of Dick Marston, 'Sydney-side native' and son of convicts, who is supposedly writing it in jail under sentence of death. This stark opening, along with Boldrewood's use of the colloquial voice of an uneducated, working-class Australian, led to the novel being rejected by both the *Town and Country Journal* and the *Australasian*. It was eventually serialised in 1882–83 by the *Sydney Mail*, attracted considerable interest and was reserialised in another Fairfax paper, the *Echo*. Book publication in London, however, did not occur until 1888 and international success only arrived with the one-volume Macmillan edition of 1889, which went through 30 reprints over the next 50 years. A stage adaptation by Alfred Dampier in 1890 was also enormously successful and no doubt helped to attract more readers to *Robbery Under Arms*. In 1907 it was adapted for Australia's second feature film and was filmed again in 1911, 1920, 1957 and 1985. Macmillan went on to publish Boldrewood's eighteen other works, which include the novels *The Squatter's Dream* (1890), *The Miner's Right* (1890), *A Sydney-Side Saxon* (1891), the memoir *Old Melbourne Memories* (1896) and collections of short stories. *EW*

From *Robbery Under Arms*
Chapter XXV

Our next chance came through father. He was the intelligence man, and had all the news sent to him—roundabout it might be, but it always came, and was generally true; and the old man never troubled anybody twice that he couldn't believe in, great things or small. Well, word was passed about a branch bank at a place called Ballabri, where a goodish bit of gold was sent to wait the monthly escort. There was only the manager and one clerk there now, the other cove having gone away on sick leave. Towards the end of the month the bank gold was heaviest and the most notes in the safe. The smartest way would be to go into the bank just before shutting-up time—three o'clock, about—and hand a cheque over the counter. While the clerk was looking at it, out with a revolver and cover him. The rest was easy enough. A couple more walked in after, and while one jumped over the counter and bailed up the manager the other shut the door. Nothing strange about that. The door was always shut at three o'clock sharp. Nobody in town would drop to what might be going on inside till the whole thing was over, and the swag ready to be popped into a light trap and cleared off with.

That was the idea. We had plenty of time to think it over and settle it all, bit by bit, beforehand.

So one morning we started early and took the job in hand. Every little thing was looked through and talked over a week before. Father got Mr. White's buggy-horses ready and took Warrigal with him to a place where a man met him with a light four-wheeled Yankee trap and harness. Dad was dressed up to look like a back-country squatter. Lots of 'em were quite as rough-looking as he was, though they drive as good horses as any gentleman in the land. Warrigal was togged out something like a groom, with a bit of the station-hand about him. Their saddles and bridles they kept with 'em in the trap; they didn't know when they might want them. They had on their revolvers underneath their coats. We were to go round by another road and meet at the township.

Well, everything turned out first-rate. When we got to Ballabri there was father walking his horses up and down. They wanted cooling, my word. They'd come pretty smart all the way, but they were middlin' soft, being in great grass condition and not having done any work to speak of for a goodish while, and being a bit above themselves in a manner of speaking. We couldn't help laughing to see how solemn and respectable dad looked.

'My word,' said Jim, 'if he ain't the dead image of old Mr. Carter, of Brahway, where we shore three years back. Just such another hard-faced, cranky-looking old chap, ain't he, Dick? I'm that proud of him I'd do anything he asked me now, blest if I wouldn't!'

'Your father's a remarkable man,' says Starlight, quite serious; 'must have made his way in life if he hadn't shown such a dislike to anything on the square. If he'd started a public-house and a pound about the time he turned his mind to cattle-duffing as one of the fine arts, he'd have had a bank account by this time that would have kept him as honest as a judge. But it's the old story. I say, where are the police quarters? It's only manners to give them a call.'

We rode over to the barracks. They weren't much. A four-roomed cottage, a log lock-up with two cells, a four-stalled stable, and a horse-yard. Ballabri was a small township with a few big stations, a good many farms about it, and rather more public-houses than any other sort of buildings in it. A writing chap said once, 'A large well-filled graveyard, a small church mostly locked up, six public-houses, gave the principal features of Ballabri township. The remaining ones appear to be sand, bones, and broken bottles, with a sprinkling of inebriates and blackfellows.' With all that there was a lot of business done there in a year by the stores and inns, particularly since the diggings. Whatever becomes of the money made in such places? Where does it all go to? Nobody troubles their heads about that.

A goodish lot of the first people was huddled away in the graveyard under the sand ridges. Many an old shepherd had hobbled into the Travellers' Rest with a big cheque for a fortnight's spree, and had stopped behind in the graveyard, too, for company. It was always a wonderful place for steadying lushingtons, was Ballabri.

Anyhow we rode over to the barracks because we knew the senior constable was away. We'd got up a sham horse-stealing case the day before, through some chaps there that we knew. This drawed him off about fifty mile. The constable left behind was a youngish chap, and we intended to have a bit of fun with him. So we went up to the garden-gate and called out for the officer in charge of police quite grand.

'Here I am,' says he, coming out, buttoning up his uniform coat. 'Is anything the matter?'

'Oh! not much,' says I; 'but there's a man sick at the Sportsman's Arms. He's down with the typhus fever or something. He's a mate of ours, and we've come from Mr. Grant's station. He wants a doctor fetched.'

'Wait a minute till I get my revolver,' says he, buttoning up his waistcoat. He was just fresh from the depôt; plucky enough, but not up to half the ways of the bush.

'You'll do very well as you are,' says Starlight, bringing out his pretty sharp, and pointing it full at his head. 'You stay there till I give you leave.'

He stood there quite stunned, while Jim and I jumped off and muzzled him. He hadn't a chance, of course, with one of us on each side, and Starlight threatening to shoot him if he raised a finger.

'Let's put him in the logs,' says Jim. 'My word! just for a lark; turn for turn. Fair play, young fellow. You're being "run in" yourself now. Don't make a row, and no one'll hurt you.'

The keys were hanging up inside, so we pushed him into the farthest cell and locked both doors. There were no windows, and the lock-up, like most bush ones, was built of heavy logs, just roughly squared, with the ceiling the same sort, so there wasn't much chance of his making himself heard. If any noise did come out the town people would only think it was a drunken man, and take no notice.

We lost no time then, and Starlight rode up to the bank first. It was about ten minutes to three o'clock. Jim and I popped our horses into the police stables, and put on a couple of their waterproof capes. The day was a little showery. Most of the people we heard afterwards took us for troopers from some other station on the track of bushrangers, and not in regular uniform. It wasn't a bad joke, though, and the police got well chaffed about it.

We dodged down very careless like to the bank, and went in a minute or two after Starlight. He was waiting patiently with the cheque in his hand till some old woman got her money. She counted it, shillings, pence, and all, and then went out. The next moment Starlight pushed his cheque over. The clerk looks at it for a moment, and quick-like says, 'How will you have it?'

'This way,' Starlight answered, pointing his revolver at his head, 'and don't you stir or I'll shoot you before you can raise your hand.'

The manager's room was a small den at one side. They don't allow much room in country banks unless they make up their mind to go in for a regular swell building. I jumped round and took charge of the young man. Jim shut and locked the front door while Starlight knocked at the manager's room. He came out in a hurry, expecting to see one of the bank customers. When he saw Starlight's revolver, his face changed quick enough, but he made a rush to his drawer where he kept his revolver, and tried to make a fight of it, only we were too quick for him. Starlight put the muzzle of his pistol to his forehead and swore he'd blow out his brains there and then if he didn't stop quiet. We had to use the same words over and over again. Jim used to grin sometimes. They generally did the business, though, so of course he was quite helpless. We hadn't to threaten him to find the key of the safe, because it was unlocked and the key in it. He was just locking up his gold and the day's cash as we came in.

We tied him and the young fellow fast, legs and arms, and laid them down on the floor while we went through the place. There was a good lot of gold in the safe all weighed and labelled ready for the escort, which called there once a month. Bundles of notes, too; bags of sovereigns, silver, and copper. The last we didn't take. But all the rest we bundled up or put into handy boxes and bags we found there. Father had come up by this time as close as he could to the back-yard. We carried everything out and put them into his express-waggon; he shoved a rug over them and drove off, quite easy and comfortable. We locked the back door of the bank and chucked away the key, first telling the manager not to make a row for ten minutes or we might have to come back again. He was a plucky fellow, and we hadn't been rough with him. He had sense enough to see that he was overmatched, and not to fight when it was no good. I've known bankers to make a regular good fight of it, and sometimes come off best when their places was stuck up; but not when they were bested from the very start, like this one. No man could have had a show, if he was two or three men in one, at the Ballabri money-shop. We walked slap down to the hotel—then it was near the bank—and called for drinks. There weren't many people in the streets at that time in the afternoon, and the few that did notice us didn't think we were any one in particular. Since the diggings broke out all sorts of travellers a little out of the common were wandering all about the country—speculators in mines, strangers, new chums of all kinds; even the cattle-drovers and stockmen, having their pockets full of money, began to put on more side and dress in a flash way. The bush people didn't take half the notice of strangers they would have done a couple of years before.

So we had our drinks, and shouted for the landlord and the people in the bar; walked up to the police station, took out our horses, and rode quickly off, while father was nearly five miles away on a cross-road, making Mr. White's trotters do their best time, and with seven or eight thousand pounds' worth of gold and cash under the driving seat. That, I often think, was about the smartest trick we ever did. It makes me laugh when I remember how savage the senior constable was when he came home, found his sub in a cell, the manager and his clerk just untied, the bank robbed of nearly everything, and us gone hours ago, with about as much chance of catching us as a mob of wild cattle that got out of the yard the night before.

Just about dark father made the place where the man met him with the trap before. Fresh horses was put in and the man drove slap away another road. He and Warrigal mounted the two brown horses and took the stuff in saddle-bags, which they'd brought with 'em. They were back at the Hollow by daylight, and we got there about an hour afterwards. We only rode sharp for the first twenty miles or so, and took it easier afterwards. [. . .]

1888

D.H. DENIEHY
1828—1865

Lawyer, politician and man of letters Daniel Henry Deniehy was born in Sydney; both his parents had been convicts. A precocious child, he attended Sydney College before being taken to England at fourteen. Refused entry to Cambridge University, he spent some time in Europe before returning to Sydney to study law. During the 1850s he became a prominent literary and political figure. Known as 'the boy orator', on 15 August 1853 he publicly derided W.C. Wentworth's proposal to establish a colonial house of peers, calling this 'a bunyip aristocracy' and ridiculing it into oblivion. From 1857 to 1860 he was a member of the NSW parliament and in 1859 founded and edited the *Southern Cross* newspaper. After moving to Melbourne to edit the *Victorian* from 1862 to 1864, he returned to Sydney but was now an alcoholic and died after a fall. He published an early novel, poetry, essays and articles in various periodicals, as well as the satirical pamphlet *How I Became Attorney-General of New Barataria* (1859). Some of his work was collected in a posthumous volume edited by E.A. Martin, *The Life and Speeches of Daniel Henry Deniehy* (1884). *EW*

Speech on Mr Wentworth's Constitutional Bill

Mr D.H. Deniehy having been called upon to second the third resolution, said:

Why he had been selected to speak to the present resolution he knew not, save that as a native of the Colony he might naturally be expected to feel something like real interest, and speak with something like real feeling on a question connected with the political institutions of the Colony. He would do his best to respond to that invitation to 'speak up', and would perhaps balance deficiencies flowing from a small volume of voice by in all cases speaking plainly and calling things by their right names. He protested against the present daring and unheard-of attempt to tamper with a fundamental popular right, that of having a voice in the nomination of men who were to make, or control the making of, laws binding on the community—laws perpetually shifting and changing the nature of the whole social economy of a given state, and frequently operating in the subtlest form on the very dearest interests of the citizen, on his domestic, his moral, and perhaps his religious relations. The name of Mr Wentworth had several times been mentioned there that day, and upon one or two occasions with an unwise tenderness, a squeamish reluctance to speak plain English, and call certain shady deeds of Mr Wentworth's by their usual homely appellations, simply because they were Mr Wentworth's. Now, he for one was no wise disposed, as preceding speakers had seemed, to tap the vast shoulders of Mr Wentworth's political recreancies—'to damn him with faint praise and mistimed eulogy'. He had listened from boyhood upwards to grey tradition, to Mr Wentworth's demagogic aeropagitas—his speeches for the liberty of the unlicensed printing *régime* of Darling; and for these and divers other deeds of a time when the honourable Member for Sydney had to the full his share of the chivalrous pugnacities of five-and-twenty, he was as much inclined to give Mr Wentworth credit as any other man. But with those *fantasias*, those everlasting varieties on the 'Light of other Days' perpetually ringing in his ears, he, Mr Deniehy, was fain to enquire by what rule of moral and political appraisal it was sought to throw in a scale directly opposite to that containing the flagrant and shameless political dishonesty of years, the democratic escapades, sins long since repented of, in early youth. The subsequent political conduct, or rather the systematic political principles of Mr Wentworth, had been of a character sufficiently outrageous to cancel the value of a century of service.

The British Constitution had been spoken of that afternoon in terms of unbounded laudation. That stately fabric, it is true, deserved to be spoken of in terms of respect; he, Mr Deniehy, respected it, and no doubt they all shared in that feeling. But his was a qualified respect at best, and in all presumed assimilations of the political hypothesis of our colonial constitution-makers, he warned them not to be seduced by mere words and phrases—sheer sound and fury. Relatively, the British Constitution was only an admirable example of slowly growing and gradually elaborated political experience applied and set in action, but it was also eminent and exemplary as a long history, still evolving, of political philosophy.

But, as he had said before, it was after all but relatively good for its wonderfully successful fusion of principles the most antagonistic. Circum-stances entirely alter cases, and he would again warn them not to be led away by vague associations, exhaled from the use of venerable phrases that had, what few phrases now-a-days seldom could boast, genuine meanings attached to them.

The patrician element existed in the British Constitution, as did the regal, for good reasons—it had stood in the way of all later legislational thought and operation as a great fact; as such it was handled, and in a deep and prudential spirit of conservatism it was allowed to stand; but as affecting the basis and foundation of the architecture of a constitution, the elective principles neutralised all detrimental influences, by conversion, practically, into a mere check upon the deliberations of the initiative section of the Legislature.

And having the right to frame, to embody, to shape it as we would, with no huge stubborn facts to work upon as in England, there was nothing but the elective principle and the inalienable right and freedom of every colonist upon which to work out the whole organisation and fabric of our political institutions. But because it was the good pleasure of Mr Wentworth, and the respectable toil of that puissant legislative body whose serpentine windings were so ridiculous, we were not permitted to form our own Constitution, but instead we were to have one and an Upper Chamber cast upon us, built upon a model to suit the taste and propriety of certain political oligarchs, who treated the people at large as if they were cattle to be bought and sold in the market, as indeed they were in American slave states, and now in the Australian colonies, where we might find bamboozled Chinese and kidnapped Coolies. And being in a figurative humour, he might endeavour to cause some of the proposed nobility to pass before the stage of our imagination as the ghost of Banquo walked in the vision of Macbeth, so that we might have a fair view of those harlequin aristocrats, those Australian magnificos. We will have them across the stage in all the pomp and circumstance of hereditary titles. First, then, stalked the hoary Wentworth. But he could not believe that to such a head the strawberry leaves would add any honour. Next comes the full-blooded native aristocrat, Mr James Macarthur, who would, he supposed, aspire to an earldom at least; he would therefore call him Earl of Camden, and he would suggest for his coat of arms a field vert, the heraldic term for green, and emblazoned on this field should be the rum keg of a New South Wales order of chivalry. There was also the much-starred Terence Aubrey Murray, with more crosses and orders—not orders of merit—than a state of mandarinhood. Another gentleman who claimed the proud distinction of a colonial title was George Robert Nichols, the hereditary Grand Chancellor of all the Australias. Behold him in the serene and moody dignity of that picture of Rodias that smiled on us in all the public-house parlours. This was the gentleman who took Mr Lowe to task for altering his opinions, this conqueror in the lists of jaw, this victor in the realms of gab. It might be well to ridicule the doings of this miserable clique, yet their doings merited burning indignation; but to speak more seriously of such a project would too much resemble the Irishman 'kicking at nothing, it wrenched one horribly'. But though their weakness was ridiculous, he could assure them that these pigmies might work a great deal of mischief; they would bring contempt upon a country whose best interests he felt sure they all had at heart, until the meanest man that walked the streets would fling his gibe at the aristocrats of Botany Bay. He confessed he found extreme difficulty in the effort to classify this mushroom order of nobility. They could not aspire to the miserable and effete dignity of the worn-out grandees of continental Europe. There, even in rags, they had antiquity of birth to point to; here he would defy the most skilled naturalist to assign them a place in the great human family. But perhaps after all it was only a specimen of the remarkable contrariety which existed at the Antipodes. Here they all knew that the common water-mole was transformed into the duck-billed platypus; and in some distant emulation of this degeneracy, he supposed they were to be favoured with a bunyip aristocracy.

However, to be serious, he sincerely trusted this was only the beginning of a more extended movement, and from its commencement he argued the happiest results. A more orderly, united, and consolidated meeting he had never witnessed. He was proud of Botany Bay, even if he had to blush for some of her children. He took the name as no term of reproach when he saw such a high, true, and manly sensibility on the subject of their political rights; that the instant the liberties of their country were threatened, they could assemble, and with one voice declare their determined and undying opposition. But he would remind them that this was not a mere selfish consideration, there were far wider interests at stake.

Looking at the gradually increasing pressure of political parties at home, they must, in the not distant future, prepare to open their arms to receive the fugitives from England, Ireland, and Scotland, who would hasten to the offered security and competence that were cruelly denied them in their own land. The interests of those countless thousands were involved in their decision upon this occasion, and they looked, and were justly entitled to look, for a heritage befitting the dignity of free men.

Bring them not here with fleeting visions and delusive hopes. Let them not find a new-fangled Brummagem aristocracy swarming and darkening these fair, free shores. It is yours to offer them a land where man is bountifully rewarded for his labour, and where a just law no more recognises the supremacy of a class than it does the predominance of a creed. But, fellow-citizens, there is an aristocracy worthy of our respect and of our admiration. Wherever human skill and brain are eminent, wherever glorious manhood asserts its elevation, there is an aristocracy that confers eternal honour upon the land that possesses it. That is God's aristocracy, gentlemen; that is an aristocracy that will bloom and expand under free institutions, and for ever bless the clime where it takes root. He hoped they would take into consideration the hitherto barren condition of the country they were legislating for. He himself was a native of the soil, and he was proud of his birthplace. It is true its past was not hallowed in history by the achievements of men whose names reflected a light upon the times in which they lived. They had no long line of poets or statesmen or warriors; in this country, Art had done nothing but Nature everything. It was theirs, then, alone to inaugurate the future. In no country had the attempt ever been made to successfully manufacture an aristocracy *pro re nata*. It could not be done; they might as well expect honour to be paid to the dusky nobles of King Kamehamaka, or to the ebony earls of the Emperor Souloque of Hayti.

The stately aristocracy of England was founded on the sword. The men who came over with the conquering Norman were the masters of the Saxons, and so became the aristocracy. The followers of Oliver Cromwell were the masters of the Irish, and so became their aristocracy. But he would enquire by what process Wentworth and his satellites had conquered the people of New South Wales, except by the artful dodgery of cooking up a Franchise Bill. If we were to be blessed with an Australian aristocracy, he should prefer it to resemble, not that of William the Bastard, but of Jack the Strapper. But he trespassed too long on their time, and would in conclusion only seek to record two things—first, his indignant denunciation of any tampering with the freedom and purity of the elective principle, the only basis upon which sound government could be built; and, secondly, he wished them to regard well the future destinies of their country. Let them, with prophetic eye, behold the troops of weary pilgrims from foreign despotism which would ere long be flocking to these shores in search of a more congenial home, and let them now give their most earnest and determined assurance that the domineering clique which made up the Wentworth party were not, and should never be, regarded as the representatives of the manliness, the spirit,

and the intelligence of the freemen of New South Wales. He had sincere
pleasure in seconding the resolution, confident that it would meet with
unanimous support and approval.

1853/1884

ANONYMOUS

A popular folk song set in the Monaro region of NSW, 'The Eumerella Shore' refers
to Sir John Robertson's land acts of 1861 that allowed free selection of land leased by
squatters. It can be read either as celebrating the opportunities for a better life thus
given to the selectors or depicting them as thieves only too ready to help themselves to
the squatters' cattle, as indeed they do in Rolf Boldrewood's (qv) *Robbery Under Arms*.
First published in the *Launceston Examiner* (7 March 1861), it was collected in Banjo
Paterson's (qv) *Old Bush Songs* (1905). *EW*

The Eumerella Shore

There's a happy little valley on the Eumerella shore,
    Where I've lingered many happy hours away,
On my little free selection I have acres by the score,
    Where I unyoke the bullocks from the dray.

To my bullocks then I say   5
No matter where you stray,
    You will never be impounded any more;
For you're running, running, running on the duffer's piece of land,
    Free selected on the Eumerella shore.

When the moon has climbed the mountains and the stars are shining bright, 10
    Then we saddle up our horses and away,
And we yard the squatters' cattle in the darkness of the night,
    And we have the calves all branded by the day.

Oh, my pretty little calf,
At the squatter you may laugh.   15
    For he'll never be your owner any more;
For you're running, running, running on the duffer's piece of land,
    Free selected on the Eumerella shore,

If we find a mob of horses when the paddock rails are down,
    Although before they're never known to stray,   20
Oh, quickly will we drive them to some distant inland town,
    And sell them into slav'ry far away.

To Jack Robertson we'll say
You've been leading us astray,
    And we'll never go a-farming any more;   25
For it's easier duffing cattle on the little piece of land
    Free selected on the Eumerella shore.

            1861/1905

ANONYMOUS

One of Australia's best-known folk songs, 'The Wild Colonial Boy' celebrates the exploits of a bushranger named Jack Doolan. Opinions are divided as to whether Doolan was an actual bushranger active in the 1860s or whether the song is a variant of ballads associated with 'Bold Jack Donohoe', a famous bushranger from the 1820s who is mentioned in both 'A Convict's Tour to Hell' and 'Jim Jones at Botany Bay'. It was first published in the *Colonial Songster* (1881). *EW*

The Wild Colonial Boy

'Tis of a wild Colonial boy, Jack Doolan was his name,
Of poor but honest parents he was born in Castlemaine.
He was his father's only hope, his mother's only joy,
And dearly did his parents love the wild Colonial boy.

Come, all my hearties, we'll roam the mountains high,   5
Together we will plunder, together we will die.
We'll wander over valleys, and gallop over plains,
And we'll scorn to live in slavery, bound down with iron chains.

He was scarcely sixteen years of age when he left his father's home,
And through Australia's sunny clime a bushranger did roam.   10
He robbed those wealthy squatters, their stock he did destroy,
And a terror to Australia was the wild Colonial boy.

In sixty-one this daring youth commenced his wild career,
With a heart that knew no danger, no foeman did he fear.
He stuck up the Beechworth mail coach, and robbed Judge MacEvoy, 15
Who trembled, and gave up his gold to the wild Colonial boy.

He bade the Judge 'Good morning,' and told him to beware,
That he'd never rob a hearty chap that acted on the square,
And never to rob a mother of her son and only joy,
Or else you may turn outlaw, like the wild Colonial boy.   20

One day as he was riding the mountain side along,
A-listening to the little birds, their pleasant laughing song,
Three mounted troopers rode along—Kelly, Davis, and FitzRoy.
They thought that they would capture him—the wild Colonial boy.

'Surrender now, Jack Doolan, you see there's three to one,   25
Surrender now, Jack Doolan, you daring highway man.'
He drew a pistol from his belt, and shook the little toy.
'I'll fight but not surrender,' said the wild Colonial boy.

He fired at Trooper Kelly, and brought him to the ground,
And in return from Davis received a mortal wound.   30
All shattered through the jaws he lay still firing at FitzRoy,
And that's the way they captured him—the wild Colonial boy.

                                                          1881

ADAM LINDSAY GORDON
1833—1870

Until well into the twentieth century, Adam Lindsay Gordon was Australia's most widely read poet. His work, especially his bush ballads, was to influence many writers of the 1890s, including Banjo Paterson, Henry Lawson and Barcroft Boake (qqv). Gordon came from an aristocratic Scottish family and was educated at the Royal Military Academy and the Royal Grammar School Worcester but seems to have preferred gambling, boxing and riding to studying. In 1853, like other ne'er-do-well sons from good families, he was packed off to the colonies. After arriving in Adelaide he joined the South Australian Mounted Police and later worked as a horse breaker and jockey, becoming known as a daring steeplechase rider. Inheriting some money from his mother, he married in 1862, and purchased a property near Penola. This and other business ventures failed, as did his attempt at a parliamentary career. During this period he also began publishing his poetry at his own expense, as was customary. *The Feud: A border ballad* (1864) and *Ashtaroth: A dramatic lyric* (1867) were attempts at the longer poetical forms then in fashion and did not attract much attention. *Sea Spray and Smoke Drift* (1867) was made up of shorter works, including some on Australian themes, such as 'Gone', about the lost explorer Robert O'Hara Burke. But it was his final collection, *Bush Ballads and Galloping Rhymes* (1870), that established Gordon's reputation as the poet of Australia. Shortly before it appeared, he learned of the failure of his claim to a Scottish estate which he hoped would solve his financial difficulties. Penniless, and unable to pay his printer's bill, he committed suicide on Brighton Beach. The manner of his death contributed to the Gordon legend, which was to culminate in 1934 when admirers arranged to have his bust installed in the Poet's Corner of London's Westminster Abbey. He is the only Australian author represented there. *EW*

The Sick Stockrider

Hold hard, Ned! Lift me down once more, and lay me in the shade.
    Old man, you've had your work cut out to guide

Both horses, and to hold me in the saddle when I sway'd,
    All through the hot, slow, sleepy, silent ride.
The dawn at 'Moorabinda' was a mist rack dull and dense,   5
    The sunrise was a sullen, sluggish lamp;
I was dozing in the gateway at Arbuthnot's bound'ry fence,
    I was dreaming on the Limestone cattle camp.
We crossed the creek at Carricksford, and sharply through the haze,
    And suddenly the sun shot flaming forth;   10
To southward lay 'Katâwa', with the sandpeaks all ablaze,
    And the flush'd fields of Glen Lomond lay to north.
Now westward winds the bridle path that leads to Lindisfarm,
    And yonder looms the double-headed Bluff;
From the far side of the first hill, when the skies are clear and calm,   15
    You can see Sylvester's woolshed fair enough.

Five miles we used to call it from our homestead to the place
    Where the big tree spans the roadway like an arch;
'Twas here we ran the dingo down that gave us such a chase
    Eight years ago—or was it nine?—last March.   20

'Twas merry in the glowing morn, among the gleaming grass,
    To wander as we've wander'd many a mile,
And blow the cool tobacco cloud, and watch the white wreaths pass,
    Sitting loosely in the saddle all the while.
'Twas merry 'mid the blackwoods, when we spied the station roofs,   25
    To wheel the wild scrub cattle at the yard,
With a running fire of stockwhips and a fiery run of hoofs;
    Oh! the hardest day was never then too hard!

Aye! we had a glorious gallop after 'Starlight' and his gang,
    When they bolted from Sylvester's on the flat;   30
How the sun-dried reed-beds crackled, how the flint-strewn ranges rang
    To the strokes of 'Mountaineer' and 'Acrobat'.
Hard behind them in the timber, harder still across the heath,
    Close behind them through the tea-tree scrub we dash'd;
And the golden-tinted fern leaves, how they rustled underneath!   35
    And the honeysuckle osiers, how they crash'd!

We led the hunt throughout, Ned, on the chestnut and the grey,
    And the troopers were three hundred yards behind,
While we emptied our six-shooters on the bushrangers at bay,
    In the creek with stunted box-tree for a blind!   40

There you grappled with the leader, man to man and horse to horse,
    And you roll'd together when the chestnut rear'd;
He blaz'd away and missed you in that shallow watercourse—
    A narrow shave—his powder singed your beard!

In these hours when life is ebbing, how those days when life was young   45
    Come back to us; how clearly I recall
Even the yarns Jack Hall invented, and the songs Jem Roper sung;
    And where are now Jem Roper and Jack Hall?

Ay! nearly all our comrades of the old colonial school,
    Our ancient boon companions, Ned, are gone;   50
Hard livers for most part, somewhat reckless as a rule,
    It seems that you and I are left alone.

There was Hughes, who got in trouble through that business with the cards,
    It matters little what became of him;
But a steer ripp'd up MacPherson in the Cooraminta yards,   55
    And Sullivan was drown'd at Sink-or-swim;
And Mostyn—poor Frank Mostyn—died at last a fearful wreck,
    In 'the horrors', at the Upper Wandinong,
And Carisbrooke, the rider, at the Horsefall broke his neck,
    Faith! the wonder was he saved his neck so long!   60

Ah! those days and nights we squandered at the Logans' in the Glen—
    The Logans, man and wife, have long been dead.
Elsie's tallest girl seems taller than your little Elsie then;
    And Ethel is a woman grown and wed.

I've had my share of pastime, and I've done my share of toil,   65
    And life is short—the longest life a span;
I care not now to tarry for the corn or for the oil,
    Or for the wine that maketh glad the heart of man.
For good undone and gifts misspent and resolutions vain,
    'Tis somewhat late to trouble. This I know—   70
I should live the same life over, if I had to live again;
    And the chances are I go where most men go.

The deep blue skies wax dusky, and the tall green trees grow dim,
    The sward beneath me seems to heave and fall;
And sickly, smoky shadows through the sleepy sunlight swim,   75
    And on the very sun's face weave their pall.

Let me slumber in the hollow where the wattle blossoms wave,
    With never stone or rail to fence my bed;
Should the sturdy station children pull the bush flowers on my grave,
    I may chance to hear them romping overhead.   80
1870

WAIF WANDER
c. 1833 — c. 1910

Very little is known about the personal life of the prolific writer who published under the pseudonyms Waif Wander and W.W. She was born Mary Helena Wilson in Ireland and emigrated with her father to Canada, where in 1851 she married Joseph Fortune. In 1855, however, with her young son, she travelled to Australia to join her father at the Victorian goldfields. Here she began to publish prose and verse in various local periodicals, including the popular and long-running magazine the *Australian Journal*, established in 1865. Fortune wrote for this journal for many years, from 1868 contributing a regular series, 'The Detective's Album', which eventually amounted to more than 500 narratives of varying length. These were published under her 'W.W.' signature and were supposedly written around the cases of a male detective, Mark Sinclair. As 'Waif Wander', Fortune also wrote a number of serialised novels for the *Australian Journal*, including 'Bertha's Legacy' and 'Dora Carleton: A tale of Australia'. For a period from the late 1860s to mid-1870s, she contributed lively journalistic essays similar in style to those written by Marcus Clarke for his 'Peripatetic Philosopher' column, though from a woman's perspective. 'The Spider and the Fly' is one of these. In the 1880s she wrote 'Twenty-Six Years Ago', a fictionalised memoir of her life on the goldfields. This, together with some of Fortune's journalism, was published as *The Fortunes of Mary Fortune* (1989). By 1909, as one learns from her one surviving letter, Mary Fortune was almost blind and in dire poverty as she could no longer write. The proprietors of the *Australian Journal* apparently provided a small annuity for her and later paid for her burial, though no record of her death has yet been found. *EW*

The Spider and the Fly

'WANTED, HOUSEKEEPER: Position of trust.'

That's the advertisement that set so many female hearts in a flutter in and around Melbourne; and as I was very much personally interested in a mythical 'place of trust', I myself was among the number of 'ladies' who donned their best bibs and tuckers, and repaired to the place appointed, at or before the time appointed.

It is astonishing what different ideas of full dress are possessed by different women; and if you want an illustration of the fact, I could not recommend you to a better observatory than one of the said places of appointment. And while upon the subject, I should like to draw your attention to the number of advertisements you will meet in *the* daily, making some hotel or other the place of rendezvous.

I have lately had some little experience in, and opportunity of, taking notes upon the way these affairs are generally conducted, and my conclusion is, that no hotel whatever, be it as respectable as it may, shall ever be honoured by the light of my countenance in search of a place of trust. I may be mistaken, as you know we are all liable to be, but I am more than suspicious that a good many of these advertisements are simply hoaxes.

It is easy for any person at all conversant with one of the many varieties of fast human nature masculine, to imagine the delightful 'fun' it must be to see forty or fifty gullible women flocking to their call, with faces more or less anxious, and with every pin in their several attires arranged to make a favourable impression upon the enviable 'gentleman'. I could have guessed all that without having seen the advertiser I am going to tell you of, so thoroughly enjoying himself and his levee.

I said forty or fifty, did I not? Well, that was about the number that, as the hour of two p.m. approached, managed to locate themselves in and around the side door of one of the first hotels in Melbourne. I have no doubt that many of the females felt as awkward as I myself did at applying in such a place, and would not have showed face near it had it not been well-known as a first-class hotel, and a noted rendezvous for country gentlemen.

Well, as I arranged my bonnet-ties, and put upon myself generally as attractive an air as I could muster, I entered the side passage, to find myself in the company of seven or eight females, every separate one of whom seemed as thoroughly uncomfortable as any woman could be. Some of them were making inquiries through a window into the hall of a barmaid, who in vain attempted to keep her countenance, and whose very face was quite a sufficient declaration that she at least considered the whole thing a most absurd farce.

Well, having received a reply from the said barmaid, the several applicants looked around for some place in which to dispose themselves until their turn came to be ushered into the presence of the great autocrat of their fates. There was little choice. On one side was a private sitting-room, already crammed with 'ladies' possessed of sufficient impertinence to intrude there. On the other, a door opening into the bar itself, on the seats of which were disposed some half score or so of persons very available for places or positions of trust.

Some vacillated between the bar and the sitting-room, afraid to encounter the number of excited persons who occupied the latter; each jealous and envious of the other, and disinclined to make so little of themselves as to seat themselves in the public bar. Indeed, there were 'ladies' who seemed to take it as a personal insult that the bar door had been left open for their accommodation, and turned up their nose visibly at those who availed themselves of it. I observed that every one of these ladies had furiously red faces, and about half a stone or so of mock jewellery on their persons.

I did not feel inclined to face the ladies in the parlour, and I could not hang about the doorway in the public streets. Certainly I might have followed the example of some confused and forward applicants, who pushed open a glass-door leading into the more private portion of the hotel, and there stood congratulating themselves, no doubt, upon the more comfortable position they had obtained.

But I didn't—I had a fancy for seeing all that was to be seen, you see, and I walked straight into the bar. Once there, I seated myself between a gentle-looking woman in deep but rusty mourning with a little pale-faced girl on her knee, and a brazen-faced lady with a 'diadem' bonnet, three quarters high, upon her head. And then I began to enjoy myself thoroughly in my own especial way. Opposite to me was the bar, and inside the counter the barmaid; the latter was affecting to arrange her glasses, etc., but her risible faculties were not under the strongest control, and sometimes overcame her altogether.

And no wonder. If you had been there you would have laughed too; that is to say if you had not been one of the 'unco guid' folk of poor Burns.[1] I was fortunate in having the advantage of the poor girl, seeing that I could observe every movement of the ladies in the mirror behind her, without being observed; while she was obliged to face the crowd, and answer the hundred and one questions put to her by fresh arrivals.

Behind the bar went one applicant after another, and returned, some looking particularly sheepish, and some bold enough to terrify a troop of dragoons. It was evident that the sanctum of the wonderful and interesting gentleman who required the person of respectability for a position of trust was somewhere inside in a corner; and do you know that for the life of me I could not help thinking of that favourably known composition, 'Will you walk into my parlour? said the Spider to the Fly.'

And such a great choice of flies had that hidden spider, that I began to have a decided curiosity to see him. I wondered if he was a huge, bloated spider, with small eyes and a grin, or a slender-limbed black, sharp chap, that seemed on all sides at once, and with long crawling limbs, that were ready to grab any fly foolish enough to put herself within his clutches. And there was such a choice of flies, too, that I can fancy the spider, of whatever stamp he might be, aggravated to death that he could not grab them all at one haul.

There was a buzzing, restless mosquito, and the ubiquitous housefly, of changeful hue and indomitable perseverance in attack. There was the ugly and disgusting big brown blow-fly, and the active and detestable, yet seemingly pretty bluebottle. There was the miserable little midge, and the silly moth, all gathering at the invitation of Mr Spider. And he was not long invisible to

1   Robert Burns (1759–96), Scottish poet who died in poverty.

me, seated in the bar parlour in a charming state of excitement, and licking his lips in a delightful state of anticipation, I could well imagine. Charming old Spider! Little he thought how open to inspection was every one of his movements, through the unpoliteness of an angry fly (of the bluebottle species), to whom his highness would not extend the top of his sceptre.

This fly was of ample proportions, and had a face of the hue of port wine stains. A number of tremulous red flowers, a profusion of metallic green silk, and blond, and beads, was raised above a quantity of shining black bepuffed hair, in the form of a bonnet wondrous to behold. A tight jacket of dark blue velvet stuck to her stout figure; and her skirt was a changeable silk, of chameleon hues. A chain—a watch—a brooch—a locket—rings upon an ungloved, puddingy hand, and *voilà*! the most dashing-looking bluebottle fly you can imagine!

'You a gentleman!' she cried, bursting from the sanctum, and dashing the intervening door open against the wall. 'A good lambing is what the likes of you wants. Gentleman indeed! Advertises for respectable ladies, and then insults 'em.'

'My good woman,' remonstrated the invisible Spider, in a deprecatory tone of voice, which had no chance amid the thunder of indignation launched at him by the parting lady.

'A position of trust, indeed. Do I look like a person to do your dirty cooking and washing, and what not? Faugh!' And, amid an indignant rustling of silks and shaking of agitated red roses, evanished that disappointed fly, leaving the door wide open behind her.

Now I could well understand why the occupant of the bar parlour left the door open. To close it, he should have been obliged to expose himself to the eager gaze of many dozens of eyes—eyes now in a state of snapping curiosity as to the occasion of the departed female's anger.

So the door remained open, and the Spider behind it, in his corner, exposed to my delighted watch, reflected in the mirror opposite the door of his den.

There he sat, I say, and in a state of unpleasant excitement, as recipient of the lady's abuse. He *was* one of the bloated, cunning-looking spiders, with small green eyes; and he had grey bristly hair, that now stood up from his low forehead, most likely where he had desperately run his fingers through it at the moment of his late attack.

He grinned, and he shuffled in his chair, and he listened; and then he tapped at the bar partition, a signal that seemed understood by the barmaid, who had not yet recovered her gravity, which had been completely upset by the bluebottle's exit.

'You can go in now,' she at length managed to articulate, indicating at the same time one of the females in the bar.

'That she won't!' exclaimed a prim, conceited-looking woman, attired in a stuff gown, a black shawl, and an old straw bonnet. 'I've been here full an hour before her, and it's my turn, whether you like it or no,' and, suiting the action to the word, the dame pushed her way into the autocrat's den.

But she was a very unattractive fly, that elderly person with the old bonnet and the wrinkled face. The Spider required but a single glance to convince him that his web would be wasted in catching a 'lady' so unsuited for a 'position of trust'.

'I have engaged a person, ma'am,' he said, with a stiff nod at the woman, as she put her screwed-up nose around the door.

'Oh!' she said, with an indescribable toss of the head, as she emerged with a vinegar visage, 'He's engaged, ye needn't wait any longer.' And she too went out of the door, shaking, I have no moral doubt, the imaginary dust from her shuffling feet at its threshold.

At this instant a loud rapping from inside assured the barmaid that our gentleman required her instant attendance. From my post I could see that his highness was exceedingly irate, and soundly rated the barmaid for something or other. When she emerged, too, she shut the door, and I think I never saw so great a want of tact as that girl displayed in a position that she doubtless felt exceedingly awkward.

'Has the gentleman engaged?', 'I never heard the like! Before he saw half the applications!'—'He had no right to do it!'—etc., etc., were some of the questions and observations with which she was assailed.

The girl looked hither and thither, and feigned to perform some extraordinary feat under the counter, casting all the time furtive looks from one to the other of the excited applicants. It amused me excessively to observe the way in which the poor girl was obliged to twist and turn her mouth, to prevent an open exhibition of her merriment; while her face was perfectly scarlet from suppressed laughter.

At this awkward juncture arose a young woman, attired cheaply in an extravagantly fashionable style. I need not describe her—you may see her type every day on the street, and the impudent stare and conceited air are not attractive. She was one of that class of foolish young ladies(?) who are happy in piling pads and bows of ribbon on their heads, and in trailing a yard of cheap material after them in the dirt, and in walking upon boots two sizes too small for them, and upon heels less comfortable than stilts. No need to describe her, is there? You know, by sight only, I hope, a round hundred of them.

Influenced by her movement, doubtless, stepped also forward an old frowsy woman of about fifty years, determined, as it would appear, not to lose any chance that might present itself of admission to *the* presence.

'I suppose I can go in?' she did not question, as she attempted to push aside the barmaid, and enter; while the fashionable 'young lady' stared at her insolent rival as if she would wither her with a look.

Again came that rap at the partition, and the poor go-between's face grew redder than ever.

'The gentleman is engaged, ma'am,' she half whispered to the frowsy woman, 'and it's no use for you to see him. He's engaged a person already.'

And she winked—yes, winked visibly with her left eye at the 'young lady'.

Another 'Oh!' from Mrs Frowsy, and out also went she, muttering as she went.

'Isn't it true that he is suited, then?' asked the smiling fashionable of the also smiling attendant of the bar and the Spider.

'Oh, he only says that to some he doesn't like the appearance of,' replied the maid. 'You can go in.'

And in swept the delighted young lady.

Now came the chief fun of the whole business. In the front door of the bar crept the most ludicrous figure you can well imagine in search of a 'position of trust'. I do not generally find much difficulty in describing to you such characters as make a forcible impression upon myself, but in this instance I confess to a fear of failure, so immeasurably beyond 'all my fancy painted her' was this old lady's absurdity of appearance, and conceit of manner.

She was tall and thin, and attired in the sparsest manner. From her appearance, it was to be judged that her dress consisted totally of the scrap of dirty black skirt and voluminous long cloak, that she drew tightly about her shoulders, always excepting the filthy muslin cap and old greasy, black*ish* bonnet, that but partially covered it.

Every line in her face had a downward tendency. From the sharp nose on her ash-coloured face, to the wrinkles at the corners of her thin mouth— even her flabby cheeks, or rather what remained of them, dropped visibly, as in a vain search to discover their proper level. But, in spite of all this, there was an impudence and a temper that asserted itself in the elevation of her sharp chin, and the twist of the most flexible nose I ever beheld in my life.

As I have said, she drew the voluminous but thin cloak tightly around her shoulders, and she drew it with both hands under her chin. That is to say, that with both hands concealed under the cloak, she clasped it across her flat chest, so that nothing remained exposed to view of her skinny person, save the ash-coloured face, and the narrow angular outline revealed by the tight black covering.

She moved toward the bar in such a noiseless manner, and with such suspicious looks at the 'ladies' in the place, that one might have come to the conclusion she had come on some errand in which she feared the intervention of the police; and as she curled up her nose, firstly at one, and secondly at another, and finally at myself, in proper person, it was but too evident that she looked down upon us separately and collectively with the most perfect contempt.

After disposing of us to her satisfaction, she leaned her old, wretched visage across the counter, and accosted the retreating barmaid in a stage whisper.

'What sort of woman does he want, my dear?'

'I don't know, indeed; he's inside with one now,' was the reply, as the speaker seized her apron and hid her face from the old hag.

It was impossible to stand it any longer—the old creature was the last straw on the risible faculties of the woman, who nearly choked in an attempt at coughing to hide a laugh, in which every one of the applicants joined as silently as they could.

'Housekeeper, eh?' in another stage whisper.

The speechless girl nodded again.

'Oh-nm!' and the old face was turned *at* us over her shoulder, as she once more examined us with a grin of ineffable disgust. 'Oh, I know what he wants! An' if I'd a known afore I cum here, you wouldn't a seen *me* wid the likes!'

And the old creature drew her drapery still more tightly around her, to avoid contact with the 'ladies', who could not help laughing aloud as she made her stately exit.

And in a few minutes forth came the 'fashionable young lady', all smiles and pride, and announced to the envying applicants who waited 'at the gate' that she had been engaged by the 'gentleman'. There is no knowing what might have been the symptoms of some of the irate and disappointed women in the bar; for sundry tossing heads and mutterings, such as, 'A person of trust indeed!', 'Pretty person for a position of trust!' were beginning to be seen and heard, when to the rescue pops in at the door the old head of the skinny old woman.

'I told ye so!' she nodded and grinned at the barmaid. 'Ha, ha! I knew what he wanted—he, he! ho, ho!' and she was gone.

Retired we all discomfited. Retired the poor widow and her pale-faced child. What impudence *she* had to suppose that one without youth, and with sense, would be eligible for a position of trust under a bloated old Spider! Retired the barmaid, to laugh heartily behind the scenes, and to repeat the whole story to the hero of the hour, who called for a glass of brandy, and chucklingly began to consider if the silly fly, who had engaged with him would require a very intricate web to entrap her.

'Will you walk into my parlour? said the Spider to the Fly,
'Tis the prettiest little parlour that ever you did spy;
The way into my parlour is up a winding stair,
And I've many pretty things to show you there.'

But I shall ever hereafter, in connection with a 'position of trust', remember the miserable old skinny face that chuckled through the doorway, and said,

'I told you so! Ha, ha! he, he!'

1870/1989

LOUISA ATKINSON
1834–1872

Louisa Atkinson was the first woman novelist to have been born in Australia. Her parents were also among our earliest authors: James Atkinson published *An Account of the State of Agriculture and Grazing in New South Wales* (1826) while Charlotte Barton produced the first Australian children's book, *A Mother's Offering to Her Children* (1841). Following James Atkinson's early death, Charlotte made an unfortunate second marriage to her farm superintendent, George Barton, who proved to be a violent alcoholic. After leaving him in 1839, she had to fight many legal battles to get custody of her children and access to funds from Atkinson's estate. Poor health, combined with the family's frequent moves, meant that Louisa was educated at home by her mother. Under Charlotte's tutorage, however, she developed her talents as a writer and illustrator as well as her strong interest in natural history. In 1853 she began to contribute illustrated articles and stories to the *Illustrated Sydney News* and later to the *Sydney Morning Herald* and *Sydney Mail*. Atkinson's first novel, *Gertrude, the Emigrant*, was published in parts in 1857, with illustrations by the author. *Cowanda, the Veteran's Grant* followed in 1859. Four other novels serialised in the *Sydney Mail* have recently been published by Mulini Press. In 1869 Atkinson married the explorer James Calvert; she died in 1872 shortly after the birth of their daughter. *EW*

Cabbage-Tree Hollow, and the Valley of the Grose[1]

'Many a cloudy morning turns out a fine day,' says a hopeful adage, which, in these misty and rainy times, it is very pleasant to believe. The day arranged for our excursion was a confirmation of its prediction, and though the ride from Fernhurst to the foot of the hill at Wheeney Creek was performed under a cloudy sky, with dewdrops sparkling on the branches by the wayside, it was soon evident that the rains of the preceding day and night were not about to return again so shortly.

The South Kurrajong is a series of undulations, extending from the foot of the higher portions of the range towards the Hawkesbury. Much

---

1   In the Blue Mountains of NSW.

of this tract is under cultivation, and offers such cheery, smiling, trite home pictures as might tempt the artist to portray: cottages nestling among the dark foliage of the orange, the higher branches of the acacia and bean-tree, or the kurrajong (*Hibiscus heterophyllus*), now starred with its white blossoms; green slopes, where sleek cows feed and horses roam at liberty, or corn, and the golden wheat, vary the hues. The plentiful moisture of the past season has added those lively greens and luxuriant tints which are so essential to such scenery. The high-wooded mountains on one side, and the glimpses of the low lands of Cumberland are accessories of great value to our picture.

Two or three miles of such scenery brought us to the forest land; the road was still good, the grass green, the trees fine and umbrageous, and the transition was from one style of beauty to another only. The owner of 'Cabbage-tree Hollow' has constructed an excellent road to his property, which winds along the side of a hill crowned with beetling masses of sandstone, fretted and excavated by the atmosphere, while below the road lies a vale through which a small stream flows, bearing its waters onwards to join the Grose River. The extreme luxuriance of the vegetation attracts the attention no less than the greenness of the leaves and the superabundance of the ferns.

The deep shade, only broken by flecks of sunlight, or occasional gleams thrown across the road, rendered the ride particularly pleasant, and became doubly grateful as the sun gained power and poured a fiery glow upon the earth. Many little streams trickled down the hill side and, crossing the path, added their tributary waters to the brook in the glen below; altogether keeping up that pleasant cool sound which only running water can make.

Man's industry has already levelled some acres of the dense brush, and we found an embryo farm and orchard in the vale. The labour of the harvest field was in progress, and the slope of a hill was dotted with shocks standing amidst the stubble.

At the cottage we alighted, and our horses were secured while we proceeded to investigate the course of the stream by which we had ridden for the last mile, and another which joined it. Having been led to this spot by what an amusing modern writer is pleased to designate the *Pseromania*, the most ferny spots had the greatest powers of attraction. By more than one fallen tree did we cross rills hastening through the wheat field between their steep high banks, till the paling fence was reached. Here for a while bidding adieu to my companions, I left the comparative civilisation of the farm for the unbroken solitude.

Rocks, impeding the course of the stream, lashed the water into puny wrath, now leaping exultingly over an obstacle, again creeping beneath it—a curious churning, gurgling sound was the result, fit music for these sylvan solitudes, sombre with heavy shadows. On the edge, and even in the stream, grow *Alsophilia Australis* and *A. affinis, Todea barbara*, &c., with numerous lesser ferns, which cluster beneath their arborescent compeers, while the stones are green with *Hymerophyllum* and *Jungermannia*.

The stems only of the large cabbage-trees remain, but numerous small palmate leaves indicate the presence of young trees. Pensile moss-woven nests, attached to the extremities of the branches of trees or creepers, swayed above the stream, and their little builders flitted about them in all the importance of nesting season. The walk through the harvest field was varied by a rather large black snake crossing the path, which little interlude kept the attention awake till we remounted.

A rather abrupt and rocky path led up the hill, and we soon passed from the luxuriant and pretty vale to the thick scrub of a sandstone range. Here the advantages of a guide who thoroughly knew the country, and who could appreciate fine scenery, was experienced.

Pursuing the top of the range I presently descried with satisfaction the fine species of dwarf palm which obtains on the Shoalhaven River. While our obliging guide was seeking for nuts, some lyre birds (*Menura superba*) were disturbed, but continued to whistle and flutter about in much agitation till we resumed the order of march. Suddenly the thick scrub gave way, and the summits of distant mountains appeared. Hardly were the words uttered 'We will alight here,' before the ground was trodden, and eager steps pressing forward to the edge of the valley of the Grose.

There are scenes which baffle description when we can only feel like

'——stout Cortes, when with eagle eyes
   He stared at the Pacific, and all his men
Looked at each other with a wild surmise,
   Silent upon a peak in Darien.'[1]

Something of that hushed wonder for a moment held us spellbound, and then came the deep heartfelt, 'Beautiful, how beautiful—how grand.'

We stood on a rock looking down into the deep gorge, through which flowed a turbulent stream, yellow and froth-laden from recent inundations, while tributaries, which in their course clove asunder the mountains, dashed down the steeps. The heights are wooded to their summits with grand masses of yellow sandstone varying them, and the rich greens of *Backhousia myrtifolia*, *Pittosporum*, and *Tasmania aromatica* indicating the course of the various rills. After having brought the sketch book into requisition, we mounted our horses and rode through a scrubby piece of country, not without interest to the botanical student, to another spur of the mountain, from whence

---

1   John Keats (1795–1821), 'On First Looking into Chapman's Homer'.

we again obtained a fine view of the Grose, perhaps hardly so striking as the first point of view, or else the repetition of the scene had lost its first startling effects.

Down the right-hand ranges fall the waters of Burrolow, and to the left is Springwood; through the furthermost part of the gorge we catch a glimpse of a distant cone—Mount Hay, perhaps.

On our return we did not descend to the lovely Cabbage-tree Hollow, but, pursuing a marshy stream, turned from thence across to a surveyor's road leading through a casuarina country till we re-entered the farmlands, and exchanged the grandeur of the vast scenes, the great depths and dense woods of the other localities for the sunny homes of the South Kurrajong.—As we purposed to devote the remainder of the day to further explorations, the kind invitation of one of our companions to dine at her house, was cordially accepted, and, having been in the saddle almost uninterruptedly from nine till after three o'clock, her hospitality was well appreciated. Quite refreshed and in excellent spirits we started up the mountain, and again bade soon farewell to the homesteads of man, and turned our backs on orange groves and vine-covered porches to pursue a shady road, which quickly led us up the range. The road, being in use to draw timber from the mountains, is broad and good, and offers a pleasant riding ground. Numerous bellbirds made the brush vocal.

After reaching the summit, the road leads over and along the opposite decline; from hence it is not in use for wheeled vehicles. It was originally cut by the former proprietor of Burrolow, and is the only means by which vehicles can gain access to the valley. The scene gains in interest as we proceed, high rocks rising on one side. Pipeclay is found in the road, and extolled as very pure, an old woman who was collecting it for the use of the cleanly housewives of the Kurrajong was recently lost, and exposed to a wet night.

The atmospherical effects upon the rocks increases in interest. In one place a mass has fallen from the cliff, and rolling so close beside the path exhibits an aperture about eighteen inches in diameter, which communicates with an extensive cavity occupying the centre of the boulder.

During a great part of this ride the forest is very dense, and the path is over arched with luxuriant vegetation, the trees being so festooned by creepers as at times to threaten to put a stop to further progress. Some rills of water cross the path, and the whole place is very humid and shady. When expecting shortly to descend into the valley, this path was found impeded by a fallen tree, and, therefore, leaving it, we wound through the scrub to the margin of the stream—the same which, much augmented, we had traced with the eye in its headlong course into the Grose. Many beautiful flowers adorn this portion of Bunolone. The vale is here contracted and wooded, but a short ride led us

to the more clear land and ruined dikes—the evidences of what had been—
and thence, by the usual narrow stoney path, we wound up the hill, leaving
the valley already grey with evening hues, though the sun shone brightly on
the mountain tops.

1861/1978

GEORGE CHANSON
1835–1898

George Chanson was the pen name of George Ettienne Loyau who was born and
educated in England before coming to Australia in 1853 at the time of the gold rushes.
He worked as a gold digger, shepherd, hut keeper, shearer, stockman and cook before
becoming a journalist in Queensland in 1861. After moving to Sydney in 1865, he
continued to write for newspapers and magazines, publishing three small collections
of poems, including *Colonial Lyrics* (1872), which drew on his experiences in the bush.
He later worked in Melbourne and in South Australia, editing newspapers and books,
including *Notable South Australians* (1885). He also wrote a fictional autobiography, *The
Personal Adventures of George E. Loyau* (1883). *EW*

Stringy Bark and Green Hide

I sing of a commodity, it's one that will not fail yer,
I mean the common oddity, the mainstay of Australia;
Gold it is a precious thing, for commerce it increases,
But stringy bark and green hide, can beat it all to pieces.

Stringy bark and green hide, that will never fail yer!   5
Stringy bark and green hide, the mainstay of Australia.

If you travel on the road, and chance to stick in Bargo,
To avoid a bad capsize, you must unload your cargo;
For to pull your dray about, I do not see the force on,
Take a bit of green hide, and hook another horse on.   10

If you chance to take a dray, and break your leader's traces,
Get a bit of green hide, to mend your broken places;
Green hide is a useful thing, all that you require,
But stringy bark's another thing, when you want a fire.

If you want to build a hut, to keep out wind and weather,   15
Stringy bark will make it snug, and keep it well together;
Green hide if it's used by you, will make it all the stronger,
For if you tie it with green hide, it's sure to last the longer.

New chums to this golden land, never dream of failure,
Whilst you've got such useful things as these in fair Australia;   20
For stringy bark and green hide will never, never fail yer,
Stringy bark and green hide is the mainstay of Australia.

                                                                1872

ERNEST GILES
1835 – 1897

Explorer Ernest Giles was born in England and educated at Christ's Hospital; he followed his parents to Australia in 1850. After having no luck at the Victorian goldfields, he became a post office clerk in Melbourne. During the 1860s he explored western NSW and in 1872 and 1873 led expeditions into central Australia. From 1875 to 1876 he finally succeeded in making an overland crossing from South to Western Australia and back, which he described in *Australia Twice Traversed* (1889). He provides a vivid account here not only of the land he crossed but of his personal struggles to overcome the many difficulties he encountered. *EW*

From *Australia Twice Traversed*
Vol II, Chapter II: From 2nd April to 6th May, 1875

On the 2nd April we departed from this friendly depot at Wynbring Rock, taking our three horses, the two camels and the calf. The morning was as hot as fire; at midday we watered all our animals, and having saddled and packed them, we left the place behind us. On the two camels we carried as much water as we had vessels to hold it, the quantity being nearly fifty gallons. The horses were now on more friendly terms with them, so that they could be led by a person on horseback. Old Jimmy, now no longer a guide, was not permitted to take the lead, but rode behind, to see that nothing fell off the camels' saddles. I rode in advance, on my best horse Chester, a fine, well-set chestnut cob, a horse I was very fond of, as he had proved himself so good. Nicholls rode a strong young grey horse called Formby; he also had proved himself to my satisfaction to be a good one. Jimmy was mounted on an old black horse, that was a fine ambler, the one that bolted away with the load of water the first night we started from Youldeh. He had not stood the journey from Youldeh at all well; the other two were quite fresh and hearty when we left Wynbring.

By the evening of the 2nd we had made only twenty-two miles. We found the country terrific; the ground rose into sandhills so steep and high, that all our animals were in a perfect lather of sweat. The camels could hardly be got along at all. At night, where we were compelled by darkness to encamp, there was nothing for the horses to eat, so the poor brutes had to be tied up, lest they should ramble back to Wynbring. There was plenty of food for the camels, as they could eat the leaves of some of the bushes, but they were too sulky to eat because they were tied up. The bull continually bit his nose-rope through, and made several attempts to get away, the calf always going with him, leaving his mother: this made her frantic to get away too. The horses got frightened, and were snorting and jumping about, trying to break loose all night. The spot we were in was a hollow, between two high sandhills, and not a breath of air relieved us from the oppression of the atmosphere. Peter Nicholls and I were in a state of thirst and perspiration the whole night, running about after the camels and keeping the horses from breaking away. If the cow had got loose, we could not have prevented the camels clearing off. I was never more gratified than at the appearance of the next morning's dawn, as it enabled us to move away from this dreadful place. It was impossible to travel through this region at night, even by moonlight; we should have lost our eyes upon the sticks and branches of the direful scrubs if we had attempted it, besides tearing our skin and clothes to pieces also. Starting at earliest dawn, and traversing formidably steep and rolling waves of sand, we at length reached the foot of the mountain we had been striving for, in twenty-three miles, forty-five from Wynbring. I could not help thinking it was the most desolate heap on the face of the earth, having no water or places that could hold it. The elevation of this eminence was over 1000 feet above the surrounding country, and over 2000 feet above the sea. The country visible from its summit was still enveloped in dense scrubs in every direction, except on a bearing a few degrees north of east, where some low ridges appeared. I rode my horse Chester many miles over the wretched stony slopes at the foot of this mountain, and tied him up to trees while I walked to its summit, and into gullies and crevices innumerable, but no water rewarded my efforts, and it was very evident that what the old black fellow Wynbring Tommy, had said, about its being waterless was only too true. After wasting several hours in a fruitless search for water, we left the wretched mount, and steered away for the ridges I had seen from its summit. They appeared to be about forty-five miles away. As it was so late in the day when we left the mountain, we got only seven miles from it when darkness again overtook us, and we had to encamp.

On the following day, the old horse Jimmy was riding completely gave in from the heat and thirst and fearful nature of the country we were traversing, having come only sixty-five miles from Wynbring. We could neither lead, ride, nor drive him any farther. We had given each horse some water from the supply the camels carried, when we reached the mountain, and likewise some on the previous night, as the heavy sandhills had so exhausted them, this horse having received more than the others. Now he lay down and stretched out his limbs in the agony of thirst and exhaustion. I was loath to shoot the poor old creature, and I also did not like the idea of leaving him to die slowly of thirst; but I thought perhaps if I left him, he might recover sufficiently to travel at night at his own pace, and thus return to Wynbring, although I also knew from former sad experience in Gibson's Desert, that, like Badger and Darkie, it was more than probable he could never escape. His saddle was hung in the fork of a sandal-wood-tree, not the sandal-wood of commerce, and leaving him stretched upon the burning sand, we moved away. Of course he was never seen or heard of after.

That night we encamped only a few miles from the ridges, at a place where there was a little dry grass, and where both camels and horses were let go in hobbles. Long before daylight on the following morning, old Jimmy and I were tracking the camels by torchlight, the horse-bells indicating that those animals were not far off; the camel-bells had gone out of hearing early in the night. Old Jimmy was a splendid tracker; indeed, no human being in the world but an Australian aboriginal, and that a half or wholly wild one, could track a camel on some surfaces, for where there is any clayey soil, the creature leaves no more mark on the ground than an ant—black children often amuse themselves by tracking ants—and to follow such marks as they do leave, by firelight, was marvellous. Occasionally they would leave some marks that no one could mistake, where they passed over sandy ground; but for many hundreds of yards beyond, it would appear as though they must have flown over the ground, and had never put their feet to the earth at all. By the time daylight appeared, old Jimmy had tracked them about three miles; then he went off, apparently quite regardless of any tracks at all, walking at such a pace, that I could only keep up with him by occasionally running. We came upon the camels at length at about six miles from the camp, amongst some dry clay-pans, and they were evidently looking for water. The old cow, which was the only riding camel, was so poor and bony, it was too excruciating to ride her without a saddle or a pad of some sort, which now we had not got, so we took it in turns to ride the bull, and he made many attempts to shake us off; but as he had so much hair on his hump, we could cling on by that as we sat behind it. It was necessary for whoever was walking to lead him by his nose-rope, or he would have bolted away and rubbed his encumbrance off against a tree, or else rolled on it. In consequence of the camels having strayed so far, it was late in the day when we again started, the two horses looking fearfully hollow and bad. The morning as usual was very hot. There not being now a horse a piece to ride, and the water which one camel had carried having been drank by the animals, Peter Nicholls rode the old cow again, both she and the bull being much more easy to manage and get along than when we started from Youldeh. Our great difficulty was with the nose-ropes; the calf persisted in getting in front of its mother and twisting her nose-rope round his neck, also in placing itself right in between the fore-legs of the bull. This would make him stop, pull back and break his rope, or else the button would tear through the nose; this caused detention a dozen times a day, and I was so annoyed with the young animal, I could scarcely keep from shooting it many times. The young creature was most endearing now, when caught, and evidently suffered greatly from thirst.

We reached the ridges in seven miles from where we had camped, and had now come ninety miles from Wynbring. We could find no water at these ridges, as there were no places that could hold it. Here we may be said to have entered on a piece of open country, and as it was apparently a change for the better from the scrubs, I was very glad to see it, especially as we hoped to obtain water on it. Our horses were now in a terrible state of thirst, for the heat was great; and the region we had traversed was dreadfully severe; and though they had each been given some of the water we brought with us, yet we could not afford anything like enough to satisfy them. From the top of the ridge a low mount or hill bore 20° north of east; Mount Finke, behind us, bore 20° south of west. I pushed on now for the hill in advance, as it was nearly on the route I desired to travel. The country being open, we made good progress, and though we could not reach it that night, we were upon its summit early the next morning, it being about thirty miles from the ridges we had left, a number of dry, salt, white lagoons intervening. This hill was as dry and waterless as the mount and ridges, we had left behind us in the scrubs. Dry salt lagoons lay scattered about in nearly all directions, glittering with their saline encrustations, as the sun's rays flashed upon them. To the southward two somewhat inviting isolated hills were seen; in all other directions the horizon appeared gloomy in the extreme. We had now come 120 miles from water, and the supply we had started with was almost exhausted; the country we were in could give us none, and we had but one, of two courses to pursue, either to advance still further into this terrible region, or endeavour to retreat to Wynbring. No doubt the camels could get back alive, but ourselves and the horses could never have re-crossed the frightful bed of rolling sand-mounds, that intervened between us and the water we had left. My poor old black companion was aghast at such a region, and also at what he considered my utter folly in penetrating into it at all. Peter Nicholls, I was glad to find, was in good spirits, and gradually changing his opinions with regard to the powers and value of the camels. They had received no water themselves, though they had laboured over the hideous sandhills, laden with the priceless fluid for the benefit of the horses, and it was quite evident the latter could not much longer live, in such a desert, whilst the former were now far more docile and obedient to us than when we started. Whenever the horses were given any water, we had to tie the camels up at some distance. The expression in these animals' eyes when they saw the horses drinking was extraordinary; they seemed as though they were going to speak, and had they done so, I know well they would have said, 'You give those useless little pigmies the water that cannot save them, and you deny it to us, who have carried it, and will yet be your only saviours in the end.' After we had fruitlessly searched here for water, having wasted several hours, we left this wretched hill, and I continued steering upon the same course we had come, viz. north 75° east, as that bearing would bring me to the north-western extremity of Lake Torrens, still distant over 120 miles. It was very probable we should get no water, as none is known to exist where we should touch upon its shores. Thus we were, after coming 120 miles from Wynbring, still nearly 200 miles from the Finniss Springs, the nearest water that I knew. It was now a matter of life and death; could we reach the Finniss at all? We could neither remain here, nor should we survive if we attempted to retreat; to advance was our only chance of escape from the howling waste in which we were almost entombed; we therefore moved onwards, as fast and as far as we could. On the following morning, before dawn, I had been lying wakefully listening for the different sounds of the bells on the animals' necks, and got up to brighten up the camp fire with fresh wood, when the strange sound of the quacking of a wild duck smote upon my ear. The blaze of firelight had evidently attracted the creature, which probably thought it was the flashing of water, as it flew down close to my face, and almost precipitated itself into the flames; but discovering its error, it wheeled away upon its unimpeded wings, and left me wondering why this denizen of the air and water, should be sojourning around the waterless encampment of such hapless travellers as we. The appearance of such a bird raised my hopes, and forced me to believe that we must be in the neighbourhood of some water, and that the coming daylight would reveal to us the element which alone could save us and our unfortunate animals from death. But, alas! how many human hopes and aspirations are continually doomed to perish unfulfilled; and were it not that 'Hope springs eternal in the human breast,' all faith, all energy, all life, and all success would be at an end, as then we should know that most of our efforts are futile, whereas now we hope they may attain complete fruition. Yet, on the other hand, we learn that the fruit of dreamy hoping is waking blank despair. We were again in a region of scrubs as bad and as dense as those I hoped and thought, I had left behind me. [. . .]

1889

HENRY KENDALL
1839—1882

Poet Henry Kendall was born near Ulladulla on the south coast of NSW. He grew up in the Clarence River region of the north coast and coastal landscapes were to inspire many of his poems and prose works. His mother, who also wrote poems, introduced her children to literature at an early age. After her husband's death in 1852, she moved the family to her father's farm near Wollongong. From 1855 to 1856, Kendall spent eighteen months at sea, an experience he did not enjoy. After the family moved to Sydney, Kendall began contributing to local newspapers and magazines from 1859; his first volume, *Poems and Songs*, was published at his own expense in 1862. By then he had begun a correspondence with fellow poet Charles Harpur (qv) and been introduced to many Sydney literary figures, including journalists D.H. Deniehy (qv) and Richard Rowe, and James Lionel Michael, a solicitor who employed Kendall as a clerk in his Grafton office from 1862 to 1863. By 1864 he was back in Sydney, working as a clerk in various government departments and writing for *Sydney Punch*. His marriage in 1868 did not help his always-precarious finances and in 1869, in debt to many friends, he resigned his post and moved to Melbourne, then the literary centre of Australia, where he hoped to make a better living through his writing. His second collection, *Leaves from Australian Forests* (1869), received favourable reviews; it included his best-known poem, 'Bell-birds'. Kendall's financial situation did not improve and he returned to Sydney in 1871, where the strain of continuous writing combined with alcoholism saw him committed to the Gladesville mental asylum for a time. From 1875 until his death, Kendall lived outside Sydney, at Gosford, Camden Haven and Broken Bay, from 1881 working as Inspector of Forests, a post arranged for him by politician Henry Parkes, despite Kendall's satirical attacks on him. His final volume, *Songs from the Mountains*, was published in 1880. While never as widely popular as Adam Lindsay Gordon (qv), whose death Kendall had mourned in 1870, he remained one of Australia's favourite writers until well into the twentieth century. *EW*

Bell-birds

By channels of coolness the echoes are calling,
And down the dim gorges I hear the creek falling;
It lives in the mountain, where moss and the sedges
Touch with their beauty the banks and the ledges;
Through breaks of the cedar and sycamore bowers   5
Struggles the light that is love to the flowers.
And, softer than slumber, and sweeter than singing,
The notes of the bell-birds are running and ringing.

The silver-voiced bell-birds, the darlings of daytime,
They sing in September their songs of the May-time.   10
When shadows wax strong, and the thunder-bolts hurtle,
They hide with their fear in the leaves of the myrtle;
When rain and the sunbeams shine mingled together
They start up like fairies that follow fair weather,
And straightway the hues of their feathers unfolden   15
Are the green and the purple, the blue and the golden.

October, the maiden of bright yellow tresses,
Loiters for love in these cool wildernesses;
Loiters knee-deep in the grasses to listen,

Where dripping rocks gleam and the leafy pools glisten.   20
Then is the time when the water-moons splendid
Break with their gold, and are scattered or blended
Over the creeks, till the woodlands have warning
Of songs of the bell-bird and wings of the morning.

Welcome as waters unkissed by the summers,   25
Are the voices of bell-birds to thirsty far-comers.
When fiery December sets foot in the forest,
And the need of the wayfarer presses the sorest,
Pent in the ridges for ever and ever,
The bell-birds direct him to spring and to river,   30
With ring and with ripple, like runnels whose torrents
Are toned by the pebbles and leaves in the currents.

Often I sit, looking back to a childhood
Mixt with the sights and the sounds of the wildwood,
Longing for power and the sweetness to fashion   35
Lyrics with beats like the heart-beats of passion—
Songs interwoven of lights and of laughters
Borrowed from bell-birds in far forest-rafters;
So I might keep in the city and alleys
The beauty and strength of the deep mountain valleys;   40
Charming to slumber the pain of my losses
With glimpses of creeks and a vision of mosses.

    1869

The Late Mr A.L. Gordon: In Memoriam

At rest! Hard by the margin of that sea
Whose sounds are mingled with his noble verse,
Now lies the shell that never more will house
The fine, strong spirit of my gifted friend.
Yea, he who flashed upon us suddenly   5
A shining soul with syllables of fire,
Who sang the first great songs these lands can claim
To be their own; the one who did not seem
To know what royal place awaited him
Within the Temple of the Beautiful,   10
He passed away; and we who knew him, sit
Aghast in darkness, dumb with that great grief,
Whose stature yet we cannot comprehend;

While over yonder churchyard, hearsed with pines,
The nightwind sings its immemorial hymn,   15
And sobs above a newly-covered grave.

The bard, the scholar, and the man who lived,
That frank, that open-hearted life which keeps
The splendid fire of English chivalry
From dying out; the one who never wronged   20
A fellow man; the faithful friend who judged
The many, anxious to be loved of him,
By what he saw, and not by what he heard,
As lesser spirits do; the brave great soul
That never told a lie, or turned aside   25
To fly from danger; he, I say, was one
Of that bright company this sin stained world
Can ill afford to lose.

                       They did not know,
The hundreds who had read the sturdy verse   30
And revelled over ringing major notes,
The mournful meaning of the undersong
Which runs through all he wrote, and often takes
The deep autumnal, half-prophetic tone
Of forest winds in March; nor did they think   35
That on that healthy-hearted man there lay
The wild specific curse which seems to cling
For ever to the Poet's twofold life!

To Adam Lindsay Gordon, I who laid
Two years ago on Lionel Michael's[1] grave   40
A tender leaf of my regard: yea, I
Who culled a garland from the flowers of song
To place where Harpur sleeps; I, left alone,
The sad disciple of a shining band
Now gone! to Adam Lindsay Gordon's name   45
I dedicate these lines; and if 'tis true
That, past the darkness of the grave, the soul
Becomes omniscient, then the bard may stoop
From his high seat to take the offering,
And read it with a sigh for human friends,   50
In human bonds, and grey with human griefs.

---

1   James Lionel Michael (1824–68), poet and lawyer.

And having wove and proffered this poor wreath,
I stand to-day as lone as he who saw
At nightfall through the glimmering moony mists,
The last of Arthur on the wailing mere,   55
And strained in vain to hear the going voice.

1870/1893

W.H.L. RANKEN
1839–1902

William Hugh Logan Ranken was born in British Guinea of Scottish parents and arrived in Australia after travelling in Europe, Asia and the Pacific. He spent time undertaking further travel in Australia before settling on a station in northern NSW. *The Dominion of Australia* (1874) is an imaginative and interesting geography handbook. *EW*

From *The Dominion of Australia*
Chapter III

[. . .] All life is thus limited by the aridity and uncertainty of the climate. There is little rain over the great bulk of the continent; there is little vegetation, little animal life, only one beast of prey, and few, very few, human creatures. But the climate is not only niggardly on the whole, it is a most capricious tyrant, destroying at uncertain intervals what it has reared in a few milder seasons. No result is gained by a rich growth in the forest, if a drought comes and withers up all young or weak life. And the interior, which has so many features in common, is so extensive in proportion to the whole, that it impresses its characteristics upon every part of the country. It reduces tropical forests to exceptional patches in sheltered nooks; it encourages one type of animal everywhere, and has forbidden the immigration of the teeming populations of the adjacent tropical archipelago to its barren shores. Floods destroy some life, they may drown some young animals, but the increased production of all life which follows them more than makes up any decrease. Drought, dry seasons, and, more than all—that deadliest weapon of the tyrant—the bush-fire, reduces and selects the life of the country.

During the long dreary months of dry heat, without rain or dew, those broad-leaved trees and herbs, which expose a large evaporating surface and require a large supply of moisture, could not survive; only the hard, thick, narrow leaves of the Australian forest, glistening like steel when they cannot hold their edges to the glaring sun, come out of the trial. On the plains and downs the acacias cluster in thickets as if to shelter one another, or singly droop their scant foliage gracefully over the parched waste. On the flats and meadows the giant eucalypti rear gaunt stems and bare boughs. The hills are timbered, but shadeless; and even in the beds of the watercourses the melaleuca is ragged and wretched-looking. All have hard, rigid, narrow leaves, and few of those. The watercourses are drying up, and the animals struggle on from one death to another. The marsupials can live for long without water, but not so the dog. He, the only foreigner of the land, cannot live without frequent water; he cannot therefore always accomplish the journey from one water to another, as the holes dry up; and he cannot remove his young to water when it is an imperative necessity. No animals are so adapted to such a trial as the marsupials; and they survive. The trees having the smallest amount of foliage, and not dependent upon a regularly returning spring to reinvigorate them—an indeciduous shadeless forest—is another result.

Then the grass is withered white, it is dry and warm night and day, and one spark of fire sets all the landscape in a blaze. This widens over the plain, gathers air in its combustion, and becomes a hurricane of fire. It sweeps the plains, storms the mountains, and rushes irresistible over watercourses, to lick up withered grass on opposite banks. The seedlings are lost, the saplings destroyed, the whole forest scorched, and every decayed giant of the wood is wreathed Laocoon-like in fire—scattering from his yielding limbs flakes and sparks on every side, from which fires spring hydra-like over the withered sward—to rise, to roar and rush on, and scale in rapid springs the grassy ranges. In the forest, it spares only the giant eucalypti, which have stems towering 30 feet without a limb, only scorching the smooth bark, which is shed and renewed annually; upon the downs, it spares only—as it lingers and lulls in the low grass—those hardy acacias which rise in iron-like columns beneath their thin graceful tresses; and upon the mountain, it spares only those eucalypti which have their veteran stems bound in an impenetrable coat of 'iron bark'. All the land is cleared except these selected trees. Hence the open forest of Australia; hence grazing and squatters and land-laws; hence wool and meat-growing are before everything else.

The jungles or 'scrubs' are not touched, for they have not grass nor sufficient tinder to lead the fire into their masses; and when the country is stocked, and bush-fires carefully kept down by man, then thickets increase upon every side. If any tract be for some years free from the visitation, then the forest will thicken; and the trees which have the most inflammable bark, like 'stringy-bark' and 'peppermint trees', grow in poor ground, and grow thickly, where fires rarely penetrate, and then only to blast the whole forest.

The fire-storm sweeps over the land, and reduces the animal kingdom; all is subject. The smaller insects and animals in their struggles are followed by flocks of birds, who snatch their prey from the flames. The small game and reptiles flee before destruction, or perish in logs and other deceptive lurking-places; and the large rodents, who survive instant destruction, have to continue the struggle for existence—without any pasture on the plain, young or old—with only the hard foliage of the thickets. Desolation is doubly desolate; the desert is burnt black and lifeless. Life has almost to begin again in the lower vegetable kingdom, and even animals lose their young. The plain depends upon the deepest roots, and the hardest of the barbed and needle-pointed grass seeds buried in the soil, to grow another crop. The forest has lost its saplings, and must plant again; and the struggle is hardest and longest with the animals. The dog, far from shelter, cannot circumvent that furious sea of fire; he cannot bound over the walls of flame and fields of cinders; nor can he remove his young, nor can they escape. If his lair is in a log upon the plain, or by the last waterhole in the valley, his life is almost worthless. The marsupial has a better chance than any other type of animal, for she can bound far over flames and scorching ground, and find a way through many fires. Her young has a much better chance; for, placed securely in its mother's pouch, it is carried high over the burning ground, over death and extermination to live, or at least to continue the struggle. The marsupials are the selected survivors; the one type of all the country. The dog has no enemy but the climate; he is not subject to any other beast of the field, and he has many varieties of victims utterly defenceless against his attacks, but is not the master. He would increase and gather into packs, like wolves and hyenas, under another climate, with the present natural stock of the country; yet he is a solitary exceptional stranger in the land. The marsupials have been selected, with hard bare trees, and all the peculiar types of the country, in that decisive struggle. And it may be conjectured that if the superior types of animals introduced by the colonists were left to continue the struggle alone, were the country at once depopulated, considering the great degeneration these animals immediately undergo if neglected, they would disappear from the climate of marsupials in a few thousand years.

1874

A. J. BOYD
1842–1928

William Alexander Jenyns Boyd was born in France and educated in England and on the Continent, where he became fluent in French, German and Italian. In 1860 he migrated to Queensland and selected a small block at Oxley Creek where he built a cotton mill. He later worked as a teacher and became headmaster of various schools. As a travelling district inspector and promoter of new schools, he toured widely in northern Queensland (1874–76). His observations of local life and characters were later published in the *Queenslander*, of which he was agricultural editor from 1874, before being collected as *Old Colonials* (1882). Boyd's sketches of bush types, especially those narrated in a colloquial first person, such as 'The Shepherd', anticipate the later work of Henry Lawson. In 1897 Boyd became the first editor of the *Queensland Agricultural Journal*, a post he held until 1921. *EW*

The Shepherd

I'm a shepherd. That's so. I've been a shepherd for nigh on twenty-five years. And I've earned good wages, too, for all I look so ragged. I remember, in the good old times, when the shepherds was the bosses. That was at the time of the big rushes to the diggings. Money was plentiful then, and we used to have some tremendous sprees. Why didn't I save my money? There never was a chance to save. First of all, when we got our wages, the cheque wasn't a right cheque: it was an order written on flimsy or soft paper, on the nearest agent of the squatter, an' cashed by the nearest publican, who, of course, never handed over a cent. A man was compelled to stay there and knock his cheque down 'like a man'. Then if the order didn't happen to be drawn on a merchant close by, it was all the same. If it was drawn on somebody in Sydney, how could a poor devil get away to Sydney—perhaps a four or five hundred mile tramp, without a farthing in his pocket? A man was obliged to go to the publican to advance him some money, and once you took a drink (for you couldn't go away without taking a nip) it was all up with you. The liquor was hocussed, and you got mad, and before you knew where you were your cheque was spent—at least so the landlord told you, and he bundled you out neck and crop. If he was at all a decent sort of fellow, he would give you a bottle of rum to help you to recover from your spree, and you returned to the station in a few days penniless. I've no heart to begin to save. I was well-to-do once—had a station of my own; but what with foot-rot and scab, and not looking after my own place, I soon went to the wall, and I've been getting lower and lower, till at last I became a shepherd. It *is* a lonely life. I never see anyone but the ration-carrier once a week, and I've no books to read. I follow the sheep, and camp when they camp. I go to sleep sometimes and lose the run of the flock. But I've been pretty well broken-in to not going to sleep. I've been made to pay for lost sheep, so that for three years I hadn't a cent of wages to take. The native dogs and the blacks worry me. Many a night I watch all night to try and get a slant at the dingoes. I used to lay baits for them, but I had my best dog poisoned through taking one of the baits, so I've given it up now and shoot them when I've a chance. It used to be fine times at night when there was a hutkeeper, but now-a-days a man has got to be his own hutkeeper, and cooking, and washing, and watching at night, and shepherding all day, mending hurdles and shifting them, takes up plenty of time. It's not such an idle life as people suppose. There's always something to do. The idlest part of it is following the sheep out at grass. Lambing time makes it pretty lively for everyone. We see more people then, and get a bit of news. Would I recognise my sheep in a crowd? Of course I could. I know every face in the flock, and there isn't two alike. People are apt to think a sheep is a sheep. So is a child a child, but no two children are exactly alike, and no two sheep are alike. I could swear to every one of 'em. I don't think I shall shepherd much longer. I'm getting on in years. Sixty, close on. I'm thinking of saving my wages next year if the publican will let me, and taking up a bit of land. I could have a home then, and only take a job with a travelling mob sometimes, or else go to shearing at shearing-time, to keep one in tucker. I'd be obliged for a bit of 'baccy. The rations ain't due till to-morrow, and I'm clean run out. Thank'e, sir.

1882

JOSEPH FURPHY
1843–1912

Joseph Furphy, the son of Protestant Irish labourers, left school at fourteen for farm work in rural Victoria and southern NSW. After marrying, he and his family farmed for ten years, but after losing both farms Furphy set up as a bullock driver in remote south-west NSW. Drought and illness wiped out his two teams, and Furphy went to work in his brother's foundry in Shepparton, Victoria. There he was influenced by the radicalism of the workers and began writing for the *Bulletin*.

Such is Life (1903), titled after Ned Kelly's (qv) reputed last words, was submitted to the *Bulletin* in 1897 under the pseudonym Tom Collins, a slang byword for the source of all rumours—a clear hint that this supposedly realist account of working life in the backblocks was not all that it seemed. Masquerading as a true account of the life and opinions of its main character, the novel is a subtle complex of ironies, yarns and subplots, described by Furphy as 'one long lie in seven chapters'.

Published six years later, after the removal and shortening of two chapters later published as *Rigby's Romance* (1921, unabridged 1946) and *The Buln Buln and the Brolga* (1948), *Such is Life* remains the strongest candidate for the 'great Australian novel'. Full as it is of hard-working, laconic bullockies without prospects but ready to help out a mate in distress, the novel is also an arcanely allusive meditation on reality and causality, informed by the Stoics as well as Furphy's Christian Socialism. It offers a critique of the labour structures of the agricultural industry, among other targets. Heavily ironised via word plays, nude frolics and satiric contests between romance and realism, the novel threads beneath its surface a tragic romance. This tells the story of a constant woman, her fate disguised from Collins by her cross-dressing, but poignantly evident to an 'observant reader', as Furphy warns us to be.

Furphy also described his novel as having a 'temper, democratic; bias, offensively Australian'. That declaration has been a touchstone for radical nationalist models of Australian literature, but, as James Wieland argues, the changing reception of *Such is Life* mirrors the changing tenor of Australian literary culture. An annotated edition (1991) has served the wealth of those readings well. *NM*

From *Such is Life*
Chapter V: Wed. Jan. 9th

[…] "'Child lost in the scrub on Goolumbulla. Dan O'Connell's little girl— five or six years old. Anybody know where there's any blackfellows?'

'Nobody knew.

"'Well, raise horses wherever you can, and clear at once," says he. "One man, for the next couple of days, will be worth a regiment very shortly. As for you, Thompson," says he; "you're your own master."

'Of course, I was only too glad of any chance to help in such a case, so I went for my horse at once. Bob had duffed his two horses into the ration paddock, on his way to the hut, and had put them along with my mare, so that he could find them at daylight by the sound of her bell. This started me and him together. He lent his second horse to one of the station chaps; and three of us got to Goolumbulla just after sunrise—first of the crowd. Twenty-five mile. There was tucker on the table, and chaff for our horses; and, during the twenty minutes or so that we stayed, they gave us the outline of the mishap.

'Seems that, for some reason or other—valuation for mortgage, I'm thinking—the classer had come round a few days before; and Spanker had called in every man on the station, to muster the ewes. You know how thick the scrub is on Goolumbulla? Dan came in along with the rest, leaving his own place before daylight on the first morning. They swept the paddock the first day for about three parts of the ewes; the second day they got most of what was left; but Spanker wanted every hoof, if possible, and he kept all hands on for the third day.

'Seems, the little girl didn't trouble herself the first day, though she hadn't seen Dan in the morning; but the second day there was something peculiar about her—not fretful, but dreaming, and asking her mother strange questions. It appears that, up to this time, she had never said a word about the man that was found dead near their place, a couple of months before. She saw that her parents didn't want to tell her anything about it, so she had never showed any curiosity; but now her mother was startled to find that she knew all the particulars.

'It appears that she was very fond of her father; and this affair of the man perishing in the scrub was working on her mind. All the second day she did nothing but watch; and during the night she got up several times to ask her mother questions that frightened the woman. The child didn't understand her father going away before she was awake, and not coming back. Still, the curious thing was that she never took her mother into her confidence, and never seemed to fret.

'Anyway, on the third morning, after breakfast, her mother went out to milk the goats, leaving her in the house. When the woman came back, she found the child gone. She looked round the place, and called, and listened, and prospected everywhere, for an hour; then she went into the house, and examined. She found that the little girl had taken about a pint of milk, in a small billy with a lid, and half a loaf of bread. Then, putting everything together, the mother decided that she had gone into the scrub to look for her father. There was no help to be had nearer than the home-station, for the only other boundary man on that part of the run was away at the muster. So she cleared for the station—twelve mile— and got there about three in the afternoon, not able to stand. There was nobody about the station but Mrs. Spanker, and the servant-girl, and the cook, and the Chow slushy; and Mrs. Spanker was the only one that knew the track to the ewe-paddock. However, they got a horse in, and off went Mrs. Spanker to give the alarm. Fine woman. Daughter of old Walsh, storekeeper at Moogoojinna, on the Deniliquin side.

'It would be about five when Mrs. Spanker struck the ewe-paddock, and met Broome and another fellow. Then the three split out to catch whoever they could, and pass the word round. Dan got the news just before sundown. He only remarked that she might have found her own way back; then he went for home as hard as his horse could lick.

'As the fellows turned-up, one after another, Spanker sent the smartest of them—one to Kulkaroo, and one to Mulppa, and two or three others to different fencers' and tank-sinkers' camps. But the main thing was blackfellows. Did anybody know where to find a blackfellow, now that he was wanted?

'Seems, there had been about a dozen of them camped near the tank in the cattle-paddock for a month past, but they were just gone, nobody knew where. And there had been an old lubra and a young one camped within a mile of the station, and an old fellow and his lubra near one of the boundary men's places; but they all happened to have shifted; and no one had the slightest idea where they could be found. However, in a sense, everyone was after them.

'But, as I was telling you, we had some breakfast at the station, and then started for Dan's place. Seven of us by this time, for another of the Kulkaroo men had come up, and there were three well-sinkers in a buggy. This was on a Thursday morning; and the little girl had been out twenty-four hours.

'Well, we had gone about seven mile, with crowds of fresh horse-tracks to guide us; and we happened to be going at a fast shog, and Bob riding a couple or three yards to the right, when he suddenly wheeled his horse round, and jumped off.

'"How far is it yet to Dan's place?" says he.

'"Five mile," says one of the well-sinkers. "We're just on the corner of his paddock. Got tracks?"

'"Yes," says Bob. "I'll run them up, while you fetch the other fellows. Somebody look after my horse." And by the time the last word was out of his mouth, he was twenty yards away along the little track. No trouble in following it, for she was running the track of somebody that had rode out that way a few days before—thinking it was her father's horse, poor little thing!

'Apparently she had kept along the inside of Dan's fence—the way she had generally seen him going out—till she came to the corner, where there was a gate. Then she had noticed this solitary horse's track striking away from the gate, out to the left; and she had followed it. However, half-a-mile brought us to a patch of hardish ground, where she had lost the horse's track; and there Bob lost hers. Presently he picked it up again; but now there was only her little boot-marks to follow.'

'A goot dog would be wort vivty men dere, I tink,' suggested Helsmok.

'Same thought struck several of us, but it didn't strike Bob,' replied Thompson. 'Fact, the well-sinkers had brought a retriever with them in the buggy; a dog that would follow the scent of any game you could lay him on; but they couldn't get him to take any notice of the little girl's track. Never been trained to track children—and how were they going to make him understand that a child was lost? However, while two of the well-sinkers were persevering with their retriever, the other fellow drove off like fury to fetch Dan's sheep-dog; making sure that we would only have to follow him along the scent. In the meantime, I walked behind Bob, leading both our horses.

'Give him his due, he's a great tracker. I compare tracking to reading a letter written in a good business hand. You must'nt look at what's under your eye; you must see a lot at once, and keep a general grasp of what's on ahead, besides spotting each track you pass. Otherwise, you'll be always turning back for a fresh race at it. And you must no more confine yourself to actual tracks than you would expect to find each letter correctly formed. You must just lift the general meaning as you go. Of course, our everyday tracking is not tracking at all.

'However, Bob run this little track full walk, mile after mile, in places where I would'n't see a mark for fifty yards at a stretch, on account of rough grass, and dead leaves, and so forth. One thing in favour of Bob was that she kept a fairly straight course, except when she was blocked by porcupine or supple-jack; then she would swerve off, and keep another middling straight line. At last Bob stopped.

'"Here's where she slept last night," says he; and we could trace the marks right enough. We even found some crumbs of bread on the ground, and others that the ants were carrying away. She had made twelve or fourteen mile in the day's walk.

'By this time, several chaps had come from about Dan's place; and they were still joining us in twos and threes. As fast as they came, they scattered out in front, right and left, and one cove walked a bit behind Bob, with a frog-bell, shaking it now and then, to give the fellows their latitude. This would be about two in the afternoon, or half-past; and we pushed along the tracks she had made only a few hours before, with good hopes of overtaking her before dark. The thing that made us most uneasy was the weather. It was threatening for a thunderstorm. At this time we were in that unstocked country south-east of the station. Suddenly Bob rose up from his stoop, and looked round at me with a face on him like a ghost.

"'God help us now, if we don't get a blackfellow quick!" says he, pointing at the ground before him. And, sure enough, there lay the child's little copper-toed boots, where she had taken them off when her feet got sore, and walked on in her socks. It was just then that a tank-sinker drove up, with Dan and his dog in the buggy.'

'Poor old Rory!' I interposed. 'Much excited?'

'Well—no. But there was a look of suspense in his face that was worse. And his dog—a dog that had run the scent of his horse for hundreds of miles, all put together—that dog would smell any plain track of the little stocking-foot, only a few hours old, and would wag his tail, and bark, to show that he knew whose track it was; and all the time showing the greatest distress to see Dan in trouble; but it was no use trying to start him on the scent. They tried three or four other dogs, with just the same success. But Bob never lost half-a-second over these attempts. *He* knew.

'Anyway, it was fearful work after that; with the thunderstorm hanging over us. Bob was continually losing the track; and us circling round and round in front, sometimes picking it up a little further ahead. But we only made another half-mile or three-quarters, at the outside—before night was on. I daresay there might be about twenty-five of us by this time, and eighteen or twenty horses, and two or three buggies and wagonettes. Some of the chaps took all the horses to a tank six or eight mile away, and some cleared-off in desperation to hunt for blackfellows, and the rest of us scattered out a mile or two ahead of the last track, to listen.

'They had been sending lots of tucker from the station; and before the morning was grey everyone had breakfast, and was out again. But, do what we would, it was slow, slow work; and Bob was the only one that could make any show at all in running the track. Friday morning, of course; and by this time the little girl had been out for forty-eight hours.

'At nine or ten in the forenoon, when Bob had made about half-a-mile, one of the Kulkaroo men came galloping through the scrub from the right, making for the sound of the bell.

"'Here, Bob!" says he. We've found the little girl's billy at the fence of Peter's paddock, where she crossed. Take this horse. About two mile—straight out there."

'I had my horse with me at the time, and I tailed-up Bob to the fence. He went full tilt, keeping the track that the horse had come, and this fetched us to where a couple of chaps were standing over a little billy, with a lump of bread beside it. She had laid them down to get through the fence, and then went on without them. The lid was still on the billy, and there was a drop of milk left. The ants had eaten the bread out of all shape.

'But Bob was through the fence, and bowling down a dusty sheep-track, where a couple of fellows had gone before him, and where we could all see the marks of the little bare feet—for the stockings were off by this time. But in sixty or eighty yards this pad run into another, covered with fresh sheep-tracks since the little girl had passed. Nothing for it but to spread out, and examine the network of pads scattered over the country. All this time, the weather was holding-up, but there was a grumble of thunder now and then, and the air was fearfully close.

'At last there was a coo-ee out to the left. Young Broome had found three plain tracks, about half-a-mile away. We took these for a base, but we didn't get beyond them. We were circling round for miles, without making any headway; and so the time passed till about three in the afternoon. Then up comes Spanker, with his hat lost, and his face cut and bleeding from the scrub, and his horses in a white lather, and a black lubra sitting in the back of the buggy, and the Mulppa stock-keeper tearing along in front, giving him our tracks.

'She was an old, grey-haired lubra, blind of one eye; but she knew her business, and she was on the job for life or death. She picked-up the track at a glance, and run it like a bloodhound. We found that the little girl hadn't kept the sheep-pads as we expected. Generally she went straight till something blocked her; then she'd go straight again, at another angle. Very rarely—hardly ever—we could see what signs the lubra was following; but she was all right. Uncivilised, even for an old lubra. Nobody could yabber with her but Bob; and he kept close to her all the time. She began to get uneasy as night came on, but there was no help for it. She went slower and slower, and at last she sat down where she was. We judged that the little girl had made about seventeen mile to the place where the lubra got on her track, and we had added something like four to that. Though, mind you, at this time we were only about twelve or fourteen mile from Dan's place, and eight or ten mile from the home-station.

'Longest night I ever passed, though it was one of the shortest in the year. Eyes burning for want of sleep, and couldn't bear to lie down for a minute. Wandering about for miles; listening; hearing something in the scrub, and finding it was only one of the other chaps, or some sheep. Thunder and lightning, on and off, all night; even two or three drops of rain, toward morning. Once I heard the howl of a dingo, and I thought of the little girl, lying worn-out, half-asleep and half-fainting—far more helpless than a sheep—and I made up my mind that if she came out safe I would lead a better life for the future.

'However, between daylight and sunrise—being then about a mile, or a mile and a half, from the bell—I was riding at a slow walk, listening and dozing in the saddle, when I heard a far-away call that sounded like "Dad-dee!". It seemed to be straight in front of me; and I went for it like mad. Hadn't gone far when Williamson, the narangy, was alongside me.

'"Hear anything?" says I.

'"Yes," says he. "Sounded like 'Daddy!' I think it was out here."

'"I think it was more this way," says I; and each of us went his own way.

'When I got to where I thought was about the place, I listened again, and searched round everywhere. The bell was coming that way, and presently I went to meet it, leading my horse, and still listening. Then another call came through the stillness of the scrub, faint, but beyond mistake, "Dad-de-e-e!". There wasn't a trace of terror in the tone; it was just the voice of a worn-out child, deliberately calling with all her might. Seemed to be something less than half-a-mile away, but I couldn't fix on the direction; and the scrub was very thick.

'I hurried down to the bell. Everyone there had heard the call, or fancied they had; but it was out to their right—not in front. Of course, the lubra wouldn't leave the track, nor Bob, nor the chap with the bell; but everyone else was gone—Dan among the rest. The lubra said something to Bob.

'"Picaninny tumble down here again," says Bob. "Getting very weak on her feet."

'By-and-by, "Picaninny plenty tumble down." It was pitiful; but we knew that we were close on her at last. By this time, of course, she had been out for seventy-two hours.

'I stuck to the track, with the lubra and Bob. We could hear some of the chaps coo-eeing now and again, and calling "Mary!" '—

'Bad line—bad line,' muttered Saunders impatiently.

'Seemed to confuse things, anyway,' replied Thompson. 'And it was very doubtful whether the little girl was likely to answer a strange voice. At last, however, the lubra stopped, and pointed to a sun-bonnet, all dusty, lying under a spreading hop-bush. She spoke to Bob again.

'"Picaninny sleep here last night," says Bob. And that was within a hundred yards of the spot I had made-for after hearing the first call. I knew it by three or four tall pines, among a mass of pine scrub. However, the lubra turned off at an angle to the right, and run the track—not an hour old—toward where we had heard the second call. We were crossing fresh horse-tracks every few yards; and never two minutes but what somebody turned-up to ask the news. But to show how little use anything was except fair tracking, the lubra herself never saw the child till she went right up to where she was lying between two thick, soft bushes that met over her, and hid her from sight'—

'Asleep?' I suggested, with a sinking heart.

'No. She had been walking along—less than half-an-hour before—and she had brushed through between these bushes, to avoid some prickly scrub on both sides; but there happened to be a bilby-hole close in front, and she fell in the sort of trough, with her head down the slope; and that was the end of her long journey. It would have taken a child in fair strength to get out of the place she was in; and she was played-out to the last ounce. So her face had sunk down on the loose mould, and she had died without a struggle.

'Bob snatched her up the instant he caught sight of her, but we all saw that it was too late. We coo-eed, and the chap with the bell kept it going steady. Then all hands reckoned that the search was over, and they were soon collected round the spot.

'Now, that little girl was only five years old; and she had walked nothing less than twenty-two miles—might be nearer twenty-five.'

There was a minute's silence. Personal observation, or trustworthy report, had made every one of Thompson's audience familiar with such episodes of new settlement; and, for that very reason, his last remark came as a confirmation rather than as an over-statement. Nothing is more astonishing than the distances lost children have been known to traverse.

'How did poor Rory take it?' I asked.

'Dan? Well he took it bad. When he saw her face, he gave one little cry, like a wounded animal; then he sat down on the bilby-heap, with her on his knees, wiping the mould out of her mouth, and talking baby to her.

'Not one of us could find a word to say; but in a few minutes we were brought to ourselves by thunder and lightning in earnest, and the storm was on us with a roar. And just at this moment Webster of Kulkaroo came up with the smartest blackfellow in that district.

'We cleared out one of the wagonettes, and filled it with pine leaves, and laid a blanket over it. And Spanker gently took the child from Dan, and laid her there, spreading the other half of the blanket over her. Then he thanked all hands, and made them welcome at the station, if they liked to come. I went, for one; but Bob went back to Kulkaroo direct, so I saw no more of him till to-night.

'Poor Dan! He walked behind the wagonette all the way, crying softly, like a child, and never taking his eyes from the little shape under the soaking wet blanket. Hard lines for him! He had heard her voice calling him, not an hour before; and now, if he lived till he was a hundred, he would never hear it again.

'As soon as we reached the station, I helped Andrews, the storekeeper, to make the little coffin. Dan wouldn't have her buried in the station cemetery; she must be buried in consecrated ground, at Hay. So we boiled a pot of gas-tar to the quality of pitch, and dipped long strips of wool-bale in it, and wrapped them tight round the coffin, after the lid was on, till it was two ply all over, and as hard and close as sheet-iron. Ay, and by this time more than a dozen blackfellows had rallied-up to the station.

'Spanker arranged to send a man with the wagonette, to look after the horses for Dan. The child's mother wanted to go with them, but Dan refused to allow it, and did so with a harshness that surprised me. In the end, Spanker sent Ward, one of the narangies. I happened to camp with them four nights ago, when I was coming down from Kulkaroo, and they were getting back to Goolumbulla. However,' added Thompson, with sublime lowliness of manner, 'that's what I meant by saying that, in some cases, a person's all the better for being uncivilised. You see, we were nowhere beside Bob, and Bob was nowhere beside the old lubra.' [. . .]

1903

ADA CAMBRIDGE
1844–1926

Novelist Ada Cambridge was born in Norfolk, England, and arrived in Melbourne in 1870 with her clergyman husband. Before leaving England she had published several volumes of religious poems, tales and hymns. While living at parishes in country Victoria, the first two of her five children died. She began contributing stories and poems to local newspapers and in 1875 the first of her Australian novels, *Up the Murray*, was serialised in the *Australasian*. It was followed by at least eighteen other serials published in the *Australasian*, the *Age* and the *Sydney Mail*, as well as shorter stories and sketches. By the end of the nineteenth century Cambridge had become a successful and well-loved novelist, with many of her novels and short stories achieving publication in England in volume form. Her best-known novels include *A Marked Man* (1890), *The Three Miss Kings* (1891), *Not All in Vain* (1892), *Fidelis* (1895), *Materfamilias* (1898) and *Sisters* (1904). While most of her fiction relies on the typical romance pattern of love and marriage, her work is distinctive for her keen sense of irony, as seen in her story 'The Wind of Destiny'. Many of her novels also question conventional religious beliefs and middle-class mores; for example, *A Marked Man* with its free-thinking hero. Later novels, like *Sisters*, increasingly subvert romance conventions, while continuing to raise questions about women's roles and male sexual desire.

Cambridge was also the first significant Australian woman poet; *Unspoken Thoughts* (1887), published anonymously in England, also challenged conventional views on marriage and religion. In 'An Answer', for example, a woman refuses to marry the man she loves since she fears what 'the bond of wedlock' will do to their relationship. Cambridge's poetry was highly regarded by many of her contemporaries; revised versions of many of the poems in *Unspoken Thoughts* were included in *The Hand in the Dark and Other Poems* (1913). Cambridge also published two memoirs later in life: *Thirty Years in Australia* (1903) and *The Retrospect* (1912). *EW*

Seeking

Bright eyes, sweet lips, with sudden fevers fill
    My strong blood, running wildly, as it must;
    But lips and eyes too soon beget distrust.
A soft touch sends a momentary thrill
Through sense unsubservient to the will;   5
    But warm caresses leave a dim disgust;
    Like Dead-Sea apples,[1] kisses turn to dust.
I kiss; I feast; but I am hungry still.

O, where is She—that straight and upright soul—
    True friend, true mate, true woman—where is She?   10
True heart—as true as needle to the pole—
    True to the truth, not only true to me—
Worth all I have to give—the best—the whole.
    When shall these eyes Her unknown beauty see?

          1887

An Answer

Thy love I am. Thy wife I cannot be,
    To wear the yoke of servitude—to take
    Strange, unknown fetters that I cannot break
On soul and flesh that should be mine, and free.
Better the woman's old disgrace for me   5
    Than this old sin—this deep and dire mistake;
    Better for truth and honour and thy sake—
For the pure faith I give and take from thee.

I know thy love, and love thee all I can—
    I fain would love thee only till I die;   10
But I may some day love a better man,
    And thou may'st find a fitter mate than I;
Some want, some chill, may steal 'twixt heart and heart.
And then we must be free to kiss and part.

          1887

The Wind of Destiny

The yachtsmen of the bay had been jubilant for months: this morning they were simply in ecstasies. Aha! it was their turn now. The sporting landsmen, magnates of the Melbourne Club and the great stations, who had had all

---

1   Fruit which looks appetising but turns to smoke and ashes when picked.

the fun of the fair hitherto, were out of it this time. Oh, no doubt the new Governor was fond of his 'bike', and of a good horse, and of golf and polo, and the usual things; and, of course, he would be pleased with the triumphal arches and many gorgeous demonstrations of civic welcome and goodwill. But it was here that his heart would be—here, on the blue water, with the brethren of his craft. The country might not know it, but they knew it—mariners all, with their own freemasonry—they and he.

Every yacht of any consequence had been on the slips quite lately—as lately as was compatible with having paint and varnish dry. One or two of the newer models, wanting extra depth for their bulbous keels, were all but too late in their desire to be spick and span for the great occasion, but happily got a west-wind tide to float them up in time. And here they all were, scores and scores of them, as smart as they could be, with their beautiful sails going up, burgee and ensign flying in the breeze of the loveliest morning that could possibly have been provided for a national festival depending wholly on the weather for success. Yesterday it had been cloudy and gloomy, threatening rain; and to-morrow the north wind was to blow a sultry hurricane, opaque with dust; but to-day was heavenly. No other adjective, as Fanny Pleydell remarked, could describe its all-round perfection.

She was putting on her new white drill with the blue sailor collar, and her new straw hat with *Kittiwake* in gold letters on its new blue ribbon, and joyously addressed her brother through a passage and two open doors. He shouted back that it—the day—was 'ripping,' which meant the same thing. The only doubt about it was whether there would be wind enough. There is always that doubt in yachting forecasts—that and the lesser fear of having too much; without which, however, yachting would be no fun at all. The *Kittiwake* (once the property of Adam Drewe, Esq.) was one of the crack boats, and Herbert Lawson—familiarly 'Bert'—was skipper and owner; and he had no mind to make himself a mere St Kilda decoration, as the land-lubbers in authority desired. Let the others tug at moorings if they chose, like wild birds tied by the legs, for hours and hours; the *Kittiwake* intended to fly when she opened her wings—weather permitting—and not submit to be treated as a slab in a canvas wall. She was going to meet the *Sunbeam* on free water, halfway down the bay, which, with any sort of wind, she could easily do, and still be back in time for the landing ceremony. And so Captain Bert kept an eye on tree branches and the set of anchored craft, while giving keen attention to his toilet, arraying himself in ducks like the driven snow and flannels like milk, waxing the curly points of his moustache till they tapered smoothly as a ram's horns, trimming his nails, and choosing a silk handkerchief to foam out of his breast pocket, as with a view to being inspected at close quarters through a strong telescope from the *Sunbeam's* deck.

But he was not dressing himself for the eyes of his vice-sovereign lady. It was for the sake of Lena Pickersgill and Myra Salter that he took such pains to render his handsome person as attractive as possible—and he did not quite know which.

Let me briefly explain. Old Lawson had died not long ago, leaving Herbert master of a good business in Melbourne, a good old family house at Williamstown (with the *Kittiwake* attached), and a most comfortable and even luxurious income for these post-boom days. Sister and brothers were sufficiently provided for—the former married, the latter studying for professions—and there was no widowed mother to take care of and defer to. Herbert was a man of domestic instincts, and turned thirty, and an arbitrary housekeeper bullied him. In short, every circumstance of the case cried aloud to him to take a wife, and he was as ready as possible to do so. But, of course, he wished to be a lover before becoming a husband, and fate had not yet clearly indicated the object he sought. He was a particular young man, as he had every right to be, and much in dread of making a mistake.

To-day he had arrived at the stage of choosing Lena and Myra, out of all the girls he knew, as the only possibles. Before night he hoped to have made up a distracted mind as to which of the two was the right one. Chaperoned by young Mrs Pleydell, both were to be guests of the *Kittiwake* for a long, fine day; and surely no better opportunity for the purpose could possibly have been devised.

Miss Salter was a Williamstown young lady, a schoolmate of Fanny Pleydell's, and was to embark with her hostess early. She was Fanny's candidate for the vacancy in the family, and rather suffered as such from the advocacy of her friend. Miss Pickersgill, belonging to a somewhat higher rank of life, lived in town, and was to be taken off from the St Kilda pier. Fanny had not wanted to have Lena asked, and for that reason Bert had firmly insisted on it. For that reason also he was inclined to promote her to the place of honour, rather than a girl whom he felt was being thrust down his throat.

But when he presently met the latter, and helped her into his dinghy with the tenderest air of strong protection, he thought her very sweet. She was a fair, slim thing, shy, unaffected, and amiable, and looked delicious in her white garb. All the ladies on board had to wear white to-day, to harmonize with the pearly enamel of the boat and her snowy new Lapthorn sails; and Myra had the neatest frock, and the prettiest figure to set it off. And, moreover, as he very well knew, *she* did not run after him when she was let alone.

He rowed her and his sister to the yacht, on which a numerous white-uniformed crew had made all ready for the start, and he sent the dinghy back in charge of his brother to pick up three more lady guests. These three were nobodies as regards this story—a homely aunt and two plain cousins, who had a family right to the suddenly valuable favours at their kinsman's disposal. They made up the number he thought would fill the cockpit comfortably—three on each side.

Mrs Pleydell, as soon as she had gained the deck, plunged below to investigate the matter of supplies; Miss Salter sat down to survey the scene, and the skipper sat down beside her. They had quite twenty minutes of quiet *tête-à-tête*, and to that extent placed Miss Pickersgill at a disadvantage.

'Isn't it a heavenly morning?'—or 'a ripping day,' as the case might be— was what they said; and 'I wonder will the breeze hold?' and 'Didn't you feel certain last night that it was changing for rain?'—conversation that had no literary value to make it worth reporting. However, it is not in words that incipient lovers explain themselves, but in the accompaniment to words played by furtive eyes and the corners of lips, and other instruments of nature inaudible to the outward ear. Myra's varying complexion confessed a lot of things, and the amount of intelligence in the horns of that moustache which had been waxed so carefully was wonderful. Indeed, it really seemed, thus early in the day, as if the die were cast. Both looked so handsome and felt so happy, and the weather and all the circumstances were so specially favourable to the development of kindly sentiments.

'I *am* so glad you were able to come,' the young man remarked, whenever they fell upon a pause, changing the emphasis to a fresh word each time. And the young woman put it in all sorts of modest but convincing ways that he was not more glad than she was. Oh, it was a heavenly morning, truly! And Mrs Pleydell and the crew were more and more careful to do nothing to mar the prospect.

But soon the fat aunt and excited cousins arrived, all in white, and as conscious of it as if dressed for a fancy ball, and it was time to make for the rendezvous across the bay. Thither were the yachts of all clubs converging in dozens and scores, like an immense flock of seabirds skimming the azure water, their sails like silver and white satin in the sun. As Bert Lawson steered his own, proudly convinced that she was queen of the company, he named his would-be rivals to his guest, keeping her so close to him that he had to apologise for touching her elbow with the tiller now and then. Occasionally he exchanged an opinion with the crew that the old so- and-so didn't look so bad, and they continually cocked their eyes aloft to where the blue ensign waved in the languid breeze. It wasn't every boat that could dip that flag to the new Governor—no, indeed!

'Isn't it a pretty sight?' the ladies cried to one another—and it certainly was. Even the prosaic shore was transfigured and glorious—in one place, at least. The St Kilda pier and the hotel, and the steep slope connecting them, smothered all over in green stuff and bunting, and packed with what appeared to be the whole population of the colony, was a striking spectacle as viewed from the sea. The most bigoted Englishman must acknowledge it.

'Oh,' exclaimed Fanny Pleydell, staring through a strong pair of glasses, 'I wouldn't have had you miss it for the world, Myra dear.'

'And yet I nearly did,' the girl replied, glancing at Bert from under her hat brim as he stood over her, intent on business. 'If mother had not been so much better this morning, I could not possibly have left her.'

The skipper ceased shouting to his too numerous men not to crowd the boat's nose so that he could not see it, and dropped soft eyes on his sister's friend. 'Dear, dutiful, unselfish little soul!' he thought. 'That's the sort of woman to make a good wife. That's the girl for me.' It was still not more than twenty minutes to eleven, and he had got as far as that.

But now Miss Pickersgill intervened. She put off from the gorgeous pier, which was not yet closed to the public, in the dinghy of a local friend, in order that the *Kittiwake* should not be burdened with its own. It afterwards transpired that she had engaged to grace the yacht of the local friend, and had thrown him over for Bert Lawson, having no scruples of pride against making use of him, nevertheless. She was a radiant vision in tailor-made cream serge, a full-blooded, full-bosomed, high-coloured, self-confident young beauty, with bold eyes and a vivacious manner, calculated to make any picnic party lively. As she approached, like a queen enthroned, all the male creatures hung forward to gaze and smile, Bert springing to the side to help her over—which was only what she expected and was accustomed to. And she jumped into the midst of the group around the cockpit,—four humble-minded admirers and one firm adversary,—chose her place and settled herself, nodding and waving salutations around, as if she were Mrs Bert already.

Myra's heart sank in presence of so formidable a rival. Myra was the daughter of a retired sea-captain in rather narrow circumstances; Lena's father was a stock-broker, and reputed to roll in money. She had fat gold bangles on her wrists, and a diamond in each ear. She lifted her smart skirt from a lace-frilled petticoat, and the serge was lined with silk. The dejected observer moved to make way for so unquestionable a superior. But Bert detained her with a quiet hand.

'Sit still,' he said. 'There is plenty of room.'

To her surprise and joy, she found he still preferred her near him. It was not money and gold bracelets that could quench her gentle charm.

And now the fun began. The yacht, with every stitch of canvas spread, set out upon her course, determined to be the first to salute her future commodore. There was just enough wind to waft her along with a motion as soft as feathers, as airy as a dream, and the heavenly morning, on the now wider waters, was more heavenly than ever.

'It's our day out, and no mistake,' quoth Miss Pickersgill, in her hearty way. 'Let's have a song, old chap'—to Bert—'or do some thing or other to improve the occasion. What do you say, Mrs Pleydell?'

'I,' said the hostess cheerfully, but with tightened lips, 'am going to get you all something to eat.'

'And I'll go and help you,' said Myra, rising hastily.

'Oh, all right—go on; I'll keep 'em alive till you come back. Now then, tune up, everybody! I'll begin. What shall I sing, Mr Lawson?' with a languishing glance at him over her shoulder. 'You shall choose.'

'I think you'd better whistle,' said Bert, whose eyes were on his sails, and his nose sniffing anxiously.

'All serene. I can do that too. But why had I better whistle?'

'Wind's dying away to nothing, I grieve to say.'

'By George, it is!' his young men echoed, in sympathetic concern. 'If we don't mind, we shall fall between two stools, and be out of everything.'

'What's the odds, so long as you're happy?' was Miss Lena's philosophic response. And they adopted that view. With every prospect of being ignominiously becalmed, out of the track of events in which they had expected to take a leading and historic part, they lolled about the deck and sang songs with rousing choruses—popular ditties from the comic operas of the day—and professed themselves as jolly as jolly could be.

'How fascinating she is!' sighed Myra Salter, listening from the little cabin to the voice of the prima donna overhead. 'I don't wonder they all admire her so much!'

'I am quite sure my brother does not admire her,' said Mrs Pleydell with decision. 'He thinks, as I do, that she is a forward minx—he must.' Bert's laugh just then came ringing down the stairs. In an interval between two songs, he and Miss Pickersgill were enjoying a bout of 'chaff'—rough wit that crackled like fireworks. 'Of course she amuses him,' said Fanny grudgingly.

'And isn't it lovely to be able to amuse people?' the girl ejaculated, envious still. 'She charms them so that they forget about the wind and everything. She is just the life and soul of the party, Fanny.'

'I think she spoils it, Myra. If we don't look out, we shall be having her serenading the Governor with "He's a jolly good fellow," or something of that sort. If she attempts to disgrace us with her vulgarity before him, clap your hand over her mouth, my dear. I shall.'

Myra laughed, and was somewhat comforted. But she still thought how lovely it would be to be able to amuse people and take them out of themselves. 'He would never be dull with her,' she thought sadly. 'I am so stupid that I should bore him to death.'

One of Miss Salter's unusual charms, perfectly appreciated by sensible

Mrs Pleydell, and not overlooked by Bert, was a sweet humble-mindedness—
a rare virtue in these days.

The first of several light luncheons was served on deck, without interrupting the concert. Between gulps of wine and mouthfuls of sandwich,
Miss Pickersgill continued to raise fresh tunes, and the crew to shout the
choruses, and the audience of fat aunt and simpering cousins to applaud
admiringly. It was a case of youth at the prow and pleasure at the helm, and
an abandonment of all responsibility. A dear little catspaw came stealing
along, and hardly excited anybody. The yacht gathered way, and began to
make knots again, faster and faster, but even that did not draw the light-
hearted young folks from their frivolous pastime. Thanks to the syren of
St Kilda, they had almost forgotten the errand they were on. It really did
not seem to matter much to any one whether he or she met Lord Brassey[1]
or not; he had become an incident of the day, rather than its main feature.

Still, the eyes of the crew continually searched the horizon, and presently
one man saw smoke where no one else saw anything, and out of that spot
a faint blur grew which resolved itself into the *Aramac* with the Governor
on board, and the *Ozone* and *Hygeia*, its consorts. The three boats in a row
advancing steadily, under all the steam they could make, were not unimpressive
in their way, but the only thing the *Kittiwake* cared to look at was the lovely
pillar of white cloud, shining like a pearl, which was recognised as the
Sunbeam with all sail set. She was bearing off from the Government flotilla,
dismissed from their company, superseded and discarded; but to yachtsmen's
eyes she was a sort of winged angel, a spirit of the sea, and they but grubby
mortals by comparison, common and gross.

'Why, why,' they exclaimed, with groans of regret, gazing on the fairy
column as if that were all the picture, '*why* didn't they let him come up
in her, and let us bring him? What does he want with a lot of cheap-jack
politicians *here*? They just spoil it all.'

'It wouldn't be them if they didn't,' some one said, voicing a rather prevalent opinion. And in fact they were spoiling it rather badly on the *Aramac* just
then, if all tales be true. They had not wanted Miss Pickersgill to show them
how to do it.

It was past the hour fixed for the landing ceremonies—and the poor
sun-baked crowds ashore would have been dropping with fatigue if there
had been room to fall in—when Bert Lawson shouted 'Dip! dip!' to his
brother, who held the ensign halliards, and was confused by the excitement
of the moment. After all, the *Kittiwake* was first, and proud was every heart
aboard when the cocked-hatted figure on the *Aramac's* bridge saluted her
and the flag as if he had known and loved the one as long as the other. Every

1   Thomas Brassey, first Earl Brassey (1836–1918), was Governor of Victoria from 1895 to 1900.

man and woman was convinced that he stood lost in admiration of her beauty and the way she was manoeuvred. Bert brought her as close as was compatible with proper respect, and they all posed to the best advantage for the Governor's eye, Miss Pickersgill in front.

'*Now*, you fellows,' she panted breathlessly. 'All at once—"See-ee the conq-'ring he-e-e-e-ero"—'

But Mrs Pleydell's hand was up like a flash, and there was a 'Hsh-sh-sh!' like the protest of a flock of geese. The fair Lena was so taken aback that she nearly fell into the captain's arms. The captain did not seem to mind; his arm went round her waist for a moment almost as if it had the habit of doing it; and he whispered an apology that restored her self-control. At the same instant he signalled to the crew, and they burst into three great solid British cheers. Another signal stopped them from further performances, and the steamers swept by. The crisis of the day was over.

Then the *Kittiwake* turned and followed the fleet, and realized her remaining ambitions. She was back at St Kilda, with the yachts that had been lying there all the morning, by the time his great excellency, transhipped once more, arrived there. Through their glasses the ladies could see the procession of little figures along the pier, and the departure of the carriages after the guns had fired the salute; and they could hear the school children singing. When all was over, a sigh of vast contentment expressed the common thought, 'What a day we're having!' The turn of the landsmen had come, but no one at sea could envy them.

'Now we'll have a look at the *Sunbeam* as she lies,' said Bert, and then headed back for Williamstown.

'And we want some refreshment after what we have gone through,' said the hospitable hostess.

Luncheon was served for the third time, and subsequently two afternoon teas. The yachts, dissolving all formation, swam aimlessly about the bay, more like seabirds than ever, and took snap-shots at each other with their kodak cameras. Miss Pickersgill's singing powers failed somewhat, but she continued to chaff and chatter with the young men, breaking off at intervals to hail her friends on passing boats. Good-natured Fanny Pleydell laughed with the rest at the fun she made; the admiring aunt and cousins could not remember when they had been so entertained; and Myra Salter was satisfied at heart because Bert had never allowed her to feel 'out of it.' And so the happy day wore through. They had had seven hours together when they began to look for Lena's dinghy, and before separating they testified with one consent that they had never had a more delightful holiday, or, as Lena neatly phrased it, 'such a jolly high old time.'

'Then I'll tell you what we must do,' said the gratified host. 'Go out together—the same party, since we suit each other so well—on the sixteenth of next month. That's our opening day, Miss Pickersgill, as of course you know; and, with the Governor for commodore, it ought to be the best we've ever had.'

'All who are in favour of this motion,' chanted Lena, 'hold up your hands!'

Every hand went up at once, except Myra's. The shy girl looked to Fanny for an endorsement of the free and easy invitation, and Mrs Pleydell was knitting her brows. But soon she smiled consent, to please her brother, who, stealing behind Miss Salter unobserved, seized her two hands and lifted them into the air.

They imagined they were going to have their good time over again. They even anticipated a better one, though only of half the length. For whereas the wind had been too light on the 25th of October, it blew like business on the 16th of November, when it was of the last importance that it should do so. No more auspicious opening day had ever dawned upon Victorian yachtsmen. The Governor, who was *their* Governor for the first time in history, had consented to direct their evolutions in person. This alone—this and a good wind—assured laurels to the clubs of Hobson's Bay which all other clubs would envy them. The *Sunbeam* had been towed to the chosen anchorage; Government House was on board. All the swells, as Miss Pickersgill termed them, indigenous to the soil, would be lone and lorn at the races, because their Lord and Lady were away. If they offered their ears for a place in viceregal company, they could not get it. 'Aha!' said the yachtsmen one to another, 'it is our turn now.'

This time the *Kittiwake* took her own dinghy to St Kilda. She towed it along with her all the afternoon, as a brake upon the pace, which threatened to carry her beyond the position assigned to her in the wheeling line, for she was faster than the boats before and behind her. And so the services of local friends were not required on Miss Lena's behalf. Bert himself, in a very ruffled sea indeed, went off to the pier to fetch her. But not altogether for the sake of paying her special honour; rather, because it was most difficult to bring anything alongside to-day without bumping off fenders and on to new paint. He had had the kindest feeling for both girls during the past three weeks, but what little love he had fallen into was love for Myra Salter. He had just left her deeply in love with him. He had given her the card of sailing directions, taught her how to read the commodore's signals, and told her she was to be his captain for the day, as he was to be the crew's. Down in the small cabin, picking pecks of strawberries, with the assistance of the aunt and cousins, Mrs Pleydell's prophetic eye saw visions of an ideal home and family—that comfortable and prosperous domestic life which is the better and not the worse for having no wildfire passions to inflame and ravage it—and a congenial sister-in-law for all time. Myra lingered on deck to follow the movements of the tossing dinghy through the captain's strong field-glasses, also assigned to her exclusive use for this occasion. He had another pair—not quite so strong—for Miss Pickersgill.

Little did that young lady suppose that she was to play second fiddle for a moment. She wore another new dress and a ravishing peaked cap, much more becoming than the sailor straw. She smiled upon the skipper, struggling to hold the dinghy to the pier, as at a faithful bond-slave merely doing his bounden duty.

'It is our opening day!' she sang, as she flourished a hand to him. 'It—is—our—opening da-ay!'

'It is, indeed,' he shouted back. 'Made on purpose. Only I think we shall have too much of a good thing this time, instead of not enough. Wind keeps getting up, and we've reefed already.'

'Oh, it's stunning!' she rejoined, gaily skipping into the boat; she was a heavy weight, and nearly tipped it over. 'Let it get up! The more the merrier.'

'Yes, if there were going to be racing. I wish there was! We should just run away from everything.'

'Then let's race,' quoth Miss Pickersgill, as if commanding it to be done. 'Let's show the old buffer'—I grieve to say it was his sacred lordship she referred to—'what the *Kittiwake* can do.'

Bert had to explain. It took him until they reached the yacht to make the young lady who looked so nautical understand what she was talking about. And after all she was inclined to be sentimentally hurt because he would not do such a little thing to please her.

The wind got up, more and more, showing that there was to be no monotonous repetition of the former circumstance. The *Kittiwake* danced and pranced as if the real sea were under her, and half a dozen dinghies trailed astern would hardly have made any difference. There was no sitting round the cockpit, as on drawing-room chairs, to flirt and sing; one side was always in the air, and the other all but under water, see-sawing sharply at uncertain intervals; and the ladies had to give their attention to holding on and keeping their heads out of the way of the swinging boom. Lena shouted to the men, who had to stick to business in spite of her, that it was the jolliest state of things imaginable, and said 'Go it!' to rude Boreas when he smacked her face, to encourage him to further efforts. But her five companions were more or less of the opinion that they had liked the first cruise better. The poor fat aunt was particularly disconcerted by the new conditions; she said she couldn't get used to the feeling of having no floor under her, and the sensation of the sea climbing up her back.

She was the first to say, 'No, thank you,' to strawberries and cream, and 'Yes, please,' to whisky.

Is there anything funny in having the toothache that people should laugh at the victim as at some inexhaustible joke? Ask the poor soul whose nerves are thus exquisitely tortured what *his* opinion is. He will tell you that it is one of the gravest elements in the tragedy of human pain; also that the heartless brute who sniggers at it ought to have thumbscrews put on him and twisted tight. Is there anything disgraceful in being sea-sick in rough weather, that those who don't happen to feel so at the moment should turn up their noses at the sufferers in contemptuous disgust? Emphatically not. It is a misfortune that may befall the best of us, and does, instead of being, as one would suppose, the penalty of a degrading vice, like delirium tremens. Why, even the *Sunbeam* was ill that afternoon—the first folks of the land, fresh from the discipline of a long and stormy voyage—which sufficiently proves the fact.

But when Myra Salter was observed to sit silent and rigid, with bleached lips and a corpse-like skin, it was with eyes that slightly hardened at the sight. Yes, even the captain's eyes! It is true he smiled at her, and said, 'Poor child!' and peremptorily ordered the useless stimulant, and was generally concerned and kind; but the traditional ignominy of her case affected him; her charm and dignity were impaired—vulgarized; and the flavour of his incipient romance began to go. Of course young men are fools—we all are, for that matter—and young love, just out of the ground, as it were, is like a baby lettuce in a garden full of slugs. And it is no use pretending that things are different from what they are. And if you want to be an artist, and not a fashionable photographer, you must not paint poor human nature, and leave the moles and wrinkles out. It is a pity that an estimable young man cannot be quite perfect, and that an admirable young woman should be unjustly despised; but so it is, and there's no more to be said.

Myra shook her head at the suggestion of whisky; only to imagine the smell of it was to feel worse at once—to feel an instant necessity to hide herself below. But Fanny Pleydell, coming upstairs at the moment when she was beginning to stagger down, caught her in her arms and held her back—a fatal blunder on Fanny's part.

'No, my dear, no!' she cried, on the spur of a humane impulse; 'you must *not* go into that horrible hole; it would finish you off at once. Besides, there isn't room for you; aunt and the girls are sprawling all over the place. Have a little spirits, darling—yes, you must; and keep in the fresh air if you want to feel better.'

She pressed whisky and water on the shuddering girl, and cruel consequences ensued. Bert turned his head away, and tried to shut his ears. Lena smiled at him in an arch and confidential manner. *She* was as bright and pretty as ever—more so, indeed, for the wind exhilarated her and deepened her bloom.

'I think,' she said, 'it is a great mistake for people who are not good sailors to go to sea in rough weather, don't you?'

Well, Bert almost thought it was. He was a very enthusiastic yachtsman, especially to-day, when he wanted the *Kittiwake* and all her appurtenances to be as correct as possible.

The drill was over, and the regiment of yachts disbanded. The *Sunbeam* had gone to a pier at Williamstown, and the commodore was receiving his new colleagues and entertaining them. The *Kittiwake* was off St Kilda, with her freight of sick on board. The aunt filled up one tiny cabin, the cousins another, and they groaned and wailed and made other unpleasant noises, to the amusement of a callous crew. Myra Salter, too helplessly ill to sit up without support while the boat rushed through the water with a slice of deck submerged, had sagged down to the floor of the cockpit, and now lay there in a limp heap, propped against Fanny's knees. She had not spoken for an hour, and during that time Bert had hardly noticed her. He had been devoting himself to Miss Pickersgill, so far as the duties of his official post allowed, as was only natural when she had become practically his sole companion, and when, as a lover of a good breeze and proper sailoring, she had proved herself so sympathetic.

Now he was rowing her home from the yacht to the shore. She sat facing him in the dinghy, with the yoke lines round her waist, and he could not keep his eyes from her brilliant person, nor keep himself from mentally comparing it with that sad wisp on the cockpit floor. She met his glance, and held it. They were both excited by the wind, the inspiring flight of the yacht, the varied interests of the opening day.

'Oh, it was splendid!' she exclaimed. 'Whatever the others may think about it, I know *I* never enjoyed myself so much in my life. And I *am* so much obliged to you for taking me, Mr Lawson.'

'You are the right sort to take,' replied Bert with enthusiasm; and he imagined a wife who would enter into his favourite pursuits like a true comrade. 'And I hope we shall have many a good cruise together.'

'It won't be my fault if we don't,' she said promptly.

'It won't be mine,' he returned. 'Consider yourself asked for every day that you'll deign to come.'

'What, for ever?'

'For ever.'

She looked at him archly, pensively, meaningly, with her head on one side. She was really very handsome in her coquettish peaked cap, and he reflected that she was evidently healthy and probably rich.

'You don't *mean* that, Mr Lawson?'

'I do mean it, literally and absolutely.'

'For every yachting day as long as I live?'

'For every yachting day, and every day that isn't a yachting day.'

She was so joyously flustered that she ran the dinghy into the pier. He had to catch her in his arms to prevent her going overboard. As there were people watching them from above, he could not kiss her, but he gave an earnest of his intention to do so at the first opportunity.

Of course she was the wrong one. He knew it no later than the next day, in his heart of hearts, though never permitting himself to acknowledge it, because he flatters himself that he is a gentleman. Equally, of course, he will go on to render his mistake irrevocable, and be miserable ever after, and make her so, from the highest motives. Already the wedding gown is bought, and they go together to ironmongers and upholsterers to choose new drawing-room furniture and pots and kettles for the kitchen. The marriage will surely take place when the bride has made her preparations, and anybody can foretell what the consequences will be. They will pull against each other by force of nature, and tear their little shred of romance to bits in no time. And then they will sink together to that sordid and common matrimonial state which is the despair and disgrace of civilization. She will grow fat and frowsy as she gets into years—a coarse woman, selfish and petty, and full of legitimate grievances; and he will hate her first, and then cease to care one way or the other, which is infinitely worse than hating. And so two lives will be utterly spoiled, and possibly three or four—not counting the children, who will have no sort of fair start.

And all because there was a bit of a breeze on the opening day of the season!

But such is life.

1897

MARCUS CLARKE
1846–1881

Although now best-known for his classic novel of the convict system, *His Natural Life* (1874), Marcus Clarke also wrote numerous essays, stories and plays, as well as editing literary journals, in an ultimately unsuccessful effort to make a living by his pen in colonial Melbourne. He was born in London and received a gentleman's education, with the expectation of entering the diplomatic service. His father's mental and financial collapse in 1862, however, saw a now-penniless young Clarke packed off to relatives in Australia. After experiencing both city and country life, including a near-fatal overland expedition to Queensland, he returned to Melbourne to try to succeed as a writer. He wrote theatrical criticism for the *Argus* before commencing a regular column for its weekly, the *Australasian*, under the heading 'The Peripatetic Philosopher'; a collection of his essays was published under this title in 1869. Readers were conducted into areas of the city they would otherwise never have entered, whether the drinking dens of lower Bohemia or the 'Nasturtium Villas' of suburbia.

Clarke edited and wrote much of the copy for a short-lived literary magazine, the *Colonial Monthly*, and for a satirical journal, *Humbug* (1869–70). In 1870, the *Argus* sent Clarke to Tasmania to research the history of the convict system. He initially produced a series of historical articles for the *Australasian*, collected in *Old Tales of a Young Country* (1871), before embarking on *His Natural Life*. The original and much longer version of the novel began its serialisation in the popular fiction magazine, the *Australian Journal*, during Clarke's time as editor (1870–71). Its length, and unpopular subject matter, apparently lost the journal sales before the serialisation concluded in 1872. Clarke then revised and substantially shortened the novel for book publication in 1874; at the instigation of friends he reluctantly killed off the wrongly convicted hero Rufus Dawes, aka Richard Devine, so giving the novel a more tragic ending. Most critics have preferred this version, though Clarke's belief in the endurance of the human spirit and the redemptive power of love are less strongly demonstrated here.

Clarke also wrote numerous short stories, many of which were collected in *Holiday Peak and Other Tales* (1873) and *Four Stories High* (1877). In 1869 Clarke married actress Marian Dunn; his works for the theatre included pantomime and operetta libretti and adaptations of popular novels. During the 1870s Clarke was employed at the Public Library of Victoria, initially as secretary to the trustees and then as sub-librarian. He hoped to be appointed principal librarian but managed to alienate influential people with *The Happy Land* (*1880/*1880), a satirical play which featured caricatures of government ministers, and his attack on conventional religion, published as *Civilisation Without Delusion* (1880). In 1881, when his creditors pressed for payment, Clarke was declared bankrupt for a second time; he collapsed and died a few days later. *EW*

From *His Natural Life*
Chapter 55: The Work of the Sea

The lift of the water-spout had saved John Rex's life. At the moment when it struck him, he was on his hands and knees at the entrance of the cavern. The wave, gushing upwards, at the same time expanded, laterally, and this lateral force drove the convict into the mouth of the subterlapian passage. The passage seemed to trend downwards, and for some seconds he was rolled over and over, the rush of water wedging him at length into a crevice between two enormous stones, which seemed to overhang a still more formidable abyss. Fortunately for the preservation of his hard-fought-for life, this very fury of incoming water prevented him from being washed out again with the recoil of the wave. He could hear the water dashing with frightful echoes far down into the depths beyond him, but it was evident that the two stones against which he had been thrust acted as breakwaters to the torrent poured in from the outside and repelled the main body of the stream in the fashion he had observed from his position on the ledge. In a few seconds the cavern was empty.

Painfully extricating himself, and feeling as yet but half doubtful of his safety, John Rex essayed to climb the twin-blocks that barred the unknown depths below him. The first movement he made caused him to shriek aloud. His left arm—with which he clung to the rope—hung powerless. Ground against the ragged entrance, it was momentarily paralysed. For an instant the unfortunate wretch sank despairingly on the wet and rugged floor of the cave; then a terrible gurgling beneath his feet warned him of the approaching torrent, and collecting all his energies, he scrambled up the incline. Though nigh fainting with pain and exhaustion, he pressed desperately higher and higher. He heard the hideous shriek of the whirlpool which was beneath him grow louder and louder. He saw the darkness grow darker as the rising water-spout covered the mouth of the cave. He felt the salt spray sting his face, and the wrathful tide lick the hand that hung over the shelf on which he fell. But that was all. He was out of danger at last! And as the thought blessed his senses, his eyes closed, and the wonderful courage and strength which had sustained the villain so long, exhaled in stupor.

When he awoke the cavern was filled with the soft light of dawn. Raising his eyes, he beheld, high above his head a roof of rock, on which the reflection of the sunbeams, playing upwards through a pool of water, cast flickering colours. On his right hand was the mouth of the cave, on his left a terrific abyss, at the bottom of which he could hear the sea faintly lapping and washing. He raised himself and stretched his stiffened limbs. Despite his injured shoulder, it was imperative that he should bestir himself. He knew not if his escape had been noticed, or if the cavern had another inlet, by which returning McNab could penetrate. Moreover, he was wet and famished. To preserve the life which he had torn from the sea, he must have fire and food. First he examined the crevice by which he had entered. It was shaped like an irregular triangle, hollowed at the base by the action of the water which in such storms as that of the preceding night was forced into it by the rising of the sea. John Rex dared not crawl too near the edge lest he should slide out of the damp and slippery orifice, and be dashed upon the rocks at the bottom of the Blow-hole. Craning his neck, he could see a hundred feet below him, the sullenly frothing water, gurgling, spouting, and creaming, in huge turbid eddies, occasionally leaping upwards as though it longed for another storm to send it raging up to the man who had escaped its fury. It was impossible to get down that way. He turned back into the cavern, and began to explore in that direction.

The twin-rocks against which he had been hurled were, in fact, pillars which supported the roof of the water-drive. Beyond them lay a great grey shadow which was emptiness faintly illumined by the sea-light cast up through the bottom of the gulf. Midway across the grey shadow fell a strange beam of dusky brilliance which cast its flickering light upon a wilderness of waving sea-weeds. Even in the desperate position in which he found himself, there survived in the Vagabond's nature sufficient poetry to make him value the natural marvel upon which he had so strangely stumbled. The immense promontory, which, viewed from the outside, seemed as solid as a mountain, was in reality but a hollow cone, reft and split into a thousand fissures by the unsuspected action of centuries of sea. The Blow-hole was but an insignificant cranny compared with this enormous chasm. Descending with difficulty the steep incline, he found himself on the brink of a gallery of rock, which, jutting out over the pool, bore on its moist and weed-bearded edges signs of frequent submersion. It must be low tide without the rock. Clinging to the rough and root-like algae that fringed the ever-moist walls, John Rex crept round the projection of the gallery, and passed at once from dimness to daylight. There was a broad loophole in the side of the honey-combed and wave-perforated cliff. The cloudless heaven expanded above him; a fresh breeze kissed his cheek, and sixty feet below him the sea wrinkled all its lazy length, sparkling in myriad wavelets beneath the bright beams of morning. Not a sign of the recent tempest marred the exquisite harmony of the picture. Not a sign of human life gave evidence of the grim neighbourhood of the prison. From the recess out of which he peered nothing was visible but sky of turquoise smiling upon a sea of sapphire.

This placidity of Nature was, however, to the hunted convict a new source of alarm. It was a reason why the Blow-hole and its neighbourhood should be thoroughly searched. He guessed that the favourable weather would be an additional inducement to McNab and Burgess to satisfy themselves as to the fate of their late prisoner. He turned from the opening and prepared to descend still further into the rocky pathway. The sunshine had revived and cheered him, and a sort of instinct told him that the cliff so honey-combed above, could not be without some gully or chink at its base, which at low tide would give upon the rocky shore. It grew darker as he descended, and twice he almost turned back in dread of the gulfs on either side of him. It seemed to him, also, that the gullet of weed-clad rock through which he was crawling doubled upon itself and led only in to the bowels of the mountain. Gnawed by hunger and conscious that in a few hours at most the rising tide would fill the subterranean passage and cut off his retreat, he pushed desperately onwards. He had descended some ninety feet, and had lost in the devious windings of his downward path all but the reflection of the light from the gallery, when he was rewarded by a glimpse of sunshine striking upwards. He parted two enormous masses of seaweed, whose bubble-beaded fronds hung curtain-wise across his path, and found himself in the very middle of the narrow cleft of rock through which the sea was driven to the Blow-hole.

At an immense distance above him was the arch of cliff. Beyond that arch appeared a segment of the ragged edge of the circular opening down which he had fallen. He looked in vain for the funnel-mouth whose friendly shelter had received him. It was now indistinguishable. At his feet was a long reft in the solid rock, so narrow that he could almost have leapt across it. This reft was the channel of a swift black current which ran from the sea for fifty yards under an arch eight feet high, until it broke upon the jagged rocks that lay blistering in the sunshine at the bottom of the circular opening in the upper cliff. A shudder shook the limbs of the adventurous convict. He comprehended that at high tide the place where he stood was under water, and that the narrow cavern became a subaqueous pipe of solid rock forty feet long, through which were spouted the league-long rollers of the Southern Sea.

The narrow strip of rock at the base of the cliff was as flat as a table. Here and there were enormous hollows like pans, which the retreating tide had left full of clear, still water. The crannies of the rocks were inhabited by small white crabs, and John Rex found to his delight that there was on this little shelf abundance of mussels, which, though lean and acrid, were sufficiently grateful to his famished stomach. Attached to the flat surfaces of the numerous stones, moreover, were coarse limpets. These, however, John Rex found too salt to be palatable, and was compelled to reject them. A larger variety, however, having a succulent body as thick as a man's thumb contained in long razor-shaped shells, were in some degree free from this objection, and he soon collected the materials for a meal. Having eaten and sunned himself, he began to examine the enormous rock to the base of which he had so strangely penetrated. Rugged and worn, it raised its huge breast against wind and wave, secure upon a broad pedestal, which probably extended as far beneath the sea as the massive column itself rose above it. Rising thus, with its shaggy drapery of sea-weed clinging about its knees, it seemed to be a motionless but sentient being—some monster of the deep, a Titan of the ocean condemned ever to front in silence the fury of that illimitable and rarely travelled sea. Yet—silent and motionless as he was—the hoary ancient gave hint of the mysteries of his revenge. Standing upon the broad and sea-girt platform where surely no human foot but his had ever stood in life, the convict saw many feet above him, pitched into a cavity of the huge sun-blistered boulders, an object which his sailor eye told him at once was part of the top hamper of some large ship. Crusted with shells, and its ruin so overrun with the ivy of the ocean, that its ropes could barely be distinguished from the weeds with which they were encumbered, this relic of human labour attested the triumph of nature over human ingenuity. Perforated below by the relentless sea, exposed above to the full fury of the tempest; set in solitary defiance to the waves, that rolling from the ice-volcano of the Southern pole, hurled their gathered might unchecked upon its iron front, the great rock drew from its lonely warfare the materials of its own silent vengeances. Clasped in iron arms, it held its prey, snatched from the jaws of the all-devouring sea. One might imagine that, when the doomed ship, with her crew of shrieking souls, had splintered and gone down, the deaf, blind giant had clutched this fragment, upheaved from the seething waters, with a thrill of savage and terrible joy.

John Rex, gazing up at this memento of a forgotten agony, felt a sensation of the most vulgar pleasure. 'There's wood for my fire!' thought he; and mounting to the spot, he essayed to fling down the splinters of timber upon the platform. Long exposed to the sun, and flung high above the water-mark of recent storms, the timber had dried to the condition of touchwood, and would burn fiercely. It was precisely what he required. Strange accident that had for years stored, upon a desolate rock, this fragment of a vanished and long-forgotten vessel, that it might aid at last to warm the limbs of a villain escaping from justice!

Striking the disintegrated mass with his iron-shod heel, John Rex broke off convenient portions; and making a bag of his shirt, by tying the sleeves and neck, he was speedily staggering into the cavern with a supply of fuel. He made two trips, flinging down the wood in the floor of the gallery that overlooked the sea, and was returning for a third, when his quick ear caught the dip of oars. He had barely time to lift the sea-weed curtain that veiled the entrance to the chasm, when the Eaglehawk boat rounded the promontory. Burgess was in the stern-sheets, and seemed to be making signals to some one on the top of the cliff. Rex, grinning behind his veil, divined the manoeuvre. McNab and his party were to search above, while the Commandant examined the gulf below. The boat headed direct for the passage, and, for an instant, John Rex's undaunted soul shivered at the thought that, perhaps after all, his pursuers might be aware of the existence of the cavern. Yet that was unlikely. He kept his ground, and the boat passed within a foot of him, gliding silently into the gulf. He observed that Burgess's usually florid face was pale, and that his left sleeve was cut open, showing a bandage on the arm. There had been some fighting, then, and it was not unlikely that his fellow-desperadoes had been captured! He chuckled at his own ingenuity and good sense. The boat, emerging from the archway, entered the pool of the Blow-hole, and, held with the full strength of the party, remained stationary. John Rex watched Burgess scan the rocks and eddies, saw him signal to McNab, and then, with much relief, beheld the boat's head brought round to the sea-board.

He was so intent upon watching this dangerous and difficult operation, that he was oblivious of an extraordinary change which had taken place in the interior of the cavern. The water, which, an hour ago, had left exposed a long reef of black hummock-rocks, was now spread in one foam-flecked sheet over the ragged bottom of the rude staircase by which he had descended. The tide had turned, and the sea, apparently sucked in through some deeper tunnel in the portion of the cliff which was below water, was being forced into the vault with a rapidity which bid fair to shortly submerge the mouth of the cave. The convict's feet were already wetted by the incoming waves, and as he turned for one last look at the boat, he saw a green, grassy billow heave up against the entrance to the chasm, and, almost blotting out the daylight, roll majestically through the arch. It was high time for Burgess to take his departure if he did not wish his whale-boat to be cracked like a nut against the roof of the tunnel. Alive to his danger, the Commandant abandoned the search after his late prisoner's corpse, and hastened to gain the open sea. The boat, carried backwards and upwards on the bosom of a monstrous wave, narrowly escaped destruction, and John Rex, climbing to the gallery, saw with much satisfaction the broad back of his outwitted gaoler disappear round the sheltering promontory. The last efforts of his pursuers had failed, and in another hour the only accessible entrance to the convict's retreat was hidden under three feet of furious sea-water.

His gaolers were convinced of his death, and would search for him no more. So far, so good. Now for the last desperate venture—the escape from the wonderful cavern which was at once his shelter and his prison. Piling his wood together, and succeeding after many efforts, by aid of a flint and the ring which yet clung to his ankle, in lighting a fire and warming his chilled limbs in its cheering blaze, he set himself to meditate upon his course of action. He was safe for the present, and the supply of food that the rock afforded was amply sufficient to sustain life in him for many days, but it was impossible that he could remain for many days concealed. He had no fresh water, and though by reason of the soaking he had received he had hitherto felt little inconvenience from this cause, the salt and acrid mussels speedily induced a raging thirst, which he could not alleviate. It was imperative that within forty-eight hours at furthest he should be on his way to the peninsula. He remembered the little stream into which—in his flight of the previous night—he had so nearly fallen, and hoped to be able under cover of the darkness to steal round the reef and reach it unobserved. His desperate scheme was then to commence. He had to run the gauntlet of the dogs and guards, gain the peninsula, and await the rescuing vessel. He confessed to himself that the chances were terribly against him. If Gabbett and the others had been recaptured—as he devoutly trusted—the coast would be comparatively clear; but if they had escaped, he knew Burgess too well to think that he would give up the chase while hope of re-taking the absconders remained to him. If indeed all fell out as he had wished, he had still to sustain life until Blunt found him—if haply Blunt had not returned, wearied with useless and dangerous waiting.

As night came on, and the firelight showed strange shadows waving from the corners of the enormous vault, while the dismal abysses beneath him murmured and muttered with uncouth and ghastly utterances, there fell upon the lonely man the terror of Solitude. Was this marvellous hiding-place that he had discovered to be his sepulchre! Was he—a monster amongst his fellow-men—to die some monstrous death, entombed in this mysterious and terrible cavern of the sea? He tried to drive away these gloomy thoughts by sketching out for himself a plan of action—but in vain. In vain he strove to picture in its completeness that—as yet vague—design by which he promised himself to wrest from the vanished son of the wealthy shipbuilder his name and heritage. His mind, filled with forebodings of shadowy horror, could not give to the subject that calm consideration which it needed. In the midst of his schemes for the baffling of the jealous love of the woman who was to save him, and the getting to England, in shipwrecked and foreign guise, as the long-lost heir to the fortune of Sir Richard Devine, there arose ghastly and awesome shapes of death and horror, with whose terrible unsubstantiality he must grapple in the lonely recesses of that dismal cavern. He heaped fresh wood upon his fire, that the bright light might drive out the grewsome things that lurked above, below, and around him. He became afraid to look behind him, lest some shapeless mass of mid-sea-birth—some voracious polyp with far reaching arms and jellied mouth ever open to devour—might not slide up over the edge of the dripping caves below and fasten upon him in the darkness. His imagination—always sufficiently vivid and spurred to unnatural effect by the exciting scenes of the previous night—painted each patch of shadow, clinging bat-like to the humid wall, as some globular sea-spider ready to drop upon him with its viscid and clay-cold body, and drain out his chilled blood, enfolding him in rough and hairy arms. Each splash in the water beneath him, each sigh of the multitudinous and melancholy sea, seemed to prelude the laborious advent of some misshapen and ungainly abortion of the ooze. All the sensations induced by lapping water and regurgitating waves took material shape and surrounded him. All creatures that could be engendered by slime and salt crept forth into the firelight to stare at him. Red dabs and splashes that were living beings, having a strange phosphoric light of their own, glowed upon the floor. The livid incrustations of a hundred years of humidity slipped from off the walls and painfully heaved their mushroom surfaces to the blaze. The red glow of the unwonted fire, crimsoning the wet sides of the cavern, seemed to attract countless blisterous and transparent shapelessnesses, which elongated themselves towards him. Bloodless and bladdery things ran hither and thither noiselessly. Strange carapaces crawled from out the rocks. All the horrible unseen life of the ocean seemed to be rising up and surrounding him. He retreated to the brink of the gulf, and the glare of the upheld brand fell upon a rounded hummock, whose coronal of silky weed out-floating in the water looked like the head of a drowned man. He rushed to the entrance of the gallery, and his shadow, thrown into the opening, seemed to take the shape of an avenging phantom, with arms upraised to warn him back.

The naturalist, the explorer, or the shipwrecked seaman would have found nothing frightful in this exhibition of the harmless life of the Australian ocean. But the convict's guilty conscience, long suppressed and derided, asserted itself in this hour when it was alone with Nature and Night. The bitter intellectual power which had so long supported him succumbed beneath imagination—the unconscious religion of the soul. If ever he was nigh repentance it was then. He deemed all the phantoms of his past crimes arising to gibber at him, and covering his eyes with his hands, he fell shuddering upon his knees. The brand, loosening from his grasp, dropped into the gulf, and was extinguished with a hissing noise. As if the sound had called up some spirit that lurked below, a whisper ran through the cavern.

'John Rex!'

The hair of the convict's flesh stood up, and he cowered to the earth.

'John Rex!'

It was a *human* voice! Whether of friend or enemy he did not pause to think. His terror over-mastered all other considerations.

'Here! here!' he cried, and sprang to the opening of the vault. [. . .]

1874

Nasturtium Villas

Did you ever wonder where live the large-jointed men with the shining hats, the elegant trousers, the red neckties, and the big coarse hands twinkling with rings? I found out one day quite accidentally, through my friend, Joseph Wapshot. They live at Nasturtium Villas.

'Come down and have a chop on Sunday,' said Mr Wapshot. He is a merchant of great respectability. 'Me and the missus'll be at home. Nasturtium Villa on the Saint Kilderkin Road.' I went at 1 o'clock—the 'chop' was to be served at 2 p.m.—and found Mr Wapshot and his friends in the garding. 'Ha, my boy,' roared Wapshot, who was painfully clean, if I may be permitted the expression; 'How are yer? Come in. 'Ave a glarse of sherry? Mr Baffatty, Mr Calimanco, Mr Blopp!' I bowed to three fat persons—who each wore a white waistcoat and elaborate watch-chain, a red necktie, and big coarse hands twinkling with rings—and followed Wapshot.

Joseph Wapshot is a good fellow—a very good fellow. He was, as you are aware, originally a clerk in the house of Hunks and Junks, the great Sandbank Ship Chandlers (Purveyors of Naval Stores they call themselves), and from that employment became a traveller for Dungaree Brown. Versed in the arts of the road, skilled in the pastimes of the commercial room, an adept at Yankee Grab, a noted hand at Loo, Poker, or 'Selling the Pony', Mr Wapshot made his mark, and soon entered into business for himself. He married, became a father, bought a villa-allotment, and settled down into an honest tradesman and a gross feeder.

Mrs Wapshot was Miss Matilda Jane Harico (of Harico, Kidney, and Company), and is a sprightly, black-eyed young person with a round, plump figure, a profusion of ringlets not altogether innocent of curl-paper, and short, chubby fingers sparkling with rings. She is an excellent mother, a good housewife, a most unentertaining companion, and plays the piano with a voluble ignorance which enchants her husband.

Into this society on a hot summer afternoon I found myself entered. Evidence of wealth without taste was all around me. The drawing-room furniture, most expensive, and therefore most excellent, was green picked out with crimson. The curtains were yellow damask (Heaven only knows how much a yard at Dungaree Brown's!), while the carpet represented daffidowndillies, roses, and sun-flowers on a pink ground. The pictures on the walls were either chromo-lithographs, or—more abominable still—oleographs of the most glaring, hideous, yellow and staring nature. There was a bad copy of the Beatrice di Cenci—every house in Nasturtium Villas has a copy of the Beatrice di Cenci—and a Guido's Magdalen, simpering at a most indecent Titian's Venus. Birket Foster, with his golden-haired rustics, eternally meditating in gowns of coloured cotton with his impossible hedgerows, his marvellous clouds, his perpetual briar hedges, was pin-pointing to admiration in every chromolithograph corner. In the dining-room we had Martin and his Satanical Architecture; in the breakfast-room Poussin feebly mezzotinted, and Watteau—poor Watteau!—more feebly mezzotinted still. On the dining-room bookshelf was Cassell's Illustrated Bible, and on the drawing-room table Doré's pale reflections of the great Spaniard Goya.[1] The house was, in fact, furnished according to Messrs Reachem and Bock's catalogue—'This splendid modern drawing-room; this dining-room replete with every convenience: sideboard, wine coolers, etc.' Nothing was wanting, not even a stained glass window, with the device J.W., and the ancient arms of Wapshot akimbo beneath it.

It was worthy of endurance to see how Joseph has aped the manners of the class he detested. His servants obey him in fear and trembling—for

---

1   Italian artist Guido Reni (1575–1642) painted both 'Beatrice di Cenci' and 'Mary Magdalene'; Titian (c. 1485–1576), also Italian, painted 'The Venus of Urbino' (1538); Myles Birket Foster (1825–99), a celebrated Victorian painter of rustic scenes; John Martin (1789–1854), English artist who specialised in images of divine punishment; Nicolas Poussin (1594–1665), French painter in the classical style; Antoine Watteau (1684–1721), French painter; Gustave Doré (1832–83), painter and engraver.

Joseph rules solely by the terrible power of the purse. His 'cut of mutton' was always admirably cooked. His 'claret' cost him as much as the wine merchant could dare to charge. His clothes were from Bilton's—the only tailor in Fawkner's Town[1]—who sneered in his sleeve as he measured the rotund good natured snob. His wife was amusing, and his cigars without peer. Do you wonder, then, that such fellows as Baffatty, Calimanco, and Blopp come and spend the evening with him? Do you wonder that Captain Phoebus, Major Busby, Jerningham Jinks, and Jemmy Jerboa are frequently found sucking-in Wapshot's wine, and leering at Wapshot's wife. If men will make their houses bachelor hotels, what other result is to be expected?

The dinner at Nasturtium Villa was an infliction under which all have suffered. Soup (*bad*), fish (*indifferent*), sherry (*very bad*), mutton (*good*), vegetables, own growing (*most excellent*), *entreés* of fowl and some other nastiness (*both infernally bad*), champagne (*that is to say moselle*), cabinet pudding, tarts, custards (*all good*), cheese (*colonial and so so*), dessert (*good*), wine (*tolerable*), cigars (*very shy, W. not being a smoker*), and brandy (*the most admirable which could be bought in the city*). This is the sort of dinner which one gets at all Nasturtium Villas, and the pure Bohemian feels inclined to say, 'Sir,—you! I didn't *ask* to dine with you? We are not sufficiently familiar for me to condescend to take "pot luck". But if you want me to feed at your expense—give me a *dinner*, sir!' Had dear, good-natured Wapshot but offered us a saddle of mutton, some reasonable claret, some Stilton cheese, and some of the Al Brandy, we should have gone home happy and satisfied. But his foolish efforts to emulate his betters, his silly assumption of rank, of good breeding, and taste not only reminded us of what he really was, but made us deem him to be a great deal worse than accident for a time had made him. In a jolly bachelor camp, in a pleasant manly meeting of friends frying a lamb chop, baking a damper, standing a drink, or uncorking a bottle, Joe Wapshot would have been excellent, charming, beneficent. But in a badly-furnished drawing-room, blocked up with a grand piano, a bird-cage, an indifferent plaster cast of the *Venus aux belles fesses*[2] (*he* doesn't know it under that name!), and five spoiled chromo-lithographs of Der Günstumper's *Windelkind Gurken-salat*, he is much out of place. Mrs Joe, who would be delightful on a desert island, is simply an unobtrusive nuisance in her own house, and the three soft-goods friends are positively indecently stupid.

After dinner we went into the veranda, drank claret, and smoked 'small Patchechos'. I have never smoked small Patchechos before, and I never wish to do so again. They are bitter and meagre and unsatisfactory. I was obliged to have a pipe to take the taste out of my mouth. Yet poor dear

---

1   Melbourne, after one of its founders, John Pascoe Fawkner (1792–1869).
2   Classical statue of Aphrodite Kallipygos.

Joseph, turning up his chin to emit the smoke in long, lingering puffs of delight, taking the filthy root from his mouth and passing the burning ash beneath his nose as if in paroxysm of chastened joy, sending smoke out of his ear and nostrils, and finally closing his eyelids in passionate abandonment as he had in the distance seen do the 'swells' at the Podiceps Cornutus.[1] The conversation was not brilliant. Baffatty related an anecdote about a sudden rise in the price of flannel, owing to a fit of the gout had by the Marquis of Welchshire. Calimanco spun a yarn concerning some ingenious swindling—broking he called it—about a shipment of tweeds, while Blopp told several old and admired spicy stories which sent the company into fits of knowing laughter. Then we went into the drawing room, and Mrs Wapshot sang 'Constance' with great feeling, Mr Blopp obliging on the flute. Then Mr Calimanco tried 'My Pretty Jane', but failed rather we thought, and it was not until Wapshot had himself sung *'Gentlemen out! Turn out! Turn out! We'll keep these Roundheads down!'* that we expressed any large satisfaction at the melodies.

After the music we had supper, and this supper was the most entertaining part of the entertainment. Joseph forgot his grandeur, and took off his coat to carve with greater ease. Blopp churned his vinegar into his mouth with his knife. Baffatty unaffectedly picked his teeth. Calimanco swallowed onions like a true British tradesman, and Mrs Wapshot swilled porter out of a pewter pot until her red cheeks shone again. During the progress of this festive meal we abused everybody of whom we could think, except his Excellency the Governor, for the Wapshots make a loyal point of satisfying all the trivial social requirements which are needed to secure invitations to the At Homes and Balls of the Queen's Representative. We abused Miss Nelly Higgins, who, as you will remember, ma'am, was so forward at the masquerade given by Wrenchem, the dentist. We discussed the bearing in society of Mrs Hockstetter, whose name was well known in Great Carib Street years ago. We whispered how Bullion, the banker, had been seen climbing over the back-garden fence of Mrs De la Touche. We told o'er again the stale story of Bangalore's misfortune with the widow. We sniggered at the threadbare calumny concerning Parson Jesse Rural, and we admitted that Mr Clipperton was not married to Mrs Clipperton, or *'report spoke falsely'*. In fact, we conducted ourselves like genuine representatives of the class of dwellers in Nasturtium Villas, and abused infamously everybody above our own rank in life.

When supper was over, the gentlemen drank brandy and water—Wapshot struggling manfully with a small Patchecho—and the ladies strolled up and down the twenty yards of garden with their arms round each other's waists.

1   Horned grebe.

Calimanco related more anecdotes of successful brokerage, and Blopp added four more spicy stories to our stock. When we wished to give a man the highest praise we spoke of him as being 'well-in', or 'having made his pile'. When we desired to express our supreme contempt for him, we hinted that he was 'rubbing along', that his 'name stunk at the bank' (this elegant metaphor was Baffatty's); or that he was 'in' someone's 'hands'. In fact, having sacrificed to the only god we owned—our belly—we set up the only idol we worshipped—Mammon—and fell down before it. At a late hour I departed, meditating upon the curious phase of civilisation which I had discovered.

Here was a whole family—a whole tribe of human beings—whose only notion of their part in life was to obtain as much money as they could by any legal means scrape together, and spend it upon eating, drinking, and decoration of their persons. They have no aspirations and few ideas. They do not read, write, or sustain one ambition which a few bank notes cannot satisfy. Deprive them of their bank-balance, and they have no resources of consolation. Place them in any place where chaffering and huckstering are not the business of life, and they would starve. And yet—how kind is Nature!—they imagine themselves to be the salt of the earth—the only fortunate people worthy to be beloved by God and man.

1874

Preface to Adam Lindsay Gordon's *Sea Spray and Smoke Drift*

The poems of Gordon have an interest beyond the mere personal one which his friends attach to his name. Written, as they were, at odd times and leisure moments of a stirring and adventurous life, it is not to be wondered at if they are unequal or unfinished. The astonishment of those who knew the man, and can gauge the capacity of this city to foster poetic instinct, is, that such work was ever produced here at all. Intensely nervous, and feeling much of that shame at the exercise of the higher intelligence which besets those who are known to be renowned in field sports, Gordon produced his poems shyly, scribbled them on scraps of paper, and sent them anonymously to magazines. It was not until he discovered one morning that everybody knew a couplet or two of 'How We Beat the Favourite' that he consented to forego his anonymity and appear in the unsuspected character of a versemaker. The success of his republished 'collected' poems gave him courage, and the unreserved praise which greeted 'Bush Ballads' should have urged him to forget or to conquer those evil promptings which, unhappily, brought about his untimely death.

Adam Lindsay Gordon was the son of an officer in the English army, and was educated at Woolwich, in order that he might follow the profession of his family. At the time when he was a cadet there was no sign of either of the two great wars which were about to call forth the strength of English arms, and, like many other men of his day, he quitted his prospects of service, and emigrated. He went to South Australia and started as a sheep farmer. His efforts were attended with failure. He lost his capital, and, owning nothing but a love for horsemanship and a head full of Browning and Shelley, plunged into the varied life which gold-mining, 'overlanding,' and cattle-driving affords. From this experience he emerged to light in Melbourne as the best amateur steeplechase rider in the colonies. The victory he won for Major Baker in 1868, when he rode Babbler for the Cup Steeplechase, made him popular, and the almost simultaneous publication of his last volume of poems gave him welcome entrance to the houses of all who had pretensions to literary taste. The reputation of the book spread to England, and Major Whyte Melville[1] did not disdain to place the lines of the dashing Australian author at the head of his own dashing descriptions of sporting scenery. Unhappily, the melancholy, which Gordon's friends had with pain observed increased daily, and in the full flood of his success, with congratulations pouring upon him from every side, he was found dead in the heather near his home with a bullet from his own rifle in his brain.

I do not propose to criticise the volumes which these few lines of preface introduce to the reader. The influence of Browning and of Swinburne upon the writer's taste is plain. There is plainly visible also, however, a keen sense for natural beauty and a manly admiration for healthy living. If in 'Ashtaroth' and 'Bellona' we recognize the swing of a familiar metre, in such poems as 'The Sick Stockrider' we perceive the genuine poetic instinct united to a very clear perception of the loveliness of duty and of labour.

> 'Twas merry in the glowing morn, among the gleaming grass,
>   To wander as we've wandered many a mile,
> And blow the cool tobacco cloud, and watch the white wreaths pass,
>   Sitting loosely in the saddle all the while;
> 'Twas merry 'mid the blackwoods, when we spied the station roofs,
>   To wheel the wild scrub cattle at the yard,
> With a running fire of stockwhips, and a fiery run of hoofs,
>   Oh! the hardest day was never then too hard!
>
> Aye! we had a glorious gallop after 'Starlight' and his gang,
>   When they bolted from Sylvester's on the flat;
> How the sun-dried reed-beds crackled, how the flint-strewn ranges
>   rang
>   To the strokes of 'Mountaineer' and 'Acrobat'.

---

1   George John Whyte-Melville (1821–78), English novelist who specialised in sporting scenes.

> Hard behind them in the timber, harder still across the heath,
>> Close behind them through the tea-tree scrub we dash'd;
> And the golden-tinted fern leaves, how they rustled underneath!
>> And the honeysuckle osiers, how they crash'd!

This is genuine. There in no 'poetic evolution from the depths of internal consciousness' here. The writer has ridden his ride as well as written it.

The student of these unpretending volumes will be repaid for his labour. He will find in them something very like the beginnings of a national school of Australian poetry. In historic Europe, where every rood of ground is hallowed in legend and in song, the least imaginative can find food for sad and sweet reflection. When strolling at noon down an English country lane, lounging at sunset by some ruined chapel on the margin of an Irish lake, or watching the mists of morning unveil Ben Lomond, we feel all the charm which springs from association with the past. Soothed, saddened, and cheered by turns, we partake of the varied moods which belong not so much to ourselves as to the dead men who, in old days, sung, suffered, or conquered in the scenes which we survey. But this our native or adopted land has no past, no story. No poet speaks to us. Do we need a poet to interpret Nature's teachings, we must look into our own hearts, if perchance we may find a poet there.

What is the dominant note of Australian scenery? That which is the dominant note of Edgar Allan Poe's poetry—Weird Melancholy. A poem like 'L'Allegro' could never be written by an Australian. It is too airy, too sweet, too freshly happy. The Australian mountain forests are funereal, secret, stern. Their solitude is desolation. They seem to stifle, in their black gorges, a story of sullen despair. No tender sentiment is nourished in their shade. In other lands the dying year is mourned, the falling leaves drop lightly on his bier. In the Australian forests no leaves fall. The savage winds shout among the rock clefts. From the melancholy gum strips of white bark hang and rustle. The very animal life of these frowning hills is either grotesque or ghostly. Great grey kangaroos hop noiselessly over the coarse grass. Flights of white cockatoos stream out, shrieking like evil souls. The sun suddenly sinks, and the mopokes burst out into horrible peals of semi-human laughter. The natives aver that, when night comes, from out the bottomless depths of some lagoon the Bunyip rises, and, in form like monstrous sea calf, drags his loathsome length from out the ooze. From a corner of the silent forest rises a dismal chant, and around a fire dance natives painted like skeletons. All is fear-inspiring and gloomy. No bright fancies are linked with the memories of the mountains. Hopeless explorers have named them out of their sufferings—Mount Misery, Mount Dreadful, Mount Despair. As when among sylvan scenes in places

> Made green with the running of rivers,
> And gracious with temperate air,[1]

the soul is soothed and satisfied, so, placed before the frightful grandeur of these barren hills, it drinks in their sentiment of defiant ferocity, and is steeped in bitterness.

Australia has rightly been named the Land of the Dawning. Wrapped in the midst of early morning, her history looms vague and gigantic. The lonely horseman riding between the moonlight and the day sees vast shadows creeping across the shelterless and silent plains, hears strange noises in the primeval forest where flourishes a vegetation long dead in other lands, and feels, despite his fortune, that the trim utilitarian civilisation which bred him shrinks into insignificance beside the contemptuous grandeur of forest and ranges coeval with an age in which European scientists have cradled his own race.

There is a poem in every form of tree or flower, but the poetry which lives in the trees and flowers of Australia differs from those of other countries. Europe is the home of knightly song, of bright deeds and clear morning thought. Asia sinks beneath the weighty recollections of her past magnificence, as the Suttee sinks, jewel-burdened, upon the corpse of dread grandeur, destructive even in its death. America swiftly hurries on her way, rapid, glittering, insatiable even as one of her own giant waterfalls. From the jungles of Africa, and the creeper-tangled groves of the islands of the South, arise, from the glowing hearts of a thousand flowers, heavy and intoxicating odours—the Upas-poison which dwells in barbaric sensuality. In Australia alone is to be found the Grotesque, the Weird, the strange scribblings of Nature learning how to write. Some see no beauty in our trees without shade, our flowers without perfume, our birds who cannot fly, and our beasts who have not yet learned to walk on all fours. But the dweller in the wilderness acknowledges the subtle charm of this fantastic land of monstrosities. He becomes familiar with the beauty of loneliness. Whispered to by the myriad tongues of the wilderness, he learns the language of the barren and the uncouth, and can read the hieroglyphs of haggard gum-trees, blown into odd shapes, distorted with fierce hot winds, or cramped with cold nights, when the Southern Cross freezes in a cloudless sky of icy blue. The phantasmagoria of that wild dreamland termed the Bush interprets itself, and the Poet of our desolation begins to comprehend why free Esau loved his heritage of desert sand better than all the bountiful richness of Egypt.

1876

---

1   Algernon Charles Swinburne (1837–1909), 'Dedication 1865'.

MARY HANNAY FOOTT
1846–1918

Poet and journalist Mary Hannay Foott was born in Scotland and migrated with her family to Melbourne in 1853. She was educated there, attending the Model School as a teacher-trainee in 1861. After teaching at various schools in Victoria and NSW, in 1874 she married Thomas Foott, a stock inspector. From 1877 until his death in 1884 they lived on his station, Dundoo, in south-west Queensland. In 1887, after moving to Brisbane, Mary Foott became editor of the women's page of the *Queenslander*, which she continued to work on for about a decade. She had been publishing poems as well as stories and articles in magazines and newspapers for many years. In 1885 her first collection appeared under the title of her best-known poem, *Where the Pelican Builds and Other Poems*. It was later expanded as *Morna Lee and Other Poems* (1890). *EW*

Where the Pelican Builds

> *The unexplored parts of Australia are*
> *sometimes spoken of by the bushmen of*
> *Western Queensland as the home of the pelican,*
> *a bird whose nesting place, so far as the*
> *writer knows, is seldom, if ever found.*

The horses were ready, the rails were down,
    But the riders lingered still,—
        One had a parting word to say,
    And one had his pipe to fill.
Then they mounted, one with a granted prayer,   5
    And one with a grief unguessed.
        'We are going' they said, as they rode away—
    'Where the pelican builds her nest!'

They had told us of pastures wide and green,
    To be sought past the sunset's glow;   10
        Of rifts in the ranges by opal lit,
    And gold 'neath the river's flow.
And thirst and hunger were banished words
    When they spoke of that unknown West;
        No drought they dreaded, no flood they feared,   15
    Where the pelican builds her nest!

The creek at the ford was but fetlock deep
    When we watched them crossing there;
        The rains have replenished it thrice since then
    And thrice has the rock lain bare.   20
But the waters of Hope have flowed and fled,

And never from blue hill's breast
    Come back—by the sun and the sands devoured—
Where the pelican builds her nest!

1885

LOUISA LAWSON
1848–1920

Journalist, poet and editor Louisa Lawson was born and raised in the bush near Mudgee in NSW. Although reputedly the possessor of a fine voice, like most bush girls of her generation her career seemed destined to be that of wife and mother. In 1866 she married Peter Larsen, a Norwegian sailor turned gold digger. The marriage was unhappy and in 1883, after the birth of five children, including the writer Henry Lawson (qv), Louisa left for Sydney with her children. There she established herself as a journalist and publisher, editing the *Republican* (1887–88) and founding and editing *The Dawn* (1888–1905), Australia's first feminist journal. In May 1889 she launched the campaign for female suffrage and founded the Dawn Club. She published a children's book, *'Dert' and 'Do'* (1904), as well as many poems, some of which were included in *The Lonely Crossing and Other Poems* (1905). Some of the numerous articles and editorials she contributed to *The Dawn* can be found in *The First Voice of Australian Feminism: Excerpts from Louisa Lawson's* The Dawn *1888–1895* (1990). A *Collected Poems* was published in 1996. *EW*

That Nonsensical Idea

'I am utterly opposed to this nonsensical idea of giving women votes,' said one of the members of parliament commenting on the proposed Electoral Bill. So are we opposed to it if it is nonsensical, but as so many reforms and discoveries of incalculable value have at first sight been declared idiotic and absurd, we may as well look at the foundation facts and see if this proposed Bill contain the essence of foolishness or whether it does, as some claim, bring us as near to pure justice and absolute freedom as any human law has yet approached.

    We are a community of men and women living in one corner of the globe which we have marked off as our own, and since the business of so many people cannot be managed by all, we select 150 men to make laws for us and manage our public offices. The laws made by these deputies are binding on women as well as men, but the women have no advocates or representatives in the Assembly, nor any means of making their wishes known. The life and work of every woman is just as essential to the good of the community as that of every man. Her work and the character she bears raise or depress the standard of the state as much as does the life of any individual man; why is she set aside and disabled from expressing her opinion as to what should be done by this community of which she is a member? Why are her rights less than her brothers? She bears a full half of the trouble when the affairs of the state are depressed, an unjust law or the lack of law brings to her life care or hardship or injury as it does to men, yet none of the deputies ask what she wishes—why should they, she has no vote. She belongs to the better behaved sex—for women only contribute one-fifth to the criminal class (four-fifths are men)—and it would therefore seem likely that her opinion would be worth having, yet she is expressly discouraged from the formation of opinions, they are declared ineffectual by the other half of this community of people. It does not seem so nonsensical after all, this idea that a woman's opinion as to the fitness of a deputy may be as just and right and worthy of weight as a man's opinion.

SUPPOSING

There are two views of the woman's suffrage question commonly discussed, the justice of the measure, and its expediency. Few doubt its justice, many question its expediency, and yet, being just, what does all else matter?

Suppose that the right to vote lay with women only, and that the progress of the world was bringing expansive thoughts and hopes of a happier future into the minds of men. When men perceived that this right was unjustly withheld from them, and felt that their individual manhood was title enough to this right to a voice in decisions affecting all, would they tolerate discussion as to the expediency or wisdom of the measure? Would they stand by and hear the women conjecture how men might perchance misuse the concession if granted, would they quietly wait while political factions summed up the chances of the support of the new voters? No, they would say 'Curse you—it is my right. What business is it of yours how I use it?'

HER PROPER SPHERE

As to expediency the arguments have been so often repeated that it seems foolish to reiterate them, especially as nothing cogent is brought forward on the opposing side. In Parliament such old phrases as these were used, viz. that 'woman should be kept in her proper sphere' and 'women have duties quite outside the political arena'. One would think the political arena consisted of the parliamentary refreshment room, they are so sure it is not a desirable place for a woman to be seen in. In the minds of these objectors 'politics' seem to consist of the petty animosities and personalities which the law-making business now gives rise to, but 'politics' in reality cover nearly all questions which thinking men or women do now consider and form opinions upon. Laws are made upon divorce, the sale of liquor, factory regulations, the employment of children, gambling, education, hours of labour, and scores of subjects upon which women do think, and respecting which they ought to have the power of giving effect to their wishes by the selection of men representing their shade of opinion. And if women do not also at once enter the 'political arena' so far as to care greatly about the land laws and mining acts, pray do men voters come to an intelligent decision on every possible subject of legislation before casting a vote? Most men do not seriously consider and decide in their own minds upon more than two or three of the many subjects which come within the wide circle of 'politics', and it would not therefore take women long to reach equality in that respect. We are inclined to believe that a woman can form as good an idea as to the best man among parliamentary candidates as the average man voter.

MORE LOGIC

But say some people, women do not want the vote, most of them would not use it if they had it. What will happen after they have the vote may be left to the prophets to say, but if A and B do not want something is that a reason why C who has a just claim should be denied?

PREMATURITY

In the debate, Mr Traill,[1] who said he was in favour of woman's suffrage, urged that the measure would be premature; that women should be first educated to the use of a vote by possessing the suffrage under a local government Act. 'Then,' said he, 'if found to be using it well they should be permitted to influence Imperial questions.'

This would be kind indeed, but this is not the method hitherto employed when new classes have been admitted to the franchise. We have not first put them through political schools; we have taken the raw material, and under the influence of its new liberty and swayed by the responsibilities of its new standing, the raw material has developed, but where has any government ever had raw material so certain to act conscientiously, so prepared already with intelligence and with a strong bias towards moderation, peace, steady reform, and moral purgation? Probably it is because they know that with women voting the men of bad character would have little chance of future election, that makes men so fearful that women 'might not use it well'.

WOMEN MEMBERS

Many of the speakers in the House contended that if women received the right to vote they should also logically have the right to sit in parliament. This is not asked for and need not at present be decided. Few women would care for such a post, but it may be safely said that if exceptional women spring up such as the world has hitherto had some examples of, they could not fail to raise the tone of the House and fill a place worthily. It is to be remembered

1   William Henry Traill (1843–1902), member of NSW parliament, 1889–94.

that men will not cease to vote when women have the suffrage, and that women are decidedly critical of their own sex. She would need to be a remarkable woman who could win the confidence of a mixed constituency of men and women. A young married woman is the usual illustration taken to show the absurdity of a woman member and a woeful picture is drawn of her deserted babies and dinnerless husband. But these pictures only show the speaker's ignorance of women, for there is no woman who would not think of her baby and the happiness of her home long before she desired in her wildest fancies the barren honour of a parliamentary seat. She would not be likely to be asked to stand, and she would not consent if asked.

Some members treated the question in the old semi-facetious way, conjecturing the effect of pretty women in parliament and the power of a lovely woman premier to win susceptible opposition members to her side. This presupposes that the political convictions of men are but wavering undecided beliefs, and easily unseated, and forgets this fact that a woman of such attainments and character that a mixed constituency of men and women esteemed her a fit parliamentary representative, would by her very nature, her modesty and quiet sense, make this silly gallantry impossible; and she would so scorn adherents won only by beauty that they would probably begin under her influence to form their opinions firmly and honestly. Another member alleged that his brother members would do no work if ladies sat beside them. If men are indeed so silly that in a place of business they must inevitably be simpering to women, it will not be so nonsensical to give a vote to a class undoubtedly not prone to publicly exhibit their weakness or their foolishness.

1890/1990

TASMA
1848–1897

Novelist and journalist Jessie Huybers, who adopted the pen name Tasma in honour of her childhood home, was born in London. When she was four, her family migrated to Van Diemen's Land (Tasmania), where her father was a wine merchant. She was educated at home by her mother, who had been a school teacher and was very widely read. In 1867 Tasma made a disastrous marriage to Charles Fraser with whom she shared few interests. Five years later she left him to travel to Europe with her family. In 1875 she returned to Australia and to her husband, but soon decided that she needed to separate from him and support herself through her writing. From 1877 her stories and articles appeared in many local publications and continued to do so after she returned to Europe in 1879. There she also found success as a lecturer, speaking about Australia and its prospects to large audiences in France and Belgium. After divorcing Fraser in 1883, she married Auguste Couvreur, a well-known Belgian journalist, in 1885. Unable to travel as widely as before, she now concentrated on writing novels, producing a number of works in rapid succession. Her best-known novel, *Uncle Piper of Piper's Hill* (1889), a gently satirical look at life among the *nouveaux riches* of 'Marvellous Melbourne', was warmly received and sold well. It was followed by a collection of her earlier stories, *A Sydney Sovereign and Other Tales* (1890) and *In Her Earliest Youth* (1890), which drew on her own marriage for its tale of an intellectual woman married to a gambler and drunkard. In *The Penance of Portia James* (1891), the heroine also makes an unfortunate marriage, which she escapes by leaving for Paris. In 1892, Auguste Couvreur had been appointed the Brussels correspondent of the London *Times*. Following his death in 1894 Tasma succeeded in taking over this role but the additional workload seems to have contributed to her early death from heart disease. She still, however, managed to write two more novels, *Not Counting the Cost* (1895) and *A Fiery Ordeal* (1897). *EW*

Monsieur Caloche

CHAPTER I

A more un-English, uncolonial appearance had never brightened the prosaic interior of Bogg & Company's big warehouse in Flinders Lane. Monsieur Caloche, waiting in the outer office, under fire of a row of curious eyes, was a wondrous study of 'Frenchiness' to the clerks. His vivacious dark eyes, shining out of his sallow face, scarred and seamed by the marks of smallpox, met their inquisitive gaze with an expression that seemed to plead for leniency. The diabolical disease that had scratched the freshness from his face had apparently twisted some of the youthfulness out of it as well; otherwise it was only a young soul that could have been made so diffident by the consciousness that its habitation was disfigured. Some pains had been taken to obviate the effects of the disfigurement and to bring into prominence the smooth flesh that had been spared. It was not chance that had left exposed a round white throat, guiltless of the masculine Adam's apple, or that had brushed the fine soft hair, ruddily dark in hue like the eyes, away from a vein-streaked temple. A youth of unmanly susceptibilities, perhaps—but inviting sympathy rather than scorn—sitting patiently through the dreary silent three-quarters of an hour, with his back to the wall which separated him from the great head of the firm of Bogg & Co.

The softer-hearted of the clerks commiserated him. They would have liked to show their good will, after their own fashion, by inviting him to have a 'drink', but—the possibility of 'shouting' for a young Frenchman, waiting for an interview with their chief! . . . Any one knowing Bogg, of Bogg & Co., must have divined the outrageous absurdity of the notion. It was safer to suppose that the foreigner would have refused the politeness. He did not look as though whisky and water were as familiar to him as a tumbler of *eau sucrée*. The clerks had heard that it was customary in France to drink absinthe. Possibly the slender youth in his loose-fitting French *paletôt*[1] reaching to his knees, and sitting easily upon shoulders that would

---

1   Coat or jacket.

have graced a shawl, had drunk deeply of this fatal spirit. It invested him with something mysterious in the estimation of the juniors, peering for traces of dissipation in his foreign face. But they could find nothing to betray it in the soft eyes, undimmed by the enemy's hand, or the smooth lips set closely over the even row of small French teeth. Monsieur Caloche lacked the happy French confidence which has so often turned a joke at the foot of the guillotine. His lips twitched every time the door of the private office creaked. It was a ground-glass door to the left of him, and as he sat, with his turned-up hat in his hand, patiently waiting, the clerks could see a sort of suppression overspreading his disfigured cheeks whenever the noise was repeated. It appeared that he was diffident about the interview. His credentials were already in the hands of the head of the firm, but no summons had come. His letter of recommendation, sent in fully half an hour back, stated that he was capable of undertaking foreign correspondence; that he was favourably known to the house of business in Paris whose principal had given him his letter of presentation; that he had some slight knowledge of the English language; that he had already given promise of distinguishing himself as a *homme de lettres*. This final clause of the letter was responsible for the length of time Monsieur Caloche was kept waiting. *Homme de lettres!*[1] It was a stigma that Bogg, of Bogg & Co., could not overlook. As a practical man, a self-made man, a man who had opened up new blocks of country and imported pure stock into Victoria—what could be expected of him in the way of holding out a helping hand to a scribbler—a pauper who had spent his days in making rhymes in his foreign jargon? Bogg would have put your needy professionals into irons. He forgave no authors, artists, or actors who were not successful. *Homme de lettres!* Coupled with his poverty it was more unpardonable a title than gaol-bird. There was nothing to prove that the latter title would not have fitted Monsieur Caloche as well. He was probably a ruffianly Communist. The French Government could not get hold of all the rebels, and here was one in the outer office of Bogg & Co. coolly waiting for a situation.

Not so coolly, perhaps, as Bogg, in his aggrieved state of mind, was ready to conclude. For the day was a hot-wind day, and Bogg himself, in white waistcoat and dust-coat, sitting in the cool depths of his revolving-chair in front of the desk in his private office, was hardly aware of the driving dust and smarting grit emptied by shovelfuls upon the unhappy people without. He perspired, it is true, in deference to the state of his big thermometer, which even here stood above 85° in the corner, but having come straight from Brighton in his private brougham, he could wipe his moist bald head without besmearing his silk handkerchief with street grime. And it was something to

---

1   Literary man.

be sitting here, in a lofty office, smelling of yellow soap and beeswax, when outside a north wind was tormenting the world with its puffs of hot air and twirling relays of baked rubbish and dirt. It was something to be surrounded by polished mahogany, cool to the touch, and cold iron safes, and maps that conveyed in their rippling lines of snowy undulations far-away suggestions of chill heights and mountain breezes. It was something to have iced water in the decanter at hand, and a little fountain opposite, gurgling a running reminder of babbling brooks dribbling through fern-tree valleys and wattle-studded flats. Contrasting the shaded coolness of the private office with the heat and turmoil without, there was no cause to complain.

Yet Bogg clearly had a grievance, written in the sour lines of his mouth, never too amiably expanded at the best of times, and his small, contracted eyes, full of shrewd suspicion-darting light. He read the letter sent in by Monsieur Caloche with the plentiful assistance of the tip of his broad forefinger, after a way peculiar to his early days, before he had acquired riches, or knighthood, or rotundity.

For Bogg, now Sir Matthew Bogg, of Bogg & Company, was a self-made man in the sense that money makes the man, and that he had made the money before it could by any possibility make him. Made it by dropping it into his till in those good old times when all Victorian storekeepers were so many Midases, who saw their spirits and flour turn into gold under their handling; made it by pocketing something like three thousand per cent, upon every penny invested in divers blocks of scrubby soil hereafter to be covered by those grand and gloomy bluestone buildings which make of Melbourne a city of mourning; made it by reaching out after it, and holding fast to it, whenever it was within spirit-call or finger-clutch, from his early grog-shanty days, when he detected it in the dry lips of every grimy digger on the flat, to his latter station-holding days, when he sniffed it in the drought which brought his neighbours low. Add to which he was lucky—by virtue of a certain inherent faculty he possessed in common with the Vanderbilts, the Stewarts, the Rothschilds of mankind—and far-seeing. He could fore-stall the news in the *Mark Lane Express*. He was almost clairvoyant in the matter of rises in wool. His luck, his foresight, were only on a par with his industry, and the end of all his slaving and sagacity was to give him at sixty years of age a liver, a paunch, an income bordering on a hundred thousand pounds, and the title of Sir Matthew Bogg.

It was known that Sir Matthew had worked his way to the colonies, acting indiscriminately as pig-sticker and deck-swabber on board the *Sarah Jane*. In his liverless, paunchless, and titleless days he had tossed for coppers with the flat-footed sailors on the forecastle. Now he was bank director, railway director, and a number of other things that formed a graceful flourish after Sir Matthew, but that would have sounded less euphonious in the wake of plain 'Bogg'. Yet 'plain Bogg' Nature had turned him out, and 'plain Bogg' he would always remain while in the earthly possession of his round, overheated face, and long, irregular teeth. His hair had abandoned its lawful territory on the top of his head, and planted itself in a vagrant fashion, in small tufts in his ears and nostrils. His eyebrows had run riot over his eyes, but his eyes asserted themselves through all. They were eyes that, without being stronger or larger or bolder than any average pair of eyes to be met with in walking down the street, had such a knack of 'taking your measure' that no one could look at them without discomfiture. In the darkened atmosphere of the Flinders Lane office, Sir Matthew knew how to turn these colourless unwinking orbs to account. To the maliciously inclined among the clerks in the outer office there was nothing more amusing than the crestfallen appearance of the applicants, as they came out by the ground-glass door, compared with the jauntiness of their entrance. Young men who wanted colonial experience, overseers who applied for managerships on his stations, youths fresh from school who had a turn for the bush, had all had specimens of Sir Matthew's mode of dealing with his underlings. But his favourite plan, his special hobby, was to 'drop on to them unawares'.

There is nothing in the world that gives such a zest to life as the possession of a hobby, and the power of indulging it. We may be pretty certain that the active old lady's white horse at Banbury Cross was nothing more than a hobby-horse, as soon as we find out in the sequel that she 'had rings on her fingers and bells on her toes,' and that 'she shall have music wherever she goes'. It is the only horse an old lady could be perpetually engaged in riding without coming to grief—the only horse that ever makes us travel through life to the sound of music wherever we go.

From the days when Bogg had the merest shred of humanity to bully, in the shape of a waif from the Chinese camp, the minutes slipped by with a symphony they had never possessed before. As fulness of time brought him increase of riches and power, he yearned to extend the terror of his sway. It was long before he tasted the full sweetness of making strong men tremble in their boots. Now, at nearly sixty years of age, he knew all the delights of seeing victims, sturdier and poorer than himself, drop their eyelids before his gaze. He was aware that the men in the yard cleared out of his path as he walked through it; that his managers up-country addressed him in tones of husky conciliation; that every eye met his with an air of deprecation, as much as to apologise for the fact of existing in his presence; and in his innermost heart he believed that in the way of mental sensation there could be nothing left to desire. But how convey the impression of rainbow-tints to eyes that have never opened upon aught save universal blackness? Sir Matthew had never seen an eye brighten, a small foot dance, at his approach. A glance of impotent defiance was the only equivalent he knew for a gleam of humid affection. He was accustomed to encounter a shifting gaze. The lowest form of self-interest was the tie which bound his people to him. He paid them as butts, in addition to paying them as servants. Where would have been his daily appetiser in the middle of the day if there had been no yard, full of regulations impossible to obey; no warehouse to echo his harsh words of fault-finding; no servile men, and slouching fast-expanding boys, to scuttle behind the big cases, or come forth as if they were being dragged by hooks, to stand with sheepish expression before him? And when he had talked himself hoarse in town, where would have been the zest of wandering over his stations, of surveying his fat bullocks and woolly merinos, if there had been no accommodating managers to listen reverentially to his loudly-given orders, and take with dejected, apologetic air his continued rating? The savour of life would have departed,—not with the bodily comfort and the consequence that riches bring, but with the power they confer of asserting yourself before your fellow-men after any fashion you please. Bogg's fashion was to bully them, and he bullied them accordingly.

But, you see, Monsieur Caloche is still waiting; in the position, as the junior clerks are well aware, of the confiding calf awaiting butchery in a frolicsome mood outside the butcher's shop. Not that I would imply that Monsieur Caloche frolicked, even metaphorically speaking. He sat patiently on with a sort of sad abstracted air; unconsciously pleating and unpleating the brim of his soft Paris hat, with long lissom fingers that might have broidered the finest silk on other than male hands. The flush of colour, the slight trembling of lips, whenever there was a noise from within, were the only signs that betrayed how acutely he was listening for a summons. Despite the indentations that had marred for ever the smoothness of the face, and pitted the forehead and cheeks as if white gravel had been shot into them, the colour that came and went so suddenly was pink as rose-coloured lake. It stained even the smooth white neck and chin, upon which the faintest traces of down were not yet visible to the scrutinising eyes of the juniors.

Outside, the north wind ran riot along the pavement, upsetting all orderly arrangements for the day with dreadful noise and fussiness, battering trimly-dressed people into red-eyed wretches heaped up with dust; wrenching umbrellas from their handles, and blinding their possessors trying to run after them; filling open mouths with grit, making havoc with people's hats and tempers, and proving itself as great a blusterer in its character of a peppery emigrant as in its original *rôle* of the chilly Boreas of antiquity.

Monsieur Caloche had carefully wiped away from his white wristband the dust that it had driven into his sleeve, and now the dust on his boots— palpably large for the mere slips of feet they inclosed—seemed to give him uneasiness; but it would seem that he lacked the hardihood to stoop and flick it away. When, finally, he extended surreptitiously a timid hand, it might have been observed of his uncovered wrist that it was singularly frail and slender. This delicacy of formation was noticeable in every exterior point. His small white ear, setting close to his head, might have been wrapped up over and over again in one of the fleshy lobes that stretched away from Sir Matthew's skull. Decidedly the two men were of a different order of species. One was a heavy mastiff of lupine tendencies—the other a delicate Italian greyhound, silky, timorous, quivering with sensibility.

And there had been time for the greyhound to shiver long with expectancy before the mastiff prepared to swallow him up.

It was a quarter to twelve by the gloomy-faced clock in the outer office, a quarter to twelve by all the clerks' watches, adjusted every morning to the patriarch clock with unquestioning faith, when Monsieur Caloche had diffidently seated himself on the chair in the vicinity of the ground-glass door. It was half-past twelve by the gloomy-faced clock, half-past twelve by all the little watches that toadied to it, when Sir Matthew's bell rang. It was a bell that must have inherited the spirit of a fire-bell, or a doctor's night-bell. It had never been shaken by Sir Matthew's fingers without causing a fluttering in the outer office. No one knew what hair-suspended sword might be about to fall on his head before the messenger returned. Monsieur Caloche heard it ring, sharply and clamorously, and raised his head. The white-faced messenger, returning from his answer to the summons, and speaking with the suspension of breath that usually afflicted him after an interview with Sir Matthew, announced that 'Mister Caloosh' was wanted, and diving into the gloomy recess in the outer office, relapsed into his normal occupation of breathing on his penknife and rubbing it on his sleeve.

Monsieur Caloche meanwhile stood erect, more like the startled greyhound than ever. To the watchful eyes of the clerks, staring their full at his retreating figure, he seemed to glide rather than step through the doorway. The ground-glass door, attached by a spring from the inside, shut swiftly upon him, as if it were catching him in a trap, and so hid him in full from their curious scrutiny. For the rest, they could only surmise. The lamb had given itself up to the butcher's knife. The diminutive greyhound was in the mastiff's grip.

Would the knife descend on the instant? Would the mastiff fall at once upon the trembling foreigner, advancing with sleek uncovered head, and hat held in front by two quivering hands? Sir Matthew's usual glare of reception was more ardent than of custom as Monsieur Caloche approached. If every 'foreign adventurer' supposed he might come and loaf upon Bogg, of Bogg & Company, because he was backed up by a letter from a respectable firm, Sir Matthew would soon let him find out he was mistaken! His glare intensified as the adventurous stripling glided with softest footfall to the very table where he was sitting, and stood exactly opposite to him.

Not so adventurous, however, but that his lips were white and his bloodless face a pitiful set-off to the cruelly prominent marks that disfigured it. There was a terror in Monsieur Caloche's expression apart from the awe inspired by Sir Matthew's glare which might have disarmed a butcher or even a mastiff. His large, soft eyes seemed to ache with repressed tears. They pleaded for him in a language more convincing than words, 'I am friendless— I am a stranger—I am—' but no matter! They cried out for sympathy and protection, mutely and unconsciously.

But to Sir Matthew's perceptions visible terror had only one interpretation. It remained for him to 'find out' Monsieur Caloche. He would 'drop on to him unawares' one of these days. He patted his hobby on the back, seeing a gratification for it in prospective, and entering shortly upon his customary stock of searching questions, incited his victim to reply cheerfully and promptly by looking him up and down with a frown of suspicion.

'What brought you 'ere?'

'Please?' said Monsieur Caloche, anxiously.

He had studied a vocabulary opening with 'Goodday, sir. What can I have the pleasure of doing for you this morning?' The rejoinder to which did not seem to fit in with Sir Matthew's special form of inquiry.

'What brought you 'ere, I say?' reiterated Sir Matthew, in a roar, as if deafness were the only impediment on the part of foreigners in general to a clear comprehension of our language.

'De sheep, Monsieur! La Reine Dorée,' replied Monsieur Caloche, in low-toned, guttural, musical French.

'That ain't it,' said Sir Matthew, scornfully. 'What did you come 'ere for? What are you fit for? What can you do?'

Monsieur Caloche raised his plaintive eyes. His sad desolation was welling out of their inmost depths. He had surmounted the first emotion that had driven the blood to his heart at the outset, and the returning colour, softening the seams and scars in his cheeks, gave him a boyish bloom. It deepened as he answered with humility, 'I will do what Monsieur will! I will do my possible!'

'I'll soon see how you shape,' said Sir Matthew, irritated with himself for the apparent difficulty of thoroughly bullying the defenceless stranger. 'I don't want any of your parley-vooing in my office—do you hear! I'll find you work—jolly quick, I can tell you! Can you mind sheep? Can you drive bullocks, eh? Can you put up a post and rail? You ain't worth your salt if you can't use your 'ands!'

He cast such a glance of withering contempt on the tapering white fingers with olive-shaped nails in front of him that Monsieur Caloche instinctively sheltered them in his hat. 'Go and get your traps together! I'll find you a billet, never fear!'

'*Mais, Monsieur*—'

'Go and get your traps together, I say! You can come 'ere again in an hour. I'll find you a job up-country!' His peremptory gesture made any protest on the part of Monsieur Caloche utterly unavailing. There was nothing for him to do but to bow and to back in a bewildered way from the room. If the more sharp-eared of the clerks had not been in opportune contiguity to the ground-glass door during Sir Matthew's closing sentences, Monsieur Caloche would have gone away with the predominant impression that 'Sir Bang' was an *enragé*, who disapproved of salt with mutton and beef, and was clamorous in his demands for 'traps', which Monsieur Caloche, with a gleam of enlightenment in the midst of his heart-sickness and perplexity, was proud to remember meant 'an instrument for ensnaring animals'. It was with a doubt he was too polite to express that he accepted the explanation tendered him by the clerks, and learned that if he 'would strike while the iron is hot' he must come back in an hour's time with his portmanteau packed up. He was a lucky fellow, the juniors told him, to jump into a billet without any bother; they wished to the Lord they were in *his* shoes, and could be drafted off to the Bush at a moment's notice.

Perhaps it seemed to Monsieur Caloche that these congratulations were based on the Satanic philosophy of 'making evil his good'. But they brought with them a flavour of the human sympathy for which he was hungering. He bowed to the clerks all round before leaving, after the manner of a court-page in an opera. The hardiest of the juniors ran to the door after he was gone. Monsieur Caloche was trying to make head against the wind. The warm blast was bespattering his injured face. It seemed to revel in the pastime of filling it with grit. One small hand was spread in front of the eyes—the other was resolutely holding together the front of his long, light *paletôt*, which the rude wind had sportively thrown open. The junior was cheated of his fun. Somehow the sight did not strike him as being quite so funny as it ought to have been.

CHAPTER II

The station hands, in their own language, 'gave Frenchy best'. No difference of nationality could account for some of his eccentricities. As an instance, with the setting in of the darkness he regularly disappeared. It was supposed that he camped up a tree with the birds. The wit of the wool-shed surmised that 'Froggy' slept with his relatives, and it would be found that he had 'croaked' with them one of these odd times. Again, there were shearers ready to swear that he had 'blubbered' on finding some sportive ticks on his neck. He was given odd jobs of wool-sorting to do, and was found to have a mania for washing the grease off his hands whenever there was an instant's respite. Another peculiarity was his aversion to blood. By some strange coincidence, he could never be found whenever there was any slaughtering on hand. The most plausible reason was always advanced for necessitating his presence in some far-distant part of the run. Equally he could never be induced to learn how to box—a favourite Sunday morning and summer evening pastime among the men. It seemed almost to hurt him when damage was done to one of the assembled noses. He would have been put down as a 'cur' if it had not been for his pluck in the saddle, and for his gentle winning ways. His pluck, indeed, seemed all concentrated in his horsemanship. Employed as a boundary-rider, there was nothing he would not mount, and the station hands remarked, as a thing 'that beat them once for all', that the 'surliest devils' on the place hardly ever played up with him. He employed no arts. His bridle-hand was by no means strong. Yet it remained a matter of fact that the least amenable of horses generally carried him as if they liked to bear his weight. No one being sufficiently learned to advance the hypothesis of magnetism, it was concluded that he carried a charm.

This power of touch extended to human beings. It was almost worth while spraining a joint or chopping at a finger to be bandaged by Monsieur Caloche's deft fingers. His horror of blood never stood in his way when there was a wound to be doctored. His supple hands, browned and strengthened by his outdoor work, had a tenderness and a delicacy in their way of going to work that made the sufferer feel soothed and halfhealed by their contact. It was the same with his manipulation of things. There was a refinement in his disposition of the rough surroundings that made them look different after he had been among them.

And not understood, jeered at, petted, pitied alternately—with no confidant of more sympathetic comprehension than the horse he bestrode— was Monsieur Caloche absolutely miserable? Granting that it were so, there was no one to find it out. His brown eyes had such a habitually wistful expression, he might have been born with it. Very trifles brought a fleeting light into them—a reminiscence, perhaps that, while it crowned him with 'sorrow's crown of sorrow',[1] was yet a reflection of some past joy. He took refuge in his ignorance of the language directly he was questioned as to his bygone life. An embarrassed little shrug, half apologetic, but powerfully conclusive, was the only answer the most curious examiner could elicit.

It was perceived that he had a strong objection to looking in the glass, and invariably lowered his eyes on passing the cracked and uncompromising fragment of mirror supported on two nails against the planking that walled the rough, attached kitchen. So decided was this aversion that it was only when Bill, the blacksmith, asked him chaffingly for a lock of his hair that he perceived with confusion how wantonly his silken curls were rioting round

---

1   From Alfred, Lord Tennyson (1809–92), 'Locksley Hall'.

his neck and temples. He cut them off on the spot, displaying the transparent skin beneath. Contrasted with the clear tan that had overspread his scarred cheeks and forehead, it was white as freshly drawn milk.

He was set down on the whole as given to moping; but, taking him all round, the general sentiment was favourable to him. Possibly it was with some pitiful prompting of the sort that the working manager sent him out of the way one still morning, when Sir Matthew's buggy, creaking under the unwelcome preponderance of Sir Matthew himself, was discerned on its slow approach to the homestead. A most peaceful morning for the initiation of Sir Matthew's blustering presence! The sparse gum-leaves hung as motionless on their branches as if they were waiting to be photographed. Their shadows on the yellowing grass seemed painted into the soil. The sky was as tranquil as the plain below. The smoke from the homestead reared itself aloft in a long, thinly-drawn column of grey. A morning of heat and repose, when even the sunlight does not frolic and all nature toasts itself, quietly content. The dogs lay blinking at full length, their tails beating the earth with lazy, measured thump. The sheep seemed rooted to the patches of shade, apathetic as though no one wore flannel vests or ate mutton-chops. Only the mingled voices of wild birds and multitudinous insects were upraised in a blended monotony of subdued sounds. Not a morning to be devoted to toil! Rather, perchance, to a glimmering perception of a golden age, when sensation meant bliss more than pain, and to be was to enjoy.

But to the head of the firm of Bogg & Company, taking note of scattered thistles and straggling wire fencing, warmth and sunshine signified only dry weather. Dry weather clearly implied a fault somewhere, for which somebody must be called to account. Sir Matthew had the memory of a strategist. Underlying all considerations of shorthorns and merinos was the recollection of a timid foreign lad to be suspected for his shy, bewildered air—to be suspected again for his slim white hands—to be doubly suspected and utterly condemned for his graceful bearing, his appealing eyes, that even now Sir Matthew could see with their soft lashes drooping over them as he fronted them in his darkened office in Flinders Lane. A scapegoat for dry weather, for obtrusive thistles, for straggling fencing! A waif of foreign scum to be found out! Bogg had promised himself that he would 'drop on to him unawares'. Physically, Bogg was carried over the ground by a fast trotter; spiritually, he was borne along on his hobby, ambling towards its promised gratification with airy speed.

The working manager, being probably of Bacon's way of thinking, that 'dissimulation is but a faint kind of policy', did not, in his own words, entirely 'knuckle down' to Sir Matthew. His name was Blunt—he was proud to say it—and he would show you he could make his name good if you 'crossed' him. Yet Blunt could bear a good deal of 'crossing' when it came to the point. Within certain limits, he concluded that the side on which his bread was buttered was worth keeping uppermost, at the cost of some hard words from his employer.

And he kept it carefully uppermost on this especial morning, when the quietude of the balmy atmosphere was broken by Sir Matthew's growls. The head of the firm, capturing his manager at the door of the homestead, had required him to mount into the double-seated buggy with him. Blunt reckoned that these tours of inspection in the companionship of Bogg were more conducive to taking off flesh than a week's hard training. He listened with docility, nevertheless, to plaints and ratings—was it not a fact that his yearly salaries had already made a nest-egg of large proportions?—and might have listened to the end, if an evil chance had not filled him with a sudden foreboding. For, pricking his way over the plain, after the manner of Spenser's knight,[1] Monsieur Caloche, on a fleet, newly broken-in two-year-old, was riding torwards them. Blunt could feel that Sir Matthew's eyes were sending out sparks of wrath. For the first time in his life he hazarded an uncalled-for opinion.

'He's a good-working chap, that, sir!'—indicating by a jerk of the head that the lad now galloping across the turf was the subject of his remark.

'Ah!' said Sir Matthew.

It was all he said, but it was more than enough.

Blunt fidgeted uneasily. What power possessed the boy to make him show off his riding at this juncture? If he could have stopped him, or turned him back, or waved him off!—but his will was impotent.

Monsieur Caloche, well back in the saddle, his brown eyes shining, his disfigured face flushed and glowing, with wide felt-hat drawn closely over his smooth small head, with slender knees close pressed to his horse's flanks, came riding on, jumping small logs, bending with flexible joints under straggling branches, never pausing in his reckless course, until on a sudden he found himself almost in front of the buggy, and, reining up, was confronted in full by the savage gleam of Sir Matthew's eyes. It was with the old scared expression that he pulled off his wideawake and bared his head, black and silky as a young retriever's. Sir Matthew knew how to respond to the boy's greeting. He stood up in the buggy and shook his fist at him; his voice, hoarse from the work he had given it that morning, coming out with rasping intensity.

'What the devil do you mean by riding my 'orses' tails off, eh?'

Monsieur Caloche, in his confusion, straining to catch the full meaning of the question, looked fearfully round at the hind-quarters of the two-year-old, as if some hitherto unknown phenomenon peculiar to Australian horses might in fact have suddenly left them tailless.

---

1   From Edmund Spenser (1552–99), *The Faerie Queen*, Book 1, 'A Gentle Knight was pricking on the plain'.

But the tail was doing good service against the flies at the moment of his observation, that, reassured, he turned his wistful gaze upon Sir Matthew.

'Monsieur,' he began apologetically, 'permit that I explain it to you. I did ga-lopp.'

'You can ga-lopp to hell!' said Sir Matthew with furious mimicry. 'I'll teach you to ruin my 'orses' legs!'

Blunt saw him lift his whip and strike Monsieur Caloche on the chest. The boy turned so unnaturally white that the manager looked to see him reel in his saddle. But he only swayed forward and slipped to the ground on his feet. Sir Matthew, sitting down again in the buggy with an uncomfortable sensation of some undue excess it might have been as well to recall, saw this white face for the flash of an instant's space, saw its desperation, its shame, its trembling lips; then he was aware that the two-year-old stood riderless in front of him, and away in the distance the figure of a lad was speeding through the timber, one hand held against his chest, his hat gone and he unheeding, palpably sobbing and crying in his loneliness and defencelessness as he stumbled blindly on.

Run-away boys, I fear, call forth very little solicitude in any heart but a mother's. A cat may be nine-lived, but a boy's life is centuple. He seems only to think it worth keeping after the best part of it is gone. Boys run away from schools, from offices, from stations, without exciting more than an ominous prognostication that they will go to the bad. According to Sir Matthew's inference, Monsieur Caloche had 'gone to the bad' long ago—*ergo*, it was well to be rid of him. This being so, what utterly inconsistent crank had laid hold of the head of the great firm of Bogg & Company, and tortured him through a lengthy afternoon and everlasting night, with the vision of two despairing eyes and a scarred white face? Even his hobby cried out against him complainingly. It was not for this that it had borne him prancing along. Not to confront him night and day with eyes so distressful that he could see nothing else. Would it be always so? Would they shine mournfully out of the dim recesses of his gloomy office in Flinders Lane, as they shone here in the wild bush on all sides of him?—so relentlessly sad that it would have been a relief to see them change into the vindictive eyes of the Furies who gave chase to Orestes.[1] There was clearly only one remedy against such a fate, and that was to change the nature of the expression which haunted him by calling up another in its place. But how and when!

Sir Matthew prowled around the homestead the second morning after Monsieur Caloche's flight, in a manner unaccountable to himself. That he should return 'possessed' to his elaborate warehouse, where he would be

---

1   In Aeschyles's *Oresteia*, Orestes is tormented by the Furies after murdering his mother Clytemnestra.

alone all day—and his house of magnificent desolation, where he would be alone all night, was fast becoming a matter of impossibility. What sums out of all proportion would he not have forfeited to have seen the white-faced foreign lad, and to be able to pay him out for the discomfort he was causing him—instead of being bothered by the sight of his 'cursed belongings' at every turn! He could not go into the stable without seeing some of his gimcracks; when he went blustering into the kitchen it was to stumble over a pair of miniature boots, and a short curl of hair, in silken rings, fell off the ledge at his very feet. There was only one thing to be done! Consulting with Blunt, clumsily enough, for nothing short of desperation would have induced Sir Matthew to approach the topic of Monsieur Caloche, he learned that nothing had been seen or heard of the lad since the moment of his running away.

'And 'twasn't in the direction of the township, neither,' added Blunt, gravely. 'I doubt the sun'll have made him stupid, and he'll have camped down some place on the run.'

Blunt's insinuation anent the sun was sheer artifice, for Blunt, in his private heart, did not endorse his own suggestion in the least degree. It was his belief that the lad had struck a shepherd's hut, and was keeping (with a show of common-sense he had not credited him with) out of the way of his savage employer. But it was worth while making use of the artifice to see Sir Matthew's ill-concealed uneasiness. Hardly the same Sir Matthew, in any sense, as the bullying growler who had driven by his side not two days ago. For *this* morning the double-seated buggy was the scene of neither plaints nor abuse. Quietly over the bush track—where last Monsieur Caloche, with his hand to his breast, had run sobbing along—the two men drove, their wheels passing over a wideawake hat, lying neglected and dusty in the road. For more than an hour and a half they followed the track, the dusty soil that had been witness to the boy's flight still indicating at intervals traces of a small footprint. The oppressive calm of the atmosphere seemed to have left even the ridges of dust undisturbed. Blunt reflected that it must have been 'rough on a fellow' to run all that way in the burning sun. It perplexed him, moreover, to remember that the shepherd's hut would be now far in their rear. Perhaps it was with a newly-born sense of uneasiness on his own account that he flicked his whip and made the trotter 'go', for no comment could be expected from Sir Matthew, sitting in complete silence by his side.

To Blunt's discerning eyes the last of the footprints seemed to occur right in the middle of the track. On either side was the plain. Ostensibly, Sir Matthew had come that way to look at the sheep. There was, accordingly, every reason for turning to the right, and driving towards a belt of timber some hundred yards away, and there were apparently more forcible reasons still for making for a particular tree—a straggling tree, with some pretensions to a meagre shade, the sight of which called forth an ejaculation, not entirely coherent, from Blunt.

Sir Matthew saw the cause of Blunt's ejaculation—a recumbent figure that had probably reached 'the quiet haven of us all'—it lay so still. But whether quiet or no, it would seem that to disturb its peace was a matter of life or death to Sir Matthew Bogg. Yet surely here was satiety of the fullest for his hobby! Had he not 'dropped on to the "foreign adventurer" unawares'? So unawares, in fact, that Monsieur Caloche never heeded his presence, or the presence of his working manager, but lay with a glaze on his half-closed eyes in stiff unconcern at their feet.

The clerks and juniors in the outer office of the great firm of Bogg & Co. would have been at some loss to recognise their chief in the livid man who knelt by the dead lad's side. He wanted to feel his heart, it appeared, but his trembling fingers failed him. Blunt comprehended the gesture. Whatever of tenderness Monsieur Caloche had expended in his short lifetime was repaid by the gentleness with which the working manager passed his hand under the boy's rigid neck. It was with a shake of the head that seemed to Sir Matthew like the fiat of his doom that Blunt unbuttoned Monsieur Caloche's vest and discovered the fair, white throat beneath. Unbuttoning still—with tremulous fingers, and a strange apprehension creeping chillily over him—the manager saw the open vest fall loosely asunder, and then—

Yes; then it was proven that Sir Matthew's hobby had gone its extremest length. Though it could hardly have been rapture at its great triumph that filled his eyes with such a strange expression of horror as he stood looking fearfully down on the corpse at his feet. For he had, in point of fact, 'dropped on to it unawares'; but it was no longer Monsieur Caloche he had 'dropped on to', but a girl, with breast of marble, bared in its cold whiteness to the open daylight, and to his ardent gaze. Bared, without any protest from the half-closed eyes, unconcerned behind the filmy veil which glazed them. A virgin breast, spotless in hue, save for a narrow purple streak, marking it in a dark line from the collar-bone downwards. Sir Matthew knew, and the working manager knew, and the child they called Monsieur Caloche had known, by whose hand the mark had been imprinted. It seemed to Sir Matthew that a similar mark, red hot like a brand, must now burn on his own forehead for ever. For what if the hungry Australian sun, and emotion, and exhaustion had been the actual cause of the girl's death? he acknowledged in the bitterness of his heart, that the 'cause of the cause' was his own bloodstained hand.

It must have been poor satisfaction to his hobby, after this, to note that Blunt had found a tiny pocket-book on the person of the corpse, filled with minute foreign handwriting. Of which nothing could be made! For, with one exception, it was filled with French quotations all of the same tenor—all pointing to the one conclusion—and clearly proving (if it has not been proved already) that a woman who loses her beauty loses her all. The English quotation will be known to some readers of Shakespeare, 'So beauty blemished once for ever's lost!'[1] Affixed to it was the faintly-traced signature of Henriette Caloche.

So here was a sort of insight into the mystery. The 'foreign adventurer' might be exonerated after all. No baser designs need be laid at the door of dead 'Monsieur Caloche' than the design of hiding the loss which had deprived her of all glory in her sex. If, indeed, the loss were a *real* one! For beauty is more than skin-deep, although Monsieur Caloche had not known it. It is of the bone, and the fibre, and the nerves that thrill through the brain. It is of the form and the texture too, as any one would have allowed who scrutinised the body prone in the dust. Even the cruel scars seemed merciful now, and relaxed their hold on the chiselled features, as though 'eloquent, just, and mightie Death'[2] would suffer no hand but his own to dally with his possession.

It is only in Christmas stories, I am afraid, where, in deference to so rollicking a season, everything is bound to come right in the end, that people's natures are revolutionised in a night, and from narrow-minded villains they become open-hearted seraphs of charity. Still, it is on record of the first Henry that from the time of the sinking of the *White Ship*, 'he never smiled again'.[3] I cannot say that Sir Matthew was never known to smile, in his old sour way, or that he never growled or scolded, in his old bullying fashion, after the discovery of Monsieur Caloche's body. But he was none the less a changed man. The outside world might rightly conjecture that henceforth a slender, mournful-eyed shadow would walk by his side through life. But what can the outside world know of the refinement of mental anguish that may be endured by a mind awakened too late? In Sir Matthew's case—relatively as well as positively. For constant contemplation of a woman's pleading eyes and a dead statuesque form might give rise to imaginings that it would be maddening to dwell upon. What a wealth of caresses those stiff little hands had had it in their power to bestow! What a power of lighting up the solemnest office, and—be sure—the greatest, dreariest house, was latent in those dejected eyes!

Brooding is proverbially bad for the liver. Sir Matthew died of the liver complaint, and his will was cited as an instance of the eccentricity of a wealthy Australian, who, never having been in France, left the bulk of his money to the purpose of constructing and maintaining a magnificent wing to a smallpox

---

1   From *The Passionate Pilgrim* (1609), stanza 13.
2   From Sir Walter Raleigh (1552–1618), *The History of the World* (1614).
3   Henry I of England lost his only son and heir William when the White Ship sank in the English Channel on 25 November 1120.

hospital in the south of France. It was stipulated that it should be called the 'Henriette' wing, and is, I believe, greatly admired by visitors from all parts of the world.

1890

BESSIE CAMERON
c. 1851 – 1895

The child of a Noongar couple, Bessie Flower spent her childhood at an Anglican boarding school in Annesfield, WA. As a young woman she travelled to Sydney and furthered her education in English literature, history, scripture and music.

In a plan devised by the Reverend Hagenauer to ensure the maintenance of Christianity in Aboriginal belief systems, Flower travelled with a group of Aboriginal women from WA to Ramahyuck Mission, Victoria, in 1867. They were to be married to Christian Kurnai men; however, Flower became the teacher at the Ramahyuck Mission school, a servant and tutor to the Hagenauer children.

Flower caught the attention of a white man who asked Hagenauer for her hand in marriage. Hagenauer disapproved, and in 1868 he quickly married Flower to Donald Cameron, a Jupagilwournditch man. The marriage was not entirely successful and, after losing the favour of Hagenauer, the Camerons moved in 1883 to Cameron's traditional lands near Ebenezer in western Victoria for some time, before returning to Gippsland, though not to the Ramahyuck or Lake Tyers missions where Bessie Cameron would have preferred to be. She wrote numerous letters requesting permission to live at Lake Tyers and in 1884 was allowed to return.

Her letters were published in the *Church of England Weekly*, *Gippsland Mercury* and *Argus*. AH/PM

Letter to the Editor

Having read in the Australasian of the 27th of March an account of 'The Vagabond's' impression of the people of Lake Tyers, I was moved to write a letter in defence.

In the first place, I will not say much on his style of calling us niggers, as he told us in his address that he was an American. Now, all respect to Mr Vagabond, but I know the way the niggers have been treated in America.

Secondly, Mr Vagabond says it was related to him that the Rev. F.A. Hagenauer knocked down a loafing blackfellow three times. Now, I have lived on Ramahyuck many years, and never in my time did it happen, nor before as I was told. Mr Hagenauer is not [of] a fighting nature; he managed us by kindness.

Thirdly, Mr Vagabond said he 'did not find the houses particularly clean and well kept.' He forgot that he went around inspecting at 9 o'clock on Saturday morning, just in the middle of cleaning.

If Mr Vagabond was a Benedict he would know all about the business of house-cleaning on a Saturday; but, then, in his own house there would be a room set apart for visitors, and we have only two rooms, so he must excuse us at not finding that house clean and tidy at 9 o'clock Saturday morning.

In conclusion, I must say the words, 'Very lazy and useless is my summary of the Lake Tyers blackfellow,' are very sad, as there is some truth in them, yet still there is some work done, or else the station could not go on as it has done. But, as Mr Vagabond asks himself, 'Would I, in this place' and goes onto say, 'As I am a truthful judge of my own character I am compelled to admit I would not,' so we will take courage from that, and go on our way, trying what is in our power to bring up our children to earn their own living, and be useful members of society, and ourselves to be grateful to the board and our missionaries for all their kindness and patience to us aboriginals.

Hoping, Sir, you will excuse my taking up a little of your valuable time, as I am writing this in the name of all my coloured brethren and sisters of Lake Tyers.

1886

E. J. BANFIELD
1852–1923

Born in Liverpool, England, Edward James Banfield worked extensively as a journalist before becoming subeditor of the *Townsville Daily Bulletin* in 1882. After a health collapse, Banfield and his wife Bertha (Golding) began searching for an island to live on, and applied for a lease of one section of Dunk Island on the Great Barrier Reef in 1897. Banfield's articles about the island, luxuriating in its tropical flora and fauna, observing the local Wangamaygan people and extolling the virtues of a life removed from society, began appearing in newspapers from 1907. They were collected as *The Confessions of a Beachcomber* in 1908.

The book was an international hit for Banfield, appealing as a combination of nature and travel writing, and bringing fame to the reef. Later collections included *My Tropic Isle* (1911) and *Tropic Days* (1918), and, posthumously, *Last Leaves from Dunk Island* (1925). *NM*

From *The Confessions of a Beachcomber*
Chapter 1: Our Island

[. . .] Our Island! What was it when we came into possession? From the sea, merely a range displaying the varied leafage of jungle and forest. A steep headland springing from a ledge of rock on the north, and a broad, embayed-based flat converging into an obtruding sand-spit to the west, enclose a bay scarcely half a mile from one horn to the other, the sheet of water almost a perfect crescent, with the rocky islet of Purtaboi, plumed with trees, to indicate the circumference of a circle. Trees come to the water's edge from the abutment of the bold eminence. Dome-shaped shrubs of glossy green (native cabbage—*Scaevola Koenigii*), with groups of pandanus palms bearing massive orange-coloured fruits; and here and there graceful umbrella-trees, with deep-red decorations, hibiscus bushes hung with yellow funnells, and a thin line of ever-sighing beech oaks (*casuarina*) fringe the clean untrodden sand. Behind is the vistaless forest of the flat.

Run the boat on the sand at high-water, and the first step is planted in primitive bush—fragrant, clean and undefiled. An empty jam tin or a broken bottle, spoors of the rude hoofs of civilisation, you might search for in vain. As difficult would it be to find either as a fellow to the nugget of gold which legend tells was used by a naked black as a sinker when he fished with hook of pearl shell out there on the edge of the coral reef.

One superficial feature of our domain is distinct and peculiar, giving to it an admirable character. From the landing-place—rather more up towards the north-east cusp than the exact middle of the crescent bay—extends a flat of black sand on which grows a dense bush of wattles, cockatoo apple-trees, pandanus palms, Moreton Bay ash and other eucalypts, and the shapely melaleuca. This flat, here about 150 yards in breadth, ends abruptly at a steep bank which gives access to a plateau 60 feet above sea-level. The regularity of the outline of this bank is remarkable. Running in a more or less correct curve for a mile and a half, it indicates a clear-cut difference between the flat and the plateau. The toe of the bank rests upon sand, while the plateau is of chocolate-coloured soil intermixed on the surface with flakes of slate; and from this sure foundation springs the backbone of the island. On the flat, the plateau, and the hillsides, the forest consists of similar trees—alike in age and character for all the difference in soil—the one tree that does not leave the flat being the tea or melaleuca. In some places the jungle comes down to the water's edge, the long antennae of the lawyer vine toying with the rod-like aerial roots of the mangrove.

The plateau is the park of the island, half a mile broad, and a mile and more long. Upon it grows the best of the bloodwoods (*Eucalyptus corynbosa*), the red stringy bark (*E. robusta*), Moreton Bay ash (*E. tessalaris*), various wattles, the gin-gee of the blacks (*Diplanthera tetraphylla*). *Pandanus aquaticus* marks the courses and curves of some of the gullies. A creek, hidden in a broad ribbon of jungle and running from a ravine in the range to the sea, divides our park in fairly equal portions.

Most part of the range is heavily draped with jungle—that is, on the western aspect. Just above the splash of the Pacific surges on the weather or eastern side, low-growing scrub and restricted areas of forest, with expansive patches of jungle, plentifully intermixed with palms and bananas, creep up the precipitous ascent to the summit of the range—870 feet above the sea. So steep is the Pacific slope that, standing on the top of the ridge and looking down, you catch mosaic gleams of the sea among the brown and grey tree-trunks. But for the prodigality of the vegetation, one slide might take you from the cool mountain-top to the cooler sea. The highest peak, which presents a buttressed face to the north, and overlooks our peaceful bay, is crowned with a forest of bloodwoods, upon which the jungle steadily encroaches. The swaying fronds of aspiring palms, adorned in due season with masses of straw-coloured inflorescence, to be succeeded by loose bunches of red, bead-like berries, shoot out from the pall of leafage. In the gloomy gullies are slender-shafted palms and tree-ferns, while ferns and mosses cover the soil with living tapestry, and strange, snake-like epiphytes cling in sinuous curves to the larger trees. The trail of the lawyer vine (*Calamus obstruens*), with its leaf sheath and long tentacles bristling with incurved hooks, is over it all. Huge cables of vines trail from tree to tree, hanging in loops and knots and festoons, the largest (*Entada scandens*) bearing pods 4 feet long and 4 inches broad, containing a dozen or so brown hard beans used for match-boxes. Along the edge of the jungle, the climbing fern (*Lygodium*) grows in tangled masses sending its slender wire-like lengths up among the trees—the most attractive of all the ferns, and glorified by some with the title of 'the Fern of God,' so surpassing its grace and beauty.

September is the prime month of the year in tropical Queensland. Many of the trees are then in blossom and most of the orchids. Nocturnal showers occur fairly regularly in normal seasons, and every sort of vegetable is rampant with the lust of life. It was September when our isolation began. And what a plenteous realisation it all was that the artificial emotions of the town had been, haply, abandoned! The blood tingled with keen appreciation of the crispness, the cleanliness of the air. We had won disregard of all the bother and contradictions, the vanities and absurdities of the toilful, wayward, human world, and had acquired a glorious sense of irresponsibleness and independence.

This—this was our life we were beginning to live—our very own life; not life hampered and restricted by the wills, wishes and whims of others; unencumbered by the domineering wisdom, unembarrassed by the formal courtesies of the crowd.

September and the gin-gee, the quaint, grey-barked, soft-wooded tree with broad, rough, sage-green leaves, and florets massed in clumps to resemble sunflowers, was in all its pride, attracting relays of honey-imbibing birds during the day, and at night dozens of squeaking flying-foxes. Within a few yards of high-water stands a flame-tree (*Erythrina indica*) the 'bingum' of the blacks. Devoid of leaves in this leafy month, the bingum arrays itself in a robe of royal red. All birds and manner of birds, and butterflies and bees and beetles, which have regard for colour and sweetness come hither to feast. Sulphur-crested cockatoos sail down upon the red raiment of the tree, and tear from it shreds until all the grass is ruddy with refuse, and their snowy breasts stained as though their feast was of blood instead of colourless nectar. For many days here is a scene of a perpetual banquet—a noisy, cheerful, frolicsome revel. Cockatoos scream with excitement and gladness; honey-eaters whistle and call; drongos chatter and scold the rest of the banqueters; the tiny sun-bird twitters feeble protests; bees and beetles maintain a murmurous soothful sound, a drowsy blending of hum and buzz from the rising of the sun until the going down thereof.

The dark compactness of the jungle, the steadfast but disorderly array of the forest, the blotches of verdant grass, the fringe of yellow-flowered hibiscus and the sapful native cabbage, give way in turn to the greys and yellows of the sand in alternate bands. The slowly-heaving sea trailing the narrowest flounce of lace on the beach, the dainty form of Purtaboi, and the varying tones of great Australia beyond combine to complete the scene, and to confirm the thought that here is the ideal spot, the freest spot, the spot where dreams may harden into realities, where unvexed peace may smile.

There is naught to remind of the foetidness, the blare and glare of the streets. None of

> 'The weariness, the fever and the fret,
> There, where men sit and hear each other groan.'[1]

You may follow up the creeks until they become miniature ravines, or broaden out into pockets with precipitous sides, where twilight reigns perpetually, and where sweet soft gases are generated by innumerable plants, and distilled from the warm moist soil. How grateful and revivifying! Among the half-lit crowded groves might not another Medea gather enchanted herbs such as 'did renew old Æson'.[2]

Past the rocky horn of Brammo Bay, another crescent indents the base of the hill. Exposed to the north-east breeze, the turmoil of innumerable gales has torn tons upon tons of coral from the out-lying reef, and cast up the débris, with tinkling chips and fragments of shells, on the sand for the sun and the tepid rains to bleach into dazzling whiteness. The coral drift has swept up among the dull grey rocks and made a ridge beneath the pendant branches of the trees, as if to establish a contrast between the sombre tints of the jungle and the blueness of the sea. Midway along the curve of vegetation a bingum flaunts its mantle—a single daub of demonstrative colouring. Away to the north stand out the Barnard Islands, and the island-like headland of Double-Point. […]

At no season of the year is the island fragrantless. The prevailing perception may be of lush grasses mingled with the soft odour of their frail flowers; or the resin and honey of blossoming bloodwoods; or the essence from

---

1   From John Keats (1795–1821), 'Ode to a Nightingale'.
2   From William Shakespeare, *The Merchant of Venice*, V. i. 14.

myriads of other eucalyptus leaves massaged by the winds. The incomparable beach-loving calophyllums yield a profuse but tender fragrance reminiscent of English meadow-sweet, and the flowers of a vigorous trailer (*Canavila obtusifolia*), for ever exploring the bare sand at high-water mark, resembles the sweet-pea in form and perfume. The white cedar (*Melia composita*) is a welcome and not unworthy substitute in appearance and perfume for English lilac. The aromatic pandanus and many varieties of acacia, each has its appointed time and season; while at odd intervals the air is saturated with the rich and far-spreading incense of the melaleuca, and for many weeks together with the honeyed excellence of the swamp mahogany (*Tristania suaveolens*) and the over-rich cloyness of the cockatoo apple (*Careya australis*). Strong and spicy are the odours of the plants and trees that gather on the edge of and crowd in the jungle, the so-called native ginger, nutmeg, quandong, milkwood, bean-tree, the kirri-cue of the blacks (*Eupomatia laurina*), koie-yan (*Faradaya splendida*), with its great white flowers and snowy fruit, and many others. Hoya, heavy and indolent, trails across and dangles from the rocks; the river mangrove dispenses its sweetness in an unexpected locality; and from the heart of the jungle come wafts of warm breath, which, mingling with exhalation from foliage and flower, is diffused broadcast. The odour of the jungle is definite—earthy somewhat, but of earth clean, wholesome and moist—the smell of moss, fern and fungus blended with balsam, spice and sweetness.

Many a time, home-returning at night—when the black contours of the island loomed up in the distance against the pure tropic sky tremulous with myriads of unsullied stars—has its tepid fragrance drifted across the water as a salutation and a greeting. It has long been a fancy of mine that the island has a distinctive odour, soft and pliant, rich and vigorous. Other mixtures of forest and jungle may smell as strong; but none has the rare blend which I recognise and gloat over whensoever, after infrequent absences for a day or two, I return to accept of it in grateful sniffs. In such a fervid and encouraging clime distillation is continuous and prodigious. Heat and moisture and a plethora of raw material, leaves, flowers, soft, sappy and fragrant woods, growing grass and moist earth, these are the essential elements for the manufacture of ethereal and soul-soothing odours—suggestive of tangible flavours. [...]

1908

TAAM SZE PUI
c. 1853–1926

Taam Sze Pui's father migrated to Far North Queensland with his two sons around 1876, in search of gold. The family came from the Sam Yap ('Three Districts') of Guangdong Province in southern China. Having no luck on the Palmer goldfield, they moved to the Johnstone River to clear land. By 1883 Taam had saved enough money to send his father back to China and set himself up as a storekeeper. Business prospered and Taam was soon sole owner of what would become See Poy & Sons, a large department store in Innisfail that stayed in the family until the 1980s. Despite the distance between China and Australia, kinship ties remained strong as funds were remitted and more relatives came to join the business. In 1897 a bride for Taam called Tue Chang-han was sent from China; she became his partner in the business. They had five children. Taam learned English from a local schoolmaster and was naturalised in 1897 and again in 1901. Towards the end of a successful life, he produced an autobiography (published bilingually in 1925) in which he gives advice to later generations, stressing traditional Chinese virtues of simplicity and right conduct. *My Life and Work* gives a rare and evocative account of early Chinese immigrant experience. NJ

From *My Life and Work*

There was a rumour then that gold had been discovered in a place called Cooktown and the source of which was inexhaustible and free to all. Without verifying the truth, my father planned to go with his two sons. We started from our village on January the 18th, 1877. On January 22nd we sailed from Hongkong and reached our destination on February 10th of the same year.

Oh, what a disappointment when we learnt that the rumour was unfounded and we were misled! Not only was gold difficult to find, the climate was not suitable and was the cause of frequent attacks of illness. As we went about, there met our gaze the impoverished condition and the starved looks of our fellow countrymen who were either penniless or ill, and there reached our ears endless sighs of sorrow. Those who arrived first not only expressed no regret for being late: on the contrary, they were thinking of departing. Could we, who had just arrived, remain untouched at these sad tales?

But since we had come, we might make an attempt. Therefore we bought hoes, shovels, provisions, utensils, etc. Carrying or balancing on the shoulders the supplies, we started on foot in a company in the direction of the mountain region on February the 16th, 1877. When we had accomplished sixteen miles, night came and we had to stop. Sleeping in the dew and exposed to the wind, the hardship is better imagined than described.

Early on the third morning, we resumed our journey. Walking sometimes slowly and sometimes briskly, we kept close to the groups, not daring to detach ourselves lest we should be set upon by the black natives and probably be devoured by them. The fear of such a fate kept one and all together, and no one dared tarry behind to rest or to regain his breath. At the 20th mile, we came upon a stream. Here we put down our burdens, prepared to cook and each attended to his own work. Thus we rested for two days before starting again.

This time, we had to climb stiff cliffs and scale over high precipices, which so exhausted us at the 26th mile that we could hardly move a step further. All wanted to rest, and this we did for three days. Then we advanced as far as the 40th mile. At this point, a torrential rain had caused the stream to rise and we had no boat to cross by. We could do nothing but sigh. Braving wind and rain, we patiently waited for the stream to dry. Our provisions had now been consumed. I was forced to return to Cooktown for supplies. The journey was resumed as soon as the water began to subside.

It was about a month after we had started when we reached the 52nd mile, where we rested. Here we came to a great plain as wide and open as a road. Proceeding to the 72nd mile, we reached a place called 'The Foot of the Great Mountain'. Behold, before us was a great mountain with the peak projecting high up into the clouds and whose height was beyond my calculation. We made our climb at a slow pace and zigzagged down on the other side. Inquiring of some companions, I was told we had travelled eighty-two miles. Completely worn out and weary, some discarded part of their supplies to lighten the burden, and some were in tears. Our limbs were numb; our shoulders were bruised and bleeding. When attempts were made to change our clothes, it was necessary to forcibly pull the clothes from the coagulated blood; the pain was unendurable. 'Alas, to suffer this torture of the flesh for no wrong doing.' I sighed bitterly.

Tarrying for a few days, we advanced again. Very soon, we reached the 96th mile, and stopped. Driven by hunger, we approached an English bakery there and begged for bread. Fortunately, the Englishman took pity on us and gave us some. Thus our hunger was appeased.

It took us fully three months to cover one hundred miles in our journey. We then began to sift sand, but to our utter disappointment, there was no gold.

… [After] five years had passed, I … realized that to search for gold was like trying to catch the moon at the bottom of the sea.

1925

AUDREY TENNYSON
1854–1916

Letter writer Audrey, Lady Tennyson, was born in England and married Hallam, eldest son of the English poet laureate Alfred, Lord Tennyson, in 1884. She accompanied him to Australia in 1899 when he was appointed governor of South Australia; he later served as Australia's governor-general from 1902 to 1903. Lady Tennyson's letters to her mother, written during this period, offer a vivid account of their travels and her reactions to the people and scenes she encountered. Edited by Alexandra Hasluck, they were published as *Audrey Tennyson's Vice-Regal Days* (1978). *EW*

Letter to Her Mother

26 July 1899. Oodnadatta

Here we are right up in Central Australia as far as the railway goes & when we looked out of the train windows this morning it really looked as if we had come to the end of the world. Just close round us ½ a dozen white, low, one-storeyed houses of wood with iron roofs, an hotel rather larger than the rest, a railway station, a most primitive little school & besides that, nothing to be seen but dreary red soil, not a plant, a tree or shrub to be seen, but far away in the distance a slight rise in the ground of some hills. But I had better begin from when we left Adelaide on Monday in our special train at 3.10. [...]

We dined the first night where we changed carriages at Terowie and had an excellent repast, I the only lady among all these men; then we went on in our new carriage & instead of our well-lit vice-regal carriage found it too dark to read. The man came in at 10 & made up the beds & I was very glad to go to bed for it was bitterly cold & to my great joy Clarke had brought my hot water bag and heated some water for it. I slept very well tho' of course waking every time the train stopped & to my great joy woke up with no headache. [...]

We were woken by children's voices singing God Save the Queen at a place called Beltana. [...] We next stopped at Leigh's Creek where we moved into the Railway Commissioner's carriage with whom we are travelling. Here at the station (a lovely morning but cold & crisp, about 8) we got out & bid goodbye to a Mr Gee. His wife and he were going to drive 600 miles to inspect the new gold mine at Worturpa which has just been found, or at least they hope so but it is doubtful yet whether it will turn out trumps or not. [...] Then on we went & next stopped at Farina about 10 & there we found about 50 schoolchildren with school mistress & master, the clergyman Mr Wilkinson, about a dozen blacks, men & women, two Afghans with turbans with their camels, & most of the leading inhabitants of the township. We got out after God Save the Queen was sung & I was given a bouquet or rather basket of flowers tied with red & yellow ribbons by one of the children, various little bunches of flowers by the other children & a basket of all the different minerals they find about there. It was quite pathetic the way they had all nearly got red & yellow rosettes. [...]

Everything, even every vegetable they have, is taken out fortnightly only by train so you may be sure they had to pay well for it. We shook hands & talked with all the adults including the blacks, all very warm & so delighted to see us, poor people, beaming. Then when the train had to go on the children sang the National Song of Australia; we got back into our carriage & were loudly cheered out of the little station.

These people are much better off than most of the townships. There are 200 inhabitants & church & school & clergyman, but many have none of these things, & have not even a store so they depend absolutely & entirely on the fortnightly train. And yet, somehow, perhaps with only two or three families, hundreds of miles from anybody they are all quite happy & contented & say they love the free bush life. All very well dressed—their parents if not they, having come from home, & are sometimes years without coming down to Adelaide. Their husbands mend the line or have the station, post & telegraph office all in one, or are store keepers or little hotel keepers—or own camels for carrying things from the train to the distant stations (farms). And at all these townships along the line the oxen & cattle are put into the trains having been driven 30, 40, 50 miles & more from the nearest stations & brought down to Adelaide either for export or for the town.

They say that drink is the curse of South Australia for although they can't get *any* out at the stations, when they come to any inn they will drink as much as £40 & £50 worth in a week & get robbed besides, & so with the wages they get, they never get rich. A head of a station told me he gives the youngest boy on his station 7/6 a week & the men up to 35/-, house *and* feed them—they are always fed on the station. Mr Ralli told me he gives 15/- the lowest & 30/- or 35/- the highest but all housed & fed & cooked for, or if they are married they have rations given them for the whole family. Government by law is not allowed to give an experienced adult less than 6/- a day but not fed or housed.

From Farina the next place of anything particular after we had stopped & gone into the Commissioner's carriage for luncheon was a place called 'Blanche Cup' where we were met by a Mr Olive & his son, with a cart called a buckboard & 4 horses in which I, H. & one of the other men drove, with the father as driver & the son riding in front to show a track to go along & 2nd vehicle with two horses in which Clarke & the other men came. The son wore spurs about 4 inches long which I was told came from England & were far less cruel than the short ones as you cannot have so much strength to prod them on—and they scarcely ever use them but must have them in case of emergency. These men had come from their station 28 miles off the day before to meet us & drive us to these springs—extremely well dressed in blue serges & very white shirts & felt hats, but burnt wasn't the word for their faces & hands.

Mr Olive told me he was the head man who lives at one & superintends the 15 stations belonging to the [blank] Company the Chairman of which is a Mr Angas, a very wealthy man who lives here in Adelaide. At this station where he & his son & 30 labourers, a female cook & her daughter, live, they have 6000 head of cattle & 1000 horses. I don't know how many sheep, & they drive cattle down every fortnight to the little station where we got out, about 150 at a time. The drovers ride & the cattle saunter along constantly stopping to eat the blue brush, & they generally only get on about 5 miles a day. They call them 'mobs', & we passed several mobs of several hundreds, sometimes a thousand, feeding in a mass; the men take it in turn two or three at a time for two hours at a time, to watch them day & night & then they are packed into these van trains, generally special ones to get them down here faster. Mr Olive told me . . . he had killed by rifle or poison 500 dingoes—wild dogs—last year, 400 the year before. [. . .]

After Blanche Cup and having left Mr Olive & his carriages of which as well as the natural springs I took some photographs, we got into the train again & went on to Coward's Creek—creek means a place where water is—& here at the little station was just the white wooden Inn & one or two houses and a water bore, which the Government sunk with others along the line 1300 feet, & from which a million million gallons of water a day pours out & has done day & night for 12 years, tepid & sometimes hot. They make use of it in building the line, and animals can drink it but it is not pure enough even to use for the engine's boiler—they tried to use it & found it impossible. [. . .]

We arrived at Oodnadatta about midnight but had long before gone to bed & only got up the next morning in time for 9 o'clock breakfast. Hallam heard what he thought was a cow bellowing but it turned out to be a camel. It was a lovely bright morning, Wednesday, but with very cold wind & on looking out on this barren place we saw a touching little decoration of festoons of mixed coloured ribbons at the station & a large Union Jack & a large yellow flag with a red lion on it, floating at the Inn whence, after all greeting each other outside our carriages, we walked across to breakfast. The Hotel kept by a Scotchman, Mr Ferguson, & we were waited on by his two daughters, everything very good—porridge delicious, bacon & eggs etc. etc. After breakfast we walked back to the station to see Mr Winter the station master who is 'boss' of the whole place, postmaster, telegraph—marries & buries the people. He had married a Chinaman & a half-caste on the 1st June—when the Chinaman asked how much it would cost & was told £3, he said, 'No, won't do, much too dear.'

He & his friend another Chinaman keep a market garden about 5 miles off and we drove to see it in the afternoon—the most enormous cauliflowers & cabbage & heaps of vegetables coming on. They found this fertile strip near a creek and have worked at it splendidly—charge 4d. for a cauliflower. We were introduced with great pride to the bride, hideously ugly, and a small boy of three very like his father & a small *white* baby, as white as my own which was rather puzzling but I made no remarks & asked no questions. The bride was fetched out of a small tent just covered with thin unbleached calico—they must freeze at night—in which stood a bedstead covered with a striped rug on which she & the children were sitting, the one sole piece of furniture in this home & at a little distance the kitchen—no tent or covering, a hole dug in the sand for the fire, two or three pots & pans & a broken white case as larder in which was a basket of fresh eggs & some bits—rag & rubbish. The partner Chinaman had another little tent with just a few bedclothes on the ground. One of these men has £250 in the Bank.

After seeing Mr Winter, Mrs Winter was brought out to be presented to me & then asked me into her house, a very nice one, & I was invited to sit by the fire in the parlour. She has 8 children . . . & was much distressed at there being no sort of service or Sunday school on Sundays & the 18 little children at the school know nothing about religion. But what struck one at all these out-of-the-way places is the happiness & content of all these people. They say they love the free life. Mrs White told me a great deal about the natives. She has two—Mary Jane & Annie—as servants to help her & evidently likes the blacks & feels for them but she says they are very trying. She can teach them all the rough work—but at any moment they may come & say 'I tired work—must go walkee-about one week or one moon etc.' and off they go to the camp which is about 1½ miles from the township if any of their tribe happen to be there. There is always a camp of some tribe or other there, for at Oodnadatta stores & blankets are given away by Government every week to any blacks who come & ask for them. They are given out every Saturday now by the trooper (the Police Sergeant) who lives there with a black police 'boy' under him. The present trooper, Mr Ireland, is the son of a Gloucestershire well-to-do Rector, & a University man. His father wanted him to take Holy Orders & he did not care for it so he came out here 18 years ago to try his fortune & loves the life. He has a thoroughly nice cheery sensible colonial wife & one child, a boy 8 years old, Stanley de Courcy Ireland! who goes to the little school with all the other children. [. . .]

Mr Ireland told me that he has made a rule that the blacks before coming for their stores have to sweep & clean up the township, & all the refuse is then burnt. If they work, they get their stores, if lazy & won't, he says, 'No, you not have flour today, you not work, you not have stores' & now they quite understand but it was very hard at first. (6 lbs flour a head, tea, sugar & tobacco.) He is devoted to his 'black boy' (policeman) & when he drives away to his distant stations to inspect he puts the house & his wife & child under his care & he would die sooner than that anything should be touched.

They *never* steal except if food is put in their way too temptingly. If once they believe that a 'white' means well to them they are devoted—but woe betide the man who treats them badly. Mr Ireland says he can go alone without any firearms anywhere among them, but many white men can't go a step without a pistol. They have been treated brutally by white men, but thank God, Government is taking up their cause very strictly this session & ill treatment will be most severely punished. They say those women I shook hands with at Farina will *never* forget it. Hallam wished one of them who could understand English to interpret to them how the Queen, he, & Government, were their friends. They are dying out fast however, & our making them wear clothes near white people & giving them blankets, alas helps to kill them for they throw off the clothes when they go off on their hunting grounds for lizards & kangaroos, emus & their eggs, rabbits & rats, & if fancy takes them, give away or leave behind their blankets. [. . .]

1899/1978

NED KELLY
1855–1880

Edward Kelly, popularly known as Ned, was born in Victoria of Irish convict parents and grew up on a selection near Glenrowan. From adolescence Kelly was in continuous trouble with the police, as were other members of his family. In 1878, after possibly false testimony from Constable Fitzpatrick, Kelly's mother was sentenced to three years' imprisonment and rewards were offered for the capture of Kelly and his younger brother Dan. They hid in the Wombat Ranges, where they were joined by Joe Byrne and Steve Hart to form what became known as the Kelly Gang. After two of the three police sent to capture them were shot, members of the gang were declared outlaws. Undeterred, they committed a number of increasingly daring raids before their final battle with the police at Glenrowan in June 1880, for which they wore homemade armour. Kelly was the only member of the gang to survive; he was executed in Melbourne on 11 November 1880 after allegedly uttering the famous last words 'Such is life'. His life has inspired numerous poems, plays, paintings, films and novels, including Peter Carey's (qv) *True History of the Kelly Gang* (2000), as well as many biographical studies such as John Molony's *I am Ned Kelly* (1980). What is now termed the 'Jerilderie Letter', Kelly's own justification for his actions, was apparently dictated to Joe Byrne, and left to be printed at Jerilderie during the gang's seizure of the town in February 1879, but to no avail. It did not appear in print until 1930. The original letter is now held in the State Library of Victoria. *EW*

The Jerilderie Letter

[. . .] I have been wronged and my mother and four or five men lagged innocent and is my brothers and sisters and my mother not to be pitied also who has no alternative only to put up with the brutal and cowardly conduct of a parcel of big ugly fat-necked wombat headed big bellied magpie legged narrow hipped splaw-footed sons of Irish Bailiffs or english landlords which is better known as Officers of Justice or Victorian Police who some calls honest gentlemen but I would like to know what business an honest man would have in the Police as it is an old saying It takes a rogue to catch a rogue and a man that knows nothing about roguery would never enter the force an take an oath to arrest brother sister father or mother if required and to have a case and conviction if possible any man knows it is possible to swear a lie and if a policeman looses a conviction for the sake of swearing a lie he has broke his oath therefore he is a perjurer either ways. A Policeman is a disgrace to his country, not alone to the mother that suckled him, in the first place he is a rogue in his heart but too cowardly to follow it up without having the force to disguise it. Next he is a traitor to his country ancestors and religion as they were all catholics before the Saxons and Cranmore yoke held sway since then they were persecuted massacred thrown into martyrdom and tortured beyond the ideas of the present generation, What would people say if they saw a strapping big lump of an Irishman shepherding sheep for fifteen bob a week or tailing turkeys in Tallarook ranges for a smile from Julia or even begging his tucker, they would say he ought to be ashamed of himself and tar-and-feather him. But he would be a king to a policeman who for a lazy loafing cowardly bilit left the ash corner deserted the shamrock, the emblem of true wit and beauty to serve under a flag and nation that has destroyed massacred and murdered their forefathers by the greatest of torture as rolling them down hill in spiked barrels pulling their toe and finger nails and on the wheel. and every torture imaginable more was transported to Van Dieman's Land to pine their young lives away in starvation and misery among tyrants worse than the promised hell itself all of true blood bone and beauty, that was not murdered on their own soil, or had fled to America or other countries to bloom again another day, were doomed to Port McQuarie, Toweringabbie Norfolk Island and Emu plains And in those places of tyrany and condemnation many a blooming Irishman rather than subdue to the Saxon yoke, Were flogged to death and bravely died in servile chains but true to the shamrock and a credit to Paddys land What would people say if I became a policeman and took an oath to arrest my brother and sisters & relations and convict them by fair or foul means after the conviction of my mother and the persecutions and insults offered to myself and people Would they say I was a decent gentleman, and yet a policeman is still in worse and guilty of meaner actions than that The Queen must surely be proud of such heroic men as the Police and Irish soldiers as It takes eight or eleven of the biggest mud crushers in Melbourne to take one poor little half starved larrakin to a watch house. I have seen as many as eleven, big & ugly enough to lift Mount Macedon out of a crab hole more like the species of a baboon or Guerilla than a man actually come into a court house and swear they could not arrest one eight stone larrakin and them armed with battens and neddies without some civilians assistance and some of them going to the hospital from the affects of hits from the fists of the larrakin and the

Magistrate would send the poor little Larrakin into a dungeon for being a better man than such a parcel of armed curs. What would England do if America declared war and hoisted a green flag as it is all Irishmen that has got command of her armies forts and batteries even her very life guards and beef tasters are Irish would they not slew around and fight her with their own arms for the sake of the colour they dare not wear for years. and to reinstate it and rise old Erins isle once more, from the pressure and tyrannism of the English yoke. which has kept it in poverty and starvation. and caused them to wear the enemys coat. What else can England expect. Is there not big fat-necked Unicorns enough paid, to torment and drive me to do thing which I don't wish to do, without the public assisting them I have never interfered with any person unless they deserved it, and yet there are civilians who take fire-arms against me, for what reason I do not know, unless they want me to turn on them and exterminate them without medicine. I shall be compelled to make an example of some of them if they cannot find no other employment

If I had robbed and plundered ravished and murdered everything I met young and old rich and poor. the public could not do any more than take firearms and assisting the police as they have done, but by the light that shines pegged on an ant-bed with their bellies opened their fat taken out rendered and poured down their throat boiling hot will be cool to what pleasure I will give some of them and any person aiding or harbouring or assisting the Police in any way whatever or employing any person whom they know to be a detective or cad or those who would be so deprived as to take blood money will be outlawed and declared unfit to be allowed human buriel their property either consumed or confiscated and them theirs and all belonging to them exterminated off the face of the earth, the enemy I cannot catch myself I shall give a payable reward for, I would like to know who put that article that reminds me of a poodle dog half clipped in the lion fashion. called Brooke. E. Smith[1] Superintendent of Police he knows as much about commanding Police as Captain Standish[2] does about mustering mosquitoes and boiling them down for their fat on the back blocks of the Lachlan for he has a head like a turnip a stiff neck as big as his shoulders narrow hipped and pointed towards the feet like a vine stake And if there is any one to be called a murderer Regarding Kennedy, Scanlan and Lonigan[3] it is that misplaced poodle he gets as much pay as a dozen good troopers, if there is any *good* in them, and what does

---

1   Alexander Brooke Smith (c. 1834–82), officer in charge of the Ovens district, 1876–78, and involved in the hunt for the Kelly Gang.

2   Frederick Charles Standish (1824–83), Chief Commissioner of Police in Victoria, 1858–80.

3   Sergeant Kennedy and Constables Scanlan and Lonigan were shot dead by Ned Kelly at Stringybark Creek in October 1878. Constable McIntyre surrendered and later escaped to report the killings.

he do for it he cannot look behind him without turning his whole frame
it takes three or four police to keep sentry while he sleeps in Wangaratta,
for fear of body snatchers do they think he is a superior animal to the
men that has to guard him *if so* why not send the men that gets big pay
and reconed superior to the common police after me and you shall soon
save the country of high salaries to men that is fit for nothing else but
getting better men than himself shot and sending orphan children to the
industrial school to make prostitutes and cads of them for the Detectives
and other evil disposed persons Send the high paid and men that received
big salaries for years in a gang by themselves after me, As it makes no
difference to them but it will give them a chance of showing whether
they are worth more pay than a common trooper or not and I think the
Public will soon find they are only in the road of good men and obtaining
money under false pretences, I do not call McIntyre a coward for I reckon
he is as game a man as wears the jacket as he had the presence of mind
to know his position, directly as he was spoken to, and only foolishness to
disobey, it was cowardice that made Lonigan and the others fight it is
only foolhardiness to disobey an outlaw as any Policeman or other man
who do not throw up their arms directly as I call on them knows the
consequence which is a speedy dispatch to Kingdom Come, I wish those
men who joined the stock protection society to withdraw their money
and give it and as much more to the widows and orphans and poor of
Greta district where I spent and will again spend many a happy day fearless
free and bold, as it only aids the police to procure false witnesses and go
whacks with men to steal horses and lag innocent men it would suit them
far better to subscribe a sum and give it to the poor of their district and
there is no fear of anyone stealing their property for no man could steal
their horses without the knowledge of the poor if any man was mean
enough to steal their property the poor would rise out to a man and find
them if they were on the face of the earth it will always pay a rich man
to be liberal with the poor and make as little enemies as he can as he shall
find if the poor is on his side he shall loose nothing by it. If they depend
in the police they shall be drove to destruction. As they can not and will
not protect them if duffing and bushranging were abolished the police
would have to cadge for their living I speak from experience as I have sold
horses and cattle innumerable and yet eight head of the culls is all ever was
found I never was interefered with whilst I kept up this successful trade.
I give fair warning to all those who has reason to fear me to sell out and
give £10 out of every hundred towards the widow and orphan fund
and do not attempt to reside in Victoria, but as short a time as possible after
reading this notice, neglect this and abide by the consequences, which shall
be worse than the rust in the wheat in Victoria or the druth of a dry season

to the grasshoppers in New South Wales I do not wish to give the order full force without giving timely warning, but I am a widows son outlawed and my orders *must* be obeyed.

1879/1930

PRICE WARUNG
1855–1911

Price Warung was the pen name adopted by journalist William Astley for his many historical stories set during the convict period. He was born in England and came to Victoria with his family in 1859. As a teenager, he met Henry Graham, who had worked as a medical officer at Port Arthur, Port Macquarie and Norfolk Island, and heard his first-hand accounts of the convict system in operation. From 1875 Astley began working as a journalist in various towns in Victoria and NSW before settling in Sydney in 1891. In May 1890 his story 'How Muster-Master Stoneman Earned His Breakfast' was published in the *Bulletin*. Over the next few years, Warung was to write more than 80 convict tales for the *Bulletin*, later collected as *Tales of the Convict System* (1892), *Tales of the Early Days* (1894) and *Tales of the Old Regime, and the Bullet of the Fated Ten* (1897). A later series written for the journal *Truth* was published as *Tales of the Isle of Death (Norfolk Island)* (1898), in the same year as *Half-Crown Bob and Tales of the Riverine*, a series set in the NSW Riverina district. In 1893 Astley became editor of *Australian Workman* but he was already suffering from a degenerative spinal condition linked to tertiary syphilis and was a morphine addict. His final years were ones of extreme poverty. *EW*

How Muster-Master Stoneman Earned His Breakfast

I

An unpretentious building of rough-hewn stone standing in the middle of a small, stockaded enclosure. A doorway in the wall of the building facing the entrance-gate to the yard. To the left of the doorway, a glazed window of the ordinary size. To its right a paneless aperture, so low and narrow that were the four upright and two transverse bars which grate it doubled in thickness no interstice would be left for the admission of light or air to the interior. Behind the bars—a face.

Sixteen hours hence that face will look its last upon the world which has stricken it countless cruel blows. In a corner of the enclosure the executioner's hand is even now busy stitching into a shapeless cap, a square of grey serge. To-morrow the same hand will use the cap to hood the face, as one of the few simple preliminaries to swinging the carcase to which the face is attached from the rude platform now in course of erection against the stockade fence and barely 20 yards in front of the stone building.

The building is the gaol—locally known as the 'cage'—of Oatlands, a small township in the midlands of Van Diemen's Land, which has gradually grown up round a convict 'muster-station', established by Governor Davey. The time is five o'clock on a September evening, 55 years ago. At nine o'clock on the following morning, Convict Glancy, No. 17,927, transportee *ex* ship Pestonjee Bomanjee (second trip), originally under sentence for seven years for the theft of a silk handkerchief from a London 'swell', will suffer the extreme penalty of the law for having, in an intemperate moment, objected to the mild discipline with which a genial and loving motherland had sought to correct his criminal tendencies. In other words, Convict Glancy, metaphorically goaded by the wordy insults and literally by the bayonet-tip of one of his motherland's reformatory agents—to wit, Road-gang Overseer James Jones—had scattered J.J.'s brains over a good six square yards of metalled roadway. The deed has been rapturously applauded by Glancy's fellow-gangers, all of whom had the inclination, but lacked the courage, to wield the crowbar that has been the means of erasing this particular tyrant's name from the pay-sheets of His Britannic Majesty's Colonial Penal Establishment. Nevertheless and notwithstanding such tribute of appreciation, H.B.M.'s colonial representatives, police, judicial and gubernatorial, have thought it rather one to be censured and have, accordingly, left Convict Glancy for execution.

This decision of the duly-constituted authorities Convict Glancy has somewhat irrelevantly (as it will seem to us at this enlightened day) acknowledged by a fervent 'Thank God!'—an ejaculation rendered the more remarkable by the fact that never before in his convict history had he linked the name of the Deity with any expression of gratitude for the many blessings enjoyed by him in that state of penal servitude to which it had pleased the same Deity to call him. On the contrary, he had constantly indulged in maledictions on his fate and on his Maker. He had resolutely cursed the benignant forces with which the System and the King's Regulations had surrounded him, and he had failed to reverence as he ought the triangles, the gang-chains, the hominy, the prodding bayonet, and the other things which would have conduced to his reformation had he but manifested a more humble and obedient spirit. No wonder, therefore, as Chaplain Ford said, that it has come about that he has qualified for the capital doom.

Upon this doom, in so far as it could be represented by the gallows, Convict Glancy was now gazing with an unflinching eye. On this September evening he stands at his cell-window looking on half-a-dozen brown-clothed figures handling saw, and square, and hammer, as they fix in the earth two sturdy uprights, and to those a projecting cross-beam; as they bind the two with a solid tie-piece of knotless hardwood; as they build a narrow platform of planks around the gallows-tree; as they fasten a rope to the notched end of the cross-beam; and as they slope to the edge of the planks, ten feet from the ground, a rude ladder. All the drowsy afternoon he had watched the working party, though Chaplain Ford had stood by his side droning of the grace which had been withheld from him in life, but might still be his in death. He had felt interested, had Convict Glancy, in these preparations for the event in which he was to act such a prominent part on the morrow. He had even laughed at the grim humour of one of the brown-garbed workers who, when the warder's eye was off him, had gone through the pantomime of noosing the rope-end round his own neck—a little joke which contributed much to the (necessarily noiseless) delight of the rest of the gang.

Altogether, Convict Glancy reflected as dusk fell, and the working party gathered up their tools, and the setting sun tipped the bayonets of the guard with a diamond iridescence, that he had spent many a duller afternoon. If the Chaplain had only held his tongue, the time would have passed with real pleasantness. He said as much to the good man as the latter remarked to the warder on duty in the cell that he would look in again after supper.

'You may save yourself the trouble, sir,' quoth, respectfully enough, Convict Glancy. 'You have spoilt my last afternoon. Don't spoil my last night!'

Chaplain Ford winced at the words. He was still comparatively new to the work of spiritually superintending a hundred or so monsters who looked upon the orthodox hell as a place where residence would be pleasantly recreative after Port Arthur Settlement and Norfolk Island; and the time lay still in the future when, being completely embruted, he would come to regard it as a very curious circumstance indeed that Christ had omitted eulogistic reference to the System from the Sermon on the Mount. Consequently he winced and sighed, not so much—to do him justice—at the utter depravity of Convict Glancy as at his own inability to reach the reprobate's heart. But he took the hint; he mournfully said he would not return that evening, but would be with the prisoner by half-past 5 o'clock in the morning.

II

When Chaplain Ford entered the enclosure immediately before the hour he had named, he at once understood, from the excitement manifested by a group assembled in front of the 'cage', that something was amiss. Voices were uttering fearful words, impetuously, almost shriekingly, and hands swung lanterns—the grey dawn had not yet driven the darkness from the stockade—and brandished muskets furiously. A very brief space of time served to inform the reverend functionary what had gone wrong.

Convict Glancy had made his escape, having previously murdered, with the victim's own bayonet, the warder who had been told-off to watch him during the night. This latter circumstance was, of course, unfortunate, but alone it would not have created the excitement, for the murder of prison-officials was a common enough occurrence. It was the other thing that galled the gesticulating and blaspheming group. That a prisoner, fettered with ten-pound irons, should have broken out of gaol on the very eve of his execution—why, it was calculated to shake the confidence of the Comptroller-General himself in the infallibility and perfect righteousness of the System. And, popular and authoritative belief in the System once shattered, where would they be?

The murdered man had gone on duty at 10 o'clock, and very shortly afterwards he must have met with his fate. How Glancy had obtained possession of the bayonet could only be conjectured. As was the custom during the day or two preceding a convict's execution, he had been left unmanacled, and ironed with double leg-chains only. Thus his hands were free to perpetrate the deed once he grasped the weapon. Glancy, on his escape, had taken the instrument with him, but there was no doubt that he had inflicted death with it, the wound in the dead man's breast being obviously caused by the regulation bayonet. Possibly the sentinel had nodded, and then a violent wrench of the prisoner's wrist and a sudden stab had extended his momentary slumber into an eternal sleep. The bayonet had been used by Glancy to prise up a flooring-flag, and to scoop out an aperture under the wall, the base-stones of which, following the slipshod architecture of the time, rested on the surface and were not sunk into the ground.

The work of excavation must have taken the convict several hours, and must have been conducted as noiselessly as the manner of committing the crime itself. A solitary warder occupied the outer guard-room, but he asserted that he had heard no sound except the exchange of whistle-signals between the dormitory guard at the convict-barracks (a quarter-of-mile away at the rear of the gaol-stockade) and the military patrol. The night routine of the 'cage' did not insist upon the whistle-signal between the men on duty, but they passed a simple 'All's well' every hour. And this the guardroom-warder maintained he had done with the officer inside the condemned cell, the response being given in a low tone, from consideration, so the former thought, for the sleeping convict so soon to die. Of course, if this man was to be believed, Glancy must have uttered the words. It was not the first time the signal which should have been given by a prison officer had been made by his convict murderer.

The murder was discovered on the arrival of the relief watch at five o'clock. The last 'All's well' was exchanged at four. Consequently the escapee had less than an hour's start. The scaling of the stockade would not be difficult even for a man in irons, and once in the bush an experienced hand would soon find a method of fracturing the links.

It must be admitted that this contumacious proceeding of Convict Glancy was most vexatious. Under-Sheriff Ropewell, now soundly reposing at the township inn, would be forthcoming at 9 o'clock with his

Excellency's warrant in his hand to demand from Muster-Master Stoneman the body of one James Glancy, and Muster-Master Stoneman would have to apologise for his inability to produce the said body. The difficulty was quite unprecedented, and Stoneman, as he stood in the midst of his minions, groaned audibly at the prospect of having to do the thing most abhorrent to the official mind—establish a precedent.

'Such a thing was never heard of!' he cried. 'A man to bolt just when he was to be turned off? And the d——d hypocrite tried to make his Honor and all of us think that he was only too happy to be scragged. It's too d——d bad!'

It certainly did seem peculiar that Glancy, who had apparently much rejoiced at the contemplation of his early decease, should give leg-bail just when he was to realise his wishes. He had told the judges that 'he was——glad they were going to kill him right off instead of by inches', and yet he had voluntarily thrown off the noose when it was virtually round his neck. Was it the mere contrariness of the convict nature that prompted the escape? Or, was it the innate love of life that becomes stronger as the benefits of living become fewer and fewer? Had the craving for existence and for freedom surged over his despair and recklessness at the eleventh hour?

Such were the enquiries which Chaplain Ford put to himself as, horrified, he took in the particulars of No. 17,927's crowning enormities from the hubbub of the group.

'Damn it!' said the Muster-Master at last, 'we are losing time. The devil can't have gone far with those ten-pounders on him. We'll have to put the regulars on the track as well as our own men. Warder Briggs, report to Captain White at the barracks, and—'

Muster-Master Stoneman stopped short. Through the foggy air there came the familiar sound as of a convict dragging his irons. What could it be? No prisoners had been as yet loosed from the dormitory. Whence could the noise proceed?

Clink—clank—s-sh—dr-g-g—clink—clank—dr-g-g. The sound drew nearer, and Convict Glancy turned in at the enclosure gateway—unescorted. He had severed the leg-chain at the link which connected with the basil of the left anklet, but had not taken the trouble to remove the other part of the chain. Thus, while he could take his natural pace with his left foot, he dragged the fetters behind his right leg.

A moment of hushed surprise, and then three or four men rushed towards him. The first who touched him he felled with a blow.

'Not yet,' said he, grimly. 'I give myself up, Mr Stoneman—you don't take me! I give myself up—you ain't going to get ten quid[1] for taking me.'

---

1   Author's note: 'Ten quid'—The reward of ten pounds paid by Government on the re-capture of an escaped prisoner.

And then Convict Glancy laughed, and held out his hands for the handcuffs. He laughed more heartily as the subordinate hirelings of the System threw themselves upon him like hounds on their prey.

'No need to turn out the sodgers now, Muster-Master—not till nine o'clock.' Once more his hideous laugh rang through the yards. 'You had an easier job than you expected, hadn't you, Stoneman, old cove?'

Muster-Master Stoneman had been surprised into silence and into an unusual abstinence from blasphemy by the re-appearance—quite unprecedented under the circumstances!—of the doomed wretch. But the desperado's jeering tones whipped him into speech.

'Curse you!' he yelled. 'I'll teach you to laugh on the other side of your mouth presently. You'd better have kept away.' He literally foamed in his mad anger.

'Do you think I couldn't have stopped away if I'd wanted to, having got clear?' A lofty scorn rang out in the words. 'But do you think I was going to run away when I was so near Freedom as that?' And the wretch jerked his manacled hands in the direction of the gallows. 'You d——d fool!'

No one spoke for a full half-minute. Then: 'Why did you break gaol then?' asked the Muster-Master.

'*Because I wanted to spit on Jones' grave!*' was the reply.

III

Muster-Master Stoneman was as good as his word. Death couldn't drive the smile from Glancy's face. That could only be done by one thing—the lash.

When next the Muster-Master spoke it was to order the prisoner a double ration of cocoa and bread. And, 'Briggs,' he continued, 'while he is getting it, see that the triangles are rigged.'

'The triangles, sir!' exclaimed Officer Briggs and Convict Glancy together.

'I said the triangles, and I mean the triangles. No. 17,927 has broken gaol, and as Muster-Master of this station, and governor of this gaol, and as a magistrate of the territory, I can give him 750 lashes for escaping. But as he has to go through another little ceremony this morning I'll let him off with a "canary"'—(a hundred lashes.)[1]

'You surely cannot mean it, sir!' exclaimed Parson Ford.

'Mean it, sir! By G——, I'll show you I mean it,' replied the M.M., whose blaspheming no presence restrained save that of his official superiors.

---

1   Author's note: Muster-Master Stoneman had doubtless in his mind's eye when he made this remark the decision of a Sydney Court which had legalised the infliction, by an official holding a plurality of offices of a sentence passed by him in each capacity, but for the one offence.

'Give him the cocoa. Warder Tuff, give the doctor my compliments, and tell him his attendance is required here. Tell him he'd better bring his smelling-salts—they may be wanted,' he sneered in conclusion.

'You devil!' cried Glancy. The reckless grin passed away, and his face faded to the pallor of the death he was so soon to die.

As Muster-Master Stoneman turned on his heel to prepare the warrant for the flogging, he looked at his watch. It was half-past six.

At seven o'clock the first lash from the cat-o'-nine-tails fell upon Convict Glancy's back.

At 7.30 his groaning and bleeding body, which had received the full hundred of flaying stripes, lay on the pallet of the cell where he had murdered the night-guard but a few hours before.

At eight o'clock Executioner Johnson entered the cell. 'I've brought yer sumthink to 'arden yer, Glancy, ol' man. I'll rub it in, an' it'll help yer to keep up.' So tender a sympathy inspired Mr Johnson's words that anyone not knowing him would have thought he was the bearer of some priceless balsam. But Convict Glancy knew him; and, maddened by pain though he was, had still sensibility enough left to make a shuddering resistance to the hangman as he proceeded to rub into the gashed flesh a handful of coarse salt. 'By the Muster-Master's orders, sonny,' soothingly remarked Johnson. 'To 'arden yer.'

At 8.45 Under-Sheriff Ropewell, who had been apprised while at breakfast of the murder and escape, appeared on the scene escorted by his javelin-men. This gentleman, too, had been greatly perplexed by Convict Glancy's proceedings. 'Really it was most inconsiderate of the man,' he said to the Muster-Master. 'I do not know whether I ought to proceed to execution, pending his trial for this second murder.'

'Oh,' said the latter functionary—flicking with his handkerchief from his coat-sleeve as he spoke a drop of Convict Glancy's blood that had fallen there from a reflex swirl of the lash, 'I think your duty is clear. You must hang him at nine o'clock, and try him afterwards for the last crime.'

And as Convict Glancy, per Pestonjee Bomanjee (second), No. 17,927, was punctually hanged at 9.5, it is to be presumed that the Under-Sheriff had accepted this solution of the difficulty.

At 10.15 a mass of carrion having been huddled into a shell, and certain formalities, which in the estimation of the System served as efficiently as a coroner's inquest, having been duly attended to, Muster-Master Stoneman bethought himself that he had not breakfasted.

'I'll see you later, Mr Ropewell,' he said, as the latter was endorsing the Governor's warrant with the sham verdict; 'I'm going to breakfast. I think I've earned it this morning.'

1892

BARBARA BAYNTON
1857–1929

Barbara Baynton was born in Scone, NSW, into a poor family: her father was a bush carpenter, though during her lifetime she told a more romantic version of her origins. Each of her three marriages saw her move higher up the social scale, but none appears to have been especially happy. While working as a governess in the Quirindi district, she met her first husband, Alexander Frater. They had three children but the marriage ended when he became sexually involved with her niece. Baynton then moved to Sydney with her children, supporting them by various jobs, including selling Bibles and making hats. Her financial troubles ended when, immediately following her divorce from Frater in 1889, she married the wealthy, 70-year-old Dr Thomas Baynton. During the fifteen years of their marriage, Baynton mixed with leading political, literary and artistic figures and began to write the stories later collected in *Bush Studies* (1902). Only one was published at this time, however: a censored version of 'The Chosen Vessel', which appeared in the *Bulletin* in 1896 under the title 'The Tramp'. As *Bulletin* literary editor A.G. Stephens (qv) later admitted when *Bush Studies* was published in London, 'its truthful glimpses of Australian life, graphically expressed, could not (would not) have been printed in any Australian paper, though they rank highly as literature'.

After Thomas Baynton's death in 1904, Baynton lived mainly in London, publishing her only novel, *Human Toll*, in 1907. During the First World War she opened her London and country homes to soldiers, and two new stories, 'Trooper Jim Tasman' and 'Toohey's Party', were added to the six from *Bush Studies* to produce *Cobbers* (1917), no doubt designed to appeal to the new interest in Australia resulting from the war. In 1921 Baynton married Lord Headley, an eccentric Englishman, but they soon separated.

Despite her relatively small output, Baynton has been increasingly recognised, especially by feminist critics, for her highly individual and completely unsentimental pictures of bush life. Drawing on her early life, she does not hesitate to stress aspects ignored by other writers: male violence, racial prejudice, sexual abuse of women, the ignorance of most of those living in the country. Her work is also read as an example of Australian Gothic. *EW*

The Chosen Vessel

She laid the stick and her baby on the grass while she untied the rope that tethered the calf. The length of the rope separated them. The cow was near the calf, and both were lying down. Feed along the creek was plentiful, and every day she found a fresh place to tether it, since tether it she must, for if she did not, it would stray with the cow out on the plain. She had plenty of time to go after it, but then there was baby; and if the cow turned on her out on the plain, and she with baby,—she had been a town girl and was afraid of the cow, but she did not want the cow to know it. She used to run at first when it bellowed its protest against the penning up of its calf. This satisfied the cow, also the calf, but the woman's husband was angry, and called her—the noun was cur. It was he who forced her to run and meet the advancing cow, brandishing a stick, and uttering threatening words till the enemy turned and ran. 'That's the way!' the man said, laughing at her white face. In many things he was worse than the cow, and she wondered if the same rule would apply to the man, but she was not one to provoke skirmishes even with the cow.

It was early for the calf to go 'to bed'—nearly an hour earlier than usual; but she had felt so restless all day. Partly because it was Monday, and the end of the week that would bring her and baby the companionship of its father, was so far off. He was a shearer, and had gone to his shed before daylight that morning. Fifteen miles as the crow flies separated them.

There was a track in front of the house, for it had once been a wine shanty, and a few travellers passed along at intervals. She was not afraid of horsemen; but swagmen, going to, or worse, coming from the dismal, drunken little township, a day's journey beyond, terrified her. One had called at the house to-day, and asked for tucker.

Ah! that was why she had penned up the calf so early! She feared more from the look of his eyes, and the gleam of his teeth, as he watched her newly awakened baby beat its impatient fists upon her covered breasts, than from the knife that was sheathed in the belt at his waist.

She had given him bread and meat. Her husband she told him was sick. She always said that when she was alone, and a swagman came, and she had gone in from the kitchen to the bedroom, and asked questions and replied to them in the best man's voice she could assume. Then he had asked to go into the kitchen to boil his billy, but she gave him tea, and he drank it on the wood heap. He had walked round and round the house, and there were cracks in some places, and after the last time he had asked for tobacco. She had none to give him, and he had grinned, because there was a broken clay pipe near the wood heap where he stood, and if there were a man inside, there ought to have been tobacco. Then he asked for money, but women in the bush never have money.

At last he had gone, and she, watching through the cracks, saw him when about a quarter of a mile away, turn and look back at the house. He had stood so for some moments with a pretence of fixing his swag, and then, apparently satisfied, moved to the left towards the creek. The creek made a bow round the house, and when he came to it she lost sight of him. Hours after, watching intently for signs of smoke, she saw the man's dog chasing some sheep that had gone to the creek for water, and saw it slink back suddenly, as if the man had called it.

More than once she thought of taking her baby and going to her husband. But in the past, when she had dared to speak of the dangers to which her loneliness exposed her, he had taunted and sneered at her. She need not flatter herself, he had coarsely told her, that anybody would want to run away with her.

Long before nightfall she placed food on the kitchen table, and beside it laid the big brooch that had been her mother's. It was the only thing of value that she had. And she left the kitchen door wide open.

The doors inside she securely fastened. Beside the bolt in the back one she drove in the steel and scissors; against it she piled the table and the stools. Underneath the lock of the front door she forced the handle of the spade, and the blade between the cracks in the flooring boards. Then the prop-stick, cut into lengths, held the top, as the spade held the middle. The windows were little more than portholes; she had nothing to fear through them.

She ate a few mouthfuls of food and drank a cup of milk. But she lighted no fire, and when night came, no candle, but crept with her baby to bed.

What woke her? The wonder was that she had slept—she had not meant to. But she was young, very young. Perhaps the shrinking of the galvanized roof—yet hardly, since that was so usual. Something had set her heart beating wildly; but she lay quite still, only she put her arm over her baby. Then she had both round it, and she prayed, 'Little baby, little baby, don't wake!'

The moon's rays shone on the front of the house, and she saw one of the open cracks, quite close to where she lay, darken with a shadow. Then a protesting growl reached her; and she could fancy she heard the man turn hastily. She plainly heard the thud of something striking the dog's ribs, and the long flying strides of the animal as it howled and ran. Still watching, she saw the shadow darken every crack along the wall. She knew by the sounds that the man was trying every standpoint that might help him to see in; but how much he saw she could not tell. She thought of many things she might do to deceive him into the idea that she was not alone. But the sound of her voice would wake baby, and she dreaded that as though it were the only danger that threatened her. So she prayed, 'Little baby, don't wake, don't cry!'

Stealthily the man crept about. She knew he had his boots off, because of the vibration that his feet caused as he walked along the verandah to gauge the width of the little window in her room, and the resistance of the front door.

Then he went to the other end, and the uncertainty of what he was doing became unendurable. She had felt safer, far safer, while he was close, and she could watch and listen. She felt she must watch, but the great fear of wakening baby again assailed her. She suddenly recalled that one of the slabs on that side of the house had shrunk in length as well as in width, and had once fallen out. It was held in position only by a wedge of wood underneath. What if he should discover that! The uncertainty increased her terror. She prayed as she gently raised herself with her little one in her arms, held tightly to her breast.

She thought of the knife, and shielded her child's body with her hands and arms. Even its little feet she covered with its white gown, and baby never murmured—it liked to be held so. Noiselessly she crossed to the other side, and stood where she could see and hear, but not be seen. He was trying every slab, and was very near to that with the wedge under it. Then she saw him find it; and heard the sound of the knife as bit by bit he began to cut away the wooden support.

She waited motionless, with her baby pressed tightly to her, though she knew that in another few minutes this man with the cruel eyes, lascivious mouth, and gleaming knife, would enter. One side of the slab tilted; he had only to cut away the remaining little end, when the slab, unless he held it, would fall outside.

She heard his jerked breathing as it kept time with the cuts of the knife, and the brush of his clothes as he rubbed the wall in his movements, for she was so still and quiet, that she did not even tremble. She knew when he ceased, and wondered why. She stood well concealed; she knew he could not see her, and that he would not fear if he did, yet she heard him move cautiously away. Perhaps he expected the slab to fall. Still his motive puzzled her, and she moved even closer, and bent her body the better to listen. Ah! what sound was that? 'Listen! Listen!' she bade her heart—her heart that had kept so still, but now bounded with tumultuous throbs that dulled her ears. Nearer and nearer came the sounds, till the welcome thud of a horse's hoof rang out clearly.

'Oh, God! Oh, God! Oh, God!' she cried, for they were very close before she could make sure. She turned to the door, and with her baby in her arms tore frantically at its bolts and bars.

Out she darted at last, and running madly along, saw the horseman beyond her in the distance. She called to him in Christ's name, in her babe's name, still flying like the wind with the speed that deadly peril gives. But the distance grew greater and greater between them, and when she reached the creek her prayers turned to wild shrieks, for there crouched the man she feared, with outstretched arms that caught her as she fell. She knew he was offering terms if she ceased to struggle and cry for help, though louder and louder did she cry for it, but it was only when the man's hand gripped her throat, that the cry of 'Murder' came from her lips. And when she ceased, the startled curlews took up the awful sound, and flew shrieking over the horseman's head.

'By God!' said the boundary rider, 'it's been a dingo right enough! Eight killed up here, and there's more down in the creek—a ewe and a lamb, I'll bet; and the lamb's alive!' And he shut out the sky with his hand, and watched the crows that were circling round and round, nearing the earth one moment, and the next shooting skywards. By that he knew the lamb must be alive; even a dingo will spare a lamb sometimes.

Yes, the lamb was alive, and after the manner of lambs of its kind did not know its mother when the light came. It had sucked the still warm breasts, and laid its little head on her bosom, and slept till the morn. Then, when it looked at the swollen disfigured face, it wept and would have crept away, but for the hand that still clutched its little gown. Sleep was nodding its golden head and swaying its small body, and the crows were close, so close, to the mother's wide-open eyes, when the boundary rider galloped down.

'Jesus Christ!' he said, covering his eyes. He told afterwards how the little child held out its arms to him, and how he was forced to cut its gown that the dead hand held.

It was election time, and as usual the priest had selected a candidate. His choice was so obviously in the interests of the squatter, that Peter Hennessey's reason, for once in his life, had over-ridden superstition, and he had dared promise his vote to another. Yet he was uneasy, and every time he woke in the night (and it was often), he heard the murmur of his mother's voice. It came through the partition, or under the door. If through the partition, he knew she was praying in her bed; but when the sounds came under the door, she was on her knees before the little altar in the corner that enshrined the statue of the Blessed Virgin and Child.

'Mary, Mother of Christ! save my son! Save him!' prayed she in the dairy as she strained and set the evening's milking. 'Sweet Mary! for the love of Christ, save him!' The grief in her old face made the morning meal so bitter, that to avoid her he came late to his dinner. It made him so cowardly, that he could not say good-bye to her, and when night fell on the eve of the election day, he rode off secretly.

He had thirty miles to ride to the township to record his vote. He cantered briskly along the great stretch of plain that had nothing but stunted cotton bush to play shadow to the full moon, which glorified a sky of earliest spring. The bruised incense of the flowering clover rose up to him, and the glory of the night appealed vaguely to his imagination, but he was preoccupied with his present act of revolt.

Vividly he saw his mother's agony when she would find him gone. At that moment, he felt sure, she was praying.

'Mary! Mother of Christ!' He repeated the invocation, half unconsciously. And suddenly, out of the stillness, came Christ's name to him—called loudly in despairing accents.

'For Christ's sake! Christ's sake! Christ's sake!' called the voice. Good Catholic that he had been, he crossed himself before he dared to look back. Gliding across a ghostly patch of pipe-clay, he saw a white-robed figure with a babe clasped to her bosom.

All the superstitious awe of his race and religion swayed his brain. The moonlight on the gleaming clay was a 'heavenly light' to him, and he knew the white figure not for flesh and blood, but for the Virgin and Child of his mother's prayers. Then, good Catholic that once more he was, he put spurs to his horse's sides and galloped madly away.

His mother's prayers were answered.

Hennessey was the first to record his vote—for the priest's candidate. Then he sought the priest at home, but found that he was out rallying the voters. Still, under the influence of his blessed vision, Hennessey would not go near the public houses, but wandered about the outskirts of the town for hours, keeping apart from the towns-people, and fasting as penance. He was subdued and mildly ecstatic, feeling as a repentant chastened child, who awaits only the kiss of peace.

And at last, as he stood in the graveyard crossing himself with reverent awe, he heard in the gathering twilight the roar of many voices crying the name of the victor at the election. It was well with the priest.

Again Hennessey sought him. He sat at home, the house-keeper said, and led him into the dimly-lighted study. His seat was immediately opposite a large picture, and as the house-keeper turned up the lamp, once more the face of the Madonna and Child looked down on him, but this time silently, peacefully. The half-parted lips of the Virgin were smiling with compassionate tenderness; her eyes seemed to beam with the forgiveness of an earthly mother for her erring but beloved child.

He fell on his knees in adoration. Transfixed, the wondering priest stood, for mingled with the adoration, 'My Lord and my God!' was the exaltation, 'And hast Thou chosen me?'

'What is it, Peter?' said the priest.

'Father,' he answered reverently, and with loosened tongue he poured forth the story of his vision.

'Great God!' shouted the priest, 'and you did not stop to save her! Have you not heard?'

Many miles further down the creek a man kept throwing an old cap into a water-hole. The dog would bring it out and lay it on the opposite side to where the man stood, but would not allow the man to catch him, though it was only to wash the blood of the sheep from his mouth and throat, for the sight of blood made the man tremble.

1902

VICTOR DALEY
c. 1858–1905

Poet Victor Daley was born in Ireland and educated there and in England. Around 1878 he migrated to Australia, working as a journalist in Adelaide and Melbourne before settling in Sydney, where he wrote for *Sydney Punch* and the *Bulletin*. In March 1882, the *Bulletin*'s J.F. Archibald hailed him as 'the rising poet of this country'. In

1898, Daley's first collection, *At Dawn and Dusk*, consisting mainly of lyrical verses in a Celtic twilight style, was produced under the guidance of A.G. Stephens (qv). Daley suffered from tuberculosis, which led to his early death, and *Poems* (1908) and *Wine and Roses* (1911) appeared posthumously. A collection of his satirical verse, including 'Correggio Jones', written under the pen name 'Creeve Roe', was published in 1947. *EW*

Correggio Jones

Correggio Jones an artist was
    Of pure Australian race,
But native subjects scorned because
    They were too commonplace.

The Bush with all its secrets grim,   5
    And solemn mystery,
No fascination had for him:
    He had no eyes to see

The long sad spectral desert-march
    Of brave Explorers dead,   10
Who perished—while the burning arc
    Of blue laughed overhead;

The Solitary Man who stares
    At the mirage so fair,
While Death steals on him unawares   15
    And grasps him by the hair;

The Lonely Tree that sadly stands,
    With no green neighbour nigh,
And stretches forth its bleached, dead hands,
    For pity to the sky;   20

The Grey Prospector, weird of dress,
    And wearied overmuch,
Who dies amidst the wilderness—
    With Fortune in his clutch;

The figures of the heroes gone   25
    Who stood forth undismayed,
And Freedom's Flag shook forth upon
    Eureka's old stockade.

These subjects to Correggio Jones
    No inspiration brought;   30
He was an ass (in semi-tones)
    And painted—as he thought.

'In all these things there's no Romance,'
    He muttered, with a sneer;
'They'd never give C. Jones a chance   35
    To make his genius clear!'

'Grey gums,' he cried, 'and box-woods pale
    They give my genius cramp—
But let me paint some Knights in Mail,
    Or robbers in a camp.   40

'Now, look at those Old Masters—they
    Had all the chances fine,
With churches dim, and ruins grey,
    And castles on the Rhine,

'And Lady Gay in miniver,   45
    And hairy-shirted saint,
And Doges in apparel fair—
    And things a man might paint!

'And barons bold and pilgrims pale,
    And battling Knight and King—   50
The blood-spots on their golden mail—
    And all that sort of thing!

'Your Raphael and your Angelo
    And Rubens, and such men,
They simply had a splendid show.   55
    Give me the same—and then!'

★

So speaks Correggio Jones—yet sees,
    When past is Night's eclipse,
The dawn come like Harpocrates,[1]
    A rose held to her lips.   60

1   Greek God of Silence.

The wondrous dawn that is so fair,
    So young and bright and strong,
That e'en the rocks and stones to her
    Sing a Memnonic song.[1]

He will not see that our sky-hue   65
    Old Italy's outvies,
But still goes yearning for the blue
    Of far Ausonian[2] skies.

        ★

He yet is painting at full bat—
    You'll say, if him you see,   70
'His body dwells on Gander Flat,
    His soul's in Italy.'

                  1898

KITTY BRANGY
c. 1859–1918

Born probably in the Upper Murray area of Victoria, Kitty Brangy was the daughter of Brangie, leader of the Oxley Flats people, near Wangaratta. In 1881, Kitty Brangy wrote several letters from Wahgunyah to her sister Edith at Coranderrk, an Aboriginal reserve established in 1816 near Healesville, Victoria. These letters demonstrate the strength of Indigenous family and kinship ties at a time when authorities were systematically trying to break them down. *AH/PM*

Letter to Edith Brangy

My dear sister I write these few lines hoping you are quite well as it leaves us All at present. My dear sister I am very sorry that I could not write before. Now my dear sister I must tell you that I am living in Wahgunyah and it is such a poor place you can hardly get anything to eat.

    I should like to come down there very much but I can never get the money to go anywhere. My dear sister I wish that you would ask Mr Briggs to lend me one pound and I will soon come and see you All. My dear sister I must tell you that I have got such a nice Little Boy and he is called Willie. My dear sister will you tell Mrs Briggs that her Uncle is dead. Tommy Read is dead. Mary send her love to her aunty and says that she would like to see you very much. My dear sister I think that the

1   Refers to an Egyptian statue said to give out a musical note when touched by the dawn.
2   Italian.

drink must of killed him he died in Corowan. My dear sister I am with Tommy McCays[?] tribe and they all send their kind love to you and would All like to see you. My dear sister I have not seen our dear Father since last year. I know not where he has got to. I should like to know very much

My dear sister I hope you will write as soon as you can for I might not be here long and then I should not get it. My dear sister I have no more to say at present but next time I hope that I will have some more to say next time. No more at present from your Loving and true sister

Kitty Brangy   kisses to you my dear sister
XXXXXXXXXXXXXXXXXXX
XXXXXXXXXXXXXXXXXX
XXXXXXXXXXXXXXXXXXXX Address Kitty Brangy
XXX XXXXXXXXXXXXXX   Wahgunyah
X·XXXXXXX   Post Office

1881

ANNIE RICH
c. 1859–1937

Born at Murat Station (Ceduna), SA, at ten Annie Rich was sent to Victoria by her white pastoralist father to work as a domestic servant. Made pregnant, probably by her employer Alexander Jeffrey, she took refuge at Lake Condah Mission Station in 1880, but after the birth of her baby the superintendent, Reverend Johann Stähle, refused to allow her to leave. Her plea to the Board for Protection of Aborigines rejected, she ran away but was captured and sent back to Lake Condah. Later she married Alf McDonald, with whom she had seven children. *AH/PM*

Letter to Solicitor, for Captain Page, Secretary of the Victorian Board for the Protection of Aborigines

Mission Station
Lake Condah
April 5th 1882.

To
The Solicitor,
Echuca

Sir,
In reply to the letter that I received from Mr Jeffrey last month, requesting me to write to you myself.

I beg you if you can apply to the Board for me to leave the Mission Station, that I do not wish to stay here.

Two years ago I came to the Mission Station, not to settle down, but to visit some of my friends, & to return home again to Echuca after my visit.

But there was an Order in Council telling me to stay on the Mission Station to settle down, But I do not wish to stay here.

Therefore will you please to investigate into the matter to the Board if they can give me permission to leave.

I remain
Sir
Yours most sincerely
Annie Rich

1882

WILLIAM COOPER
c. 1861–1941

Born in Yorta Yorta country in Victoria, William Cooper spent his early life working in the pastoral industry. He was married four times and had several children, including a daughter who was matron of the first Aboriginal Hostel in Melbourne, a son who fought and died in the First World War, and another who was a gifted sprinter. As a member of the Australian Workers' Union in the late 1920s, Cooper became a spokesperson for the Aboriginal peoples of central Victoria and western NSW. In 1933, he moved to Melbourne where he became secretary of the Australian Aborigines League and a leader in the 1930s campaigns against state Protection Acts and for constitutional change. He began a petition for change, and in 1935 led a delegation to the Minister of the Interior, the first Aboriginal meeting with a Commonwealth Minister. With members of the Aborigines Progressive Association, Cooper led the first Aboriginal delegation to a prime minister in 1938. Their claims rejected, and having collected over 1814 signatures from Aboriginal Australians, Cooper addressed his petition to King George VI. The Commonwealth refused to forward his petition or to change the status quo. Cooper was a leader of the Aboriginal Day of Mourning Conference and Protest in Sydney on 26 January 1938. In 1940 he established National Aborigines Day, a forerunner to NAIDOC week celebrations. *AH/PM*

Petition to the King[1]

Whereas it was not only a moral duty, but also a strict injunction included in the commission issued to those who came to people Australia that the original occupants and we, their heirs and successors, should be adequately cared for; and whereas the terms of the commission have not been adhered to, in that (a) our lands have been expropriated by your Majesty's Government in the Commonwealth, (b) legal status is denied to us by your Majesty's

1 This petition was produced by Cooper and the Australian Aborigines League and published during the reign of King George V. In 1937 a version was presented to the Commonwealth during the early reign of King George VI.

Government in the Commonwealth; and whereas all petitions made in our behalf to your Majesty's Government in the Commonwealth have failed: your petitioners therefore humbly pray that your Majesty will intervene in our behalf and through the instrument of your Majesty's Government in the Commonwealth grant to our people representation in the Federal Parliament, either in the person of one of our own blood or by a white man known to have studied our needs and to be in sympathy with our race.

1933

BANJO PATERSON
1864–1941

Andrew Barton Paterson adopted the pen name The Banjo for some of his contributions to the *Bulletin*. Thanks to the popularity of his poems, it was to become the name by which Paterson is best known. He was born on a family property near Orange in NSW and later lived on a station near Yass before moving to Sydney to attend Sydney Grammar School and then train as a solicitor. From 1885 he began to have verse and prose published in the *Bulletin*. 'Clancy of the Overflow' (1889), apparently based on a real letter from the bush sent to his law firm, quickly became popular thanks to the way it strongly contrasted the spacious, sunny bush with the drabness of city life. Even more successful was 'The Man from Snowy River' (1890), which built on the continuing popularity of Adam Lindsay Gordon's (qv) horsy ballads as well as on Australians' fondness for the underdog, symbolically representing the triumph of the young Australian-born man from Snowy River over the older, presumably British, station owner. In 1895, while on a visit to northern Queensland, Paterson wrote the words for 'Waltzing Matilda', another celebration of the battler spirit and resistance to authority, which has now become Australia's national song.

The new publishing firm of Angus & Robertson capitalised on the growing appeal of Paterson's work by issuing *The Man from Snowy River and Other Verses* (1895), with a preface by Rolf Boldrewood (qv). It was an outstanding success, selling 7000 copies in a month, and brought Paterson literary celebrity. In 1899 he reported on the Boer War for the *Sydney Morning Herald* and a few years later travelled to China and London. In 1903, after a brief dalliance with the young Miles Franklin (qv), Paterson resigned from his law practice to edit the Sydney *Evening News* and later the *Town and Country Journal*. His *Old Bush Songs* (1905) collected traditional ballads for the first time and *The Collected Verse of A.B. Paterson* (1921) confirmed Paterson's status at the time as Australia's leading poet. He remains one of our most celebrated writers and is featured on the ten-dollar note. *The Man from Snowy River* was made into a successful film in 1982. In the 2000 Sydney Olympics, 'The Man from Snowy River' began the opening ceremony, while 'Waltzing Matilda' was sung to conclude the closing ceremony. *EW*

The Man from Snowy River

There was movement at the station, for the word had passed around
That the colt from old Regret had got away,
And had joined the wild bush horses—he was worth a thousand pound,
So all the cracks had gathered to the fray.

All the tried and noted riders from the stations near and far   5
Had mustered at the homestead overnight,
For the bushmen love hard riding where the wild bush horses are,
And the stock-horse snuffs the battle with delight.

There was Harrison, who made his pile when Pardon won the cup,
The old man with his hair as white as snow;   10
But few could ride beside him when his blood was fairly up—
He would go wherever horse and man could go.
And Clancy of the Overflow came down to lend a hand,
No better horseman ever held the reins;
For never horse could throw him while the saddle-girths would stand, 15
He learnt to ride while droving on the plains.

And one was there, a stripling on a small and weedy beast,
He was something like a racehorse undersized,
With a touch of Timor pony—three parts thoroughbred at least—
And such as are by mountain horsemen prized.   20
He was hard and tough and wiry—just the sort that won't say die—
There was courage in his quick impatient tread;
And he bore the badge of gameness in his bright and fiery eye,
And the proud and lofty carriage of his head.

But still so slight and weedy, one would doubt his power to stay,   25
And the old man said, 'That horse will never do
'For a long and tiring gallop—lad, you'd better stop away,
'Those hills are far too rough for such as you.'
So he waited sad and wistful—only Clancy stood his friend—
'I think we ought to let him come,' he said;   30
'I warrant he'll be with us when he's wanted at the end,
'For both his horse and he are mountain bred.

'He hails from Snowy River, up by Kosciusko's side,
'Where the hills are twice as steep and twice as rough,
'Where a horse's hoofs strike firelight from the flint stones every stride, 35
'The man that holds his own is good enough.
'And the Snowy River riders on the mountains make their home,
'Where the river runs those giant hills between;
'I have seen full many horsemen since I first commenced to roam,
'But nowhere yet such horsemen have I seen.'   40

So he went—they found the horses by the big mimosa clump—
They raced away towards the mountain's brow,

And the old man gave his orders, 'Boys, go at them from the jump,
'No use to try for fancy riding now.
'And, Clancy, you must wheel them, try and wheel them to the right.   45
'Ride boldly, lad, and never fear the spills,
'For never yet was rider that could keep the mob in sight,
'If once they gain the shelter of those hills.'

So Clancy rode to wheel them—he was racing on the wing
Where the best and boldest riders take their place,   50
And he raced his stock-horse past them, and he made the ranges ring
With the stockwhip, as he met them face to face.
Then they halted for a moment, while he swung the dreaded lash,
But they saw their well-loved mountain full in view,
And they charged beneath the stockwhip with a sharp and sudden dash,   55
And off into the mountain scrub they flew.

Then fast the horsemen followed, where the gorges deep and black
Resounded to the thunder of their tread,
And the stockwhips woke the echoes, and they fiercely answered back
From cliffs and crags that beetled overhead.   60
And upward, ever upward, the wild horses held their way,
Where mountain ash and kurrajong grew wide;
And the old man muttered fiercely, 'We may bid the mob good day,
'*No* man can hold them down the other side.'

When they reached the mountain's summit, even Clancy took a pull,   65
It well might make the boldest hold their breath,
The wild hop scrub grew thickly, and the hidden ground was full
Of wombat holes, and any slip was death.
But the man from Snowy River let the pony have his head,
And he swung his stockwhip round and gave a cheer,   70
And he raced him down the mountain like a torrent down its bed,
While the others stood and watched in very fear.

He sent the flint stones flying, but the pony kept his feet,
He cleared the fallen timber in his stride,
And the man from Snowy River never shifted in his seat—   75
It was grand to see that mountain horseman ride.
Through the stringy barks and saplings, on the rough and broken ground,
Down the hillside at a racing pace he went;
And he never drew the bridle till he landed safe and sound,
At the bottom of that terrible descent.   80

He was right among the horses as they climbed the further hill,
And the watchers on the mountain standing mute,
Saw him ply the stockwhip fiercely, he was right among them still,
As he raced across the clearing in pursuit.
Then they lost him for a moment, where two mountain gullies met 85
In the ranges, but a final glimpse reveals
On a dim and distant hillside the wild horses racing yet,
With the man from Snowy River at their heels.

And he ran them single-handed till their sides were white with foam.
He followed like a bloodhound on their track, 90
Till they halted cowed and beaten, then he turned their heads for home,
And alone and unassisted brought them back.
But his hardy mountain pony he could scarcely raise a trot,
He was blood from hip to shoulder from the spur;
But his pluck was still undaunted, and his courage fiery hot, 95
For never yet was mountain horse a cur.

And down by Kosciusko, where the pine-clad ridges raise
Their torn and rugged battlements on high,
Where the air is clear as crystal, and the white stars fairly blaze
At midnight in the cold and frosty sky, 100
And where around the Overflow the reedbeds sweep and sway
To the breezes, and the rolling plains are wide,
The man from Snowy River is a household word to-day,
And the stockmen tell the story of his ride.

  1895

Waltzing Matilda

Oh! there once was a swagman camped in the Billabong,
  Under the shade of a Coolabah tree;
And he sang as he looked at his old billy boiling,
  'Who'll come a-waltzing Matilda with me?'

Who'll come a-waltzing Matilda, my darling, 5
  Who'll come a-waltzing Matilda with me?
Waltzing Matilda and leading a water-bag—
  Who'll come a-waltzing Matilda with me?

Down came a jumbuck to drink at the water-hole,
  Up jumped the swagman and grabbed him in glee; 10

And he sang as he put him away in his tucker-bag,
 'You'll come a-waltzing Matilda with me!'

Down came the Squatter a-riding his thorough-bred;
 Down came Policemen—one, two, and three.
'Whose is the jumbuck you've got in the tucker-bag?   15
 You'll come a-waltzing Matilda with me.'

But the swagman, he up and he jumped in the water-hole,
 Drowning himself by the Coolabah tree;
And his ghost may be heard as it sings in the Billabong,
 'Who'll come a-waltzing Matilda with me?'   20
             1895/1917

Mulga Bill's Bicycle

'Twas Mulga Bill, from Eaglehawk, that caught the cycling craze;
He turned away the good old horse that served him many days;
He dressed himself in cycling clothes, resplendent to be seen;
He hurried off to town and bought a shining new machine;
And as he wheeled it through the door, with air of lordly pride,   5
The grinning shop assistant said, 'Excuse me, can you ride?'

'See, here, young man,' said Mulga Bill, 'from Walgett to the sea,
'From Conroy's Gap to Castlereagh, there's none can ride like me.
'I'm good all round at everything, as everybody knows,
'Although I'm not the one to talk—I *hate* a man that blows.   10
'But riding is my special gift, my chiefest, sole delight;
'Just ask a wild duck can it swim, a wild cat can it fight.
'There's nothing clothed in hair or hide, or built of flesh or steel,
'There's nothing walks or jumps, or runs, on axle, hoof, or wheel,
'But what I'll sit, while hide will hold and girths and straps are tight: 15
'I'll ride this here two-wheeled concern right straight away at sight.'

'Twas Mulga Bill, from Eaglehawk, that sought his own abode,
That perched above the Dead Man's Creek, beside the mountain road.
He turned the cycle down the hill and mounted for the fray,
But ere he'd gone a dozen yards it bolted clean away.   20
It left the track, and through the trees, just like a silver streak,
It whistled down the awful slope, towards the Dead Man's Creek.

It shaved a stump by half an inch, it dodged a big white-box:
The very wallaroos in fright went scrambling up the rocks,

The wombats hiding in their caves dug deeper underground,   25
As Mulga Bill, as white as chalk, sat tight to every bound.
It struck a stone and gave a spring that cleared a fallen tree,
It raced beside a precipice as close as close could be;
And then as Mulga Bill let out one last despairing shriek
It made a leap of twenty feet into the Dead Man's Creek.   30

'Twas Mulga Bill, from Eaglehawk, that slowly swam ashore:
He said, 'I've had some narrer shaves and lively rides before;
'I've rode a wild bull round a yard to win a five pound bet,
'But this was the most awful ride that I've encountered yet.
'I'll give that two-wheeled outlaw best; it's shaken all my nerve   35
'To feel it whistle through the air and plunge and buck and swerve.
'It's safe at rest in Dead Man's Creek, we'll leave it lying still;
'A horse's back is good enough henceforth for Mulga Bill.'

1902

A.G. STEPHENS
1865–1933

Critic and editor Alfred George Stephens was born in Toowoomba, Queensland, and educated at Toowoomba Grammar School. In 1880 he was apprenticed as a typographer; after moving to Sydney he studied at Sydney Technical College. Returning to Queensland, he edited the *Gympie Miner* (1888–90) and then worked briefly for the Brisbane *Boomerang*, together with the young Henry Lawson (qv). He later moved to Cairns to edit the *Argus*, and published *Why North Queensland Wants Separation* (1893). Travel to North America and Europe resulted in another work, *A Queenslander's Travel Notes* (1894). While in London, Stephens was offered a position on the Sydney *Bulletin*. Initially he was responsible for conducting the 'Book Exchange', a column about recent publications, which by 1896 he had expanded into his famous 'Red Page', featuring poems, essays, reviews, correspondence and other literary material. From 1897 to 1906 he also ran the *Bulletin*'s book-publishing arm, and produced Steele Rudd's (qv) *On Our Selection!* (1899), Joseph Furphy's (qv) *Such is Life* (1903), anthologies and many collections of poems. In 1899 Stephens also edited a short-lived literary monthly, *The Bookfellow*; in the April issue poet Victor Daley (qv) mocked him as the 'Red Page Rhadamanthus' in his satire 'Narcissus and Some Tadpoles'.

In 1906, following changes in ownership, Stephens left the *Bulletin* and, after an unsuccessful attempt to run a bookshop, moved to Wellington, New Zealand, to work for the *Evening Post*. There he established a regular 'Bookfellow' page, which he continued to write after returning to Sydney in 1909. In 1911 he revived the monthly *Bookfellow*, which appeared anything but monthly until 1925. Among his many other publications were *The Red Pagan* (1904), a collection of his essays, *Victor Daley: A biographical and critical notice* (1905), *Henry Kendall* (1928) and *Chris: Brennan* (1933). He also edited and published John Shaw Neilson's (qv) first four collections of poetry. Stephens's interview with Louisa Lawson (qv) shows just how skilled a journalist he was, someone able to bring scenes and characters to life in a few well-chosen words. *EW*

A Poet's Mother

Many gifted men have had remarkable mothers, and Henry Lawson's mother, Mrs Peter Larsen (better known as Louisa Lawson), is in many ways a remarkable woman. Born at Guntawang, near Mudgee, New South Wales, she has suffered all her life from that craving for knowledge and culture which one sees in so many bush girls—often suppressed in deference to their not understanding men-folk, sometimes fighting hopelessly against the round of trivialities in which Custom circumscribes a woman, rarely succeeding to reach an enlightened plane of thought or performance. Louisa Lawson's mother burnt her books; her husband, a clever, capable man, frowned down her impulse to imaginative work; friends and relatives looked askance at her 'queer ways'. The energy of a magnificent physical constitution enabled her to struggle on. She read, and wrote, and occasionally talked. When she came to Sydney a dozen years ago, a poor little wooden cross marked the grave of poet Kendall in Waverley cemetery. Maybe the sentiment was a foolish one, for Kendall's monument is in his work, but Mrs Lawson initiated a movement which replaced the shabby little cross with a handsome monument. Then she started *The Dawn*, a journal for the household, edited, printed, and published by women. The paper is living yet, and in its heyday spoke many brave and true words. Then she organised the first Woman's Suffrage League established in Sydney. Then she was chosen a member of Sydney School of Arts committee, and for several years her strong sense was a force in its deliberations. Recently she has become a Government contractor—and inventor. For twenty-one years New South Wales mail-bags have been fastened with a strap, sealed by a device invented by Superintendent Davies. Mrs Lawson took a contract for supplying these straps, and it struck her at once that the contrivance for fastening was slow and cumbrous. So it was, undoubtedly; the astonishing thing is that in twenty-one years the consensus of male wisdom among postal officials should not have bettered it. In odd moments Mrs Lawson thought out an improved buckle, had a model made from her description, and took it to the Post Office authorities, who instantly recognised its ingenuity and adopted it. It saves two-thirds of the time formerly needed to fasten the bags, and many hundreds of pounds annually in value of string and wax. Mrs Lawson's portrait in another part of this issue barely does her justice. The expression is too hard. Despite all, Louisa Lawson is essentially a womanly woman, of a characteristically feminine type. Her nature is the groundwork of her son Henry's; but there is in him the additional element of restless male intensity. And now Mrs Lawson may speak a little space for herself.

'Something about myself? Oh, dear! Won't it look very conceited? Well, if it does don't blame me. Are you sure *The Bulletin* wants it? Do you know, I'd much rather not.

'I'm forty-eight. But you don't want to tell the people my age, do you? I was married when I was eighteen—and what I've gone through since then! It would fill a book. You know my husband's name was Peter Larsen, but Henry's name is really Lawson—he was registered Lawson—that was the way people always spoke of my husband.

'He is dead years now. Of the children, I think Bert takes after him more; Henry is like me: Gertie is more like my mother. You have heard how clever Bert is at music? And everybody knows Henry. Gertie is with me now, working on *The Dawn*. Henry and Bert are in Westralia.

'My father is alive still—such a fine old man!—he must be about seventy-five now: mother died only the other day. Father's father and mother were such good old people—that's my grandfather and mother—Henry's great-grand-parents. The old lady—she had worked hard all her life, poor soul!—she could reap her three-quarters of an acre of wheat in a day—and when she felt herself going to die she got out of bed and washed herself, dressed in clean clothes, lay down again, and folded her hands on her breast—"so as not to give trouble", she said.

'Father is a born poet; they tell me I take after him. You can see the likeness in this portrait: Henry is the same. He is a good old Kentish yeoman, is father; a big, strong, handsome man. You think I'm handsome? Do you really? I suppose I am taller and stronger than most women: I'd need to be, for what I've gone through.

'And why shouldn't a woman be tall and strong? I feel sorry for some of the women that come to see me sometimes: they look so weak and helpless—as if they expected me to pick 'em up and pull 'em to pieces and put 'em together again. I try to speak softly to them, but sometimes I can't help letting out, and then they go away and say, "Mrs Lawson was so unkind to us!"

'And whose fault is it but men's? Women are what men make them. Why, a woman can't bear a child without it being received into the hands of a male doctor; it is baptised by a fat old male parson; a girl goes through life obeying laws made by men; and if she breaks them, a male magistrate sends her to a gaol where a male warder handles her and looks in her cell at night to see she's all right. If she gets so far as to be hanged, a male hangman puts the rope round her neck; she is buried by a male gravedigger; and she goes to a Heaven ruled over by a male God or a hell managed by a male devil. Isn't it a wonder men didn't make the devil a woman?

'Run down the men? Don't you go away with that idea. Men are gods—and women are angels. And do you know what you make them suffer? I declare, it's the most pitiful thing in the world. When I come sometimes to a meeting of these poor working women—little, dowdy, shabby things all worn down with care and babies—doing their best to bring up a family on the pittance they get from their husbands—and keep those husbands at home and away from the public-house—when I see their poor lined faces I feel inclined to cry. They suffer so much.

'And listen to their talk! So quiet and sensible. If you want real practical wisdom, go to an old washerwoman patching clothes on the Rocks with a black eye, and you'll hear more true philosophy than a Parliament of men will talk in a twelve-month.

'No, I don't run down men, but I run down their vanity—especially when they're talking and writing about women. A man editing a ladies' paper! Or talking about a woman's question in Parliament! I don't know whether to laugh or cry: they know so little about us. *We* see it. Oh, why don't the women laugh right out—not quietly to themselves; laugh all together; get up on the housetops and laugh, and startle you out of your self-satisfaction.

'Men are so self-satisfied. Why, would you believe it! I was talking a while ago to a member of Parliament and sympathising with him about his wife—he's separated from her, poor thing!—and saying how hard people were on a woman that's alone, and he looked up at me so innocently and said, "I'm not in the market, Mrs Lawson." The fool thought I wanted to marry him! And to this day I believe he thinks he had a narrow escape. Poor men!

'*Did* you ever think what it was to be a woman, and have to try to make a living by herself, with so many men's hands against her. It's all right if she puts herself under the thumb of a man—she's respectable then; but woe betide her if she strikes out for herself and tries to compete with men on what they call "their own ground". Who made it their own ground?

'Why, when I started out ten years ago to make a woman's paper—*The Dawn*—this is the last number of it—the compositors boycotted me, and they even tried to boycott us at the Post Office—wouldn't let it go through the post as a newspaper. I knew nothing about printing, but I felt I could write—or, anyhow, I felt I could *feel*—so I scraped a few pounds together and got a machine and some type, and I and the girls began to print without knowing any more about it than Adam.

'How did we learn to set type and lock up a forme? Goodness knows! Just worked at it till we puzzled it out! And how the men used to come and patronise us, and try to get something out of us! I remember one day a man from the *Christian World* came round to borrow a block—a picture. I wouldn't lend it to him; I said we had paid a pound for it, and I couldn't afford to go and buy blocks for other papers. Then he stood by the stone and sneered at the girls locking up the formes. We were just going to press, and you know locking-up isn't always an easy matter—particularly for new-chums like we were.

'Well, he stood there and said nasty things and poor Miss Greig—she's my forewoman—and the girls, they got as white as chalk: the tears were in their eyes. I asked him three times to go, and he wouldn't, so I took up a watering-pot full of water that we had for sweeping the floor, and I let him have it.

'It went with a s-swish, and you should just have seen him! he was so nicely dressed—all white flannel and straw-hat, and spring flowers in his button-hole; and it wet him through—knocked his hat off and filled his coat-pocket full of water. He was brave, I'll say that; he wouldn't go; he just wiped himself and stood there getting nastier and nastier, and I lost patience. "Look here", I said, "do you know what we do in the bush to tramps that come bothering us? We give 'em clean water first, and then, if they won't go, we give 'em something like this." And I took up the lye-bucket that we used for cleaning the type: it was thick, with an inch of black scum on it like jelly, that wobbled when you shook it. I held it under his nose, and said: "Do you see this?" And he went in a hurry.

'Did Henry help me? He did that. His father thought a lot of Henry; he used to call him a tiger for work. Poor boy! when we were starting *Dawn* he used to turn the machine for us; he would just get some verse in his head and go on turning mechanically, forgetting all about us. He didn't like to be interrupted when he was thinking, so often when the issue was all printed off we would go upstairs to supper and leave him there turning away at the empty machine, with his eyes shining.

'Are you married? I am glad: a bachelor is only half a man. But so many of you think that a wife is bought by a wedding-dress and a ring. No! a woman is bound to a man only by her love for him, her respect for him, to the extent of her trust and faith in him. O, if men would permit us to trust and honour them! We do so wish to.'

1896/1978

MARY GILMORE
1865—1962

At her death, Dame Mary Gilmore had published around 600 uncollected poems in journals, as well as eight major collections, but in 1988 her biographer could describe her work as almost unknown. A two-volume *Collected Poems* (2004 and 2007), edited by Jennifer Strauss (qv), promises a significant reassessment of this once nationally renowned figure whose image appears on the ten-dollar note.

She was born Mary Jean Cameron near Goulburn, NSW. Gilmore's lifelong socialist views were formed by her working-class rural childhood and time spent as a teacher in mining towns during the late 1880s, when she began publishing poetry. She moved to Sydney in 1890. A sentimental friend of Henry Lawson (qv), she was also committed to the utopian socialism of William Lane and in 1895 was one of the few single women to migrate to the cooperative commune established in Paraguay. There she married the 'handsome but scantily educated' William Gilmore, and their son Billy was born.

They returned to Australia in 1902, where Gilmore slowly resumed her career as a poet and journalist committed to social change. She particularly directed her efforts to women, collecting recipes for *The Worker Cook Book* (1915), which was very popular. Her later collections thread a concern for the environment and for the treatment of Indigenous Australians with a nostalgia for pioneering often expressed as such. *NM*

Eve-Song

I span and Eve span
A thread to bind the heart of man;
But the heart of man was a wandering thing
That came and went with little to bring:
Nothing he minded what we made,   5
As here he loitered, and there he stayed.

I span and Eve span
A thread to bind the heart of man;
But the more we span the more we found
It wasn't his heart but ours we bound.   10
For children gathered about our knees:
The thread was a chain that stole our ease.
And one of us learned in our children's eyes
That more than man was love and prize.
But deep in the heart of one of us lay   15
A root of loss and hidden dismay.

He said he was strong. He had no strength
But that which comes of breadth and length.
He said he was fond. But his fondness proved
The flame of an hour when he was moved.   20
He said he was true. His truth was but
A door that winds could open and shut.

And yet, and yet, as he came back,
Wandering in from the outward track,
We held our arms, and gave him our breast,   25
As a pillowing place for his head to rest.
I span and Eve span,
A thread to bind the heart of man!

1918

The Measure

Must the young blood for ever flow?
Shall the wide wounds no closing know?
Is hate the only lantern of the stars?
And honour bastard but to scars?
And yet, the equal sun looks down   5
On kingly head and broken clown,
And sees, not friend and foe, but man and man
As when these years began.

These are the days of all men's tears—
Tears like the endless drop that wears   10
The rock, and rusts the steel, and frets the bones
Of dead men lying under stones:
And yet, the stars look on the earth
As in the hour of Christ His birth,
And see, not friend and foe, but man and man   15
As when these years began.

Weeds on the garden pathways grow
Where the swift feet were wont to go;
Closed are the doors that stood so wide—
The white beds empty, side by side.   20
                                                1918

Old Botany Bay

I'm old
Botany Bay;
Stiff in the joints,
Little to say.

I am he   5
Who paved the way,
That you might walk
At your ease today;

I was the conscript
Sent to hell   10
To make the desert
The living well;

I bore the heat,
I blazed the track—
Furrowed and bloody   15
Upon my back.

I split the rock;
I felled the tree:
The nation was—
Because of me!   20

Old Botany Bay
Taking the sun
From day to day …
Shame on the mouth
That would deny   25
The knotted hands
That set us high!

                                       1918

Australia

I

There was great beauty in the names her people called her,
Shaping to patterns of sound the form of their words;
They wove to measure of speech the cry of the bird,
And the voices that rose from the reeds of the cowal.[1]

There, when the trumpeting frog boomed forth in the night,   5
Gobbagumbalin! he said, *Gobbagumbalin!*
And even as Aristophanes heard in the far-off deeps
Of his Grecian marshes, the frogs, so we in that word.
'*Gobbagumbalin! … Gobbagumbalin! … Gobbagumbalin! …*'
Hearken, and measure the sound!   10

II

Mark where, fallen, the tribes move in the shadow;
Dark are the silent places where Arunta walks—
Dark as the dim valleys of Hades, where stalk,

---

1   An Aboriginal word meaning 'a small, tree-grown, swampy depression', C.E.W. Bean (qv).

Grey-shaped, the heroes and the gods of the Greeks.
These were the young, for even then Arunta was old.   5

Very old was Arunta when Alexander wept;
Old, old was Arunta when over Bethlehem
Was seen the star that told the birth of Christ;
Old, old was Arunta when upward from the deep
Was swung the hammer-symbol of Poseidon.   10
Troy rose and fell, but Arunta lived on.
Then was Arunta put out in a night.

                                                                    1932

Fourteen Men

Fourteen men,
And each hung down
Straight as a log
From his toes to his crown.

Fourteen men,   5
Chinamen they were,
Hanging on the trees
In their pig-tailed hair.

Honest poor men,
But the diggers said 'Nay!'   10
So they strung them all up
On a fine summer's day.

There they were hanging
As we drove by,
Grown-ups on the front seat,   15
On the back seat I.

That was Lambing Flat,[1]
And still I can see
The straight up and down
Of each on his tree.   20
                                                                    1954

---

1   The anti-Chinese goldfields riots at Lambing Flat (now Young) occurred in 1861 and resulted in the
    passage of the NSW *Chinese Immigration Act* restricting Chinese migration.

BARCROFT BOAKE
1866–1892

Poet Barcroft Boake was born and educated in Sydney, where he began work as a surveyor in 1883. In 1886 he moved to the Monaro district of southern NSW and later worked as a boundary rider in the central-west of the state, before travelling further north to Queensland where he worked as a drover. During these years in the bush, he read Adam Lindsay Gordon's (qv) poems, which were then highly popular. He began to write his own poems while working as a surveyor near Wagga Wagga in southern NSW, publishing many of them in the *Bulletin*. At the end of 1891 he returned to Sydney to find his father bankrupt and his family in disarray. Depressed, and unable to find work in the city, he committed suicide by hanging himself from a gum tree with his stockwhip. In 1897 the *Bulletin*'s A.G. Stephens (qv) edited and published a collection of Boake's poems, under the title of his best-known piece, 'Where the Dead Men Lie'. *EW*

Where the Dead Men Lie

Out on the wastes of the Never Never—
 That's where the dead men lie!
There where the heat-waves dance for ever—
 That's where the dead men lie!
That's where the Earth's loved sons are keeping   5
Endless tryst: not the west wind sweeping
Feverish pinions can wake their sleeping—
 Out where the dead men lie!

Where brown Summer and Death have mated—
 That's where the dead men lie!   10
Loving with fiery lust unsated—
 That's where the dead men lie!
Out where the grinning skulls bleach whitely
Under the saltbush sparkling brightly;
Out where the wild dogs chorus nightly—   15
 That's where the dead men lie!

Deep in the yellow, flowing river—
 That's where the dead men lie!
Under the banks where the shadows quiver—
 That's where the dead men lie!   20
Where the platypus twists and doubles,
Leaving a train of tiny bubbles;
Rid at last of their earthly troubles—
 That's where the dead men lie!

East and backward pale faces turning—   25
    That's how the dead men lie!
Gaunt arms stretched with a voiceless yearning—
    That's how the dead men lie!
Oft in the fragrant hush of nooning
Hearing again their mothers' crooning,   30
Wrapt for aye in a dreamful swooning—
    That's how the dead men lie!

Only the hand of Night can free them—
    That's when the dead men fly!
Only the frightened cattle see them—   35
    See the dead men go by!
Cloven hoofs beating out one measure,
Bidding the stockmen know no leisure—
That's when the dead men take their pleasure!
    That's when the dead men fly!   40

Ask, too, the never-sleeping drover:
    He sees the dead pass by;
Hearing them call to their friends—the plover,
    Hearing the dead men cry;
Seeing their faces stealing, stealing,   45
Hearing their laughter, pealing, pealing,
Watching their grey forms wheeling, wheeling
    Round where the cattle lie!

Strangled by thirst and fierce privation—
    That's how the dead men die!   50
Out on Moneygrub's farthest station—
    That's how the dead men die!
Hardfaced greybeards, youngsters callow;
Some mounds cared for, some left fallow;
Some deep down, yet others shallow;   55
    Some having but the sky.

Moneygrub, as he sips his claret,
    Looks with complacent eye
Down at his watch-chain, eighteen carat—
    There, in his club, hard by: 60
Recks not that every link is stamped with

Names of men whose limbs are cramped with
Too long lying in grave mould, camped with
Death where the dead men lie.

1897

BERNARD O'DOWD
1866–1953

A radical socialist influenced by his Irish heritage and the Eureka Stockade, Bernard O'Dowd was a powerful voice in the dynamic Melbourne literary scene of the early twentieth century. His first volume of poetry, *Dawnward?* (1903), posed the problem of Australia's future and his 1909 address 'Poetry Militant' employed strong notes from his correspondence with Walt Whitman in emphasising the importance of poetic engagement with the social world. *The Bush* (1912), O'Dowd's most significant collection, manifested a radical nationalist aesthetic for the new century. He shared his life with fellow poet Marie Pitt. *NM*

Australia

Last sea-thing dredged by sailor Time from Space,
Are you a drift Sargasso, where the West
In halcyon calm rebuilds her fatal nest?
Or Delos of a coming Sun-God's race?
Are you for Light, and trimmed, with oil in place,   5
Or but a Will o' Wisp on marshy quest?
A new demesne for Mammon to infest?
Or lurks millennial Eden 'neath your face?

The cenotaphs of species dead elsewhere
That in your limits leap and swim and fly,   10
Or trail uncanny harp-strings from your trees,
Mix omens with the auguries that dare
To plant the Cross upon your forehead sky,
A virgin helpmate Ocean at your knees.

1900

HENRY LAWSON
1867–1922

Poet and short-story writer Henry Lawson was born at Grenfell, NSW, and grew up in the nearby goldfields town of Gulgong. His father, a Norwegian sailor named Peter Larsen, had jumped ship to try his luck as a gold miner but by the time of Lawson's birth was struggling to make a living on a small selection. While still a boy, Lawson became profoundly deaf; he received a few years' education at a local school before leaving to help his father. His mother, Louisa Lawson (qv), herself an aspiring writer, left the marriage and the bush in 1883 for Sydney, accompanied by her children. In Sydney, Lawson worked as a coach painter and attempted to study. He began contributing poems and stories to magazines and newspapers, including the *Bulletin*, where his first story, 'His Father's Mate', was published in 1888. In 1892 *Bulletin* editor J.F. Archibald funded Lawson's trip to Bourke, which resulted in some notable works, including 'The Union Buries Its Dead' and 'In a Dry Season'.

Lawson's first collection, *Short Stories in Prose and Verse* (1894), was published by his mother's press. In 1896, buoyed by the success of Banjo Paterson's (qv) *The Man from Snowy River and Other Verses* (1895), the new publishing firm of Angus & Robertson brought out two collections by Lawson: *While the Billy Boils*, which included many of his best stories, and *In the Days When the World was Wide*, a volume of his poems. In the same year, Lawson married Bertha Bredt, with whom he was to have two children. Their marriage was, however, dogged by Lawson's continued difficulty in finding work and his fondness for alcohol. After living in Western Australia and New Zealand, in 1900 the Lawsons left for London, hoping for literary success. Lawson managed to publish three collections there, *The Country I Come From* (1901), a selection of previously published work, *Joe Wilson and His Mates* (1901), which includes a sequence of autobiographically based stories about the marriage of Joe and Mary Wilson, and *Children of the Bush* (1902). But London did not solve either Lawson's financial or marital problems. In 1902 the family returned to Sydney, and Lawson soon separated from his wife.

While Lawson was to continue writing, and would publish several more collections of both prose and verse, his best work was behind him. He spent time in prison for drunkenness and failure to pay family maintenance, and was also admitted to mental hospitals. But his legend was already well established and after his death in 1922 he became the first Australian writer to be honoured with a state funeral. Lawson's work has remained in print and there have been numerous books, plays, films, and television and radio shows written about him. His best stories are the equal of any written internationally at the time and have played a significant role in the development of Australian literature. *EW*

Faces in the Street

They lie, the men who tell us in a loud decisive tone
That want is here a stranger, and that misery's unknown;
For where the nearest suburb and city proper meet
My window-sill is level with the faces in the street—
    Drifting past, drifting past,   5
    To the beat of weary feet—
While I sorrow for the owners of those faces in the street.

And cause I have to sorrow, in a land so young and fair,
To see upon those faces stamped the marks of Want and Care;
I look in vain for traces of the fresh and fair and sweet, 10
In sallow, sunken faces that are drifting through the street—
    Drifting on, drifting on,
    To the scrape of restless feet;
I can sorrow for the owners of the faces in the street.

In hours before the dawning dims the starlight in the sky   15
The wan and weary faces first begin to trickle by,
Increasing as the moments hurry on with morning feet,
Till like a pallid river flow the faces in the street—
    Flowing in, flowing in,
    To the beat of hurried feet—   20
Ah! I sorrow for the owners of those faces in the street.

The human river dwindles when 'tis past the hour of eight,
Its waves go flowing faster in the fear of being late;
But slowly drag the moments, whilst, beneath the dust and heat,
The city grinds the owners of the faces in the street—   25
    Grinding body, grinding soul,
    Yielding scarce enough to eat—
Oh! I sorrow for the owners of the faces in the street.

And then the only faces till the sun is sinking down
Are those of outside toilers and the idlers of the town,   30
Save here and there a face that seems a stranger in the street
Tells of the city's unemployed upon his weary beat—
    Drifting round, drifting round,
    To the tread of listless feet—
Ah! My heart aches for the owner of that sad face in the street.   35

And when the hours on lagging feet have slowly dragged away,
And sickly yellow gaslights rise to mock the going day,
Then flowing past my window like a tide in its retreat,
Again I see the pallid stream of faces in the street—
    Ebbing out, ebbing out,   40
    To the drag of tired feet,
While my heart is aching dumbly for the faces in the street.

And now all blurred and smirched with vice the day's sad pages end,
For while the short 'large hours' towards the longer 'small hours' trend,
With smiles that mock the wearer, and with words that half entreat,   45
Delilah pleads for custom at the corner of the street—
    Sinking down, sinking down,
    Battered wreck by tempests beat—
A dreadful, thankless trade is hers, that Woman of the Street.

But, ah! To dreader things than these our fair young city comes,   50
For in its heart are growing thick the filthy dens and slums,

Where human forms shall rot away in sties for swine unmeet,
And ghostly faces shall be seen unfit for any street—
  Rotting out, rotting out,
  For the lack of air and meat—   55
In dens of vice and horror that are hidden from the street.

I wonder would the apathy of wealthy men endure
Were all their windows level with, the faces of the Poor?
Ah! Mammon's slaves, your knees shall knock, your hearts in terror beat,
When God demands a reason for the sorrows of the street!   60
  The wrong things and the bad things
  And the sad things that we meet
In the filthy lane and alley, and the cruel, heartless street.

I left the dreadful corner where the steps are never still,
And sought another window overlooking gorge and hill;   65
But when the night came dreary with the driving rain and sleet,
They haunted me—the shadows of those faces in the street,
  Flitting by, flitting by,
  Flitting by with noiseless feet,
And with cheeks but little paler than the real ones in the street. 70

Once I cried: 'Oh, God Almighty! if Thy might doth still endure,
Now show me in a vision for the wrongs of Earth a cure.'
And, lo! with shops all shuttered, I beheld a city's street,
And in the warning distance heard the tramp of many feet,
  Coming near, coming near,   75
  To a drum's dull distant beat,
And soon I saw the army that was marching down the street.

And, like a swollen river that has broken bank and wall,
The human flood came pouring with the red flags over all,
And kindled eyes all blazing bright with revolution's heat,   80
And flashing swords reflecting rigid faces in the street—
  Pouring on, pouring on,
  To a drum's loud threatening beat,
And the war-hymns and the cheering of the people in the street.

And so 'twill be while e'er the world goes rolling round its course, 85
The warning pen shall write in vain, the warning voice grow hoarse,
But not until a city feels Red Revolution's feet
Shall its sad people miss awhile the terrors of the street—

The dreadful everlasting strife
For scarcely clothes and meat   90
In that pent track of living death—the city's cruel street.

1888/1896

The Drover's Wife

The two-roomed house is built of round timber, slabs, and stringy bark, and floored with split slabs. A big bark kitchen standing at one end is larger than the house itself, verandah included.

Bush all round—bush with no horizon, for the country is flat. No ranges in the distance. The bush consists of stunted, rotten native apple trees. No undergrowth. Nothing to relieve the eye save the darker green of a few sheoaks which are sighing above the narrow, almost waterless creek. Nineteen miles to the nearest sign of civilisation—a shanty on the main road.

The drover, an ex-squatter, is away with sheep. His wife and children are left here alone.

Four ragged, dried-up-looking children are playing about the house. Suddenly one of them yells: 'Snake! Mother, here's a snake!'

The gaunt, sun-browned bushwoman dashes from the kitchen, snatches her baby from the ground, holds it on her left hip, and reaches for a stick.

'Where is it?'

'Here! gone into the wood-heap!' yells the eldest boy—a sharp-faced, excited urchin of eleven. 'Stop there, mother! I'll have him. Stand back! I'll have the beggar!'

'Tommy, come here, or you'll be bit. Come here at once when I tell you, you little wretch!'

The youngster comes reluctantly, carrying a stick bigger than himself. Then he yells, triumphantly:

'There it goes—under the house!' and darts away with club uplifted. At the same time the big, black, yellow-eyed dog-of-all-breeds, who has shown the wildest interest in the proceedings, breaks his chain and rushes after that snake. He is a moment late, however, and his nose reaches the crack in the slabs just as the end of its tail disappears. Almost at the same moment the boy's club comes down and skins the aforesaid nose. Alligator takes small notice of this, and proceeds to undermine the building; but he is subdued after a struggle and chained up. They cannot afford to lose him.

The drover's wife makes the children stand together near the dog-house while she watches for the snake. She gets two small dishes of milk and sets them down near the wall to tempt it to come out; but an hour goes by and it does not show itself.

It is near sunset, and a thunderstorm is coming. The children must be brought inside. She will not take them into the house, for she knows the snake is there, and may at any moment come up through the cracks in the rough slab floor; so she carries several armfuls of firewood into the kitchen, and then takes the children there. The kitchen has no floor—or, rather, an earthen one—called a 'ground floor' in this part of the bush. There is a large, roughly-made table in the centre of the place. She brings the children in, and makes them get on this table. They are two boys and two girls—mere babies. She gives them some supper, and then, before it gets dark, she goes into the house, and snatches up some pillows and bedclothes—expecting to see or lay her hand on the snake any minute. She makes a bed on the kitchen table for the children, and sits down beside it to watch all night.

She has an eye on the corner, and a green sapling club laid in readiness on the dresser by her side; also her sewing basket and a copy of the *Young Ladies' Journal*. She has brought the dog into the room.

Tommy turns in, under protest, but says he'll lie awake all night and smash that blinded snake.

His mother asks him how many times she has told him not to swear.

He has his club with him under the bedclothes, and Jacky protests:

'Mummy! Tommy's skinnin' me alive wif his club. Make him take it out.'

Tommy: 'Shet up, you little—! D'yer want to be bit with the snake?'

Jacky shuts up.

'If yer bit,' says Tommy, after a pause, 'you'll swell up, an' smell, an' turn red an' green an' blue all over till yer bust. Won't he, mother?'

'Now then, don't frighten the child. Go to sleep,' she says.

The two younger children go to sleep, and now and then Jacky complains of being 'skeezed'. More room is made for him. Presently Tommy says: 'Mother! listen to them (adjective) little opossums. I'd like to screw their blanky necks.'

And Jacky protests drowsily:

'But they don't hurt us, the little blanks!'

Mother: 'There, I told you you'd teach Jacky to swear.' But the remark makes her smile. Jacky goes to sleep.

Presently Tommy asks:

'Mother! Do you think they'll ever extricate the (adjective) kangaroo?'

'Lord! How am I to know, child? Go to sleep.'

'Will you wake me if the snake comes out?'

'Yes. Go to sleep.'

Near midnight. The children are all asleep and she sits there still, sewing and reading by turns. From time to time she glances round the floor and wall-plate, and, whenever she hears a noise, she reaches for the stick. The thunderstorm comes on, and the wind, rushing through the cracks in the slab wall, threatens to blow out her candle. She places it on a sheltered part of the dresser and fixes up a newspaper to protect it. At every flash of lightning, the cracks between the slabs gleam like polished silver. The thunder rolls, and the rain comes down in torrents.

Alligator lies at full length on the floor, with his eyes turned towards the partition. She knows by this that the snake is there. There are large cracks in that wall opening under the floor of the dwelling-house.

She is not a coward, but recent events have shaken her nerves. A little son of her brother-in-law was lately bitten by a snake, and died. Besides, she has not heard from her husband for six months, and is anxious about him.

He was a drover and started squatting here when they were married. The drought of 18— ruined him. He had to sacrifice the remnant of his flock and go droving again. He intends to move his family into the nearest town when he comes back, and, in the meantime, his brother, who keeps a shanty on the main road, comes over about once a month with provisions. The wife has still a couple of cows, one horse, and a few sheep. The brother-in-law kills one of the sheep occasionally, gives her what she needs of it, and takes the rest in return for other provisions.

She is used to being left alone. She once lived like this for eighteen months. As a girl she built the usual castles in the air; but all her girlish hopes and aspirations have long been dead. She finds all the excitement and recreation she needs in the *Young Ladies' Journal*, and, Heaven help her! takes a pleasure in the fashion-plates.

Her husband is an Australian, and so is she. He is careless, but a good enough husband. If he had the means he would take her to the city and keep her there like a princess. They are used to being apart, or at least she is. 'No use fretting,' she says. He may forget sometimes that he is married; but if he has a good cheque when he comes back he will give most of it to her. When he had money he took her to the city several times—hired a railway sleeping compartment, and put up at the best hotels. He also bought her a buggy, but they had to sacrifice that along with the rest.

The last two children were born in the bush—one while her husband was bringing a drunken doctor, by force, to attend to her. She was alone on this occasion, and very weak. She had been ill with a fever. She prayed to God to send her assistance. God sent Black Mary—the 'whitest' gin in all the land. Or, at least, God sent 'Jimmy' first, and he sent Black Mary. He put his black face round the door post, took in the situation at a glance, and said cheerfully: 'All right Missis—I bring my old woman, she down alonga creek.'

One of her children died while she was here alone. She rode nineteen miles for assistance, carrying the dead child.

★

It must be near one or two o'clock. The fire is burning low. Alligator lies with his head resting on his paws, and watches the wall. He is not a very beautiful dog to look at, and the light shows numerous old wounds where the hair will not grow. He is afraid of nothing on the face of the earth or under it. He will tackle a bullock as readily as he will tackle a flea. He hates all other dogs—except kangaroo-dogs—and has a marked dislike to friends or relations of the family. They seldom call, however. He sometimes makes friends with strangers. He hates snakes and has killed many, but he will be bitten some day and die; most snake-dogs end that way.

Now and then the bushwoman lays down her work and watches, and listens, and thinks. She thinks of things in her own life, for there is little else to think about.

The rain will make the grass grow, and this reminds her how she fought a bush fire once while her husband was away. The grass was long, and very dry, and the fire threatened to burn her out. She put on an old pair of her husband's trousers and beat out the flames with a green bough, till great drops of sooty perspiration stood out on her forehead and ran in streaks down her blackened arms. The sight of his mother in trousers greatly amused Tommy, who worked like a little hero by her side, but the terrified baby howled lustily for his 'mummy'. The fire would have mastered her but for four excited bushmen who arrived in the nick of time. It was a mixed-up affair all round: when she went to take up the baby he screamed and struggled convulsively, thinking it was a 'black man'; and Alligator, trusting more to the child's sense than his own instinct, charged furiously, and (being old and slightly deaf) did not in his excitement at first recognise his mistress's voice, but continued to hang on to the moleskins until choked off by Tommy with a saddle-strap. The dog's sorrow for his blunder, and his anxiety to let it be known that it was all a mistake, was as evident as his ragged tail and a twelve-inch grin could make it. It was a glorious time for the boys; a day to look back to, and talk about, and laugh over for many years.

She thinks how she fought a flood during her husband's absence. She stood for hours in the drenching downpour, and dug an overflow gutter to save the dam across the creek. But she could not save it. There are things that a bushwoman cannot do. Next morning the dam was broken, and her heart was nearly broken too, for she thought how her husband would feel when he came home and saw the result of years of labour swept away. She cried then.

She also fought the *pleuro-pneumonia*—dosed and bled the few remaining cattle, and wept again when her two best cows died.

Again, she fought a mad bullock that besieged the house for a day. She made bullets and fired at him through cracks in the slabs with an old shot-gun. He was dead in the morning. She skinned him and got seven-and-sixpence for the hide.

She also fights the crows and eagles that have designs on her chickens. Her plan of campaign is very original. The children cry 'Crows, mother!' and she rushes out and aims a broomstick at the birds as though it were a gun, and says, 'Bung!' The crows leave in a hurry; they are cunning, but a woman's cunning is greater.

Occasionally a bushman in the horrors, or a villainous-looking sundowner, comes and nearly scares the life out of her. She generally tells the suspicious-looking stranger that her husband and two sons are at work below the dam, or over at the yard, for he always cunningly enquires for the boss.

Only last week a gallows-faced swagman—having satisfied himself that there were no men on the place—threw his swag down on the verandah, and demanded tucker. She gave him something to eat; then he expressed his intention of staying for the night. It was sundown then. She got a batten from the sofa, loosened the dog, and confronted the stranger, holding the batten in one hand and the dog's collar with the other. 'Now you go!' she said. He looked at her and at the dog, said 'All right, mum,' in a cringing tone, and left. She was a determined-looking woman, and Alligator's yellow eyes glared unpleasantly—besides, the dog's chawing-up apparatus greatly resembled that of his namesake.

She has few pleasures to think of as she sits here alone by the fire, on guard against a snake. All days are much the same to her, but on Sunday afternoon she dresses herself, tidies the children, smartens-up baby, and goes for a lonely walk along the bush-track, pushing an old perambulator in front of her. She does this every Sunday. She takes as much care to make herself and the children look smart as she would if she were going to do the block in the city. There is nothing to see, however, and not a soul to meet. You might walk for twenty miles along this track without being able to fix a point in your mind, unless you are a bushman. This is because of the everlasting, maddening sameness of the stunted trees—that monotony which makes a man long to break away and travel as far as trains can go, and sail as far as ships can sail—and further.

But this bushwoman is used to the loneliness of it. As a girl-wife she hated it, but now she would feel strange away from it.

She is glad when her husband returns, but she does not gush or make a fuss about it. She gets him something good to eat, and tidies up the children.

She seems contented with her lot. She loves her children, but has no time to show it. She seems harsh to them. Her surroundings are not favourable to the development of the 'womanly' or sentimental side of nature.

It must be near morning now; but the clock is in the dwelling-house. Her candle is nearly done; she forgot that she was out of candles. Some more wood must be got to keep the fire up, and so she shuts the dog inside and hurries round to the woodheap. The rain has cleared off. She seizes a stick, pulls it out, and—crash! the whole pile collapses.

Yesterday she bargained with a stray blackfellow to bring her some wood, and while he was at work she went in search of a missing cow. She was absent an hour or so, and the native black made good use of his time. On her return she was so astonished to see a good heap of wood by the chimney, that she gave him an extra fig of tobacco, and praised him for not being lazy. He thanked her, and left with head erect and chest well out. He was the last of his tribe and a King: but he had built that woodheap hollow.

She is hurt now, and tears spring to her eyes as she sits down again by the table. She takes up a handkerchief to wipe the tears away, but pokes her eyes with her bare fingers instead. The handkerchief is full of holes, and she finds that she has put her thumb through one, and her forefinger through another.

This makes her laugh, to the surprise of the dog. She has a keen, very keen, sense of the ridiculous; and some time or other she will amuse bushmen with the story.

She has been amused before like that. One day she sat down 'to have a good cry,' as she said—and the old cat rubbed against her dress and 'cried too'. Then she had to laugh.

It must be near daylight now. The room is very close and hot because of the fire. Alligator still watches the wall from time to time. Suddenly he becomes greatly interested; he draws himself a few inches nearer the partition, and a thrill runs through his body. The hair on the back of his neck begins to bristle, and the battle-light is in his yellow eyes. She knows what this means, and lays her hand on the stick. The lower end of one of the partition slabs has a large crack on both sides. An evil pair of small, bright, bead-like eyes glisten at one of these holes. The snake—a black one—comes slowly out, about a foot, and moves its head up and down. The dog lies still, and the woman sits as one fascinated. The snake comes out a foot further. She lifts her stick, and the reptile, as though suddenly aware of danger, sticks his head in through the crack on the other side of the slab, and hurries to get his tail round after him. Alligator springs, and his jaws come together with a snap. He misses this time, for his nose is large, and the snake's body close down in the angle formed by the slabs and the floor. He snaps again as the tail comes round. He has the snake now, and tugs it out eighteen inches. Thud, thud comes the woman's club on the ground. Alligator pulls again. Thud, thud. Alligator pulls some more. He has the snake out now—a black brute, five feet long. The head rises to dart about, but the dog has the enemy close to the neck. He is a big, heavy dog, but quick as a terrier. He shakes the snake as though he felt the original curse in common with mankind. The eldest boy wakes up, seizes his stick, and tries to get out of bed, but his mother forces him back with a grip of iron. Thud, thud—the snake's back is broken in several places. Thud, thud—its head is crushed, and Alligator's nose skinned again.

She lifts the mangled reptile on the point of her stick, carries it to the fire, and throws it in; then piles on the wood, and watches the snake burn. The boy and dog watch, too. She lays her hand on the dog's head, and all the fierce, angry light dies out of his yellow eyes. The younger children are quieted, and presently go to sleep. The dirty-legged boy stands for a moment in his shirt, watching the fire. Presently he looks up at her, sees the tears in her eyes, and, throwing his arms round her neck, exclaims:

'Mother, I won't never go drovin'; blast me if I do!'

And she hugs him to her worn-out breast and kisses him; and they sit thus together while the sickly daylight breaks over the bush.

1894

The Union Buries Its Dead

While out boating one Sunday afternoon on a billabong across the river, we saw a young man on horseback driving some horses along the bank. He said it was a fine day, and asked if the water was deep there. The joker of our party said it was deep enough to drown him, and he laughed and rode farther up. We didn't take much notice of him.

Next day a funeral gathered at a corner pub and asked each other in to have a drink while waiting for the hearse. They passed away some of the time dancing jigs to a piano in the bar parlour. They passed away the rest of the time sky-larking and fighting.

The defunct was a young union labourer, about twenty-five, who had been drowned the previous day while trying to swim some horses across a billabong of the Darling.

He was almost a stranger in town, and the fact of his having been a union man accounted for the funeral. The police found some union papers in his swag, and called at the General Labourers' Union Office for information about him. That's how we knew. The secretary had very little information to give. The departed was a 'Roman', and the majority of the town were otherwise—but unionism is stronger than creed. Drink, however, is stronger than unionism; and, when the hearse presently arrived, more than two-thirds of the funeral were unable to follow. They were too drunk.

The procession numbered fifteen, fourteen souls following the broken shell of a soul. Perhaps not one of the fourteen possessed a soul any more than the corpse did—but that doesn't matter.

Four or five of the funeral, who were boarders at the pub, borrowed a trap which the landlord used to carry passengers to and from the railway station. They were strangers to us who were on foot, and we to them. We were all strangers to the corpse.

A horseman, who looked like a drover just returned from a big trip, dropped into our dusty wake and followed us a few hundred yards, dragging his pack-horse behind him, but a friend made wild and demonstrative signals from a hotel verandah—hooking at the air in front with his right hand and jobbing his left thumb over his shoulder in the direction of the bar—so the drover hauled off and didn't catch up to us any more. He was a stranger to the entire show.

We walked in twos. There were three twos. It was very hot and dusty; the heat rushed in fierce dazzling rays across every iron roof and light coloured wall that was turned to the sun. One or two pubs closed respectfully until we got past. They closed their bar doors and the patrons went in and out through some side or back entrance for a few minutes. Bushmen seldom grumble at an inconvenience of this sort, when it is caused by a funeral. They have too much respect for the dead.

On the way to the cemetery we passed three shearers sitting on the shady side of a fence. One was drunk—very drunk. The other two covered their right ears with their hats, out of respect for the departed—whoever he might have been—and one of them kicked the drunk and muttered something to him.

He straightened himself up, stared, and reached helplessly for his hat, which he shoved half off and then on again. Then he made a great effort to pull himself together—and succeeded. He stood up, braced his back against the fence, knocked off his hat, and remorsefully placed his foot on it—to keep it off his head till the funeral passed.

A tall, sentimental drover, who walked by my side, cynically quoted Byronic verses suitable to the occasion—to death—and asked with pathetic humour whether we thought the dead man's ticket would be recognized 'over yonder'. It was a G.L.U. ticket, and the general opinion was that it would be recognized.

Presently my friend said:

'You remember when we were in the boat yesterday, we saw a man driving some horses along the bank?'

'Yes.'

He nodded at the hearse and said:

'Well, that's him.'

I thought awhile.

'I didn't take any particular notice of him,' I said. 'He said something, didn't he?'

'Yes; said it was a fine day. You'd have taken more notice if you'd known that he was doomed to die in the hour and that those were the last words he would say to any man in this world.'

'To be sure,' said a full voice from the rear. 'If ye'd known that ye'd have prolonged the conversation.'

We plodded on across the railway line and along the hot, dusty road which ran to the cemetery, some of us talking about the accident, and lying about the narrow escapes we had had ourselves. Presently someone said:

'There's the Devil.'

I looked up and saw a priest standing in the shade of the tree by the cemetery gate.

The hearse was drawn up and the tail-boards were opened. The funeral extinguished its right ear with its hat as four men lifted the coffin out and laid it over the grave. The priest—a pale, quiet young fellow—stood under the shade of a sapling which grew at the head of the grave. He took off his hat, dropped it carelessly on the ground, and proceeded to business. I noticed that one or two heathens winced slightly when the holy water was sprinkled on the coffin. The drops quickly evaporated, and the little round black spots they left were soon dusted over; but the spots showed, by contrast, the cheapness and shabbiness of the cloth with which the coffin was covered. It seemed black before;—now it looked a dusky grey.

Just here man's ignorance and vanity made a farce of the funeral. A big, bull-necked publican, with heavy, blotchy features and a supremely ignorant expression, picked up the priest's straw hat and held it about two inches over the head of his reverence during the whole of the service. The father, be it remembered, was standing in the shade. A few shoved their hats on and off uneasily, struggling between their disgust for the living and their respect for the dead. The hat had a conical crown and a brim sloping down all round like a sunshade, and the publican held it with his great red claw spread over the crown. To do the priest justice, perhaps he didn't notice the incident. A stage priest or parson in the same position might have said, 'Put the hat down, my friend; is not the memory of our departed brother worth more than my complexion?' A wattlebark layman might have expressed himself in stronger language, none the less to the point. But my priest seemed unconscious of what was going on. Besides, the publican was a great and important pillar of the church. He couldn't, as an ignorant and conceited ass, lose such a good opportunity of asserting his faithfulness and importance to his church.

The grave looked very narrow under the coffin, and I drew a breath of relief when the box slid easily down. I saw a coffin get stuck once, at

Rookwood, and it had to be yanked out with difficulty, and laid on the sods at the feet of the heart-broken relations, who howled dismally while the grave-diggers widened the hole. But they don't cut contracts so fine in the West. Our grave-digger was not altogether bowelless, and, out of respect for that human quality described as 'feelin's', he scraped up some light and dusty soil and threw it down to deaden the fall of the clay lumps on the coffin. He also tried to steer the first few shovelsful gently down against the end of the grave with the back of the shovel turned outwards, but the hard dry Darling River clods rebounded and knocked all the same. It didn't matter much—nothing does. The fall of lumps of clay on a stranger's coffin doesn't sound any different from the fall of the same things on an ordinary wooden box—at least I didn't notice anything awesome or unusual in the sound; but, perhaps, one of us—the most sensitive—might have been impressed by being reminded of a burial of long ago, when the thump of every sod jolted his heart.

I have left out the wattle—because it wasn't there. I have also neglected to mention the heart-broken old mate, with his grizzled head bowed and great pearly drops streaming down his rugged cheeks. He was absent—he was probably 'Out Back'. For similar reasons I have omitted reference to the suspicious moisture in the eyes of a bearded bush ruffian named Bill. Bill failed to turn up, and the only moisture was that which was induced by the heat. I have left out the 'sad Australian sunset' because the sun was not going down at the time. The burial took place exactly at mid-day.

The dead bushman's name was Jim, apparently; but they found no portraits, nor locks of hair, nor any love letters, nor anything of that kind in his swag—not even a reference to his mother; only some papers relating to union matters. Most of us didn't know the name till we saw it on the coffin; we knew him as 'that poor chap that got drowned yesterday'.

'So his name's James Tyson,' said my drover acquaintance, looking at the plate.

'Why! Didn't you know that before?' I asked.

'No; but I knew he was a union man.'

It turned out, afterwards, that J.T. wasn't his real name—only 'the name he went by'.

Anyhow he was buried by it, and most of the 'Great Australian Dailies' have mentioned in their brevity columns that a young man named James John Tyson was drowned in a billabong of the Darling last Sunday.

We did hear, later on, what his real name was; but if we ever chance to read it in the 'Missing Friends Column', we shall not be able to give any information to heart-broken Mother or Sister or Wife, nor to anyone who could let him hear something to his advantage—for we have already forgotten the name.

1894

In a Dry Season

Draw a wire fence and a few ragged gums, and add some scattered sheep running away from the train. Then you'll have the bush all along the New South Wales Western line from Bathurst on.

The railway towns consist of a public house and a general store, with a square tank and a schoolhouse on piles in the nearer distance. The tank stands at the end of the school and is not many times smaller than the building itself. It is safe to call the pub 'The Railway Hotel', and the store 'The Railway Stores', with an 's'. A couple of patient, ungroomed hacks are probably standing outside the pub, while their masters are inside having a drink—several drinks. Also it's safe to draw a sundowner sitting listlessly on a bench on the veranda, reading the *Bulletin*.

The Railway Stores seem to exist only in the shadow of the pub, and it is impossible to conceive either as being independent of the other. There is sometimes a small, oblong weatherboard building—unpainted, and generally leaning in one of the eight possible directions, and perhaps with a twist in another—which, from its half-obliterated sign, seems to have started as a rival to the Railway Stores; but the shutters are up and the place empty.

The only town I saw that differed much from the above consisted of a box-bark humpy with a clay chimney, and a woman standing at the door throwing out the wash-up water.

By way of variety, the artist might make a water-colour-sketch of a fettler's tent on the line, with a billy hanging over the fire in front, and three fettlers standing round filling their pipes.

Slop sac suits, red faces, and old-fashioned, flat-brimmed hats, with wire round the brims, begin to drop into the train on the other side of Bathurst; and here and there a hat with three inches of crape round the crown, which perhaps signifies death in the family at some remote date, and perhaps doesn't. Sometimes, I believe, it only means grease under the band. I notice that when a bushman puts crape round his hat he generally leaves it there till the hat wears out, or another friend dies. In the later case, he buys a new piece of crape. This outward sign of bereavement usually has a jolly red face beneath it. Death is about the only cheerful thing in the bush.

We crossed the Macquarie—a narrow, muddy gutter with a dog swimming across, and three goats interested.

A little farther on we saw the first sundowner. He carried a Royal Alfred,[1] and had a billy in one hand and a stick in the other. He was dressed in a tail-coat turned yellow, a print shirt, and a pair of moleskin trousers, with big square calico patches on the knees; and his old straw hat was covered

---

1   A large rolled swag.

with calico. Suddenly he slipped his swag, dropped his billy, and ran forward, boldly flourishing the stick. I thought that he was mad, and was about to attack the train, but he wasn't; he was only killing a snake. I didn't have time to see whether he cooked the snake or not—perhaps he only thought of Adam.

Somebody told me that the country was very dry on the other side of Nevertire. It is. I wouldn't like to sit down on it anywhere. The least horrible spot in the bush, in a dry season, is where the bush isn't—where it has been cleared away and a green crop is trying to grow. They talk of settling people on the land! Better settle *in* it. I'd rather settle on the water; at least, until some gigantic system of irrigation is perfected in the West.

Along about Byrock we saw the first shearers. They dress like the unemployed, but differ from that body in their looks of independence. They sat on trucks and wool-bales and the fence, watching the train, and hailed Bill, and Jim, and Tom, and asked how those individuals were getting on.

Here we came across soft felt hats with straps round the crowns, and full-bearded faces under them. Also a splendid-looking black tracker in a masher uniform[1] and a pair of Wellington boots.

One or two square-cuts and stand-up collars struggle dismally through to the bitter end. Often a member of the unemployed starts cheerfully out, with a letter from the Government Labour Bureau in his pocket, and nothing else. He has an idea that the station where he has the job will be within easy walking distance of Bourke. Perhaps he thinks there'll be a cart or a buggy waiting for him. He travels for a night and day without a bite to eat, and, on arrival, he finds that the station is eighty or a hundred miles away. Then he has to explain matters to a publican and a coach-driver. God bless the publican and the coach-driver! God forgive our social system!

Native industry was represented at one place along the line by three tiles, a chimney-pot, and a length of piping on a slab.

Somebody said to me, 'Yer wanter go out back, young man, if yer wanter see the country. Yer wanter get away from the line.' I don't wanter; I've been there.

You could go to the brink of eternity so far as Australia is concerned and yet meet an animated mummy of a swagman who will talk of going 'out back'. Out upon the out-back fiend!

About Byrock we met the bush liar in all his glory. He was dressed like—like a bush larrikin. His name was Jim. He had been to a ball where some blank had 'touched' his blanky overcoat. The overcoat had a cheque for ten 'quid' in the pocket. He didn't seem to feel the loss much. 'Wot's ten quid?' He'd been everywhere, including the Gulf country. He still had three

1 Clothes suitable for wearing in one's courting days.

or four sheds to go to. He had telegrams in his pocket from half-a-dozen squatters and supers offering him pens on any terms. He didn't give a blank whether he took them or no. He thought at first he had the telegrams on him, but found that he had left them in the pocket of the overcoat aforesaid. He had learned butchering in a day. He was a bit of a scrapper himself and talked a lot about the ring. At the last station where he shore he gave the super the father of a hiding. The super was a big chap, about six foot three, and had knocked out Paddy Somebody in one round. He worked with a man who shore 400 sheep in nine hours.

Here a quiet-looking bushman in a corner of the carriage grew restless, and presently he opened his mouth and took the liar down in about three minutes.

At 5.30 we saw a long line of camels moving out across the sunset. There's something snaky about camels. They remind me of turtles and iguanas.

Somebody said, 'Here's Bourke.'

1896

STEELE RUDD
1868–1935

Steele Rudd was the pen name used by Arthur Hoey Davis for his highly popular stories about the Rudd family and their life on a small Queensland selection; they began appearing in the *Bulletin* in 1895. Davis was born in Queensland—his Welsh father had been transported for stealing. In 1875 the Davis family took up a selection at Emu Creek, and Rudd's experiences growing up there were to form the basis of his first stories, in which Dad Rudd and his family struggle to make a living from the land. Unlike Dad's son Dave, Rudd himself left the selection when he was seventeen for a job as a public service clerk in Brisbane. He worked in various posts there until retrenched in 1903, when he attempted to support his wife and family through his writing. Thanks in part to assistance from the *Bulletin*'s literary editor, A.G. Stephens (qv), Rudd's first collection, *On Our Selection!* (1899), was a great success, with 20,000 copies sold by the time its successor, *Our New Selection!*, appeared in 1903. From 1904 Rudd began to sell his material to A.C. Rowlandson, whose NSW Bookstall Company sold cheap and colourful paperback books at railway stations. The paperback version of *On Our Selection!* sold an estimated quarter of a million copies but since Rudd had sold his copyright to Rowlandson he did not share in this success. Rudd's characters became even better known following the success of the stage adaptation of *On Our Selection!* in 1912, though again without much financial benefit to Rudd himself. The original stage Dad, Bert Bailey, went on to star in a cinematic adaptation of the play in 1932 and in three later films which moved the characters further away from Rudd's originals. From 1937 to 1952, a radio serial, 'Dad and Dave from Snake Gully', was performed without any acknowledgement of Rudd or his stories. By then the characters had become part of Australian folklore and their originator was forgotten. Although Rudd published a further 22 books, as well as running *Steele Rudd's Magazine* (1903–07), he was never able to repeat the success of his first two collections. In 1930 he was granted a Commonwealth Literary Fund pension. *EW*

From *On Our Selection!*
Chapter 3: Before We Got the Deeds

Our selection adjoined a sheep-run on the Darling Downs, and boasted of few and scant improvements, though things had gradually got a little better than when we started. A verandahless four-roomed slab-hut now standing out from a forest of box-trees, a stock-yard, and six acres under barley were the only evidence of settlement. A few horses—not ours—sometimes grazed about; and occasionally a mob of cattle—also not ours—cows with young calves, steers, and an old bull or two, would stroll around, chew the best legs of any trousers that might be hanging on the log reserved as a clothes-line, then leave in the night and be seen no more for months—some of them never.

And yet we were always out of meat!

Dad was up the country earning a few pounds—the corn drove him up when it didn't bring what he expected. All we got out of it was a bag of flour—I don't know what the storekeeper got. Before he left we put in the barley. Somehow, Dad didn't believe in sowing any more crops, he seemed to lose heart; but Mother talked it over with him, and when reminded that he would soon be entitled to the deeds he brightened up again and worked. How he worked!

We had no plough, so old Anderson turned over the six acres for us, and Dad gave him a pound an acre—at least he was to send him the first six pounds got up country. Dad sowed the seed; then he, Dan and Dave yoked themselves to a large dry bramble each and harrowed it in. From the way they sweated it must have been hard work. Sometimes they would sit down in the middle of the paddock and 'spell' but Dad would say something about getting the deeds and they'd start again.

A cockatoo-fence was round the barley; and wire-posts, a long distance apart, round the grass-paddock. We were to get the wire to put in when Dad sent the money; and apply for the deeds when he came back. Things would be different then, according to Dad, and the farm would be worked properly. We would break up fifty acres, build a barn, buy a reaper, ploughs, cornsheller, get cows and good horses, and start two or three ploughs. Meanwhile, if we (Dan, Dave and I) minded the barley he was sure there'd be something got out of it.

Dad had been away about six weeks. Travellers were passing by every day, and there wasn't one that didn't want a little of something or other. Mother used to ask them if they had met Dad? None ever did until an old grey man came along and said he knew Dad well—he had camped with him one night and shared a damper. Mother was very pleased and brought him in. We had a kangaroo-rat (stewed) for dinner that day. The girls didn't want to lay

it on the table at first, but Mother said he wouldn't know what it was. The
traveller was very hungry and liked it, and when passing his plate the second
time for more, said it wasn't often *he* got any poultry.

He tramped on again, and the girls were very glad he didn't know it
was a rat. But Dave wasn't sure that he didn't know a rat from a rooster, and
reckoned he hadn't met Dad at all.

The seventh week Dad came back. He arrived at night, and the lot of us
had to get up to find the hammer to knock the peg out of the door and let
him in. He brought home three pounds—not enough to get the wire with,
but he also brought a horse and saddle. He didn't say if he bought them.
It was a bay mare, a grand animal for a journey—so Dad said—and only
wanted condition. Emelina, he called her. No mistake, she was a quiet mare!
We put her where there was good feed, but she wasn't one that fattened
on grass. Birds took kindly to her—crows mostly—and she couldn't go
anywhere but a flock of them accompanied her. Even when Dad used to
ride her (Dan or Dave never rode her) they used to follow, and would fly on
ahead to wait in a tree and 'caw' when he was passing beneath.

One morning when Dan was digging potatoes for dinner—splendid
potatoes they were, too, Dad said; he had only once tasted sweeter ones, but
they were grown in a cemetery—he found the kangaroos had been in the
barley. We knew what *that* meant, and that night made fires round it, thinking
to frighten them off, but didn't—mobs of them were in at daybreak. Dad
swore from the house at them, but they took no notice; and when he ran
down, they just hopped over the fence and sat looking at him. Poor Dad!
I don't know if he was knocked up or if he didn't know any more, but he
stopped swearing and sat on a stump looking at a patch of barley they had
destroyed, and shaking his head. Perhaps he was thinking if he only had a
dog! We did have one until he got a bait. Old Crib! He was lying under the
table at supper-time when he took the first fit, and what a fright we got!
He must have reared before stiffening out, because he capsized the table
into Mother's lap, and everything on it smashed except the tin-plates and
the pints. The lamp fell on Dad, too, and the melted fat scalded his arm. Dad
dragged Crib out and cut off his tail and ears, but he might as well have
taken off his head.

Dad stood with his back to the fire while Mother was putting a stitch
in his trousers. 'There's nothing for it but to watch them at night,' he was
saying, when old Anderson appeared and asked 'if I could have those few
pounds.' Dad asked Mother if she had any money in the house? Of course
she hadn't. Then he told Anderson he would let him have it when he got
the deeds. Anderson left, and Dad sat on the edge of the sofa and seemed
to be counting the grains on a corn-cob that he lifted from the floor, while
Mother sat looking at a kangaroo-tail on the table and didn't notice the cat

drag it off. At last Dad said, 'Ah, well!—it won't be long now, Ellen, before we have the deeds!'

We took it in turns to watch the barley. Dan and the two girls watched the first half of the night, and Dad, Dave and I the second. Dad always slept in his clothes, and he used to think some nights that the others came in before time. It was terrible going out, half awake, to tramp round that paddock from fire to fire, from hour to hour, shouting and yelling. And how we used to long for daybreak! Whenever we sat down quietly together for a few minutes we would hear the dull *thud! thud! thud!*—the kangaroo's footstep.

At last we each carried a kerosene tin, slung like a kettle-drum, and belted it with a waddy—Dad's idea. He himself manipulated an old bell that he had found on a bullock's grave, and made a splendid noise with it.

It was a hard struggle, but we succeeded in saving the bulk of the barley, and cut it down with a scythe and three reaping-hooks. The girls helped to bind it, and Jimmy Mulcahy carted it in return for three days' binding Dad put in for him. The stack wasn't built twenty-four hours when a score of somebody's crawling cattle ate their way up to their tails into it. We took the hint and put a sapling fence round it.

Again Dad decided to go up country for a while. He caught Emelina after breakfast, rolled up a blanket, told us to watch the stack, and started. The crows followed.

We were having dinner. Dave said, 'Listen!' We listened, and it seemed as though all the crows and other feathered demons of the wide bush were engaged in a mighty scrimmage. 'Dad's back!' Dan said, and rushed out in the lead of a stampede.

Emelina was back, anyway, with the swag on, but Dad wasn't. We caught her, and Dave pointed to white spots all over the saddle, and said—'Hanged if they haven't been ridin' her!'—meaning the crows.

Mother got anxious and sent Dan to see what had happened. Dan found Dad, with his shirt off, at a pub on the main road, wanting to fight the publican for a hundred pounds, but he couldn't persuade him to come home. Two men brought him home that night on a sheep-hurdle, and he gave up the idea of going away.

After all, the barley turned out well—there was a good price that year, and we were able to run two wires round the paddock.

One day a bulky Government letter came. Dad looked surprised and pleased, and how his hand trembled as he broke the seal! 'The Deeds!' he said, and all of us gathered round to look at them. Dave thought they were like the inside of a bear-skin covered with writing.

Dad said he would ride to town at once, and went for Emelina.

'Couldn't y' find her, Dad?' Dan said, seeing him return without the mare.

Dad cleared his throat, but didn't answer. Mother asked him.

'Yes, I *found* her,' he said, slowly, '*dead.*'

The crows had got her at last.

He wrapped the deeds in a piece of rag and walked.

There was nothing, scarcely, that he didn't send out from town, and Jimmy Mulcahy and old Anderson have many and many times after that borrowed our dray.

Now Dad regularly curses the deeds every mail-day, and wishes to Heaven he had never got them.

1899

MARY E. FULLERTON
1868–1946

After growing up on a Gippsland farm without a formal education, Mary Fullerton became involved with literature, progressive politics and the women's suffrage campaigns of the late 1890s and early 1900s. She wrote on women's issues and against conscription, and released three verse collections—*Moods and Melodies* (1908), *The Breaking Furrow* (1921) and *Bark House Days* (1921)—before moving to England in 1922.

There she lived with fellow women's activist Mabel Singleton and met Miles Franklin (qv), with whom she sustained a twenty-year correspondence. Fullerton wrote three novels under her own name and two under a male pseudonym. After returning to Australia she released two poetry collections—*Moles Do So Little with Their Privacy* (1942) and *The Wonder and the Apple* (1946)—under the pseudonym E, with Franklin's help. *NM*

War Time

Young John, the postman, day by day,
In sunshine or in rain,
Comes down our road with words of doom
In envelopes of pain.

What cares he as he swings along   5
At his mechanic part,
How many times his hand lets fall
The knocker on a heart?

He whistles merry scraps of song,
Whate'er his bag contain—   10
Of words of death, of words of doom
In envelopes of pain.

1921

ETHEL TURNER
1870–1958

Fame came to Ethel Turner very early, with the publication of her best-known children's novel, *Seven Little Australians* (1894), when she was only 24. She had been born in England; her father died in 1874 and, when her stepfather Henry Turner also died, her mother Sarah Jane decided to move to Australia, where in 1880 she married for a third time. Turner was a foundation pupil of Sydney Girls' High School where, with her older sister Lilian, she ran a magazine, the *Iris*, in opposition to the *Gazette* run by Louise Mack. After leaving school, the sisters founded a monthly magazine, the *Parthenon*, which they continued for three years; Turner wrote the serial romances and ran the children's page. In 1893 her first story appeared in the *Bulletin* and she edited the children's page for the *Illustrated Sydney News*. When it appeared the following year, *Seven Little Australians* won praise for its humour, domestic realism and refusal to idealise or sentimentalise its portrayal of Australian children. It has never been out of print and has been adapted many times for film, radio, television and the stage. A sequel, *The Family at Misrule* (1895), was less successful, perhaps because it lacked Judy's rebellious spark. Turner revived her for her final novel, *Judy and Punch* (1928).

Between 1894 and 1928, Turner produced 42 books, mainly children's novels but also collections of stories and poems. In 1896 she married a barrister, Herbert Curlewis. They had two children, Jean and Adrian. After the death of her daughter from tuberculosis in 1930, Turner's writing career came to an end. For a remarkable 62 years, she kept personal diaries which reveal the incidents and events that influenced her life and writing career. Extracts from these were published in 1979, edited by her granddaughter, Philippa Poole. *EW*

From *Seven Little Australians*
Chapter II: Fowl for Dinner

'Oh, don't the days seem lank and long
When all goes right and nothing wrong?
And isn't your life extremely flat
With nothing whatever to grumble at?'[1]

I hope you are not quite deafened yet, for though I have got through the introductions, tea is not nearly finished, so we must stay in the nursery a little longer. All the time I have been talking Pip has been grumbling at the lack of good things. The table was not very tempting, certainly; the cloth looked as if it had been flung on, the china was much chipped and battered, the tea was very weak, and there was nothing to eat but great thick slices of bread and butter. Still, it was the usual tea, and everyone seemed surprised at Pip's outburst.

'My father and Esther' (they all called their young stepmother by her Christian name) 'are having roast fowl, three vegetables, and four kinds of pudding,' he said angrily; 'it isn't fair!'

---

1   From W.S. Gilbert (1836–1911), *Princess Ida* (1884).

'But we had dinner at one o'clock, Pip, and yours is saved as usual,' said Meg, pouring out tea with a lavish allowance of hot water and sugar.

'Boiled mutton and carrots and rice pudding!' returned her brother witheringly. 'Why shouldn't *we* have roast fowl and custard and things?'

'Yes, why shouldn't we?' echoed little greedy Bunty, his eyes lighting up.

'What a lot it would take for all of us!' said Meg, cheerfully attacking the bread loaf.

'We're only children; let us be thankful for this nice thick bread and this abundance of melting butter,' said Judy in a good little tone.

Pip pushed his chair back from the table.

'I'm going down to ask for some roast fowl,' he said, with a look of determination in his eyes. 'I can't forget the smell of it, and they'd got a lot on the table; I peeped in the door.'

He took up his plate and proceeded downstairs, returning presently, to the surprise of everyone, with quite a large portion on his plate.

'He couldn't very well refuse,' he chuckled; 'Colonel Bryant is there; but he looked a bit mad. Here, Fizz, I'll go you halves.'

Judy pushed up her plate eagerly at this unusually magnanimous offer, and received a very small division, a fifth part, perhaps, with great gratitude.

'I just *love* fowl,' said Nell longingly; 'I've a great mind to go down and ask for a wing—I believe he'd give it to me.'

These disrespectful children, as I am afraid you will have noticed, always alluded to their father as 'he'.

Nell took up another plate, and departed slowly to the lower regions. She followed into the dining room at the heels of the housemaid, and stood by the side of her father, her plate well behind her.

'Well, my little maid, won't you shake hands with me? What is your name?' said Colonel Bryant, tapping her cheek playfully.

Nell looked up with shy, lovely eyes.

'Elinor Woolcot, but they call me Nell,' she said, holding out her left hand, since her right was occupied with the plate.

'What a little barbarian you are, Nell!' laughed her father; but he gave her a quick, annoyed glance. 'Where is your right hand?'

She drew it slowly from behind her and held out the cracked old plate. 'I thought perhaps you would give me some fowl too,' she said; 'just a leg or a wing, or a bit of breast would do.'

The Captain's brow darkened. 'What is the meaning of this? Pip has just been to me too. Have you nothing to eat in the nursery?'

'Only bread and butter, very thick,' sighed Nellie.

Esther suppressed a smile with difficulty.

'But you had dinner, all of you, at one o'clock.'

'Boiled mutton and carrots and rice pudding,' said Nell mournfully.

Captain Woolcot severed a leg almost savagely and put it on her plate.

'Now run away; I don't know what has possessed you two to-night.'

Nellie reached the door, then turned back.

'Oh, if you would just give me a wing for poor Meg; Judy had some of Pip's, but Meg hasn't any,' she said, with a beautiful look of distress that quite touched Colonel Bryant.

Her father bit his lip, hacked off a wing in ominous silence, and put it upon her plate.

'Now run away, and don't let me have any more of this nonsense—dear.' The last word was a terrible effort.

Nell's appearance with the two portions of fowl was hailed with uproarious applause in the nursery; Meg was delighted with her share, cut a piece off for Baby, and the meal went on merrily.

'Where's Bunty?' said Nell, pausing suddenly with a very clean drumstick in her fingers. 'Because I *hope* he hasn't gone too; someway I don't think father was very pleased, especially as that man was there.'

But that small youth had done so, and returned presently crestfallen.

'He wouldn't give me any; he told me to go away, and the man laughed, and Esther said we were very naughty; I got some feathered potatoes, though, from the table outside the door.'

He opened his dirty little hands and dropped the uninviting feathered delicacy out upon the cloth.

'Bunty, you're a pig!' sighed Meg, looking up from her book. She always read at the table, and this particular story was about some very refined, elegant girls.

'Pig yourself; all of you've had fowl but me, you greedy things!' retorted Bunty fiercely, and eating up his potato very fast.

'No, the General hasn't,' said Judy, and the old mischief light sprang up suddenly into her dark eyes.

'Now, Judy!' said Meg warningly; she knew too well what that particular sparkle meant.

'Oh, I'm not going to hurt you, you dear old thing,' said Miss Judy, dancing down the room and bestowing a pat on her sister's fair head as she passed. 'It's only the General, who's after havin' a bit o' fun.'

She lifted him up out of the high chair, where he had been sitting drumming on the table with a spoon and eating sugar in the intervals.

'It's real action you're going for to see, General,' she said, dancing to the door with him.

'Oh, Judy, what *are* you going to do?' said Meg entreatingly.

'Ju-Ju!' crowed the General, leaping almost out of Judy's arms, and scenting fun with the instinct of a veteran.

Down the passage they went, the other five behind to watch proceedings. Judy sat down with him on the last step.

'Boy want chuck-chuck, pretty chuck-chuck?' she said insidiously.

'Chuck-chuck, chuck-a-chuck,' he gurgled, looking all around for his favourite friends.

'Dad got lots, all *this* many,' said Judy, opening her arms very wide to denote the number in her father's possession. 'Boydie go get them!'

'Chuck-chuck,' crowed the General delightedly, and struggling to his feet; 'find chuck-chuck.'

'In there,' whispered Judy, giving him a gentle push into the half-open dining-room door; 'ask dad.'

Right across the room the baby tottered on his fat, unsteady little legs.

'Are the children *all* possessed to-night, Esther?' said the Captain as his youngest son clutched wildly at his leg and tried to climb up it.

He looked down into the little dirty, dimpling face. 'Well, General, and to what do we owe the honour of *your* presence?'

'Chuck-chuck, chuck-a-chuck, chuck, chuck, chuck,' said the General, going down promptly upon all fours to seek for the feathered darlings Judy had said were here.

But Esther gathered up the dear dirty-faced young rascal and bore him struggling out of the room. At the foot of the stairs she nearly stumbled over the rest of the family.

'Oh, you scamps! You bad, wicked imps!' she said, reaching out to box all their ears, and of course failing.

She sat down on the bottom stair to laugh for a second, then she handed the General to Pip.

'To-morrow,' she said, standing up and hastily smoothing the rich hair that the General's hands had clutched gleefully—'to-morrow I shall beat every one of you with the broomstick!'

They watched the train of her yellow silk dress disappear into the dining room again, and returned slowly to the nursery and their interrupted tea.

1894

CHRISTOPHER BRENNAN
1870–1932

The son of Irish emigrants, Christopher Brennan was born in Sydney into a poor Catholic family. Early in life he demonstrated a flair for languages that earned him a scholarship to St Ignatius' College, Riverview, a selective Jesuit secondary school, where he began to read widely in both classical and English literature. He then studied arts at the University of Sydney with a particular focus on philosophy and classics. At university Brennan soon lost his religious faith and began his search for an alternative system of belief, reading Romantic, mystical and esoteric literature, all of which was to fuel his later poetry. After completing his master's thesis in 1891, Brennan won a university scholarship to study for his doctorate in Germany. In Berlin, however, he neglected his academic work in favour of writing poetry and conducting a love affair with his landlady's daughter, Anna Werth, whom he eventually married in 1897.

While in Berlin, Brennan had begun to read contemporary European literature and in 1892 wrote to the French symbolist poet Mallarmé about the availability of his published work. Later, he sent Mallarmé a copy of his *XXI Poems: (1893–1897) Towards the source* (1897), receiving an enthusiastic response. Most of these poems reappeared in Brennan's major work, *Poems*, usually referred to as *Poems [1913]*, published by subscription in 1914. Following Mallarmé, it takes the form of a *livre composé* in which each poem makes a contribution to the whole while also being able to be read separately. *Poems* consists of three major sections—'Towards the Source', 'The Forest of Night', in which Lilith is a central figure, and 'The Wanderer'—and two shorter concluding ones, 'Pauca Mea' and 'Epilogues'. While critics have offered differing interpretations, there is general agreement that the central concern of *Poems* is the quest for the Absolute, the Eden.

After returning to Sydney in 1894 without his doctorate, Brennan worked as a cataloguer at the Public Library of NSW before finally being given a teaching post at the University of Sydney in 1909, becoming an associate professor in German and comparative literature in 1921. Although a popular lecturer, over the years he became increasingly erratic and an alcoholic. In 1925, when his wife sued for divorce on the grounds of adultery, the university took advantage of this to dismiss Brennan from his post. In 1931 he was given a Commonwealth Literary Fund pension. *EW*

'She is the night: all horror is of her'

She is the night: all horror is of her
heap'd, shapeless, on the unclaim'd chaotic marsh
or huddled on the looming sepulchre
where the incult and scanty herb is harsh.

She is the night: all terror is of her   5
when the distemper'd dark begins to boil
with wavering face of larve and oily blur
of pallor on her suffocating coil.

Or majesty is hers, when marble gloom
supports her, calm, with glittering signs severe   10
and grandeur of metallic roof of doom,
far in the windows of our broken sphere.

Or she can be all pale, under no moon
or star, with veiling of the glamour cloud,
all pale, as were the fainting secret soon   15
to be exhaled, bride-robed in clinging shroud.

For she is night, and knows each wooing mood:
and her warm breasts are near in the charm'd air
of summer eve, and lovingly delude
the aching brow that craves their tender care.   20

The wooing night: all nuptials are of her;
and she the musky golden cloud that hangs
on maiden blood that burns, a boding stir
shot thro' with flashes of alluring pangs,

far off, in creeks that slept unvisited   25
or moved so smoothly that no ripple creas'd
their mirror'd slip of blue, till that sweet dread
melted the air and soft sighs stole, releas'd;

and she the shame of brides, veiling the white
of bosoms that for sharp fulfilment yearn;   30
she is the obscure centre of delight
and steals the kiss, the kiss she would return

deepen'd with all the abysm that under speech
moves shudderingly, or as that gulf is known
to set the astonied spouses each from each   35
across the futile sea of sighs, alone.

All mystery, and all love, beyond our ken,
she woos us, mournful till we find her fair:
and gods and stars and songs and souls of men
are the sparse jewels in her scatter'd hair.   40

1898–99/1914

'Fire in the heavens, and fire along the hills'

Fire in the heavens, and fire along the hills,
and fire made solid in the flinty stone,
thick-mass'd or scatter'd pebble, fire that fills
the breathless hour that lives in fire alone.

This valley, long ago the patient bed   5
of floods that carv'd its antient amplitude,
in stillness of the Egyptian crypt outspread,
endures to drown in noon-day's tyrant mood.

Behind the veil of burning silence bound,
vast life's innumerous busy littleness   10
is hush'd in vague-conjectured blur of sound
that dulls the brain with slumbrous weight, unless

some dazzling puncture let the stridence throng
in the cicada's torture-point of song.

                                                                    1899/1914

'O desolate eves along the way, how oft'

O desolate eves along the way, how oft,
despite your bitterness, was I warm at heart!
not with the glow of remember'd hearths, but warm
with the solitary unquenchable fire that burns
a flameless heat deep in his heart who has come   5
where the formless winds plunge and exult for aye
among the naked spaces of the world,
far past the circle of the ruddy hearths
and all their memories. Desperate eves,
when the wind-bitten hills turn'd violet   10
along their rims, and the earth huddled her heat
within her niggard bosom, and the dead stones
lay battle-strewn before the iron wind
that, blowing from the chill west, made all its way
a loneliness to yield its triumph room;   15
yet in that wind a clamour of trumpets rang,
old trumpets, resolute, stark, undauntable,
singing to battle against the eternal foe,
the wronger of this world, and all his powers
in some last fight, foredoom'd disastrous,   20
upon the final ridges of the world:
a war-worn note, stern fire in the stricken eve,
and fire thro' all my ancient heart, that sprang
towards that last hope of a glory won in defeat,
whence, knowing not sure if such high grace befall   25
at the end, yet I draw courage to front the way.

                                                                          1914

'The land I came thro' last was dumb with night'

The land I came thro' last was dumb with night,
a limbo of defeated glory, a ghost:
for wreck of constellations flicker'd perishing

scarce sustain'd in the mortuary air,
and on the ground and out of livid pools   5
wreck of old swords and crowns glimmer'd at whiles;
I seem'd at home in some old dream of kingship:
now it is clear grey day and the road is plain,
I am the wanderer of many years
who cannot tell if ever he was king   10
or if ever kingdoms were: I know I am
the wanderer of the ways of all the worlds,
to whom the sunshine and the rain are one
and one to stay or hasten, because he knows
no ending of the way, no home, no goal,   15
and phantom night and the grey day alike
withhold the heart where all my dreams and days
might faint in soft fire and delicious death:
and saying this to myself as a simple thing
I feel a peace fall in the heart of the winds   20
and a clear dusk settle, somewhere, far in me.

1914

HENRY HANDEL RICHARDSON
1870–1946

Ethel Robertson grew so attached to her pseudonym that she eventually required her friends and family to call her Henry. This was perhaps unsurprising, since her powerfully detailed, intellectual and psychological novels accorded her expansive recognition from American, British and European readerships by the early 1930s, while the Australian critic Nettie Palmer (qv) hailed her as 'our most famous writer' in 1929.

Ethel Florence Lindesay Richardson was born in Melbourne to older parents, whose mining wealth collapsed early in her life. She based her famous trilogy, *The Fortunes of Richard Mahony* (1930), on the experiences of the family in the Australian colonies in the nineteenth century, as well as her father's madness and death, and her life informed her other novels in direct ways. She met her husband J. George Robertson while they were both students in Leipzig, Germany, and they sustained a long partnership of interest in European culture while he served as professor of German literature at London University.

Her first novel, *Maurice Guest* (1908), concerns the lives of music students in Leipzig. A novel about love and art, it explores questions of individual fulfilment, with a candid focus on the possibilities for women artists, even as the main character's desolately hopeless obsession with Louise, an Australian, results in his suicide. It pushed boundaries of expression with its representation of feminist and openly homosexual characters. *The Getting of Wisdom* (1910), a lighter, satirical take on girlhood in Australia, is based on Richardson's schooling at Melbourne's Presbyterian Ladies College, and is characterised by an adult irony even though it was a book of choice for adolescents.

Of the three volumes of her trilogy—*Australia Felix* (first published as *The Fortunes of Richard Mahony* in 1917), *The Way Home* (1925) and *Ultima Thule* (1929)—only the last was an undisputed success with both readers and critics. The trilogy was released in one volume in 1930, while her previous novels were re-released as her acclaim grew. As a flawed but appealing man of intense self-reflection, Richard Mahony is a study of the influence of economic forces and national circumstance on subjectivity and character. Set against the pragmatism and emotional honesty of his wife Mary, whose point of view becomes more dominant as the trilogy progresses, Mahony's struggle to maintain sanity is both a subtle portrait of the development of syphilis and an exploration of the nature of understanding and existence. *NM*

From *The Fortunes of Richard Mahony*
'Australia Felix', Part 4, Chapter 3

It had struck two before the party began to break up. The first move made, however, the guests left in batches, escorting one another to their respective house-doors. The Henry Ococks' buggy had been in waiting for some time, and Mrs Henry's pretty head was drooping with fatigue before Henry, who was in the vein, could tear himself from the card-table. Mahony went to the front gate with them; then strolled with the Longs to the corner of the road.

He was in no hurry to retrace his steps. The air was balmy, after that of the overcrowded rooms, and it was a fabulously beautiful night. The earth lay steeped in moonshine, as in the light of a silver sun. Trees and shrubs were patterned to their last leaf on the ground before them. What odd mental twist made mortals choose rather to huddle indoors, by puny candle-light, than to be abroad laving themselves in a splendour such as this?

Leaning his arms on the top rail of a fence, he looked across the slope at the Flat, now hushed and still as the encampment of a sleeping army. Beyond, the bush shimmered palely grey—in his younger years he had been used, on a night like this when the moon sailed full and free, to take his gun and go opossuming. Those two old woody gods, Warrenheip and Buninyong, stood out more imposingly than by day; but the ranges seemed to have retreated. The light lay upon them like a visible burden, flattening their contours, filling up clefts and fissures with a milky haze.

'Good evening, doctor!'

Spoken in his very ear, the words made him jump. He had been lost in contemplation; and the address had a ghostly suddenness. But it was no ghost that stood beside him—nor indeed was it a night for those presences to be abroad whose element is the dark.

Ill-pleased at the intrusion, he returned but a stiff nod: then, since he could not in decency greet and leave-take in a breath, feigned to go on for a minute with his study of the landscape. After which he said: 'Well, I must be moving. Good night to you.'

'So you're off your sleep, too, are you?' As often happens, the impulse to speak was a joint one. The words collided.

Instinctively Mahony shrank into himself; this familiar bracketing of his person with another's was distasteful to him. Besides, the man who had sprung up at his elbow bore a reputation that was none of the best. The owner of a small chemist's shop on the Flat, he contrived to give offence in sundry ways: he was irreligious—an infidel, his neighbours had it—and of a Sabbath would scour his premises or hoe potatoes rather than attend church or chapel. Though not a confirmed drunkard, he had been seen to stagger in the street, and be unable to answer when spoken to. Also, the woman with whom he lived was not generally believed to be his lawful wife. Hence the public fought shy of his nostrums; and it was a standing riddle how he managed to avoid putting up his shutters. More nefarious practices no doubt, said the relentless *vox populi*.—Seen near at hand, he was a tall, haggard-looking fellow of some forty years of age, the muscles on his neck standing out like those of a skinny old horse.

Here, his gratuitous assumption of a common bond drew a cold: 'Pray, what reason have you to think that?' from Mahony. And without waiting for a reply he again said good night and turned to go.

The man accepted the rebuff with a meekness that was painful to see. 'Thought, comin' on you like this, you were a case like my own. No offence, I'm sure,' he said humbly. It was evident he was well used to getting the cold shoulder. Mahony stayed his steps. 'What's the matter with you?' he asked. 'Aren't you well? There's a remedy to be found for most ills under the sun.'

'Not for mine! The doctor isn't born or the drug discovered that could cure me.'

The tone of bragging bitterness grated anew. Himself given to the vice of overstatement, Mahony had small mercy on it in others. 'Tut, tut!' he deprecated.

There was a brief silence before the speaker went on more quietly: 'You're a young man, doctor, I'm an old one.' And he looked old as he spoke; Mahony saw that he had erred in putting him down as merely elderly. He was old and grey and down-at-heel—fifty, if a day—and his clothes hung loose on his bony frame. 'You'll excuse me if I say I know better'n you. When a man's done, he's done. And that's me. Yes,'—he grew inflated again in reciting his woes—'I'm one o' your hopeless cases, just as surely as if I was being eaten up by a cancer or a consumption. To mend me, you doctors 'ud need to start me afresh—from the mother-egg.'

'You exaggerate, I'm sure.'

'It's that—knowin' one's played out, with by rights still a good third of one's life to run—that's what puts the sleep away. In the daylight it's none so hard to keep the black thoughts under; themselves they're not so daresome;

and there's one's pipe, and the haver o' the young fry. But night's the time! Then they come tramplin' along, a whole army of 'em, carryin' banners with letters a dozen feet high, so's you shan't miss rememberin' what you'd give your soul to forget. And so it'll go on, et cetera and ad lib., till it pleases the old Joker who sits grinnin' up aloft to put His heel down—as you or me would squash a bull-ant or a scorpion.'

'You speak bitterly, Mr. Tangye. Does a night like this not bring you calmer, clearer thoughts?' and Mahony waved his arm in a large, loose gesture at the sky.

His words passed unheeded. The man he addressed spun round and faced him, with a rusty laugh. 'Hark at that!' he cried. 'Just hark at it! Why, in all the years I've been in this God-forsaken place—long as I've been here—I've never yet heard my own name properly spoken. You're the first, doctor. You shall have the medal.'

'But, man alive, you surely don't let that worry you? Why, I've the same thing to put up with every day of my life. I smile at it.' And Mahony believed what he said, forgetting, in the antagonism such spleen roused in him, the annoyance the false stressing of his own name could sometimes cause him.

'So did I, once,' said Tangye, and wagged his head. 'But the day came when it seemed the last straw; a bit o'mean spite on the part o' this hell of a country itself.'

'You dislike the colony, it appears, intensely?'

'You like it?' The counter question came tip for tap.

'I can be fair to it, I hope, and appreciate its good sides.' As always, the mere hint of an injustice made Mahony passionately just.

'Came 'ere of your own free will, did you? Weren't crowded out at home? Or bamboozled by a pack o' lying tales?' Tangye's voice was husky with eagerness.

'That I won't say either. But it is entirely my own choice that I remain here.'

'Well, I say to you, think twice of it! If you have the chance of gettin' away, take it. It's no place this, doctor, for the likes of you and me. Haven't you never turned and asked yourself what the devil you were doin' here? And that reminds me ... There was a line we used to have drummed into us at school—it's often come back to me since. *Coelum, non animum, mutant, qui trans mare currunt.*[1] In our green days we gabbled that off by rote; then, it seemed just one more o' the eel-sleek phrases the classics are full of. Now, I take off my hat to the man who wrote it. He knew what he was talkin' about—by the Lord Harry, he did!'

---

1   A line from the Roman poet Horace, which can be translated as 'the sky, not the heart, they change, those who cross the sea'. See also Robert Hughes (qv).

The Latin had come out tentatively, with an odd, unused intonation. Mahony's retort: 'How on earth do you know what suits me and what doesn't?' died on his lips. He was surprised into silence. There had been nothing in the other's speech to show that he was a man of any education—rather the reverse.

Meanwhile Tangye went on: 'I grant you it's an antiquated point o' view; but doesn't that go to prove what I've been sayin'; that you and me are old-fashioned, too—out-o'-place here, out-o'-date? The modern sort, the sort that gets on in this country, is a prime hand at cuttin' his coat to suit his cloth; for all that the stop-at-homes, like the writer o' that line and other ancients, prate about the Ethiopian's hide or the leopard and his spots. They didn't buy their experience dear, like we did; didn't guess that if a man *don't* learn to fit himself in, when he gets set down in such a land as this, he's a goner; any more'n they knew that most o' those who hold out here—all of 'em at any rate who've climbed the ladder, nabbed the plunder—have found no more difficulty in changin' their spots than they have their trousers. Yes, doctor, there's only one breed that flourishes, and you don't need me to tell you which it is. Here they lie'—and he nodded to right and left of him—'dreamin' o' their money-bags, and their dividends, and their profits, and how they'll diddle and swindle one another afresh, soon as the sun gets up to-morrow. Harder 'n nails they are, and sharp as needles. You ask me why I do my walkin' out in the night-time? It's so's to avoid the sight o' their mean little eyes, and their greedy, graspin' faces.'

Mahony's murmured disclaimer fell on deaf ears. Like one who had been bottled up for months, Tangye flowed on. 'What a life! What a set! What a place to end one's days in! Remember, if you can, the yarns that were spun round it for our benefit, from twenty thousand safe miles away. It was the Land o' Promise and Plenty, topful o' gold, strewn over with nuggets that only waited for hands to pick 'em up.—Lies!—lies from beginnin' to end! I say to you this is the hardest and cruellest country ever created, and a man like me's no more good here than the muck—the parin's and stale fishguts and other leavin's—that knocks about a harbour and washes against the walls. I'll tell you the only use I'll have been here, doctor, when my end comes: I'll dung some bit o' land for 'em with my moulder and rot. That's all. They'd do better with my sort if they knocked us on the head betimes, and boiled us down for our fat and marrow.'

Not much in that line to be got from *your* carcase, my friend, thought Mahony, with an inward smile.

But Tangye had paused merely to draw breath. 'What I say is, instead o' layin' snares for us, it ought to be forbid by law to give men o' my make ship room. At home in the old country we'd find our little nook, and jog along decently to the end of our days. But just the staid, respectable, orderly sort I belonged to's neither needed nor wanted here. I fall to thinkin' sometimes on the fates of the hundreds of honest, steady-goin' lads, who at one time or another have chucked up their jobs over there—for this. The drink no doubt's took most: they never knew before that one *could* sweat as you sweat here. And the rest? Well, just accident … or the sun … or dysentery … or the bloody toil that goes by the name o' work in these parts—you know the list, doctor, better'n me. They say the waste o' life in a new country can't be helped; doesn't matter; has to be. But that's cold comfort to the wasted. No! I say to you, there ought to be an Act of Parliament to prevent young fellows squanderin' themselves, throwin' away their lives as I did mine. For when we're young, we're not sane. Youth's a fever o' the brain. And I *was* young once, though you mightn't believe it; I had straight joints, and no pouch under my chin, and my full share o' windy hopes. Senseless truck these! To be spilled overboard bit by bit—like on a hundred-mile tramp a new-chum finishes by pitchin' from his swag all the needless rubbish he's started with. What's wanted to get on here's somethin' quite else. Horny palms and costive bowels; more'n a dash o' the sharper; and no sickly squeamishness about knockin' out other men and steppin' into their shoes. And I was only an ordinary young chap; not over-strong nor over-shrewd, but honest—honest, by God I was! That didn't count. It even stood in my way. For I was too good for this and too mealy-mouthed for that; and while I stuck, considerin' the fairness of a job, some one who didn't care a damn whether it was fair or not, walked in over my head and took it from me. There isn't anything I haven't tried my luck at, and with everything it's been the same. Nothin's prospered; the money wouldn't come—or stick if it did. And so here I am—all that's left of me. It isn't much; and by and by a few rank weeds 'ull spring from it, and old Joey there, who's paid to grub round the graves, old Joey 'ull curse and say: a weedy fellow that, a rotten, weedy blackguard; and spit on his hands and hoe, till the weeds lie bleedin' their juices—the last heirs of me … the last issue of my loins!'

'Pray, does it never occur to you, you fool, that *flowers* may spring from you?'

He had listened to Tangye's diatribe in a white heat of impatience. But when he spoke he struck an easy tone—nor was he in any hesitation how to reply: for that, he had played devil's advocate all too often with himself in private. An unlovely country, yes, as Englishmen understood beauty; and yet not without a charm of its own. An arduous life, certainly, and one full of pitfalls for the weak or the unwary; yet he believed it was no more impossible to win through here, and with clean hands, than anywhere else. To generalise as his companion had done was absurd. Preposterous, too, the notion that those of their fellow-townsmen who had carried off the prizes owed their success to some superiority in bodily strength … or sharp dealing ... or thickness of skin. With Mr. Tangye's permission he would cite himself as an example. He was neither a very robust man, nor, he ventured to say, one of any marked ability in the other two directions. Yet he had managed to succeed without, in the process, sacrificing jot or tittle of his principles; and to-day he held a position that any member of his profession across the seas might envy him.

'Yes, but till you got there!' cried Tangye. 'Hasn't every superfluous bit of you—every thought of interest that wasn't essential to the daily grind—been pared off?'

'If,' said Mahony stiffening, 'if what you mean by that is, have I allowed my mind to grow narrow and sluggish, I can honestly answer no.'

In his heart he denied the charge even more warmly; for, as he spoke, he saw the great cork-slabs on which hundreds of moths and butterflies made dazzling spots of colour; saw the sheets of pink blotting-paper between which his collection of native plants lay pressed; the glass case filled with geological specimens; his Bible, the margins of which round Genesis were black with his handwriting; a pile of books on the new marvel Spiritualism; Colenso's *Pentateuch*; the big black volumes of the *Arcana Coelestia*; Locke on Miracles:[1] he saw all these things and more. 'No, I'm glad to say I have retained many interests outside my work.'

Tangye had taken off his spectacles and was polishing them on a crumpled handkerchief. He seemed about to reply, even made a quick half-turn towards Mahony; then thought better of it, and went on rubbing. A smile played round his lips.

'And in conclusion let me say this,' went on Mahony, not unnettled by his companion's expression. 'It's sheer folly to talk about what life makes of us. Life is not an active force. It's we who make what *we* will, of life. And in order to shape it to the best of our powers, Mr. Tangye, to put our brief span to the best possible use, we must never lose faith in God or our fellow-men; never forget that, whatever happens, there *is* a sky, with stars in it, above us.'

'Ah, there's a lot of bunkum talked about life,' returned Tangye dryly, and settled his glasses on his nose. 'And as a man gets near the end of it, he sees just *what* bunkum it is. Life's only got one meanin', doctor; seen plain, there's only one object in everything we do; and that's to keep a sound roof over our heads and a bite in our mouths—and in those of the helpless creatures who depend on us. The rest has no more sense or significance than a nigger's hammerin' on the tam-tam. The lucky ones o' this world don't grasp it; but we others do; and after all p'raps, it's worth while havin'

---

1   Freethinker Bishop J.W. Colenso's *Pentateuch and the Book of Joshua Critically Examined* (1862), Emanual Swedenborg's *Arcana Coelestia* (8 vols, 1749–56), John Locke's, *A Discourse on Miracles* (1706).

gone through it to have got at *one* bit of the truth, however small. Good night.'

He turned on his heel, and before his words were cold on the air had vanished, leaving Mahony blankly staring.

The moonshine still bathed the earth, gloriously untroubled by the bitterness of human words and thoughts. But the night seemed to have grown chilly; and Mahony gave an involuntary shiver. 'Some one walking over my ... now what would that specimen have called it? Over the four by eight my remains will one day manure!'

'An odd, abusive, wrong-headed fellow,' he mused, as he made his way home. 'Who would ever have thought, though, that the queer little chemist had so much in him? A failure? ... yes, he was right there; and as unlovely as failures always are—at close quarters.' But as he laid his hands on the gate, he jerked up his head and exclaimed half aloud: 'God bless my soul! What he wanted was not argument or reason but a little human sympathy.' As usual, however, the flash of intuition came too late. 'For such a touchy nature I'm certainly extraordinarily obtuse where the feelings of others are concerned,' he told himself as he hooked in the latch.

'Why, Richard, where *have* you been?' came Mary's clear voice—muted so as not to disturb John and Jinny, who had retired to rest. Purdy and she sat waiting on the verandah. 'Were you called out? We've had time to clear everything away. Here, dear, I saved you some sandwiches and a glass of claret. I'm sure you didn't get any supper yourself, with looking after other people.'

Long after Mary had fallen asleep he lay wakeful. His foolish blunder in response to Tangye's appeal rankled in his mind. He could not get over his insensitiveness. How he had boasted of his prosperity, his moral nicety, his saving pursuits—he to boast!—when all that was asked of him was a kindly: 'My poor fellow-soul, you have indeed fought a hard fight; but there *is* a God above us who will recompense you at His own time, take the word for it of one who has also been through the Slough of Despond.' And then just these ... these hobbies of his, of which he had made so much. Now that he was alone with himself he saw them in a very different light. Lepidoptera collected years since were still unregistered, plants and stones unclassified; his poor efforts at elucidating the Bible waited to be brought into line with the Higher Criticism; Home's levitations and fire-tests called for investigation; while the leaves of some of the books he had cited had never even been cut. The mere thought of these things was provocative, rest-destroying. To induce drowsiness he went methodically through the list of his acquaintants, and sought to range them under one or other of Tangye's headings. And over this there came moments when he lapsed into depths ... fetched himself up again—but with an effort ... only to fall back.... .

But he seemed barely to have closed his eyes when the night-bell rang. In an instant he was on his feet in the middle of the room, applying force to his sleep-cogged wits.

He threw open the sash. 'Who's there? What is it?'

Henry Ocock's groom. 'I was to fetch you out to our place at once, governor.'

'But—Is Mrs. Henry taken ill?'

'Not as I know of,' said the man dryly. 'But her and the boss had a bit of a tiff on the way home, and Madam's excited-like.'

'And am I to pay for their tiffs?' muttered Mahony hotly.

'Hush, Richard! He'll hear you,' warned Mary, and sat up.

'I shall decline to go. Henry's a regular old woman.'

Mary shook her head. 'You can't afford to offend the Henrys. And you know what he is—so hasty. He'd call in some one else on the spot, and you'd never get back. If only you hadn't stayed out so long, dear, looking at the moon!'

'Good God! Mary, is one never to have a moment to oneself? Never a particle of pleasure or relaxation?'

'Why, Richard!' expostulated his wife, and even felt a trifle ashamed of his petulance. 'What would you call to-night, I wonder? Wasn't the whole evening one of pleasure and relaxation?'

And Mahony, struggling into shirt and trousers, had to admit that he would be hard put to it to give it another name.

1930

LOUIS STONE
1871–1935

Declared the best novel of 1912 by the *Bulletin*, Louis Stone's *Jonah* (1911) is a revelatory portrait of working-class life in Sydney's inner city. Its main character, Jonah Jones, is a larrikin leader of a street 'push'. His desperate ruthlessness sees him succeed as a businessman, owner of a large shoe shop, but fail to find happiness. Born in England, Stone lived in Sydney at Redfern and Waterloo as a boy and taught high school for 40 years, interrupted by chronic illnesses that may have stunted his career as a writer. He published one other novel, *Betty Wayside* (1915), and *The Lap of the Gods* (*1928/1923*), one of three published plays, won second place in a *Daily Telegraph* competition in 1923. NM

From *Jonah*
Chapter 1: Saturday Night at the Corner

One side of the street glittered like a brilliant eruption with the light from a row of shops; the other, lined with houses, was almost deserted, for the people, drawn like moths by the glare, crowded and jostled under the lights.

It was Saturday night, and Waterloo, by immemorial habit, had flung itself on the shops, bent on plunder. For an hour past a stream of people had flowed from the back streets into Botany Road, where the shops stood in shining rows, awaiting the conflict.

The butcher's caught the eye with a flare of colour as the light played on the pink and white flesh of sheep, gutted and skewered like victims for sacrifice; the saffron and red quarters of beef, hanging like the limbs of a dismembered Colossus; and the carcasses of pigs, the unclean beast of the Jews, pallid as a corpse. The butchers passed in and out, sweating and greasy, hoarsely crying the prices as they cut and hacked the meat. The people crowded about, sniffing the odour of dead flesh, hungry and brutal—carnivora seeking their prey.

At the grocer's the light was reflected from the gay labels on tins and packages and bottles, and the air was heavy with the confused odour of tea, coffee and spices.

Cabbages, piled in heaps against the door-posts of the greengrocer's, threw a rank smell of vegetables on the air; the fruit within, built in pyramids for display, filled the nostrils with the fragrant, wholesome scents of the orchard.

The buyers surged against the barricade of counters, shouting their orders, contesting the ground inch by inch as they fought for the value of a penny. And they emerged staggering under the weight of their plunder, laden like ants with food for hungry mouths—the insatiable maw of the people.

The push was gathered under the veranda at the corner of Cardigan Street, smoking cigarettes and discussing the weightier matters of life—horses and women. They were all young—from eighteen to twenty-five—for the larrikin never grows old. They leaned against the veranda posts, or squatted below the windows of the shop, which had been to let for months.

Here they met nightly, as men meet at their club—a terror to the neighbourhood. Their chief diversion was to guy the pedestrians, leaping from insult to swift retaliation if one resented their foul comments.

'Garn!' one was saying, 'I tell yer some 'orses know more'n a man. I remember old Joe Riley goin' inter the stable one day to a brown mare as 'ad a derry on 'im 'cause 'e flogged 'er crool. Well, wot does she do? She squeezes 'im up agin the side o' the stable, an' nearly stiffens 'im afore 'e cud git out. My oath, she did!'

'That's nuthin' ter wot a mare as was runnin' leader in Daly's 'bus used ter do,' began another, stirred by that rivalry which makes talkers magnify and invent to cap a story; but he stopped suddenly as two girls approached.

One was short and fat, a nugget, with square, sullen features; the other, thin as a rake, with a mass of red hair that fell to her waist in a thick coil.

''Ello, Ada, w'ere you goin'?' he inquired, with a facetious grin. 'Cum 'ere, I want ter talk ter yer.'

The fat girl stopped and laughed.

'Can't—I'm in a 'urry,' she replied.

'Well, kin I cum wid yer?' he asked, with another grin.

'Not wi' that face, Chook,' she answered, laughing.

'None o' yer lip, now, or I'll tell Jonah wot yer were doin' last night,' said Chook.

'W'ere is Joe?' asked the girl, suddenly serious. 'Tell 'im I want ter see 'im.'

'Gone ter buy a smoke; 'e'll be back in a minit.'

'Right-oh, tell 'im wot I said,' replied Ada, moving away.

''Ere, 'old 'ard, ain't yer goin' ter interdooce yer cobber?' cried Chook, staring at the red-headed girl.

'*An' 'er ginger 'air was scorchin' all 'er back,*' he sang in parody, suddenly cutting a caper and snapping his fingers.

The girl's white skin flushed pink with anger, her eyes sparkled with hate.

'Ugly swine! I'll smack yer jaw, if yer talk ter me,' she cried.

'Blimey, 'ot stuff, ain't it?' inquired Chook.

'Cum on, Pinkey. Never mind 'im,' cried Ada, moving off.

'Yah, go 'ome an' wash yer neck!' shouted Chook, with sudden venom.

The red-headed girl stood silent, searching her mind for a stinging retort.

'Yer'd catch yer death o' cold if yer washed yer own,' she cried; and the two passed out of sight, tittering.

Chook turned to his mates.

'She kin give it lip, can't she?' said he, in admiration.

A moment later the leader of the Push crossed the street, and took his place in silence under the veranda. A first glance surprised the eye, for he was a hunchback, with the uncanny look of the deformed—the head, large and powerful, wedged between the shoulders as if a giant's hand had pressed it down, the hump projecting behind, monstrous and inhuman. His face held you with a pair of restless grey eyes, the colour and temper of steel, deep with malicious intelligence. His nose was large and thin, curved like the beak of an eagle. Chook, whose acquaintance he had made years ago when selling newspapers, was his mate. Both carried nicknames, corrupted from Jones and Fowles, with the rude wit of the streets.

'Ada's lookin' fer yous, Jonah,' said Chook.

'Yer don't say so?' replied the hunchback, raising his leg to strike a match. 'Was Pinkey with 'er?' he added.

'D'ye mean a little moll wi' ginger hair?' asked Chook.

Jonah nodded.

'My oath, she was! Gi' me a knockout in one act,' said Chook; and the others laughed.

'Ginger fer pluck!' cried someone.

And they began to argue whether you could tell a woman's character from the colour of her hair; whether red-haired women were more deceitful than others.

Suddenly, up the road, appeared a detachment of the Salvation Army, stepping in time to the muffled beat of a drum. The procession halted at the street corner, stepped out of the way of traffic, and formed a circle. The Push moved to the kerbstone, and, with a derisive grin, awaited the performance.

The wavering flame of the kerosene torches, topped with thick smoke, shone yellow against the whiter light of the gas-jets in the shops. The men, in red jerseys and flat caps, held the poles of the torches in rest. When a gust of air blew the thick black smoke into their eyes, they patiently turned their heads. The sisters, conscious of the public gaze, stood with downcast eyes, their faces framed in grotesque poke-bonnets.

The Captain, a man of fifty, with the knotty, misshapen hands of a workman, stepped into the centre of the ring, took off his cap, and began to speak.

'Oh friends, we 'ave met 'ere again tonight to inquire after the safety of yer everlastin' souls. Yer pass by, thinkin' only of yer idle pleasures, w'en at any moment yer might be called to judgment by 'Im Who made us all equal in 'Is eyes. Yer pass by without 'earin ' the sweet voice of Jesus callin' on yer to be saved this very minit. For 'E is callin' yer to come an' be saved an' find salvation, as 'E called me many years ago. I was then like yerselves, full of wickedness, an' gloryin' in sin. But I 'eard the voice of 'Im Who died on the Cross, an' saw I was rushin' 'eadlong to 'ell. An' 'Is blood washed all my sins away, an' made me whiter than snow. Whiter than snow, friends—whiter than snow! An' 'E'll do the same fer you if yer will only come an' be saved. Oh, can't yer 'ear the voice of Jesus callin' to yer to come an' live with 'Im in 'Is blessed mansions in the sky? Oh, come tonight an' find salvation!'

His arms were outstretched in a passionate gesture of appeal, his rough voice vibrated with emotion, the common face flamed with the ecstasy of the fanatic. When he stopped for breath or wiped the sweat from his face, the Army spurred him on with cries of 'Hallelujah! Amen!' as one pokes a dying fire.

The Lieutenant, who was the comedian of the company, met with a grin of approval as he faced the ring of torches like an actor facing the footlights, posing before the crowd that had gathered, flashing his vulgar conceit in the public eye. And he praised God in a song and dance, fitting his words to the latest craze of the music-hall:

> *'Oh! won't you come and join us?*
> *Jesus leads the throng,'*

snapping his fingers, grimacing, cutting capers that would have delighted the gallery of a theatre.

'Encore!' yelled the Push as he danced himself to a standstill, hot and breathless.

The rank and file came forward to testify. The men stammered in confusion, terrified by the noise they made, shrinking from the crowd as a timid bather shrinks from icy water, driven to this performance by an unseen power. But the women were shrill and self-possessed, scolding their hearers, demanding an instant surrender to the Army, whose advantages they pointed out with a glib fluency as if it were a Benefit Lodge.

Then the men knelt in the dust, the women covered their faces, and the Captain began to pray. His voice rose in shrill entreaty, mixed with the cries of the shopmen and the noise of the streets.

The spectators, familiar with the sight, listened in nonchalance, stopping to watch the group for a minute as they would look into a shop window. The exhibition stirred no religious feeling in them, for their minds, with the tenacity of childhood, associated religion with churches, parsons and hymn-books.

The Push grew restless, divided between a desire to upset the meeting and fear of the police.

'Well I used ter think a funeral was slow,' remarked Chook, losing patience; and he stepped behind Jonah.

''Ere, look out!' yelled Jonah the next minute, as, with a push from Chook, he collided violently with one of the soldiers and fell into the centre of the ring.

''E shoved me,' cried Jonah as he got up, pointing with an injured air to the grinning Chook. 'I'll gi' yer a kick in the neck, if yer git me lumbered,' he added, scowling with counterfeit anger at his mate.

'If yer was my son …' said the Captain severely. 'If yer was my son …' he repeated, halting for words.

'I should 'ave trotters as big as yer own,' cried Jonah, pointing to the man's feet, cased in enormous bluchers. The Push yelled with derision as Jonah edged out of the circle, ready for flight.

The Captain flushed angrily, and then his face cleared.

'Well, friends,' he cried, 'God gave me big feet to tramp the streets and preach the Gospel to my fellow men.' And the interrupted service went on.

Jonah, who carried the brains of the Push, devised a fresh attack, involving Chook, a broken bottle, and the big drum.

'It'll cut it like butter,' he was explaining; when suddenly there was a cry of 'Nit! 'Ere's a cop!' and the Push bolted like rabbits.

Jonah and Chook alone stood their ground, with reluctant valour, for the policeman was already beside them. Chook shoved the broken bottle into his pocket, and listened with unusual interest to the last hymn of the Army. Jonah, with one eye on the policeman, looked worried, as if he were struggling with a desire to join the Army and lead a pure life. The policeman looked hard at them and turned away.

The pair were making a strategic movement to the rear, when the two girls who had exchanged shots with Chook at the corner passed them. The fat girl tapped Jonah on the back. He turned with a start.

'Nit yer larks!' he cried. 'I thought it was the cop.'

'Cum 'ere, Joe; I want yer,' said the girl.

'Wot's up now?' he cried, following her along the street.

They stood in earnest talk for some minutes, while Chook complimented the red-headed girl on her wit.

'Yer knocked me sky-'igh,' he confessed, with a leer.

'Did I?'

'Yer did. Gi' me one straight on the point,' he admitted.

'Yous keep a civil tongue in yer head,' she cried, and the curious pink flush spread over her white skin.

'Orl right, wot are yer narked about?' inquired Chook.

He noticed, with surprise, that she was pretty, with small regular features; her eyes quick and bright, like a bird's. Under the gaslight her hair was the colour of a new penny.

'W'y, I don't believe yer 'air is red,' said Chook, coming nearer.

'Now then, keep yer 'ands to yerself,' cried the girl, giving him a vigorous push. Before he could repeat his attack, she walked away to join Ada, who hailed her shrilly.

Jonah rejoined his mate in gloomy silence. The Push had scattered—some to the two-up school, some to the dance-room. The butcher's flare of lights shone with a desolate air on piles of bones and scraps of meat—the debris of battle. The greengrocer's was stripped bare to the shelves, as if an army of locusts had marched through with ravenous tooth.

'Comin' down the street?' asked Chook, feeling absently in his pockets.

'No,' said Jonah.

'W'y, wot's up now?' inquired Chook in surprise.

'Oh, nuthin'; but I'm goin' ter sleep at Ada's tonight,' replied Jonah, staring at the shops.

''Strewth!' cried Chook, looking at him in wonder. 'Wot's the game now?'

'Oh! the old woman wants me ter put in the night there. Says some blokes 'ave bin after 'er fowls,' replied Jonah, hesitating like a boy inventing an excuse.

'Fowls!' cried Chook, with infinite scorn. 'Wants yer to nuss the bloomin' kid.'

'My oath, she don't,' replied Jonah, with great heartiness.

'Well, gimme a smoke,' said Chook, feeling again in his pockets.

Jonah took out a packet of cigarettes, counted how many were left, and gave him one.

'Kin yer spare it?' asked Chook, derisively. 'Lucky I've only got one mouth.'

'Mouth? More like a hole in a wall,' grinned Jonah.

'Well, so long. See yer tomorrer,' said Chook, moving off. 'Ere, gimme a match,' he added.

'Better tell yer old woman I'm sleepin' out,' said Jonah.

He was boarding with Chook's family, paying what he could spare out of fifteen shillings or a pound a week.

'Oh, I don't suppose you'll be missed,' replied Chook, graciously.

'Rye buck!'[1] cried Jonah.

1911

JOHN LE GAY BRERETON
1871–1933

Professor of English at the University of Sydney, Brereton was a close friend of writers Henry Lawson and Christopher Brennan (qqv), and sustained an active interest in Sydney's literary culture as well as publishing his own lyrical poetry. His academic work centred on Elizabethan drama, while his poetry was often whimsical, celebrating the bush school and its nostalgia, as the titles of his collections suggest: *The Song of Brotherhood and Other Verses* (1896), *Sea and Sky* (1908) and *Swags Up!* (1928). 'ANZAC' and 'Transports', first published in 1915 soon after the landings at Gallipoli, are now his best-remembered poems. *NM*

ANZAC

Within my heart I hear the cry
Of loves that suffer, souls that die,
And you may have no praise from me
For warfare's vast vulgarity;
Only the flag of love, unfurled   5
For peace above a weeping world,
I follow, though the fiery breath
Of murder shrivel me in death.
Yet here I stand and bow my head
To those whom other banners led,   10
Because within their hearts the clang

1   Slang for 'good'.

Of Freedom's summoning trumpets rang,
Because they welcomed grisly pain
And laughed at prudence, mocked at gain,
With noble hope and courage high,   15
And taught our manhood how to die.
Praise, praise and love be theirs who came
From that red hell of stench and flame,
Staggering, bloody, sick, but still
Strong with indomitable will,   20
Happy because, in gloomiest night,
Their own hearts drummed them to the fight.

                                                    1919

Transports

Behind us lay the homely shore
        With youthful memories aureoled;
A sky of dazzling blue before,
        We sailed a sea of molten gold.

To our old haven we return;   5
        By smoky hills as grey as mud
We see the sullen sunset burn
        Malignant on a lake of blood.

Yes, we return: but memory roams
        A foul, bleak age of pain that yields   10
The smoke and flame of ruined homes,
        The muck of cannon-pitted fields.

                                                    1919

MAGGIE MOBOURNE
c. 1872–1917

Maggie Mobourne was a Keerrupjmara woman from the Lake Condah region, Victoria. She married Ernest Mobourne in 1893, and together they vigorously protested against Reverend Johann Stähle's treatment of Aboriginal people at the Lake Condah Mission. She wrote many letters, including one published in the *Hamilton Spectator*, and as a result of their protests Mobourne and her husband were removed from Lake Condah Mission by the Victorian Board for the Protection of Aborigines in 1900.

In 1907, Mobourne eloped with Henry Albert, but she returned to Ernest in 1910. They moved back to Lake Condah Mission but Mobourne was again forced to leave. She spent her remaining years near Lake Tyers. Although she was in poor health the Board for the Protection of Aborigines refused to allow her to return to Lake Condah. *AH/PM*

Petition to D.N. McLeod, Vice-Chairman
of the Victorian Board for the Protection of Aborigines

Mission Station
Lake Condah
February 27th, 1900
D.N. McLeod, Esqre. M.L.A.
and Vice Chairman

Sir

Having returned in September last to the Mission Station with the object of endeavouring to live in peace and in accordance with the rules of the Station I am sorry to inform you that Mr Stahle seems to take every opportunity to find fault with us, and it seems as if our efforts to live peacefully are of no use here because Mr Stahle seems determined to annoy us and to take every opportunity of reporting us to the Board for insubordination.

On the 18th inst. Mr Stahle spoke in a threatening manner to me and stopped our rations, which he denies and I say that he is a liar and has always been. (See full particulars in another letter). and he doesn't treat us justly. I would ask you to get up an impartial Board of Inquiry to investigate and see fairness and justice.

I am prepared to substantiate my statements to be true and also can get the majority here as witnesses to prove that we have been living peacefully.

I am
Sir
Yours respectfully
Maggie Mobourne

(We the following corroborate the statements given above)
Signatures

Ernest Mobourne	Isaac McDuff his X mark	
Robert Turner	his X mark	Bella Mobourne
Thomas Willis	his X mark	
James Cortwine	his X mark	
Jenny Green	her X mark	
Albert White		
Fred Carmichael		
Louisa White	her X mark	
Edward P Cortwine		

1900

CONSTANCE CAMPBELL PETRIE
1872–1926

Constance Campbell Petrie was one of the nine children of Tom Petrie and Elizabeth Campbell, whose property Murrumba ('Good Place') in the Pine River district north of Brisbane was one of the first freehold properties in Queensland. Tom Petrie arrived in Sydney with his parents in 1831 and moved to Moreton Bay in 1837. He grew up as an accepted companion of the local Aboriginal people and learned to speak Turrabal, the language of the country between the Brisbane and Pine rivers. He accompanied his father on expeditions into unsettled country and at fourteen was taken to the triennial Bunya feast in the mountains west of Brisbane. As overseer of the first Aboriginal reserve in Queensland, on Bribie Island in 1877, his report on the people's experiences led to its closure the next year.

In 1904, Constance published a record of her father's experiences with the Aboriginal people of the Brisbane area, narrated in her voice and titled *Tom Petrie's Reminiscences of Early Queensland (Dating from 1837) Recorded by His Daughter*. A detailed, empathetic account, it includes extraordinary detail about everyday life, often comparing Aboriginal activities to similar European habits. *NM*

From *Tom Petrie's Reminiscences of Early Queensland*
Chapter XIV

Games.—As a boy my father has often joined in with the games of the blacks. One of them, called 'Murun Murun', was played a great deal in the early days of Brisbane on the road to and from camp. As they came along their pathway into Brisbane the natives played this; then again as they returned in the evening. It was carried out so:—The men and boys picked sides, and each player had a small waddie, made for the purpose, which he hit on the ground to make it bounce. The object was to see who could make the instrument bounce furthest—there was a knack about it. The menfolk were very fond of this game; women never played with waddies or spears.

Another game was 'Purru Purru'. It was played with a ball made from kangaroo skin stuffed with grass, and sewn up. 'Purru' meant ball. As in the first game, sides were picked, but the women joined in. The ball was thrown up in the air, and caught here and there, each side trying to keep it to themselves or to catch it from the opposite one.

'Murri Murri' was yet another game, and boys generally played it, though sometimes men joined in. The players picked a clear space, and stood in two lines, each holding a couple of small, sharp spears in their hands. In the open space between the lines a man stood. In his hand he held a piece of bark (generally gum), cut into a circular shape and some eighteen inches across. This, when the game started, he would throw on the ground, causing it to bowl along like a hoop about eight or nine yards from both lots of boys. As it passed they all threw their spears at it, trying to see who was best at hitting it. 'Murri' was the native name for kangaroo, and this was really playing at spearing one of those animals.

The toy boomerang has been already mentioned—the natives spent hours with it.

Another instrument ('Birbun-Birbun') made from two lengths of wood tied together in the middle crosswise, was thrown and returned in the same manner. The lengths were about one and a-half inches wide, and eighteen inches long (or they were smaller), and one side of both was more rounded than the other. In throwing, one end of the cross was held. Often sides were taken for this and for boomerang throwing, to see who was cleverest at getting the return. This game is met with at present in the Cairns and Cardwell districts (Dr. Roth's Bulletin, No. 4).[1]

Yet another toy (which does not appear to have been hitherto drawn attention to or described) played with like the boomerang, was just a small piece of bark, obtained from the top branches of the fig-leaf box. The bark was taken six or seven inches long and an inch and a-half wide, then was rounded at both ends, and put into hot ashes. While hot it was bent into almost a half-circle, and kept so till, when cold and hard, it had taken on that shape. The bark mentioned is the only kind suitable for these toys, and they could only be made at one time in the year, when the sap was up, and allowed the bark to peel off easily. Father as a boy has made numbers of them, and, of course, has often thrown them and had lots of fun in the game. For sides could be taken for this also. These toys were thrown with the first finger and thumb, and circled and returned as a boomerang.

It may not be generally known that skipping with a vine was an amusement with the Brisbane blacks before ever they saw the white man's skipping-rope used. But so it was, and the vine was circled round and round just as we do a rope, and also, like us, either one person or two could skip at a time. Men or women went in for the amusement, and it was a great thing to skip on the hard sea beach when near the water. Whatever kind of vine was handiest at the time was used—either those of the scrub or a creeper which grew on the seashore. And the blacks skipped away, keeping things going for a long time, amidst great interest and amusement from the onlookers. Some natives were splendid skippers, notably 'Governor Banjo' of whom I will speak later. It seemed almost impossible to trip this man out, and my father says one could notice how his eyes watched every movement of the hands of those who turned the vine—for, of course, they did their best to get him off his guard. An extra-determined attempt at this caused roars of laughter always, for Banjo was sure to be ready.

Another amusement which seems European, yet which was common to the blacks in their primitive state, is that known to us as 'cat's cradle'. An

---

1   Dr Walter Roth, the first Northern Protector of Aborigines from 1898, published eighteen bulletins on North Queensland Aboriginal culture from 1901 to 1910.

aboriginal held the string on his hands, while another took it off, and so on till they worked it into all sorts of shapes and forms. To the natives these shapes could be made to represent a turtle, a kangaroo, or, indeed, almost any animal or thing. They were very clever at it. The amusement was called 'Warru Warru', and with the white man's appearance, his fences got the same name, because of the resemblance of posts and rails to the shape of the string when held in one way across the hands.

In hot weather the natives had lots of fun in the water, and would stay there for hours. It was remarkable that they always jumped in feet foremost, and the women all had a peculiar habit of bending up both legs and holding with their hands to each ankle before they 'plopped' in. Many games were played in the water. 'Marutchi', or 'black swan', caused great fun. One man (the swan) would jump in, and when he had gone some thirty yards from the bank, several watchers would give chase. When they got within catching distance he would dive under, and they followed. If the bird were caught, he was held and tapped lightly on the head, and so died, and was taken ashore. However, he often escaped, because the captors laughed so much at the antics he went on with that they could not hold him. He would cry out like a swan, and clap his arms up and down frantically as though they were wings. Father says it was great fun to watch this game, and when one bird was disposed of another was ready, and so on, for perhaps hours. He himself played the swan sometimes, but, being a white one, was easily seen among the dark forms, and so was captured quickly.

In some thing the same sort of way turtle-hunting was played at. Shallow water (about eight or nine feet deep) in creek or river, with a white sandy bottom, was chosen for this sport, so that the players could see down through it. Three or four people getting into a canoe would paddle about, and presently a man who had in the meantime quietly slipped into the water, would come up blowing as a turtle does not far from the boat. Immediately he popped down again, but the boat gave chase in his direction, one man standing up ready to jump in on the next appearance, which would not be long in coming. The 'turtle' would hardly show himself this second time when he would be gone again, but the man on the alert would jump in and dive after the prey, and then another would help bring him to the surface, and lift him into the boat, when he was taken ashore. During all the time laughing and joking went on, indeed the blacks in those days were as 'happy as princes'.

Often when playing in the water the blacks would dive down, and stay under to see who had the best wind, and could remain longest beneath the surface, or they would try their swimming powers in a race. And they were fond of getting hold of white stones or bones in order to dive for these. Throwing them in some yards apart, where the water was about ten feet deep, the object was to see who could find the most and bring them to the surface again. Father has spent hours thus in diving with the blacks; indeed, splendid as they must have been in the water, I hardly think their white companion was behind hand at all, judging from his after years.

Aboriginal children learnt to swim at a very early age. Small 'kiddies' (really babies) were thrown into the water, and they seemed to take to it at once; swimming came naturally to them evidently. Their elders stood round bent on rescue if necessary, and they laughed heartily at the way the child, to prevent himself sinking, would paddle with his hands and feet. My father's brothers taught him to swim in this same way by throwing him into the water.

As I have mentioned before, the blacks were very clever as 'mimics'. They would amuse each other in that way for long hours together. Generally it would be when they were all lying lazily in the shade after a good meal or swim that some lively members would start with their antics. They perhaps imitated two fighters, or a man hunting, or a bird, or a kangaroo, etc.; indeed, everything they could think of; and they never failed to cause a laugh. At those times, too, they sometimes played with balls of mud in this way: Mud was rolled up into balls, and then two men, apparently solely to amuse the others, got hold of these, and dancing, with their bodies half-stooped all the time, they pelted each other. First one man in the dance turned and held out his cheek for a mud ball, then, receiving it, he threw one back, and held out the other cheek, and so on till they both would be smothered all over with mud.

Though their faces were grave they must have enjoyed the fun (fun with a question after it), and the onlookers, of course, were convulsed with laughter.

Often the young boys had sham fights, with the men joining them. Sides were taken as in the real thing, and everything was carried out after the same style, but the weapons were harmless enough. Tambil meant 'blunt'—hence the name of the sport, 'Tambil Tambil'. The spears used were fashioned from small oak saplings about five feet long and half-an-inch thick, or from strong reeds (*Gahnia aspera*) growing in the swamps or waterholes. All of them, however, were chewed in the mouth at one end into a sort of brush, so that when they hit they did not hurt. The shields were made from a piece of gum bark about eighteen inches long and seven or eight inches wide; two small holes were made in the centre on the under side, and a piece of split wattle branch was bent and put through these holes to form a handle. Sham fights taught the boys how to manage when their turn came to take part in a real one.

My father has fought with the little darkies many a time in a 'Tambil Tambil'. Once during one held in the hollow below Beerwah on Gregory

Terrace, a boy throwing a small sharp spear, which he should not have used in play, hit the white boy with it on the cheek immediately below his left eye. Though the wound was not a severe one and soon healed, a slight scar remains to this day. At the time the little blackfellow got such a scare at what he had done that he cleared out, and did not show himself again for two years. Afterwards, however, when they were both men, my father had a good deal to do with him; his name was 'Dulu-marni' (creek-caught), and he was one of the twenty-five to be mentioned later, who bore P as a brand.

As well as the boys, girls were taught to fight and use the 'kalgur', so that they could protect themselves later on. The blacks had their way of teaching children even as we have. And they seemed to derive fun from the task. For instance, it was a source of amusement showing the lads how to climb. They picked a leaning tree first, and would instruct the youngster how to hold an end of the climbing vine with his big toe, etc. And then they had games in which they practised throwing spears or waddies at small saplings, seeing who was best at it. All this helped the boys to learn.

Aboriginal children delighted in imitating their elders in every way, and played much as white children do. And they were mischievous, of course. One rather cruel habit they had was to catch a March fly, and sticking a piece of grass through its body, watch with delight how it flew off with its burden. If the March flies were as plentiful and as troublesome as mosquitoes are to-day, one could not wonder at the delight even multiplied one thousandfold. But, alas! one could not treat mosquitoes so.

1904

JOHN SHAW NEILSON
1872–1942

John Shaw Neilson is recognised by many as one of the finest lyric poets writing in English during the first half of the twentieth century. The son of itinerant rural workers in the Wimmera region of Victoria, he grew up in a strict but loving Presbyterian household. His formal schooling was limited and much of his understanding of language, imagery and poetic form was acquired from the King James Bible, the Psalter and Hymnal, as well as poetry in Palgrave's *Golden Treasury* and the *Bulletin*. During a life of unrelenting hardship, spent in farm labouring, road work and grinding poverty, Neilson actively sought publication.

From the beginning his poetry attracted the interest of many writers, while an original, synaesthesic use of colour and imagery in his work has appealed to artists. The themes in Neilson's lyrics—as with his thoughtful and neighbourly crane, 'the gentle water bird'—'ripple out to the edges of a dream', compelling composers to set the words to music.

The contrast between Neilson's life and his total commitment to the bardic tradition has attracted stage and film productions while scholarly attention, since the 1940s, has secured a position for Neilson in the literary canon. Research and critical work dating from the 1990s has, however, succeeded in debunking many of the romantic myths associated with this enigmatic poet. A variorum edition of his collected poems was released in 2003. *HH*

Honeythirst

'Twas yesterday I walked abroad
So that mine eyes might see
The yellow world, to calm and cure
This honeythirst in me.

The sun like a fierce player stood   5
Chiding his violin;
Loves were the songs that came to him,
Red as an orange skin.

And as he ceased, two simple stars
Like tender brides and shy   10
Stood mournfully, and 'Oh,' I cried,
'This honeythirst have I.'

As they were mourning, slow the moon
Walked in her gown of gold,
And in me woke the bitterness,   15
The honeythirst of old.

1912/1970

The Girl With the Black Hair

Her lips were a red peril
    To set men quivering,
And in her feet there lived the ache
    And the green lilt of Spring.

'Twas on a night of red blossoms,   5
    O, she was a wild wine!
The colours of all the hours
    Lie in this heart of mine.

I was impelled by the white moon
    And the deep eyes of the Spring,   10
And the voices of purple flutes
    Waltzing and wavering.

Of all the bloom most delicate,
　　Sipping the gold air
Was the round girl with round arms—　　　　15
　　The girl with the black hair!

Her breath was the breath of roses,
　　White roses clean and clear;
Her eyes were blue as the high heaven
　　Where God is always near.　　　　　　20

Her lips were a red peril
　　To set men quivering,
And in her feet there lived the ache
　　And the green lilt of Spring.

　　　　　　　　　　　　　　　　1913/1964

The Orange Tree

The young girl stood beside me. I
　　Saw not what her young eyes could see:
—A light, she said, not of the sky
　　Lives somewhere in the Orange Tree.

—Is it, I said, of east or west?　　　　　5
　　The heartbeat of a luminous boy
Who with his faltering flute confessed
　　Only the edges of his joy?

Was he, I said, borne to the blue
　　In a mad escapade of Spring　　　　10
Ere he could make a fond adieu
　　To his love in the blossoming?

—Listen! the young girl said. There calls
　　No voice, no music beats on me;
But it is almost sound: it falls　　　　15
　　This evening on the Orange Tree.

—Does he, I said, so fear the Spring
　　Ere the white sap too far can climb?
See in the full gold evening
　　All happenings of the olden time?　　　20

Is he so goaded by the green?
    Does the compulsion of the dew
Make him unknowable but keen,
    Asking with beauty of the blue?

—Listen! the young girl said. For all   25
    Your hapless talk you fail to see
There is a light, a step, a call
    This evening on the Orange Tree.

—Is it, I said, a waste of love
    Imperishably old in pain,   30
Moving as an affrighted dove
    Under the sunlight or the rain?

Is it a fluttering heart that gave
    Too willingly and was reviled?
Is it the stammering at a grave,   35
    The last word of a little child?

—Silence! the young girl said. Oh, why,
    Why will you talk to weary me?
Plague me no longer now, for I
    Am listening like the Orange Tree.   40

                                                 1921/1934

The Poor, Poor Country

Oh 'twas a poor country, in Autumn it was bare,
The only green was the cutting grass and the sheep found little there.
Oh, the thin wheat and the brown oats were never two foot high,
But down in the poor country no pauper was I.

My wealth it was the glow that lives forever in the young,   5
'Twas on the brown water, in the green leaves it hung.
The blue cranes fed their young all day—how far in a tall tree!
And the poor, poor country made no pauper of me.

I waded out to the swans' nest—at night I heard them sing,
I stood amazed at the Pelican, and crowned him for a King;   10
I saw the black duck in the reeds, and the spoonbill on the sky,
And in that poor country no pauper was I.

The mountain-ducks down in the dark made many a hollow sound,
I saw in sleep the Bunyip creep from the waters underground,

I found the plovers' island home, and they fought right valiantly.   15
Poor was the country, but it made no pauper of me.

My riches all went into dreams that never yet came home,
They touched upon the wild cherries and the slabs of honeycomb;
They were not of the desolate brood that men can sell or buy:
Down in that poor country no pauper was I.   20

The New Year came with heat and thirst and the little lakes were low,
The blue cranes were my nearest friends and I mourned to see them go;
I watched their wings so long until I only saw the sky;
Down in that poor country no pauper was I.

1934

DAVID UNAIPON
1872–1967

David Unaipon was a gifted Ngarrindjeri man born at the Point McLeay (Raukkan) Mission, SA. He attended the mission school until 1885, then worked as a servant for a family that encouraged his interest in philosophy, science and music, returning to the mission in 1890, where he continued to read widely, practise music and learn practical skills for employment. He married in 1902.

Unaipon was known as 'Australia's Leonardo' because of his intellectual capacity and inventions, which included a modified handpiece for shearing and nine other patents. Becoming a prominent Aboriginal voice in state and Commonwealth politics, he appeared as his people's spokesperson before government commissions and inquiries into the treatment of Aborigines, arguing throughout his life that Aboriginal people should be extended the benefits of education and Christianity.

From the early 1920s, Unaipon studied western mythology and began to compile his own people's myths and legends. He wrote for the Sydney *Daily Telegraph* from 1924 and, with the assistance of the Aborigines' Friends Association, began publishing his collected myths from 1927. His *Native Legends* (1929) is considered to be the first book authored by an Aboriginal person. Without Unaipon's permission, publisher Angus & Robertson onsold the copyright to his stories to William Ramsay Smith, who published *Myths and Legends of the Australian Aborigines* in London without acknowledging their original author.

Unaipon continued to travel widely, speaking and lecturing in schools and churches on traditional Aboriginal legends and contemporary Aboriginal affairs. He received a Coronation medal in 1953. Returning to Point McLeay Mission, he worked on inventions and his lifelong quest for the key to perpetual motion.

Since 1988, the David Unaipon Award, an annual literary competition, has honoured his memory with a prize for an unpublished manuscript by an Aboriginal or Torres Strait Islander author. Unaipon's portrait appeared on the Australian $50 note in 1995. His manuscript of Aboriginal legends was edited and published as *Legendary Tales of the Australian Aborigines* (2001), adopting his original title and finally acknowledging his authorship. *AH/PM*

Aborigines, Their Traditions and Customs:
Where Did They Come From?

[...] Since coming to Australia thousands of years ago, there has been probably little or no change in the habits and the customs of my people. They have kept the balance of Nature; for centuries they have neither advanced nor retrogressed. Our tribal laws and customs are fixed and unchangeable. Generation after generation has gone through the same rigid tribal training.

Every race has had its great traditional leader and law-giver who has given the race its first moral training, as well as its social and tribal customs. Narroondarie was our great traditional leader. The laws of Narroondarie are taught to the children in their infancy. The hunting-grounds were given out to the different families and tribes by Narroondarie. The boundaries of the tribal hunting-grounds have been kept the same from remotest time. Whilst the children of the tribes are hearing from their elders all the traditions and legends of our race, they are learning all the knowledge and skill of bush craft and hunting, as well as undergoing the three great tests or initiations, to Kornmund (full manhood) and Meemund (full womanhood), which is generally completed at the age of eighteen.

The first test is to overcome the appetite, by doing a two-day walk or hunt without food, and then to be brought suddenly before a fire, on which is cooking some choice kangaroo steak or other native delicacy. The next test is to overcome pain. The young boys and girls submit to having their noses pierced, their bodies marked, and to lying down upon hot embers, thinly covered with boughs. The third test is to overcome fear. The young people are told fearful and hair-raising stories about ghosts and the Muldarpi (Evil Spirit or devil-devil). After all this, they are put to sleep in a lonely place or near the burial-places of the tribe. During the night the elders, made hideous with white clay and bark head-dresses, appear, making weird noises. Those who show no signs of having had a disturbed night are then admitted as fully initiated members of the tribe.

No youth or maiden is allowed to marry until he, or she, has passed through these tests. The marriage is talked over first by all the old members of the tribe, and it is always the uncle of the young man who finally selects the wife. The uncle on the mother's side is the most important relative. The actual marriage ceremony takes place during the time of festivals. The husband does not look or speak at his mother-in-law, although he is husband in name to all his sisters-in-law. Under native conditions, the sex-laws are very strict.

A fully developed Aboriginal has, in his own way, a vast amount of knowledge. Although it may not be strictly scientific learning, still it is a very exact knowledge, and his powers of physical observation are developed to the utmost. For instance, an Aboriginal living under primitive life knows the habits and the anatomy and the haunts of every animal in the bush. He knows all the birds, their habits, and even their love, or mating, notes. He knows the approach of the different seasons of the year from various signs, as well as from the positions of the stars in the heavens. He has developed the art of tracking the human footprint to the highest degree. There is a whole science in footprints. Footprints are the same evidence to a bush native as fingerprints are in a court of law.

He knows the track of every individual member of the tribe. There is as much difference and individuality in footprints as in fingerprints. Of course, it will be readily understood that the Aboriginal language and customs vary a great deal according to the nature of the country the tribes are living in, although there is a great common understanding running through us all. Our legends and traditions are all the same tales, or myths, told slightly differently, with local colouring, etc. […] There is not the slightest hint in any of our traditions that there were any other previous inhabitants in Australia.

The greatest time of the year, to my people, is the Par bar rarrie (springtime). It is then that all the great traditional corroborees take place. All our sacred traditions are then chanted and told.

All the stars and constellations in the heavens, the Milky Way, the Southern Cross, Orion's Belt, the Magellan Cloud, etc., have a meaning. There are legends connected with them all. We call the heavens the Wyerriewarr and the ruler of the heavens Nebalee.

From time immemorial we have understood the subtle art of hypnotic suggestion. Our medicine men (the Mooncumbulli) have used charms, etc. to drive out pain.

It will be seen from the foregoing account, and from other sources, that my race, living under native and tribal conditions, has a very strict and efficacious code of laws that keeps the race pure. It is only when the Aborigines come in contact with white civilisation that they leave their tribal laws, and take nothing in place of these old and well-established customs. It is then that disease and deterioration set in.

1924

Hungarrda

JEW LIZARD

Thus and thus spake Nha Teeyouwa (blackfellow). Nhan-Garra Doctor: Children, I have many strange stories to tell you. All came to me whilst I slumbered in deep sleep.

Enfolding itself from its appointed place my Spirit Self gently stepped outside my body frame with my earthly body subjective consciousness. And this is my experience.

First I stood outside my mortal frame undecided what to do, and my Spirit consciousness revealed to me that I was encased within a bubble substance and as frail. Now if my bubble frame did burst, I'd be still within that Spirit World.

Then a vapour enclosed me round about like a shroud. And I moved away from my body and the earth upon the wings of a gentle breeze, towards the deep blue sky, far beyond the distant clouds. Then my progress ceased, suspended for awhile. With my earthly mind which I still retained, I thought of my body, home and environment, with Spirit vision clear, far excelling the King of Birds.

I looked toward the earth, sought my body frame, and saw its heaving breast still breathing deep in sleep. Then I thought of loved ones, kindred and my tribes. The aged honourable Ah Yamba and my people Harrunda. The landscape west, south and east, a radius of two hundred miles from the Mountain Ah Yamba. In panoramic order lay Ellureecha, Kokacha, Hunmajarra, Deiree and Allu Wharra Tribes. All under the swaying influence and Laws of the Harrunda.

Then by some unseen, compelling force I was carried swiftly onward until the bright sunlight grew dim, as I went through period after period of ten thousand, thousand years of ages past.

In the Early Dawn of Life, I stood upon the bounds and coastline of a slimy sea, and transparent. In wonderment I gazed into its depth, and saw a state of infinitesimal rippling. And yet the surface was undisturbed.

Suddenly out of the silent, slimy sea myriads of living creatures came pushing, jostling and struggling up the rugged incline, eager to reach the sunlight that shone with threadlike ray, twinkling in the distance through the misty age, beckoning them onward to the million years ahead to accomplish that life for which they were designed.

Up and up along the winding pathway of the Gulf of Time, like pilgrims this great mass moves o'er the earth in a living stream, until ten thousand years arrive, when some living species reach their appointed span and silently pass from the rank and file and die by the wayside. Embalmed and preserved by the kindly hand of Time, they were buried in a tomb of strata for a thousand years.

Thus Life with the world moved on, with seasons ever changing all living forms and creatures adapting themselves to conditions and seasons and environment too.

As we approached to the realm of the Day-light, all the great living creatures passed into the Land of the Dead, and a new order of Creatures came to take possession of the Earth.

They were strange living forms, ridiculously shaped, some with human body, legs and arms, with head, eyes and mouth of birds, reptile and fish, some with body of fish and human head.

But what amazed me most, the intelligence they possessed was like the culture of our present day.

I was interested in one particular being. As I approached him I saw that he returned the interest, and came toward me, and when about ten paces away he placed his right hand upon his belly, then closing the fingers, as if extracting something. Quickly extending his arm toward my stomach and opening his hand, a sign of offering of goodwill.

And then we sat upon a ledge of rock. He spake unto me in my tongue, Harruna, explaining the secret code of initiation. The origin and the adoption of Totemism and its laws that marriage custom must obey. And in parting said, Speak unto your neighbouring tribes the things I have told you. It is the word of Hungarrda, the great prophet who came out of the slimy sea, the Land of Mist.

In remembrance of our meeting take this stone; on it is inscribed the song I sang to the Kangaroo, Emu, Goanna, Snakes, and Insect Tribes.

THE SONG OF HUNGARRDA

Bright, consuming Spirit. No power on earth so great as Thee,
First-born child of the Goddess of Birth and Light,
Thy habitation betwixt heaven and earth within a veil of clouds dark as night.

Accompanied by furious wind and lashing rain and hail. Riding majestically upon the storm, flashing at intervals, illumining the abode of man.

Thine anger and thy power thou revealest to us. Sometimes in a streak of light, which leaps upon a great towering rock, which stood impregnable and unchallenged in its birth-place when the earth was formed, and hurls it in fragments down the mountain-side, striking terror into man and beast alike.

Thus in wonder I am lost. No mortal mind can conceive. No mortal tongue express in language intelligible. Heaven-born Spark, I cannot see nor feel thee. Thou art concealed mysteriously wrapped within the fibre and bark of tree and bush and shrubs.

Why dost thou condescend to dwell within a piece of stick?
As I roam from place to place for enjoyment or search of food,
My soul is filled with gratitude and love for thee.
And conscious, too, of thine all pervading spirit presence.

It seems so strange that thou wilt not hear or reveal thyself nor bestow a blessing unless I pray.

But to plead is not enough to bring thee forth and cause thy glowing smiles to flicker over my frame.

But must strive and wrestle with this piece of stick pressing and twirling into another stick with all the power I possess, to release the bonds that bind thee fast.

Then shall thy living spark leap forth in contact with grass and twig.

Thy flame leaps upward like waves that press and roll.

Radiant sister of the Day, I cannot live without thee. For when at twilight and in the depth of midnight; before the morning dawns, the mist hangs over the valley like death's cold shroud, And dewdrops chill the atmosphere. Ingee Too Ma.

Then like thy bright Mother shining from afar,

Thy beaming smiles and glowing energy radiates into this frail body.

Transfusing life, health, comfort, and happiness too.

1929

Narrinyeri Saying

Like children at play we begin Life's journey,
Push our frail bark into the stream of Time,
That flows from snow-capped Mountain.
With no care; Singing and laughing as our boat glides
Upon the tide wending its way through steep rocky banks,
And meadows with bushes and plants all abloom, with sweet fragrant flowers.
Until we arrive in the Great Ocean where we are battled and tossed by the
    angry waves. Onward and onward.
For three score years and ten. Then we are cast forlorn and shipwrecked upon
    the shore of a strange land.

1929

The Voice of the Great Spirit

It is interesting to learn how all races of men have wrestled with the problem of good and evil. The Australian Aborigines have a greater and deeper sense of morality and religion than is generally known. From a very early age the mothers and the old men of the tribe instruct the children by means of tales and stories. This is one of the many stories that is handed down from generation to generation by my people.

In the beginning, the Great Spirit spoke directly everyday to his people. The tribes could not see the Great Spirit but they could hear his voice, and they assembled early every morning to hear him. Gradually, however, the tribes grew weary of listening to the Great Spirit and they said one to the other: 'Oh, I am tired of this listening to a voice I cannot see; so let us go and enjoy ourselves by making our own corroborees.'

The Great Spirit was grieved when he heard this, and as the tribes did not assemble to hear him but went and enjoyed themselves at the corroborees, the Great Spirit said: 'I must give the people a sign that they will understand.'

He sent his servant Narroondarie to call all the tribes together again once more. Narroondarie did so, saying: 'The Great Spirit will not speak again to you but he wishes to give you a sign.'

All the tribes came to the meeting. When every one was seated on the ground, Narroondarie asked them all to be very silent. Suddenly a terrific rending noise was heard. Now, Narroondarie had so placed all the tribes that the meeting was being held around a large gum tree. The tribes looked and saw this huge tree being slowly split open by some invisible force. Also, down out of the sky came an enormous Thalung (tongue), which disappeared into the middle of the gum tree, and the tree closed up again.

After this wonderful performance Narroondarie said to the tribes: 'You may go away now to your hunting and corroborees.'

Away went the tribes to enjoy themselves. After a long time some of them began to grow weary of pleasure and longed to hear again the Great Spirit. They asked Narroondarie if he would call upon the Great Spirit to speak to them again.

Narroondarie answered: 'No, the Great Spirit will never speak to you again.'

The tribes went to the sacred burial grounds to ask the dead to help them but the dead did not answer. Then they asked the great Naboolea [...], who lives in the Milky Way, if he would help them but still there was no answer and the tribes at last cried aloud with sorrow and regret. They cut their bodies with sharp stones and painted themselves white. They began to fear that they would never get in touch again with the Great Spirit.

The tribes finally appealed to Wy young gurrie, the wise old blackfellow who lives in the South Cross. He told them to gather about the big gum tree again. When all were there, Wy young gurrie asked: 'Did you not see the Thalung go into this tree?'

'Yes,' answered the tribes.

'Well,' said Wy young gurrie, 'take that as a sign that the Thalung of the Great Spirit is in all things.'

Thus it is today that the Aborigines know that the Great Spirit is in all things and speaks through every form of Nature. Thalung speaks through the voice of the wind; he rides on the storm; he speaks out from the thunder. Thalung is everywhere, and manifests through the colour of the bush, the birds, the flowers, the fish, the streams; in fact, everything that the Aboriginal sees, hears, tastes, and feels—there is Thalung.

1930/1959

ANNA MORGAN
1874—1935

Anna Morgan spent her early childhood in north-west Victoria and worked in domestic service from the age of eleven. In her twenties she moved near Cummeragunja Aboriginal Reserve, NSW, where she met and married Caleb Morgan in 1899. They had three children. Early in her marriage Morgan needed assistance but was rejected by the Board for the Protection of Aborigines. Later her application for a Commonwealth pension was also rejected. Morgan was a member of the Australian Aborigines League, and promoted Aboriginal women's education when part of the 1935 delegation to the Minister of the Interior. *AH/PM*

Under the Black Flag

What flag flies over the Australian Aborigines? Some say it is the British flag. We say that we live under the Black Flag of the Aborigines 'Protection' Board. We have not the same liberty as the white man, nor do we expect the same justice. For twelve years we lived on a mission station in New South Wales. My husband was given a 30-acre block of land; he cleared and fenced it, and then waited for implements to break it up. There were only two teams of horses to do all the work for ten such farms, and no assistance from outside was allowed. When at last we did get in a crop the Board took away the land from us. We wanted to remain on the land and make our living however we could. But, no; the Board would not have that; we must live on the mission station.

After the men had cleared and fenced about 90[0] acres of virgin soil the manager wrote to the Board, saying that the men were too lazy to work the land. Those who protested against this injustice were classed as agitators, an expulsion order was made out against them, and it was served by the local police. My husband was among the victims. Soon after, he went away, but because we had no way of removing our belongings, we left some at his father's place.

A few months later we came, prepared to take our belongings away. We stayed one night at his father's place, and the next day my husband got a summons for trespassing. He was taken and gaoled for fourteen days. Did he break any of the British laws? No. He broke the laws of the Black Flag. When a white man is charged with a crime, he is taken to court and judged. If innocent, he is allowed to go home to his family, and there the matter ends. A black man is expelled from the mission—the land reserved for him and his people—and can never go back to his own people again. Perhaps the family, unwilling to be separated from him, shares his exile until it pleases the mighty 'Protectors' of the Aborigines, or their managers, to give them a gracious pardon, and allow them to return home again. My husband and I have been expelled for all time.

Here we are! Taken from the bush, placed in compounds, told, 'This is your home and your children's as long as there is an Aboriginal left'; put under managers, scarcely allowed to think for ourselves. We were suppressed. We were half-educated. We lived on what white people call 'sustenance'. We bought our own clothes. We cleared Crown lands. At the age of fourteen our girls were sent to work—poor, illiterate, trustful little girls to be gulled by the promises of unscrupulous white men. We all know the consequences. But, of course, one of the functions of the Aborigines' Protection Board is to build a white Australia. Those who pride themselves on 'British fair play' should think of us who live under the Black Flag. We want a home. We want education. You have taken our beautiful country from us—'a free gift'.

Even a worm will turn, and we, the down-trodden of the earth, at last raise a feeble protest, and dare to ask for better conditions and the abolition of the rule of the 'Black Flag'. Will you help us?

1934

FRED BIGGS and ROLAND ROBINSON
c. 1875–1961   1912–1992

Of Ngiyampaa descent, Frederick Biggs grew up in his traditional country near Ivanhoe in western NSW. The Aborigines Protection Board moved his community to Menindee in 1934 and then to Murrin Bridge, near Lake Cargelligo, in 1949, far from his traditional country. Biggs was an active advocate for his culture, and an educator of both children and non-Indigenous researchers. He recorded stories and songs, some of which were collected by Roland Robinson in his *Aboriginal Myths and Legends* (1966).

Roland Robinson is described by *The Oxford Companion to Australian Literature* as 'the best and most dedicated of the Jindyworobak movement'. The non-Indigenous writers associated with the Jindyworobak anthologies, published between 1938 and 1953, looked to Indigenous Australian culture as the source of a truly Australian culture. Robinson received Commonwealth funding to collect and record Aboriginal stories and law, and released five prose collections both recording and inspired by this material. His eight volumes of poetry begin with *Beyond the Grass-Tree Spears* (1944), and include *Language of the Sand* (1949), *Tumult of the Swans* (1953), *Deep Well* (1962) and *Selected Poems* (1989). *Altjeringa and Other Aboriginal Poems* (1970) is a collection of collaborative poems, such as 'The Star-Tribes', written with Fred Biggs, which have been ascribed to Robinson alone in the past. *NM*

The Star-Tribes

Look, among the boughs. Those stars are men.
There's Ngintu, with his dogs, who guards the skins
of Everlasting Water in the sky.
And there's the Crow-man, carrying on his back
the wounded Hawk-man. There's the Serpent, Thurroo,

5

glistening in the leaves. There's Kapeetah,
the Moon-man, sitting in his mia-mia.

And there's those Seven Sisters, travelling
across the sky. They make the real cold frost.
You hear them when you're camped out on the plains.　　10
They look down from the sky and see your fire
and, 'Mai, mai, mai!' they sing out as they run
across the sky. And, when you wake, you find
your swag, the camp, the plains all white with frost.

1960/1970

C.J. DENNIS
1876–1938

Clarence Michael James Dennis was born in Auburn, SA, and was discharged from his first job at an Adelaide stock and station agent for reading Rider Haggard instead of attending to his duties. He made a thin living as an editor and journalist, and began publishing his first verses at nineteen. In 1908 he camped with an artist friend at Toolangi, in the hills north-east of Melbourne. He made literary friends there and wrote much of *The Songs of a Sentimental Bloke* in his hut at Kallista, the first verses of which were published in the *Bulletin* in 1909.

The Songs of a Sentimental Bloke was first released as a full rhyming narrative in 1915, and republished in 1932 as *The Sentimental Bloke*, by which title it has remained popular ever since. More than 300,000 copies have been produced in 60 editions. Despite Dennis's strong attachments to bush life, his 'Bloke' was a city 'larrikin'. Much of the appeal of the poem lies in its ironic treatment of the opposing values of working-class and ruling-class culture. In its best-known episode, the Bloke takes Doreen to see *Romeo and Juliet*, narrating it in his own vividly vernacular style and drawing conclusions from it about his own activities.

Bill the Bloke drinks, gambles and fights while mooning after Doreen but gives up his larrikinism for love and marriage, moving to a berry farm with their young son. The love story at its heart was repeated in its sequel, *The Moods of Ginger Mick* (1916), about one of the Bloke's more disreputable mates who is sent off to fight, and discovers that activities that would have seen him in jail now bring him honour. In 1919, Raymond Longford released a fine film version of *The Sentimental Bloke*, starring Lottie Lyell as Doreen, with the tagline 'Adapted from the world-famous verses of C.J. Dennis'. *NM*

From *The Songs of a Sentimental Bloke*
The Play

'Wot's in a name?' she sez … An' then she sighs,
An' clasps 'er little 'ands, an' rolls 'er eyes.
'A rose,' she sez, 'be any other name
Would smell the same.

Oh, w'erefore art you Romeo, young sir?   5
Chuck yer ole pot, an' change yer moniker!'

Doreen an' me, we bin to see a show—
The swell two-dollar touch. Bong tong, yeh know.
A chair apiece wiv velvit on the seat;
A slap-up treat.   10
The drarmer's writ be Shakespeare, years ago,
About a barmy goat called Romeo.

'Lady, be yonder moon I swear!' sez 'e.
An' then 'e climbs up on the balkiney;
An' there they smooge a treat, wiv pretty words   15
Like two love-birds.
I nudge Doreen. She whispers, 'Ain't it grand!'
'Er eyes is shinin'; an' I squeeze 'er 'and.

'Wot's in a name?' she sez. 'Struth, I dunno.
Billo is just as good as Romeo.   20
She may be Juli-er or Juli-et—
'E loves 'er yet.
If she's the tart 'e wants, then she's 'is queen,
Names never count ... But ar, I like 'Doreen!'

A sweeter, dearer sound I never 'eard;   25
Ther's music 'angs around that little word,
Doreen! ... But wot was this I starts to say
About the play?
I'm off me beat. But when a bloke's in love
'Is thorts turns 'er way, like a 'omin' dove.   30

This Romeo 'e's lurkin' wiv a crew—
A dead tough crowd o' crooks—called Montague.
'Is cliner's push—wot's nicknamed Capulet—
They 'as 'em set.
Fair narks they are, jist like them back-street clicks,   35
Ixcep' they fights wiv skewers 'stid o' bricks.

Wot's in a name? Wot's in a string o' words?
They scraps in ole Verona wiv the'r swords,
An' never give a bloke a stray dog's chance,
An' that's Romance.   40

But when they deals it out wiv bricks an' boots
In Little Lon.,[1] they're low, degraded broots.

Wot's jist plain stoush wiv us, right 'ere to-day,
Is 'valler' if yer fur enough away.
Some time, some writer bloke will do the trick   45
Wiv Ginger Mick,
Of Spadger's Lane. *'E'll* be a Romeo,
When 'e's bin dead five 'undred years or so.

Fair Juli-et, she gives 'er boy the tip.
Sez she: 'Don't sling that crowd o' mine no lip;   50
An' if you run agin a Capulet,
Jist do a get.'
'E swears 'e's done wiv lash; 'e'll chuck it clean.
(Same as I done when I first met Doreen.)

They smooge some more at that. Ar, strike me blue!   55
It gimme Joes to sit an' watch them two!
'E'd break away an' start to say good-bye,
An' then she'd sigh
'Ow, Ro-me-o!' an' git a strangle-holt,
An' 'ang around 'im like she feared 'e'd bolt.   60

Nex' day 'e words a gorspil cove about
A secret weddin'; an' they plan it out.
'E spouts a piece about 'ow 'e's bewitched:
Then they git 'itched ...
Now, 'ere's the place where I fair git the pip!   65
She's 'is for keeps, an' yet 'e lets 'er slip!

Ar! but 'e makes me sick! A fair gazob!
'E's jist the glarsey on the soulful sob,
'E'll sigh and spruik, an' 'owl a love-sick vow—
(The silly cow!)   70
But when 'e's got 'er, spliced an' on the straight
'E crools the pitch, an' tries to kid it's Fate.

Aw! Fate me foot! Instid of slopin' soon
As 'e was wed, off on 'is 'oneymoon,

_____
1   Little Lonsdale Street, Melbourne.

'Im an' 'is cobber, called Mick Curio,   75
They 'ave to go
An' mix it wiv that push o' Capulets.
They look fer trouble; an' it's wot they gets.

A tug named Tyball (cousin to the skirt)
Sprags 'em an' makes a start to sling off dirt.   80
Nex' minnit there's a reel ole ding-dong go—
'Arf round or so.
Mick Curio, 'e gets it in the neck,
'Ar rats!' 'e sez, an' passes in 'is check.

Quite natchril, Romeo gits wet as 'ell.   85
'It's me or you!' 'e 'owls, an' wiv a yell,
Plunks Tyball through the gizzard wiv 'is sword,
'Ow I ongcored!
'Put in the boot!' I sez. 'Put in the boot!'
''Ush!' sez Doreen … 'Shame!' sez some silly coot.   90

Then Romeo, 'e dunno wot to do.
The cops gits busy, like they allwiz do,
An' nose around until 'e gits blue funk
An' does a bunk.
They wants 'is tart to wed some other guy.   95
'Ah, strike!' she sez. 'I wish that I could die!'

Now, this 'ere gorspil bloke's a fair shrewd 'ead.
Sez 'e 'I'll dope yeh, so they'll *think* yer dead.'
(I tips 'e was a cunnin' sort, wot knoo
A thing or two.)   100
She takes 'is knock-out drops, up in 'er room:
They think she's snuffed, an' plant 'er in 'er tomb.

Then things gits mixed a treat an' starts to whirl.
'Ere's Romeo comes back an' finds 'is girl
Tucked in 'er little coffing, cold an' stiff,   105
An' in a jiff,
'E swallows lysol, throws a fancy fit,
'Ead over turkey, an' 'is soul 'as flit.

Then Juli-et wakes up an' sees 'im there,
Turns on the water-works an' tears 'er 'air,   110

'Dear love,' she sez, 'I cannot live alone!'
An' wiv a moan,
She grabs 'is pockit knife, an' ends 'er cares …
'*Peanuts or lollies!*' sez a boy upstairs.

1915

LOUIS ESSON
1878–1943

A meeting with Irish poet W.B. Yeats is said to have inspired Louis Esson, often credited as the 'father of Australian drama', to produce distinctively Australian theatre. Esson's first full-length play, *The Time is Not Yet Ripe* (1912/1912), is instead an urbane, cosmopolitan comedy, influenced by George Bernard Shaw and Oscar Wilde. Other plays, however, especially the one-act *Dead Timber* (1911/1920), *The Battler* (1922/unpublished), *The Drovers* (1923/1920) and *Mother and Son* (1923/1946), look to rural experience in portraying tragedy and human failure. With Vance Palmer and Stewart Macky, Esson and his wife Hilda (Bull) established the Pioneer Players in Melbourne, which performed sixteen plays in seven seasons, all with local content. Australian content in melodrama and the music hall had never been lacking but the Pioneer Players saw their work as serious theatre. *NM*

From *The Time is Not Yet Ripe*
Act 1, Scene 1

The Prime Minister's Drawing Room. After Dinner.
　　[*Enter* SIR JOSEPH QUIVERTON, *followed by* DORIS.]
SIR JOSEPH: Not another word. I refuse to give the matter further consideration. I tell you, Doris, finally, irrevocably—
DORIS: Listen a moment, father! You haven't finished your coffee.
SIR JOSEPH: I will not listen. I should have forbidden you to speak. This thing is preposterous, impossible,—
DORIS: I know it is difficult for a politician to preserve an open mind.
SIR JOSEPH: At present I am not a politician. I am your father.
DORIS: Why do you raise these technical points! We will sit down quietly and have a little chat on the subject. Shall I bring in your coffee?
SIR JOSEPH: No. And I don't want to debate with my own daughter. I am shocked, Doris, and deeply wounded.
DORIS: Wasn't I right to tell you I was engaged?
SIR JOSEPH: Yes—No! Not to a man like that. Never in all my experience have I heard of such a thing. If you have no self-respect, you might at least think of the dignity of my position.
DORIS: Father!
SIR JOSEPH: Don't answer me. Barrett is a Socialist, a revolutionary Socialist. That is sufficient.

DORIS: He has a big station in the Riverina, and goodness knows how many sheep. I love sheep.

SIR JOSEPH: He proposes to confiscate land and capital.

DORIS: Not his own, father. Sydney may be a Socialist, and an advanced Atheist, but he is not a philanthropist.

SIR JOSEPH: I thank you for the information. It deeply gratifies me to learn that my prospective son-in-law is not only a revolutionary Socialist, but also an advanced Atheist—a most promising young man, a credit to his country.

DORIS: Father, have I your consent or not?

SIR JOSEPH: My consent, never! I mean to fight the next election on this very issue of Socialism versus Private Enterprise. You know I am no Tory. I am a progressive man, and believe in a policy of progress and reform.

DORIS: Everybody says that before an election.

SIR JOSEPH: Doris, for the sake of the party, for the sake of the country, for the sake of the Empire—for my sake—you must give up this folly.

DORIS: Love is not folly. Plato says that love is the highest wisdom.

SIR JOSEPH: Plato is wrong. And that's the stuff they want to introduce into the University. Have I no authority left! No, I am the last one to be considered. Now, Doris, children must obey their parents.

DORIS: You are mistaken, father. In the natural cause of evolution parents must be sacrificed to their children; not children to their parents. It is a law of nature.

SIR JOSEPH: There is such a thing as a moral law, Doris.

DORIS: No, there isn't, father. That is a popular fallacy. People used to think there was, but there isn't.

SIR JOSEPH: I have always given you your own way, and this is my reward. Don't you realise that the country is in a critical condition? I want you to understand my aims, my policy.

DORIS: I am sorry, father, but I don't believe in your policy.

SIR JOSEPH: What!

DORIS: I would like to, but I can't.

SIR JOSEPH: You can't?

DORIS: No, father. Once I used to believe in the things you do, but I have got beyond that stage.

SIR JOSEPH: That is good, very good indeed. I have devoted thirty years of my life to formulating a progressive Liberal policy that has won the confidence of the country, and now my own daughter tells me to my face that she has got beyond it. What is the world coming to!

DORIS: Sydney says the Liberal policy is an anachronism.

SIR JOSEPH: You must put Sydney out of your thoughts. His influence is immoral.

DORIS: Listen, father!

SIR JOSEPH: Please don't interrupt me! This is a pretty situation for the leader of a great party! What will the Opposition say when it learns that my daughter is engaged to a Socialist, a revolutionary Socialist. I will retire at once. I will give up public life. My day is past. I won't be made a laughing stock by my unscrupulous opponents. And we are on the eve of an election. The country needs my services—so much to do, so little done.

[*Enter* BUTLER.]

BUTLER: Sir Henry and Lady Pillsbury.

[*Enter* SIR HENRY and LADY PILLSBURY. *Exit* BUTLER.]

SIR JOSEPH: Good evening!

DORIS: Delighted you have come!

LADY PILLSBURY: I would have called before only I had a touch of neuralgia.

SIR HENRY: My wife enjoys the most extraordinary bad health.

LADY PILLSBURY: Nerves! Strikes always upset me. I loathe paid agitators.

[*They take seats.*]

These Salons are sure to have a great educational influence. It is so pleasant to drop in and exchange ideas on the great political problems.

SIR JOSEPH: The educated classes must be organised to protect their rights.

DORIS: What do you think of the bakers' strike, Sir Henry?

SIR HENRY: I can only trust that wise counsels will prevail.

LADY PILLSBURY: Is it going to last for ever?

SIR HENRY: One never knows. One never knows.

LADY PILLSBURY: I refuse to use cake on principle. It is encouraging the bakers.

SIR HENRY: I notice Barrett made another inflammatory speech this afternoon.

LADY PILLSBURY: That is a dangerous man, most dangerous.

SIR HENRY: And he is a Rhodes Scholar, if I remember rightly.

SIR JOSEPH: That makes his conduct all the more uncalled for.

LADY PILLSBURY: I have never met the young man.

DORIS: Mr. Barrett holds very advanced views, and that unfits him for fashionable society. He may look in to-night.

SIR JOSEPH: Surely you didn't invite him!

DORIS: I thought it would do him good.

LADY PILLSBURY: How can a squatter be a Socialist, even if he has been educated at Oxford?

SIR JOSEPH: I am not a Spiritualist, Lady Pillsbury. I do not pretend to explain the supernatural.

SIR HENRY: [*airily*] We are all Socialists now-a-days.

SIR JOSEPH: But Barrett is an extremist, a revolutionary Socialist. At the Wagga Wagga Agricultural Show dinner he said the present land tax was a farce, and should be raised to fifteen shillings in the pound.

DORIS: Yes, I know. He is inclined to exaggerate a little.

SIR JOSEPH: That is not all. He is setting class against class, and where is it going to end? If our squatters adopt such views, what can be expected from the Trades Unionists?

DORIS: Please don't worry, father. It is becoming a mannerism. We must convert Mr. Barrett.

SIR HENRY: We must always hope for the best.

SIR JOSEPH: [*ready for long speech*] The situation is grave. Great issues are at stake. What do we see around us—unrest and discontent. We are standing, as it were, at the parting of the ways.

DORIS: [*breaking in*] Bridge or music?

LADY PILLSBURY: You might play something.

DORIS: Stravinsky or Bach?

LADY PILLSBURY: I loathe classical music. Neither, dear—a little American piece. I have a slight headache.

DORIS: I am so sorry.

    [*The ladies rise.*]

LADY PILLSBURY: It is always a strain listening to intellectual conversation.

    [*Exeunt* DORIS *and* LADY PILLSBURY.]

SIR JOSEPH: How is Lady Pillsbury keeping now?

SIR HENRY: Much better, thanks. She complains only about half her time.

SIR JOSEPH: That Barrett is a violent young man.

SIR HENRY: Indeed he is. I heard a rumour he was going to stand for Parliament.

SIR JOSEPH: What! How! Why!

SIR HENRY: It was only a rumour.

SIR JOSEPH: Standing for Parliament! Ah, well, nothing surprises me now.

    [*Enter* BUTLER, *followed by* JOHN K. HILL.]

BUTLER: Mr. John K. Hill.

    [*Exit* BUTLER.]

SIR JOSEPH: Sir Henry Pillsbury—our Attorney-General—Mr. Hill. Mr. Hill is an ambassador of Commerce.

JOHN K. HILL: No, sir, I am a plain man of figures.

SIR JOSEPH: And a maker of nations.

JOHN K.: I just financed that little revolution in Uruguay.

SIR HENRY: There usually seems to be trouble in that part of the world.

SIR JOSEPH: And there will be trouble here, too, if the Socialists have their way. This country is on the eve of changes, Mr. Hill, startling changes.

JOHN K.: You don't say.

SIR JOSEPH: We are moving too fast.

JOHN K.: Well, I wouldn't have guessed that now. I am only a visitor, but I was kept waitin' in a hat store yesterday afternoon close on one minute and a half before the young man behind the counter woke up.

SIR HENRY: The new unionism.

JOHN K.: Australia's an extraordinary country.

SIR HENRY: This is a holiday trip, I presume.

JOHN K.: No, sir, I never take holidays. I have sert'n propositions to consider. Your Northern Territory interests me. It is virgin soil. I am a missionary—a missionary traveller. I represent a little Chicago syndicate that wants scope for investment. But I can't advise it to shovel money into a noo country without sert'n concessions.

SIR JOSEPH: Do you propose to establish industries, Mr. Hill?

JOHN K.: Yes, sir. That is my business. I want to develop this country, bring it up to time, Americanise it. It has golden possibilities. Take your bêche-de-mer—regarded by epicures as superior to turtle—why, it's a beat—it's just crying out to be canned! All we want is freezin' works—and cheap labour—and no public banquet will be complete without it.

SIR HENRY: Our fisheries have so far been somewhat neglected.

JOHN K.: And there's your forests of cypress pine, wonderful forests, absolutely goin' to waste. Most valuable timber, sir, put to its legitimate use—specially adapted for makin' Chinese coffins—they use up quite a number over there in China—10,000 a day, I have the exact figures—unlimited market—easy transit to Hong Kong! Revolution is China's long suit now-a-days, and it's me to deliver the goods. I'm goin' to bring death within the reach of all.

SIR JOSEPH: This country can develop only with the aid of capital. Capital is as necessary as labour. One is the complement of the other.

JOHN K.: That's so. But if your Socialist party gains a majority, won't it pass Anti-Trust legislation?

SIR HENRY: It is difficult to say what it would not do.

JOHN K.: And nationalise the Chinese coffin monopoly and the canned slug monopoly?

SIR JOSEPH: You can rely on the Government, Mr. Hill, to assist you in every way.

JOHN K.: Thanks, Sir Joseph. We'll stand or fall together.

[*Enter* DORIS.]

DORIS: How do you do? Mr. Hill and I are old friends.

JOHN K.: I'm honoured, Miss Quiverton.

DORIS: And what do you think of Australia now?

JOHN K.: You have lots of space, I guess.

DORIS: Our sheep require it. Our population is mostly sheep.

SIR JOSEPH: You forget Mr. Hill has not yet seen the country.

DORIS: I hope you will not be disappointed. Australia is still uncultivated nature. Our scenery, of course, is not so smooth and highly finished as the English, but we can hardly expect that in such a young country. Will you make one for a small game?

SIR HENRY: Lady Pillsbury is devoted to bridge.

[*Exeunt* SIR HENRY *and* SIR JOSEPH.]

DORIS: We are all keenly interested in politics. It's the latest thing. There is a Salon almost every week.

JOHN K.: As an American it's all most fascinating to me.

[*Enter* SYDNEY BARRETT *as* DORIS *shows* JOHN K. HILL *into card-room, and returns.* BARRETT *advances.*]

DORIS: O, Syd! What nice rough cloth! It suits you very well.

BARRETT: I am a man of the people.

DORIS: How did you get in?

BARRETT: By what you call the tradesmen's entrance. But Doris—

DORIS: Why are you so absurdly bashful! You are making yourself positively ridiculous … I told father.

BARRETT: Was he pleased?

DORIS: Pleased! He went off.

BARRETT: I am glad of that. He so seldom does.

[*He goes to kiss her.*]

DORIS: Wait till I shut the door! I can give you only a few minutes alone.

[*She shuts card-room door, and returns.* BARRETT *embraces her.*]

[*With head on his shoulder*] O, Sydney, this is all I want. No more. [*Putting him away*]

Sit down. Now! [*Taking a seat*] Do you admire me immensely?

BARRETT: I do. You are quite perfect. But Doris—

DORIS: But what?

BARRETT: You are still wearing jewellery.

DORIS: One can express oneself in jewellery.

BARRETT: Did I not tell you to discard those pearls?

DORIS: Three times.

BARRETT: Have you never thought of the Ceylon diver who held his breath, and went all naked to the hungry shark?

DORIS: Does he mind? You said once you would feel transcendently happy if I permitted you to die for me.

BARRETT: So I would, in a romantic mood. But, Doris, it is time we had a definite understanding. You must give up your jewellery and bridge and salons and other forms of fashionable frivolity.

DORIS: Does Socialism mean that?

BARRETT: Of course it does.

DORIS: I am not a Socialist, then. I don't believe in it.

BARRETT: You are pursuing an illusory existence. It must end.

DORIS: I wish, Syd, you wouldn't try to reform me. It will be much better for us both if I reform you.

BARRETT: Listen, Doris, you must do as I tell you.

DORIS: You are getting as bad as father.

BARRETT: What an atmosphere! Bridge and bad politics!

DORIS: Sydney!

BARRETT: Here am I after a four years' absence, returned to my native land, full of a fine enthusiasm, to find the country stagnant, decadent,—and the young Australian, with his bright, fresh mind, untramelled by the traditions of the past—that is the current phrase—repeating all the popular superstitions, from beer to bishops, of his fogbound ancestors. Australia is an outer suburb of Brixton. That explains its amazing school of architecture. That explains everything. We are unoriginal, therefore uninteresting.

DORIS: That's all so abstract, isn't it!

BARRETT: We prate of progress, and what is Australia's chief contribution to civilisation? Frozen mutton and the losing hazard. Can you wonder that I am dissatisfied!

DORIS: You always are. You're an idealist.

BARRETT: Every country must have a national ideal. We have nothing, absolutely nothing. Australia is an empty country. We produce wool and cricketers and factory butter and legislative councillors, but we do not produce ideas. Why, the national intelligence has not yet invented one new drink. Things can't go on like this. But where are our leaders? Look at your worthy father. He certainly seems troubled about many things, but he goes on uttering empty phrases, meaning nothing, suggesting nothing,—

DORIS: Yes, I know. Father is very tiresome. But what are you proposing to do?

BARRETT: Everything. I propose change, disorder, revolution. We will have to make a fresh start. I attended the Socialist Congress tonight.

DORIS: That explains your behaviour.

BARRETT: We had a stormy meeting. I was accused of being an intellectual. There was nearly a split in the party. That shows how earnest we are. We are going to do things. You must give up this empty life, Doris.

DORIS: Don't dare me, Sydney. I might do something rash.

BARRETT: I have no fear. You are not in revolt.

DORIS: Don't tempt me to prove you are wrong.

BARRETT: You don't realise my position. I haven't told you my plans yet. I have something most important to tell you. I decided to-night—

    [*Enter* MISS PERKINS.]

Great Caesar! Who is that?

DORIS: Miss Perkins.

BARRETT: I'm off. I'll tell you my secret later.

DORIS: Mr. Barrett—Miss Perkins. Miss Perkins is the energetic secretary of the Women's Anti-Socialist League. Please sit down.

MISS PERKINS: [*taking a chair*] I have hurried round from the League. The business was most important.

BARRETT: [*escaping*] Pray, don't let me disturb you.

[*Exit* BARRETT.]

DORIS: [*tired and languid*] Was it a pleasant evening?

MISS PERKINS: We had a prolonged discussion. You must help us, Miss Quiverton.

DORIS: I shall be delighted.

MISS PERKINS: I don't know what the country is coming to. The domestic helps have formed a union.

DORIS: I prefer men servants. They are more docile.

MISS PERKINS: They will demand a day at home next. You must assist us, Miss Quiverton.

DORIS: Certainly.

MISS PERKINS: You will promise to stand by the League?

DORIS: I shall promise anything, with pleasure.

[*Enter* LADY PILLSBURY.]

MISS PERKINS: We have decided on a most momentous step.

LADY PILLSBURY: How are you, Miss Perkins?

MISS PERKINS: Well, I thank you. How are you? We have decided—

LADY PILLSBURY: Bridge is too exciting. Heart! Mr. Barrett has arrived. He is wearing a red tie.

MISS PERKINS: [*going ahead*] The matter was exhaustively discussed by all our ablest speakers. We came to the conclusion that there was only one way to save the country.

LADY PILLSBURY: And what may that be?

MISS PERKINS: Women must take their place in the political arena.

LADY PILLSBURY: You are right, Miss Perkins. We have been kept down for centuries by a man-made law. But we are quite capable of directing the destiny of a great nation. All we need is more opportunity to display our ability. That is why I never allow my husband to make up his mind on any public question till he has first consulted me.

MISS PERKINS: I have an important announcement to make. May I see Sir Joseph?

DORIS: [*going to door*] Father! Miss Perkins has an important communication to deliver.

[*Enter* SIR JOSEPH *and* SIR HENRY, *followed later by* JOHN K. HILL *and* SYDNEY BARRETT.]

MISS PERKINS: The Committee of the League held its fortnightly meeting this evening, Mrs. Jasper Jones occupying the chair. After a short debate, it was decided that it was the duty of every lady in the land to take an active and intelligent interest in the coming elections… The time has arrived when women's refining influence should extend over a wider sphere.

SIR HENRY: I incline to that view myself, but we must not go too far.

MISS PERKINS: We must go far enough, Sir Henry, to reach a logical conclusion. The country is in a dreadful condition. Men have not the requisite knowledge to deal adequately with the problem of social reform. That is women's special province. The morality of the nation is in our keeping. Shall we forsake our trust?

DORIS: No!

LADY PILLSBURY: Certainly not!

MISS PERKINS: I'm glad we agree on that point. Certain names were forwarded for our approval, but after due consideration we came to the conclusion that there was not one man whom we could conscientiously support. The League decided that the women of this electorate must be represented by a woman.

[*Applause.*]

SIR HENRY: It is so difficult to decide on any definite line of action.

MISS PERKINS: Therefore, in the best interests of the country I have been requested to ask Miss Quiverton to stand for Parliament.

[*Mild sensation.*]

DORIS: Me!

MISS PERKINS: The proposal was carried by acclamation, and with only one dissentient voice.

[*Loud applause.*]

DORIS: But I don't understand politics.

MISS PERKINS: It is not a question of mere politics. It is a question of morality.

DORIS: Of course, that makes a considerable difference.

LADY PILLSBURY: All the difference, my dear.

DORIS: But please tell me how I can promote the morality of the nation. I should be only too delighted.

MISS PERKINS: By defeating the Socialist candidate.

SIR HENRY: What constituency has been selected for Miss Quiverton?

MISS PERKINS: Wombat.

DORIS: Wombat! That doesn't sound particularly moral.

MISS PERKINS: O, yes, it is only the name of a local bird. There is no time for hesitation. Tomorrow is the last day for nominations. The Socialists are selecting their candidate to-night.

DORIS: Will you give me a few moments to think it over?

MISS PERKINS: Do try to persuade Miss Quiverton to save the country. It is a most anxious time for us all.

[DORIS *is surrounded.*]

LADY PILLSBURY: It is your duty, my dear, to protect our rights. I would overcome my natural feeling of modesty and contest the seat myself, only my uncertain health could not endure the strain of an election.

SIR HENRY: I opposed votes for women, when the subject was first broached, but I have been converted to the opinion that women have every right to take their place in our legislatures.

LADY PILLSBURY: I converted my husband to that opinion.

SIR JOSEPH: I do not wish to advise you in any way, but I may say that the situation is grave, very grave. We have reached a crisis.

DORIS: What is your advice, Mr. Hill? Do you think, as an American, that it is wrong for women to take part in political agitation?

JOHN K.: Well, Miss Quiverton, it is a very delicate subject. I know good American citizens negotiating dangerous propositions in order that their elegant wives and daughters might stroll through Rome and Florence, with a calm expression on their face, and the 'Beauties of Ruskin' under their arm, tracin' the influence of Leonardo on Perugino. That, Miss Quiverton, is the American ideal.

DORIS: How chaste and beautiful.

LADY PILLSBURY: We couldn't trust our husbands to that extent.

DORIS: Now, Mr. Hill, would you be very shocked if I went into Parliament?

JOHN K.: On the contrary, Miss Quiverton. I would leave home at once to live in any country that had the honour of being governed by you.

DORIS: [*bringing him forward*] Mr. Barrett … As my father observed, we are standing at the parting of the ways.

BARRETT: That is the usual position of a politician.

MISS PERKINS: You have extraordinary personal popularity, Miss Quiverton. You will gain a large sympathetic masculine vote.

DORIS: But—

MISS PERKINS: O, you must. You must really. It is a patriotic duty. Think of the state of the country.

DORIS: What do you think of the state of the country, Mr. Barrett? Don't be so shy.

BARRETT: [*affably*] Socialism is still spreading, you know.

MISS PERKINS: You see, Miss Quiverton, Mr. Barrett agrees with me.

DORIS: I am glad Mr. Barrett agrees with somebody. What are we going to do, then? We must do something, I suppose.

MISS PERKINS: You will have a strong committee to help you.

DORIS: Thanks very much.

MISS PERKINS: I shall attend to all the secretarial work.

DORIS: But—

MISS PERKINS: That will be all right, Miss Quiverton. Leave that entirely to me.

DORIS: Is it State or Federal?

MISS PERKINS: Federal.

BARRETT: Excuse me, are you arranging a sale of gifts?

MISS PERKINS: This is not a bazaar.

DORIS: I have been asked to stand for Parliament.

BARRETT: As a Syndicalist, I presume.

DORIS: I really couldn't say. What is our policy, Miss Perkins?

MISS PERKINS: Social reform.

DORIS: I thought so. We are going to reform Society. You believe in that, I hope.

MISS PERKINS: Purity of the home is our guiding principle. The League has drawn up a complete manifesto.

DORIS: What is the funny name of the constituency?

MISS PERKINS: Wombat.

BARRETT: Wombat!

DORIS: It is a most respectable district.

BARRETT: I trust so. For, curiously enough, I myself am standing for this eminently respectable district of Wombat.

[*Sensation.*]

DORIS: Are you? Why didn't you tell me before?

BARRETT: I was trying to.

DORIS: O! that was your great secret.

MISS PERKINS: Miss Quiverton is the Good Woman candidate.

BARRETT: And I am the Bad Man candidate.

DORIS: That is only a personal distinction. Have you any policy?

BARRETT: I have, but it is not so daring as yours. My policy does not propose in any way to vaccinate the community against the complaint called joy. Its tendency, indeed, is distinctly immoral.

SIR HENRY: Shame!

SIR JOSEPH: If you have no moral feelings, you might at least have the decency to—

BARRETT: Excuse me, Sir Joseph, I have no desire to listen to your opinions. I prefer to give you mine.

SIR HENRY: There are ladies present.

BARRETT: [*pleasantly*] I occupy the soap box. You say Socialism will destroy the purity of the home. Of course, it will. That will be one of the chief glories of Socialism. To the devil with the purity of the home! Purity is a disease, and the suburban home is a horror.

JOHN K.: Up and away to the woods!

SIR HENRY: I am surprised to hear a young man—

BARRETT: Be calm, Sir Henry. There is no necessity for heated argument. It is our intention simply to overthrow the present form of bourgeois society.

SIR JOSEPH: Silence!

BARRETT: Ladies and gentlemen, I beg to inform you that a Reign of Terror is at hand. But what can you expect! I am standing, you see, in the interests of revolutionary Socialism.

SIR HENRY: Who will vote for you?

MISS PERKINS: You won't get in.

BARRETT: But I shall take it as a personal matter if any here present may have the effrontery to cast one such worthless vote in my favour.

SIR JOSEPH: Leave my house, sir.

BARRETT: A new era begins tomorrow. Beware! Yours for the revolution.

    [*Exit* BARRETT. *Uproar and babble.*]

ALL: {
    Now you see our danger.
    Disgraceful.
    This is anarchy.
    Who would have believed it!

DORIS: [*to various people*] If you really wish it. Quite a pleasure, I assure you.

MISS PERKINS: [*voice rising above din*] Our first committee meeting tomorrow afternoon, three sharp.

    [*General confusion.*]

CURTAIN

        1912

P.J. HARTIGAN
1878–1952

A Catholic parish priest in western NSW, Patrick Joseph Hartigan published two volumes of verse under his pseudonym John O'Brien. *Around the Boree Log and Other Verses* (1921) includes 'Said Hanrahan': its refrain of 'We'll all be rooned' has passed into the Australian vernacular as a comic expression of the extreme pessimism of farmers faced with an unpredictable climate. With *The Parish of St Mel's* (1954), a tribute to his Narrandera parish, the often simple balladry of P.J. Hartigan centres on Irish-Australian, Catholic rural community life. *NM*

Said Hanrahan

'We'll all be rooned,' said Hanrahan,
    In accents most forlorn,
Outside the church, ere Mass began,
    One frosty Sunday morn.

The congregation stood about,   5
    Coat-collars to the ears,
And talked of stock, and crops, and drought,
    As it had done for years.

'It's lookin' crook,' said Daniel Croke;
    'Bedad, it's cruke, me lad,   10
For never since the banks went broke
    Has seasons been so bad.'

'It's dry, all right,' said young O'Neil,
    With which astute remark
He squatted down upon his heel   15
    And chewed a piece of bark.

And so around the chorus ran
    'It's keepin' dry, no doubt.'
'We'll all be rooned,' said Hanrahan
    'Before the year is out.   20

'The crops are done; ye'll have your work
    To save one bag of grain;
From here way out to Back-o'-Bourke
    They're singin' out for rain.

'They're singin' out for rain,' he said,   25
    'And all the tanks are dry.'
The congregation scratched its head,
    And gazed around the sky.

'There won't be grass, in any case,
    Enough to feed an ass;   30
There's not a blade on Casey's place
    As I came down to Mass.'

'If rain don't come this month,' said Dan,
    And cleared his throat to speak—
'We'll all be rooned,' said Hanrahan,   35
    'If rain don't come this week.'

A heavy silence seemed to steal
    On all at this remark;

And each man squatted on his heel,
    And chewed a piece of bark.   40

'We want a inch of rain, we do,'
    O'Neil observed at last;
But Croke 'maintained' we wanted two
    To put the danger past.

'If we don't get three inches, man,   45
    Or four to break this drought,
We'll all be rooned,' said Hanrahan,
    'Before the year is out.'

In God's good time down came the rain;
    And all the afternoon   50
On iron roof and window-pane
    It drummed a homely tune.

And through the night it pattered still,
    And lightsome, gladsome elves
On dripping spout and window-sill   55
    Kept talking to themselves.

It pelted, pelted all day long,
    A-singing at its work,
Till every heart took up the song
    Way out to Back-o'-Bourke.   60

And every creek a banker ran,
    And dams filled overtop;
'We'll all be rooned,' said Hanrahan,
    'If this rain doesn't stop.'

And stop it did, in God's good time;   65
    And spring came in to fold
A mantle o'er the hills sublime
    Of green and pink and gold.

And days went by on dancing feet,
    With harvest-hopes immense,   70
And laughing eyes beheld the wheat
    Nid-nodding o'er the fence.

And, oh, the smiles on every face,
  As happy lad and lass
Through grass knee-deep on Casey's place   75
  Went riding down to Mass.

While round the church in clothes genteel
  Discoursed the men of mark,
And each man squatted on his heel,
  And chewed his piece of bark.   80

'There'll be bush-fires for sure, me man,
  There will, without a doubt;
We'll all be rooned,' said Hanrahan,
  'Before the year is out.'

                                          1921

MILES FRANKLIN
1879–1954

Miles Franklin was a legend in her lifetime and remains so today. The legend rests firmly on her first novel, the audacious *My Brilliant Career* (1901), her ongoing commitment to Australian literature through the establishment of the Miles Franklin Literary Award (first awarded to Patrick White (qv) in 1957), and an increasing appreciation of her life experiences and quirky personality.

Miles Franklin's principal published works amount to 21 novels, plays and non-fiction titles, plus some 160 topical writings. She also sponsored the publication of two volumes of the poetry of her friend Mary E. Fullerton (qv). Several volumes of letters and diaries have been published posthumously, and more of her writings remain in manuscript form.

After *My Brilliant Career*, success as a writer evaded her. Seeking publishers for works such as *My Career Goes Bung* (published in Australia in 1946), she left for America and England. Only two of numerous writings during the years away have appeared to date: the 'New Woman' novels *The Net of Circumstance* (1915, by 'Mr & Mrs Ogniblat L'Artsau', a play on Austral Talbingo, the southern NSW town where she was born) and *On Dearborn Street* (1981).

The turning point came with the First World War, when Franklin served briefly as a hospital orderly in Macedonia. In London in the dying days of empire, she was drawn to historical fiction and Australian themes. *Old Blastus of Bandicoot* (1931) was the first book to appear under her own name since the Penrith suffrage novel *Some Everyday Folk and Dawn* (1909), followed by three titles in the now under-appreciated 'Brent of Bin Bin' historical series set in the Southern Highlands of NSW.

When she returned to Australia in 1932, she joined the Fellowship of Australian Writers and became a strong advocate of Australian writing and writers, and of free speech. Her most popular work was the prize-winning pastoral saga *All That Swagger* (1936), and she made significant contributions to literary scholarship: *Joseph Furphy: The man and his book* (1944, with Kate Baker) and *Laughter, Not for a Cage* (Commonwealth Literary Fund lectures delivered in Perth in 1950).

Franklin's penchant for secrecy irritated people. However, pseudonyms were not unusual in her day, and she believed that publishers would lose interest in the remaining Brent volumes if she revealed Brent's identity. The entire six-volume Brent series was published by Angus & Robertson (1950–56). Brent's identity was finally established when her personal papers, donated to the State Library of NSW, were opened in 1966.

Miles Franklin is thought of as an 1890s writer. While nationalism and feminism shaped her approach and she remained a realist, her wide experience, gift for friendship and quick mind ensured a cosmopolitan perspective. She never felt she achieved her full potential. Her struggle to do so is one of the reasons her writings still appeal to so many readers. *JR*

From *My Brilliant Career*
Chapter 5: Disjointed Sketches and Grumbles

A DROUGHT IDYLL

'Sybylla, what are you doing? Where is your mother?'

'I'm ironing. Mother's down at the fowl-house seeing after some chickens. What do you want?'

It was my father who addressed me. Time, 2 o'clock p.m. Thermometer hung in the shade of the veranda registering 105½ degrees.

'I see Blackshaw coming across the flat. Call your mother. You bring the leg-ropes—I've got the dog-leg. Come at once; we'll give the cows another lift. Poor devils—might as well knock 'em on the head at once, but there might be rain next moon. This drought can't last for ever.'

I called mother, got the leg-ropes, and set off, pulling my sunbonnet closely over my face to protect my eyes from the dust which was driving from the west in blinding clouds. The dog-leg to which father had referred was three poles, about eight or ten feet long, strapped together so they could be stood up. It was an arrangement father had devised to facilitate our labour in lifting the cows. A fourth and longer pole was placed across the fork formed by the three, and to one end of this were tied a couple of leg-ropes, after being placed round the beast, one beneath the flank and one around the girth. On the other end of this pole we would put our weight while one man would lift with the tail and another with the horns. New-chum cows would sulk, and we would have great work with them; but those used to the performance would help themselves, and up they'd go as nice as a daisy. The only art needed was to draw the pole back quickly before the cows could move, or the leg-ropes would pull them over again.

On this afternoon we had six cows to lift. We struggled manfully, and got five on their feet, and then proceeded to where the last one was lying, back downwards, on a shadeless stony spot on the side of a hill. The men slewed her round by the tail, while mother and I fixed the dog-leg and adjusted the ropes. We got the cow up, but the poor beast was so weak and knocked about that she immediately fell down again. We resolved to let her have a few minutes' spell before making another attempt at lifting. There was not a blade of grass to be seen, and the ground was too dusty to sit on. We were too overdone to make more than one-worded utterances, so waited silently in the blazing sun, closing our eyes against the dust.

Weariness! Weariness!

A few light wind-smitten clouds made wan streaks across the white sky, haggard with the fierce relentless glare of the afternoon sun. Weariness was written across my mother's delicate careworn features, and found expression in my father's knitted brows and dusty face. Blackshaw was weary, and said so, as he wiped the dust, made mud with perspiration, off his cheeks. I was weary—my limbs ached with the heat and work. The poor beast stretched at our feet was weary. All nature was weary, and seemed to sing a dirge to that effect in the furnace-breath wind which roared among the trees on the low ranges at our back and smote the parched and thirsty ground. All were weary, all but the sun. He seemed to glory in his power, relentless and untiring, as he swung boldly in the sky, triumphantly leering down upon his helpless victims.

Weariness! Weariness!

This was life—my life—my career, my brilliant career! I was fifteen—fifteen! A few fleeting hours and I would be old as those around me. I looked at them as they stood there, weary, and turning down the other side of the hill of life. When young, no doubt they had hoped for, and dreamed of, better things—had even known them. But here they were. This had been their life; this was their career. It was, and in all probability would be, mine too. My life—my career—my brilliant career!

Weariness! Weariness!

The summer sun danced on. Summer is fiendish, and life is a curse, I said in my heart. What a great dull hard rock the world was! On it were a few barren narrow ledges, and on these, by exerting ourselves so that the force wears off our finger-nails, it allows us to hang for a year or two, and then hurls us off into outer darkness and oblivion, perhaps to endure worse torture than this.

The poor beast moaned. The lifting had strained her, and there were patches of hide worn off her the size of breakfast-plates, sore and most harrowing to look upon.

It takes great suffering to wring a moan from the patience of a cow. I turned my head away, and with the impatience and one-sided reasoning common to fifteen, asked God what He meant by this. It is well enough to heap suffering on human beings, seeing it is supposed to be merely a probation for a better world, but animals—poor, innocent animals—why are they tortured so?

'Come now, we'll lift her once more,' said my father. At it we went again; it is surprising what weight there is in the poorest cow. With great struggling we got her to her feet once more, and were careful this time to hold her till she got steady on her legs. Father and mother at the tail and Blackshaw and I at the horns, we marched her home and gave her a bran mash. Then we turned to our work in the house while the men sat and smoked and spat on the veranda, discussing the drought for an hour, at the end of which time they went to help someone else with their stock. I made up the fire and we continued our ironing, which had been interrupted some hours before. It was hot unpleasant work on such a day. We were forced to keep the doors and windows closed on account of the wind and dust. We were hot and tired, and our feet ached so that we could scarcely stand on them.

Weariness! Weariness!

Summer is fiendish and life is a curse, I said in my heart.

Day after day the drought continued. Now and again there would be a few days of the raging wind before mentioned, which carried the dry grass off the paddocks and piled it against the fences, darkened the air with dust, and seemed to promise rain, but ever it dispersed whence it came, taking with it the few clouds it had gathered up; and for weeks and weeks at a stretch, from horizon to horizon, was never a speck to mar the cruel dazzling brilliance of the metal sky.

Weariness! Weariness!

I said the one thing many times but, ah, it was a weary thing which took much repetition that familiarity might wear away a little of its bitterness! [. . .]

Chapter 23: 'Ah! For One Hour Of Burning Love, 'Tis Worth An Age Of Cold Respect'

We walked in perfect silence, Harold not offering to carry my little basket. I did not dare lift my eyes, as something told me the face of the big man would not be pleasant to look upon just then. I twirled the ring he had given me round and round on my finger. I occasionally put it on, wearing the stones on the palm-side of my finger, so that it would not be taken for other than one of two or three aunt Helen had lent me, saying I was at liberty to use them while at Caddagat, if it gave me any pleasure.

The Caddagat orchard contained six acres, and being a narrow enclosure, and the cherries growing at the extreme end from the house, it took us some time to reach them. I led the way to our destination—a secluded nook where grape-vines clambered up fig-trees, and where the top of gooseberry bushes met the lower limbs of cherry-trees. Blue and yellow lupins stood knee-high, and strawberries grew wild among them. We had not uttered a sound, and I had not glanced at my companion. I stopped; he wheeled abruptly and grasped my wrist in a manner which sent the basket whirling from my hand. I looked up at his face, which was blazing with passion, and dark with a darker tinge than Nature and the sun had given it, from the shapely swelling neck, in its soft well-turned-down collar, to where the stiff black hair, wet with perspiration, hung on the wide forehead.

'Unhand me, sir!' I said shortly, attempting to wrench myself free, but I might as well have tried to pull away from a lion.

'Unhand me!' I repeated.

For answer he took a firmer hold, in one hand seizing my arm above the elbow, and gripping my shoulder with the other so tightly that, through my flimsy covering, his strong fingers bruised me so severely that in a calmer moment I would have squirmed and cried out with pain.

'How dare you touch me!' He drew me so closely to him that, through his thin shirt—the only garment on the upper part of his figure—I could feel the heat of his body, and his big heart beating wildly.

At last! at last! I had waked this calm silent giant into life. After many an ineffectual struggle I had got at a little real love or passion, or call it by any name—something wild and warm and splendidly alive that one could feel, the most thrilling, electric, and exquisite sensation known.

I thoroughly enjoyed the situation, but did not let this appear. A minute or two passed and he did not speak.

'Mr Beecham, I'll trouble you to explain yourself. How dare you lay your hands upon me?'

'Explain!' he breathed rather than spoke, in a tone of concentrated fury. 'I'll make *you* explain, and I'll do what I like with you. I'll touch you as much as I think fit. I'll throw you over the fence if *you* don't explain to *my* satisfaction.'

'What is there that I can explain?'

'Explain your conduct with other men. How dare you receive their attentions and be so friendly with them!'

'How dare you speak to me like that! I reserve the right of behaving as I please without your permission.'

'I won't have a girl with my engagement-ring on her finger going on as you do. I think I have a right to complain, for I could get any amount of splendid women in every way to wear it for me, and behave themselves properly too,' he said fiercely.

I tossed my head defiantly, saying, 'Loose your hold of me, and I'll quickly explain matters to my own satisfaction and yours, Harold Beecham.'

He let me go, and I stepped a pace or two away from him, drew the costly ring from my finger, and, with indifference and contempt, tossed it to his feet, where the juice of crushed strawberries was staining the ground, and facing him, said mockingly—

'Now, speak to the girl who wears your engagement-ring, for I'll degrade myself by wearing it no more. If you think I think you as great a catch as you think yourself, just because you have a little money, you are a trifle mistaken, Mr Beecham, that is all. Ha! ha! ha! So you thought you had a right to lecture me as your future slave! Just fancy! I never had the slightest intention of marrying you. You were so disgustingly conceited that I have been attempting to rub a little of it out of you. Marry you! Ha! ha! Because the social laws are so arranged that a woman's only sphere is marriage, and because they endeavour to secure a man who can give them a little more ease, you must not run away with the idea that it is yourself they are angling for, when you are only the bothersome appendage with which they would have to put up, for the sake of your property. And you must not think that because some women will marry for a home they all will. I trust I have explained to your satisfaction, Mr Beecham. Ha! ha! ha!'

The jealous rage had died out of his face and was succeeded by trembling and a pallor so ghastly, that I began to have a little faith in descriptions of love which I had hitherto ridiculed.

'Are you in earnest?' he asked in a deadly calm voice.

'Most emphatically I am.'

'Then all I can say is that I haven't much respect for you, Miss Melvyn. I always considered that there were three classes of women—one, that would marry a black-fellow if he had money; another, that were shameless flirts, and who amuse themselves by flirting and disgracing the name of woman; and a third class that were pure and true, on whom a man could stake his life and whom he could worship. I thought you belonged to this class, but I have been mistaken. I know you always try to appear heartless and worthless, but I fancied it was only your youth and mischief, and imagined you were good underneath; but I have been mistaken,' he repeated with quiet contempt.

His face had regained its natural colour, and the well-cut pleasant mouth, clearly seen beneath the soft drooping moustache, had hardened into a sullen line which told me he would never be first to seek reconciliation—not even to save his life.

'Bah!' I exclaimed sarcastically. 'It appears that we all labour under delusions. Go and get a beautiful woman to wear your ring and your name. One that will be able to say yes and no at the right time; one who will know how to dress properly; one who wouldn't for the world do anything that other women did not also; one who will know where to buy the best groceries and who will readily sell herself to you for your wealth. That's the sort of woman that suits men, and there are plenty of them; procure one, and don't bother with me. I am too small and silly, and have nothing to recommend me. I fear it speaks little for your sense or taste that you ever thought of me. Ta-ta, Mr Beecham,' I said over my shoulder with a mocking smile, and walked away.

When about half-way down the orchard reflection pulled me up shortly under an apple-tree.

I had said what I had said because, feeling bitter for the want of love, and because full of pain myself, I rejoiced with a sort of revenge to see the same feeling flash across another's face. But now I was cool, and, forgetting myself, thought of Harold.

I had led him on because his perpetually calm demeanour had excited in me a desire to test if it were possible to disturb him. I had thought him incapable of emotion, but he had proved himself a man of strong and deep emotion; might he not also be capable of feeling—of love? He had not been mean or nasty in his rage, and his anger had been righteous. By accepting his proposal of marriage, I had given him the right of expressing his objection to any of my actions of which he disapproved. I on my part had the liberty of trying to please him or of dissolving our engagement. Perhaps in some cases there was actually something more than wounded vanity when a man's alleged love was rejected or spurned. Harold had seemed to suffer, to really experience keen disappointment. I was clearly in the wrong, and had been unwomanly beyond a doubt, as, granting that Harold Beecham was conceited, what right had I to constitute myself his judge or to take into my own hands the responsibility of correcting him? I felt ashamed of my conduct; I was sorry to have hurt any one's feelings. Moreover, I cannot bear to be at ill-will with my fellows, and am ever the first to give in after having quarrelled. It is easier than sulking, and it always makes the other party so self-complacent that it is amusing as well as convenient, and—and—and—I found I was very, very fond of Harold Beecham.

I crept noiselessly up the orchard. He had his back to me, and had moved to where a post of the fence was peeping out among the greenery. He had his elbow placed thereon, and his forehead resting on his hand. His attitude expressed dejection. Maybe he was suffering the torture of a broken ideal.

His right hand hung limply by his side. I do not think he heard me approach.

My heart beat quickly, and a fear that he would snub me caused me to pause. Then I nerved myself with the thought that it would be only fair if he did. I had been rude to him, and he had a right to play tit-for-tat if he felt so disposed. I expected my action to be spurned or ignored, so very timidly slipped my fingers into his palm. I need not have been nervous, for the strong brown hand, which had never been known to strike a cowardly blow, completely enfolded mine in a gentle caressing clasp.

'Mr Beecham, Harold, I am so sorry I was so unwomanly, and said such horrible things. Will you forgive me, and let us start afresh?' I murmured. All flippancy, bitterness, and amusement had died out of me; I was serious and in earnest. This must have expressed itself in my eyes, for Harold, after gazing searchingly right there for a time, seemed satisfied, and his mouth relaxed to its habitually lovable expression as he said—

'Are you in earnest? Well, that is something more like the little woman.'

'Yes, I'm in earnest. Can you forgive me?'

'There is nothing to forgive, as I'm sure you didn't mean and don't remember the blood-curdling sentiments you aired.'

'But I did mean them in one sort of a way, and didn't in another. Let us start afresh.'

'How do you mean to start afresh?'

'I mean for us to be chums again.'

'Oh, chums!' he said impatiently; 'I want to be something more.'

'Well, I will be something more if you will try to make me,' I replied.

'How? What do you mean?'

'I mean you never try to make me fond of you. You have never uttered one word of love to me.'

'Why, bless me!' he ejaculated in surprise.

'It's a fact. I have only flirted to try and see if you cared, but you didn't care a pin.'

'Why, bless me! didn't you say I was not to show any affection yet awhile. And talk about not caring—why, I have felt fit to kill you and myself many a time the last fortnight, you have tormented me so; but I have managed to keep myself within bounds till now. Will you wear my ring again?'

'Oh no; and you must not say I am flirting if I cannot manage to love you enough to marry you, but I will try my best.'

'Don't you love me, Syb? I have thought of nothing else but you night and day since I saw you first. Can it be possible that you don't care a straw for me?' and a pained expression came upon his face.

'Oh, Harold! I'm afraid I very nearly love you, but don't hurry me too much. You can think me a sort of secretly engaged to you if you like, but I won't take your ring. Keep it till we see how we get on.' I looked for it, and finding it a few steps away, gave it to him.

'Can you really trust me again after seeing me get in such a vile beast of a rage? I often do that, you know,' he said.

'Believe me, Hal, I liked it so much I wish you would get in a rage again. I can't bear people who never let themselves go, or rather, who have nothing in them to carry them away—they cramp and bore me.'

'But I have a frightful temper. Satan only knows what I will do in it yet. Would you not be frightened of me?'

'No fear,' I laughed; 'I would defy you.'

'A tomtit might as well defy me,' he said with amusement.

'Well, big as you are, a tomtit having such superior facilities for getting about could easily defy you,' I replied.

'Yes, unless it was caged,' he said.

'But supposing you never got it caged,' I returned.

'Syb, what do you mean?'

'What could I mean?'

'I don't know. There are always about four or five meanings in what you say.'

'Oh, thanks, Mr Beecham! You must be very astute. I am always thankful when I am able to dish one meaning out of my idle gabble.'

The glorious summer day had fallen asleep on the bosom of the horizon, and twilight had merged into dusk, as, picking up the basket, Harold and I returned cherry- and strawberry-less to the tennis court. The players had just ceased action, and the gentlemen were putting on their coats. Harold procured his, and thrust his arms into it, while we were attacked on all sides by a flood of banter.

My birthday tea was a great success, and after it was done we enjoyed ourselves in the drawing-room. Uncle Jay-Jay handed me a large box, saying it contained a present. Every one looked on with interest while I hurriedly opened it, when they were much amused to see—nothing but a doll and materials to make its clothes! I was much disappointed, but uncle said it would be more in my line to play with that than to worry about tramps and politics.

I took care to behave properly during the evening, and when the good-byes were in full swing had an opportunity of a last word with Harold, he stooping to hear me whisper—

'Now that I know you care, I will not annoy you any more by flirting.'

'Don't talk like that. I was only mad for the moment. Enjoy yourself as much as you like. I don't want you to be like a nun. I'm not quite so selfish as that. When I look at you and see how tiny you are, and how young, I feel it is brutal to worry you at all, and you don't detest me altogether for getting in such an infernal rage?'

'No. That is the very thing I liked. Good night!'

'Good night!' he replied, taking both my hands in his. 'You are the best little woman in the world, and I hope we will spend all your other birthdays together.'

'It's to be hoped you've said something to make Harry a trifle sweeter than he was this afternoon,' said Goodchum. Then it was—

'Good night, Mrs Bossier! Good night, Harry! Good night, Archie! Good night, Mr Goodchum! Good-bye, Miss Craddock! Ta-ta, Miss Melvyn! So long, Jay-Jay! Good-bye, Mrs Bell! Good-bye, Miss Goodjay! Good night, Miss Melvyn! Good night, Mr Goodjay! Good night, Mrs Bossier! Good-bye, Miss Melvyn! Good night all!'

I sat long by my writing-table that night—thinking long, long thoughts, foolish thoughts, sad ones, merry ones, old-headed thoughts, and the sweet, sweet thoughts of youth and love. It seemed to me that men were not so invincible and invulnerable as I had imagined them—it appeared they had feelings and affections after all.

I laughed a joyous little laugh, saying, 'Hal, we are quits,' when, on disrobing for the night, I discovered on my soft white shoulders and arms—so susceptible to bruises—many marks, and black.

It had been a very happy day for me.

1901

Letter to Katharine Susannah Prichard

20 November 1947
26 Grey Street,
Carlton, NSW

My dearest Katharine,

I'm in need of a little dissipation such as writing to you. I hope you are keeping up your strength, and the kind of fizz necessary for literary work.

We are having quite a bit of fun with *Tomorrow and Tomorrow*.[1] It went to J B Miles[2] from me with all my ribaldries thick upon it, and he added to them with deeper and more political, if less scintillatory, observations. It became a game to me to find out the word 'pattern'.[3] J B Miles found a good many and marked them missed by MF. Then the book went to Marjorie Pizer,[4] and she is very cocky because she found several 'patterns' which she marked missed by both JBM and MF. In one spot I noticed JBM had put MBE = MF. I must investigate whether that is an insult or a compliment. I made an additional entry that I had missed the 'patterns' through kangarooing. I shd read the book properly to be sure I'm not doing it an injustice, but my snap judgement is that it is a great piece of composition but no creation.

Glen [Mills Fox] has gone to Melb for perhaps three months. She and Nettie [Palmer] went on the same train. Their sleepers were even in the same car and Glen, restless as ever, insisted that they shd be together, so we swopped Nettie and a dear little lady after both were settled in for the night. Nettie's eyes flashed, and no wonder. She said she was very tired, and wanted to go to bed immediately. Glen was hailing her as a companion that she could stay up all night with and smoke as much as she wishes, which is continuously. Nettie said, Glen is a pest. I said, of course she is a confisticated infernal pest. Glen said that was not nice of me, and I said, not until you realise that our friends endear themselves to us not by their perfections but

1   M. Barnard Eldershaw's (qv) novel *Tomorrow and Tomorrow* (1947).
2   John Branwell Miles (1888–1969), communist.
3   'This annotated copy is in the Mitchell [Library]. The incidence of the word "pattern" is indeed startling, it is marked 21 times in the first 34 pages' (Ferrier, p. 180).
4   Writer (b. 1920).

by their pestiferations. The phrase and the fact seemed to cheer Nettie. Glen wrote me that, next day, she and Nettie were discussing Aust Lit when a priest opposite said, I hear you mention a Miles, if that's Miles Franklin she's the best writer in Australia, isn't she. Glen finished there and left me curious. The delight of the anecdote is that the priest had a rosary of quandong seeds!!!!!

I've met that Billy Wentworth,[1] since you left, at a wedding of my young cousin. The bride was given all the linen, etc. by Packer or Theodore who were both at the church with some ladies, I don't know if they were all wives. They were too busy for the reception. Wentworth hailed me and we began to talk, and then I remembered and said, Ha ha, me boy, I've been meaning to go for you for a long time, and now's my chance. I told him: A member of *my gestapo* informed me that *your Ogpu*[2] takes the form of a black list of certain people, and that my name is on it, and a certain publisher said it might be necessary to ban my books because I'm a communist. I said, 'I am not a communist.' 'I shd hope not', said he. Then he said, 'I never said you were a communist, tho I have lots of others on my list, I said you were a stooge for communists.' I said I accepted that as quite fair, because communists were sure to quote advanced thinkers, such as I hoped I was, whereas the blimps would fly to him for backing. I told him I had said something pretty stiff about him. Pretty blasting I expect said he. No, brilliant, said I—you know I *can* be brilliant if I bestir myself. I said my remark was that *I* did not matter, I was frail and obscure and of no account, it wd be easy to obliterate me, but my one axe to grind, my great love, was Australia, and what alarmed me was that our business men, who would have to meet the business men of other countries for Australia's sake, shd depend for information upon any informer who cd be guilty of such misinformation.

I think he's cracked. I put up with him to have straight from the ass's mouth the wisdom of a blimp, but he was such a bore that I soon tried to escape him. In vain! He pursued me. So I gave him my favourite who dun it Joe Stalin, because in one slap he had taken women off the midden and put them into parliament. Wentworth said blandly that that was not true. I said one must believe the Dean of Westminster. He said the need to free women is all hooey, they have always been free. You can guess how he endeared himself to me. He's such a bore in his half-wittedness, is the trouble. Says he's going into parliament, or to try to get there again. The most hrrumphing, moustached, barnacled Anglo-Indian of yesterday would be a bolshevist compared with this museum specimen. I like his little wife, and am sorry

1 William Charles Wentworth (1907–2003) was a Liberal Party member of the House of Representatives and fiercely anti-communist.
2 OGPU were the 'initials by which the state security service in the Soviet Union was known in the 1920s and 1930s' (Ferrier, p. 181).

she has such material to labor with. It wound up by them asking me to dine with them at Prince's. I came home to Glen, whom I had here then, and Marg [Pizer] too, to work on *Fellowship*. Oh, why was I such a fool as to miss my chance of sitting between Mrs and Mr Bill W at Prince's, when they had photographers laid on! It might have saved my life when I'm to be hanged for associating with communists. I must try to make up for such a miss by going to Canberra, and being clasped to the bosom of R G M[enzies] on the steps of Parliament House.

I've just read Gavin Casey's book.[1] How did such a thing get into print? I read about three words to a page. It's just as if a greedy pig wrote a book as long as a novel, on one night's swilling in an overfull trough with his mates and equals. There's not one glint of suggestion that the author is one nth of an inch above the fellow swillers, in culture, ideals, experience, or intelligence. Yet C H[artley] G[rattan] hails him as an important Australian writer.

On 29th, there is to be a party for Rod Quinn's birthday,[2] by his nieces out at Summer Hill, and the FAW is going, and going to give him a copy of Mrs Holman's *Memoirs*[3] just out, because so immediately contemporaneous to Rod. The *Memoirs* are readable macaroon, but I do not trust her judgements of people—M Bondfield for instance, with whom I was intimate. I acted as entrepreneuse to get her to USA on her first trip. Good heavens, she must be 76 now! I wonder why Dalton[4] made a fool of himself, and why was he taken grinning so happily to the crowd about it. He has always had an idiotic grin on him lately—too much of a good thing for the conditions over there. I have heard it rumored that he drinks—perhaps that is the truth. I used to meet him and his wife privately in London. Poor Mrs Holman has been at death's door again with pneumonia: she has had it more times than I've had influenza. I don't know how she survives. Her *Memoirs* are an exposé of the grand times the wives of representatives have among the mighty, whom I, the nonentity, have to support. No wonder they drive their husbands, and that the husbands sell their souls to become officials of the State, the only way to achieve pomp greater than that open to a millionaire per se. And it doesn't matter if they are hereditary parasites, or a fresh State crop every few years, the junketing is as gaudy and the paying for it as heavy on the small people.

Well, royalty is now on its way to the Abbey. I wonder why they didn't wait for summer weather. Philip of Spain tried to take the great Elizabeth of

---

1   *The Wits Are Out* (1947).
2   Roderic Quinn (1867–1949), poet.
3   Ada Holman, *Memoirs of a Premier's Wife* (1947).
4   Probably Hugh Dalton (1887–1962), British Chancellor of the Exchequer, who was forced to resign in 1947 for negligently leaking budget secrets.

England, and lost his Armada. Philip of Greece had better luck with a lesser Elizabeth—has made a great match. I wonder what is his private fortune, or is he a comparative pauper like [Princess] Marina. The people have to have someone to worship—silly mugs! One grows cynical about the whole silly gallimauphry. Did you hear Hartley Grattan in the international quiz for the latest loan? I have no news, so will end this screed with much love, dear.

1947

C.E.W. BEAN
1879–1968

The journalist and historian Charles Edwin Woodrow Bean has been a key figure in creating the masculine legends of Australian national identity.

Although born a schoolmaster's son in Bathurst, NSW, Bean was a child of the British empire, living from 1889 to 1904 in England. With a public school education and an Oxford law degree, when he returned to Australia he became a journalist on the *Sydney Morning Herald*. In 1909 he was sent outback to write about the wool industry. The resulting articles were republished as *On the Wool Track* (1910). A second series became *The 'Dreadnought' of the Darling* (1911).

From 1914, as an official correspondent, Bean was with Australian troops on First World War battlefronts, surviving a wound in the leg at Gallipoli and carnage in the trenches in France. In 1919 his recommendation to the government for a national war memorial and a history of Australia during the war resulted in his appointment as official historian, based at first in Canberra. *The Official History of Australia in the War of 1914–1918* was completed in 1942; he had written six volumes and edited a further six.

Bean married Ethel Young, a nursing sister, in 1921. He died in Sydney in 1968. *On the Wool Track* was republished several times. In spare yet poetic reportage, it describes a vacant, pitiless landscape, evoked in his famous line: 'Only there happened—nothing.' Bean's rural Australia, like his Gallipoli, was peopled by 'outstanding national types'— there, bosses managed 'strong, independent, sometimes unruly men' and 'people had no respect for any "claims of birth"'. *CC*

From *On the Wool Track*
Chapter 1: The Maker of a Continent

There was death in the paddock. For nine days the police had followed a man's footsteps. Once and again the footmarks would turn back upon themselves. Now they would lead round and round a tree. Now they would shoot off at right angles. At long intervals the searchers had found towards evening clear signs that his feet had begun to drag. They could see clearly the long scrape of the toe before each heel-mark. They quickened pace, following the tracks with all the skill that was in them. Presently they came to his hat. There the dark closed in upon them. It was too black to follow, and they had to camp.

That night down came the rain. By the morning every trace of the tracks had been sponged away as from a slate. All day they searched—both the trooper and the black tracker—but found nothing. Months later, a boundary rider came upon his coat. There were letters in it from some man in Scotland; from that day to this no other trace of him has been discovered.

Long afterwards a letter came back from the man in Scotland, to whom the police had written. He was a doctor, and the dead man's brother. The dead man had been working his way through the far West from station to station on foot. He had suddenly announced that he meant to walk to Sydney. Probably he drank. Certainly he went mad.

Now, the paddock where that man was lost was not twenty miles out of Menindie. He never got out of the one paddock. It was no larger than most other enclosures in the west of New South Wales—ten miles by ten miles. Yet, either in that or in the one which we drove through next to it, the boundary riders have at one time or another, ridden across the skeletons of three men, with their swags scattered near them, just as they lay down when they came to the end of their strength. The truth is that a great part of New South Wales outback there, though it is marked off into little squares on the map and has well-known names written over it and even roads drawn through it—and therefore is not pictured by us city-folk as different from other civilized lands—is not really, as yet, a country in which a man can be sure of keeping his life.

When the first white men pushed out from the fringe of the known districts into this 'outside' region, each took his life in his hands, and knew that he did so. There was some danger from blacks—not a very great risk. The real danger was from the country itself. The white men—Burke and Wills and others—went provided against that danger, with stock and water-bags and provisions, even with camels. And then, despite all their preparations, sometimes those men gave out and died.[1]

One has seen the country where men have died; and if the place had not actually done them to death, one would not have dreamed that there could be any cruelty in the heart of it. There were no Alpine precipices, no avalanches or volcanoes or black jungles full of wild beasts, no earthquakes, not even a flood or a bushfire. The countryside looked like a beautiful open park, with gentle slopes and soft grey tree-clumps. Nothing appalling or horrible rushed upon these men. Only there happened—nothing. There might have been a pool of cool water behind any one of those tree-clumps; only—there was not. It might have rained, any time; only—it did not. There

1 Author's note: For example, the paper—this morning on which I write—contains the following message. It was sent along the wires by one of a party that was making for the Tanami goldfield—which is in a particularly distant and desolate corner. 'Failed to reach field via Treuer Ranges, got out sixty miles, driven back, no water. Terribly hot, all native wells and holes dried up. Frayne (leader) perished while trying to locate water. Made back to line at Barrow Creek. I had to leave loading and ride on, perishing. As a last resource, cut wires and worked north, hoping to meet linesman for repairs. Got water on the road. Further particulars next station.'

might have been a fence or a house just over the next rise; only—there was not. They lay down, with the birds hopping from branch to branch above them and the bright sky peeping down at them. No one came. Nothing happened. That was all.

What even Australians do not realize—sometimes until it is past mattering whether they realize it or not—is that in the greater part of this 'outside' region there has been wrought only one change since the explorers first came out upon it. It is the same beautiful, endless, pitiless country that it was when they found it—except for just one difference. Sheep have come there.

Men have transformed that region into one in which there exist—as a general rule—the living conditions for sheep. That is all.

Men cannot live there. It is when they imagine they can that they come to grief. They have made themselves homesteads—little redoubts fifty or a hundred miles apart, where they can defend themselves securely enough when they get there. But over the wide spaces in between they have to stage from water to water, from tank to tank or well to well. And it was not for them that the water was dammed or the wells sunk. It was for the sheep. Except for the sheep, and the provision that is made for them, the 'outside' country is to-day as the untamed centuries left it—as the first white man, emerging from the pine-scrub and over the red sand-hill on the horizon, found it.

Some way out of Menindie we happened to drive through a paddock which had been unstocked for many years. It gave one a fleeting vision of what those white men did find. It was almost impossible to get out of one's head the notion that we were driving through a park. One could swear that a glimpse of the house, or the white pinafores of the children playing in the grass, or the ornamental water, or the pet Jersey cows must turn up round the next corner. As a matter of fact, there was not a house or a pinafore or even a cow within twenty miles. We saw that day the tracks of one boundary rider; of two buggies which had been through a fortnight before; and of a wild dog and his mate. We passed—miles away—the low sandy dam or parapet of a 'tank.' Its bottom, we happened to know, was at that time dry sand. We were following those buggy tracks over the horizon for three hundred miles, and at times they were the only thing to follow. One of us was a skilled bushman, or the chances are that the other would not have found the marks of the buggy wheels, and would have lain down under the trees and the blue sky; and—perhaps they might have found him later.

But one could not help believing it was a park, in spite of all. Pretty pine-trees, blue clumps of applewood, needlewood, belar, grey-blue mulga, with the exquisite black tracery of its delicate branches showing under the leaves, sailed by in groups on either side of us. Up a shallow glade between them the long white beards of spear-grass, three seasons old, were standing, in parts knee-deep. The track—the one sign of man's existence—wound through the grass away out of sight. And along it, far ahead of us, startled by the trotting horses, bounced two kangaroos, mother and young one, furlong after furlong. Others we started and sent off into the scrub, a dozen or more of them, grey and brown. But these two stuck to the 'road' as though it were made for them—disappearing sometimes where it wound behind the trees, but always turning up, still bumping along it, where it wound out again beyond. No wonder men thought the land would carry any stock they liked to cram upon it.

Emu and kangaroo swarmed throughout that paddock. How they had discovered it, Heaven knows. What we saw there impressed us with the notion that the first white men must have found the back country teeming with life. To our surprise one of them told us afterwards that they did not. Life teemed around the lakes—duck, teal, swans, kangaroo, emu, brolga, pelican, ibis, and all the rest. But on the waterless back-country—he said—they came out into an almost ghastly stillness, long white grass, soft blue trees, no animals, few blacks.

'Why, there wasn't enough water even for the blacks, at some times,' he said. 'The Mulga blacks—those that lived in the mulga scrub, away from the river—had to come down to the Darling for water, so they told me, sneaking down by night and getting back again before daybreak for fear of the Darling blacks. There were great battles if they were caught, for their law was never to trespass on each other's grounds.

'As for the animals, you would not see a beast or even a bird. The only ones we did see were those "twelve apostles", and I'm sure I don't know what they did for water. That was before we dug the tanks in the paddocks. As soon as the tanks began to gather water, the game began to find it out— the animals became thick enough after that.'

Those tanks were put down for the sheep. So the sheep were actually responsible for making this country to some extent liveable not only for men or for tame beasts, but even for its own wild animals.

Some of the main features of the country which even some of the inhabitants assume to be natural, have been brought into existence, apparently, by sheep. For example, we spent one night at the homestead of a man who was the first to take a homestead lease in the Central West. He was a grand fellow, the only one of all in that part—squatters and selectors— who had survived the great drought. It was a very isolated little home, the farthest-back selection in the district. That night, at first from far in the scrub, afterwards, of all places, from just outside my window, came the most dismal, alarming, long-drawn howl that one has ever listened to. It was a wild dog, which had killed a sheep the day before and had come back under cover of dark, howling after the station dogs. It was a lonely place and no mistake.

At the back of that house, stretching away acre beyond acre to the hills, and also for miles along the road to the south, was a thick pine-forest. But with a few exceptions here and there, where the roots happened to tap some hidden watercourse, every pine-tree in the whole area was dead—leafless and almost branchless. The forest which had died was the main feature of the country thereabouts. According to the man who had watched it from its beginning, it was the sheep that had caused its birth. The only thing they were not responsible for was its death. The drought caused that.

'It was this way,' said the old man. 'When first I rode my horse on to this red country, it was all beautifully-grassed open land away to the hills— not a pine-tree on it. And the soil was so loose that my horse sank up to his fetlocks at every step and the sheep drove their feet deep into it as they walked.

'As I'm telling you, it was open country then; but in a year or two the sheep had trodden in the whole face of it, and I think its hardening must have affected some seed that was hidden there all the time; for no sooner was the ground solid than up came this pine-scrub thick all over the surface. It grew and grew into this forest, as you see it. And then came the drought and killed every pine-tree for miles.'

And there you see the relics at this day—acre after acre of bare grey poles. There is nowhere any trace of such destruction having previously occurred; which makes it probable, though not certain, that there had not for centuries been any such drought. One cannot be certain, however, because during those previous centuries the sheep were not there; and they may have been responsible for some change—the hardening of the ground, for example—which may have helped this last drought to destroy a forest that would otherwise have survived.

Providence only knows what the sheep are not responsible for in the outside country—it is such a region to play with. In places they have trampled a drafting-yard to dust for twenty years; and after they have departed the first spring rain has brought up grasses that had not been seen for a generation. In other places (during a dry spell, with the rabbits to help them) they have eaten out the roots of the grass and saltbush, and so trampled and trodden and powdered the face of the country, that it has blown clean away and piled itself up behind tree clumps and over fences and old stockyards, where you can see it to-day, and drive your buggy over it, fences and all, if you care to. And where the earth was once grass-covered you will find great piebald patches of shiny bare clay, which, if the sheep go on with their work and trample it to powder, may possibly bear grass and saltbush again some day—or may not. At least, that is perhaps the most general of the utterly conflicting opinions expressed by those best qualified to prophesy.

Whatever the sheep may or may not have done, they have done this for the Western District of New South Wales. As far as the West is liveable for men, it is the sheep and they alone that have made it so. You cannot wander away to nowhere in that country nowadays. There are at least fences across the plain—though the next one may be over the horizon. And there is at least water nowadays every thirty miles or so, if only you know where to find it. The first thing an owner does is to find depressions, dam them, and run drains from them like the spokes of a wheel for as much as two miles in various directions to catch every precious drop that falls. Once caught, he does all he can to keep it—builds high mounds round the banks to give shelter from the dry winds; plants a break of trees; even tries covering the tanks with water-weeds to protect them from the sun. They say there are days on which in these parts as much as an inch of water evaporates: and seeing that, in an average year, the rainfall on the plain around the tank is only nine or ten inches, they have to husband every drop.

So the early white men made their preparations, and stocked this beautiful country with millions of sheep—with a sheep to three acres in some places. And then came three years in which seven inches, all told, of rain fell.

[…]

Even as near to Sydney as the centre of New South Wales there exist 'main roads' of which a town man can barely see the traces. We struck one like that. 'There's been a lot of traffic along here,' said the driver, when we cut it. You could see all the wheel marks of years past—there appeared (when, from curiosity, we afterwards counted them) to be exactly fourteen. Another road was traceable by the ruts which stood out of the ground—instead of being driven into it: some waggon had hardened the sand beneath its wheels, and the years had worn away the softer sand on either side of the wheel-marks. Another road across some grassland was marked by a white line of wild oats, sprung from seed which had caught in the old ruts and grown there.

Those are the landmarks which human beings follow in these parts. By one who is not used to them they are apt to be overlooked—to his peril. But then the provision around him is not for men but for sheep—sheep which may go six weeks without water. Where the Australian country has actually turned the tables on the sheep, and driven him back, as it has from South Australian runs over the border, it has driven the white man too—*a fortiori*—and the land is desolate, fences down, homesteads ruined.

There, around Lake Eyre, and over some part of Central Australia, you may see them to-day—deserted homesteads standing out from the desert with the marks of old settlement around them. That is what sheep mean to Australia.

1910

NORMAN LINDSAY
1879–1969

A rhyming children's book about a walking, talking, inexhaustible pudding is perhaps an unlikely achievement to be remembered by. That is certainly so for an artistic polymath such as Norman Lindsay, who as a distinctive figure in Australian art and letters through the 1920s and '30s produced a significant body of art, fiction and writing on cultural aesthetics, and was never far from controversy. *The Magic Pudding* (1918) is only one of his contributions to Australian culture, but it is one of the best-loved pieces of children's literature ever produced and Lindsay's own illustrations are a large part of its appeal.

Born in Creswick, Victoria, Lindsay moved to Melbourne in 1895 and to Sydney in 1900. His pen drawings, etchings and watercolours, often of classical and mythic scenes, characteristically highlight erotic situations and feature nudes, usually women, but also satyrs, mythical beasts and cherubs. Lindsay's interest in the relation between sex and art was informed by Nietzschean philosophy transformed into an anti-modern 'vitalism', with an emphasis on classical form and paganism. He was a dominating influence on a small coterie of prominent writers, including Kenneth Slessor, Robert D. FitzGerald and Douglas Stewart (qqv) as well as Lindsay's son Jack, and combined a prodigious output with a love of display and frolics. *Creative Effort* (1920), an essay that rejects modernism and the separation of art from society has been much debated as a force for cultural conservatism, even as Lindsay's bohemian publishing and art practice challenged some social conventions. Lindsay's fiction for adults is marked by a comic lightness of touch and again a provocative interest in sexual appetites, which saw his novels *Redheap* (1930) and *The Cautious Amorist* (1932) banned by Australian Customs. *NM*

From *The Magic Pudding*

SECOND SLICE

The Society of Puddin'-Owners were up bright and early next morning, and had the billy on and tea made before six o'clock, which is the best part of the day, because the world has just had his face washed, and the air smells like Pears' soap.

'Aha,' said Bill Barnacle, cutting up slices of the Puddin', 'this is what I call grand. Here we are, after a splendid night's sleep on dry leaves, havin' a smokin' hot slice of steak-and-kidney for breakfast round the camp fire. What could be more delightful?'

'What indeed?' said Bunyip Bluegum, sipping his tea.

'Why, as I always say,' said Bill, 'if there's one thing more entrancin' than sittin' round a camp fire in the evenin' it's sittin' round a camp fire in the mornin'. No beds and blankets and breakfast tables for Bill Barnacle. For as I says in my 'Breakfast Ballad'—

> 'If there's anythin' better than lyin' on leaves,
>   It's risin' from leaves at dawnin',
> If there's anythin' better than sleepin' at eve,
>   It's wakin' up in the mawnin'.

> 'If there's anythin' better than camp firelight,
>> It's bright sunshine on wakin'.
> If there's anythin' better than puddin' at night,
>> It's puddin' when day is breakin'.
> 'If there's anythin' better than singin' away
>> While the stars are gaily shinin',
> Why, it's singin' a song at dawn of day,
>> On puddin' for breakfast dinin''.'

There was a hearty round of applause at this song, for, as Bunyip Bluegum remarked, 'singing at breakfast should certainly be more commonly indulged in, as it greatly tends to enliven what is on most occasions a somewhat dull proceeding'.

'One of the great advantages of being a professional puddin'-owner,' said Sam Sawnoff, 'is that songs at breakfast are always encouraged. None of the ordinary breakfast rules, such as scowling while eating, and saying the porridge is as stiff as glue and the eggs are as tough as leather, are observed. Instead, songs, roars of laughter, and boisterous jests are the order of the day. For example, this sort of thing,' added Sam, doing a rapid back-flap and landing with a thump on Bill's head. As Bill was unprepared for this act of boisterous humour, his head was pushed into the Puddin' with great violence, and the gravy was splashed in his eye.

'What d'yer mean, playin' such bungfoodlin' tricks on a man at breakfast?' roared Bill.

'What d'yer mean,' shouted the Puddin', 'playing such foodbungling tricks on a Puddin' being breakfasted at?'

'Breakfast humour, Bill, merely breakfast humour,' said Sam, hastily.

'Humour's humour,' shouted Bill, 'but puddin' in the whiskers is no joke.'

'Whiskers in the Puddin' is worse than puddin' in the whiskers,' shouted the Puddin', standing up in his basin.

'Observe the rules, Bill,' said Sam hurriedly. 'Boisterous humour at the breakfast table must be greeted with roars of laughter.'

'To Jeredelum with the rules,' shouted Bill. 'Pushing a man's face into his own breakfast is beyond rules or reason, and deserves a punch in the gizzard.'

Seeing matters arriving at this unpromising situation, Bunyip Bluegum interposed by saying, 'Rather than allow this happy occasion to be marred by unseemly recriminations, let us, while admitting that our admirable friend, Sam, may have unwittingly disturbed the composure of our admirable friend, Bill, at the expense of our admirable Puddin's gravy, let us, I say, by the simple act of extending the hand of friendship, dispel in an instant these gathering clouds of disruption. In the words of the poem—

"Then let the fist of Friendship
  Be kept for Friendship's foes.
Ne'er let that hand in anger land
  On Friendship's holy nose".'

These fine sentiments at once dispelled Bill's anger. He shook hands warmly with Sam, wiped the gravy from his face, and resumed breakfast with every appearance of hearty good humour.

The meal over, the breakfast things were put away in the bag, Sam and Bill took Puddin' between them, and all set off along the road, enlivening the way with song and story. Bill regaled them with portions of the 'Ballad of the *Salt Junk Sarah*', which is one of those songs that go on for ever. Its great advantage, as Bill remarked, was that as it hadn't got an ending it didn't need a beginning, so you could start it anywhere.

'As for instance,' said Bill, and he roared out—

'Ho, aboard the *Salt Junk Sarah*,
  Rollin' home across the line,
The Bo'sun collared the Captain's hat
  And threw it in the brine.
Rollin' home, rollin' home,
  Rollin' home across the foam,
The Captain sat without a hat
  The whole way rollin' home.'

Entertaining themselves in this way as they strolled along, they were presently arrested by shouts of 'Fire! Fire!' and a Fireman in a large helmet came bolting down the road, pulling a fire hose behind him.

'Aha!' said Bill, 'Now we shall have the awe-inspirin' spectacle of a fire to entertain us,' and, accosting the Fireman, he demanded to know where the fire was.

'The fact is,' said the Fireman, 'that owing to the size of this helmet I can't see where it is; but if you will kindly glance at the surrounding district, you'll see it about somewhere.'

They glanced about and, sure enough, there was a fire burning in the next field. It was only a cowshed, certainly, but it was blazing very nicely, and well worth looking at.

'Fire,' said Bill, 'in the form of a common cowshed, is burnin' about nor'-nor'-east as the crow flies.'

'In that case,' said the Fireman, 'I invite all present to bravely assist in putting it out. But,' he added impressively, 'if you'll take my advice, you'll shove that Puddin' in this hollow log and roll a stone agen the end to keep him in, for if he gets too near the flames he'll be cooked again and have his flavour ruined.'

'This is a very sensible feller,' said Bill, and though Puddin' objected strongly, he was at once pushed into a log and securely fastened in with a large stone.

'How'd you like to be shoved in a blooming log,' he shouted at Bill, 'when you was burning with anxiety to see the fire?' but Bill said severely, 'Be sensible, Albert, fires is too dangerous to Puddin's flavours.'

No more time was lost in seizing the hose and they set off with the greatest enthusiasm. For, as everyone knows, running with the reel is one of the grand joys of being a fireman. They had the hose fixed to a garden tap in no time, and soon were all hard at work, putting out the fire.

Of course there was a great deal of smoke and shouting, and getting tripped up by the hose, and it was by the merest chance Bunyip Bluegum glanced back in time to see the Wombat in the act of stealing the Puddin' from the hollow log.

'Treachery is at work,' he shouted.

'Treachery,' roared Bill, and with one blow on the snout knocked the Fireman endways on into the burning cinders, where his helmet fell off, and exposed the countenance of that snooting, snouting scoundrel, the Possum.

The Possum, of course, hadn't expected to have his disguise pierced so swiftly, and, though he managed to scramble out of the fire in time to save his bacon, he was considerably singed down the back.

'What a murderous attack!' he exclaimed. 'O, what a brutal attempt to burn a man alive!' and as some hot cinders had got down his back he gave a sharp yell and ran off, singeing and smoking. Bill, distracted with rage, ran after the Possum, then changed his mind and ran after the Wombat, so that, what with running first after one and then after the other, they both had time to get clean away, and disappeared over the skyline.

'I see it all,' shouted Bill, casting himself down in despair. 'Them low puddin'-thieves has borrowed a fireman's helmet, collared a hose, an' set fire to a cowshed in order to lure us away from the Puddin'.'

'The whole thing's a low put-up job on our noble credulity,' said Sam, casting himself down beside Bill.

'It's one of the most frightful things that's ever happened,' said Bill.

'It's worse than treading on tacks with bare feet,' said Sam.

'It's worse than bein' caught stealin' fowls,' said Bill.

'It's worse than bein' stood on by cows,' said Sam.

'It's almost as bad as havin' an uncle called Aldobrantifoscofornio,' said Bill, and they both sang loudly—

> 'It's worse than weevils, worse than warts,
> It's worse than corns to bear.

It's worse than havin' several quarts
    Of treacle in your hair.

'It's worse than beetles in the soup,
    It's worse than crows to eat.
It's worse than wearin' small-sized boots
    Upon your large-sized feet.

'It's worse than kerosene to boose,
    It's worse than ginger hair.
It's worse than anythin' to lose
    A Puddin' rich and rare.'

Bunyip Bluegum reproved this despondency, saying 'Come, come, this is no time for giving way to despair. Let us, rather, by the fortitude of our bearing prove ourselves superior to this misfortune and, with the energy of justly enraged men, pursue these malefactors, who have so richly deserved our vengeance. Arise!

'The grass is green, the day is fair,
    The dandelions abound.
Is this a time for sad despair
    And sitting on the ground?

'Our Puddin' in some darksome lair
    In iron chains is bound,
While puddin'-snatchers on him fare,
    And eat him by the pound.

'Let gloom give way to angry glare,
    Let weak despair be drowned,
Let vengeance in its rage declare
    Our Puddin' must be found.

'Then let's resolve to do and dare.
    Let teeth with rage be ground.
Let voices to the heavens declare
    Our Puddin' MUST be found.'

'Bravely spoken,' said Bill, immediately recovering from despair.

'Those gallant words have fired our blood,' said Sam, and they both shook hands with Bunyip, to show that they were now prepared to follow the call of vengeance. [. . .]

1918

FREDERIC MANNING
1882–1935

Frederic Manning died of pneumonia in England in 1935 largely unknown to Australians, but his novel *The Middle Parts of Fortune: Somme and Ancre 1916* (1929) is cited around the world as one of the most significant and memorable novels of the First World War. Manning left Sydney for England when he was fifteen with his tutor Arthur Galton, former private secretary to the governor of NSW. He lived his adult life with Galton in England as a writing recluse, publishing volumes of poetry—*The Vigil of Brunhild* (1907), *Poems* (1910) and *Eidola* (1917)—and a book of prose, *Scenes and Portraits* (1909).

Often grouped with Ernest Hemingway's *A Farewell to Arms* (1929) and Erich Remarque's *All Quiet on the Western Front* (1929), *The Middle Parts of Fortune* is a terse, sometimes bitter, complexly reflective account of the experiences of a private on the battlefields of the Western Front in 1916. Based on Manning's own service in the King's Shropshire Light Infantry Regiment, the main character's nationality is not made explicit, in keeping with the novel's deflation of military hierarchies and nationalism. Exploring the effect of war on reason and selfhood, Manning's novel is an existentialist study of the extremes of human experience.

The first anonymous edition was published privately in London and issued under subscription by Peter Davies' Piazza Press in 1929. An expurgated edition released soon after, by 'Private 19022', removed the soldiers' expletives that strongly punctuate the text. It has been reprinted many times as *Her Privates We,* while the original was not republished until 1977. *NM*

From *The Middle Parts of Fortune*
Chapter 1

'By my troth, I care not; a man can die but once;
we owe God a death … and let it go which way it will,
he that dies this year is quit for the next.'

SHAKESPEARE

The darkness was increasing rapidly, as the whole sky had clouded, and threatened thunder. There was still some desultory shelling. When the relief had taken over from them, they set off to return to their original line as best they could. Bourne, who was beaten to the wide, gradually dropped behind, and in trying to keep the others in sight missed his footing and fell into a shell-hole. By the time he had picked himself up again the rest of the party had vanished; and, uncertain of his direction, he stumbled on alone. He neither hurried nor slackened his pace; he was light-headed, almost exalted, and driven only by the desire to find an end. Somewhere, eventually, he would sleep. He almost fell into the wrecked trench, and after a moment's hesitation turned left, caring little where it led him. The world seemed extraordinarily empty of men, though he knew the ground was alive with them. He was breathing with difficulty, his mouth and throat seemed to be cracking with dryness, and his water-bottle was empty. Coming to a dug-out, he groped his way down, feeling for the steps with his feet; a piece of Wilson canvas, hung across the passage but twisted aside, rasped his cheek; and a few steps lower his face was enveloped suddenly in the musty folds of a blanket. The dug-out was empty. For the moment he collapsed there, indifferent to everything. Then with shaking hands he felt for his cigarettes, and putting one between his lips struck a match. The light revealed a candle-end stuck by its own grease to the oval lid of a tobacco-tin, and he lit it; it was scarcely thicker than a shilling, but it would last his time. He would finish his cigarette, and then move on to find his company.

There was a kind of bank or seat excavated in the wall of the dug-out, and he noticed first the tattered remains of a blanket lying on it, and then, gleaming faintly in its folds a small metal disk reflecting the light. It was the cap on the cork of a water-bottle. Sprawling sideways he reached it, the feel of the bottle told him it was full, and uncorking it he put it to his lips and took a great gulp before discovering that he was swallowing neat whiskey. The fiery spirit almost choked him for the moment, in his surprise he even spat some of it out; then recovering, he drank again, discreetly but sufficiently, and was meditating a more prolonged appreciation when he heard men groping their way down the steps. He recorked the bottle, hid it quickly under the blanket, and removed himself to what might seem an innocent distance from temptation.

Three Scotsmen came in; they were almost as spent and broken as he was, that he knew by their uneven voices; but they put up a show of indifference, and were able to tell him that some of his mob were on the left, in a dug-out about fifty yards away. They, too, had lost their way, and asked him questions in their turn; but he could not help them, and they developed among themselves an incoherent debate, on the question of what was the best thing for them to do in the circumstances. Their dialect only allowed him to follow their arguments imperfectly, but under the talk it was easy enough to see the irresolution of weary men seeking in their difficulties some reasonable pretext for doing nothing. It touched his own conscience, and throwing away the butt of his cigarette he decided to go. The candle was flickering feebly on the verge of extinction, and presently the dug-out would be in darkness again. Prudence stifled in him an impulse to tell them of the whiskey; perhaps they would find it for themselves; it was a matter which might be left for providence or chance to decide. He was moving towards the stairs, when a voice, muffled by the blanket, came from outside.

'Who are down there?'

There was no mistaking the note of authority and Bourne answered promptly. There was a pause, and then the blanket was waved aside, and an officer entered. He was Mr Clinton, with whom Bourne had fired his course at Tregelly.

'Hullo, Bourne,' he began, and then seeing the other men he turned and questioned them in his soft kindly voice. His face had the greenish pallor of crude beeswax, his eyes were red and tired, his hands were as nervous as theirs, and his voice had the same note of over-excitement, but he listened to them without a sign of impatience.

'Well, I don't want to hurry you men off,' he said at last, 'but your battalion will be moving out before we do. The best thing you can do is to cut along to it. They're only about a hundred yards further down the trench. You don't want to straggle back to camp by yourselves; it doesn't look well either. So you had better get moving right away. What you really want is twelve hours solid sleep, and I am only telling you the shortest road to it.'

They accepted his view of the matter quietly, they were willing enough; but, like all tired men in similar conditions, they were glad to have their action determined for them; so they thanked him and wished him good-night, if not cheerfully, at least with the air of being reasonable men, who appreciated his kindliness. Bourne made as though to follow them out, but Mr Clinton stopped him.

'Wait a minute, Bourne, and we shall go together,' he said as the last Scotsman groped his way up the steeply pitched stairs. 'It is indecent to follow a kilted Highlander too closely out of a dug-out. Besides I left something here.'

He looked about him, went straight to the blanket, and took up the water-bottle. It must have seemed lighter than he expected, for he shook it a little suspiciously before uncorking it. He took a long steady drink and paused.

'I left this bottle full of whiskey,' he said, 'but those bloody Jocks must have smelt it. You know, Bourne, I don't go over with a skinful, as some of them do; but, by God, when I come back I want it. Here, take a pull yourself; you look as though you could do with one.'

Bourne took the bottle without any hesitation; his case was much the same. One had lived instantaneously during that timeless interval, for in the shock and violence of the attack, the perilous instant, on which he stood perched so precariously, was all that the half-stunned consciousness of man could grasp; and, if he lost his grip on it, he fell back among the grotesque terrors and nightmare creatures of his own mind. Afterwards, when the strain had been finally released, in the physical exhaustion which followed, there was a collapse, in which one's emotional nature was no longer under control.

'We're in the next dug-out, those who are left of us,' Mr Clinton continued. 'I am glad you came through all right, Bourne. You were in the last show, weren't you? It seems to me the old Hun has brought up a lot more stuff, and doesn't mean to shift, if he can help it. Anyway we should get a spell out of the line now. I don't believe there are more than a hundred of us left.'

A quickening in his speech showed that the whiskey was beginning to play on frayed nerves: it had steadied Bourne for the time being. The flame of the candle gave one leap and went out. Mr Clinton switched on his torch, and shoved the water-bottle into the pocket of his raincoat.

'Come on,' he said, making for the steps, 'you and I are two of the lucky ones, Bourne; we've come through without a scratch; and if our luck holds we'll keep moving out of one bloody misery into another, until we break, see, until we break.'

Bourne felt a kind of suffocation in his throat: there was nothing weak or complaining in Mr Clinton's voice, it was full of angry soreness. He switched off the light as he came to the Wilson canvas.

'Don't talk so bloody wet,' Bourne said to him through the darkness. 'You'll never break.'

The officer gave no sign of having heard the sympathetic but indecorous rebuke. They moved along the battered trench silently. The sky flickered with the flash of guns, and an occasional star-shell flooded their path with light. As one fell slowly, Bourne saw a dead man in field grey propped up in a corner of a traverse; probably he had surrendered, wounded, and reached the trench only to die there. He looked indifferently at this piece of wreckage. The grey face was senseless and empty. As they turned the corner they were challenged by a sentry over the dug-out.

'Good night, Bourne,' said Mr Clinton quietly.

'Good night, sir,' said Bourne, saluting; and he exchanged a few words with the sentry.

'Wish to Christ they'd get a move on,' said the sentry, as Bourne turned to go down.

The dug-out was full of men, and all the drawn, pitiless faces turned to see who it was as he entered, and after that flicker of interest relapsed into apathy and stupor again. The air was thick with smoke and the reek of guttering candles. He saw Shem lift a hand to attract his attention, and he managed to squeeze in beside him. They didn't speak after each had asked the other if he were all right; some kind of oppression weighed on them all, they sat like men condemned to death.

'Wonder if they'll keep us up in support?' whispered Shem.

Probably that was the question they were all asking, as they sat there in their bitter resignation, with brooding enigmatic faces, hopeless, but undefeated; even the faces of boys seeming curiously old; and then it changed suddenly: there were quick hurried movements, belts were buckled, rifles taken up, and stooping, they crawled up into the air. Shem and Bourne were among the first out. They moved off at once. Shells travelled overhead; they heard one or two bump fairly close, but they saw nothing except the sides of the trench, whitish with chalk in places, and the steel helmet and lifting swaying shoulders of the man in front, or the frantic uplifted arms of shattered trees, and the sky with the clouds broken in places, through which opened the inaccessible peace of the stars. They seemed to hurry, as though the sense of escape filled them. The walls of the communication trench became gradually lower, the track sloping upward to the surface of the ground, and at last they emerged, the officer standing aside, to watch what was left of his men file out, and form up in two ranks before him. There was little light, but under the brims of the helmets one could see living eyes moving restlessly in blank faces. His face, too, was a blank from weariness, but he stood erect, an ash-stick under his arm, as the dun-coloured shadows shuffled into some sort of order. The words of command that came from him were no more than whispers, his voice was cracked and not quite under control, though there was still some harshness in it. Then they moved off in fours, away from the crest of the ridge, towards the place they called Happy Valley.

They had not far to go. As they were approaching the tents a crump dropped by the mule-lines, and that set them swaying a little, but not much. Captain Malet called them to attention a little later; and from the tents, camp-details, cooks, snobs, and a few unfit men, gathered in groups to watch them, with a sympathy genuine enough, but tactfully aloof; for there is a gulf between men just returned from action, and those who have not been in the show as unbridgeable as that between the sober and the drunk. Captain Malet halted his men by the orderly-room tent. There was even a pretence to dress ranks. Then he looked at them, and they at him for a few seconds which seemed long. They were only shadows in the darkness.

'Dismiss!'

His voice was still pitched low, but they turned almost with the precision of troops on the square, each rifle was struck smartly, the officer saluting; and then the will which bound them together dissolved, the enervated muscles relaxed, and they lurched off to their tents as silent and as dispirited as beaten men. One of the tailors took his pipe out of his mouth and spat on the ground.

'They can say what they bloody well like,' he said appreciatively, 'but we're a fuckin' fine mob.' [. . .]

1929

WILLIAM FERGUSON and JOHN PATTEN
1882–1950   1905–1957

Trade unionist and Aboriginal activist William Ferguson was born in Darlington Point in the Riverina, NSW, and worked as a shearer from 1896, becoming shed organiser for the Australian Workers' Union. In 1916 he settled with his family in Gulargambone, where he reformed the local branch of the Australian Labor Party and was its secretary for two years. He moved to Dubbo in 1933, where he launched the Aborigines Progressive Association (APA) on 27 June 1938.

John Thomas Patten was born in Moama, NSW. Educated in both mission and public schools, he worked as a labourer and boxer. Patten became politically active from the early 1930s when he settled near Sydney and started organising political groups and protests, including his frequent Sunday lectures on Aboriginal rights at the Sydney Domain.

Patten joined the APA in October 1938 and with Ferguson began coordinating Aboriginal political protest. They first contributed to the NSW Legislative Assembly's inquiry into the Aborigines Protection Board, Patten visiting Aboriginal reserves to collect affidavits as evidence and Ferguson representing the APA at the inquiry. The failure of reform prompted them to co-write the pamphlet 'Aborigines Claim Citizen Rights!' and, with William Cooper (qv), organise the 1938 Day of Mourning. They later presented Prime Minister Joseph Lyons with a ten-point plan for national Aboriginal policy and Aboriginal equality. Ferguson and Patten's political relationship ended when Ferguson objected to an APA constitution published in the first issue of the newspaper *Australian Abo Call*, believing Patten was influenced by the non-Indigenous publisher, W.J. Miles.

Patten left the APA after Ferguson led a vote of no confidence, but continued to tour NSW reserves encouraging Aboriginal resistance to the Protection Board. Patten healed the rift with Ferguson by calling for Aboriginal unity at the APA annual conference in 1940. He served in the Australian army during the Second World War and was discharged injured in 1942, settling in Melbourne where he did clerical work and volunteered with the Australian Aborigines League.

During the 1940s, Ferguson's political interventions escalated but were consistently unsuccessful. In 1943 he was voted one of two Aboriginal members of the first NSW Aborigines Welfare Board, but was forced to resign in 1946 before being as quickly reinstated. In 1949, as vice-president of the NSW branch of the Australian Aborigines League, he drafted a number of reforms that were presented to the Commonwealth Minister for the Interior. Ignored, Ferguson resigned from the Labor Party and unsuccessfully contested the December federal election as an independent in Dubbo. He collapsed and died after delivering his final speech. *AH/PM*

Aborigines Claim Citizen Rights!

ONE HUNDRED AND FIFTY YEARS

The 26th of January, 1938, is not a day of rejoicing for Australia's Aborigines; it is a day of mourning. This festival of 150 years' so-called 'progress' in Australia commemorates also 150 years of misery and degradation imposed upon the original native inhabitants by the white invaders of this country. We, representing the Aborigines, now ask you, the reader of this appeal, to pause in the midst of your sesquicentenary rejoicings and ask yourself honestly whether your 'conscience' is clear in regard to the treatment of the Australian blacks by the Australian whites during the period of 150 years' history which you celebrate?

THE OLD AUSTRALIANS

You are the New Australians, but we are the Old Australians. We have in our arteries the blood of the Original Australians, who have lived in this land for many thousands of years. You came here only recently, and you took our land away from us by force. You have almost exterminated our people, but there are enough of us remaining to expose the humbug of your claim, as white Australians, to be a civilised, progressive, kindly and humane nation. By your cruelty and callousness towards the Aborigines you stand condemned in the eyes of the civilised world.

PLAIN SPEAKING

These are hard words, but we ask you to face the truth of our accusation. If you would openly admit that the purpose of your Aborigines Legislation has been, and now is, to exterminate the Aborigines completely so that not a trace of them or of their descendants remains, we could describe you as brutal, but honest. But you dare not admit openly that your hope and wish is for our death! You hypocritically claim that you are trying to 'protect' us; but your modern policy of 'protection' (so-called) is killing us off just as surely as the pioneer policy of giving us poisoned damper and shooting us down like dingoes!

We ask you now, reader, to put your mind, as a citizen of the Australian Commonwealth, to the facts presented in these pages. We ask you to study the problem, in the way that we present the case, from the Aborigines' point of view. We do not ask for your charity; we do not ask you to study us as scientific freaks. Above all, we do not ask for your 'protection'. No, thanks! We have had 150 years of that! We ask only for justice, decency and fair play. Is this too much to ask? Surely your minds and hearts are not so callous that you will refuse to reconsider your policy of degrading and humiliating and exterminating Old Australia's Aborigines? [...]

ABORIGINES PROTECTION ACTS

All Aborigines, whether nomadic or civilised, and also all half-castes, are liable to be 'protected' by the Aborigines Protection Boards, and their legal status is defined by Aborigines Protection Acts of the various States and of the Commonwealth. Thus we are for the greater part deprived of ordinary civil legal rights and citizenship, and we are made a pariah caste within this so-called democratic community.

The value of the Aborigines Protection Acts in 'protecting' Aborigines may be judged from the fact that at the 1933 census there were no Aborigines left to protect in Tasmania; while in Victoria there were only 92 full-bloods, in South Australia 569 full-bloods, in New South Wales 1,034 full-bloods.

The Aborigines of full-blood are most numerous, and most healthy, in the northern parts of Australia, where white 'protection' exists in theory, but in practice the people have to look after themselves! But already the hand of official 'protection' is reaching out to destroy these people in the north, as it has already destroyed those in the southern states. We beg of you to alter this cruel system before it gets our 36,000 nomadic brothers and sisters of North Australia into its charitable clutches!

WHAT 'PROTECTION' MEANS

The 'protection' of Aborigines is a matter for each of the individual States; while those in the Northern Territory come under Commonwealth ordinances.

This means that in each State there is a different 'system', but the principle behind the Protection Acts is the same in all States. Under these Acts the Aborigines are regarded as outcasts and as inferior beings who need to be supervised in their private lives by Government officials.

No one could deny that there is scope for the white people of Australia to extend sympathetic, or real, protection and education to the uncivilised blacks, who are willing and eager to learn when given a chance. But what can be said for a system which regards these people as incurably 'backward' and does everything in its power to keep them backward?

Such is the effect of the Aborigines Protection Acts in every State and in the Northern Territory.

No real effort is being made to bring these 'backward' people forward into the national life. They are kept apart from the community, and are being pushed further and further 'backward'.

'PROTECTION' IN NEW SOUTH WALES

We take as an example the Aborigines Protection Act (1909–1936) of New South Wales, the Mother State of Australia, which is now so proudly celebrating its 150th Anniversary.

This Act sets up a Board, known as the 'Board for Protection of Aborigines', of which the Commissioner of Police is *ex officio* Chairman. Other members—not exceeding 10 in number—are appointed by the Governor. The Board has power to distribute moneys voted by Parliament for the relief of Aborigines, and has power 'to exercise a general supervision and care over all Aborigines and over all matters affecting the interests and welfare of Aborigines, and to protect them against injustice, imposition and fraud'.

The arbitrary treatment which we receive from the A.P. Board reduces our standards of living below life-preservation point, which suggests that the intention is to exterminate us. In such circumstances it is impossible to maintain normal health. So the members of our community grow weak and apathetic, lose desire for education, become ill and die while still young.

ABORIGINAL WITHIN THE MEANING OF THE ACT

An 'Aborigine' is defined in the New South Wales Act as 'any full-blooded or half-caste Aboriginal who is a native of Australia, and who is temporarily or permanently resident in New South Wales'.

It will be noted that the Board's 'protection' extends to half-castes as well as to full-bloods.

Under certain provisions of the Act, the Board has power to control 'any person apparently having an admixture of Aboriginal blood', and may order any such person 'apparently' of Aboriginal blood (under a Magistrate's order) to live on an Aboriginal Reserve, and to be under the control of the Board.

By an amendment of the Act (1936) an averment that a person is an 'Aborigine' is regarded as 'sufficient evidence of the truth of such averment … unless the contrary is shown to the satisfaction of the Court'. The onus of disproof is thus on the accused, contrary to the traditional practice of 'British' law.

HALF-CASTES, QUADROONS AND OCTOROONS

The Aboriginal Protection Board, which has 'protected' the full-bloods of New South Wales so well that there are now less than a thousand of them remaining, has thus recently acquired the power to extend a similar 'protection' to half-castes, quarter-castes, and even to persons with any 'admixture' of Aboriginal blood whatever.

Its powers are so drastic that merely on suspicion or averment it can continue its persecuting protection unto the third, fourth and fifth generation of those so innocently unfortunate as to be descended from the original owners of this land.

POWERS OF THE BOARD

The Protection Act gives the Board an almost unlimited power to control the private lives of Aborigines as defined by that Act.

For example, the Board may order any Aboriginal into any Reserve or out of any Reserve at its own discretion.

The Board may prevent any Aboriginal from leaving New South Wales.

The Board may prevent any non-Aboriginal person from 'lodging or wandering in company' with Aborigines (thus keeping the Aborigines away from white companionship)!

The Board may prosecute any person who supplies intoxicating liquor to any 'Aborigine, or person having *apparently* an admixture of Aboriginal blood'.

The Board may cause the child of any Aborigine to be apprenticed to any master, and any child who refuses to be so apprenticed may be removed to a home or institution.

The Board may assume full control and custody of the child of any Aborigine.

The Board may remove any Aborigine from his employment.

The Board may collect the wages of any Aborigine, and may hold them in trust for the Aborigine.

The Board may order any Aborigines to move from their camp to another camp-site, and may order them away from towns or townships.

The Board may authorise the medical inspection of any Aborigine and may order his removal to any institution for treatment.

The Board may issue blankets, clothing and rations to Aborigines but blankets and other articles so issued are 'considered to be on loan only'.

The Board may make regulations to 'apportion amongst *or for the benefit of Aborigines*' the earnings of any Aboriginal living upon a Reserve.

DEPRIVED OF CITIZEN RIGHTS

The effect of the foregoing powers of the Aborigines Protection Board in New South Wales is to deprive the Aborigines and half-castes (and other 'admixtures') of ordinary citizen rights.

By a curious twist of logic, the Aborigines of New South Wales have the right to vote—for the State Parliament! They are considered worthy of the franchise, but not worthy of other citizen rights. They are officially treated either as a menace to the community (similar to criminals) or as incapable of looking after themselves (similar to lunatics)—but yet they are given a vote! […]

ABOLITION OF THE A.P. BOARD

We, representing the Aborigines and half-castes of New South Wales, call for the abolition of the A.P. Board in New South Wales, and repeal of all existing legislation dealing with Aborigines.

We ask to be accorded full citizen rights, and to be accepted into the Australian community on a basis of equal opportunity.

Should our charges of maladministration and injustice be doubted, we ask for a Royal Commission and Public Inquiry into the conditions of Aborigines, to be held in public.

We can show that the Report of the Aborigines Protection Board omits to state relevant facts, bearing on the 'care and protection' which the Board is supposed to give our people.

The Aborigines themselves do not need or want this 'protection'.

NO 'SENTIMENTAL SYMPATHY', PLEASE!

We do not wish to be regarded with sentimental sympathy, or to be 'preserved', like the koala bears, as exhibits; but we do ask for your *real* sympathy and understanding of our plight.

We do not wish to be 'studied' as scientific or anthropological curiosities. All such efforts on our behalf are wasted. We have no desire to go back to primitive conditions of the Stone Age. We ask you to teach our people to live in the Modern Age, as modern citizens. Our people are very good and quick learners. Why do you deliberately keep us backward? Is it merely to give yourselves the pleasure of feeling superior? Give our children the same chances as your own, and they will do as well as your children!

We ask for equal education, equal opportunity, equal wages, equal rights to possess property, or to be our own masters—in two words: *equal citizenship!* How can you honestly refuse this? In New South Wales you give us the vote, and treat us as equals at the ballot box. Then why do you impose the other unfair restriction of rights upon us? Do you really think that the 9,884 half-castes of New South Wales are in need of your special 'protection'? Do you really believe that these half-castes are 'naturally backward' and lacking in natural intelligence? If so, you are completely mistaken. When our people are backward, it is because your treatment has made them so. Give us the same chances as yourselves, and we will prove ourselves to be just as good, if not better, Australians, than you!

Keep your charity! We only want justice.

A NATIONAL QUESTION

If ever there was a national question, it is this. Conditions are even worse in Queensland, Northern Territory and Western Australia than they are in New South Wales; but we ask New South Wales, the Mother State, to give a lead in emancipating the Aborigines. Do not be guided any longer by religious and scientific persons, no matter how well-meaning or philanthropic they may seem. Fellow-Australians, we appeal to you to be guided by your own common sense and ideas of fair play and justice! Let the Aborigines themselves tell you what they want. Give them a chance, on the same level as yourselves, in the community. You had no race prejudice against us when you accepted half-castes and full-bloods for enlistment in the A.I.F. We were good enough to fight as Anzacs. We earned equality then. Why do you deny it to us now?

EXPLOITATION OF LABOUR

For 150 years the Aborigines and half-castes throughout Australia have been used as cheap labour, both domestic and out-of-doors. We are to-day beyond the scope of Arbitration Court awards, owing to the A.P. Board system of 'apprenticeship' and special labour conditions for Aborigines. Why do the Labour Unions stand for this? We have no desire to provide coolie labour competition, but your Protection Acts force this status upon us. The Labour Parties and Trade Unions have given us no real help or support in our attempts to raise ourselves to citizen level. Why are they so indifferent to the dangers of this cheap, sweated labour? Why do they not raise their voices on our behalf? Their 'White Australia' policy has helped to create a senseless prejudice against us, making us social outcasts in the land of our ancestors!

COMIC CARTOONS AND MISREPRESENTATION

The popular Press of Australia makes a joke of us by presenting silly and out-of-date drawings and jokes of 'Jacky' or 'Binghi', which have educated city-dwellers and young Australians to look upon us as sub-human. Is this not adding insult to injury? What a dirty trick, to push us down by laws, and then make fun of us! You kick us, and then you laugh at our misfortunes. You keep us ignorant, and then accuse us of having no knowledge. Wake up, Australians, and realise that your cruel jokes have gone over the limit!

WINDOW-DRESSING

We appeal to young Australians, or to city-dwelling Australians, whose knowledge of us is gained from the comic Press or from the 'window-dressing' Aboriginal Settlement at La Perouse, to study the matter more deeply, and to realise that the typical Aboriginal or half-caste, born and bred in the bush, is just as good a citizen, and just as good an Australian, as anybody else. Aborigines are interested not only in boomerangs and gum leaves and corroborees! The overwhelming majority of us are able and willing to earn our living by honest toil, and to take our place in the community, side by side with yourselves.

RACIAL PREJUDICE

Though many people have racial prejudice, or colour prejudice, we remind you that the existence of 20,000 and more half-castes in Australia is a proof that the mixture of Aboriginal and white races are practicable. Professor Archie Watson, of Adelaide University, has explained to you that Aborigines can be absorbed into the white race within three generations, without any fear of a 'throw-back'. This proves that the Australian Aboriginal is somewhat similar in blood to yourselves, as regards inter-marriage and inter-breeding. We ask you to study this question, and to change your whole attitude towards us, to a more enlightened one. Your present official attitude is one of prejudice and misunderstanding. We ask you to be proud of the Australian Aboriginal, and to take his hand in friendship. The New Zealanders are proud of the Maoris. We ask you to be proud of the Australian Aborigines, and not to be misled any longer by the superstition that we are a naturally backward and low race. This is a scientific lie, which has helped to push our people down and down in to the mire.

At worst, we are no more dirty, lazy, stupid, criminal, or immoral than yourselves. Also, your slanders against our race are a moral lie, told to throw all the blame for your troubles on to us. You, who originally conquered us by guns against our spears, now rely on superiority of numbers to support your false claims of moral and intellectual superiority.

A NEW DEAL FOR ABORIGINES!

After 150 years, we ask you to review the situation and give us a fair deal—a New Deal for Aborigines. The cards have been stacked against us, and we now ask you to play the game like decent Australians. Remember, we do not ask for charity, we ask for justice.

J. T. PATTEN,
        President,
        La Perouse.
W. FERGUSON,
        Organising Secretary,
        Dubbo.

1938

ANNA WICKHAM
1883–1947

An overtly feminist poet, Anna Wickham wrote of the difficulties of balancing the demands of marriage, motherhood and a literary career. Following an unorthodox Australian childhood, she left for London where she married Patrick Hepburn. Believing her poetry to be a symptom of mental illness, Hepburn had her committed for four months. While in London, she established friendships with Harold Monro, David Garnett and D.H. Lawrence but remained unaligned with any poetic movement. By the early 1920s, Wickham had established an international reputation. She travelled regularly to Paris where she became part of Natalie Barney's circle. Besides two early children's books, Wickham published a number of poetry collections in free and rhymed verse, notably *The Contemplative Quarry* (1915) and *The Man with a Hammer* (1916) as well as *Anna Wickham* (1936). Largely forgotten until Virago published an extensive collection of her writing in 1984, she has only recently received detailed scholarly attention. *AV*

The Sick Assailant

I hit her in the face because she loved me.
It was the challenge of her faithfulness that moved me;
For she knew me, every impulse, every mood,
As if my veins had run with her heart's blood.
She knew my damned incontinence, my weakness—   5
Yet she forbore with her accursèd meekness.
I could have loved her had she ever blamed me;
It was her sticky, irritating patience shamed me.
I was tired-sick. It was her business to amuse me:
Her faith could only daunt me and confuse me.   10
She was a fine great wench, and well I knew
She was one good half panther, one half shrew—
Then why should my love, more than any other,
Induce in her the silly human Mother?
She would have nursed me, bathed me, fed me, carried me;   15
She'd have burned her soul to thaw me—she'd have married me!
I hit her in the face because she loved me;
It was her sticky, irritating patience moved me.

1936

KATHARINE SUSANNAH PRICHARD
1883–1969

Born in Fiji, 'the child of a hurricane' as she later described it, Katharine Susannah Prichard was one of Australia's most distinguished writers of the first half of the twentieth century, as well as one of its most politically engaged. Part of a group that established a Western Australian branch of the Communist Party, she remained a member until her death. Her writing was always informed by a broad-reaching socialism that embraced anti-racism, feminism and anti-colonial nationalism, and sometimes drew from Soviet models to explore the representation of working-class life and economic justice in Australia.

Prichard published many major novels, including *Working Bullocks* (1926), hailed on publication as the first properly Australian modern novel, and *Coonardoo* (1929), joint winner of the *Bulletin* Prize, which attracted some hostile criticism for its portrait of a loving sexual relationship between a young Aboriginal woman and a white man. Among the earliest Australian fiction to self-consciously address race relations as its central subject, *Coonardoo* has remained an important text of the Australian tradition, even though its central portrait is crucially ambiguous, in ways somewhat similar to Prichard's short story 'Marlene'.

Other novels such as *Haxby's Circus* (1930) and *Intimate Strangers* (1937) explore self-determination for white women caught in social roles they are not completely able to repudiate, set in contexts in which women's individuation is seen within a broader need for societal change. Her goldfields trilogy from the later 1940s brings together Prichard's representation of working-class traditions with a Marxist modelling of necessary economic transformation. Earlier novels and her short stories explore connections between character and environment, especially the natural world. *NM*

Marlene

Coming out from the trees, the camp on the hillside was almost invisible. It crouched among rocks and wet undergrowth, with the township lying under mists in the valley below. The wurlies of bark, bagging and matted leaves had taken on the colouring of the rocks and tree-trunks. They were shaped like mounds of earth: crude shells with open mouths. A breath of smoke betrayed them. It hung in the air and drifted away among the trees.

Two women riding along the bush track detected the first humpy, then another and another, until half a dozen were in sight about a rough open space. Dogs flew out, barking fiercely. Two or three children, barelegged, lean, sallow, bright-eyed, with black tousled hair, slid out from before the wurlies. A man lying beside a fire sat up and glanced at the women.

'Hullo, Benjy,' the elderly woman on a grey horse called. 'Sleeping in this morning? Where's Mollie?'

The man grunted, starting sullenly over the rain-sodden clearing. Men and women appeared at the open mouths of other wurlies, all dressed as they had been sleeping, in faded dungarees and khaki trousers, shirts and skirts grey with grime and grease, threadbare woollen jackets and coats—cast-off clothing of the townspeople.

'Hullo, Mrs Boyd,' some of the women called.

'This is Miss Cecily Allison,' Mrs Boyd explained, introducing the girl on the chestnut colt. 'Miss Allison's from England; going to write a book about the aborigines. She wanted to see your camp.'

'We're half-castes here—not abos,' a morose, middle-aged man replied.

'And not "at home" so early in the day,' one of the young men added sarcastically. 'It's a hell of a place to see, anyhow.'

'Y're fergettin' y'r manners, Albert—swearin' before ladies!' one of the women said.

She giggled shyly.

'How's yerself, Mrs Boyd?'

'I'm well, Tilly. But you're looking like drowned rats, the lot of you. Why don't you shift camp for the winter, George?'

Mrs Boyd sat her upstanding mount squarely, as well-conditioned as he was. A good horsewoman, capable of managing her own affairs, it was evident. Her manner was authoritative, but kind and friendly.

'Where'd we shift to?' a fat, youngish woman asked jocosely. Barefooted, she stood, a once-white dress dragged across her heavy breast and thighs, a youngster slung on one hip. A little laugh nibbled its way through the crowd.

'This is the only place we're allowed to camp in the district,' the man who had first spoken said sourly. 'You know that, Mrs Boyd.'

'The rain's been comin' down steady for two months.' One of the other women raised a flat, uncomplaining treble.

'How on earth do you manage to get a dry spot in the humpies or keep your clothes dry?'

'We don't.' The crowd laughed as though that were a good joke. 'Our clothes are all soakin'. There's not a dry blanket in the camp.'

'We ought to be ducks. The rain'd run off our backs then.'

'It's a disgrace you should have to live like this,' Mrs Boyd declared. 'But what I came about this morning is Mollie. Where is she?'

The crowd shifted uneasily. Eyes encountered and glanced aside. A wild crew they looked in their shabby clothes, the women wearing remnants of finery, a bright scarf or coloured cardigan over their draggled dresses.

Brown-eyed, black-haired, they all were, but their skin varied from sickly yellow to weathered bronze. The women were sallow and tawny, the men darker. On most of the faces, thick noses and full lips denoted the aboriginal strain; a few others had sharp, neat features, showing no trace of aboriginal origin except in their eyes.

'Where is Mollie?' Mrs Boyd demanded. 'I've been letting Mr Edward drive her in to the pictures on Saturday nights when he goes into town himself. But she didn't come back with him last week. He waited an hour for her.'

'She's fair mad about the pictures, Mollie,' Ruby burbled.

'That's all very well, but it's not very considerate of her to run away like this. She knows how busy we are just now with all the cows coming in. Mr Phillip and Mr Edward've got their hands full. I had to ride in with the mail myself this morning. And Mollie was very useful, helping with the milking and feeding poddies.'

'She's a fine kid, Mollie,' Albert declared.

'But where is she? What's the matter?'

The crowd surged. Obviously the question was disturbing: it had to be evaded. Exclamations and suggestions clattered. There was no surprise, no consternation, although everybody seemed upset, a little nervous and amused at Mrs Boyd's query.

Mrs Boyd guessed they were hiding Mollie. The child had got a quirk about something: one of those mysterious urges to go bush with her own kind.

'Did y'know Bill Bibblemun took bad with the p'monia and died in hospital, Sunday week?' somebody asked.

Others joined in eagerly.

'It was a grand funeral, Mrs Boyd.'

'The Salvation Army captain said Bill'd go straight to glory because he was a good Christian.'

'He was, too. Testified at street meetings and sang hymns—even when he was drunk.'

'They said some beautiful prayers.'

'All about his bein' washed in the blood of the lamb and his sins bein' whiter than snow.'

'And the kids have all had measles,' Ruby boasted.

'What's happened to Wally Williams?' Mrs Boyd inquired, willing to humour them. 'He was to come over and cut fencing-posts for me last month.'

There was a lull in the rattle of voices, eyelids fell, wary glances slid under them. Coughing, a hoarse whispering, filled the pause.

'He's gone up-country,' George said.

'You mean, he's in jail. What's he been up to now?'

'Well, you see, Mrs Boyd, it wasn't hardly Wally's fault,' Tilly Lewis explained. 'Jo Wiggins said some steers had got out of his holding-paddocks, and he offered Wally two bob for every steer he could track and bring in. Wally took in a couple of cleanskins. He thought they were Mr Wiggins's steers, natcherly—'

'Naturally—at two bob apiece,' Mrs Boyd agreed.

'But when the mounted trooper found a couple of red poley steer skins in Jo Wiggins's slaughteryard, Mr Wiggins put the blame on to Wally—and Wally got two years.'

'Everybody knows Jo Wiggins's game,' Mrs Boyd admitted. 'But Wally ought to keep his hands off clean-skins.'

'Oh, he's not like that, Wally, Mrs Boyd. He's a real good stockman. But if he can't get a job, he doesn't know what to do with hisself. He's jest got to be workin' cattle—'

'I know.' Mrs Boyd laughed good-humouredly. 'I suspect he's "worked" calves from our back hills before now. We had an epidemic of milkers coming in without calves last year.'

'If a cow drops a calf in the bush, Mrs Boyd, the dingoes are as likely to get it as—'

'Wally! Of course. But my money's on Wally. I reckon Jo Wiggins has had more of our calves than the dingoes.'

Her horse, cropping the young grass, swung Mrs Boyd sideways. She saw the figure of a man sleeping before a smouldering fire at the entrance of his shack. Steam was rising from the damp blanket that covered him.

'Who's that?' she asked.

'It's Charley,' a woman who had been coughing incessantly said. 'He's not well.'

'Better put that bottle away then,' Mrs Boyd advised. 'If the trooper comes round somebody'll be getting into trouble for selling Charley plonk again. Where does he get the money to buy drink, anyhow?'

'The shopkeepers take his drawings for showcards sometimes.'

'He's quite an artist in his own way, Charley,' Mrs Boyd explained to her companion. 'Self-taught. Could you show Miss Allison some of Charley's drawings, Lizzie?'

Charley's wife slipped away, burrowed into the wurley, and returned with a black exercise-book in her hands. Miss Allison dismounted to look at the drawings, crude outlines of people and animals, a football match, the finish of a race.

Pleasure in Charley's drawings, awed interest and expectancy animated his friends and relations.

'Well'—Mrs Boyd yanked her horse's head round and straightened her back, smiling but implacable—'have you made up your minds yet to tell me about Mollie?'

The faces about her changed. There was a moment of sombre, unresponsive silence.

Then Tilly Lewis exclaimed delightedly: 'Why, it's Mrs Jackson! She's been bad with the rheumatics; but got up—and put on her hat for the visitors!'

A withered little woman, a neat black hat perched on her head, walked across the clearing, wearing a dingy black dress and frayed grey cardigan with an air of forlorn propriety.

'Good morning, Myrtle,' Mrs Boyd said. 'I'm sorry to hear you've been having rheumatism.'

'What can you expect, Miss Ann?' The half-caste held herself with some dignity: her faded eyes, ringed like agates, looked up at the pleasantly smiling, healthy, fresh-complexioned woman on the big horse. 'I'm not used to living out of doors.'

'No, of course not,' Mrs Boyd replied.

'You know I was brought up at the mission station. And I've worked in some of the best homes in the district; but now—you wouldn't keep a sow in the place where I've got to live.'

'It's not right, Mrs Boyd,' George muttered.

'No, it's not right,' Mrs Boyd agreed. 'But what can I do about it? Would you go into the Old Women's Home if I could get you in, Myrtle?'

'I've been there. The police took me from the hospital after I had rheumatic fever. But I ran away—'

'She did, Mrs Boyd!' eager voices chimed.

'She walked near on a hundred and thirty miles till she got here.'

'Cooped up in the city—with a lot of low-down old women treatin' me like dirt. I've always kept myself to myself. I've always been respectable, Miss Ann.'

'Oh, yes, she's terrible respectable, Mrs Boyd,' the chorus went up.

'Nobody can't say Mrs Jackson isn't respectable!'

'All I want's to die in my own place—like any respectable person. It *is* my own place, Miss Ann, the house your father gave Tom and me; and Mr Henry had no right to turn us out.'

'She's breaking her heart, like any old abo, for the hunting-grounds of her people,' Albert said cynically. 'They always want to go home to die, but, being half-and-half, it's a roof over her head Mrs Jackson wants, and a bed to lie on.'

'I'll see what I can do about it, Myrtle,' Mrs Boyd promised.

'Funny, isn't it?' Albert's lounging, graceful figure tilted back as he gazed at her. 'You're the granddaughter of one of the early settlers who shot off more blacks than any other man in the country. Mrs Jackson is the granddaughter of one of the few survivors, and related to the best families in the district. But you've got the land and the law on your side. They put the dogs onto her if she goes round the homesteads asking for a bit of tucker or old clothes.'

'And this is the only spot where we're allowed to camp in the district.'

'Something will have to be done about it,' Mrs Boyd declared.

'What?' Albert demanded. 'All the land about has been taken up. It's private property now. We're not allowed to work in the mines. We're not allowed to sell the fish we catch—not allowed to shoot or trap. They don't want us on the farms. They won't let us work on the roads. All we're allowed to do is draw rations and rot … though there is some talk of packing us off to one of those damned reservations "where the diseased and dying remnants of the native race are permitted to end their days in peace". Excuse me quoting the local rag.'

'You can't say I haven't tried to help you,' Mrs Boyd protested. 'I've always given you work on my farm when I could.'

A wry smile twisted the young man's mouth. 'And paid us less than half you'd have had to pay other workers.'

'Albert!' one of the women objected. 'Don't take any notice of him, Mrs Boyd.'

'You're talking like one of those crazy agitators, Albert,' Mrs Boyd cried hotly. 'If you're not careful you'll find yourself being moved on.'

'I'll remember you said so, Mrs Boyd.' Albert grinned maliciously.

'It's hard on Albert not being able to get work, Mrs Boyd,' Ruby expostulated. 'He's real clever: can read and write as good as any white man. When he went to school he could beat any of the boys.'

'Lot of good it's ever done me,' Albert sneered. 'If I'd been a myall I'd've had a better life. The blacks of any tribe share all they've got with each other. The whites grab all they can for themselves—and let even their own relations starve.'

'Do the aboriginals treat half-castes better?' Miss Allison's voice rose clear and chilly against his wrath.

'They don't treat us like vermin.' Albert might have been admiring the gleam of her hair or the horse she was holding. 'Up in the nor'-west, when I was a kid, I went around with my mother's tribe. Never knew I was any different from the rest. Then my father got interested in me. Sent me down here to school. He died—and I've been trying to get a job ever since.'

'Do you want to go back to your own people?'

Albert's anger resurged. 'My own people!' he jeered. 'Who are they? My father was as fair as you are. I couldn't live in a blacks' camp now—though this is as bad. But I don't belong there. I think differently. We all do. We like soap and clean clothes when we can get them, and books. We want to go to the pictures and football matches. I want to work and have a house to live in, a wife and kids. But this is all I've got. These are my only people—mongrels like myself.'

'You shouldn't talk bitter like that, Albert,' Mrs Jackson reproved. 'It does no good.'

'Nothing does any good.' He flung away from the crowd and stalked off behind the wurlies.

'He's sore because he can't get work and the Protector won't let Penny Carnarvon marry him,' Ruby said. 'Penny's in service, and she's such a good servant they don't want to lose her. But she's fond of Albert. She says she'll learn the Protector.'

'She will, too.'

'Stella did, didn't she?'

'Too right, she did.'

'She dropped a trayload of dishes to get herself the sack because she wanted to marry Bob. But the missus forgave her and took it out of her wages. Stella had to get herself in the family way, and make up to the boss, before the Protector decided she'd better marry Bob.'

'Penny'll be going for a little holiday soon, Albert says. Then perhaps they can get married and go up north. He's almost sure he can get a job on one of the stations.'

'But where's Mollie?' Mrs Boyd returned to the attack. The crowd closed down on their laughter and gossip. There was a disconcerted shuffling and searching for something to say.

'Mollie?'

'Yes, Mollie. It's no use pretending you don't know where she is. If she's hiding, doesn't want to come home, I'm not going to worry about her. But I'll have to let the Department know—'

'Hullo, Mrs Boyd!' A girl in a pink cotton frock stood in the opening of a wurley behind the horses. A pretty little thing, sturdy and self-possessed, but rather pale, she stood there, a small bundle wrapped in a dirty shawl in her arms.

'Mollie,' Mrs Boyd gasped. 'Have you been getting a baby?'

The girl nodded, smiling.

'But you're only a child,' Mrs Boyd cried. 'You're not sixteen.'

'I was sixteen last month,' Mollie replied calmly.

'It's scandalous,' Mrs Boyd exclaimed indignantly. 'Who's the father?'

Mollie's eyes smiled back at her. 'I been going with two or three boys in town.'

The little crowd before her quivered to breathless excitement: a sigh, as of relief, and a titter of suppressed mirth escaped.

'You ought to be ashamed of yourself,' Mrs Boyd declared furiously. 'You know, I thought better of you, Mollie. I thought you were different from the other girls. You've lived with me for so many years, and I trusted you to behave yourself.'

'Don't be angry,' Mollie said quietly. 'I couldn't help it … and I like the baby.'

'When did it happen?'

'Last night.'

Mrs Boyd stared at the girl. She looked a little wan, but quite well.

'Is she all right?' she asked the crone who had come out of the hut behind Mollie. 'Had I better get the doctor to come out and see her, or arrange for her to go into hospital?'

'I've never felt better in my life,' Mollie said. 'Aunty May can look after me.'

'No need to bother,' the old half-caste beside Mollie mumbled soothingly. 'She hadn't a bad time. I'd have sent her to the hospital—but everything happened in such a hurry.'

'Let me see the child,' Mrs Boyd demanded: turned her horse and rode to Mollie.

'She's very little and red,' Mollie apologized, tenderly lifting the dirty shawl that covered the baby.

Mrs Boyd leaned down from her saddle. It was the ugliest scrap of humanity she had ever seen; but there was something vaguely familiar in its tiny crumpled face. Cecily Allison dragged her horse over the grass to look at the baby, too.

'Ra-ther sweet, isn't she?' she murmured mechanically. 'What are you going to call her?'

Mollie drew the shawl over the baby's face again.

'Marlene,' she said happily.

The rain descended in a gusty squall, driving the half-castes into their wurlies, the horsewomen back among the trees. As they rode, the older woman sagged in her saddle, curiously aged and grim.

'The sooner they're cleaned out of the district the better,' she said viciously. 'They're an immoral lot, these half-castes.'

'What about the whites who are responsible for them?' the girl on the chestnut colt asked.

She wondered whether it was a tragedy or a comedy she had been witnessing. These people might live like dogs in their rotten wurlies, with the dark bush behind them and the prosperous little township spread at their feet; but their aspirations were all towards the ways and ideas of the white race. The exotic film-star,[1] and that baby in this dump of outcasts—what an indictment! Yet Miss Allison suspected they had tried to spare the baby's grandmother, with simple kindliness, knowing the truth behind Mollie's bravado. Had they altogether succeeded?

The camp on the hillside was moved on before the end of the month.

1938

Letter to Miles Franklin[2]

11 December 1947
Greenmount

My darling Miles,

I was just feeling I needed a word from you. The sort of uplift & glow, that follows a letter from MF!

And truly, it came. I could look out of my window on to a jacaranda waving its mauvy plumes, & tell it just what a darling Miles is—and my confidences spill out, all over the wide plains which stretch from this hillside towards Perth & the far horizon.

It was good coming home after a month on the goldfields—though the house wasn't like home. Looking so delapidated & dishevelled with strangers in it, & as if no one had cared for it, for a long time. Still, they've allowed me to resume my old bed room, and I can be alone in my work room at the bottom of the orchard. All that's left of it, a few orange trees, lemons, figs, plums, almonds and apricots. With the wild oats five feet high & pale gold everywhere!

I've been living on apricots—making jam & drying them. Lovely things—colour & perfume so exquisite—to say nothing of the taste, in the early morning under a tree, with the birds & bees in possession.

---

1   The baby has been named after Marlene Dietrich (1901–92).
2   In reply to Miles Franklin's letter of 20 November 1947: see Miles Franklin (qv).

On the goldfields, found some material I'd been researching for a long time, & did all I wanted to before settling down to Vol. III.[1] Ernestine Hill & her son were camped at Coolgardie with a big truck & caravan, & I spent an interesting night with them.[2] But in the hot weather, I do appreciate the mod cons—baths & decent sanitary arrangements. Afraid I'm not so fond of the simple life as I used to be. Particularly when it includes flies & red-backed spiders galore. Ernestine seems to take them in her stride though. She's a strange, otherwhereish creature with big beautiful eyes, a hoarse voice & curious incapacity to argue logically about anything. Talking or arguing logically, that's what I find wrong with *To-morrow and To-morrow*, chiefly. If people will deal with communism, at least they shd know something about it. The Marxian dialectic does give a logical basis for thought, & the characters & conditions described by MB & FE have no relation to either Communist mentality or methods. I think that Flora, at least, intended to be sympathetic, but the result wd be damaging if anybody thought a nitwit like her Communist could be responsible for Communist policy. After all, some of the best brains in the world to-day are associated with it, including Professor Joliot-Curie, JBS Haldane, but there are many others. Flora is ill, & I'm so sorry for her. She attaches a lot of importance to the book. Says she put everything she's got into it. And I think she has. There's some fine writing in the first descriptions of Sydney.

For the love of Mike how cd you be bothered with a Type—as the French say—like Wentworth! He's just an egocentric idiot, psychopathic really. I couldn't have imagined a man wd make such a fool of himself, publicly, as he did in the debate with Sharkey.[3] Just indulged in vicious abuse, & never even mentioned the subject of the debate until the last round. It doesn't matter what he says, one way or the other. Even his own side regard him as an embarrassment & futile wind-bag.

I haven't read Gavin's book. Am too fed up with beer, to even read about it. (Mustn't offend your eyes with a split infinitive, darling,[4] although I am writing on the edge of my bed, & so tired my mind won't spell correctly.) My tenant likes beer: has beery parties, what time I retire to my work room to escape the stinking stuff.

Has there been any discussion about the *Telegraph* prize yet?[5] What a nerve to keep the MSS so long, and hang-up a decision.

---

1   Third volume of Prichard's goldfields trilogy, published as *Winged Seeds* (1950).
2   Ernestine Hill was a popular travel writer and novelist who spent much of her life travelling and research-ing in remote parts of Australia.
3   Lawrence Sharkey was general secretary of the Australian Communist Party from 1948 to 1965. In 1949 he was convicted of sedition and served an eighteen-month sentence.
4   In the original 'the previous sentence is corrected, removing the split infinitive' (Ferrier, p. 182).
5   *Daily Telegraph* novel competition. Dymphna Cusack and Florence James (qqv) entered *Come in Spinner* under the name Sydney Wybourne and won.

Have you read *Rachel,* by March Cost—quite a relief from most of the overseas tripe. It's well-written, & gives an intriguing version of a French actress I've always been interested in.

What are you doing? Do tell me. Hope you're getting down to some of the writing I love to read from MF. There's nobody has your exquisite wit and sense of humour, my dear. First priest I've heard of, for a long time, who has anything to recommend him—the one who appreciated your work & told his rosary with quandongs, I mean.

Love to you, Miles dear, and all honour and glory to your creative work. Please remember me to Jack—with best wishes for the New Year, too.

Cheers—with homage—always,
Katharine
1947

DOROTHEA MACKELLAR
1885–1968

The second verse of Dorothea Mackellar's 'My Country' is the most often recited piece of poetry in Australia. Isobel Marion Dorothea Mackellar was born into a well-established Sydney family and travelled widely. Her poem 'Core of My Heart' was published in the London *Spectator* in 1908, and was revised and retitled 'My Country' when it was published in her collection *The Closed Door and Other Verses* in 1911. She published three other volumes of poetry—*The Witch-Maid and Other Verses* (1914), *Dreamharbour and Other Verses* (1923) and *Fancy Dress and Other Verse* (1926)—as well as three minor novels in the mid-1920s. A collection of her poetry was published in 1971, but she remains familiar to many Australians as the author of one poem only. She co-founded the Sydney Centre of International PEN in 1931. *NM*

My Country

The love of field and coppice,
   Of green and shaded lanes,
Of ordered woods and gardens
   Is running in your veins.
Strong love of grey-blue distance   5
   Brown streams and soft, dim skies—
I know but cannot share it,
   My love is otherwise.

I love a sunburnt country,
   A land of sweeping plains,   10
Of ragged mountain ranges,
   Of droughts and flooding rains.

I love her far horizons,
  I love her jewel-sea,
Her beauty and her terror—   15
  The wide brown land for me!

The stark white ring-barked forests,
  All tragic to the moon,
The sapphire-misted mountains,
  The hot gold hush of noon.   20
Green tangle of the brushes,
  Where lithe lianas coil,
And orchids deck the tree tops
  And ferns the warm dark soil.

Core of my heart, my country!   25
  Her pitiless blue sky,
When sick at heart, around us,
  We see the cattle die—
But then the grey clouds gather,
  And we can bless again   30
The drumming of an army,
  The steady, soaking rain.

Core of my heart, my country!
  Land of the Rainbow Gold,
For flood and fire and famine,   35
  She pays us back three-fold.
Over the thirsty paddocks,
  Watch, after many days,
The filmy veil of greenness
  That thickens as we gaze …   40

An opal-hearted country,
  A wilful, lavish land—
All you who have not loved her,
  You will not understand—
Though earth holds many splendours,   45
  Wherever I may die,
I know to what brown country
  My homing thoughts will fly.

                 1911

NETTIE PALMER
1885—1964

Warmly praised during her lifetime as an inspirational critic, enabling mentor and perceptive, lively correspondent, Nettie Palmer is now remembered as a key figure of Australian literary and cultural life during the 1920s, '30s and '40s. Two early volumes of poetry—*The South Wind* (1914) and *Shadowy Paths* (1915)—show clear promise as a poet. Debate as to whether Palmer's life as a writer was redirected by her marriage to the novelist and critic Vance Palmer and her care for their children, or whether her work as a critic was her real talent, is ongoing.

Her early years in Melbourne saw her active in feminist, socialist and literary causes, gaining work as a language teacher, before her marriage to Palmer in 1914. Theirs was one of the great literary partnerships of Australia, Vance achieving significant recognition for his novels through the 1930s. He was the most prominent representative of a revived interwar literary nationalism rooted in the values of the 1890s. Nettie's writing, however, was the main source of income for the family through the 1920s. She published critical essays in many journals throughout the decade, and her study *Modern Australian Literature 1900–1923* (1924) was the first critical work on twentieth-century Australian literature. She wrote on many topics and many writers, both Australian and international, and developed a profile as the most interesting and influential non-academic critic of her day. Her journals, however, remain her most significant work. Kept between 1925 and 1939, collating events, encounters, reading, literary life and reflections on aesthetics, they are an extraordinarily vivid slice of cosmopolitan Australian cultural life, marked by both acute discernment and a generously detailed eye for the future. *NM*

From *Fourteen Years*

PARIS

April 23rd, 1935. It's really too early in the year to make a rendezvous with yourself—there's nobody else about—on one of the chairs by the side of the Medici Fountain. There's a biting wind, and I feel all the colder from watching the group of little waterproof tent-like objects—some sort of Girl Guides, their hands red-shivery, with sheaves of bluebells from a hike— as they cross the corner of the Boul' Mich' just outside the Luxembourg Gardens. A new type of 'jeune fille bien élevée'.

Yes, it's early in the year, but this is the centre of Paris for me, and here on my first morning I sit for a while. When I used to come here before (1911, was it?) it was high summer, so that every drop of water falling from the superb fountain into its oblong basin was welcome. The rows of chairs on each side were crowded, but I'd manage to find myself one. I had always bolted from lunch after the morning session at Bourg la Reine; the laborious steam tram had seemed as slow as a steam-roller and nearly as loud, and here was a moment of quiet. I was impatient each day for Jeanne to come and lead me away, yet hardly wanted the spell under the thick trees to be broken. Further on in the Gardens, the children's theatres were waking up for the afternoon; outside, the wide rue Soufflot ran shortly to the Panthéon straddling across its square, the great words gleaming across its pediment: *Aux grands morts la patrie reconnaissante.*[1] Punch and Judy—and the Panthéon: from this chair you could have both in view. As well as an occasional small comedy. See if I can remember one, over the years.

(... On a chair opposite, across the oblong basin, sits a good-looking young woman. Almost too good-looking, she is profuse in colouring and figure, though dressed with extreme discretion—small, dark hat, dark-blue tailleur, white jabot. Just sitting there. A man, obviously a stranger, takes the chair next to her. Any ordinary, preoccupied middle-aged man. The young woman turns slightly towards him, at the same time staring emphatically into some vast distance. He is looking through some papers, and takes no notice of her; why should he? But she finds this neglect intolerable, and takes steps. Rising from her chair, she sits down again sideways, her back violently turned to the man, as if she had boxed his ears. At the same time she lowers her chin and smiles at him, like a black pansy; but her smile is somehow directed at him through the back of her head—or gradually, relentingly, over her shoulder. It becomes too much, even for a preoccupied, unadventurous man; he begins to respond, his papers now in his pocket. There develops an exchange of contemptuous pleasantries; or is it unpleasantries? No one would know, for a large lady sails into view, not seeking a chair for herself, merely a husband. 'Ah, there you are Adolphe! Sorry I'm late.' He gets up and follows her. As for the young woman, she arranges herself squarely on the chair, with all her work to be done over again.)

Twenty-five years and a long war have made very little change in Paris, except for the women's fashions. And not so much in those. At least it seems so to me as I sit here, trying to remember what was worn in those days, and particularly what it was to be a student, coming in every afternoon from Bourg la Reine with a breathless eagerness for new experience.

April 25th, 1935. Spent most of yesterday looking at bookshops. One at the Odéon is marked Larousse, as a watchmaker's might be marked Greenwich, where time is made. Poking into its shelves, rich not only with dictionaries, I said to the young salesman, without first noticing his languid eyes, that it must be wonderful to be where knowledge comes from—Larousse! He wasn't pleased by my bungling enthusiasm.

But how many ways there are of bungling in a foreign city! It's a long while since I shopped in Paris, and I'd forgotten about the business siesta from twelve till two. Walking from that Larousse down the narrow, neat, quiet Rue de l'Odéon, I came on Sylvia Beach's bookshop and library—Shakespeare

---

1 The inscription reads 'Aux grands hommes la patrie reconnaissante' ('To great men a grateful country'). Palmer's mistake suggests she was writing from memory.

and Company, in distinguished lettering. An impressive shop-front showing American and English classics and moderns in good editions; Shakespeare, Hemingway, Gertrude Stein, Whitman, Quixote (English), Christina Stead, Thackeray. In a frame, a striking piece of embroidery, showing a ship, a sunset …

I made to enter the shop and found myself banging at a shut door, my bump sounding like a knock. The door was opened by a dark-eyed American woman, with a forgiving voice: 'Did you *specially* want anything?' Of course not: I wanted everything in time and nothing now: I'd come later.

In the afternoon I found that the gentle dark woman was Sylvia Beach herself. The photograph I'd seen of her discussing proofs with Joyce had made her springy hair look fair, her eyes blue. (These preconceptions!). As she told me the story of Shakespeare and Company from its beginning in the twenties when American and other English-speaking people came in droves to Paris, I soon understood that from the first it was no perfunctory library and bookstore, but a workshop and a treasure-house. A leaflet she gave me, explaining library subscription terms, carried a brief testimonial, signed 'A.M.' Who? It was cautiously translated, its French bones showing through:

'… Is the student eager to pore over the great Elizabethans? He need not cross the Channel; in the rue de l'Odéon he will find them all … English novels from the earliest to 'Ulysses', writers of the Victorian Age and the Irish Renaissance. Those who follow the latest literary events know that the book that London and New York is discussing is always to be found at the same moment at Shakespeare and Company.'

So it seems that from being an English library for the foreign colony, it has become an institution for French readers, its value recognized by the French Government, which gives it a small subsidy now that bad times have come and the American invasion has receded like a tide.

Sylvia Beach's biggest single exploit has been the publication of 'Ulysses' a dozen years ago, when both American and English publishers were afraid to touch the book. She has done other publishing, issuing novels (not only Lawrence's), and then, the tiniest exploit, that perfect book with a dozen poems by Joyce, 'pomes penyeach'. I remember ordering half-a-dozen copies of this shilling book when we were at Caloundra, seeing it mentioned in the *Times*. Sylvia Beach agreed that, of course, the title as spelt was taken from some kerbside barrow in Dublin, laden with perhaps penny broadside ballads. It was all part of Joyce's memory—Dublin photographed in his eyes, echoing in his ears, till he's made the whole world aware of this old shabby city on the Liffey.

Sylvia Beach has a good many of Joyce's papers—transcripts, corrected proofs, letters about details of production—the kind of thing that would gather in the course of publishing such an extraordinarily complex work as 'Ulysses'. At the present crisis she'd be willing to sell them in England for the sake of Shakespeare and Company, taking them to Christie's herself, but a very high authority has assured her this wouldn't be possible; any Joyce papers would be seized by the Customs and burnt! So Shakespeare and Company limps along gloriously, providing not only the most stimulating books in the English-speaking world but a rendezvous for writers. Not only for foreign ones. As a dark black-hatted, heavy-shouldered man enters the shop and begins moving round the shelves she whispers: 'Excuse me a moment; there's Paul Valéry. I must see if there's something he specially wants.'

As a library and a place for the interchange of ideas the shop has its definite functions. Sylvia Beach said she didn't pretend to handle French books much; she's going to show me why to-morrow.

April 26th, 1935. As I crossed the little street from No. 12 with S.B. this morning, she said: 'There really ought to be an underground tunnel here; Adrienne and I go backwards and forwards so often.'

Adrienne, I found, was M'lle Monnier, the proprietor of No. 7, with its sign, 'La Maison des Amis du Livre'—a woman as markedly French as Sylvia Beach is American. And if the one is twentieth century in her looks, the other is deliberately medieval. Adrienne Monnier's full gown of heavy woollen grey stuff (duffel grey?) seemed a habit of some order—oh, a secular order. Her round face with its large lambent eyes and good brow looks what is called spiritual—in a secular way again. As for the habit, it wasn't austere and lank, but bunchy and merry, not worn by a 'sainte triste'.

(... I've often wondered if the rationalists, the humanists, the defenders of the rights of man—if they couldn't develop a secular-religious approach. There was that secular monastery in Henry James's story, 'The Great Good Place', but it was too much like a gentleman's club. There was Guyau's, 'Esquisse d'une Morale', mapping out a moral equivalent for orthodoxy—equivalent, not ersatz. All this zig-zagged through my head while I looked at Adrienne Monnier, with her world-rejecting clothes, her lambent eyes, her illuminated face.)

She explained the various functions of her Maison; the recent publication of pamphlets on folk-lore (olk, as in polka); the occasional publication of literary reviews, especially, ten years ago, her monthly, *Le Navire d'Argent*, edited by Sylvia and herself—Sylvia the gatherer of foreign material, the two of them often collaborating as its translators—Whitman, Blake, Disraeli (letters), young Americans like Robert McAlmon; and Adrienne Monnier collecting rare work, often work-in-progress, from French writers of the time.

But what interested me most in the old copies of their review that they gave me was the standing statement on its back-covers about the final, basic function of the Friends of the Book:

This House stands as the unchallenged initiator of the present library movement. Its two great principles have by now stood the test. The first is moral: that a librarian must not only be well-read, but must conceive his task as a sacred one; the second is practical, and consists of the management of selling and lending.

This Library is the most complete and well-stocked of all lending libraries. It contains many out-of-print books, all the moderns right up to the vanguard, and all the old classics.

What an achievement! I have been thinking of my feelings in the presence of Adrienne Monnier—and not merely because of her duffel-grey, either. '*De savoir prendre sa tache comme une véritable sacerdoce*';[1] and Sylvia Beach is equally consecrated to her task. They are the two vestals of the rue de l'Odéon, and their undying fire is the spirit of the book.

April 28th, 1935. If I hadn't known about the world depression, *la crise*, I'd have guessed it from Paris, where its wave actually broke later than with us—and is lasting longer. For instance, there are the books in English for sale, mostly printed for emigré Americans, remaindered now for next to nothing. Little Crosby editions—Kay Boyle's short stories, Hemingway's 'In Our Time', Robert McAlmon, and then Saint Exupéry's 'Night Flight', excellently translated by that remarkable man, Stuart Gilbert.

Who is Stuart Gilbert? Translator, into English, of 'Vol de Nuit', and much else. Translator of 'Ulysses' into French. Author of 'Ulysses—an Interpretation'. And a convinced admirer of H.H.R. [Henry Handel Richardson (qv)] I've something in a notebook he wrote to the publisher of her 'Two Studies' a couple of years ago: 'There is no book previous to "Ulysses" that I have read so often, and so often recommended, as "Maurice Guest". To my mind, it is the best novel written in the twenty years preceding the war …'

But still, who is he, this perceptive critic, this bi-linguist, translator, interpreter? Every country needs such men.

These nuggety American books, in paper covers and with excellent print, are now to be found heaped up in the most unlikely places. This week I've bought perhaps a dozen copies of 'Night Flight' (with Gide's preface) at about fourpence each. Their primary public has left France; no wonder Paris shivers a little. 'Good Americans when they die go to Paris'; not now. New Dealers will hope for some different Champs Elysées, with a valuta more tempting for men in hard times.

April 29th, 1935. These haunting open-and-shut book-barrows, guarded by old men, that stretch along the Left Bank! This morning, rummaging

---

1 'To be able to assume one's task as a true religious calling.' Palmer's French is not perfect.

among them, I came across a selection of Australian short stories from Dr. Mackaness's anthology,[1] translated into rather prim French. A little further on, a very clean copy of Léon Daudet's novel of 1922 about a military dictator, 'Sulla': too clean, hardly cut, and with a clean visiting-card inside: *Léon Daudet, Deputé de Paris, 12 rue de Rome.* Did he name that street in his image: was it part of his *action* française? And who sold his book unread—a friend or a reviewer? Anyhow I bought it. I'm prepared to believe that Daudet wrote the book with an eye on his own rue de Rome rather than on Sulla's city: in fact, he has pointed this out before the book begins. On the cover. 'Sulla et son destin'; the subtitle, 'A tale of long ago and always'; and the dedication, 'To Frenchmen who can see, this true tale is warmly dedicated'.

June 15th, 1935. With daylight saving, and in June, even the most determined late-diner can't dine after dark. So in sunset light you recognize Heinrich Mann in a Boul' Mich' pavement café. He is dining alone, thoughtfully, and with a napkin tucked amply round his neck. In another café is Alfred Kerr, looking like a dignified poet of 1860—wing collar, black cravat, sideboards, frock coat; exiled in time as in place. Then in a bistro near the Deux Magots there is a group of youngish people, mixed French and German, gathered round little Gustav Reger, anxious and passionate; probably speaking of friends, worse off than himself, left behind in Germany. In an Italian group is Gaetano Salvemini, challenging beard raised with his voice, his head gleaming in baldness after his exile that began more than ten years ago.

You wonder, as you move round, if there are no writers but exiles—refugees—in Paris now. Maybe the French ones are invisible, dining in private; but it's certain the refugees are very many. How do they live? Heinrich Mann, I suppose, can keep on with his novels wherever he is, and they'll be translated and published. Writers of literary criticism, like Alfred Kerr, or political opinion, like Gustav Reger, contribute to the various free journals that went into exile when they did. Ossietsky's *Weltbühne* left Germany in 1933 for Prague, Zürich, and, I think, Amsterdam. And here there are German periodicals—some short-lived—a *Weltwoche*, a *Wochenblatt*, written for and by refugees. There's also at least one antifascist Italian weekly.

But what is life for all these refugee-writers? 'By the waters of Babylon I sat down and wept.' It's true they're not captives; they're guests in a country still free; yet how can they sing the songs of Zion in a strange land! What they write will surely be a poetry militant—not triumphant—and tragic, revolutionary tales like those of Anna Seghers.[2]

---

1 George Mackaness (1882–1968) edited several anthologies of Australian literature, including *Australian Short Stories* (1928).
2 Anti-fascist German writer of part-Jewish descent (1900–83).

Her memorable face is one you will not see among refugees in the cafés. A friend of hers tells me that with a husband and two lively children she keeps house in a suburban flat, somehow managing to write her books, too. With her political record, she'd have long ago reached a concentration camp if she hadn't come away from Hitler's Germany. As it is, her parents in Germany are apt to be endangered if she's conspicuously outspoken here, in writing or speech—which she wistfully remembers when she opens her sewing-basket and looks at their photographs fastened inside the lid.

June 21st, 1935. Talks at odd intervals with Christina Stead. I feel rather ashamed of having brought her, with some others, to this Hotel des Grands Hommes, just because I knew it and they asked for a suggestion. It's suddenly burning midsummer, and the Panthéon makes this the hottest square in Paris. Christina, who knows her way everywhere, would have chosen better. But it has meant that we've seen a good deal of one another, going out for meals and walks, as well as sitting together in conference sessions.[1] Her voice is easy to remember:

'My father wanted me to be a scientist like himself. When I was very tiny he used to tell me the names of what interested him most—fishes with frightening faces. It was all right, but when he saw I learnt easily he took me to science meetings. I suppose I was about ten by then. I wasn't frightened of fish with ugly faces, but those science women who didn't know how to do their hair or put their clothes on! I ran away from science forever.'

Or on Sunday morning, as we set out on a walk from our hotel, which is near an important police headquarters:

'Now *why* are all these gendarmes being sent out in lorries from the barracks to-day? What meeting of the people are they going to break up? Would it be that big communal picnic at St. Cloud? Look, there's another lorry being loaded with them. Who's going to be crushed?'

And later, in the Luxembourg Gardens, coming back to the dread science-women:

'… I was determined to make enough money some day to have the right clothes. I must admit that I've got rather a weakness for shoes. And gloves. Yes, and hats. I buy my hats in London, but it does seem a pity not to be able to take one back from Paris now. It's not the best part of the season, though; it's too late. You see, in Paris when hats come in at the beginning of the season you don't think of buying those. Hats in the first wave are bound to be exaggerated, put out to attract people who are bound to be caught by anything showy. You just wait till that short wave's over and then the good

---

1   The 1935 Writers' Congress in Paris.

hats appear—the serious ones; you simply must have one of those. Yes, of course there's a third wave later in the season, as now; it consists partly of failures, rather cheap. It's not safe to buy one of them, but it's not at all safe to buy from the first wave, either.'

All this carefully-adjusted wisdom uttered by this lightly-elegant young woman in a voice of homely realism; a voice without accent, but slightly coloured by her recent pan-European years.

1948

LESBIA HARFORD
1891–1927

One of the first women to graduate in law at the University of Melbourne, Lesbia Keogh was involved in the anti-conscription movement. Attracted to the radical labour movement the Industrial Workers of the World (known as the 'Wobblies'), she followed the policy of direct action and was, at various times, an art teacher, a servant and a factory worker. She was the first female vice-president of the Clothing Trades Union's industry section in Victoria. After entertaining significant relationships with activist Guido Baracchi and university tutor Katie Lush, she ended up unexpectedly marrying post-impressionist artist Pat Harford. Lesbia Harford's poetry remained largely unpublished during her lifetime although some would feature in a special issue of *Birth* edited by her friend Nettie Palmer (qv) in 1921. Suffering from defective heart valves, Harford died prematurely.

While a small selection of her poetry would be published by Palmer in 1941, it was not until the 1985 publication of Drusilla Modjeska (qv) and Marjorie Pizer's more extensive collection, *The Poems of Lesbia Harford*, that Harford's work began receiving critical recognition. Her novel, *The Invaluable Mystery*, was located and published in 1987. Often minimalist, Harford's poetry focuses on the everyday, the colloquial and the particular. It is underwritten by a sharp awareness of class oppression and vividly represents aspects of female sexuality. Her novel portrays Australia's culture of suspicion during the First World War and explores the emergence of female independence. *AV*

In the Public Library

Standing on tiptoe, head back, eyes and arm
Upraised, Kate groped to reach the higher shelf.
Her sleeve slid up like darkness in alarm
At gleam of dawn. Impatient with herself
For lack of inches, careless of her charm,   5
She strained to grasp a volume; then she turned
Back to her chair, an unforgetful Eve
Still snatching at the fruit for which she yearned
In Eden. She read idly to relieve
The forehead where her daylong studies burned,   10

Tales of an uncrowned queen who fed her child
On poisons, till death lurked, in act to spring,
Between the girl's breasts; who with soft mouth smiled
With soft eyes tempted the usurping King
Then dealt him death in kisses. Kate had piled   15
Her books three deep before her and across
This barricade she watched an old man nod
Over a dirty paper, until loss
Of life seemed better than possession. Shod
With kisses death might skid like thistle floss   20
Down windy slides, might prove at heart as gay
As Cinderella in glass slippers.
Life goes awkwardly so sandalled. Had decay
Been the girl's gift in that Miltonic strife
She would have rivalled God, Kate thought. A ray   25
Of sunshine carrying gilded flecks of dust
And minutes bright with fancies, touched her hair
To powder it with gold and silver, just
As if being now admitted she should wear
The scholar's wig, colleague of those whose lust   30
For beauty hidden in an outworn tongue
Had made it possible for her to read
Tales that were fathered in Arabia, sung
By trouvères and forgotten with their creed
Of love and magic. Beams that strayed among   35
Kate's fingers lit a rosy lantern there
To glow in twilight. Suddenly afraid
She seemed to see her beauty in a flare
Of light from hell. A throng of devils swayed
Before her, devils that had learned to wear   40
The shape of scholar, poet, libertine.
They smiled, frowned, beckoned, swearing to estrange
Kate from reflection that her soul had been
Slain by her woman's body or would change
From contact with it to a thing unclean.   45
Woman was made to worship man, they preached,
Not God, to serve earth's purpose, not to roam
The heavens of thought … A factory whistle screeched,
Someone turned up the lights. On her way home
Kate wondered in what mode were angels breeched.   50

1912/1985

'My heart is a pomegranate full of sweet fancies'

My heart is a pomegranate full of sweet fancies,
To crimson with sunshine and swell with the dew.
Warmed by your smile and besprent by your glances
See, it has opened for you!

1914/1985

Machinist's Song

The foot of my machine
Sails up and down
Upon the blue of this fine lady's gown.

Sail quickly, little boat,
With gifts for me,—   5
Night and the goldy streets and liberty.

1917/1953

Grotesque

My
Man
Says
I weigh about four ounces,
Says I must have hollow legs.   5
And then say I,
'Yes.
I've hollow legs and a hollow soul and body.
There is nothing left of me.
You've burnt me dry.   10

You
Have
Run
Through all my veins in fever,
Through my soul in fever for   15
An endless time.
Why,
This small body is like an empty snail shell
All the living soul of it
Burnt out in lime.'   20

1918/1974

MARTIN BOYD
1893–1972

Martin à Beckett Boyd was born in Lucerne, Switzerland, while his peripatetic family was travelling; his parents were Arthur Merric Boyd and Emma Minnie Boyd, both Australian artists of note. Two of Boyd's brothers were also artists—Merric a potter, Penleigh a painter—and he was the uncle of the major Australian painter Arthur Boyd, while his great-grandfather William à Beckett was the first Chief Justice of Victoria.

The story of this gifted and flamboyant family is retold a number of times in Boyd's fiction and again in two books by Brenda Niall, *Martin Boyd: A life* (1988) and *The Boyds: A family biography* (2002). Boyd himself is the author of two autobiographical works, *A Single Flame* (1939) and *Day of My Delight: An Anglo-Australian memoir* (1965). Boyd grew up travelling with his family between Australia and Europe and served in the Royal Flying Corps during the First World War, an experience that was to make him a pacifist. His novel *The Montforts* (1928) was published under the pseudonym Martin Mills.

He published *Lucinda Brayford*, one of his best-known works and regarded by many critics as his most accomplished novel, in 1946, and shortly afterwards returned home to Australia from England, buying back the old Boyd family home at Berwick in Victoria. There he found his grandmother's old diaries, a trove of family secrets that led directly to the writing of the 'Langton Quartet'. This is a tetralogy in which the young narrator, Guy, tells the story of his family from various angles: *The Cardboard Crown* (1952), *A Difficult Young Man* (1955), *Outbreak of Love* (1957) and *When Blackbirds Sing* (1962).

Boyd's work was unusual for its time in that his view was far from the radical nationalism of many of his Australian contemporaries. He favoured the retention of what he saw as civilised European values in an Australian setting, an argument made implicitly or explicitly in several of his novels. He was also concerned with the tension between individual freedoms and the external pressure, sometimes based on dubious values, placed on individuals by familial or social norms and rules. *KG*

From *Outbreak of Love*
Chapter 10

Diana was waiting in the house at Brighton for Russell to call for her. She felt wretched. She had let the two servants go out after tea, and at six o'clock Wolfie went to Melbourne, ostensibly to a 'Saturday night reunion of musicians', a fixture for many years, which she now realized had been a cover for visits to Mrs Montaubyn or her precursors. She half hoped that tonight he *was* going to see her, as it would give stronger justification to her own departure, but she was not cheered by the possibility.

He came to tell her that he was leaving. He did not look smart, but as usual like a village boy who has tidied himself up under protest to go to Sunday School. Normally she supervised his dressing, fixing his collar, pulling his coat straight, and brushing him down; but since the ball she had left him to himself, and he showed signs of her neglect.

A week or so earlier she had lent him a pound as he was setting out on one of these jaunts. He now took a handful of coins from his pocket and picked out from them the only sovereign. He handed it to her saying: 'Here is the pound I borrowed from you.'

It was unusual for him to return money he had borrowed from her, unless she asked for it, which she only did in an emergency. Clearly he wanted to end their strained relations and to be reconciled. Perhaps, after all, he was not going to Mrs Montaubyn, as, if he gave her the pound it would only leave him a few shillings, not enough to take her out to dinner. She felt confused and ashamed and did not want to take anything from him even though it was her own.

'Oh, don't give it to me now,' she said.

'I may have it?' asked Wolfie, looking pleased, both at keeping the money and at a sign that Diana was relenting. This sudden change from an air of pompous guilt to naïve pleasure was so characteristic of him that it made vivid in a moment all the long years of their life together, and the anger which she had been laboriously sustaining, became dangerously weak. She thought: 'This may be the last time I'll see him,' and she went with him to the door, and then, impulsively, she kissed him.

She turned into the empty house which she was to leave in an hour. She had been quietly packing in her room since tea-time. She was not taking many things. The clothes she left behind could be given away. She had written a note for Wolfie and a letter to Josie, and she had nothing to do but wait.

She thought she had been idiotic to kiss Wolfie, and yet she could not feel sorry that she had done so. It would make him think that she was utterly treacherous, when he came back and found her gone. Josie too must think her treacherous, when she found that she had said good-bye to her as if for four days, when it was for a year or perhaps longer. For twenty years she had been the strength and stay of the family. They would be bewildered to find her gone. She felt as if she had arranged to commit a murder.

She went round the house saying good-bye to the different rooms, and in every one she was overwhelmed with memories. She went into Josie's room, and into Daisy's and again felt in them all the love and amusement and anxiety the children had given her. In an hour it would be ended for ever. 'I can't go,' she told herself. She certainly would not be able to go, she thought, if she continued to give way to these feelings, and she returned to the drawing-room where she lighted a jet in the chandelier, and sat down to reason with herself.

'What will happen if I don't go?' she thought. 'Wolfie will never change. People will go on pitying me, Josie may marry soon, and I shall be here alone. Russell offers me the most wonderful life, the sort of life I have always wanted. We get on perfectly together. It would be outrageous to fail him after all his kindness.' She repeated these arguments to herself, but they did not change her feelings. 'It has been arranged too suddenly,' she thought. 'I really need more time to become used to the idea.' But it was she who had wanted to make the sharp break. 'I don't know myself,' she thought, and her wretchedness came near to panic.

She could not sit still, and she began to walk about the darkening house again. The walls seemed to reproach her, to send out emanations they had absorbed from the children's lives. All their laughter and their pains seemed to have been absorbed into their surroundings, into the things they used.

The house was full of ghosts, but ghosts of the living, and of the living who were most dear to her. They poured on her, as on myself at Westhill forty years later, with full hands, their treasures and their calamities. It was not, as it has been claimed a house should be, a machine to live in. It was a material substance that absorbed life from the lives and feelings of those who lived in it, and which gave out again to console them for vanished time, the life that it had absorbed. When she left it, she would cut her life in half, and with a sense of desperation, she went from room to room, choosing various small objects to take with her so that her loss would not be absolute. From Josie's room she took a small watercolour of Westhill. It was really Josie's but when she found it had gone, she would know, Diana hoped, that the theft was an act of love. She thought of taking the reputed Parmigiano from the drawing-room, but it might be valuable, and she thought it might be a mean thing to do. There had always been speculations and jokes about it, and she could imagine their dismay, not at its loss, but at some kind of repudiation of one of those many trivial causes of amusement which together added so much to the substance of family affection, when they came in and said: 'Mummy's taken the Old Master.'

From Wolfie's room she took a blue vase which Harry had given her at Christmas when he was twelve, and she collected photographs of the children from various parts of the house. She took a Florentine pottery bowl which her mother had brought back from Europe for her when she was a child. It was of no value and she would probably be going where she could buy hundreds of such things, but she had known it nearly all her life and it would help to give her a feeling of continuity. She put these things on her bed and looked at the pitiful array; all the material evidence she would have of her past life.

She tried to encourage herself by feeling angry with Wolfie, but she did not feel angry, even when she thought of Mrs Montaubyn. Then she thought of Russell, all his attractive qualities and his kindness, but they seemed irrelevant. She could only think of the children and of her life being cut in half. [. . .]

1957

JEAN DEVANNY
1894–1962

A feminist and communist activist, Jean Devanny produced fifteen novels between 1926 and 1949, long unpublished works on gender, sexuality and race relations, much journalism for the left press on topics such as birth control and censorship, regular film reviews for the *Worker's Weekly*, activist writing and speeches, two volumes of atmospheric travel writing, as well as a play and an autobiography published after her death.

Born Jane Crook in a small mining town in New Zealand, she got married in 1911 to miner Hal Devanny, with whom she had three children. Her first novel, *The Butcher Shop* (1926), about a New Zealand sheep station, was banned for its exploration of women's sexuality outside marriage and caused a minor scandal. A number of highly original New Woman novels and a volume of short stories were published by Duckworth in London. In 1929 the family migrated to Sydney. There, all of them joined the Communist Party of Australia.

Devanny was a charismatic platform agitator and organiser, and divided her time between writing and Party work for most of the rest of her life. Her Australian novels continue her interest in women's experience and sexuality, interleaved with an interest in the politics of class conflict and the history of race relations. *Sugar Heaven*, about the 1935 cane-cutters' strike in North Queensland, where Devanny moved in the mid-1930s, is regarded by many as Australia's most successful socialist realist novel. *NM*

From *Sugar Heaven*
Chapter 4

So passed Saturday. Sunday followed with Hefty in the clutches of a pervasive restlessness connected with the close approach of the cut. Dulcie sweated with the winter heat and tried valiantly to bring order out of the chaos of her mind. Shame was still uppermost in the ruffled reservoir of her emotions. Shame, not so much at what Hefty had done, as at her own eventual acquiescence and response. When Hefty's warm blue eyes met hers, expressing his heightened love, she turned from him swiftly, feeling bad. He was considerate and extraordinarily tender. He couldn't keep still that day. 'I'm full of silk,' he told her, knotting the muscles of his great arms and swinging the heavy cane knife.

'I suppose you're glad to start work,' Dulcie remarked. 'I like work, too. At least, I like some kinds of work. I hated being a waitress. There's nothing to it. I'd like to be a farmer. A cane farmer, I think.'

'Yes, work's great if you've got a choice. God knows why I feel like this. It's energy, I suppose. I've had a pretty good spin in the cane. Been cutting for seven years now and am good for several seasons yet. Most cutters are done at my age.'

'Done? Why?'

'You wait and see. But today I can't get into it quick enough. Six months loafing puts the silk into a man. Yet I dread it, too.' Simply. 'You needn't put me out in the morning. You wouldn't know how to fill in your days if you rose so early. Fill my tucker tin tonight and I'll get my own breakfast.'

'No. My job is the home. I'll put you out.'

The amount of food he took for smoko amazed her. Since the first run was only a mile and a half away his bicycle would enable him to come home for lunch. 'Get's a pound of steak for lunch, Dulce. And how about some cakes for afternoon smoko?'

It appeared that cutters ate five full meals a day. The hours of work varied according to the weather. To begin with, Hefty's gang would cut from seven till twelve in the morning and from two till five later. 'I don't know how you can digest such an amount of food,' Dulcie commented.

'Come out in the paddocks some day and you'll find out. The amount of food we eat is one reason why there are no old men on the knife. The digestive system won't stand the racket. In the slack men lacking the stomach of an ostrich get ill. The body works like a machine during the cut and when the slack comes we slump to half food and idleness. You heard Mowls say that he'd about "had it." He's been one of the champions in the paddocks. To cut with Mowls a man had to *cut*. He was one of a gang of three that cut and loaded, in rough scrub land, thirteen tons a day for three and a half days, in the Tully. That's a record. George Hinkler, Bert Hinkler's brother, was one of the three.'

'Oh!' Dulcie conceived a new respect for their neighbour. 'Yet he's not a very big man. Not nearly as big as you.'

'That's so. The biggest men are not always the best cutters. Some chaps are muscle bound. Seems to be a matter of energy and stamina, and organisation, than muscle. It's a pleasure to see Mowls cut. Sorta poetry of motion.'

It seemed that Hefty had to carry a change of flannels to the paddocks, too; to change into when they loaded the cane. 'The one we wear cutting gets saturated with sweat,' he explained. 'The bundles of heavy cane chafe the shoulder and if we don't change the sweat and dirt gets us in a nice mess of festers and sores.'

'How can you bear to work in heavy flannel in this heat?' Dulcie, watching him cut thick sandwiches for his smoko before retiring at eight o'clock that night (her finger was still sore), found herself interested in these aspects of a cane cutter's life; an interest she welcomed as relief from the emotional stress which had beset her.

'Suits me. Some chaps work in a Jackie Howe and shorts—.'

'What on earth is that?'

'A Jackie Howe? This.' He indicated the athletic singlet he wore. 'Lots of chaps cut with bare feet, too, but I'm wise to that. It's asking for Weil's disease.'

'Weil's disease. That's what you and Mr. Mowls were discussing yesterday—.' Dulcie's inquiries came to an abrupt conclusion as the phrase

'Weil's disease' revived the implications of yesterday's discussion. Her friendly interest changed to restraint. 'My leg pains me,' she added briefly. 'I'll attend to it and go to bed.' She went into the other room.

Hefty packed the sandwiches into his tucker tin, placed it with his tea billy and followed her.

When the alarm clock turned him out of bed at 5.30 in the morning the powerful pressure of traditional concepts urged Dulcie to activity, too. However, she saw plainly enough that Hefty was well able to prepare his own breakfast so agreed with him that she might as well stay in bed for the future. While he fried the bacon and eggs she stood in the doorway and watched the covers of night lift from the body of the cane. A gentle sighing seemed to emanate from it; a waking fluttering of breath. Broad bands of rose satin were painted by the heralds of the sunrise on the encircling belt of dark hills. The air was cool.

'She's on the table.' Hefty came and stood beside her. 'Look at it! It's alive, begod! Waiting for the knife.'

Dulcie glanced at him curiously. Did he hate the cane or did he love it? He was drawing her over to the table, his arm about her shoulders. 'Let's eat. I'll say I'll need it.'

At 6.30 he was gone with Mowls, leaving his wife blankly facing her first day in the rôle of a cane cutter's wife. What could one do? She would skip over the household duties in an hour. And then nothing till twelve; and after that nothing from two till five. She must get books. Was there a library in Silkwood? Mrs. Mowls would know.

A practical talk with Gladys disclosed the possibilities of cultural and social life in the place. A few books were available in a store in Old Silkwood. Gladys played a part in the Country Women's Association, which occasionally ran dances. Also, during the season the cutters ran a dance every Saturday night in Smith's hall near the station. Did Dulcie dance?

'Oh, yes. But Hefty doesn't.'

'Neither does Jake. But that's nothing to worry about here. There are always three men to one woman.'

Hefty and Mowls joined the rest of their gang at the cutting paddock a few minutes before the time to start. The ganger shook hands with Lee, whom he had not seen since last season, and introduced two new-comers, both Jugoslavs from Cairns. Then: 'Let's go,' he said shortly.

Each man took his place at the head of a row of cane; the left hand grasped the thick stick; the broad-bladed short-handled knife was wielded to sever the stalk on a level with the ground. No time for waste motion. Another stroke with the knife severed the top; two downward motions cleaned the trash from the stalk. The fifth motion heaped the sticks. Bundles of wine-red Badilla were bedded down in rows on the green trash, to be loaded in due time onto the trucks sent out by the cane inspector from the mill.

With automatic precision the knives rose and fell, the hook which was its head raking any undergrowth clear. The 'hairy Mary', fine prickles which clothed leaves and cane, penetrated every pore of the cutters' arms and hands. Some faces, too, for individuals cut differently. Some burrowed into the cane and consequently sustained innumerable cuts and scratches on face, neck and arms. Some cut from beneath; others bent the stick down and smashed through it from above. For heavy 'outside' cane, rich and swollen with the caresses of the sun from top to stool, at times three blows were needed.

No talk; no rest. The cutters paced each other. A heavy drill or row next to a light one was the general order. The best strike in the plants took the growth and the heavy row took the sun. This meant that the man on the light drill, all other things being equal, would finish ahead of his mate on the heavy drill, unless the latter exerted herculean efforts. The pride of the cutter demanded equal work. A 'lag' despised himself. When the man on the heavy drill got onto the light one he 'got his own back'. Two men pacing each other in this way would sool the whole gang on.

Before long the cutters' bodies streamed with filthy sweat that stung as it dribbled into the scratches and cuts. Backs suffered the exaggerated ache of the new season's time. Cut low! Cut lower! Cut right into the ground! It's every last vestige of sugar content harvested or the 'sack'. Gone the days when stumps six inches high could be left to burn with the trash. Hack into the roots, now! The heavy sugar content lies low in the stick. Big Boss Ratoon needs a clean stump to spring from! And Big Boss Sugar Baron hears the sweet chink of gold emanate from clean fields!

Dust from the cane filled the mouth, filled the nostrils, as the cutter drew his fierce breath. It got into the back of the throat and forced constant raucous coughing. With the progress of the season the mass of the cutters would suffer heartburn in dry weather, the result of the dust and the bending. It got into the stomach and caused havoc there.

Smoko came at nine-thirty. The ganger threw down the knife and shouted. Nine men slouched to their tucker tins and dropped limply beside them. They grabbed at their billies and gustily swilled great draughts of tea. They spat and they coughed. They disposed of the contents of the tins. Their sweat dappled the scarlet lining of the trash upon which they sprawled. Thirty minutes and then back to the knife. 'Trucks will be in about three o'clock,' said the ganger as he rose. The man beside him picked his teeth with the sharp end of a stick, then unloosed a stream of filth. Turgid obscenity expressed as nothing else could the squalor, the stresses, the brutal finality of life on the end of the knife.

1936

ROBERT MENZIES
1894–1978

Prime minister of Australia (1939–1941 and 1949–1966), Robert (Bob) Gordon Menzies, in his famous speech from 1942, articulates the rhetorical power given to 'middle Australia'. It was delivered to wartime Australia from the demoralised back benches, after Menzies had lost power to the Curtin Labor government. An attempt to deny the influence of class in Australia, it also posited the middle class as a forgotten force in Australian politics, carving out its interests as separate from working-class organisation, and emphasising home life, moral values and individualism as the 'backbone of this country'.

While interested in literature, Menzies is not always remembered as a friend to Australian writers. While he was prime minister, his government's anti-communist stance saw recipients of Commonwealth Literary Fund grants threatened with retraction of funding and extensive surveillance of other writers by ASIO through the 1950s and '60s. *NM*

The Forgotten People

Quite recently, a bishop wrote a letter to a great daily newspaper. His theme was the importance of doing justice to the workers. His belief, apparently, was that the workers are those who work with their hands. He sought to divide the people of Australia into classes. He was obviously suffering from what has for years seemed to me to be our greatest political disease—the disease of thinking that the community is divided into the rich and relatively idle, and the laborious poor, and that every social and political controversy can be resolved into the question: what side are you on?

Now, the last thing that I want to do is to commence or take part in a false war of this kind. In a country like Australia the class war must always be a false war. But if we are to talk of classes, then the time has come to say something of the forgotten class—the middle class—those people who are constantly in danger of being ground between the upper and the nether millstones of the false class war; the middle class who, properly regarded, represent the backbone of this country.

We do not have classes here as in England, and therefore the terms do not mean the same; so I must define what I mean when I use the expression 'the middle class'. Let me first define it by exclusion. I exclude at one end of the scale the rich and powerful: those who control great funds and enterprises, and are as a rule able to protect themselves. I exclude at the other end of the scale the mass of unskilled people, almost invariably well-organised, and with their wages and conditions safeguarded by popular law.

These exclusions being made, I include the intervening range—the kind of people I myself represent in Parliament—salary-earners, shopkeepers, skilled artisans, professional men and women, farmers, and so on. These are, in the political and economic sense, the middle class. They are for the most part unorganised and unselfconscious. They are envied by those whose social benefits are largely obtained by taxing them. They are not rich enough to have individual power. They are taken for granted by each political party in turn. They are not sufficiently lacking in individualism to be organised for what in these days we call 'pressure politics'. And yet, as I have said, they are the backbone of the nation.

Now, what is the value of this middle class, so defined and described? First, it has 'a stake in the country'. It has responsibility for homes—homes material, homes human, homes spiritual.

I do not believe that the real life of this nation is to be found either in great luxury hotels and the petty gossip of so-called fashionable suburbs, or in the officialdom of organised masses. It is to be found in the homes of people who are nameless and unadvertised, and who, whatever their individual religious conviction or dogma, see in their children their greatest contribution to the immortality of their race. The home is the foundation of sanity and sobriety; it is the indispensable condition of continuity; its health determines the health of society as a whole. The material home represents the concrete expression of the habits of frugality and saving 'for a home of our own'. Your advanced socialist may rage against private property even while he acquires it; but one of the best instincts in us is that which induces us to have one little piece of earth with a house and a garden which is ours: to which we can withdraw, in which we can be among our friends, into which no stranger may come against our will.

If you consider it, you will see that if, as in the old saying, 'the Englishman's home is his castle', it is this very fact that leads on to the conclusion that he who seeks to violate that law by violating the soil of England must be repelled and defeated. National patriotism, in other words, inevitably springs from the instinct to defend and preserve our own homes.

Then we have homes human: a great house, full of loneliness, is not a home. 'Stone walls do not a prison make', nor do they make a house. They may equally make a stable or a piggery. Brick walls, dormer windows and central heating need not make more than an hotel. My home is where my wife and children are. The instinct to be with them is the great instinct of civilised man; the instinct to give them a chance in life—to make them not leaners but lifters—is a noble instinct.

And, finally, we have homes spiritual. Human nature is at its greatest when it combines dependence upon God with independence of man.

We offer no affront—on the contrary we have nothing but the warmest human compassion—for those whom fate has compelled to live upon the bounty of the state, when we say that the greatest element in a strong people is a fierce independence of spirit. This is the only *real* freedom, and it has as its corollary a brave acceptance of unclouded individual responsibility.

Second, the middle class, more than any other, provides the intelligent ambition which is the motive power of human progress. The idea entertained by many people that, in a well-constituted world, we shall all live on the state is the quintessence of madness, for what is the state but *us*? We collectively must provide what we individually receive. The great vice of democracy—a vice which is exacting a bitter retribution from it at this moment—is that for a generation we have been busy getting ourselves on to the list of beneficiaries and removing ourselves from the list of contributors, as if somewhere there was somebody else's wealth and somebody else's effort on which we could thrive.

To discourage ambition, to envy success, to hate achieved superiority, to distrust independent thought, to sneer at and impute false motives to public service, these are the maladies of modern democracy, and of Australian democracy in particular. Yet ambition, effort, thinking, and readiness to serve are not only the design and objectives of self-government but are the essential conditions of its success. Where do we find these great elements most commonly? Among the defensive and comfortable rich? Among the unthinking and unskilled mass? Or among what I have called 'the middle class'?

Third, the middle class provides more than perhaps any other the intellectual life which marks us off from the beast: the life which finds room for literature, for the arts, for science, for medicine and the law. Consider the case of literature and art. Could these survive as a department of state? Are we to publish our poets according to their political colour? Is the state to decree surrealism because surrealism gets a heavy vote in a key electorate? The truth is that no great book was ever written and no great picture ever painted by the clock or according to civil service rules. These things are done by *man*, not men. You cannot regiment them. They require opportunity, and sometimes leisure. The artist, if he is to live, must have a buyer; the writer, an audience. He finds them among frugal people to whom the margin above bare living means a chance to reach out a little towards that heaven which is just beyond our grasp.

Fourth, this middle class maintains and fills the higher schools and universities, and so feeds the lamp of learning. What are schools for? To train people for examinations? To enable people to comply with the law? Or to produce developed men and women?

Are the universities mere technical schools, or have they as one of their functions the preservation of pure learning, bringing in its train not merely riches for the imagination but a comparative sense for the mind, and leading to what we need so badly—the recognition of values which are other than pecuniary?

Now, have we realised and recognised these things, or is most of our policy designed to discourage or penalise thrift, to encourage dependence on the state, to bring about a dull equality on the fantastic idea that all men are equal in mind and needs and deserts: to level down by taking the mountains out of the landscape, to weigh men according to their political organisations and power—as votes and not as human beings? These are formidable questions, and we cannot escape from answering them if there is really to be a new order for the world.

I have been actively engaged in politics for fourteen years. In that period I cannot readily recall many occasions upon which any policy was pursued which was designed to help the thrifty, to encourage independence, to recognise the divine and valuable variations of men's minds. On the contrary, there have been many instances in which the votes of the thriftless have been used to defeat the thrifty. On occasions of emergency, as in the depression and during the present war, we have hastened to make it clear that the provision made by a man for his own retirement and old age is not half as sacrosanct as the provision which the state would have made for him had he never saved at all.

We have talked of income from savings as if it possessed a somewhat discreditable character. We have taxed it more and more heavily. We have spoken slightingly of the earnings of interest at the very moment when we have advocated new pensions and social schemes. I have myself heard a minister of power and influence declare that no deprivation is suffered by a man if he still has the means to fill his stomach, clothe his body and keep a roof over his head! And yet the truth is, that frugal people who strive for and obtain the margin above these materially necessary things are the whole foundation of a really active and developing national life.

Are you looking forward to a breed of men after the war who will have become boneless wonders? Leaners grow flabby; lifters grow muscles. Men without ambition readily become slaves. Indeed, there is much more slavery in Australia than most people imagine. How many hundreds of thousands of us are slaves to greed, to fear, to newspapers, to public opinion—represented by the accumulated views of our neighbours? Landless men smell the vapours of the street corner. Landed men smell the brown earth, and plant their feet upon it and know that it is good.

To all of this many of my friends will retort: 'Ah, that's all very well, but when this war is over the levellers will have won the day.' My answer is that, on the contrary, men will come out of this war as gloriously unequal in many things as when they entered it. Much wealth will have been destroyed; inherited riches will be suspect; a fellowship of suffering, if we really experience it, will have opened many hearts and perhaps closed many mouths. Many great edifices will have fallen, and we will be able to study foundations as never before, because war will have exposed them.

But I don't believe that we shall come out into the overlordship of an all-powerful state on whose benevolence we shall live, spineless and effortless—a state which will dole out bread and ideas with neatly regulated accuracy; where we shall all have our dividend without subscribing our capital; where the government, that almost deity, will nurse us and rear us and maintain us and pension us and bury us; where we shall all be civil servants, and all presumably, since we are equal, heads of departments.

If the new world is to be a world of men we must be not pallid and bloodless ghosts, but a community of people whose motto shall be, 'To strive, to seek, to find, and not to yield.'[1] Individual enterprise must drive us forward. That does not mean that we are to return to the old and selfish notions of laissez faire. The functions of the state will be much more than merely keeping the ring within which the competitors will fight. Our social and industrial obligations will be increased. There will be more law, not less; more control, not less.

But what really happens to us will depend on how many people we have who are of the great and sober and dynamic middle class—the strivers, the planners, the ambitious ones. We shall destroy them at our peril.

1942

A.B. FACEY
1894–1982

A.B. Facey's fame is based on his autobiography, *A Fortunate Life* (1981). The work has been adapted into a children's book, stage play, audio book and television film. It has been translated into Chinese and was voted as Australia's tenth favourite book in the ABC television program *Australia's Favourite Book* (2004).

A Fortunate Life, written in plain, laconic language, details the harsh conditions of Facey's childhood, his wartime experiences, and his life as a farmer and unionist. After the death of their father, Facey and his siblings were left in the care of their grandmother. Moving to Western Australia in 1899, Facey (who was born in Victoria) went to work at the age of eight, beginning a life often marked by hardship and itinerant employment. Facey served in the First World War, and after being wounded at Gallipoli returned to Perth in 1915. Two of his brothers died in the war, including one at Gallipoli. He taught himself to read and write, and began making notes for what became *A Fortunate Life*. DM

From *A Fortunate Life*
Chapter LV: Fighting On

Our position in the trenches became a stalemate, a kind of cat-and-mouse affair. We had to work hard digging new trenches. Some of the trenches were tunnelled and we carried the dirt out in small bags, tipping it into the valleys and gullies. The Turks would not know about the tunnelled trenches until they were finished and opened up. After we had carried all the earth

---

1   From Alfred, Lord Tennyson (1809–92), 'Ulysses'.

out from underground, we would open them at night and put sand-bags in front to form parapets every twenty feet or so. When daylight came the Turks would see that our line had moved closer. They would shell hell out of the new trench for a day or two.

It was during one of these shellings that I received a nasty wound. A piece of shrapnel struck me on the left side of my face, knocking four of my teeth out and loosening several others. It made a cut some three inches long, level with my teeth, then embedded itself in the roof of my mouth and right jaw, loosening some teeth on that side as well.

I had to go to our frontline dressing-station. The doctor there had a look at my face, and after a lot of pulling and working the shrapnel about, he got the piece out. However, my mouth was in a mess so I was sent down to the beach dressing-station near where the first landing took place. There another doctor made an examination, then said he would have to pull out the broken teeth and the very loose ones. 'Or,' he said, 'better still, we will send you over to the hospital ship and they can fix you up.' I asked the doctor not to send me away and suggested that he go ahead and pull the teeth himself as I didn't want to leave my mates—we were very short-handed. In fact, my battalion was only half strength at that time. I said that it hadn't knocked me out and I felt okay, only a little sore.

After speaking to another doctor he agreed to pull the teeth out there. Three big strapping orderlies held me in a sitting position, and without any anaesthetic, the doctor, who was a big strong man, pulled the teeth out. This was very painful while it lasted. The doctor washed my mouth out with some kind of solution and made me lie on a bunk in a dugout for about two hours while the bleeding eased. He then painted my mouth and the wounds with some kind of antiseptic paste and made a cradle out of bandages to hold my face and jaws firmly in place. He said I would only be allowed to have liquid foods until my face healed. I was then allowed back to join my mates.

I looked a fright; the bandage cradle covered nearly all my head. The doctor gave me several tins of condensed sweetened milk and some soft biscuits and ordered me to report back every two days. My face healed quickly and at the end of two weeks I was nearly okay again. They put some kind of strapping around the left side of my face covering the scar and gave me an ointment to put on the scar twice a day. With this treatment I was able to remain at the front and cope with the bully beef and hard dog biscuits again.

It was some time in June when the fourth and fifth reinforcements arrived and my brother Roy was with the fourth. He thought I was in 'A' Company and asked to be drafted there. When he found out that I was with 'D' Company he made an application to be transferred. It was an army regulation that when a transfer of this nature was required the older brother had to make the application. Roy's officer told him that it would take about fourteen days before this could be arranged and the elder brother had to move to the younger.

The routine continued: observing, tunnelling, a little sniping, killing lice, doing water-carrying duty, and guarding the donkey trains carrying food and ammunition up to our position.

On a date I will always remember—the twenty-eighth of June—word came through to our Commanding Officer to the effect that the English were hard-pressed at Cape Helles a few miles right of our position, and we were to make an attack on the Turks in front of our trenches to draw them away.

At some time in the afternoon we got an order to go over the top and attack the Turks. I was in the first lot to go. We had to run down hill as our trenches were on a higher position than the Turks'. Below the hill there was a dry watercourse—it was some distance from our position but only about thirty yards from the Turks' trenches. Some twenty of us reached this watercourse and we were quite safe there from rifle-fire, but the Turks gave us a bad time with shelling. A lot of the boys were killed and many wounded. We waited for the shelling to ease off before we charged the Turks' trenches. Just before we made our move we picked up a signal to retire back as we had achieved our objective—the Turks had broken off the attack on the English at Cape Helles. We had to get back as best we could and were ordered not to take any unnecessary risks. We decided to stay in the watercourse until after dark as we were sitting ducks in the daylight.

We got back safely to our fire-line after dark (that is our little group), and on arriving back I was told that Roy had been killed. He and his mate had been killed by the same shell.

This was a terrible blow to me. I had lost a lot of my mates and seen a lot of men die, but Roy was my brother. We had been through a lot together and always got along fine. I had been looking forward to having him with me.

I helped to bury Roy and fifteen of our mates who had also been killed on the twenty-eighth. We put them in a grave side by side on the edge of a clearing we called Shell Green. Roy was in pieces when they found him. We put him together as best we could—I can remember carrying a leg—it was terrible. He was to have been transferred to my company the next day.

A few days before Roy was killed, my eldest brother Joseph had arrived. He had enlisted with the Tenth Light Horse and they had gone to Egypt with their horses, but owing to the shortage of men for Gallipoli, the authorities turned them into infantry to help us out. My job was now to find him and tell him the terrible news.

My Commanding Officer gave me permission to visit Joseph. I found out from Headquarters at the beach where he was; his unit had taken up a position away to the left of our bridge-head at a high, hilly spot called the Apex. He was very upset and swore revenge for Roy. He promised to come and see me later.

July was passing and Joseph hadn't turned up—my battalion was ordered out of the trenches for a few days' rest and our position near Lone Pine was held by another battalion. We rested under the protection of a steep cliff in dugouts prepared for the purpose, just above Shell Green where Roy was buried.

While we were resting I got permission to visit Joseph again. I found him without any trouble and asked why he hadn't come to see me. He said that his Commanding Officer had given him permission to visit me but while he was walking up along the valley that leads to Lone Pine, a huge shell had come from nowhere and exploded into the hill on the left, sending tons of earth and rocks tumbling down into the valley. 'That was enough for me,' he said, 'so I came back.' I explained that this often happened. Every day those shells (they were thirteen-inch shells and made a hell of an explosion) came over. They seemed to come from a fort on the narrows some seven or eight miles away and were trying to silence the battery of Australian Artillery that had dug in on top of the hill on the left-hand side of the valley. (This battery was called Browne's Battery, after its Commanding Officer. The Turks had tried all kinds of shelling to put it out of action.)

We weren't safe even while we were resting. Browne's Battery used to fire over our resting place and one day one of their eighteen pounders had a premature burst, killing and wounding twenty-one of our mates.

When we were resting we were allowed to go down to the beach and have a swim, but only near Headquarters. The beach nearest to our position was within range of Turkish snipers and would have been too dangerous. The bay was continually under shell-fire but this didn't worry us because we could hear a shrapnel shell coming and would dive under the water just before it exploded.

We used to go on these swimming trips a section at a time under the command of a sergeant. We enjoyed them very much and were able to get ourselves clean.

One day we got a shock. It had been reported that several men who had gone on one of these trips hadn't returned. Army Headquarters had set up a military police patrol, whose job was to guard the supplies and Headquarters, and also to watch the beaches at night. We heard talk that the Turks had tried to land spies from the sea under the cover of darkness, using small row-boats.

But one day, when our section was swimming near the end of a jetty, a sailor suddenly called a warning to us to get out of the water quickly. I was the furthest away from the end of the jetty and he yelled to me to look around. I looked and spotted something—the head and body of a creature I had never seen before. It had, I thought at a glance, one big eye! It was moving towards me. I gave a terrified yell of, 'Look—get out!!' Being a good, strong swimmer it didn't take me many seconds before I reached the end of the jetty and climbed on. My mates had done the same, and when we were all safe on the jetty I asked the sailor what it was. He said it was what they called an 'old man squid'. He told us that the eye I had seen was really two eyes but that it looked like one. The body was about three feet across and around and it had very long tentacles with suckers all along them. The sailor said that if it got its tentacles around you it would pull you under.

We decided that that was probably what happened to the missing men. That was the last time our section went swimming at Gallipoli.

1981

MARJORIE BARNARD
1897–1987

Perhaps best known for the fiction she co-authored with Flora Eldershaw under the pseudonym M. Barnard Eldershaw (qv), Marjorie Barnard published short stories, history, literary criticism and biography under her own name. She referred to her short stories as 'the most private sector of my literary output' and struggled across the 1930s to perfect this challenging literary form. *The Persimmon Tree and Other Stories* (1943) represents her most accomplished writing. Although she sought advice from both Vance Palmer and Frank Dalby Davison on short fiction and modelled her own work after theirs, her stories largely depart from their nationalist-inspired rural subject matter. Instead, she explores the realms of femininity and modernity against a largely urban backdrop. Educated at the University of Sydney, Barnard maintained strong interests in history and in debates concerning the formation of a national literature. She published some of the earliest criticism on Patrick White (qv), who subsequently became a strong supporter of hers. Barnard characterised her life as 'sheltered' and, although she participated actively in Sydney literary circles throughout the 1930s and early '40s and worked for many years as a librarian, she continued to live at home with her parents throughout her adult life. *MD*

Australian Literature

If you set out to give a very short talk it is generally safest to choose for it a very large subject. In ten minutes, or at least so it seems to me, I can say something about Australian literature as a whole, taking the subject in the round and dealing in point blank generalizations whereas, if I tried to talk to you about an individual Australian writer, who as likely as not you have not read, I would never get past the uninteresting preamble. So, let us repair to the wide open spaces at once.

The really fascinating thing about Australian literature is that we can still catch it at it. It is in active evolution before our very eyes and there is not yet so much timber that we cannot get a clear view of the bush. There are processes happening in our literature, in the full day-light of our consciousness, that in the case of the parent English literature happened long ago in an unwatched past. No literature can be transplanted holus bolus, it is something that has to grow, like any other plant in the earth. To produce it man's mind must be mated with his environment. Pioneering periods do not produce art. Men's energies run in other channels, but that is not the only reason, or perhaps a reason at all. Periods of great national activity, such as the Elizabethan, are almost always great in arts and letters. Pioneers—and this is the point—are still unadjusted to their environment, they possess only half the magic formula. They can express themselves no wit less than other men, but not the country about them; they might write books but not Australian books.

When in the 1820s the cultivated Mr. Justice Field, a man of some literary pretentions, friend of Charles Lamb, set himself to write what he ambitiously called 'The First Fruits of Australian Poetry'—he was reduced to bathos. The continent grimaced behind his back and twitched his pen to comic results. Simpler men, like Alexander Harris, the sawyer, did better having fewer pretensions and preconceived ideas, but all books written in Australia in those early days remained onlooker books and their place is in Australian history not Australian literature.

Australian literature began as all literatures have as a floating anonymous body of tales and songs. Drovers moving cattle and sheep in the great unfenced inland, camped at the waterholes, yarning under the stars to the clink of hobble chains; diggers going from field to field in the roaring days of the gold rush; bullock wagons toiling up the country; sundowners on the track; the flotsam of the bush meeting in the shanties and bark huts, carried stories and ballads as the wind carries pollen. As they forgot the songs they had brought with them from England, Scotland and Ireland, they replaced them with new ones of their own rough manufacture, new words fitted to the old tunes, shanties of that inland sea, the bush. These men were the equivalents of the folk story tellers of all ancient cultures, the bards of the Middle Ages. Out of just such material long ago, Homer sprang. This was the period of Australian folklore, the matrix of her literature.

Australian literature has followed the same line of evolution as other literatures, foreshortened and speeded up by modern conditions. First poetry then prose, ballads and short stories then the more complex literary forms, the vernacular creeping out from behind the formal language of educated men. You know, in the middle ages all really nice people wrote in Latin, Chaucer and Dante were revolutionaries when they wrote in the vernacular. It wasn't done. So the idiom of the Australian bush with its new words and local turns of phrase, selected by conditions from a great many sources, including convict slang and the argot of unlettered men from all over the world, had to make its way in the face of elegant and educated speech. The paddock ousted the field and the bush the forest. In the transition period it used to be thought necessary to attach glossaries to Australian books. Even as late as 1909 when Miles Franklin published 'Some Everyday Folk and Dawn', she added a glossary of Australianisms with their English and American equivalents for the benefit of overseas readers.

Such writers as Joseph Furphy and Henry Lawson, A.B. Paterson and the balladists generally drew directly on the treasury of anonymous bush tales and rhymes. They were genuine Australian writers because they had the deep sea lift of the continent behind them. They had background in the sense that the most cultivated imported writer could not have it. In them the man and the continent were mated. The process is authentic. Time is telescoped and the scale reduced. For the Iliad we have 'Such is Life'. For Chevy Chase, 'Waltzing Matilda'. The romantic and picaresque, and their combination in the romantic rogue, abound. The bushranger is our Robin Hood.

Australian literature today—in this decade—reaches its maturity— the maturity, shall we say of a young man of 21 years. It is ready to take its place among the literatures of the world, having safely accomplished its normal infancy and adolescence. I speak, not of individual writers, but of the bulk of writing. Today there is the variety [...] the abundance of work to lift our literature out of the hands of the few into a second socialization. It does not any longer depend on a few small scale giants but is carried by many hands.

This literature that has evolved has its well marked characteristics and is a commentary on our social life and development. The majority of Australians are city dwellers but the bulk of our writing is still about the bush and bush ways. It is one of the most naturally and effortlessly democratic literatures in the world. It, equally with the American, is the literature of and for the man in the street and on the track. It belongs far more than, for instance, current English literature does to the world of men. The freedom of the great open spaces is in it and the mateship of the bush. It is, as a corollary to this, remarkably devoid of affectations. There is no cult of writing here, few professional writers. Writing is rarely done in book-lined studies. Our incomes don't run to them. It is done in the intervals of living, a literature of action, drawn from life, very very rarely escapist. The continent in all its natural aspects plays a large part in it. Because our world is still new and strange, background is important and intriguing. We are absorbed in our wonder book.

One more important point. Not only has the Australian writer had to evolve from scratch, the Australian reader also had to evolve not so much from scratch as from a handicapped position. The handicap has been his advantage of having older and richer literatures to divert and hold his attention. The Australian reader is some distance behind the Australian writer and this is a bitter disadvantage to the latter. Reading and writing are two halves of the same process. The backwardness of the Australian reader, in regard to his own literature, causes a serious cultural loss to the community. If the writer has mated with his environment it still remains for him to effect contact with his audience. It is a local audience that he needs, not an overseas one; for an Australian book to succeed it must succeed here, anything else is beside the point. Australian literature is the property of the Australian people; they as a whole have contributed to make it; it is a national emanation and therefore our natural cultural food.

1941

The Persimmon Tree

I saw the spring come once and I won't forget it. Only once. I had been ill all the winter and I was recovering. There was no more pain, no more treatments or visits to the doctor. The face that looked back at me from my old silver mirror was the face of a woman who had escaped. I had only to build up my strength. For that I wanted to be alone, an old and natural impulse. I had been out of things for quite a long time and the effort of returning was still too great. My mind was transparent and as tender as new skin. Everything that happened, even the commonest things, seemed to be happening for the first time, and had a delicate hollow ring like music played in an empty auditorium.

I took a flat in a quiet, blind street, lined with English trees. It was one large room, high ceilinged with pale walls, chaste as a cell in a honey comb, and furnished with the passionless, standardised grace of a fashionable interior decorator. It had the afternoon sun which I prefer because I like my mornings shadowy and cool, the relaxed end of the night prolonged as far as possible. When I arrived the trees were bare and still against the lilac dusk. There was a block of flats opposite, discreet, well tended, with a wide entrance. At night it lifted its oblongs of rose and golden light far up into the sky. One of its windows was immediately opposite mine. I noticed that it was always shut against the air. The street was wide but because it was so quiet the window seemed near. I was glad to see it always shut because I spend a good deal of time at my window and it was the only one that might have overlooked me and flawed my privacy.

I liked the room from the first. It was a shell that fitted without touching me. The afternoon sun threw the shadow of a tree on my light wall and it was in the shadow that I first noticed that the bare twigs were beginning to swell with buds. A water colour, pretty and innocuous, hung on that wall. One day I asked the silent woman who serviced me to take it down. After that the shadow of the tree had the wall to itself and I felt cleared and tranquil as if I had expelled the last fragment of grit from my mind.

I grew familiar with all the people in the street. They came and went with a surprising regularity and they all, somehow, seemed to be cut to a very correct pattern. They were part of the mise en scene, hardly real at all and I never felt the faintest desire to become acquainted with any of them. There was one woman I noticed, about my own age. She lived over the way. She had been beautiful I thought, and was still handsome with a fine tall figure. She always wore dark clothes, tailor made, and there was reserve in her every movement. Coming and going she was always alone, but you felt that that was by her own choice, that everything she did was by her own steady choice. She walked up the steps so firmly, and vanished so resolutely into the discreet muteness of the building opposite, that I felt a faint, a very faint, envy of anyone who appeared to have her life so perfectly under control.

There was a day much warmer than anything we had had, a still, warm, milky day. I saw as soon as I got up that the window opposite was open a few inches, 'Spring comes even to the careful heart,' I thought. And the next morning not only was the window open but there was a row of persimmons set out carefully and precisely on the sill, to ripen in the sun. Shaped like a young woman's breasts their deep, rich, golden-orange colour, seemed just the highlight that the morning's spring tranquillity needed. It was almost a shock to me to see them there. I remembered at home when I was a child there was a grove of persimmon trees down one side of the house. In the autumn they had blazed deep red, taking your breath away. They cast a rosy light into rooms on that side of the house as if a fire were burning outside. Then the leaves fell and left the pointed dark gold fruit clinging to the bare branches. They never lost their strangeness—magical, Hesperidean trees. When I saw the Fire Bird danced my heart moved painfully because I remembered the persimmon trees in the early morning against the dark windbreak of the loquats. Why did I always think of autumn in springtime?

Persimmons belong to autumn and this was spring. I went to the window to look again. Yes, they were there, they were real. I had not imagined them, autumn fruit warming to a ripe transparency in the spring sunshine. They must have come, expensively packed in sawdust, from California or have lain all winter in storage. Fruit out of season.

It was later in the day when the sun had left the sill that I saw the window opened and a hand come out to gather the persimmons. I saw a woman's figure against the curtains. *She* lived there. It was her window opposite mine.

Often now the window was open. That in itself was like the breaking of a bud. A bowl of thick cream pottery, shaped like a boat, appeared on the sill. It was planted, I think, with bulbs. She used to water it with one of those tiny, long-spouted, hand-painted cans that you use for refilling vases, and I saw her gingerly loosening the earth with a silver table fork. She didn't look up or across the street. Not once.

Sometimes on my leisurely walks I passed her in the street. I knew her quite well now, the texture of her skin, her hands, the set of her clothes, her movements. The way you know people when you are sure you will never be put to the test of speaking to them. I could have found out her name quite easily. I had only to walk into the vestibule of her block and read it in the list of tenants, or consult the visiting card on her door. I never did.

She was a lonely woman and so was I. That was a barrier, not a link. Lonely women have something to guard. I was not exactly lonely. I had stood my life on a shelf, that was all. I could have had a dozen friends round me all day long. But there wasn't a friend that I loved and trusted above all the others, no lover, secret or declared. She had, I suppose, some nutrient hinterland on which she drew.

The bulbs in her bowl were shooting. I could see the pale new-green spears standing out of the dark loam. I was quite interested in them, wondered what they would be. I expected tulips, I don't know why. Her window was open all day long now, very fine thin curtains hung in front of it and these were never parted. Sometimes they moved but it was only in the breeze.

The trees in the street showed green now, thick with budded leaves. The shadow pattern on my wall was intricate and rich. It was no longer an austere winter pattern as it had been at first. Even the movement of the branches in the wind seemed different. I used to lie looking at the shadow when I rested in the afternoon. I was always tired then and so more permeable to impressions. I'd think about the buds, how pale and tender they were, but how implacable. The way an unborn child is implacable. If man's world were in ashes the spring would still come. I watched the moving pattern and my heart stirred with it in frail, half-sweet melancholy.

One afternoon I looked out instead of in. It was growing late and the sun would soon be gone, but it was warm. There was gold dust in the air, the sunlight had thickened. The shadows of trees and buildings fell, as they sometimes do on a fortunate day, with dramatic grace. *She* was standing there just behind the curtains, in a long dark wrap, as if she had come from her bath and was going to dress, early, for the evening. She stood so long and so still, staring out,—at the budding trees, I thought—that tension began to accumulate in my mind. My blood ticked like a clock. Very slowly she raised her arms and the gown fell from her. She stood there naked, behind the veil of the curtains, the scarcely distinguishable but unmistakeable form of a woman whose face was in shadow.

I turned away. The shadow of the burgeoning bough was on the white wall. I thought my heart would break.

1943

M. BARNARD ELDERSHAW
1897−1987 (Barnard); 1897−1956 (Eldershaw)

Marjorie Barnard's (qv) writing partnership with Flora Eldershaw is recognised as one of the most successful and enduring collaborations in Australian literary history. Eldershaw was born in Sydney but grew up in the Riverina district. She and Barnard met while students at the University of Sydney and in a shared career spanning nearly twenty years, under the pseudonym of M. Barnard Eldershaw, they co-authored five novels, in addition to writing short stories, critical articles, volumes of history and a significant collection of literary criticism.

While their first novel, *A House is Built* (1929), enjoyed enormous popular success in Australia and England, recent critical attention has focused primarily upon their controversial final novel, *Tomorrow and Tomorrow and Tomorrow*. An ambitious dystopian fiction which was unfairly subjected to wartime censorship prior to its publication as *Tomorrow and Tomorrow* in 1947, it only appeared in full in 1983. That novel is distinguished not only by its innovative structure and its sustained meditation on the social role of the writer, but also by its haunting evocation of the city of Sydney.

The two authors made few public statements about their shared writing routine, leading to substantial speculation over each author's part in the collaboration. Initially lacking confidence in her own writing ability, Barnard preferred to hide behind Eldershaw's more robust personality; however, it is clear she later took a leading role in their joint works.

Barnard and Eldershaw were influential figures in Sydney literary circles of the 1930s and '40s and played significant roles in the Fellowship of Australian Writers. Eldershaw served as the first female president of the organisation. *MD*

From *Tomorrow and Tomorrow and Tomorrow*
Part 4: Afternoon

[...] This was the day of the great hegira. The pouring forth of the people. It was hard to believe there were so many people in the city, just as it is hard to believe there can be so much blood in a human body when it spurts forth. Thousands had already left, snatching at any foothold on the conveyances that had poured along the western roads in the last few days. But the great bulk remained. The trains went out in steady succession jammed to their roofs, their last journey. By dawn the roads west and south had begun to move. There were all the hitches and troubles usual to such an occasion, people who had lost their evacuation cards and forgotten the number of their vehicle, who failed to arrive or came late, who tried to smuggle out prohibited articles and resisted when these were taken from them and thrown upon the wayside fires that burned for this purpose, children who strayed and got lost, women who fainted and old people who collapsed. All these were dealt with quickly and ruthlessly because that was the only way. The tragic part was that families were being torn apart, the men staying, the women and children going, and in the formless future there was no means of reuniting them. Only a tithe of the refugees realised this. For the most part they went quietly, calmly, making the best of things, helping one another, trusting.

Sometimes they got a laugh. There was the middle-aged woman with a baby and the man with a broken arm, for instance. She was a stout strong woman, but she bent under the weight of the baby swathed in shawls despite the heat. The guard, a family man, didn't like the shape of the baby. He tried to pull aside the shawl. The woman resisted. 'Arnie,' she yelped. The man pulled harder, the sagging shawl gave way, a medley of small tins and packets fell to the ground. As he kicked at them, some burst open. They contained money, jewellery, securities. 'So that's your little game,' shouted the guard. The woman was scarlet with rage, not shame, the man's face had gone a dirty white with apprehension. The crowd laughed, even people who hadn't rightly seen what happened laughed and stood to stare.

'I suppose that's a fake, too,' said the guard, roughly tearing the sling from Arnie's arm. But it was genuinely broken, for the safe, the precious safe, that had been their child, had fallen on Arnie's arm as he was levering it out of its niche for burial in a safe place. He screamed with pain and Chris burst into a flood of shrill curses.

'Keep moving,' yelled the guard, as two of his offsiders hauled the culprits away. The valuables were scattered by many feet, the jewellery ground into the pavement. None dared pick them up.

'Don't amount to a bunch of curses, not now,' an old man muttered, not knowing himself whether he was triumphant or bitter.

All the incidents were not amusing. There was the old man and his book. The people who saw that remembered it afterwards. It smouldered in their minds, they were hurt and ashamed because of it. He was haggard and dirty, but it was easy to imagine that he had not always been like that. As recently as twenty-four hours ago, he might have been a dapper elderly gentleman with polished speech and a tailored suit. He had a large roughly wrapped package held to his chest, no other luggage.

'What you got there?' the guard asked him as he checked his card.

'A book,' said the old man.

'A book?' asked the guard, who thought of such things only in connection with the racecourse. 'Show it here.'

'Not exactly a book, but I thought that is what you'd call it. It's a manuscript.' With trembling fingers he opened the package while the man waited impatiently.

For a moment the pages glowed in their gold, vermilion, and blue, between their dusky covers.

'I saved it from the University library,' the old man explained.

'Loot,' said the guard.

'It's twelfth century. A beautiful example. It's priceless.' The old man said in a soft voice as if he spoke of a sleeping child.

'Capital goods,' said the guard and tossed the manuscript into the fire where the ancient pages ignited at once.

A hoarse terrible cry rose from the old man as if it were he who burned. He would have snatched it, burning, out of the flames if he had not been held. He fought for an instant with long vanished strength and went limp. The tears were running down his cheeks. He turned blindly, dumbly, and tried to go back the way he had come.

The guard was after him. 'You can't go back. You're evacuated, see? Move along now. Hi,' he called to a group with the same number, 'take him along.'

'Poor old bugger,' one said for all, 'why couldn't they let him keep it? Wouldn't do no one any harm.'

A little hunchback who used to sell him tobacco recognised him. 'He's a professor up at the University,' he explained.

A girl took the old man's arms. 'Come on, pop,' she said kindly. 'We'll look after you,' and so she led him away.

The guard, feeling himself unpopular, shouted truculently to everyone to keep moving.

Mrs Blan, Mrs Nelson, and Ally had got away early. Their bus was bowling through the morning across the littoral plain. The thirty passengers and their bundles had shaken down into some sort of comfort.

'We're still neighbours,' said Mrs Blan, with her old rich laugh. She had carried out her threat and piled on every garment she possessed. Her face was crimson and she was like a stove for heat in the seat beside Ally. In vain did Ally dig her with sharp elbows, she never reached the flesh. When she laughed, she wobbled all over Ally in waves of already odorous heat.

Mrs Nelson on the seat behind pushed her large pale face between them. She had at last resolved the problem that had been troubling her. 'If government force us to evacuate,' she said, 'it'll have to look after us, won't it?'

'That's right,' agreed Mrs Blan, nodding vigorously. Mrs Nelson sat back and gave herself up to placid contemplation of the scenery, drawn effortlessly past her eyes. She didn't much mind where she was so long as she was 'looked after.' It was only the thought of fending for herself that flummoxed her.

'I wonder if they've got round to Carnation Street yet,' Mrs Blan shouted to Ally above the rattle, when, looking back east from a bend in the road, the pall over Sydney suggested that her fires were already alight.

Ally shook her head. 'We only went there temporary,' she shouted back, 'it never was home.'

Fire sprang up simultaneously all over the city and through the suburbs. From the air it would have looked like the very perfection of pattern bombing. Every area had its squad and its ration of combustible material. In every gang there was at least one expert to direct the work and ensure its effectiveness. It was surprising how many experts in destruction the city could muster—professional wreckers, trained N.E.S. men who had only to invert their knowledge, soldiers who had had experience in scorching the earth, the handful who, in the long brooding hatred, had worked out their own methods. … The new disorder had been strong in the fire brigades and they had come over with their tackle, their stores of dynamite, their skills. To them fell the big work of blasting out the rocklike buildings that could not readily be dissolved in fire. It was they who broke into the sealed banks, the smooth invulnerable insurance offices, the other bulwarks of the old world, and reduced them at last to fountains of dust, smoke, and flame, whose core was twisted girders, shattered stone, fallen pillars, and rubble. It was they who broke open the strong heart of the city against which fanaticism with bare hands would have been futile. For labourers Sid Warren gave them the men from the Labour Camps, that conglomeration of beaten and defaced men, the ever multiplying rejects of the crumbling order that had now fallen.

They were a ramshackle lot but they had to serve, and in forcing the work from their degenerate bodies and exhausted minds only strong measures were effective. Not for them the future. The realists of the caucus knew, as the realists of the capitalist regime had known, that these were not the People. They were wastage, there was no road back for them, the only profit was in using what capacity for work was left in them, ruthlessly and at once, cutting their losses for them.

With them came Bowie. There was a little to distinguish him from the others. He was bearded, shaggy, his clothes stiff with dirt and worn to rags, his trousers held up on his bony loins with a length of rope. His eyes were a little wild. But he didn't know it. He didn't view himself critically any longer. Where everyone was rather queer, they looked on him as a bit odd. He didn't have occasion to talk much, but when he did speak it was still with the voice of an educated man. He was too tired to think, but occasionally memories—a lifeless curdlike scud—passed across the mind.

They worked before and after the dynamite, preparing the way for it and then completing its work. Most of them found it oddly comforting to be tearing something down. Bowie didn't. It went against the grain. The original grain of the man was still there. Suddenly, in the middle of the morning, he said to the man working next to him, 'We're destroying the city. It's bad to destroy things. It isn't natural. I'm not going to do it.' It was a long speech. The man shot him a suspicious sidelong glance and grunted. Bowie threw down his pick and walked away. No one tried to stop him. The foreman wasn't looking. His action had no significance. He might just have been stepping aside for a natural purpose.

He walked straight on. Every now and then he stopped and looked about him. He could feel change in the air, the sick cloud hanging over the city. He came to Parramatta Road and found it running a banker with people going west. Refugees. He joined them. His hands were empty, his pockets were empty. He had nothing at all but the torn caked clothes he wore. It didn't worry him, he didn't even think it strange. For so long now he had been either in prison or the concentration camp where meals, however meagre and rough, were always provided, that to take any thought for his future seemed superfluous. At sunset he was still walking west.

The westerlies blowing a half gale drove on the fires. 'The weather is helping us,' said Sid Warren. To Ruth, who was still beside him, his calm was terrible and inhuman. Never afterwards could she quite forgive him for it. He never lost his hold on the situation, never deviated into uncertainty or fear. He was as little touched by physical danger as by imaginative horror. He continued to plan and correlate, to receive reports and issue orders, as if it were a government in the ordinary sense that he had set up. As little came into the city in the way of news as left it. From the north there was nothing. The invading force continued to bide its time. The miners appeared to have missed their moment, not to have risen or to have been crushed before they could develop any strength. From the south, like a thin echo, came the news that the men at Port Kembla had risen, sabotaged the plant and marched away, leaving it burning like a lonely volcano by the sea. The government having declared Melbourne an open city was continuing its deliberations on the 'terms'. Sid, his mind strained to envelop so much, was totally unaware of what was going on in the thoughts of the woman beside him. In the proportions of his world it would only be unimportant.

Ruth knew that Sid would stay till the very last and that she would stay with him. But she was possessed by fear, saturated and interpenetrated by fear and grief, to the last cell of her brain. Her body was frightened by the stench of fire, by the furnace-like heat, the darkness even at noon when the sky was black with smoke and red with volcanic fire, by the choking air. Her mind was overwhelmed by the magnitude of the wreck and the knowledge that it was beyond control. All that was human and normal in her revolted against destruction as destruction, not for the value of what burned but because, however corrupted, it was a shape of human effort, a palimpsest of men's minds.

In her imagination pictures rose and became fixed like barbs in her brain, tormenting her to the outer edge of her endurance. One of these pictures, the most terrible, the most persistent, was of a dog, forgotten, left chained, without water, maddened with fear as the fires came closer and closer, straining at his chain till the blood flowed, howling in a terrible elemental fear when there was none to hear, till at last he was buried living in the burning debris.

There was no night or day. Time had melted and run together in an indistinguishable mass.

It could not have been that day but the next, for Sydney was then far gone, that Sid, wanting to make a survey, had ascended the A.W.A. tower. Ruth went with him. He did not ask her to go, but since she did, he took it for granted that she would endure what he endured without comment.

They climbed higher and higher. The heat was intense. Ruth thought that their clothing would ignite from contact with the fiery air, and the tears that coursed down her cheeks seemed to cut the flesh till they felt like blood flowing from raw wounds.

The guttering city was spread out beneath them, layered to the horizon in smoke and flame. It was immense and unrecognisable. Death and transfiguration. It boiled with smoke, black, grey, brown, white. Here and there, there were great coils of fire where a timber yard was burning, or a paint factory, a chemical works, or a very dry old building. Against brief curtains of flame, gaunt black shells of buildings stood out in relief. As they watched, walls dissolved, facades swayed fantastically and crashed, opening craters of living fire in the smoke, roofs fell in and fountained stars that were red hot metal and incandescent cinders. All that happens in the grate on a winter night was happening here on a panoramic scale.

Macquarie Street burned with great dignity, each building as it were a set piece. Parliament House, so old, so wheezy, made a fine bonfire. The hospital arcaded with red fire was a spectacle people would have walked five miles to see, were there not so many rivals. There was a bushfire in the Botanic Gardens, flying over the grass, climbing the trees, hanging them with leaves of flame, shrivelling in an instant all the little bushes, blackening the statues and leaving them hideously extruded, like corpses, from the scene whose natural beauty they had once been expected to leaven with culture. The bushfire lapped round Government House as water flows round a sand castle.

Down on the water front, wool stores burned with heavy greasy smoke though there was not much wool in them. Fiery particles floated in the water of the harbour. The bridge which had been dynamited hung half-destroyed, leviathan wounded.

Whole streets were obliterated, reduced to black dead ruin. Here and there fire seemed to have died of satiety and little clusters of buildings barely touched were left standing, only the most perishable parts burned away. Trees planted in the streets had lit like candles and burned to the earth. The old Port Jackson figs of the Domain, which had watched the city grow up, were first desiccated and then burned. The dispossessed birds of the city, the sparrows, the pigeons, the doves, the starlings, the ducks, the swans, had risen in clouds at the first breath of fire. Who would have thought there were so many birds in the city? Their cries as they wheeled in the sky were the city's only valediction. The trees that had sheltered them were gone now.

Sid noted the landmarks that yet stood. Greenway's church, St James's, was still unscathed like Shadrach in the fiery furnace. He could see the cupola of Queen Victoria Markets like hard bubbles in the smoke, and the tower of the Town Hall was still in the sky. The clock tower at Central Railway was gone.

Immediately beneath him Martin Place was a cauldron, the post-office full of bright fire like a box with eyes, a bank facade blown right out blocked the George Street end with a mountain of rubble. Jagged, fragmentary, unrecognisable buildings rose out of the smoke and dust of explosions, the cenotaph was overthrown, its sailor and soldier caught in a second holocaust of death, the lillipilli trees—who would remember them?—gone like matchwood.

Ruth stared out over the ruined city and breathed its hot black breath. She was a rag of flesh, no more, alive, able to understand what she saw, still sentient. She had known the strangling tragedy of her home and it had marked her. In her father she had glimpsed the crucifixion of Everyman and it had impacted her will. Now, not only her heart, but her very self, the matrix of her spirit, was broken open by pity and despair—pity for the people who must now be forced to learn, if they could learn, through new sacrifices, who would be relentlessly winnowed till only the strongest and most steadfast were left to be the stones of the new world, despair for herself. There was no road back. The irremediable that the plastic human spirit dreads had come to pass. She still believed that what had been done was the best that could be done, that the road, the only road through, lay that way, that there was courage and hard logic in it. The people were again the scapegoat. By their suffering, the sins—not the sins they had committed, but that, being committed against them, they had condoned—would be atoned. No, it was harder even than that. Suffering was nothing, bought nothing, brought no compensation, it was a byproduct, and even when it destroyed it was of no account in the logic of event. The people would not be purged or saved by suffering, they would only be selected, freed of the weak and the irresolute, reduced at last to a sticking point. For those who died, for those who despaired, for those who suffered too much and were destroyed in their heart or courage by it, there was no redress. No future would give them back what they had lost. They and their pain would be as meaningless as grains of dust. Ruth consented, and, knowing that she consented with her mind and will, she must bear upon her heart the burden of it, be destroyed, having served her turn. Gethsemane is commemorated and the Son of Man did not watch alone. Down through time there has been here and there one who saw in anguish the suffering of Man and his own destruction—humble people who did not know they kept a vigil—a man perhaps, walking up his street in the twilight from his profitless work to his wretched home, while his imagination widened to the knowledge that his world was doomed, and pain and bitterness flowed in him like blood; or a woman, looking down on a burning city, acknowledging it, realising what it would mean to a million people unprepared for change, unintegrated, who must nevertheless bear the wastage to an end they might never accomplish.

Ruth wanted, not hysterically but out of the same hard and bitter logic that had brought her so far, to throw herself down from the tower. The gulf of fiery air drew her, the dead gulf in her own mind drew her. Only the discipline that had become the unrelenting habit of her mind held her back. She had incurred the future. She must go on into it. She knew in her heart that the destroyer could never be the builder. He was conditioned by his role and must in the nature of things be scrapped. If they had not destroyed more than the city their work and all its consequences were in vain. If they had cast down with the stones of the city a social system or a corrupt way of life, then life in its own defence must rid itself of them. This Ruth knew, as the spirit may sometimes teach the brain.

Ruth tried to pick out King's Cross in the wreck, but all was smoke and chaos. She could not pin the spot with any landmark. The spire of St John's must have fallen, the high buildings had altered their shape. Carnation Street would be a tributary of fire flowing down into the river of William Street, or, perhaps, by now only the blackened banks where fire had flowed remained. To look for it, to look back on it, was utterly vain. Blinded, choking, she turned away. The past had fallen in, the future did not exist. There was only this moment that impaled her like a sword.

As the Cross had lived, so it burned, with greater gusto than any other part of the city, as if it were more inflammable, as if the very stones and concrete of its material body from a constant contact with life had lost their hard inanimate surface and become friable. Once the fire had taken hold it was up and away with banners, out of control. The hill became a volcano and streams of fire flowed down its sides to the waterfront. It had majesty and even, while the fire was new and bright, beauty. Its last beauty was the legitimate child of its first beauty, that had been lavish, brilliant, vainglorious, and so thinly laid over shabby ugliness.

The blocks of flats that had been congeries of little boxes, so packed with life that it bulged from the windows and sprouted on to the roofs, became craters of fire, each one burning stormily of itself. The matchwood partitions, the lattices, the tawdry ornaments, the awnings, the paints, the lacquers of hasty smartness, the hangings, the detritus of habitation, the greasy dirt, spread a gargantuan banquet for the flames. There was plenty of marrow fat. The fiery tongues licking into corners and hiding places uncovered and consumed a thousand trumpery secrets. Facades fell out, and the dens and love nests, the tabernacles and the secret places, the abodes of respectability, vice, dirt, and eccentricity of the great rookery were for an instant revealed in section and laid bare, not to curious gaze but to destruction.

The starving poet of King's Cross had left in great haste and fear. When the fire reached his home it found confusion, as if thieves had ransacked the place, everything in disorder, drawers pulled out, the contents spilled and scattered, the papers from his desk littering the floor, doors and windows left open. The hot wind and the breath of the fire preceding it dried everything to tinder and gave a dancing lightness to fabrics and papers before they perished. The closely written sheets of the Spring Symphony, the epic that had cost the poet so much of his heart's blood and that he now no longer valued nor even remembered, since he was brought face to face with what he conceived to be reality, trembled where they lay on the floor. They began to flutter and struggle for life. Some were blown into corners and stayed there flickering ineffectually against the walls, but others rose and eddied, sank, rose again each time higher, like a ballet when the intoxication of the music begins to work, some escaped into the street. The street was utterly deserted, loud with the noise of fire, distant and at hand. It was undestroyed but on the verge of destruction. The whole street seemed about to explode. There was wind but no air, as it might be inside a furnace. The pages were carried along like dry autumn leaves. Some rose above the houses and were consumed by fires in neighbouring streets. Others took fire in mid-air, burned for a second and fell. No word of it escaped.

The narrow lanes and alleys provided admirable draught. It was dry fire. It did not have to fight with columns of water as fires usually do, but went proudly in unbroken conquest. It smelled different. It made terrific heat, windows burst like bubbles. From the continents of flame, islands broke loose and sailed into the sky. Among the terraces of the meanest and most congested parts the fire lost individuality. Their wreckage fused in a vast anonymity. The fires sent the men who had made them scuttling away like ants. Theirs was work that, begun prosaically or in fanatic hatred, ended by overawing them and driving them before it. The gangs broke and fled. Here and there a man, negligent, exhausted, overcome by fumes, or not quick enough, was cut off and perished as surely, and almost as quickly as the frail sheets of paper had. His companions, preoccupied by their own escape, rarely missed him in time to save or even to search for him.

Timmy Andrews, maintaining his beatific state, continued to ride the holocaust. He did towering sums in his head, reckoning the amount of bourgeois property destroyed and the capital value of the city. He announced the results from time to time to the labouring sweating gang beside which he was camped. He had constituted himself a morale department of one. They were, however, too busy to listen to him. They waved to him good-naturedly when he made a speech. Every now and then when they were particularly hard pressed—they were mining a big block of buildings—he would rush in among them and with flailing energy lend a hand till, going limp with exhaustion, he retired again to his vantage place and stoked up with more liquor. Once the man in charge of the gang, young and cold sober, expostulated with him.

'You'll get hurt if you stay round here, mate, we'll be blowing her soon. Better hop it.'

Timmy drew himself up in his dignity. 'Young man,' he said, 'I was a revolutionary before you were born or thought of. When you were saluting the bloody flag in the bloody playground I was instructing the masses in the duties of the socialist state.'

They liked having him about. When they took a spell he was ready with a joke and a bottle.

'Decent old Toby.'

He humanised the situation, though they would not have put it that way.

It was after one of his bursts of energy that Timmy slipped and fell in a world gone black as eternal night. Nobody noticed at the moment, but when the fuses were lit and they were scattering to safety they saw him. His face was purple and congested, his eyes rolled up, his breath coming in uneven jerks. The ganger picked him up and ran with him to safety. They gathered round him, their grimy faces heavy with concern.

'Poor old bugger, he's for it.'

''Ad a stroke, that's wot.'

'Ought ter get him to orspital.'

'The hell we can.'

Someone remembered that there were still ambulance stations and ran to find one, but before the stretcher-bearers could arrive Timmy was gone. The men stood round bareheaded, disconcerted, moved.

'Poor old bugger.'

'In the movement all his life.'

'One of the old timers.'

'Gone before he could say knife.'

'What are we gonna do with him?'

'What the bleeding hell did this have to happen to him for?'

'The drink done it.'

'No, he busted himself using the pick.'

If Timmy could have commented he would have said that it was a good proletarian death. He died for the revolution in the beatitude of strong drink and among his mates.

Others perished less happily.

Gwen awoke. She was lying among the fluff and dust under her bed, the empty whisky bottle on her chest. There was light so it must be day. She shut her eyes and rolled her head, which felt as if it had been battered to a pulp, from side to side. She didn't want to wake up, she didn't want to go on living, she was afraid of everything, even of crawling out from under the bed. But it was suffocating there. She could not breathe and there was a strange noise that she did not recognise, something like a high wind in an open place, battering on her brain. Before she had willed it her body had crept out of its refuge. Everything rocked and reeled, even the light flowed to and fro like a tide. It wasn't daylight and it wasn't electric light. It was red.

'Some hangover,' thought Gwen.

She looked out of the window. The window had gone, there was only a hole in the wall. What she saw sent a stiffness of terror through her limbs. It dissolved. Screaming, she rushed from the room and down the stairs. Through her terror she could feel that the house was empty. It was not yet alight, but, dry as tinder, it waited and seemed about to explode.

In the street the buildings opposite were blazing. They were melting in fire and gobbets of burning wood were falling from them to the pavements. She ran to the end of the street to find it blood-red with fire. She ran back. Her mouth was wide open but no cries came, only a hoarse growling. The other end of the street was blocked with ruins. There was no way through. There was a little alley way between two burning buildings. She ran the gauntlet, but the street beyond was so well alight that she had to return the way she had come. She thought she was on fire and beat at herself with frenzied hands, but it was only the blistering roaring heat that surrounded her. She ran to the house where she lived with some wild idea of taking refuge there, but now it was alight too. She was hemmed in. She ran hither and thither in blind panic. The whole area was deserted, she was quite alone among the burning ruins. They were immense, she was like an ant.

A facade bulged towards her, she saw it coming. Standing there she knew the final madness of terror. The inescapable thing was upon her. She lived for perhaps five minutes more. Then her agony was blotted out. [...]

1947/1983

NORMAN HARRIS
c. 1898–1968

Norman Harris was born at Mount Helena, WA, and became a Noongar activist. His family were pioneer farmers in the Morawa region. In 1926, with his uncle, the civil rights leader William Harris, he formed an Aboriginal union, protesting against the treatment of Aboriginal Australians by state authorities. In 1934 he gave evidence before the Moseley Royal Commission. A farmer, gold miner and, later, a property owner in Perth, Harris married Eva Mary Phillips. Their children continued the family tradition of community leadership. *AH/PM*

Letter to Jim Bassett

We have been looking out for you some time now but I don't think you are much of a swimmer and I know that you haven't got a boat and now that the lakes are running you can't come per road or water and perhaps not by train, so I don't expect to see you this winter.

Now, Jim, we are trying to get some of the natives and half-castes together has a deporation to the Premier has you know what for.

So we can get a vote in the county also one law for us all that is the same law that governs the whites also justice and far play.

I suppose you know that Perth is a prohibiterd around Perth for natives and half cast it is in Saturdays pappie of March 19th, 1927, and last year Tindale Cpt. said that the Government ought to put all the natives out of Australia onto a island out from Kimberly thats rotten what do you say Jim.

Last year in Parliament House they disgust where they should give halfcasts a vote or not anyhow their was hell to pop over that so they would not let them have it.

They are afraid of the native wanting the same has the halfcast why shouldn't he if he is respectable or any person.

Now you see yourself where is the Abo. got a fare go.

He is not alowed in a Pub, not to have a gun, not to camp on revers because squatters stock are there, he is not to have dogs near stock. He is not to grow grapes because he may make wine and get drunk. They bar him in football and cricket must not be in town to long after dark. All Police are in the bush a sort of proctor I have never heard of them protecting the native yet.

In the North has you know they were never given wages just work for kick in the sturn and a little tucker such has it is, and still the same.

A native can't leave this state without getting the permission from the Proctor (Mr. A.O. Neville) a rotten B. The white Police can do just has they like. The native is a prisiner wherever he is. He can be brought from any part of the State put in a Compond such has Mogumber, a rotten prison for alsorts just fancy young girls and boys brought up among them sort and for a certain they dont learn them much *and no moral trainning atal.* Thoes children are there being brought up among all the black cut throats the Police can lay their hands on from all parts of the country. They say they are trying to send them out in the world to do good for themsselves. How cant they when this Aboriginal Act is over them if a girl or boy goes out to work they get the money, if the girls have the misfortune to have a kidie she is got by the Police and sent strait back to Mogumber in most case death release them. So Jim you see they are blocked whatever way they go.

Now it is comonly known that while girls were in Carolup they were tired up floged some time four and five at a time. All thoes that were in Carolup Mission were brought to Mogumber. They never got payed for the work they done their. Now this is the question who got that land and place if it were sold what hapend the money I dont know does anyone know I never heard of any natives getting a holiday out of the money.

Now Mogumber, a native name Bob Lookenglass tryed to run away from that prison, he was caught near Moora belted by the Black Police of Mongumba. Then he got or was brought back to Mongumber he was tired to a tree and was belted by the white officer in charge put into the boob that they have ther I think of cause we cant say for a certain he was brought out of the boob *dead* or nearly.

Yet their are hundreds of halfcast send their children there for schooling and trainning think they are doing good if they only stop and think they can see enough. Then again if they dont send them the Police come along and sends them along to Mongumba or the Prison I should say The Police can take the children without a warrant or ask their perants permission. They are quite within the Act to take any Aborinal or Halfcast.

Someone goes up North getting all the half cast girls and boys off all the stations nitives to if they want them. They have got a motor truck with seats along the sides and big rings bolted to the centure chains from rings to natives.

The South Australian League for Natives are trying for a native State up in the Northern Territory that will be no good because they will have to keep them their that is the same has Mongumba only on a biger scale.

Mr. Neville gave a lecture in Perth and he said that it was no good giveing natives land because they would not work it they only use it for camping ground and he went on to say that he could not name a single native where he has got land and done good. So you see they will not let the native have land next. Not letting have land is quite easey when they make Perth Prohibited against natives and halfcast.

I have got a headache thinking about this Act. Uncle Bill has just gone from here in to Morawa I am at Dads place now but will be going back to my place next week. Uncle Bill is going down to Perth at about the end of the month he is going to Yalgoo now. Uncle Bills is going to have a go at the Aborigal Department. I think he will smash it up also all these Componds of cause he wants help from all the natives and h.c. He is not setting their for his own good because we all can do alright there are some halfcast yourself and us we get not a bad deal but it not the think we dont want to be under that Act atal, the one law is quite enough so if all the natives and halfcast pay a little in to him for a lawyer if we can get every one it will only run into a few shillings, anyhow thoes who dont pay what do you think ought to be done to them. So think this is enough about this question.

How are you getting on with your cropping, we haven't started putting any in yet. I was doing some rolling before that rain it settled the burn, although I set it alight last Sunday I may be able to plough it in. We are all doing alright has regards health my little fellow has got two teeth also walking about now so I think I have told you all the news this time hoping I will see you before I die and that you will get a good crop.

Questions within the meaning of the Act[1]

Why should the abo. Act be over us, it is only a By Law?
Isnt the one law good enough it is hard enough to live under?
Why shouldn't a native have land?
The country belongs to him?
Why segregation in his own land?
Why can't he be alowd in a public Hotel?
Why is he a prisnor in any part of the State?
He can be arrested without a warrant.
Why shouldn't he have a voise in the making of the Laws?
How do they suppose keeping natives in a big reserve?
Why shouldn't a native mother demand Freedom for her child?
Why should the Aboriginal Department put quadroons in Morgumba?
How many schollars have they turned out of Morgumba?
Why is it that the fairest are to the blackest?
Why is it that all letters are opened before going and out to?
Is it so that all girls and boy are found a job by the Dept?
Is it so that all from their have to send their money back?
Is it so that girls are lock up in Dormotorys?
Does children have to work?
There are about 300 people in Morgumba what do they do?
Do they get any money for their work?

1 Attwood and Markus (1999) note that these questions were undated and bundled together with this and other letters between the correspondents.

What dose their food consist of, I bleave Billy Goats?
Do they encourage young people to come their?
Do they stop card playing or gambling their?
Why does anyone who leaves their have to report his movements?
Why is the Act still over anyone who comes from Morgumba?
Why was thoes people shifted from Carrollup to Morgumba?
Who has got Carrollup now how much was it sold for?
Who has got the money for it?
I bleave that girls were tied with chains to get punished.
I bleave that girls were made bend forward while the kick them from behind
    Jist fancy that.
Why was the name change to Aboriginal Department from a Chief Proctor of
    Aborigines?
Where does the money go to that is set aside for the Aborigines?
In the early day a white person who married a native woman was aword a
    bit of land and never lost cast.
Now a white man who is caught near a camp is heavily find or
    imprisoned.

I could write a lot more but I have got to go on to home this afternoon so
    will ring off.
Burn this when you are finished with it or send it back to me.

1927

RICKETTY KATE
1898–1971

Paralysed and bedridden for much of her adult life, Minnie Agnes Filson (Cole), who wrote as Ricketty Kate (also published as R. Kate and Rickety Kate) produced three collections of poetry. With the long poem of the title work powerfully foregrounding the gender dynamics of an Aboriginal tale, *Bralgah: A legend* (1944) was published by the Jindyworobak movement. More of Ricketty Kate's poems appear in Jindyworobak anthologies. While much of her work engages with the Australian bush, it also describes new urban creations such as the Sydney Harbour Bridge and the cigarette-toting, pants-wearing New Woman. Other poems touch on fairy and spiritual worlds and a number reveal strong anti-war sentiments. Her autobiographical novel *Feet on the Ground*, from the 1940s, was published by her granddaughter in 2008. Although Ricketty Kate had a relatively small output, her best poems demonstrate a memorable lyricism. *AV*

Via the Bridge

If you come to Sydney often
Via the Bridge,
And have already scanned

The racing notes
Or the social gossip,   5
You may glance at the cables
Or the crimson pointed nails
Of the woman opposite.
But, if you have not passed that way before,
You will look at the pylons   10
And you will say to yourself:
'How regular these pinnacles are,
And
How alien!'
And, when they are behind,   15
'I am treading upon the smoke
Of a ship that perhaps
Sailed out from Brazil;'
Or you will whisper to yourself:
'This is the way the winds walk   20
Above the sea,
Where the gulls flicker like silver moths.'
Then you will want to put your hands
Out of the window
And let them flutter   25
With all the things that move
Above the waters.
And, when you are in the centre—
That enormous centre
Moulded of concrete and steel—   30
And the sweat of hands
And the labour of minds—
And there is nothing beneath
But the wind and the smoke and the gulls,
Nothing to the east and nothing to the west   35
But the flowing gossamer of the skies
Looping it with two horizons,
'This is a great wonder.'
Your spirit will sing:
'I shall not pass   40
This way again, too soon,
That I may keep
This vast astonishment.'

                                                               1942

A.A. PHILLIPS
1900–1985

Arthur Angell Phillips was born in Melbourne. After attending the universities of Melbourne and Oxford he became a schoolmaster at Wesley College, Melbourne (1925–71). As well as editing a number of anthologies, Phillips had a major impact as a critic. His essay 'The Cultural Cringe' (a phrase that has become idiomatic) is a statement on the cultural servility of Australia in the 1950s. His influential collection of essays *The Australian Tradition* (1958) argued that the democratic nature of 1890s writing laid the foundations of an Australian literary tradition. As well as writing for journals, such as *Meanjin*, and newspapers, Phillips edited editions of Bernard O'Dowd and Barbara Baynton, and wrote a study of Henry Lawson (qqv). He was made founding patron of the Association for the Study of Australian Literature in 1978. *DM*

The Cultural Cringe

The Australian Broadcasting Commission has a Sunday programme, designed to cajole a mild Sabbatarian bestirment of the wits, called 'Incognito'. Paired musical performances are broadcast, one by an Australian, one by an overseas executant, but with the names and nationalities withheld until the end of the programme. The listener is supposed to guess which is the Australian and which the alien performer. The idea is that quite often he guesses wrong or gives it up because, strange to say, the local lad proves to be no worse than the foreigner. This unexpected discovery is intended to inspire a nice glow of patriotic satisfaction.

I am not jeering at the ABC for its quaint idea. The programme's designer has rightly diagnosed a disease of the Australian mind and is applying a sensible curative treatment. The dismaying circumstance is that such a treatment should be necessary, or even possible: that in any nation, there should be an assumption that the domestic cultural product will be worse than the imported article.

The devil of it is that the assumption will often be correct. The numbers are against us, and an inevitable quantitative inferiority easily looks like a qualitative weakness, under the most favourable circumstances—and our circumstances are not favourable. We cannot shelter from invidious comparisons behind the barrier of a separate language; we have no long-established or interestingly different cultural tradition to give security and distinction to its interpreters; and the centrifugal pull of the great cultural metropolises works against us. Above our writers—and other artists—looms the intimidating mass of Anglo-Saxon culture. Such a situation almost inevitably produces the characteristic Australian Cultural Cringe—appearing either as the Cringe Direct, or as the Cringe Inverted, in the attitude of the Blatant Blatherskite, the God's-Own-Country and I'm-a-better-man-than-you-are Australian Bore.

The Cringe mainly appears in an inability to escape needless comparisons. The Australian reader, more or less consciously, hedges and hesitates, asking himself: 'Yes, but what would a cultivated Englishman think of this?' No writer can communicate confidently to a reader with the 'Yes, but' habit; and this particular demand is curiously crippling to critical judgment. Confronted by Furphy, we grow uncertain. We fail to recognise the extraordinarily original structure of his novel because we are wondering whether perhaps an Englishman might not find it too complex and self-conscious. No one worries about the structural deficiencies of *Moby-Dick*. We do not fully savour the meaty individualism of Furphy's style because we are wondering whether perhaps his egotistic verbosity is not too Australianly crude; but we accept the egotistic verbosity of Borrow[1] as part of his quality.

But the dangers of the comparative approach go deeper than this. The Australian writer normally frames his communication for the Australian reader. He assumes certain mutual preknowledge, a responsiveness to certain symbols, even the ability to hear the cadence of a phrase in the right way. Once the reader's mind begins to be nagged by the thought of how an Englishman might feel about this, he loses the fine edge of his Australian responsiveness. It is absurd to feel apologetic towards *Such is Life*, or *Coonardoo* or *Melbourne Odes* because they would not seem quite right to an English reader; it is part of their distinctive virtue that no Englishman can fully understand them.

I once read a criticism which began from the question 'What would a French classicist think of *Macbeth*?' The analysis was discerningly conducted and had a certain paradoxical interest; but it could not escape an effect of comic irrelevance.

A second effect of the Cringe has been the estrangement of the Australian Intellectual. Australian life, let us agree, has an atmosphere of often dismaying crudity. I do not know if our cultural crust is proportionately any thinner than that of other Anglo-Saxon communities; but to the intellectual it seems thinner because, in a small community, there is not enough of it to provide for the individual a protective insulation. Hence, even more than most intellectuals, he feels a sense of exposure. This is made much worse by the intrusion of that deadly habit of English comparisons. There is a certain type of Australian intellectual who is forever sidling up to the cultivated Englishman, insinuating: '*I*, of course, am not like these other crude Australians; *I* understand how you must feel about them; *I* should be spiritually more at home in Oxford or Bloomsbury.'

It is not the critical attitude of the intellectual that is harmful: that could be a healthy, even creative, influence, if the criticism were felt

---

1   George Borrow (1803–81), English novelist.

to come from within, if the critic had a sense of identification with his subject, if his irritation came from a sense of shared shame rather than a disdainful separation. It is his refusal to participate, the arch of his indifferent eye-brows, which exerts the chilling and stultifying influence.

Thinking of this type of Australian Intellectual, I am a little uneasy about my phrase 'Cultural Cringe'; it is so much the kind of missile which he delights to toss at the Australian mob. I hope I have made it clear that my use of the phrase is not essentially unsympathetic, and that I regard the denaturalised Intellectual as the Cringe's unhappiest victim. If any of the breed use my phrase for his own contemptuous purposes, my curse be upon him. May crudely-Dinkum Aussies spit in his beer, and gremlins split his ever to be preciously agglutinated infinitives.

The Australian writer is affected by the Cringe because it mists the responsiveness of his audience, and because its influence on the intellectual deprives the writer of a sympathetically critical atmosphere. Nor can he entirely escape its direct impact. There is a significant phrase in Henry Handel Richardson's *Myself When Young*. When she found herself stuck in a passage of *Richard Mahony* which would not come right, she remarked to her husband, 'How did I ever dare to write *Maurice Guest*—a poor little colonial like me?' Our sympathies go out to her—pathetic victim of the Cringe. For observe that the Henry Handel Richardson who had written *Maurice Guest* was not the raw girl encompassed by the limitations of the Kilmore Post Office and a Philistine mother. She had already behind her the years in Munich and a day-to-day communion with a husband steeped in the European literary tradition. Her cultural experience was probably richer than that of such contemporary novelists as Wells or Bennett.[1] It was primarily the simple damnation of being an Australian which made her feel limited. Justified, you may think, by the tone of Australian life, with its isolation and excessively material emphasis? Examine the evidence fairly and closely, and I think you will agree that Henry Handel Richardson's Australian background was a shade richer in cultural influence than the dingy shop-cum stuffy Housekeeper's Room-cum sordid Grammar School which incubated Wells, or than the Five Towns of the eighteen-eighties.[2]

By both temperament and circumstance, Henry Handel Richardson was peculiarly susceptible to the influence of the Cringe; but no Australian writer, unless he is dangerously insensitive, can wholly escape it; he may fight it down or disguise it with a veneer of truculence, but it must weaken his confidence and nag at his integrity.

---

1   H.G. Wells (1866–1946) and Arnold Bennett (1867–1931), English writers.
2   Fictionalised towns in the novels of Arnold Bennett.

It is not so much our limitations of size, youth and isolation which create the problem as the derivativeness of our culture; and it takes more difficult forms than the Cringe. The writer is particularly affected by our colonial situation because of the nature of his medium. The painter is in some measure bound by the traditional evolution of his art, the musician must consider the particular combinations of sound which the contemporary civilised ear can accept; but ultimately paint is always paint, a piano everywhere a piano. Language has no such ultimate physical existence; it is in its essence merely what generations of usage have made it. The three symbols m-a-n create the image of a male human being only because venerable English tradition has so decreed. The Australian writer cannot cease to be English even if he wants to. The nightingale does not sing under Australian skies; but he still sings in the literate Australian mind. It may thus become the symbol which runs naturally to the tip of the writer's pen; but he dare not use it because it has no organic relation with the Australian life he is interpreting.

The Jindyworobaks are entirely reasonable when they protest against the alien symbolisms used by O'Dowd, Brennan or McCrae; but the difficulty is not simply solved. A Jindyworobak writer uses the image 'galah-breasted dawn'. The picture is both fresh and accurate, and has a sense of immediacy because it comes direct from the writer's environment; and yet somehow it doesn't quite come off. The trouble is that we—unhappy Cringers—are too aware of the processes in its creation. We can feel the writer thinking: 'No, I mustn't use one of the images which English language tradition is insinuating into my mind; I must have something Australian: ah, yes—' What the phrase has gained in immediacy, it has lost in spontaneity. You have some measure of the complexity of the problem of a colonial culture when you reflect that the last sentence I have written is not so nonsensical as it sounds.

I should not, of course, suggest that the Australian image can never be spontaneously achieved; one need not go beyond Stewart's *Ned Kelly* to disprove such an assumption. On the other hand, the distracting influence of the English tradition is not restricted to merely linguistic difficulties. It confronts the least cringing Australian writer at half-a-dozen points.

What is the cure for our disease? There is no short-cut to the gradual processes of national growth—which are already beginning to have their effect. The most important development of the last twenty years in Australian writing has been the progress made in the art of being unself-consciously ourselves. If I have thought this article worth writing, it is because I believe that progress will quicken when we articulately recognise two facts: that the Cringe is a worse enemy to our cultural development than our isolation, and that the opposite of the Cringe is not the Strut, but a relaxed erectness of carriage.

1950

KENNETH SLESSOR
1901–1971

Kenneth Slessor's early collections *Thief of the Moon* (1924) and *Earth Visitors* (1926) evidence Norman Lindsay's (qv) 'vitalist' aesthetic, after Slessor's involvement in the short-lived *Vision* magazine with Norman and Jack Lindsay. But they also sustain some of the chilled melancholy that features in his work, in its preoccupation with time and memory, apprehension and alienation, death and meaning. These themes lead critics to claim Slessor as a pioneer of modernism in Australia, even though his work is not always formally experimental. A portion of his poetry is also popular in approach and notably this work displays more engagement with the energies of modern urban life.

    Darlinghurst Nights and Morning Glories: Being 47 strange sights observed from eleventh storeys, in a land of cream puffs and crime, by a flat-roof professor (1933) collected Slessor's 'light verse', which had been originally published in *Smith's Weekly* where he worked as a journalist. These deft and whimsical poems about 'girls' were accompanied by Virgil Reilly's drawings and display Slessor's facility with rhyme and metre. *Cuckooz Contrey* (1932) contains some of his most celebrated poems, exhibiting an intensified imagism. *Five Bells: XX poems* (1939) was his last full collection and includes one of Australia's best-known poems, his beautiful 128-line elegy for the drowned artist Joe Lynch. After 1939, Slessor added few new poems to his body of work. These included 'Beach Burial' (1944), which drew on his experience as a war correspondent. *NM*

Up in Mabel's Room

The stairs are dark, the steps are high—
    Too dark and high for YOU—
Where Mabel's living in the sky
    And feeding on the view;
Five stories down, a fiery hedge,   5
    The lights of Sydney loom,
But the stars burn on the window-ledge
    Up in Mabel's room.

A burning sword, a blazing spear,
    Go floating down the night,   10
And flagons of electric beer
    And alphabets of light—
The moon and stars of Choker's Lane,
    Like planets lost in fume,
They roost upon the window-pane   15
    Up in Mabel's room.

And you with fifty-shilling pride
    Might scorn the top-floor back,
But, flaming on the walls outside,
    Behold a golden track!   20

Oh, bed and board you well may hire
    To save the weary hoof,
But not the men of dancing fire
    Up on Mabel's roof.

There Mr Neon's nebulae   25
    Are constantly on view,
The starlight falls entirely free,
    The moon is always blue,
The clouds are full of shining wings,
    The flowers of carbon bloom—   30
But you—YOU'll never see these things
    Up in Mabel's room.

                                   1933

Backless Betty from Bondi

The beach is not entirely free,
The sands are far from trackless,
When Betty dances to the sea,
So rapturously backless;
By this, we don't impute a lack   5
In one whose back is peerless—

    FOR WHO,
    POSSESSING SUCH A BACK,
    COULD BE DESCRIBED
    AS REARLESS?   10

And, oh, the Euclid of her spine,
The trills, divine and deathless,
That ripple down a magic line
And leave the watcher breathless!
A thousand feet her feet pursue,   15
With hopeless tread and tireless—

    HER BACK IS FULL
    OF POOH-FOR-YOU,
    HER EYES ARE FULL
    OF WIRELESS.   20

You aldermen who thunder out
Damnation for the Backless,
Your waists, no doubt, are rather stout,

Which makes you somewhat tactless;
And you, arch-bulldogs of the sand,   25
So big and brown and artless,

    WHO PUT THE BELLOW
    IN THE BANNED—
    INSPECTORS,
    DON'T BE HEARTLESS!   30

Oh, make the great Pacific dry,
And drive the council speechless,
Remove the breakers from Bondi—
The beach, and leave us beachless,
The fair, the bare, the naked-backed,   35
The beer, the pier, the jetty—

    TAKE ANYTHING AT ALL,
    IN FACT,
    BUT LEAVE,
    OH LEAVE US BETTY!   40
                                                           1933

Five Bells

Time that is moved by little fidget wheels
Is not my Time, the flood that does not flow.
Between the double and the single bell
Of a ship's hour, between a round of bells
From the dark warship riding there below,   5
I have lived many lives, and this one life
Of Joe, long dead, who lives between five bells.

Deep and dissolving verticals of light
Ferry the falls of moonshine down. Five bells
Coldly rung out in a machine's voice. Night and water   10
Pour to one rip of darkness, the Harbour floats
In air, the Cross hangs upside-down in water.

Why do I think of you, dead man, why thieve
These profitless lodgings from the flukes of thought
Anchored in Time? You have gone from earth,   15
Gone even from the meaning of a name;

Yet something's there, yet something forms its lips
And hits and cries against the ports of space,
Beating their sides to make its fury heard.

Are you shouting at me, dead man, squeezing your face   20
In agonies of speech on speechless panes?
Cry louder, beat the windows, bawl your name!

But I hear nothing, nothing ... only bells,
Five bells, the bumpkin calculus of Time.
Your echoes die, your voice is dowsed by Life,   25
There's not a mouth can fly the pygmy strait—
Nothing except the memory of some bones
Long shoved away, and sucked away, in mud;
And unimportant things you might have done,
Or once I thought you did; but you forgot,   30
And all have now forgotten—looks and words
And slops of beer; your coat with buttons off,
Your gaunt chin and pricked eye, and raging tales
Of Irish kings and English perfidy,
And dirtier perfidy of publicans   35
Groaning to God from Darlinghurst.
                                                Five bells.
Then I saw the road, I heard the thunder
Tumble, and felt the talons of the rain
The night we came to Moorebank in slab-dark,   40
So dark you bore no body, had no face,
But a sheer voice that rattled out of air
(As now you'd cry if I could break the glass),
A voice that spoke beside me in the bush,
Loud for a breath or bitten off by wind,   45
Of Milton, melons, and the Rights of Man,
And blowing flutes, and how Tahitian girls
Are brown and angry-tongued, and Sydney girls
Are white and angry-tongued, or so you'd found.
But all I heard was words that didn't join   50
So Milton became melons, melons girls,
And fifty mouths, it seemed, were out that night,
And in each tree an Ear was bending down,
Or something had just run, gone behind grass,
When, blank and bone-white, like a maniac's thought,   55
The naphtha-flash of lightning slit the sky,

Knifing the dark with deathly photographs.
There's not so many with so poor a purse
Or fierce a need, must fare by night like that,
Five miles in darkness on a country track,   60
But when you do, that's what you think.

                                                        Five bells.

In Melbourne, your appetite had gone,
Your angers too; they had been leeched away
By the soft archery of summer rains   65
And the sponge-paws of wetness, the slow damp
That stuck the leaves of living, snailed the mind,
And showed your bones, that had been sharp with rage,
The sodden ecstasies of rectitude.
I thought of what you'd written in faint ink,   70
Your journal with the sawn-off lock, that stayed behind
With other things you left, all without use,
All without meaning now, except a sign
That someone had been living who now was dead:
'At Labassa. Room 6 × 8   75
On top of the tower; because of this, very dark
And cold in winter. Everything has been stowed
Into this room—500 books all shapes
And colours, dealt across the floor
And over sills and on the laps of chairs;   80
Guns, photoes of many differant things
And differant curioes that I obtained …'

In Sydney, by the spent aquarium-flare
Of penny gaslight on pink wallpaper,
We argued about blowing up the world,   85
But you were living backward, so each night
You crept a moment closer to the breast,
And they were living, all of them, those frames
And shapes of flesh that had perplexed your youth,
And most your father, the old man gone blind,   90
With fingers always round a fiddle's neck,
That graveyard mason whose fair monuments
And tablets cut with dreams of piety
Rest on the bosoms of a thousand men
Staked bone by bone, in quiet astonishment   95
At cargoes they had never thought to bear,
These funeral-cakes of sweet and sculptured stone.

Where have you gone? The tide is over you,
The turn of midnight water's over you,
As Time is over you, and mystery,   100
And memory, the flood that does not flow.
You have no suburb, like those easier dead
In private berths of dissolution laid—
The tide goes over, the waves ride over you
And let their shadows down like shining hair,   105
But they are Water; and the sea-pinks bend
Like lilies in your teeth, but they are Weed;
And you are only part of an Idea.
I felt the wet push its black thumb-balls in,
The night you died, I felt your eardrums crack,   110
And the short agony, the longer dream,
The Nothing that was neither long nor short;
But I was bound, and could not go that way,
But I was blind, and could not feel your hand.
If I could find an answer, could only find   115
Your meaning, or could say why you were here
Who now are gone, what purpose gave you breath
Or seized it back, might I not hear your voice?

I looked out of my window in the dark
At waves with diamond quills and combs of light   120
That arched their mackerel-backs and smacked the sand
In the moon's drench, that straight enormous glaze,
And ships far off asleep, and Harbour-buoys
Tossing their fireballs wearily each to each,
And tried to hear your voice, but all I heard   125
Was a boat's whistle, and the scraping squeal
Of seabirds' voices far away, and bells,
Five bells. Five bells coldly ringing out.

Five bells.
1939

Last Trams

I

That street washed with violet
Writes like a tablet
Of living here; that pavement
Is the metal embodiment
Of living here; those terraces   5

Filled with dumb presences
Lobbed over mattresses,
Lusts and repentances,
Ardours and solaces,
Passions and hatreds   10
And love in brass bedsteads …
Lost now in emptiness
Deep now in darkness
Nothing but nakedness,
Rails like a ribbon   15
And sickness of carbon
Dying in distances.

II

Then, from the skeletons of trams,
Gazing at lighted rooms, you'll find
The black and Röntgen diagrams
Of window-plants across the blind

That print their knuckleduster sticks,   5
Their buds of gum, against the light
Like negatives of candlesticks
Whose wicks are lit by fluorite;

And shapes look out, or bodies pass,
Between the darkness and the flare.   10
Between the curtain and the glass,
Of men and women moving there.

So through the moment's needle-eye,
Like phantoms in the window-chink,
Their faces brush you as they fly,   15
Fixed in the shutters of a blink;

But whose they are, intent on what,
Who knows? They rattle into void,
Stars of a film without a plot,
Snippings of idiot celluloid.   20
                                                          1939

South Country

After the whey-faced anonymity
Of river-gums and scribbly-gums and bush,

After the rubbing and the hit of brush,
You come to the South Country

As if the argument of trees were done,   5
The doubts and quarrelling, the plots and pains,
All ended by these clear and gliding planes
Like an abrupt solution.

And over the flat earth of empty farms
The monstrous continent of air floats back   10
Coloured with rotting sunlight and the black,
Bruised flesh of thunderstorms:

Air arched, enormous, pounding the bony ridge,
Ditches and hutches, with a drench of light,
So huge, from such infinities of height,   15
You walk on the sky's beach

While even the dwindled hills are small and bare,
As if, rebellious, buried, pitiful,
Something below pushed up a knob of skull,
Feeling its way to air.   20
                                                                         1939

Beach Burial

Softly and humbly to the Gulf of Arabs
The convoys of dead sailors come;
At night they sway and wander in the waters far under,
But morning rolls them in the foam.

Between the sob and clubbing of the gunfire   5
Someone, it seems, has time for this,
To pluck them from the shallows and bury them in burrows
And tread the sand upon their nakedness;

And each cross, the driven stake of tidewood,
Bears the last signature of men,   10
Written with such perplexity, with such bewildered pity,
The words choke as they begin—

'Unknown seaman'—the ghostly pencil
Wavers and fades, the purple drips,

The breath of the wet season has washed their inscriptions   15
As blue as drowned men's lips,

Dead seamen, gone in search of the same landfall,
Whether as enemies they fought,
Or fought with us, or neither; the sand joins them together,
Enlisted on the other front.   20

El Alamein
1944/1956

XAVIER HERBERT
1901–1984

Xavier Herbert is best known for two prize-winning novels, *Capricornia* (1938) and *Poor Fellow My Country* (1975). *Capricornia* was his first book, a sprawling, caustically satiric and vitally energetic epic that made Herbert's reputation. Herbert himself called it 'that old botch', in a reference perhaps to its genre-busting form. Set in a fictionalised, frontier NT, *Capricornia*'s central concern is with what governmental regimes and newspaper debates termed the 'half-caste problem'. It can be read as a scathing critique of the brutalising contempt for Aboriginal inheritance, family, belonging and culture demonstrated in white/black relations.

Herbert researched it in periods of working in Darwin and elsewhere. He was employed as acting superintendent of Darwin's Kahlin compound, with his wife Sadie as matron, from October 1935 to June 1936. Described ironically in *Capricornia* as 'the Nation's pride, a miniature city of whitewashed hovels crowded on a barren hill above the sea', it was a fenced reserve impounding 'half-castes'. Herbert's satire introduces a pervasive ambiguity to the novel's critique, however. Its portrait of the sexual exploitation of Aboriginal women in particular combines a revelatory silence with a masculinist verbiage that Elizabeth Lawson, in 'Oh, Don't You Remember Black Alice? or How Many Mothers Had Norman Shillingsworth?' *Westerly* (1987), calls 'endemically depraved'.

Herbert himself was a yarn spinner, adventurer, bushman and blatherer—his account of his life is full of concoctions and overstatements. He was a notorious womaniser and also a misogynist, his autobiographical *Disturbing Elements* (1963) boasting of the rape of a teenager. He published short stories with outback themes, one expanded into the novella *Seven Emus* (1959), and published the novel *Soldiers' Women* in 1961, set during the Second World War. But it was his final opus, *Poor Fellow My Country*, which was his life's work—the longest novel in Australian literature at 800,000 words. Published during the constitutional crisis that led to the sacking of the Whitlam government in 1975, it was acclaimed as an Australian classic. With another mixed-heritage Aboriginal hero, like *Capricornia,* it is a novel about Australia's potential, and failure, to realise a new model for society, a 'true commonwealth'. *NM*

From *Capricornia*
Chapter 1: The Coming of the Dingoes

Although that northern part of the Continent of Australia which is called Capricornia was pioneered long after the southern parts, its unofficial early history was even more bloody than that of the others. One probable reason for this is that the pioneers had already had experience in subduing Aborigines in the South and hence were impatient of wasting time with people who they knew were determined to take no immigrants. Another reason is that the Aborigines were there more numerous than in the South and more hostile because used to resisting casual invaders from the near East Indies. A third reason is that the pioneers had difficulty in establishing permanent settlements, having several times to abandon ground they had won with slaughter and go slaughtering again to secure more. This abandoning of ground was due not to the hostility of the natives, hostile enough though they were, but to the violence of the climate, which was not to be withstood even by men so well equipped with lethal weapons and belief in the decency of their purpose as Anglo-Saxon builders of Empire.

The first white settlement in Capricornia was that of Treachery Bay—afterwards called New Westminster—which was set up on what was perhaps the most fertile and pleasant part of the coast and on the bones of half the Karrapillua Tribe. It was the resentment of the Karrapilluas to what probably seemed to them an inexcusable intrusion that was responsible for the choice of the name of Treachery Bay. After having been driven off several times with firearms, the Tribe came up smiling, to all appearances unarmed and intending to surrender, but dragging their spears along the ground with their toes. The result of this strategy was havoc. The Karrapilluas were practically exterminated by uncomprehending neighbours into whose domains they were driven. The tribes lived in strict isolation that was rarely broken except in the cause of war. Primitive people that they were, they regarded their territorial rights as sacred.

When New Westminster was for the third time swept into the Silver Sea by the floods of the generous Wet Season, the pioneers abandoned the site to the crocodiles and jabiroos and devil-crabs, and went in search of a better. Next they founded the settlement of Princetown, on the mouth of what came to be called the Caroline River. In Wet Season the river drove them into barren hills in which it was impossible to live during the harsh Dry Season through lack of water. Later the settlements of Britannia and Port Leroy were founded. All were eventually swept into the Silver Sea. During Wet Season, which normally lasted for five months, beginning in November and slowly developing till the Summer Solstice, from when it raged till the Equinox, a good eighty inches of rain fell in such fertile places on the coast as had been chosen, and did so at the rate of from two to eight inches at a fall. As all these fertile places were low-lying, it was obviously impossible to settle on them permanently. In fact, as the first settlers saw it, the whole vast territory seemed never to be anything for long but either a swamp during Wet Season or a hard-baked desert during the Dry. During the seven months of a normal Dry Season never did a drop of rain fall and rarely did a cloud appear. Fierce suns and harsh hot winds soon dried up the lavished moisture.

It was beginning to look as though the land itself was hostile to anyone but the carefree nomads to whom the Lord gave it, when a man named Brittins Willnot found the site of what came to be the town of Port Zodiac, the only settlement of any size that ever stood permanently on all the long coastline, indeed the only one worthy of the name of Town ever to be set up in the whole vast territory. Capricornia covered an area of about half a million square miles. This site of Willnot's was elevated, and situated in a pleasantly unfertile region where the annual rainfall was only about forty inches. Moreover, it had the advantage of standing as a promontory on a fair-sized navigable harbour and of being directly connected with what came to be called Willnot Plateau, a wide strip of highland that ran right back to the Interior. When gold was found on the Plateau, Port Zodiac became a town.

The site of Port Zodiac was a Corroboree Ground of the Larrapuna Tribe, who left the bones of most of their number to manure it. They called it Mailunga, or the Birth Place, believing it to be a sort of Garden of Eden and apparently revering it. The war they waged to retain possession of this barren spot was perhaps the most desperate that whitemen ever had to engage in with an Australian tribe. Although utterly routed in the first encounter, they continued to harass the pioneers for months, exercising cunning that increased with their desperation. Then someone, discovering that they were hard-put for food since the warring had scared the game from their domains, conceived the idea of making friends with them and giving them several bags of flour spiced with arsenic. Nature is cruel. When dingoes come to a waterhole, the ancient kangaroos, not having teeth or ferocity sharp enough to defend their heritage, must relinquish it or die.

Thus Civilisation was at last planted permanently. However, it spread slowly, and did not take permanent root elsewhere than on the safe ground of the Plateau. Even the low-lying mangrove-cluttered further shores of Zodiac Harbour remained untrodden by the feet of white men for many a year. It was the same with the whole maritime region, most of which, although surveyed from the sea and in parts penetrated and occupied for a while by explorers, remained in much the same state as always. Some of the inhabitants were perhaps amazed and demoralized, but still went on living in the way of old, quite unaware of the presumably enormous fact that they had become subjects of the British Crown. [. . .]

Chapter 22: Song of the Golden Beetle

It was shame of his folly that drove Norman from home. He dared not face those who had witnessed it. But he did not admit as much. He went angrily, insisting that he had been wronged. He intended to ride to the

Melisande. Thus he would avoid having to meet the guests again, and Oscar and Marigold, who would surely be angry, and also the people of the Siding, who would surely know all about the affair with Ket and want to know more; and by travelling thus he would be occupied during the couple of weeks for which he must wait for the opening of the Construction. So actually he chose the precipitate mode of departure for very practical reasons, though he preferred to consider it dramatic. That New Year's Day he travelled twenty-seven miles, first stopping at his water-works on the southern boundary, where he had dinner and slept for several hours, then at Purruwunni Creek near the railway, where he pitched his camp for the night. The day was calm and dry, as had been every day for a week past. As yet Wet Season had been mild.

Darkness put an end to his conceit. Never before had night found him out of earshot of his kind. It was long before he slept. He heaped up the fire, heaped it up, not for warmth nor for illumination, since the night was hot and the blaze roused sinister shadows, but for companionship. Squatting—no, crouching—at the bottom of a grey-and green-walled well of light, he sensed the Spirit of the Land to the full. Phantoms came crowding, wailing afar off, whispering as they neared, treading with tiny sounds, flitting like shadows. He felt afraid. His scalp crept. His black eyes rolled.

A golden beetle shot into the firelight, for a while dashed blindly round, then settled in a bush, began to sing: Whirrrree — whirrrree — whirrrreeyung — eeyung — eeyung — eeyong — eeyung — eeyahng — eeyah — eeyah — eeyahn, eeyung — eeyong — eeyong — eeyong — eeyah — eeyah — eeyah — eeyah—reverberating droning rising rising in compelling volume into miniature boom of didjeridoo diminishing to momentary pause then rising rising waxing waxing seizing mind compelling limb—eeyung — eeyung — eeyong — eeyong — eeyah — eeyah — eeyah—voice of the spirit of Terra Australis—eeyah-eeyah-eeyah—and Norman, wrapt, with eyes on Southern Cross, took up a stick and beat upon a log—click-click — clickaclick-click — click-click — clickaclick-click — eeyung-eeyung-eeyong-eeyahng-eeyah-eeyah-eeyah—O mungallini kurritai, ee-tukka wunni wurri-gai, ee-minni kinni tulli-yai—ee-yah-eeyah-eeyah!

He dropped the stick. His skin was tingling. He looked at his hand, ashamed. Then he snatched up the stick and hurled it at the beetle. The beetle fled. But for long its song went on.

He sought companionship of stars that formerly had been as familiar as street-lamps, to find them strange, utterly strange, vastly remote, infinite, arranged now to form mysterious designs of frightening significance. The cry of the kwiluk—Kwee-luk!—Kwee-luk!—Kweeee-luk!—which he had heard every night since coming home but scarcely heeded, became the lamenting of the wandering Devils of the Dead. He heaped up the fire, heaped it up, poked it to make it blaze and crackle, tried by staring into it to burn from his mind his tingling fears. But the higher the fire blazed the greater grew his own black shadow, which he knew without turning round to see was reared above him, menacing. He had to restrain himself from seeking relief in the Song of the Golden Beetle. Then for the first time he realized his Aboriginal heritage. He was mighty pleased to hear occasionally the clink of hobbles and the clank of the bell and the clump of the horses' hoofs. When the horses came to the smoke of the fire to rid themselves of flies he was delighted. He hailed them as fellows, rose, went to them, fondled them and talked to them for hours. It was past midnight when he fell asleep. He slept badly, dreaming that he was lost with some sort of silent nomadic tribe among moving shadows in a valley of mountainous walls.

He woke at dawn to see through his mosquito-net a pair of red-eyed crows making furtive examination of the pack-bags. He stared at the familiar surroundings in surprise. He rose and went down to the creek to drink and bathe. By the time he returned he had abandoned all thought of riding to the Melisande.

But much as loneliness had increased his love of kind and home, it had not engendered any illusions in him about the reception awaiting at Red Ochre. Undecided what to do, he set off up the creek towards the Lonely Ranges. By noon he had stifled the inclination to return. After dinner he set out with purpose to find the pad to Tatlock's Pool, having decided to spend a day or two there with Joe Backhouse and Bill Donniken, who lived on the late Pat O'Hay's property, and whom he had met at the Siding, to spend another day or two in hunting cattle along the Lonely River, and then to go home with a handful of beasts with which to appease Oscar. But though he had, as he supposed, arranged matters satisfactorily, he was far from happy. Throughout the afternoon he was haunted by thoughts of his debasement, and that night was more sensitive to the Spirit of the Land than ever.

On the third day he became quite cheerful, as the result of discovering for the first time in his life that he was thinking deeply. This he did through solving with a minute's thought a problem in mechanics that had been puzzling him for weeks. Encouraged to ponder other problems with what he thought remarkable success, he began to feel for the first time in his life that he was clever. Soon he forgot his debasement. And he found himself marvelling at the phenomenon of his existence as a creature, of the existence of Mankind, and of nature's contrariety to Man that made Man's ingenuity essential. And for the first time in his life he began consciously to doubt the existence of the conventional Divinity in which he had been trained to believe, and to wonder about the Something he could see in the stars. So he came to marvel at Infinity instead of fearing it. That third night he forgot the phantoms roused by his fire in pondering over the phenomenon of combustion.

He retained this pleasant state of mind till he reached Tatlock's Pool. He arrived there at noon on the fifth day, loving all Mankind. He departed two hours later cursing the Universe. For Backhouse and Donniken received him as they might any wandering yeller-feller, questioned him as rudely as they might a nigger, and as though he were a nigger did not ask him in to dinner but sent a portion out to him on a tin plate to eat on the veranda. He was amazed at first. For a while he sat staring at the nigger's dollop, then rose and went away. Backhouse and Donniken were surprised to find him gone, then annoyed to find his food aswarm with ants.

He rode eastward blindly. Natives in a camp he passed rose up and shouted. He did not heed. Blindly he went on, following a pad to the Lonely River. So he came to a crossing, wide and turbulent, over which the yellow water boomed as rage was booming in his heart. He did not halt. He wished to put a barrier between himself and the hated world. Barrier! He shouted the word through yellow spray while flogging the horses over. Barrier! Barrier! The river boomed the word. Jabiroo and ibis swept up croaking it. Barrier! Barrier! As though he were not barriered off already!

Loving the river because its violence suited his mood, he rode up its grassy western bank till sundown, camped beside it, and slept soundly with its booming in his ears. Night held no terrors for him now; and loneliness no longer troubled him. He spent the hours between sundown and ten o'clock in working out a problem in mechanics and studying his map.

Having in the last few hours lost all desire to go home, he was reconsidering the idea of riding to the Melisande, this time by following a route that appeared on the map to be much shorter than the railway, that is, the course of the Lonely River, of which the Melisande River was a tributary. According to the map the Melisande joined the Lonely at a point about fifty miles above Tatlock's, and the railway bridge was no more than thirty miles above this point. Thus he was now but eighty miles from the construction-camp, a three or four days' quiet ride, whereas at Purruwunni Creek, which now lay forty miles to east of him, he had been one hundred and sixteen miles from it.

Scanning the map, he observed that the railway ran through what appeared to be a chain of hills. This was the backbone of the Willnot Plateau. He wondered why it had not been built along the Lonely River, knowing enough about the country to suppose that little difference would be made to the cattle-industry, the country's only staple one, if the road ran anywhere to east or west within fifty miles of the position chosen. What he did not know was that the Plateau was about the only part of Capricornia of much extent within three hundred miles of the sea that was not completely flooded in Wet Season. The Plateau extended from Port Zodiac to the

Leichhardt Tableland, a distance of three hundred miles, and was, on average, some thirty-five miles wide. He had descended from it when he rode away from the settlement at Tatlock's.

He had often been told that it was impossible to travel in low country during the Wet. Not knowing exactly what low country was and having forgotten how violent the Wet was when it set in properly, he had never appreciated the information.

Next morning he had to hunt far for his horses. He found them back at the crossing trying to cross. The river was there quite shallow, and the strength of it not great for all the turbulence. But the horses were short-hobbled and unable to negotiate the rocks and holes. Never in his experience with them had they wandered more than a hundred yards or so from camp. The fact that they went as far as possible on this occasion might have struck one more conversant with the whims of horses and the ways of Capricornia as significant, especially as the air was heavy with humidity and dark with clouds. He merely thought that they had gone back with intent to join the horses at Tatlock's.

Above the crossing, as far as he had seen as yet, the river was about a chain in width, not half as wide as at the crossing, though obviously much deeper. That it was swollen much above Dry-Season volume was apparent, as also that the volume had increased through comparatively light showers that had fallen in the last two days. This much he realized. What he did not realize was the river's capability of swelling rapidly and mightily. He could not have realized the rapidity without seeing it for himself; but he might have understood its potentiality for rising mightily if he had studied the scored and snag-littered bed of the grassy spaces flanking it. The space on his side was a good six chains wide near the crossing, bound by a ridge a good thirty feet above the level of the river, which meant that the river was capable of spreading to a width of at least twelve chains and rising thirty feet. The grassy space was actually the river's flood-bed. The western flood-bank was the distant bush-grown ridge.

The vegetation hedging the river's normal bed comprised such semi-aquatic growths as banyan, swamp-mahogany, leichhardt, paper-bark, bamboo, and pandanus palms. A cataclysm could not uproot such growths. But for all their sturdiness they never could have lived a week in earth so dry as that in which the common gum-trees grew in the Dry Season. The grassy spaces flanking the river were strips of no-tree's land, being too wet in the Wet for eucalypts, too dry in the Dry for aquatics. The fact that they were treeless was significant. Norman considered it merely fortunate, since it made travelling easy. The fact that he saw no kangaroos in the vicinity, whereas he had seen hundreds on the banks of watercourses on The Plateau, was also significant and also lost on him. There was no sign even of the almost amphibious buffalo.

He might also have realized how mightily the river swelled by simply looking into trees and noting the old flood-debris thirty feet above, instead of noting only cockatoos and nuttagul geese and cranes. Thus, though lately he had become well-skilled in the art of using his eyes, all unconscious of the river's dangerous potentialities, he rode up the grassy flood-bank, under a rain-filled sky, towards a destination that to him was only an inscription on a map, as careless as he would have been if riding to Red Ochre from the rail. During that day's march he came upon another crossing, but ignored it, preferring the western bank because the map described the eastern further up as swampy. He thought the western would be easy all the way, since it was dealt with on the map with much less detail. The country eastward of the river, that is on The Plateau-side, was fully detailed on the map, while that to the westward was for the most part marked *Not Surveyed*.

He noticed as he went along that the grassy space he rode in widened gradually, that the ridge that bounded it declined, and that the vegetation there grew denser. Thus till noon, when he crossed a tributary creek, which brawled through tangled growths like those along the river, and came upon a very different scene. The ridge had disappeared; the vegetation on the right, or west, had, as it were, closed in; the river had become much wider; and the grass that grew in the now restricted space was six feet high instead of three or four as it had been. The vegetation on the right was now of the aquatic type, composed mainly of paper-barks so closely crowded that their trunks looked from a distance like palings of a huge white fence. And the grassy space was only three chains wide instead of six, and the earth of it moist and steaming. He stopped on the further side of the creek and pitched his dinner-camp beneath a shady tree. Though he had ridden neither far nor fast his clothes were soaked with sweat and he was weary. The heat was overpowering. One-third of the sky was packed with voluminous black and woolly-white clouds, the rest of it blazing blue. Sunbeams peeping through the leaves stung him like rays from a burning-glass, forcing him to rig his ground-sheet as an additional shelter and stifle himself still more. After a meal of tinned peaches and biscuit and tea he covered himself with the mosquito-net and fell asleep.

He was wakened by the sound of crashing foliage. He jumped up, thinking of buffaloes. Soon he heard a horsey snort and clink of hobbles. He found The Policeman in the middle of the creek, caught by the pack-saddle in bamboos. Later he found Juggler and False on the other side, waiting for The Policeman to come. Still the fact that there was significance to be found in their attempted desertion was lost on him. He made haste to be on his way, annoyed to find that he had slept for more than two hours. Now the sky was pitchy black behind him. Thunder was rumbling far away. Wind was moaning in the jungle to the right. Obviously a storm was brewing. But he went on fearlessly, not realizing how violent a Capricornian storm could be, since the few he had experienced so far had been moderate.

That storm was a cockeye bob. It was not long in coming. It began with a gust of wind that smote him like a club and sent him and horse staggering into the scrub beside the river, that for a moment crushed the tall grass flat, that filled the sky with leaves. Then lightning streamed down the black wall in the north like water down the face of a bursting dam. Then a mighty cannonade. Then bursting of the dam. He leant upon his horse's neck, helpless while the deluge flogged him.

The squall blew itself out in a minute or two. But the rain did not stop; indeed, as with the falling of the wind it descended perpendicularly, it seemed to increase in volume, and with a roar as steady as that of a waterfall poured down for half an hour. Norman soon dismounted and sought the shelter of a tree. He was troubled about the pack-horses, afraid that they might have bolted. He could not see a yard ahead for rain, could not even see his top-boots for water racing to the river. Then the rain stopped dead. The surroundings were revealed as though by the drawing of a silver curtain. He saw The Policeman and Juggler at once. And they saw him and whinnied. For all their powers of prescience they evidently lacked the sense to hate him for his folly in frustrating their wise endeavours.

He mounted, and in bright sunshine went on his way, intending before night to cross another fair-sized creek that was, according to the map, some eight miles distant. Now a great cascade was flowing from the jungle to the river. And the river had begun to race and murmur. By nightfall the river was spilling over its banks and surging. Norman crossed the creek. It was worthy of the name of river, so big and strong was it. He took care to camp well away from its spreading waters, and from those of the river too, though he was not yet aware of danger. And he hobbled the horses fore and hind.

Being unable to make a fire on the streaming ground, he went to bed early, to lie on a stretcher rigged with saplings, pack-saddles, and the ground-sheet. Sleep did not come to him till the accustomed hour of ten, though not so much because he was troubled by the custom as by scores of tiny frogs that set up an ear-piercing chorus as soon as the sun went down, and by swarms of mosquitoes and fireflies that whined and flashed about his net, and by the din of running water. He was proof against the insects, but not against the frogs, which burrowed under the net and crawled on him. The frogs were not so friendly as they were cunning. They were seeking insects, not his company. Scores climbed the net like sailors climbing rigging, piping as though they were all bosuns.

Though the sky was starry, the early moon he had expected did not appear; so he supposed that the eastern sky, hidden from him by the river-trees, was clouded, and feared that another cockeye bob might come and blow his bed away. This fear helped to keep him wakeful too, and persisted even when at last he slept, so much so that he woke with starts from dreaming of thunder. The rainstorm that came down in the small hours of the morning and raged till nearly dawn crept on him silently and dumped the net and canvas shelter over him before he woke. He did not sleep again till dawn.

He rose at eight, tired and sodden and stiff, to eat a breakfast of mouldy damper and butter sprinkled fluid from the tin. He had tinned meat and preserved potato-starch, but did not fancy them. For a moment he thought of going out to shoot one of a flock of nuttaguls that were yelling in the river-trees near by. But he could not see the tops of the trees for a mist of steam; and then he could not make a fire. Everything was sodden except his waterproof wax matches and tobacco in its rubber pouch. And mildew had set in, growing in patches on his clothes and boots and saddles. The heat was stifling.

When he went to the river to drink and bathe he found to his surprise that he had much less distance to go to it than he expected. It was gushing through the grass within six yards of the camp, having increased by a good ten yards in width since last he saw it, or rather, since it must have spread an equal distance on the other side as well, by a good twenty. And it was spreading still. But he did not realize his danger. He bathed while the river spread by inches. He struck camp at ten, and with his sleeping-nap spread out to dry on The Policeman's saddle and wood and grass for a fire on Juggler's, went squelching on his way up stream.

The jungle on the right was described but briefly on the map, set down as a line of dots running parallel with the river for thirty miles or so, behind which were the words *Dense Jungle*. Norman calculated, making allowance for the increased bogginess and height of grass and the fact that seven creeks lay in his path, that he would pass the jungle before sundown of next day. He rode easily, letting the horses pick their way, thinking more about the past than of the future. He rode easily only for a while. Two hours after setting out he stopped to cook a meal and rest the horses. By then the fuel was dry and the horses tired out. He had covered about five miles, only half the distance he had reckoned, and had done so with difficulty, finding the earth boggier and the grass taller and tougher as he went, and that there were six times as many creeks to cross as the map-makers predicted. He reckoned he had gone five miles because the first creek marked on the map was about that distance from the one from which he had set out, and since this creek was much bigger than the five unmapped ones he had crossed, which was saying a good deal for its size, and was, unlike the others, screened by trees, he supposed it was the mapped one. Evidently, he decided, that part of the country was surveyed in the Dry, when the smaller creeks did not exist. He never thought that the surveyors would not expect to have to serve

Wet-Season travellers. Then he began to wish that he had crossed the river when he might have done so. Still he was not alarmed, thinking that he had merely come upon an inordinately well-watered stretch that he would soon put behind.

It took him long to cross this creek, so deep was it and vigorous and cluttered with snags and beset with tangled vegetation. In the middle, which was shoulder-deep, False fell and spilled his rider twice, and the second time, becoming entangled in the sword-sharp leaves of a low clump of pandanus palms, sustained deep cuts about the neck. It took them all a good half-hour to recover normal breathing. Norman patched up False's wounds as best he could, and made a pack-horse of him. When he went on he rode Juggler. Progress became even slower. The horses were tired and dejected. Covering the six miles to the next big creek took a good four hours.

Norman had decided that if the second creek should appear to be as difficult to cross as the other was, he would follow it into the jungle till he came, as he thought he would come without having far to go, to a point where crossing would be easier. And this he did, finding the creek all he had feared and more. But he did not find the easy-crossing point, though doubtless he would have had he gone on far enough. He gave up the search when it occurred to him that it was harder to enter the jungle than to cross the creek. He turned back on his tracks. It might have been easier to cross at the point he reached; but had he crossed there he would have had the difficulty of breaking another track through the jungle on the other side. As it was, his clothes and flesh were torn through his having to ride ahead and hack a path for the widely-saddled pack-horses. The horses were torn and tired too, and obviously glad to have done with what to them must have seemed sheer madness. Their legs and bellies were chafed raw by grass before they entered the jungle. They had gone in with great reluctance. They almost trotted out. The creek was crossed, with a great struggle, near the river. Camp was made in twilight. An hour after darkness fell a cockeye bob roared down.

Norman was not prepared for the prodigious display he saw in the storm that night. The fulminations of the other cockeye were rendered mild by the light of day and the sense of security engendered by that blessing. This one had the pitch-black night to blast and blaze in. Norman was badly scared, not only by the blasting and the blazing but by the sheeting rain and surging water at his feet. While blasting and blazing was at its height he crouched beneath the ground-sheet, waiting to be shattered. And while the deluge was at its worst he staggered about calf-deep in water, blinded, fighting for his breath. He staggered into the river, yelled when he felt it pulling at his legs, ran from it, staggered into it again. He splashed about madly, sliding, falling, till at length he crashed into a tree and nearly brained himself. Thus by sheer luck he reached the jungle. Lucky for him that he did not reach it earlier. He discovered in the morning that lightning had struck close to where he stood. He spent the night squatting with back to trees, and even slept a little.

At dawn he was relieved to see the horses in the jungle. He had feared that the booming river had engulfed them, hobbled as they were. And he was relieved to find that the river had not risen nearly as high as he expected, had not even reached his camp. But not all his discoveries were relieving. The creek he crossed the night before had swelled enormously, which made him fear that those ahead might be impassable. And he found that though the river had not yet filled the entire grassy space it soon would do so, and not only that, would flood the jungle, submerge it. He saw the debris in the trees.

He thought of turning back, but after consideration decided that, since he would have to cover at least fifteen miles in that direction before he would regain high ground, he might as well cover the fifteen miles ahead. He had no map to help him now. That, together with many other things in the pack-bag with it, razor, nap, clothing, his hat, net, and some food, had been washed into the river. The loss caused him no dismay. He was thankful he had not been lost with it. After a breakfast of biscuits and tinned meat, eaten in drizzling rain, he saddled up and went his way.

To his great delight he found that the third big creek, which he reached after three or four hours of laborious travelling, was not impassable. But his delight soon passed. Crossing the river cost him False, his favourite, who, while plunging wildly, scared of pandanus palms and floating logs, tripped over a snag and broke a leg. Norman shot him. It was a miserable cavalcade that carried on. Norman was troubled by the memory of False's eyes, Juggler and The Policeman by the memory of screaming and the consciousness of False's absence.

Before he reached that creek the rain had stopped and the sky had cleared. He had believed as he crossed that the journey ahead would be less arduous. But everything was changed with the death of False. Clouds swept up and blotted out the sun; rain poured down again; Norman felt that he was doomed. And soon he had good cause to feel so. The fourth big creek, which he reached at two o'clock, proved to be impassable, to be so big, indeed, that at first he thought it was a sudden bend of the river. It required no trial to prove it was impassable. That was proclaimed in the creek's own booming voice. The horses would not go near it. Norman went to it on foot, and stared at it long, seeing little more through silver mist of rain than blackish water surging over flattened grass. He turned from it shuddering, splashed back to the horses, led them into the jungle.

Now he must travel up the creek if need be to the source to cross it. And he must do so quickly. But first he must eat and rest and shelter for a while from the incessant rain. He was ravenous, tired to the point of falling when he walked, and sodden to the bone. He stopped beneath a paper-bark where the earth was not awash, and took the pack off The Policeman, saddle and all, intending, after he had rested, to arrange the pack so as to make it as narrow as possible in preparation for the struggle through the jungle. He did not unsaddle Juggler, nor hobble either horse. They were as tired as he was.

He made himself a gunyah by first cutting a strip of bark from the tree with the tommy-axe and stripping it to the base in such a way as to leave the bottom still attached, then by pegging out the free ends and propping up the middle with the rifle. He threw in a few loose sheets of bark and the pack-bags to make a floor, then stripped himself and wrung his clothes and put them on again, then crawled into the gunyah to eat. He had scarcely done eating when he fell asleep.

He woke with a start to find the moon staring in his face. He sat up blinking, absently striking at mosquitoes. Then he leapt up. Water was winking at him from the grassy corridor crushed by his horses in entering the jungle. He rushed to see. The river was in the jungle!

He looked for the horses. No sign of them or of their having gone further into the jungle. He shouted. Bursting foliage and hasty flap of wings replied. He listened long, unconscious of the boom of the creek and river, but well aware of the chuckling of water in the grass. He shouted again. A kwiluk answered—Kwee-luk!—Kwee-luk!—Kweeee-luk!

His clothes were dry. He looked at the moon. It was nearly overhead. He went to the gunyah, groped for his tobacco-pouch, found his watch. The time was half-past twelve.

After searching widely for the horses, he climbed a tree and looked out over the space he had ridden in. Except for the swaying tops of scrub and grass in the foreground and in the background a black line of half-submerged trees, there was nothing to be seen but water, water in a vast, booming, scintillating, silver flood. When he got back to the gunyah he found the water licking at his belongings. He snatched the things away as from a thief.

The horses were gone, perhaps back to look for False. At any rate, there was no time to look for them. Thus Norman reasoned while he packed a few things and watched the advancing water. But he did not hurry. For much as he feared the chuckling assassin before him he was wondering about the wilderness behind. What if he should get lost in the jungle? What if he should struggle through to meet with the assassin on the other side? What if he should escape a death by drowning in low country, to meet one by starvation in high? He did not leave till he saw the bark flooring float out of the gunyah. Then he took up the rifle, shouldered the pack-bag, and fled.

He travelled till the moon went down behind the trees and left him in pitch darkness. For three hours or more, sunk to the tops of boots in foetid mud and with the same filth plastered over hands and face and places where his ragged clothes exposed his flesh to protect him from mosquitoes, he squatted waiting for the dawn, fearful not so much of the creeping waters now as of the Devils of the Dead. Time and again he broke into the Song of the Golden Beetle.

He resumed his painful way with dawn of day and travelled till the night. The jungle grew thicker and boggier as he went; but because the roar of the river was decreasing and no roar rose ahead to second it, he was grateful, and grateful also because the sky was clear and because he found dry wood with which to make a fire. The second night he camped on a bed of leaves beside a roaring fire and sang himself to sleep with the Beetle's Song before the moon rose. Next day was also fine, and made more pleasant by the fact that the jungle was becoming thinner and less boggy. The third day was wet, but was made the best of all those countless days of wandering because it was the day of his deliverance, of his deliverance not only from the jungle and the fear of death, but from unutterable loneliness.

Soon after nightfall of the third day, six or seven hours after leaving the jungle, he was squatting by a fire under a gum-tree in a pleasantly sterile spot, grilling a turkey he had shot, when he heard a sound behind, and turned to behold a savage.

He dropped the turkey in the fire, leapt up with a startled cry.

The savage was tall, broad, bearded, naked but for a belt of human hair, painted hideously, white from head to foot, and striped with red and yellow, and armed with a handful of spears. Norman was terrified, open-mouthed, breathless, crouched.

For a moment the savage eyed him, then shocked him more by saying mildly, 'Goodday.'

Norman exhaled, gaping at the death's-head face.

Then the savage smiled eagerly and said, 'By cripes—Norman!'

Norman gaped. He caught sight of other savages stealing up. The first, looking him over, noting burst boots and rags and beard and matted hair, said, 'Wha' name—you go walkabout?'

Norman swallowed.

'Me Bootpolish,' replied the savage. 'You no savvy?'

'Bootpolish?' breathed Norman. 'W-what—old Bootpolish work longa Red Ochre?'

'Yu-i,' said the savage, and skipped to the fire and retrieved the burning bird.

Norman caught him by a shoulder, and looking wide-eyed at his death's-head face, cried, 'Bootpolish—Bootpolish—what you doing here?'

Bootpolish grinned and answered, 'Belong me country. Me go walkabout. Me fella bin hearim rifle, come look see.'

'Oh God!' cried Norman. 'Ol' Bootpolish—ol' cobber! Well I'll be damned!'

'What you doin' here, Norman?'

'Me? God—I been through hell!'

When Bootpolish heard the tale he said, 'Too bad! Yeah—him proper cheeky bukka dat one chungle. No good. Dibil-dibil country—Aint it?' he asked of his friends. They nodded gravely.

'Now I wanter get back home,' said Norman.

'Carn do it,' said Bootpolish. 'Big-fella Wet come properly.'

'Eh—can't I get round somewhere?'

'Too muchee water.'

'But I gotter get home,' cried Norman.

'Carn do it,' said Bootpolish. 'Dis one wet-time. Can't go nowhere. You askim Muttonhead. Him ol' man boss belonga me-fella. Him savvy.'

Norman's old friend Muttonhead grinned at him and told him that he could not hope to reach home for four or five more moons.

'But—but I gotter get back South,' gasped Norman. 'Or lose me job.'

Muttonhead picked up the rifle and eyeing it said, 'More better you stop long me-fella.'

'But I can't—'

'More better stop. You harcarse. Plenty harcarse stop longa bush longa blackfella.'

'I—I mean I gotter—'

'Proper good country dis one. Plenty kangaroo, plenty buffalo, plenty bandicoot, plenty yam, plenty goose, plenty duck, plenty lubra, plenty corroboree, plenty fun, plenty ebrytings. Number-one good country. More better you sit down all-same blackfella—eh Norman? Dat lo—ng lo—ng time you gotter wait—You gottim plenty baccy?'

1938

ELEANOR DARK
1901–1985

A candidate for the most highly regarded writer of the 1930s and '40s, Eleanor Dark has since been in danger of neglect and obscurity, only to be rescued at periodic intervals by readers struck by the combination of intellectualism and warmth characteristic of her ten novels.

The Timeless Land (1941), the first volume of Dark's historical trilogy, was acclaimed internationally and was a Book of the Month Club bestseller in the US. The three volumes recreated the first years of European settlement in Australia, establishing a popular historical imaginary for those now-mythic events. Dark's humanist portrait of

Governor Phillip, as a coloniser with a conscience (drawn from the journals of Watkin Tench (qv)), has strongly influenced contemporary constructions of the first moments of armed conflict with Indigenous Australia.

Her other novels are characterised by an almost opposite modernist sensibility, asserting the importance of contemporary experience and foregrounding many of the political, aesthetic and philosophical questions of the 1930s and '40s, with an interest in challenging the form of the novel. *Prelude to Christopher* (1934) is a self-conscious and experimental novel interested in the tensions between eugenic determinism and free will, women's intellectual life and sexuality, and relocates the political questions of William Lane's New Australia to a 1930s context. *The Little Company* (1945) grapples with the responsibilities of intellectuals in a time of war; *Sun Across the Sky* (1937) and *Waterway* (1938) both feature artists struggling to find new forms to express new social conditions.

Dark also wrote short fiction, essays, radio scripts and poetry. She was married to Eric Dark, a medical doctor and leftist social thinker. They were both involved in early forms of environmentalism in the Blue Mountains, and Varuna, their house in Katoomba, NSW, was gifted by their son Michael as a haven for writers. *NM*

From *The Timeless Land*
Part III: 1790

[. . .] Such disturbances, he decided philosophically, were, after all, but a small price to pay for the goodwill of a people who were essentially generous, and endlessly willing to be of service to those whom they liked and trusted. As instances of this generosity multiplied he became increasingly optimistic. The tale of a soldier, who had lost himself in the woods, added to his already high opinion of their integrity. Falling in with a party of natives, and begging their assistance, this man had been informed that they would take him to the settlement if he would first give up his musket, which they would return to him upon arrival. With considerable misgivings, he had agreed. No sooner had he surrendered his weapon, however, than all the natives had laid their own upon the ground, and bidding him accompany them had escorted him to the settlement, returned him his gun, and bade him a friendly farewell.

Upon another occasion, seeing a boatload of white men overturn on the harbour, Bennilong and several of his friends had plunged to the rescue, and saved all the occupants. Not content with dragging them ashore, they had kindled a fire to dry their clothes, and finished by seeing them safely home.

Remembering such incidents, the Governor dared to hope more and more that this one of his many problems was solved. He was still far from believing that he understood this primitive race, but he felt that at least a hopeful stage had been reached, in which each was confident of the good intentions of the other.

It was, therefore, with a shock of utter dismay that he learned, early in December, that his gamekeeper, McEntire, had been brought into the settlement with a spear through his body. The Governor was at Rose Hill when the news was brought to him, and he spent a sleepless night wondering what action he must take upon his return to Sydney Cove. Such an outrage could not be ignored, but he was loath to risk undoing, at a stroke, what it had taken him nearly three years to achieve, and he was continually haunted by the conviction that, in all his dealings with the natives, he was never able to find out more than half of the truth.

This man, McEntire, he thought, had always been the object of their particular and consistent hatred. Why? Phillip had not forgotten that Bennilong, ordinarily so friendly and gregarious, could never be persuaded to speak to him or to approach him. He had not forgotten how the man had been shunned and repulsed by the natives upon that unlucky occasion when he himself had been attacked, and he could not avoid the suspicion that he might have earned his death. As a game-killer, he had been one of those authorised to carry a musket out into the woods in search of emus and kangaroos, and it was impossible to escape the knowledge that he might not have used it only in pursuit of game. Nevertheless, the natives could not be allowed to kill his men and escape unpunished. He told himself that he had tried indulgence and kindness, subduing because he must the itching suspicion that a little kindness cannot wipe out a great injustice, that land and liberty and livelihood cannot be paid for with a few fish-hooks and beads, that the humiliation of captivity is not forgotten in the honour of a seat at his Excellency's table. ...

The inward conflict, half unconscious, sharpened his temper and frayed his nerves. He sat alone upon his return from Rose Hill, wrestling with his problem and hating it as he had never hated any problem before. He was tired; in this relentless heat, these dry and drought-stricken days, the mere effort of forming a coherent thought seemed a labour, and he rested his forehead on his hands and then lifted it and snatched irritably at his handkerchief because his palms were wet with perspiration. He knew himself entangled with two irreconcilable ideas. Duty pushed him one way, and humanity the other, but it was an unequal contest; he had been bred to revere the former. He had lived all his life in a world which admitted no arguing with Orders. Orders, certainly, had bidden him treat the natives with indulgence. He had been told to *'conciliate their affections'*. Had he not tried to do so? He had been instructed to see that his own people lived *'in amity and kindness with them'*. This also he had attempted. *'And if any of our subjects shall wantonly destroy them, or give them any unnecessary interruption in the exercise of their several occupations, it is our will and pleasure that you do cause such offenders to be brought to punishment ...'*

He pushed his chair back with a clatter and began to walk about the room. For the first time he felt a stirring of resentment that such impossible commands should have been laid upon him. No physical hardship, no material obstacle would have so roused him, but now he felt his inner self threatened by division, and was angered. Easy enough, he thought, to sit in London and pen humanitarian words! It was left to him to attempt the impossible—to find, in trying to obey them, that they rang hollow—hollow! *'Unnecessary'* interruption! Unnecessary—for whom? Am I to convince these people that it was 'necessary' to steal their land from them? That it is 'necessary', having stolen it, to hunt their game, to haul nets in their waters? That it is 'necessary' now to send an armed force against them? What is this 'necessity'? The necessity for a distant jail in which to herd our criminals! The necessity for another colonial possession! The necessity for empire and dominion, for power and glory …

Inevitably, those two words refrained themselves in a familiar context. He found his tired, stampeding brain repeating: 'For Thine is the Kingdom, the Power and the Glory …' and turned back to his table and his chair, startled by the labyrinths into which his undisciplined thoughts were leading him. Deliberately he brought them back to order. Deliberately he refused to acknowledge that out of that large conception of his settlement, which had sustained him, there had resulted a new and inevitable widening of his whole mental horizon. For a man cannot plan nobly and remain narrow; he cannot build for the future and remain mentally wedged in his little present; he cannot admit dreams of human advancement and exclude nightmares of human suffering; he cannot hold power, and wield it justly within limitations imposed upon him, without becoming ever more humble, more conscious of those limitations, more tortured by them, more rebelliously determined to break through them to some higher plane of conduct, unhampered by custom—by … Orders—by Duty…

But these were impossible, incredible thoughts for a middle-aged naval captain, bred and set in the mould of his times, trained from childhood to see obedience to Authority as the first of all the virtues. What Authority? That was a question one did not need to ask, for the answer had been so often repeated that it rang in one's ears, deafening, shutting out all other sound. King and Country! King and Country! King and Country! Who could hear beyond that clarion call? Who would seek to do so?

Duty reared itself in his thoughts like a blank brick wall, and comforted him. You could put your back against that wall and fight till you died, seeing no enemies but those clearly enough defined for you by Authority, no cause but that which Authority handed to you ready-made, with your Instructions. Thus was life simplified. He sent for Tench, and sat down wearily at his table again.

Tench, facing him across it a few minutes later, wondered whether it were anxiety, anger, or physical pain which was making his pallor leaden, and fold-ing into deep grooves the two creases between his eyes. Phillip said abruptly:

'This business of McEntire …'

Tench thought with rueful but unsurprised apprehension: 'So that's it!' There had been a good deal of conjecture as to how the Governor would deal with this latest assault, and Captain Tench, glancing out the window at the yellow blaze of sunlight, found himself suspecting cynically that a punitive expedition, if such were in his Excellency's mind, would probably turn out to be punishment for the avengers rather than the culprits. However, he only said: 'Yes, sir?' and waited attentively for the Governor to continue.

'I have decided,' Phillip said slowly, 'to send out a force against the tribe responsible. Colbee and other natives about the settlement seem agreed that the assailant was a man named Pemulwy, of the Bideegal. You are to assume this command, Captain Tench, choosing two subalterns to accompany you, and taking the sergeant and the two convicts who were with McEntire when the incident occurred as guides. And about forty men.'

He was sitting forward in his chair, staring at his clasped hands on the desk before him, so Tench permitted himself the shadow of a wry grimace while he answered again dutifully:

'Yes, sir.'

'You will proceed,' Phillip went on, 'to the peninsula at the head of Botany Bay, which is, I understand, the headquarters of this tribe, and bring back two native prisoners'—Tench brightened a little—'and put to death ten.'

There was another pause. For two seconds Captain Tench's usually imperturbable countenance showed a flash of utter consternation. Ten! Put to death, in cold blood, ten of those poor devils, those cheerful, amusing, inoffensive creatures! … He said again, mechanically: 'Yes, sir,' but there was a different tone in his voice. Phillip heard it, and looked up at him. Without words there passed between them a knowledge of the detestation with which they both regarded this task. Phillip went on grimly:

'You are to take them by surprise or by open force. In no circumstances are signs of friendship or invitation to be used. You are to destroy all weapons of war, but nothing else. You are not to burn huts or to injure women or children, I think—that's all.'

For the fourth time Tench replied: 'Yes, sir.' But as he turned to go the Governor stopped him. Since the arrival of the Second Fleet, and the influx of new personalities into his domain, Phillip had found himself relying more than ever upon the little group which had been with him from the beginning of this arduous adventure; and of them all, he felt, none was more to be depended upon than this rather worldly young man, whose very worldliness, tempered as it was with humour and humanity, seemed to lend to all his judgments a balance, an indestructible good sense, which his commander had found useful upon more than one occasion. He said now:

'One moment, Captain Tench. Sit down.'

'Thank you, sir.'

Phillip's voice became a little sharper, his manner a little primmer and more precise, as it always did when he spoke under the stress of an emotion.

'This is an unpleasant necessity, Captain. I regret it. It has always been my hope that no such measures would ever be needed. But since our arrival no fewer than seventeen of our people have been killed or wounded by the natives. Those that live on the north arm of Botany Bay—the Bideegal—have always seemed, I think, the most hostile, the most likely to prove troublesome. One sharp lesson may be enough to convince them that our people are not to be molested with impunity.'

'No doubt you are right, sir.' Tench's tone was politely and beautifully calculated to convey a quite considerable doubt. Phillip stood up and walked across to the window.

'I have noticed this about them, Tench. As individuals they regard death lightly enough. But the strength of their tribes is of the utmost importance to them. Nothing seems to give them more concern than a prospect of the weakening of their numerical strength. That is why I think that the loss of ten warriors would be the sharpest form of penalty which I could inflict.' He came back to his chair, but stood behind it, resting his hands on its carved back. 'I have delayed this as long as I could. Now something must be done.'

'You do not think, sir,' Tench suggested, 'that they may have been—provoked—to their attack on McEntire?'

Phillip shook his head.

'No. On former occasions, yes. Sometimes they have retaliated upon our people for some injury or insult. Sometimes it has been—as in the case of my own wound—the result of a pure misapprehension. But this time there seems to have been no such reason. Our people were peacefully asleep in their tent, and were awakened to find natives creeping towards them with spears in their hands. McEntire himself, when he was speared, was doing no more than speak to them. I have questioned him …'

Tench's expressive eyebrows lifted a fraction of an inch. The Governor added emphatically:

'… *and* the sergeant who was with him, of whose veracity I have the highest opinion, and the convicts. Their stories are short and simple and bear each other out in every detail.'

Tench sighed.

'Did you not make some effort, sir, to enlist the help of Bennilong and Colbee? Is nothing to be hoped for in that direction?'

Phillip made a little gesture of impatience.

'I don't understand them. They are utterly unreliable. Only yesterday they promised to go in search of the aggressor and bring him in, and went off, too, as if bent on that errand. But to-day—what do I find …?'

Tench, who knew very well, lowered his eyes to hide their flicker of amusement, and answered:

'Colbee, certainly, is still about the settlement.'

'He has been loitering round the lookout house all day. And Bennilong has gone across the harbour in his canoe to draw the teeth of some young men on the other side. I have never known a people with less stability of purpose.'

'They might, all the same, sir, give us some useful information about the culprit. There was some rumour that he was a man with a blemish in his left eye.'

'I have no doubt of knowing the man once he is taken. The sergeant and the convicts all say they can identify him, and they all agree about his eye. But Bennilong—looking me in the face with the utmost assurance—swore that the man had a deformed foot, which is obviously a lie. No, we shall have to depend on ourselves in this matter. But …' he drew his chair out again, and sat down wearily, '… if you can propose any alteration in my plan, Captain, which you would consider an improvement, let me hear it. I am most willing to listen.'

Tench, thus encouraged, sat forward in his chair with a trace of eagerness.

'Thank you, sir. If I might suggest—would it not answer the purpose equally well if, instead of putting ten to death, I were to capture six? Out of this number some—as many as your Excellency thought proper—might be put to death, and the rest set at liberty after having seen the fate of their companions.'

Phillip reflected only for a moment, and then adopted this humaner proposition with an inward sigh of relief.

'Very well, Captain. If you can't capture six, shoot that number. If you can, I'll hang two of them and send the rest to Norfolk Island for a while, so that their companions will think they also have been killed. I shall make out an order, and you must be ready to march to-morrow morning, at daylight.'

'Yes, sir.'

'And—Captain Tench …'

'Yes, sir?'

'Don't forget—no signs of friendship are to be made to entice the natives near you.'

'No, sir, I won't forget.'

He went out into the blazing heat, reflecting that after the method of capture which had been used in the case of Arabanoo, and later of Bennilong and Colbee, this admonition was, perhaps, a little belated.

But the representatives of His Majesty, sitting in conclave over the fate of the ignorant savages, had reckoned without their victims. By nightfall there was no man, woman or child in the neighbouring tribes who did not know all about the expedition. They looked at each other, puzzled, amused, even a little embarrassed by the stupidity of these white people. Let them come, tramping and crashing through the bush, laden with their gooroobeera and all their unwieldy gear, the noise of their progress waking the echoes for a mile around, the glare of their red coats ablaze through the tree trunks in the dappled light. What would they find? Quiet, bare feet would move lightly about them and they would hear nothing. Naked bodies, motionless, shadow-coloured, would lie near their path watching them pass, and they would not know. They would get very hot beneath all their coverings, very tired and bad tempered beneath their loads, and they would not see a single black man all day long. It would be all very amusing, a source of much cheerfulness and merriment among the tribes. Indeed, yes—let them come! [. . .]

1941

PEARL GIBBS
1901–1983

Pearl Gibbs (Gambanyi) was born near Sydney and grew up near Yass, NSW. She became politically active, supporting Aboriginal workers affected by the Depression and gathering information against the NSW Aborigines Protection Board. Gibbs joined the Aborigines Progressive Association (APA) and assisted in organising the 1938 Day of Mourning, becoming APA secretary until 1940. With William Ferguson (qv) she established the Dubbo branch of the Australian Aborigines League. During the 1950s, she co-founded the Australian Aboriginal Fellowship with Faith Bandler and was the only Aboriginal member of the NSW Aborigines Welfare Board. In later life Gibbs enjoyed great prominence as an Aboriginal spokesperson. *AH/PM*

Radio Broadcast

Good evening listeners,

I wish to express my deepest gratitude to the Theosophical Society of Sydney in granting me this privilege of being on the air this evening. It is the first time in the history of Australia that an Aboriginal woman has broadcast an appeal for her people. I am more than happy to be that woman. My grandmother was a full-blood Aborigine. Of that fact I am most proud. The admixture of white blood makes me a quarter-caste Aborigine. I am a member of the Committee for Aboriginal Citizenship.

My people have had 153 years of the white man's and white woman's cruelty and injustice and unchristian treatment imposed upon us. My race is fast vanishing. There are only 800 full-bloods now in New South Wales due to the maladministration of previous governments. However, intelligent and educated Aborigines, with the aid of good white friends, are protesting against these conditions. I myself have been reared independently of the Aborigines Protection Board now known as the Aborigines Welfare Board.[1] I have lived and worked amongst white people all my life. I've been in close contact with Aborigines and I have been on Aboriginal stations in New South Wales for a few weeks and months at a time. I often visit them. Therefore I claim to have a thorough knowledge of both the Aboriginal and white viewpoints. I know the difference between the status of Aborigines and white men. When I say 'white man' I mean white women also. There are different statuses for different castes. A person in whom the Aborigine blood predominates is not entitled to an old-age, invalid or returned soldier's pension. There are about thirty full-blooded returned men in this state whom I believe are not entitled to the old-age pension. A woman in whom the Aborigine blood predominates is not entitled to a baby bonus.

Our girls and boys are exploited ruthlessly. They are apprenticed out by the Aborigines Welfare Board at the shocking wage of a shilling to three and six per week pocket money and from two and six to six shillings per week is paid into a trust fund at the end of four years. This is done from fourteen years to the age of eighteen. At the end of four years a girl would, with pocket money and money from the trust, have earned £60 and a boy £90. Many girls have great difficulty in getting their trust money. Others say they have never been paid. Girls often arrive home with white babies. I do not know of one case where the Aborigines Welfare Board has taken steps to compel the white father to support his child. The child has to grow up as an unwanted member of an apparently unwanted race. Aboriginal girls are no less human than my white sisters. The pitiful small wage encourages immorality. Women living on the stations do not handle endowment money, but the managers write out orders. The orders are made payable to one store in the nearest town—in most cases a mixed drapery and grocery store. So you will see that in most cases the mother cannot buy extra meat, fruit or vegetables. When rations and blankets are issued to the children, the value is taken from the endowment money. The men work sixteen hours per week for rations worth five and six-pence. The bad housing, poor water supply, appalling sanitary conditions and the lack of right food, together with unsympathetic managers, make life not worth living for my unfortunate people.

It has now become impossible for many reasons for a full-blood to own land in his own country. On the government settlements and in camps around the country towns, the town people often object to our children attending the school that white children attend. This is the unkindest and cruelest action I know. Many of the white people call us vile names and

---

1   The *New South Wales Aborigines Protection Act* (1909) was amended in 1940, and the Board for the Protection of Aborigines was replaced by the Aborigines Welfare Board.

say that our children are not fit to associate with white children. If this is so, then the white people must also take their share of the blame. I'm very concerned about the 194 full-blooded Aboriginal children left in this State. What is going to happen to them? Are you going to give them a chance to be properly educated and grow up as good Australian citizens or just outcasts? Aborigines are roped off in some of the picture halls, churches and other places. Various papers make crude jokes about us. We are slighted in all sorts of mean and petty ways. When I say that we are Australia's untouchables you must agree with me.

You will also agree with me that Australia would not and could not have been opened up successfully without my people's help and guidance of the white explorers. Hundreds of white men, women and children owe their very lives to Aborigine trackers and runners—tracking lost people. Quite a few airmen owe their lives to Aboriginals. I want you to remember that men of my race served in the Boer War, more so in the 1914–18 War and today hundreds of full-bloods, near full-bloods and half-castes are overseas with the AIF. More are joining each day. My own son is somewhere on the high seas serving with the Australian Navy. Many women of Aborigine blood are helping with war charities. Many are WRANS. We the Aborigines are proving to the world that we are not only helping to protect Australia but also the British Empire. New South Wales is the mother State and therefore should act as an inspiration to the rest of Australia. So we are asking for full citizenship and the status to be granted to us. We are asking that the 800 full-bloods in New South Wales be included in the claim—all those who are deprived of all federal social services to be granted, through the state, the old age pension and the maternity bonus until this injustice can be reformed by a federal law. We want an equal number of Aborigines as whites on the Welfare Board.

My friends, I'm asking for friendship. We Aborigines need help and encouragement, the same as you white people. We need to be cheered and encouraged to the ideals of citizenship. We ask help, education, encouragement from your white government. But the Aborigines Welfare gives us the stone of officialdom. Please remember, we don't want your pity, but practical help. This you can do by writing to the Hon. Chief Secretary, Mr. Baddeley, MLA Parliament House, Sydney and ask that our claims be granted as soon as possible. Also that more white men who understand my people, such as the chairman, Mr Michael Sawtell, be appointed to the Board—not merely government officials. We expect more reforms from the new government. By doing this you will help to pay off the great debt that you, the white race, owe to my Aboriginal people. I would urge, may I beg you, to hand my Aboriginal people the democracy and the Christianity that you, the white nation of Australia, so proudly boast of. I challenge the white nation to make these boasts good. I'm asking your practical help for a new and better deal for my race. Remember we, the Aboriginal people, are the creditors. Do not let it be said of you that we have asked in vain. Will my appeal for practical humanity be in vain? I leave the answer to each and every one of you.

1941

J.M. HARCOURT
1902–1971

Upsurge caused a sensation in 1934. It was Western Australian John Mewton Harcourt's second novel, after *The Pearlers* (1933)—which was set among the pearl divers of Broome and provocative in its own radical politics and frank treatment of sexuality. *Upsurge* was hailed by Katharine Susannah Prichard (qv) as 'the first proletarian novel in Australia', and denounced by newspaper reviews for its obscenity, one reviewer sniffing at its 'overpowering taint of the sexual'. Seized by police in Perth and the subject of obscenity charges in Sydney, the novel was banned by the Commonwealth Book Censorship Board in November 1934. It was not released until 1958.

Harcourt's empathy for the struggles of working-class Australians during the Depression was forged during his time as a pearl-shell opener in Broome, and during a period living on the road in his early adulthood. Describing himself as a fellow traveller with the organised left, he was the first president of the Book Censorship Abolition League, but the banning of *Upsurge* saw him unsuccessfully abandon political content in favour of romance and adventure—*It Never Fails* (1937) was described by the critic Richard Nile as 'a monumental failure'—and eventually cease writing altogether. *NM*

From *Upsurge*
Chapter 31

[. . .] There was a surging movement in the crowd. The red banners moved together. McClintock shouted from the rostrum:

'Come on, Comrades! The old formation! We're going to *march* to the Treasury …'

A cheer like the roar of a waterfall went up, and the banners, in ranks, moved slowly forward. Behind the banners a broad column of men began to draw out of the crowd like a colossal snake from the pile of its own coils.

'Stay with me,' Peter Groom said, clutching Theodora's arm. 'You shouldn't be in this, you know. There's going to be trouble.'

She nodded, conscious of an upwelling excitement that made her heart thump. She moved forward at Groom's side, borne along by the irresistible current of the crowd …

4

A small knot of police under the charge of a burly inspector waited alertly on the broad steps of the Treasury Building. There were no other uniforms in sight. The little knot waited as the unemployed advanced—a broad column marching along the centre of the street bearing aloft their red flags, flanking columns streaming along the footpaths on either side and overflowing them into the gutters. At last the unemployed halted before the Treasury Building, and their leaders advanced. The knot of police stepped forward to meet them.

'Where do you think you're going?' the inspector inquired grimly.

'We're going to see the Premier,' one of the men answered.

'No you're not.'

'I said: we're going to see the Premier,' repeated the leader deliberately. 'Stand aside!'

'Arrest them,' said the inspector to his subordinates.

They moved forward briskly.

The man Gruder, one of the several leaders, shouted: 'Stand firm, comrades. We're going to see the Premier, and we've got thousands behind us!'

A weak cheer went up from the unemployed.

The inspector's eyes glittered and his lips curled back a little from his teeth. He took a step forward and with all the weight of his great frame behind it, drove his fist into Gruder's face. The man stumbled and fell.

For an instant there was an astounded silence, then, beginning as a murmur, like a distant flood, a great roar of rage went up from the unemployed. At the same moment police whistles shrilled stridently, and from every gate and alleyway in the vicinity police appeared. Foot-police appeared with their batons gripped purposefully, and there was a clatter of the hoofs of troopers' horses.

'A trap!' someone shouted.

'Break 'em up!' said the inspector, and the police charged.

The next moment the street was filled with shouting, struggling unemployed and police. A park fence across the street gave way beneath the press, and men tore the pickets from the fallen lengths of fence to use as weapons. Whistles shrilled again and more police came running. Nearby the road was up for work on a watermain, and beside the excavation lay a heap of diorite and lumps of concrete and bitumen. In a moment the air was thick with a hail of flying stones. The street echoed with shouts, curses, screams, and cries of rage and pain and fear.

Yet more police reinforcements arrived, and, working to a plan, cleared a space of a few score yards before the Treasury steps. Troopers formed up quickly in the space and charged the crowd. The unemployed went down before the horses. A flying stone struck a trooper on the temple and he rolled out of his saddle. Others were dragged from their horses. But the troopers reformed and charged again. Each time they charged they cleared a further few yards. Under the shock of the charges those who were unhurt began to struggle to get away, to break through the jam of humanity behind. The crowd surged and swayed like a wounded thing that cried out in its death agonies.

With Theodora beside him, Peter Groom was flung this way and that by the convulsions of the crowd like a sodden chip in a torrent. Suddenly, the crowd in front of him seemed to melt away. A trooper bore down upon him. The crowd closed in behind like a wall. Desperately Groom swung the girl behind him, with his eye on the trooper. The crowd thrust him forward against the legs of the trooper's horse. The man swung up his baton. Groom ducked and felt in his hair the wind of the baton as it descended. And in his ears sounded a dull crunch. Theodora crumpled up at his feet. The murderous devil, he thought. The trooper swung up his baton again. The young idler felt a tremendous shock, and the trooper and his horse, and Theodora, and the street and the crowd flowed together and exploded into darkness.

By and by, when the street was clear, the erstwhile idler Peter Groom, and the girl Theodora Luddon, and several others, were placed on stretchers and conveyed in an ambulance to the Perth Public Hospital.

In the meantime, and throughout the day, the police were quelling minor riots all over the city.

1934

CHRISTINA STEAD
1902—1983

One of Australia's most distinguished writers, Christina Stead is recognised as among the most interesting novelists of the twentieth century. Her more than a dozen novels sustain a complex, highly original narrative mode that can be at once polyphonic and polysemic, vivifying the detailed surface of interaction while simultaneously critiquing her characters' self-regard. Her work is noted for talkative, even monstrous characters who both overwhelm her books and are extraordinary portraits of postwar life, satirising materialism while exploring alienation and desire.

After growing up in Sydney's Watsons Bay on Sydney Harbour, Stead trained to be a teacher and then left for London. Her first novel, *Seven Poor Men of Sydney* (1934), and *For Love Alone* (1944) are both set in Sydney, and both offer detailed realisations of the harbour suburbs and inner city of the interwar years. *For Love Alone* is an Australian postcolonial, feminist odyssey, its heroine Teresa's quest for love, knowledge and independence framed by a reactive distaste for Australian snobbery.

Married to a Marxist banker, Stead embraced a non-humanist Marxism in a European mode, which informs her interest in the surface of relations, while her characters are always embedded in economic situations to which they must relate, as in her early European novels *The Beauties and Furies* (1936) and *The House of All Nations* (1938). The short stories of *The Salzburg Tales* (1934), many of them elaborate allegories, show Stead's interest in the gothic and fantastic, which she developed in later novellas and stories.

The Man Who Loved Children (1940) was hailed by US critics as a masterpiece and is counted among the great novels of the twentieth century. A harrowing and closely observed study of the constrictions of bourgeois family life, it evinces both savage black humour and poignant sympathy for Louise, the teenager at its centre. Stead's short story extracted here is a study for it, although published much later.

Letty Fox: Her luck (1946), a satirical New York novel about an adventurous and cynical young woman, was banned in Australia as obscene. Later novels continued Stead's interest in social and family groups, removed to a British context, while her posthumously published *I'm Dying Laughing* (1986) is set in McCarthyite Hollywood. *NM*

From *For Love Alone*
Preface: The Sea People

In the part of the world Teresa came from, winter is in July, spring brides marry in September, and Christmas is consummated with roast beef, suckling pig, and brandy-laced plum pudding at 100 degrees in the shade, near the tall pine-tree loaded with gifts and tinsel as in the old country, and old carols have rung out all through the night.

This island continent lies in the water hemisphere. On the eastern coast, the neighbouring nation is Chile, though it is far, far east, Valparaiso being more than six thousand miles away in a straight line; her northern neighbours are those of the Timor Sea, the Yellow Sea; to the south is that cold, stormy sea full of earth-wide rollers, which stretches from there without land, south to the Pole.

The other world—the old world, the land hemisphere—is far above her as it is shown on maps drawn upside-down by old-world cartographers. From that world and particularly from a scarcely noticeable island up toward the North Pole the people came, all by steam; or their parents, all by sail. And there they live round the many thousand miles of seaboard, hugging the water and the coastal rim. Inside, over the Blue Mountains, are the plains heavy with wheat, then the endless dust, and after outcrops of silver, opal, and gold, Sahara, the salt-crusted bed of a prehistoric sea, and leafless mountain ranges. There is nothing in the interior; so people look toward the water, and above to the fixed stars and constellations which first guided men there.

Overhead, the other part of the Milky Way, with its great stars and nebulae, spouts thick as cow's milk from the udder, from side to side, broader and whiter than in the north; in the centre the curdle of the Coalsack, that black hole through which they look out into space. The skies are sub-tropical, crusted with suns and spirals, as if a reflection of the crowded Pacific Ocean, with its reefs, atolls, and archipelagos.

It is a fruitful island of the sea-world, a great Ithaca, there parched and stony and here trodden by flocks and curly-headed bulls and heavy with thick-set grain. To this race can be put the famous question: 'Oh, Australian, have you just come from the harbour? Is your ship in the roadstead? Men of what nation put you down—for I am sure you did not get here on foot?' [...]

Chapter 6: *Lance with His Head in His Hand*

Lance, with his head in his hand, was at the dining-room table poring over his engineering books. She stood in the doorway and asked: 'Did you get your dinner off the stove? If you stay out with the fishermen, you can't get it fresh.'

He turned slowly towards her, flashed a look at her bathing-suit, and then spoke to one side of her, his eyes downcast. 'Of course.'

'Was it all right? It was kept from lunch.'

'Of course.'

With misgiving and a real touch of pity for him, she looked over his lemon-coloured face, its hollows and long lines from nose to mouth. His pale-red lips were slightly apart and showed the two gaps where his front teeth had fallen out. He was still dirty after his afternoon. His long ash-blond hair, slicked back, dark-green with water, was coming down over his forehead again. His skin was very fair, his neck and all his features long and soft; his neck and face drooped easily under trouble and fatigue. He had docile brown eyes, so that however despising or sarcastic he looked, he seemed gentle too. He had a changeable face that he could never control—just when he was trying to be harsh, superior, cold, a sheepish or reluctant look upset the expression. He was estranged from them all, a young man of twenty-two, who had already spent several years on the treadmill of working boys, college at night. He worked in the daytime as a chemist in a factory where the men were always nauseated at lunch-time with the smells. He did not eat his lunches. In the week-ends, Lance lighted out early with a friend, cycling furiously for long distances, practising for reliability trials on his motor-bike, or exercising for marathons. He was an intolerant faddist. Tess searched his dusty face until he withdrew his sidelong glance and went back to his books. She knew why he careered all over the country that way in the week-ends, wearing himself out.

'You ought to go to bed,' she ventured.

'Shut up,' he said softly, working at his figures.

'You'll be all in.'

He turned slowly and looked at her with eyes great and unfocused.

'You'd better go and get that off, there's a split on the side, anyhow,' he said with quiet dignity. She giggled.

'You get out of here,' he shrieked, leaping out of his chair, starting towards her. She vanished. He fell back on his books. Going up the stairs, slowly lifting each bare foot and putting it down voluptuously on the dusty wood, she thought vaguely of Leo's shouts of wrath in the mornings, when Kitty packed his lunch and blacked his boots, Kitty, in tears, rarely answering back, the father quietly letting it pass over him, drinking his black tea off the hob. Lance also mistreated the young woman who did everything for him.

'She oughtn't to clean their boots,' said Tess to herself, lifting her fingers one by one out of the dust of the balustrade. Why did Dad let the boys rave and never intervene? 'Least said, soonest mended?'

Lance even hit Kitty, knocked her roughly out of his way as he plunged in to breakfast, a desperate look in his eyes. Leo, flaming with anger, red-cheeked, bright-eyed, leaped into the kitchen, his shirt half on, shouting complaints. Tess did nothing for them except some housework, but she did, of course, earn money, while poor Kitty seemed a burden to them, a mouth to fill. Thinking of this, Teresa remembered that she had not paid her money to Kitty this week. She went into her room and took it out of her drawer, all in silver. At this moment she heard Kitty come in and waited with some curiosity till Kitty had explained herself to her father and gone up to her room. Then she went in, still in her bathing-suit, which had now dried on her.

Kitty was sitting by the lamp, her hat still on, her short-sighted eyes looking off vaguely, a faint silly smile on her face. Teresa put down the money on Kitty's work-table. Kitty looked up with a smile of gratitude that had nothing to do with the regularly paid money. She had been a very pretty little girl, slightly cross-eyed with large black pupils; she had become a stocky adolescent with pleasant little cries and laughs when playing with the village children she was fond of, then a dull, clumsy, and slow housekeeper for the family. Teresa looked at her in her new mood with curiosity, thinking:

'I don't know what goes on in her head!'

Kitty said: 'It was a nice wedding, wasn't it?'

'Not bad.'

'I thought you'd forgotten,' said Kitty, pointing. 'You get paid on Thursdays.'

'I know, I'm sorry, I forgot. What's that?'

Kitty showed her a crocheted cap, emerald green.

'It's for Joycie Baker. Her mother provides the wool, I only get two shillings for that. If I provide the wool, I make them for three and six. I made them for a few of the mothers. It's the style now.'

'You can't make anything on them?'

'Two shillings, but of course I don't get many and it's only a fad.'

'I'll give you some money,' said Teresa, in shame.

Kitty laughed eagerly, but said: 'No, no. I ought to earn some. You pay enough.'

'We ought to pool some pocket-money for you.'

The younger girl's lip curled as she looked at her sister's dress. That brown! If she had real money, she'd make her wear different things, but Kitty was obstinate; she wanted to be safe, respectable. Teresa sighed and went back to her room, and had forgotten her sister before she was half-way along the passage.

The room! She literally jumped across the threshold and stood panting with pleasure near the middle of the room. Then with a silent, shivering, childish laugh, she closed the door, quickly and softly. She stripped off the bathing-suit, which she hung out the window to get completely dry and felt her flesh, cold as marble in the warm air. She shivered again with excitement and went to kneel at the uncurtained window looking out on the back road, the road into the camp and the hill. This hill was half a hill. On the other side it fell straight into the sea, part of South Head; the open sea was not more than two or three hundred feet away from where she stood. She envisioned it tonight, a water floor out to the horizon, with a passage strewn with moonrushes and barely breaking at the base of the cliffs.

'Oh, God, how wonderful, how wonderful!' she muttered half-intelligible exclamations which were little more than cries of ecstasy as she stood in the window. If someone was crouching among the rocks on the hill, he could see her, but otherwise she was safe here. She leaned over the sill, her round arms and full breasts resting on the woodwork. Her flesh was a strange shade in that light, like the underside of water beasts. Or like—She began to think like what. She did not care if she never went to bed; the night stretched before her. 'I know every hour of the night,' she said joyfully and repeated it. It seemed to her that she knew more of the night and of life than they all did down there; hunched Kitty, cheesy Lance, girl-mad Leo, slow Andrew Hawkins, entombed in their lives. She heard footfalls in the Bay, far off—people going home—voices, a pair of lovers perhaps, climbing higher up on the cliffs. The footsteps of anyone going home late to the camp, the permanent staff, going by the paved road, could be heard long before he came in sight and so too in the blind road underneath the house.

She was free till sunrise. She was there, night after night, dreaming hotly and without thinking of any human beings. Her long walks at night through the Bay, in which she had discovered all the lost alleys, vacant lots and lonely cottages, her meditation over the poor lovers from the city, her voluptuous swimming and rolling by herself in the deep grass of the garden and her long waking nights were part of the life of profound pleasure she had made for herself, unknown to them. She was able to feel active creation going on around her in the rocks and hills, where the mystery of lust took place; and in herself, where all was yet only the night of the senses and wild dreams, the work of passion was going on.

She had a vague picture of her future in her mind. Along the cliffs on a starlit night, very dark, strolled two figures enlaced, the girl's hair, curled as snail-shells, falling back over the man's shoulders, but alive of itself, as she leaned against him walking and all was alive, the revolute leaves, the binding roots. This she conceived happened in passion, a strange walking in harmony, blood in the trees. The playful taps and squeezes, wrestling and shrieking which Leo had with the girls was not what she expected and she did not think of this as love. She thought, dimly, that even Leo when he sat on the beach at Maroubra with his girl, made some such picture; a turbulent, maddening, but almost silent passion, a sensual understanding without end.

She abandoned herself and began to think, leaning on the window-sill. In a fissure in a cliff left by a crumbled dike, a spout of air blew up in new foam and spray, blue and white diamonds in the moon, and in between the surges the ashy sky filled the crack with invisible little stars. Hundreds of feet beneath, the sea bursting its skin began to gush up against the receding tide; with trumpet sounds, wild elephants rose in a herd from the surf and charged the cliffs; the ground trembled, water hissed in the cracks.

The full moon shone fiercely on the full-bellied sea. A woman who had known everything, men's love and been deserted, who had the vision of a life of endless work and who felt seedy, despairing, felt a bud growing on its stalk in her body, was thirsty; in her great thirst she drank up the ocean and was drowned. She floated on it now in a wooden shell, over her a white cloth and over all the blazing funeral of the sky, the moon turning its back, sullen, calloused.

What the moon saw. The beaches, the shrubbery on the hills, the tongues of fire, the white and dark of bodies rolling together in snaky unions. Anne—Malfi, 'Don't think too badly of me!'—herself! She sighed, shivered and drew in. All the girls dimly knew that the hole-in-a-corner marriages and frantic petting parties of the suburbs were not love and therefore they had these ashamed looks; they lost their girlish laughter the day they became engaged, but those who did not get a man were worse off. There was a glass pane in the breast of each girl; there every other girl could see the rat gnawing at her, the fear of being on the shelf. Beside the solitary girl, three hooded madmen walk, desire, fear, ridicule. 'I won't suffer,' she said aloud, turning to the room to witness. 'They won't put it upon me.' She thought, a girl who's twenty-seven is lost. Who marries a woman of thirty-five to get children? She's slightly ridiculous to marry at that age. Look at Aunt Maggie, everyone laughed. Take Queenie, few marry at fifteen. Say eighteen, eighteen to thirty; twelve years, whereas men have eighteen to—any time at all, fifty at least, well, forty-eight, they can have children at forty-eight. They can marry then; thirty years. A woman is a hunter without a forest. There is a short open season and a long closed season, then she must have a gun-licence, signed and sealed by the state. There are game laws, she is a poacher, and in the closed season she must poach to live. A poor man, a serf say, clears himself a bit of land, but it's the lord's land. As soon as it's cleared, he grows a crop on it, but it isn't his crop, only partly, or perhaps not at all, it isn't in his name; and then there must be documents, legalities, he must swear eternal fealty to someone. A woman is obliged to produce her full quota on a little frontage of time; a man goes at it leisurely and he has allotments in other counties too. Yes, we're pressed for time. We haven't time to get educated, have a career, for the crop must be produced before it's autumn. There are northern countries where the whole budding, leafing, and fruiting take place in three months. A farmer said: 'What do they bother to put out leaves for, when they must go in so soon?' We put out leaves and flowers in such a brief summer and if it is a bad summer? We must do it all ourselves, too, just like wild animals in the bush. Australian savages arrange all that for their women, they don't have women going wanting, but we do. Girls are northern summers, three months long; men are tropical summers. But then there are the savage women, and the Italian, Spanish women—do they have as short a time? The women of ancient Greece, the Romans, so corrupt and so libertine, but happy no doubt—there might be other women. It isn't necessary—Malfi, Anne, Ray, Ellie, Kitty—me! But they won't even rebel, they're afraid to squander their few years. The long night of spinsterhood will come down. What's to be done? But one thing is sure, I won't do it, they won't get me.

How about the boys, too, Lance and Leo? They were different, but they were pressed too; nothing that was, suited them. If nothing that is, suits people, why do they all take it lying down? Because they have so little time, no money—but is that enough excuse?

Standing upright at the window, thinking, thinking, feeling rage at her floundering and weakness, and at seeing all the issues blocked, she thought of how cocksure she had been at school. Awkward, easily faced down, of course, but confident about the future. The things she wanted existed. At school she first had news of them, she knew they existed; what went on round her was hoaxing and smooth-faced hypocrisy. Venus and Adonis, the Rape of Lucrece, Troilus and Cressida were reprinted for three hundred years, St Anthony was tempted in the way you would expect; Dido, though a queen, was abandoned like a servant-girl and went mad with love and grief, like the girl in the boat outside. This was the truth, not the daily simpering on the boat and the putting away in hope chests; but where was one girl who thought so, besides herself? Was there one who would not be afraid if she told them the secret, the real life? Since school, she had ravaged libraries, disembowelled hundreds of books, ranged through literature since the earliest recorded frenzies of the world and had eaten into her few years with this boundless love of love, this insensate thirst for the truth above passion, alive in their home itself, in her brothers and sister, but neglected, denied, and useless; obnoxious in school, workshop, street.

Teresa knew all the disorderly loves of Ovid, the cruel luxury of Petronius, the exorbitance of Aretino, the meaning of the witches' Sabbaths, the experiments of Sade, the unimaginable horrors of the Inquisition, the bestiality in the Bible, the bitter jokes of Aristophanes and what the sex-psychologists had written. At each thing she read, she thought, yes, it's true, or no, it's false, and she persevered with satisfaction and joy, illuminated because her world existed and was recognized by men. But why not by women? She found nothing in the few works of women she could find that was what they must have felt. By comparison, history, with its lies to discourage the precocious, and even the inspired speculative stuff, meant nothing. But it was either rigmarole or raving, whereas the poets and playwrights spoke the language she knew, and the satirists and moralists wrote down with stern and marvellous precision all that she knew in herself but kept hidden from family and friends.

In her bare room, ravished, trembling with ecstasy, blooming with a profound joy in this true, this hidden life, night after night, year after year, she reasoned with herself about the sensual life for which she was fitted. She smelled, heard, saw, guessed faster, longed more than others, it seemed to her. She listened to what they brought out with a galling politeness, because what she had to say she could not tell them. It was not so that life was and they were either liars or stupid. At the same time, how queer that she understood what was going on in their minds so well! For it seemed to her that they were all moved by the same passion, in different intensities.

The newspapers made it appear so. Even the most sedate and crusty newspapers recounted at length, in divorce suits, what happened on worn divans in broken-down old office buildings, they all laughed together over those unlucky paramours who had been followed and caught in degrading positions, the schoolchildren gulped down the stories of bathing parties in the bushy reaches, mad cohabitations in the little bays, dives where sailors and black men went, miserable loves of all kinds, the naked dancing in the sweltering Christmas days and the nights of pale sand. Love panted in and out of their young nostrils, and the adolescents dreaming of these orgies, maddened by the tropical sun and these dissolute splendours of the insolent flesh, spent their nights in a bath of streaming sweat and burning blood.

A faint breeze had risen, rather damp. A mosquito sang windily. 'What have I done yet?' said Teresa to herself. She had had a dream the night before. This dream made her realize her age and she felt the shame of being unmarried. She had given the breast to her child, she dreamed, a small dark-haired baby. Everything was as clear as life, the nuzzling, sucking, and the touch of the child's spread hand. She was a woman, she was nineteen. Funny that at fourteen she had felt quite old! Her life was dull and away from men. Where would she get a husband?

She made a fretful gesture and accidentally pushed the bathing-suit off the window-sill into the yard. She pulled on a sweater and skirt and went downstairs.

There was no light in the back as she passed between the boys' rooms to the kitchen. Leo's room looked out on the grass slope and Lance's on the small alley by the neighbour's house. The moon had passed over, the kitchen was dark, only the yard shone. She went out into the yard, picked up her suit, hung it over the saw-horse and sniffed around for a while in the toolshed, fresh with sawdust. When she came in, Lance was at the old ice-chest, near the back door, munching and pulling out bits of food.

'It stinks in here,' he said cheerfully.

'You stink in there,' responded Tess.

'Good job I like sour milk, there always is plenty,' continued her brother, holding up a bottle towards the lighted yard.

'Sour milk is good for pigs and goats,' observed Teresa, coming into the kitchen and lounging against the table. Lance had a furtive smile in his long cheeks.

'What were you doing out there?'

'Getting my bathing-suit, it fell out the window.'

He thoughtfully munched for a while, standing side on and giving her meaningless glances; then he grinned to himself. 'You pushed it out.'

'What for? Don't be silly.'

'You're lying.'

'What!' She sprang forward.

Lance turned round and smirked, 'You're a liar. You threw it out.' It was the signal for battle. Teresa felt the blood rush to her head. Lance was the only one who dared to give her the lie.

'You're a liar,' repeated Lance lusciously, waiting. She flung herself upon him, pounding his chest, his long neck, and his head.

'Hey, hey!' said Lance, turning his head from side to side. She panted. He could see, even in the gloom, the dark flush over her face and neck.

'Don't you dare say that.'

'You're a liar,' he panted.

As if delighted, though puffing and writhing in her grasp, he merely fended off her clumsy blows, his face now stark and serious. Teresa punched his face on each cheek and temple and grasped his hair. Suddenly he groaned and staggered away from her. 'You got my boil.'

She stood back, dark with anger, furious with him, heaving and ready to rush in again and beat him. He staggered down the hall, moaning, holding his hand to his head. 'Oh, my boil.'

She looked after him contemptuously; he was always a coward. It did not occur to her that he had not hit her.

She saw him in the ghastly hall light. Blood trickled from his temple, two threads reached his neck. Fists clenched, astride and full of fight, the girl watched him go towards his bedroom. Kitty was half-way down the stairs, asking him questions, getting no answer. She clattered down the rest of the way, ran in after him. She came into the kitchen for water and put on the light. 'What were you doing?'

Teresa frowned at her and muttered: 'He called me a liar.'

Kitty said nothing to that. She went in again and said to Lance, as she bathed him: 'How did it happen?'

Lance said: 'The fool! I called her a liar for a joke, just because it gets her goat.' Teresa choked. She stood in the kitchen door and shouted: 'That's no joke, it's no joke. You knew what you were saying.'

Kitty said reproachfully: 'You knew he was joking.'

'It wasn't a joke! I'll kill anyone for that,' shouted Teresa. 'I'll kill him if he says it.'

Lance, satisfied, said nothing, only moaned as Kitty washed him.

'Poor Lance,' said Kitty, looking at her sideways.

'I'll smash him to pieces for that,' said the girl. 'He knows it, too.'

Lance groaned. Teresa went away furious. He had said it with a grin and kept grinning right through. That was a knife in her gall. She knew that out of malice he enjoyed the fight. She moved off sulkily. When she got up to her room, she sat down on the little sewing-box and thought about it, clenching her fists and grinding her teeth. She would kill anyone for that! She would kill for honour. A scene flew up in her mind in which she killed in hot blood, for honour and was glad of it, saw the spilt blood spreading. Ha-ha, that paid him off! For twenty minutes she sat there, her breath coming quickly and then her other thoughts began to creep in. She flung herself on her bed. Downstairs she heard the noises of the house as Kitty put things away and she heard her father beginning to lock up, leaving the door unbarred for Leo. Presently he came upstairs. He saw her open door and looked in. 'You hit Lance?'

'Yes.' Her temper rose again.

'You hurt him, you know, Terry.'

'Let him look out.'

Andrew Hawkins said quietly: 'Good night, Terry,' and went away towards his room. Terry felt rather flat. He called out: 'Early to bed, early to rise.'

'Yes,' she muttered, 'yes.'

Her father called from his room: 'Terry? You get Leo up?'

'Yes,' she answered impatiently.

His door shut. She heard him wind his clock. This time she left her door open.

1944

Uncle Morgan at the Nats

'You may notice the noise I am making,' said Uncle Morgan, champing with his jaws. 'You know what I have told you: masticate, denticate, chump, chew, and swallow. Now all together, masticate, denticate, chump, chew, AND swallow.'

The five children chumped, chewed, and swallowed in rhythm with pleasure. There was a loud noise like a hippopotamus eating sugarcane.

'That loud noise,' said Uncle, 'is a healthy noise and if you were in some countries, they would take it as a compliment, that you were pleased with the food; and you would be obliged to smack your lips, smack your bellies, and belch; and in fact,' he said, becoming excited, 'explode with greed and satisfaction in all directions, ears, eyes, nose, mouth, belly, and lower down. We will now smack our lips, roll our eyes, shake our ears, heave with our lungs, and belch if we can. Those who can't belch must try. It relieves the stomach of gases which accumulate and which if not relieved will go down lower, ro-oll around the large and the small intestines and rumble in the rumble-seat.'

The children broke out into cries, chuckles, and guffaws. Aunt Mildred rolled her black eyes in revolt. Her beautiful, black-fringed eyes rolled in her thin, yellow face, she shut her purplish red lips and with a look of disgust went out to the kitchen.

The orgy degenerated into horseplay, which Uncle Morgan took in hand. 'Enough,' he commanded, 'Gilbert the Filbert!'

'Morgan the Gorgon,' answered Gilbert cheekily but with his charming little grin. Morgan relaxed and sent a sparkling blue glance to the boy.

'Now when I was young I had digestive troubles,' pursued Uncle Morgan, with an agreeable air. 'I was a vegetarian, I wrongly believed that it was meat that upset me. Never say I don't change my mind. When facts present themselves to me, I change my mind. If I like the taste. In this case it was a meat-stew brought to a Nats' picnic by a lovely, serious young woman, who admired your Uncle Morgan. I did not know it then; I was too serious.'

'It was my friend Nellie,' said Morgan's younger sister, Beatrix, 'you were keeping company.'

Morgan passed this over, 'Morgan has never been known to ignore a fact. Aunt Mildred he MAY ignore when she is in one of her whimsies and whim-men have whimsies; Aunt Beatrix he MAY ignore when she forgets to collect the porridge plates—' Beatrix got up hastily '—and when her hair is sticking up—'

'Now, Morgan,' began Beatrix with chatty ire, 'you have twisted your own hair into horns, into yellow horns.' This was a habit of Uncle Morgan's.

The children looked at the horns but did not laugh; but Aunt Beatrix giggled and her timid, little, brown-haired, three-year-old daughter, Renee, broke down and giggled too. It was pretty to see how her round face changed, broke, mottled, dimpled, shifted, as she bent her head down, bashfully.

'Now, Grandmother,' said Morgan, gravely addressing the three-year-old.

Her eyes shone, she flushed.

'Now, Grandmother,' he said ominously, 'will you do everything your Uncle Morgan tells you? Do you love your Uncle Morgan?'

'Yes,' she piped.

'Then,' he said looking gravely at her, 'put your hand in the fire for your Uncle Morgan. Will you, Grandmother?'

This was before Uncle Morgan took down the chimney and dug out the fireplace, to avoid fire risks; and at that moment, half the breakfast fire was still blazing away in the grate, behind Aunt Mildred's armchair. Renee (Grandmother) looked from her uncle to her mother; she paled.

'Grandmother?' he said sternly.

'Will you, Gilbert the Filbert?' he enquired.

'No,' said Gilbert.

'But Grandmother *will*!' said Uncle Morgan gravely. 'Grandmother, get down from your chair!' She slipped off her chair and leaned over the seat, her face already working; but she did not dare to cry yet.

'Morgan, don't be so stupid,' said Beatrix.

'I mean it,' he said instantly, 'Trixie, I am training the child to obey, I know what I am doing. Leave it to me.' She waited.

'Grandmother, go to the grate.'

She tottered away from the chair, looked at her mother; she was crying now, but not loudly.

'Go to the grate and stand in front of the fire.'

She did so.

Her mother looked at her and said gently, 'Don't cry, my lamb. It's only fun.'

'Grandmother,' said Uncle Morgan, 'this is one of the most serious moments of your life. You are now learning something that will affect your whole life.'

'Morgan,' burst out Beatrix, 'how can you tease the baby?'

'Grandmother is not a baby,' said Morgan. 'Grandmother! Put your hand in the fire.'

She was sobbing loudly now, but she bent forward slowly and held out her pudgy hand with one fat finger advanced.

A thunderbolt tore into the room from the kitchen, the curtains blew about. Aunt Mildred, blazing black fury, was there.

'Morgan,' she shouted, 'how dare you tease the children!'

Uncle Morgan lifted the milk jug off the table and with a sweet laugh, parting his lips and showing many of his white teeth, he made as if to hurl the jug at Mildred.

'Let's see if I can land it right on her nose,' said he.

Aunt Mildred rushed forward and Aunt Beatrix rose to her feet. There was confusion. Morgan sat there, sanguine, grinning. 'Down, women!' said he, putting down the milk jug.

'You see,' he remarked in a pathetic, gentle tone to the children, 'when a child is getting social training, when its character is being formed, the women interfere and ruin its character. Now my character fortunately was not ruined, because my mother was a stern old Methody woman, good, loving but firm—'

'She was our mother too, Morgan,' said Beatrix, 'and she made me promise to obey those rules she believed in and which have kept me straight and true ever since.'

Aunt Mildred was now retiring to the kitchen and Beatrix said, 'Come here, lamb, to its mother.' But Morgan instantly changing his tune, commanded. 'Grandmother, back to the fire! You have not done what I told you.'

'Oh, Morgan,' said Beatrix.

'And you, Beatrix, don't butt in,' he said rudely, 'ideas come before sentiment. Granny,' he began in an ingratiating drone, 'do what your little Uncle asks, Granny, your little Uncle is asking you. Granny, do what oo is told! Granny be a dood girl. Granny, put your hand in the fire for Uncle Morg!'

Trembling and weeping the child put her hand out, felt the heat that surrounds the flame, blindly weeping, unquestioning, while Uncle Morgan ducking his head and grinning whispered to left and right, 'She'll do it,' gleefully, 'Granny will do it!'

'Renee!' shrieked her mother and fell on the baby, pulling the poor thing from the fire.

'She touched the fire, she touched the fire,' the children shouted, jubilating, dismayed.

'Granny did not al-to-gether touch the fire, Granny let her Uncle down, Granny did not obey her Uncle,' said Morgan, in a repulsive weeping tone.

Aunt Mildred was marching up and down the cemented kitchen floor with her arms folded, her eyes black. She stared through the window like a witch and if the crooked, smooth, silver arms of the fig trees had been broomsticks, she would have flown off on them.

Aunt Beatrix, weeping with her child, rushed into the kitchen to Aunt Mildred. 'Mildred! My poor fatherless baby!'

'You're a pack of fools, all of you,' said Mildred.

She went into the boys' room next to the kitchen and started throwing the mattresses about in a rage. Beatrix sat down on the rickety kitchen chair and began combing Granny's soft, curly brown hair. She soon smiled, her eyes rounded and shone and she whispered, 'Uncle Morgan didn't mean you to do it, love, Uncle Morg was having fun, Uncle Morg loves you, darling.'

Aunt Mildred could be heard hissing. She turned the mattress with such a thump that the iron bedstead of Sid, her eldest, slid halfway across the cement floor bringing to light Sid's heterogeneous collections and also a board he had cut loose in the wall to make a secret cupboard. Aunt Mildred surveyed this with contempt, pushed the bed back and muttered, 'What a pack!'

In the breakfast room, Uncle Morgan was saying cheerfully, 'But all this interrupted what I was going to tell you about the Nats' Dinner.'

The Nats were the Naturalists. The night before they had had their annual dinner and Uncle Morgan had not been re-elected Chairman. They had instead made a rule, the week before, saying that no chairman should serve more than two terms consecutively; and Uncle Morgan had already served three. He felt injured. At the same time, he held the Nats in contempt for having to pass a new law to get rid of him.

'At the Nats' Dinner, Ratty Atty,' by which he referred to Mr Atkinson, a lively naturalist, tall, thin, dark, whom he regarded as a rival (though of no account), 'was in the chair and sat at the head of the table, so that your Uncle Morgan—'

'—Morgan the Organ,' contributed Gilbert the Filbert. Uncle Morgan smiled in the corner of his mouth, not wishing to acknowledge this hit, but proud of it, '—had to sit at the side of the banquet table; and since I am left-handed,' he said, illustrating with knife and fork, 'I was inconvenienced; and my right-hand and left-hand neighbours were also inconvenienced. When I eat, I cut with my left hand and my elbow sticks into my neighbour's elbow or his side or shoulder, or his eye, it depends on his size,' said Uncle Morgan with a spiteful twinkle, for he was tall, large, and strong, 'and the eating rhythm of the table is disturbed, whereas when I am Chairman, if my arm moves to left or right, no one is disturbed.

'Last night I was sitting by a lady, it is true she was only an old schoolteacher with a bun, but a very fine woman, a woman of intellect, who admires your Uncle Morgan—' he continued with a marvellous genial expression of malice, for Aunts Mildred and Beatrix were not women of intellect, but read the bestsellers and the women's magazines; and Aunt Mildred called intellectual talk 'snobbish talk by gasmen', while Aunt Beatrix did not listen at all, only waiting to 'chip in', as she herself said.

'—and because my right arm was only holding the fork and her sharp elbow was coming my way; in fact, she was continually nudging me in the elbow!—because my elbow stuck out to wrestle with a tough bit of gristle and I made the fork twang and the plate whistle, and her elbow would be poked out as she went for a juicy tendon, for it was prime wether mutton about fifteen years old, though not so old as Miss Wetherby and perhaps that is why he bought wether, or I don't know whether. And on my other side, was Miss Rosemary Atkinson, Ratty Atty's daughter, beautiful as a rose, so that when the old lady with the bun jabbed my elbow and I jabbed hers, my chop skittered across my plate on to Sweet Rosemary's plate and I had to fly after it with my fork and we both said at the same time, "Not much chop!" and laughed. But it was difficult for your Uncle Morgan to laugh because at that identical moment I had in the side of my cheek, my right cheek, on her side that is, a large ball of half-chewed tendon and gristle, with a little bit of bone in the middle. I didn't want to swallow the bone, and I didn't want to spit it out, so I had embedded it in a ball of refuse, much as the dung beetle builds up his precious hoard from droppings, and I could smile but I could hardly speak. I carried that ball about in my mouth for an hour after dinner and it was only when I was walking in the back of the house, in the conservatory with Lady Wassail and she asked me, "What is the name of that little plant with the heartshaped leaves, Mr Jackstraw?" that I could turn round, while pretending to look, and could rid myself of the downy greyish ball. For by now, it had been completely chewed up and also had bits of salad and strawberry in it. For a whole hour I had been rolling that ball between my plate and my tongue and cheek.'

'What plant was it, Uncle?' said Gilbert.

'Of course she knew, she just asked to please me, to get my attention. It was *Orosera rotundifolia*, a sundew,' said Morgan carelessly.

'Another thing, when I am President and hence Chairman of the Nats and sit at the head of the table, no one can hear my plate clicking. Your poor Uncle Morg—'

'Morg the Dorg,' said Gilbert who had been only waiting for this.

'—Morgan,' said Uncle Morgan firmly, 'no matter what certain smarties who think themselves very witty may say,' (Gilbert the Filbert grinned conceitedly), 'was a very poor boy and is an autodidact, that is to say, he gained his education at night school and in the Library of Life and also of Knife.'

This was greeted with the usual appreciation and he proceeded, 'And Morgan Jackstraw did not have the chance you children have; hence he had to have his teeth out by the roots, when they could have been stopped from going, but they went.'

He smiled at the titter and continued, 'And I who am a natural speaker and have great natural charm, especially with the ladies; and with any men and boys,' he turned an eye on the boys, 'who believe in reason, logic, the true, the beautiful, was obliged to learn to speak through impedimenta, the impediment of my ivories. They click. You children know that however poor the fare at home, for a man like me, who has eaten in the company of lords and magnates,' (he said, ridiculing himself), 'I prefer to eat at home, because I can click at ease.' He clicked not only at ease but demonstratively and went through a series of denture acrobatics, wobbling, tossing, clicking, and pretending to shoot his plates out on the table. 'Plates to the plate,' said he. The children greeted this with a roar of laughter, while Aunt Mildred, rushing through the room, groaned and tossed her head. He replaced his dentures with a lick of his agile tongue.

'Lady Wassail then asked me the name of another plant, which incidentally was a *Hardenbergia sydniensis*. I believe, children, that she feels for your Uncle Morg. She told me something I could quite agree with,' he said artfully, 'that she did not enjoy this banquet anything like the last two, for she loves to see me shining at the head of the table. "The head is my natural element," I said to her modestly. At which she tittered. For your Uncle Morg,' he said mournfully, looking round the table and especially at Renee, 'may not be appreciated by Lilliputians at home; but many is the beautiful woman who has wanted to run her long slender fingers through his golden hair. Your Aunt Mildred may pretend to be in tantrums, but time was when she used to sit and dream over your Uncle Morgan's golden hair.'

At this grotesque idea, the children burst into laughter. Uncle Morgan shook his head sadly, '*Tempus he fugit*,' he said. 'You kids have no idea how I was as a boy. You girls have no idea. Trixie there has an idea; but you don't know now, with my beard getting rough, my plate clicking, my catarrh, my digestive troubles, my appendix, my photophobia, my antrum, my torticollis, the pain in the small of my back, all of which I fight bravely, what I was like as a boy, a young god; only that there aren't gods; but man is a god. Ah, kids, you missed me as a boy. When I went to work, a boy there named Nunneally, I was thirteen, he was seventeen, used to stroke my arms and say "Like satin, Morg, like white satin, like a duchess!" '

Beatrix giggled and then seeing her brother's astonished eye on her, she said apologetically, 'Yes, Morg, you were a handsome boy and with such a dreamy look as if you were too good for this world.'

'And so I was,' he assented, 'I was too good for the world, I didn't know there were evil men; I thought, if I was good, people would be good to me. But you see, kids, what happens? The Nats,' he said lugubriously, 'the Nats do not see me as I am. Can I blame them? They are naturalists but also men, and men have failings. Well, let me tell you, these dinners are an ordeal for a sensitive man, but next year Ratty Atty will have to vacate the seat and you will see the Padrone Morgan, the Patroon, at the head of the banquet table.'

'Morgan,' cried Beatrix breathlessly, 'do you know what I dreamed last night? I dreamed I was at the dentist's and he put out his tongue—'

'When I am going to have trouble, I dream of a yellow-bellied sea eagle; he comes to warn me,' said Morgan.

'Mowed down by a bird of ill-omen,' said Beatrix rushing to get in, 'and the funny thing is that though I knew it was Nell, I kept calling her Mrs File—'

'The sausages are burning, Trix,' called Aunt Mildred sourly.

'Yes, Millie dear,' said Trixie eagerly, 'and I woke up and it came to me out of a blue sky—'

'—in the middle of the night,' contributed Gilbert.

'The sausages are burned to a cinder,' said Aunt Mildred glaring.

'Trixie's cooking is a pillar of cloud by day and a pillar of fire by night,' said Uncle Morgan.

'And the dentist scratched my stocking and the funny thing is there is a run in my stocking.'

'Those are my stockings,' said Aunt Mildred.

'Mill's stockings are on Trix's last legs,' said Uncle Morgan.

Trixie brought in the sausages. It was Sunday. The children did not have to get ready for school.

'I adore Sunday,' said Trixie, and sang.

The kitchen became full of her sprightly chatter, the clash of dishes, and her gay soprano. Uncle Morgan had retired to the cane lounge where he lay at full length, 'expatiating', as he said.

1976/1985

ALAN MARSHALL
1902—1984

A writer with an ear for the rhythms of Australian speech, Melbourne-based Alan Marshall published in the dominant social realist tradition of the 1940s and '50s. The author of short stories, journalism, children's books, novels and advice columns, he is best remembered for the first book of his autobiography, *I Can Jump Puddles* (1955). This was praised by Vance Palmer as a 'warm and human book' and translated into many languages. His work is marked by a deep interest in rural and working-class life, with an emphasis on shared experience. *NM*

The Grey Kangaroo

She knew the old prospector. From a cleared patch on the hillside she often noticed him washing for gold in the creek that ran through the valley.

Sometimes he stopped his swirling and sat on the bank watching her while he filled his pipe.

He had known her for two years. She was his friend. She was smaller than her companions, and differed from them in colour. She was grey; they were almost black—'scrubbers', the old man called them.

Each morning the creaking of his cart, as he followed the winding track round the mountain side, would cause them to stand erect for a moment, nostrils twitching.

But they did not fear him. He was one with the carol of the magpies and the gums.

When his 'Whoa there!' stayed the old black horse, they knew he only wished to look at them. They continued feeding. Their movements were like music—rhythmical—an undulating rise and fall of symmetrical bodies against a background of slender trees.

Occasionally they stopped and, sitting upright, looked back at him, a look of intense interest, of watchfulness.

Their flanks, wet with the dew from sweet-smelling leaves, glistened in the morning sun. They seemed like children of the trees.

There was a day when the old prospector approached within a few yards of the grey kangaroo. She awaited his coming, standing with head extended, eyes half-closed, nostrils working with curiosity. He remained motionless, and they regarded each other.

She turned and hopped slowly away from him. She moved with grace and dignity, despite her burden. She carried a joey.

A mile from the spot where the old prospector worked, two boys were cutting timber. Their axe-heads glittered in the sun. When for a moment the eager steel poised motionless above their heads, the muscles on their uncovered backs stood out in little, smooth brown hills. Their skin had the unblemished gloss of eggshells.

Beside the log on which they worked lay a blue kangaroo dog. His powerful, rib-lined chest rose and fell. His narrow loins had the delicacy of a stem.

Suddenly he lifted his head and, turning, bit at the smooth hair on his shoulder to ease an irritation. His lips, pushed up and back, revealed red gums and the smooth, ivory daggers of his teeth. He snuffled and worked his jaws. His jowls flowed with saliva. He expelled a deep breath and lay back again. Flies hovered over his head. He snapped and moved restlessly.

The boys called him Springer—Springer, the killer. In the shade from surrounding trees lay other dogs. They formed a pack, the existence of which was due to the boys' love of hunting. They had no beauty of line, as had Springer. They were a rabble. They barked at nights and howled at the moon. They ran down rabbits with savage joy and, in the pack, were relentless in their pursuit. They looked to Springer to bring down the larger game. They were content to be in at the kill.

One of them, Boofer, a half-bred sheep dog, rose and stretched herself. She yawned with a whine and walked into the sunlight. She stood there a moment meditatively. She looked back over her shoulder. A flying chip fell beside her. She sniffed it. She was bored. She turned and trotted off among the trees.

Some time later her excited barking caused the other dogs to jump to their feet. They stood with their necks erect, their heads moving alertly from side to side.

Boofer tore past, some distance away, running at speed, her nose to the ground. The dogs yelped with delight and, scattering dry gum leaves and crashing through scrub, sped after her.

The boys stopped work and watched.

'There they are, up on the hill!' cried one. 'Look, quick, look!'

He pointed.

He put two fingers to his mouth and whistled shrilly.

Springer, having disregarded the yelping of the pack, leaped to his feet at the sound, as to a clarion call.

He sprang forward with short, stiff bounds, craning his neck as if to see over obstacles. He stopped and grew tense, one forefoot raised in the air. His panting had ceased. He looked eagerly from side to side.

The boy who had whistled jumped from the log. He ran to the blue dog and, grasping his head between his hands, half lifted him from the ground. The dog's neck was stretched and rolls of skin half-closed his eyes.

'See 'em. See 'em,' he whispered excitedly.

But no responsive quickening of muscle stirred the dog. The boy ran forward dragging Springer with him.

Then Springer saw. With a mighty bound he parted the boy's hands. He leaped with a terrific releasing of energy, doubling like a spring until, having attained speed, he moved with effortless beauty.

The boy sprang again to the log. He stood with his lips slightly parted, eyes wide, his hands clenched by his side.

'Boy!' he breathed to his companion. 'Look at him.'

Upon the hillside the mob of kangaroos had heard the yapping of Boofer on their trail. The little grey kangaroo lifted her head quickly. For a long, tense moment she stood in frozen immobility looking down into the valley. Her joey, nibbling at the grass some distance from her, jumped in sudden panic and made for his mother with single-purposed speed. With her paws she held her pouch open like a sugar bag. He tumbled in headlong, his kicking legs projecting a moment before he disappeared.

How safe he felt in there; how secure from dogs with teeth and men with guns. His little heart, swift-beating at the excited barking of the pack, became even and content. He turned and his head popped forth with childish curiosity.

His mother was already on the move. The does were in haste; the old men were more leisured.

With a clamour the pack broke through the trees. Ahead of them, like the point of a spear, Springer ran silently.

The kangaroos leaped into frantic speed, but before they gained their top Springer was among them and they scattered wildly.

Perhaps it was because of her conspicuous colour, perhaps because she was so very small, the kangaroo dog singled her out from her companions and set after her relentlessly. And, recognising his leadership, the pack followed eagerly, joyfully, the hills echoing their exultation.

She had intended making up the hill to thicker timber, but, as if suddenly realising her desperate plight and the heavy responsibilities of motherhood, she turned her flight towards the old prospector.

Through the fragrant hazel, past the mottled silver-wattles, by sad tree-ferns and across chip-strewn clearings she sped; and behind her Springer cleared as she the fallen trunks, the scattered limbs, swerved as she did from the pointed stakes, flew wombat holes and trickling water-courses with equal ease. He rode the air like Death itself.

The clutch of some mimosa hampered the grey kangaroo. She lost ground. The blue dog gathered himself and sprang, but the rough take-off spoiled his leap and he wobbled in mid-air. His teeth closed on the skin of her shoulder, his body struck her. She staggered and collided with a sapling. The dog shot past her, scarring the moist earth with tearing feet.

With heroic endeavour the grey kangaroo recovered her balance and in a violent, concentrated effort, she drew away from the dog, a tattered banner of red skin draggling from her naked shoulder.

She made for some crowded gum suckers. They brushed her as she passed. With a swift and desperate movement she tore her joey from her pouch and flung him, almost without loss of speed, into their shelter. She turned at right angles, leading the blue dog away from him.

The joey staggered to his feet and hopped away distractedly. But the following pack, with triumphant cries, bore down on him. He gave one helpless glance back at them and tried to flee. They swept over him like a wind. He was lost in their midst.

Their howl of triumph reached the little grey mother as she strained ahead of Springer, the killer. Their unleashed savagery, fleeing from them in bloody glee, broke upon her in waves.

The old prospector heard it too, and, dropping his dish, he clambered in clumsy haste from the creek. When his head and shoulders appeared over the bank, he stopped a moment with dazed eyes and open mouth watching the approach of the grey kangaroo and her pursuer.

He raised himself swiftly and ran towards them. His eyes were wide open, distraught. He raised his hand in the air and cried hoarsely, 'Come be'ind 'ere! Come be'ind 'ere!'

When the grey kangaroo reached the clearing she was all but spent. The blue dog, with mouth open and silken strands of saliva blowing free, raced behind her across a patch of fern. He was but a length away when, with painful bounds, she reached the cool sweetness of young grass.

He made a last, terrific burst. He left the ground with all the glorious energy of a skin-clad dancer, his body modelled in clean curves of muscle. His teeth locked deep in her shoulder. His hurtling body seemed to arrest its speed as if suddenly braked. He met the ground stiff-legged and taut.

The grey kangaroo, her head jerked downwards, spun in the air. She turned completely over. Her long tail whipped in a circle above her head. She landed with a dull crash on her back. Before the shock of her falling had released her breath, Springer was at her throat. With demoniac savagery he tore at the soft, warm fur. With braced forelegs and tail erect, he shook her in a frenzy.

She kicked helplessly.

He sprang back, keyed for further conflict.

Her front paws, like little hands, quivered in unconscious supplication. She relaxed, sinking closer to the earth as to a mother.

He turned and walked away from her, panting, with red drops dripping from his running tongue.

With half-closed eyes he watched the old prospector running towards them, his heavy, wet boots flop-flopping on the grass.

1946

DYMPHNA CUSACK and FLORENCE JAMES
1902–1981　　　　　　　　1902–1993

The playwright and novelist Ellen Dymphna Cusack was born in West Wyalong, NSW, and went to school in the provincial city of Armidale before taking an honours degree in history and the new discipline of psychology at the University of Sydney. Like the other famous collaborators of Australian fiction, Marjorie Barnard (qv) and Flora Eldershaw, Cusack and her friend and collaborator Florence James, with whom she wrote *Come in Spinner* (1951), met through the Sydney University Dramatic Society.

Cusack graduated in 1925 and taught in high schools across country NSW for almost twenty years. From 1928 onwards she wrote plays and poems that were broadcast on radio, and for which she won prizes. She published her first novel, *Jungfrau*, in 1936 and many of the topics and themes to be found in *Come in Spinner* were first tried out there: the restrictions placed on women's lives, and their struggles with education, work, love, marriage and parenthood.

Cusack's first literary collaboration was with Miles Franklin (qv); they co-wrote *Pioneers on Parade* (1939). She was also active as a playwright, particularly during the 1940s and '50s; her best-known plays are *Red Sky at Morning* (1935/1942), *Morning Sacrifice* (1942/1943), *Comets Soon Pass* (1943/1950) and *The Golden Girls* (1955/1955).

In 1944 Cusack, whose health was always fragile, was pensioned off by the NSW Education Department and rented a cottage in the Blue Mountains. Here, with James, she wrote *Come in Spinner*, which won the 1948 Sydney *Daily Telegraph* novel competition. Because of its length and the controversial nature of some of its subject matter—prostitution, black-marketeering, war profiteering, abortion—it was not finally published in book form, with the original manuscript severely cut, until 1951. It was published in the original unabridged version for the first time in 1988.

Always a committed left-wing writer and social reformer, Cusack met up in Europe after the war with her lover Norman Freehill, a journalist and leading member of the Communist Party of Australia. They travelled together for twenty years, including three years in China, and married in 1962. Cusack remained prolific, writing non-fiction and novels about the lives of women and workers, and recording her travels in China, Russia and elsewhere.

Florence James was born in Gisborne, NZ. As a Quaker with a strong commitment to the cause of pacifism, her world view was complemented by Cusack's commitment to social reform. After graduating from the University of Sydney in 1926, she went to London, where for a time she shared a flat with Christina Stead (qv). James returned to Sydney in 1938 and married the same year. She later returned to London, where she gained a solid reputation as an editor and critic. In 1963 she returned again to Australia and remained active in its literary affairs, including the establishment of the Australian Society of Authors.

Come in Spinner was dramatised for ABC television in 1989 by Nick Enright and Lissa Benyon in a popular and critically acclaimed production. *KG*

From *Come in Spinner*
Saturday V

(i)

For an hour, Deb had played the hose on the roof and walls of the house, soaking the veranda and showering the dusty Christmas bushes in the garden below. The hot wind brought with it a choking smell of smoke and the scent of burning gum trees. She was streaming with sweat and Nolly's old cotton frock stuck to her back and thighs. She felt the moisture gather and run down her body, little rivulets dripped off the end of her nose, and her hair, under the old cabbage tree hat, was gummed together in draggled wisps. Her shoulders and back were aching and her arms felt as if they would drop off.

At last the sun was sinking down to the bush-covered hills. Deb turned her face to the wind and watched the yellow haze in the western sky deepen to menacing red-gold. At one minute, the hot wind in her face was like a blast from some great oven, at the next it had dropped and there was only the still heat around her.

'No-o-olly,' she called, 'the wind's gone down!' She held the hose upright and the water shot up like a flagstaff and fell back again on her head and shoulders.

The children heard her voice and came running round the veranda.

'Look,' Andrew called, 'Auntie Deb's having a shower.' He was down the steps in a flash and plunging into the spray.

'You little scamp, you'll get your clothes wet.'

'I don't care, I don't care. Shower me, Auntie Deb,' he begged.

Nolly came and looked over the veranda.

'The wind's gone down,' Deb called up.

'That's a relief. They must have stopped the fire beyond the far ridge. Good heavens,' she laughed as she caught sight of Deb's bedraggled figure. 'You look a wreck.'

'Well, I've cooled the place down at least, even if I've nearly drowned myself.'

Andrew hopped up and down in the spray and the other three came tearing round the corner. 'Hose us too,' they shouted, leaping round her.

'Go on,' Nolly called down, 'it doesn't matter about their clothes.'

Deb made an arch of spray for the children, who ran in dancing and squeaking with delight. Durras kicked off his shorts, Luen tossed her shirt and shorts into the air and little Jack came to have the buttons of his sun-suit undone, before he danced into the spray. The children dodged in and out, shrieking and chasing each other, their naked brown bodies glistening in the red glow, their hair stuck to their heads like tight, glossy caps.

Dusk was settling down when at last Deb turned off the water. 'Come on,' she called to them, 'we'll all go and have a good rub down.' But the children scattered in front of her, darting among the orange trees, calling to her to catch them.

She gathered up the sopping clothes and looked up at Nolly. 'I'm all in. You'll have to use your authority now.' She came up the steps with the water dripping from her hat, her shoulders drooping and her sodden frock flapping against her legs.

Nolly took the bundle of small garments. 'The children can romp for a while. You get out of that frock and give yourself a rub down. There's an old dirndl of mine at the back of the bathroom door you can put on; then stretch out on Lu's bed on the veranda, it's coolest there. I'll just see that Debby's asleep and then I'll get you some tea.'

When Nolly came out with the tray, Deb was propped up on her elbow looking over the veranda railing at the rounded edge of the moon which was just showing above the bush. Nolly's gaze followed hers and together they watched in silence while a copper moon lifted itself above the tree-tops.

'It's a bush-fire moon,' Deb broke the silence.

Nolly spoke the troubled thought that she had put aside all the afternoon; 'I do hope Tom'll be all right.'

'Of course he will. It's not an hour since the wind dropped. It'll take longer than that to get a big fire under control and, judging by the glare in the sky, it's been a pretty big blaze.'

'I know it's silly to worry. Tom's not the one to leave while there's anything to be done.'

'Of course he won't. You can't really expect him for hours yet.'

'No, I suppose not.'

Deb could hear the droop in Nolly's voice. 'You're just tired, that's the only reason you're worrying. Drink up your tea and come and lie down beside me.' She put her cup on the tray and moved against the wall to make room. 'Do you remember the last time we watched a bush-fire moon? We were really worried then . . . and we needn't have been.'

'I'll never forget it,' Nolly stretched herself out beside Deb. 'I'll never forget a single minute of that holiday. If it hadn't been for you and Jack, I don't think Tom and I would have had the courage to get married.'

'Oh yes, you would. You were made for each other.'

'But we might have wasted so many precious years saving up if we hadn't seen how happy you two could be on nothing . . . and after that bush fire, I could hardly bear to let him out of my sight. The moon was copper that night, too. Remember how it rose out of the sea, and you and me sitting at the foot of the cliff with the water lapping at our feet and all our camping gear around us?'

Deb nodded.

'And we talked and talked all night, until the moon went down behind the blazing ridge.'

'Why, Nolly, the moon's making you quite poetic,' Deb cut across the emotion she heard in Nolly's voice.

'I knew that night I would marry Tom. Although I could hardly speak of him for fear, somehow my mind worked perfectly clearly. If he came out of that fire alive, I knew I would marry him. I knew then that we belonged to each other and nothing in the world mattered but having the man you loved.'

Deb stirred restlessly. Her physical tiredness and the moon shining on her face drew her back into the memory of that first Christmas after she and Jack were married when Tom and Nolly had spent a week with them at the Camp.

On New Year's Eve the heat had been unbearable with the same oppressive feeling as tonight. Next morning they had all wakened up heavy and tired and not even a dip in the surf could cool them for more than half an hour. After Jack and Tom had set out along the forest track with their rucksacks full of fish to sell up on the Princes Highway, Nolly suggested taking a last look from the top of Durras Mountain before she went back to Sydney next day.

It was a steep pull up the side of the mountain and they took their time. When at last they broke out of the forest, the sun was high overhead and veiled in a golden mist, and the fiery breath of a wind newly sprung from the west scorched their faces and brought with it an acrid scent.

Nolly wrinkled her nose and sniffed the wind. 'Smells like a bush fire.'

'It is too. Let's climb up a bit higher and see where it is.'

They scrambled up the wall of boulders that brought them out above the tree-tops and a rising westerly whipped the hair back from their faces. They shaded their eyes with their hands and looked into the wind. The forest ridges were wrapped in a thick haze, and far off a smother of blue smoke shot with flashes of yellow flame curled like a trail from an enormous engine. Nearer, they could hear the crackling as the tree-tops caught.

Nolly had turned to Deb, her eyes wide and panic in her voice: 'The boys. Suppose they're in that.'

They had taken one last look at the fire leaping towards them, then they'd run, slithering down the giant boulders until they reached the bush, plunging down the mountain side, slipping, steadying themselves against the tree-trunks, tripping over the undergrowth, unconscious of scratches and cuts, sweat running down their faces, their shirts sticking to their backs, hearts pounding, breath coming short. When at last they reached the camp there was no sign of the boys and the fire was still beyond the ridge that bounded the bay.

All the afternoon and all night they had sat in unendurable suspense on the rocks at the foot of the cliff, the forest behind them a wall of flame against a lurid sky. They watched the tide go out as the moon rose higher bleaching the sand and the cliffs and paling the leaping flames. They watched until the sun came up, a flaming ball in the smoky haze that the wind had blown out to sea.

Then at last they saw the boys, two small figures rounding the far headland, and they leapt up shouting and raced along the sand to meet them. Deb could still feel Jack's prickly cheek against hers and his arms tight around her. His face was streaked and dirty and his eyes reddened, and he smelled of smoke and singeing . . . and he was safe!

Deb found that she was lying stiff and tense on the bed and her heart was thumping as it had thumped that morning. If Jack had been in that fire it would have been the end of everything for her. That was how she'd felt too when he left for the Middle East, as though she was torn in half . . . She made herself relax. How stupid it was to get worked up like this.

Nolly began to talk. 'You know, Deb, I've been thinking of the fun we had that year, bush fire or no bush fire. I never told you, did I, how shocked I was that first day when the boys were fishing round the headland and we went into the surf without our bathing suits. I saw you were tanned all over and I realised that you and Jack must have spent most of your time naked.'

'Oh! That all began when I lost my costume. There was no harm in it.'

'I never felt there was. After the first surprise, it seemed a perfectly natural part of your Garden of Eden.'

'Garden of Eden! That's all very well when you're young, but it's a different matter when you have responsibilities.'

But the old enchantment was strong upon Nolly and she went on: 'Remember the Christmas pudding we made in the billy?'

'Yes, and I remember too that our dole rations and our few shillings would never have run to the ingredients if everybody back at home hadn't sent down something towards it. Goodness, what a pair of beggars we must have seemed.'

'You seemed wonderful to Tom and me. I remember it awfully well, nobody could afford much. Tom's mother sent half a dozen eggs that I carried carefully packed with paper in our billy and Jack's mother sent currants and sultanas and I had bought a tin of condensed milk so we could make mother's recipe.'

Deb was touched in spite of herself. She remembered how thrilled she'd been as the packages came out of Nolly's rucksack. And when the oranges and apples were added from Tom's, she could hardly believe her eyes. 'We can't just eat them,' she'd said as she picked up the oranges and smelled the pungent oil in their rinds. 'We must hang them on our Christmas tree.' [. . .]

1951

ROBERT D. FITZGERALD
1902–1987

Born in Sydney, and the nephew of the poet John Le Gay Brereton (qv), Robert D. FitzGerald discontinued his studies at the University of Sydney to become a surveyor. Influenced in the 1920s by Norman Lindsay (qv), he helped produce the Lindsayite journal *Vision* (1923–24). As a surveyor he worked in Fiji for the Native Lands Commission for much of 1931–36, and in 1940 joined the Commonwealth Department of the Interior, where he held a number of positions before retiring in 1965. FitzGerald was also a critic, publishing *The Elements of Poetry* in 1963.

FitzGerald's longer poems, such as 'The Hidden Bole' and 'Essay on Memory' from *Moonlight Acre* (1938), established him as one the most important poets of the

1930s. The poem 'Voyager' in *Heemskerck Shoals* (1949) is a dramatic monologue concerning the Dutch explorer Abel Tasman. FitzGerald's historical and Oceanic interests come together in the long poem *Between Two Tides* (1952). The relationship between historical guilt and contemporary identity is the concern of 'The Wind at Your Door' (1958), based on a convict-flogging incident that involved FitzGerald's ancestor Martin Mason.

In 1965 FitzGerald published *Forty Years' Poems*, which contained most of his later work, and the earlier work (in revised form) that he wished to retain. FitzGerald's poetry, which has received divergent responses from critics, is often abstract, philosophical and attracted to the metaphysical. Not a popular poet as such, FitzGerald played an important role in modernising and broadening the scope of Australian poetry. FitzGerald also edited the letters of Mary Gilmore (qv), the dedicatee of 'The Wind at Your Door', and Hugh McRae. He is the subject of monographs by G.A. Wilkes (1981) and A. Grove Day (1974). *DM*

The Wind at Your Door[1]

To Mary Gilmore

My ancestor was called on to go out—
a medical man, and one such must by law
wait in attendance on the pampered knout
and lend his countenance to what he saw,
lest the pet, patting with too bared a claw,   5
be judged a clumsy pussy. Bitter and hard,
see, as I see him, in that jailhouse yard.

Or see my thought of him: though time may keep
elsewhere tradition or a portrait still,
I would not feel under his cloak of sleep   10
if beard there or smooth chin, just to fulfil
some canon of precision. Good or ill
his blood's my own; and scratching in his grave
could find me more than I might wish to have.

Let him then be much of the middle style   15
of height and colouring; let his hair be dark
and his eyes green; and for that slit, the smile
that seemed inhuman, have it cruel and stark,
but grant it could be too the ironic mark
of all caught in the system—who the most,   20
the doctor or the flesh twined round that post?

---

1   The poem is based on the uprising of Irish convicts at Castle Hill in 1804, though the flogging depicted in the poem occurred at Toongabbie in 1800.

There was a high wind blowing on that day;
for one who would not watch, but looked aside,
said that when twice he turned it blew his way
splashes of blood and strips of human hide   25
shaken out from the lashes that were plied
by one right-handed, one left-handed tough,
sweating at this paid task, and skilled enough.

That wind blows to your door down all these years.
Have you not known it when some breath you drew   30
tasted of blood? Your comfort is in arrears
of just thanks to a savagery tamed in you
only as subtler fears may serve in lieu
of thong and noose—old savagery which has built
your world and laws out of the lives it spilt.   35

For what was jailyard widens and takes in
my country. Fifty paces of stamped earth
stretch; and grey walls retreat and grow so thin
that towns show through and clearings—new raw birth
which burst from handcuffs—and free hands go forth   40
to win tomorrow's harvest from a vast
ploughland—the fifty paces of that past.

But see it through a window barred across,
from cells this side, facing the outer gate
which shuts on freedom, opens on its loss   45
in a flat wall. Look left now through the grate
at buildings like more walls, roofed with grey slate
or hollowed in the thickness of laid stone
each side the court where the crowd stands this noon.

One there with the officials, thick of build,   50
not stout, say burly (so this obstinate man
ghosts in the eyes) is he whom enemies killed
(as I was taught) because the monopolist clan
found him a grit in their smooth-turning plan,
too loyally active on behalf of Bligh.[1]   55
So he got lost; and history passed him by.

1   Sir William Bligh (1754–1817), controversial governor of New South Wales, 1806–08.

But now he buttons his long coat against
the biting gusts, or as a gesture of mind,
habitual; as if to keep him fenced
from stabs of slander sticking him from behind,   60
sped by the schemers never far to find
in faction, where approval from one source
damns in another clubroom as of course.

This man had Hunter's[1] confidence, King's[2] praise;
and settlers on the starving Hawkesbury banks   65
recalled through twilight drifting across their days
the doctor's fee of little more than thanks
so often; and how sent by their squeezed ranks
he put their case in London. I find I lack
the hateful paint to daub him wholly black.   70

Perhaps my life replies to his too much
through veiling generations dropped between.
My weakness here, resentments there, may touch
old motives and explain them, till I lean
to the forgiveness I must hope may clean   75
my own shortcomings; since no man can live
in his own sight if it will not forgive.

Certainly I must own him whether or not
it be my will. I was made understand
this much when once, marking a freehold lot,   80
my papers suddenly told me it was land
granted to Martin Mason. I felt his hand
heavily on my shoulder, and knew what coil
binds life to life through bodies, and soul to soil.

There, over to one corner, a bony group   85
of prisoners waits; and each shall be in turn
tied by his own arms in a human loop
about the post, with his back bared to learn
the price of seeking freedom. So they earn
three hundred rippling stripes apiece, as set   90
by the law's mathematics against the debt.

1   John Hunter (1737–1821), governor of New South Wales, 1795–1800.
2   Philip Gidley King (1758–1808), governor of New South Wales, 1800–1806.

These are the Irish batch of Castle Hill,
rebels and mutineers, my countrymen
twice over: first, because of those to till
my birthplace first, hack roads, raise roofs; and then   95
because their older land time and again
enrolls me through my forebears; and I claim
as origin that threshold whence we came.

One sufferer had my surname, and thereto
'Maurice', which added up to history once;   100
an ignorant dolt, no doubt, for all that crew
was tenantry. The breed of clod and dunce
makes patriots and true men: could I announce
that Maurice as my kin I say aloud
I'd take his irons as heraldry, and be proud.   105

Maurice is at the post. Its music lulls,
one hundred lashes done. If backbone shows
then play the tune on buttocks! But feel his pulse;
that's what a doctor's for; and if it goes
lamely, then dose it with these purging blows—   110
which have not made him moan; though, writhing there,
'Let my neck be,' he says, 'and flog me fair.'

One hundred lashes more, then rest the flail.
What says the doctor now? 'This dog won't yelp;
he'll tire you out before you'll see him fail;   115
here's strength to spare; go on!' Ay, pound to pulp;
yet when you've done he'll walk without your help,
and knock down guards who'd carry him being bid,
and sing no song of where the pikes are hid.

It would be well if I could find, removed   120
through generations back—who knows how far?—
more than a surname's thickness as a proved
bridge with that man's foundations. I need some star
of courage from his firmament, a bar
against surrenders: faith. All trials are less   125
than rain-blacked wind tells of that old distress.

Yet I can live with Mason. What is told
and what my heart knows of his heart, can sort

much truth from falsehood, much there that I hold
good clearly or good clouded by report;   130
and for things bad, ill grows where ills resort:
they were bad times. None know what in his place
they might have done. I've my own faults to face.

1965

LENNIE LOWER
1903–1947

Jack Gudgeon, the principal character of Leonard Waldemere Lower's only novel, *Here's Luck* (1930), is a drunken psychopath who debauches his son and his brother-in-law, neglects his wife, tries to slaughter his mother-in-law's pets, frequents sly grog joints, hangs out with prostitutes (whose company he shares with his son), and spends time in jail (also with his son). The book culminates with him burning down his house whilst in the grip of delirium tremens. But it is still, arguably, one of the funniest Australian books ever written.

While his humour might be considered sexist by the contemporary reader—indeed Gudgeon does call his mother-in-law 'a senseless, whining, nagging, leather-faced old whitlow not fit to cohabit with a rhinoceros beetle'—it could be argued that someone with no respect or affection for women would be incapable of describing Gudgeon's reconciliation with his wife so tenderly. Its continuing appeal is evidenced by the fact that *Here's Luck* has been reprinted more than twenty times, and has sold well over 200,000 copies.

Although Lower published only one novel, he wrote much journalism—initially for Packer publications such as the *Telegraph* and *Women's Weekly*, then for *Smith's Weekly*. He wrote up to eight columns a week in the 1930s and '40s, and his comic writing has been collected in seven separate anthologies, from *Here's Another* (1932) to *The Legends of Lennie Lower* (ed. Tom Thompson, 1988), themselves frequently republished. *MC*

Where the Cooler Bars Grow

I'm only a city boy. Until a short time ago I'd never seen a sheep all in one piece or with its fur on. That's why, when people said to me, 'Go west, young man, or east, if you like, but go,' I went.

Truth to tell, I thought it would be safer. I had a shotgun and a rifle, and a bag of flour, and two sealed kerosene tins of fresh water in the luggage van. I thought of taking some coloured beads for the natives, but decided it was too expensive.

I forget now where it was I went to. Anyhow, it was full of wheat silos and flies, and there was a horse standing on three legs under a tree. There were no other signs of life except a faint curl of smoke coming from the hotel chimney.

When I walked into the bar there was nobody there, so I walked out the back to the kitchen and there was nobody there. I went out to the front veranda again, and saw a little old man picking burrs off his socks.

'Good-day!' I said.

'Day!' he replied.

'Where's everybody?' I asked.

'Never heard of him. Unless you mean old Smith. He's down by the crick. You're a stranger, aren't you?'

'Just got off the train. Where's the publican?'

'Do you want a drink?'

'Yes.'

'Orright!'

So we went into the bar and had a drink.

'I want to book a room here,' I told him.

'Don't be silly!' he replied. 'Sleep out on the veranda with the rest of us if you've got blankets. They're decoratin' the School of Arts with the sheets. You going to the dance?'

'I can't dance!'

'Strike me pink, who wants to! We leave that to the women. There ought to be some good fights at this one. When I was younger there wasn't a man could stand up to me on the dance floor. Here comes somebody now.'

'Day.'

'Day. Don't you bring that horse into the bar! Hang it all, you've been told about that before.'

'He's quiet. I broke him in yesterday. Hear about Snowy? Got his arm caught in the circular saw up at the timber mill.'

'That's bad.'

'Too right it is! They've got to get a new saw. Whoa there!'

'Take him out into the kitchen. The flies are worryin' him.'

'Goodo. Pour me out a beer.'

'Pour it out yourself.'

'Go to bed, you old mummified ox!'

'I'll give you a belt in the ear, you red-headed son of a convict!'

'Give it to your uncle, Giddap!'

'One of me best friends,' said the old man, as the horse was led into the kitchen.

'I suppose,' said the red-headed one, returning, 'it'll be all right if he eats that cake on the kitchen table? Won't do him any harm, will it?'

'That's for supper at the dance!'

'Well, I'll go and take it off him. There's a good bit of it left.'

Outside on the veranda voices were heard.

'I wouldn't sell that dog for a thousand pounds.'

'I wouldn't give you two bob for 'im.'

'You never had two bob in your life! You ever seen a sheep dog trial? That dog has won me more prizes at the Show than ten other dogs.

'Why,' he continued, 'you could hang up a fly-veil, point out one particular hole in it and that dog could cut a fly out of a bunch and work him through that hole.'

'Good-day!'

'Day!'

'No sign of rain yet.'

'No. I heard of a swaggie who had to walk eighty miles to get water to boil his billy, and when he got there he found he'd forgotten his cup and saucer, and by the time he'd walked back for his cup and saucer there was a bushfire started in the water-hole, it was that dry.'

'Don't bring your horses into the bar!'

'Don't take any notice of the old crank. Why don't you put this beer out in the sun to get cool? If it was any flatter you'd have to serve it in a plate. Going to the Show this year?'

'Of course I am. Why don't you teach that horse manners?'

'Good-day, Mrs. Smith.'

'Who put that horse in my kitchen?'

'Is he in the kitchen? Well, what do you think of that!'

'Fancy him being in the kitchen!'

'In the kitchen, of all places!'

'Who could have let him in?'

'Never mind about that. Get him out at once, Jack! Wipe up that counter, I told you to cut some wood this morning. And put that dog outside and get the broom and sweep up the bar. Wash those glasses first.'

By this time we were all out on the veranda.

'She hasn't found out about the horse eating the cake yet,' said somebody.

'Better go for a walk somewhere, eh?'

But that was years ago. They've got radios and refrigerators in the bush now, and that's why you see me mournfully wandering about the cattle stalls at Show time. I'm thinking of the good old days before the squatters took up polo, and started knitting their own berets. When men were men, and women were useful about the farm when the plough horse took sick.

> Wrap me up in my stockwhip and blanket
>   And bury me deep down below
> Where the farm implement salesmen won't molest me,
>   In the shades where the cooler bars grow.

Ah, me!

c. 1930s/1963

EVE LANGLEY
1904—1974

Born in Forbes, NSW, Eve Langley died a reclusive death in a mountain hut near Katoomba. Her two published novels, *The Pea Pickers* (1942) and *White Topee* (1954), demonstrate a heightened lyricism that is distinctive in Australian literature and exceptional for the period. Despite this, Langley wrote more than ten other novels, as well as poetry, prose sketches and plays, which remained unpublished until their 2500 interrelated pages were edited to 304, in a collection titled *Wilde Eve: Eve Langley's story* (1999), by Lucy Frost.

Langley's biographer, Joy Thwaite, describes her as a writer 'dogged constantly by the limitations of conventional ideas and sexual roles'. Her early adulthood was spent travelling as an itinerant fruit picker in Gippsland with her sister, when both often dressed as men, and in 1929 she rode alone on horseback across the Australian Alps. In the 1930s she lived, married and had four children in New Zealand, but after the publication of *The Pea Pickers* she was institutionalised for seven years for mental disturbance. She sent writing to her publisher for more than two decades but did not gain the success heralded by her early promise, and spent her later life in isolation and poverty. In 1954, she changed her name by deed poll to Oscar Wilde, reflecting her long interest in both appropriating and questioning gender roles and artistic personae. *NM*

Native-born

In a white gully among fungus red
    Where serpent logs lay hissing at the air,
I found a kangaroo. Tall, dewy, dead,
So like a woman, she lay silent there.
Her ivory hands, black-nailed, crossed on her breast,   5
    Her skin of sun and moon hues, fallen cold.
Her brown eyes lay like rivers come to rest
    And death had made her black mouth harsh and old.
Beside her in the ashes I sat deep
    And mourned for her, but had no native song   10
To flatter death, while down the ploughlands steep
    Dark young Camelli whistled loud and long,
'Love, liberty, and Italy are all.'
    Broad golden was his breast against the sun.
I saw his wattle whip rise high and fall   15
    Across the slim mare's flanks, and one by one
She drew the furrows after her as he
    Flapped like a gull behind her, climbing high,
Chanting his oaths and lashing soundingly,
    While from the mare came once a blowing sigh.   20
The dew upon the kangaroo's white side
    Had melted. Time was whirling high around,

Like the thin wommera, and from heaven wide
    He, the bull-roarer, made continuous sound.
Incarnate lay my country by my hand: 25
    Her long hot days, bushfires, and speaking rains,
Her mornings of opal and the copper band
    Of smoke around the sunlight on the plains.
Globed in fire-bodies the meat-ants ran
    To taste her flesh and linked us as we lay,   30
For ever Australian, listening to a man
    From careless Italy, swearing at our day.
When, golden-lipped, the eagle-hawks came down
    Hissing and whistling to eat of lovely her,
And the blowflies with their shields of purple brown   35
    Plied hatching to and fro across her fur,
I burnt her with the logs, and stood all day
    Among the ashes, pressing home the flame
Till woman, logs, and dreams were scorched away,
    And native with night, that land from whence they came.   40
                                        1940

From *The Pea Pickers*
Chapter XXIX

The paddocks were lonely that season. I was like a blind person feeling about in the dark for a beloved hand. All day we toiled in the light spring weather and the white flowers of the peas tossed their green-veined petals among us. Over the stones, we crawled, filling the tins and dreaming of love, Blue of her faithful youth who in his weekly letters begged for marriage, and I, forsaken, dreaming of Macca, lost in the Black Mountains.

When evening came with the cold winds, we filled our hats with peas and took them home for the evening meal. Afterward, we crawled into bed and slept, to rise and work again next day. It was impossible to sit by the fire at night, for the chimney smoked furiously. The only way cooking could be done was by breaking down a big bundle of tea-tree, flinging it on the hearth, lighting it, placing the billy on a hook above it, and rushing outside. From a distance we watched the smoke rising and when no more came out of the chimney, the room was considered safe to enter and eat in.

The working days of a pea-picker depended on the extent of the crop. A first picking in a small paddock took only a few days, for the plants were carefully handled and only the full pods taken off. When the first paddock had been gone over, we were idle for a week or so.

★

What a morning it was! The sunshine from it promised to penetrate all the coming years of sadness and shine through the mind, carrying with it a remembrance of cool bracken ferns, stiff and dark with dew, and dappled with sunlight.

Peppino stood at the door of the hut.

'Dis morning I go see one my countryman, Leonardo della Vergine. Why you no come wit me? Dis a fonny man. We have tea and cake fill your bell', like-a Mrs 'Ardy.' Peppino jumped with joy at the thought of the virtuous family. 'Quick, too quick, you come wit me, Steve and Blue.'

Dressing with due solemnity, we argued over who was to wear Willie Gray's wrist watch and red flannel rheumatic belt. I said, 'No, I will not go unless I can wear them. You will remember, Blue, that you wore them to the Swanreach sale.'

I felt that with the surgical appliance worn over my trousers and the large leather watch-case on my small wrist, I should appear more handsome than Adonis. Blue disagreed bitterly. 'You wore it last time, Steve, and anyhow, the red belt doesn't suit your colouring.'

'It suits me and you know it,' I said obstinately. 'That's why you want it.'

'But it's only for people with rheumatics.'

'It is not. It suits me.' I buckled it on, tenderly.

Peppino stood outside whistling 'O Sole Mio' and patting Teddy. 'Carm arn. You good dog, eh? Ow … doncha bite me … Gerrout!'

Blue gave in; handed me the wrist watch and, with the red flannel belt in place, I stepped out, satisfied, into the glory of the day.

The sun laid its hand on us, and we fell into a dream of beauty, as mystical as religion. On and on, we wandered, over old roads red with spring, trees crimson with it, saplings bloody with it. We took short cuts over rival pea paddocks where the pickers were working among the crops. Such was the harsh light of the day, that the clods looked enormous and golden, cracked fascinatingly, and carrying blue-grey peas, coloured like the Greek hills of the alpine district. Teddy scampered in front of us; the silky rags of his hide flying in the wind.

Walking under flowering trees near the lake, we came to the residence of a retired judge, who had the reputation of being considerate enough to have travellers rowed across the creek that separated them from the rest of the foreshore; otherwise a long walk through harsh bush and a cold wade through shallow waters were indicated.

We looked around for the judge. Seeing a long low shed, we knocked at its door. No one answered; we opened the door and walked into a workshop. An old man dressed in fine black clothes, with petulance and bewilderment written on his little aristocratic face, walked up to us.

'Well?' he asked.

We said politely that we wanted to cross the creek. But he was as deaf as a beetle. So we bellowed courteously the request to be rowed out of his sight. The old man looked around, his little red eyes sparkling irritably.

'My man is not here. You want to cross the creek?'

'Yes,' we cried jovially and hopefully. 'Can he row us over, please?'

'Troublesome devils,' muttered the old man.

Awed and saddened, we crawled away and took to the bush.

It was not so difficult after all. The sand gleamed in the sunlight, and the short stiff grass bounced under our feet. Some sheep grazed in a paddock. Here it was that Teddy revealed his true trade of sheep-killing. After them he coursed in true dingo style, pulling them down by the ears and looked around for a larger dog to come along and finish them off. I aimed my pea-rifle at him, but it had no bullets in it, so with a laughing yelp he coursed after another. Peppino threw oaths and stones and at last, red-mouthed and gay, Teddy romped back to a kick in the ribs.

Rounding a point of land, we were in the backyard of the old farm at Bell's Point where we had bought the blue jug last year.

'Why, we've been here before, Peppino! We know this place! What is your friend like? Is he an old man with a brown shining face, all dwarfed and grotesque?'

'*Si, il grotesco* … that's Leonardo!' replied Peppino.

We walked through the unpainted gate under the squat green cedar; the skin of the water-rat was still hanging on its branches. Peppino knocked at the back door.

The short broad man came out, with a boyish sweet smile that was scarcely recognizable. On that wet day we first saw him, he had appeared a ragged, but serenely smiling dwarf, his large grotesque features looming up like a seventh party in a drawing by Dürer, so that we had a sense of him being in the picture at some one else's pleasure.

A year of proprietorship had changed him into a firm, red-cheeked brown-eyed man, with sensual moist underlip lying loose and laughing beneath watchful benevolent eyes. Whitely shone his teeth as he smiled at us, and his rounded belly made his white shirt and khaki trousers swell out firmly.

'*Buon giorno, Peppino,*' he remarked in the slow lazy voice of an Italian Yorkshireman. '*Come sta-a-a!*' And to us sweetly and slowly. '*Buon giorno, come sta, Lei?*'

'*Bene grazie,*' we answered.

'Come in. Sid down.' He added laboriously in English. '*Un minuto!*' he added, disappearing to an inner room.

The old kitchen looked unchanged. The long rough wooden table was there, the form behind it, under the window; a box beside the fireplace, and, the sign of the proprietor, a large guitar on the wall. We sat with our backs to the window that looked out on the misty blue lake; the fine cobwebs across the panes gave this natural canvas an appearance of age and the cracking-up of paints. The form was firm under us. We spread our legs and watched comfortably the preparations for our lunch. Leonardo talked in his lazy easy-going dialect to Peppino. '*Ho preso il crops st' anno; ho venduto it primo sacco al Mr Jonson,*'[1] with English words thrown in easily and nicely.

Moving around the kitchen with a frying-pan full of oil in his hand, he murmured in his luxurious Italian of crops and prices, while his big coarse fingers gesticulated awkwardly, showing the palm all the time. He broke several eggs into the pan, chopped up some parsley and flung it in on top of the oil and the raw yellow globes of the eggs. '*Ma, credo che non posso venire a Melbourne st' anno! Non è sicuro il crops.*'[2]

He stopped at the fire, blowing its red flame higher, and the red handkerchief tucked in his belt at the back bobbed as he worked. Through the window the lake gleamed under the misty wind, and we eyed the guitar and wondered if he would play it later. I followed his every movement with delight, through the large shadowy room. '*Un minuto, un minuto!*' he repeated.

A few tomatoes were cut up and added to the eggs and parsley. He waddled from the room and returned with several bottles of wine. Lifting the pan from the fire, he dished up in big old plates the delicately cooked mixture, and poured out wine for us. Fumbling among the glasses he tipped one over.

'*Ah, una festa!*' he and Peppino cried, and we nodded and smiled. For the spilt glass was a sign that the day should be one of feasting and music. Another glass was filled, '*Un minuto!*' Leonardo went away again, returning with bottles of pickles, glasses of honey, jars of nuts and sweets, and a lump of cake. Stripped kidney beans and fennel roots were added to the *salata*, and cups of weak black coffee were placed, slopping over, at our right hands.

From a shelf he took down round loaves of hard bread. '*Questo pane ho fornato, io stesso!*' he cried proudly.

'What? You cook dis yourself?' said Peppino, proud to air his English.

'*Per sicuro!*' Lazily he took down from a board swinging above the table on wires a large round ball of cheese, of a pink and white colour, streaked like marble. It was so hard that he had to cut the pieces off with a hatchet. 'This ... whatchum callem ... cheese,' he said slowly and delicately, 'I make from milk my sheep.'

---

1 'I have gathered crops this year; I sold the first sack to Mr Jonson.'
2 'Well, I do not think that I will be able to come to Melbourne this year! The crops are not reliable this year.'

We nibbled the salty slices and found them so much to our liking that Leonardo was soon tearing off slice after slice. The tomatoes and eggs went to find it and, after them, five glasses of wine apiece, followed by beans, fennel, nuts, pickles, lollies and cakes. Talking and eating, we sat fatly around the table, dreaming dazedly of the mistral-covered waters seen through the cobwebs; of the amiable Leonardo whose face now shone like polished furniture, with a dish of apples standing a few feet off from it and indistinctly reflected on the shine. Listening to his slow ruminative accent, we fell into a trance of joy. For the first time, in years, I felt happy, truly happy. Love hurt me no more.

'Ah, Italy,' I cried, sipping the wine, 'what joys you bring! I give up my dreams of being a great Australian, a pioneer in racial purity and a passionate single-hearted lover of my country. The Australians despise me; they have nothing to give but awkward suspicions. Therefore, I shall forsake them and cling to Italy, to her wine, her slow rich dialects, her foods and her beautiful simian people, faintly savage, faintly over-civilized … and old, so old, with Dante, Tasso and Petrarch as marks for their periods of magnificence.'

I fell in love with Italy that day, as I sipped the wine. Ah, Italy, you have not loved me well! Perhaps you did not forgive me for holding you lightly when we first met. No matter, your sin against me has bound us together for all eternity.

Their natures made open and free with wine, Peppino and Leonardo laughed loudly as they talked, and we bemusedly stared at the poetry of their faces. Peppino took out his mouth-organ and, leaping to his feet, played a furious dance, 'for the old men', as he said. He danced it with Leonardo. They faced each other, Peppino, with his finely cut ivory face sweating out the wine, the black curls hanging over his slanting eyes that glared merrily at Leonardo. This ancient *ballerino* pointed his toes and stepped briskly, clapped his hands and spun around and around, with the red handkerchief bobbing an excited tail in the rear.

While they danced, we kept time with stamping feet. The dust rose from the cracks in the floor, and beyond the cobwebbed windows rose the blue waters and the glassy wind.

Tearing down the guitar from the wall, Leonardo sat on the box by the fire and, plucking the strings clumsily but masterfully, sang in a harsh crow-like voice to the thrum of the music.

Gently we disengaged ourselves from the company and strolled off, with full stomachs, to lie down on the shore. Above in the sky, a large eagle flew glittering against the sun.

At twilight, we were back in the hut with a bottle of wine, a bunch of flowers, and the memory of Leonardo della Vergine bursting in our veins.

Impetuously, we said to Peppino, 'Let us continue the night further, Peppino. We will go with you to your hut and sing there, the old songs of Italy.'

'Sorry, Steve and Blue,' said Peppino in his soft bass voice, 'but Mr Whitebeard son, he tell his fader that he have seen you come dat first night in my plice for see me. And Mr Whitebeard, he tell me, "Peppino, I no want dis young girl come near my house." '

'Ah, Gippsland! Gippsland!' I said, and the joy of the day left me; I was a poet no more.

But the thought of Leonardo persisted; the memory of his lonely gaunt farmhouse was sweet. As I toiled in the paddocks I saw through the rainbow showers of the morning, the spilt wine of the *festa* and the glitter of fruits, vegetables and eggs.

Within my heart, Peppino leapt to his feet again, chanting on the mouth-organ, with the deep swift Italian accompaniment; Leonardo's red handkerchief flapped up and down, and above all, the huge eagle flew piercingly in the sky against the escaping cloud and the flying sun. All was evanescent!

'Ah, Macca, you don't come to me!' I cried, and from the torture of my mind, I made poetry. 'Macca rides in the Black Mountain, and he sings this song. It was in his heart, really, and I took it from him, and shaped it so that I, too, might know what he thought of the past. Ah, the past. Ah, the past, the past! He knows that I, at night, haunt the bark hut, mourning for him. In dreams he sees me and feels my sorrow. Who can help me? I must suffer alone.'

I thought I had made manifest in this song those days when I lay in the old bark hut and listened to the rain drifting across the yellow paddocks, from the Tambo River.

> I cropped the true love from her lips
> As we lay close pressed together,
> When the stallion rains came in from the sea,
> Treading the ploughlands pitilessly,
> As I caught her closer into me,
> In the wild September weather.
> I cropped the true love from her lips,
> From her eyes that opened never,
> And while I kissed, the stallion, rain,
> Came thundering in from the sea again …
> Swiftly I caught him by his mane,
> And we left her alone for ever.

1942

JOHN MORRISON
1904–1998

First published in trade union magazines, John Morrison's short stories and novels employ a naturalistic mode to observe social situations, with acute attention to the felt impact of social and economic hierarchies. Born in England, Morrison migrated to Australia in 1923 and joined the Melbourne Realist Writers Group in the 1940s. His evocations of the industrial conflicts of Melbourne's waterfront are the object of most continuing interest, as well as his portrait of the impact of football on domestic life in his popular story 'Black Night in Collingwood'. His publications include the short-story collections *Sailors Belong Ships* (1947), *Black Cargo and Other Stories* (1955), *Twenty-Three* (1962) and *North Wind* (1982), and a memoir, *Australian By Choice* (1973). NM

The Nightshift

Eight o'clock on a winter's evening.

Two men sit on the open section of a tramcar speeding northwards along St Kilda road. Two stevedores going to Yarraville—nightshift—'down on the sugar'. One—old, and muffled to the ears in a thick overcoat—sits bolt upright, his tired eyes fixed on the far end of the car with that expression of calm detachment characteristic of the pipe-smoker. His companion, a much younger man, leans forward with hands clasped between his knees, as if enjoying the passing pageant of the famous road.

'It'll be cold on deck, Joe,' remarks the young man.

'It will that, Dick,' replies Joe. And they both fall silent again.

At Toorak Road a few passengers alight. A far greater number crowd aboard. Mostly young people going to dances and theatres. Smoothly groomed heads and white bow-ties. Collins Street coiffures and pencilled eyebrows and rouged lips. Creases and polished pumps. Silk frocks and bolero jackets. They fill the tram right out to the running-boards. The air becomes heavily scented.

The young wharfie, mindful of past rebuffs, keeps his seat. He can still see the road, but within twelve inches of his face a remarkably small hand is holding a pink silk dress clear of the floor. He finds it a far more interesting study than the road. Reflects that he could enclose it completely and quite comfortably within his own big fist. Little white knuckles, the fingers of a schoolgirl, painted nails—like miniature rose-petals. He sniffs gently and appreciatively. Violets. His gaze moves a little higher to where the wrist—a wrist that he could easily put thumb and forefinger around—vanishes into the sleeve of the bolero. Higher still. Violets again. Real flowers this time, to go with the perfume. From where he's sitting, a cluster of purple on a pale cheek. She's talking to a young fellow standing with her; her smile is a flicker of dark eyelashes and a flash of white teeth.

Dick finds himself contrasting his own immediate future with that of the girl's escort. Yarraville and the Trocadero. Sugar-berth and dance-floor. His eyes fall again to the little white hand so near his lips, and he sits back with an exclamation of contempt as he catches himself wondering what she would do if he suddenly kissed it. Sissy!

Old Joe's thoughts also must have been reacting to the impact of silks and perfumes.

'The way they get themselves up now,' he hisses into Dick's ear, 'you can't tell which is backside and which is breakfast.'

Dick eyes him with mild resentment. 'What's wrong with them? They look good to me.'

Joe snorts his disagreement, and the subject drops. Dick is only amused. He understands Joe. The old man has shown no disapproval of similar passengers who joined the tram at Alma Road and in Elsternwick. It's the name: 'Toorak'. It symbolizes something. Poor old Joe! Too much courage and not enough brain. Staunch as ever, but made bitter and pig-headed with the accumulation of years. Weary of 'The Struggle'. Left behind. A trifle contemptuous of the young bloods carrying the fight through its final stages. A grand mate, though. And a good hatchman. That means a lot on a sugar job. With the great bulk of the old stevedore at his elbow, and the little white hand before his face, Dick is sensitive of contact with two worlds. Shoddy and silk. Strong tobacco and a whiff of violets. Yesterday and Tomorrow.

Flinders Street-Swanston Street intersection. They get off and push through the pleasure-seeking crowd on the wide pavement under the clocks. Another tram. Contrast again. Few passengers this time. One feels the cold more. Swift transition from one environment to another. Swanston Street to Spencer Street. Play to work. Light to darkness. No more silks and perfumes. Shadowy streets almost deserted. Groups of men, heavily wrapped against the cold, tramping away under the frowning viaduct.

'It'll be a fair bitch on deck,' says Joe, quite unconscious of his lack of originality.

'Yes, you can have it all on your own.'

No offence intended; none taken. They walk in silence. Joe isn't the talking kind. Dick is, but the little white hand and the glimpse of violets on a pale cheek have set in motion a train of thought that makes him irritable. He keeps thinking: 'Cats never work, and even horses rest at night!'

Berth Six, River. Passing up the ramp between the sheds they come out on to the wharf. Other men are already there. Deep voices, and the stamping of heavy boots on wood. The mist is thick on the river, almost a fog. Against the bilious glow of the few lights over on south side dark figures converge on one point, then vanish one at a time over the edge of the wharf.

Dick and Joe join their mates on the floating landing-stage. Rough greetings are exchanged.

'How are you, Joe?'

'What the hell's that got to do with you?'

'You old nark! Got a needle on the hip?'

'I don't need no needle. How's the missus, Sammy?'

'Bit better, Joe. She was up a bit today.'

'Line up there!—here she comes.'

As the little red light appears on the river the men crowd the edge of the landing-stage, each anxious to get a seat in the cabin on such a night. The water is very black and still, and the launch moves in with hardly a ripple. The night is full of sounds. Little sounds, like the rattle of winches at the distant timber berths; big sounds, like the crash of the coal-grabs opposite the gasworks. All have the quality of a peculiar hollowness, so that one still senses the overwhelming silence on which they impinge. In some strange way sound never quite destroys the portentous hush which goes with fog. Dick feels it as he follows old Joe over the gunwale and gropes his way through the cabin, to the bows.

'It's quiet tonight, Joe. Can't be many ships working.'

'Quiet be damned. There's four working on north side. Where the hell're you going, anyway?'

'I'm going to sit outside.'

'You can sit on your own, then. This ain't no Studley Park tour.'

Dick doesn't mind that; all the same he isn't left alone. Other men are forced out beside him as the cabin fills. He finds it hard to dodge conversation. Racing. Football. Now if it was politics … The Struggle! Just a humour, of course. He has no fixed antipathies to nightwork, the waterfront or his mates. Nightwork means good money; three pounds a shift. A real saver sometimes. Many a time he's stood idle for days, then picked up a single night—enough to keep landlord and tradesmen quiet, at least. Two hours less work than the dayshift too. Nevertheless it's all wrong. Surely to Christ the work of the world could be carried on in daylight. So much waste and idleness during the day, and toil at night. Only owls, rats and men work at night.

'What's wrong, Dick? You're not saying much.'

'Just a bit dopey, Bluey. Not enough shut-eye.'

Damn them!—why can't they mind their own business?

The launch travels smoothly and swiftly. Quite safe. The mist is thickening, but there's a bit of light in the river here from the ships working on north side. Small ships, as ships go, but monstrous seen from the passing launch. Beautiful in a way of their own, too, with the clusters of lights hanging from masts and derricks. Little cities of industry resting on towering black cliffs. One can't tell where the black hulls join the black water.

Nameless bows, but still familiar to the critical stevedores.

'That's the *Bundaleera*. Good job. She worked the weekend.'

'The *Era*. She'll finish tonight.'

'The *Montoro*. They say there's only one night in her.'

Strange twentieth-century code of values. A collier which works Sundays is a good ship; a deep-water liner which works only one night is a bad ship.

'They can stick their Sunday work for mine!' Joe's voice.

'I suppose you get more out of the collection-box, you bloody old criminal!'

'That's all right. I only been to church twice in my life. The first time they tried to drown me, and the second time they married me to a crazy woman.'

Dick smiles to himself. A smile of affection for the old warrior. Joe's a good Christian, whether he knows it or not. There's a word for him: 'Nature's gentleman'. A hard doer and a bit of a pagan, that's all. Three convictions: one for stealing firewood during the Depression, one for punching a policeman during the '28 strike, and one for travelling on an expired railway ticket— also during the Depression. Across one cheek the scar of a wound received on Gallipoli. A limp in his right leg from an old waterfront accident. 'Screwy' arms and shoulders from too much freezer work in the days when every possible job had to be stood up for. 'Sailor Joe'. Dick loves him as any healthy youth can love a seasoned guide and mentor. They work together, ship after ship. They travel together, live near each other.

With a mutter of deep voices the launch chugs its way across the Swinging Basin. The mist continues to thicken. South side is just visible. Haloes of brassy yellow around lonely lights. Dismal rigging of idle coal lighters—grimy relics of the white wings of other days. North side can be heard but not seen. Beyond the veil ageing winches clatter at the coal berths and railway trucks crash against each other in Dudley Street yards. A man's voice hailing another comes across the water with extraordinary distinctness.

A few minutes later everything vanishes and the speed of the launch drops to a walking pace. Real fog now. Dick's eyes have been fixed on the ridge of water standing out from the bows. Twice since leaving Berth Six it has fallen in height; now it is but a ripple. Voices in the cabin are still cursing the cold, speculating lightly on the chances of reaching shore in the event of a collision. Dick wishes they'd all shut up. He's cold himself, but some of his irritation has gone. Here again is beauty—of a kind, like ships working at night, and the little white hand. Just three feet away the sooty water flows slowly past. It's easy to imagine that only the water moves, that the launch is motionless, a boatload of men resting in the perpetual night of a black river.

To port, south side has ceased to exist; to starboard, north side is only the distant clamour of a lost world.

Nine o'clock.

The green navigation light of Coode Island.

Only the light. A bleary green eye, neither suspended nor supported. Green eye and grey fog. They pass fairly close. Too close, they realize, as the launch swings sharply off to port. New sounds come out of the night. Sounds of a working ship. Dead ahead, and not far away. Yarraville. Conversation, which has languished, flickers into life again.

'What the hell's that?'

'Don't tell me it ain't nine o'clock yet!'

'Just turned. Maybe there's a rockboat in.'

'There is. They picked up for her this morning.'

'We won't be long now—thank Christ! I'm as cold as a frog.'

'Listen to the dayshift howl when we pull in. It'll be ten o'clock when they get up the river.'

In two places, one on each bow, the fog changes colour. Two glowing caves open up, as if a giant had puffed holes in a drop-curtain. And in each cave the imposing superstructure of a ship materializes with all the bewildering play of light and shadow characteristic of ships at night. Rockboat and sugarboat. The *Trienza* and the *Mildura*. The comparatively graceful lines of the bigger ship don't interest the approaching stevedores. Their eyes are all on the *Mildura*, their minds all grappling with one question: how many nights?

'By God, she's low!'

'She's got a gutsful all right.'

'Three or four nights—you beaut!'

Under a barrage of jeers and greetings from the dayshift the launch noses in to the high wharf.

'You were a long time coming!'

'What're you growling at? You're getting paid for waiting.'

'Ho there, Bluey, you old scoundrel!'

'How are you, Jim? Left a good floor for us?'

'Good enough for you, anyhow. She ain't a bad job.'

'How many brands?'

'Five in Number Two Hatch. Grab the port-for'ard corner if you're down there. You'll get a good run till supper. Two brands.'

'Good on you, son!'

The nightshift swarms up the face of the wharf, cursing a Harbour Trust which provides neither ladder nor landing-stage. Dick is last up, for no other reason than that Joe is second last. The strain imposed on the old man to reach the top angers his young mate. Damn their hides! All ugliness again.

A man can never get away from it for long. The strange charm of the fog-bound river has gone. The black beams of the wharf, with the shrouded men clinging to them like monstrous beetles, symbolize all the galling dreariness of the ten hours just beginning. Symbolism also in the tremendous loom of the coal-gantry. Toiling upwards, always toiling upwards, with just a little glimpse of beauty now and then, like the mist, and the little white hand, and the ridge of black water streaming away from the bows of the launch.

'Shake it up, old-timer!' someone cries from above.

Joe's big boots are just above Dick's head. One of them is lifted on to the next beam. He waits for the other to move, but the old man is still feeling for a higher grip for his hands. Dick's own fingers are getting numb. The beams are covered with wet coal-dust and icy cold. At either side the dayshift men are swarming down. Noise, confusion, and black shapes everywhere.

A sudden anxiety seizes Dick as Joe's higher foot comes down again to the beam it has just left.

'On top there!' he yells. 'Help this man up!'

Too late. Even as he moves to one side and reaches upwards in an endeavour to get alongside his mate, the old man's tired fingers give in. A big clumsy bundle hurtles down, strikes the gunwale of the launch with a sickening thud, and rolls over the side before anyone can lay a hand on it.

An hour later another launch noses away into the fog. Only two men. Both are within the cabin, one standing behind the little steering wheel, the other crouched near the open doorway with eyes fixed on the grey pall beyond the bows. Coode Island is astern before the boatman speaks.

'He was your mate?'

'Yes, he was my mate.'

'You got him out pretty quick.'

'Not quick enough. He hit the launch before he went into the water, you know.'

After a minute's silence. 'Does the buck know you've left?'

'I'm not worried. I wouldn't work tonight, not for King George. And somebody's got to tell his old woman.'

'I'm going right up to Berth Two. Will that do you?'

'Yes, anywhere.'

Anywhere indeed. And the further and slower the better.

Not so much different from an hour ago. Mist, black water, and the crash of trucks over in the railway yards. But no men. One of them embarked now on a longer journey than he ever dreamed of. And in a few minutes there will be lights, and more lights. And voices, and the faces of many people. And not one of them will know a thing of what has happened. Princes Bridge, and the bustle of the great intersection. Trams, and St Kilda Road.

And the big cars rolling along beneath the naked elms. The other world—violets—and the little white hand.

The little white hand. Funny. She'll be dancing somewhere now, and the grand old man with whom she very nearly rubbed shoulders—

'What was that?' asks the boatman.

Dick is startled to find he has spoken aloud.

'We don't know much about each other, do we?' he says without hesitation.

'What d'you mean?'

'Oh, nothing …'

1947

DOUG NICHOLLS
1906–1988

Pastor Doug Nicholls of the Yorta Yorta people was born on Cummeragunja Mission in NSW, and was schooled according to strict religious principles. At the age of eight he saw the police forcibly remove his sixteen-year-old sister Hilda from the family to take her to the Cootamundra Training Home for Girls.

Nicholls worked as a tar boy and a general sheep hand before becoming a professional footballer. He was recruited by the Carlton Football Club but because of the players' racist attitudes did not compete with the team. In 1932 he joined Fitzroy Football Club where, in 1935, he became the first Aboriginal player to be selected to play for the Victorian Interstate Team. Nicholls also boxed with Jimmy Sharman's Boxing Troupe, and earned an income running races, preparing him for the role of inaugural chairman of the National Aboriginal Sports Foundation.

Nicholls was a social worker, the pastor of the first Aboriginal Church of Christ in Australia, and a field officer for the Aboriginal Advancement League. He edited their magazine, *Smoke Signals*, helped set up hostels for Aboriginal children and holiday homes for Aboriginal people at Queenscliff, and was a founding member and Victorian secretary of FCAATSI.

In 1968 Nicholls became a member of the new Ministry of Aboriginal Affairs in Victoria. In 1976 he was appointed Governor of South Australia and in 1991 the Canberra suburb of Nicholls was named after him. *AH/PM*

Letter to the Editor

In expressing our appreciation of Dr. Donald Thomson's[1] public statement (*The Age*, 23/5) of the position we have known he maintains, may I give some illustrations from my own experience.

Our birth place means much to our people.

Whenever possible I return to my home at Cummeroogunja, on the Murray. Like the people of Lake Tyers, we, too, wished to develop our land.

---

1 An anthropologist who worked with the Yolngu people in Arnhem Land.

522 | A.D. HOPE

On each visit as I walk across the small part of the reserve still available to us, I see again the fine old people who were our parents, I remember the pride they had in their flourishing wheat fields, grown on land they had cleared.

Many families owned their own horse and jinker. We were proud of our homes, our church and our school.

Gradually the N.S.W. Government made it clear we had not titled right to the land. White neighbours were leased sections of the reserve.

We became dispirited and depressed. As the station commenced to break up the blame was put on to the people and it was said we were lazy and irresponsible.

Destroyed.

It was the Government's policy and bad administration which destroyed us.

A self-respecting, independent people became dependent on charity and hand-outs.

Many families, refusing to live under the Government's system, attempted to make their way in the white community. Descendants of these folk now walk the streets, live on the fringes of nearby towns and the banks of the Murray.

Other families who put up with conditions were ultimately offered homes in the nearest country centre, where, it was alleged, employment would be available and their children would receive a better standard of education.

The three families who accepted the offer found how difficult life is for unskilled aboriginal labourers in white society, in spite of assistance from well-intentioned people.

They became demoralised and disintegrated. Their children finished up in Government institutions.

This is what I have seen and I will fight to the end to prevent it happening to the Lake Tyers families.

The retaining of Lake Tyers as a basis for creation of employment through community development must be seen as a practical humane plan which can offer security, shelter and stability to family life.

1963

A.D. HOPE
1907–2000

For many years A.D. Hope was Australia's best-known poet internationally. He was born in Cooma, NSW, the son of a Presbyterian minister, and spent his early years in Tasmania. He was educated at the universities of Sydney and Oxford. After a period of school teaching, he became a lecturer in 1937 at the Sydney Teachers College. In 1945 he moved to the University of Melbourne, and in 1951 became professor of English at Canberra University College, later part of the ANU, where Hope worked—and where a building was named after him—until his retirement in 1968 when he became professor emeritus. Hope's early career is notable for his caustic literary criticism (some of which can be found in *Native Companions*, 1974), which included a notorious review of Patrick White's (qv) *The Tree of Man* (1955).

Although Hope had been publishing poems since the 1930s, his first collection, *The Wandering Islands*, was not published until 1955, a delay possibly caused by the work's erotic content. By this time Hope's reputation was assured. His *Collected Poems 1930–1965* appeared in 1966, and was expanded in 1972. His later poems appeared in *The Age of Reason* (1985) and *Orpheus* (1991). He also wrote the mock-epic *Dunciad Minor* (1970), which satirised modern literary criticism. Hope was the author of a number of studies on poetry, including *The Cave and the Spring* (1965) and *The New Cratylus* (1979). He also wrote a memoir, *Chance Encounters* (1992). Hope's selected notebooks have been published as *Dance of the Nomad* (2005), edited by Ann McCulloch.

Hope's poetry relies heavily on literary and biblical precedents and emphasises sexuality. It is generally uninterested in putatively 'Australian' themes and is often brutally satirical about modernity, especially as a force of standardisation and conformity. As Hope's poetry is also formalist and relies heavily on mythology he has been described as 'classical' in style. Nevertheless, Hope's view of poetry as quasi-sacred, his knowledge of symbolism and surrealism, and his interest in the unconscious make him a more complex and modern poet than such a description would allow. Accusations of misogyny in Hope's poetry are harder to refute. Certainly there is a noted ambivalence in Hope's writings on love and sex, a duality that is found generally in his sophisticated poetry. *DM*

Australia

A Nation of trees, drab green and desolate grey
In the field uniform of modern wars,
Darkens her hills, those endless, outstretched paws
Of Sphinx demolished or stone lion worn away.

They call her a young country, but they lie: 5
She is the last of lands, the emptiest,
A woman beyond her change of life, a breast
Still tender but within the womb is dry.

Without songs, architecture, history:
The emotions and superstitions of younger lands,   10
Her rivers of water drown among inland sands,
The river of her immense stupidity

Floods her monotonous tribes from Cairns to Perth.
In them at last the ultimate men arrive
Whose boast is not: 'we live' but 'we survive',   15
A type who will inhabit the dying earth.

And her five cities, like five teeming sores,
Each drains her: a vast parasite robber-state
Where second-hand Europeans pullulate
Timidly on the edge of alien shores.   20

Yet there are some like me turn gladly home
From the lush jungle of modern thought, to find
The Arabian desert of the human mind,
Hoping, if still from the deserts the prophets come,

Such savage and scarlet as no green hills dare   25
Springs in that waste, some spirit which escapes
The learned doubt, the chatter of cultured apes
Which is called civilization over there.

                                                1939/1966

Ascent into Hell

Little Henry, too, had a great notion of singing.
—History of the Fairchild Family[1]

I, too, at the mid-point, in a well-lit wood
Of second-rate purpose and mediocre success,
Explore in dreams the never-never[2] of childhood,
Groping in daylight for the key of darkness;

Revisit, among the morning archipelagoes,   5
Tasmania, my receding childish island;
Unchanged my prehistoric flora grows
Within me, marsupial territories extend:

There is the land-locked valley and the river,
The Western Tiers[3] make distance an emotion,   10
The gum trees roar in the gale, the poplars shiver
At twilight, the church pines imitate an ocean.

There, in the clear night, still I listen, waking
To a crunch of sulky wheels on the distant road;
The marsh of stars reflects a starry croaking;   15
I hear in the pillow the sobbing of my blood

---

1   A series of best-selling didactic and evangelical works for children by Mary Martha Sherwood (1818, 1842, 1847).
2   'The Never Never' is the vast inland area of Northern Australia.
3   A mountainous area of Tasmania.

As the panic of unknown footsteps marching nearer,
Till the door opens, the inner world of panic
Nightmares that woke me to unawakening terror
Birthward resume their still inscrutable traffic.   20

Memory no more the backward, solid continent,
From island to island of despairing dream
I follow the dwindling soul in its ascent;
The bayonets and the pickelhauben[1] gleam

Among the leaves, as, in the poplar tree,   25
They find him hiding. With an axe he stands
Above the German soldiers, hopelessly
Chopping the fingers from the climbing hands.

Or, in the well-known house, a secret door
Opens on empty rooms from which a stair   30
Leads down to a grey, dusty corridor,
Room after room, ominous, still and bare.

He cannot turn back, a lurking horror beckons
Round the next corner, beyond each further door.
Sweating with nameless anguish then he wakens;   35
Finds the familiar walls blank as before.

Chased by wild bulls, his legs stick fast with terror.
He reaches the fence at last—the fence falls flat.
Choking, he runs, the trees he climbs will totter.
Or the cruel horns, like telescopes, shoot out.   40

At his fourth year the waking life turns inward.
Here on his Easter Island the stone faces
Rear meaningless monuments of hate and dread.
Dreamlike within the dream real names and places

Survive. His mother comforts him with her body   45
Against the nightmare of the lions and tigers.
Again he is standing in his father's study
Lying about his lie, is whipped, and hears

---

1   Spiked helmets of the German army.

His scream of outrage, valid to this day.
In bed, he fingers his stump of sex, invents   50
How he took off his clothes and ran away,
Slit up his belly with various instruments;

To brood on this was a deep abdominal joy
Still recognized as a feeling at the core
Of love—and the last genuine memory   55
Is singing 'Jesus Loves Me'—then, no more!

Beyond is a lost country and in vain
I enter that mysterious territory.
Lit by faint hints of memory lies the plain
Where from its Null took shape this conscious I   60

Which backward scans the dark—But at my side
The unrecognized Other Voice speaks in my ear,
The voice of my fear, the voice of my unseen guide;
'Who are we, stranger? What are we doing here?'

And through the uncertain gloom, sudden I see   65
Beyond remembered time the imagined entry,
The enormous Birth-gate whispering, *'per me,*
per me si va tra la perduta gente.'[1]

          1955

The Death of the Bird

For every bird there is this last migration:
Once more the cooling year kindles her heart;
With a warm passage to the summer station
Love pricks the course in lights across the chart.

Year after year a speck on the map, divided   5
By a whole hemisphere, summons her to come;
Season after season, sure and safely guided,
Going away she is also coming home.

And being home, memory becomes a passion
With which she feeds her brood and straws her nest,   10

---

1 'Through me, through me is the way to join the lost people': from the inscription on the gates of hell in the third canto of Dante's *Inferno*. The last line of the inscription reads 'Abandon all hope, you who enter!'

Aware of ghosts that haunt the heart's possession
And exiled love mourning within the breast.

The sands are green with a mirage of valleys;
The palm-tree casts a shadow not its own;
Down the long architrave of temple or palace   15
Blows a cool air from moorland scarps of stone.

And day by day the whisper of love grows stronger;
That delicate voice, more urgent with despair,
Custom and fear constraining her no longer,
Drives her at last on the waste leagues of air.   20

A vanishing speck in those inane dominions,
Single and frail, uncertain of her place,
Alone in the bright host of her companions,
Lost in the blue unfriendliness of space,

She feels it close now, the appointed season: 25
The invisible thread is broken as she flies;
Suddenly, without warning, without reason,
The guiding spark of instinct winks and dies.

Try as she will, the trackless world delivers
No way, the wilderness of light no sign,   30
The immense and complex map of hills and rivers
Mocks her small wisdom with its vast design.

And darkness rises from the eastern valleys,
And the winds buffet her with their hungry breath,
And the great earth, with neither grief nor malice,   35
Receives the tiny burden of her death.
                                                                 1955

Crossing the Frontier

Crossing the frontier they were stopped in time,
Told, quite politely, they would have to wait:
Passports in order, nothing to declare,
And surely holding hands was not a crime;
Until they saw how, ranged across the gate,   5
All their most formidable friends were there.

Wearing his conscience like a crucifix,
Her father, rampant, nursed the Family Shame;
And, armed with their old-fashioned dinner-gong,
His aunt, who even when they both were six,   10
Had just to glance towards a childish game
To make them feel that they were doing wrong.

And both their mothers, simply weeping floods,
Her head-mistress, his boss, the parish priest,
And the bank manager who cashed their cheques;   15
The man who sold him his first rubber-goods;
Dog Fido, from whose love-life, shameless beast,
She first observed the basic facts of sex.

They looked as though they had stood there for hours;
For years; perhaps for ever. In the trees   20
Two furtive birds stopped courting and flew off;
While in the grass beside the road the flowers
Kept up their guilty traffic with the bees.
Nobody stirred. Nobody risked a cough.

Nobody spoke. The minutes ticked away;   25
The dog scratched idly. Then, as parson bent
And whispered to a guard who hurried in,
The customs-house loudspeakers with a bray
Of raucous and triumphant argument
Broke out the wedding march from *Lohengrin*.   30

He switched the engine off: 'We must turn back.'
She heard his voice break, though he had to shout
Against a din that made their senses reel,
And felt his hand, so tense in hers, go slack.
But suddenly she laughed and said: 'Get out!   35
Change seats! Be quick!' and slid behind the wheel.

And drove the car straight at them with a harsh,
Dry crunch that showered both with scraps and chips,
Drove through them; barriers rising let them pass;
Drove through and on and on, with Dad's moustache   40
Beside her twitching still round waxen lips
And Mother's tears still streaming down the glass.

1963/1972

Inscription for a War

Stranger, go tell the Spartans
we died here obedient to their commands.
Inscription at Thermopylae

Linger not, stranger; shed no tear;
Go back to those who sent us here.

We are the young they drafted out
To wars their folly brought about.

Go tell those old men, safe in bed,   5
We took their orders and are dead.

1971

The Mayan Books

Diego de Landa, archbishop of Yucatán[1]
—The curse of God upon his pious soul—
Placed all their Devil's picture-books under ban
And, piling them in one sin-heap, burned the whole;

But took the trouble to keep the calendar   5
By which the Devil had taught them to count time.
The impious creatures had tallied back as far
As ninety million years before Eve's crime.

That was enough: they burned the Mayan books,
Saved souls and kept their own in proper trim.   10
Diego de Landa in heaven always looks
Towards God: God never looks at him.

1991

JUDAH WATEN
1911–1985

Judah Waten was born in Odessa in the Ukraine, his birth date uncertain because of
the confusion of calendars—Russian, Jewish and Ottoman—created by his family's
circumstances at the time. Waten himself claimed 29 July 1911 as his date of birth; if this
is correct, he died on his 74th birthday.

Soon after his birth, his family emigrated from Tsarist Russia to Palestine to escape
the pogroms; the family then immigrated to Australia when Waten was three years old.
He was educated in Perth and then in Melbourne.

---

1 Diego de Landa Calderón (1524–79), charged with bringing the Roman Catholic faith to the Mayans after
   the Spanish conquest of Yucatán.

Always a highly politicised writer, he began to write in his teens, mainly about the unemployed. Between 1931 and 1933 he lived in England, where he co-edited *The Unemployed Worker*. After his return to Australia he worked in the public service and resumed writing fiction, becoming, with his Hungarian-born contemporary David Martin, one of the earliest Australian writers to record the postwar migrant experience in fiction.

As a Russian Jewish communist writer, he was regarded as a suspicious character both by the conservative Menzies (qv) government and by the Communist Party of Australia, with which he had a difficult relationship. His best-known work is *Alien Son* (1952), an early version of what Frank Moorhouse (qv) calls 'discontinuous narrative'— in which separate stories are loosely connected by common characters and settings— detailing the life of a European Jewish migrant family in Australia. His other novels include *The Unbending* (1954), *Time of Conflict* (1961) and *Distant Land* (1964). David Carter's detailed account of his life and work, *A Career in Writing: Judah Waten and the cultural politics of a literary career*, was published in 1997. KG

From *Alien Son*
Mother

[. . .] Mother was very concerned about how she could give us a musical education. It was out of the question that we both be taught an instrument, since Father's business was at a low ebb and he hardly knew where he would find enough money to pay the rent, so she took us to a friend's house to listen to gramophone records. They were of the old-fashioned, cylindrical kind made by Edison and they sounded far away and thin like the voice of a ventriloquist mimicking far off musical instruments. But my sister and I marvelled at them. We should have been willing to sit over the long, narrow horn for days, but Mother decided that it would only do us harm to listen to military marches and the stupid songs of the music-hall.

It was then that we began to pay visits to musical emporiums. We went after school and during the holidays in the mornings. There were times when Father waited long for his lunch or evening meal, but he made no protest. He supposed Mother knew what she was doing in those shops and he told his friends of the effort Mother was making to acquaint us with music.

Our first visits to the shops were in the nature of reconnoitring sorties. In each emporium Mother looked the attendants up and down while we thumbed the books on the counters, stared at the enlarged photographs of illustrious composers, and studied the various catalogues of gramophone records. We went from shop to shop until we just about knew all there was to know about the records and sheet music and books in stock.

Then we started all over again from the first shop and this time we came to hear the records.

I was Mother's interpreter and I would ask one of the salesmen to play us a record she had chosen from one of the catalogues. Then I would ask him to play another. It might have been a piece for violin by Tchaikowsky or Beethoven or an aria sung by Caruso or Chaliapin. This would continue until Mother observed the gentleman in charge of the gramophone losing his patience and we would take our leave.

With each visit Mother became bolder and several times she asked to have whole symphonies and concertos played to us. We sat for nearly an hour cooped up in a tiny room with the salesman restlessly shuffling his feet, yawning and not knowing what to expect next. Mother pretended he hardly existed and, making herself comfortable in the cane chair, with a determined, intent expression she gazed straight ahead at the whirling disc.

We were soon known to everyone at the shops. Eyes lit up as we walked in, Mother looking neither this way nor that with two children walking in file through the passage-way towards the record department. I was very conscious of the humorous glances and the discreet sniggers that followed us and I would sometimes catch hold of Mother's hand and plead with her to leave the shop. But she paid no heed and we continued to our destination. The more often we came the more uncomfortably self-conscious I became and I dreaded the laughing faces round me.

Soon we became something more than a joke. The smiles turned to scowls and the shop attendants refused to play us any more records. The first time this happened the salesman mumbled something and left us standing outside the door of the music-room.

Mother was not easily thwarted and without a trace of a smile she said we should talk to the manager. I was filled with a sense of shame and humiliation and with downcast eyes I sidled towards the entrance of the shop.

Mother caught up with me and, laying her hand upon my arm, she said, 'What are you afraid of? Your mother won't disgrace you, believe me.' Looking at me in her searching way she went on, 'Think carefully. Who is right—are they or are we? Why shouldn't they play for us? Does it cost them anything? By which other way can we ever hope to hear something good? Just because we are poor must we cease our striving?'

She continued to talk in this way until I went back with her. The three of us walked into the manager's office and I translated Mother's words.

The manager was stern, though I imagine he must have had some difficulty in keeping his serious demeanour.

'But do you ever intend to buy any records?' he said after I had spoken.

'If I were a rich woman would you ask me that question?' Mother replied and I repeated her words in a halting voice.

'Speak up to him,' she nudged me while I could feel my face fill with hot blood.

The manager repeated his first question and Mother, impatient at my hesitant tone, plunged into a long speech on our right to music and culture and in fact the rights of all men, speaking in her own tongue as though the manager understood every word. It was in vain; he merely shook his head. [...]

1952

HAL PORTER
1911–1984

As recounted in his autobiography, *The Watcher on the Cast-Iron Balcony* (1963), Hal Porter was born in Melbourne and grew up in Bairnsdale. Until the early 1940s he worked as a school teacher. A severe traffic accident in 1939 led to him being unable to take part in the Second World War. After the war he worked as a teacher and at various other occupations, was attached as a teacher to the Occupied Forces in Japan (1949–50), and was librarian at Bairnsdale and Shepparton (1953–61), after which he became a full-time writer. He died after being hit by a car.

Porter's reputation was slow to establish, but by the time of his death he had won critical success and numerous literary awards. Porter's most important role was as a writer of short stories and autobiography, of which he wrote two more volumes, *The Paper Chase* (1966) and *The Extra* (1975). He also wrote poetry, novels—*The Tilted Cross* (1961) being the most significant—plays, history, travel writing and essays. Porter was a prose stylist of a kind rarely seen in Australia. His writings are both highly mannered and documentary-like in their ability to represent Australia. Like other anti-realist writers (not least Katherine Mansfield, one of Porter's influences), Porter's anti-realist style is in service to a realist project. In *Contemporary Novelists* (1972) he writes of a 'wish to record clearly an extraordinary country and ... its unique-enough inhabitants'. He is the subject of a controversial biography by Mary Lord (1993). *DM*

From *The Watcher on the Cast-Iron Balcony*

In a half-century of living I have seen two corpses, two only. I do not know if this total is conventional or unconventional for an Australian of my age.

The first corpse is that of a woman of forty. I see its locked and denying face through a lens of tears, and hear, beyond the useless hullabaloo of my début in grief, its unbelievable silence prophesying unbelievable silence for me. It is not until twenty-eight years later that I see, through eyes this time dry and polished as glass, my second corpse, which is that of a seventy-three-year-old man. Tears? No tears, not any, none at all. The silence of this corpse is as credible as my own silence is to be, and no excuse for not lighting another cigarette. I light it, tearless, while the bereaved others scatter their anguish in laments like handbills. I am tearless because twenty-eight years have taught that it is not the dead one should weep for but the living.

Once upon a time, it seems, but in reality on or about the day King Edward VII died, these two corpses have been young, agile and lustful enough to mortise themselves together to make me. Since the dead wear no ears that hear and have no tongues to inform, there can now be no answer, should the question be asked, as to where the mating takes place, how zestfully or grotesquely, under which ceiling, on which kapok mattress—no answer anywhere, ever.

In time, the woman, Mother, is six months large with me, and Dr Crippen is hanged. In time, and missing Edwardian babyhood by nine months, I am born. I am born a good boy, good but not innocent, this two-sided endowment laying me wide open to assaults of evil not only from without but also from within. I am a Thursday's child with far to go, brought forth under the sign of Aquarius, and with a cleft palate. This is skilfully sewn up. In which hospital? When I am how few months old? By whom now dead or nearing death? No one, I think, no one living now knows. Thus secretly mended, and secretly carrying, as it were, my first lie tattooed on the roof of the mouth that is to sound out so many later lies, I grow. I am exactly one week old when the first aeroplane ever to do so flies over my birthplace. On aesthetic grounds or for superstitious reasons I am unvaccinated; I am superstitiously and fashionably uncircumcised, plump, blue-eyed and white-haired. I have a silver rattle, Hindu, in the shape of a rococo elephant hung on a bone ring. I crawl. The *Titanic* sinks. I stand. The Archduke is assassinated at Sarajevo, and I walk at last into my own memories.

These earliest memories are of Kensington, a Melbourne suburb, and one less elegant than that in which I am born between the tray-flat waters of Albert Park Lake and the furrowed and wind-harrowed waters of Port Phillip Bay. The memories are centred in a house then 36 Bellair Street, Kensington. Of this house and of what takes place within it until I am six, I alone can tell. That is, perhaps, why I must tell. No one but I will know if a lie be told, therefore I must try for the truth which is the blood and breath and nerves of the elaborate and unimportant facts.

At the age of six I physically leave Kensington and 36 Bellair Street for ever, lightly picking up and taking with me Kensington and 36 Bellair Street. Until this very point in time a baggage of memories has travelled with me.

The moment of unpacking at hand I am astounded by the size and complexity of this child's luggage. Even now, a middle-aged man, I cannot unpack all: I have not yet the skill to unlade what a happy egocentric little boy skilfully jammed into invisible nothing.

Let me immediately reveal, in my largely visual recollections of this pre-six era, that my father and my mother are not visually alive to me as the young woman and young man they then are. I cannot see them. I remember the face of Father's gold pocket-watch, and the hair-line crack across its enamel, but not his; I remember exactly the pearls and rubies in Mother's crescent brooch but not her eyes. Except for Mother's singing, I cannot hear them; a mere little litter of words blows down the galleries of time, some of it aesthetically haunting, more of it unforgettably trite. I do remember his fatherliness and her motherliness, essences informed by their youth and vitality and simplicity in which I have every trust. Fatherliness, motherliness, youth, vitality and simplicity I would not now trust for a moment. Each can destroy. Each helps destroy my parents; each helps them lay waste about them. But, however omniscient the child, he dares not, particularly if he be first born, further blind the parents he has already blinded with his existence by showing that he knows they are dupes not only of himself but of nature. So, my parents, imagining their physical selves as clearly seen as they think they see themselves in looking-glasses, move with blind instinct about me and always towards me and my imperious ego. They play the fool for me. They put on voices. They spend money on rubbish, toys for their toy. They cannot know that they themselves are clouds only, symbolic blurs meaning certainty and warmth and happiness, slaves without faces in a small universe where everything else is exquisitely clear.

The detail!

The colour!

Except in dreams, neither detail nor colour has ever since been so detailed or coloured; the fine edge of seeing for the first time too early wears blunt. But the first seeing is so sure that nothing smudges it. Take Bellair Street.

Bellair Street, built about 1870, is a withdrawn street overhung by great plane-trees and is on the way to nowhere else. It is only several blocks long and, so far as houses are concerned, one-sided. This is because it is the last street, three-quarters of the way down, of several streets lying horizontally along the eastern slope of a ridge crowned with Norfolk Island pines, non-conformist churches of brick the colour of cannas or gravy-beef, and a state school of brick the colour of brick. The slope makes it necessary to ascend from the front gate of 36 along a path of encaustic tiles, next by eight wooden steps on to a front veranda which is therefore a long balcony balustraded with elaborately convoluted cast-iron railings. From this balconic veranda I look over the plane-trees towards a miles-off miles-long horizon composed of the trees of the Zoo, Prince's Park, Royal Park and the Melbourne University. There are the towers and domes of the University and the Exhibition Buildings, and countless nameless spires.

This prospect is less colonial Australian than eighteenth-century English in quality: billowy green trees, misty towers, even a shallow winding stream that starts and ends in obscurity like a painter's device. Southern Hemisphere clouds pile themselves up, up above, and take on Englishy oil-landscape tones, or steel-engraving shafts of biblical light strike down, or incandescent Mississippis of lightning. Between this romantic or dramatic background and the watcher at the cast-iron lace of the balustrade innumerable more sordid elements are disposed: paltry municipal parks like seedy displays of parsley; endless terraces of houses; endless perspectives of ignoble streets and, strange as palaces, many three-storeyed stucco hotels whose baroque façades topped with urns and krateres[1] protrude here and there above an agitation of humbler roofs of slate or terracotta but largely of unpainted corrugated iron. Sometimes, brilliant and perfectly executed hailstorms load the gulches of the roofs with white. Sometimes, a sunset behind Kensington ridge is reflected in sumless distant windows like spots of golden oil. I seem to be often watching, now and again with Mother a shape behind my shoulder, but most often alone. This watching, this down-gazing, this faraway staring, is an exercise in solitude and non-involvement. Perhaps my relish for aloneness, that deep and quenching draught, a content I have at times wrestled ferociously with circumstances to pluck from the hubbub of gregariousness, explains why no human beings appear in memories of that fanned out landscape. Disdain and self-sufficiency have sponged them off. This landscape, transfixed and unpeopled, untouchable and mute and mine, is my first glimpse of a world I am to see far too much and yet not nearly enough of and into. Let my eyes, so sated and so deprived, turn from the scene and peer at closer matters.

Behind the watcher's back lies a more restricted world, tangible, cluttered, comfortable, a world from which I can pick up sections and smash them to smithereens. I am too much of a good boy to do this. It is, moreover, a sensual world I like more than my view but love less although it contains more love than I shall ever need or ever need to seek.

My parents are generous with their natural love, and exact no more from me than the barest minimum of sensible behaviour in gratitude for not eating me in a *fricassée* or giving me to the old-clothes-man. This lop-sided bargain, of whatever advantage to them then and none now, is of lasting advantage to me. It has fattened my confidence to the point where I can be treacherous to their conception of privacy. Had I been less loved, I could not drag them from their graves without warning, for the dead cannot wash behind their ears before appearing in public.

Behind the watcher's back, one each side of the wooden front door painted and grained to resemble some other wasp-coloured wood, lie the front bedroom (right) and the front room (left).

I am child of an era and a class in which adults are one tribe and children another, each with its separate rights and duties, freedoms and restrictions, expected gentlenesses and condoned barbarities, each with its special reticences and sacred areas. One area taboo to children is the front room. I am, of course, sometimes permitted to enter the congested sanctuary, a magnanimity that leaves me now, so far as I know, the one creature living who knows what was within. Its contents and their stylized arrangement are equally an aspect of the Australian lower middle class of the Great War

---

1   Unusual spelling of 'kraters', ancient Greek vases.

years and my mother, an indictment of suburban vulgarity and my mother, and an indictment, too, of my father, marking him down as an indubitable Australian, one of a nation of men willing to live in a feminized house. My mother says, as Australian women say to this day, *my* dinner service, *my* doormats, *my* umbrella-stand, *my* pickle-fork.

Outside the door of *her* front room, Japanese wind-bells hang from the passage ceiling, a dangle on threads of triangular and rectangular slices of glass from which air in motion splashes delicious scraps of sound. Thirty years later, in a brothel street by a canal in Osaka, I hear wind-bells through the giggles of drunkards and the sound of the samisen and, there, under paper lanterns large as oil-drums, see again the front room and its ritual garnishings.

There is the richly fringed saddlebag and Utrecht velvet suite. On its mainly magenta sofa leans a magenta velvet cushion on which three padded white velvet arum lilies poke out their yellow velvet phalli. A be-bobbled mantel-drape of magenta plush skirts the chimney-shelf burdened with Mary Gregories.[1] There are an eight-sided occasional table on which an antlered buck of fake bronze attitudinizes sniffily, two gipsy tables, a bamboo music canterbury, a Renardi upright grand of Italian walnut before which sits a tri-legged revolving piano-stool. A dog-ended nickel fender and a yard-long set of nickel fire-irons, never used, weekly burnished, the shovel pierced almost to filigree, occupy the hearth. It is a room that bruises sound; in its air that suffers an inflammation the hoofs of horses passing on the asphalt roadway come wooden and weary to the ear.

On the other hand, the front bedroom, the parental one, is filled with a luminosity that seems to swing and sway like a bird-cage, white with a tinge of jade. Through this the hoof-beats click sharply and swiftly as though the roadway of Bellair Street is ivory, and the hoofs of carved ivory. This pretty-pretty evocation suggests that Mother has taste after all. It is scarcely so. It is what can be afforded of what offers when a young woman from the country becomes a suburban bride.

Nottingham lace curtains, whereon a self-conscious liaison of bracts of white fern and pendent bunches of white muscatels occurs, hang at the window, their scalloped edges skimming the leek-green linoleum blotched with white chrysanthemums. In the centre of one wall, and rigidly at right angles to it, a Venetian double bed of white enamel columns banded and curlicued with nickel asserts an importance as of a sacrificial altar or an operating-theatre table. On each side of the bed, dead parallel to the dead-straight hems of the dead-white quilt, lies a shaggy white mohair mat. A

---

1   The name given to glassware with idyllic depictions of Victorian-era children. Mary Gregory (1856–1908) was an American glass painter.

fourfold Japanese screen, reeds and cranes embroidered in greenish gold on linen, conceals a cabinet that contains the chamber-pot into which, sometimes, from my own next-door bedroom, I half-asleep hear, dispassionately yet with some interest, my father or my mother urinating. Sometimes, one later than the other, I hear them both. For some atavistic reason or because of some information obtained in the womb, it is easy to recognize who is engaged. It is only during this brief period of their and my lives that such opportunities to use my untainted animal hearing happen. Very little later, the ability to distinguish without hesitation or mistake whether, for example, Mother, unseen in the next room, is talking while lying down or talking while standing or talking while moving about or talking while sitting and brushing her hair, is an ability I lose. A child is forced to abandon purely animal faculties such as this one.

Now that the eye and the ear of the watcher have been brought closer enough to these humans who made my body it seems that Mother is revealed, in the furnishings of the front bedroom, as guilty of an intention to an inhuman scheme of Austral-*japonoiserie* until the eye swivels to the walnut duchesse dressing-table with its central swing-mirror and hinged side-mirrors, its many brass-handled drawers and bracketed shelves. On this piece of furniture, set out on doilies or crocheted runners, are evidences of humanity. Here lies the last of Mother's girlish vanity, although not the last of her girlishness. Here are the tag-ends of courting devices. Here are many objects soon to disappear, not because the fashion for them changes or Mother's vanity grows less but because, as the number of my brothers and sisters increases disproportionately to my father's income, time strikes them from her hands to replace them with more brutal weapons: the vaginal syringe, the breast-pump, the preserving-pan, the vegetable garden hoe, the sewing-machine nibbling stitches into boys' galatea blouses and flannel under-shirts, into girls' corduroy velvet dresses, serge skirts and pink cotton sunbonnets. Here, for a little longer, and to me for ever, lie tortoise-shell-backed brushes and tortoise-shell combs, curling-tongs, hair-curlers, hairpins, hairnets, and those soft sausages of hair-padding Mother calls rats. Here hangs the embroidered hair-tidy plump with combings; here hang three horse-tail-like switches of her own made-up hair. Here are all the other humble artifices she needs to construct a woman of the conventional shape of coiffure, smell and colour to appear, without diffidence, publicly as young wife and mother. Here are the hock-bottle-green flask of eau-de-Cologne, the atomizer, the two circular boxes of Swansdown Adhesive Powder, White and *Rosée*, the prism of French nail-polish, the disc of dry rouge, the cake of Castile soap in its china dish decorated with moss roses.

Because, already scrubbed, combed and decorated, I am often made to sit on the white Dante chair while my parents finish decorating themselves, my memories of the bedroom are detailed and accompanied by memories of those gesticulations that immediately preface outings: Mother's hands and arms soaring with sure and accidentally graceful movements to skewer on her hat with foot-long hatpins knobbed with enamelled flowers, imitation cairngorms, pear-shaped *Ballet Russe* pearls or *ersatz* cameos; Father trimming his nails with a mother-of-pearl-handled penknife; Mother buttoning her kid gloves; Father fixing through its special vertical buttonhole in his waistcoat either the gold watchchain from which hangs a sovereign or his silver chain which bears a shark's tooth rooted in agate. Gestures of going out—how indicative it is of three-, four- and five-year-old greed for experience that I should remember, forty years later, the gestures themselves but not the faces and voices of the man and woman making them, enlarged and brilliantly lit gestures, close-ups cut from context by the knife of a selfish, pleasure-seeking eye.

Going where?

Going in steam-trains or cable-trams, sometimes in cabs, sometimes walking hand-in-hand with Mother or Father across streets where the crossing-sweeper pushes piles of horse-manure from before our feet, going to the places little Melbourne suburban boys of those years go with their mummies and daddies: the Museum, the Botanical Gardens, the Waxworks, Wirth's Circus, Punch and Judy shows, the Aquarium in the Exhibition Buildings, the Royal Park Zoo. The final stage in travelling to the Zoo is done in the last horse-drawn tram left over from an earlier age. Before I have seen a sheep or a cow, and many years before I see a kangaroo, I am familiar with elephants, camels, lions and leopards, with middle-class animals like the giraffe and the hippopotamus, old-fashioned nineteenth-century creatures. Indeed, all these entertainments are, in a sense, left-overs from Victoria's reign. Other animals like Charlie Chaplin are taking their places. The middle- and late-Victorian auras of the London originals on which they are modelled emanate from these pleasure places. Cole's Book Arcade, of which the lofty cast-iron galleries bisect two Melbourne blocks, has the common-sense yet engaging eccentricity that is Edward Lear's and the Englishman's. At the great entrance to the arcade with its architectural air of Waterloo Station, two small mechanical puppets, earnestly and rosily grinning like pot-boys from Dickens, jerk ceaselessly at crank handles which rotate into view successive boards advertising in rainbow colours The Largest Book Arcade In The World and its subsidiary attractions. These attractions have not always to do with books. I remember indoor cages of monkeys, tropical palms and tree-ferns, and an afternoon tea of cream horns eaten to the music of a small whining orchestra and, upstairs, in a first floor gallery supported by brass columns, tiers and seeming miles of gilt-poxed china figurines and curly vases with gilded handles.

Going where else?

Going to visit Grandfather Porter at seaside Williamstown, and being able to remember nothing of him externally except his wheelchair, the afghan that covers his knees, and his white military moustache nicotined tawny at the centre and smelling of wine. I remember my instant perception that, inwardly, he cares nothing for me. I consequently find him valueless even though he gives me a bronze statuette of Kwannon, the Goddess of Mercy. Behind the smudged façades of my parents are stacked almost visible quantities of security, of the emotional fodder and spiritual information I assume to be the truth and everlasting. Behind Grandfather's afghan and stained moustache stretches an emptiness I have not the need, tricks nor impulse to imprint with the patter of childish cloven feet. Anyway, babyish tricks and winning wiles would, I see now, have been of no avail; a blown-off leg, a Boer War medal and a voice like a bittern might have won him back from no man's land to the idiocy of affection, for Grandfather is consciously a Warrior and a Fine Old Gentleman and, deliberately, a Character. English, starting as a drummer-boy in the Crimean War, he has progressed to the wheel chair by such military steps as taking part in the looting of the Summer Palace in Peking, taking for his second wife a crack rifle-shot, and naming one of my uncles Martini-Henry. Militarism seems all to him; his hobby, before the wheel chair, is painting battle scenes. These large canvases illustrate no aspect of his own experience that is unfit to hang on a wall. Rape, gangrene, cholera, blown-out guts and bloody slaughter are absent. The paintings, in every shade of glossy brown, show neat soldiers, their helmets and plumes and cloaks and sabres exquisitely fresh, dreamily involved in some nineteenth-century battle. Caught at a moment of horrorless cessation, the finespun horses curvet like statue horses, their eyes limpid as madonnas'. The warriors pose in attitudes of languor. Here and there a brow is bandaged, the bandage immaculate except for one tiny carnation of rosewood-coloured blood. Usually these picnic-like siestas occupy the well-swept bed of a romantically rocky pass at whose gothic extremity is a golden-brown glaze of sky behind which no one but a superannuated God can be drowsing.

Uncle Martini-Henry, my father's brother, is married to Aunt Rosa Bona, my mother's sister. They too, as Grandfather does, live in Williamstown but in a new house in fashionable Victoria Street. Grandfather Porter and his rifle-shooting second wife, Father's stepmother, occupy an older, shabby, wind-tormented house at the edge of the Rifle Ranges on the bay's edge. The house seems guarded by two small cannon, and filled with cedar sideboards, wine decanters, glass-fronted bookcases and tarnished silver meat-dish covers. Where the walls are not covered with Grandfather's paintings there hang crossed swords and racks of muskets and rifles. Nothing grows in the sandy garden but tamarisks all leaning away from the sea.

Uncle Martini-Henry's and Aunt Rosa Bona's house, Australian Queen Anne in style, is of blood-orange-red tuck-pointed bricks. At the end of

Victoria Street, which is lined by immature date-palms in picket enclosures, sand drifts on to the asphalt road from the beach with its tide-lines of shells and its wheeling and marching blue soldier crabs. On this beach Mother and Aunt Bona, squealing and holding up great handfuls of skirts and petticoats, take me paddling. Port Phillip Bay flickers many fringed, age-white eyebrows behind our backs as we return to Aunt Bona's house, the ridge ends of its alp-steep roof and false gables of Marseilles tiles infested by terracotta griffins, its bay windows and fanlights enriched by *art nouveau* leadlights.

At this stage of my recollections Aunt Bona appears continuously to wear a salver-sized black hat occupied by a whirlpool of yellow ostrich feathers. A string-thin golden chain hangs down her front. She and Mother call this front a bust. On the chain is a gold heart, fat as a fuchsia bud, with a ruby in it. Aunt Bona contains love and safety, not merely because of tribal relationship, but on her own account. The watcher perceives this, and that the brew, more diluted than that brimming Mother, and with a dash of wormwood, is nevertheless much the same brew and contains no poison of danger, of withdrawal or denial.

Uncle Tini has a large beetle-shaped opal on his watchchain, a jinker with dahlia-red spokes, a jinker-rug of simulated ocelot lined by waterproofed black, and a horse called Dolly. I find this mystifying because Father calls Mother Dolly which is mystifying enough as her real name is Ida. With a mocking intention I am later to recognize as part of her character she calls him Curly. His hair is as unrelentingly straight as mine.

Just as Aunt Bona's fund of certainty is noted by the watcher to be a paler extension of Mother's, the paleness expressed in empty garrulity, so too Uncle Tini's offering of simplicity is seen to be an extension of Father's. Obscurely puzzled and dubious as I am, even then, I am never puzzled or dubious enough to be wary of this simplicity in Father, nor aroused enough from my inborn placidity, when wariness does much later come, to fight it face to face until it is too late, and lives have been mildewed by it. The danger in Father's simplicity is that, years later, step by hidden ruthless step, it has transmuted itself to stubbornness, thence to simon-pure indifference, the final and most killing of self-treacheries. His ultimate destruction of himself and others by unfortified simplicity is something not foreseeable, but instinct, and observation of Father, warn me in time to give attention to my own inherited simplicity and indifference lest they shrivel me too down to an inhuman actor. When I do, much later, guess at the danger Father has passed from his body through Mother's into mine, I watch myself closely. It is hardly necessary. I have been watching myself, by this time, for too long, since the days of the cast-iron balcony. I have watched myself watching the small suburban creature, the uninnocent good boy.

1963

KYLIE TENNANT
1912–1988

In her autobiography *The Missing Heir* (1986), Kylie Tennant recounts that she was sued for libel over the scene anthologised below from her 1943 novel *Ride on Stranger*. In her satire of the social life of the Communist Party of Australia, she included a character with a real false 'Party name'. 'I felt I could not invent a better name, and carelessly put it in.' Angus & Robertson withdrew the edition and paid the claimant £250. ' "But it was a *false* name," I kept insisting. "It wasn't his real name at all." '

The author of nine novels, plus short stories, plays, journalism, criticism and biography, as well as much writing for children, including plays and novels, Tennant was a versatile writer of both wit and compassion. She is noted for her social realist studies of urban and rural working-class life from the 1930s that began with *Tiburon* (1935) and included *Foveaux* (1939), named after a street in the slums of Sydney's Surry Hills, *The Battlers* (1941) and *Time Enough Later* (1943). The hard-bitten, bitter liveliness of her battlers was sourced in Tennant's research, which included taking to the road with itinerant workers in the worst years of the Depression. A Christian Socialist, she was criticised by more politicised writers while the conservative politician W.C. Wentworth accused her of being a communist after her receipt of a grant from the Commonwealth Literature Fund.

Tell Morning This (1967) was first published in abridged form as *The Joyful Condemned* (1953) and is similar to *Ride on Stranger* in its lively portrayal of young women's experiences in bohemian Sydney. Her later novels *The Honey Flow* (1956) and *Tantavallon* (1983) celebrate small-town life. *NM*

From *Ride on Stranger*
Chapter XIV

Joe, Olly's brother, was a fair sample of the members of the Proletarian Club. Jewish, a smart boy on the make, with long dark hair and brooding eyes like a spaniel, he did his desperate best to keep from his friends the knowledge that his mother had a small stall in the markets to make the money on which he went to the University and loafed away his time. Later, he became a gigolo in London and was kept by a series of wealthy women who pampered him much as his mother had done.

There was also in the Club Mary Hatton who wrote weird poetry about old maids nursing poodles and repressions, and wore a hibiscus over her ear; merry little Josephine McCrea who kept a pet duck and fed it with spoonfuls of wine; and the producer of the drama group, John Charteris, which was, of course, a fake name he had picked out for himself. His real name was Harrigan. He had a white, tense face with nerves that stood trembling under his eyes. He knew literature backwards and, at times, took drugs, drank, and went raving mad. Seamen would shamble up to him and hold mysterious conversations with him in some dark doorway. When he got drunk, he would get wild, and decide to denounce everybody and have a splendid time doing it.

Many of the members were the dregs of the paper *Torrent*, which had died out a short time before in the desert sands of bourgeois ignorance. The most competent journalist of them all was Clarry Stokes who was addicted to writing stories about a staid, suburban resident, who woke up in the night with a vague yearning and stole out on the front lawn to let the rain beat on his naked flesh. He was greatly prized as a find, and orders came through from those Higher Up which read: 'Now that this great soul has been brought into the Movement, let your treatment of him be tender and soft.'

With him, as the leading lights of the Proletarian Club, shone the poet, Chaverin Brome, also a fake name (these aliases became such a nuisance that the wall-paper of the Club sarcastically gave notice that 'Every one is forbidden to change his name more than once a day'). Chaverin Brome wrote poems about the black teeth of the factories grinding the workers into red meat. He wore a black velour hat and a small black moustache, and later married money and went to America with it where he interviewed Trotsky.

It was he who invented a new religion for a member who had to go into hospital and state his religion on a form. The religious sect was the Tarsinians who followed Paul of Tarsus and only worshipped one day a year, which was the twenty-ninth of June, when they had to genuflect twenty-nine times with their backs to the sun. Brome had one devoted satellite, a little shabby chap called Nobby, a kindly friendly soul, who would buttonhole you and talk by the hour. His conversation was like some sort of soup; bits and pieces of all sorts of things floated to the top, and were usually so broken up that it was hard to say how they had come into his repertoire or whence.

Chaverin Brome's cousin, Harry, a tall bad-tempered lad, the son of a rich family, had a muddy, unscrupulous face and a voice like someone speaking through tinfoil, thin, nasal, and hard on the ear. Harry, who was in charge of the artists' group, went around quoting James Joyce. He had a collection of camera snaps of a very surrealist type, and he chanted poetry aloud, not always his own, and usually beginning: 'You are a fawn, slant-eyed, remote.' There were also more cynical pieces describing a garbage heap under a hot sun. He had an unscrupulous habit of lifting wise-cracks, such as: 'These women, they use communism as a cosmetic.'

The majority of the members of the Proletarian Club were young men, but there was always a drifting crew of society girls who thought it would be fun to languish their looks on the intellectuals; and these last, regrettable to relate, were mercilessly exploited in the matter of small cash loans and donations to funds. There were other drifters who found the Proletarian Club a convenient address when they had no other. Of these was a mysterious member who would put his head in at the door and say: 'If any one asks for Norman Lindsay or Cashel Byron, tell them I'll be back later.'

The caretaker, Wodgers, who lived in a little dark hole under the stairs, in a smell of horses, rats and the onion brew he was always cooking, was also a member of the Club, except on those occasions when the Club had paid no rent for a long time, and then he padlocked the door against them. The members filed the padlock off and streamed in gaily as of yore. Wodgers had dirty, crinkled underpants hanging down below his upper garments. He chewed his false teeth. It was rather startling to hear this strange clicking noise from the very odorous darkness under the stairs. He had once been a gardener, had a manner at once cringing and domineering, and was always being hauled off to the lock-up for participating in unlicensed demonstrations and disturbances. If the police made a baton charge, he never failed to get his head in the way, and, with overweening vanity, wore dirty pieces of old bandage around it long after the bump had gone down.

The girls did not like him, because he was a sneaking talebearer against them and thought they ought to fall in love with him. One of the first rows in the Proletarian Club was over the long, abusive letters he wrote to Olly, who treated Wodgers kindly because she was sorry for him. He carried tales to the District Commissars about Shannon, asserting that she was a police spy, and he was given gracious permission to watch and report.

'Of course she may be a police spy,' Comrade Leggatt agreed, when he was reproached with electing a spy as secretary of the Club. 'There are men in this Movement who have been doing solid work for years and are still police spies. She's valuable as long as we can use her. What the Proletarian Club needs is not so many of these Bohemians, and a lot more solid middle-class. One thing about this Shannon Hicks, she is middle-class to the core.'

This was also the rancorous opinion of the wilder section of the Proletarian Club, who were unable to see why Shannon was secretary at all. The way she guarded the money that came in was most obnoxious. Instead of the old glad way in which every member had dipped for himself, the collection at the door for plays and lectures was strictly watched and listed. Dreary, trustworthy people like Mac were put in charge, and there were no more little suppers or private loans from the Club funds. There was a banking account, and those members who believed in the hatefulness of saving money were incensed. Comrade Leggatt, who, every one knew, had been sent to 'clean up' the Club, backed Shannon vigorously and instructed the President to expel the opposition.

Then there was the matter of morals. Privately, they called Comrade Hicks 'The Virgin', and took reckless bets on the chances of gentlemen members. Quite a number of otherwise feckless young men brisked up and worked assiduously, until they found that Shannon only smiled at them while they worked, and never when they tried to hold her hand. John Charteris brought off a brilliant coup when he insisted one night on seeing her home. Having been bidden good-bye at her door, he returned to the

Club and gave such a wealth of circumstantial evidence that he collected all bets and was drunk for a week. After that, the members only grinned at Shannon's preaching, until John Charteris was made to admit that he had once more embezzled funds to which he had no right. There was no chance, however, of members getting their bets back.

Money came into the Proletarian Club from the weekly dance, from lectures, from meetings, and, most surprisingly, from the poster artists. Under Mac and Bert, who were hard workers, the poster department was paying its way. They even landed a contract, of course not as the Proletarian Club, but simply as themselves, to supply a series of posters for the National Assets Party which was running candidates for the elections. These posters showed bolsheviks in whiskers and fur caps stretching gorilla paws over Australia. They urged all right-thinking Australians to save their country by voting for a red-faced, choleric, old gentleman who was fond of roaring out that he and his party would not be: 'Abused, spat upon, ground down, trampled upon, by those who abused our National Acids.'

With the money from the posters of horrific bolsheviks, the Proletarian Club blossomed out in a bright, new set of red banners for itself, which were carried gaily in many a procession, either by the Proletarian Club or borrowers from unions and leagues with like opinions.

The drama group was giving excellent shows, and actors of Shannon's acquaintance were only too pleased to work for nothing in plays that could never have been put over the air. John Charteris and Joe might be unreliable and emotional but, as producers, they knew what they were about. All Shannon had to do was find the money for lighting, costumes, props, printing programmes, and the hire of theatres, when the crowds they drew were too big for their own hall. She had started in the Proletarian Club with a bank balance of her own, but so many calls were made on it that this soon became a thing of the past. None of the loans were ever repaid, because there never was a time when the money was not needed, and for a time the drama group was financially on the edge of extinction.

Then, luckily, a couple of the Club's plays were banned, and this allowed them to hold protest meetings, collect funds for appeals, and give invitation performances to packed houses, so that there was enough in hand to carry them on when the ban was lifted and every one rushed to see the play. In a twelve-month the Proletarian Club had one of the best teams of amateurs in Sydney, had lost three of their best men to a film company, and won two gold cups of which the actors were publicly derisive and privately proud. The membership had grown to the point where it became necessary to move from the Club's tiny loft to more convenient quarters.

'I'll be sorry to leave the old place,' Shannon told Mervyn Leggatt. 'It's been such good fun here.'

Shannon had grown so devoted to the drama activities of the Club that for the magnificent sum of a pound a week she had become its full-time secretary. She had been taking parts in radio plays and in anything Bleeby Peverill wanted her for. She had even made extra money in a mannequin show Beryl staged, and by writing script for advertising firms with whom she had formed a connexion at 2RQ. She meant to continue in these money-bringing odd jobs, but more and more she found herself dropping out until she was existing solely on the pound a week from her labours at the Pro Club. All her energies were absorbed by it. She had struggled for it, sacrificed her own funds that it might flourish, guarded its reputation, wooed into it good actors, thrown out people like Chaverin Brome who were no use. The Proletarian Club was hers.

Yes, with the devoted Olly, Bert and Mac and Joe, she had built it up.

She was not very keen on the lectures, which were usually by some palmer returned from the Holy Land of Russia. But one, at least, had given her a sardonic enjoyment; when a returned lady novelist cried enthusiastically: 'And, oh comrades! Sexual intercourse in the Soviet Union is so delightful!'

Shannon's view of the Working Class Movement was more than half cynical, but she did not obtrude her view on the believers. There were quite a few of the members who were more interested in the poster work or the drama group than they were in the holy land, but night after night the hall was jammed by people who listened without stirring to the wonders of this other world.

They sat for hours in the foul air, solid with blue smoke; they put their hard-earned pennies in the china saucers passed down the close-packed rows of sweaty people. They sat with their faces upturned to the speaker on the little stage; hard, careworn faces; grim, dark faces; old faces; young faces; listening to the news of the Promised Land to which they too might enter in; and always Shannon's heart was stirred with pity. Even if it wasn't all so delightful, even if it was just another fake, why shouldn't they believe and hope? Surely it couldn't do any harm.

'I'm going to miss this place,' she repeated sentimentally to Mervyn Leggatt.

1943

PATRICK WHITE
1912–1990

Novelist and playwright Patrick White was born in London to Australian parents and educated in Australia and England. After his graduation from Cambridge in 1935, White lived in London, writing for the stage and working on his first novel, *Happy Valley* (1939). He left England in 1939 to travel in the US, where he wrote his second, *The Living and the Dead* (1941). He enlisted in the RAF in 1941 and was posted to the Middle East.

He returned to Australia with his life partner Manoly Lascaris in 1948; they settled in a house on the outskirts of Sydney where they bred dogs and goats.

White's third novel, *The Aunt's Story*, was published the same year; its elaborated, modernist interest in the structures of subjectivity or interior life establishes a keynote in his work. Through the later 1950s and early '60s, he wrote a set of ambitious novels that rework major settler preoccupations, such as dislocation, pioneering, exploration and identity, weighting everyday experience with ontological and philosophical questions. As he explains in his essay 'The Prodigal Son' (1958), his next novel, *The Tree of Man* (1955), was an attempt 'to discover the extraordinary behind the ordinary', according psychological gravitas to the society he critiqued and satirised as shallow, materialist and mundane. *Voss* (1957), an imaginative retelling of the story of explorer Ludwig Leichhardt and an investigation into the foundations of contemporary Australia, won the inaugural Miles Franklin Literary Award. These novels, with *Riders in the Chariot* (1961) and a collection of stories, *The Burnt Ones* (1964), established him as a writer with both an extraordinary voice and a dominating presence in Australian culture.

During this period several of his plays were produced; *The Ham Funeral* (*1961*/1965), *The Season at Sarsaparilla* (*1962*/1965), *A Cheery Soul* (*1963*/1965) and *Night on Bald Mountain* (*1964*/1965) undo the conventions of naturalism with wit, symbolism and adventurous staging. *The Solid Mandala* (1966), a dark novel exploring White's fascination with duality, was followed by *The Vivisector* (1970), White's 'portrait of the artist' novel. In 1973, shortly after the publication of *The Eye of the Storm*, White won the Nobel Prize for Literature; he was the first Australian to do so, and used some of the prize money to set up the Patrick White Award, for Australian writers who have 'not received adequate recognition'.

A Fringe of Leaves (1976) is a postcolonial novel rewriting captivity narratives; *The Twyborn Affair* (1979), White's last major novel, revisits themes of personal and national identity, presenting an explicit challenge to gender boundaries and fixed notions of sexuality. He remained productive throughout the 1980s, writing the autobiographical *Flaws in the Glass* (1981), a short, self-parodying *jeu d'esprit* entitled *Memoirs of Many in One* (1986), two collections of essays and speeches and a handful of late plays.

Much of White's work can be seen as a form of mythopoesis, a body of work that, taken as a whole, seems to be mapping the country and trying to make sense of contemporary Australian society and its short post-settlement history, often explored through his abiding interest in the figure of the outsider. White died in 1990, but not before he had read and approved the manuscript of a biography by David Marr (qv), *Patrick White: A life* (1991), that was itself to become a landmark in Australian literature. *KG/NM*

From *Voss*
Chapter 16

[. . .] Just then, rather late, for she had been detained at her school by a problem of administration, Miss Trevelyan, the headmistress, arrived. Her black dress, of a kind worn by some women merely as a covering, in no way detracted from the expression of her face, which at once caused the guests to differ sharply in opinion. As she advanced into the room, some of the ladies, glittering and rustling with precious stones, abandoned their gauzy conversations and greeted her with an exaggerated sweetness or girlishness. Then, resentful of all the solecisms of which they had ever been guilty, and it appeared their memories were full of them, they seized upon the looks of this woman after she had passed, asking one another for confirmation of their own disgust:

'Is she not plain? Is not poor Laura positively ugly? And such a freakish thing to do. As if it were not enough to have become a schoolmistress, to arrive late at Belle's party in that truly hideous dress!'

In the meantime Miss Trevelyan was receiving the greetings of those she recognized. Her face was rather white. Holding her head on one side, she murmured, with a slight, tremulous smile, that could have disguised a migraine, or strength:

'Una, Chattie, Lizzie. Quite recovered, Elinor, I hope.'

'Who is this person to whom all the ladies are curtseying?' asked Mr Ludlow, an English visitor, recommended to the Radclyffes by a friend.

'That is Miss Trevelyan. I must attempt to explain her,' volunteered the Englishman's neighbour.

The latter immediately turned away, for the object of their interest was passing them. It happened that the speaker was Dr Kilwinning. Even more richly caparisoned than in the past, the physician had continued to resent Miss Trevelyan as one of the few stumbling blocks he had had the misfortune to encounter in his eminently successful career.

'I will tell you more presently,' he said, or whispered loudly into the wall. 'Something to do with the German explorer, of whom they have just been speaking.'

'What a bore!' guffawed Mr Ludlow, to whom every aspect of the colonial existence was incredible. 'And the young girl?'

'The girl is the daughter,' whispered Dr Kilwinning, still to the wall.

'Capital,' laughed the Englishman, who had already visited the supper room. 'A green girl. A strapping, sonsy girl. But the mother!'

People who recognized Miss Trevelyan, on account of her connexions and the material glories of the past, did not feel obliged to accept Mercy. They received her with flat smiles, but ignored her with their eyes. Accustomed to this, she advanced with her chin gravely lowered, and an expression of some tolerance. Her glance was fixed on that point in her mother's vertebrae at which enemies might aim the blow.

Then Laura met Belle, and they were sisters. At once they erected an umbrella in the middle of the desert.

'Dearest Laura, I would have been here to receive you, but had gone up to Archie, who is starting a cold.'

'I could not allow you to *receive* me in our own house.'

'Do you really like the gas? I loved the lamps.'

'To sit reading beside the lamps!'

'After the tea had been brought in. You are tired, Laura.'

'I am rather tired,' the schoolmistress admitted.

It was the result of her experience of that afternoon, for Mr Sanderson had been so kind as to send Miss Trevelyan a card for the unveiling of the memorial.

'You should have come, too, Belle.'

'I could not,' Belle replied, and blushed.

Small lies are the most difficult to tell.

The cousins had arrived at a stiff and ugly chair. It was one of those pieces of furniture that become cast up out of an even life upon the unknown, and probably perilous shores of a party, there to stay, marooned for ever, it would seem.

'I shall sit here,' said Laura.

No one else would have dared, so evident was it that the stern chair belonged to its absent owners.

'Now you can see,' people were saying.

'Is she not a crow?'

'A scarecrow, rather!'

'Do not bring me anyone,' Laura Trevelyan enjoined. 'I would not care to be an inconvenience. And I have never succeeded in learning the language. I shall sit and watch them wearing their dresses.'

This woman, of the mysterious, the middle age, in her black clothes, was now commanding the room that she had practically repudiated. One young girl in a dream of white tarlatan, who was passing close enough to look, did so, right into the woman's eyes and, although never afterwards was she able to remember exactly what she saw, had been so affected at the time that she had altered her course immediately and gone out into the garden. There she was swept into a conspiracy of movement, between leaf and star, wind and shadow, even her own dress. Of all this, her body was the struggling core. She would have danced, but her heels were still rooted, her arms had but reached the point of twitching. In her frustration the young person attempted, but failed, to remember the message of the strange woman's eyes, so that it appeared as though she were intended to remain, at least a little longer, the victim of her own inadequacy.

Laura Trevelyan continued to sit in the company of Mercy, who did not care to leave her mother. Bronze or marble could not have taken more inevitable and lasting shapes than the stuff of their relationship. The affection she received from one being, together with her detachment from all others, had implanted in the daughter a respectful love for the forms of all simple objects, the secrets of which she was trying perpetually to understand. Eventually, she must attempt to express her great preoccupation, but in what manner, it was not yet clear. That its expression would be true was obvious, only from looking at her neat brown hair, her strong hands, and completely pleasing, square face.

In the meantime, seated upon a little stool at the feet of her mother, she was discussing with the latter the war between Roman Catholic and Protestant maids that was disturbing the otherwise tranquil tenor of life at their school.

'I did not tell you,' Mercy informed, 'Bridget has blackened Gertrude's eye, and told her it will match the colour of her soul.'

'To decide the colour of truth! If I but had Bridget's conviction!'

The two women were grateful for this humble version of the everlasting attempt. Laura was smiling at Mercy. It was as though they were seated in their own room, or at the side of a road, part of which they had made theirs.

Strangers came and went, of course. Young people, moved by curiosity. An Englishman, a little drunk, who wished to look closely at the school-mistress and her bastard daughter. A young man with a slight talent for exhibiting himself had sat down at the piano and was reeling off dreamy waltzes, whereupon Mrs de Courcy persuaded the Member of the Legislative Assembly to take a turn, and several youths were daring to drift with several breathless girls.

At one stage, the headmistress began to knead the bridge of her nose. She had, indeed, been made very tired by the episode in the Domain.

The platform had groaned with officials and their wives, to say nothing of other substantial citizens—old Mr Sanderson, who was largely responsible for the public enthusiasm that had subscribed to the fine memorial statue, Colonel Hebden, the schoolmistress who had been a friend of the lost explorer, and, of course, the man they had lately found. All of these had sat listening to the speeches, in the pleasant, thick shade.

Johann Ulrich Voss was by now quite safe, it appeared. He was hung with garlands of rarest newspaper prose. They would write about him in the history books. The wrinkles of his solid, bronze trousers could afford to ignore the passage of time. Even Miss Trevelyan confessed: it is agreeable to be safely dead. The way the seats had been fixed to the platform, tilted back ever so slightly, made everybody look more official; hands folded themselves upon the stomach, and chins sank in, as if intended, for repose. The schoolmistress was glad of some assistance towards the illusion of complacency. Thus, she had never thirsted, never, nor felt her flesh shrivel in crossing the deserts of conscience. No official personage has experienced the inferno of love.

So that she, too, had accepted the myth by the time the Premier, still shaky from the oratory prescribed for an historic occasion, pulled the cord, and revealed the bronze figure. Then the woman on the platform did lower her eyes. Whether she had seen or not, she would always remain uncertain, but applause informed her that here was a work of irreproachable civic art.

Soon after this everyone regained solid ground. Clothes were eased, civilities exchanged, and Miss Trevelyan, smiling and receptive, observed the approach of Colonel Hebden.

'You are satisfied, then?' he asked, as they were walking a little apart from the others.

'Oh, yes,' she sighed. 'I am satisfied.' She had to arrange the pair of little silken acorns that hung from the handle of her parasol. 'Though I do wish you had not asked it.'

'Our relationship is ruined by interrogation,' laughed the Colonel, rather pleased with his command of words.

Each recalled the afternoon in Mrs de Courcy's summer-house.

'Years ago I was impressed by your respect for truthfulness,' he could not resist saying, although he made of it a very tentative suggestion.

'If I am less truthful now, it is owing to my age and position,' she cried with surprising cynicism, almost baring her teeth at him.

'No.' She recovered herself. 'I am not dishonest, I hope, except that I am a human being.'

Had he made her tremble?

To disguise the possibility, she had begun speaking quickly, in an even, kind voice, referring not so much to the immediate case as to the universal one:

'Let none of us pass final judgement.'

'Unless the fellow who has returned from the grave is qualified to judge. Have you not spoken to him?'

As her appearance suggested that she might not have heard, the Colonel added:

'He appears to share the opinion you offered me at our first meeting: that Voss was, indeed, the Devil.'

Now, Miss Trevelyan had not met the survivor, although old Sanderson, all vague benevolence since time had cast a kinder light upon the whole unhappy affair, had gone so far as to promise him to her. Seated, on the platform, listening to the official speeches, she had even been aware of the nape of a neck, somewhere in the foreground, but, deliberately, she had omitted to claim her right.

'I do not wish to meet the man,' she said, and was settling her shawl against a cold wind that was springing up.

'But you must!' cried Hebden, taking her firmly by the elbow.

Of dreadful metal, he towered above her, with his rather matted, grizzled hair, and burning desire for truth. Her mouth was dry. Was he, then, the avenging angel? So it appeared, as they struggled together.

If anybody had noticed, they would have made an ugly group, and he, of course, the stronger.

'Leave me,' she strained, out of her white mouth, 'I beg of you, Colonel Hebden!'

At that moment, however, old Sanderson, whom no one of any compassion would willingly have hurt, emerged from the group still gathered round the statue, bringing with him a man.

'Miss Trevelyan,' said the grazier, smiling with genuine pleasure, 'I do believe that, after all, I have failed to bring the two of you together, and you the most important.'

So it was come to pass.

Mr Sanderson smiled, and continued:

'I would like you to meet my friend Judd.'

The leaves of the trees were clapping.

She was faced with an elderly, or old-looking man, of once powerful frame, in the clothes they had provided for him, good clothes, fashionable even, to which he had not accustomed himself. His large hands, in the absence of their former strength, moved in almost perpetual search for some reassuring object or position, just as the expressions were shifting on his face, like water over sand, and his mouth would close with a smile, attempt briefly to hold it, and fail.

'So this is Judd, the convict,' said Miss Trevelyan, less harshly than stating a fact, since she must stand on trial with him.

Judd nodded.

'I earned my ticket-of-leave two years, no, it would be four years before the expedition left.'

All the old wounds had healed. He could talk about them now. He could talk about anything.

His lips parted, Colonel Hebden watched quite greedily. Old Sanderson was bathed in a golden glow of age. Such warmth he had not experienced since the lifetime of his dear wife.

'Yes, yes,' he contributed. 'Judd was a neighbour of mine in the Forties. He joined the expedition when it passed through. In fact, I was responsible for that.'

Miss Trevelyan, whose attention had been engaged by the ferrule of her parasol, realized that she was expected to speak. Judd waited, with his hands hanging and moving. Since his return, he had become accustomed to interrogation by ladies.

'And were you able to resume your property?' Miss Trevelyan asked, through her constricted throat.

There was something that she would avoid. She would avoid it to the end. So she looked gravely at the ferrule of the parasol, and continued to interrogate a man who had suffered.

'Resume?' asked Judd, managing his tongue, which was round like that of a parrot. 'No. It was gone. I was considered dead, you know.'

'And your family?' the kind woman asked.

'All dead. My wife, she went first. It was the heart, I think they told me. My eldest boy died of a snakebite. The youngest got some sickness, I forget what.' He shook his head, which was bald and humble above the fringe of white hair. 'Anyways, he is passed on.'

The survivor's companions expressed appropriate sympathy.

But Judd had lived beyond grief. He was impressed, rather, by the great simplicity with which everything had happened.

Then Colonel Hebden took a hand. He could still have been holding the lady by an elbow. He said:

'You know, Judd, Miss Trevelyan was a friend of Mr Voss.'

'Ah,' smiled the aged, gummy man. 'Voss.'

He looked at the ground, but presently spoke again.

'Voss left his mark on the country,' he said.

'How?' asked Miss Trevelyan, cautiously.

'Well, the trees, of course. He was cutting his initials in the trees. He was a queer beggar, Voss. The blacks talk about him to this day. He is still there—that is the honest opinion of many of them—he is there in the country, and always will be.'

'How?' repeated Miss Trevelyan. Her voice was that of a man. She dared anyone.

Judd was feeling his way with his hands.

'Well, you see, if you live and suffer long enough in a place, you do not leave it altogether. Your spirit is still there.'

'Like a god, in fact,' said Colonel Hebden, but laughed to show his scepticism.

Judd looked up, out of the distance.

'Voss? No. He was never God, though he liked to think that he was. Sometimes, when he forgot, he was a man.'

He hesitated, and fumbled.

'He was more than a man,' Judd continued, with the gratified air of one who had found that for which he had been looking. 'He was a Christian, such as I understand it.'

Miss Trevelyan was holding a handkerchief to her lips, as though her life-blood might gush out.

'Not according to my interpretation of the word,' the Colonel interrupted, remorselessly, 'not by what I have heard.'

'Poor fellow,' sighed old Sanderson, again unhappy. 'He was somewhat twisted. But is dead and gone.'

Now that he was launched, Judd was determined to pursue his wavering way.

'He would wash the sores of the men. He would sit all night with them when they were sick, and clean up their filth with his own hands. I cried,

I tell you, after he was dead. There was none of us could believe it when we saw the spear, hanging from his side, and shaking.'

'The spear?'

Colonel Hebden behaved almost as though he himself were mortally wounded.

'But this is an addition to the story,' protested old Mr Sanderson, who also was greatly perturbed. 'You did not mention the spear, Judd. You never suggested you were present at the death of Voss, simply that you mutinied, and moved off with those who chose to follow you. If we understood you rightly.'

'It was me who closed his eyes,' said Judd.

In the same instant that the Colonel and Mr Sanderson looked across at each other, Miss Trevelyan succeeded in drawing a shroud about herself.

Finally, the old grazier put an arm round the convict's shoulders, and said:

'I think you are tired and confused, eh, Judd? Let me take you back to your lodgings.'

'I am tired,' echoed Judd.

Mr Sanderson was glad to get him away, and into a hired brougham that was waiting.

Colonel Hebden became aware that the woman was still standing at his side, and that he must recognize the fact. So he turned to her awkwardly at last, and said:

'Your saint is canonized.'

'I am content.'

'On the evidence of a poor madman?'

'I am content.'

'Do not tell me any longer that you respect the truth.'

She was digging at the tough roots of grass with the ferrule of her parasol.

'All truths are particoloured. Except the greatest truth of all.'

'Your Voss was particoloured. I grant you that. A perfect magpie!'

Looking at the monstrous ants at the roots of the grass, Miss Trevelyan replied:

'Whether Judd is an impostor, or a madman, or simply a poor creature who has suffered too much, I am convinced that Voss had in him a little of Christ, like other men. If he was composed of evil along with the good, he struggled with that evil. And failed.'

Then she was going away, heavily, a middle-aged woman, over the grass.

Now, as they sat in the crowded room, full of the deceptive drifts of music and brutal explosions of conversation, Mercy Trevelyan alone realized the extent to which her mother had been tried by some experience of the afternoon. If the daughter did not inquire into the origin of the mother's distress, it was because she had learnt that rational answers seldom do explain. She was herself, moreover, of unexplained origin.

In the circumstances, she leaned towards her mother from where she sat upon her stool, the whole of her strong young throat swelling with the love she wished to convey, and whispered:

'Shall we not go into another room? Or let us, even, go away. It is simple. No one will miss us.'

Then Laura Trevelyan released the bridge of her nose, which her fingers had pinched quite white.

'No,' she said, and smiled. 'I will not go. I am here. I will stay.'

Thus she made her covenant.

Other individuals, of great longing but little daring, suspecting that the knowledge and strength of the headmistress might be accessible to them, began to approach by degrees. Even her beauty was translated for them into terms they could understand. As the night poured in through the windows and the open doors, her eyes were overflowing with a love that might have appeared supernatural, if it had not been for the evidence of her earthly body: the slightly chapped skin of her neck, and the small hole in the finger of one glove, which, in her distraction and haste, she had forgotten to mend.

Amongst the first to join Miss Trevelyan was the invertebrate Willie Pringle, who, it transpired, had become a genius. Then there was Topp, the music-master. Out of his hatred for the sour colonial soil upon which he had been deposited many years before had developed a perverse love, that he had never yet succeeded in expressing and which, for that reason, nobody had suspected. He was a grumpy little man, a failure, who would continue to pulse, none the less, though the body politic ignore his purpose. To these two were added several diffident persons who had burst from the labyrinth of youth on that night, and were tremblingly eager to learn how best to employ their freedom.

The young person in the gown of white tarlatan, for instance, came close to the group and spread her skirts upon the edge of a chair. She balanced her chin upon her hand and blushed. Although nobody knew her, nobody asked her name, since it was her intention that mattered.

Conversation was the wooden raft by which their party hoped eventually to reach the promised shore.

'I am uncomfortably aware of the very little I have seen and experienced of things in general, and of our country in particular,' Miss Trevelyan had just confessed, 'but the little I have seen is less, I like to feel, than what I know. Knowledge was never a matter of geography. Quite the reverse, it overflows all maps that exist. Perhaps true knowledge only comes of death by torture in the country of the mind.'

She laughed somewhat painfully.

'*You* will understand that. Some of you, at least, are the discoverers,' she said, and looked at them.

That some of them did understand was the more marvellous for their realization of it.

'Some of you,' she continued, 'will express what we others have experienced by living. Some will learn to interpret the ideas embodied in the less communicative forms of matter, such as rock, wood, metal, and water. I must include water, because, of all matter it is the most musical.'

Yes, yes. Topp, the bristling, unpleasant little thing, was sitting forward. In the headmistress's wooden words, he could hear the stubborn music that was waiting for release. Of rock and scrub. Of winds curled invisibly in wombs of air. Of thin rivers struggling towards seas of eternity. All flowing and uniting. Over a bed of upturned faces.

The little Topp was distracted by the possibility of many such harmonies. He began to fidget and snatch at his trouser leg. He said:

'If we do not come to grief on our mediocrity as a people. If we are not locked for ever in our own bodies. Then, too, there is the possibility that our hates and our carnivorous habits will unite in a logical conclusion: we may destroy one another.'

Topp himself was sweating. His face was broken up into little pinpoints of grey light under the globes of blue gas.

It fascinated Willie Pringle.

'The grey of mediocrity, the blue of frustration,' he suggested, less to inform an audience than to commit it to his memory. He added at once, louder and brisker than before: 'Topp has dared to raise a subject that has often occupied my mind: our inherent mediocrity as a people. I am confident that the mediocrity of which he speaks is not a final and irrevocable state; rather is it a creative source of endless variety and subtlety. The blowfly on its bed of offal is but a variation of the rainbow. Common forms are continually breaking into brilliant shapes. If we will explore them.'

So they talked, while through the doorway, in the garden, the fine seed of moonlight continued to fall and the moist soil to suck it up.

Attracted by needs of their own, several other gentlemen had joined the gathering at the farther end of the large room. Old Sanderson, arrived at the very finish of his simple life, was still in search of tangible goodness. Colonel Hebden, who had not dared approach the headmistress since the episode at the unveiling, did now stalk up, still hungry for the truth, and assert:

'I will not rest, you know.'

'I would not expect it,' said Miss Trevelyan, giving him her hand, since they were agreed that the diamonds with which they cut were equal both in aim and worth.

'How your cousin is holding court,' remarked Mrs de Courcy, consoling herself with a strawberry ice.

'Court? A class, rather!' said and laughed Belle Radclyffe. Knowing that she was not, and never would be of her cousin's class, she claimed the rights of love to resent a little.

At one stage, under pressure, Mrs Radclyffe forgot her promise and brought the headmistress Mr Ludlow. Though fairly drunk with brandy punch, the latter had remained an Englishman and, it was whispered by several ladies in imported poult-de-soie, the younger brother of a baronet.

Mr Ludlow said:

'I must apologize for imposing on you, madam, but having heard so much in your favour, I expressed a wish to make your acquaintance and form an opinion of my own.'

The visitor laughed for his own wit, but Miss Trevelyan looked sad.

'I have been travelling through your country, forming opinions of all and sundry,' confessed Mr Ludlow to his audience, 'and am distressed to find the sundry does prevail.'

'We, the sundry, are only too aware of it,' Miss Trevelyan answered, 'but will humbly attempt to rise in your opinion if you will stay long enough.'

'How long? I cannot stay long,' protested Mr Ludlow.

'For those who anticipate perfection—and I would not suspect you of wishing for less—eternity is not too long.'

'Ohhhh dear!' tittered Mr Ludlow. 'I would be choked by pumpkin. Do you know that in one humpy I was even faced with a stewed crow!'

'Did you not also sample baked Irish?'

'The Irish, too ? Ohhh dear!'

'So, you see, we are in every way provided for, by God and nature, and consequently, must survive.'

'Oh, yes, a country with a future. But when does the future become present? That is what always puzzles me.'

'Now.'

'How—*now*?' asked Mr Ludlow.

'Every moment that we live and breathe, and love, and suffer, and die.'

'That reminds me, I had intended asking you about this—what shall we call him?—this familiar spirit, whose name is upon everybody's lips, the German fellow who died.'

'Voss did not die,' Miss Trevelyan replied. 'He is there still, it is said, in the country, and always will be. His legend will be written down, eventually, by those who have been troubled by it.'

'Come, come. If we are not certain of the facts, how is it possible to give the answers?'

'The air will tell us,' Miss Trevelyan said.

By which time she had grown hoarse, and fell to wondering aloud whether she had brought her lozenges.

1957

The Prodigal Son

This is by way of being an answer to Alister Kershaw's recent article 'The Last Expatriate', but as I cannot hope to equal the slash and dash of Kershaw's journalistic weapons, I shall not attempt to answer him point by point. In any case, the reasons why anybody is an expatriate, or why another chooses to return home, are such personal ones that the question can only be answered in a personal way.

At the age of 46 I have spent just on twenty of those years overseas. During the last ten, I have hardly stirred from the six acres of 'Dogwoods', Castle Hill. It sounds odd, and is perhaps worth trying to explain.

Brought up to believe in the maxim: Only the British can be right, I did accept this during the earlier part of my life. Ironed out in an English public school, and finished off at King's, Cambridge, it was not until 1939, after wandering by myself through most of Western Europe, and finally most of the United States, that I began to grow up and think my own thoughts. The War did the rest. What had seemed a brilliant, intellectual, highly desirable existence, became distressingly parasitic and pointless. There is nothing like a rain of bombs to start one trying to assess one's own achievement. Sitting at night in his London bed-sitting room during the first months of the Blitz, this chromium-plated Australian with two fairly successful novels to his credit came to the conclusion that his achievement was practically nil. Perhaps significantly, he was reading at that time Eyre's *Journal*.[1] Perhaps also he had the wind up; certainly he reached rather often for the bottle of Calvados in the wardrobe. Any way, he experienced those first sensations of rootlessness which Alister Kershaw has deplored and explained as the 'desire to nuzzle once more at the benevolent teats of the mother country'.

All through the War in the Middle East there persisted a longing to return to the scenes of childhood, which is, after all, the purest well from which the creative artist draws. Aggravated further by the terrible nostalgia of the desert landscape, this desire was almost quenched by the year I spent stationed in Greece, where perfection presents itself on every hand, not only the perfection of antiquity, but that of nature, and the warmth of

---

1   Edward John Eyre (1815–1901), *Journals of Expedition of Discovery: Into Central Australia and overland from Adelaide to King George's Sound, in the years 1840–1* (1845).

human relationships expressed in daily living. Why didn't I stay in Greece? I was tempted to. Perhaps it was the realisation that even the most genuine resident Hellenophile accepts automatically the vaguely comic role of Levantine beachcomber. He does not belong, the natives seem to say, not without affection; it is sad for him, but he is nothing. While the Hellenophile continues humbly to hope.

So I did not stay in my elective Greece. Demobilisation in England left me with the alternative of remaining in what I then felt to be an actual and spiritual graveyard, with the prospect of ceasing to be an artist and turning instead into that most sterile of beings, a London intellectual, or of returning home, to the stimulus of time remembered. Quite honestly, the thought of a full belly influenced me as well, after toying with the soft, sweet awfulness of horsemeat stew in the London restaurants that I could afford. So I came home. I bought a farm at Castle Hill, and with a Greek friend and partner, Manoly Lascaris, started to grow flowers and vegetables, and to breed Schnauzers and Saanen goats.

The first years I was content with these activities, and to soak myself in landscape. If anybody mentioned Writing, I would reply: 'Oh, one day, perhaps.' But I had no real intention of giving the matter sufficient thought. *The Aunt's Story*, written immediately after the War, before returning to Australia, had succeeded with overseas critics, failed as usual with the local ones, remained half-read, it was obvious from the state of the pages, in the lending libraries. Nothing seemed important, beyond living and eating, with a roof of one's own over one's head.

Then, suddenly, I began to grow discontented. Perhaps, in spite of Australian critics, writing novels was the only thing I could do with any degree of success; even my half-failures were some justification of an otherwise meaningless life. Returning sentimentally to a country I had left in my youth, what had I really found? Was there anything to prevent me packing my bag and leaving like Alister Kershaw and so many other artists? Bitterly I had to admit, no. In all directions stretched the Great Australian Emptiness, in which the mind is the least of possessions, in which the rich man is the important man, in which the schoolmaster and the journalist rule what intellectual roost there is, in which beautiful youths and girls stare at life through blind blue eyes, in which human teeth fall like autumn leaves, the buttocks of cars grow hourly glassier, food means cake and steak, muscles prevail, and the march of material ugliness does not raise a quiver from the average nerves.

It was the exaltation of the 'average' that made me panic most, and in this frame of mind, in spite of myself, I began to conceive another novel. Because the void I had to fill was so immense, I wanted to try to suggest in this book every possible aspect of life, through the lives of an ordinary man and woman. But at the same time I wanted to discover the extraordinary behind the ordinary, the mystery and the poetry which alone could make bearable the lives of such people, and incidentally, my own life since my return.

So I began to write *The Tree of Man*. How it was received by the more important Australian critics is now ancient history. Afterwards I wrote *Voss*, possibly conceived during the early days of the Blitz, when I sat reading Eyre's *Journal* in a London bed-sitting room. Nourished by months spent traipsing backwards and forwards across the Egyptian and Cyrenaican deserts, influenced by the arch-megalomaniac of the day, the idea finally matured after reading contemporary accounts of Leichhardt's expeditions and A.H. Chisholm's *Strange New World* on returning to Australia.

It would be irrelevant to discuss here the literary aspects of the novel. More important are those intentions of the author which have pleased some readers without their knowing exactly why, and helped to increase the rage of those who have found the book meaningless. Always something of a frustrated painter, and a composer *manqué*, I wanted to give my book the textures of music, the sensuousness of paint, to convey through the theme and characters of *Voss* what Delacroix and Blake might have seen, what Mahler and Liszt might have heard. Above all I was determined to prove that the Australian novel is not necessarily the dreary, dun-coloured offspring of journalistic realism. On the whole, the world has been convinced, only here, at the present moment, the dingoes are howling unmercifully.

What, then, have been the rewards of this returned expatriate? I remember when, in the flush of success after my first novel, an old and wise Australian journalist called Guy Innes came to interview me in my London flat. He asked me whether I wanted to go back. I had just 'arrived'; who was I to want to go back? 'Ah, but when you do,' he persisted, 'the colours will come flooding back onto your palette.' This gentle criticism of my first novel only occurred to me as such in recent years. But I think perhaps Guy Innes has been right.

So, amongst the rewards, there is the refreshed landscape, which even in its shabbier, remembered versions has always made a background to my life. The worlds of plants and music may never have revealed themselves had I sat talking brilliantly to Alister Kershaw over a Pernod on the Left Bank. Possibly all art flowers more readily in silence. Certainly the state of simplicity and humility is the only desirable one for artist or for man. While to reach it may be impossible, to attempt to do so is imperative. Stripped of almost everything that I had considered desirable and necessary, I began to try. Writing, which had meant the practice of an art by a polished mind in civilised surroundings, became a struggle to create completely fresh forms out of the rocks and sticks of words. I began to see things for the first time. Even the boredom and frustration presented avenues for endless exploration; even the ugliness, the bags and iron of Australian life, acquired a meaning. As for the cat's cradle of human intercourse, this was necessarily simplified, often bungled, sometimes touching. Its very tentativeness can be a reward. There is always the possibility that the book lent, the record played, may lead to communication between human beings. There is the possibility that one may be helping to people a barely inhabited country with a race possessed of understanding.

These, then, are some of the reasons why an expatriate has stayed, in the face of those disappointments which follow inevitably upon his return. Abstract and unconvincing, the Alister Kershaws will probably answer, but such reasons, as I have already suggested, are a personal matter. More concrete, and most rewarding of all, are the many letters I have received from unknown Australians, for whom my writing seems to have opened a window. To me, the letters alone are reason enough for staying.

1958

Miss Slattery and Her Demon Lover

He stood holding the door just so far. A chain on it too.

'This,' she said, 'is Better Sales Pty Ltd.' Turning to a fresh page. 'Market research,' she explained. 'We want you to help us, and hope, indirectly, to help you.'

She moistened her mouth, easing a threat into an ethical compromise, technique pushed to the point where almost everyone was convinced. Only for herself the page on her pad would glare drearily blank.

Oh dear, do not be difficult, she would have said for choice to some old continental number whose afternoon sleep she had ruined.

'Faht do you vornt?' he asked.

'I want to ask you some questions,' she said.

She could be very patient when paid.

'Kvestions?'

Was he going to close the door?

'Not you. Necessarily. The housewife.'

She looked down the street, a good one, at the end of which the midday sun was waiting to deal her a blow.

'Housevife?'

At least he was slipping the chain.

'Nho! Nho! Nho!'

At least he was not going to grudge her a look.

'No lady?' she asked. 'Of any kind?'

'Nho! Nefer! Nho! I vould not keep any vooman of a permanent description.'

'That is frank,' she answered. 'You don't like them.'

Her stilettoes were hurting.

'Oh, I *lihke*! How I lihke! Zet is *vhy*!'

'Let us get down to business?' she said, looking at her blank pad. 'Since there is no lady, do you favour Priceless Pearl? Laundry starch. No. Kwik Kreem Breakfast Treat? Well,' she said, 'it's a kind of porridge that doesn't get lumps.'

'Faht is porritch?'

'It is something the Scotch invented. It is, well, just *porridge*, Mr Tibor.'

'Szabo.'

'It is Tibor on the bell.'

'I am Hoongahrian,' he said. 'In Hoongary ze nimes are beck to front. Szabo Tibor. You onderstend?'

He could not enlist too much of himself, as if it were necessary to explain all such matters with passionate physical emphasis.

'Yes,' she said. 'I see. Now.'

He had those short, but white teeth. He was not all that old; rather, he had reached a phase where age becomes elastic. His shoes could have cost him a whole week's pay. Altogether, all over, he was rather suède, brown suède, not above her shoulder. And hips. He had hips!

But the hall looked lovely, behind him, in black and white.

'Vinyl tiles?' Her toe pointed. 'Or lino?'

After all, she was in business.

'Faht? Hoh! Nho! Zet is all from marble.'

'Like in a bank!'

'Yehs.'

'Well, now! Where did you find all that?'

'I brought it. Oh, yehs. I bring everysing. Here zere is nossing. Nossing!'

'Oh, come, Mr Tibor—Szabo—we Australians are not all that uncivilized. Not in 1961.'

'Civilahsed! I vill learn you faht is civilahsed!'

She had never believed intensely in the advantages of knowledge, so that it was too ridiculous to find herself walking through the marble halls of Tibor Szabo Tibor. But so cool. Hearing the door click, she remembered the women they saw into pieces, and leave in railway cloak-rooms, or dispose of in back yards, or simply dump in the Harbour.

There it was, too. For Szabo Tibor had bought a View. Though at that hour of day the water might have been cut out of zinc, or aluminium, which is sharper.

'You have got it good here,' she said.

It was the kind of situation she had thought about, but never quite found herself in, and the strangeness of it made her languid, acting out a part she had seen others play, over life-size.

'Everysing I hef *mosst* be feuhrst class,' Szabo Tibor was explaining. 'Faht is your nime, please?'

'Oh,' she said 'Slattery. Miss Slattery.'

'Zet is too match. Faht little nime else, please?'

Miss Slattery looked sad.

'I hate to tell you,' she said. 'I was christened Dimity. But my friends,' she added, 'call me Pete.'

'Vitch is veuorse? Faht for a nime is zet? Pete!'

'It is better than going through life with Dimity attached.'

'I vill call you nossing,' Szabo Tibor announced.

Miss Slattery was walking around in someone else's room, with large, unlikely strides, but it made her feel better. The rugs were so easy, and so very white, she realized she hadn't taken her two-piece to the cleaner.

'A nime is not necessary,' Szabo Tibor was saying. 'Tike off your het, please; it is not necessary neither.'

Miss Slattery did as she was told.

'I am not the hatty type, you know. They have us wear them for business reasons.'

She shook out her hair, to which the bottle had contributed, not altogether successfully, though certain lights gave it a look of its own, she hoped: tawnier, luminous, dappled. There was the separate lock, too, which she had persuaded to hang in the way she wanted.

An Australian girl, he saw. Another Australian girl.

Oh dear, he was older perhaps than she had thought. But cuddly. By instinct she was kind. Only wanted to giggle. At some old teddy bear in suède.

Szabo Tibor said:

'Sit.'

'Funny,' she said, running her hands into the depths of the chair, a habit she always meant to get out of, 'I have never mixed business and pleasure before.'

But Szabo Tibor had brought something very small and sweet, which ran two fiery wires out of her throat and down her nose.

'It is goot. Nho?'

'I don't know about *that*'—she coughed—'Mr Szabo. It's effective, though!'

'In Australien,' Mr Szabo said, and he was kneeling now, 'peoples call me Tibby.'

'Well! Have you a sense of humour!'

'Yehs! Yehs!' he said, and smiled. '*Witz!*'

When men started kneeling she wanted more than ever to giggle.

But Tibby Szabo was growing sterner.

'In Australien,' he said, 'no *Witz*. Nho! Novair!'

Shaking a forefinger at her. So that she became fascinated. It was so plump, for a finger, banana-coloured, with hackles of little black hairs.

'Do you onderstend?'

'Oh, yes, I understand all right. I am nossing.'

She liked it, too.

'Then faht is it?' asked Tibby Szabo, looking at his finger.

'I am always surprised,' she answered, 'at the part texture plays.'

'Are you intellectual girl?'

'My mind,' she said, re-crossing her legs, 'turned to fudge at puberty. Isn't that delicious?'

'Faht is futch?'

'Oh dear,' she said, 'you're a whale for knowing. Aren't there the things you just accept?'

She made her lock hang, for this old number who wouldn't leave off kneeling by the chair. Not so very old, though. The little gaps between his white teeth left him looking sort of defenceless.

Then Tibby Szabo took her arm, as though it didn't belong to her. The whole thing was pretty peculiar, but not as peculiar as it should have been. He took her arm, as if it were, say, a cob of corn. As if he had been chewing on a cob of corn. She wanted to giggle, and did. Supposing Mum and Wendy had seen! They would have had a real good laugh.

'You have the funniest ways,' she said, 'Tib.'

As Tibby Szabo kept on going up and down her arm. When he started on the shoulder, she said:

'Stoput! What do you think I *am*?'

He heard enough to alter course.

A man's head in your lap somehow always made you feel it was trying to fool itself—it looked so detached, improbable, and ridiculous.

He turned his eyes on then, as if knowing: here is the greatest sucker for eyes. Oh God, nothing ever went deeper than eyes. She was a goner.

'Oh God!' she said, 'I am not like this!'

She was nothing like what she thought she was like. So she learned. She was the trampoline queen. She was an enormous, staggery spider. She was a rubber doll.

'You Australhlian girls are visout *Temperament*,' Tibby Szabo complained. 'You are all gickle and talk. Passion is not to resist.'

'I just about broke every bone in my body not resisting,' Miss Slattery had to protest.

Her body that continued fluctuating overhead.

'Who ever heard of a glass ceiling!'

'Plenty glass ceiling. Zet is to see vis.'

'Tibby,' she asked, 'this wouldn't be—mink?'

'Yehs. Yehs. Meenk beds are goot for ze body.'

'I'll say!' she said.

She was so relaxed. She was half-dead. When it was possible to lift an arm, the long silken shudders took possession of her skin, and she realized the southerly had come, off the water, in at the window, giving her the goose-flesh.

'We're gunna catch a cold,' she warned, and coughed.

'It is goot.'

'I am glad to know that something is good,' she said, sitting up, destroying the composition in the ceiling. 'This sort of thing is all very well, but are you going to let me love you?'

Rounding on him. This fat and hairy man.

'Lof? Faht execkly do you mean?'

'Oh, Tibby!' she said.

Again he was fixing his eyes on her, extinct by now, but even in their dormancy they made her want to die. Or give. Or was it possible to give and live?

'Go to sleep,' he ordered.

'Oh, Tibby!'

She fell back floppy whimpery but dozed. Once she looked sideways at his death-mask. She looked at the ceiling, too. It was not unlike those atrocity pictures she had always tried to avoid, in the papers, after the War.

It was incredible, but always had been.

By the time Miss Slattery stepped into the street, carrying her business hat, evening had drenched the good address with the mellower light of ripened pears. She trod through it, tilted, stilted, tentative. Her neck was horribly stiff.

After that there was the Providential, for she did not remain with Better Sales Pty Ltd; she was informed that her services would no longer be required. What was it, they asked, had made her so unreliable? She said she had become distracted.

In the circumstances she was fortunate to find the position with the Providential. There, too, she made friends with Phyllis Wimble.

'A Hungarian,' Phyllis said, 'I never met a Hungarian. Sometimes I think I will work through the nationalities like a girl I knew decided to go through the religions. But gave up at the Occultists.'

'Why?'

'She simply got scared. They buried a man alive, one Saturday afternoon, over at Balmoral.'

When old Huthnance came out of his office.

'Miss Slattery,' he asked, 'where is that Dewhurst policy?'

He was rather a sweetie really.

'Oh yes,' Miss Slattery said. 'I was checking.'

'What is there to check?' Huthnance asked.

'Well,' Miss Slattery said.

And Huthnance smiled. He was still at the smiling stage.

Thursday evenings Miss Slattery kept for Tibby Szabo. She would go there Saturdays too, usually staying over till Sunday, when they would breakfast in the continental style.

There was the Saturday Miss Slattery decided to give Tibby Szabo a treat. Domesticity jacked her up on her heels; she was full of secrecy and little ways.

When Tibby asked:

'Faht is zet?'

'What is what?'

'Zet stench! Zet blue *smoke* you are mecking in my kitchenette. Faht are you prepurring?'

'That is a baked dinner,' Miss Slattery answered. 'A leg of lamb, with pumpkin and two other veg.'

'Lemb?' cried Tibby Szabo. 'Lemb! It stinks. Nefer in Budapest did lemb so much as cross ze doorways.'

And he opened the oven, and tossed the leg into the Harbour.

Miss Slattery cried then, or sat, rather, making her handkerchief into a ball.

Tibby Szabo prepared himself a snack. He had *Paprikawurst*, a breast of cold paprika chicken, paprikas in oil, paprika in cream cheese, and finally, she suspected, paprika.

'Eat!' he advised.

'A tiny crumb would choke me.'

'You are not crying?' he asked through some remains of paprika.

'I was thinking,' she replied.

'So! *Sink*-ing!'

Afterwards he made love to her, and because she had chosen love, she embraced it with a sad abandon, on the mink coverlet, under the glass sky.

Once, certainly, she sat up and said:

'It is all so *carnal*!'

'You use zeese intellectual veuords.'

He had the paprika chicken in his teeth.

There was the telephone, too, with which Miss Slattery had to contend.

'Igen! *Igen!* IGEN!' Tibby Szabo would shout, and bash the receiver on somebody anonymous.

'All this *iggy* stuff!' she said.

It began to get on her nerves.

'Demn idiots!' Tibby Szabo complained.

'How do you make your money, Tib?' Miss Slattery asked, picking at the mink coverlet.

'I am Hoongahrian,' he said. 'It come to me over ze telephown.'

Presently Szabo Tibor announced he was on his way to inspect several properties he owned around the city.

He had given her a key, at least, so that she might come and go.

'And you have had keys cut,' she asked, 'for all these other women, for Monday, Tuesday, Wednesday, and Friday, in all these other flats?'

How he laughed.

'At least a real *Witz*! An Australian *Witz*!' he said on going.

It seemed no time before he returned.

'Faht,' he said, 'you are still here?'

'I am the passive type,' she replied.

Indeed, she was so passive she had practically set in her own flesh beneath that glass conscience of a ceiling. Although a mild evening was ready to soothe, she shivered for her more than nakedness. When she stuck her head out the window, there were the rhinestones of Sydney glittering on the neck of darkness. But it was a splendour she saw could only dissolve.

'You Austrahlian girls,' observed Tibby Szabo, 'Ven you are not all gickle, you are all cry.'

'Yes,' she said. 'I know,' she said, 'it makes things difficult. To be Australian.'

And when he popped inside her mouth a kiss like Turkish delight in action, she was less than ever able to take herself in hand.

They drove around in Tibby's Jag. Because naturally Tibby Szabo had a Jag.

'Let us go to Manly,' she said. 'I have got to look at the Pacific Ocean.'

Tibby drove, sometimes in short, disgusted bursts, at others in long, lovely demonstrations of speed, or swooning swirls. His driving was so much the expression of Tibby Szabo himself. He was wearing the little cigar-coloured hat.

'Of course,' said Miss Slattery through her hair, 'I know you well enough to know that Manly is not Balaton.'

'Balaton?'

Tibby jumped a pedestrian crossing.

'Faht do you know about Balaton?'

'I went to school,' she said. 'I saw it on the map. You had to look at *some*thing. And there it was. A gap in the middle of Hungary.'

She never tired of watching his hands. As he drove, the soft, cajoling palms would whiten.

Afterwards when they were drawn up in comfort, inside the sounds of sea and pines, and had bought the paper-bagful of prawns, and the prawn-coloured people were squelching past, Tibby Szabo had to ask:

'Are you trying to spy on me viz all zese kvestions of Balaton?'

'All these questions? One bare mention!'

Prawn-shells tinkled as they hit the asphalt.

'I wouldn't open any drawer, not if I had the key. There's only one secret,' she said, 'I want to know the answer to.'

'But Balaton!'

'So blue. Bluer than anything we've got. So everything,' she said.

The sand-sprinkled people were going up and down. The soles of their feet were inured to it.

Tibby Szabo spat on the asphalt. It smoked.

'It isn't nice,' she said, 'to spit.'

The tips of her fingers tasted of the salt-sweet prawns. The glassy rollers, uncurling on the sand, might have raked a little farther and swallowed her down, if she had not been engulfed already in deeper, glassier caverns.

'Faht is zis secret?' Tibby asked.

'Oh!'

She had to laugh.

'It is us,' she said, 'What does it add up to?'

'Faht it edds up to? I give you a hellofa good time. I pay ze electricity and ze gess. I put you in ze vay of cut-price frocks. You hef arranged sings pretty nice.'

Suddenly too many prawn-shells were clinging to Miss Slattery's fingers.

'That is not what I mean,' she choked. 'When you love someone, I mean. I mean it's sort of difficult to put. When you could put your head in the gas-oven, and damn who's gunna pay the bill.'

Because she did not have the words, she got out her lipstick, and began to persecute her mouth.

Ladies were looking by now into the expensive car. Their glass eyes expressed surprise.

'Lof!' Tibby Szabo laughed. 'Lof is viz ze sahoul!' Then he grew very angry; he could have been throwing his hand away. 'Faht do zay know of lof?' he shouted. 'Here zere is only stike and bodies!'

Then they were looking into each other, each with an expression that suggested they might not arrive beyond a discovery just made.

Miss Slattery lobbed the paper-bag almost into the municipal bin.

'I am sursty,' Tibby complained.

Indeed, salt formed in the corners of his mouth. Could it be that he was going to risk drinking deeper of the dregs?

'This Pacific Ocean,' Miss Slattery said, or cried, 'is all on the same note. Drive us home, Tibby,' she said, 'and make love to me.'

As he released the brake, the prawn-coloured bodies on the asphalt continued to lumber up and down, regardless.

'Listen,' Miss Slattery said, 'a girl friend of Phyllis Wimble's called Apple is giving a party in Woolloomooloo. Saturday night, Phyllis says. It's going to be bohemian.'

Szabo Tibor drew his lower lip.

'Austrahlian-bohemian-proveenshul. Zere is nossing veuorse zan bohemian-proveenshul.'

'Try it and see,' Miss Slattery advised, and bitterly added: 'A lot was discovered only by mistake.'

'And faht is zis Epple?'

'She is an oxywelder.'

'A vooman? Faht does she oxyveld?'

'I dunno. Objects and things. Apple is an artist.'

Apple was a big girl in built-up hair and pixie glasses. The night of the party most of her objects had been removed, all except what she said was her major work.

'This is *Hypotenuse of Angst*,' she explained. 'It is considered very powerful.' And smiled.

'Will you have claret?' Apple asked. 'Or perhaps you prefer Scotch or gin. That will depend on whoever brings it along.'

Apple's party got under way. It was an old house, a large room running in many directions, walls full of Lovely Textures.

'Almost everybody here,' Phyllis Wimble confided, 'is doing something.'

'What have you brought, Phyl?' Miss Slattery asked.

'He is a grazier,' Phyllis said, 'that a nurse I know got tired of.'

'He is all body,' Miss Slattery said, now that she had learnt.

'What do you expect?'

Those who had them were tuning their guitars.

'Those are the Spanish guitarists,' Phyllis explained. 'And these are English teddies off a liner. They are only the atmosphere. It's Apple's friends who are doing things.'

'Looks a bit,' the grazier hinted.

Phyllis shushed him.

'You are hating it, Tib,' Miss Slattery said.

Tibby Szabo drew down his lip.

'I vill get dronk. On Epple's plonk.'

She saw that his teeth were ever so slightly decalcified. She saw that he was a little, fat black man, whom she had loved, and loved still. From habit. Like biting your nails.

I must get out of it, she said. But you didn't, not out of biting your nails, until you forgot; then it was over.

The dancing had begun, and soon the kissing. The twangling of guitars broke the light into splinters. The slurp of claret stained the jokes. The teddies danced. The grazier danced the Spanish dances. His elastic-sides were so authentic. Apple fell upon her bottom.

Not everyone, not yet, had discovered Tibby Szabo was a little, fat, black man, with serrated teeth like a shark's. There was girl called Felicia who came and sat in Tibby's lap. Though he opened his knees and she shot through, it might not have bothered Miss Slattery if Felicia had stayed.

'They say,' Phyllis Wimble whispered, 'they are all madly queer.'

'Don't you know by now,' Miss Slattery said, 'that everyone is always queer?'

But Phyllis Wimble could turn narky.

'Everyone, we presume, but Tibby Szabo.'

Then Miss Slattery laughed and laughed.

'Tibby Szabo,' she laughed, 'is just about the queerest thing I've met.'

'Faht is zet?' Tibby asked.

'Nossing, darling,' Miss Slattery answered. 'I love you with all my body, and never my soul.'

It was all so *mouvementé*, said one of Apple's friends.

The grazier danced. He danced the Spanish dances. He danced bareheaded, and in his Lesbian hat. He danced in his shirt, and later, without.

'They say,' whispered Phyllis Wimble, 'there are two men locked in the lavatory together. One is a teddy, but they haven't worked out who the other can be.'

'Perhaps he is a social-realist,' Miss Slattery suggested.

She had a pain.

The brick-red grazier produced a stockwhip, too fresh from the shop, too stiff, but it smelled intoxicatingly of leather.

'Oh,' Miss Stattery cried, 'stockwhips are never *made*, they were there in the beginning.'

As the grazier uncoiled his brand-new whip, the lash fell glisteningly. It flicked a corner of her memory, unrolling a sheet of blazing blue, carpets of dust, cattle rubbing and straining past. She could not have kept it out even if she had wanted to. The electric sun beating on her head. The smell of old, sweaty leather had made her drunker than bulk claret.

'Oh, God, I'm gunna burn up!' Miss Slattery protested.

And took off her top.

She was alarmingly smooth, unscathed. Other skins, she knew, withered in the sun. She remembered the scabs on her dad's knuckles.

She had to get up then.

'Give, George!' she commanded. 'You're about the crummiest crack I ever listened to.'

Miss Slattery stood with the stockwhip. Her breasts snoozed. Or contemplated. She could have been awaiting inspiration. So Tibby Szabo noticed, leaning forward to follow to its source the faintest blue, of veins explored on previous expeditions.

Then, suddenly, Miss Slattery cracked, scattering the full room. She filled it with shrieks, disgust, and admiration. The horsehair gadfly stung the air. Miss Slattery cracked an abstract painting off the wall. She cracked a cork out of a bottle.

'Brafo, Petuska!' Tibby Szabo shouted. 'Vas you efer in a tseerkoos?'

He was sitting forward.

'Yeah,' she said, 'a Hungarian one!'

And let the horsehair curl round Tibby's thigh.

He was sitting forward. Tibby Szabo began to sing:

> 'Csak egy kislány
> van a világon,
> az is az én
> drága galambo-o-om!'

He was sitting forward with eyes half-closed, clapping and singing.

> 'Hooray for love,
> it rots you, . . .'

Miss Slattery sang.

She cracked a cigarette out of the grazier's lips.

> 'A jó Isten
> de nagyon szeret,'

sang Tibby Szabo,

> 'hogy nékem adta
> a legszebbik-e-e-et!'[1]

---

1 'Only one little girl/in the world/and she is/my dear little dove!/The good God/must love me indeed/to have given me/the most beautiful one!'

Then everybody was singing everything they had to sing, guitars disintegrating, for none could compete against the syrup from Tibby Szabo's compulsive violin.

While Miss Slattery cracked. Breasts jumping and frolicking. Her hair was so brittle. Lifted it once again, though, under the tawny sun, hawking dust, drunk on the smell of the tepid canvas water-bags.

Miss Slattery cracked once more, and brought down the sun from out of the sky.

It is not unlikely that the world will end in thunder. From the sound of it, somebody must have overturned *Hypotenuse of Angst*. Professional screamers had begun to scream. The darkness filled with hands.

'Come close, Petuska.'

It was Tibby Szabo.

'I vill screen you,' he promised, and caressed.

When a Large Person appeared with a candle. She was like a scone.

'These studios,' the Large Person announced, 'are let for purposes of creative arts, and the exchange of intellectual ideas. I am not accustomed to louts—and worse,' here she looked at Miss Slattery's upper half, 'wrecking the premises,' she said. 'As there has never been any suspicion that this is a Bad House, I must ask you all to leave.'

So everybody did, for there was the Large Person's husband behind her, looking as though he might mean business. Everybody shoved and poured, there was a singing, a crumbling of music on the stairs. There was a hugging and a kissing in the street. Somebody had lost his pants. It was raining finely.

Tibby Szabo drove off very quickly, in case a lift might be asked for.

'Put on your top, Petuska,' he advised. 'You vill ketch a colt.'

It sounded reasonable. She was bundling elaborately into armholes.

'Waddayaknow!' Miss Slattery said. 'We've come away with the grazier's whip!'

'Hef vee?' Tibby Szabo remarked.

So they drove in Tibby's Jag. They were on a spiral. 'I am so tired,' Miss Slattery admitted.

And again:

'I am awful tired.'

She was staring down at those white rugs in Tibby's flat. The soft, white, serious pile. She was propped on her elbows. Knees apart. Must be looking bloody awful.

'Petuska,' he was trying it out, 'vill you perhaps do vun more creck of ze whip?'

He could have been addressing a convalescent.

'Oh, but I am tired. I am done,' she said.

'Just vun little vun.'

Then Miss Slattery got real angry.

'You and this goddam lousy whip! I wish I'd never set eyes on either!'

Nor did she bother where she lashed.

'*Ach! Oh! Aÿ-ÿaÿ-ÿaÿ! Petuska!*'

Miss Slattery cracked.

'What are the people gunna say when they hear you holler like that?'

As she cracked, and slashed.

'*Aÿ!* It is none of ze people's business. *Pouff! Yaÿ-ÿaÿ-ÿaÿ-ÿaÿ!*' Tibby Szabo cried. 'Just vun little vun more!'

And when at last she toppled, he covered her very tenderly where she lay.

'Did anyone ever want you to put on boots?'

'What ever for?' asked Phyllis Wimble.

But Miss Slattery found she had fetched the wrong file.

'Ah, dear,' she said, resuming. 'It's time I thought about a change,' she said. 'I'm feeling sort of tired.'

'Hair looks dead,' said Phyllis Wimble. 'That is always the danger signal.'

'Try a new rinse.'

'A nice strawberry.'

Miss Slattery, whose habit had been to keep Thursday evening for Tibby Szabo, could not bear to any more. Saturdays she still went, but at night, for the nights were less spiteful than the days.

'Vair vas you, Petuska, Sursday evening?' Tibby Szabo had begun to ask.

'I sat at home and watched the telly.'

'Zen I vill install ze telly for here!'

'Ah,' she said, 'the telly is something that requires the maximum of concentration.'

'Are you changing, Petuska?' Tibby asked.

'Everything is changing,' Miss Slattery said. 'It is an axiom of nature.'

She laughed rather short.

'That,' she said, 'is something I think I learned at school. Same time as Balaton.'

It was dreadful, really, for everyone concerned, for Tibby Szabo had begun to ring the Providential. With urgent communications for a friend. Would she envisage Tuesday, Vensday, Friday?

However impersonally she might handle the instrument, that old Huthnance would come in and catch her on the phone. Miss Slattery saw that Huthnance and she had almost reached the point of no return.

'No,' she replied. 'Not Thursday. Or any other day but what was agreed. Saturday, I said.'

She slammed it down.

So Miss Slattery would drag through the moist evenings. In which the scarlet hibiscus had furled. No more trumpets. Her hair hung dank, as she trailed through the acid, yellow light, towards the good address at which her lover lived.

'I am developing a muscle,' she caught herself saying, and looked round to see if anyone had heard.

It was the same night that Tibby Szabo cried out from the bottom of the pit:

'Vhy em I condemned to soffer?'

Stretched on mink, Miss Slattery lay, idly flicking at her varnished toes. Without looking at the view, she knew the rhinestones of Sydney had never glittered so heartlessly.

'Faht for do you *torture* me?'

'But that is what you wanted,' she said.

Flicking. Listless.

'Petuska, I vill gif you *any*sink!'

'Nossing,' she said. 'I am going,' she said.

'*Gowing?* Ven vee are so suited to each ozzer!'

Miss Slattery flicked.

'I am sick,' she said, 'I am sick of cutting a rug out of your fat Hungarian behind.'

The horsehair slithered and glistened between her toes.

'But faht vill you do visout me?'

'I am going to find myself a thin Australian.'

Tibby was on his knees again.

'I am gunna get married,' Miss Slattery said, 'and have a washing-machine.'

'*Yaÿ-yaÿ-yaÿ! Petuska!*'

Then Miss Slattery took a look at Tibby's eyes, and re-discovered a suppliant poodle, seen at the window of an empty house, at dusk. She had never been very doggy, though.

'Are you ze Defel perheps?' cried Tibby Szabo.

'We Australians are not all that unnatural,' she said.

And hated herself, just a little.

As for Tibby Szabo, he was licking the back of her hand.

'Vee vill make a finenshul arrangement. Pretty substenshul.'

'No go!' Miss Slattery said.

But that is precisely what she did. She got up and pitched the grazier's stockwhip out of the window, and when she had put on her clothes, and licked her lips once or twice, and shuffled her hair together—she went.

1964

GEORGE JOHNSTON
1912 – 1970

Novelist George Johnston was born in the Melbourne suburb of Malvern and educated in state schools. After an apprenticeship as a lithographer he gained a job as a cadet journalist on the Melbourne *Argus*, for which he became a senior war correspondent after the outbreak of the Second World War.

Johnston is best known for his 1964 classic *My Brother Jack*, one of the best-known and most widely read Australian novels of the twentieth century. Much of this novel is semi-autobiographical and events and characters from Johnston's own life can be identified in it in some form of disguise. A fictionalised version of his second wife, the writer Charmian Clift (qv), appears towards the end of the novel as the beautiful young Lieutenant Cressida Morley. In this novel traditional Australian values are tested by the effects of the Depression and the two world wars, a drama played out by the contrast between the two brothers who are the novel's main characters.

Johnston and Clift's relationship was one of the great romances of Australian literary life, and their careers as writers were intricately bound together. They met at the end of the Second World War when they were both working as journalists on the Melbourne *Argus* and Johnston was married with a small child. When their affair became public knowledge, Clift was sacked, whereupon the experienced and highly valued Johnston resigned in protest.

Johnston and Clift married in 1947, the same year that they collaborated on the novel *High Valley*, which won what was then Australia's most lucrative literary prize. In 1951 they moved to London, where Johnston was European correspondent for the Sydney *Sun*. Three years later the Johnstons moved to the Greek islands, where they lived in poverty, raised three children including Martin Johnston (qv), pursued a noisy bohemian lifestyle at the centre of a shifting expatriate population, and wrote fiction.

After ten years in Greece they moved back to Australia, partly because of the tubercular Johnston's deteriorating state of health. *My Brother Jack* was published the same year, 1964; the first of two sequels, *Clean Straw for Nothing*, was published in 1969 but the success of that novel was overshadowed by Clift's suicide the same year. The third novel in Johnston's trilogy, *A Cartload of Clay*, was published posthumously in 1971. Garry Kinnane's *George Johnston: A biography* was published in 1986. *KG*

From *My Brother Jack*
Chapter 13

[. . .] On this Sunday morning I had to get up on the roof to fit the stubby tubular mast which would take the new long aerial, and it had to be made fast to the chimney with the bolted metal straps which had come with the set, and for this I borrowed the Solomons' ladder. When I had finished the job—which didn't take long because the pamphlet which had come with the radio gave detailed illustrated instructions for fixing what was called the Quicktite Patent Antenna Clamp, and added, 'Even a child can do it!'—I stayed up on the roof, sitting on the sloping, terracotta tiles with my back wedged against the chimney because for the first time in weeks I had an odd feeling, not only of being alone and away from everything, but of being in some way unassailable as well, and I had not been up on the roof of a house since the time, more than twenty years before, when I had looked down in the rain on old Grandma Emma raging around the back garden brandishing the castor-oil bottle.

This second experience was even more terrifying, in a different way, because my elevation provided me with the first opportunity I had had to look out over all the Beverley Park Gardens Estate, and there was nothing all around me, as far as I could see, but a plain of dull red rooftops in their three forms of pitching and closer to hand the green squares and rectangles of lawns intersected by ribbons of asphalt and cement, and I counted nine cars out in Beverley Grove being washed and polished. In the slums, I reflected, they had a fetish about keeping front doorknobs polished, but here in the 'good' respectable suburbs the fetish was applied to cars and to gardens, and there were fixed rituals about this, so that hedges were clipped and lawns trimmed and beds weeded, and the lobelia and the mignonette were tidy in their borders, and the people would see that these things were so no matter what desolation or anxiety or fear was in their hearts, or what spiritless endeavours or connubial treacheries were practised behind the blind neat concealment of their thin red-brick walls. The doorknobs and this more elaborate ritual were part of a similar thing, of course, the public 'front', but it occurred to me suddenly that the door-knob people might be a worthier tribe, really, because they still grappled with existence where audacities were possible, and even adventure.

I stayed up on the roof because once I had worked this out a great many other things began to follow. Strange things. Terrifying things. Wondering things. (I could even stay up here for years, I thought, like some Stylite of the suburbs, on terracotta building tiles in place of a Syrian pillar, and ruminate on all the problems of the world. The ancient Stylites had liked desert places for their meditations.)

The realisation that I did not love Helen, and never had loved her, came to me quite dispassionately at first; so dispassionately that I was able to examine the revelation with a kind of clear careful logic, and find it sound, and put it aside for later. 'Later', of course, would be another thing altogether, when I would want to blame *her* for the predicament we were in, and then passion and anger would need to be invoked. But not yet.

Still, it was the thought of Helen, busy at her casserole in the kitchen, that diverted my reflections at once to all the disturbing little problems and quandaries which up until so recently had baffled and troubled me—politics and Spain and the German ships and the interviews on the liners—because I saw that I had been wrong to allow Helen to work these things out for me. I should have seen for myself that a lot of the dissonance of the world had nothing whatever to do with 'downtrodden masses' or any of Helen's other clichés, but was there because half the world lived in mental deserts very much like the Beverley Park Gardens Estate, and that the real enemy was not the obvious embodiment of evil, like Hitler or his persecution of the Jews or the Russian purges or the bombs on Guernica, but was this awful fetish of a respectability that would rather look the other way than cause a fuss, that hated 'scenes', that did not *want* to know because *to know* might somehow force them into a situation which could take the polish off the duco and blight the herbaceous borders and lay scabrous patches across the attended lawns.

But there were gradations of this respectability—this was the next thing I worked out as Meredith Stylites of the Garden Suburb—and I knew that there had been more things of true value in the shabby house called *Avalon*, from which I had fled, than there ever would be, or could be, in this villa in Beverley Grove. This was where my meditations began to turn in and maul me. I stared around over the whole of the sterile desolation, and I realised with a start of panic that I had got myself into the middle of this red and arid desert, and there was nobody to bring me water.

I had chosen it, of my own free will. I had planned for it, approved of it, connived at it, worked for it, and paid for it. But no!—I winced as the mauling became more brutal—the whole point was that *I had not paid for it!* Oh no, I had not *paid* for it, not yet . . . I had mortgaged my life and my career for years ahead simply for the privilege of living between Mr Phyland and Mr Treadwell and directly opposite Wally and Sandra Solomons!

And the console-radio, the hated new acquisition of the console-radio, inclusive of the Quicktite Patent Antenna Clamp against which my back rested, was another seventy-five pounds, thirteen shillings and elevenpence to be added to all those other precise and handsomely-printed documents with which the top drawer of my study desk was stuffed. My guarantees! Diplomas! Some of them even looked like diplomas, with their Old English type and the copperplate flourishes and the big red impressive seals. Diplomas conferred in testimony of some inalienable right to live on in the soft warmth of these empty plains where heads could always be hidden in the comforting granular sand of an unimpeachable respectability. Gavin Turley's guarantees . . .

(This was the point where Meredith Stylites of the Garden Suburb abandoned his red brick chimney-pillar and eased himself down the pitch of the tiled roof, and was transformed into the qualified Meredith, Bachelor of Deserts, Doctor of Sterile Studies, Master of the Empty Soul, by the time he reached the point where the borrowed Solomons' ladder poked two rungs above the eaves, and there he sat for a few more minutes with his long legs dangling over the guttering, staring around at the desert of his choice as if he might memorise forever its every shade and contour, and this was when the really forceful realisation came to him . . .)

There was not one tree on the whole estate.

Yet there must have been trees once, I thought, because when you closely examined the layout of the estate there were little folds to it and faint graceful rises and declivities, not anywhere near definite enough to be thought of as hills or gullies, but the place was not really *flat*, that was the point, and at one side, a little distance beyond Dr Felton Carradine's house, there was almost a real knoll. Once—I felt absolutely sure about this—there would have been trees growing here and there, and I pictured this knoll as having two or three good sturdy blue-gums or stringybarks on the crest, and slopes brown with bracken, and some sandy chewed-out patches where rabbits would have made little squats scattered with the liquorice-black pellets of their droppings and where they would have hopped about at dusk, flickering the pale cotton tufts of their tails. The place could have been really beautiful at one time in a tranquil sort of way, I thought—before Bernie Rothenstein came in with his bulldozers and graders and grubbed out all the trees and flattened everything out so that the subdivision pegs could be hammered in and his lorries could move about without hindrance—because there was a blur of higher ground much farther out, and beyond that the bluish bulk of the Dandenongs sat up there against a good bright sky in nice shapes and colours. And now there was nothing but a great red scab grown over the wounds the bulldozers had made, and not a single tree remaining, because by no stretch of the imagination could anybody count the spindly little sticks which had been stuck in at intervals along the footpaths, because they really were only sticks, and too hidden behind their ugly little tree-guards for anyone to know whether they were leafing or whether they were dead. [. . .]

1964

JOE TIMBERY
1912–1978

Poet, storyteller and world champion boomerang thrower, Joe Timbery spent much of his life at La Perouse near Sydney. His ancestors included Timbere, King of the Five Islands, and his Dharawal grandmother, Emma, a gifted traditional shellmaker. Timbery was highly regarded for his boomerangs, which were decorated with carved images of animals and the Sydney Harbour Bridge. He demonstrated his boomerang throwing beneath the Eiffel Tower, and in 1954 presented Queen Elizabeth II with one of his boomerangs during her visit to Australia. *AH/PM*

The Boomerang Racket

Boomerangs are now being manufactured by the thousand by people with very little (or no) experience of how such weapons should be made.

In Sydney, it will soon be hard to find a boomerang made by an Australian Aborigine. Some Aboriginals who really have the experience and can make good boomerangs are out of business, or soon will be. Most of the shops are to blame for this. They want boomerangs so cheap they don't care who makes them.

When an Aboriginal takes his boomerang to try and sell them as before, most of the shops say 'We buy our boomerangs from agents now'—but the agents haven't been handling boomerangs made by Aborigines. It doesn't matter to the shops if the boomerangs offered to them are good throwing types—they won't pay any more money for them. They don't even know what are good throwers. But if you go to buy a boomerang from them, they say the ones they have are good throwing boomerangs.

How can Aborigines compete with their genuine, quality boomerangs? No wonder some dark people live the way they do.

The public are being caught all the time. I feel sorry for them. They have been good to me—that is why I write this warning.

Now to try and help you, remember this—

The cross on one end of the boomerang, and the arrow at the other is often a gimmick to help sell it. Such marks don't always mean that a boomerang is a genuine throwing kind.

If shown how, almost any person can throw a boomerang and make it return, if it has been made right. But it does not matter how good a boomerang thrower may be, it won't return to you correctly if it has not been made right. The instruction on how to throw it is of no use to you— only a gimmick to help sell it.

If your boomerang is faulty, don't muck around with it unless you know the cause of the trouble. A boomerang is a weapon and could be dangerous when thrown.

If the boomerang is made from good natural coloured wood, and is about a quarter of an inch thick, in the first place it may be warped. A good boomerang should, when thrown correctly, spin very fast, and not lose its spin until it lands. If it does lose its spin, don't blame yourself, it's not made right. There could be many things wrong with it. For instance, the less angle the boomerang has, the harder it is to make it return.

More experience is needed in making a boomerang from heavy timber than making one from light wood.

There are very, very few living in Sydney today who have the kind of experience needed to make boomerangs correctly.

Your children would have a much better chance of throwing a good boomerang made by an expert, than the cheap, mass-produced ones sold in most shops. And when they are successful, they will have the fun of their lives. You will be happy too.

1968

DOUGLAS STEWART
1913–1985

A highly influential literary figure, as well as a deftly adaptable writer, Douglas Stewart is remembered both for his finely observed nature poetry and his verse dramas. Born in New Zealand, he moved to Australia as a young man to work on the *Bulletin* and sustained a long association with it, editing the literary pages from 1940 to 1960. He was also a long-term literary adviser to publisher Angus & Robertson, initiating the yearly anthologies *Australian Poetry* and *Coast to Coast*.

The Fire on the Snow (1944), a verse drama about Scott's ill-fated Antarctic expedition (1910–1913) was broadcast on ABC radio in 1941 and is Stewart's most significant and successful work. Other verse dramas include *Ned Kelly* (1943), *The Golden Lover* (1943), *The Earthquake Shakes the Land* (1944), about the New Zealand wars of 1840, and *Shipwreck* and *Glencoe* (both 1947).

From 1936 Stewart published nine collections of poetry, *Sun Orchids and Other Poems* (1952) containing his most anthologised poems. In the 1950s he was commissioned by the Shell Film Unit to provide a scripted narration for the award-winning, highly poetic documentary *Back of Beyond* (1954), about the Birdsville Track. A suite of poems first published in the *Bulletin* in 1952 form part of this script and were collected in *The Birdsville Track and Other Poems* (1955). Five of these poems are published as a sequence here. *NM*

The Green Centipede

Whatever lies under a stone
Lies under the stone of the world:
That day of the yellow flowers
When out of moss and shale
The cassia bushes unfurled   5
Their pale soft yellow stars
And lit the whole universe,
Out from the same deep source
Like some green shingly rill
From the grey stone dislodged   10
The big green centipede ran
Rippling down from the hill:
And fringed with silvery light,
So beautiful, not to be touched,
In its green grace had power   15
—Down where all rivers meet
Deep under stony ground—
To make the most gentle flower
Burn, burn in the hand.

1952

The Fierce Country

Three hundred miles to Birdsville from Marree
Man makes his mark across a fierce country
That has no flower but the whitening bone and skull
Of long-dead cattle, no word but 'I will kill'.

Here the world ends in a shield of purple stone   5
Naked in its long war against the sun;
The white stones flash, the red stones leap with fire:
It wants no interlopers to come here.

Whatever it is that speaks through softer earth
Still tries to stammer indeed its broken phrases;   10
Between some crack in the stone mosaic brings forth
Yellow and white like suns the papery daisies;

The cassia drinks the sky in its gold cup,
Straggling on sandhills the dwarf wild-hops lift up
Their tufts of crimson flame; and the first hot wind   15
Blows out the suns and smothers the flames in sand.

And man too like the earth in the good season
When the Diamantina floods the whole horizon
And the cattle grow fat on wildflowers says his proud word:
Gathers the stones and builds four-square and hard: 20

Where the mirage still watches with glittering eyes
The ruins of his homestead crumble on the iron rise.
Dust on the waterless plains blows over his track,
The sun glares down on the stones and the stones glare back.

1955

Marree

Oh the corrugated-iron town
In the corrugated-iron air
Where the shimmering heat-waves glare
To the red-hot iron plain
And the steel mirage beyond: 5

The blackfellow's squalid shanty
Of rags and bags and tins,

The bright-red dresses of the gins
Flowering in that hot country
Like lilies in the dust's soft pond: 10

The camels' bones and the bullocks',
The fierce red acre of death
Where the Afghan groans beneath
His monstrous concrete blankets
That peel in the heat like rind: 15

Where life if it hopes to breathe
Must crawl in the shade of a stone
Like snake and scorpion:
All tastes like dust in the mouth,
All strikes like iron in the mind.   20
                                                        1955

Afghan

Mopping his coppery forehead under his turban,
Old Bejah in baggy trousers, bearded, immense:
'Oh ya, oh ya, the young man dead in the sands,
I dig with my hands, I find him, and fifty yards further
The other, both dead, so young; no water, no water.'   5
The gestures, the voice, all larger and wilder than human,
Some whirlwind out of the desert. 'Two days in the sun,
Done when I sight the camp. I shoot off my gun
And Larry Wells he carry me over his shoulder;
Looking for water out there; oh ya, no water.'   10
Old camel-driver, explorer, the giant Afghan
Who steered his life by compass and by Koran,
'Oh ya, believe in God; young man no care;
God save, God help; oh ya, need help out there!'
And fondled his box of brass and kissed his book   15
So passionately, with such a lover's look,
He whirled in deserts still, too wild for human.
                                                        1955

Place Names

Ethadinna, Mira Mitta,
Mulka, Mungerannie—
Dark shadows blown

With the dust away,
Far from our day   5
Far out of time,
Fill the land with water.
Where the blue sky flames
On the bare red stone,
Dulkaninna, Koperamanna,   10
Ooroowilanie, Kilalpaninna—
Only the names
In the land remain
Like a dark well
Like the chime of a bell.   15
                                                1955

Sombrero

In a cowboy hat and a dark-green shirt,
Lithe on a piebald pony,
The blackfellow rode through the coolabah-trees
Where the creek was dry and stony.

Here's fifty horses from Pandie Pandie   5
To drove to far Marree
But before I start on the track again
I'll boil up a billy of tea.

Oh he was dark as the gibber stones
And took things just as easy   10
And a white smile danced on his purple lips
Like an everlasting daisy.

The horses strayed on the saltbush plain
And he went galloping after,
The green shirt flew through the coolabah-trees 15
Like budgerigars to water.

And then what need had he to sigh
For old men under the gibbers
When he was free as the winds that blow
Along the old dry rivers?   20

He had the lubras' hot wild eyes,
His green shirt and sombrero,
He rode the plains on a piebald horse
And he was his own hero.

1955

BILL NEIDJIE
c. 1913—2002

Bill Neidjie was born at Alawanydajawany on the East Alligator River in Arnhem Land, NT. Prior to the Second World War, Neidjie had a variety of jobs for which he was paid in tea, sugar, meat, flour and tobacco. After the 1942 bombing of Darwin, he assisted affected Aboriginal people. Around this time he was initiated in a Ubarr ceremony at Paw Paw Beach. For nearly 30 years Neidjie worked on a lugger along the north coast of WA. In 1979 he returned home to his Bunitj clan land, becoming a claimant in the Alligator Rivers Stage II land claim.

He was an author of 'Indjuwanydjuwa: A report on Bunitj clan sites in the Alligator Rivers region' (1982), which helped the Bunitj people of the Gagadju language group gain title to their land. Neidjie was instrumental in the decision to lease the traditional lands to the Commonwealth of Australia so it could be managed as a resource for all Australians. He became a senior elder of Kadaku National Park and was a keen conservationist throughout his life. On his death the Gagadju tongue died with him. He died near Kakadu, the park named after his language. He is the author of two works, *Australia's Kakadu Man* (1985) and *Story About Feeling* (1989). *AH/PM*

Ahh ... Bush-Honey There!

You cannot see.
I cannot see but you feel it.
I feel it.
E can feeling.
I feeling.   5

Spirit longside with you.
You sit ... e sit. Telling you.
You think ...
   'I want to go over there.'
E tell im you ... before!   10
Anything you want to look ...
   'Ahh ... go tree.'

But e say ...
   'Hey! You go look that tree.
   Something e got there.'   15

You look … well you look straight away.
You might look snake, you might look bush-honey.
E telling you to have a look …
    'Look up!'
    'Ahh … bush-honey there.'   20

Alright, you say …
    'I go somewhere else. I go look painting.'

All that painting, small mark …
they put cross, cross and over again.
White, yellow and little bit charcoal, little bit red clay …   25
that's the one all small meaning there.
They put it meaning.
They painting fish … little mark they make im, you know.
That's the one same as this you look newspaper.
Big mob you read it all that story,   30
e telling you all that meaning.
All that painting now, small,
e tell im you that story.

That meaning that you look … you feel im now.
You might say …   35
    'Hey! That painting good one!
    I take im more picture.'

That spirit e telling you …
    'Go on … you look.'

Taking picture.   40

Well all that meaning there.
E say mother, granny, grandpa, grass, fire, bird, tree.
All that small thing, little thing,
all that mark they make it, when you go sleep
you dream …   45
going through your feeling.
You might sleep. Well you feel …
    'Hey, I bin dream good dream!'
White paint might be big hawk … before.
Yellow clay where sunset … e tell im you that secret.   50
You got to put im on yellow clay
because all that dream, all that story is there.
You got to put charcoal
because e got 'business' there, what we call Dhuwa.

Yellow clay … Yirridtja. 55
Well all that piece, piece they paint im, all that story
secret, grandpa, granny, back, chest, head …
e coming through your feeling.
That painting you say …
'That lovely painting.' 60

Finger prints …
E put finger prints because hand e put it.
Where you grab it thing, you know.
Fruit or cutting it anykind … with your fingers!
They put it finger prints. 65
They said …
    'They can look.'

Some foot prints …
That's the one they feel it.
They used to feel it turtle there 70
or might be water-python, snake.
They feel …
    'Hey! Snake!'

That way all that painting they left it behind,
dead … on the rock. 75

No matter who is.
E can feel it way I feel it in my feeling.
You'll be same too.
You listen my story and you will feel im
because spirit e'll be with you. 80
You cannot see but e'll be with you and e'll be with me.
This story just listen careful.

Spirit must stay with us. E longside us.
E can feel it spirit e's there.
That way all that dreaming they left … to see. 85
1989

DONALD FRIEND
1914–1989

The artist, writer and diarist Donald Friend was born in Sydney to a privileged landed family, though he largely grew up in the artistic circles surrounding his mother. He studied art formally in Sydney and London and embarked on a trip to Nigeria prior to the Second World War. On returning to Australia, he enlisted in the army and in 1945 became an official war artist, serving in Labuan and Borneo. After the war, he lived in Australia between extensive trips to Europe (in the early 1950s), Sri Lanka (1957–61) and Bali (from the later 1960s to the end of the 1970s). In 1980, partly for health reasons, he returned home permanently. He continued to exhibit till near the end of his life, though the predominantly figurative style of his work, appraised in a 1965 study by the young Robert Hughes (qv), has not helped keep him in high artistic fashion. Friend's consummate skills as a draughtsman are well recognised, however, and are nowhere more evident than in his richly illustrated diaries, which he kept from the age of thirteen; four volumes of extracts have been published by the National Library of Australia (2001–06). *IB*

From *The Diaries of Donald Friend*

2 OCTOBER 1952

Toledo

Alas—the first day the Prado was closed because of a fiesta. Dick had gone off to the university to meet some of the scientists, so we wandered around the big city, expensive, glittering and dull. We did see one gem, the hermitage of Santa Maria de Florida, with frescoes by Goya, painted with crazy verve—great swathes of paint broomed on—the colour very subdued and subtle, and what was a miracle, it was in the rococo manner—cherubs and angels and so on, but its tremendous virility soared infinitely beyond the limits of the style of that epoch. The Majas and whores who were the angels of his painting expressed the man's great gusto with brilliant gestures, with violence. But apart from that, we had begun to regret Barcelona and the gay Catalans recalling incident by incident songs and dances and gestures from that night there, and certain fantastic mimes done by the waiters, and a hugely fat, superbly tight-laced dancer, whose figure, an hourglass expanded and contracted according to some very especial Catalan taste, encased in a tight green frock, and others, and our own company, Miguel the writer, and a mad young man whose hair had been cropped to the skull for some misdemeanour during army service—they were all such marvellous people. In contrast, these Madrilènes seemed drearily bourgeois.

So they were right, those who said that Madrid was an expensive bore, to be tolerated only on account of the Prado.

Ah—but that Prado. One reeled away from the place, positively battered by the impact of those tremendous, magnificent, ill-preserved, horribly-lit and badly-preserved masterpieces. El Grecos that flamed through black and brown treacle of bad varnish, Goyas that by the miracle of their mastery only managed to overcome the ill-treatment they had received. Velasquez at his superb greatest, and the realisation of a dream that has waited since my student days to be realised—to see the Bosch *Garden of Earthly Delights* that was finer even than merited the long expectation.

So at nearly midnight we arrived, by the light of a full moon which gave to the town an incomparable dreamy eeriness, in Toledo. Too late to eat dinner, we took some wine and a plate of mixed oddities in a bar in a back street, and there was a drunk, an amiable rather brutal-looking fellow who bought us drinks and told us once he had been a famous toreador.

3 OCTOBER 1952

I felt as much alarm as pleasure when Dick announced we'd stay another night here. This because ever since the first of the month I've been very conscious that I ought soon to be back in London. At our present rate of progress it will take at least 10 days, which is cutting it very fine. My show opens on the 15th, and I ought to be there now seeing to things. Nevertheless, this town is so wonderful one cannot become too upset over anything but waste of precious time. I've managed to see the sights of the place, and by dint of getting up at six this morning got one drawing of the town done before breakfast, and did two more, from a point in the rocks above the Tagus, of the town. The place is sheer enchantment, magic. I won't speak of the Grecos, which are beyond belief. As much of his art, I imagine, grew out of this environment as was born in his Byzantine origin. The folds of hills and rocks suggest, quite as much as the enclosing womb shapes of ikons, the peculiar swooping and folding-in forms he used.

Dick's reason for deciding to stay was that an amiable shoeshine boy he had met during the morning had told him there was flamenco singing to be heard that night. Accordingly, we met this chap who took us to a tiny bar full of wine barrels and work people. Presently two of his friends turned up, and in no time, with carafes of the Toledan dry white wine on the table, were snapping fingers, stamping, clapping hands and singing, in that typical agonised way, indicative of great personal effort and strain, the weird cadences of flamenco.

From there we went on to other bars, and others again, and consumed enormous quantities of wine which they utterly refused to allow us to pay for. It developed into a riotous night. Somewhere about 10.30 we all dined, and went on for more wine-bibbing and singing. [. . .]

2005

27 APRIL 1975

Bali
I have no intention of allowing myself to fall in love. At this time of life it would be a grotesquery: however, there is no doubt I enjoy pleasurable stirrings and questionable emotions that hover on the verge of becoming something stronger and yet more unstable when I contemplate Michael Komendi.

And toward me he beams waves of affection. Listens to my old man's babble, demands more, and thinks me wise when I am merely entertaining. I wish my spirit could release itself from this battered obese old body and enter some lithe and vigorous form—take on a shape companion to his uncalculating grace.

Coming home late after dining out he stayed overnight with me: In that enormous ancient pavilion of a bed, all carved and painted, we lay side by side talking for long before sleeping. But I lay long wakeful thinking things over to myself. And imagined a mere touch would bring him to me all warm and fresh as new baked bread. The desire was certainly there to embrace the generous affections of youth. It probably would have needed no more than a gesture to stir up a fire such as I could not cope with, but I was afraid to start anything that might disillusion or disgust him. It is easy to believe that he would remain happier in his affection and admiration, drawing from me stories and poetry and words of wisdom and humour: which are what he already loves me for, and which are such as may be lost during interludes of sensuality. Youth is easily disgusted by passion. It revolts even against its own passion—how much more against the sweaty transports of an old satyr in the tropic night?

These cogitations thankfully float about a situation that as yet demands no solution or decision at all, because tonight he returns to Australia. He has just learned his father is ill, probably with cancer.

How practical—unpractical, folly-wise and admirable they are, the young whose quixotisms have not been eliminated by experience!

Michael told me: 'A Balinese family in a bamboo hut: I used to pass by there every day, and stop to talk. They are wonderful. Very poor, the man and his wife and three children. They would all run out and greet me, and make me go in, and give me tea to drink. They never asked me for anything. I loved talking with them. The children were so *small*. Thin. You could see their diet was not right. Then I found out they'd *never ever* ever *tasted* milk. Can you believe it? So I didn't tell them what I meant to do. I went with a friend of mine to a cattle auction. We bought a milking cow in calf and took it back and gave it to them. They just simply couldn't believe it. They were so happy, so astonished.'

I'll bet they were. Milk is no part of Balinese diet. I wonder what those poor people will do with the cow!—but one cannot help being charmed with his motive and the deed. And who knows, the Balinese may actually milk the cow. There is a tale I heard somewhere of someone who remarked in the hearing of a cranky old yankee that you can lead a horse to water, but not make him drink.

'Most horses drink water,' the yankee observed.

2006

J.S. MANIFOLD
1915–1985

John Streeter Manifold was a prominent figure in cultural life of the mid-twentieth century, although his varied and lively poetry is now neglected. He published his first volume of poetry in 1933 while still a schoolboy and continued to write at Cambridge, where he joined the Communist Party of Great Britain. He graduated with a degree in French and German, and worked for a German publishing house. During the Second World War he served with the British army in Nigeria and France, working for British Intelligence. His best-known poem, 'The Tomb of Lieutenant John Learmonth, A.I.F', was written in this period.

By the time he returned to Australia in 1949, Manifold had received international recognition for his four volumes of poetry. A *Selected Verse* was released in 1946. Tension with his wealthy family led Manifold and his wife Katherine to move to Brisbane, where they became involved with the local branches of the Communist Party of Australia and helped found the Brisbane Realist Writers Group. He published two more collections of poetry and *Collected Verse* was released in 1978.

Manifold was an influential champion of folk music and bush ballads, editing significant collections, including the much-reprinted *Penguin Australian Song Book* (1964). *Who Wrote the Ballads? Notes on Australian folksong* (1964) is an important study of the origins of Australian ballads. NM

The Tomb of Lieutenant John Learmonth, A.I.F.

At the end on Crete he took to the hills, and said he'd fight
    it out with only a revolver. He was a great soldier …
                                           One of his men in a letter

This is not sorrow, this is work: I build
A cairn of words over a silent man,
My friend John Learmonth whom the Germans killed.

There was no word of hero in his plan;
Verse should have been his love and peace his trade,   5
But history turned him to a partisan.

Far from the battle as his bones are laid
Crete will remember him. Remember well,
Mountains of Crete, the Second Field Brigade!

Say Crete, and there is little more to tell   10
Of muddle tall as treachery, despair
And black defeat resounding like a bell;

But bring the magnifying focus near
And in contempt of muddle and defeat
The old heroic virtues still appear.   15

Australian blood where hot and icy meet
(James Hogg and Lermontov were of his kin)
Lie still and fertilize the fields of Crete.

★

Schoolboy, I watched his ballading begin:
Billy and bullocky and billabong,   20
Our properties of childhood, all were in.

I heard the air though not the undersong,
The fierceness and resolve; but all the same
They're the tradition, and tradition's strong.

Swagman and bushranger die hard, die game,   25
Die fighting, like that wild colonial boy—
Jack Dowling, says the ballad, was his name.

He also spun his pistol like a toy,
Turned to the hills like wolf or kangaroo,
And faced destruction with a bitter joy.   30

His freedom gave him nothing else to do
But set his back against his family tree
And fight the better for the fact he knew

He was as good as dead. Because the sea
Was closed and the air dark and the land lost,   35
'They'll never capture me alive,' said he.

★

That's courage chemically pure, uncrossed
With sacrifice or duty or career,
Which counts and pays in ready coin the cost

Of holding course. Armies are not its sphere   40
Where all's contrived to achieve its counterfeit;
It swears with discipline, its volunteer.

I could as hardly make a moral fit
Around it as around a lightning flash.
There is no moral, that's the point of it,   45

No moral. But I'm glad of this panache
That sparkles, as from flint, from us and steel,
True to no crown nor presidential sash

Nor flag nor fame. Let others mourn and feel
He died for nothing: nothings have their place.   50
While thus the kind and civilized conceal

This spring of unsuspected inward grace
And look on death as equals, I am filled
With queer affection for the human race.

                                                        1946

JUDITH WRIGHT
1915–2000

A poet whose work spanned the second half of the twentieth century, Judith Wright has attracted national and international acclaim. She was nominated for the Nobel Prize and in 1999 was declared a National Treasure. Her poetry combines philosophical enquiry and an intense interest in the relations between words and things, image and being, with a passionate belief in writing's responsibility to the world, particularly in an Australian landscape.

She published more than eleven volumes of poetry, significant volumes of criticism on Australian writing, and some breakthrough environmental, historical and political writing. Her work has been profoundly influential in the Australian environmental movement, while her political volumes, calling for the recognition of Aboriginal sovereignty and exploring her responsibilities to Aboriginal people as a daughter of settler Australia, are a logical extension of earlier themes in her poetry. A tension between activism and aesthetics has been traced by many critics, some negatively, but recently with clearer recognition of their mutual constitution.

Wright grew up on a pastoral station in the New England region of NSW, the daughter of a family who could trace their holdings to squatted runs in the Hunter Valley in the 1820s. Her interest in poetry was fired by a period spent working on the station during the Second World War, and her first volume of poetry, *The Moving Image* (1946), drew strongly on that landscape. Containing many of her best-loved poems, this collection both celebrates a double inheritance, of British and settler Australian heritage, and questions its legitimacy.

Subsequent volumes of her poetry, especially *Woman to Man* (1949), *The Two Fires* (1955) and *Birds* (1962), contain well-recognised poems, ranging in subject from a questing eroticism to studies of an othered, yet intensely desired natural world, to an almost tender guilt about colonial violence. Angry bitterness about the ongoing loss of a natural landscape, sometimes called 'hortatory', reads as prophetic now. Her later work continued these concerns but reflects a more direct engagement with attempts at social change and politics. Her poem 'Skins' (1985), like so much of her work, wonders at the processes of time, using as its central image worn, 66-year-old 'skin gloves', the poet's hands. *NM*

South of My Days

South of my days' circle, part of my blood's country,
rises that tableland, high delicate outline
of bony slopes wincing under the winter,
low trees blue-leaved and olive, outcropping granite—
clean, lean, hungry country. The creek's leaf-silenced,   5
willow-choked, the slope a tangle of medlar and crabapple
branching over and under, blotched with a green lichen;
and the old cottage lurches in for shelter.

O cold the black-frost night. The walls draw in to the warmth
and the old roof cracks its joints; the slung kettle   10
hisses a leak on the fire. Hardly to be believed that summer
will turn up again some day in a wave of rambler roses,
thrust its hot face in here to tell another yarn—
a story old Dan can spin into a blanket against the winter.
Seventy years of stories he clutches round his bones.   15
Seventy summers are hived in him like old honey.

Droving that year, Charleville to the Hunter,
nineteen-one it was, and the drought beginning;
sixty head left at the McIntyre, the mud round them
hardened like iron; and the yellow boy died   20
in the sulky ahead with the gear, but the horse went on,
stopped at the Sandy Camp and waited in the evening.
It was the flies we seen first, swarming like bees.
Came to the Hunter, three hundred head of a thousand—
cruel to keep them alive—and the river was dust.   25

Or mustering up in the Bogongs in the autumn
when the blizzards came early. Brought them down; we brought them
down, what aren't there yet. Or driving for Cobb's on the run
up from Tamworth—Thunderbolt at the top of Hungry Hill,
and I give him a wink. I wouldn't wait long, Fred,   30
not if I was you; the troopers are just behind,
coming for that job at the Hillgrove. He went like a luny,
him on his big black horse.
                    Oh, they slide and they vanish
as he shuffles the years like a pack of conjuror's cards.   35
True or not, it's all the same; and the frost on the roof
cracks like a whip, and the back-log breaks into ash.

Wake, old man. This is winter, and the yarns are over.
No-one is listening.
                South of my days' circle   40
I know it dark against the stars, the high lean country
full of old stories that still go walking in my sleep.

                                                 1946

The Surfer

He thrust his joy against the weight of the sea;
climbed through, slid under those long banks of foam—
(hawthorn hedges in spring, thorns in the face stinging).
How his brown strength drove through the hollow and coil
of green-through weirs of water!   5
Muscle of arm thrust down long muscle of water;
and swimming so, went out of sight
where mortal, masterful, frail, the gulls went wheeling
in air as he in water, with delight.

Turn home, the sun goes down; swimmer, turn home.   10
Last leaf of gold vanishes from the sea-curve.
Take the big roller's shoulder, speed and swerve;
Come to the long beach home like a gull diving.

For on the sand the grey-wolf sea lies snarling,
cold twilight wind splits the waves' hair and shows   15
the bones they worry in their wolf-teeth. O, wind blows
and sea crouches on sand, fawning and mouthing;
drops there and snatches again, drops and again snatches
its broken toys, its whitened pebbles and shells.

                                                 1946

Nigger's Leap, New England

The eastward spurs tip backward from the sun.
Night runs an obscure tide round cape and bay
and beats with boats of cloud up from the sea
against this sheer and limelit granite head.
Swallow the spine of range; be dark, O lonely air.   5
Make a cold quilt across the bone and skull
that screamed falling in flesh from the lipped cliff
and then were silent, waiting for the flies.

Here is the symbol, and the climbing dark
a time for synthesis. Night buoys no warning   10
over the rocks that wait our keels; no bells
sound for her mariners. Now must we measure
our days by nights, our tropics by their poles,
love by its end and all our speech by silence.
See in these gulfs, how small the light of home.   15

Did we not know their blood channelled our rivers,
and the black dust our crops ate was their dust?
O all men are one man at last. We should have known
the night that tided up the cliffs and hid them
had the same question on its tongue for us.   20
And there they lie that were ourselves writ strange.

Never from earth again the coolamon
or thin black children dancing like the shadows
of saplings in the wind. Night lips the harsh
scarp of the tableland and cools its granite.   25
Night floods us suddenly as history
that has sunk many islands in its good time.
                                                      1946

Woman to Man

The eyeless labourer in the night,
the selfless, shapeless seed I hold,
builds for its resurrection day—
silent and swift and deep from sight
foresees the unimagined light.   5

This is no child with a child's face;
this has no name to name it by:
yet you and I have known it well.
This is our hunter and our chase,
the third who lay in our embrace.   10

This is the strength that your arm knows,
the arc of flesh that is my breast,
the precise crystals of our eyes.
This is the blood's wild tree that grows
the intricate and folded rose.   15

This is the maker and the made;
this is the question and reply;
the blind head butting at the dark,
the blaze of light along the blade.
Oh hold me, for I am afraid.   20
                                                                1949

Eroded Hills

These hills my father's father stripped,
and beggars to the winter wind
they crouch like shoulders naked and whipped—
humble, abandoned, out of mind.

Of their scant creeks I drank once   5
and ate sour cherries from old trees
found in their gullies fruiting by chance.
Neither fruit nor water gave my mind ease.

I dream of hills bandaged in snow,
their eyelids clenched to keep out fear.   10
When the last leaf and bird go
let my thoughts stand like trees here.
                                                                1953

The Two Fires

Among green shades and flowering ghosts, the remembrances of love,
inventions of the holy unwearying seed,
bright falling fountains made of time, that bore
through time the holy seed that knew no time—
I tell you, ghosts in the ghosts of summer days,   5
you are dead as though you never had been.
For time has caught on fire, and you too burn:
leaf, stem, branch, calyx and the bright corolla
are now the insubstantial wavering fire
in which love dies: the final pyre   10
of the beloved, the bridegroom and the bride.
These two we have denied.

In the beginning was the fire;
Out of the death of fire, rock and the waters;
and out of water and rock, the single spark, the divine truth. 15

Far, far below, the millions of rock-years divide
to make a place for those who were born and died
to build the house that held the bridegroom and the bride.
Those two, who reigned in passion in the flower,
whom still the hollow seasons celebrate,   20
no ritual now can recreate.
Whirled separate in the man-created fire
their cycles end, with the cycle of the holy seed;
the cycle from the first to the last fire.
These too time can divide;   25
these too have died.

And walking here among the dying centuries—
the centuries of moss, of fern, of cycad,
of the towering tree—the centuries of the flower—
I pause where water falls from the face of the rock.   30
My father rock, do you forget the kingdom of the fire?
The aeons grind you into bread—
into the soil that feeds the living and transforms the dead;
and have we eaten in the heart of the yellow wheat
the sullen unforgetting seed of fire?   35

And now, set free by the climate of man's hate,
that seed sets time ablaze.
The leaves of fallen years, the forest of living days,
have caught like matchwood. Look, the whole world burns.
The ancient kingdom of the fire returns.   40
And the world, that flower that housed the bridegroom and the bride,
burns on the breast of night.
The world's denied.

                                                                      1955

At Cooloolah

The blue crane fishing in Cooloolah's twilight
has fished there longer than our centuries.
He is the certain heir of lake and evening,
and he will wear their colour till he dies,

but I'm a stranger, come of a conquering people.   5
I cannot share his calm, who watch his lake,
being unloved by all my eyes delight in,
and made uneasy, for an old murder's sake.

Those dark-skinned people who once named Cooloolah
knew that no land is lost or won by wars,   10
for earth is spirit: the invader's feet will tangle
in nets there and his blood be thinned by fears.

Riding at noon and ninety years ago,
my grandfather was beckoned by a ghost—
a black accoutred warrior armed for fighting,   15
who sank into bare plain, as now into time past.

White shores of sand, plumed reed and paperbark,
clear heavenly levels frequented by crane and swan—
I know that we are justified only by love,
but oppressed by arrogant guilt, have room for none.   20

And walking on clean sand among the prints
of bird and animal, I am challenged by a driftwood spear
thrust from the water; and, like my grandfather,
must quiet a heart accused by its own fear.

                                                                        1955

Eve to Her Daughters

It was not I who began it.
Turned out into draughty caves,
hungry so often, having to work for our bread,
hearing the children whining,
I was nevertheless not unhappy.   5
Where Adam went I was fairly contented to go.
I adapted myself to the punishment: it was my life.

But Adam, you know …!
He kept on brooding over the insult,
over the trick They had played on us, over the scolding.   10
He had discovered a flaw in himself
and he had to make up for it.
Outside Eden the earth was imperfect,
the seasons changed, the game was fleet-footed,
he had to work for our living, and he didn't like it.   15
He even complained of my cooking
(it was hard to compete with Heaven).

So he set to work.
The earth must be made a new Eden
with central heating, domesticated animals,   20
mechanical harvesters, combustion engines,
escalators, refrigerators,
and modern means of communication
and multiplied opportunities for safe investment
and higher education for Abel and Cain   25
and the rest of the family.
You can see how his pride had been hurt.

In the process he had to unravel everything,
because he believed that mechanism
was the whole secret—he was always mechanical-minded.   30
He got to the very inside of the whole machine
exclaiming as he went, So this is how it works!

And now that I know how it works, why, I must have invented it.
As for God and the Other, they cannot be demonstrated,
and what cannot be demonstrated   35
doesn't exist.
You see, he had always been jealous.

Yes, he got to the centre
where nothing at all can be demonstrated.
And clearly he doesn't exist; but he refuses   40
to accept the conclusion.
You see, he was always an egotist.

It was warmer than this in the cave;
there was none of this fall-out.
I would suggest, for the sake of the children,   45
that it's time you took over.

But you are my daughters, you inherit my own faults of character;
you are submissive, following Adam
even beyond existence.
Faults of character have their own logic   50
and it always works out.
I observed this with Abel and Cain.

Perhaps the whole elaborate fable
right from the beginning

is meant to demonstrate this; perhaps it's the whole secret.   55
Perhaps nothing exists but our faults?

But it's useless to make
such a suggestion to Adam.
He has turned himself into God,
who is faultless, and doesn't exist.   60
                                              1966

Memory

Yesterday wrapped me in wool; today drought's changeable weather
sends me down the path to swim in the river.

Three Decembers back, you camped here; your stone hearth
fills with twigs and strips peeled from the candlebark.

Where you left your tent, the foursquare patch is unhealed.   5
The roots of the kangaroo-grass have never sprouted again.

On the riverbank, dead cassinias crackle.
Wombat-holes are deserted in the dry beds of the creeks.

Even in mid-summer, the frogs aren't speaking.
Their swamps are dry. In the eggs a memory lasts.   10

They will talk again in a wet year, a year of mosquitoes.
The grass will seed on that naked patch of earth.

Now only two dragonflies dance on the narrowed water.
The river's noise in the stones is a sunken song.
                                              1985

Skins

This pair of skin gloves is sixty-six years old,
mended in places, worn thin across the knuckles.

Snakes get rid of their coverings all at once.
Even those empty cuticles trouble the passer-by.

Counting in seven-year rhythms I've lost nine skins   5
though their gradual flaking isn't so spectacular.

Holding a book or a pen I can't help seeing
how age crazes surfaces. Well, and interiors?

You ask me to read those poems I wrote in my thirties?
They dropped off several incarnations back.   10

1985

DAVID CAMPBELL
1915–1979

With Judith Wright, Roland Robinson and Douglas Stewart (qqv), David Campbell
was among a group of poets who returned to a rural and balladeering tradition in the
years after the Second World War. Vincent Buckley (qv) lamented this return, even as he
acknowledged that they brought to it a new formal sophistication as well as a pessimism,
informed in Campbell's case by his war service in the RAAF. Campbell flew many
missions over New Guinea and Timor, and 'Men in Green' is sourced directly from that
experience, as are his later short stories published in *Evening Under Lamplight* (1959).

Speak with the Sun (1949), his first collection of poetry, was acclaimed, and Campbell
won significant awards for his poetry, developing what Chris Wallace-Crabbe (qv) has called
a 'squatter pastoral'. He published more than fifteen books in thirty years. Philip Mead and
others note a distinct change in Campbell's work of the 1970s, however, in the wake of his
opposition to the Vietnam War, as his poetry became more experimental. *NM*

Men in Green

There were fifteen men in green,
Each with a tommy-gun,
Who leapt into my plane at dawn;
We rose to meet the sun.

Our course lay to the east. We climbed   5
Into the break of day,
Until the jungle far beneath
Like a giant fossil lay.

We climbed towards the distant range
Where two white paws of cloud   10
Clutched at the shoulders of the pass.
The green men laughed aloud.

They did not fear the ape-like cloud
That climbed the mountain crest
And rode the currents of the air   15
And hid the pass in mist.

They did not fear the summer's sun
In whose hot centre lie
A hundred hissing cannon shells
For the unwatchful eye.   20

And when at Dobadura we
Set down, each turned to raise
His thumb towards the open sky
In mockery and praise.

But fifteen men in jungle green   25
Rose from the kunai grass
To come aboard, and my green men
In silence watched them pass:
It seemed they looked upon themselves
In a prophetic glass.   30

There were some leaned on a stick
And some on stretchers lay,
But few walked on their own two feet
In the early green of day.

They had not feared the ape-like cloud   35
That climbed the mountain crest;
They had not feared the summer's sun
With bullets for their breast.

Their eyes were bright, their looks were dull,
Their skin had turned to clay.   40
Nature had met them in the night
And stalked them in the day.

And I think still of men in green
On the Soputa track
With fifteen spitting tommy-guns   45
To keep a jungle back.
                                                           1949

Winter

When magpies sing in sky and tree
And colts like dragons snuff the air
And frosts paint hollows white till three

And lamp-lit children skip their prayer;
Then Meg and Joan at midnight lie   5
And quake to hear the dingoes cry
Who nightly round the white church stone
Snap at their tails and the frosty moon.

When stockmen lapped in oilskin go
And lambing ewes on hill-tops bleat   10
And crows are out and rain winds blow
And kettles simmer at the grate;
Then Meg and Joan at midnight lie
And quake to hear the dingoes cry
Who nightly round the white church stone   15
Snap at their tails and the weeping moon.

                                       1949

Kelly Country

I POWER'S LOOKOUT

At Power's Lookout a boy
Chases his girl up iron rungs.
Eagle Rock drops one way
To the King River and tobacco crops.

Here a boy wagging school, young Ned,   5
Kept nit[1] and held a horse for Power:
The mild waistcoated bushranger
Gazes through camera and police,
His watchchain slipped below his knees.

Here Mrs Quinn drew in her breath;   10
And Aaron Sherritt thick as thieves
With Superintendent Hare,
Read in her Irish eyes his death.

Below, is that Quinn's peacock screams?
The sunset spreads its eastern tail   15
And gum-tree shadows slip behind the gums.

Giant pylons stalk from range to range,
The King is dammed. Make love not war.
Beyond the polished tourist rail
A young man lies beside his girl.   20

---

1   Kept watch.

II PEACOCK AT QUINN'S

Peacock
Be my eyes
Or with stretched neck
I shall die.

In the night spread   5
A zodiac
Of fine fire
Over your back.

With trembling fan
In the east   10
Like ironbark
Plant your feet.

In the thin shade
And blaze of noon
Be my hot sun,   15
My daylight moon.

Fold your wings
Like the purples
Vanishing
From hill to hill.   20

Peacock
Fire crowned,
Pride and men
Will bring you down.

III THE ELEVEN MILE CREEK

Eagles nest in a tall tree,
Swallows in a chimney.

Two chimneys of apricot
At the Eleven Mile the Kellys built.

The Eleven Mile Creek is black,   5
Through river-gums a face looks back.

Of river-gum they built their stable:
Two-foot slabs are serviceable.

Three horses nod therein:
The sun shines through wood and bone.   10

Two gnarled pears and a fig-tree
Gave sweet meat and milk to me.

Between twin hills as white as breasts
Violence and beauty have their nests.

Four eagle-nests in the one tree: 15
A country rich in poverty.

IV KELLY'S TREE: STRINGYBARK CREEK

A sense of silence listening.
Trees rub together. From the creek
The singing of the thrush is like
Sunlight in water over stone.

But from a trunk the words jump out: 5
Kelly shot Lonigan and death
Has still the power to still the breath.
A century takes you by the throat.

The horses' hooves move in the mind,
And who are we to plead or shout?   10
The whip-bird cracks a rifle shot
And twice his mate replies in kind.

V GLENROWAN

They've burnt the grass beneath the pepper-trees
Where Mrs Jones' hotel
Once flared between the railway and the hill.
A roadsign says *Police.*

Under the trees there is a dump for cars: 5
Their wry pathetic shells
Stripped and forgotten, rust among old bottles,
Victims of other wars.

Behind stand two new churches. As the hard
Dawn tips the steepled hills,   10
On time the *Spirit* yells upon its rails,
Passing the scrapper's yard.

VI IF IT MOVES

If it moves,
Draw a bead.
There's a price
On the hawk's head.

There's a ghost   5
In the squatters' oats:
A shilling a scalp
For bandicoots.

They nailed the fox
To the jail door   10
For dodging pullets
In the green dawn.

They tied Ned's eyes
With a handkerchief:
His dying words were,   15
'Such is life!'

They hanged Kelly
Until he was dead:
Businessmen
Sleep quiet in bed.   20

'If I'd my way
I'd shoot or hang
All thinking men
While they are young.'

                                                                1974

The Australian Dream

The doorbell buzzed. It was past three o'clock.
The steeple-of-Saint-Andrew's weathercock
Cried silently to darkness, and my head

Was bronze with claret as I rolled from bed
To ricochet from furniture. Light! Light   5
Blinded the stairs, the hatstand sprang upright,
I fumbled with the lock, and on the porch
Stood the Royal Family with a wavering torch.

'We hope,' the Queen said, 'we do not intrude.
The pubs were full, most of our subjects rude.   10
We came before our time. It seems the Queen's
Command brings only, "Tell the dead marines!"
We've come to you.' I must admit I'd half
Expected just this visit. With a laugh
That put them at their ease, I bowed my head.   15
'Your Majesty is most welcome here,' I said.
'My home is yours. There is a little bed
Downstairs, a boiler-room, might suit the Duke.'
He thanked me gravely for it and he took
Himself off with a wave. 'Then the Queen Mother?   20
She'd best bed down with you. There is no other
But my wide bed. I'll curl up in a chair.'
The Queen looked thoughtful. She brushed out her hair
And folded up *The Garter* on a pouf.
'Distress was the first commoner, and as proof   25
That queens bow to the times,' she said, 'we three
Shall share the double bed. Please follow me.'

I waited for the ladies to undress—
A sense of fitness, even in distress,
Is always with me. They had tucked away   30
Their state robes in the lowboy; gold crowns lay
Upon the bedside tables; ropes of pearls
Lassoed the plastic lampshade; their soft curls
Were spread out on the pillows and they smiled.
'Hop in,' said the Queen Mother. In I piled   35
Between them to lie like a stick of wood.
I couldn't find a thing to say. My blood
Beat, but like rollers at the ebb of tide.
'I hope your Majesties sleep well,' I lied.
A hand touched mine and the Queen said, 'I am   40
Most grateful to you, Jock. Please call me Ma'am.'

1978

MANNING CLARK
1915–1991

Charles Manning Hope Clark, probably Australia's most famous historian, is the author of the epic *A History of Australia* (six volumes, 1962–87), which covers Australian history from 1788 to 1945. Clark was educated at the universities of Melbourne and Oxford, and was professor of history at the ANU (1949–75). He was an especially literary historian. His tone was often prophetic and he relied heavily on the Bible, the Book of Common Prayer and Western literature (especially the classic Russian novelists). His history, which relies on large themes and symbols, such as the clash between the 'Old Dead Tree' of European culture and the 'Young Tree Green' of Australian nationalism, has attracted numerous admirers and detractors. In part this was because of his partisan politics. In 1960 he published a sympathetic account of his travels in the Soviet Union, and by the 1970s he was a supporter of the Labor Party. As well as history, Clark wrote a biography of Henry Lawson, a collection of short stories, and three volumes of autobiography, the first volume of which, *The Puzzles of Childhood* (1989), was especially successful. He was named Australian of the Year in 1980. In 1988 the unlikely *Manning Clark's History of Australia: A musical* was produced, and in 1993 Michael Cathcart abridged the six-volume history. *DM*

From *A History of Australia*
Volume 1, Chapter 3: The Sons of Enlightenment

[. . .] The *Endeavour* sailed from Plymouth on 26 August 1768, for which day the entry [Captain] Cook wrote in his diary sharpens the contrast between him and his predecessors, whether from Catholic or Protestant Christendom. For where Magellan's and Quiros' men had taken the sacrament, and Tasman had beseeched God Almighty to vouchsafe His blessing on his work, Cook recorded the facts: 'At 2 p.m. got under sail and put to sea . . .' They rounded the Horn and sailed for Tahiti, arriving there on 12 April 1769. While the scientists observed the transit of Venus, Cook spent much of his time observing the life of the natives, measuring it as he put it against the first principles of human nature. For Cook wrote of this people, not with that enthusiasm or delight of a man who believed civilization was an evil, or that noble savages had preserved the secret of human happiness, but rather with a strong inclination to insert in his journal every scrap of knowledge he could obtain of a people who for many centuries had been shut off from almost every other part of the world.

All the early observers of the Tahitians tended to project on to them the tensions in their own minds. Bougainville, who was less driven than Cook to dispense praise or blame, noted their addiction to spending their whole lives in pleasure, which gave them a marked taste for that gentle raillery born of ease and joy. It also gave their character a degree of levity which astonished the Frenchmen daily, for the slightest degree of reflection seemed unbearable toil to them, and they avoided fatigue of the mind even more than fatigue of the body. The missionaries on the *Duff*, who arrived at Tahiti in 1797, saw them in quite a different light. These men believed that man at the beginning of the world had been seduced by Satan to eat of the fruit of a tree and, having thereby lost the image of God, had involved the whole human race in ruin and imparted to it a nature wholly corrupted and depraved. They found the Tahitians dissolute, and their society a sink of lewdness and cruelty. On the day they first mentioned the name of the saviour of mankind from the consequences of this transgression, they sang to them the hymn: 'O'er the gloomy hills of darkness'.

Some of these missionaries settled in Sydney in 1798, where they influenced Protestant attitudes to primitive people—to the aborigines, the Maoris, and the Pacific islanders. It was not until Cook reached the east coast of New Holland that he was ready to put down on paper his thoughts on the advantages of the life of a savage over those of a civilized human being. While at Tahiti he confined himself to such a generalization as that the mysteries of most religions were very dark and not easily understood even by those who professed them.

On 15 August 1769 he decided to stand directly to the southward from Tahiti in search of the southern continent, though not expecting to find one, for paradoxically enough, Cook was one of the greatest sceptics concerning its very existence. From 15 August on they sighted nothing till 7 October, when Cook, the man of coolness and precision, noted in his journal: 'At 2 p.m. saw land from the mast head bearing WBN.' That was Poverty Bay, on the south-east coast of the north island of New Zealand. Cook spent from October 1769 to March 1770 charting the coasts of the two islands of New Zealand, and making occasional entries in his journal on the way of life and beliefs of the Maoris, though again, as at Tahiti, the experience did not stimulate in his mind any comparison between the savage and the civilized. By March, having finished his work on the coasts of New Zealand, he began to turn over in his mind the route to be followed on the way home.

To go by Cape Horn had its attractions as by taking this route he would have been able to prove or disprove the existence of a southern continent, which, he added with his customary dry scepticism on that point, yet remained doubtful. But the Cape Horn route would have meant sailing in a high latitude in the very depth of winter, and the condition of the ship was not thought sufficient for such an undertaking. No human discomfort could influence the intrepid Cook. To sail direct to the Cape of Good Hope was laid aside as no discovery of any moment could be hoped for in that route. After consulting the officers, Cook resolved to return by way of the East Indies, by the following route: to steer westward until they fell in with the east coast of New Holland (a name also used by the Dutch for the Southland from as early as the 1630s). He was then to follow the direction of that coast till they arrived at its northern extremity, or if this were found to be impracticable, to fall in with the lands or islands discovered by Quiros.

So Cook sailed westward. One fact which he omitted to mention in his discussion of his motives, was that on the *Endeavour* he had a map on which a dotted line traced the course of Torres in 1607, for just as the mysteries of religions may be very dark, so are the motives which move men to those decisions from which flow such singular events as the coming of European civilization to Australia.

Again chance played its part. Cook was sailing for the east coast of Van Diemen's Land, but the great swell of the ocean nudged the *Endeavour* northwards. On 17 April 1770 a small land bird was seen to perch upon the rigging, but Cook, as unromantic as ever about significance or possibility, sandwiched this in between his nautical observations. Two days later they sighted land, but again Cook restricted himself to a typical cautious aside on the unlikelihood of land between Van Diemen's Land and New Holland, adding modestly that anyone who compared his journal with that of Tasman would be as good a judge as he. 'I have Named it *Point* Hicks,' Cook wrote in his journal, 'because Leuit [*sic*] Hicks was the first who discover'd this land.' Again he used the simple language of the observer; for Cook, the occasion demanded neither majesty of language nor sanguine sentiments. He then sailed northward looking for a place to land, and on 28 April at last decided on a place which appeared to be tolerably well sheltered from the winds, but ran into difficulty in deciding on a name. He plumped first for Sting-ray's Harbour, Botanist Harbour, and Botanist Bay, before finally choosing Botany Bay on Sunday, 6 May.

On 29 April, just after one of the aborigines threw a stone at the small boat as a mark of their resolution to oppose a landing, Cook replied with light musket shot, while the wives and children of the aborigines on the beaches set up a most horrid howl. In this way the European began his tragic association with the aborigines on the east coast. A few minutes later Cook turned to Isaac Smith: 'Isaac, you shall land first', and the white man waded ashore.

From 29 April to 6 May they examined the hinterland of Botany Bay, finding in many places a deep black soil which produced, besides timber, as fine meadow as ever was seen and which Cook believed was capable of producing any kind of grain. This burst of enthusiasm was to perplex all subsequent visitors to Botany Bay as well as to embarrass those who wanted to raise Cook above criticism as an observer, though this temporary aberration was destined to carry more weight than his cautious summing up after passing the northern extremity of the coast. During his stay in Botany Bay, Cook caused the English colours to be displayed ashore every day and an inscription to be cut upon one of the trees near the watering place setting forth the ship's name, and the date of their arrival. So the English began their ceremonies in Australia, though, apart from Cook's own words and the diaries of his companions, the sole memorial of their coming lived on in the minds of the aborigines, who weaved into the songs in which they commemorated the story of their people the memory of the winged bird which came over the mighty ocean, and, they believed, would one day return. But they were the only ones to entertain such a faith at the time.

For on 6 May, having decided that they had seen everything this place afforded, Cook weighed anchor and sailed north, noting that at latitude 33° 50' by observation they were abreast of a bay or harbour wherein there appeared to be safe anchorage, which he called Port Jackson. Between Botany Bay and the northern extremity they landed at Bustard Bay, Thirsty Sound and Endeavour River, by which time the rigour of their experiences, the harshness of the country and the implacable hostility of the aborigines almost certainly caused those more unfavourable comments by Cook which contrast sharply with the cry of delight he had allowed himself during those halcyon autumn days at Botany Bay, when they were recuperating after the green swell and swing of the Tasman Sea.

On 22 August 1770 at Possession Island, off the northern tip of Cape York peninsula, having satisfied himself that New Guinea was separate from New Holland, acknowledging he could make no new discoveries on the west coast the honour of which belonged to the Dutch navigators, and being confident that the eastern coast had never been seen or visited by any European before them, Cook hoisted the English colours and in the name of His Majesty King George III took possession of the whole eastern coast from the latitude of 38° south to Possession Island by the name of New South Wales, and fired three volleys of small arms which were answered by a like number from the ship. From that day the western half of Australia was known as New Holland, and the eastern half as New South Wales; it was still unknown whether a passage divided them, or whether a passage divided Van Diemen's Land from New South Wales.

Between Cape York and Timor, Cook summed up in his journal his impressions of the country and the aborigines. In his remarks on the country he distinguished between its condition in a state of nature, and what it might become at the hand of industry. In its state of nature the land was indifferently watered and indifferently fertile; the trees were hard and ponderous and could not be applied to many purposes. By nature the land produced hardly anything fit for man to eat; nor did it produce any one thing that could become an article in trade to invite Europeans to fix a settlement upon it. Yet to Cook this eastern side was not that barren and miserable country that Dampier and others had described the western side to be. Fruits and roots of every kind would flourish were they once brought thither and planted and cultivated by the hand of industry, as there was provender for more cattle at all seasons of the year than ever could be brought into the country. Substitute sheep for cattle, and this becomes a prophecy in broad outline of the pastoral period in the history of Australia.

At that time, however, Cook alone entertained hopes of turning the hard rock into a standing water by the hand of industry. The sameness and the barrenness had overwhelmed the other articulate ones on the *Endeavour.* Banks complained of the sameness to be observed in the face of the country, that its soil was uncommon barren and so far devoid of the helps derived from cultivation as not to be supposed to yield much towards the support of man. Another man on the *Endeavour* described the shore as barbarous and inhospitable.

To the Aborigines they felt more kindly. Of their character Cook wrote with surprising fondness: a timorous and inoffensive race, he found them, in no ways inclinable to cruelty. Of their achievements in culture he wrote more unfavourably, finding their tools very bad, their houses mean small hovels not much bigger than an oven, and their canoes very bad and mean. Then, in a passage for which the reader of his journal is not prepared by any previous hints, Cook, in words befitting the majesty of his theme, reflected on the connection between the way of life of the aborigines and human happiness:

> From what I have seen of the Natives of New-Holland, they may appear to some to be the most wretched people upon Earth, but in reality they are far more happier than we Europeans; being wholy unacquainted not only with the superfluous but the necessary Conveniencies so much sought after in Europe, they are happy in not knowing the use of them. They live in a Tranquillity which is not disturb'd by the Inequality of Condition: The Earth and sea of their own accord furnishes them with all things necessary for life, they covet not Magnificent Houses, Household-stuff &c, they live in a warm and fine Climate and enjoy a very wholesome Air, so that they have very little need of Clothing and this they seem to be fully sencible of, for many to whome we gave Cloth &c to, left it carlessly upon the Sea beach and in the woods as a thing they had no manner of use for. In short they seem'd to set no Value upon any thing we gave them, nor would they ever part with any thing of their own for any one article we could offer them; this in my opinion argues that they think themselves provided with all the necessarys of Life and that they have no superfluities.

Cook wrote these words on the eve of a declaration in another place that all men had a right to pursue happiness, when the high-minded were dreaming of those better things in what had hitherto been accepted as a vale of tears, while others subscribed to the view that civilization was the enemy of human happiness. For the achievement has informed his words with an occasional majesty, just as it has puffed up that flaw in his make-up, that point where the hand of the potter faltered.

On 22 October 1770 they arrived at Batavia, where Cook again essayed a generalization that whoever gave a faithful account of this place must in many things contradict all the authors he had had the opportunity to consult. But most of the time there his mind was on quite other things: on repairs to the ship, and on the well-being of his crew, for Batavia threatened to take a terrible toll on health, even on life. They left at last on 26 December for the Cape of Good Hope. As the ship rose and fell on the green swell of the Indian Ocean, events in Asia and North America were preparing the way for the voyage to acquire a significance which no member of the crew could ever have pondered. In India and the Indonesian archipelago a new era of territorial conquest and occupation had begun in response to the change in the economic use of those areas to the commercial companies exploiting their wealth. During the long pull home after rounding the Cape of Good Hope they heard again of news from the English colonies in America, as they had heard earlier in Batavia that the American disputes were made up. So Cook, almost at journey's end, brushed up against an event, or the prelude to an event, which was to lead to an attempt to found a penal colony at Botany Bay, on the site of that meadow as fine as ever was seen. He was brushing up against the prelude to an event in which a new vision of human life was to be brought to birth. In this vision all men were born equal, and all men had a right to life, liberty and the pursuit of happiness. By which they did not mean that happiness, that hope of re-union with God, which had inspired Quiros, nor that happiness which Cook had detected in the aborigine, but a happiness here on earth, a vision of a day when men should neither hurt nor destroy. This new vision of human life was emerging as Cook sailed home from a country in which the European would in time rejoice in its promise, and dream that this millennial Eden was actually drawing nigh.

But no such thoughts, no such hopes, crossed Cook's mind as he anchored in the Downs on Saturday 13 July 1771 and, as he put it, 'soon after I landed in order to repair to London'. With this simple statement he characteristically ended his journal, adding later a postscript on how to search for a southern continent, supposing it were to exist.

1962

YIRRKALA PEOPLE

Situated in Arnhem Land on the north-eastern tip of the NT, Yirrkala is a small community of predominantly Yolngu people. In 1963, Prime Minister Robert Menzies announced that 390 square kilometres of Yirrkala land would be leased to a bauxite mining company. The Yirrkala people protested the lease by presenting a petition to the Commonwealth Parliament signed by seventeen elders. Typed on paper in both

Yolngu and English, the petition was glued to a sheet of stringy-bark bordered by paintings expressing Yirrkala law. The petition protested the government's secrecy and failure to consult, and requested an inquiry into the lease. A parliamentary committee acknowledged the Yirrkala people's moral rights to their land, but failed to stop the mine. As the first traditional document by an Aboriginal community to be recognised in the Australian Parliament, the Yirrkala Bark Petition represents the first recognition in Australian law of Aboriginal language and culture. *AH/PM*

Yirrkala Bark Petition

The Humble Petition of the Undersigned Aboriginal people of Yirrkala, being members of the Balamumu, Narrkala, Gapiny and Miliwurrwurr people and Djapu, Mangalili, Madarrpa, Magarrwanalinirri, Gumatj, Djambarrpuynu, Marrakula, Galpu, Dhaluaya, Wangurri, Warramirri, Maymil, Rirrtjinu tribes, respectfully sheweth.

1. That nearly 500 people of the above tribes are residents of the land excised from the Aboriginal Reserve in Arnhem Land.

2. That the procedures of the excision of this land and the fate of the people on it were never explained to them beforehand, and were kept secret from them.

3. That when Welfare Officers and Government officials came to inform them of decisions taken without them and against them, they did not undertake to convey to the Government in Canberra the views and feelings of the Yirrkala Aboriginal people.

4. That the land in question has been hunting and food gathering land for the Yirrkala tribes from time immemorial; we were all born here.

5. That places sacred to the Yirrkala people, as well as vital to their livelihood are in the excised land, especially Melville Bay.

6. That the people of this area fear that their needs and interests will be completely ignored as they have been ignored in the past, and they fear that the fate which has overtaken the Larrakeah tribe will overtake them.

7. And they humbly pray that the Honourable the House of Representatives will appoint a Committee, accompanied by competent interpreters, to hear the views of the people of Yirrkala before permitting the excision of this land.

8. They humbly pray that no arrangements be entered into with any company which will destroy the livelihood and independence of the Yirrkala people.

And your petitioners as in duty bound will ever pray God to help you and us. (English translation)

Bukudjulni gonga'yurru napurrunha Yirrkalalili Yulnunha malanha Balamumu, Narrkala, Gapiny, Miliwurrwurr nanapurru dhuwala mala, ga Djapu, Mangalili, Madarrpa, Magarrwanalinirri, Djambarrpuynu, Gumaitj, Marrakula, Galpu,

Dhabuayu, Wangurri, Warramirri, Maymil, Ririfjinu malamanapanmirri djal dhunapa.

1. *Dhuwala yulnu mala galki 500 nhina ga dhiyala wananura. Dhuwala wanga Arnhem Land yurru djaw'yunna naburrungala.*

2. *Dhuwala wanga djaw'yunna ga nhaltjana yurru yulnungunydja dhiyala wanga nura nhaltjanna dhu dharrpanna yulnu walandja yakana lakarama madayangumuna.*

3. *Dhuwala nunhi Welfare Officers ga Government bungawa lakarama yulnuwa malanuwa nhaltjarra nhuma gana wanganaminha yaka nula napurrungu lakarama wlala yaka'lakarama Government-gala nunhala Canberra nhaltjanna napurruga guyana yulnuyu Yirrkala.*

4. *Dhuwala wänga napurrungyu balanu Iarrunarawu napurrungu näthawa, guyawu, miyspunuwu, maypalwu nunhi napurru gana nhinana bitjarrayi näthilimirri, napurru dhawalguyanana dhiyala wänganura.*

5. *Dhuwala wänga yurru dharpalnha yurru yulnuwalandja malawala, ga dharrpalnha dhuwala bala yulnuwuyndja nhinanharawu Melville Bathurru wänga balandayu djaw'yun nyumukunin.*

6. *Dhuwala yulnundja mala yurru nhämana balandawunu nha mulkurru nhämä yurru moma ga darangan yalalanumirrinha nhaltjanna dhu napurru bitjarra nhakuna Larrakeahyu momara wlalanguwuy wänga.*

7. *Nuli dhu bungawayu House of Representatives djaw'yn yulnuwala näthili yurru nha dhu lakarama interpreteryu bungawawala yulnu matha, yurru nha dhu djaw'yun dhuwala wängandja.*

8. *Nunhiyina dhu märrlayun marrama'-ndja nhinanharawu yulnuwu marrnamathinyarawu. Dhuwala napurru yulnu mala yurru liyamirriyama bitjan bili marr yurru napurru hha gonga' yunna wangarr'yu.*

(Australian *matha* original)

1963

NARRITJIN MAYMURU
c. 1916–1981

A prominent member of the Maymuru family, Manggali clan—bark painters, printmakers and sculptors of north-eastern Arnhem Land, NT—Narritjin (Narrijin) was active in developing relationships between the Yolngu and outsiders. He worked for a pearler and for the missionary Wilbur Chaseling and produced paintings for the anthropologist Ronald Berndt. In the 1950s he lived in Darwin. Narritjin helped to paint the Yirrkala Bark Petition presented to the House of Representatives in 1963. After mining was established at Nhulunbuy in 1971, he worked with film-maker Ian Dunlop to document Yolngu life. In 1978, with his son Banapana, Narritjin was offered a Visiting Artistic Fellowship at the Australian National University. He played a major role in encouraging women to produce sacred paintings and his daughters became well-known painters. *AH/PM*

Letter to Mr H.E. Giese, Director of Aboriginal Welfare, NT

Mr Gise who looking after for all the Aborigines in the N.T. We want to help us belong to this country Yirrkala, please Mr Gise? Because the Maining campany will be here soon. All the Aborigines in Yirrkala are wondering about this country. What we are going to do Mr Gise? You think us a funny? or you think us a good people. You going to help us Mr Gise? or no. These maining people will chasing us to other places, we don't like that. Please sir? We like Yirrkala best. This is a word for all the people in Yirrkala. We want Yirrk. open country. So we may go hunting for meat. We don't like the maining campany will come close to the Mission area, please Mr Gise? Our children are in school. They will grow up belong to this country. They may [tell] us what they were learned in school. They will help the fathers, mothers, sisters, brothers, or their relations about the white man laws, white man way to living, white man ways to eat. White man way to cook, and wash our plates. This time we don't understand about the white man ways yet. We going to ask you for this country Yirrkala. We are don't like to come near to the Mission. If the maining people like to use this country, alright they will stay away from the Mission, Mr Gise? This is a words for Narrijin and all the Aborigines in Yirrkala Mission, says this.

Thankyou Mr Gise, Goodbye.

1963

JESSICA ANDERSON
b. 1916

Novelist and short-story writer Jessica Anderson was born Jessica Queale in Gayndah, Queensland, and was educated in Brisbane. She then moved to Sydney where she has lived ever since, apart from a few years in London. During the 1960s and '70s she worked on the adaptation of literary works for radio and wrote original radio dramas. She is the mother of screenwriter Laura Jones, who was born in 1951.

Anderson's first novel, *An Ordinary Lunacy*, was published in 1963; her second was a crime novel, *The Last Man's Head* (1970). In her third novel Anderson shifted from crime to historical fiction and produced the extraordinarily subtle and powerful *The Commandant* (1975), a fictionalised account of the murder of the notorious Captain Patrick Logan, commandant of the Moreton Bay penal settlement, in 1830. The story is seen and told through the eyes of the female characters, particularly Logan's wife Letty and her sister Frances; the white women of the settlement function as mediators between the strictness and inflexibility of the military command and the uncontrollable forces of the convicts and the Aborigines. Anderson's experience as a radio dramatist stands her in good stead in this novel, where pauses, hints and silences must often suffice as a means of communication.

But it was the publication of *Tirra Lirra by the River* in 1978 that made Anderson's name well known nationally. This is a brilliantly crafted, jewel-like novella narrated by its elderly heroine, Nora, who has come home to Brisbane after spending most of her adult life in London. The story is about Nora's quest for 'real life' as she imagines it, symbolised by Europe and by the life of art; it shifts back and forth in time as Nora's memory, jarred by age and illness, takes her back to her childhood, her painful marriage, her years away from Australia, and her life's work as a dressmaker and designer.

The Impersonators (1980) continues the theme of the relationship between Australia and Europe and the way that individual lives are shaped by attitudes towards them, particularly in the lives of women. Stories from the Warm Zone (1987) again features Anderson's preoccupation with the relationship between place and experience, juxtaposing semi-autobiographical stories set in Brisbane in the 1920s with stories set in Sydney 60 years later. Her last book was the novel One of the Wattle Birds (1994), after which she expressed her intention to write no more fiction. KG

From *Tirra Lirra by the River*

[...] It is wonderful to be able to stop smiling. I feel that ever since setting foot in Australia I have been smiling, and saying, 'Thank you' and 'So kind'. I have one rather contemptible characteristic. In fact, I have many. But never mind the others now. The one I am talking about is my tendency to be a bit of a toady. Whenever I am in an insecure position, that is what happens. I massage the smile from my face by pressing the flesh with my fingertips, over and over again, as I used to do when I had that facelift, all those years ago. I long more than ever for that hot bath, but am too tired to move. I am troubled, too, by guilt, because I was irritable with Jack Cust, who was so kind. I shut my eyes, and when, after a few minutes, I open them again, I find myself looking through the glass on to a miniature landscape of mountains and valleys with a tiny castle, weird and ruined, set on one slope.

That is what I was looking for. But it is not richly green, as it used to be in the queer drenched golden light after the January rains, when these distortions in the cheap thick glass gave me my first intimation of a country as beautiful as those in my childhood books. I would kneel on a chair by this window, and after finding the required angle of vision, such as I found just now by accident, I would keep very still, afraid to move lest I lose it. I was deeply engrossed by those miniature landscapes, green, wet, romantic, with silver serpentine rivulets, and flashing lakes, and castles moulded out of any old stick or stone. I believe they enchanted me. Kneeling on that chair, I was scarcely present at all. My other landscape had absorbed me. And later, when I was mad about poetry, and I read The Idylls of the King and The Lady of Shallot,[1] and so on and so forth, I already had my Camelot. I no longer looked through the glass. I no longer needed to. In fact, to do so would have broken rather than sustained the spell, because that landscape had become a region of my mind, where infinite expansion was possible, and where no obtrusion, such as the discomfort of knees imprinted by the cane of a chair, or a magpie alighting on the grass and shattering the miniature scale, could prevent the emergence of Sir Lancelot.

1   Poems by Alfred, Lord Tennyson (1809–92).

From underneath his helmet flowed
His coal-black curls as on he rode,
As he rode down to Camelot.
From the bank and from the river
He flashed into the crystal mirror,
'Tirra lirra,' by the river
Sang Sir Lancelot.

The book was one of my father's. It used to open at the right page because I had marked the place with a twist of silk-worm floss, a limp and elongated figure-of-eight. Many readings must have been necessary to drive it into my mind so that I still retain it, because I was—am—a person of undisciplined mind, and in spite of the passion I had for poetry, I could seldom hold more than a few consecutive lines in my head. The poetry in my head was like a jumble of broken jewellery. Couplets, fragments, bits of bright alliteration, and some dark assonance. These, like Sir Lancelot's helmet and his helmet feather, burned like one burning flame together. Often, I used to walk by the river, the real river half a mile from the house. It was broad, brown, and strong, and as I walked beside it I hardly saw it, and never used it as a location for my dreams. Sometimes it overran its banks, and when the flood water receded, mud would be left in all the broad hollows and narrow clefts of the river flats. As soon as this mud became firm, short soft thick tender grass would appear on its surface, making on the green paddocks streaks and ovals of a richer green. One moonlit night, coming home across the paddocks from Olive Partridge's house, I threw down my music case, dropped to the ground, and let myself roll into one of these clefts. I unbuttoned my blouse, unlaced my bodice, and rolled over and over in the sweet grass. I lay on my back and looked first at the moon, then down my cheeks at the peaks of my breasts. My breasts did not have (nor did they ever develop) obtrusive nipples, but the moon was so bright that I could clearly distinguish the two pink discs that surmounted them. I fell into a prolonged trance. I heard the sound of trampling and tearing, but it seemed to come from a long way off. I was astonished when I saw the horse moving along the edge of the cleft. I see him now, a big bay, walking slowly and pulling grass with thievish and desperate-looking jerks of his head. When he had passed I jumped to my feet and quickly laced my bodice. I buttoned my blouse and tucked it into my skirt. My brown hair ribbon lay shining on the grass where my head had been. It was before I put my hair up. I must have been less than sixteen.

I wish I had recalled the incident earlier. I should have liked to have recounted it at number six. It would have had to be told at a time when Fred was not there. Fred had that horror of what he called 'fuggy female talk', and although he made a great comedy of it, we all knew that those exaggerated sour mouths, and all that hissing and head-ducking, covered a real detestation, and so we were careful to spare him. No, I should never have recounted the incident in his presence. It would have been told when he was out, or downstairs, and we three were gossiping in Liza's quarters, perhaps, before her new electric fire. And after I had finished, I know what Hilda and Liza would have said. I can hear Liza's voice, with its touch of dogmatism.

'Of course, Nora, you were looking for a lover.'

And Hilda. 'But of course! As girls did in those days, without even knowing it.'

And I would probably have said, yes, of course, because in these times, when sexuality is so very fashionable, it is easy to believe that it underlies all our actions. But really, though I am quite aware of the sexual nature of the incident, I don't believe I was looking for a lover. Or not only for a lover. I believe I was also trying to match that region of my mind, Camelot.

If that sounds laughable, do consider that this was a long time ago, and that I was a backward and innocent girl, living in a backward and unworldly place. And consider, too, that the very repression of sex, though it produced so much that was warped and ugly and cruel, let loose for some natures, briefly, a luminosity, a glow, that I expect is unimaginable now, and that for those natures, it was possible to love and value that glow far beyond the fire that was its origin.

I am going to put down a strange word. Beauty. I was in love with beauty. [...]

1978

JAMES McAULEY
1917–1976

James McAuley rose to prominence in Australian poetry as one of the two perpetrators of the Ern Malley (qv) hoax, drawing on his training in symbolism and surrealism to create a plausible oeuvre for Malley, in order to debunk such modernism. His own first volume, *Under Aldebaran* (1946), demonstrated his skills in both satire and symbolism, which were turned to more specific ends in his middle years with several faith-inspired volumes. His late poetry evidenced a new phase, in four collections which were more humane and worldly, and displayed a detailed appreciation of the Tasmanian landscape.

After his conversion to Catholicism in 1952, McAuley became a dominating conservative figure in Australian cultural life. He was founding editor of *Quadrant*, the magazine of the Australian Congress for Cultural Freedom, which controversially sourced its funding from the CIA for a period. *The End of Modernity: Essays on literature, art and culture* (1959) argued for the need for a return to spiritualism and divine inspiration in poetry, while elsewhere McAuley proselytised more broadly. Appointed as reader in English at the University of Tasmania in 1961, he later assumed the chair and contributed significant scholarly work to the field of Australian literary studies. *NM*

Envoi

There the blue-green gums are a fringe of remote disorder
And the brown sheep poke at my dreams along the hillsides;
And there in the soil, in the season, in the shifting airs,
Comes the faint sterility that disheartens and derides.

Where once was a sea is now a salty sunken desert,   5
A futile heart within a fair periphery;
The people are hard-eyed, kindly, with nothing inside them,
The men are independent but you could not call them free.

And I am fitted to that land as the soul is to the body,
I know its contractions, waste, and sprawling indolence;   10
They are in me and its triumphs are my own,
Hard-won in the thin and bitter years without pretence.

Beauty is order and good chance in the artesian heart
And does not wholly fail, though we impede;
Though the reluctant and uneasy land resent   15
The gush of waters, the lean plough, the fretful seed.

                                                                    1946

Terra Australis

Voyage within you, on the fabled ocean,
And you will find that Southern Continent,
De Quiros'[1] vision—his hidalgo heart
And mythical Australia, where reside
All things in their imagined counterpart.   5

It is your land of similes; the wattle
Scatters its pollen on the doubting heart;
The flowers are wide-awake; the air gives ease;
There you come home; the magpies call you Jack
And whistle like larrikins at you from the trees.   10

And there, too, the angophora preaches on the hillsides
With the gestures of Moses; and the white cockatoo,
Perched on his limbs, screams with demoniac pain;

---

1   Pedro Fernandes de Queirós (1563–1615), a Portuguese seaman and explorer. In 1605–06 he led an
    expedition that crossed the Pacific in search of Terra Australis.

And who shall say on what errand the insolent emu
Walks between morning and night on the edge of the plain? 15

And northward, in valleys of the fiery Goat
Where the sun like a centaur vertically shoots
His raging arrows with unerring aim,
Stand the ecstatic solitary pyres
Of unknown lovers, featureless with flame. 20

1946

Dialogue

There was a pattering in the rafters, mother,
My dreams were troubled by the sounds above.

—That is just a young man's fancy, son,
Lightly turning now to thoughts of love.

I heard things moving in the cellar, mother, 5
And once I thought that something touched my side.

—Your father used to hear those noises, son,
About the time that I became a bride.

And when I woke up in the cold dawn, mother,
The rats had come and eaten my face away. 10

—Never mind, my son, you'll get another,
Your father he had several in his day.

1946

St John's Park, New Town

Often I walk alone
Where bronze-green oaks embower
John Lee Archer's[1] tower
Of solid Georgian stone.

Tradition is held there, 5
Such as a land can own

---

1   John Lee Archer (1791–1852), architect and engineer, who was born in Ireland and emigrated to Tasmania
    in 1827, where he took up the position of Civil Engineer and Architect.

That hasn't much of one.
I care—but do I care?

Not if it means to turn
Regretful from the raw   10
Instant and its vow.

The past is not my law:
Queer, comical, or stern,
Our privilege is now.

                                                          1969

Credo

That each thing is a word
Requiring us to speak it:
From the ant to the quasar,
From clouds to ocean floor—

The meaning not ours, but found   5
In the mind deeply submissive
To the grammar of existence,
The syntax of the real;

So that alien is changed
To human, thing into thinking: 10
For the world's bare tokens
We pay golden coin,

Stamped with the king's image;
And poems are prophecy
Of a new heaven and earth,   15
A rumour of resurrection.

                                                          1969

Father, Mother, Son

From the domed head the defeated eyes peer out,
Furtive with unsaid things of a lifetime, that now
Cannot be said by that stiff half-stricken mouth
Whose words come hoarse and slurred, though the mind is sound.

To have to be washed, and fed by hand, and turned   5
This way and that way by the cheerful nurses,

Who joke, and are sorry for him, and tired of him:
All that is not the worst paralysis.

For fifty years this one thread—he has held
One gold thread of the vesture: he has said   10
Hail, holy Queen,[1] slightly wrong, each night in secret.
But his wife, and now a lifetime, stand between:

She guards him from his peace. Her love asks only
That in the end he must not seem to disown
Their terms of plighted troth. So he will make   15
For ever the same choice that he has made—

Unless that gold thread hold, invisibly.
I stand at the bed's foot, helpless like him;
Thinking of legendary Seth who made
A journey back to Paradise, to gain   20

The oil of mercy for his dying father.
But here three people smile, and, locked apart,
Prove by relatedness that cannot touch
Our sad geometry of family love.

                                                                          1969

JACK DAVIS
1917−2000

The grandfather of Aboriginal theatre, Jack Leonard Davis grew up at Yarloop, WA. His many plays and poems were inspired by the experiences of his family and the Noongar people—his mother was forcibly removed from her parents, and on the death of his father Davis was sent to Moore River Native Settlement to learn farming at the age of fourteen. He left after nine months, having experienced the appalling conditions in Aboriginal reserves that would be the focus of much of his work.

The young Davis worked as a stockman, boxer, horse breeder, train driver and truck driver. While living at the Brookton Aboriginal Reserve he started to learn the language and culture of his people. He discovered the details of his mother's family history, and later spent time in tribal society while working as a stockman.

Davis's writing spans the genres of drama, poetry, short fiction, autobiography and criticism, reflecting a lifelong commitment to Aboriginal literature and activism. He was the director of the Aboriginal Centre in Perth from 1967 to 1971 and became the first chair of the Aboriginal Lands Trust in WA. His first book of poetry was *The First-born and Other Poems* (1970). In 1973 he moved to Sydney to join the Aboriginal Publications Foundation as editor of *Identity*, soon moving the magazine back with him to Perth. He published further books of poetry and wrote a series of groundbreaking plays, such as

---

1   First words of the Catholic prayer, 'Salve, Regina'.

No Sugar (*1985/1986*), *Kullark* (*1979/1982*) and *The Dreamers* (*1982/1982*), defining modern Aboriginal theatre's exploration of colonisation and cultural dislocation, the search for identity and meaning by Aboriginal youth, and the clash of Aboriginal and white law. His works include *Jagardoo: Poems from Aboriginal Australia* (1977), *Honey Spot* (1987), *John Pat and Other Poems* (1988), *Barungin: Smell the wind* (1989), *A Boy's Life* (1991), *Black Life: Poems* (1992) and *Moorli and the Leprechaun* (1994).

Davis also made a significant contribution to Aboriginal literary life as a cultural activist and administrator. In the 1980s he co-founded the Aboriginal Writers, Oral Literature and Dramatists' Association, and was a member of the council of the Australian Institute of Aboriginal Studies and the Aboriginal Arts Board. Davis was named an Australian Living National Treasure in 1998. *AH/PM*

The First-born

Where are my first-born, said the brown land, sighing;
They came out of my womb long, long ago.
They were formed of my dust—why, why are they crying
And the light of their being barely aglow?

I strain my ears for the sound of their laughter.   5
Where are the laws and the legends I gave?
Tell me what happened, you whom I bore after.
Now only their spirits dwell in the caves.

You are silent, you cringe from replying.
A question is there, like a blow on the face.   10
The answer is there when I look at the dying,
At the death and neglect of my dark proud race.

                                                                     1970

The Black Tracker

He served mankind for many a year
Before the jeep or the wireless.
He walked, he loped, no thought of fear,
Keen-eyed, lithe and tireless.

He led Eyre[1] to the western plains;   5
He went with Burke and Wills;[2]
He put Nemarluk[3] back in chains:
He found the lost in the hills.

---

1   Edward John Eyre (1815–1901), English explorer of SA and WA.
2   Irishman Robert O'Hara Burke (1821–61) and Englishman William John Wills (1834–61) led an ill-fated expedition from Melbourne to the Gulf of Carpentaria (1860–61).
3   An Aboriginal warrior active in the NT during the early twentieth century.

He found hair and spittle dry:
He found the child with relief.   10
He heard a mother's joyful cry
Or a mother's wail of grief.

He found the lost one crawling south,
Miles away from the track.
He siphoned water, mouth to mouth,   15
And carried him on his back.

He heard the white man call him names,
His own race scoffing, jeering.
'A black man playing white man games,'
They laughed and pointed, sneering.   20

No monument of stone for him
In your park or civilized garden.
His deeds unsung, fast growing dim—
It's time you begged his pardon.

                                                   1970

Warru

Fast asleep on the wooden bench,
Arms bent under the weary head,
There in the dusk and the back-street stench
He lay with the look of the dead.

I looked at him, then back through the years,   5
Then knew what I had to remember—
A young man, straight as wattle spears,
And a kangaroo hunt in September.

We caught the scent of the 'roos on the rise
Where the gums grew on the Moore;[1]   10
They leaped away in loud surprise,
But Warru was fast and as sure.

He threw me the fire-stick, oh what a thrill!
With a leap he sprang to a run.

---

1   The government of WA administered Moore River Native Settlement near Mogumber between 1918
    and 1951.

He met the doe on the top of the hill,   15
And he looked like a king in the sun.

The wattle spear flashed in the evening light,
The kangaroo fell at his feet.
How I danced and I yelled with all my might
As I thought of the warm red meat.   20

We camped that night on a bed of reeds
With a million stars a-gleaming.
He told me tales of Noongar deeds
When the world first woke from dreaming.

He sang me a song, I clapped my hands,   25
He fashioned a needle of bone.
He drew designs in the river sands,
He sharpened his spear on a stone.

I will let you dream—dream on, old friend—
Of a boy and a man in September,   30
Of hills and stars and the river's bend—
Alas, that is all to remember.

                                                          1970

Integration

Let these two worlds combine,
Yours and mine.
The door between us is not locked,
Just ajar.
There is no need for the mocking   5
Or the mocked to stand afar
With wounded pride
Or angry mind,
Or to build a wall to crouch and hide,
To cry or sneer behind.   10

This is ours together,
This nation—
No need for separation.
It is time to learn.
Let us forget the hurt,   15
Join hands and reach
With hearts that yearn.

Your world and mine
Is small.
The past is done.   20
Let us stand together,
Wide and tall
And God will smile upon us each
And all
And everyone.   25
                                                   1970

Walker

To Kath[1]

Fight on, Sister, fight on,
Stir them with your ire.
Go forward, Sister, right on,
We need you by the fire.

Your mind is no flat desert place,   5
But like serrated spears;
You must lead the talk, talk for our race
And help dispel our fears.

You were not born to walk on by
Or rest in sheltered bower,   10
But to fight until the ink is dry,
Until the victory hour.
                                                   1978

ERN MALLEY

In 1944, Adelaide editor Max Harris opened a bundle of poems addressed to the modernist literary magazine, *Angry Penguins*. They had been forwarded to him by Ethel Malley, the sister of Ern Malley, who provided these details about her poet brother: born in Liverpool, England, in March 1918, he moved to Australia with his family in 1920 after his father's death; he was schooled in Sydney and had worked as a mechanic, and in Melbourne as an insurance salesman and watch repairer; he suffered from Graves disease, however, and returned to Sydney where he died in July 1943.

Ethel included seventeen poems designed to be read in sequence, as 'The Darkening Ecliptic', and asked for Harris's opinion. Harris was elated by them—they were exactly what his new magazine was looking for. He would publish all of them in a special issue,

---

1 Kath Walker, Aboriginal poet and activist also known as Oodgeroo Noonuccal (qv).

and commissioned the modernist artist Sidney Nolan to paint the cover. The Autumn 1944 issue of *Angry Penguins* introduced a new poet to the Australian scene with fanfare, including a lengthy critical piece on Malley from Harris.

In June 1944, however, poets James McAuley (qv) and Harold Stewart pounced. Ern Malley was a hoax. They had cobbled together his poetry from materials they had to hand, including a manual on mosquitoes, as well as their own classical training as poets, and had spiked it with a few give-away jokes. In their public explanation, published in the *Sun*, they declared it had been a 'serious literary statement' to debunk the principles of modernism. To further Harris's ignominy, the Malley issue was successfully prosecuted for obscenity under the South Australian *Police Act*.

Ironically, of course, Malley's suggestive, surrealist, pondering poetry has much to recommend it, especially for contemporary readers, and the notoriety has given it more life than the work of the hoaxers. Inspiring imitators, recreators and novelists such as Peter Carey (qv) in his novel *My Life as a Fake* (2003), the non-existent Ern Malley's contribution to Australian literature has been significant. *NM*

Dürer: Innsbruck, 1495

I had often, cowled in the slumberous heavy air,
Closed my inanimate lids to find it real,
As I knew it would be, the colourful spires
And painted roofs, the high snows glimpsed at the back,
All reversed in the quiet reflecting waters—   5
Not knowing then that Dürer perceived it too.
Now I find that once more I have shrunk
To an interloper, robber of dead men's dream,
I had read in books that art is not easy
But no one warned that the mind repeats   10
In its ignorance the vision of others. I am still
the black swan of trespass on alien waters.

1944

Night Piece

The swung torch scatters seeds
In the umbelliferous dark
And a frog makes guttural comment
On the naked and trespassing
Nymph of the lake.   5

The symbols were evident,
Though on park-gates
The iron birds looked disapproval
With rusty invidious beaks.

Among the water-lilies   10
A splash—white foam in the dark!
And you lay sobbing then
Upon my trembling intuitive arm.

                                                                    1944

Petit Testament

In the twenty-fifth year of my age
I find myself to be a dromedary
That has run short of water between
One oasis and the next mirage
And having despaired of ever   5
Making my obsessions intelligible
I am content at last to be
The sole clerk of my metamorphoses.
Begin here:

In the year 1943   10
I resigned to the living all collateral images
Reserving to myself a man's
Inalienable right to be sad
At his own funeral.
(Here the peacock blinks the eyes   15
of his multipennate tail.)
In the same year
I said to my love (who is living)
Dear we shall never be that verb
Perched on the sole Arabian Tree   20
Not having learnt in our green age to forget
The sins that flow between the hands and feet
(Here the Tree weep gum tears
Which are also real: I tell you
These things are real)   25
So I forced a parting
Scrubbing my few dingy words to brightness.

Where I have lived
The bed-bug sleeps in the seam, the cockroach
Inhabits the crack and the careful spider   30
Spins his aphorisms in the corner.
I have heard them shout in the streets

The chiliasms of the Socialist Reich
And in the magazines I have read
The Popular Front-to-Back.   35
But where I have lived
Spain weeps in the gutters of Footscray
Guernica is the ticking of the clock
The nightmare has become real, not as belief
But in the scrub-typhus of Mubo.   40

It is something to be at last speaking
Though in this No-Man's-language appropriate
Only to No-Man's-Land.
Set this down too:
I have pursued rhyme, image, and metre,   45
Known all the clefts in which the foot may stick,
Stumbled often, stammered,
But in time the fading voice grows wise
And seizing the co-ordinates of all existence
Traces the inevitable graph   50
And in conclusion:
There is a moment when the pelvis
Explodes like a grenade. I
Who have lived in the shadow that each act
Casts on the next act now emerge   55
As loyal as the thistle that in session
Puffs its full seed upon the indicative air.
I have split the infinite. Beyond is anything.

                                                                1944

VINCENT LINGIARI
1919–1988

Vincent Lingiari was the 'Kadijeri man' (leader) of the Gurindji people, Kalkaringi, NT. In 1966 he led the Wave Hill walk-off, protesting against poor conditions and pay for Aboriginal workers on the cattle station, owned since 1914 by the British pastoral company Vesteys. Lingiari's thumbprint was the first signature on the petition to the station owner, and he successfully expanded the protest to include a claim for traditional land rights. After years of struggle, the Gurindji were handed inalienable title to their land in 1975 by Prime Minister Gough Whitlam, who, in an iconic gesture, poured sand from his hand into Lingiari's. The Gurindji success was further reflected in the *Aboriginal Land Rights (Northern Territory) Act* 1976 (Cth). Lingiari is remembered in the song 'From Little Things Big Things Grow', by Paul Kelly and Kev Carmody (qv). *AH/PM*

Gurindji Petition to Lord Casey, Governor General

MAY IT PLEASE YOUR EXCELLENCY

We, the leaders of the Gurindji people, write to you about our earnest desire to regain tenure of our tribal lands in the Wave Hill–Limbunya area of the Northern Territory, of which we were dispossessed in time past, and for which we received no recompense.

Our people have lived here from time immemorial and our culture, myths, dreaming and sacred places have evolved in this land. Many of our forefathers were killed in the early days while trying to retain it. Therefore we feel that morally the land is ours and should be returned to us. Our very name Aboriginal acknowledges our prior claim. We have never ceased to say amongst ourselves that Vesteys should go away and leave us to our land.

On the attached map, we have marked out the boundaries of the sacred places of our dreaming, bordering the Victoria River from Wave Hill Police Station to Hooker Creek, Inverway, Limbunya, Seal Gorge, etc. We have begun to build our own new homestead on the banks of beautiful Wattie Creek in the Seal Yard area, where there is permanent water. This is the main place of our dreaming only a few miles from the Seal Gorge where we have kept the bones of our martyrs all these years since white men killed many of our people. On the walls of the sacred caves where these bones are kept, are the painting of the totems of our tribe.

We have already occupied a small area at Seal Yard under Miners Rights held by three of our tribesmen. We will continue to build our new home there (marked on the map with a cross), then buy some working horses with which we will trap and capture wild unbranded horses and cattle. These we will use to build up a cattle station within the borders of this ancient Gurindji land. And we are searching the area for valuable rocks which we hope to sell to help feed our people. We will ask the N.T. Welfare Department for help with motor for pump, seeds for garden, tables, chairs, and other things we need. Later on we will build a road and an airstrip and maybe a school. Meanwhile, most of our people will continue to live in the camp we have built at the Wave Hill Welfare Centre twelve miles away and the children continue to go to school there.

We beg of you to hear our voices asking that the land marked on the map be returned to the Gurindji people. It is about 500 square miles in area but this is only a very small fraction of the land leased by Vesteys in these parts. We are prepared to pay for our land the same annual rental that Vesteys now pay. If the question of compensation arises, we feel that we have already paid enough during fifty years or more, during which time, we and our fathers worked for no wages at all much of the time and for a mere pittance in recent years.

If you can grant this wish for which we humbly ask, we would show the rest of Australia and the whole world that we are capable of working and planning our own destiny as free citizens. Much has been said about our refusal to accept responsibility in the past, but who would show initiative working for starvation wages, under impossible conditions, without education for strangers in the land? But we are ready to show initiative now. We have already begun. We know how to work cattle better than any white man and we know and love this land of ours.

If our tribal lands are returned to us, we want them, *not* as another 'Aboriginal Reserve', but as a leasehold to be run cooperatively as a mining lease and cattle station by the Gurindji Tribe. All practical work will be done by us, except such work as bookkeeping, for which we would employ white men of good faith, until such time as our own people are sufficiently educated to take over. We will also accept the condition that if we do not succeed within a reasonable time, our land should go back to the Government.

(In August last year, we walked away from the Wave Hill Cattle Station. It was said that we did this because wages were very poor (only six dollars per week), living conditions fit only for dogs, and rations consisting mainly of salt beef and bread. True enough. But we walked away for other reasons as well. To protect our women and our tribe, to try to stand on our own feet. We will never go back there.)

Some of our young men are working now at Camfield, and Montejinnie Cattle Stations for proper wages. However, we will ask them to come back to our [own] Gurindji Homestead when everything is ready.

These are our wishes, which have been written down for us by our undersigned white friends, as we have had no opportunity to learn to write English.

Vincent Lingiari. Pincher Manguari. Gerry Ngaljardji. Long-Johnny Kitgnaari. Transcribed, witnessed and transmitted by Frank J. Hardy. J. W. Jeffrey.

1967

OLGA MASTERS
1919–1986

Olga Masters was born Olga Lawler in Pambula, NSW. She grew up during the Depression and worked as a journalist from the age of fifteen on the *Cobargo Chronicle*. In 1937 she moved to Sydney, where she wrote advertising copy for radio and married Charles Masters, a teacher, in 1940. They had seven children, including high-profile rugby league coach Roy Masters and award-winning ABC journalist Chris Masters.

In 1955 she resumed work as a journalist, writing for the women's pages of country newspapers in what she regarded as a 'long apprenticeship' for her late career as a fiction writer. After a positive public response to a humorous piece commissioned by her editor in 1974 about her son, 'My Boy Roy', Masters considered seriously the idea of writing fiction and in 1977 began to do so full time, establishing the same kind of late-blooming career as Elizabeth Jolley (qv) at the beginning of the period when second wave feminism had caused a revolution in the publishing of Australian women's writing.

Her first book was a collection of short stories, *The Home Girls* (1982), followed by the novels *Loving Daughters* (1984) and *A Long Time Dying* (1985). Her burgeoning career as a fiction writer was cut short when she died of a brain tumour. Two books were published posthumously: *The Rose Fancier* (1987), which she had been working on at the time of her death, and *Collected Stories* (1996). A biography, *Olga Masters: A lot of living* by Julie Lewis, was published in 1991.

Masters's novels and stories are deceptively simply written, and profoundly emotive without being in any way sentimental. Much of her fiction is set in the period of her own childhood and youth, and uses the material details of ordinary people's lives as a way of obliquely suggesting their circumstances, emotions and likely fates. *KG*

The Christmas Parcel

Christmas in 1935 would have been a dreary affair for the Churchers but for a parcel, more like a small crate, sent from the eldest, Maxine, in Sydney.

Maxine was eighteen, and had been away two years. The first Christmas she sent a card, and the Churchers were delighted with this and stood it against the milk jug on the table for Christmas dinner, which was baked stuffed rabbit, for they were plentiful, but money was not.

The next Christmas Eve the driver of the mail car gave several long blasts on the horn passing the paddocks where the Churcher children were standing, spindly legged among the saplings and tussocks, trying to invent a game to ward off disappointment that there would be no presents.

Their mother had warned them. Sometimes she cried softly as she told them, sometimes she was angry and blamed their father for his inability to find work, sometimes she was optimistic, indulging in a spasm of house cleaning, washing curtains and bed clothes, whitewashing the fireplace ready to fill with gum tips, and scrubbing the floorboards until they came up a grey white, like sand on some untouched beach.

Who knows, something might turn up, she would say as she worked. Her better off sisters in distant towns might send a ten shilling note in their Christmas cards, which would buy lollies, cordial, oranges, bananas, and raisins for a pudding, and be damned to Fred Rossmore who would expect it paid off the account, owing now for half a year.

The clean house gave her spirits a lift, as if they were cleansed too, and she would finish off the day by bathing all the children in a tub in front of the stove, adding a kettle of hot water with each one, washing their heads as well, and sending them out to sit on the edge of the veranda and share a towel, very threadbare, to dry.

Their old skimpy shirts and dresses were usually not fastened properly; it didn't matter, it would be bedtime soon.

The young Churchers would feel lighter in spirit too, sniffing at the soap lingering on them, although it was the same Mrs Churcher used to wash the clothes. They would look forward to fried scones for tea, and some stewed peaches, a small greenish variety, sour near the stone, eaten bravely while trying to avoid thinking of the sugar and cream that would make them so much more palatable.

Mr and Mrs Churcher were sitting on the woodheap when the mail car driver blew the horn through a cloud of dust.

'And a Merry Christmas to you too!' Mrs Churcher shouted. She was in a black mood, and Mr Churcher feared it and feared for the children, soon to trail home, not giving in readily to the futility of hanging stockings. While she angrily shuffled a foot among the chips, he looked at the children like stringy saplings themselves, some like small scarecrows, for they were playing a game with arms outstretched, their ragged old shapeless clothes flapping in the wind that had sprung up, kindly cooling the air after one of the hottest days of the summer.

Mr Churcher watched as one of them suddenly tore off to the track that led to the road. It was Lionel, racing hard and soon lost to sight where the track disappeared into a patch of myrtle bush. Mr Churcher was surprised at the energy with which Lionel ran. He worried about the children's not getting enough to eat, but perhaps they were doing better than he thought. Anyone who could run like that after tearing about all day must be suitably fuelled. He felt a little happier, and looked at Mrs Churcher, surprised she was not sharing this feeling. She looked over the top of their grey slab house at some puffed up clouds, but not seeing them, he was sure, for the clouds had a milky transparency and he foolishly thought they would have a softening effect upon her. But her face wore a cloud of another kind, dark and thunderous. There was mutiny in her dark eyes, creased narrowly, not wide and soft, not even her body was soft, but gone tight in the old morrocain dress, practically the only one she owned.

'I'll chop the head off the wyandotte,' Mr Churcher said. He was proud of his knowledge of poultry, and they had a cross breeding in their meagre fowl run, comprising cast offs from other, fussier, farmers who pitied the impoverished state of the Churchers.

They rented their old place from the Heffernans, who had built it as their first home when they settled on the land fifty years earlier. Heffernan bought an adjoining property as fortunes improved and used the old place to run cattle. Since the house wasn't fenced in it was difficult, due to wandering steers, to grow produce to feed the eight children, or seven, now that Maxine had gone.

Mr Churcher was in constant conflict with Jim Heffernan. He (Mr Churcher) considered the five shillings a week rent unreasonable; he was actually doing the Heffernans a favour living there in a caretaking capacity, stopping the house from falling into ruin. He never tired of pointing out the work he put into the fowl run, although he had actually stolen some wire netting from a bundle delivered to the roadside for the Heffernans to extend their kitchen garden. Mr Churcher saw the heap and sent Lionel for pliers to snip a length from a roll, which he was sure would escape the notice of the Heffernans.

Mrs Churcher was distressed to see the children a witness to theft, but put those feelings to one side when she saw Mr Churcher had made a good job of the pen and more eggs appeared, since the fowls did not continue to lay in obscure places like inside blackberry bushes and up hollow logs.

Mr Churcher was thinking now of making some reference to the fowl pen to expose (once again) a more commendable side of his character and get him into his wife's good graces, although he did not think there was much chance of this. He took up the axe and spat on the blade, rubbing the spittle along the edge.

'I'll chop off its head before they get here,' he said, seeing the ragged little army, still several hundred yards off.

'It'll be tough as an old boot,' Mrs Churcher said looking at his. Her own feet were bare.

'It'll make good gravy and there's plenty of 'taters,' he said, injecting cheer into his voice.

Mrs Churcher was going to say the dripping to roast the fowl in was needed for their bread, for they had not eaten butter in weeks, when a shrill cry made her look towards the myrtle patch on the rise.

Lionel came screaming out of it, like a brown leaf bowling along, aided by a strong wind, his feet beating so hard upon the earth, Mr and Mrs Churcher expected the vibrations to be felt at the woodheap. They stood up.

'He's bitten! A snake's got him!' she cried out. (Her mood would not allow for anything but the worst news.)

But Lionel had stopped yelling to fly towards the woodheap, with the other children breaking into a run and shouting wildly too.

Lionel flung himself upon his father. He was a skinny boy of eight, so red of face now his freckles had disappeared in what looked like a wash of scarlet sweat. His brown straight hair, in need of a cut, was standing upright in spikes or plastered to his wet ears. His chest, no bigger it seemed than a golden syrup can, heaved and thudded and his little stick-like arms were trembling.

'It's a parcel! The biggest I've ever seen! With Dad's name on it! Mr Barney Churcher, it says. And there's a million stamps!'

That was as much as he could say. He breathed and puffed and held his father's waist for support.

'Barney Churcher! That's me!' Mr Churcher said. He stroked down his front and looked up the track. 'That's me alright!'

Lionel sat panting on a block of wood. 'Oh, it's big, it's so big!'

The other children, all six of them, had reached the woodheap by this time. Ernestine was first. She was thirteen, and fairly fleet of foot too. 'The mail car left us a parcel!' she called back to the running knot.

'Big!' Lionel cried now, with enough breath back to stand and throw his arms wide. 'Take the slide for it!'

'Hear that boy!' said Mr Churcher looking at Mrs Churcher, watching for the film of ugliness to slide from her face. He's a smart boy and he's ours, was the pleading message in his eyes.

'Go and get whatever it is, and I'll stoke the stove, for God knows what we'll eat,' Mrs Churcher said, walking off. Mr Churcher told himself her body was softening up a little and that was something.

'Come on!' he called, sounding no older than Lionel, and seizing the rope attached to the slide standing on its end by the tank-stand. The slide flew wide with the great tug Mr Churcher gave it, and the children laughed as they jumped out of its way.

'Lionel should get a ride!' Ernestine cried. She was brown haired and slender like Maxine, and would be a beauty too.

'He should and will!' Mr Churcher shouted and steadied the slide while Lionel climbed on and made a small heap of himself in the middle. Raymond, who was fifteen, took a part of the rope, and like two eager horses with heads down, father and son raced ahead, the slide flying over the brittle grass, barely easing its pace up the rise.

The parcel was from Maxine. They knew her writing. The contents were enclosed in several sheets of brown paper, then the lot wedged into a frame of well spaced slats. Mr Churcher's name and their address was written on a label nailed to one side. Above the writing was a line of stamps, some heavily smudged with the stamp of the post office through which it was sent.

Mr Churcher and the children crowded around it, sitting by the slip rails, the gate long gone, unhinged by the Heffernans and used on their new property. All of them, even four year old Clifford who had ridden to the road on Ernestine's back, bent over the parcel, stroking the paper, patting the wood, jumping back to keep their eyes on it, as if it might disappear. How different the road, the sliprails, the deeply rutted track leading to the house, looked with it there. Leave it, leave it! cried part of the minds of the Churchers. Take it away and the emptiness will be more than we can bear!

'Come on!' called Mr Churcher, as if he too had to discipline himself to break the spell. He flung the parcel onto the slide and put Clifford beside it.

'Not too fast!' cried six year old Josephine, who was not as sturdy as the others and suffered bronchitis every winter. Ernestine took her on her back for she was no heavier than Clifford. She whispered into Ernestine's neck that the parcel might be opened before everyone was there, for Mr Churcher and Raymond were flying down the track with the wind taking all of Clifford's hair backwards.

'No, no!' cried Ernestine, breaking into an energetic jog. 'We'll all be there!'

Mrs Churcher was watching the track. 'There's Mum!' Clifford shouted.

'We got it!' screamed Lawrence, who was nine and between Gloria and Lionel in age. (Which accounts for all the Churcher children.)

Mrs Churcher watched, as if mesmerized, the parcel sliding to a stop at the edge of the veranda. Mr Churcher took his eyes off it to fasten them on her face. A crease at each corner of her mouth kept any threatened softness at a distance.

'From Maxine,' Mr Churcher said, pleading. He looked down on it beside Clifford, who was still on the slide reluctant to climb off.

'The stamps,' Mr Churcher said, touching them with his boot. 'Look what it cost even to send it.'

'It's a parcel for us for Christmas, Mum!' Ernestine said, brown eyes like her mother's begging with some impatience for her excitement.

'There'll be nothing to eat in it,' Mrs Churcher said. 'Toys and rubbish, I'll bet.' She looked hard at it, perhaps to avoid the eyes of the children, every pair on her she felt.

'I'll knock the old chook's head off!' Mr Churcher said.

'Not Wynie!' came in a chorus from most of them.

Gloria, who had wild red hair, sat on the edge of the veranda and held her bare feet. 'We can eat anything,' she murmured dreamily.

'Anything you'll be eating too!' Mrs Churcher said.

'It's soft,' Lionel said. 'So I reckon it's clothes. Clothes.' The light in his eyes ran like a small and gentle fire setting alight the eyes of the others.

'It's heavy, even for Dad,' Ernestine said. 'There's something in there for you Mum, I reckon. New plates, like you want.'

'Plates! They'd smash to smithereens. We'll be sticking with the tin ones!' Her eyes rested briefly on Mr Churcher. It's your fault they're only tin, they said.

Mr Churcher looked down on his hands wishing for a cigarette to use them, but he had no tobacco. There might be tobacco in the parcel. Yes! A packet of Log Cabin and papers. Two packets. Maxine used to sit on his knee and watch him roll cigarettes when she was a little thing, no more than two and the only one. They thought there would be no more and life would be fairly easy with the Great War finished and not too many joined up from Cobargo, thank heavens, to show him up. (He had no sense of adventure where war was concerned, no inclination to join in fighting.)

They had rented a little place in the town for six shillings a week (one shilling more than this and a palace in comparison, as he was always threatening to inform Jim Heffernan) and he had work, stripping bark, cutting eucalyptus, navvying on the road now and again. But the Depression came, and so did the children. Sometimes he went away for work, down as far as Moruya, coming home with his clothes in one sugar bag and some produce in another, oysters one time which the children had never tasted and passionfruit, which had been growing wild on the side of a mountain cleared for a new road. Mrs Churcher waited hopefully for him to produce some money, but there was always little of this. Once there was a pound note which the children looked upon as a fortune. It was a terrible disappointment to them when Mrs Churcher gave it to Fred Rossmore to ensure credit for a few more weeks.

Mr Churcher was thinking of past homecomings now, looking at the parcel, still on the slide with Clifford, irrelevant thoughts, for they concerned Maxine, not likely to come home herself, spending all that money on things for them. The children saw. They found other things to look at momentarily, but in a while their glances strayed back.

'Did any of you find any eggs today?' Mrs Churcher said. (For the fowls had found means of escaping the pen and were reverting to former laying habits.) They had not, it seemed. They stared at the parcel, as if the remark had insulted it.

'Then what do we eat?' Mrs Churcher said. She did not look at Mr Churcher, who turned his face towards the paddocks, hard and dry like his throat.

'You'll find something, Mum,' Ernestine said. 'You always do.'

'There comes a time when you don't!' Mrs Churcher said. 'It's come at Christmas. A good time to arrive!'

Her voice, hard as the baked, brittle paddocks, gave the words a ringing sound like an iron bar striking earth it couldn't penetrate.

Mr Churcher longed for an early evening, for long striped shadows to bring a softness to the hard, harsh day.

'Will we have nothing for Christmas dinner?' Clifford said, huddled and dreamy on the slide. The others felt their bodies twitch, hungrier suddenly than they were before.

'Remember last year?' Gloria said. 'We had baked rabbit and Maxie's card.'

'This year is better,' Lionel said. 'We got the parcel.'

'If Mum will let us open it,' Gloria said.

Mr Churcher looked at Mrs Churcher's set face.

'It's not addressed to me,' she said.

Mr Churcher slapped a top pocket as if tobacco were already there. 'It's not Christmas yet,' he said. They looked at the setting sun filling the sky with salmon and peach jam and beaten egg white.

'We'll go into town and ask Fred Rossmore for some stuff!' Now he was patting his pockets as if money were there. He put his hands down and his face away. 'We can pay after Christmas.'

'With the endowment money I want for something for the kids to wear back to school!' Mrs Churcher cried.

The children wondered briefly which of them might have got something new.

'There might be things in here we could wear,' Lionel said, with a gentle toe on the brown paper.

'Come on!' Mr Churcher said, and began to walk rapidly off. He was taking the short cut through the bush, cutting off a quarter of a mile of road. Lionel ran to him and they both stopped and looked back to see who else was coming. Even with distance Mr Churcher's face showed he wanted Ernestine.

'I'll get my shoes and carry them!' she said, and was in and out of the room where the girls slept before Mr Churcher turned his head towards the track again. She ran to her father, not looking back.

Raymond, after standing with legs apart for a moment, holding his braces with fingers hooked in them, let the braces snap back into place and followed, racing past the little group to sit on a log some hundred yards ahead and wait, picking up bits of dead wood, rabbit dung and anything big enough to throw at nothing.

After a while they were lost to sight of those on the veranda, the gums and wattles and grey white logs, their roots exposed like a mouthful of rotten teeth, swallowing them up.

'I wonder what they'll bring back?' murmured Gloria. Clifford stood up and jumped off the slide, a very small jump he tried to make big. Lawrence moved along from his place on the veranda and put both feet on the slide.

'I'll stay with the parcel and mind it,' he said.

Mrs Churcher padded to the kitchen, opening the stove door and shutting it with a clatter of metal so loud Gloria came uneasily inside.

'Did you see that?' Mrs Churcher said, sitting with her knees spread, stretching the morrocain until you saw through it.

Gloria did not know what she should have seen.

'Him!' Mrs Churcher said.

That meant Mr Churcher. That much she did know.

'Do you know why he made Ernestine go?'

No, Gloria didn't. Her chest went tight. Perhaps Ernie was his favourite. She (Gloria) was ugly (she thought). She and Lawrence were the two heavily freckled and with bright red hair. She had only sandshoes and could not have gone to town on Christmas Eve. Not that she would cry about it. There might be shoes in the parcel for her. She sat forward in her chair so that she saw a corner of it, watched by Lawrence, Josephine and Clifford, close together on the veranda edge. She was sorry she had come inside. Her mother strode to the stove now and put in a piece of wood Gloria thought too big and green to burn properly.

When Mrs Churcher went back to sit by the kitchen table she put her head on her arm and began to cry. 'Rotten men' she said, sitting up suddenly and wiping her eyes with her fingers.

A thin smoke began to bathe the log in the stove and some of it ran out of the stove door. 'You need some chips,' Gloria said, anxious that her father should not be blamed too harshly for the wood he had brought in. Perhaps it was the smoke that sent more tears running down Mrs Churcher's cheeks.

'He took her with him to get stuff easier from Fred Rossmore!' Mrs Churcher said. 'I know Fred Rossmore!'

Of course, Gloria thought. Everyone in Cobargo did. Even children knew he was a powerful man in the town.

'He's fond of girls,' Mrs Churcher said. That seemed alright in Gloria's view, except for the tone of her mother's voice (like an iron bar on hard dry earth it couldn't penetrate).

'Huh!' Mrs Churcher said, which could be interpreted as meaning that Gloria knew precious little about Fred Rossmore's character. 'Not for their good, but for his!' Mrs Churcher said.

Gloria pondered this. It appeared to mean that without Ernestine there, Fred Rossmore would not be handing out goods from his shelves. Her heart was troubled for her father coming in empty handed.

'He touches diddies if you let him,' Mrs Churcher said. 'And up here.' She touched the morrocain stretched across her chest.

Gloria considered this a small price for butter, bacon, tinned peaches and biscuits, but dared not say so.

'And that parcel,' Mrs Churcher said. 'I wonder about that.'

Gloria bent forward again to see it, the most innocent thing in all the world.

'To start with, a man would put it in a frame like that. Not her.'

I wish she wouldn't say her, Gloria thought. Maxine had the nicest name of them all. Ernestine was next. After that it seemed Mrs Churcher's selection of names was clouded by her worries at feeding and clothing them all. Gloria had been told an aunt, a sister of her father, had named her after the film star Gloria Swanson. Gloria felt a deep shame that she failed to turn out looking anything like Miss Swanson.

The green wood was filling the kitchen with smoke and Mrs Churcher got up and rubbed it into the hot ashes for it to burn quicker.

'For all we know a man might have bought what's in it. I reckon he did.'

'For touching her diddie?' Gloria said.

Mrs Churcher was across the room in a second with a slap across Gloria's face so violent, Gloria lost her balance on the chair, and the noise brought the three from the veranda running to the door. They returned almost at once.

'Only Mum whacking Gloria,' Clifford said, sitting down even closer to the parcel.

'There!' Mrs Churcher said, working the legs of the chair into the floor as she sat down. Gloria lay her face on her knee and cried softly. Mrs Churcher also cried. She allowed the tears to run in a great hurry down her cheeks, and when Gloria lifted her head she was surprised to see her mother's eyes quite bright and her face quite soft. She left her chair and went and sat on her knee. The fold of her stomach was soft as a mattress, and her shoulder a pillow, a fragrant fleshy pillow.

Mrs Churcher began to rock Gloria and this appeared to set them both crying without sound. When the others came in, tired of waiting by the parcel, Gloria lowered her face and Mrs Churcher turned hers. But they saw enough to make their eyes water too, so they moved together in a little bunch and stood giving all their attention to the stove fire.

Lawrence went off and returned with his old hat full of peaches. Gloria brought in some spindly wood that helped the green piece burn. Josephine asked if she could set the table, and Gloria, frowning on her, said to bring in some clothes from the line. The peaches were not as small and hard as those usually found, and when they had rolled to a stop on the table and Gloria brought a saucepan and a knife, Mrs Churcher said: 'You'd better let me.'

The four of them pressed their small chests against the edge of the table as they watched the peeling. It was a miracle of thinness, the furry skin falling from the knife like pale green tissue paper. Look at our Mum, said their eyes to each other. If only there was sugar to shake on some spoonfuls, without spilling a grain.

Mr Churcher brought some. Clifford, going out to check on the parcel, saw them come out of the bush and start their troop across to the house. He yelled as loud as Lionel when he found the parcel.

'They've got something!' he cried, flying inside then out again. The others followed except Mrs Churcher, who went to the stove with the saucepan of peaches and stayed there, making sure the lid was tight and they were on the right part of the stove to cook gently. Gloria allowed herself a brief look at the returning party, then when her mother had hung up the hessian oven rag, she went and hooped both arms around her and lay her face in the hollow of her breasts.

'They're coming,' Mrs Churcher said, not actually pushing her off.

'Sugar, Mum!' Lawrence cried, as Mr Churcher put the little brown bag on the table with two tins of herrings in tomato sauce, some cheese, cut into such a beautiful triangle it would be a shame to disturb it, and a half pound packet of tea and some dried peas.

'And look what Ernie's got!' Lionel cried, stepping aside from in front of her to reveal her holding clasped against her waist a paper bag. Everyone knew, by the little squares and rolls and balls making little bulges in the paper, it could be nothing else but sweets.

'Lollies!' screamed Clifford, and Mrs Churcher turned to the stove again and they saw by the neck showing under the thick straggling bun of her grey and black hair that she was crying.

'Stop crying, Mum,' Josephine said. 'Ernie will give you one.'

'They're for all of us to share,' Raymond said, in case anyone should begin to think differently. He sat on the doorstep with a glance backwards at the parcel, the afternoon sun making diamonds of the tacks holding the label in place.

'Mum's not well,' Mr Churcher said. He was standing in the middle of the room, one hand near his waist, the fingers spread as if a cigarette was there. 'She's having another one.'

Mrs Churcher sat and found the hem of her petticoat to wipe her nose.

'It'll be the last,' Mr Churcher said.

The eyes of the children said this might or might not be so. Ernestine put the bag of sweets at the end of the top shelf of the dresser and snapped the glass doors shut. She moved to the table and put the other things from Fred Rossmore's inside the food safe. Mrs Churcher's wet eyes followed her. Ernestine's old sleeveless print dress showed her round tanned arms, and her hair heavy as a bird's nest showed bits of her neck, pure white inside dark brown slits. She brought out flour to make fried scones, holding the bag between breasts beginning to pout. Tears ran over Mrs Churcher's cheeks as Ernestine lowered the flour to the table and took a mixing bowl from a crude shelf above her head.

'There's four boys and four girls in this family,' Lionel said. 'So the next one can be anything it likes.'

Mr Churcher was on a chair with his elbows on his knees. 'Well said, Lionel. A smart boy that.' He longed to be brave enough to look into Mrs Churcher's eyes. 'You're all smart, all of you,' he said.

Raymond looked at the kitchen floor boards between his feet. He had left school a year ago, and still had no job except for trapping rabbits in the winter and selling the skins, a great pile of them for only five shillings. The tips of his ears were very red.

'Next year things are going to be better,' Mr Churcher said. Everyone half believed it, and Mrs Churcher, as if her mind were on something else, took out the sugar, and carrying it to the stove tipped a little onto the peaches. They all watched her fold the top of the bag down letting nothing escape.

'Yes, I reckon next year will be better,' Mr Churcher said, putting a hand to a back pocket and moving it around there, as if making room for a packet of tobacco.

'And there's the parcel!' he said, throwing back his head suddenly like a terrier about to bark.

Josephine flung herself on Ernestine, as if the excitement was too much to bear alone. Raymond drew himself into a tight ball with his face crushed between his knees.

Lionel and Lawrence went to the veranda to each put a light foot on the parcel. Clifford climbed onto his father's knee, and Gloria leaned against her mother, with the cheek still red from the slap rubbing gently into her morrocain shoulder.

'And it's Christmas tomorrow!' Mr Churcher said, with his head back again and the words coming out like a terrier's bark. Out of the corner of his eye he saw Mrs Churcher's face start to go soft, then tighten again. She stood, taller than normal, he thought and looked across at him. Her eyes swept the children to one side. She might have sent them from the room, though all were there, faces tipped up at her, eyes begging for harmony.

'That parcel was sent from the place where the bad girls are,' she said.

There was a rush for the veranda to look at the parcel again. Even Mr Churcher screwed his head towards it, but turned it back almost at once. His face did not believe it.

Gloria had a vision of a great mass of girls with pinched and sorrowful faces and their skirts dented deeply in the region of their diddies. She looked at Ernestine, who was measuring flour into a bowl with lowered eyes, but there was nothing to be seen past her waist, which was level with the table.

'Make sure you sift that flour properly,' Mrs Churcher said. Then she sat on a chair with her head up, not looking at Mr Churcher. 'You can see on the stamps where it was sent from.'

'She could have given it to anyone to post. It's a great thing to lug herself,' Mr Churcher said.

'She never writes,' Mrs Churcher said.

'She was saving up for all those stamps,' Mr Churcher answered. He got up and went and pulled the label from the parcel, looking at the stamps and postmark.

'You see it? Kings Cross! That's where she is!' Mrs Churcher took the bowl of flour from Ernestine and buried her hands in it. She began to cry again.

Mr Churcher put the label in the dresser next to the lollies from Fred Rossmore.

'Now it doesn't matter where it came from,' Lionel said. Mr Churcher's eyes told Lionel this was wisely said.

Josephine went to Ernestine to cry into her waist. 'We'll never know what's in the parcel!' she wailed.

'That's right!' Mrs Churcher was mixing dough fast with a knife, her tears temporarily halted. 'We'll send it back!'

Josephine wept louder and Ernestine, checking that her mother's hands were covered with dough, and Josephine seemed safe from a blow, held her very tight.

Raymond went pale, and the freckles stood out on Gloria and Lawrence for their faces had a pallor too. Lionel, sitting suddenly beside Raymond, turned the sole of one foot up and looked long and intently on it.

'You're a cruel woman, Maudie,' Mr Churcher said.

The children were not as frightened by his words as they might have been. He called Mrs Churcher Maudie in the soft moments.

Mrs Churcher, her face clear of tears, tossed her head high and banged the frying pan on the stove. It was not a terribly loud bang though.

'I know my Maxie,' Mr Churcher said. He was seated with his elbows on his knees. He held two fingers near his face and the children looked hard to be sure he had no cigarette.

'Your Maxie!' Mrs Churcher said.

'Our Maxie!' Mr Churcher said. 'A good girl!'

'Yes, yes, yes!' came in different voices, Josephine's the strangest, for she was laughing as well as sobbing. Ernestine wandered outside, still holding Josephine, and Gloria followed.

Under the old apricot tree, from which the fruit had been early and hungrily stripped, they put their backs to the trunk.

'I'm frightened,' Gloria said. 'If there are gold and jewels in that parcel, what will we do?'

Ernestine tried to shrink the parcel in her vision. Mr Churcher came to the back door and filled the opening. Ernestine, Gloria and Josephine went and sat at his feet on the slabs laid on the earth to make a rough veranda.

Ernestine bound her body in her arms and rocked herself a little while, looking away to the mountains gone black to show the sunset up all the brighter.

She lifted her face, no less lovely, to her father. 'You open the parcel, Dad. Like Mum said, it's addressed to you.'

'By jove I think I might!' Mr Churcher said, loud enough to swing Mrs Churcher's face from the food safe to which she was returning the flour.

'I'm setting the table here,' Mrs Churcher said. 'Without any help as usual!'

'Leave the table setting!' Mr Churcher said. 'I'm bringing in the parcel!'

He didn't go through the kitchen but strode around the house with Ernestine, Gloria and Josephine clinging to him.

Raymond, Lawrence, Lionel and Clifford were around the slide when they reached it. Mr Churcher lifted the parcel as if it were a pillow.

'Our Dad's so strong!' cried Lawrence. They stepped back like a guard of honour for him to go to the kitchen. He laid it on the table end.

'Don't break the box!' Lionel said. 'It'll be handy for something!'

'A doll's cradle!' Gloria said. 'If there's a doll in there for Josie!' Her eyes then sent an agonized apology to her mother.

There was no doll in there. But Josephine forgot her disappointment when the paper was pulled away and Ernestine held up a quilt, a snowy white fringed quilt with the honeycomb pattern broken up with a design of roses as big as cabbages, and trailing stems and leaves.

'Look at that!' someone cried.

'For Mum's bed!'

'And Dad's!'

Ernestine put it tenderly on a chair.

'Towels!' shrieked Gloria as four were found inside and four sheets with only a little fraying at the hems.

After that came a tablecloth, heavy and white, a beautiful thing for Christmas dinner, and several tea towels.

Ernestine held them up against the open doorway and there was hardly any wear showing.

'Give them all to Mum!' Gloria cried.

Mrs Churcher was on a chair, hands on her thighs, trying to keep the hardness in her eyes.

Mr Churcher sat on the door step where Raymond had been. He was watching Ernestine, Gloria and Lionel come to the end of the parcel.

Lionel shrieked when he held up a single page with Maxine's writing on it.

'I hope you like these things,' she wrote, 'I work for these people called Pattens. Mr Patten has a shop. He brought home some new sheets and things, all in colours which is the new fashion now. Mrs Patten decided to give me the old ones, or some of them, to send to you. She is not paying me this week, but says she has a Christmas present for me. They are having roast pork for Christmas dinner here, but I would rather be having what you are.'

Lionel read the letter and everyone hearing it was quiet.

Mrs Churcher bent down to look into the stove fire, which was smoking again, so she needed to find her petticoat hem to wipe her eyes and nose.

Mr Churcher stared at his hands as if for the first time he realized they were holding nothing.

1985

IDA WEST
1919–2003

Ida West was born on an Aboriginal reserve on Cape Barren Island. In the 1920s the family moved to Killiecrankie, Flinders Island. She married Marcus Sydney West, had one daughter and two sons, and divorced in 1960.

West spent much of her life as a tireless advocate for the Tasmanian Aboriginal community's rights to land and cultural self-determination. In 1987 West published her autobiography *Pride Against Prejudice: Reminiscences of a Tasmanian Aborigine.* Her many years of struggle finally resulted in the Wybalenna Aboriginal Community's acquisition of land title on Flinders Island on 18 April 1999. She was named Tasmanian of the Century by the *Mercury* and NAIDOC National Female Aboriginal Elder of the Year (2002) and NAIDOC Elder of the Year (2003). *AH/PM*

From *Pride Against Prejudice*
Chapter 2: The Middle Years

BROTHER-IN-LAW AND BILLY SAMUEL

My brother-in-law, Andy, was bringing a heifer over from Pine Scrub one day. He was riding a horse and he took a short cut from Tanners Bay to Killiecrankie. He was going around the bushes, but the heifer was going through the bushes. Andy was going to give it up when he saw another man on a horse. The horse belonged to Charlie Jones and was being ridden bareback by Billy Samuel. The horse was called Tunny. Mr Billy Samuel, an Aborigine from Queensland, was a boxer. The heifer was going through the bushes, so Billy Samuel went through the bushes too. Billy Samuel was an expert in the bush, and they got the heifer to Killiecrankie.

Billy Samuel used to be at the Quoin with us doing some work. He would put on a clean shirt each evening and go over to another man and his wife and little girl to listen to the boxing on the wireless. The champion, Mr Samuel, would bob his head and put his fist out during the fighting. The little girl was looking at him and she said to him, 'Why don't you go home and wash your hands and face?' He told me, 'That's the best line ever put over me.' He said he had been called 'old smoke' or a 'big thunder cloud', but he reckoned that was the best. The little girl's father was going to hit her and Billy told him, 'You have never explained to her about coloured people.' So he did that and they were friends then, Mr Samuel and the little girl.

Mr Samuel told me that up in Queensland they saw white people rounding their cows and calves, and branding them. The Aboriginal people saw this, and the Aboriginal children had the branding irons in a fire ready to start branding their little brothers and sisters. I think that they did do one! There's a lot that should have been learnt years ago.

He also told me about his Uncle, Gerry Jerome, when he won his first fight, they asked him what he wanted in money. Instead of saying so much money, he said he wanted a new horse, saddle and bridle. That was what he wanted.

ABORIGINES SWIMMING

I was on Killiecrankie Beach with Aunty Sarah Beeton and her children, and Billy Samuel was on the beach somewhere as well. Billy, a full-blood Aborigine, was staying with us and he was a champion boxer in his day. Dad liked him very much. I was sitting with Aunt Sarah when I looked towards the bay and saw three small boys, they seemed to be sitting on the water, but they were moving. I said to Aunt Sarah, 'Look at your boys.' The reason they looked like they were sitting on the water was because they were sitting on Billy's back. Billy was like a whale. He put his head up, blew out his nose and would then go under a little way. The boys were having a wonderful time. Billy was a very good swimmer, he and his brothers had taught themselves to swim, he said.

FLOODS AT KILLIECRANKIE

Girlie and Tim lived in a hut near a swamp and we lived in a tent not far away. Aunty Sarah Beeton, Elvin and Les had a tent in the scrub towards the beach at Killiecrankie. We were all snaring for kangaroo and wallaby. Wallaby snares were called footies because we caught them by the foot, and the ones for roos were neckies as they were caught by the neck. The rain came—it rained and rained and the swamp filled up. Markie and I were in bed. We were roused up because the tent was leaking and water was coming in underneath. We got up, dressed, put knee boots on and went over to Girlie and Tim's hut thinking that they would be dry. When we were nearly there Markie said, 'The water is nearly up to the hut.' We had a lantern and we knocked at the door noticing the water coming through the door, Girlie said, 'Come in'. We told her that we were flooded out and that the water was coming through their door. Tim and Girlie had been in bed asleep. We lit the lamp and they couldn't believe that the water was coming through the door. They opened their eyes when the two, unused, jerry pots came floating out from under the bed and across the floor! They got dressed and then we talked it over, we had to go over to Aunty Sarah and the boys' tent. We started through the bush to Aunty Sarah when we heard someone cooee-ing. It was raining very hard. We listened. It was coming from up the track, cooee, cooee, again. We found Aunty Sarah with a blanket around her shoulders wet through. She had got off the track and was trembling all over. We took her back to her tent. Aunty Sarah's tent was dry so we didn't know why she left it. It was up a little hill and she had a big fire going outside. We put dry clothes on her and the men built up the fire. We stayed there all night.

It was a flood all right.

ELDERLY GENTLEMEN

Mr Frank Boyes left Robertdale and built a hut in the bush at North East River. He was a great age. He would cut wood and pile it up for when he got old. He used to talk to himself. Mr Jack Gardner, who kept the store at Lughrata, would bring food up to him, and another man, Mr Wattie Archer, who lived alongside for a while. This man was brother to Mr Archer on Cape Barren Island and he died before Mr Boyes. They lived like hermits, but you were always sure of a cup of tea when you called there. The Robinsons from Five-Mile used to take a short cut from Five-Mile to see these elderly gentlemen. Frank and George Boyes were well educated. Mr Frank was the best. He had a wireless and would argue with the men on the wireless and tell them that they were wrong.

We were going down the road, Mum and I. Our wireless was broken at the old home so we had to go down to Esma's to hear the serial, 'It Walks by Night'. There were gum-tree roots all over the road. It was a dark night and I had my hand around Mum's arm. The torch wasn't very good because the batteries were nearly out. I said to her, 'Jump.' She said, 'What are you jumping for?' I said, 'There's an extra gum root on the road.' I said, 'I think it's a snake. At certain times they travel of a night.' So we jumped and we turned around to have a look. When we put the torch on it, it was moving. We kind of knew how many gum roots there were on the road—so there was always these stories.

COOKING

Mutton-birds can be cooked several different ways. We used to make a brown stew in the old iron pots. There is grilled mutton-birds, fried mutton-birds, baked mutton-birds with onions and stuffing, curried mutton-birds with rice, sea pie, and salted birds.

For smoked mutton-birds we used to thread the birds on a stick and put them over a drum and keep the fire in the drum for four to six weeks.

We made kangaroo tail soup and brawn. We would dip the kangaroo tails in hot water and scrape the skin off.

We had coupons to buy meat, sugar, tea, butter and clothes. We made our own soap out of dripping and we used mutton-bird oil for rubbing our chests for flu. Garlic in your shoes was a remedy for whooping cough. We would boil the buzzies from the vine of the bush and bottle. We ate grass tree bread which is the meat of the tree—white in colour and sweet in taste. We loved it.

All my people cooked fruit cakes with mutton-bird fat dripping. The women were good cooks.

They used to cook bread, damper and johnny cake in bakers [camp ovens]. Uncle Bun Beeton used to make his damson jam in the baker. Uncle Bun used to have an orchard at Pine Scrub which had peaches, damson, grapes and a vegetable garden. On my school holidays I used to stay with Johnny Maynard, his wife Nellie and their children, Hazel, Phillip, and Ruby. They lived on top of the hill at Pine Scrub. They had a cow which was the best I have seen for producing cream. They would boil the milk and skim the cream off it. Nellie used to make butter, but it was just about butter before we started. We used to take it to the salt water to wash it. When we cooked our crayfish we put them straight into boiling water—all Aboriginal people do it that way.

One of the prettiest sights I ever saw in my life was in about 1937, on my first trip out to Babel Island. As I was going past Cat Island I saw it smothered with lovely white gannets. It was a picture. The last time I was out at Babel there were only a few there. It's a shame seeing these lovely white birds disappearing but it was a sight to see when the island was full of them.

1987

ROSEMARY DOBSON
b 1920

Rosemary Dobson was born in Sydney. Her father died when she was five, leaving her mother to raise two daughters. Dobson was educated at Frensham School, attended the University of Sydney as a non-award student, and studied drawing with the artist Thea Proctor. In her early twenties Dobson began working for the publishers Angus & Robertson, where she met numerous important literary figures of the day, including the editor Beatrice Davis. She also met her husband, Alec Bolton (1926–96), who later worked at the National Library of Australia, and who in 1972 established Brindabella Press, which published work by Dobson and other poets.

Dobson's first mature collection of poems was *In a Convex Mirror* (1944). She has written nine other major collections, including *Child With a Cockatoo and Other Poems* (1955), *Over the Frontier* (1978) and *The Three Fates* (1984), and has translated, with David Campbell (qv), two collections of Russian poetry. She has also edited a number of anthologies, published one novel for young adults, and written a study of the painter Ray Crooke. In 1991 her *Collected Poems* appeared. She has received numerous awards, including the *Age* Book of the Year Award in 2001 for *Untold Lives and Later Poems* (2000). Since 1972 she has lived in Canberra.

Many of Dobson's earlier poems show an interest in visual art, while her later poems meditate on subjects as diverse as the type of a printing press, classical Chinese poetry and ancient Greek coins. Her poetry is lucid, while being deeply aware of the darker notes of history and personal experience. Like other poets of her generation, her earlier poetry is marked by its formality and rationality. In the 1970s she modernised her style by turning to essentials, as well as the work of artists such as Ben Nicholson. Her later poems often meditate on the loss of her husband. *DM*

Child With a Cockatoo

Portrait of Anne, daughter of the Earl of Bedford, by S. Verelst

'Paid by my lord, one portrait, Lady Anne,
Full length with bird and landscape, twenty pounds
And framed withal. I say received. Verelst.'

So signed the painter, bowed, and took his leave.
My Lady Anne smiled in the gallery   5
A small, grave child, dark-eyed, half turned to show
Her five bare toes beneath the garment's hem,
In stormy landscape with a swirl of drapes.
And, who knows why, perhaps my lady wept
To stand so long and watch the painter's brush   10
Flicker between the palette and the cloth
While from the sun-drenched orchard all the day
She heard her sisters calling each to each.
And someone gave, to drive the tears away,
That sulphur-crested bird with great white wings,   15
The wise, harsh bird—as old and wise as Time
Whose well-dark eyes the wonder kept and closed.
So many years to come and still, he knew,
Brooded that great, dark island continent
Terra Australis.   20
                  To those fabled shores
Not William Dampier, pirating for gold,
Nor Captain Cook his westward course had set
Jumped from the longboat, waded through the surf,
And clapt his flag ashore at Botany Bay.   25
Terra Australis, unimagined land—
Only that sulphur-crested bird could tell

Of dark men moving silently through trees,
Of stones and silent dawns, of blackened earth
And the long golden blaze of afternoon.   30
That vagrant which an ear-ringed sailor caught
(Dropped from the sky, near dead, far out to sea)
And caged and kept, till, landing at the docks,
Walked whistling up the Strand and sold it then,
The curious bird, its cynic eyes half closed,   35
To the Duke's steward, drunken at an inn.
And he lived on, the old adventurer,
And kept his counsel, was a sign unread,
A disregarded prologue to an age.
So one might find a meteor from the sun   40
Or sound one trumpet ere the play's begun.

                                                          1955

Over the Frontier

Reverie on a poem by Zbigniew Herbert[1]

The object that exists
a glass, say, or a bottle
is one step away from the object that does not exist,
it has crossed over the outermost rim
and between light and darkness   5
it has assumed shape and purpose.

And the poem that exists
will never equal the poem that does not exist.
Trembling, it crosses the frontier at dawn
from non-being to being   10
carrying a small banner,
bearing a message,

bringing news of the poem that does not exist,
that pulses like a star, red and green, no-colour,
blazing white against whiteness.   15
Listen to the universe—
those are the possibilities of order
buzzing and humming.

---

1 Polish author (1924–88).

The outline of non-existence
can be held by the inner eye,   20
always moving, it assumes the shape of stillness.
So a plate spinning on a stick
is the essence of plate, a still one,
absolute plate with a fish on it.

1978

The Almond-tree in the King James Version

White, yes, pale with the pallor of old timbers,
Thistle-stalks, shells, the extreme pallor of starlight—

It is the almond-tree flourishing,
An image of Age in the Book of Ecclesiastes.

Premonitions, like visitors turning the door-handle,   5
Cry out, 'It's us. It's only us.'

And I, opening the door from the other side, reply
'Of course. You are expected.'

To memory I say: 'You must be disciplined.'
To hands: 'Do not tremble. Be still.'   10
To bones: 'Do not ache. Remain flexible.'
To ears: 'Do not be affrighted
It is only the voice of the bird.'

To eyes I say: 'Be faithful. Stay with me.
Do not, looking out of the window, be darkened.'   15

Yes, it is as I have always been led to believe:
Premonitions, recognitions, the need for acceptance.

The almond-tree shall flourish, and the grass-hopper shall be a burden
It is all in the twelfth chapter of Ecclesiastes.

1991

Who?

Who, then, was 'Auntie Molly'? No one now
Can tell me who she was: or how it was
She and my mother shared a rented house

One summer for a fortnight—we took a train
And from the station trudged a country road.   5
I know she worked year-long and lived alone
Somewhere with a strange name, like Rooty Hill.

Postoffice-Store-in-one sold bread and milk.
Returning to our house we scuffed along
Cloth-hatted, sandalled, kicking at the stones.   10
Mother and Auntie Molly walked ahead
And suddenly Mother stopped, threw back her head
And laughed and laughed there in the dusty road.
We were amazed to hear our mother laugh.

The fowl-yard fence sagged with ripe passion-fruit,   15
We bought cream in a jug. At night we sat
Around the lamp-lit table, colouring in.
In bed, near sleep, we'd hear the rise and fall
Of their grave voices—hers, and Auntie Molly's,
Whom no one now would know; who made my mother   20
Laugh joyfully in the middle of the road.

                                                              1991

Reading Aloud

Low, clear and free of self your voice went on
At night you read, and for how many years
From Sterne to Kipling, Flaubert, Boswell, Proust—
Proust a whole year, and finishing you said
'One of the great experiences of my life.'   5
And mine, and mine.

Intent to listen, quieting my hands
With plain and purl, I followed your low voice,
Knitting unmindfully long scarves for friends
Sent off as signs of that shared calm content   10
Still looked for in the un-shared books I choose
Reading alone.

Well, we gave up once, stalled on Chuzzlewit.
How wrong it felt. You sensed a binding need
To take books to the end. Faced with reverses said,   15

'We must press on.'

                From books to life, your thought:

'Forgive, learn from the past. Press on.'

And I press on.

2000

COLIN THIELE
1920–2006

Novelist, poet and educator Colin Thiele was born in Eudunda on the edge of SA's Barossa Valley. He was a bilingual child in a German farming community and one of his best-known books, *The Sun on the Stubble* (1961), affectionately recalls this childhood; it would probably now be classified as young adult fiction. Thiele was educated at Kapunda High School and the University of Adelaide, from where he graduated in 1941, then serving as a radar mechanic in northern Australia with the RAAF for the rest of the Second World War.

After ten postwar years as a high school teacher Thiele joined Wattle Park Teachers College, of which he was appointed principal in 1965, going on to a long and distinguished career in the field of education. He wrote over 90 books, including poetry, fiction, children's books, biography, radio plays and educational texts, but the three for which he is best known are some of his own favourites: *The Sun on the Stubble*, the children's book *Storm Boy* (1963)—later made into a highly successful feature film of the same title (1976)—and his biography of the South Australian artist Hans Heysen, *Heysen of Hahndorf* (1968). *KG*

From *The Sun on the Stubble*
Chapter 1: The Possum in the Kitchen

Bruno stopped pulling the possum's tail and sat back. It was time to think things over.

From his perch in the fork of the big gum he could see the whole farm. The sun was setting like a gong of gold on the Range. Shadows half a mile long crossed the home-paddock and made straight for the house in flat lines till they came to the trees and sheds where they seemed to turn suddenly upwards at right angles. It was like looking across at dozens of big, dark carpenters' squares stacked upright between layers of gold foil. On the far side of the home-paddock where the slope had just been combed out by the cultivator, the strands of the fallow furrows ran up and down with shadows too. As he watched, the last of the sun's rays streamed down in sloping planks, clear and bold enough for him to want to run up them and cross high over the valley to the rim of the hills beyond. Then the sun dipped away and the world was soft and grey.

Bruno looked at the taut tail he held, and dragged back against it. About nine inches of it ran from his hand and disappeared into the hollow branch in front of him, but if he leant forward until his chest pressed against the smooth bark, he could see that a little way inside the hole the tail joined a set of sinewy hindquarters. On either side, too, he could just make out a set of claws curving deep and desperately into the wood. Pulling against four legs like that was like pulling against the tree itself.

Bruno could feel the tail gripping him as firmly as he was gripping it. It seemed to be shaking hands with him, frantically. Although the top and sides were blue-grey with smoky fur, soft and fluffy to the touch, a strip of tough, supple skin ran like a thong of green-hide along the underside. It tapered to a point just short of the end of the tail and wrapped itself around the middle knuckles on the back of his hand. That was how things stood now. In fact, that was how things had been standing ever since Bruno, looking for hawks' eggs on the way back from his rabbit traps, had surprised the possum in the short hollow branch nearly half an hour earlier. He had come back empty-handed, the hessian sugar-bag that should have been weighed down with rabbits, rolled up inside his pullover, puffing him out in front like a pouter pigeon. And then he had seen the hawk fly from the big gum and had gone up looking for its nest, reckoning that a hawk's egg in the hand was worth two rabbits in the burrow. Instead, he had found something even better—the possum—but all that he had been able to win so far was a foot of tail. For one thing, he didn't want to be cruel. In fact the whole idea of hurting the possum repelled him. What he did want, and want very badly, was the warm contented excitement that the thought of catching a live possum gave him—he could almost feel the soft fur between his hands.

He looked round once more. There was just time for one more try. Risking safety for success, he brought up his left leg and braced it against the branch in front of him. The angle of the fork was fairly steep, so that, even with his back pressed firmly against the tree-trunk behind him, his left knee came up past his ear like a grasshopper's in reverse. Then, tensing all his muscles, he gave a quick pull upwards. It took the possum by surprise and forced him to change the position of a back leg. Bruno, seeing his chance, quickly gave another tug sideways so that the leg missed its hold and scrabbled frantically in the air. Risking everything, he grabbed the tail with his left hand and thrust his right under the two legs. Although the claws scarified his arm he pushed in deeper, running his hand along the possum's underbelly, trying to unhook the front claws. Suddenly he winced with pain and whipped out his hand. Blood dripped from his forefinger where the possum's teeth had bitten deeply and fiercely, and in the sting of the bite Bruno lost the initiative and the hollow swallowed up the base of the tail once more. But the attempt had shown him a new way.

Thrusting his bleeding hand down his shirt-front he pulled out the empty bag, wrapped it round his fist and so, well-gloved, felt along the possum's belly again towards the front claws. There he at last unhooked them and, pulling mightily, brought the creature out into the open, one hand still clutching the tail and the other holding him firmly by the neck. Sweet victory! It was not often that anyone caught a fully-grown possum alive—not even a man.

It was no easy job to get him inside the bag, but he did it in the end, climbed down perilously, and set off in triumph for the house. This would be something to show Mum and Dad and Grandpa, Herbert and Lottie and the rest of his doubting brothers and sisters. In the mornings whenever he walked in and tipped his bagful of rabbits on the kitchen floor for their inspection Herbert and Oscar sniffed patronisingly as if it were just by luck that young brothers like Bruno caught rabbits at all. What would they say now! This would set them back in their places. Delicious anticipation!

Beacon-straight he hurried across the home-paddock towards the warm light in the kitchen window. The August twilight was gathering round him as he went, softly and imperceptibly covering the world like dark dew. The men were clumping up through the yard to the house. He could hear the iron ring of Dad's heels on the limestone paving, the clang of the empty wash-basins, the wet coughing of the pump and the prodigious snorts and wheezes of Dad's evening wash, scarcely distinguishable through the distant gloom from the wallowings of the cows in the dam.

By the time Bruno came up through the house-yard gate everyone was already in the kitchen. Mum and the girls in their aprons looked ceremoniously arranged for scuffles with food, Dad and the boys ridiculously clean and overwashed, wet beads still gleaming on the spikes of their hair. Lottie, holding a wooden ladle, was filling the nine plates on the table with niagaras of hot soup and noodles from Mum's black saucepan. Herbert, Oscar, Victor and Anna were seated expectantly, Grandpa was busy dunking brown bread in his soup, and Dad was standing with his back to the stove, completely obliterating the fireplace. When Lottie had filled the last plate, Mum circumnavigated Dad with the pot to get it back on the fire.

She took a log from the wood-box and manoeuvred adroitly round Dad again to put it into the stove. He eyed her steadily but didn't move.

'We need more wood,' said Lottie. 'Better cut some tomorrow.'

Oscar gave his face an agonised wrench. 'What, *again?*'

'The way the big wood-heap by the dam is going down,' said Herbert tartly, 'you'd think someone was *stealing* the stuff.'

Dad stiffened at the word stealing: 'Don't talk stupid, Herbert! Who right by the house here would steal our wood away?'

He moved like an uneasy mountain and looked at the clock. 'Where's young Bruno? Time he was in!'

'He went down to his traps,' said Mum gently, 'he won't be long.'

'Tea time is time to be home,' said Dad. 'It's dark!'

'I s'pose,' said Herbert, 'he's frightened to show his nose with an empty bag.'

And then Bruno walked in. Curiosity! Silence! Astonishment!

'*Mein Gott*, Bruno! You hurt?' Mum always recoiled at the sight of blood. A long association with five brothers, a husband and four sons had convinced her that men and boys squandered their blood so prodigally that only the strictest vigilance by wives and mothers could prevent them from letting it drain away altogether. She seemed to think that every one of them was born with a fixed reservoir of blood in his body, and that if any was allowed to leak away during his lifetime it couldn't be replaced and therefore reduced by so much the level of what was left; and if that was the case it was obvious that Dad must be very nearly empty by now, and even Bruno, young as he was, could not possibly be more than half full.

Yet here was Bruno with long red claw-marks up one arm and his right hand hidden in a sodden handkerchief that looked as if it had just been used to wipe up a cup of spilt raspberry.

'You didn't take the rifle, Bruno? I said never to take the rifle!' Mum's thoughts always jumped to whatever was most wicked and gruesome.

'Using steel traps when you shouldn't have been,' Herbert said weightily. 'Get your fingers caught?'

Bruno brushed them aside. 'Ah, it's nothin',' he said. Then his voice took on the proud eagerness of secrets about to be revealed; he looked round at them confidingly.

'See what I've caught.'

The boys strained forward inquisitively across the table, Oscar's shirt-front soaking up his soup almost as greedily as if it had been his mouth; the girls formed a fidgety half-circle; even Dad leant forward indulgently. Only Mum, from deep instinct or arduously-trained mistrust of things in bags, retreated a step towards the wood-box in the corner.

'What is it?'

'Tip it out!'

'Go on, hurry up!'

Advice was thick in Bruno's ears. He took the bag by the two bottom corners and upended it with a flourish. Everyone craned forward, even Mum. Nothing happened.

'It's nothin'.'

'Is it a lizard?'

'A wombat? I'll bet you it's a wombat!'

'It's not a snake? Bruno, you haven't brought a snake into the house?' Mum edged nearer to the wood-box, eyeing the pieces of wood for a likely weapon.

'It won't come out, whatever it is.'

'Shake it!'

Bruno shook the bag vigorously. Still nothing, except the sound of scrabbling claws on hessian. He gave a sudden impatient flick and at last the possum fell out soundlessly onto the kitchen floor and crouched there, motionless.

'What is it?'

There was a general crowding forward—much craning and peering in the shadows thrown by the lamp on the cupboard!

'It's a blue rabbit!'

'It's a chinchilla!'

'It's got a long tail!'

'Well, I'm blowed!'

Dad was obviously impatient at the ignorance of his family. He stepped forward imperiously to settle the thing once and for all, just as the right answer dawned on everyone else.

'It's a *possum*!'

The combined shout seemed to rouse the captive. Perhaps it was just that it was beginning to recover from its daze, or that its eyes were growing used to the light. Whatever the cause, it suddenly seemed to become aware of Dad's boots beside it, each one bigger than it was itself, and, above them, towering up towards the ceiling, something tall and straight and soft.

Everyone agreed afterwards that it was hard to remember any definite movement that started it. There was a sort of blue-grey shadow running up Dad's side, and that was all. But in an instant the set tableau of the whole family was broken into whirling bits.

'Look out!'

'He's on Dad!'

'Phui, you devil!'

The possum, which had fled up to the top of Dad's head, paused there for only a second, its little hands clutching him tightly by one ear, before it realised that it had chosen a very unsteady tree. Even before Dad could begin flapping wildly at his head, yelling and dancing about as if he were on fire, the possum had seen the danger of its situation and jumped for the mantelpiece. It caught the edge, hung there for an instant, then scrabbled up and ran swiftly along to the far end where it climbed onto the canister marked SAGO. Here it turned round and faced them.

'Oh, it's pretty,' said little Anna.

'Poor little thing,' said Lottie, 'it's frightened. Isn't it a pet!'

'It's a *pest*!' Dad rubbed his ear resentfully and glared at the possum with insulted dignity. And up on the canister the little animal that was the cause of it all sat quite motionless. Perhaps not quite 'sat'; rather did it seem to be balanced on fur, cushioned and spongy, resting on nothing in particular. Its four feet were all tucked away somewhere; its furry tail curled round into a ringlet on the side of the tin. But it was far from sleepy-looking. Its little pointed face was more peaked than ever, its button-nose thrust forward on the verge of a twitch, and its eyes, big and soft and wise, fixed full on them.

'Grab him!' Herbert yelled, coming out from behind the table. 'Now's your chance.'

He and Dad lunged simultaneously, the soft feel of fur already tingling in their imaginations. But the possum was gone. It skittered along to the other end of the shelf; Big Ben, the alarm clock whose iron roar had woken Dad and half the farm each morning for the past fourteen years, tilted under the momentary pressure of its passing. It toppled over on its side, rocked there once on the very edge, then fell with a crash of glass and an expiring clang of bells. Dad made a leap to the left like a slips-fieldsman, but again he was too late.

'*Verdammt!*' he shouted. 'Get him out of here before everything is in pieces.'

But the possum, seeing the trend of things, leapt for the top of the dresser before he could be hemmed in on the shelf. From the dresser he climbed to the top of the open door and from there scrabbled crab-wise across the flywire looking for an opening onto the dark verandah and the freedom beyond it.

'I'll get him!' cried Oscar, and grabbed.

To his astonishment he found himself with both hands momentarily round the possum's middle, very much like a child holding a tame tabby. But only momentarily! Four sets of claws and two rows of sharp teeth instantly needling him were too much for Oscar. He dropped the possum with a yell. Before anyone could recover, the possum had fled up the table-leg, flashed across the tea-things with a clatter of cups, sugar-bowls and cutlery, scalded a leg in somebody's hot noodle soup and, with a little squeak of pain and fear, raced up on top of the dresser again.

'Heh! Heh! Heh!' laughed Grandpa, more delighted than surprised, 'he's a jolly quick insect ain't he!'

'Get him out! Get him out!' Mum cried in anguish, 'or into the fire he'll jump.'

Dad came forward purposefully.

'Look out!' he said, pushing Oscar aside. 'Let me.'

Dad was a big man—six feet tall and an axe handle across the shoulders. Each of his hands was like a leg of mutton. With fine strategy he crouched against the side of the dresser ready to surprise the possum with a sudden grab. To the others he looked rather like a hippopotamus trying to hide behind a water-lily, but no one argued with Dad, especially when his blood was up. For a moment they all stood tense and silent. The whole kitchen was motionless, rigid. A burning twig snapped in the stove, the kettle hummed gently in an undertone.

'Got you!'

Dad's shout was more of a challenge to battle than a roar of triumph. His shoulder crashed against the dresser in his fearful upward grasp and the whole thing rocked precariously. Four plates standing on edge inside it fell forward on their faces with a crash. Mum shrieked, Anna cried out, and Oscar and Herbert leapt forward to stop the whole dresser from falling on its face too. As for Dad, he felt the tingle of fur running along his fingertips, but nothing more. His attack, so to speak, had fallen short, and the quarry was back on the mantel—this time on the very top of the highest canister, marked FLOUR.

'You hairy moke!' Dad, breathing heavily, made straight for the mantelpiece. Battle was now fully joined. The boys whooped, the girls shrieked, Dad flailed. And the possum, terrified beyond belief, fled from place to place like a grey shadow, always just one instant ahead of its pursuers. The air was full of hands, always descending or charging from front or rear or from this side or that or coming up from below. It darted and dived, scuttled and ran, leapt and clung, in a mad merry-go-round of noise and fear. Beads of perspiration began to stand out on Dad's face; his breath wheezed.

'Get the broom!' he cried, panting. 'Get the broom!'

'Which broom? Where?'

'Any broom! Any broom! Something to poke him down with!'

Herbert, who could never remember where the broom was kept if he had some sweeping to do, was back with it instantly. He made a dart at the possum but aimed too low and merely crumpled the sides of the canister with a crackling thud.

As more and more weapons were brought to bear, the threat to everyone increased. The kitchen began to look more and more like a riot-torn cafe. But it was on the fourth time round that the real danger suddenly threatened. Tired and terrified, the possum became less sure of its way, clumsier in its movements—and, racing along the top of the cupboard, collided with the lamp and sent it hurtling down.

'Look out! The lamp!'

In an emergency Dad was always reliable. He was strong and quick, even if no one could possibly describe him as cool. He was out to the verandah and back with two empty bags that were used as boot-mats there, almost before the first surge of flame flared from the spilt kerosene among the broken glass. And in another moment he had both bags down to smother the flames and was jumping and stamping about on them with his great boots, crackling and pounding the glass into fragments as he did so, as if the flames were living things and he was crushing their bones into little bits as he pounded the life out of them.

It was all over quickly. In the light of the stove Dad threw monstrous shadows against the walls as he stamped and smote. His face and hands glowed red. It was an eerie, satanic sight. Mum quaked visibly in the corner. The white smoke and the stinging tang of kerosene and burnt hessian filled the kitchen, and the linoleum bubbled and heaved tackily like toasted cheese. But it wasn't really serious. In ten minutes the worst of the mess had been cleared up. Mum got a candle-holder and stood it on the table—well in towards the middle.

'Possums!' said Dad in a fierce whisper to himself—a tone he only adopted in times of extreme emotion. 'Blasted insects! Burn the place down around our ears next.' In moments of great stress everything—fur, fin and feather—became 'insect' to Dad and Grandpa.

'Where is he?' asked Herbert. 'Where's the possum?'

But the possum had gone. The screen door having been flung open in the turmoil, he had fled out into the safety of the dark. And the storm in the kitchen died out in rumbles and mutterings now that its storm-centre, that little grey nucleus of energy, had disappeared into the night. All that was left was the aftermath.

Out by the edge of the verandah Bruno slunk to the pump and doused the smart of the possum's claws in the cold water from the underground tank. If he could have taken out his heart, how gladly he would have held that in the cool plunge and shock of the water too, to take away the burn of the shame and wrong that he felt. Life was inscrutable. From the triumph of a possum captured to the disgrace of a kitchen in shambles and, greatest sin of all, the evil of fire set loose in his own home. It had been so quick. It was something he could not have foreseen. As he crept along the verandah to the towel-rail he could hear Mum's voice remonstrating gently with Dad.

'But Marcus, it was not really his fault.'

'Don't talk stupid, woman! Of course it was his fault! Did the possum want to come in by himself, to pay us a visit?'

'He couldn't help it, Marcus! You know that!'

'Of course he could help it! He could have left the possum where it was.'

'And the rabbits too?'

'Rabbits are different.'

'The same thing you would have done when you were a boy. You would have caught the possum too.'

'Ahhh . . .' Dad's voice trailed off into an exasperated grumble. A big tear started suddenly in Bruno's eye and he dabbed it hastily with the towel. Dear old Mum! He knew she was near tears herself, but she had a great love in her small body—more than Dad would ever know—and Bruno felt it suddenly like a warm and living thing. If she had come out into the darkness of the verandah at that moment he would have behaved like Anna or Lottie and flung himself on her and kissed her. Some day, Bruno felt, Mum would die for them, and perhaps they would never even know. Yet by comparison with Dad she seemed as small and spindly as the underfed-looking stick figures drawn in the school primer—as angular and jerky too. But that was where it ended. Her strong instinct of motherly protection, inherited from her Silesian ancestors, was something she had brought to South Australia, along with the Lutheranism, the gregariousness and the astonishing capacity for hard work that her forebears had brought with them when they had fled from Germany in Pastor Kavel's flock to the freedom of the new wilderness in Australia. And so, when it came to a question of defending her younger children she could stand up even in the face of Dad's anger.

There was silence for a moment. Then Dad's voice took up the train of his silent thinking.

'When do the holidays end?'

'On Monday.'

'He goes back to school on Tuesday morning?'

'Yes.'

'With the new school-teacher?'

'Miss Gent, she is called. After the holidays Mr. Robinson's place she is taking. His kidneys were too sick to come back.' Mum observed a moment's silence in memory of Mr. Robinson's kidneys before continuing about Miss Gent.

'They say she is a good teacher, a real fine teacher.'

Dad was brusque. 'Might do Bruno a bit of good, then! He mightn't have so much time to muck about, for a change.' But Bruno was a boy, and so he still managed to find time to muck about.

1961

OODGEROO NOONUCCAL
1920–1993

Describing herself as an educator and storyteller, Oodgeroo (meaning 'paperbark tree') of the Noonuccal tribe of Minjerriba (North Stradbroke Island, Queensland) was an Aboriginal poet, environmentalist and leader in the struggle for Aboriginal rights.

She was educated at Dunwich State School, became a domestic servant at thirteen and joined the army during the Second World War. In 1942 she married her childhood friend Bruce Walker. She had two sons. In 1988, Kath Walker readopted her tribal name as a protest against Australia's Bicentenary celebrations and a symbol of her Aboriginal pride.

Oodgeroo was politically active from the late 1940s and became one of the most prominent Aboriginal voices. She joined the Communist Party of Australia, the only political party opposed to the White Australia policy at the time, and from the early 1960s held key positions in the Aboriginal civil rights movement. She was a founding member and Queensland state secretary of FCAATSI, and a leader of the successful 1967 referendum campaign. She later chaired the National Tribal Council, the Aboriginal Arts Board, the Aboriginal Housing Committee and the Queensland Aboriginal Advancement League.

We Are Going, the first book of poetry by an Aboriginal writer and the first book by an Aboriginal woman, was published in 1964. In the following years Oodgeroo wrote numerous volumes of poetry, books for children, a play, essays, speeches and books illustrated with her own artworks, including *The Dawn is at Hand* (1966), *My People: A Kath Walker collection* (1970), *Stories from Stradbroke* (1972), *Kath Walker in China* (1988), *The Rainbow Serpent* (1988) and *Australia's Unwritten History: More legends of our land* (1992). She travelled widely overseas, representing Aboriginal writing and culture. For many years Oodgeroo lived at Moongalba ('sitting-down place'), her home on Minjerriba, where she established the Noonuccal-Nughie Education and Cultural Centre and for over two decades shared her culture and way of life with thousands of visitors. The grandmother of Aboriginal poetry was buried on Minjerriba with great ceremony. *AH/PM*

Speech Launching the Petition of the Federal Council for Aboriginal Advancement

[…] I feel now that I must bring in two very important words, they are integration and assimilation. There seems to be much confusion around these two words, the policy of the government up till now has been that of assimilation for my people. Now, boiled down, assimilation means the swallowing up by a majority group of a minority group. My people, the Aboriginal people, are the minority group and they can only be assimilated by the final wiping out of this minority group. Now it is not our desire to have this happen, they have tried hard to do this, but it has not been successful and we feel that this is the most inhuman way of bringing my people forward, we feel that something must be done about it, so picture if you can, in my attempt to explain to you these two very important words, picture if you can a river which we will call the river of ignorance with two banks, the one on the right side we shall call the civilisation side of the bridge, the other side—stone age. Imagine a span from the civilised side of the bridge up and we shall call that span assimilation. Now my people on the stone age side of the bridge have to jump the big gap to the assimilation side span of the bridge. Some made it, I was fortunate enough to be one of them, to have made this big jump, but there are thousands of my people who did not, and they fell to the river bank below and were forced to live like scavengers on the rubbish dumps of the white race. These are our fringe dwellers, they have come too far and cannot climb back to what used to be, but they have not yet reached the stage where they can stand side by side with the white race. Of all my people, I'm most upset about the fringe dwellers. Much help is needed for them. How then, can we help the fringe dwellers?

Now then, let us put the other span of the bridge in, the span from the stone age side of the bridge, and we'll call it integration. Integration means the bringing forward of a race of people with their own identity and their own pride intact. They would come forward onto the integration side of the bridge with such things as their culture and their language. No doubt the old people would want to stay at the integration side of the bridge, so let it be. Let the choice be that of my people, they should be allowed to stay there. But the young people who are forever pushing on, would no doubt cross to the assimilation side of the bridge and so on to the assimilation side of the river. But when they crossed this bridge, the young people would do so, proud of the fact that they were of Aboriginal blood, happy to be what they are, and not going forward as replicas of the white race. Assimilation can only bring us forward as replicas of the white race; this is not what we desire, we desire to be Aboriginals, proud of this fact, and when they stood on the other side of the bridge amongst the civilised people, the white people, they would stand there as a friend and neighbour alongside the white man, respecting his way of life and expecting him in return to respect the Aboriginal's way of life. Now I find in my tour through, that the Aboriginal's knowledge is much greater than that of the white man in one respect. He knows more about the white man than the white man knows about us, and this is something that we must get together and rectify. We took time off, we, the Aboriginals took time off to understand what the white man wanted and to respect his views, this has not happened on the white man's side of the bridge and now the time has come when he himself must get to know us and understand us and respect us for what we want. I know that the present generation is not responsible for the past, I cannot blame the present white man or woman nor will I hold him or her responsible for what has happened in the past. I care not about the past, but the future I am worried about. The future is what we want, a bigger and brighter future for both races. I will however, and I feel I'm justified, I will hold the present white man and woman responsible for what happens to my people in the future. This I feel is their responsibility as well as mine.

1962

Aboriginal Charter of Rights

> We want hope, not racialism,
> Brotherhood, not ostracism,
> Black advance, not white ascendance:
> Make us equals, not dependants.

We need help, not exploitation,   5
We want freedom, not frustration;
Not control, but self-reliance,
Independence, not compliance,
Not rebuff, but education,
Self-respect, not resignation.   10
Free us from a mean subjection,
From a bureaucrat Protection.
Let's forget the old-time slavers:
Give us fellowship, not favours;
Encouragement, not prohibitions,   15
Homes, not settlements and missions.
We need love, not overlordship,
Grip of hand, not whip-hand wardship;
Opportunity that places
White and black on equal basis.   20
You dishearten, not defend us,
Circumscribe, who should befriend us.
Give us welcome, not aversion,
Give us choice, not cold coercion,
Status, not discrimination,   25
Human rights, not segregation.
You the law, like Roman Pontius,
Make us proud, not colour-conscious;
Give the deal you still deny us,
Give goodwill, not bigot bias;   30
Give ambition, not prevention,
Confidence, not condescension;
Give incentive, not restriction,
Give us Christ, not crucifixion.
Though baptized and blessed and Bibled   35
We are still tabooed and libelled.
You devout Salvation-sellers,
Make us neighbours, not fringe-dwellers;
Make us mates, not poor relations,
Citizens, not serfs on stations.   40
Must we native Old Australians
In our own land rank as aliens?
Banish bans and conquer caste,
Then we'll win our own at last.

                                                                1964

The Dispossessed

For Uncle Willie McKenzie

Peace was yours, Australian man, with tribal laws you made,
Till white Colonials stole your peace with rape and murder raid;
They shot and poisoned and enslaved until, a scattered few,
Only a remnant now remain, and the heart dies in you.
The white man claimed your hunting grounds and you could not remain, 5
They made you work as menials for greedy private gain;
Your tribes are broken vagrants now wherever whites abide,
And justice of the white man means justice to you denied.
They brought you Bibles and disease, the liquor and the gun:
With Christian culture such as these the white command was won. 10
A dying race you linger on, degraded and oppressed,
Outcasts in your own native land, you are the dispossessed.

When Churches mean a way of life, as Christians proudly claim,
And when hypocrisy is scorned and hate is counted shame,
Then only shall intolerance die and old injustice cease, 15
And white and dark as brothers find equality and peace.
But oh, so long the wait has been, so slow the justice due,
Courage decays for want of hope, and the heart dies in you.

1964

We Are Going

For Grannie Coolwell

They came in to the little town
A semi-naked band subdued and silent,
All that remained of their tribe.
They came here to the place of their old bora ground
Where now the many white men hurry about like ants. 5
Notice of estate agent reads: 'Rubbish May Be Tipped Here'.
Now it half covers the traces of the old bora ring.
They sit and are confused, they cannot say their thoughts:
'We are as strangers here now, but the white tribe are the strangers.
We belong here, we are of the old ways. 10
We are the corroboree and the bora ground,
We are the old sacred ceremonies, the laws of the elders.
We are the wonder tales of Dream Time, the tribal legends told.
We are the past, the hunts and the laughing games, the wandering
    camp fires.
We are the lightning-bolt over Gaphembah Hill 15

Quick and terrible,
And the Thunderer after him, that loud fellow.
We are the quiet daybreak paling the dark lagoon.
We are the shadow-ghosts creeping back as the camp fires burn low.
We are nature and the past, all the old ways   20
Gone now and scattered.
The scrubs are gone, the hunting and the laughter.
The eagle is gone, the emu and the kangaroo are gone from this place.
The bora ring is gone.
The corroboree is gone.   25
And we are going.'

                                                                        1964

Assimilation—No!

Pour your pitcher of wine into the wide river
And where is your wine? There is only the river.
Must the genius of an old race die
That the race might live?
We who would be one with you, one people,   5
We must surrender now much that we love,
The old freedoms for new musts,
Your world for ours,
But a core is left that we must keep always.
Change and compel, slash us into shape,   10
But not our roots deep in the soil of old.
We are different hearts and minds
In a different body. Do not ask of us
To be deserters, to disown our mother,
To change the unchangeable.   15
The gum cannot be trained into an oak.
Something is gone, something surrendered, still
We will go forward and learn.
Not swamped and lost, watered away, but keeping
Our own identity, our pride of race.   20
Pour your pitcher of wine into the wide river
And where is your wine? There is only the river.

                                                                        1966

Integration—Yes!

Gratefully we learn from you,
The advanced race,
You with long centuries of lore behind you.

We who were Australians long before
You who came yesterday,   5
Eagerly we must learn to change,
Learn new needs we never wanted,
New compulsions never needed,
The price of survival.
Much that we loved is gone and had to go,   10
But not the deep indigenous things.
The past is still so much a part of us,
Still about us, still within us.
We are happiest
Among our own people. We would like to see   15
Our own customs kept, our old
Dances and songs, crafts and corroborees.
Why change our sacred myths for your sacred myths?
No, not assimilation but integration,
Not submergence but our uplifting,   20
So black and white may go forward together
In harmony and brotherhood.

                                                                                    1966

The Dawn is at Hand

Dark brothers, first Australian race,
Soon you will take your rightful place
In the brotherhood long waited for,
Fringe-dwellers no more.

Sore, sore the tears you shed   5
When hope seemed folly and justice dead.
Was the long night weary? Look up, dark band,
The dawn is at hand.

Go forward proudly and unafraid
To your birthright all too long delayed,   10
For soon now the shame of the past
Will be over at last.

You will be welcomed mateship-wise
In industry and in enterprise;
No profession will bar the door,   15
Fringe-dwellers no more.

Dark and white upon common ground
In club and office and social round,
Yours the feel of a friendly land,
The grip of the hand.   20

Sharing the same equality
In college and university,
All ambitions of hand or brain
Yours to attain.

For ban and bias will soon be gone,   25
The future beckons you bravely on
To art and letters and nation lore,
Fringe-dwellers no more.

                                                               1966

No More Boomerang

No more boomerang
No more spear;
Now all civilized—
Colour bar and beer.

No more corroboree,   5
Gay dance and din.
Now we got movies,
And pay to go in.

No more sharing
What the hunter brings.   10
Now we work for money,
Then pay it back for things.

Now we track bosses
To catch a few bob,
Now we go walkabout   15
On bus to the job.

One time naked,
Who never knew shame;
Now we put clothes on
To hide whatsaname.   20

No more gunya,
Now bungalow,
Paid by higher purchase
In twenty year or so.

Lay down the stone axe,   25
Take up the steel,
And work like a nigger
For a white man meal.

No more firesticks
That made the whites scoff.   30
Now all electric,
And no better off.

Bunyip he finish,
Now got instead
White fella Bunyip,   35
Call him Red.

Abstract picture now—
What they coming at?
Cripes, in our caves we
Did better than that.   40

Black hunted wallaby,
White hunt dollar;
White fella witch-doctor
Wear dog-collar.

No more message-stick;   45
Lubras and lads
Got television now,
Mostly ads.

Lay down the woomera,
Lay down the waddy.   50
Now we got atom-bomb,
End *every*body.

                                                1966

Ballad of the Totems

My father was Noonuccal man and kept old tribal way,
His totem was the Carpet Snake, whom none must ever slay;
But mother was of Peewee clan, and loudly she expressed
The daring view that carpet snakes were nothing but a pest.

Now one lived right inside with us in full immunity,   5
For no one dared to interfere with father's stern decree:
A mighty fellow ten feet long, and as we lay in bed
We kids could watch him round a beam not far above our head.

Only the dog was scared of him, we'd hear its whines and growls,
But mother fiercely hated him because he took her fowls.   10
You should have heard her diatribes that flowed in angry torrents
With words you never see in print, except in D.H. Lawrence.

'I kill that robber,' she would scream, fierce as a spotted cat;
'You see that bulge inside of him? My speckly hen make that!'
But father's loud and strict command made even mother quake;   15
I think he'd sooner kill a man than kill a carpet snake.

That reptile was a greedy-guts, and as each bulge digested
He'd come down on the hunt at night as appetite suggested.
We heard his stealthy slithering sound across the earthen floor,
While the dog gave a startled yelp and bolted out the door.   20

Then over in the chicken-yard hysterical fowls gave tongue,
Loud frantic squawks accompanied by the barking of the mung,
Until at last the racket passed, and then to solve the riddle,
Next morning he was back up there with a new bulge in his middle.

When father died we wailed and cried, our grief was deep and sore,   25
And strange to say from that sad day the snake was seen no more.
The wise old men explained to us: 'It was his tribal brother,
And that is why it done a guy'—but some looked hard at mother.

1966

ROBIN DALTON
b. 1920

Born in England, Robin Dalton grew up in Sydney. Her childhood is discussed in *Aunts Up the Cross* (1965), a comic recreation of an eccentric family published under her unmarried name, Robin Eakin. This was followed much later by *An*

Incidental Memoir (1998). This second volume covers the author's time in England as a film producer. Her credits include the adaptation of Peter Carey's (qv) *Oscar and Lucinda*. DM

From *Aunts Up the Cross*
Chapter 8

Although my father appeared in the role of resigned provider to a household of permanent guests, I think his enjoyment of their continual company equalled, in his much quieter way, my mother's. At least he could escape, and frequently did—not far, to be sure, for to reach his bed he had to undress in one room and make his way in striped pyjamas through the crowded sitting-room to the verandah where he slept. But he had no inhibitions about doing this and the evening's conversation continued to the accompaniment of his ferocious snores. He became, at this time, quite an established 'club man' and keen billiards player. His championship status ended on the day he shot himself; ever after, he found it painful and difficult to bend the affected knee into the prescribed position.

Actually his first two adventures with firearms weren't too serious: only on the third occasion was any bodily damage done. The pistol was of very small, very smart Spanish manufacture—just large enough to lie in the palm of his hand, and affording a more comforting and solid feel than the thin jingle of key rings or the like with which some men fidget. He first came to carry one of these on the advice of the police, who were concerned over his lone night calls into the underworld areas of dock and slum land. Sydney had during the Thirties a crime wave of serious proportions, terrorised by a gang of slashers known as the Razor Gang, and it was against the possibility of attack by these assailants that the gun was bought. On his first day home with his new toy, my father indulged in a little quiet target practice in the surgery, but beyond a ricochetting bullet which gouged some plaster out of the surgery wall, splintered a glass case full of instruments and bounced harmlessly out into the light area, no untoward incidents occurred. Secure in the assumption that he now knew when it was liable to go off, and when it was not, he took the gun out with him at night for as long as the situation lasted, and occasionally fondled it by day as it lay in his desk drawer. When war broke out, all licences to own firearms were reviewed: my father took his pistol up to No. 3 Police Station where, over a cup of tea with the Station boys, he missed the sergeant's leg by inches.

On the afternoon he finally shot himself, my mother was upstairs and as usual entertaining some friends to tea. It was a humid, somnolent day, enervating; and the patient who was sitting by my father's desk cataloguing her woes was one of his regular and more boring hypochondriacs, whose long list of ailments needed no further response than an occasional murmur of sympathy. Whilst making these reassuring noises, he idly fingered the pistol in the middle drawer of his desk, lying in its accustomed nest of old papers, tobacco pouches, and pipe cleaners. As usual it was loaded, and, as usual, my father hadn't quite got the hang of it.

'I get these terrifying palpitations, Doctor—sometimes when I lie down I think I'm going to choke. And then, suddenly, I'll get a feeling of something awful about to happen—it's my nerves, I suppose. Don't you think I should have something to calm my nerves?'

'Mmmm,' said my father, and pulled the trigger.

The bullet made a deafening report, in the doubly-confined space of the drawer, and of the consulting room. The initial impact of the drawer-bottom probably lightened the blow, which nevertheless neatly blew off part of my father's kneecap. The patient swooned—my father cursed and bellowed—the nurse ran in, first to mop up the blood and call an ambulance into which she assisted my father; then, to revive the patient and put her in a taxi. Upstairs my mother's guests exclaimed at the noise, but my mother assured them, 'Don't worry. The doctor's probably shot himself.'

It was not until some hours later that she learnt that her husband was in hospital, where he stayed for two weeks, the central figure of a good deal of amused attention.

Later that night, I opened the door to two plain-clothes policemen.

'Miss Eakin,' they said, 'you can tell that father of yours that if he doesn't learn to use that gun properly soon, we're going to take it away from him.'

While he was in hospital, the patient who had witnessed the accident recovered sufficiently to ring him for further professional advice. In fact, the hospital switchboard operators were pestered by the wretched woman, and finally agreed to ask the doctor for his opinion. The Sister on duty came one day, 'Mrs So-and-so is on the telephone. She says to tell you she has that sinking feeling again, and please, what should she do?'

'Tell her,' said my father, 'to strike out for the shore.'

1965

GWEN HARWOOD
1920–1995

The poet and librettist Gwen Harwood was born in Brisbane. Upon her marriage, she moved to Hobart. Harwood loved music. She studied piano and composition, and held the position of organist at All Saints Church, Brisbane. She also had a deep interest in philosophy, especially that of Ludwig Wittgenstein. Harwood's musico-philosophical interests come together in the ironic personae Professor Eisenbart and Professor Kröte, who figure in Harwood's first collections, *Poems* (1963) and *Poems: Volume two* (1968).

In addition to the use of poetic personae, until the early 1970s Harwood published and submitted poems to editors pseudonymously, and throughout her career she was attracted to parody, as seen in 'The Sick Philosopher'. Such practices illustate Harwood's attraction to puzzles and mischief. Such mischievous literary practices are most obviously expressed in Harwood's hoaxing of the *Bulletin* in 1961 with two uncomplimentary acrostic sonnets.

Harwood's lyric poetry deals with 'universal' themes regarding ageing, death and issues to do with identity. A number of Harwood's poems detail the lives of women submerged in domesticity and suburbia. As Elizabeth Lawson notes in *The Oxford Companion to Australian Literature* (1994), Harwood's wide-ranging poems have an 'unusual capacity to blend opposing feelings: the painful with the funny, exhilaration with rue, black jokiness with the death's head, warmth and fun with nostalgia'. Harwood's poems are also formally controlled, and deeply rooted in a sense of place. Despite being an unwilling traveller to Tasmania, she became that island-state's representative poet.

In 2003 Harwood's *Collected Poems 1943–1995* appeared, edited by Alison Hoddinott and Gregory Kratzmann. A collection of her letters, edited by Kratzmann, appeared as *A Steady Storm of Correspondence* (2001). Harwood also wrote libretti for a number of composers, especially Larry Sitsky. A recipient of numerous literary awards herself, Harwood has a poetry prize named after her. *DM*

Father and Child

I. BARN OWL

Daybreak: the household slept.
I rose, blessed by the sun.
A horny fiend, I crept
out with my father's gun.
Let him dream of a child   5
obedient, angel-mild—

old No-Sayer, robbed of power
by sleep. I knew my prize
who swooped home at this hour
with daylight-riddled eyes   10
to his place on a high beam
in our old stables, to dream

light's useless time away.
I stood, holding my breath,
in urine-scented hay,   15
master of life and death,
a wisp-haired judge whose law
would punish beak and claw.

My first shot struck. He swayed,
ruined, beating his only   20
wing, as I watched, afraid

by the fallen gun, a lonely
child who believed death clean
and final, not this obscene

bundle of stuff that dropped,   25
and dribbled through loose straw
tangling in bowels, and hopped
blindly closer. I saw
those eyes that did not see
mirror my cruelty   30

while the wrecked thing that could
not bear the light nor hide
hobbled in its own blood.
My father reached my side,
gave me the fallen gun.   35
'End what you have begun.'

I fired. The blank eyes shone
once into mine, and slept.
I leaned my head upon
my father's arm, and wept,   40
owl-blind in early sun
for what I had begun.

                                                   1975

Matinee

Kröte[1] plays for a tenor bleating
Schubert songs at an Afternoon.
Some idiot biscuit-nibbler beating
time on a saucer with a spoon
makes him accelerate his pace.   5
Annoyance clouds the tenor's face.

He sings, 'My heart is like the sea',[2]
frowning at his accompanist,
but at 'where many a pearl may be'
glows, to imply he can't resist   10

1   A character who appears in a number of Harwood's poems. A European professor of music, he is alienated
    by the conventionality and materialism of Australia.
2   From Schubert's *Schwanengesang* (Swan Song).

the charm of music-loving girls
who plainly think he's crammed with pearls.

Applause! The singer's head is turned
with praise. Kröte's ignored. 'I am
where those young ladies are concerned   15
only a giant human clam
in whose unlovable inside
dull pearls the size of golf-balls hide.'

Hoping by instinct to locate
some drink better than tea, he snatches   20
the choicest cream-cake from a plate,
and wanders off while no one watches,
licking his fingers, opening doors,
dropping odd crumbs on polished floors

or bedroom carpets. His vain prying   25
leads him into a nursery
where in its cot a child is crying.
Kröte looks round him guiltily.
Mother? or nurse? No one at all.
How tenderly he lifts the small   30

creature and soothes it; rearranges
its shawl; so, comforted and kissed,
the fretful baby's crying changes
to trembling smiles. From its plump wrist
dangles a heart-shaped locket set   35
with pearls. Engraved is: *Margaret.*

'My child. My sister.' Kröte sits
beside the window with his prize,
marvelling how her frail skull fits
the hollow of his arm, how wise   40
yet innocent her glances seem.
He takes her, in his waking dream,

to be his own. Sober, inspired
by his enchanting child, his days
are prodigies of work; admired   45
by all, he writes, composes, plays

as no one's played before. He sees
his image in the glass, and he's

himself, the man he knows, the same
suburban Orpheus reflected   50
against a darkening sky, whose name
is called, who knows that he's expected
to play more swan songs. So he lays
his sleeping beauty down, but stays

one moment longer to make sure   55
her sleep is sound. 'So was I, long
ago,' he mourns, losing the pure
translucence of her face among
those ignorant of what wonders rest
in his obscure, unfathomed breast.   60
                                                            1975

Carnal Knowledge II

Grasshoppers click and whirr.
Stones grow in the field.
Autumnal warmth is sealed
in a gold skin of light
on darkness plunging down   5
to earth's black molten core.

Earth has no more to yield.
Her blond grasses are dry.
    Nestling my cheek against
    the hollow of your thigh
    I lay cockeyed with love   10
    in the most literal sense.

Your eyes, kingfisher blue.
This was the season, this
the light, the halcyon air.   15
Our window framed this place.
If there were music here,
insectile, abstract, bare,

it would bless no human ear.
Shadows lie with the stones.   20

Bury our hearts, perhaps
they'll strike it rich in earth's
black marrow, crack, take root,
bring forth vines, blossom, fruit.

    Roses knocked on the glass.   25
    Wine like a running stream
    no evil spell could cross
    flowed round the house of touch.
God grant me drunkenness
if this is sober knowledge,   30

song to melt sea and sky
apart, and lift these hills
from the shadow of what was,
and roll them back, and lie
in naked ignorance   35
in the hollow of your thigh.

                                  1975

Andante

    New houses grasp our hillside,
    my favourite walks are fenced.
    Still there's the foreshore, still
    transparent overlappings
    seaward, let there be space   5
    for the demon's timeless patience
    with myself and my dying.

    Silence fixes our loves.
    Let me cultivate silence.
    What's my head but a rat's nest   10
    of dubious texts? Let water
    ask me, what have you learned?
    I tell the plush deeps, nothing.
    Nightfall, an old vexed hour.

    Why do I have an image   15
    of owls with silver bells
    hung from the tarsus, hunting
    fieldmice round the new houses?

Hunger, music and death.
And after that the calm   20
full frontal stare of silence.

                                                           1981

Dialogue

If an angel came with one wish
I might say, deliver that child
who died before birth, into life.
Let me see what she might have become.
He would bring her into a room   5
fair skinned   the bones of her hands
would press on my shoulderblades
in our long embrace
                        we would sit
with the albums spread on our knees: 10
now here are your brothers   and here
your sister   here the old house
among trees and espaliered almonds.
—But where am I?
                        Ah my dear   15
I have only one picture
                    here
in my head   I saw you lying
still folded   one moment   forever
your head bent down to your heart   20
eyes closed on unspeakable wisdom
your delicate frog-pale fingers
                                    spread
apart as if you were playing
a woodwind instrument.   25
          —My name?
                        It was never given.
          —Where is my grave?
                        In my head   I suppose
the hospital burnt you.   30
          —Was I beautiful?
                        To me.
          —Do you mourn for me every day?
Not at all   it is more than thirty years
I am feeling the coolness of age   35
the perspectives of memory change.

Pearlskull   what lifts you here
from night-drift to solemn ripeness?
Mushroom dome? Gourd plumpness?
The frog in my pot of basil?[1]   40
    —It is none of these, but a rhythm
    the bones of my fingers   dactylic[2]
    rhetoric smashed from your memory.
    Forget me again.
              Had I lived   45
    no rhythm would be the same
    nor my brothers and sister feast
    in the world's eternal house.

Overhead   wings of cloud
    burning   and under my feet   50
        stones marked with demons' teeth.
          1981

Mother Who Gave Me Life

Mother who gave me life
I think of women bearing
women. Forgive me the wisdom
I would not learn from you.

It is not for my children I walk   5
on earth in the light of the living.
It is for you, for the wild
daughters becoming women,

anguish of seasons burning
backward in time to those other   10
bodies, your mother, and hers
and beyond, speech growing stranger

on thresholds of ice, rock, fire,
bones changing, heads inclining
to monkey bosom, lemur breast,   15
guileless milk of the word.

1   A reference to John Keats's macabre poem 'Isabella, or the Pot of Basil' (1820).
2   In poetry: a metrical foot of one stressed syllable followed by two unstressed syllables.

I prayed you would live to see
Halley's Comet a second time.
The Sister said, When she died
she was folding a little towel.   20

You left the world so, having lived
nearly thirty thousand days:
a fabric of marvels folded
down to a little space.

At our last meeting I closed   25
the ward door of heavy glass
between us, and saw your face
crumple, fine threadbare linen

worn, still good to the last,
then, somehow, smooth to a smile   30
so I should not see your tears.
Anguish: remembered hours:

a lamp on embroidered linen,
my supper set out, your voice
calling me in as darkness   35
falls on my father's house.

                                                   1981

Bone Scan

Thou hast searched me and known me.
Thou knowest my downsitting and mine uprising.
                                    Psalm 139

In the twinkling of an eye,
in a moment, all is changed:
on a small radiant screen
(honeydew melon green)
are my scintillating bones.   5
Still in my flesh I see
the God who goes with me
glowing with radioactive
isotopes. This is what he
at last allows a mortal   10
eye to behold: the grand

supporting frame complete
(but for the wisdom teeth),
the friend who lives beneath
appearances, alive   15
with light. Each glittering bone
assures me: you are known.

                                                                    1988

The Sick Philosopher[1]

Hold hard, Fred, lift me down once more, I think I need some Ayer.[2]
    I thought my brain would last me to the end,
But I've caught the Scepticisms and I can't be sure you're there,
    So I'll put my wits together and pretend.

'Twas merry in the glowing morn among the campus trees   5
    With dialogic problems far behind,
To engage in textual intercourse with pretty PhDs,
    Or to wander in a pleasant frame of mind.

'Twas merry in the staff club where we sat all afternoon
    While the chardonnay was running like a creek,   10
And waited after dinner for the rising of the moon,
    Discussing that whereof one cannot speak.

I wonder what's become of Schopenhauer's little Will
    And that herd of Monads Leibniz used to keep,
And are there signs of trespassing on Hegemonic Hill   15
    Where the Hart[3] leaps and the students flock like sheep?

When I lie beneath the pasture as an unexamined given
    Will my monoglossic nationalism die?
And can I wear a seamless textual robe at last in heaven
    When there's nothing left on earth to signify?   20

O bury me in hyper-space and fence me round with Posts,
    And leave me where the gentle grasses wave.
May the post-colonial forces drive away the angry ghosts
    From the charismatic statue on my grave.

                                                                    1992

1   See Adam Lindsay Gordon's (qv) 'The Sick Stockrider'.
2   A.J. Ayer (1910–89), philosopher.
3   Possibly Kevin Hart (qv) or H.L.A. Hart (1907–92), philosopher.

Letter to Tony Riddell

23.8.95

Dearest T,

Perhaps the last letter. I'm very weak and shaky though I fear the liberation I long for is still far off. A university student has just rung me to say she was organizing a 'Bluestocking Breakfast'. Invasion by telephone—'I am *terminally ill*,' I replied. 'I cannot come to any kind of breakfast,' and hung up. O for the day of invitation cards and courtesy.

Tony Staley[1] was on early TV today talking about near-death experiences he enjoyed when he was in hospital after his terrible accident. Three times he nearly died, twice he had the now often-reported light & presence of old friends and total bliss. He said it didn't make him believe in an after-life, it was just overwhelmingly delightful. As he observed, it may result from changes in the oxygen supply. I hope it happens to me!

I am listening to a treasure Mary brought me from New York: Handel's 'Teseo', a dramatic tragedy. I didn't know about it—of course it's full of Handelian delights and surprises. The CD player is my source of refreshment. Tom Shapcott has sent me the Brahms string quintets; he sends me delightful cards and letters to cheer me. Fay Zwicky writes delightful letters that need no reply. Chris Wallace-Crabbe writes me witty poems—how different from the theatrical phone calls: 'DARLING! We all love you!'[2]

It's strange to be in a strange weak drug-affected body. As you observe, the handwriting remains intact. That's a surprise, as I drop things from my shaky hands. My legs are so weak I cannot lift myself up a step. I don't know how long I'll be able to walk at all. Odd things occur to me: why not re-read *Coriolanus*? Why not? I shall do so this afternoon. O for the days when I'd jump from my chair and get the book off the shelf—how great a journey it seems now ...

Fond love, G
1995

RAY LAWLER
b. 1921

Ray Lawler was born in the working-class Melbourne suburb of Footscray and worked in a foundry from the age of thirteen, becoming interested in amateur dramatics and playwriting in his early twenties. His masterpiece *Summer of the Seventeenth Doll* (1957), one of the iconic texts of Australian literature, was first staged in Melbourne in 1955 after being declared a joint winner, with Oriel Gray's *The Torrents*, of the Playwrights Advisory Board's play competition the previous year.

1   Tony Staley (b. 1939), Australian politician and businessman.
2   Tom Shapcott, Fay Zwicky, Chris Wallace-Crabbe (qqv), poets.

The play toured internationally in 1957 and Lawler lived in Ireland for many years in the wake of its success, making a living writing for television and for the stage. In 1975 he returned to Australia and was involved in the production of his two new plays, 'prequels' to *Summer of the Seventeenth Doll*—*Kid Stakes* (1975) and *Other Times* (1976)—with a marathon whole-day production of the complete trilogy by the Melbourne Theatre Company in 1977.

The combination of the classic three-act structure with the bold and unprecedented use of the Australian vernacular in a play that was extremely frank for its time about the sexuality of its characters made *Summer of the Seventeenth Doll* unusually powerful and memorable. In 1996 the play was adapted as an opera by composer Richard Mills and librettist Peter Goldsworthy (qv), a form that highlighted its emotional power and demonstrated its timeless appeal. *KG*

From *Summer of the Seventeenth Doll*

Act 1, Scene 1

It is five o'clock on a warm Sunday afternoon. The room of the play has a dressed up look that is complementary to, and yet extending beyond, the usual decorative scheme. A table is heavily set for the big meal of the week, Sunday tea.

BUBBA RYAN, *a shy-looking girl of twenty-two, is busily tying wide blue ribbons to two of the red-and-white-striped candies known as walking-sticks. At the same time she is chatting with a touch of wistful authoritativeness to* PEARL CUNNINGHAM, *who is sitting smoking nearby on a sofa, ostensibly looking through a magazine, but listening rather suspiciously.* PEARL *is a biggish woman, well corseted, with dyed hair. She is a widow driven back to earning a living by the one job she knows well, that of barmaid, though she would infinitely prefer something more classy—head saleswoman in a frock salon, for instance. The pub game, she feels, is rather crude. She is wearing what she refers to as her 'good black', with a double string of artificial pearls. Very discreet.*

BUBBA: . . . So I was the only one went to the wedding. August it was, and the boys were away, though of course when Olive wrote up and told them, they sent down money for a present. But I had to buy it and take it along, Olive wouldn't have anythin' to do with it. Wouldn't even help me pick anythin' out.

PEARL: [*questioningly*] The . . . boys . . . didn't mind her getting married, then?

BUBBA: [*frowning a little*] I dunno. I s'pose they did, in a way—'specially Barney, it must have been a bit of a shock to him—but like I said, they wouldn't do anythin' to stand in her way. That's how they are, see. Olive was the one really kicked up a fuss. She wouldn't believe, even up till the Saturday afternoon, that Nance'd ever go through with it.

PEARL: If you ask me, I'd say this Nancy had her head screwed on the right way.

BUBBA: [*slowly, forgetting the walking-sticks for a moment*] She got tired of waiting, I think. Olive doesn't mind it, she just looks forward to the next time, but it used to get on Nance's nerves a bit. 'N of course, she reads a lot, and this feller, this Harry Allaway—he works in a book shop, and he'd bring books into the pub for her. I s'pose that's how he got around her, really. I don't reckon Barney's ever read a book in his life.

PEARL: [*broodingly*] Mmmmm. Well, I'm fond of a good book myself now and then.

BUBBA: [*smilingly tolerant*] You won't need any till after April. Even Nancy, she only used to read in the winter . . .

[OLIVE'*s voice, nervously importunate, calls from upstairs.*]

OLIVE: Bubba.

BUBBA: [*moving up to the arch*] Yes?

OLIVE: Those earrings of mine with the green stones . . .

BUBBA: Haven't seen 'em.

OLIVE: Ooh, I'll bet the old girl's taken a loan of them, she knew I wanted to . . . [*With a change of voice*] No, it's all right, here they are. Couldn't see 'em for looking.

[BUBBA *comes back into room, smiles at* PEARL *and speaks half apologetically.*]

BUBBA: Olive always gets nervous. We used to have to joke her out of it, Nancy and me. Only this time I think she's got it worse'n usual. I mean she's probably worryin' a bit how you're going to fit in.

PEARL: [*sharply*] I don't have to fit in. What I'm here for is a . . . a visit, and if Olive's told you it's anythin' else . . .

BUBBA: [*hastily*] Oh, she hasn't. She's hardly said a word.

PEARL: In that case, then, there's no need for you to get nasty.

BUBBA: [*surprised*] I wasn't being nasty.

PEARL: You were. Nasty-minded. What you said before 'bout not needing any books till after April was bad enough. It strikes me you know too much of this place for your own good.

BUBBA: I've lived next door all my life, why shouldn't I know?

PEARL: I'm not going to argue, you just shouldn't, that's all.

BUBBA: But you said I was being nasty—what made you say that?

[*Under the directness of her gaze,* PEARL *shifts uneasily, not willing to implicate herself further.* BUBBA *returns to table and continues quietly.*]

I'll bet Olive never told you there was anythin' nasty 'bout the lay-off season.

PEARL: [*staring straight ahead*] That's none of your business.

OLIVE: [*off*] Hang on to your hats and mittens, kids, here I come again.

[*She comes downstairs, wearing a crisp green and white summer frock, and moves with a trace of excitement into the room, showing herself off.*]

Well, whaddya think this time? Snazzy enough? It mightn't knock your eye out, but it's nice and cool, and it's the sort of thing Roo likes. Y'know . . . fresh and green . . .

[*She postures, waiting for their comments. Despite a surface cynicism and thirty-nine years of age, there is something curiously unfinished about* OLIVE, *an eagerness that properly belongs to extreme youth. This is intensified at the moment by her nervous anticipation. She is a barmaid at the same city hotel as* PEARL, *but, unlike the latter, she enjoys the job.* BUBBA, *still a little unsettled by her spat with* PEARL, *blurts hastily:*]

BUBBA: Yes, it's—it's lovely.

[OLIVE *gives a nervous laugh and embraces her.*]

OLIVE: Pearl?

PEARL: [*reluctantly*] Yes, not my taste, but it suits you.

OLIVE: [*crossing to the mirror and making last-minute adjustments*] Well, it'll have to do, anyway. I haven't got time to change again. [*Turning to survey the room*] Now, what else is there? I know—get the beer in!

BUBBA: [*quickly*] I'll do it.

OLIVE: [*after her retreating figure*] Would yer, love? In the fridge. God, she's a good kid, that.

PEARL: Yeah. I'd say she knows more than her prayers, just the same.

OLIVE: [*mildly astonished*] Bubba? Don't be silly, she's only a baby.

PEARL: Not too much of a baby. If Vera ever spoke to me like that, I'd put her straight back across my knee. And I don't think it's nice the way this one acts . . .

OLIVE: How?

PEARL: Just as if she owns the place.

OLIVE: Well, whaddya expect? She's been runnin' in and out ever since she was old enough to walk. Roo and Barney she treats as if they were uncles. [*Laughing suddenly, turning to shake her head at* PEARL] God, you're a wag. Talk about cautious Kate!

PEARL: Why?

OLIVE: Look at them suitcases by the stairs. You'd think someone was getting ready for a moonlight flit.

PEARL: [*firmly*] That's different. I've taken my overnighter up, and I'm not taking anythin' else till I'm certain.

OLIVE: Don't be silly. I told yer, he's all right.

PEARL: Yes. Well, I'll find that out for meself, if you don't mind.

OLIVE: Oh, nobody's trying to talk you into anything. Just don't take too long to decide, that's all.

PEARL: Where's that photo you said you were gunna show me?

OLIVE: Oh, yeah. [*Collecting a framed enlargement from the side-board and taking it to her*] You can see him much better in this one, those others he was always clownin' about.

[PEARL *takes the photograph and studies it.*]

It's the four of us at Luna Park the year before last, Nance is on the end there. Can you see what I mean?

PEARL: What?

OLIVE: You're a bit alike, you two.

PEARL: [*frowning*] How d'you mean?

OLIVE: Somethin' in the way you look. I noticed it the first time that we met.

PEARL: Can't see it myself. She looks to me like she was drunk.

OLIVE: Oh well, she was. Yes. She'd been on the whisky. Right after that was taken she got sick on the Ocean Wave.

PEARL: [*nodding distastefully*] Mmm. I can imagine she'd be the sort to get sick on an Ocean Wave.

OLIVE: She wasn't like that, really. Nance was a—[*a hundred memories*]—she was a real good sport. Barney was pretty mad about her.

PEARL: [*snorting*] You can see that, the way he's holding her. Bit intimate, isn't it?

OLIVE: Listen, lovey, you better make up your mind. These are a coupla sugarcane-cutters fresh from the tropics, not two professors from the university. [*She carries the picture back to the sideboard.*]

PEARL: I know one thing, he'll never lay hands on me like that in public.

OLIVE: Won't he? Honest, you've never met a bloke like Barney. Only about so big, and yet—I dunno—the women go mad on him.

PEARL: I'll believe it when I see it. Didn't seem to stop her goin' off and gettin' married.

OLIVE: She made a mistake.

PEARL: Who says?

OLIVE: I say. Marriage is different, and Nancy knew it. Just because there was no hope of hooking on with Barney . . .

PEARL: Her own fault. I'll guarantee she made herself cheap. So long as a woman keeps her self-respect, any man will marry her.

OLIVE: I wouldn't bank on that, Pearl. Not with Barney.

PEARL: Oh, I'm not anticipating anythin', believe me. But from all you've said, it's about time some decent woman took this feller in hand. I don't reckon I've ever heard of anyone with more reasons to get married in all my life.

OLIVE: Maybe I shouldna told you.

PEARL: [*darkly*] Oh, don't worry, I would've found out. I'm a mother. A thing like that—you couldn't trick me.

OLIVE: He'll probably tell you himself, anyway; he doesn't make any secret of it—

[BUBBA *enters quickly, her arms full of bottles of beer.*]

BUBBA: Oh golly, these are cold . . .

OLIVE: Here, let me help you.

PEARL: Put 'em on the table and you'll get rings on the cloth.

OLIVE: [*as they set out bottles at regular intervals*] Doesn't matter. A few bottles make a party look a party, I think. [*To* BUBBA] Did you do your walking-sticks?

BUBBA: Yes, I haven't put 'em up yet. [*She moves to collect them.*]

PEARL: What are they for?

OLIVE: Tell her, Bubba.

BUBBA: [*lamely*] Oh, they're just a bit of a joke. One's for Roo and one's for Barney.

OLIVE: It started off the first year they came down, she was only a little thing—how old were you, Bub?

BUBBA: [*as she takes walking-sticks to set them up on mantelpiece*] Five.

OLIVE: She was always in and out here, and when Roo bought me the first lot of presents and she saw the doll among 'em she howled her eyes out. She wanted a doll on a walkin'-stick too, she said. So out the two of them go—after eight o'clock at night it was—tryin' to bang up a shop to get her one. But all they could buy were these lolly walkin'-sticks, and in the end that's what they had to bring her back. Well, she was as happy as Larry; off she went to bed, one in each hand. After that they always brought 'em down every year . . .

BUBBA: Till I was fifteen . . .

OLIVE: Oh yes, this is funny, listen. They didn't seem to wake up that she was gettin' too old for lollies, see, they kept on bringin' 'em down, bringin' 'em down, so Nancy put her up to a dodge. The year after the War, when she was fifteen, and they arrived with their bundles of presents, there she had a walking-stick for each of *them*, tied up with blue ribbons, sitting on the mantelpiece. It taught 'em a lesson all right. Ever since, whenever they've brought me a doll, they've always brought her down gloves, or scent, or—or something like that.

> [*There is a faint pause.* PEARL *is clearly unimpressed by the story, and makes little attempt to hide it.*]

PEARL: I see.

BUBBA: [*a trifle ashamed*] I said it was only a bit of a joke. Is there anything else you want me to do, Ol?

OLIVE: No, I don't think so, love . . . but you're gunna stay and meet them, aren't yer?

BUBBA: No. I've got to change and everything. I—I think I'll come in after tea.

OLIVE: [*understandingly*] Just as you like. [*Moving to verandah with* BUBBA] What about comin' in and havin' tea with us?

BUBBA: [*anxious to escape*] No, I'll come in after.

OLIVE: Well, don't forget now.

BUBBA: I won't.

> [*She goes.* OLIVE *surveys the sky.*]

OLIVE: It's starting to get dark. I wonder where that mother of mine can have got to?

PEARL: Where's she supposed to have gone?

OLIVE: The community singin'. But that oughta been out long ago.

PEARL: [*consulting her watch, and rising with alarm*] It's after six.

OLIVE: [*dashing back into the room*] Yeah. Oh, she's an old shrewdy, that one. I wouldn't mind betting she's gone down to the terminal to meet them. She'll get a fiver each out of them before they find a taxi.

PEARL: You shouldn't say things like that about your mother.

OLIVE: Listen, a fiver's nothing. She shakes them down for all they're worth the whole time they're here. [*Switching on the radio which presently plays a dreamy waltz*] Course they're awake up, but they don't seem to mind. Fact, I think Roo likes it. [*Looking at the photograph*] Good old Roo. I reckon he's got the best-looking mouth in the world.

PEARL: [*inspecting her make-up at the mantelpiece*] He's certainly a better proposition than the other one.

OLIVE: Oh, but you can't compare them, they're different types. I mean Roo's the big man of the two, but it's Barney makes you laugh. And like I said, it's Barney the women go for.

PEARL: [*aggrieved*] I dunno why I always have to get tangled up with little men, just the same. Even Wallie, he was shorter than me. The day we got married I had to wear low heels . . .

OLIVE: Barney's not all that short. You wait, you'll see.

PEARL: Yeah. Well, he'd better not start countin' on anythin', I haven't made up me mind yet. How do you reckon my hair looks?

OLIVE: [*taking a cursory glance*] Pretty good.

PEARL: I don't think that new girl round at Rene's knows how to handle it, she doesn't seem to get down to the roots. [*Turning suddenly*] What do they call him Barney for, anyway?

OLIVE: Barney's bull, I think. His right name's Arthur.

PEARL: Oh.

OLIVE: [*enjoyably*] Did I ever tell you 'bout Roo's name? I used to think at first that it was short for Kanga, and that's what I called him once. He just looked at me silly like, and said: Kanga? Well, I said, isn't that what the Roo's part of? You should've seen him—he roared! Then he told me what Roo was, short for his real name, and just see if you can guess what that is?

> [PEARL *shakes her head.* OLIVE *continues delightedly.*]

Reuben—wouldn't it kill yer? Reuben!

PEARL: It's out the Bible.

OLIVE: [*ironically*] Is it? I didn't know that.

> [*There is the sound of a car horn offstage.* OLIVE *reacts excitedly and swoops to the window.*]

Oooh, me beads . . . that's not them, is it? No. Car up the road. Nearly died. [*Surveying the table*] Not that there's much more to do. I'll get some glasses out 'n' bring the salad in.

> [*She exits, a second or two later breaking into a faulty soprano offstage, taking up the melody from the radio.* PEARL *stares the room over, then crosses to close the French windows. She moves to pick up the photograph, and studies it closely.* OLIVE *re-enters, carrying glasses. The daylight is gradually fading from the room.*]

Hey, did you hear that Charlie in the saloon bar last night? All the time we was cleanin' up he kept whistlin' 'Old Black Magic'. [*Placing glasses*] Havin' a go at me, a course; he's known about Roo for years, and he always gets in a crack every time. Not that I ever let on, mind yer.

> [*She looks across at* PEARL *who is frowning over the photograph, and speaks with a note of reserve.*]

Well, what's the matter now?

PEARL: Nothin'. I'm just havin' another look.

OLIVE: [*moving in and taking the photograph from her*] If you don't watch out you're gunna start hating the poor bloke before he even gets here.

> [*She goes back to sideboard with it.*]

PEARL: No I won't. [*Sitting, righteously*] At the same time, I'm not letting myself in for any nasty mess, either.

OLIVE: [*contemptuously*] Nasty mess! What makes you think I'd have anythin' to do with it if there was any mess about it?

PEARL: It doesn't matter for you, you haven't got a daughter to think of. Vera's just at that age I gotta be careful. If she cottons on to me doing anything wrong, she's likely to break out the same way.

OLIVE: [*in quick hostility, snapping off the radio*] Now look, that's one thing I'm not gunna stand for. Right from the start!

PEARL: What?

OLIVE: You know what! That respectable mother stunt. Don't you try and put that over on me.

PEARL: I didn't say a word.

OLIVE: You said wrong, didn't yer? 'N' nasty mess? That's enough. I've told yer over 'n' over again what this lay-off is, yet every time you open your mouth you make it sound like something—low and dirty. Well, if that's the way you look at it, you don't have to stay, y'know—nobody's forcin' you to make any decisions about it—you can get your bags from the hall and clear out before they get here.

PEARL: [*defensively*] Just because I don't think it's altogether proper.

OLIVE: Yeah. Just because of that.

PEARL: Nobody would say it was a decent way of living.

OLIVE: Wouldn't they? I would! I've rubbed shoulders with all sorts from the time I was fourteen, and I've never come across anything more decent in my life. Decency is—it depends on the people. And don't you say it doesn't!

PEARL: I meant decent like marriage. That's different, you said yourself it was.

OLIVE: [*with a slight shudder*] It's different all right. Compared to all the marriages I know, what I got is . . . [*groping for depth of expression*] is five months of heaven every year. And it's the same for them. Seven months they spend up there killin' themselves in the cane season, and then they come down here to live a little. That's what the lay-off is. Not just playing around and spending a lot of money, but a time for livin'. You think I haven't sized that up against what other women have? [. . .]

1957

DONALD HORNE
1921–2005

Donald Horne was born in Muswellbrook, NSW. He attended the University of Sydney, but did not gain a degree. After army service in the Second World War he was a reporter for the *Daily Telegraph* (1945–49). From the 1950s he edited a number of magazines, most notably the *Bulletin* (1961–62 and 1967–72). In 1973 he became an academic at the University of NSW. He was chair of the Australia Council (1985–90). After being a notable conservative polemicist, Horne turned to supporting the Labor opposition in the late 1960s. He was the author of countless essays, reviews and articles, as well as several significant works of social and political commentary, most famously *The Lucky Country* (1964), a critique of Australian culture. Its title has become idiomatic (usually shorn of its irony). Horne also wrote social history, travel literature, three novels and a multi-volume autobiography, the best-known volume of which is the first, *The Education of Young Donald* (1967). Dispassionate, ironic and self-reflexive, Horne's memoirs are generally considered his most important literary achievement. The first three volumes were revised and republished as *An Interrupted Life* (1998). Two more volumes subsequently appeared, *Into the Open* (2000) and the posthumous *Dying: A memoir* (2007), co-written by Horne's wife, Myfanwy. *DM*

From *The Education of Young Donald*
Country, King, God

In the bottom right-hand drawer of his side of the dressing-table Dad kept the symbols of his most important beliefs. When there was no one in the house I sometimes took them out and wondered at them. There was his Masonic apron, his bible, his war medals, a Bedouin's knife he had brought back from the Palestine campaign, an army revolver, his spurs. One day I put on the Masonic apron and the medals. Holding the revolver in my hand, with the Bedouin's knife at my waist and the spurs on my feet, I looked at myself in the mirror and saw an Australian.

In the photographs he kept in this drawer columns of horses marched along the desert; Dad, in his hat with the emu plumes, rode down a desert wadi; a desert plain was studded with Australian bivouacs; in Cairo there were men in sun helmets and Sam Brownes[1] or fezes and galabeahs; there was a background of mosques, minarets and British lions; in Sydney the troopship was leaving for Suez, its paper streamers billowing up in the air. There was also a newspaper clipping of pictures of Dad and four of his brothers in their uniforms—a private, a sapper, a trooper, a lance-corporal, a sergeant—and a photograph of the grave of one of them.

The Great War and the ethos of the Australian soldier cast a bright light over our house. We lived not only with clear memories of the past war but with thoughts of the wars to come. It was assumed that when my turn came I would also play my part. One night, when we came home from a pacifist movie, as we had our cup of tea Dad was silent. Then he looked at me anxiously and said: 'You'd fight if you had to, wouldn't you?' Often there were rumours of war in the Sunday papers and, home from a day's rabbit-shooting, we might discuss the prospects of war before I went to bed.

The only day of ceremony in our year was Anzac Day, the day we commemorated the Australian landing at Gallipoli in 1915, seen as the occasion when Australia 'came of age'. On Anzac Day Dad would put on his three medals and join the other 'returned men' who were forming up in the main street behind the Muswellbrook brass band, the Boy Scouts and the Junior Red Cross. They would march up and down the street to the music of wartime marching tunes, then bifurcate—the Catholics to St James's Church, where the priest would remind his congregation that life was eternal and that they should pray for the souls of the dead soldiers; the Protestants to St Alban's Church, where, as the rector processed, with the gold cross held before him, and the choir sang 'Onward Christian Soldiers', we knew that soldiers like Dad and his brothers, by volunteering to sail across the Indian Ocean to fight the Turk, had given the word 'Australia' meaning. The rector would remind us that Australia was young in the company of nations but that its nationhood had been earned in the glorious epic of Anzac bravery. 'The history of Australia begins with a blank space on the map and ends with the record of a new name on the map, that of Anzac.' While we sang 'Fight the good fight with all thy might' the returned men would move in procession to the Soldiers' Chapel, where in front of the flame of remembrance the roll of the Muswellbrook dead would be called. The Last Post would sound, then the Protestant returned men would march to the war memorial, where the mayor would preside over another ceremony and we would sing 'O God, our help in ages past, our hope in years to come'. One of the Protestant

---

1   A type of belt usually worn as part of a military uniform.

clergymen would then remind us that Anzac Day was a solemn sacrament of mateship, commemorating our heroes as a band of brothers who for the first time in history had shown a final understanding of the essential humanness of mankind. However impatient they were of saluting and ceremonial, they could rise to the occasion, do the right thing and never let down a mate. We would observe two minutes' silence in honour of the men who had escaped calculation and ambition by dying blameless and young, in the simple act of men following their destiny. The Last Post would be sounded; wreaths would be laid; we would sing Kipling's 'Recessional'; then the bugler would blow Reveille and the ceremonies would be over until the reunion dinner at night, when the rector would again remind his audience that Anzac Day was the birthday of our nation, commemorating for ever the nobility of men who took something on and saw it through without whinging; other speakers would remind themselves that Australian soldiers were uniquely independent-minded and adventurous, uniquely able to display initiative, uniquely healthy in body and bold in spirit, uniquely *men*. Australian soldiers were the greatest men in the world.

Dad had fought in the desert with the Australian Light Horse. It was not on the Western Front and with the infantry, but only in the desert and with the cavalry, that war seemed fully to assume the heroic meaning we gave it, that things renewed themselves when young men went off to risk death. Dad had not reached Gallipoli; he had got sick on the island of Lemnos and by the time he was better the Gallipoli campaign was over. When he campaigned in Palestine he was so reduced by the sicknesses of the desert that at the end of the war it was noted on his discharge certificate that his physical condition was one of 'general debility'.

Much of the Australian history we learned at school, particularly the disastrous record of exploration, seemed to concern itself with virtues similar to those of the Anzac spirit—endurance, commitment, the expression of will. (The school syllabus spoke of liberating the child's life force.) As men struggled across deserts of stone or sandy wastes Australia seemed the dead frontier, the land of the dogged gesture. Even the Gallipoli expedition, the savage act of national self-recognition, had failed.

We were living through a run-down time. I was seven when prices fell in Wall Street. The worst the Depression did to our own family was that Uncle Loy, who had been an agent for Borsalino hats and a few other Italian lines, was put out of business by high tariffs and for a while was forced to work as a floorwalker at a city department store, another Carpenter forced to eat his pride. But the Depression seemed to drain the whole country of its spirit, and for some years most of what I was likely to hear was pessimistic. There was an occasional flash of sardonic wit: merely to say 'Prosperity is just around the corner' could set a roomful of people laughing. But despite the happiness with which I was immediately surrounded, there was nothing invigorating to hear about Australia. Australians may have been the best people in the world, but the best, apparently, was no longer very good. The Depression had a sense of inevitable calamity about it, like floods farther down the valley, or bushfires on the coast.

The main contemporary enthusiasms lay in admiration for our sportsmen and aviators, particularly the cricketer Don Bradman and the aviator Kingsford Smith. Even here it was their will that was most admired. Bradman was the boy from the bush who had battled his way to the top; he was a calculating, implacable batsman; a granite idol. Kingsford Smith showed more dash. As he and other Australian aviators crossed continents and oceans in their improvised aeroplanes we marked their positions on maps and pasted their pictures in scrapbooks. This was 'exploring'—very Australian. When some of them died, lost with their planes, no one knew where. This also seemed very Australian. They were great men, capable of iron-willed Australian failures.

Perhap the most human thing we felt at school for our newly established nation was an admiration of our plants and animals. We were proud of kangaroos and platypuses and koala bears, gumtrees and flannel flowers. These were ours. The waratah seemed a proud symbol; we celebrated spring by festooning the classrooms with wattle; at Christmas we decorated the table with Christmas bells and put a sprig of Australian Christmas bush on the plum pudding instead of holly. Along with the English nature verse we also learned poems that boasted that our Australian seasons and countryside were different from those of England. The Anzac spirit had its place in the school syllabus, but it did not carry conviction at school; you needed a father at home with a secret drawer to do that. And it did not finally carry conviction anywhere. It was just a belief. We believed in the Anzac spirit. But we didn't believe it *existed*. Not any longer. The Anzac spirit was a failure too. On the evening of each Anzac Day the daughter of one of the old families subsidised the attendance at the reunion dinner of any 'old diggers' down on their luck who were passing through town. After their free dinner they could go back to sleep under the bridge or in the pig pens. [. . .]

1967

RITA HUGGINS and JACKIE HUGGINS
1921–1996   b. 1956

Rita Huggins (née Holt) was born at Carnarvon Gorge, Queensland. The Holt family was forcibly removed from their traditional Bidjaraher country in the late 1920s, and were taken to what was then known as Barambah Mission (known today as the Cherbourg Aboriginal Reserve). From that time Rita worked for herself, her family and her people, and was an active member of the One People of Australia League. Thousands attended her funeral, a testimony to her standing in the Aboriginal community and beyond.

Her daughter Jackie Huggins, born in Ayr, Queensland, is an author, historian and activist dedicated to reconciliation, social justice, literacy and women's issues within Indigenous communities. Jackie has been involved in many organisations at local, state and national levels, ranging from reconciliation and Aboriginal welfare forums to appointments on editorial and performing arts boards. She co-wrote the auto/biography *Auntie Rita* (1994) with her mother. A collection of her political writings, *Sister Girl: The writings of Aboriginal activist and historian Jackie Huggins*, was published in 1998. *AH/PM*

From *Auntie Rita*

Chapter 1: Don't Cry, Gunduburries

I was only a small child when we were taken from my born country. I only remember a little of those times there but my memories are very precious to me. Most of my life has been spent away from my country but before I tell you any more of my story I want to tell you what I remember about the land I come from. It will always be home, the place I belong to.

My born country is the land of the Bidjara–Pitjara people, and is known now as Carnarvon Gorge, 600 kilometres northwest of Brisbane. This was also the land of the Kairi, Nuri, Karingbal, Longabulla, Jiman and Wadja people. Our people lived in this land since time began. In our land are waterfalls, waterholes and creeks where we swam and where the older people fished. Our mob always seemed cool, even on the hottest days, because the country was like an oasis. There were huge king ferns. I believe they have been described as living fossils because their form has not changed for thousands of years.

We were never left with empty bellies. The men hunted kangaroos, goannas, lizards, snakes and porcupines with spears and boomerangs. The women gathered berries, grubs, wild plums, honey and waterlilies, and yams and other roots with their digging sticks. Children stayed with the women when the men hunted so that they wouldn't be close to the hunt and frighten away the animals. The creeks gave us lots of food, too—yellow belly and jew, perch and eel.

My mother would use leaves from trees to make soap for washing our bodies with, and unfortunately for us kids there was no excuse not to take a bogey.[1] I remember goanna fat being used for cuts and scratches as well as being a soothing ointment for aches and pains. Eucalyptus leaves were used for coughs, and the bark of certain trees for rashes and open wounds. Witchetty grubs helped babies' teething, and we used charcoal for cleaning teeth.

There were huge cliffs and rocks, riddled with caves where many of my people's paintings were. Most caves and rock faces showed my people's

---

1   A Dharawal word meaning bath or swim.

stencilled hands, weapons and tools, and there were engravings here, too. Fertility symbols and the giant serpent tell us of the spiritual significance of the place. This place is old. My people and their art were here long before the whiteman came.

The caves were cool places in summer and warm places in winter, and offered shelter when the days were windy or when there was rain. They offered a safe place for the women bringing new life into the world. As had happened for my mother and her mother before her, going back generation after generation, I was born in the sanctuary of one of those caves. My mother would tell us how my grandmother would wash my mother's newborn babies in the nearby creek, place them in a cooliman and carry them back to suckle on my exhausted mother's breast.

We lived in humpies, or gunyahs, that the men built from tree branches, bark and leaves. Gum resin held them together. We would sleep inside the gunyahs, us children arguing for the warm place closest to Mama, a place usually kept for the youngest children. More gunyahs would be built as they were needed in this serene valley that had nurtured my people since time began.

My mother, Rose, had a Bidjara–Pitjara mother known as Lucy Conway from the Maranoa River and a white father who was never married to her mother. I never knew who her father was. I don't know much about the contact my mother had with whites. She had a whiteman's name, but she also had a tribal name, Gylma, and she spoke language and knew the old ways. My father, Albert Holt, was the son of a Yuri woman known as Maggie Bundle and a whiteman, the owner of Wealwandangie Station. My father was named after that man. My grandmother may have been working at the homestead. Dadda was brought up on the station, away from his mother's people. When he grew older he wanted to be with Aboriginal people, and started visiting the camps. He saw my mother there and wanted to marry her. After that, he stayed in the camp with her, and then the children started coming.

One winter's night, troopers came riding on horseback through our camp. My father went to see what was happening, and my mother stayed with her children to try to stop us from being so frightened. One trooper I remember clearly. Perhaps he was sorry for what he was doing, because he gave me some fruit—a banana, something as unknown to me as the whiteman who offered it. My mother saw, and cried out to me, 'Barjun! Barjun!'

Dadda and some of the older men were shouting angrily at the officials. We were being taken away from our lands. We didn't know why, nor imagined what place we would be taken to. I saw the distressed look on my parents' faces and knew something was terribly wrong. We never had time to gather up any belongings. Our camp was turned into a scattered mess—the fire embers still burning.

What was to appear next out of the bush took us all by surprise and we nearly turned white with fright. It was a huge cage with four round things on it which, when moved by the man in the cabin in front, made a deafening sound, shifting the ground and flattening the grass, stones and twigs beneath it. We had never seen a cattle truck before. A strong smell surrounded us as we entered the truck and we saw brown stains on the wooden floor.

They packed us in like cattle with hardly any room to move. The troopers threw a few blankets over us (we thought they were strange animal skins). There weren't enough blankets for all of us, and so the older people gave them to us younger ones while they went without. The night was cold and colder still on the back of the open truck.

It took the whole night across rough dirt tracks to reach our first destination of Woorabinda Aboriginal Settlement. Woori was a dry and dusty place compared to the home we were forced to leave. My memory of the place at that time is not clear but I do remember seeing some gunyahs and some people there watching us. The people were not smiling—just like us. Although curious to see us, the people did not come too far outside their gunyahs but watched from a safe distance as our older people were unloaded by the troopers.

I will never forget how they huddled, frightened, cold and crying in their blankets. Some of our old relations were wrenched from our arms and lives that day and it is for them that I shed my tears. One old lady broke away from the others and screamed, 'Don't take my gunduburries! Don't take my gunduburries!' as the truck moved off, taking us away from her. After running a small distance she was stopped and held by the officials who wanted to keep 'wild bush Blacks' on these reserves.

My father's ashen face told the story and we were never to see our old people again. Dadda could never bring himself to speak about it. Our tribe was torn away—finished. Perhaps the hurt and pain always remained for him. It was understandable then why he would hate and rebel against the authorities for the rest of his days after what they did to our people.

The old people from both Cherbourg and Woorabinda always told the story that the 'full bloods' were sent to Woorabinda and the fairer-skinned to Cherbourg. Both my parents were considered 'half-castes' because they both had white fathers. I had always wondered why our people were split up and found out sometime in my twenties that the government people thought that those of us who looked whiter would more easily assimilate than the darker ones, but this was not so. Sometimes it was vice versa. But skin never mattered to us. It was how we felt about being Aboriginal that counted. It was when I was in my twenties, too, that I was given a certificate which specified my 'breed'. 'Cross out description not required', it said. 'Full blood, half caste, quadroon.'

The truck went on, travelling for two terrible days, going further south. As if in a funeral procession, we were loud in our silence. We were all in mourning. I can't remember what we had to eat or drink, or where we stopped on the journey, but by the time we reached our destination we were numb with cold, tiredness and hunger. And this new country was so different from our country—flat, no hills and valleys, arid and cleared of trees.

It was Barambah Reserve (renamed Cherbourg in 1932) that we'd been brought to, just outside Murgon on the Barambah River. Here we were separated from each other into rough houses—buildings that seemed so strange to me then, with their walls so straight. Each family was fenced off from the others into their own two little rooms where you ate and slept. The houses were little cells, all next to each other in rows. A prison. No wonder that, along with 'mission', 'reserve', 'settlement', 'Muddy Flats' and 'Guna Valley', Cherbourg has been named 'prison' and 'concentration camp' by Aboriginal people. The place in fact had its own gaol. A prison in a prison. There were white and Aboriginal areas. Government authorities and teachers stayed away from us, and their areas were off-limits to all Aboriginal people.

One of the Aboriginal living areas was called top camp, and it was dotted with gunyahs. It was here that Annie Evans lived with her large family. She was the first person to greet us when we arrived, and gave us food. Her generosity was never forgotten by my parents or by myself. Her daughter Barbara was my age and we became best friends and stayed that way all our lives.

No one had the right to remove us from our traditional lands and to do what they did to us. We were once the proud custodians of our land and now our way of life became controlled by insensitive people who knew nothing about us but thought they knew everything. They even chose how and where we could live. We had to stay in one place now while the whiteman could roam free.

We took a trip back to my born country in 1986. It was the first time I had been back since that night we were taken over sixty years before. Tourism has taken its toll in the area, but the place still has its wild beauty. I felt the call of my people billowing through the trees and welcoming me home again. I saw the smiling faces of my elders, the embers of the campfire, heard the women singing. In my heart was such a deep happiness because I knew I was home again. 'Rita Huggins was born somewhere out there,' I said over and over again in my mind.

Returning to my mother's born country as she refers to it complemented my own sense of identity and belonging, and my pride in this. It was important that together we make this trip as she had been insisting for quite some time, pining for her homelands. We shared a special furthering of our mother–daughter bond during this time, although we argued incessantly about nothing as usual or, as she calls it, 'fighting with our tongues'. I began to gain an insight into and understanding of her obvious attachment and relationship to her country and how our people had cared for this place way before the Royal Geographic Society and park rangers ever clapped eyes on it. The way my mother moved around, kissed the earth and said her prayers will have a lasting effect on my soul and memory because she was paying homage and respect to her ancestors who had passed on long ago but whose presence we could both intensely feel.

The land of my mother and my maternal grandmother is my land, too. It will be passed down to my children and successive generations, spiritually, in the manner that has been carried on for thousands of years. Fate dictates that nothing will ever change this. As Rita's daughter, I not only share the celebration and the pain of her experience but also the land from which we were created.

Like most Aboriginal people, it is my deeply held belief that we came from this land, hence the term 'the land is my mother'. The land is our birthing place, our cradle; it offers us connection with the creatures, the trees, the mountains and the rivers, and all living things. There are no stories of migration in our dreamtime stories. Our creation stories link us intrinsically to the earth. We are born of the earth and when we die our body and spirit go back there. This is why land is so important to us, no matter where and when we were born.

The removal of Aboriginal people from their lands has gone on since the arrival of the whiteman, and it still goes on. Alienation from traditional lands has just taken different forms at different times. Reserves like Cherbourg and Woorabinda onto which my mother's people were placed were set up under the Queensland Aborigines Protection and Restriction of the Sale of Opium Act *of 1897. The decades that followed the introduction of the Act were a period of acute isolation and control of Aboriginal people. Aboriginals were deliberately and systematically cut off from their traditional ways of life and made to conform to, and become dependent on, European ways. The reserves refused Aboriginals the rights to their own languages, ceremonies, religious beliefs and marriage laws, and in their place was put a culture of control and surveillance. Every action and association was monitored; employment—including any wages—was managed by the reserves' superintendents; personal relations were intervened in. Punishment, including days and nights in the gaol, sometimes in solitary confinement, was meted out with imperialist assurance.*

Reserves were supposedly established for the care and protection of Aboriginal people, and there is a double irony in that. Not only were Aboriginals subjected to humiliating treatment in the reserves, but if they needed protection it was from whites. In the decades preceding the introduction of the Act, bloody massacres had taken place in Carnarvon Gorge, and all across the country. The massacres were ritualised violence, intended to demonstrate white superiority and power. The poisoning of flour and waterholes may be common knowledge; burying Blackfellas alive in sand, tying them to trees for use in shooting practice, is less so. Who were the barbarians?

The history of violence on the frontier has only been partially addressed. More orthodox historians have tended to downplay the extent of the violences committed against Aboriginal people, and revisionist historians, such as Ray Evans and Gordon Reid, who have attempted to reconstruct the massacres around my family's area, are marginalised.

In 1857, the Jiman of the Carnarvon Gorge area, reacting against the rape of Jiman women, the dispossession of hunting grounds, and the destruction of sacred sites, killed the whites present at the Fraser homestead at the Hornet Bank Station. In revenge, whites conducted the six-month 'little war' over a vast area unrelated to the Gorge, shooting down men, women and children as they ran. No measures were taken to stop this slaughter.

The killings went on long after, and all over Australia. Aboriginal people were nearly wiped out and it is a wonder that we are alive to tell the story. Because our beginnings as Black and white Australians were steeped in bloodshed and murder, and Black survival depended on such flimsy pieces of fate, it makes it almost impossible for us to pick up the pieces, forget about it and make up.

1994

JACOB G. ROSENBERG
1922–2008

Jacob G. Rosenberg grew up in Łódź, Poland, and moved to Melbourne in 1948. His prize-winning memoir *East of Time* (2005) uses various vernacular genres—the anecdote, the fairytale, gossip, song and the parable—to recreate the Jewish ghetto in Łódź before Rosenberg and his family were transported to Auschwitz. As *East of Time* relates, the author's family (with the exception of one sister, who committed suicide shortly afterwards) were all murdered on the day of their arrival at Auschwitz. Rosenberg's memoir is an elegy for his family and, by association, all of those who died in the Holocaust. *Sunrise West* (2007) is a sequel to *East of Time*. He has written poetry and fiction in English and Yiddish. His poetry collections include *Behind the Moon* (2000) and his prose works include *Lives and Embers* (2003). DM

From *East of Time*

MY SISTER IDA

There was something contradictory about my sister Ida. On the one hand, she was a quiet, unassuming, polite little girl; on the other, a restless, frolicking child, mischievous almost to the extreme. Her history and literature teacher, Yuda Reznik, once told father, presumably in jest: 'If you won't take her out of school, I'm going to kill myself.' Perhaps, like all the girls in her class, my sister was in love with this charismatic man.

Ida was of slender build but well-shaped, with a wave of auburn hair that danced alluringly over her forehead, her black eyebrows and her deep brown eyes. She carried herself with a pleasing, lingering quietude. Ida passed through our shadowy world like a pale ray of some mysterious hope. But every mystery conceals a story.

She was only fifteen, and just three months from obtaining her school certificate, when her sister Pola's marital life ran into difficulties. Putting aside her own needs and feelings, Ida left the school she loved and her friends there to look after Pola's two-year-old infant girl.

After that, life took a new turn.

Young men were readily attracted to Ida. At the outbreak of war in 1939, as booted hordes from the west descended on the country of my birth, there was the young fine-looking carpenter, the Bundist Grinszpan, who loved her dearly and begged her to run away with him to the east. But Ida shook her head. 'No,' she told him. 'I wouldn't leave mother behind.'

Of course, there were plenty of others—among them a fellow who, if not too prudent, was certainly persistent. He kept hanging around, endeared himself to our mother, and finally found a place in my sister's heart. Possibly this changed the course of her life. I know that one shouldn't point the finger, that life is serendipitous; that he who guards his tongue (as it is written) guards himself from evil. Nonetheless, I believe there are times when even the cruellest truth is preferable to the gentlest lie.

When Ida became pregnant she was barely twenty-two years old. I still recall the duel of eyes as she broke the news to mother, and then father's blunt but pragmatic remark: 'It's not too late . . .' For quite a few days, the spirit of the Pharaoh who didn't know Joseph struggled against the spirit of Shifra and Puah.[1] Obviously, however, a foetus was not a sufficient offering to our Almighty—He desired much more.

I vividly remember the unlit carriage of a screaming cattle-train, and Ida hushing her whining little Chayale to sleep:

There once was a king,
There once was a page,
There once was a beautiful queen . . .

The lullaby told of the terrible death that befell the royal threesome: the king was eaten by a dog, the page by a cat, and the queen by a little mouse!

---

1   See Exodus 1.

But the child should not grieve, the song concluded—for the king was made of sugar, the page of gingerbread, and the queen was of marzipan . . .

We arrived at our destination on a hot August day of barking dogs. There, beneath an unblemished sky, dressed in black and with gloves of white, stood a man called Mengele who was convinced that he was God's deputy. [. . .]

SUICIDE

Like a wet smear, a rumour ran through the ghetto. A fearful and tangible murmur.

The Hunt.

The Germans, employing the Jewish police as their sniffer dogs, were about to strike at the very essence of our being. Nobody knew when; we knew only that all ghetto children under the age of ten and all adults over sixty-five would be taken, to be 'resettled'. We were accustomed to confronting death on a daily basis, but this latest perfidy caused the ghetto, that surreal asylum, to go berserk. Between 5 August and 5 September 1942, a plague of suicides—a spit in the face of creation—swept through our community.

Among these suicides was 27-year-old Kuna Leska, known after she married as Kuna Rotsztajn, who lived with her infant daughter Rifkele and her brother Gedaliah in a one-room apartment on the fifth floor of a nearby block. Like many others, Kuna had become acutely aware that her life was dangling from a cobweb's thread over a dark, bottomless abyss. She was alone: in 1940 the Germans had conscripted her husband Michael to forced labour; a year later she was notified that he had 'died' in the course of his 'work'. Kuna was devastated; no doubt the blow nourished her psyche with murky solutions. And so, on that defeated sunny afternoon of 19 August, she jumped from her window into the liberating arms of death. Why she left her child behind is a question to which no one should seek an answer. Nothing will become clearer through explanation, and for the sake of a survivor's sanity it is dangerous even to ask.

Within a few minutes the paramedics (whose children, like those of the sniffer dogs, were exempt from the Hunt) arrived on the scene. Kuna's eyes were still open. The older of the two men gave her one glance, struck a match, sheltering the cigarette in the shell of his hands, and said: 'As good as gone. Take her away.'

The Hunt began on the morning of 5 September. As the huge high-sided truck rolled into the yard of 22 Lagiewnicka Street to collect the petrified little children, Gedaliah grabbed his niece, ran up to the roof, and roped her to the chimney in such a way that, for the duration of the search of their yard, she would appear as one with that structure. (He didn't have to warn the three-year-old fugitive not to cry.) Then Gedaliah turned his face to the sky: 'Almighty Lord,' he prayed, 'grant this child at least seven days of what my people granted You for all eternity—make her invisible!'

And He, may His name be forever blessed, did.

By the twelfth day of the month, the Hunt had come to a temporary pause. Gedaliah was just nineteen, his sister was dead, his parents in some nowhere, and he with a little girl to shelter, feed and protect. He decided to seek the help of his sister's sister-in-law, Dora Blatt. But as he entered her flat, holding Rifkele's thin hand in his, the woman and her husband Israel—a man who, once known for his composure, now resembled an asylum escapee—crumpled before him. 'Oh, Gedaliah, Gedaliah,' cried Dora. 'They took away *our* two children too, they've slaughtered us! We are dead!'

The young man understood the situation and left.

A few hours later, as the night was closing in, Dora unexpectedly appeared on Gedaliah's doorstep. She was dishevelled and her face bled from self-inflicted scratches, 'How will I sleep, Gedaliah? How *can* I sleep?' she wailed, taking the bewildered Rifkele by the hand and hugging her tightly to her breast. 'Maybe someone out there will have mercy on *my* children. After all, God is great . . .'

The little one, white as a ghost and trembling all over, as if suffering from an attack of malaria, could not contain herself any longer. 'Mummy!' she screamed. 'Mummy, *where are you, Mummy?*'

Her heart-wrenching plea would reverberate in her uncle's soul for the rest of his life.

So it was that, thanks to a distraught woman's nobility—and to Gedaliah's food-ration card, which he left with Dora—the good Lord endowed Rifkele with two more years of life and dread.

2005

DOROTHY HEWETT
1923–2002

An awarded poet, playwright and prose writer, Dorothy Hewett distinguished herself in multiple genres, making her work difficult to discuss as a single thread. By the time she was twenty-two she had won a national poetry competition and a drama competition. A complex romanticism is often traced through her work, even as much of her early work is directly political, and her theatre radical and formally experimental.

Hewett's political ballads, which recall Australia's folk tradition, were collected with work by her husband Merv Lilley in *What About the People!* (1962), while her 1959 novel about women workers in a Sydney textile mill, *Bobbin Up*, is now regarded as one of Australia's most innovative pieces of working-class literature.

Having grown up on a farm in the Western Australian wheatbelt, Hewett drew on her childhood there and teenage years in Perth for inspiration. She joined the Communist Party of Australia when she was nineteen. In the late 1960s, she turned to playwriting and resigned from the Party, bringing an iconoclastic, feminist experimentalism to the stage in plays like *The Chapel Perilous* (1971/1972) and *Bon-Bons and Roses for Dolly* (1972/1976). Hewett wrote more than fifteen plays, including *The Man from Mukinupin*, commissioned for the WA sesquicentenary in 1979, as well as film scripts, and saw many of them produced, including the NIDA staging of her abridged trilogy *The Wire Fences of Jarrabin* in 2004, in a posthumous tribute.

In 1975, Hewett published a collection of poetry called *Rapunzel in Suburbia*, announcing an ongoing preoccupation with scripted femininity and role playing. She published five collections of poetry, including *Halfway Up the Mountain* (2001) after her collected poems had drawn together her work from the 1940s to 1995. *Wild Card* (1990), the first volume of her autobiography, was a celebrated return to writing prose. Her novels *The Toucher* (1993) and *Neap Tide* (1999) followed, while her short stories were collected as *A Baker's Dozen* in 2001. *NM*

Clancy and Dooley and Don McLeod

Clancy and Dooley and Don McLeod
Walked by the wurlies when the wind was loud,
And their voice was new as the fresh sap running,
And we keep on fighting and we keep on coming.

Don McLeod beat at a mulga bush,   5
And a lot of queer things came out in a rush.
Like mongrel dogs with their flattened tail,
They sneaked him off to the Hedland jail.

In the big black jail where the moonlight fell
Clancy and Dooley sat in a cell.   10
In the big white court crammed full with hate,
They said: 'We wouldn't scab on a mate.'

In the great hot quiet they said it loud,
And smiled in the eyes of Don McLeod,
And the working-men all over the land,   15
Heard what they shouted and shook their hand.

The sheep's wool dragged and the squatters swore
And talked nice words till their tongues got sore,
And their bellies swelled with so much lies,
But the blackfellers shooed them off like flies.   20

The sheep got lost on the squatters' run,
The shearing season was nearly done.
Said the squatters eaten up with greed:
'We'll pay good wages and give good feed.'

The blackfellers sheared the wool and then 25
Got their wages like working-men.
The squatters' words were stiff and sore:
'We won't pay wages like that no more.'

The white boss said: 'STAY OUT OF TOWN,'
And they ground with their boots to keep us down. 30
'We'll starve them out until they crawl
Back on their bellies, we'll starve 'em all.'

The sun was blood on the bare sheep-runs.
The women whispered: 'They'll come with guns.'
But we marched to our camp, and our step was proud, 35
And we sat down there and we laughed out loud.

Clancy and Dooley and Don McLeod,
Walked by the wurlies when the wind was loud,
And their voice was new as the fresh sap running,
And we keep on fighting and we keep on coming. 40

Don McLeod beat at a mulga bush,
And a lot of queer things came out in a rush,
Like mongrel dogs with their flattened tail,
They sneaked him off to the Hedland jail.

The young men marched down the road like thunder, 45
Kicked up the dust and padded it under.
They marched into town like a whirlwind cloud:
OPEN UP THE JAIL AND LET OUT DON McLEOD.

The squatters are riding round in the night
Crying: 'Load up your guns and creep out quiet. 50
Let's teach these niggers that they can't rob
The big white bosses of thirty bob.'

Our young men are hunters our old men make songs,
And the words of our people are whiplashed with wrongs.
In the tribes of our country they sing, and are proud 55
Of the Pilbara men and the white man, McLeod.

Our voice is lighting all over the land,
And we clench up our fists on the sweat of our hands,

For the voice of the workers is thundering loud:
FIGHT WITH CLANCY AND DOOLEY AND DON McLEOD.   60

Don McLeod beat at a mulga bush,
And a lot of queer things came out in a rush.
Like mongrel dogs with their flattened tail,
They've sneaked him off to the Hedland jail.

But Clancy and Dooley and Don McLeod   65
Walk by the wurlies when the wind is loud,
And their voice is new as the fresh sap running,
And we keep on fighting and we keep on coming.

1946/1962

Grave Fairytale

I sat in my tower, the seasons whirled,
the sky changed, the river grew
and dwindled to a pool.
The black Witch, light as an eel,
laddered up my hair   5
to straddle the window-sill.

She was there when I woke, blocking the light,
or in the night, humming, trying on my clothes.
I grew accustomed to her; she was as much a part of me
as my own self; sometimes I thought, 'She *is* myself!'   10
a posturing blackness, savage as a cuckoo.

There was no mirror in the tower.

Each time the voice screamed from the thorny garden
I'd rise and pensively undo the coil,
I felt it switch the ground, the earth tugged at it,   15
once it returned to me knotted with dead warm birds,
once wrapped itself three times around the tower—
                              the tower quaked.
Framed in the window, whirling the countryside
with my great net of hair I'd catch a hawk,   20
                     a bird, and once a bear.
One night I woke, the horse pawed at the walls,
the cell was full of light, all my stone house

suffused, the voice called from the calm white garden,
                           'Rapunzel'.   25
I leant across the sill, my plait hissed out
                        and spun like hail;
he climbed, slow as a heartbeat, up the stony side,
we dropped together as he loosed my hair,
his foraging hands tore me from neck to heels: 30
the witch jumped up my back and beat me to the wall.

Crouched in a corner I perceived it all,
the thighs jack-knifed apart, the dangling sword
                        thrust home,
pinned like a specimen—to scream with joy.   35

I watched all night the beasts unsatisfied
roll in their sweat, their guttural cries
made the night thick with sound.
Their shadows gambolled, hunchbacked, hairy-arsed,
and as she ran four-pawed across the light,   40
the female dropped coined blood spots on the floor.

When morning came he put his armour on,
kissing farewell like angels swung on hair.
I heard the metal shoes trample the round earth
                        about my tower.   45
Three times I lent my hair to the glowing prince,
hand over hand he climbed, my roots ached,
the blood dribbled on the stone sill.
Each time I saw the framed-faced bully boy
                        sick with his triumph.   50

The third time I hid the shears,
a stab of black ice dripping in my dress.
He rose, his armour glistened in my tears,
the convex scissors snapped,
the glittering coil hissed, and slipped   55
                        through air to undergrowth.
His mouth, like a round O, gaped at his end,
his finger nails ripped out, he clawed through space.
His horse ran off flank-deep in blown thistles.
Three seasons he stank at the tower's base.   60
A hawk plucked out his eyes, the ants busied his brain,

the mud-weed filled his mouth, his great sword rotted,
his tattered flesh-flags hung on bushes for the birds.

Bald as a collaborator I sit walled
                          in the thumb-nosed tower,   65
wound round three times with ropes of autumn leaves.
And the witch … sometimes I idly kick
a little heap of rags across the floor.
I notice it grows smaller every year.

                                                        1975

Living Dangerously

O to live dangerously again,
meeting clandestinely in Moore Park,
the underground funds tucked up between our bras,
the baby's pram stuffed with illegal lit.
We hung head down for slogans on the Bridge,   5
the flatbed in the shed ran ink at midnight.

Parked in the driveway, elaborately smoking,
the telltale cars, the cameras, shorthand writers.
Plans for TAKING OVER … 3 YRS THE REVOLUTION.
The counter revs. out gunning for the cadres.   10
ESCAPE along the sea shelf, wading through
                warm waters soft with Blood.
WOW! WHAT A STORY! … guerilla fighters
wear cardigans and watch it on The Box,
lapsed Party cards, and Labor's in again.   15
Retired, Comrade X fishes Nambucca Heads,
& Mrs Petrov, shorthand typist,
                hiding from reporters
                brings home the weekly bacon.

But   O   O   O   to live   20
                so dangerously again,
their Stamina trousers pulling at the crutch.

                                                        1975[1]

1   This poem is part of the sequence 'O! Baby, Baby it's a Wild World'.

From *The Man From Mukinupin*
Act 1

[...] POLLY *whirls about the room in her new negligee while* CECIL *talks to* EDIE, *showing off his wares up-stage.* JACK *has re-entered during the song and stands downstage left, glowering at* POLLY.

JACK: Take it off.
POLLY: Why?
JACK: It's . . . indecent, that's why.
POLLY: Why?
JACK: Because it . . . shows.
POLLY: Shows what?
JACK: Everything!
POLLY: Don't you like it?
JACK: No.
POLLY: Liar!
JACK: *He* gave it to you.
POLLY: Mr Brunner.
JACK: [*mocking*] Cecil!
POLLY: He likes me.
JACK: D'ya want to be an old man's darlin'?
POLLY: I'm not an old man's—anything.
JACK: Then take it off.
POLLY: No. I'm not a young man's—anything, either.
JACK: I thought you was.
POLLY: Then you thought wrong. Mother says—
JACK: [*mocking*] Mother says!
POLLY: You're too . . . familiar.
JACK: You didn't used to think so.
POLLY: When?
JACK: Behind the floursacks in the storeroom after closin' time.
POLLY: You're not a gentleman.
JACK: Mother says!
POLLY: I shouldn't waste myself.
JACK: [*angry*] Don't, then.
POLLY: I don't intend to.
    [*She tosses her head.*]
JACK: You'll soon be rid of me.
POLLY: What's that mean?
JACK: Miss Polly with her hair up.
POLLY: [*hurt*] Don't you like *it*, either?
JACK: It's nothin' to me.

POLLY: That's all right, then.

   [*She turns away.*]

JACK: I got other fish, bigger fish . . .

POLLY: What, then?

JACK: Joined up.

POLLY: Joined up!

   [*She turns back.*]

JACK: Goin' to the war . . . [*a laugh*] to be a hero.

POLLY: What for?

JACK: To fight the Hun. Better than a grocer's boy. Or a—nightie traveller.

POLLY: You're not going.

   [*She crosses and confronts him.*]

JACK: Goodbye, Polly.

   [*He takes off his apron and begins to move away.*]

POLLY: Come back.

JACK: Can't come back. The war'll be over in a month or two.

CECIL: England needs you, Jack.

EEK: The only good German is a dead German.

EDIE: Keep clean and fight fairly.

   [*Re-enter the two* MISSES HUMMER *with a large Australian flag. They stand downstage well in view and wave it. As* JACK *puts on his Army uniform, slouch hat and leather leggings and hoists his kitbag on his shoulder,* EEK, EDIE, CECIL *and* POLLY *dance and sing him off to the war. The two* MISSES HUMMER *join in the singing.*]

    YOUR COUNTRY NEEDS YOU IN THE TRENCHES

ALL: [*except* JACK]

   Your country needs you in the trenches,
   Follow your masters into war,
   And if you cop it we'll remember
   You at the Mukinupin Store.

   Economic domination
   That's what we're fighting for,
   Join up and save the Empire,
   We've got to win this war.

   You'll murder them at Wipers.
   And at Bathsheba Wells,
   Only one more stunt, boys,
   And then you'll get a spell.

   Face the test of nationhood,
   Keep Australia free,

                England needs you, Jack, to fight
                For me, and me, and me.

EDIE AND POLLY:

                Your mothers and your sisters,
                Your sweethearts and your wives,
                Won't hand you a white feather,
                If you'll only look alive.

EEK AND CECIL:

                Look alive, for Crissake look alive,
                The brasshats are all toffs,
                But we've gotta beat the Boch,
ALL: For England Home and Beauty look alive.

                Your country needs you in the trenches,
                Follow your masters into war
                And if you cop it we'll remember
                You at the Mukinupin Store.

EEK: Fight for the West, laddie.

JACK: The West, why it's the freest, richest, happiest land on earth. I'll fight for it. [. . .]

                                                                    1979

From *Wild Card*
Prologue

The first house sits in the hollow of the heart, it will never go away. It is the house of childhood become myth, inhabited by characters larger than life whose murmured conversations whisper and tug at the mind. Enchanted birds and animals out of a private ark sail out on tides of sleep, howling, whistling, mewing, neighing, mooing, baaing, barking, to an endless shimmer of wheat and cracked creek beds. Through the iron gate on the edge of Day's paddock we enter the farm, and drive past the giant she-oak split in two by a strike of lightning. The house lies in the bend of two creeks. The sheepdogs are barking from the verandahs. Beyond is the stable yard with the well in the centre where you let down the bucket to bring up fresh clear water. Large animals move there, draught horses big as the Spanish Armada champing forever at mangers full of oats, licking at rock salt, or rolling ridiculously in grey sand, hoofs waving in air. Liquid or wild-eyed, the cows file into the cow bails with curled horns and names like Strawberry, Buttercup and Daisy. The sheep jostle together in the pens, the kelpie running and snapping across their backs. The sun reflects off the corrugated iron of the shearing shed till it tilts and topples, crazy as a glasshouse. In the chaff house it makes eyes that glitter and run like mice across the floor.

The haystacks prickle and gleam behind the 'chunk chunk chunk' of the chaff cutter feeding an endless belt through cogs and wheels. Magpies are sitting carolling on the York gums. At the back of the stable yard is an old, half-rotted horse race where Yarriman, the Aboriginal horse-breaker, drove the wild horses down from the low hills before we were born. To the right of the path through the house paddock where our father staggered with a bloody eye kicked in by Jack, the rogue horse, there is the married couple's flat-fronted, flat-roofed weatherboard humpie, with one door and two eyes for windows like a child's drawing. The red-headed Pommy, Mrs Rogers, is running in and out of the house like a weather woman bringing her underclothes in off the line so that my father won't see them; inside Peggy Rogers is eating her peas off her knife, because 'the fork might prick me tongue'. Outside in the yard their electric-blue Tin Lizzie is parked waiting to carry them away for ever.

Near the high wire stable gate are the murderous gallows, dripping blood and fat; where the sheep hang with their throats cut. On the other side of the gate is the blacksmith's shop with the grinder and the forge and the black anvil shooting sparks, the floor littered with curls of wood shavings. We hang them over our ears like Mary Pickford. On the left is the ant-heap tennis court where I tried to jump the tennis net and broke my arm and had to be driven fourteen miles over bush roads to the local doctor, with a deal splint my father cut from the wood heap bound round my elbow. My mother sits on the sidelines barracking 'good shot' and 'butterfingers'. Past the tennis court is a dry abandoned dam full of rusty tins where Nancy the black-and-white cow fell in and had to be hauled out, mad-eyed and lowing, with ropes and a pulley.

The little gate opens into the garden with the pink Dorothy Perkins rose climbing on the wire fence, the Geraldton wax bush blooming. The house is ringed with almond and fig trees. In spring the almond blossom falls in white bruised drips on the couch-grass lawn. In summer the twenty-eight parrots crack nuts over our heads till our father goes for the shotgun. At Christmas time we sit on the verandah preparing the nuts for the cake with a silver nutcracker. The twenty-eight parrots flash green and black as they fly away, the nutcracker flashes silver in the sun. We carry the almonds into the kitchen, plunge them in boiling water and peel off the skins, till they curl like brown tissue paper and the almonds emerge smooth and creamy white.

The fig leaves are rough like cows' tongues and the fig skins tingle and burn in our mouths. At night time our father carries us shoulder high to the outside dunny singing 'When the moon shines over the cow shed' and 'There's a little black cupid in the moon'.

The house is built with two wings, the old house and the new. The old house has two corrugated-iron rooms. In the ramshackle sleepout, my grandparents live in an old iron bedstead with silver balls for decoration. The shelves are made of butterboxes filled with paperbacks, and copies of *Bleak House* and *Little Dorrit*, with the ominous Phiz drawings. The Swiss Family Robinson build their tree-house, menaced by giant snakes and jungle. My grandmother's tin trunks are crammed with eyelet-embroidered petticoats with yards of handmade lace, pale leather button-up boots, pearl-buttoned kid gloves and VAD nurses' uniforms from the First World War.

Beside the old sleepout is the little back verandah where the quinces and Jonathan apples are stored to ripen on open wooden shelves. I hide there reading *All Quiet on the Western Front*, and a paperback stolen out of the butterboxes with a cover drawing of a droopy, yellow-haired girl playing the piano, mooned over by a handsome Catholic priest.

Go through the French doors, pleated and dark with dusty muslin curtains, into the enchanted centre, the playroom, the children's domain packed with forty-three dolls and a huge box full of *Alice in Wonderland*, *Tom the Water Baby*, *Treasure Island*, *Wind in the Willows*, *Peter Pan*, *Emily of New Moon*, *A Child's Garden of Verses*, Ida Rentoul Outhwaite's *Elves and Fairies*, Andersen's and Grimm's *Fairy Tales*, *A Child's History of England*, *What Katy Did* and *What Katy Did at School*, *Seven Little Australians*, *Norah of Billabong*, *Dot and the Kangaroo*, *Pollyanna*, *Daddy Long Legs*, *Anne of Green Gables*, *The Tales of Pooh*, *Robin Hood*, *Robinson Crusoe*, *Gulliver's Travels*, *The Arabian Nights*, *Little Women* and *Good Wives*, *Coral Island* and *Tom Brown's School Days*, *Lamb's Tales from Shakespeare* and all my mother's English *Schoolgirl Annuals*.

The dolls are made of rag, celluloid and china. The china dolls' eyes fall in and rattle about in their heads. On the rag dolls' plaster faces the painted eyes run blue when they are left out in the rain. A black mechanical toy car called Leaping Lena bucks across the playroom floor. There is a train set with tangled rails, a double-storeyed, butterbox dolls' house with wicker furniture and a magic lantern, its wavering images clicking on and off across the wall.

Here is the open whitewashed fireplace where our father roasts potatoes in their jackets under the coals in winter, and in summer piles up gum branches to break the fall of Father Christmas as he tumbles down the chimney. We put out a bottle of beer and a piece of Christmas cake, iced and decorated with silver cashews, to reward him for his trouble.

In summer we sleep in the big sleepout completely enclosed in flywire so that at night we feel as if we are floating in air above the garden and the quiet orchard, borne away by the call of the mopokes. In the morning we wake to a wash of light, a magpie perched on the clothes prop, a rooster crowing from the chook yard at the bottom of the garden. In the dim light we watch the cured hams swaying from the iron hooks above our heads.

An old weatherboard verandah runs right through the centre of the house where the sheep carcasses hang in blood-spotted calico. A big water bag with a long spout swings by the tank stand, the rainwater tasting of wet hessian. The bathroom has a claw-footed enamel bath and a chip heater, where our mother develops her sepia photographs in an enamel dish on the marble washstand.

The new wing of weatherboard and fibro was built when I was five. There is a big farm kitchen, a black stove with two huge boiling kettles, a long lino-covered pine table, and a jarrah dresser with a recess underneath where we can crawl and hide. Our father sits in the corner, puts the headphones on, and listens to the test cricket on the crystal set.

In the pantry there are sacks of flour, nuts, sugar and potatoes, rows of home-made preserves and jars of jam. The kettles hiss on the blackened stove, the bread rises in the pans set out on the hob, the wheat is ground into meal for our morning porridge, the sheep's head floats in the white basin, muslined from the flies, the cream is slapped into butter between the wooden pats.

The flypaper hangs from the ceiling and catches in our hair. Blowflies buzz angrily outside the flywire door. Through the kitchen window you can look out on the cannas growing beside the drain, the wattles marking the orchard boundary and the edge of the creek.

In the hall there is an etching of Gladstone, who always chewed every mouthful thirty-six times, and two oil paintings, 'The Stag at Bay' by Great-Aunt Eva and 'The Deer in the Snow' by Great-Aunt Dora, who died of TB in Wooroloo Sanatorium. Eva's stag has a crooked leg.

The hall is the best place to be when the temperature hits 114 in the shade. We lie on our bellies on the jarrah boards listening to *In a Monastery Garden*, *Cavalleria Rusticana*, *Humoresque* and *The Laughing Policeman* on the wind-up His Master's Voice gramophone. Sometimes we play lady wrestlers, or impersonate Two-Ton Tony Galento on the strip of Persian-patterned carpet.

On the other side of the hall is Great-Aunt Eva's bedroom, all polished lino, cheval mirror and oak bedroom suite, reflecting the light. When Aunty Eva comes, once or twice a year, she lies in bed with us reciting *The Schooner Hesperus*, *Hiawatha*, *Horatius at the Bridge* and *Little Jim*, while we pull out her grey hairs one by one.

In the bedroom next door that I share with my mother and sister I have a little single bed where I lie sweating at night, keeping one eye on the griffins on the wardrobe door, which are likely to metamorphose into real monsters, and the other eye on the square of light from the bedroom window, which is likely to let in all things that go bump in the night. The little oil night-light with its round milky glass floats luminous above the dressing-table, where my mother sits singing … 'There's a long, long trail awinding into the land of my dreams.'

On the right of the hall is the sitting room where we are allowed to go only on special occasions, or when the Salvation Army chaplain calls in overnight. Then my mother plays hymns and makes mistakes on the iron-framed German piano. My grandfather's favourite is 'Rock of Ages', my father's is 'Abide with Me'. There is a leatherette sofa and two armchairs, an oval jarrah table and six high-backed dining chairs. The table is always draped in an orange tasselled cover with a leather centrepiece in a cut-out design of fruit and flowers. On the walls are prints of 'The Watcher on the Hill', a group of wild horses with flying manes and rolling eyes, a herd of Highland cattle fording a stream, some Victorian English girls in frilly muslin pinafores toasting chestnuts in front of a fire grate, a sunflower painted on glass, and Great-Aunt Eva's out-of-perspective painting of a huge Newfoundland, paws outstretched under a half-drowned girl, a ship's funnel smoking in the distance.

The fire grate has fleur-de-lis tiles, and elephants from Bombay on the mantelpiece. The bow windows are hung with pale yellow linen curtains bordered with William Morris fruit. They frame the lightning-struck she-oak and the line of salmon gums, shiny and creaking in the wind, their bark hanging in rags like giant beggar women.

Under a broken-backed wattle in the orchard we have our cubby: an old dunny, cement-floored with a row of tulip tiles behind the seat, and a tent made of sewn wheatbags. By the swing is the wrecked Willy's Knight chassis that once belonged to our grandfather. I play Death and the Maiden laid out on the cracked leather seat, dressed up in my mother's crepe de Chine wedding dress, pleated from neck to hem, with the remnants of a gossamer train.

The orchard is heavy with peach and apricot, nectarine and mandarin, quince and pear. A silver balloon hangs for a moment on the quince tree and floats away. The grapevines are pendulous with pale green ladies' fingers. The orchard is thick with paddy and pig melons. I suck the transparent globule of gum prised off the jam tree. The moon rests on the stable roof like a great ruby bubble. My mountain pony Silver steps out daintily, pulling up clumps of cape-weed, her hoofs curling like Arabian slippers. She has foundered in the wheat.

Every spring the magpies nest in the almond tree, raising naked-necked fledglings, their beaks gaping for worms. The tomtit builds its hanging nest and lays three warm speckled eggs amongst dry grass and feathers. A wagtail balances on the toprail of the wire fence hung with dew drops, chirping 'sweet pretty creature'. The drops hang, glisten and slide. The plover nests in the furrows made by the plough. The quail settles down in the long grass over her eggs. The peewits are crying over the wheat. Rain's coming—the black cockatoos sweep down from the rock hill and collect like black rags on the gums. The racehorse goannas are racing through the orchard, switching their tails. A silver-green tree frog leaps into the pink ivy geranium hanging by the tank stand. I am running to the end of the farm, I am running to the end of the rainbow where there is, apparently, a pot of gold. I am holding the silver balloon on the end of a long string. 'The crow flies home to the rooky wood',[1] and Trix, the sixteen-year-old shearers' tabby, sits patiently in the doll's pram under the almond trees, a frilled baby-doll's bonnet tied under her white whiskers. [...]

1990

CHARMIAN CLIFT
1923–1969

Born in Kiama, NSW, Charmian Clift joined the army in the Second World War, during which time she began to write fiction and met the writer George Johnston (qv), whom she later married and with whom she wrote a number of novels. After living in London from 1951 to 1954, Clift and Johnston moved with their children to Greece, where Clift wrote fiction and travel writing. The family returned to Australia in 1964. In the next five years Clift's weekly columns in the *Sydney Morning Herald* and the Melbourne *Herald* attracted a large readership. A number of these essays, which eventually tackled significant issues such as the war in Vietnam, were published in 1965 in *Images in Aspic* (as well as in a number of posthumous collections). Alcohol and conflict between the couple led to Clift dying after taking an overdose of sleeping pills. She is the subject of two biographical works, *Searching for Charmian* (1994), by Clift's first daughter Suzanne Chick, who had been adopted at birth, and *The Life and Myth of Charmian Clift* (2001), by Nadia Wheatley. The poet Martin Johnston (qv) was Clift's son. *DM*

Images in Aspic

There has been a lot of interested, if not quite animated, talk lately in our Alice in Wonderland film circles (shrunk-and-still-shrinking: oh *why* did they eat the wrong side of the mushroom?) about the two big foreign feature films to be made here soon. The one about drovers. The other—still in the stage of preliminary reconnaissance—about a kangaroo.

Oh dear!

I knew a funny story once, which (mercifully) I have forgotten. Only the tag-line seems appropriate here. 'Hang on to your beaver hats, kids! Here we go again!'

Not that one has anything against drovers, or kangaroos either for that matter. The lean man on the big horse gazing out through sun-creased eyes across the spinifex is a romantic image, and home-grown rather than imported, which is something, and our furry marsupial friend is quaint enough to warrant even enhanced celebrity overseas. But when did *you* last sit loosely

---

1   Echoes William Shakespeare, *Macbeth*, III. ii. 50–51.

in the saddle? And what do you keep in your pouch, anyway? I am Australian born and bred, and I can't ride a horse at all. And I've never seen a kangaroo outside a zoo.

Eighty-two per cent of the population of Australia lives in cities or towns. Surely that suggests an alternative national image, or even images, not *instead* of the drover one, but as well as. I am not necessarily thinking of a paunchy man with a briefcase (although according to the statistics he would be a far truer image than the man on the horse), but of the unique aspects of Australian life that could be so excitingly dramatised.

Nobody yet has exploited cinematically our stupendous beaches, or sought to portray the neo-paganism of the surf cult, which is utterly contemporary, utterly Australian, and so very intriguing with its rituals and hierarchies, its austerity of physical discipline, its more-than-liberal morals, the orgiastic quality of its songs and dances, the physical beauty of its devotees. The bronzed man on the surfboard is at least as authentic an image as the bronzed man on the horse, and much more familiar to most of us.

Neither has anybody touched upon our particular contemporary problem of the integration of hundreds of thousands of Europeans into our communities. There is yeast enough there to ferment a dozen films, without formula or cliché.

We have the strongest trade union movement in the world. Our industries are expanding at a fantastic rate. Every element of drama is present, not American drama, not British drama, but Australian drama, as the story of Mount Isa so dramatically illustrates.

And on the heroic scale, what stories might not be dug out of the grand conception of the Snowy Scheme, or the Ord, or the Cape York peninsula? Or for glamour take the jazzy Gold Coast, or the romantic islands of the Great Barrier Reef. And haven't we tuna fisheries, giant meat-works, enormous road trains, gem-fields, wharves and shipping, whale-spotters, a rocket range, radio telescopes? . . . the possibilities are endless. Above the Nullarbor there are small groups of hunters who live in isolation for months at a time, filling up modern freezer-trucks with the carcasses of rabbits they shoot at night from Landrovers. It is a strange country, an exciting country, an original country, from the stupefying immensity of its scale to the most delicate of its particular nuances.

Ever since I have been back here I have been conscious that Australians, caught in international cross-currents of ideas and manners and fashions, twisted about by reassessments of their own old myths, bewildered by elusive and changing standards, are desperate to be redefined.

But it is for us to define ourselves, to reveal ourselves unself-consciously in our many facets, before the aspic of the overseas conception sets firmly around the jolly swagman and the overlander and condemns us to be served up forever in jellied garnish. Because one thing is certain: if we are incapable of presenting ourselves in our own true image and images, the huge overseas companies, on whom we seem to be relying rather optimistically to do it for us, will carry on with the safe cliché that conforms so glibly to the prefabricated notion.

Lately I have been talking with film people, or listening to them, rather, and one particular conversation was a striking illustration of this very point. A British film director, a good one, and a perceptive sensitive man, was advising an American director, newly arrived and scouting locations for his kangaroo film. The British director strongly recommended a location (quite remote) which I swear not one per cent of Australians have ever seen or are ever likely to. The British director had himself made a film there. So had an earlier American company. You couldn't go wrong, said the Britisher. He strongly recommended it for the American's purposes, even though the story would certainly have to be altered a little to fit the locale. It wasn't perfect, he said, but it was quite the closest thing he had been able to find to what he had imagined Australia to be like *before he came here.* And he thought that it was most important to portray that preconceived idea as nearly as possible. After all, he summed up, that's what people overseas *expected* to see.

And another highly successful American script-writer, again a sensitive, intelligent (although disenchanted) man, came here looking for Australian material and went back to Hollywood empty-handed. He said, with a little deprecating grin, that what his company really wanted was another Australian 'Western', and it wasn't much good presenting them with anything more subtle. It makes one wish, he said, that you had a film industry of your own. There is so much you could do here on a modest scale in that intimate and wise way the Italians have. And what is so sad, he said, is that you have the people here, and all the technical equipment and the technical knowledge to do it.

It's true too. The studios, the equipment, the labs, the cameras, the cameramen, who must long to do something bigger than TV and film commercials, or even the quality sponsored documentaries that seem to be the only hopeful thing happening here in the film industry.

There must be an answer somewhere. Even in the depressing realities of finance and distribution and profits and markets and all the reasons put forward by the people who should be making the films as to why it is absolutely impossible to do anything at all. In my ignorance of big business and high finance I tend to believe that image-making could be more important than profit-making. Perhaps I am wrong.

In Sydney recently a taxi-driver asked me what I thought of the Opera House, glimpsed just then with the gaunt framework of its skeletonic sails fantastic against the water. If they could finance such an undertaking by means of a lottery, he said, why couldn't someone start another lottery—a more modest one perhaps—for the benefit of a native film industry. It wouldn't cost anybody anything, would it? And then we could get the industry back on its feet again without begging the Government for subsidies.

'What makes you so interested in the film industry?' I asked curiously, and in the driving mirror he gave me a small, lenient smile. 'I'm an actor,' he said. 'Resting.'

1965

ERIC ROLLS
1923–2007

Poet, historian, farmer and environmentalist Eric Charles Rolls was born into a farming family in western NSW. After primary schooling at home through Blackfriars Correspondence School, he won his way into the selective Fort Street Boys' High School in Sydney. In the Second World War he served with the AIF in Papua New Guinea and Bougainville. From 1948 to 1986 he farmed in central-northern NSW, the area about which he wrote in some of his most important works. An idiosyncratic writer of many moods and styles, and always highly energetic, Rolls was a pioneer of environmental writing in Australia in books such as *They All Ran Wild: The story of pests on the land in Australia* (1969), *The River: A chronicle of life on the land* (1974) and *A Million Wild Acres: 200 years of man and an Australian forest* (1981). Other major works include *Celebration of the Senses* (1984) and his two-volume history of the Chinese in Australia, *Flowers and the Wide Sea: Sojourners* (1992) and *Citizens* (1996). His *Selected Poems* appeared in 1990. *A Million Wild Acres* tells the epic story of the Pilliga Scrub. Les Murray said of it, 'Through a fusion of vernacular elements with fine-grained natural observation, and a constant movement of back-reference, he breaks through sequential time not to timelessness but to a sort of enlarged spiritual present in which no life is suppressed.' *NJ*

From *A Million Wild Acres*
Chapter 8: Timber and Scrub

If the forest had been as dense in 1900 as it is in the 1980s, Jimmy Governor[1] might have had an even better game with his pursuers. He could have boxed them up in huge impenetrable thickets of Spurwing Acacia or lost them on hands and knees in tangles of fallen dead Spearwood and varying live scrub. He could have hidden there for years and, if he had deigned to live off the country, it would have supported him.

It would be sensible to sum up the scattered references I have made to the marvellous growth of the forest. When the first squatters sent their stock in, the ridgy country on the east and south carried the same heavy growth as it does now, a remarkably coastal scrub which I shall specify later. Not all the growth extended to the flats, not all the ridges were covered. The rest, apart from the great arc of Brigalow in the north, was grassland dominated in the east by three to four big ironbarks (*Eucalyptus crebra*) to the hectare, and in the centre and west—about half a million hectares—by three to four big pines

1   Outlaw (1875–1901), subject of Thomas Keneally's (qv) novel *The Chant of Jimmy Blacksmith* (1972).

to the hectare. The White Cypress pine is known in 1980 as *Callitris columellaris*. It has persisted unchanged through numerous Latin tags. A few pines that were seedlings in the 1830s were still alive in the 1970s to show how big the pines grew before profuse growth crowded them. John Grosser who owned a one-man sawmill and 400 hectares of timber on the eastern edge of the Pilliga Nature Reserve had three or four old pines he kept as seed trees. In the 1970s they were nearing the end of their lives of about 200 years. North-west of Kenebri off Dry Sand Road grew two big pines. These trees were twenty to twenty-five metres high and up to ninety centimetres in diameter at breast height. That is not big by coastal standards where Blackbutt logs two metres in diameter come in on the trailers as single riders. But the biggest pine milled in modern times is less than half the size of those old pines.

The old ironbarks were ever bigger. Some would have fitted two only to a modern trailer. There are giants that died in the 1902 drought still standing as witness. Among the ironbarks and the pines grew their scattered seedlings. In places there were small belts of dense saplings. And there were belts of Bull Oak and Belar (*Casuarina luehmannii* and *C. cristata*), of Western Black Wattle (*Acacia hakeoides*), and especially of Curracabah, once known as *Acacia cunninghamii*, a name recently found to cover three species. The early reports of dense patches of it were not misidentification. Bert Ruttley who knew individual trees among myriads of the same kind told me that a wattle with long flowers and red stems, common when he was a boy, no longer grew. He knew it by no name, but he gave a good description of Curracabah. Other trees and shrubs—several hundred species—grew singly or in sparse clumps.

The first change noticed throughout Australia, and the principal change, was in the texture of the soil. Cloven hooves destroyed the mulch of thousands of years in five to ten years. So the grasses changed. As the Aborigines were displaced they ceased their husbandry of the land by fire. For varying periods over Australia there was no more regular burning. In the Pilliga forest the period was about twenty-five years from the late 1840s to the early 1870s. Then the seeds of spear or corkscrew grasses (*Stipa* spp.) and of wire grasses (*Aristida* spp.) began to worry sheep. The profuse long-tailed seeds depreciated the wool. But worse, they bored into flesh. These seeds move when dampened: the long straight tails twist into spirals on the first few drops of rain and turn the long pointed seeds into the ground like augers or down through wool into skin. It was common to find spear grass seed in mutton chops just as the broken-off heads of Aboriginal spears were sometimes found in the carcasses of cattle cut up for boiling-down.

So sheep owners shore in the autumn before the seed ripened, then burnt the dried off grass in the winter. In the spring it grew from the butts and gave a month or two of clean grazing before beginning to set its vicious seeds. Some men burnt again in late spring.

After the hard drought of 1877 the soil was bare and powdered. Extreme rains in 1879 brought away a dense growth of grass from butts and from seed. These herbaceous perennial grasses can appear quite dead after months of drought, then shoot green in three or four days after ten millimetres of rain. The old pines seeded well in the lush spring. When the stockowners burnt, pine seedlings came up thickly in the ash. Rat-kangaroos, eaters of seedlings, were in low numbers after the drought. Sheep had destroyed their cover as well as their feed. The pine grew unchecked.

In one of the periodic depressions in cattle prices that still trouble Australian graziers, thousands of extra sheep were brought into the forest area. The burning increased. More pockets of pine came away in good years in the early 1880s. Many runs were abandoned. When the 1902 drought ended there were more bursts of pine growth here and there. Scrub extended off the ridges and belts of oak came away.

Then the rabbits built up. Management of the area changed. Burning was irregular. The wandering shepherds burnt pockets here and there. Those cattlemen who used the abandoned forest as a giant common rode out and lit big fires ahead of rain. What seedlings these fires started were eaten by rabbits.

In 1917 the Pilliga West and Pilliga East State forests were dedicated and the New South Wales Forestry Commission took control. Although fire germinates pine seeds, it kills growing pines of all ages, so the Forestry Commission stopped the burning where it had authority. For forty-five years there was little fresh growth.

The thick pine grew in belts. Much of the forest area was still fairly open. 'Look at that!' an old man will say. 'Sixty, seventy years ago I shepherded a thousand sheep out there. I could let 'em all feed out and I could stand in one place and watch the whole flock. Only twenty year ago I could walk out there and shoot a kangaroo a hundred yards off easy. Now if I walked in there twenty yards and didn't watch where I was going I'd bloody get lost.'

By the long wet of 1950 years of litter had accumulated: natural fall, natural deaths, and the tops, branches and stripped bark that log-fallers and sleeper cutters leave behind them. Grass grew up among it and hayed off in the hot November of 1951.

Fire started near the Rocky Creek sawmill north-east of Kenebri on 16 November. It swept in double tongues south and south-east. The two tongues attracted one another. Fire is always sucked towards fire because of the displaced hot air. When they met, 'they went up like a masonic bomb', said one old resident of Baradine. The fire continued on a wider front. It is the worst yet known in the area. I lived then east of the Namoi about ninety kilometres from the fire. At midday the sun was a dull orange circle in a green sky. Our eyes watered from the smoke. [...]

1981

ELIZABETH JOLLEY
1923–2007

Elizabeth Jolley was born in the English Midlands to an Austrian mother 'with aristocratic pretensions' (as Jolley describes her) and an English father, who was a pacifist teacher imprisoned for his beliefs in the First World War and disowned by his father because of them. Jolley was brought up in a household she described with characteristic wry humour as 'half-English and three-quarters Viennese'; she went to a Quaker boarding school and then trained as a nurse in London during the Second World War, where she met her husband Leonard Jolley. Some of Jolley's fiction draws on these experiences, especially her moving trilogy *My Father's Moon* (1989), *Cabin Fever* (1990) and *The Georges' Wife* (1993).

In 1959 Jolley moved to Perth when her husband became chief librarian of the University of Western Australia. While Jolley liked to mention a number of jobs she held at this time, including 'door to door salesman (failed), real estate salesman (failed) and a flying domestic', which helped to create the impression that she came late to authorship, she was always writing and had some early success with radio plays. However, her first collection of stories, *Five Acre Virgin*, did not appear until 1976, and her first novel, the dramatic and (to some) disturbing story of lesbian desire *Palomino*, was not published until 1980. From her first published stories, Jolley created a unique genre of black comedy, semi-Gothic drama, enigmatic and at times opaque characters, and a style that moves like lightning between pathos and dry humour.

During the 1980s, when a range of powerful work was being published by women writers in Australia, Jolley constantly surprised her readers with what seemed like an avalanche of idiosyncratic books (at the rate of almost one every year), from the excoriating comedy of *Mr Scobie's Riddle* (1983), set in an eccentric nursing home, and the somewhat more genial *Miss Peabody's Inheritance* (1983), which plays gentle games with the reality of the narrative, through to the brilliant use of Gothic conventions in her award-winning narrative of thwarted desire, *The Well* (1986, filmed in 1997). In the more conventionally Gothic *Milk and Honey* (1984) and the faintly distorted comedy of manners *The Sugar Mother* (1988), Jolley showed that she could create male protagonists every bit as unusual and convincing as her female protagonists.

In the 1990s Jolley published four novels and a perfect, polished novella, *The Orchard Thieves* (1995)—an unflinching but touching examination of family tensions, especially those between mothers and daughters and sisters. In her final three novels, *Lovesong* (1997), *An Accommodating Spouse* (1999) and *An Innocent Gentleman* (2001), she returns to the interlocking themes of love, desire and a sense of estrangement—occasionally ameliorated by glimpses of understanding that are fleetingly produced by music, memories and landscapes. *PS*

Night Runner

Night Sister Percy is dying. It is my first night as Night Runner at St Cuthbert's. Night Sister Bean, grumbling and cackling, calls the register and, at the end, she calls my name.

'Nurse Wright.'

'Yes Sister,' I reply, half rising in my chair as I have seen the others do. The Maids' Dining Room, where we eat, is too cramped to do anything else.

'Night Runner,' she says and I sit down again. The thought of being Night Runner is alarming. Nurse Dixon has been Night Runner for a long time. All along I have been hoping that I would escape from these duties and responsibilities, the efficient rushing here and there to relieve on different wards; every night bringing something new and difficult.

The Night Runner has to prepare the Night Nurses' meal too; one little sitting at twelve midnight and a second one at twelve forty five and, of course, the clearing up and the washing up.

Every night I admire Nurse Dixon in the tiny cramped kitchen where we sit close together, regardless of rank, in the hot smell of warmed up fish or mince and the noise of the jugs of strong black coffee, keeping hot, in two black pans of boiling water. We eat our meal there in this intimacy with these two hot saucepans splashing and hissing just behind us. The coffee, only a little at the bottom of each jug, looks thick and dark and I wonder how it is made. Tonight I will have to find out and have it ready when the first little group of nurses appears.

When I report to Night Sister Bean in her office, she tells me to go for the oxygen.

'Go up to Isolation for the oxygen,' she says without looking up from something she is writing. I am standing in front of her desk. I have never been so close to her before, not in this position, that is, of looking at her from above. She is starch-scented, shrouded mysteriously in the daintily severe folds of spotted white gauze. She is a sorceress disguised in the heavenly blue of the Madonna; a shrivelled, rustling, aromatic, knowledgeable, Madonna-coloured magician; she is a wardress and a keeper. She is an angel in charge of life and in charge of death. Her fine white cap, balancing, nodding, a grotesque blossom flowering forever in the dark halls of the night, hovers beneath me. She is said to have powers, an enchantment, beyond the powers of an ordinary human. For one thing, she has been on night duty in this hospital for over thirty years. As I stand there I realise that I do not know her at all and that I am afraid of her.

'Well,' she says, 'don't just stand there. Go up to Isolation for the oxygen and bring it at once to Industry.'

'Yes, Sister,' I say and I go as quickly as I can. The parts of the hospital are all known by different names; Big Boys, Big Girls, Top Ward, Bottom Ward, Side Ward and Middle, Industry, Peace, Chapel and Nursery. I have a room on the Peace Corridor, so named because it is above the Chapel and next to Matron's Wing.

Industry is the part over the kitchens. There are rooms for nurses there too. Quite often there is a pleasant noise and smell of cooking in these rooms. The Nurses' Sick Bay is there and it is there that I have to take the oxygen.

★

I am frightened out here.

For one thing, Isolation is never used. It is, as the name suggests, isolated. It is approached by a long, narrow covered way sloping up through a war-troubled shrubbery where all the dust bins are kept. Because of not being able to show any lights it is absolutely dark there. When I go out into the darkness I can smell rotting arms and legs, thrown out of the operating theatre and not put properly into the bins. I gather my apron close so that I will not get caught by a protruding maimed hand.

When I flash my torch quickly over the bins I see they are clean and innocent and have their lids firmly pressed on. In the torchlight there is no smell.

The sky at the end of the covered passage is decorated with the pale moving fans of search lights. The beams of light are interwoven with the sounds of throbbing engines. The air raid warning might sound at any moment. In the emergency of being made Night Runner so suddenly, I have forgotten to bring my tin hat and gas mask from the Maids' Dining Room.

I am worried about the gas mask and the tin hat. I have signed for them on arrival at the hospital and am completely responsible for them. I will have to hand them back if I leave the hospital or if this war comes to an end. Usually I never leave either of them out of my care. I have them tied together with thick string. I put them under my chair at meal times and I hang them up in the nurses' cupboard in the ward where I am working.

It is hard to find the oxygen. My torch light picks up stacks of pillows, shelves of grey blankets, rolls of waterproof sheets, and some biscuit tins labelled Emergency Dressings, all with dates on them. There are two tea chests filled with tins and bottles. The chests are marked Emergency. Iron Rations. Doctors Only in red paint. There do not seem to be similar boxes marked for nurses or patients.

At last I find the oxygen cylinder and I rush with the little trolley up to Industry.

Sister Percy is dying. She is the other Night Sister and is very fat. She is propped, gasping, on pillows, a blue trout with eyes bulging, behind the floral screens made by Matron's mother for sick nurses.

It is the first time I have seen someone who is dying. Night Sister Bean is there and the RMO and the Home Sister. They take the oxygen and Sister Bean tells me I need not stay. She pulls the screens closer round Sister Percy.

In the basement of the hospital I set about the secrets of making the coffee and having it come only so far up the jugs.

Later Night Sister Bean comes and says why haven't I lit the gas, which, when you think about it, is a good thing to say as they will surely want that potato and mince stuff hot. Before she leaves she makes me get down on my knees to hunt behind the pipes for cockroaches. She has a steel knitting needle for this and we knock and scrape and rattle about, Night Sister Bean on her knees too, and we chase them out, the revolting things, and sprinkle some white powder which, she says, they love to eat without knowing it is absolutely fatal to them.

It is something special about night duty, this little meal time in the middle of the night, with everyone sitting together, even Night Sister Bean, herself, coming to one or the other of the sittings. She seems almost human, in spite of the mysterious things whispered about her, at these meals. Sometimes she even complains about the sameness of them, saying that one thing the war cannot do is to make these meals worse than they are and that it is sheer drudgery to eat them night after night. When I think about this I realise she has been eating stewed mince and pounded fish for so many years and I can't help wishing I could do something about it.

This first night it takes me a long time to clear up in the little pantry. When at last I am finished Night Sister Bean sends me to relieve on Bottom Ward. There is a spinal operation in the theatre recovery room just now, she says, and a spare nurse will be needed when the patient comes back to the ward.

On my way to Bottom Ward I wish I could be working with Staff Nurse Ramsden.

'I will play something for you,' she said to me once when I was alone and filled with tears in the bleak, unused room which is the nurses' sitting room.

She ran her fingers up and down the piano keys. 'This is Mussorgsky,' she said, 'it's called Gopak, a kind of little dance,' she explained. She played and turned her head towards me nodding and smiling, 'do you like this?' she asked, her eyes smiling. It is not everyone who has had Mussorgsky played for them; the thought gives me courage as I hurry along the unlit passage to the ward.

There is a circle of light from the uncurtained windows of the office in the middle of the ward. I can see a devout head bent over the desk in the office. I feel I am looking at an Angel of mercy who is sitting quietly there ready to minister to the helpless patients.

Staff Nurse Sharpe is seated in the office with an army blanket tucked discreetly over her petticoat. Her uniform dress lies across her lap. She explains that she is just taking up the hem and will I go to the kitchen and cut the bread and butter. As I pass the linen cupboard I see the other night nurse curled up in a heap of blankets. She is asleep. This is my friend Ferguson.

I sink slowly into the bread cutting. It is a quiet and leisurely task. While I cut and spread I eat a lot of the soft new bread and I wonder how Sharpe will manage to wear her uniform shortened. Matron is so particular that we wear them long, ten inches off the ground, so that the soldiers do not get in a heightened excitement about us.

Sharpe comes in quite soon. She seems annoyed that I have not finished. She puts her watch on the table and says the whole lot, breakfast trays all polished and set, and bread and butter for sixty men, must be finished in a quarter of an hour. I really hurry up after this and am just ready when the operation case comes back and I have to go and sit by him in the small ward. I hope to see Ferguson but S/N Sharpe has sent her round changing the water jugs.

Easily I slip into my dream of Ferguson. She owes me six and sevenpence. I have written it on the back of my writing pad. I'll go out with her and borrow two and six.

'Oh Lord!' I'll say, 'It's my mother's birthday and I haven't a thing for her and here I am without my purse. Say, can you lend me two and six?' And then I'll let her buy a coffee and a bun for me—that will bring it to three shillings and I won't ever pay it back and, in that way, will recover some of the six and sevenpence.

'Cross my heart, cut me in two if my word is not true,' I say to myself and I resolve to sit in Ferguson's room as soon as I am off duty. I'll sit there till she pays me the money. I'll just sit and sit there till it dawns on her why I am there.

The patient, quite still as if dead, suddenly moves and helps himself to a drink of water. He vomits and flings the bowl across the room. He seems to be coming round from his anaesthetic. I grope under the bed clothes. I should count his pulse but I am unable to find his wrist.

'Oh I can't,' he groans, 'not now I can't.'

He seems to be in plaster of Paris from head to foot. He groans again and sleeps. Nervously I wait to try again to find some place on his body where I can feel his pulse.

High on the wall in the Maids' Dining Room is an ancient wireless. It splutters and gargles all day with the tinny music of workers' play time and Vera Lynn plaintively announcing there'll always be an England. Sometimes in the early mornings, while we have our dinner, the music is of a different kind. Sometimes it is majestic, lofty and sustaining.

'Wright!' Staff Nurse Ramsden calls across the crowded tables. 'Mock Morris? Would you say?' She waves a long fingered hand.

'No', I shake my head, 'not Mock Morris, it's Beethoven.' She laughs. She knows it is not Beethoven. It is a little joke we have come to share. It is the only joke I have with anyone. Perhaps it is the same for Ramsden. She has a slight moustache and I have noticed, in her room, an odour, a heaviness which belongs with older women perhaps from the perfumed soap she has and the material of well made underwear. Her shoes and stockings, her suits and blouses and hats have the fragrance of being of a better quality. Ramsden asked me once about the violin I was carrying. She has said to me to choose one of her books, she has several in her room, as a present from her to me. Secretly I think, every day, that I admire Ramsden. I love her. Perhaps, I think, I will tell her, one day, the truth about the violin case.

A special quality about working during the night is the stepping out of doors in the mornings, the first feeling of the fresh air and the sun which is hardly warm in its brightness.

We ride our bicycles. Not Ramsden. There is a towing path along the river. I, not knowing it before, like the smell of the river, the muddy banks and the cattle-trodden grass. Water birds, disturbed, rise noisily. Our own voices echo.

Though we have had our meal we want breakfast. Ferguson hasn't any money. Neither has Queen. Ferguson says she will owe Queen if Queen will owe me for them both. We agree and I pay. And all the way back I am trying to work out what has to be added to the outstanding six and sevenpence.

Ferguson's room, when I go to sit there, looks as if it should be roped off as a bomb crater. Her clothes, and some of mine, are scattered everywhere. There is a note from the Home Sister on her dusty dressing table. I read the note, it is to tell Ferguson to clean her hair brush.

Bored and sleepy I study the note repeatedly, and add 'Neither a Borrower nor a Lender be' in handwriting so like the Home Sister's it takes my breath away.

I search for Ferguson's writing paper. It is of superior quality and very suitable. I write some little notes in this newly learned handwriting and put them carefully in my pocket. I continue to wait for Ferguson, hardly able to keep my eyes open.

I might have missed my sleep altogether if I had not remembered in time that Ferguson has gone home for her nights off.

I do not flash the torch for fear of being seen. I grope in the dark fishing for something, anything, in the cavernous tea chest, and hasten back down the covered way.

Night Sister Bean says to me to go to Bottom Ward to relieve and I say, 'Yes Sister,' and leave her office backwards, shuffling my feet and bending as if bowing slightly, my hands, behind my back, clasping and almost dropping an enormous glass jar.

It is bottled Chinese gooseberries, of all things, and I put one on each of the baked apples splashing the spicy syrup generously. Night Sister Bean smiles, crackling starch, and says the baked apples have a piquant flavour. She has not had such a delicious baked apple for thirty years. 'Piquant!' she says.

S/N Sharpe sits in the office all night with nursing auxiliary Queen. Queen has put operation stockings over her shoes to keep warm. Both Sharpe and Queen are wrapped up in army blankets. Sharpe has to let down the hem of her dress. Sister Bean asked her to stay behind at breakfast.

Whenever I come back to the office Sharpe says, 'take these pills to bed twelve' or 'get the lavatories cleaned', and, 'time to do the bread and butter—and don't leave the trays smeary like last night'.

At the end of the ward I pull out the laundry baskets and I move the empty oxygen cylinders and the fire equipment; the buckets of water and sand. I simply move them all out from their normal places, just a little way out, and later, when Sharpe and Queen go along to the lavatory, they fall over these things and knock into each other, making the biggest disturbance ever heard in a hospital at night. Night Sister Bean comes rushing all the way up from her office in the main hall. She is furious and tells Sharpe and Queen to report to Matron at nine a.m. She can see that I am busy, quietly with my little torch, up the other end of the ward, pouring the fragrant mouth-wash in readiness for the morning.

The tomato sauce has endless possibilities. The dressed crab is in such a small quantity that the only thing I can do is to put a tiny spoonful on top of the helpings of mashed potato. Night Sister Bean is appreciative and says the flavour seeps right through. Tinned bilberries, celery soup and custard powder come readily to my experienced hands.

I do not see S/N Ramsden very often. She has not asked me in to her room again to choose the book. Perhaps she has changed her mind. She is, after all, senior to me.

There are times when an unutterable loneliness is the only company in the cold early morning. The bicycle rides across the heath or along the river are over too quickly and, because of this, are meaningless. With a sense of inexplicable bereavement my free time seems to stretch ahead in emptiness. I go to bed too soon and sleep badly.

I am glad when Ferguson comes back; very pleased. In the pantry I am opening a big tin, the biggest thing I have managed to lift out so far. I say 'Hallo,' to Ferguson as she sits down with the other nurses; they talk and laugh together. I go on with my work.

'Oh, you've got IT,' I say to Ferguson. 'Plenty of S.A. Know what that is? Sex appeal, it's written all over you.' And seeing, out of the corner of my eye, Night Sister Bean coming in, I go on talking as if I haven't seen her.

'How you do it beats me Fergie,' I say. 'How is it you have all the men talking about you the way they do? You certainly must have given them plenty to think about. They all adore you. Corporal Smith's absolutely mad about you, really!' Unconcernedly I scrape scrape at the tin. 'He never slept last night. Sharpe had to slip him a Mickey Finn, just a quick one. He's waiting for another letter from you and I think he's sending the poem you asked for. Who on earth is your go between?' So I go on and scrape scrape at the tin.

I know why there is silence behind me. I turn round.

'Oh, here you are at last Sister,' I say to Night Sister Bean. Ferguson is a dull red colour, pity, as she was looking so well after her nights off.

'Here we are Sister,' I say, 'on the menu we have Pheasant Wing in aspic. Will you have the fish pie with it?' I serve all the plates in turn. The coffee hisses and spits behind us.

'Matron's office, nine o'clock,' Night Sister Bean says to Ferguson.

'Yes, Sister.'

Ferguson is sent to Big Girls for the rest of the night and I am to relieve, as usual, on Bottom Ward. I wake Corporal Smith at four a.m. and urge him to write to Nurse Ferguson. 'Every day she waits for a letter,' I tell him, 'she'll get ill from not eating if you don't write.' S/N Sharpe finds me by his bed and sends me to scrub the bathroom walls.

'And do out all the cupboards too, and quickly,' she says.

In the morning when I see Sharpe safely in the queue for letters I rush up to the Peace corridor and find her room. I cram her curtains into her messy wet soap dish and leave one of my neatly folded notes on her dressing table.

Do not let your curtains dangle in the soap dish. Sister.

There is not much I can do with the cherry jam. I serve it with the stewed mince as a sweet and sour sauce. It is a favourite with the royal family, I tell them, but I can see I shall have to risk another raid on my secret store.

The next night I have a good dig into both chests and load myself up with tinned tomato soup, a tinned chicken, some sardines and two tins of pears.

Nurse Dixon is mystified. Her eyes are full of questions.

'Where d'you get all . . .' her lips form whispered words.

'No time to chat now, sorry,' I say. I am hastily setting a little tray for Night Sister Bean. I have started taking an extra cup of coffee along to her office. It seems the best way to use up a tin of shortbread fingers. Balancing my tray I race up the dark stairs and along the passage to Night Sister Bean's office.

'Bottom Ward,' Night Sister Bean says without looking up. Again I am at the mercy of Sharpe.

'Wash down the kitchen walls,' she says, 'and do all the shelves and cupboards and quickly—before you start the blanket baths.' She gives me a list of the more disagreeable men to do; she says to change their bottom sheets too. All the hardest work while N/A Queen, who is back there, and herself sit wrapped up in the office, smoking, with a pot of hot coffee between them on the desk.

I go into the small ward and give the emergency bell there three rings bringing Night Sister Bean to the ward before Sharpe and Queen realise what is happening.

'Is it an air raid?' Queen asks anxiously.

'Nurses should know why they ring, Nurse,' Sister Bean says and she makes them take her round to every bed whispering the diagnosis and treatment of every patient. Night Sister Bean rustling and croaking, fidgeting and cursing, disturbs all the men trying to find out who rang three times.

'Someone must be haemorrhaging,' she says, 'find out who it is.'

Peering maliciously into the kitchen, Sister Bean sees me quietly up the step ladder with my little pail of soapy water. The wet walls gleam primrose yellow as if they have been freshly painted. She tells Sharpe and Queen to report to matron's office nine a.m. for smoking on duty.

Once again Sharpe is in the letter queue. I take the loaded ash tray from the Porters' Lodge and spill it all over her room.

Your room is disgusting. Take some hot water and disinfectant and wash down. Sister.

The folded note lies neatly on her dressing table.

I try listening to Beethoven but it reminds me of my loneliness. I wish Corporal Smith would write to me. I wish someone would write to me. Ferguson is going to The Old Green Room for coffee. She is popular, always going out.

In my room I have a list.

1. Listen to Beethoven
2. Keep window wide open. If cold sleep in school jersey.
3. Ride bicycle for complexion. (care of)
4. Write and Think.

'I can't come out,' I say to Ferguson, 'I'm listening to Beethoven,' I say, ignoring the fact that she has not asked me.

'It's only one record,' she says, 'you've only got one record.'

'It's Beethoven all the same,' I beat time delicately and wear my far away look.

Ferguson goes off out and I add number 5 with difficulty to the list. The paper is stuck in at the side of the dressing table mirror and uneven to write on.

5. Divine N.S.B.'s nature and discover exactly the extent of her powers.

I take my white windsor, bath size, to the wash room and fill a basin with hot water to soften the soap. I set to work with my nail file and scissors. I'll take my torch tonight, I'm thinking, a tin of powdered milk would be useful. Whipped up, it makes very good cream; delicious with the baked apples.

The likeness is surprising. It is the distinction of the shape and the tilt of the cap, the little figure is emerging perfectly. I work patiently for a long time. I am going to split the image in half very carefully and torture one half keeping the other half as a control, as in a scientific experiment, and observe the effect on the living person.

The idea is so tremendous I feel faint. Already I foresee results, the upright, crisp little blue and white Bean totters in the passage, she wilts and calls for help.

'Nurse Wright! Help me up, Dear. What a good child you are, so gentle too. Just help me to that chair, thank you, dear child. Thank you!'

The Peace corridor is very quiet. Another good thing about the night duty is that we all may sleep in our beds during the day. Every morning I long for this sleep. Up until this time I, like the others, have had to carry bedclothes down to the basement every night because of the air raids. There are no beds in the basement, only some sack mattresses of straw. There is no air there either.

I love the smell of the clean white windsor. I am sculpting carefully with the file. The likeness is indeed perfect. My hands are slippery and wrinkled and I am unable to stop them from shaking. I feel suddenly that I possess some hitherto unknown but vital power to be able to make this—this effigy.

And then, all at once, Night Sister Bean is there in the doorway of the washroom, peering about to see who it is not in bed yet and it is after twelve noon already. Because I am thinking of the moment when I will split the image and considering which tool will be most suitable for this, the sudden appearance of Sister Bean is, to say the least, confusing.

I plunge my head into the basin together with Her I am so carefully fashioning, saying:

'Oh, I can never get the soap out of my hair!' delighted at the sound of weariness achieved.

She says to remember always to have the rinsing water hotter than the washing water. 'Hot as you can bear it,' she says.

'Thank you Sister.'

She is rustling and cackling, crackling and disturbing, checking every corner of the washroom, quickly looking into all the lavatories, saying as she leaves:

'And it is better to take off your cap first.'

So there I am with the soaked limp thing, frothed and scummed all over with the white windsor, on my head, still secure with an iron foundry of hair grips and useless for tonight. My work of art too is ruined, the outlines blurred and destroyed before being finished. It is a solemn moment of understanding that from a remote spot, namely the door, she has been able to spoil what I have made and add a further destruction of her own, my cap.

My back aches with bending over the stupid little sink. These days I am missing too much sleep. In spite of being so tired I go down to the ramp where the milk churns are loaded and unloaded. It is the meeting place of the inside of the hospital with the outside world. The clean laundry boxes are there, neatly stacked. Fortunately Ferguson's box is near the edge. I open it and remove one of her fresh clean caps. My box is there too but I don't want to take one of mine as it will leave me short later in the week.

The powdered household milk is in the chest as I hoped, tins of it and real coffee too. I find more soup, mushroom, cream of asparagus, cream of chicken, vegetable and minestrone. I am quite reckless with my torch. Christmas is coming, I take a little hoard of interesting tins.

I discover that Night Sister Bean has a weakness for hot broth and I try, every night, to slip a cup along to her office in the early part of the night before I start on anything else.

Several things are on my mind, mostly small affairs. For some time I have Corporal Smith's love letter to Ferguson, sixteen pages, in my pocket. It is not sealed and her name does not appear anywhere in the letter. It is too long for one person so I divide the letter in half and address two envelopes in Corporal Smith's handwriting, one to Sharpe and one to Ferguson. Accidentally I drop them, unsealed, one by the desk in Night Sister Bean's office and the other in the little hall outside Matron's room. We are not supposed to be intimate with the male patients and I feel certain too that Corporal Smith is a married man . . . but there is something else on my mind; it is whether a nurse should send a Christmas card to the Matron. It is something entirely beyond my experience.

In the end I buy one, a big expensive card, a Dutch Interior. It costs one and ninepence. I sit a whole morning over it trying to think what I should write.

A very Happy Christmas to Matron from Nurse Wright

Nurse Wright sounds presumptuous. I haven't taken an external exam yet. She may not regard me as nurse.

A Very Happy Event . . . that would be quite wrong.

A Very Happy Christmas to You from Guess Who. She might think that silly.

Happy Christmas. Vera. Too familiar. *Veronica.* I have never liked my name.

A Happy Christmas to Matron from one of her staff and in very small writing underneath *N/V Wright.*

I keep wondering if all the others will send Matron a Christmas card. It is hardly a thing you can ask anyone. Besides I do not want, particularly, to give Ferguson the idea. She will never think of it herself. And who can I ask if I don't ask her.

I put the card in Matron's correspondence pigeon hole. The card is so big it has to be bent over at the top to fit in. I am nervous in case someone passing will see me.

Again I am relieving on Bottom Ward. Always it is this Bottom Ward. This time I have to creep round cleaning all the bed wheels.

'And quietly,' Sharpe says, 'Nurse Queen and I don't want everyone waking up!'

The card worries me. I will take it out in the morning. The message is all wrong.

One of her staff! I can't bear to think about it. The card is still there, bending, apologising and self conscious in the morning. I want to remove it but there are people about and correspondence must not be tampered with.

Twice during the day I get dressed and creep down from the Peace corridor, pale, hollow-eyed and drab; all night nurses are completely out of place in the afternoons. I feel conspicuous, sick nearly, standing about in the hall waiting to be alone there so that I can remove that vulgar card and its silly message. It is still bending there in the narrow compartment.

Even when the hall is free of people there are two nurses chattering together by the main door. Why ever do they stand in this cold place to talk. I have to give up and go back to bed, much too cold to sleep. Ferguson has my hot water bottle for her toothache. It seems I can never get even with her. Never ever.

The card is still there in the evening when we go down to the Maids' Dining Room for breakfast. I can hardly eat as I am thinking of a plot to retrieve the card.

The register is finished.

'Nurse Wright.'

'Yes Sister?' half rising in my chair as we all do in that cramped place.

'Matron's office nine a.m. tomorrow.'

'Yes Sister', I sit down again. It can't be to thank me for the card as it hasn't been received yet. A number of reasons come to mind, for one thing there are the two deep caves of dark emptiness; perhaps they have been discovered . . .

In spite of a sense of foreboding I go, with my little torch hidden beneath my apron, up the long covered way. I need more powdered milk. The path seems endless. The night sky has the same ominous decoration; throbbing engines alternate with sharp anti-aircraft guns and the air raid sirens wail up and down, up and down. The soft searchlights move slowly. They make no noise and are helpless. I feel exposed and push my hands round the emptiness of the nearest tea chest. Grabbing a tin of powdered milk I rush back down past the festering bins and on down towards an eternity of the unknown.

I have a corner seat in this train by a mistake which is not entirely my fault. The woman, who is in this seat, asks me if I think she has time to fetch herself a cup of tea. I can see that she badly wants to do this and, in order that she does not have to go without the tea, I agree that, though she will be cutting it fine, there is a chance that she will have time. So she goes and I see her just emerging from the refreshment room with a look on her face which shows how she feels. She has her tea clutched in one hand and I have her reserved seat because it is silly, now that the train has started, to stand in the corridor being crushed by army greatcoats and kit bags and boots, simply looking at the emptiness of this comfortable corner.

I have some household milk for Mother, it is always useful in these days of rationing. I have the tinned chicken also. At the last minute I could not think what to do with it as Night Sister Bean will not be naming the next Night Runner till this evening, and, of course, I shall not be there to know who it is and so am not able to hand on either the milk or the chicken.

There is too the chance that the new Night Runner might be my friend Ferguson. It would not do to give her these advantages.

This is my first holiday from St Cuthbert's, my nights off and ten days holiday. Thirteen days off.

'Shall I take my tin hat, I mean my helmet, and my gas mask?' I ask Matron.

'By all means if you would like to,' she says and wishes me a pleasant holiday and a happy Christmas.

The tin hat and the gas mask are tied to my suitcase. My little sister will be interested to see them.

My father will be pleased with his Christmas card. He has always liked the detail and the warm colours of a Dutch Interior. He will not mind the crossing out inside. The card will flatten if I press it tonight in the dictionary.

For some reason I am thinking about Staff Nurse Ramsden. Last night, in the doorway of the Maids' Dining Room, I stood aside to let her go in first.

'Thank you,' she said and then she asked me what my first name was.

'First name?'

'Yes, your Christian name, what is it?' her voice, usually low, was even lower. Like a kind of shyness.

I did not have the chance to answer. We had to squeeze through to our different tables quickly as Night Sister Bean was already calling the register.

If Ramsden could be on the platform to meet my train at the end of this journey I would be able to answer her question. Perhaps I would be able to explain to her about the violin case. I would like to see Ramsden, I would like to be going to her. Thinking about her and seeing her face, in my mind, when she turned to smile at me, the time when she played Mussorgsky on the piano in the nurses' sitting room, makes me think that it is very probable, though no one has ever spoken about it, that Night Sister Bean might very well be missing her life-long friend Night Sister Percy. Missing her intolerably.

1983

MONICA CLARE
1924—1973

Born near Goondiwindi, Queensland, Monica McGowan was the daughter of an Aboriginal shearer and an English woman. Following the death of her mother in 1931, Monica and her brother Dan lived in various homes in Sydney before being fostered to the Woodbury family on a farm near Spencer, NSW. Although treated with affection by the Woodburys, the children were removed to a home by government officials in 1935 and separated. Monica worked in domestic service for numerous families before beginning work at a cigarette factory. Following this she became a waitress and studied at night school to become a secretary.

Her interest in Aboriginal social justice grew from the late 1940s when she became a regular visitor to the Bellwood Aboriginal Reserve while staying with the Woodburys, who had retired to Nambucca Heads. In 1953 she married and had a daughter, the marriage later ending in divorce. In 1962 she married union official and Aboriginal rights advocate Leslie Forsyth Clare and became actively involved in the union's women's committee. She and Les travelled around NSW, highlighting the appalling living conditions and racial discrimination inflicted upon Aboriginal people.

Prior to the 1967 referendum, Clare became secretary of the Aboriginal committee of the South Coast Labor Council, often writing to politicians and passing on complaints of discrimination. She helped to establish housing and low-interest loans for Aborigines, and in 1968, as secretary to the South Coast Illawarra tribe, led the campaign to re-house the Aboriginal communities there. A delegate to many FCAATSI conferences, she was also active on the International Women's Day, May Day and National Aborigines Day committees. Her autobiographical novel *Karobran: The story of an Aboriginal girl* (1978) was published posthumously. *AH/PM*

From *Karobran*
Chapter 4

On the train, the woman welfare officer who was seated opposite Isabelle and Morris could do nothing to lessen the shock they were in, as the children stared backwards at the long shiny railway lines that were taking them further and further away from their Dad.

Days later in Sydney, the woman rang a bell that seemed to open a small gate in a high wooden fence at the girls' home. She handed Isabelle and her brother over to the Matron, who sternly told them that if they did not behave and stop their crying, she would send Morris to the boys' home.

Then the Matron rang a bell, and another girl much older than Isabelle appeared. Hand in hand, and bewildered at what was going on, Isabelle and Morris were led down stone steps through another gate and into a big bathroom, where the bath was built up high. Standing beside it was a woman the children very quickly learned to call 'Nurse'.

'Come along!' Nurse said sharply to the older girl. 'Get those rags off them, and burn them at once.'

Then she looked down her nose at the two naked figures standing in front of her, and without a sound she made signs for them to climb the steps into the bath. She told the older girl to scrub them hard with the brush, while she stood stiffly by and watched them with disgust.

For most of the day, Isabelle had to go to the school that was built in the same grounds but sometimes she could look out the window, and see Morris and other smaller children being taken by an older girl for a walk around the huge lawn.

At mealtime the two children would be seated in the same dining room, but talking was forbidden and no one dared to ask for more than was put in front of them; and when the nurse who was always seated at a table near the door said, 'Start!' or 'Finish!' everyone obeyed immediately.

Never before had Isabelle and Morris been put to bed so early, so that when their beds were near each other, they would laugh and talk loudly, forgetting that there were others nearby who wanted to sleep, until they would either hear the stern voice of the nurse or feel her hand on their bottoms.

One day the nurse told Isabelle that she was to fetch Morris and take him around to Matron's office. Isabelle was frightened because she had heard other girls say that when anyone played up, they were sent to Matron's office for punishment. Hand in hand they were dawdling along, when Matron's white uniform flashed around the corner in front of them and she said, 'Come along now!'

'Please Matron, what have we done wrong?' asked Isabelle as Matron took hold of Morris's hand.

Matron looked down and smiled at Isabelle. 'You haven't done anything wrong, Isabelle!' she said. 'I just want you both to meet someone.' Then as Isabelle looked towards Matron's office, she could see a strange woman sitting in a chair smiling at them. Matron went and sat in her chair before telling the children:

'This lady's name is Miss Manbury, and she lives in the country and she would like to take both of you up there, to live with her.' Neither of the children spoke for a few seconds: then Morris asked in a shy voice, 'Yer got any sheep?'

The women smiled at each other. Then Miss Manbury said, 'No lad, but we have got cows, horses, ducks, chooks and dogs; and a big river that you can catch some fish in sometimes—if you're lucky—and we've got pigs, too.'

'That's great,' said Morris with a broad grin, and he felt for his sister's hand to get her approval.

'Mind you,' said Matron, 'you'll have to be good, otherwise Miss Manbury will bring you back here again.'

They talked more about it.

'Right,' said Matron, as she rose from her chair. 'Come along, and let's see what's in the store. We'll have to fit you out now, because Miss Manbury wants to leave early in the morning.'

Carrying smart new suitcases filled with new clothes, Isabelle and Morris were so excited as they sat in the train. When Miss Manbury led them from the railway station towards a broad river, they were anxious until she assured them that the launch was safe. Neither of them had even seen one before, but they soon settled down.

'Look Isabelle, look at the crayfish!' shouted Morris in the launch, getting excited again.

'No, lad, they're not crayfish,' Miss Manbury told him, 'they are called crabs. You can pick them up, but be careful, because they have nippers and they bite sometimes, so watch out.'

Morris leaned further over the side to get a better look, and Miss Manbury caught hold of him just in time to stop him from falling overboard.

Isabelle settled down beside Miss Manbury and smiled up at her, asking, ''Ave yer got any kids?'

Miss Manbury smiled back and said, 'Just you and Morris me girl, but there's only my brother and me, and it gets very lonely sometimes. So we are looking forward to both of you being with us for a long time. We do have a lot of visitors though, mostly relatives, and then the house is not big enough! But you'll find out all about that, when you start to help me clean it out.'

Isabelle felt contentment for the first time in a long while; and Morris, sliding closer to the other side of Miss Manbury, put a hand through her arm, asking: 'What's your name again?'

As she put a gloved hand on Morris's hand Miss Manbury said, 'Carmel's my first name, and Manbury's far too long isn't it? How would you like to call me Auntie?'

'Yeah, Aunt,' they shouted out together, so loud that the man who was driving the launch turned around and smiled. Then they settled back and enjoyed the scenery.

Isabelle looked about her, and thought how beautiful it all really was, with the wide river going on for miles and miles, and the tall mountains on both sides of them. Everything was lovely and green, and now and then they would go past a house with lots of fruit on the trees. She really had not seen anything like this before.

Aunt broke her silence and brought Isabelle's thoughts back to the present by saying:

'See that house up there, the one with the red roof on it? Well, that's your new home.'

'It's gone, it's gone!' shouted Morris, as he stood up in the launch, and for the second time Aunt saved him from falling overboard.

'No son, it's not gone, we just went round a bend in the river,' said Aunt, 'you'll see it again in a minute. Look, there it is now.'

'I can see it,' Morris shouted, then as he looked over at his sister, he asked, 'Isabelle, can you see it? It's on top of a hill.'

Isabelle had been looking in silence, but the only thing that she could really see was the verandah that went right around the house. She was still seeing the verandah even after they had left the launch and were walking up the hill towards it, but as she got closer, she could see the flower garden that was in front of it; and she smiled to herself. This verandah could not be sad for her, because the flowers were too beautiful.

A man came hurrying down the hill towards them. Isabelle liked him at once, and as he smiled, Aunt introduced them all affectionately.

'This is my brother, and your new Uncle,' she said.

'We'll have to feed them up, won't we?' said Uncle, as he ruffled Morris's hair. 'Come on, young man, let you and me go down to the wharf, and get your cases, and we can have a yarn about your trip.'

Then he and Morris hurried off chatting together as though they had always known each other. Aunt and Isabelle continued up the hill to the house; and as Isabelle was being shown from one room to the other she knew that she and Morris would be all right here, as she could feel the love in it.

The kitchen which was built separate from the house, was almost as big. The long dining table and stools that went with it suddenly reminded Isabelle of the ones that Ma had in the cook-house on the station, and her mind went back. Aunt, noticing that something was wrong, tried to cheer her up.

'See all these pictures on the walls, Isabelle, it's due to be papered again, and you can give me a hand just as soon as we get enough newspapers saved up.'

Isabelle could not help smiling at that. Then on the river side of the kitchen Aunt opened a small board window, and there at the bottom of the hill sat Uncle and Morris yarning away.

Just then Isabelle noticed under the window the lovely pink flowers growing along a small garden fence, and she said: 'Gee, Aunt, they're pretty.'

'Yes, Isabelle, I call them button roses,' replied Aunt, and she pointed out to Isabelle things that were growing in the garden. 'Over there is where I grow things I need for cooking, like parsley, sage and mint.'

All that afternoon was spent showing Isabelle and Morris over the farm. The dairy came first, where the cream was separated from the milk and made into butter, the shed where feed was kept and where pumpkins and gramma and melons were put to ripen, then to the orchard where almost every kind of fruit tree was laden with fruit; then to the cow bails and pig pens, the big patch of peas and beans that were growing from one side of the rise in the hill to the other. Above the vegetable garden Isabelle found a flat rock with a big hole in the middle of it, which still held water from the last rains. As she stood on top of it, she found out that she could see for miles and miles everywhere, almost to the top of the big mountain behind her.

She was reluctant to leave.

The two adults smiled at each other when they saw the happiness in Isabelle's face.

'Do you like that rock?' asked Uncle.

'Oh yes!' replied Isabelle. 'I can see everything from up here, and when I look down, I can see myself in the water.'

'You can have the rock, if you like,' said Uncle, still smiling at her, and he winked at Aunt.

'You mean it!' exclaimed Isabelle, sounding surprised.

'Yes: and we'll call it Isabelle's rock, if you like,' said Uncle.

Isabelle bounded off the rock, and pulled Uncle and Aunt down to her size and kissed them on the cheek, and they blushed. As they were walking back to the house, Isabelle kept turning back to look at her rock, when she heard Uncle say:

'We'll have to find you something now, won't we, Morris?'

'I know what he'd like,' said Aunt with a smile, as Morris, all excited, ran backwards down the hill in front of her.

'What's that?' asked Uncle.

'A bent pin, and some dough to go fishing with,' said Aunt.

1978

FRANCIS WEBB
1925–1973

Often characterised as a poet's poet, Francis Webb produced poetry with a distinctive blend of emotional intensity, technical complexity and highly developed intellectual and religious reference, making his work both obscure at times and revered. His deeply held Catholicism provided a rich source for the spiritualism and 'meditative purposefulness' that Bill Ashcroft in *DLB* names as his art's mien, while a struggle with schizophrenia throughout his adult life resonates in the poetry's interest in immanence and experience.

His first long poem, 'A Drum for Ben Boyd' (1946), was hailed by his mentor Douglas Stewart (qv) as 'without parallel', and was the beginning of a preoccupation with explorers that was shared by many significant Australian writers in the 1940s and '50s, allegorically investigating the heroic man in time and space, particularly colonial space. Later poetry, such as the sequence 'Ward Two' from Webb's collection *The Ghost of the Cock* (1964), which was written while he was an inmate at a Parramatta psychiatric centre, exhibits a facility with startling metaphor and densely inscribed ambiguity, sustaining a profoundly affective register. His poems were collected in 1969. *NM*

The Explorer's Wife

Never more than a thought at all.
Fables return: the thunderhead
Reversing what earlier stars had said
For the yellow ears of careened ships;
The clock with its brassy nymph in bed   5
Ticks blandly back; claims of eclipse
Dispute our somehow lighted wall.
How had I wished it?—more than style
For a malign unplotted mile
Of weathers; stronger than summer's will.   10
It does not show now nor hold still.
Perhaps no more than a thought at all.

Or was it a lamp I had trimmed well,
Oil of bread and linen and wit?
Our One—intense raft centring it—   15
Shivers now while a boy creates
Again his darkness and will not eat.
I waver: unanswered, a letter waits
Whitely nagging in the close hall.
These omens and dusty memories,   20
Sly hillocks, writhen trees,
Pry at the knocker, twitch the bell.
O a tall world trying! I see and feel
The light between my hands is dull.

1952

End of the Picnic[1]

When that humble-headed elder, the sea, gave his wide
Strenuous arm to a blasphemy, hauling the girth
And the sail and the black yard
Of unknown *Endeavour* towards this holy beach,
Heaven would be watching. And the two men. And the earth,   5
Immaculate, illuminant, out of reach.

It must break—on sacred water this swindle of a wave.
Thick canvas flogged the sticks. Hell lay hove-to.
Heaven did not move.
Two men stood safe: even when the prying, peering   10
Longboat, the devil's totem, cast off and grew,
No god shifted an inch to take a bearing.

It was Heaven-and-earth's jolting out of them shook the men.
It was uninitiate scurf and bone that fled.
Cook's column holds here.[2]   15
Our ferry is homesick, whistling again and again;
But still I see how the myth of a daylight bled
Standing in ribbons, over our heads, for an hour.

     1953

Eyre All Alone[3]

1. SOUTH AUSTRALIAN SETTLER

East to west. Our little township is a lesion
On the plump hinder parts of nothing. Scratching, scratching,
The moody nails of the sun. Or say, our stony
Brain and gullet wobble corroboree
With London, tall lady Exeter, Broad Devon,   5
And other tender ghosts swaying towards the palate:
Comes always that militant toothpick of such good weather.
We are isolated. Is man man?

---

1   Author's note: 'It is likely that at the time of Cook's landing, Kurnell was holy ground to the local Aboriginals' (*Cap and Bells*, p. 250). Kurnell, the southern headland of Botany Bay, is the place where Captain Cook landed in 1770 when navigating Australia in the *Endeavour*. It has consequently been described as 'the birthplace of modern Australia'. Recreational visits (such as picnics) were made there in light of its historical significance.
2   The commemorative Cook obelisk in Kurnell.
3   Edward John Eyre (1815–1901), explorer.

He shrugs among guffaws, transports of old jailbird dayshine
Riotous in the stocks, and drooling.   10
Listen, man, watch for the seamstress, the yawning mildewed whaler.
Unwinding east to west a slack cotton of news:
Man to man: brave golden organic thread
Nibbled to nothing between teeth of mother sea.

So we dream of the stock route, east to homely west,   15
To Perth, and the Sound, and the river of elder swans:
Now a huge cable of winged sheep and bullocks
Whirls through vast fords, milky ways, lies coiled
Upon fat pastures. Man to man. Which is sometimes
God to man, under all seven stars, westward.   20

Walk, walk. From dubious footfall one
At Fowler's Bay the chosen must push on
Towards promised fondlings, dancings of the Sound.
Fourth plague, of flies, harries this bloodless ground.
Cliff and salt balance wheel of heathen planet   25
Tick, twinkle in concert to devise our minute.
But something on foot, and burning, nudges us
Past bitter waters, sands of Exodus. [. . .]

1961

Ward Two

1. PNEUMO-ENCEPHALOGRAPH[1]

Tight scrimmage of blankets in the dark;
Never fluxions, flints coupling for the spark;
Today's guilt and tomorrow's blent;
Passion and peace trussed together, impotent;
Dilute potage of light   5
Dripping through glass to the desk where you sit and write;
Hour stalking lame hour . . .
May my every bone and vessel confess the power
To loathe suffering in you
As in myself, that arcane simmering brew.   10

---

1   An early, painful and dangerous method of medical imaging in which cerebrospinal fluid from around the
    brain is replaced with air to allow the structure of the brain to appear more clearly on an X-ray picture.

Only come to this cabin of art:
Crack hardy, take off clothes, and play your part.
Contraband enters your brain;
Puckered guerrilla faces patrol the vein;
The spore of oxygen passes   15
Skidding over old inclines and crevasses,
Hunting an ancient sore,
Foxhole of impulse in a minute cosmic war.
Concordat of nature and desire
Was revoked in you; but fire clashes with fire.   20

Let me ask, while you are still,
What in you marshalled this improbable will:
Instruments supple as the flute,
Vigilant eyes, mouths that are almost mute,
X-rays scintillant as a flower,   25
Tossed in a corner the plumes of falsehood, power?
Only your suffering.
Of pain's amalgam with gold let some man sing
While, pale and fluent and rare
As the Holy Spirit, travels the bubble of air.   30

2. HARRY

It's the day for writing that letter, if one is able,
And so the striped institutional shirt is wedged
Between this holy holy chair and table.
He has purloined paper, he has begged and cadged
The bent institutional pen,   5
The ink. And our droll old men
Are darting constantly where he weaves his sacrament.

Sacrifice? Propitiation? All are blent
In the moron's painstaking fingers—so painstaking.
His vestments our giddy yarns of the firmament,   10
Women, gods, electric trains, and our remaking
Of all known worlds—but not yet
Has our giddy alphabet
Perplexed his priestcraft and spilled the cruet of innocence.

We have been plucked from the world of commonsense,   15
Fondling between our hands some shining loot,

Wife, mother, beach, fisticuffs, eloquence,
As the lank tree cherishes every distorted shoot.
What queer shards we could steal
Shaped him, realer than the Real: 20
But it is no goddess of ours guiding the fingers and the thumb.

She cries: *Ab aeterno ordinata sum.*[1]
He writes to the woman, this lad who will never marry.
One vowel and the thousand laborious serifs will come
To this pudgy Christ, and the old shape of Mary.   25
Before seasonal pelts and the thin
Soft tactile underskin
Of air were stretched across earth, they have sported and are one.

Was it then at this altar-stone the mind was begun?
The image besieges our Troy. Consider the sick   30
Convulsions of movement, and the featureless baldy sun
Insensible—sparing that compulsive nervous tic.
Before life, the fantastic succession,
An imbecile makes his confession,
Is filled with the Word unwritten, has almost genuflected.   35

Because the wise world has forever and ever rejected
Him and because your children would scream at the sight
Of his mongol mouth stained with food, he has resurrected
The spontaneous thought retarded and infantile Light.
Transfigured with him we stand   40
Among walls of the no-man's-land
While he licks the soiled envelope with lover's caress

Directing it to the House of no known address.

                                                                       1964

VINCENT BUCKLEY
1925–1988

Vincent Buckley attended the universities of Melbourne and Cambridge, after having served in the RAAF during the Second World War. From 1951 he taught and researched at the University of Melbourne, where he held a personal chair in Poetry from 1967 to 1987. One of the so-called university poets, Buckley was also an

---

1 'Ages ago, I was set up', words spoken by Wisdom (Proverbs 8:23). In Christian liturgy the words apply to Mary.

important critic (especially of Australian poetry), often writing on matters to do with politics and religion. He had considerable influence in Catholic intellectual debate during the Cold War. From 1958 to 1964 he edited *Prospect* and from 1961 to 1963 he was poetry editor for the *Bulletin*. He increasingly identified with his Irish background, spending considerable amounts of time in Ireland, something discussed in his memoir, *Cutting Green Hay: Friendships, movements and cultural conflicts in Australia's great decades* (1983). The title sequence in *Golden Builders and Other Poems* (1976) is a complex, autobiographical tribute to Melbourne. His *Last Poems* (1991) brings together various concerns, including ageing and illness. He edited *The Faber Book of Modern Australian Verse* (1991). *DM*

Golden Builders

What are those Golden Builders doing? Where was the
                                      burying place
Of soft Ethinthus? near Tyburn's fatal tree? Is that
Mild Zion's hill's most ancient promontory, near mournful
Ever-weeping Paddington?

                       [William Blake: *Jerusalem*]

                    I

The hammers of iron glow down Faraday.[1]
Lygon and Drummond shift under their resonance.
Saws and hammers drawn across the bending air
shuttling like a bow; the saw trembles
the hammers are molten, they flow with quick light   5
striking; the flush spreads and deepens on the stone.
The drills call the streets together
stretching hall to lecture-room to hospital.

But prop old walls with battens of old wood.

Saturday work. Sabbath work. *On this day*   10
we laid this stone
to open this Sabbath School. Feed My Lambs.

The sun dies half-glowing in the floating brickdust,
suspended between red and saffron.
The colours resonate like a noise; the muscles of mouth   15
neck shoulders loins arm themselves against it.
Pavements clink like steel; the air soft,

---

1   Faraday, Lygon, Drummond, Pelham, Grattan, Cardigan, Queensberry and Elgin are streets near the University of Melbourne.

palpable as cork, lets the stone cornices
gasp into it. Pelham surrenders, Grattan
runs leading forward, seeking the garden's breadth, the   20
                                            fearful
edge of green on which the sexes lay.

We have built this Sabbath School. Feed My Lambs.

Evening wanders through my hands and feet
my mouth is cool as the air that now thins   25
twitching the lights on down winding paths. Everything
leans on this bright cold. In gaps of lanes, in tingling
shabby squares, I hear the crying of the machines.

O Cardigan, Queensberry, Elgin: names of their lordships.
Cardigan, Elgin, Lygon: Shall I find here my Lord's grave?   30
                                                      1976

THEA ASTLEY
1925—2004

Thea Astley was born in Brisbane and educated at Catholic schools and the University of Queensland, from where she graduated in 1947, marrying Jack Gregson the following year. Astley worked as a teacher; she taught in schools until 1967, and then at Macquarie University from 1968 to 1980.

Her first novel, *Girl With a Monkey* (1958), heralded the beginning of one of the longest and most distinguished fiction careers in the history of Australian literature. With Peter Carey (qv), she holds the record for the largest number of Miles Franklin Literary Awards: for *The Well Dressed Explorer* (1962), *The Slow Natives* (1965), *The Acolyte* (1972) and *Drylands* (1999), her final novel, as co-winner with Kim Scott (qv) for *Benang* (1999).

Astley continued to publish novels and short stories throughout the 1960s and '70s, a period almost completely dominated in Australia by male writers, with only a handful of Australian women publishing literary novels. Her second novel, *A Descant for Gossips* (1960), was dramatised for ABC television in 1983.

A Kindness Cup (1974), which featured for years on school syllabi around the country, was well ahead of its time in its recognition of the country's dark history of colonisation and the many instances of criminal mistreatment of Aboriginal people by white settlers. Astley's sympathetic and indignant attitude to Australia's race relations history has been a major feature of her work throughout her writing career, notably in this novel and in *It's Raining in Mango* (1987).

When Helen Garner's (qv) *Monkey Grip* was published in 1977, followed by Jessica Anderson's (qv) *Tirra Lirra by the River* in 1978, their extensive critical and commercial success heralded a transformation of Australian fiction. From this point on, Australian women writers began to flourish and Astley herself was given a new lease of life by these changed conditions; her 1982 novel *An Item From the Late News* was the first she had written from a female point of view, something she has said she found alien and strange: 'I grew up believing that women weren't really people, and didn't matter in the scheme of things.'

Astley was a major and influential Australian writer over a period of 40 years, during which her work addressed the issues of her time and place, and evolved in style as well as content. She is known as a regional writer, with much of her work set in Far North Queensland, but her concerns are also national and international. Her writing is highly allusive and erudite, written in a style that can be densely ornate. While her work is often witty and sometimes downright comic, many of her plots have the shape of classical tragedy, moving towards some disastrous yet seemingly inevitable end point.

In her lifetime she published a total of fourteen novels, two novellas and two collections of short stories. *KG*

From *It's Raining in Mango*
Heart is Where the Home is

The morning the men came, policemen, someone from the government, to take the children away from the black camp up along the river, first there was the wordless terror of heart-jump, then the wailing, the women scattering and trying to run dragging their kids, the men sullen, powerless before this new white law they'd never heard of. Even the coppers felt lousy seeing all those yowling gins. They'd have liked the boongs to show a bit of fight, really, then they could have laid about feeling justified.

But no. The buggers just took it. Took it and took it.

The passivity finally stuck in their guts.

Bidgi Mumbler's daughter-in-law grabbed her little boy and fled through the scrub patch towards the river. Her skinny legs didn't seem to move fast enough across that world of the policeman's eye. She knew what was going to happen. It had happened just the week before at a camp near Tobaccotown. Her cousin Ruthie lost a kid that way.

'We'll bring her up real good,' they'd told Ruthie. 'Take her away to big school and teach her proper, eh? You like your kid to grow up proper and know about Jesus?'

Ruthie had been slammed into speechlessness.

Who were they?

She didn't understand. She knew only this was her little girl. There was all them words, too many of them, and then the hands.

There had been a fearful tug-o'-war: the mother clinging to the little girl, the little girl clutching her mother's dress, and the welfare officer with the police, all pulling, the kid howling, the other mothers egg-eyed, gripping their own kids, petrified, no men around, the men tricked out of camp.

Ruthie could only whimper, but then, as the policeman started to drag her child away to the buggy, she began a screeching that opened up the sky and pulled it down on her.

She bin chase that buggy two miles till one of the police he ride back on his horse an shout at her an when she wouldn take no notice she bin run run run an he gallop after her an hit her one two, cracka cracka, with his big whip right across the face so the pain get all muddle with the cryin and she run into the trees beside the track where he couldn follow. She kep goin after that buggy, fightin her way through scrub but it wasn't no good. They too fast. An then the train it come down the line from Tobaccotown an that was the last she see her little girl, two black legs an arms, strugglin as the big white man he lift her into carriage from the sidin.

'You'll have other baby,' Nelly Mumbler comforted her. 'You'll have other baby.' But Ruthie kept sittin, wouldn do nothin. Jus sit an rock an cry an none of the other women they couldn help, their kids gone too and the men so angry they jus drank when they could get it an their rage burn like scrub fire.

Everything gone. Land. Hunting grounds. River. Fish. Gone. New god come. Old talk still about killings. The old ones remembering the killings.

'Now they take our kids,' Jackie Mumbler said to his father, Bidgi. 'We make kids for whites now. Can't they make their own kids, eh? Take everythin. Land. Kids. Don't give nothin, only take.'

So Nelly had known the minute she saw them whites comin down the track. The other women got scared, fixed to the spot like they grow there, all shakin and whimperin. Stuck. 'You'll be trouble,' they warned. 'You'll be trouble.'

'Don't care,' she said. 'They not takin my kid.'

She wormed her way into the thickest part of the rain forest, following the river, well away from the track up near the packers' road. Her baby held tightly against her chest, she stumbled through vine and over root, slashed by leaves and thorns, her eyes wide with fright, the baby crying in little gulps, nuzzling in at her straining body.

There'd bin other time year before she still hear talk about. All then livin up near Tinwon. The govmin said for them all to come long train. Big surprise, eh, an they all gone thinkin tobacco, tucker, blankets. An the men, they got all the men out early that day help work haulin trees up that loggin camp and the women they all excited waitin long that train, all the kids playin, and then them two policemen they come an start grabbin, grabbin all the kids, every kid, and the kids they screamin an the women they all cryin an tuggin an some, they hittin themselves with little sticks. One of the police, he got real angry and start shovin the women back hard. He push an push an then the train pulls out while they pushin an they can see the kids clutchin at the windows and some big white woman inside that train, she pull them back.

Nelly dodged through wait-a-while, stinging-bush, still hearing the yells of the women back at the camp. Panting and gasping, she came down to the water where a sand strip ran half way across the river. If she crossed she would only leave tracks. There was no time to scrape away telltale footprints. She crept back into the rain forest and stood trembling, squeezing her baby tightly, trying to smother his howls, but the baby wouldn't hush, so she huddled under a bush and comforted him with her nipples for a while, his round eyes staring up at her as he sucked while she regained her breath.

Shouts wound through the forest like vines.

Wailing filtered through the canopy.

Suddenly a dog yelped, too close. She pulled herself to her feet, the baby still suckling, and went staggering along the sandy track by the riverbank, pushing her bony body hard, thrusting between claws of branch and thorn, a half mile, a mile, until she knew that soon the forest cover would finish and she'd be out on the fence-line of George Laffey's place, the farm old Bidgi Mumbler had come up and worked for. She'd been there too, now and then, help washin, cleanin, when young Missus Laffey makin all them pickles an things.

For a moment she stood uncertain by the fence, then on impulse she thrust her baby under the wire and wriggled through after him, smelling the grass, smelling ants, dirt, all those living things, and then she grabbed him up and stumbled through the cow paddock down to the mango trees, down past the hen yard, the vegetable garden, down over a lawn with flower-blaze and the felty shadows of tulip trees, past Mister Laffey spading away, not stopping when he looked up at her, startled, but gasping past him round the side of the house to the back steps and the door that was always open.

Mag Laffey came to the doorway and the two young women watched each other in a racket of insect noise. A baby was crying in a back room and a small girl kept tugging at her mother's skirts.

The missus was talkin, soft and fast. Nelly couldn't hear nothin and then hands, they pull her in, gently, gently, but she too frightened hangin onto Charley, not lettin go till the white missus she put them hands on her shoulders and press her down onto one them kitchen chairs an hold her. 'Still, now,' her voice keep sayin. 'Still.'

So she keep real still and the pretty white missus say, 'Tell me, Nelly. You tell me what's the matter.'

It took a while, the telling, between the snuffles and the coaxing and the gulps and swallowed horrors.

'I see,' Mag Laffey said at last. 'I see,' she said again, her lips tightening. 'Oh I see.'

She eased the baby from Nelly's arms and put him down on the floor with her own little girl, watching with a smile as the children stared then reached out to touch each other. She went over to the stove and filled the teapot and handed the black girl a cup, saying, 'You drink that right up now and then we'll think of something. George will think of something.'

It was half an hour before the policemen came.

They rode down the track from the railway line at an aggressive trot, coming to halt beside George as he rested on his spade.

Confronted with their questions he went blank. 'Only the housegirl.' And added, 'And Mag and the kids.'

The police kicked their horses on through his words and George slammed his spade hard into the turned soil and followed them down to where they were tethering their horses at the stair rails. He could see them boot-thumping up the steps. The house lay open as a palm.

Mag forestalled them, coming out onto the veranda. Her whole body was a challenge.

'Well,' she asked, 'what is it?'

The big men fidgeted. They'd had brushes with George Laffey's wife before, so deceptively young and pliable, a woman who never knew her place, always airing an idea of some sort. Not knowing George's delight with her, they felt sorry for that poor bastard of a husband who'd come rollicking home a few years back from a trip down south with a town girl with town notions.

'Government orders, missus,' one said. 'We have to pick up all the abo kids. All abo kids have got to be taken to special training schools. It's orders.'

Mag Laffey inspected their over-earnest faces. She couldn't help smiling.

'Are you asking me, sergeant, if I have any half-caste children, or do I misunderstand?' She could hardly wait for their reaction.

The sergeant bit his lower lip and appeared to chew something before he could answer. 'Not you personally, missus.' *Disgusting,* he thought, *disgusting piece of goods, making suggestions like that.* 'We just want to know if you have any round the place? Any belonging to that lot up at the camp?'

'Why would I do that?'

'I don't know, missus.' He went stolid. 'You've got a housegirl, haven't you? Your husband said.'

'Yes, I do.'

'Well then, has she got any kids?'

'Not that I'm aware of,' Mag Laffey lied vigorously. Her eyes met theirs with amused candour.

'Maybe so. But we'd like to speak to her. You know it's breaking the law to conceal this.'

'Certainly I know.' George was standing behind the men at the foot of the steps, his face nodding her on. 'You're wasting your time here, let me tell you. You're wasting mine as well. But that's what government's for, isn't it?'

'I don't know what you mean, missus.' His persistence moved him forward a step. 'Can we see that girl or not?'

Mag called over her shoulder down the hall but stood her ground at the doorway, listening to Nelly shuffle, unwilling, along the lino. When she came up to the men, she still had a dishcloth in her hands that dripped suds onto the floor. Her eyes would not meet those of the big men blocking the light.

'Where's your kid, Mary?' the sergeant asked, bullying and jocular. 'You hiding your kid?'

Nelly dropped her head and shook it dumbly.

'Cat got your tongue?' the other man said. 'You not wantem talk, eh? You lying?'

'She has no children,' Mag Laffey interrupted coldly. 'I told you that. Perhaps the cat has your ears as well. If you shout and nag and humiliate her, you'll never get an answer. Can't you understand something as basic as that? You're frightening her.'

She looked past the two of them at her husband who was smiling his support.

'Listen, lady,' the sergeant said, his face congested with the suppressed need to punch this cheeky sheilah right down her own hallway, 'that's not what they tell me at the camp.'

'What's not what they tell you?'

'She's got a kid all right. She's hiding it some place.'

George's eyes, she saw, were strained with affection and concern. *Come up,* her own eyes begged him. *Come up.* 'Sergeant,' she said, 'I have known Nelly since she was a young girl. She's helped out here for the last four years. Do you think I wouldn't know if she had a child? Do you? But you're free to search the house, if you want, and the grounds. You're thirsting for it, aren't you, warrant or not?'

The men shoved roughly past her at that, flattening Nelly Mumbler against the wall, and creaked down the hallway, into bedrooms and parlor and out into the kitchen. Cupboard doors crashed open. There was a banging of washhouse door.

George came up the steps and took his wife's arm, steering her and Nelly to the back of the house and putting them behind him as he watched the police come in from the yard.

'Satisfied?'

'No, we're not, mate,' the sergeant replied nastily. 'Not one bloody bit.'

Their powerful bodies crowded the kitchen out. They watched contemptuously as Nelly crept back to the sink, her body tensed with fright.

'We don't believe you, missus,' the sergeant said. 'Not you or your hubby. There'll be real trouble for both of you when we catch you out.'

Mag held herself braced against infant squawls that might expose them at any minute. She made herself busy stoking the stove.

'Righto,' George said, pressing her arm and looking sharp and hard at the other men. 'You've had your look. Now would you mind leaving. We've all got work to get on with.'

The sergeant was sulky. He scraped his boots about and kept glancing around the kitchen and out the door into the back garden. The Laffeys' small girl was getting under his feet and pulling at his trouser legs, driving him crazy.

'All right,' he agreed reluctantly. 'All right.' He gave one last stare at Nelly's back. 'Fuckin' boongs,' he said, deliberately trying to offend that stuck-up Mrs. Laffey. 'More trouble than they're worth. And that's bloody nothing.'

The two women remained rooted in the kitchen while George went back up the track to his spadework. The sound of the horses died away.

At the sink Nelly kept washing and washing, her eyes never leaving the suds, the dishmop, the plate she endlessly scoured. Even after the thud of hoof faded beyond the ridge, even after that. And even after Mag Laffey took a cloth and began wiping the dishes and stacking them in the cupboard, even after that.

Mag saw her husband come round the side of the house, toss his hat on an outside peg and sit on the top step to ease his earth-stuck clobbers of boots off. Nelly's stiffly curved back asked question upon question. Her long brown fingers asked. Her turned-away face asked. When her baby toddled back into the kitchen, taken down from the bedroom ceiling manhole where George had hidden him with a lolly to suck, Nelly stayed glued to that sink washing that one plate.

'Come on, Nelly,' Mag said softly. 'What's the matter? We've beaten them, haven't we?'

George had picked up the small black boy and his daughter and was bouncing a child on each knee, waggling his head lovingly between them both while small hands pawed his face.

Infinitely slowly, Nelly turned from the sink, her fingers dripping soap and water. She looked at George Laffey cuddling a white baby and a black but she couldn't smile. 'Come nex time,' she said, hopeless. 'Come nex time.'

George and his wife looked at her with terrible pity. They knew this as well. They knew.

'And we'll do the same next time,' Mag Laffey stated. 'You don't have to worry.'

Then George Laffey said, 'You come live here, Nelly. You come all time, eh?' His wife nodded at each word. Nodded and smiled and cried a bit. 'You and Charley, eh?'

Nelly opened her mouth and wailed. *What is it?* they kept asking. *What's the matter? Wouldn't you like that?* They told her she could have the old store shed down by the river. They'd put a stove in and make it proper. Nelly kept crying, her dark eyes an unending fountain, and at last George became exasperated.

'You've got no choice, Nelly,' he said, dropping the baby pidgin he had never liked anyway. 'You've got no choice. If you come here we can keep an eye on Charley. If you don't, the government men will take him away. You don't want that, do you? Why don't you want to come?'

'Don't want to leave my family,' she sobbed. 'Don't want.'

'God love us,' George cried from the depths of his nonunderstanding, 'God love us, they're only a mile up the river.' He could feel his wife's fingers warning on his arm. 'You can see them whenever you want.'

'It's not same,' Nelly insisted and sobbed. 'Not same.'

George thought he understood. He said, 'You want Jackie, then. You want your husband to come along too, work in the garden maybe? Is that it?'

He put the baby into her arms and the two of them rocked sombrely before him. He still hadn't understood.

The old men old women uncles aunts cousins brothers sisters tin humpies bottles dogs dirty blankets tobacco handouts fights river trees all the tribe's remnants and wretchedness, destruction and misery.

Her second skin now.

'Not same,' she whispered. And she cried them centuries of tribal dream in those two words. 'Not same.'

1987

JESSIE LENNON
c. 1925–2000

Daughter of Nylatu and Kutin (Rosie Austin), Jessie Lennon, a Matutjara woman, was born in the station country of outback South Australia. Through her mother she has links with Tjalyiri or Tallaringa, north-west of present-day Coober Pedy. As a child, Jessie Lennon travelled on foot and by 'jumping' the train with her father Nylatu, her sisters Mollie (Angkal) and Linda (Wantjiyla) and her niece Edna and family, visiting North Well, near Kingoonya and Ooldea Soak. Daisy Bates was living in her tent at Ooldea siding, not far from the Soak. Later on, her father took them travelling again, sometimes on foot and sometimes on camels, to Lake Pirinya (Phillipson) and Kupa Piti (Coober Pedy), while her mother and stepfather stayed at Kingoonya. When she met Barney Lennon their families would not allow them to live together because they were too young. Later, Barney found her again and they were married. Jessie Lennon had six children and many grandchildren and great-grandchildren. *MM*

From *And I Always Been Moving!*

Wilgena, I born Wilgena, I grewed up there:
mother had me there—baby.
Carried me round there—grow me up.
Big sister, Molly born there too—*Angkal*, her *Anangu*—
Aboriginal name, again.   5

After that we came to Kingoonya.
Mum married to my stepfather, Willie Austin's father.
We stopped there, Kingoonya.
Looked after me there.

We always go where they want.   10
'We'll go back to Wilgena working, shearing sheep.'
We'll go back to the place where I was born.

★

Old people used to camp there—at Lake Pirinya—Lake Phillipson.
Kanku—wurlies—nice *kanku* they made there. Shady.

Lake Pirinya full of water.   15
Yes, *malu*—kangaroo—there every day, all hanging up on the tree.
They killed them, cook 'em, they cut 'em up and hang 'em out.
They eat that part there.

Emu, they sometimes come—*kalaya*.
One time I saw, Old People say,   20
'Don't you fellas make too much noise!'
They wait for emu too—a lot of sweet tucker they want.
Kalaya come to the water and 'BANG!'
Kill two or three—so a big lot of people, you know, can eat.

                                                                           1995

ALAN SEYMOUR
b. 1927

Playwright Alan Seymour was born in Fremantle, WA, and from his teenage years
worked in radio as a writer and announcer, first in Perth and then in Sydney, including
for the ABC. He later worked in Sydney as an opera director. His play *The One Day
of the Year* (1960/1962) is a landmark in the history of Australian literature. It marked
a shift in Australian popular attitudes to Anzac Day in particular and to war in general,
emphasising and dramatising the generational nature of that shift. *The One Day of the
Year* sparked passionate debate when it was first staged and continued to do so for several
years, as a set text in schools across the country.

Seymour left Australia in 1961 and did not return until 1995. He has strong associations with the long-running Australian literary magazine *Westerly* and received an honorary doctorate from the University of Western Australia in 2002. *KG*

From *The One Day of the Year*
Act 2, Scene 3

[. . .] [HUGHIE *has joined them. He stands looking a little defiantly at his mother, then relents.*]

HUGHIE: Hullo.

MUM: What y'bin doing all day?

HUGHIE: Had a ball! [*Going to lounge, flops into it.*] Oh, the pictures I got! You oughta see the pictures I got.

MUM: What pictures?

HUGHIE: For our story. I told you—for the Uni paper, story on Anzac Day. Jan's writing it.

MUM: You started late enough, it was all over practically before you even left.

HUGHIE: What was all over?

MUM: The march and everything.

HUGHIE: I wasn't after the march. You'll see half a page of all that crap in the paper tomorrow. Oh, golly, and to think I nearly didn't want to go. Came to my senses all right once I saw it again.

[*Slight pause.* MUM *and* WACKA *exchange a glance.*]

WACKA [*tentatively*]: What sort of pictures did you take, son?

HUGHIE [*sitting up, faces them seriously*]: Anzac Day. As it is. I got some beauties.

MUM: How do you know if they're any good?

HUGHIE: When we finished this arvo we shot in to a mate of mine, runs a photography place in town, and we could see right away.

MUM [*irritably*]: But what was they pictures of?

HUGHIE: Everything. [*Sarcastically*] The celebration. There's one, one terrific one—pure fluke how I got it—of an old man lying flat on his back in a lane near a pub. Boy, had he had it.

[WACKA *starts to laugh, picturing it.* MUM *silences him with a look.*]

MUM: What'd y'want to take a picture of that for?

HUGHIE: That's the point of it. They're all like that. Outside a pub near Central there was a character sitting on the footpath leaning up against a post. He had the most terrific face, hadn't shaved, few teeth missing, very photogenic. I snuck up near him and squatted down and . . . oh, just as I got it framed up, it was wonderful. He vomited. Just quietly. All down his chin, all down the front of his coat. I took it.

[WACKA *has been about to drink from his glass of wine, lowers it and pushes it away from him.*]

MUM [*evenly*]: You're goin' to put that in a paper?

HUGHIE: Are we ever!

MUM [*after a blank pause*]: Why?

HUGHIE: Because we're sick of all the muck that's talked about on this day . . . the great national day of honour, day of memory, day of salute to the fallen, day of grief . . . It's just one long grog-up.

MUM: But—

HUGHIE: No buts. I know what you lot think about it, everyone your age is the same. Well, I've seen enough Anzac Days to know what I think of them. And that's what I got today with my little camera. What I think of it.

MUM: You can't put that sort of thing in a paper.

HUGHIE: Just watch us.

MUM: It's more than that. Anzac Day's more than that.

HUGHIE: Yeah, it's a lot of old hasbeens getting up in the local R.S.L. and saying . . . Well, boys, you all know what we're here for, we're here to honour our mates who didn't come back. And they all feel sad and have another six or seven beers.

MUM: Hughie.

HUGHIE: Look, no argument. You think what you like, I've had to put up with that all my life, well now you can just put up with my views. If they don't agree, bad luck.

MUM: Y'd better not let yr father hear y'talkin' like this. 'E'd better not know nothin' about this thing goin' in the paper.

HUGHIE: He's got to know sooner or later.

MUM: Yr gettin' carried away. Just because a coupla blokes get a few in –

HUGHIE: Couple? Everywhere you look—every suburb you go through—and we went through them today—every pub, every street—all over this damned country today men got rotten. This is THE day. [*In a dinkum-Aussie speech-maker's voice*] 'When Awstrylia first reached maturity as a nation.' [*His own voice*] Maturity! God!

WACKA [*shyly*]: 'Scuse me, lad.

HUGHIE: What?

WACKA: That's not all it is.

HUGHIE: Oh, Wacka.

WACKA [*gently*]: Can't you let 'em enjoy it? You don't have to agree. But they've got a right to their feelings.

HUGHIE: Wacka—you've been brought up on the speeches. They say what it's officially supposed to be. I've been looking at what it is. As far as I'm concerned, that's all it is. A great big meaningless booze-up. Nothing more.

MUM [*snapping*]: Well, y'r wrong.

[*From outside a crash. Then* ALF's *voice in a burst of drunken profanity.*]

HUGHIE [*gently*]: Am I?

[*Another crash. A burst of bawdy song.*]

MUM: Alf.

WACKA [*listening*]: 'E'ad too much?

[ALF *roars again.*]

MUM: No. Not enough. [*To* HUGHIE] Now, you be careful what you say.

[*The door flies open.* ALF *totters in. He is dishevelled, hair flies wild, face is heavy with grog, trousers hang below his waist, shirt hangs half out. Clothes are sodden with spilt grog. He carries bottles, wrapped and unwrapped and lurches to table, starting his dissertation as soon as he gets in.*]

ALF: 'Ullo? You buggers on the plonk? [*Wags a finger at* MUM.] Y'know what it says on the wiless, when y'driving' don't drink when y' drivin' don't drive. [*Unaware he's muddled it, forges on*]: Christ, 've I 'ad a day? I've had a bloody lovely day. I seen everybody, Dot—Wack—Wack—I seen everybody, what y' doin',—Ughie, siddown yr makin' me giddy, I seen everybody. Old Bert Charles, y'oughter seen old Bert Charles, eighteen stone an' pisspot, c'n 'e drink? Oh Jeez, we started at a pub in King Street straight after the march, I was with Bluey Norton an' Ginger Simms, did we get on it? We bin there 'bout an hour in comes ole Fred Harvey, I sung out You old bastard and 'e come up t' me y'know wot 'e did, 'e put on a voice like a bloody panz and 'e sez up high like, 'Darl, 'ow ARE yer?' An' 'e kisses me, right in the bloody public bar, front of everyone, laugh, thought we'd bloody die, I hit him one and then we all 'ad a couple of grogs and then Ginge said I gotta meet me ole mate down the Quay, come'n meet me ole mate down the Quay so we goes, whole lot of us goes and all the way down Fred does this act makin' up to the other blokes, laugh, I never laughed so much, on the way we picks up Johnny 'Opkins with 'is gammy leg—[*A foggy glare towards* WACKA.] *He* marched, *he* was in the march—and 'e was sittin' in the gutter lookin' for the lav so we got 'im to 'is feet and shot 'im into a public lav and in the lav there was a brawl, broken bottles flyin' everywhere and blood, Gawd, blood, and off we all went to Plasto's and there's Ginge's mates, we was there hours, hours, then we says let's get out'f'ere and we're off up Pitt Street, we went into every pub, every pub we come to, we went in every pub, there was ten of us by then, ten of us so someone says Come on let's get some other bastards 'n' make it a round dozen, so we grabs two ole blokes and turned out they was real old diggers, real Anzacs, 'ear that 'Wack, Anzacs, they was sittin' 'avin' a quiet yarn to themselves, we soon fixed that—we got 'em and shouted 'em and Ginge 'e made a speech, 'e said these are the blokes wot started the Anzac legend, these done the trick, soldiers and bloody gentlemen and we poured bloody beer into the poor old cows till they couldn't stand up, they was rotten, then silly bloody Johnny 'Opkins 'as to go 'n' muck things, 'e turns round too quick and gets all dizzy and spews, did 'e spew, brought it all up all over the bloody bar, all over the mob, in their beer, all over the floor, all over 'mself, laugh . . . Jeez, I never laughed so much in all me . . .

[*Very early on* HUGHIE *has turned to face his mother and* WACKA. *As* ALF *drives remorselessly on* HUGHIE *watches their faces gradually change.* MUM, *who has been laughing at first, looks at* HUGHIE *long and steadily then slowly sits.* WACKA *looks completely embarrassed, not at first but very gradually, finally drops his glance, can't face* HUGHIE, *makes feeble attempt to quieten* ALF, *then stands looking down uncomfortably.* ALF *has at last realised something is wrong. His voice dies away. He turns, looks groggily at them all.*]

ALF: What's the matter? What's up?

[*Nobody speaks.*]

HUGHIE: You've just proved something.

ALF: What? [*Sways, tries to focus.*] What'd I prove?

HUGHIE: Forget it. You had a great day, that's all that matters.

ALF [*suddenly swinging* HUGHIE *around*]: You bein' funny? You playin' up again, Mr Bloody Brains Trust?

HUGHIE [*quietly*]: Why couldn't you leave them alone? Those two poor old boys having their quiet talk? Does everyone have to be as rotten as you are before you can enjoy Anzac Day?

ALF [*very quietly*]: Watch y'self. Watch y'self, mister. [*To* MUM] Is that what he's on now? 'E's pickin' on the old diggers now?

HUGHIE [*Breaking away in sudden burst of complete exasperation*]: Oh, frig the old diggers.

ALF [*weaving after him unsteadily*]: Why—you . . . you . . .

HUGHIE [*swinging on him*]: Do you know what you're celebrating today? [*To* MUM] Do you? Do you even know what it all meant? Have you ever bothered to dig a bit, find out what really happened back there, what this day meant?

MUM: I bin talkin' to Wacka about it just tonight—

HUGHIE: Oh, Wacka—what would he know about it?

ALF: Don't you insult my mate, don't you insult him. He was there, wasn't he?

HUGHIE: What does the man who was there ever know about anything? All he knows is what he saw, one man's view from a trench. It's the people who come after, who can study it all, see the whole thing for what it was—

ALF [*with deepest contempt*]: Book-learnin'. [*Points to* WACKA.] He bloody suffered, that man. You sayin' to me book-learnin' after the event's gunna tell y'more about it than he knows?

HUGHIE: Wacka was an ordinary soldier who did what he was told. He and his mates became a legend, OK. But did any of them ever sit down and look at that damn stupid climb up those rocks to see what it meant?

ALF: How do you know so bloody much?

HUGHIE: How do I know? Didn't you shove it down my throat? [*He has plunged over to bookcase against wall, drags out large book.*] It's all here. Encyclopaedia for Australian kids. You gave it to me yourself. Used to make me read the Anzac chapter every year. Well, I read it. The official history, all very glowing and patriotic. I read it—enough times to start seeing through it. [*He has been leafing through book, finds the place.*] Do you know what that Gallipoli campaign meant? Bugger all.

ALF [*lunging at him*]: You—

HUGHIE [*dodging him*]: A face-saving device. An expensive shambles. The biggest fiasco of the war. [*He starts to read rapidly.*] 'The British were in desperate straits. Russia was demanding that the Dardanelles be forced by the British Navy and Constantinople taken. The Navy could not do it alone and wanted Army support.' [*His father by now has stopped weaving groggily and stands watching him, trying to take it in.*] 'Kitchener said the British army had no men available.' [*He looks up.*] So what did they do? The Admiralty, in fact, your great favourite, Dad, Winston Churchill at the Admiralty, *insisted* it be done no matter what the risk. Britain's Russian ally was expecting it. So your Mr Churchill, Dad, big bloated blood-sucker that he was, found the solution. Australian and New Zealand troops had just got to Cairo for their initial training . . . Untrained men, untried. [*He looks quickly back at book.*] 'Perhaps they could be used.'

[*He snaps the book shut.*]

Perhaps. Perhaps they could be pushed in there, into a place everybody knew was impossible to take from the sea, to make the big gesture necessary . . . to save the face of the British. [*He turns on his father.*] . . . the British, Dad, the bloody Poms. THEY pushed those men up those cliffs, that April morning, knowing, KNOWING it was suicide. [. . .]

1962

BRUCE BEAVER
1928–2004

Bruce Beaver was born in the Sydney beachside suburb of Manly, where—apart from some years working in New Zealand—he spent most of his life. He worked in surveying, radio, journalism and publishing and was a contributing editor for *Poetry Australia*. From the age of seventeen, he was diagnosed with manic depression (bipolar disorder), a condition with which he struggled for much of his life, as detailed in his poetry.

Beaver's fourth collection of poetry, *Letters to Live Poets* (1969), established his reputation and, in its use of American models, its freeing up of prosody and its confessional turn, is commonly seen as prefiguring the poetics of the Generation of '68. Indeed, Beaver is included—as a kind of 'godfather' figure—in John Tranter's (qv) defining anthology *The New Australian Poetry* (1979). As the epistolary turn of *Letters to Live Poets* also suggests, Beaver's poems were commonly auto/biographical in nature. Beaver was long recognised as a progressive force in Australian poetry. His last book, *The Long Game* (2005), published posthumously, ranges widely in terms of tone and subject matter, from the commonplace to the metaphysical. *DM*

Letters to Live Poets

I

God knows what was done to you.
I may never find out fully.
The truth reaches us slowly here,
is delayed in the mail continually
or censored in the tabloids. The war[1]   5
now into its third year
remains undeclared.
The number of infants, among others, blistered
and skinned alive by napalm
has been exaggerated   10
by both sides we are told,
and the gas does not seriously harm;
does not kill but is merely
unbearably nauseating.
Apparently none of this   15
is happening to us.

I meant to write to you more than a year
ago. Then there was as much to hear,
as much to tell.
There was the black plastic monster   20
prefiguring hell
displayed on the roof
of the shark aquarium at the wharf.
At Surfers' Paradise were Meter Maids
glabrous in gold bikinis.   25
It was before your country's
president came among us like a formidable
virus. Even afterwards—
after I heard (unbelievingly)

---

1   The Vietnam War (1964–75).

you had been run down on a beach   30
by a machine
apparently while sunning yourself;[1]
that things were terminal again—
even then I might have written.

But enough of that. I could tell by the tone   35
of your verses there were times
when you had ranged around you,
looking for a lift from the gift horse,
your kingdom for a Pegasus.
But to be trampled by the machine   40
beyond protest . . .

I don't have to praise you; at least
I can say I had ears for your voice
but none of that really matters now.
Crushed though. Crushed on the littered sands.   45
Given the *coup de grâce* of an empty beer can,
out of sight of the 'lordly and isolate satyrs'.
Could it have happened anywhere else
than in your country, keyed to obsolescence?

I make these words perform for you   50
knowing though you are dead, that you 'historically
belong to the enormous bliss of American death',
that your talkative poems remain
among the living things
of the sad, embattled beach-head.   55

Say that I am, as ever, the young-
old fictor of communications.
It's not that I wish to avoid
talking to myself or singing
the one-sided song.   60
It's simply that I've come to be
more conscious of the community
world-wide, of live, mortal poets.
Moving about the circumference

1   The American poet Frank O'Hara (1926–66) died the day after being hit by a beach vehicle on Fire Island, New York.

I pause each day   65
and speak to you and you.
I haven't many answers, few
enough; fewer questions left.
Even when I'm challenged 'Who
goes there?' I give ambiguous   70
replies as though the self linking
heart and mind had become a gap.

You see, we have that much in common
already. It's only when I stop
thinking of you living I remember   75
nearby our home there's an aquarium
that people pay admission to,
watching sharks at feeding time:
the white, jagged rictus in the grey
sliding anonymity,   80
faint blur of red through green,
the continually spreading stain.

I have to live near this, if not quite with it.
I realize there's an equivalent
in every town and city in the world.   85
Writing to you keeps the local, intent
shark-watchers at bay
(who if they thought at all
would think *me* some kind of ghoul);
rings a bell for the gilded coin-slots   90
at the Gold Coast;
sends the president parliament's head on a platter;
writes Vietnam like a huge four-letter
word in blood and faeces on the walls
of government; reminds me when   95
the intricate machine stalls
there's a poet still living at this address.

VI

Pain, the problem of, not answered
by dogma, orthodox or otherwise. The only problem being
how to bear with. You may have an
answer ready. I, only the   5

long-winded question breaking words
up and down the crooked line,
the graph of pain. Burns got it
in the neck. That's where it gets me.
Coleridge wrote 'My sole sensuality   10
was *not* to be in pain!'

Some of us are supposed to sing
when it's bad. Old Graves[1] says he
whistled once with it white-hot.
Beethoven maybe wrote the 'even'   15
symphonies when he was at odds with
feeling. At midnight Nietzsche's eyes
turned red with it. Valéry cracked his
knuckles, succumbing at mid-day.
Freud chewed aspirin,   20
his cancered jaw half-plastic.
Whatever else it isn't, pain's
feeling. Maybe the most intimate
experience we're capable of.

Tonight my head's clamped and hearing's   25
affected. Rheumatism's in the
neck. We knew it was in the air
today. All day the surf roared
till the spray was thick as fog.
Everything's salted down. I like it—   30
the primal salt-lick in the air.
Both of us like the old sea breath,
but she with her sinusitis, I with
rheumatics, ache and gasp, winded
before the big crass statement of pain.   35

And its talent for metaphors:
it piles up a tide of breakers
then subsides leaving pools
full of little twinges. But there's
this much to be said for it: 40
there's no falsity in it at all.
There's no ambiguity to pain.

---

1   Robert Graves (1895–1985), poet, critic and novelist.

You've got to fight it to the death—
its own, or yours. You don't relieve
yourself of it, you use a pain   45
killer on the understanding
it's born and reborn again.
Pain shows eternity as hell, but
without it you're dead. How does it feel
to be without any pain?   50

                                                                1969

PETER PORTER
b. 1929

Peter Porter was born in Brisbane. After his mother died in 1938, Porter, an only child, was sent to boarding school. He was a cadet journalist for the *Courier-Mail* (1947–48) before moving to England in 1951 where he became associated with 'The Group', and published his first collection of poems in 1961.

Before 1968, when he became a full-time freelance writer, Porter worked as a bookseller, journalist and advertising copywriter. Porter has edited anthologies (including *The Oxford Book of Modern Australian Verse*, 1996), written libretti, collaborated with the Australian artist Arthur Boyd (1920–99) and translated the classical poet Martial. Since 1974 he has regularly returned to Australia for short stays, where he is recognised as a non-resident 'Australian poet'. Porter has a major international reputation, and has won a number of awards, including the Queen's Gold Medal for Poetry in 2002.

The emotions associated with the suicide of his wife in 1974 led to the elegiac poems of *The Cost of Seriousness* (1978), generally considered Porter's best single volume. 'An Exequy' (along with 'The Delegate') is an important addition to modern elegy. Porter is both an urbane and an urban poet. His poetry habitually alludes to European high culture (often music), and has become increasingly concerned with stanzaic forms and the linguistic construction of reality. *DM*

Sydney Cove, 1788

The Governor[1] loves to go mapping—round and round
The inlets of the Harbour in his pinnace.
He fingers a tree-fern, sniffs the ground

And hymns it with a unison of feet—
We march to church and executions. No one,   5
Even Banks,[2] could match the flora of our fleet.

---

1   Captain Arthur Phillip (1738–1814).
2   Joseph Banks (1743–1820), English botanist who sailed with Cook on his first voyage of discovery.

Grog from Madeira reminds us most of home,
More than the pork and British weevils do.
On a diet of flour, your hair comes out in your comb.

A seaman who tried to lie with a native girl   10
Ran off when he smelt her fatty hide.
Some say these oysters are the sort for pearls.

Green shoots of the Governor's wheat have browned.
A box of bibles was washed up today,
The chaplain gave them to two Methodists. Ross[1] found   15

A convict selling a baby for a jug of rum.
Those black hills which wrestle with
The rain are called Blue Mountains. Come

Genocide or Jesus we can't work this land.
The sun has framed it for our moralists   20
To dry the bones of forgers in the sand.

We wake in the oven of its cloudless sky,
Already the blood-encircled sun is up.
Mad sharks swim in the convenient sea.

The Governor says we mustn't land a man   25
Or woman with gonorrhoea. Sound felons only
May leave their bodies in a hangman's land.

Where all is novel, the only rule's explore.
Amelia Levy and Elizabeth Fowles spent the night
With Corporal Plowman and Corporal Winxstead for   30

A shirt apiece. These are our home concerns.
The cantor curlew sings the surf asleep.
The moon inducts the lovers in the ferns.

                                                          1964

---

1   Major Robert Ross (c. 1740–94), Lieutenant Governor and officer of the marines.

On This Day I Complete My Fortieth Year[1]

Although art is autonomous
somebody has to live in the poet's body
and get the stuff out through his head,
  someone has to suffer

especially the boring sociology of it   5
and the boring history, the class war
and worst of all the matter of good luck,
  that is to say bad luck—

for in the end it is his fault, i.e. your fault
not to be born Lord Byron and saying   10
there has already been a Lord Byron is no excuse—
  he found it no excuse—

to have a weatherboard house and a white
paling fence and poinsettias and palm nuts
instead of Newstead Abbey[2] and owls and graves   15
  and not even a club foot;

above all to miss the European gloom
in the endless eleven o'clock heat among
the lightweight suits and warped verandahs,
  an apprenticeship, not a pilgrimage—   20

the girl down the road vomiting dimity
incisored peanuts, the bristly boss speaking
with a captain's certainty to the clerk,
  'we run a neat ship here':

well, at forty, the grievances lie around   25
like terminal moraine and they mean
nothing unless you pay a man in Frognal
  to categorize them for you

but there are two sorts of detritus, one a pile
of moon-ore, the workings of the astonished   30
mole who breathes through your journalism
  'the air of another planet',

---

1 Cf 'On this Day I Complete My Thirty-Sixth Year' by Byron and the poem by John Tranter (qv).
2 Byron inherited Newstead Abbey, the subject of one of his poems, in 1798.

his silver castings are cherished in books and papers
and you're grateful for what he can grub up
though you know it's little enough beside   35
      the sea of tranquillity—

the second sort is a catalogue of bitterness,
just samples of death and fat worlds of pain
that sail like airships through bed-sit posters
      and never burst or deflate;   40

far more real than a screaming letter,
more embarrassing than an unopened statement
from the bank, more memorable than a small
      dishonesty to a parent—

but to make a resolution will not help,   45
Greece needs liberating but not by me,[1]
I am likely to find my Sapphics not verses
      but ladies in Queensway,

so I am piling on fuel for the dark,
jamming the pilgrims on tubular chairs   50
while the NHS[2] doctor checks my canals,
      my ports and my purlieus,

praying that the machine may work a while
longer, since I haven't programmed it
yet, suiting it to a divisive music   55
      that is the mind's swell

and which in my unchosen way
I marked out so many years ago
in the hot promises as a gift I must follow,
      'howling to my art'   60

as the master put it while he was still young—
these are the epiphanies of a poor light,
the ghosts of mid-channel, the banging doors
      of the state sirocco.

      1970

1   Lord Byron supported the Greeks in the Greek War of Independence.
2   National Health Service (UK).

Sex and the Over Forties

It's too good for them,
they look so unattractive undressed—
let them read paperbacks!

A few things to keep in readiness—
a flensing knife, a ceiling mirror, 5
a cassette of *The Broken Heart*.[1]

More luncheons than lust,
more meetings on Northern Line stations,
more discussions of children's careers.

A postcard from years back— 10
I'm twenty-one, in Italy and in love!
Wagner wrote *Tristan* at forty-four.

Trying it with noises and in strange positions,
trying it with the young themselves,
trying to keep it up with the Joneses! 15

All words and no play,
all animals fleeing a forest fire,
all Apollo's grafters running.

Back to the dream in the garden,
back to the pictures in the drawer, 20
back to back, tonight and every night.

1972

An Exequy[2]

In wet May, in the months of change,
In a country you wouldn't visit, strange
Dreams pursue me in my sleep,
Black creatures of the upper deep—
Though you are five months dead, I see 5
You in guilt's iconography,
Dear Wife, lost beast, beleaguered child,

1   A play by John Ford (1586–c. 1640).
2   Cf 'An Exequy for his Matchless never to be forgotten Friend' by Henry King (1592–1669), written for King's wife Anne who died in 1624.

The stranded monster with the mild
Appearance, whom small waves tease,
(Andromeda upon her knees   10
In orthodox deliverance)
And you alone of pure substance,
The unformed form of life, the earth
Which Piero's brushes brought to birth
For all to greet as myth, a thing   15
Out of the box of imagining.
This introduction serves to sing
Your mortal death as Bishop King
Once hymned in tetrametric rhyme
His young wife, lost before her time;   20
Though he lived on for many years
His poem each day fed new tears
To that unreaching spot, her grave,
His lines a baroque architrave
The Sunday poor with bottled flowers   25
Would by-pass in their mourning hours,
Esteeming ragged natural life
('Most dearly loved, most gentle wife'),
Yet, looking back when at the gate
And seeing grief in formal state   30
Upon a sculpted angel group,
Were glad that men of god could stoop
To give the dead a public stance
And freeze them in their mortal dance.

The words and faces proper to   35
My misery are private—you
Would never share your heart with those
Whose only talent's to suppose,
Nor from your final childish bed
Raise a remote confessing head—   40
The channels of our lives are blocked,
The hand is stopped upon the clock,
No one can say why hearts will break
And marriages are all opaque:
A map of loss, some posted cards,   45
The living house reduced to shards,
The abstract hell of memory,
The pointlessness of poetry—

These are the instances which tell
Of something which I know full well,   50
I owe a death to you—one day
The time will come for me to pay
When your slim shape from photographs
Stands at my door and gently asks
If I have any work to do   55
Or will I come to bed with you.
O *scala enigmatica*,[1]
I'll climb up to that attic where
The curtain of your life was drawn
Some time between despair and dawn—   60
I'll never know with what halt steps
You mounted to this plain eclipse
But each stair now will station me
A black responsibility
And point me to that shut-down room,   65
'This be your due appointed tomb.'

I think of us in Italy:
Gin-and-chianti-fuelled, we
Move in a trance through Paradise,
Feeding at last our starving eyes,   70
Two people of the English blindness
Doing each masterpiece the kindness
Of discovering it—from Baldovinetti[2]
To Venice's most obscure jetty.
A true unfortunate traveller, I   75
Depend upon your nurse's eye
To pick the altars where no Grinner

Puts us off our tourists' dinner
And in hotels to bandy words
With Genevan girls and talking birds,   80
To wear your feet out following me
To night's end and true amity,
And call my rational fear of flying
A paradigm of Holy Dying—
And, oh my love, I wish you were   85
Once more with me, at night somewhere

1   An invented musical scale. Guiseppe Verdi used it for his 'Ave Maria' in *Four Sacred Pieces* (1889).
2   A Florentine painter (c. 1427–99).

In narrow streets applauding wines,
The moon above the Apennines
As large as logic and the stars,
Most middle-aged of avatars,   90
As bright as when they shone for truth
Upon untried and avid youth.

The rooms and days we wandered through
Shrink in my mind to one—there you
Lie quite absorbed by peace—the calm   95
Which life could not provide is balm
In death. Unseen by me, you look
Past bed and stairs and half-read book
Eternally upon your home,
The end of pain, the left alone.   100
I have no friend, or intercessor,
No psychopomp or true confessor
But only you who know my heart
In every cramped and devious part—
Then take my hand and lead me out,   105
The sky is overcast by doubt,
The time has come, I listen for
Your words of comfort at the door,
O guide me through the shoals of fear—
'Fürchte dich nicht, ich bin bei dir.'[1]   110
                                                                    1978

What I Have Written I Have Written[2]

It is the little stone of unhappiness
which I keep with me. I had it as a child
and put it in a drawer. There came
a heap of paper to put beside it,
letters, poems, a brittle dust   5
of affection, sallowed by memory.

Aphorisms came. Not evil, but
the competition of two goods
brings you to the darkened room.
I gave the stone to a woman   10

1 A motet by J.S. Bach (1685–1750) for double chorus: 'Fear not, I am with you' (Isaiah 43:1).
2 See John 19:22.

and it glowed. I set my mind
to hydraulic work, lifting words
from their swamp. In the light from the stone
her face was bloated. When she died
the stone returned to me, a present   15
from reality. The two goods
were still contending. From wading pools
the children grew to darken
gardens with their shadows. Duty
is better than love, it suffers no betrayal.   20

Beginning again, I notice
I have less breath but the joining
is more golden. There is a long way to go,
among gardens and alarms,
after-dinner sleeps peopled by toads   25
and all the cries of childhood.
Someone comes to say my name
has been removed from the Honourable
Company of Scribes. Books in the room
turn their backs on me.   30

Old age will be the stone and me together.
I have become used to its weight
in my pocket and my brain.
To move it from lining to lining
like Beckett's tramp,   35
to modulate it to the major
or throw it at the public—
all is of no avail. But I'll add
to the songs of the stone. These words
I take from my religious instruction,   40
complete responsibility—
let them be entered in the record,
What I have written I have written.

                                                                 1981

R.A. SIMPSON
1929–2002

The poet, artist and editor R.A. (Ron) Simpson was born in Melbourne, a city with which he was profoundly associated: as one of the 'university poets' (with Chris Wallace-Crabbe (qv) and others) in the 1950s; as a lecturer in art at Melbourne's Chisholm Institute of Technology (1968–87); and as the poetry editor of the *Age* (1969–97). Like his artwork (which decorated a number of his collections of poetry), Simpson's poetry is clear, minimalist and often melancholic in tone, though this is sometimes offset by a satirical and comic edge. *DM*

Evening

There is little to recommend this light
at evening as the tall men return
like undertakers from the railway station.

Children have moonstruck mouths—and wives
pour their clarity into saucepans   5
and watch themselves boil away for minutes.

There is a sharp moon in the pine-tree
where so many lines are credible
and where the answers are impossible to guess.

Tonight some wives will be unwrapped in rooms   10
and some may lie awake, hoping
no-one has come to repossess the Milky Way.

1976

Parallels

1846 Lincoln comes to Congress
President-elect in 1860

1946 Kennedy walks into Congress
finally President-elect in 1960

They're succeeded by Andrew Johnson   5
born 1808 and Lyndon Johnson 1908

1839 Lincoln's killer is born
1939 Kennedy's

Both Southerners
shot before their trials   10

Booth fires in a theatre
escaping via a warehouse

Oswald fires from a warehouse
and runs into a theatre

History never repeats itself   15
exactly
                                            1999

K.S. INGLIS
b. 1929

A historian of public culture, Ken Inglis has written on hospitals, churches and the Anzac tradition. In addition to his prize-winning history of war memorials, *Sacred Places* (1998, assisted by Jan Brazier), he is the author of an acclaimed two-volume history of the ABC (1983/2006). In 1966 he became foundation professor of history at the University of Papua New Guinea, where he was vice-chancellor from 1972 to 1975. He returned to Australia in 1977 as research professor at the ANU. He conceived and edited the twelve-volume Bicentennial history *Australians: A historical library* (1987). *DM*

From *Sacred Places*
Introduction: Holy Ground

The Shrine of Remembrance was a new and mysterious presence in the Melbourne of my childhood. Rising from a mound in the Domain, just south of the city, the building proclaimed itself the most important object in the landscape. The king's son, the Duke of Gloucester, dedicated the Shrine on 11 November, Armistice Day, 1934, when I was five, at a ceremony timed to coincide with the city's centenary celebrations.

What was a Shrine? In remembrance of what? The makers, sensing that elucidation was necessary, had answers carved into the grey granite wall. Every visitor, everybody who passed along the grand boulevard of St Kilda Road, was addressed by a solemn command.

LET ALL MEN KNOW THAT THIS IS HOLY GROUND

THIS SHRINE ESTABLISHED IN THE HEARTS OF MEN AS ON
THE SOLID EARTH COMMEMORATES A PEOPLE'S FORTITUDE
AND SACRIFICE

YE THAT COME AFTER GIVE REMEMBRANCE.

The archaic language signalled tradition. What tradition? To the most educated of readers the message sounded Greek, and therefore in harmony with the architecture. Other monumental buildings on holy ground in Melbourne, the two Christian cathedrals named for St Paul and St Patrick, the Scots and Methodist churches, were Gothic. This one was Athenian. To receive any Christian message you had to go inside. In the centre of the pavement was set a Stone of Remembrance inscribed 'GREATER LOVE HATH NO MAN'. Readers were expected to recognize these words as Jesus' and to supply for themselves the rest of the verse: 'than this, that a man lay down his life for his friends'.[1] Written on that stone, the text was clearly intended to speak of the war dead. Their names were written on parchment in books housed in glass cases. But not only the names of the dead: every man who had gone to the Great War from the state of Victoria was honoured in those books. We who came after were to give remembrance to all who had exhibited that fortitude and sacrifice, the men who returned as well as those whose bodies were buried on the other side of the earth. My own earliest memory of the Shrine connects it with the occult. I learned with wonder that on Armistice Day every year, at the eleventh hour of the eleventh day of the eleventh month, a ray of light would fall on the Stone of Remembrance. Had some capricious supernatural power chosen to stop the war at exactly that moment?

Greek building, Christian inscription, ancient pagan theatre of the sun: 'Shrine' was a name chosen to embody complex understandings of war, death, sacrifice, the nation, the universe.

My first experiences of the Shrine inspired awe and confusion and fear: awe in the presence of the holy, confusion about what to think and feel and do in response, fear of I don't know what. I met in the grounds the wholly intelligible, attractive and unfrightening little statue of two men and a donkey. Private Simpson, the Man with the Donkey, saviour of comrades at Gallipoli, I had learned about already, probably at church (where preachers of children's sermons would connect two kinds of sacred story by comparing Simpson with the Good Samaritan), certainly at school in the Fourth Grade Reader, where the Victorian Education Department placed him to initiate us into the Anzac tradition. Here was the one story from the war which all our mentors, the most bellicose and the most peace-loving, could agree was entirely edifying. (The Reader did not tell us about the most famous Australian fighter of the war, Albert Jacka, from Melbourne, awarded the Victoria Cross for killing seven Turks the day Simpson died.) *Find Gallipoli on the map,* said the Notes and Exercises. *Was Simpson brave? What does his story teach us? Write a composition entitled 'Their Mission is to Save'.*

The time for that assignment was around Anzac Day, which to school children as to everybody else meant more than Armistice Day. 25 April was a state school and public holiday; 11 November was not. On the last working day before 25 April some children were delivered to the Shrine for a special service, and the rest of us were gathered in quadrangles to be addressed

1 John 15:13.

by teachers and returned soldiers (and some men who were both) on the meanings of Anzac. Birth and/or baptism of the nation; sacrifice; rallying to the empire; holding on against impossible odds; fighting to defend the right, and being prepared to do it again. In my class at North Preston, most of us, born in 1928 or 1929, had fathers who had been just too young for the war; an envied minority wore their dads' medals, and the most admired of all, my friend Wally, wore medals of a dad who was dead. Anzac Eve speakers drew our attention to the honour board bearing the names of old boys. Above the blackboard in one classroom hung a print of Will Longstaff's painting *Menin Gate at Midnight*, showing the great British monument to dead men 'Missing' in Belgium, among them thousands of Australians, and in the foreground, ghostly soldiers rising among the poppies.

Simpson, Menin Gate, the old soldiers' sermons, the honour board: we were being thoroughly schooled in the values the Shrine was created to signify. My age-mate Peter Shrubb, born in New South Wales, recalls that like perhaps most children of our time he grew up in the culture of the Great War. 'Anzac Day', he writes, 'was the only day of the year that had any kind of holiness in it'. And not only for boys. Joan Colebrook, growing up in Herberton, north Queensland, remembers 'the sacred letters' which 'had about them the unforgettable aura of the 1914 that we had not experienced', and the days when she marched to the monument with fellow-pupils for wreath-laying, singing and 'tears of pain and patriotism'.

On the actual day some of us took tram or train with parents into town and watched the march to the Shrine; some attended ceremonies at the nearest local war memorial (an arch outside the Preston Town Hall); some listened to wireless descriptions of the march, some just had a holiday—a dour one, like a Sunday, for no public pleasures were yet permitted on the sacred day. If you visited the Shrine after the march and the service, you could inspect a pile of wreaths laid around the Stone of Remembrance. On Armistice Day classes were suspended between morning playtime and lunch while we stood in line, heard addresses like those of Anzac eve but dwelling more on death than birth and on the world rather than the nation; and we bowed our heads in silence at the moment the ray of sunlight was lighting up the Stone of Remembrance.

On the steps of the Shrine, day in and day out, stood a man dressed in the Great War uniform of the Australian Light Horse—leggings, emu-plumed Digger hat, rifle to shoulder—guarding the Shrine and when necessary reminding visitors, especially young ones, to keep their voices down, stop running about and generally show proper respect. Wally and I once got a stern reproach from him on a holiday visit, for fooling about. He was actually a policeman dressed up: a living statue, an incarnation of all the Shrine enjoined us to remember. One Anzac eve more than thirty years later the Light Horseman told my daughter Louise, sitting innocently on the steps, to stand up.

There is a vivid description of a war memorial in *Kangaroo*, the novel D.H. Lawrence dashed off while he and his wife Frieda were living at Thirroul (in the novel 'Mullumbimby') on the south coast of New South Wales in 1922.

> It was really a quite attractive little monument: a statue in pale, fawnish stone, of a Tommy standing at ease, with his gun down at his side, wearing his puttees and his turned-up felt hat. The statue itself was about life size, but standing just overhead on a tall pedestal it looked small and stiff and rather touching. The pedestal was in very nice proportion, and had at eye level white inlet slabs between little columns of grey granite, bearing the names of the fallen on one slab, in small black letters, and on the other slabs the names of all the men who served: 'God Bless Them'. The fallen had 'Lest we forget', for a motto. Carved on the bottom step it said, 'Unveiled by Grannie Rhys'. A real township monument, bearing the names of everybody possible: the fallen, all those who donned khaki, the people who presented it, and Grannie Rhys. Wonderfully in keeping with the place and its people, naive but quite attractive, with the stiff, pallid, delicate fawn-coloured soldier standing forever stiff and pathetic.

A sensitive observer—novelist, poet, painter—is here responding to the local variant of a monumental form new to the world. What does he see? First, pathos, not triumph. That may be why Lawrence prefers the homely English word 'Tommy' to the hard 'Digger', which he knows well but saves for darker purposes. Or he may simply have wanted to keep it simple for English readers: Frieda calls it in letters an 'Anzac'. Second, Lawrence notices the monument's communal character, naming townspeople and bearing on separate white slabs the names of the fallen and of men who served: at Thirroul as in the Shrine of Remembrance, the survivors as well as the dead are honoured. Finally, he likes it. Lawrence had discovered an Australian icon. For once the word can be used with no stretch of meaning: a bodily image, created to be revered.

1998

GEOFFREY BLAINEY
b. 1930

Geoffrey Blainey, the son of a Methodist clergyman, is a popular, prolific and sometimes controversial Australian historian. Blainey was educated at the University of Melbourne, where, after a decade of earning a living as a freelance historian, he later held chairs in economic history (1968–76) and history (1976–88). Many of his historical works have gained considerable popularity, and the phrase 'the tyranny of distance' (the name of his 1966 study of Australian geographic history) has become idiomatic. Blainey is often iconoclastic, as seen in his account of the Eureka Stockade (in *The Rush that Never Ended*, 1963) as a tax revolt of small capitalists, rather than as a workers' rebellion. Blainey's success has made him a public figure. He made a television series, *The Blainey View* (1982), chaired the Literature Board of the Australia Council (1977–81) and served on the Australian Heritage Commission. In 1984 he caused controversy by calling for a cut in the level of Asian immigration. In 1988 he resigned from the University of Melbourne, becoming again a freelance historian and commentator. He coined the phrase 'black-armband history' to describe what he saw as a model of Australian history that focused unduly on Indigenous dispossession, environmental damage, and a culture of sexism and racism. *DM*

From *The Rush that Never Ended*
Chapter 4: Ballarat's Ditch of Perdition

[. . .] On the Friday, 1 December, blue smoke piped from thousands of breakfast fires in the mild morning air, a day for action on Ballarat. One of the busiest places that morning was the Eureka Lead, a buried watercourse that ran south for a mile and then turned west. The Irishmen had most of the shafts and tent-stores and restaurants at the place where the lead changed course, and their ground was chosen as defensive post by Lalor's rebels.[1] During the day hundreds of armed men gathered there, organizing patrols to tour the other leads and collect arms and protect the miners. They surrounded their parade ground and tents with a simple fence, made from the slabs of timber 4 to 6 feet long with which they lined the sides of their deep shafts. In the yard the miners drilled and planned, awaiting the next military raid on working miners or on themselves.

On Saturday evening, 2 December, more than a thousand men were in the stockade at Eureka, and more than four hundred soldiers and police were in their camps on the hills two miles away. The miners' stockade lacked sufficient tents to house its armed men, and late in the evening many men went to sleep in their own tents along the leads. Lalor went to bed in the stockade at midnight. At 1.50 a.m. on the Sunday morning whisky was freely given to the rebels, and some were intoxicated on their last night. A few captains were suspicious that the issue of whisky was a government plot, so they led their armed miners from the stockade. By 3 a.m. only 120 men armed with guns and pistols and pikes remained behind the slab fence. Ballarat lay in darkness, hardly a light from the tents and huts where thousands slept.

A few stirred in their sleep, awakened by the noise of a company of men moving past. In the pale light before the sunrise soldiers and police

---

1   Peter Lalor (1827–89), leader of the Eureka Stockade rebellion, one of Australia's few armed uprisings.

attacked the stockade. A hail of shots fell on the defenders. Captain Wise of the 40th Regiment was mortally wounded and 'as he lay on his back he cheered them on to the attack'. Lalor was wounded with a musket ball in the left shoulder and was concealed under a pile of mining slabs while the slaughter went on. The fighting lasted less than half an hour but killed an uncounted number of miners, perhaps thirty, and five soldiers. The troops wrecked the stockade and set fire to tents and fired on unarmed miners nearby, and by breakfast that Sunday morning the rebellion was bleeding.

On Monday the miners' funerals were followed for miles by thousands to the burial ground by the swamp. That day there were isolated clashes and indiscriminate firing by the soldiers. Martial law was proclaimed in the district for a few days, and captured rebels were taken to Melbourne to face trial for high treason.

The spirit of rebellion lived on, and few miners or diggers throughout Victoria bought new licences.[1] In Melbourne juries refused to convict the Eureka prisoners. Finally in the winter of 1855 the government reformed its goldfields laws. Instead of the digger's licence it issued for £1 a year a 'miner's right' that entitled the miner to dig gold and vote at parliamentary elections and make his own mining laws. To raise revenue which the licences had once provided, the government collected 2s. 6d. on each ounce of gold exported, a duty equivalent to about 3 per cent. And so the rigid system of controlling the diggings that had been born in the crisis across the Blue Mountains in 1851 was abolished in Victoria, and soon wiped from the lawbooks in the other auriferous colonies.

In Australia's quiet history Eureka became a legend, a battlecry for nationalists, republicans, liberals, radicals, or communists, each creed finding in the rebellion the lessons they liked to see. Collectively their fascination magnified the effects of the episode. The effects were easy to magnify, because from 1856 four of the five existing Australian colonies gained the essentials of the British parliamentary system and virtual control of their domestic affairs, and to many this seemed one of Eureka's achievements. In fact the colonies' political constitutions were not affected by Eureka, but the first parliament that met under Victoria's new constitution was alert to the democratic spirit of the goldfields, and passed laws enabling each adult man in Victoria to vote at elections, to vote by secret ballot, and to stand for the Legislative Assembly.

The Ballarat riot probably quickened political democracy in Victoria but its mark was clearest on the goldfields. In 1855 the miners began to make their own mining laws and settle disputes in their own courts.

---

1   A miner's licence, the expense of which was one of the grievances that led to the uprising.

Such in essence was the Californian system, but whereas it had arisen in California because there was at first no mining law and no authority to make or administer laws, it arose in Victoria at the command of the central government. The government created local courts in the main mining districts, and all men who held a miner's right could elect the nine members of the court. The local court made all mining laws for its district, decided how much ground each man could hold, on what conditions he could retain it, and even interpreted its own laws. This system was probably the high tide of Australian democracy. The miner in moleskins, for long hunted and herded, was lord of his own goldfields.

In 1857 the Victorian government wisely handed the judicial powers of the local court to a new court of mines, with a judge presiding and miners or storekeepers acting as assessors to assess the damages or compensation in disputes; and the local courts themselves became known as 'mining boards', with the same strong powers of law making over a wide area. In southern New South Wales the new goldfields of Kiandra, Adelong, Young, Forbes, and Araluen elected local courts, and Gympie in Queensland elected its own court, and they tended to adopt the liberal Victorian rules during their brief life. Their influence, however, was faint compared to that of the Victorian mining boards which together with the judicial decisions of the Victorian mining judge, Robert Molesworth, shaped mining law for most of Australia. And when Arthur C. Veatch came to study Australia's mining code half a century later as the personal representative of Theodore Roosevelt, President of the United States, he praised a code which seemed to him in advance of America's code.

The miners' moots that first sat at Ballarat and Bendigo and the Victorian gold towns in the winter of 1855 rapidly granted larger areas of ground to men who had to combat water or great depth. Ballarat's court encouraged the mining of its deep leads by allowing miners to unite their claims and by permitting one man to hold shares in many claims. Its court and mining board were so liberal in difficult areas that by 1863 a man could hold 120 times the maximum area of a decade previously.

The new mining code was flexible, imposing duties and privileges on the miner in relation to the nature of the ground he worked. It usually aided the humble digger in areas where he could win gold with his primitive methods, and it helped large parties of working miners in deeper ground where an alliance of capital and labour alone could succeed. The Eureka rebellion thus paved the way for the rapid and orderly growth of capitalist mining and the accumulation of large fortunes in few hands. This was most marked on Ballarat, the scene of the rebellion, and significantly one of the driving capitalists of the new era was the chief rebel, Peter Lalor.

1963

MENA ABDULLAH and RAY MATHEW
b. 1930   1929–2002

Short-story writer Mena Abdullah was born in Bundarra, NSW, an Indian Hindu of Punjabi background. She spent her early years on her parents' rural property before going to school at Sydney Girls High School, and then worked for the CSIRO for 40 years. In the short-story collection *The Time of the Peacock* (1965), which she wrote with Ray Mathew, most of the stories are narrated by an Indian girl called Nimmie. Representing an early foray into literary multiculturalism, these stories deal with a mixed Moslem and Hindu Indian-Australian community.

Ray Mathew was born in Leichhardt, NSW. During the 1950s he wrote a number of plays and worked in a variety of jobs, including freelance journalist and lecturer at the University of Sydney, before moving first to Italy and then to London, finally settling in New York in 1968 to work as a freelance writer and art critic. As well as collaborating on *The Time of the Peacock*, he published three volumes of poetry, but is best known in Australia as a playwright. *KG*

The Dragon of Kashmir

It was the heat of summer, the holiday time, and all of us—Ama, Father, we children—had come away from the farm and its bare, glazed hills. We had come to the North Coast country, the world near Nambucca. The grass was green and gentle and the blue of Krishna was everywhere—in the sky, in the sea, in the puddles after rain, in every drop of water that you held to look at. We stayed with the Shahs.

They were nice people. Everyone liked them, but not really me. The children were brave, when I was shy. They were quick, when I was slow. They were Australian, and not like me. They had always had white friends, when I had had only Rashida. Rashida liked them. Sometimes it frightened her—the games they played, the way they talked—but she could do the same. She was braver than I, she was older. It was Grandmother Shah that I liked.

She was old and gentle. And I think that she was sad. She had come to Australia from Kashmir. She had come a long time ago, when she was young and Grandfather Shah was young, too. And now he was dead and her children were grown, and her grandchildren were brittle with Australian ways and Australian talk and had no time to listen to her. There was no one alive who remembered her. She was *Grandmother* Shah—even to Ama, my mother, who had also come from Kashmir.

But I listened to her. I asked her questions and pestered her to tell of the old days and the old ways, to tell me stories of Grandfather Shah and the days when he trained camel-drivers for the long rides through Australia, stories of Kashmir and the jewels that the Indian Maharanis wore. She scolded me and called me a Bengali, said that I chattered like monkeys, that I was wearing her out, that I should play with the other children and I should be quiet—the way Kashmiri children were quiet—and should never ask questions. But, always, she answered me. Only, sometimes, her answers were so long and so slow, so full of memories that she seemed to forget that I was there. She would look at me and not see me, so that I had to chatter again and to prod her with words to bring her back to the story. I had to call her 'Grandmother' to make her look at me.

She was not my grandmother. She was not related to my family at all, except by friendliness.

It was for friendliness, or to keep me quiet, that she let me look through the old cardboard boxes that held her memories—ribbons and letters, photographs and brooches. We were in the garden. Grandmother Shah sat in her chair in the shade of the tamarind-tree and crocheted. I sat on the grass near her and went through one of the boxes.

It was a warm day, but nice and lazy, and I pulled the old things out tiredly and looked at them as though looking were a very hard job. I was watching how slowly my hand moved when I was lifting them—the envelopes with their faded stamps and the letters covered with writing in Hindi. It was then, under a heap of letters, that I found the fan.

It was old. Some of the sticks were broken. But it was silk, and big. It was bright, but faded. I opened it and fanned myself like an Indian lady or a Maharani. But it was full of dust that made me sneeze. So, sneezing, and laughing, and chattering like a monkey, I jumped up and dropped it on Grandmother Shah's lap, on her crochet work. She did scold me then. I had made her white work dirty. I was stupid and thoughtless. I was Australian and not well bred. And what was I doing with a filthy old fan?

'But, Grandmother, it's yours. It was in your box. Wasn't it yours? Who did it belong to? Did she have a story? Can you remember?'

Grandmother Shah had brushed the fan to the ground, but now she picked it up and looked at it. She looked for a long time. I was bored.

'Grandmother Shah!'

'Bring me that box. It was in that box?'

She looked through the things in the box, and then pulled out an envelope that had a photograph inside it. It was very old and faded, but she held it and looked at it as if it were new. I leant on the arm of her chair and looked at it, too. It was very old and faded. It was not new at all.

It showed two girls in a garden. They stood very close to one another and the hems of their saris were touching. They both had long black plaited hair and caste-marks on their foreheads. One of them held the fan—but it was a new fan then.

'There's something on it,' I said. I opened it—the real fan—and looked hard at the faded silk. 'It's a dragon.'

'The dragon of Kashmir,' said Grandmother. 'I remember it now.' She took the open fan from me, and held it. 'It was bright green then, and the dragon was silver. It was not the kind of fan that a young girl should have.'

'Did you know them, Grandmother—the girls in the picture?'

'That one is me,' she said. 'That was when I was Farida, and not Grandmother. That was when I was fourteen, and not here. That was in Kashmir.' She laughed, at the picture. 'They are Kashmiri roses,' she said.

'They're withered and brown.'

'It is the photograph that has withered,' said Grandmother Shah. 'That was the garden of our house in Kashmir, my father's house. I remember it all now—the day the photograph was taken. It was my brother. He had come back from Oxford, from the big school there. He had come back the night before. He was wearing English clothes. He forgot to take off his shoes at the door. He was like a stranger, but he was still ours. And in the morning he said, 'I will photograph you all.' But we didn't know what that meant and we thought that photographed might be like—baptized, or vaccinated, or something nasty. And then he came out of the house with the box on legs and he made us all stand still and look at it. He said that we would see a bright yellow bird. But we did not. None of us did.'

'The other girl is holding the fan.' I knew all about photographs.

'It is hers,' said Grandmother Shah. 'We were both fourteen—Lala and I.'

'You're smiling,' I said. 'You're smiling in the photograph, and now, too.'

'We were both fourteen. We thought that wonderful things would happen.'

'And didn't they? You came to Australia.'

'I came to Australia,' said Grandmother Shah. 'But I never wanted to go away. I wanted to be home. I wanted to be married, with children, a house with servants and the people that I knew. Lala is the one that should have come away. She wanted never to stay at home. She used to say—I remember how she used to tell me about countries a long way off where women walked like men. I used to say to her, "The woman is the sole of the husband's foot." It made her angry. Every time, it made her angry. I said it to her that morning. "My brother is home," I said. "He is very fierce and white and handsome. He will make you want to be the sole of his foot."'

'Did he?'

'No. Yes. She was very shy with him. Perhaps she loved him. She was shyer every day. Every day we saw him. She was my great friend, but she was the one who talked. She was very grown up. She used to talk no matter who was in the room—even if there were real adults there, even if there were men. But when my brother came into the room, she was quiet. All that summer she carried this fan. It was not the kind of fan that a young girl should have had, but it had been her mother's before it was hers. I remember now, when he was there, how slowly she used it; how she held it almost to hide her face. And the next year I came to Australia to be married, and Lala came with her father to the ship.'

'Did she give you the fan then? As a present?'

'I cannot remember. I remember how I cried and how she told me that I was silly, a child, that I should be proud to be free and going away—even if it did mean that I had to be married and become nothing.'

'Was your brother there?'

'He was there. With his wife.'

'Was Lala his wife?'

'Oh, Nimmi, child! Nothing wonderful ever happens, ever.'

'Did she get married?'

'Who should she marry? She was more clever than any man in Kashmir. Her father used to let her help him. She would never have been Grandmother, and not Lala.'

'Is she dead then?'

Grandmother looked at the photograph. 'We were fourteen then,' she said. 'We are both dead now. I am Grandmother Shah and no one remembers Farida. She is as old as I am and she has never left Kashmir.'

'But I remember you!'

'You remember what I tell you, and that is all you will remember.'

I waved the fan, slowly, almost hiding my face. I peeped at Grandmother Shah. 'Do I look like Lala?' I said.

But grandmother was looking at the photograph with its brown faded flowers in Kashmir, and its brown faded faces.

'Why do they have dragons on Kashmiri things?' I was peering at the design on the fan.

'Because they eat everything. Because they live for ever.' She put the photograph down on the ground and picked up her crochet work.

'If she didn't give you the fan, then you ought to send it back.'

'Stop chattering, child.'

The wind picked at the photograph. I moved to grab it.

'Let it go,' said Grandmother. Almost, she shouted. 'Let it go!'

And the two of us sat there—as though it were that time again—and watched the wind lift the photograph and then drop it, tug it and push at it, lift it and lever it till suddenly it went up high, high, and whirled round in the sky that was as blue as Krishna.

'It will blow away,' I said. 'You will never see it again.'

'The dragon will eat it,' said Grandmother Shah. She went back to her crochet work.

1965

BRUCE DAWE
b. 1930

After an itinerant childhood in Victoria, Bruce Dawe left school at sixteen to work as a labourer, farmhand, clerk and postman. He attended the University of Melbourne in 1954 where he developed his interest in poetry. From 1959 to 1968 he served in the RAAF, completing his first degree and publishing his first three volumes of poetry. In 1972 Dawe became a lecturer in literature at the Darling Downs Institute of Advanced Education (later the University of Southern Queensland). In 1990, after completing his master's and doctoral degrees, he was made an associate professor of the University of Southern Queensland, and was appointed honorary professor in 1993.

Dawe is a prolific and popular poet. His poetry is notable for its attention to social issues, often being critical of governments, Australian insularity and oppressive elements of modernity. His comic or satirical poems are notable for their attention to Australian suburbia and the domestic sphere. His style is characteristically a mix of lyricism and Australian colloquial speech. Les Murray (qv) has noted that Dawe's work shows a 'wonderfully modulated command of vernacular language and concerns'. It is perhaps not surprising that so many of Dawe's successful poems take the form of dramatic monologues. Dawe's selected/collected poems, *Sometimes Gladness*, has been enormously successful, and he is one of Australia's best-selling poets. In recent times Dawe has written numerous poems on the Iraq War. *DM*

A Victorian Hangman Tells His Love

Dear one, forgive my appearing before you like this,
in a two-piece tracksuit, welder's goggles
and a green cloth cap like some gross bee—this is the State's idea . . .
I would have come
arrayed like a bridegroom for these nuptials   5
knowing how often you have dreamed about this
moment of consummation in your cell.
If I must bind your arms now to your sides
with a leather strap and ask if you have anything to say
—these too are formalities I would dispense with: 10
I know your heart is too full at this moment
to say much and that the tranquilliser which I trust
you did not reject out of a stubborn pride
should by this have eased your ache for speech, breath
and the other incidentals which distract us from our end.   15
Let us now walk a step. This noose
with which we're wed is something of an heirloom, the last three
members of our holy family were wed with it, the softwood beam
it hangs from like a lover's tree notched with their weight.
See now I slip it over your neck, the knot   20
under the left jaw, with a slip ring

to hold the knot in place . . . There. Perfect.
Allow me to adjust the canvas hood
which will enable you to anticipate the officially prescribed darkness
by some seconds. 25
The journalists are ready with the flash-bulbs of their eyes
raised to the simple altar, the doctor twitches like a stethoscope
—you have been given a clean bill of health, like any
modern bride.
        With this spring of mine 30
from the trap, hitting the door lever, you will go forth
into a new life which I, alas, am not yet fit to share.
Be assured, you will sink into the generous pool of public feeling
as gently as a leaf—accept your rôle, feel chosen.
You are this evening's headlines. Come, my love. 35
        1968

Homecoming

All day, day after day, they're bringing them home,
they're picking them up, those they can find, and bringing them home,
they're bringing them in, piled on the hulls of Grants, in trucks, in convoys,
they're zipping them up in green plastic bags,
they're tagging them now in Saigon, in the mortuary coolness 5
they're giving them names, they're rolling them out of
the deep-freeze lockers—on the tarmac at Tan Son Nhut
the noble jets are whining like hounds,
they are bringing them home
—curly-heads, kinky-hairs, crew-cuts, balding non-coms 10
—they're high, now, high and higher, over the land, the steaming *chow mein*
their shadows are tracing the blue curve of the Pacific
with sorrowful quick fingers, heading south, heading east,
home, home, *home*—and the coasts swing upward, the old
        ridiculous curvatures 15
of earth, the knuckled hills, the mangrove-swamps, the desert emptiness . . .
in their sterile housing they tilt towards these like skiers
—taxiing in, on the long runways, the howl of their homecoming rises
surrounding them like their last moments (the mash, the splendour)
then fading at length as they move 20
on to small towns where dogs in the frozen sunset
raise muzzles in mute salute,
and on to cities in whose wide web of suburbs

telegrams tremble like leaves from a wintering tree
and the spider grief swings in his bitter geometry   25
—they're bringing them home, now, too late, too early.

1969

And a Good Friday Was Had by All

You men there, keep those women back
and God Almighty he laid down
on the crossed timber and old Silenus
my offsider looked at me as if to say
nice work for soldiers, your mind's not your own   5
once you sign that dotted line Ave Caesar
and all that malarkey Imperator Rex

well this Nazarene
didn't make it any easier
really—not like the ones   10
who kick up a fuss so you can
do your block and take it out on them
                                        Silenus
held the spikes steady and I let fly
with the sledge-hammer, not looking   15
on the downswing trying hard not to hear
over the women's wailing the bones give way
the iron shocking the dumb wood.

Orders is orders, I said after it was over
nothing personal you understand—we had a   20
drill-sergeant once thought he was God but he wasn't
a patch on you

then we hauled on the ropes
and he rose in the hot air
like a diver just leaving the springboard, arms spread   25
so it seemed
over the whole damned creation
over the big men who must have had it in for him
and the curious ones who'll watch anything if it's free
with only the usual women caring anywhere   30
and a blind man in tears.

1971

FRANK MALKORDA
c. 1930–1993

Djambidj singer and ritual leader Frank Malkorda grew up in the Blyth River region of Arnhem Land, NT. His father was Nakarra and his mother a member of the Anbarra ('River Mouth') people. Together with Frank Gurrmanamana, Malkorda recorded *Djambitj: An Aboriginal song series from Northern Australia* (1981), songs from the people of the Blyth River near Maningrida. Djambidj is a collection of thematically associated songs that has the actions and characteristics of the Djambidj spirits as its subject. There is often a mythological connection between the song subjects, for example between White Cockatoo and Crow. The songs were translated by Margaret Clunies Ross (b. 1942) as part of her research into Aboriginal songs and oral literature. The cockatoo song mentions the names of two wells at places where the cockatoo lives. The crow song, which is often performed at funeral rites, mentions two types of hollow log coffin, Badurra and Maraych, which are used as repositories for the bones of the dead. They are also conceived of as living, totemic spirits. *NJ/MCR*

Ngalalak/White Cockatoo

Wang-gurnga guya, wang-gurnga guya, gulob'arraja,
    ngwar-ngwar larrya, maningala rarey Ngaljipa.
Jamburr bujarinya, blayriber larrya, garrarra-garrarra,
    Ngwar-ngwar larrya, blayriber larrya, jamburr bujarinya,
        Ngaljipa guya, garambak mbana.   5
Yeliliba guya, ngwar-ngwar larrya, garrarra-garrarra,
    rarrchnga guya, blayriber larrya.
Ga-garrarra rarrchnga guya.
Ngaljipa guya, ngwar-ngwar worrya, jamburr bujarinya,
    blayriber larrya, ngwar-ngwar worrya, maningala rarey,   10
    rarrchnga guya, Gulgulnga guya.
Ngwar-ngwar worrya, yirpelaynbelayn, rarrchnga guya
    Ngaljipa guya
Ngwayrk, ngwayrk, Gulgulngam.

White cockatoo, white cockatoo gorging on grass seeds,
    dancing and leaping in the sky
        at Ngaljipa.
At his upland forest home he eats corms and dry grass
    seeds,   5
        his crest bobbing up and down.
He dances and leaps, greedy for grass seeds at his forest
    home, at Ngaljipa where he plays didjeridu.
See him leap, his crest rising and falling, see him eat
    rarrcha grass and corms!   10
See his crest bob up and down as he eats the *rarrcha* grass!

At Ngaljipa he dances, his crest bobbing, gorges and
   belches, dances again and leaps, eats *rarrcha*
      at his birthplace Gulgulnga;
See him dance in the sky, see him eat *rarrcha* grass at   15
   Ngaljipa!
He calls *ngwayrk ngwayrk* at Gulgulnga.

1978/1990

Muralkarra/Crow

Daunyiley-nyiley, gaya barrnga, gulbi birrirra warralanga,
   wardupalma, birrirra borja, Wakwakwak, jirnbangaya.
Birrirra borja, garma borja, Garanyula-nyula, Warduba
   jirnbanga.
Birrirra borja, wandalanga, gurta birrirala.
   wak wak wak   5
Bianga borja, jirnbanga.
Badurra borja, wandalanga, a Maraychnga, daunyiley-
   nyiley,
      Badurra Wardupalmam.   10

Crow plays and sings, rubs his firesticks together—see his
   track in the skies!—gets up to dance and tap
   his sticks—Wakwak's a dancing man.
Crow taps his sticks, perches on hollow log, dances at
   Garanyula, his camp in the upland forest—   5
      Wardupalma's his clan.
He climbs on Badurra—see his heavenly track! he's
   dancing up above.
   wak wak wak
A flock of crows caw to each other as they eat, then rise   10
   to dance.
Crow perches on Badurra—see his heavenly track!—on
   Maraych; he plays and sings, Wardupalma clansman
   dancing on Badurra.

1982/1990

SHIRLEY HAZZARD
b. 1931

Novelist and short-story writer Shirley Hazzard was born in Sydney but left Australia in 1947, travelling with her diplomat parents, and has spent her adult life living mainly in the US and Italy. She was engaged by British Intelligence at sixteen while living in Hong Kong and was involved in monitoring the civil war in China in 1947–48. From

1952 to 1962 she worked as a clerical employee for the United Nations and later wrote several highly critical books about that institution, including *Defeat of an Ideal* (1973) and *Countenance of Truth* (1990). Her best-known book on the subject is the fictionalised account *People in Glass Houses* (1967).

Hazzard began her career as a writer in the 1950s with short stories published in the *New Yorker*. Her first book was the short-story collection *Cliffs of Fall* (1963); her other novels are *The Bay of Noon* (1970), *The Transit of Venus* (1980) and *The Great Fire* (2003).

Hazzard maintained only an intermittent connection with Australia but was invited to deliver the 1984 Boyer lectures, published the following year as *Coming of Age in Australia*. Her only two works featuring Australia or Australian characters are *The Transit of Venus* and *The Great Fire*. KG

From *People in Glass Houses*
Chapter 2: *The Flowers of Sorrow*

'In my country,' the great man said, looking out over hundreds of uplifted faces, 'we have a song that asks, "Will the flowers of joy ever equal the flowers of sorrow?"'

The speech, up to then, had been the customary exhortation—to uphold the Organization, to apply oneself unsparingly to one's work—and this made for an interesting change. Words like joy and, more especially, sorrow did not often find their way into that auditorium, and were particularly unlooked-for on Staff Day, when the Organization was at its most impersonal. The lifted faces—faces of a certain fatigued assiduity whose contours, dinted with the pressure of administrative detail, suggested habitual submergence beneath a flow of speeches such as this—responded with a faint, corporate quiver. Members of the staff who had been half sleeping when the words reached them were startled into little delayed actions of surprise, and blew their noses or put on their glasses—to show they had been listening. In the galleries, throats were cleared and legs recrossed. The interpreters' voices hesitated in the earphones, then accelerated to take in this departure from the Director-General's prepared text. '*Les fleurs du chagrin*,' said the pretty girl in Booth No. 2; '*Las flores del dolor*,' said the Spanish interpreter, with a shrug towards his assistant.

The man on the rostrum now repeated the words from the song, in his own language—and apparently for his own satisfaction, since throughout the hall only a few very blond heads nodded comprehendingly. He went on in English. 'Perhaps,' he said, 'perhaps the answer to that question is No.' Now there was a long pause. 'But we should remember that sorrow does produce flowers of its own. It is a misunderstanding always to look for joy. One's aim, rather, should be to conduct oneself so that one need never compromise one's secret integrity; so that even our sufferings may enrich us—enrich us, perhaps, most of all.' He had laid his hand across his mimeographed text, which was open at the last page, and for a moment it seemed that he meant to end the speech there. The précis-writers were still scribbling 'our sufferings may enrich us.' However, he looked down, shifted his hand, and went on. He thanked them all for continued devotion to their duties in the past year, and for the productivity illustrated by an increased flow of documentation in the five official languages. There would be no salary raise this year for the Subsidiary Category. The Pension Plan was under review by a newly appointed working group, and the proposed life-insurance scheme would be studied by an impartial committee. It was hoped to extend recreational facilities along the lines recommended by the staff representatives . . . He greatly looked forward to another such meeting with the staff before long.

The speaker stood a few moments with his speech in his hand, inclined his head politely to applause, and withdrew. In the eyes of the world he was a personality—fearless, virtuous, remote—and the ovation continued a little longer without reference to the content of the speech, although some staff members were already filing out and others had begun their complaints while still applauding.

'Scarcely a mention of the proposed change in retirement age.' A burly Belgian youth from Forms Control gave a last angry clap as he moved into the aisle. 'And not a word about longevity increments.' This he said quite fiercely to a Canadian woman, Clelia Kingslake, who had a modest but unique reputation for submitting reports in advance of deadlines.

'That might come under the pension review,' she suggested.

'He would have said so. It's just a move to hold the whole thing over for another year.' He held the heavy glass exit door for her. The vast hallway into which they passed was brightly lit, and thickly carpeted in a golf-links green, 'And what in God's name was all that about flowers?'

They were joined by Mr Matta from Economic Cooperation. 'Yes, what was that?' Mr Matta, from the Punjab, had a high lilting voice like a Welshman's and often omitted the article. 'Has D.G. gone off his head, I wonder?'

A group passed them heading for the elevators. Someone said violently, '. . . not even on the agenda!'

When they arrived at the escalator leading to the cafeteria, Miss Kingslake asked the two men, 'Are you coming up for tea?'

'Maybe later,' said the Belgian boy. 'Must go back to the office and see what's come in with the afternoon distribution.'

'Back to the shop, I'm afraid,' said Mr Matta from Economic Cooperation. 'Our workload has reached the point of boiling.'

Clelia Kingslake, who had greying hair and a light-grey dress, got on the moving stair alone and went up to the cafeteria.

The cafeteria was full. It usually was—and invariably after a staff meeting. Miss Kingslake joined the queue and when her turn came took a tray from the rack and a fork and spoon from the row of metal boxes. First there was a delay (someone ahead was buying containers of coffee for an entire office—a breach of good faith), and then the line moved along so quickly that she found herself at the cake before she had decided what to have. She would have preferred a single piece of bread with jam, but she had passed the butter and it would have been unthinkable to go back for it. So she took down from the glass shelf what seemed to be the largest piece of cake there. A sweet-faced Spanish woman at the tea counter fixed her up with a cup of boiling water and a tea-bag, and she paid.

She wandered out into the centre of the room looking for an empty table. There did not seem to be one, and certainly not one by the windows on the river side. She moved along beside the tables with the unfocused, purposeful step of a sleep-walker. Hot water spilled over into the saucer of her cup.

'Miss Kingslake. Miss Kingslake.'

'Oh Mr Willoughby.'

'I've got a table at the window, if someone hasn't taken it.'

'I thought you'd gone to the Field. I heard your assignment to mission went through.'

'I leave tomorrow night. But not for Santiago after all. That was changed. Let me have your tray. They're sending me to Kuala Lumpur.'

'Thanks, but I'd better not let go. I hadn't heard.'

They made their way through to the windows. She balanced her tray on a corner of his table while he cleared it of the cups, plates and tea-bags discarded by the previous occupants. When he had stacked these on the heating equipment, they sat down.

Claude Willoughby was a spare, fair-haired Anglo-Saxon who resembled nothing so much as a spar of bleached wood washed up on a beach. He was, for so industrious a man, remarkably able. He and Clelia Kingslake had been thrown together in Interim Reports, before her upgrading to Annual Reports and his lateral transfer to the World Commodity Index.

'I might—' he began.

She said at the same moment, 'I'm so glad—'

They both said, 'I'm sorry.'

'You might?' she enquired, squeezing her tea-bag and putting it in the ashtray.

'I was going to say that I might have enquired whether you really wanted to join me. You seemed to be in a trance.'

'I was afraid of seeing someone I didn't want to sit with. Instead, what a nice surprise.' She took two paper napkins from the metal dispenser on the table, and gave him one.

'You were going to say?' he asked. 'Something about being glad?'

'How glad I am, that's all, to see you before you go. I thought you must have left without saying good-bye.'

'I've been terribly busy. Forms, clearances, briefing—and of course my replacement hasn't even been appointed. They're holding the post for an African candidate—or so I'm told. And then, at home—you can imagine— all the packing and storing, added to which we've already taken the children out of school.' Mr Willoughby, having four children of school age, was a substantial beneficiary of the Staff Education Grant. 'But don't let's get into that. And of course I wouldn't have gone without saying good-bye.'

When he had said this, she stared out the window and he turned his head towards the next table, where two officials of the Department of Personnel were getting up from their coffee.

'Shouldn't have said that about the flowers,' one of them remarked—a ginger-haired Dutchman in charge of Clerical Deployment. 'Unnecessary.'

'I should think,' agreed his friend, Mr Andrada from Legal Aspects. 'If I may say so, not good for morale.'

'Particularly that part about the answer being No.'

'Isn't it curious,' Mr Willoughby said to Miss Kingslake, 'how uneasy people are made by any show of feeling in official quarters?' He placed his paper napkin under his cup to absorb spilt tea. 'I suppose they find it inconsistent. What did you think of those remarks today—I mean, about the flowers?'

Miss Kingslake was still looking out at the broad river and the wasteland of factories on its opposite bank. She held the teacup in both hands, her elbows on the table. 'I don't quite know. I think I felt heartened to hear something said merely because it was felt. Something that—wasn't even on the agenda. Still, I did find all that stuff about one's integrity a bit Nordic. After all, it would hardly be possible for most people to get through a working day without compromising their idea of themselves.'

'I think he said "*secret* integrity".' Mr Willoughby drank his tea. 'We can check it tomorrow in the Provisional Verbatim Record.'

'I suppose,' she conceded, 'it would depend on how secret one was prepared to let it become.'

The noise in the cafeteria, like that of a great storm, was beyond all possibility of complaint or remedy. It was a noise in some ways restful to staff members from quiet offices, and Clelia Kingslake was one of these. Eating her cake with a fork, resting her cheek on her left hand, she looked quite at ease—more at ease, in fact, than was appropriate to her type.

'You busy at present?' Mr Willoughby asked her.

'Oh yes,' she said. (It was a question which had never in the Organization's history been known to meet with a negative reply.) 'We're finishing up the report on Methods of Enforcement.'

'How is it this year?'

'A much stronger preamble than the last issue. And some pretty tough recommendations in Appendix III.'

Someone leant over their table. 'You using this chair?'

A group of the interpreters had come in. The interpreters were always objects of interest, their work implying an immediacy denied to the rest of the staff. They stacked their manila folders on the heaters and pushed up extra chairs to the table vacated by the officers of Personnel. Two of them went to fetch tea for the entire table. The rest sat down and began to talk loudly, like children let out of the examination room.

'One could see something was coming when he looked up like that.'

'*Les fleurs du chagrin* . . . I suppose one could hardly have said *Les fleurs du mal* . . .'

A Russian came back with a loaded tray. 'What are you laughing at?'

One of the English interpreters said, 'It would be better not to give us a prepared text at all than to make all these departures from it.'

'What did you think of the speech?' Mr Willoughby asked a white-haired Frenchman who paused to greet him.

'Most interesting.' Mr Raymond-Guiton bowed to Miss Kingslake over his tray. 'And particularly well calculated—that interpolation about the flowers.'

Miss Kingslake said, 'I rather thought that seemed extempore.'

Mr Raymond-Guiton smiled. 'Most interesting.' The repetition of the remark had the effect of diminishing its significance. He passed on with his tray and disappeared behind a screen of latticed plants.

'Now wasn't it he,' Miss Kingslake asked, wrinkling up her brow, 'who refused to go to the Bastille Day party because of his aristocratic connections?'

'You're thinking of that fat chap in the Development Section. This one's too well-bred to do a thing like that. Miss Kingslake, shall we go?'

No sooner had they risen from their chairs than two pale girls in short skirts came up with their trays of tea and cake and started to push the empty dishes aside. Miss Kingslake and Mr Willoughby lost one another briefly in the maze of tables and met again outside the glass doors, in the relative shelter of a magazine stand.

'May I see you to your elevator bank, Miss Kingslake?'

'That would be lovely,' she said.

They went down a short flight of steps and walked slowly along a grey-tiled, grey-walled corridor lined with blue doors.

'I wonder,' she said, 'if we will ever meet again.'

'I have been wondering that too,' he answered without surprise. 'In a place like this there are so many partings and reunions—yet one does find one's way back to the same people again. Rather like those folk dances they organize at Christmas in the Social and Anthropological Department. I feel we shall meet.'

They reached a row of elevator doors. Mr Willoughby pushed the Up button.

She said, as if they were on a railway platform, 'Don't wait.'

'I really should get back to the office,' he said, 'and see if my Travel Authorization's come in yet.'

'Of course.'

'Shall we say good-bye, then?'

'Why yes,' she said, but did not say good-bye.

A Down elevator stopped but no one got off. A messenger boy went slowly past wheeling a trolley of stiff brown envelopes.

'Miss Kingslake,' Mr Willoughby said. 'Miss Kingslake. Once, in this corridor, I wanted very much to kiss you.'

She stood with her back to the grey wall as if she took from it her protective colouring.

He smiled. 'We were on our way to the Advisory Commission on Administrative and Budgetary Questions.'

Now she smiled too, but sadly, clasping her fingers together over the handle of her bag. This prevented him from taking her hand, and he merely nodded his farewell. She had not spoken at all—he had gone quite a way down the corridor before that occurred to her. He was out of sight by the time the elevator arrived.

'Thirty-seven,' she announced, getting in.

Someone touched her shoulder. 'So good to see you, Miss Kingslake,' It was Mr Quashie from Archives.

'Oh, Mr Quashie.'

Mr Quashie, wearing a long, light-coloured robe and scrolling a document lightly between his palms, moved up to stand beside her. 'I suppose you were at the meeting?'

'I was, yes.'

'I thought the D.-G. looked tired.' Mr Quashie stepped aside to let someone get out. 'But then—I hadn't seen him since he addressed the staff last Human Dignity Day.'

'Nor had I.'

'What a job he has. One wonders how anyone stands it. No private life at all. What did you think of the speech, by the way?'

'Quite good. And you?'

'Oh—here's my floor.' Mr Quashie glanced up at the row of lighted numbers. 'I didn't hear much of it. We were busy in the office, and I stayed to answer the phones. Getting off, please. Getting off. And then I took the wrong staircase in the conference building. So I only came in at the very end. I was just in time to hear about the flowers, you know. About how we need more flowers of joy.'

1967

CHRISTOPHER KOCH
b. 1932

Christopher Koch was born and educated in Hobart. After two years in England, the first of many travels abroad, he returned to Australia in 1957 and joined the ABC as a producer of radio broadcasts for schools. As with many Tasmanian writers, his home state—its unique geography, dramatic history and metaphorical power as an island—looms large in his work, as reflected by the title of his first novel, *The Boys in the Island* (1958). His second, *Across the Sea Wall* (1965), is set partly in India and marks the beginning of Koch's extensive treatment in his fiction of Australia's relationship with Asia.

This was further extended, and Koch's reputation firmly established, by *The Year of Living Dangerously* (1978), which was made into a feature film in 1982. This novel is set in Indonesia in 1965, just before the fall of Suharto, and encompasses a number of the features that characterise Koch's work: Asian–Australian relations, spirituality, doubleness and balance, the responsibilities of journalism and reportage, and the fate of individual lives caught up in the forces of history.

After *The Doubleman* (1985), which has some of these features and which the Catholic Koch has described as his 'most Catholic' book, Koch published a collection of essays, *Crossing the Gap* (1987), which investigates such issues further. The highly successful *Highways to a War* (1995), whose doomed hero Mike Langford is partly modelled on the legendary cameraman Neil Davis, is set during and after the wars that ravaged Vietnam and Cambodia and revisits that history in its representation of a particular kind of single-mindedness and dedication to an idea.

Highways to a War and Koch's next novel, *Out of Ireland* (1999), form a diptych entitled *Beware the Past*. The same narrative trope is employed in *Out of Ireland*; each is a tale with its roots in Tasmania, where the elusive hero has left a documentary trail—diaries, written or taped—for his investigator and double to follow. Koch continued his writerly investigation of the Irish strand of his heritage with the travel memoir *The Many-Coloured Land: A return to Ireland* (2002). KG

From *The Year of Living Dangerously*
Chapter 17

[. . .] It was just a flat stretch of road beside a row of small Dutch-style commercial buildings, with galvanised-iron veranda awnings: beyond them were the houses of a kampong. Nothing unusual; he had seen a hundred similar scenes in the past four days; yet tonight the dark doorways of these little shops, where coconut-oil and kerosene lamps burned, were mysterious and novel to Hamilton. An old pedlar in a conical straw hat sat behind a tray of gleaming red peppers and beans, his slyly humorous, upturned face seeming to wait for applause, as though the trays contained gems; and Hamilton was enchanted by him, and by everything here; by the gentle evening heat, and the composite odour of Java: clove-smoke of the *kreteks*, and nutty tang of human flesh, innocent as that of the high-piled vegetables.

He saw a light, from the corner of his eye. Looking past the end of the line of shops, he found that it was the screen of a *wayang kulit* show, floating in the dark near the kampong.

He had seen these before, from the car, but had always passed them by: he knew that the *wayang* was in old Javanese, and thus completely incomprehensible. It had never occurred to him to look at one; they had not interested him, and anyway he had felt vaguely that they were out of bounds, an experience he could not enter. But tonight he had a sudden desire to approach the screen and watch with the village crowd: he was drawn towards the light.

The *wayang* had been set up in a clearing beyond the last shop, its lit screen hanging in the dark like that of a drive-in cinema. Approaching, Hamilton heard the gonging of *gamelan* instruments, and the guttural cries of the puppets. When he came to the edges of the crowd, brown faces turned and studied him briefly; then, grave and intent, they turned back to the screen, re-entering their ancient dream of the Kingdom of Dwarawati, Gate of the World, Kresna's kingdom, whose mountains are highest, women most beautiful, soil most fertile, men most noble. This had been their cinema since the time of Java's ancient Hindu kingdoms, and it seemed to Hamilton to have a weird modernity: a video-machine from an unknown civilisation. At the edges of the *wayang* show's arc of light were other small lights, where little stalls sold *saté* and cigarettes. People laughed together; came and went; children dodged among their legs. A line of flying-foxes glided overhead, like magic animals which had escaped from the screen into the air.

He had approached from the side of the screen where the priestly puppet-master worked, with his humble *gamelan* orchestra behind him. Three white-clad men played a wooden xylophone, a fiddle, and drums, while a thin woman with an infant at the breast and a cigarette slanting from her mouth worked with her free hand on a set of bronze gongs. The *dalang* was a small, stern man in spectacles and a ceremonial cap of midnight blue: above his head, a pressure-lamp, the source of the radiance, hung from a rope; rows of *wayang* puppets were stuck into yellow-green banana logs below the screen, waiting for their entrances, from the left and the right. Sheaves of rice (tribute for Dewi Sri) hung from each end of the screen. In the *dalang's* upraised hands two of the flat, ornate figures in which Billy Kwan had tried vainly to interest Hamilton were moving now with uncanny life. With a chock held between his toes, the master of the shadows knocked constantly for attention on the side of his puppet-box: *tun-tun*; *tuk-tuk*.

People pressed close to watch the sacred theatre's mysteries; but Hamilton drifted away to the other side of the screen, to the magic side, where only the filigreed silhouettes could be seen, their insect profiles darting, looming into hugeness, or dwindling to vanishing-point. Their voices chattered things he could never understand, rising into the warm dark: but the schoolroom rapping on the puppet-box commanded his attention. Standing behind solemn elders from the kampong, for whom chairs had been placed on the grass, he seemed to be watching the deeply important activity of dreams.

The *dalang* was singing. His wailing, almost female voice climbed higher and higher, while the little drum pattered on underneath, and the gongs bubbled. On one wavering note, his voice was drawn out and out, until Hamilton, transfixed, seemed to see it like a bright thread against eternal sky; until it connected with Heaven. What was the *dalang* singing about? He would never know. Usually bored by things he could not understand, he could not now bring himself to return to the car; he lingered, locked in delight. The figures of this dream of Java's childhood tantalised him with the notion that he *ought* to know them, *ought* to recall them, from some other life. And they woke in him now a long-buried memory of his own.

At eight years old, he said, in hospital with appendicitis, he had been alarmed by the noises of the ward at night: agonised coughing, groans, distant crashes. And he had hidden behind comic books his elder brother had brought him, erecting them on his chest like screens between himself and the unthinkable landscape beyond his bed. He had not wanted to hear the coughing of the old man dying in the bed next to him; he had not wanted to smell his bedpan, or hear the bubbling of his bowels. And there came back to him now the peculiar affection he had felt for those little figures in the comic books which could make him forget what lay beyond their pages. He had followed Mickey Mouse and Tarzan and the Phantom from frame to frame (as he now followed the darting figures in the lit frame of the *wayang*) with mysterious pleasure, but without comprehension, whispering like runes the phrases they spoke. And it occurred to him now, Hamilton said, that the *wayang* frame was perhaps erected here for the same reason that he had propped his comic-book-screen on his chest: so that the people of the kampong could forget, for a whole night, the presences of hunger and pain and threat at the edges of their green world. He glanced about at the still brown faces with an affectionate compassion which was new to him. And he would ask me later: 'What can we *do* for them, Cookie?' The question was rhetorical, but it was genuinely felt.

A delicately built, Hindu-faced man of about thirty, with oiled, curly hair and a small moustache, was standing at Hamilton's elbow; suddenly he held out the rolled leaf of a *kretek*, speaking softly in Bahasa. Hamilton did not hear what he said; but he took the *kretek*, and thanked him. It tasted not unpleasant, he found, this clove-spiced cigarette of the poor. He had never smoked one before.

The moustached man spoke again, and Hamilton's limited Bahasa was sufficient for him to understand that he was being asked if he liked the *wayang*; he said that he did, and they watched for a time in intimate silence. Smiling at him from time to time with an appearance of remarkable fondness, the moustached man offered soft remarks about the story, some of which Hamilton understood. This was the first part, his companion said, which would run until midnight. (They were watching the court scenes, which correspond to the period of man's foolish youth.) At midnight, the hero Arjuna would enter, and the comical dwarf, Semar: you should wait for this, he told Hamilton.

The figures of India's great Pandava story, transformed into weird cartoons, formally addressed each other, laughed and wept, prepared for battle in their chariots. Ogres who were coarse as Westerners ranted and broke wind, while the audience laughed derisively. Hamilton was introduced to the *Wayang* of the Right and the *Wayang* of the Left, who are in constant conflict. Kings with butterfly wings ascended into the air; evil spirits invaded the screen from the bottom, while the *dalang* narrated all in the deep tones of a father; growled; was shrill; sang.

But Hamilton would not be there when the Pandava brothers, led by Arjuna (a saturnine gnat, bow in hand), did battle with their cousins, the 99 evil Kaurawas; and he would never learn how Arjuna, through deep meditation, upsets the whole balance of nature—building up his *sakti*, the spirit-power which animates the universe—to bring on storms and earthquakes. Neither would he see Dwarf Semar, the god in mis-shapen form, whose breasts are female, sitting in tears: he would never understand Dwarf Semar's grief. All these things would come after midnight, at their appointed time; but Hamilton decided he must leave to book into a hotel in the city. [...]

1978

VIVIAN SMITH
b. 1933

Vivian Smith was born in Hobart. He graduated with a master's degree from the University of Tasmania, where he taught French for ten years. In 1967 he moved to Sydney to work in the English department of the University of Sydney. He retired, as reader in English, in 1996. Smith is a poet, and a noted critic and anthologist. He has published monographs on James McAuley (qv), Vance and Nettie Palmer (qv), and the American poet Robert Lowell. Among his many anthologies, Smith edited a number of important 'regional' anthologies, including *Sydney's Poems* (1992, with Robert Gray (qv)) and *Windchimes: Asia in Australian poetry* (2006, with Noel Rowe). He also wrote the poetry section of *The Oxford History of Australian Literature* (1981).

Although he is not a prolific poet, or one attracted to literary fashion, Smith's work has been especially popular with critics and other poets. His collections include *Tide Country* (1982) and *Along the Line* (2006). His poetry is precise in observation, rooted in a sense of place (especially Tasmania and Sydney), and sometimes melancholy in tone. His work can also be satirical, and the darkness of history or the unknown regions of the self can often be intuited in his light-filled poems. His poems' clarity should not blind the reader to their complexity. He has also published a number of skilful translations. *DM*

Balmoral Summer

All day the weight of summer and the shrill
spaced flight of jet planes climbing north.
The news at half past twelve brought further crimes.
Insane dictators threaten new disasters.

The light of summer with its bone white glare   5
and pink hibiscus in the yacht club garden.
The beach is strewn with bodies of all sizes.
How the sight of human nudity surprises—
cleft buttock, shaved armpit, nipple hair.

The heat haze hovers over Grotto Point   10
and skiers skim the violent flat water;
incredible the feats that art demands.

Submarines surface to refuel
around this headland in a small bay's stillness.
History encroaches like an illness.   15
And children chase the gulls across the sand.

1978

Tasmania

Water colour country. Here the hills
rot like rugs beneath enormous skies
and all day long the shadows of the clouds
stain the paddocks with their running dyes.

In the small valleys and along the coast,   5
the land untamed between the scattered farms,
deconsecrated churches lose their paint
and failing pubs their fading coats of arms.

Beyond the beach the pine trees creak and moan,
in the long valley poplars in a row,   10
the hills breathing like a horse's flank
with grasses combed and clean of the last snow.

1982

Sydney Perhaps

I

Equivalent in feeling, light and sky,
a Roman morning, fifteen years ago
returns with the clear weight of summer air,
the tang of something dry in copied pines,
dust or oil, a rustling feathered palm,   5
the heat haze hanging over Mosman Bay.

II

Often reminded now of somewhere else,
my growing stock of slow comparisons
holds in this down sloping narrow street
the remnants of a walk towards the *Fram*:[1]
a suburb garden trim with picket fence,   5
assorted shrubs, a violence of flowers.

III

Jacarandas and huge moreton bays
with elephants still hiding behind trunks
open the gardens to the Library.
The botany, equestrian monuments,
the relics of colonial heritage: 5
it could be Buenos Aires in November.

2006

KEVIN GILBERT
1933–1993

Born in Wiradjuri country at Condobolin, NSW, Kevin Gilbert was a leading poet, playwright, essayist, editor and political activist. Raised by relatives and in welfare homes after he was orphaned at seven, he worked as a seasonal agricultural worker and station manager. In 1957 he was sentenced to life imprisonment when his wife was killed in a domestic dispute.

Gilbert learned to read while in prison and became interested in art and literature. He discovered a gift for lino printmaking and is considered to be the first Aboriginal printmaker. In 1968, while still in prison, he wrote the first play by an Aboriginal author: *The Cherry Pickers* (1971/1988). Gilbert was paroled in 1971 and *The Cherry Pickers* was performed in August that year in Sydney, the first production of an Aboriginal play. He disowned the 1971 publication of his poems, *End of Dreamtime*, as his editor made significant alterations without permission. The corrected volume, *People Are Legends: Aboriginal poems* (1978), is considered to be Gilbert's first authorised collection of poetry.

---

1   A ship used in Arctic and Antarctic expeditions by Norwegian explorers between 1893 and 1912.

Gilbert joined the Aboriginal Black Power movement and played an important role in establishing the 1972 Aboriginal Tent Embassy in Canberra. Beginning with *Because a White Man'll Never Do It* (1973), he wrote and edited a number of political works arguing for Aboriginal land rights and the restoration of Aboriginal cultural and spiritual autonomy. His oral history *Living Black: Blacks talk to Kevin Gilbert* (1977) won the 1978 National Book Council Award. In 1988 he coordinated the Treaty '88 Campaign and wrote *Aboriginal Sovereignty: Justice, the law and the land*, promoting Aboriginal sovereignty and a treaty.

Many of Gilbert's books combine art, photography and language. He helped to organise the photographic exhibition *Inside Black Australia*, and used this title for a ground-breaking anthology of Aboriginal poetry, which won HREOC's 1988 Human Rights Award for Literature. Gilbert refused the award, protesting that his people were still deprived of human rights in their own land. The Kevin Gilbert Memorial Trust was established in 1993 to advance his political, literary and artistic aspirations. His other books include *Child's Dreaming* (1992) and *Black from the Edge* (1994). *AH/PM*

People *Are* Legends

Kill the legend
Butcher it
With your acute cynicisms
Your paternal superfluities
With your unwise wisdom   5
Kill the legend
Obliterate it
With your atheism
Your fraternal hypocrisies
With your primal urge of miscegenation   10
Kill the legend
Devaluate it
With your sophistry
Your baseless rhetoric
Your lusting material concepts   15
Your groundless condescension
Kill it
Vitiate the seed
Crush the root-plant
All this   20
And more you must needs do
In order
To form a husk of a man
To the level and in your own image
Whiteman   25

1978

From *The Cherry Pickers*
Act 3, Scene 2

At the old Cherry Tree—King Eagle.

King Eagle stands down stage, right of centre. He is a huge old cherry tree with twisted boughs wrought with life's growth. His leaves are plentiful but brown and dying off.

Lighting simulates a hot parched atmosphere. Tall sparse tussocks of grass are wilted and browned by the summer heat.

A breeze moves the leaves and small eddies of dust.

A whisper of Aboriginal tribal music is heard, didgeridoo and bullroarer. Faint voices moan in corroboree, spirits from the past.

TOMMLO enters. Looking directly at audience, he stares unseeing, discomfortingly hard at them. He glances around the orchard and stares again at audience with look of despair, pain, hopelessness, as his face reflects his inner loss and uncertainty. In his left hand is an old carved Churinga stone. Bullroarer sounds softly as he places the stone on the ground reverently. He faces King Eagle, rips at his clothes and discards upper sections. He approaches King Eagle in small quick nimble steps, whirls around, facing audience, and angrily throws away his belt and trousers. He whirls around in several flexing leaps. Tempo and volume of tribal music ascends. He scoops up a handful of earth, swirls it towards base of tree, slaps leg with right hand in time to haunting didgerridoo and corroboree chants. As he faces audience, music fades.

TOMMLO: [*yelling*] ZEENA! Zeena—ZEEEENNNAAA!!!! What the bloody hell is taking you so long? ZEENNAAA!!!

ZEENA: [*off-stage*] Alright, ALRIGHT! I'm coming Tommlo.

[*Enter ZEENA, carrying a cumbersome bundle: A sugar-bag, a brown paper parcel and two spears under her arms.*]

I get on OK in my rightful role as your gin and your wife Tommlo, but I am *not* accustomed to acting as a bloody myall bush donkey or workhorse for you!

TOMMLO: It's the woman's place to carry the family possessions, Zeena.

ZEENA: Since when has the woman have to carry the flamin' spears? You didn't carry any.

TOMMLO: Zeena, I had to carry the Bullroarer and the Sacred Churinga stone that I found on Corroboree Hill.

ZEENA: How do you know it *is* a Sacred Churinga? Just because you 'found' it in the old place?

TOMMLO: This is *not* the time—or the place to argue. I *know*—I—*feel* it, woman. I feel it an' recognise it for what it *is*!

ZEENA: Recognise it do you? *Your* feelings have been wrong before today. Remember Kathy and your feelings that you were *meant* for each other?

That was until I smashed a wine bottle on your thick head for being so damned silly!

TOMMLO: OK OK!! I was wrong then—but that feeling sprung from my guts. This one is straight from my heart!

ZEENA: [*laughing*] Not your *guts* Tommlo, but from what hangs from it! I never realised that you'd grown so you could tell the difference between the heart and the other part of the body that makes you do the things you do!

TOMMLO: [*pained, accusing*] Zeena, Zeena, *our* People are dying. We've lost our way. Their hearts are breaking because they have been denied justice and human rights, because they have been denied their rightful place in this our land and—the only thing you can contribute is your silly laughter!!

ZEENA: [*hurt*] Tommlo? That's not right, Tommlo. I'll do anythin' to help them. I want to stop the starvation, the needless dyin', the endless pain too. I *do*!!

TOMMLO: Undress! Get those skirts off!

ZEENA: This is impossible! Tommlo, we can't go back in time!

TOMMLO: We can *change* things. We *have* to change things. It is our destiny to find our human way.

ZEENA: I *want* to help. I would do any thing Tommlo to have stopped our babies from dying. I would do anything to bring my babies back to life and make our living easier—*but we can't!! We can't go back. We can't change what has happened!!*

TOMMLO: We've got to. We've *got to find our place*!! Our rightful place. Not a 'place' where we've been kicked and trodden, smashed and starved, killed and conquered until we take the shape of whitemen—*imitation whitemen*. I'm a *man*!! I'm gunna *live* as a man, and by the livin' Jesus I'm gunna *die* as a man! I'm gunna *fight* for the right for my kids to *live*, and to live as *whole* human beings!!!

ZEENA: They were *my* babies too, Tommlo. Mine too!!!

[TOMMLO *springs towards the base of the huge tree, he pulls the tussocks of grass together then springs back and rips open the brown paper parcel.* ZEENA *sits slumped with head in hands, emotionally overcome, near the parcels and spears.* TOMMLO *tears a small decorated shield from parcel, picks up bullroarer, leaps to pile of grass. He rubs the bullroarer on the shield to spark off the fire.* ZEENA *has slowly, tiredly, risen and removed her blouse.*]

TOMMLO: Enough!! This *has* to be done!

ZEENA: [*defiantly*] If it *has* to be done, then why ain't you and I, two Australian Aborigines, dancing this Sacred Dance under an Australian gum-tree? A gum-tree with the Sacred Bora Ground symbols carved deep into its guts? *We* two are corroboreeing beneath a cherry-tree. Doesn't this prove

that *some* advance has been made because 'cherry tree' means money—
and food?

> [TOMMLO *leaps up in fury and cuffs* ZEENA *across the head with his open hand.*]

TOMMLO: Shut up!!

> [*He goes to the sugar-bag, picks up a wooden boondi and a glass jar containing gum 'blood'. He passes the boondi and jar to* ZEENA *and commands—*]

Now!!

ZEENA: This blood has jellied together!

TOMMLO: Use it!

> [*He kneels, facing audience, hands at side, head back.* ZEENA's *face twists as she dips the boondi applicator into the jar of 'blood' and taps it rapidly on his shoulders. As sufficient 'blood' flows on, she quickly presses featherdown onto the 'blood' to form patterns.*]

TOMMLO: [*pained*] *You* don't believe our culture should exist, either?!!

ZEENA: [*tremulous, positive*] I! Of *course* I believe our old culture should exist!—Culture is the development of man, it is the outward expression of man's inner beauty and is relevant to—and through *every* age!

> [ZEENA *rapidly taps his arms, his thighs and decorates with down.*]

TOMMLO: Then *what* are you complaining about?

ZEENA: Oh, I'm not complaining. I am merely trying to tell you that we can't live, nor find a new life, by embracing a stone-age identity in this nuclear age. We should be rightfully proud of our old culture for it was the expression, the cry, the search for beauty by man. *This truth* we should hold and advance by, not revert to that cultural age. We must advance, must mature and must never, never revert back, for life is a constant process of growth.

TOMMLO: Our growth has been stopped—through this we can grow again! We have nothing save our culture. We *must* git back our culture!!

ZEENA: [*sorrowfully, gently*] Our culture, the age of our culture has passed for we have outgrown it! Man must go forward, must advance with the times, the age!

TOMMLO: We *must* keep our identity! Without it we have *lost all. Do* you see us advance?

> [TOMMLO *attempts to light fire again.*]

ZEENA: [*listlessly*] I have some Federal safety matches here, Tommlo. They'll be much quicker.

TOMMLO: [*savagely*] *This* is how it *has* to be done. Now shut up and git undressed!!

ZEENA: *No. No!!* Not everything. *Not Everything!!*

TOMMLO: Everything! The lot! Git the bloody lot orf! Are you frightened that God made your body black, ugly and unclean so it can't face the clean air of day without shame!! *Are you ashamed of your black body?!*

ZEENA: I—No! It's not *that* but I—

TOMMLO: Then show yourself as you were made, woman!

> [TOMMLO *leaps to the hessian sugar-bag, pulls out rings of red, white, black feathered symbols placing them either side of the tussock at the base of the tree, parallel with a perpendicular blaze of a white feathered shaft, as* ZEENA *slowly, hesitantly undresses.*]

Help me. Come on woman, help me with these!

ZEENA: No woman is allowed to touch the Sacred Churinga symbols. To touch is to die.

TOMMLO: It is *different* now. There is no one left out of our tribespeople to help me!

> [TOMMLO *moves at a furious leaping pace, kicking aside sticks, leaves, grass and pushes the circlet symbols into the earth. He leaps to the paper parcel, grabs several feathers and forms arm-leg patterns on circlets, while* ZEENA, *in a leaping crouch, places the other symbols beside him. She squats on ground, hands between legs, and zig-zags in kangaroo hops between the symbols. Occasionally she sits up, scratches ribs with forepaws, nibbles at grass.* TOMMLO *has begun his corroboree. Aboriginal ghost music ascends.* ZEENA *sits upright, scratches rib in kangaroo pose.*]

ZEENA: This is wrong, only *learned* ones can do this!

TOMMLO: [*corroboreeing*] Uh—uh—gnhuuu—there are *no* Learned Ones left, therefore *we* must do it!!

> [ZEENA *moves again in the Kangaroo dance.*]

ZEENA: But I am a *woman* and the sacred ceremonies would not produce miracles if a woman was even present in the old days.

> [TOMMLO *leaps behind her, spear upraised as he stalks his sacrificial victim, corroboreeing, leaping thrusting the aim of the spear.*]

TOMMLO: The old days have *gone!*

> [TOMMLO *leaps forward, twirls, springs again toward her his spear ready to thrust—he stops, as if confused, as she glances up at him.*]

ZEENA: No!! No!!! What are you doing?? If the old days are gone, then what are you doin', what *are* we doin' here???

TOMMLO: It's alright! We're doin' what we *must*, now *shut up!!—Dance!!*

ZEENA: Six strong warriors and the Songman must attend these rites. You are no Songman an' I am no Warrior.

TOMMLO: Our Songmen have all died. Only you and I believe, and it is said: 'Where two or three are gathered together in *my* name …'

ZEENA: God said that, *not* the Corroboree Men.

TOMMLO: This dance isn't for the Corroboree Men either. It's for *us*, a People. It's for us *blacks* and our right to live!!!

ZEENA: This is wrong, Tommlo. We can't go back in time and change things!

TOMMLO: We can't go back in time—but we can bring time back to us. Dance, dance!! Keep movin' or so help me Christ!!

[*Tribal music ascends.*]

ZEENA: [*afraid*] Those were cave-age days, the Stone Age. This—this is an anachronism! The truths from the beginning of time—the truth of two hundred years ago can't be given rebirth and become the truth applicable to today!

TOMMLO: *This* is not the time to argue! What are you trying to say?

ZEENA: I can't say it. Do you remember the poem that Bidjarng wrote? The one about true *truth* and each man's right being another's wrong?

TOMMLO: So what the hell does that mean?

ZEENA: [*reciting*]

> I *know* you're right—when you claim I'm wrong
> that I'm out of tune with your own sad song
> For you *believe* and to me, it seems
> that your feet of clay keeps your heart from dreams
> and away from a Nobler Truth.
> Yet you believe, and I know I know
> that man must crawl before he grows
> and man must *leap* and often fall
> yet aeons pass and *still* you crawl
> *still* you believe
> and I know, I grieve—I know.

[*The last words are uttered as a sob-sighing of spirit.*]

TOMMLO: What does all that supposed to mean?

ZEENA: It means the Jews shouldn't go and build a Golden Calf again, just because it belongs to a story in Moses' time. Nor should we attempt to imprison the spirit of man, nor his attempts to mature. Just because we *believe* something, doesn't necessarily mean it is right. It is little more than one hundred years ago since a high court in England tried a pig, yes, an animal on a charge of witchcraft. The pig had to stand in the dock—and the court found it guilty as charged and sentenced it to be burnt!!!

The poem means we should grow out of superstition. It means we should not crawl forever, nor leap, then crawl back into the protective past and become blinded by cowardice and bigotry, too afraid to grow again, to leap again. It means we should leap to our full height. We might fall, but we must be prepared to fall and leap again. We must hold to a truth only until such time as we can think it out and then supersede it by a higher truth.

TOMMLO: Zeena, this is not just for the old culture. This is for the goin' forward. This is our hope for a People. It means we find we're trapped—and we've *got to leap*. Without hope, without justice, without *true identity* a People die! *Come dance!! Dance!! Dance!!!*

[ZEENA *remains squatting.*]

Don't you understand, Zeena? I've looked at life, the world, the whiteman's way. I've looked through a whiteman's eyes and I was lost. [*Pause.*] I ain't lost anymore. I am a *nothing*. The trees, the grass, the river, the earth is life, is *everything*. I am *nothing*, a *nothing*. Now that tree is *me*. It is all of me. I am that tree. I am nothing, yet I am somethin' because the earth is me. These rocks are me and I am the movin' soul of them all. See, I looked at the tree and said that is a tree. I kept it all separate and alien, but now, like the old days, I am a nothing but that *tree* is me and I am a something and when I die I will flow into the creative essence that made *me*, the tree and all created life, for we are all inseparable. I have come home, Zeena. I am *me*, a nothing, that tree is *me*. I have come home because the infinite living immortal *essence* of all life is *me*. I am the moving soul and the truth of me is the truer truth that Our People will find.

It's not going back to the 'Stone Age', it's flowing our soul back to the Beginning, the Dreaming, being one with the Presence of the undying Spirit. Why did them Old People of ours sit in the ashes and chant their chants? Whitemen call it 'yuckaiing', but our Old Ones know it's calling the Spirit. You want to talk in poems, hey? Listen then to this:

> By my campfire at night with the heavens in sight
> with the Great Serpent Spirit a-star
> I sing songs of love to the Presence within
> as it plays with the sparks in my fire!

[*Silence.*]

That's what we had. That's what we have to regain. *Now dance!! Dance!! Dance!!!*

[TOMMLO *follows* ZEENA *with spear poised—she moves into a frenzied tempo—the kangaroo trying to evade its hunter—*TOMMLO *leaps to the small fire, picks up the Churinga stone, rubs the designs quickly. Background tribal music and chanting heightens.* TOMMLO *holds Churinga in left hand, pulls* ZEENA *back by grasping her hair. He cuts her upper arms in initiation, her breasts. He hauls her to her feet, springs away in a weaving corroboree midst the circlets—their tempo increases as* ZEENA *follows him in the dance. He now weaves in high stepping, feet stamping, kangaroo hopping motion.*]

TOMMLO: Yuck—aiee—Ba—ai—mee—Yulangarrah—God—Doungudieeee. Dance— dance—dance—dance. Zeena—dance!!

PHONSO: [*off-stage*] Johnollo—John-o-llo—John-o-llo—o—John-o-llo—

ZEENA: They are comin'! Oh, oh my dress!!

[*She snatches her dress.*]

TOMMLO: You spoke of Truth and the times, Zeena. Your body is not a shameful thing. This land is *our* Garden of Eden. We were created here in this land. We'll restore our place, we'll restore our place, we'll find *our* God again, a new and true way, Zeena, and no man will stop us!

[ZEENA *drops the dress, places her arms about him in a quick embrace. He caresses her hair, gently pushes her away. He picks up the bullroarer, the sacred circlets, places them quickly back on the ground, gathers his pants, leaps to pick up* ZEENA's *dress, clasps his spears.* TOMMLO *and* ZEENA *move slowly gracefully and exit.*]

1988

Redfern

In the savage streets of Redfern
where the 'cockatoo' and turk
peer from the doors of porno dens
while dealers do their work
dicing out a score or two   5
and wait with bated breath
the coins or coppers to descend
in thrills of sudden death

A country girl in fear subdued
reels bloodied from a lane   10
to strains of raucous laughter
boomeranging 'come again'
the crows with forks awaiting
thin strips of lusting meat
to pay the bill of vice-squad men   15
grown fat on Redfern street

In the ghetto streets of Redfern
prowls the battler on the dole
the Blacks still free come morning
who survived the night patrol   20
and paddy-wagon coffins
who only ply their trade
where politicians don't count votes
police training grounds are made

From the ghetto streets of Redfern   25
which abound with rats and mice
comes a wail—a human wailing
that is surging strong and nice
of people grown angry
tired of horror and the pain   30
marching to a bicentenary
armed to blow apart the chains

with a mop in hand
a bucket and something more besides
in the grandest celebration   35
for the 'free' door opening wide
In the savage streets of Redfern
coils a Taipan poised to strike
the fangs are readied, gleaming
in the alley-ways at night.   40
    1990

Me and Jackomari Talkin' About Land Rights

He said
Don't be like the rest of 'em bud
a big loose mouth or a pen
Who's gonna lead us ... and lead ya must
to git us our right place again   5
we're sick of the pain and the sneerin'
tired of bein' treated like dirt
we ain't fifth-raters—we're human
'cept they keep up the cripplin' an' hurt ...
say what is the *word* for us Blacks now   10
where are we goin' to turn
if you're like the rest Christ help us—

I replied
Men have died in less hope brother
LAND justice is our cause   15
don't tremble at the sound of drums
or cringe at thought of wars
stand yourself up fiercely
gather strength from all your grief
and terrorise injustice if you must   20
to cure the thief ...
and we'll stand there beside you
our land will glow applause
the big mouths too will join and lead
and pens turn into swords   25
our women with their eyes aglow
their suckling babes at breast
will MARCH AND BURN AND BLEED AND WEEP
AND WIN before we rest.
    1990

Tree

I am the tree
the lean hard hungry land
the crow and eagle
sun and moon and sea
I am the sacred clay   5
which forms the base
the grasses vines and man
I am all things created
I am you and
you are nothing   10
but through me the tree
you are
and nothing comes to me
except through that one living gateway
to be free   15
and you are nothing yet
for all creation
earth and God and man
is nothing
until they fuse   20
and become a total sum of something
together fuse to consciousness of all
and every sacred part aware
alive
in true affinity   25
                                               1990

Speech at the Aboriginal Tent Embassy, Canberra

It's twenty-five years since we Aboriginal People have had Australian citizenship imposed upon us, very much against the will of the Aboriginal People, for we have always been Australian Aborigines, not Aboriginal Australians.

We have never joined the company. We have never claimed citizenship of the oppressor, the people who have invaded our country.

Twenty-five years after this citizenship, which was supposed to give us some sort of rights and equality we see that instead of lifting us to any sort of degree of place or right it has only given us the highest infant mortality rate, the highest number of Aboriginal people in prison, the highest mortality rate, the highest unemployment rate.

And after twenty-five years we still have Aboriginal children and people dying from lack of clean drinking water, lack of medication, lack of shelter.

We have still had twenty-five years of economic, political and medical human rights apartheid in Australia. And it hasn't worked for Aboriginal People.

At the end of the twenty-five years, we have seen the Australian Government and the Australian people try and get off the hook of responsibility by saying, ten years down the track, we'll have Reconciliation.

And Reconciliation doesn't promise us human rights, it doesn't promise us our Sovereign rights or the platform from which to negotiate, and it doesn't promise us a viable land base, an economical base, a political base, or a base in which we can again heal our people, where we can carry out our cultural practices.

It is ten more years of death! There must be something better.

Australia is calling for a Republic and a new flag, a new vision. It cannot have a vision. It cannot have a new flag. It cannot have a Sovereign nation until it addresses the right of Aboriginal People, the Sovereign Land Rights of Aboriginal people.

You cannot build a vision, you cannot build a land, you cannot build a people, on land theft, on massacre, on continuing apartheid and the denial of the one group of Aboriginal people.

We have committed no crime, we have done no wrong except own the land which the churches and white society want to take from us.

It must change.

And we can never become, and we never will become, Australian citizens. For we are Aboriginal People. We are Sovereign Aboriginal People. […]

1992

Song of Dreamtime

With our didgeridoos
in the heart of night
we piped to our God our song
our sacred chants filled the ever-Now
The Beginning covenant   5
The Essence of the presence
Our Dreaming Spirits Flow
and we held His hands
in the heart of night
and walked by His side at day   10
we rejoiced with His sacred angels
as they danced in the trees and clay

and leapt with love in the quivering stars
shimmered the trembling leaves
became a part of pirouetting waves   15
and the roar of the sea's great heaves.
Our sacred chants filled the ever-Now
we sang and danced with God
and loved with Him creation's gift
Our Dreaming Spirits Flow.   20
Hand in hand to the hunt were we
knee to knee in love
heart to heart in our sacred chant
all sacred our sacred mud
eye to eye in our testament   25
hand in hand the Son
we children of the one Great God
who fell to the vandals' gun.
Their poisoned flour sapped our lives
their greed stole our sacred land   30
but they couldn't change our chants to hate
our love to a less than grand
they could not steal our sacred song
nor make our God depart
nor raise His hand in vengeance   35
to those who kill our heart
while ever our pipes speak to His Being
while ever our camp-fires glow
He'll dance and laugh and cry with us
while His lost white children grow   40
and seek and learn to know His face
where the fire's red embers leap
He'll bring them yet to His covenant
and a Dreaming that they'll keep.

1994

FAY ZWICKY
b 1933

Fay Zwicky was born in Melbourne in 1933. She began studying the piano at the age of four, and was playing in public from the age of six. She studied at the University of Melbourne (1950–54) and subsequently worked as both a concert pianist (until 1965) and a literature teacher. She has worked in Indonesia, America and Europe, and at the University of Western Australia, where she was a lecturer and senior lecturer in English (1972–87). Zwicky began publishing poems regularly in 1969. She has published six volumes of poetry, a volume of short stories, a collection of essays, *The Lyre in the Pawnshop* (1986), and edited a number of poetry anthologies, including *Journeys* (1982), an anthology of poems by Judith Wright, Rosemary Dobson, Gwen Harwood and Dorothy Hewett (qqv). Since *Poems 1970–1992* (1993) Zwicky has published two collections of poetry: *The Gatekeeper's Wife* (1997) and *Picnic* (2006). Her work often concerns a tension between the life of the artist and the life of the person. As seen in 'Makassar, 1956', Zwicky's poems often deal with issues to do with identity (especially with regard to displacement and exile) and responsibility. Culturally wide-ranging, Zwicky's poems are often elegiac, as seen in her elegy for her father, 'Kaddish', which links Zwicky's Jewish and Anglo-Saxon legacies. *DM*

Tiananmen Square June 4, 1989

Karl Marx, take your time,
looming over Highgate on your plinth.[1]
Snow's falling on your beard,
exiled, huge, hairy, genderless.
Terminally angry, piss-poor,   5
stuffed on utopias and cold,
cold as iron.

I'm thinking of your loving wife,
your desperate children and your grandchild
dead behind the barred enclosure of your brain.   10
Men's ideas the product, not the cause
of history, you said?

The snow has killed the lilacs.
Whose idea?
The air is frozen with theory.   15

What can the man be doing all day
in that cold place?
What can he be writing?
What can he be reading?
What big eyes you have, mama!   20
Next year, child, we will eat.

I'm thinking of my middle-class German grandmother
soft as a pigeon, who wept
when Chamberlain declared a war.
Why are you crying, grandma?   25

---

1   The political economist and revolutionary is buried in Highgate Cemetery, London.

It's only the big bad wolf, my dear.
It's only a story.

There's no end to it.
The wolves have come again.
What shall I tell my grandchildren?   30

No end to the requiems, the burning trains,
the guns, the shouting in the streets,
the outraged stars, the anguished face
of terror under ragged headbands
soaked in death's calligraphy.   35

Don't turn your back, I'll say.
Look hard.
Move into that frozen swarming screen.
How far can you run with a bullet in your brain?

And forgive, if you can, the safety of a poem   40
sharpened on a grieving night.

A story has to start somewhere.
                                                       1992

Makassar, 1956

We didn't fly the homeland in those days.
Lumbering P & O Orient liners slid sedately off
to postwar bliss in England; we spoke with English
vowels, revered our teachers, grieved for Hamlet
and the star-crossed lovers.   5
Parents, relatives and friends cried and waved,
the streamers strained, snapped, collapsed
in lollypop tangles on the wharf. Pulling away
from the tumbled web, we didn't care about
falling behind, getting ahead, dry-eyed and   10
guiltless, went as everything was happening
somewhere else. I wouldn't have seen the signs.

Mine was someone else's colonial route,
heading for the magic islands learnt from Conrad.
I took instead a trampy old Dutch steamer,   15
the *Nieuw Holland* plying the spicy archipelago

for Koninklijke Paketvaart Maatschappij, the
Royal Packet Navigation Company: wood-slatted cabin doors,
cork-chequered mats in *Badkamers*, tin dippers,
tubs for dousing, cold water tasting salty, three green   20
bottles in the toilet: paper was for infidels.

Decks buzzed with students going home, new
graduates from our Colombo Plan,[1] old hands from
what was called The Indies in *tempo dulu*,[2] stiff-backed
older lady teachers, nurses like grey Mrs Marshall from   25
Ballarat who'd been in prison camp and knew the ropes.
Mr Tisnadi Wiria with his wife, four children; Som and
Suparpol, the plump Thai dentists; shiny avuncular Mr Doko,
cultural superintendent from North Bali and pretty Enni
from Kadiri. And big-boned Mrs Stecklenburg with a   30
Victory Roll[3] and pale apologetic daughter—the way
that woman sang! We all got into the act but respectful,
celebrating all hours and lining up for nasi goreng,
flower-cut beetroot, lobster-men, oranges and apples
for our games. The ship's lights caught us frolicking   35
in their benign glare.

Mornings found the sharp-nosed Aussie horse trainer,
Mr Young, rakish-angled felt hat bound for Singapore.
He used to take a daily turn around the deck, smashing
his thin Malayan wife against the rails like a rag doll.   40
She never made a sound. We heard he had horses and a cockatoo
on board. Later, in shock I watched her hurl a dipper
against the bathroom wall, weeping. She lived what I
had only seen on stage or read about in penny novels,
what my Nana called 'hot stuff': other peoples' lives.   45
Betrayal, death and homicidal rage were opera.
It must have flicked my mind to wonder how you stuck
with someone slamming your bones on what passes for
a normal morning walk, stay silent, letting it happen
over and over. Marriage, after all, meant love, an infinity   50
of calm water shining for miles under a new moon,
our kindly southern stars. My thoughts were virtuous,

1   An international cooperative effort in the Asia-Pacific region that emerged from a Commonwealth
    Conference of Foreign Ministers held in Colombo, Sri Lanka (then Ceylon), in 1950.
2   Indonesian: 'the old times', usually a reference to the Dutch colonial era.
3   A hairstyle of the Second World War.

naive, each nerve geared to heartless young imaginings,
how much better I would do it.

I ate a poisoned oyster on the Brisbane stop,   55
puked the north-east coast as far as the Arafura Sea.
Jovial Dr Chi's bulk filled my tiny cabin as he poked
my gut with some contempt: 'Gas, my girl, just gas!'
Offended, I lay flattened for a day, revived with Chinese
powders of a suspect green, began a letter to my mother,   60
tore it up: my life or what I thought was called a life
had just been launched, the world my oyster.
Never let them know and don't give up.
Dolphins and flying fish leaped and soared in the wake.
Hypnotised in hazy warmth, we dozed the afternoons   65
away and nightly watched Orion shift his shape.

The night before Makassar Mr Doko sang a song from Timor
about an Australian soldier with an Indonesian girlfriend.
Hearing he's been wounded by the Japanese
she rushes off to find him, takes him to the hospital   70
where he dies of wounds. The tears were in our eyes
for such devotion. The girl then dresses in a soldier's
uniform, goes off to fight and gets killed too. How I
remember how we listened, how it cast us into unexpected
silence, grieving for the two young star-crossed lovers.   75
Mr Doko beamed with pride in his song and its effect.
Mr Eisenring looked impatient, Mr Nasiboe folded his hands:
they were getting off in the morning.

I woke to calm, the shuddering engines stopped and
through the cabin porthole saw the sea, flat, metallic,   80
sage-green, the ship becalmed as if in oil, still as a dream.
On deck, the soft rain fell, spindly palms fringed the
shoreline, little prahus and rowing boats swished
silently between the harbour's knolls, each marked with
a coconut palm or two just like the comic strips.   85
Steady rain fell on the upturned faces of the children
dotted red and yellow, blue and green waving from the wharf,
skinny arms outstretched for oranges and apples we threw.
Any minute now we'd be on land. I couldn't wait.

Boys scampered under giant banana leaves held dripping   90
above their heads, darting and calling. Steel-helmeted

young militia men lounged near our enchanted ship,
rifle-bayonets slung casually over one shoulder, smooth
and nerveless features gazing past us: boy-men so they seemed.
I'd never seen a gun and felt no fear: just something else   95
we'd read about at home. Our fathers used them in the War.
It would never happen again, we said.

After the unloading of the flour, each lumpy bag carted
down the gangway by a tribe of scrawny men, legs bowed
under the weight, scrambling fast like a moving spider's nest,   100
we were let out. Through Imigrasi and the stampings, permits,
questions, then released into the rain, the fragrant air
of frangipani, coconut oil, clove-scented Kretek cigarettes.
Blue smoke rose from street corner braziers charring
kambing saté sticks: our senses reeled and charged,   105
the crowd milling, jostling us into town while Mr Eisenring
and Mr Nasiboe disappeared for ever in a heap of luggage,
gesticulating porters and two burdened *betjaks.*

A wedding procession threaded its way along
Djalan Pintu Dua at a fine clip, embroidered silks   110
and gold-fringed parasols, crimson, blue and green.
First came a tall big drum, bicycle attached, the
pedals dangling from the skin, its rider thumping
forward, trombone, flutes and trumpets blaring.
My heart stood open like a door—the bride looked   115
very nervous sitting, eyes downcast, beside her thin
proud groom in a little cart bringing up the rear.
As it jolted past us in the warm rain, I felt a poem
starting to take shape under the reedy rhythms of the band.
It settled on my heart for nearly fifty years.   120

Later, looking up the Indonesia-Inggeris pocket
dictionary given me by Fong Chi Hang as I sheltered
from the driving rain in his Shanghai Sport Shop, the
phrase 'the West Monsoon' was rumoured. Can't remember how
I got to be out back eating a soup of fermented rice   125
and octopus with Mr Fong, his wife and lots of curious
kids or how I came to have his dictionary.
Must have needed a word for how I felt and looked up
'happy' announced 'Saja senang hati' while everybody laughed.
But I was relishing the darkened vowels, the alien softness   130

that spelled out my state however topsy-turvy it might be.
For once sound matched sense.

'Bahagian' was happiness and as I spoke the word,
three women passed in purdah in the street, thickly veiled
from head to toe in black like mourners. Their burning eyes   135
arrested me, speaking soundless of an older, fiercer order
of things. Haunted eyes that followed me in dreams—I see
them still—their black concealment hinting how
it's possible to be in one place, also somewhere else,
possible to let things happen over and over, possible   140
to stick in silence to pain's colours and, if it's in you,
transmit poems: burning, angry, frightened, loving, yearning
poems, rock-grooved water poems, poems of flame and
moon-flute poems, poems of the ocean and volcano's crater,
poems repeating dreams from darkness, remembering darkness.   145

Never in my life had I been so near to growing up
as on that day in Makassar back in 1956 watching
a wedding in the rain and the women passing.

2006

JENNIFER STRAUSS
b. 1933

Born in Heywood, Victoria, Jennifer Strauss was educated at the universities of
Melbourne and Glasgow, and Monash University. From the mid-1960s she worked at
Monash University, where she became an associate professor and later an honorary senior
research fellow. An important critic, Strauss has written major studies on Australian
poetry, Judith Wright and Gwen Harwood (qqv), as well as editing two anthologies,
including *The Oxford Book of Australian Love Poems* (1993), co-editing *The Oxford
Literary History of Australia* (1998) and editing *The Collected Verse of Mary Gilmore* (2 vols,
2004/2007), presenting the definitive edition of that writer's poetry. Strauss's poetry
shows a particular interest in women's experiences, families and death, combining wit
with realism. She is the author of four collections, including *Tierra del Fuego: New and
selected poems* (1997). DM

Discourse in Eden

'I think I'll call it giraffe'—
He speaks: she smiles; is
always smiling, but won't
discriminate—just
watches the wide garden   5
with boundless pleasure.

'Giraffe!' he says, emphatic,
making her look; then sighs
'It isn't easy, having to find
so *many* different names.'   10
Lively now, she offers help:
he's unconvinced.

'Well really it was me God told
to name the creatures . . . but p'rhaps
you could try something small . . .'   15
'But my ideas are large.'
He takes her hand,
'We'll see . . . my love . . . tomorrow . . .'

Tomorrow she basks in sunlight,
grass tickling her toes,   20
'Where is giraffe?' he asks.
'Why here,' she says 'somewhere here.'
'Nonsense! Look there—
(finger stabbing) there, there,

there's no giraffe.' 'But,   25
surely there's enough.'
'That's not the point—he's lost
if I can't see him, lost,
or somewhere else.'
So Adam goes off, questing.   30

And though the sky's still blue,
the leaves densely green,
there is a blank,
a space within creation—
inscribed giraffe, it signifies   35
the other, absence, lack.

Eve feels, for the first time,
hollow . . . bespoken
(above her head on the branch
but ripe to a hand's reach)   40
the fruit shines,
round, substantial.

                                                              1997

A Mother's Day Letter: Not for Posting

When you were small you'd fall,
graze a knee, break a collar-bone,
nothing that could not be kissed
and mended—except the blow
death struck, we never spoke of.   5

I wanted you brave, concerned,
intelligent. Fifteen years late
you tell of fearing your dead
father's anger. What of my pride
that would not consider happiness   10

in the mere three wishes we get?
Swan-grown you ruffle your plumage
on history's polluted tide.
And I'm like any goose-girl now,
crying 'Come back! Come back!'   15

'The woods of love are wild
with beasts. In politics' swamp
your sinking feet will hit
toe-breaking boulders of stupidity,
strike razor edges of spite.'   20

No. Marshal the necessary march.
But if you come back shieldless,
remember I've no appetite for Spartan
deaths. I want you brave,
concerned, intelligent, alive.   25
                                                              1997

BARRY HUMPHRIES
b. 1934

While not as famous as his comic persona, Dame Edna Everage (the source of films, and numerous theatrical shows, books, and television programs), Barry Humphries is an internationally recognised performer. He was born in Melbourne and attended the University of Melbourne but discontinued his studies to tour with Ray Lawler's (qv) theatrical group, which led to the invention of Edna Everage. He left Australia in 1959 to continue his theatrical career in England. In the 1960s Humphries found his métier with his one-man satirical stage revues in which he appeared as Edna Everage and other satirical characters devised by him, including the Rabelaisian Les Patterson. In the same decade he wrote the text for the *Private Eye* cartoon strip, 'The Adventures of Barry McKenzie', which became a film in 1972 (co-scripted by and co-starring Humphries).

As discussed in the first volume of his autobiography, *More Please* (1992), Humphries's drinking became a major problem and he gave up alcohol in the early 1970s. Humphries's attraction to satire, subversion and discomforting audiences began with a series of Dadaesque stunts while he was a student. Since then, his ongoing success as Dame Edna may have overshadowed his other achievements. In addition to writing his own comic material, he has written light verse (collected as *Neglected Poems*, 1991), two novels, and co-authored a study of the artist Thea Proctor. *DM*

Maroan

For Elizabeth Jolley

You've read in all the magazines
About the Colour Question:
Should we be black, off-white or beige?
May I make a suggestion:
Maroan's my favourite colour,   5
It's a lovely shade I think—
It's a real hard colour to describe,
Not purple—and not pink.

All our family loves it and
You ought to see our home,   10
From the bedroom to the laundry—
Every room's maroan!
When we bought our home in Moonee Ponds
It didn't have a phone,
But it had one thing to offer: 15
The toilet was maroan.

Look, I fell in love with it at once,
I felt the place was mine.
You see the day I married Norm
My bridesmaids were in wine.   20
Our wedding cake was iced to match
And glowed in splendour lonely,
And they drank our toast in burgundy
Which sparkled so maroanly.

The day my mother had her turn   25
We heard an awful groan,
I dropped young Ken, dashed to her room
And there she was—maroan.

And now she's in the twilight home,
We're going to England soon   30
But one English custom gets my goat:
They call maroan 'maroon'??

1955/1990

Edna's Hymn

Australia is a Saturday
With races on the trannie,
Australia is the talcy smell
Of someone else's granny.
Australia is a kiddie   5
With zinc cream on his nose,
Australia's voice is Melba's[1] voice,
It's also Normie Rowe's.[2]
Australia's famous postage stamps
Are stuffed with flowers and fauna,   10
Australia is the little man
Who's open round the corner.
Australia is a sunburnt land
Of sand and surf and snow;
All ye who do not love her   15
Ye know where ye can go.

1968/1990

Letter to Richard Allen

DEAR MR ALLEN

Thank you for inviting me to subscribe to a fund to build a tennis court for the students at Clyde House. Regret that I am unable to do what you so kindly propose since I am deeply opposed to all forms of sporting activity, which I have always felt receive far too much emphasis in our 'better schools'. I always found it tiresome at dinner parties in Australia finding myself seated next to ladies who think of little else but sport, and I think we parents should do all in our power to prevent another generation of muscle-bound, bone-headed girls from infesting society.

The dangers of encouraging tennis have been forcibly brought home to me in recent months by the disclosures about the life of the American tennis star Billie-Jean King, who has admitted to the press that the game of

---

1 Dame Nellie Melba (1861–1931), Australian opera soprano.
2 Normie Rowe (b. 1947), Australian popular singer.

tennis contributed to her grievous sexual disorder. Under these circumstances, I am very sorry that I cannot be a party to this scheme, although I would always be happy to make a generous financial contribution to any proposal which involved the dismantling of Geelong Grammar's sporting facilities.

May I wish you the compliments of the season.

SINCERELY YOURS/BARRY HUMPHRIES

1981

From *More Please*
Licking the Beaters

[. . .] The South Camberwell State School was a raw red-brick two-storey building in a small street off Toorak Road. It stood in an extensive asphalt wasteland, bounded by the palings of adjacent houses. This was the playground. Far away, against the back fence and partly shaded by a mutilated peppercorn, stood the only other structure in that desolate schoolground, the shelter shed. This was a sort of wooden box with one wall missing in which children presumably sheltered from the extremes of the Melbourne climate. At lunchtime on a wet day it would be packed with damp urchins delving into their sandwich tins and screaming at the tops of their voices. The noise in that confined space under a reboant tin roof was appalling, but worse was the overpowering and nauseating stench of gooey brown banana sandwiches and other nameless fillings. It did not surprise me in the least, when years later I learnt that the artless expression, 'Who opened their lunch?' was 1930s Australian slang for 'Who farted?' Only then did I realize that others before me had reeled back from the effluvia of cut lunches.

My parents sent me there for about a year until I was old enough to attend a nice Junior School. I had seen the brochure for Camberwell Grammar in my father's den. It had a sky-blue crinkly cover, embossed with the school's mitred crest, and glossy pages with pictures of some brand-new manganese brick buildings photographed from oblique angles to make them look more monumental than they actually were. It was supposed to be a 'very good school' and it charged *fees*. It catered for boys only, and mostly boys from 'comfortable homes'.

But Camberwell State, which I was forced to attend in the meantime, was free and co-ed. The hardships of life in Mrs Flint's back-yard jungle were nothing compared with the shrieking, thumping, yelling, wrestling maelstrom of human maggots into which I had been hurled.

Quickly I became aware of the gulf that divided me from them; the gulf that separated the Australian working class from the newly arisen 'affluent' middle class. It was wider, bleaker and more inimical than the grey tundra of the playground. In my effeminate little blue Aertex shirt which laced at the neck, pleated linen shorts, fawn cotton socks and leather sandals with side buckles, I felt uncomfortably alien to the other boys. Many of them wore scuffed and splitting sandshoes and a few even arrived at school barefoot. Our classroom was full of densely darned and threadbare maroon sweaters, patched britches, grubby lacunose stockings, scabby knees, bloody noses, verminous hair and ears erupting with bright pumpkin wax. The slatternly girls were no less alarming to a mollycoddled little Lord Fauntleroy from the Golf Links Estate.

The first form was presided over by a gorgon called Miss Jensen. She was the first woman I ever met with her hair in a bun, and she had a knack of making the chalk squeal on the blackboard. She favoured bottle-green 'twin sets' and fawn tweed skirts and she looked uncannily like Mrs Bun the Baker's wife in Happy Families.[1] Miss Jensen and I took an instant dislike to one another.

We lived only about half a mile from the school, so I was mostly spared the ordeal of sandwiches in the shelter shed. Instead, punctually at 12.30, my father would collect me in the big putty-white Oldsmobile and drive me home for a peaceful lunch at my own little table on the lawn, or with my mother in the sun-room amongst her new cane furniture and shining brass knick-knacks. Everything in our house was new, or 'up-to-date' as they said in the thirties. We had a new Frigidaire with a light inside which went on when you opened the door. Every now and then it shuddered rather violently, as if from the cold. Most other people we knew still had ice-chests, and I rather envied them the iceman's visit as he shouldered those great glassy blocks up their sideways. On top of the fridge stood our new Sunbeam Mixmaster. This was a streamlined bullet-shaped appliance rather like a Buck Rogers spaceship, in the popular colour combination of cream and black. We had all the attachments and the brochure, but we only used it for juicing oranges and making cakes. When the twin whisks plunged into the bowl of glutinous sponge mixture my mother tweaked a mammiform control knob to the appropriate speed and the engine whirred into action, the whisks churning so that their blades seemed to vanish until they were just two chrome rods suspended in a fragrant yellow vortex. The kitchen filled with a miraculous aroma of heating machinery, compounded with vanilla essence. Once the Mixmaster was silenced and the whisks detached, I was allowed to lick off the ambrosial emulsion. Licking the beaters was one of the great privileges of an Australian childhood.

Our other modern appliance was a Radiola 'mantel model' wireless set. Chubbily ziggurattish in moulded brown Bakelite, it had a vertically fluted front panel rather like the fascia of a modernistic building. Behind the

1 A traditional card game.

organ-pipe grille could be glimpsed a curtain of sheeny brown cretonne through which the music and the voices shrilly filtered. 'The Girl on the Pink Police Gazette' and 'My Merry Oldsmobile' were popular airs of the period, and it seemed strange and inexplicable that the radio could be singing so intimately about our family car.

> Come away with me Lucile
> In my merry Oldsmobile,
> Down the road of life we'll fly
> Automobubbling you and I.
> To the church we'll swiftly steal,
> Then our wedding bells will peal,
> You can go as far as you like with me,
> In my merry Oldsmobile.

I had been given a toy submarine made in Japan, containing a clockwork mechanism which, when wound up, propelled it realistically along the bottom of the bath. One day I took it to school, a big mistake. It was one of those rare days when I didn't go home for lunch, so, avoiding the hellish shelter shed, I took my sub and my sandwiches to a peaceful corner of the playground. Soon I found myself encircled by a group of rough kids who demanded my submarine. A tussle ensued in which my lunch got trodden into the asphalt and as the jeering circle of larrikins drew closer and more threatening I picked up a handful of gravel ready to defend myself. The bullies fled, but they did not disperse. They must have formed a delegation to Miss Jensen because immediately after recess she hauled me out in front of the class for 'throwing stones', a heinous violation of the school rules. I denied doing any such thing, but the testimony of the smirking yahoos carried more weight than my tearful protestations, and I was pushed in the corner for the rest of the afternoon with a sign on my back: I AM A BULLY. Much later, when the class had been dismissed for the afternoon, Miss Jensen told me that if I persisted in denying my guilt she would take me to see Mr Fraser, the headmaster, a ginger-haired functionary whom I had privately nicknamed 'Duckface'. I stuck to my guns, however, and only at the entrance to his study, and threatened with imminent expulsion, did I finally break down and recant, confessing to a crime I had never committed. Grudgingly, clemency supervened, and I was allowed to go home, my heart pounding with shame and rage. For some reason which remains obscure, I never told my parents of this incident—perhaps I feared that they might share Miss Jensen's view of the matter.

Since then I have entertained fantasies of vengeance. Supposing Miss Jensen had been, say, twenty-five at the time, she might now, in 1992, be a sprightly seventy-seven-year-old living with her daughter, sitting peacefully knitting in some honeysuckled garden bower, or quietly watching television in a Melbourne suburb. For my purposes it would be more convenient if she were installed in a sunset facility or oldsters' terminary. There I could visit her, explaining to the nursing staff that I was a concerned relation who required a few moments' privacy with the titubating inmate. I would need very little time to attach the small placard, concealed under my raincoat, to the back of old Miss Jensen's bobbing matinée jacket.

1992

CHRIS WALLACE-CRABBE
b. 1934

Chris Wallace-Crabbe is deeply associated with Melbourne, the city of his birth. One of the so-called university poets, Wallace-Crabbe was educated at the University of Melbourne, where he became a lecturer, reader and, in 1988, professor. He was founding director of the Australian Centre at the University of Melbourne (1989–94), general editor of the Oxford University Press Australian Writers series (1992–96), and an editorial board member of *Australian Book Review* and *Meanjin*. Since 1998 he has been professor emeritus at the Australian Centre. He is an important critic and has published four major works of criticism, most recently *Read it Again* (2005). He has edited and co-edited numerous anthologies and critical works, including *The Golden Apples of the Sun: Twentieth century Australian poetry* (1980). He has also written one novel and supplied the text for numerous artists' books (especially by Bruno Letti).

Wallace-Crabbe was one of the first poets in the late 1950s to represent Australian suburbia, but he is notably cosmopolitan. He has held international academic fellowships and professorships (such as at Yale and Harvard), and has travelled widely. Cosmopolitan poetic interests are visible in his engagements with American poetry and prose poetry, both early in the Australian context. Published in the 1980s and '90s by Oxford University Press, and later by Carcanet, Wallace-Crabbe has a significant international reputation.

Wallace-Crabbe's poetry has developed from ethical-formalist beginnings to a widening interest in politics and the self. Strongly attracted to the Australian vernacular and the quotidian, Wallace-Crabbe's lyrics often contain more sombre, metaphysical concerns. This is seen in *For Crying Out Loud* (1990), with its moving elegies for the poet's adult son. Ultimately, however, the poet looks to the multiplicity of daily life, the world of ideas and nature as sources of replenishment and joy. *The Universe Looks Down* (2005), a postmodern quest poem, illustrates Wallace-Crabbe's erudition, playfulness and originality. DM

The Swing

On a swing at midnight in the black park. Between poplars which are towers of light for a hidden street lamp and inky she-oaks my arc is maintained. From lighter to darker I go, from dark to light; but only, as ever, to return.

Here we live in the imperfect syntax of light and darkness; wanting to write a sentence as perfect as the letter o in praise of things. For things exist supremely; all our values cohere in things.

The austere prose which could outline the world with a physicist's clarity never arrives. We move through the fugal elaboration of leaves, through centuries of drowning flowers. Unsatisfied, uncertain, I am swinging again tonight in the park.

1963

Introspection

Have you ever seen a mind
thinking?
It is like an old cow
trying to get through the pub door
carrying a guitar in its mouth;   5
old habits keep breaking in
on the job in hand;
it keeps wanting
to do something else:
like having a bit of a graze   10
for example,
or galumphing round the paddock
or being a café musician
with a beret and a moustache.
But if she just keeps trying   15
the old cow, avec guitar,
will be through that door
as easy as pie
but she won't know how it was done.
It's harder with a piano.   20

Have you heard the havoc
of remembering?
It is like asking
the local plumber
in to explore a disused well;   25
down he goes in on a twisting rope,
his cloddy boots
bumping against
that slimed brickwork,
and when he arrives at bottom   30
in the smell of darkness,
with a splash of jet black water
he grasps a huge fish,

slices it open
with his clasp-knife   35
and finds a gold coin inside
which slips
out of his fingers
back into the unformed unseeing,
never to be found again.   40
                                                          1980

God

That is the world down there.
It appears that I made it
but that was way back,
donkey's years ago, children,
when I spoke like a solar lion   5
beguiling physics out of chaos.

I spun my brilliant ball in air.
Such thought was new to me
though I had not guessed at my lack
in the old indigo days,   10
children, before you fell—
to use a technical verb.

It is full of beautiful flair,
a jewel and a garden at once,
bluish-green with the track   15
of silver engraving its veins . . .
Shit, but it's lovely
and no end of trouble at all.

Children, it once was bare
of all salacious language,   20
of goats and bladderwrack,[1]
of banksia trees and wrens.
I endeavoured to bring it up rich.
I reckon it's my museum.

I gave a big party   25
and the name of the party

___
1   A type of seaweed.

kept slipping clean away
from my wooden tongue
but I reckon it was
called history.   30

Some honoured guests
took off their names
or left them impaled like scarecrow rags
on my staggy front hedge.
I thought of it as being   35
a party for my son.
                                                           1988

An Elegy

Everything turns out more terrible
than they had said, or what I thought
at midnight they had said,

but the dark marks
tracking across clean snow   5
way down there must be people,

that is,
if anything on earth can be human
when eighteen storeys below,

so that I wish again   10
it were possible to pluck my son
out of dawn's moist air

by the pylon-legs
in that dewy-green slurred valley
before he ever hit the ground,   15

to sweep under his plunge
like a pink-tinged angel
and gather him gasping back into his life.
                                                           1990

Puck Disembarks

That sun is glazing and glaring from the wrong direction.
In his government regulation gear
And cultural arsy-turvitude

Puck steps ashore in a grammar of ti-tree.
>He rocks the pinnace.
>The foliage looks pretty crook.   5

Even a spirit can fail to be gruntled
Standing on his northern hemisphere head
In a wilderness without fairies or dairies,
Whose Dreaming he cannot read.   10
>He tweaks a tar's pigtail.
>This land is all wombat-shit.

The mosquitoes lead him to think of swallows,
The dipping swallows of Devon
And these alien magpies can sing like Titania   15
In love with a kangaroo.
>Puck waters the gin,
>Peddling the balance to snubnosed natives.

The glittering wavelets throw on yellow sand
Big shells like Wedgwood ware   20
As the imp rises inside him, getting ready
To rewrite Empire as larrikin culture.
>He daubs a first graffito on
>The commissary tent, GEORGE THE TURD.[1]

Against the pale enamel sky   25
Rebel cockatoos are screaming
New versions of pleasure:
This is the paradise of Schadenfreude.
>He begins to adore
>The willy wagtail's flirting pirouettes.   30
1990

New Year

As when the locality darkens,
earth odours rise up
and colour has bled away

while the lit clouds yet

>   sail sweetly over us   5
inhabiting a daylight of their own.

2001

1 George III (1738–1820), who reigned from 1760 to 1820, was king in the early years of Australia's settlement.

DAVID MALOUF
b. 1934

Poet and novelist David Malouf was born and educated in Brisbane. His father's family had come to Australia in the 1880s from Lebanon; his mother's were Sephardic Jews and had come from Spain via England. His childhood is recalled in the memoir *12 Edmondstone Street* (1985), four essays that form an affectionate tribute to his home city as well as a more abstract and complex meditation on the relation between place and self, which is a theme that runs through much of his work.

He left Australia at 24 and was away for ten years, teaching in England and travelling in Europe. In 1968 Malouf returned to Australia and was appointed tutor and then lecturer in English at the University of Sydney; ten years later he resigned from the academy to become a full-time writer, from then on living alternately in Tuscany and Australia until 1985, when he settled back in Sydney.

Malouf was known as a poet before he began to write fiction, publishing his first book, *Bicycle and Other Poems*, in 1970 and his second, *Neighbours in a Thicket: Poems*, in 1974. His first novel, *Johnno* (1975), which critic Ivor Indyk in his book *David Malouf* (1993) has called 'the most deliberately autobiographical of Malouf's fictional works', is also a very 'Brisbane' book, vividly recalling the city during the Second World War. *Johnno* is the first of many Malouf novels to represent contrasting modes and styles of masculinity, particularly in wartime. It also introduced what was to become a very familiar Malouf motif, the use of literary models and allusions as an integral part of his fiction.

He has continued to write poetry, with the major collection *Poems 1959–89* appearing in 1992, but during the 1980s became better known for his fiction. The short novels *An Imaginary Life* (1978) and *Child's Play* (1982) were followed by the weightier *Harland's Half Acre* (1984), and in 1985 Malouf published his first collection of short stories, the award-winning *Antipodes*. He then began to write for the stage: Patrick White's (qv) novel *Voss* was adapted and produced as an opera, first staged in 1986, for which Malouf wrote the libretto, and the following year saw the production of his play *Blood Relations* (1988). Malouf has since written three more libretti for contemporary opera, most recently *Jane Eyre* (2000).

His Second World War novel *The Great World* (1990) won a number of significant national and international awards, and was followed in 1993 by *Remembering Babylon*, one of a number of Australian novels in recent years to tackle the difficult and controversial topic of Australian contact and settlement history and race relations. *The Conversations at Curlow Creek* (1996) also deals with Australian colonial history. The small, quirky *Untold Tales* (1999) was followed by two substantial volumes of short stories, *Dream Stuff* (2000) and *Every Move You Make* (2006) and a collection of poems, *Typewriter Music* (2007). Malouf was awarded the Neustadt International Prize for Literature in 2000. *KG*

The Year of the Foxes

For Don Anderson

When I was ten my mother, having sold
her old fox-fur (a ginger red bone-jawed
Magda Lupescu[1]

---

1   Elena (Magda) Lupescu (1896–1977), mistress of King Carol II of Romania, and (after his abdication) his wife.

of a fox that on her arm played
dead, cunningly dangled   5
a lean and tufted paw)

decided there was money to be made
from foxes, and bought via
the columns of the *Courier Mail* a whole
pack of them; they hung from penny hooks   10
in our panelled sitting room, trailed from the backs
of chairs; and Brisbane ladies, rather
the worse for war, drove up in taxis wearing
a GI on their arm
and rang at our front door.   15

I slept across the hall, at night hearing
their thin cold cry. I dreamed the dangerous spark
of their eyes, brushes aflame
in our fur-hung, nomadic
tent in the suburbs, the dark fox-stink of them   20
cornered in their holes
and turning

                    Among my mother's show pieces—
Noritake teacups, tall hock glasses
with stems like barley sugar,   25
goldleaf *demitasses*—
the foxes, row upon row, thin-nosed, prick-eared,
dead.

        The cry of hounds
was lost behind mirror glass,   30
where ladies with silken snoods and fingernails
of chinese lacquer red
fastened a limp paw;
went down in their high heels
to the warm soft bitumen, wearing at throat   35
and elbow the rare spoils
of '44; old foxes, rusty red like dried-up wounds,
and a GI escort.

                                                            1970

Poem

You move by contradictions:
out of a moment
of silence far off
in Poland or January
you smile and your body   5
returns to my touch.

Entering a winter
room I find myself
dazzled: all summer
in the throats of vases, windows   10
ablaze with air, our pear-tree
brimming with wasps.

My dull hands follow
at night your unseasonable
kindling and cooling   15
through twelve dreams and the twelve
colours of darkness
between midnight and dawn.

                                                    1970

A First Place

My purpose is to look at the only place in Australia that I know well, the only place I know from inside, from my body outwards, and to offer my understanding of it as an example of how we might begin to speak accurately of where and what we are. What I will be after is not facts—or not only facts, but a description of how the elements of a place and our inner lives cross and illuminate one another, how we interpret space, and in so doing make our first maps of reality, how we mythologise spaces and through that mythology (a good deal of it inherited) find our way into a culture. You will see, I hope, how a writer might be particularly engaged by all this, and especially a writer of fiction; and you will see too why any one man might have only a single place he can speak of, the place of his earliest experience. For me that was Brisbane. It has always seemed to me to be a fortunate choice—except that I didn't make it. But then the place you get is always, in the real sense of the word, fortunate, in that it constitutes your fortune, your fate, and is your only entry into the world. I am not suggesting that Brisbane is unique in offering the sort of reading I mean to make. The city is unique, as all places are, but the reading, the method I hope, is not.

To begin then with topography.

The first thing you notice about this city is the unevenness of the ground. Brisbane is hilly. Walk two hundred metres in almost any direction outside the central city (which has been levelled) and you get a view—a new view. It is all gullies and sudden vistas. Not long views down a street to the horizon—and I am thinking now of cities like Melbourne and Adelaide, or Manchester or Milan, those great flat cities where you look away down endless vistas and the mind is drawn to distance. Wherever the eye turns here it learns restlessness, and variety and possibility, as the body learns effort. Brisbane is a city that tires the legs and demands a certain sort of breath. It is not a city, I would want to say, that provokes contemplation, in which the mind moves out and loses itself in space. What it might provoke is drama, and a kind of intellectual play that delights in new and shifting views, and this because each new vista as it presents itself here is so intensely colourful.

The key colour is green, and of a particular density: the green of mangroves along the riverbanks, of Moreton Bay figs, of the big trees that are natives of this corner of Queensland, the shapely hoop-pines and bunyas that still dominate the skyline along every ridge. The Australian landscape here is not blue-grey, or grey-green or buff, as in so much of southern Australia; and the light isn't blond or even blue. It is a rich golden pink, and in the late afternoon the western hills and the great flat expanse of water that is the Bay create an effect I have seen in other places only before or after a storm. Everything glows from within. The greens become darkly luminous. The sky produces effects of light and cloud that are, to more sober eyes, almost vulgarly picturesque. But then, these are the subtropics. You are soon made aware here of a kind of moisture in the air that makes nature a force that isn't easily domesticated—everything grows too fast, too tall, it gets quickly out of control. Vegetation doesn't complement the man-made, it fiercely competes with it; gardens are always on the point of turning themselves into wilderness, hauling down fences, pushing sheds and outhouses over, making things look ramshackle and halfway to ruin. The weather, harsh sunlight, hard rain, adds to the process, stripping houses of their paint, rotting timber, making the dwellings altogether less solid and substantial, on their high stumps, than the great native trees that surround them.

I'll come back to those houses in a moment. It is no accident that they should have invaded a paragraph that is devoted to nature, since they are, in this place, so utterly of it, both in form and substance. Open wooden affairs, they seem often like elaborated tree-houses, great grown-up cubby-houses hanging precariously above ground.

Now what you abstract from such a landscape from its greenness, its fierce and damply sinister growth, its power compared with the flimsiness of the domestic architecture, its grandeur of colour and effect, its openness upwards to the sky—another consequence of all those hills—is something other, I would suggest, than what is abstracted from the wide, dry landscapes of southern Australia that we sometimes think of as 'typical'. It offers a different notion of what the land might be, and relates it to all the daily business of life in a quite different way. It shapes in those who grow up there a different sensibility, a different cast of mind, creates a different sort of Australian.

So much then for the lay of the land; now for that other distinctive feature of the city, its river. Winding back and forth across Brisbane in a classic meander, making pockets and elbows with high cliffs on one side and mud-flats on the other, the River is inescapable. It cuts in and out of every suburb, can be seen from every hill. It also keeps the Bay in mind, since that, clearly, is where all its windings, its odd turns and evasions, lead. But this river does not have the same uses for the citizen as the rivers that flow through other towns.

We think of the Thames, or the Seine or the Tiber or the Arno, and it is clear how they are related to the cities they have growing up on their banks. They divide them, north and south. They offer themselves as a means of orientation. But the river in Brisbane is a disorienting factor. Impossible to know which side of it you are on, north or south, or to use it for settling in your mind how any place or suburb is related to any other.

So the topography of Brisbane, broken up as it is by hills and by the endless switching back and forth upon itself of the river, offers no clear map for the mind to move in, and this really is unusual—I know of no other city like it. Only one thing saves you here from being completely mapless, and that is the net—the purely conceptual net—that was laid down over the city with the tramline system. Ideally it is a great wheel, with the business centre as the hub and a set of radial spokes that push out into the suburbs. The city is conceived of in the minds of its citizens in terms of radial opposites that allow them to establish limits, and these are the old tram termini: Ascot/ Balmoral, Clayfield/Salisbury, Toowong/the Grange, West End/New Farm Park, to mention only a few; and this sense of radial opposites has persisted, and continues to be worked with, though the actual tramlines have long since been replaced with 'invisible' (as it were) bus routes. The old tramline system is now the invisible principle that holds the city together and gives it a shape in people's minds.

But that wheel-shape, as I said at the beginning, was ideal—not actual. I lived at Ascot. I have always thought of Balmoral as being at the other end of the city geographically—say, an hour's tram journey or twelve to fifteen miles away. But when I looked at a map recently I discovered that it is, in fact, only half a mile away on the opposite side of the river. Space, in this city, is unreadable. Geography and its features offer no help in the making of a mental map. What you have to do here is create a conceptual one. I ask myself again what habits of mind such a city may encourage in its citizens, and how, though taken for granted in this place, they may differ from the habits of places where geography declares itself at every point as helpful, reliable, being itself a map.

I have already referred briefly to the Brisbane house, setting its insubstantiality for a moment against the solidity of the big local trees, evoking the oddness with which it places itself, reared high on tree-stumps, on the side of its hill.

The houses are of timber, that is the essence of the thing, and to live with timber is to live with a material that yields at every step. The house is a living presence as a stone house never can be, responding to temperature in all its joists and floorboards, creaking, allowing you to follow every step sometimes, in every room. Imagine an old staircase and magnify its physical presence till it becomes a whole dwelling.

Children discover, among their first sensual experiences in the world of touch, the feel of tongue-and-groove boards, the soft places where they have rotted, the way paint flakes and the wood underneath will release sometimes, if you press it, a trickle of spicy reddish dust. In earlier days they often made themselves sick by licking those walls and poisoning themselves with lead.

You learn in such houses to listen. You build up a map of the house in sound, that allows you to know exactly where everyone is and to predict approaches. You also learn what not to hear, what is not-to-be-heard, because it is a condition of such houses that everything can be heard. Strict conventions exist about what should be listened to and these soon become habits of not-listening, not-hearing. So too, habits grow up of not-seeing.

Wooden houses in Brisbane are open. That is, they often have no doors, and one of the conventions of the place (how it came about might be a study in itself) is that doors, for the most part, are not closed. Maybe it is a result of the weather. Maybe it has something to do with the insistence that life as it is lived up here has no secrets—or should have none. Though it does of course.

Whatever the reason, bedroom doors in a Brisbane house are kept open—you get used to that. Even bathroom doors have no locks and are seldom closed. The proximities are dealt with, and privacy maintained, by just those subtle habits of not-seeing, not-hearing that growing up in such a house creates in you as a kind of second nature. There is something almost Indian about all this. How different from life as it is lived in solid brick houses, with solid walls and solid doors and the need to keep them sealed against the air. Brisbane houses are unsealable. Openness to the air, to the elements, is one of the conditions of their being—and you get used to that too.

So there it is, this odd timber structure, often decorated with wooden fretwork and scrolls of great fantasy, raised on tree-stumps to leaf level and still having about it some quality of the tree—a kind of tree-house expanded. At the centre a nest of rooms, all opening on to a hallway that as often as not runs straight through from front to back, so that when you step up to the front door of the house you can see right through it to trees or sky. Around the nest of rooms, verandahs, mostly with crossed openwork below and lattice or rolled venetians above; an intermediary space between the house proper, which is itself only half closed in, and the world outside—garden, street, weather.

Verandahs have their own life, their own conventions, but serve, for the most part, to make the too-open interior seem closed, therefore safe and protected. Weather beats in on the verandah and the house stays dry. Hawkers and other callers may be allowed up the front steps on to the verandah, but the house, utterly visible and open right through, remains inviolate. There are conventions about this too. You develop a keen sense, from early on, if you grow up in such a house, of what is inside and safe and what is out there at the edge, a boundary area, domestic but exposed.

Inside and out—that is one aspect of the thing: the nest of rooms at the centre and the open verandah. But there is also upstairs and down, and this doesn't at all mean the same thing here as in the two-storeyed terrace, where upstairs means sleeping and downstairs is public life. Upstairs in the Brisbane house is everything: the division between night and day might at the very least be established as one side or the other of a hall. Downstairs here means under-the-house, and that is in many ways the most interesting place of all.

It comes into existence as a space because of the need to get those houses up on stumps, to get them level on the hills it might be, or to keep them cool by providing a buffer of cool air underneath. There are several explanations, no one of them definitive.

So the space down there may be a cube, but is more often a wedge of deepening dark as the high house-stumps at the back diminish till they are as little at the front as a metre or half-a-metre high.

The stumps are capped with tin and painted with creosote against termites. The space they form is closed in with lattice, sometimes all the way to the ground, sometimes to make a fringe a half-metre or so below floor level. The earth is bare, but flooring boards being what they are, a good deal of detritus falls down there from the house above: rusty pins and needles, nails, tacks, occasionally a peachstone or some other rubbish where a child has found a crack big enough to push it through. And a good deal of what the house rejects in other ways also finds its way down there: old sinks or cisterns or bits of plumbing, bed-frames, broken chairs, a superannuated ice-box or meat safe, old toys.

It's a kind of archaeological site down there, and does in fact develop a time dimension of its own that makes the process of falling below, or sending below, or storing below, a passage out of the present into limbo, where things go on visibly existing as a past that can be re-entered, a time-capsule underworld. Visiting it is a way of leaving the house, and the present and daylight and getting back to the underside of things.

It's a sinister place and dangerous, but you are also liberated down there from the conventions. It's where children go to sulk. It's where cats have their kittens and sick dogs go. It's a place to hide things. It is also, as children discover, a place to explore; either by climbing up, usually on a dare, to the dark place under the front steps—exploring the dimensions of your own courage, this is, or your own fear—or by exploring, in the freedom down there, your own and other people's bodies. There can be few Brisbane children who do not associate under-the-house, guiltily or as a great break-out of themselves, with their first touch or taste of sex.

A landscape and its houses, also a way of life; but more deeply, a way of experiencing and mapping the world. One of our intellectual habits, it seems to me, is the visualising, in terms drawn from the life about us, of what is not visible but which we may need to see. One such entity is what we call mind or psyche. One observes in Freud's description of how the mind works how essential architectural features are, trapdoors, cellars, attics, etc. What I mean to ask here is how far growing up in the kind of house I have been describing may determine, in a very particular way, not only habits of life or habits of mind but the very shape of the psyche as Brisbane people conceive it, may determine, that is, how they visualise and embody such concepts as consciousness and the unconscious, public and private areas of experience, controlled areas and those that are pressingly uncontrollable or just within control—and to speak now of my own particular interest, how far these precise and local actualisations may be available to the writer in dealing with the inner lives of people. What I mean to suggest, at least problematically, is ways in which thinking and feeling may be intensely local—though that does not necessarily make them incomprehensible to outsiders, and it is the writer's job, of course, so long as we are in the world of his fiction, to make insiders of all of us.

We have tended, when thinking as 'Australians', to turn away from difference, even to assume that difference does not exist, and fix our attention on what is common to us; to assume that some general quality of Australianness exists, a national identity that derives from our history in the place and from the place itself. But Australians have had different histories. The states have produced, I would want to claim, very different social forms, different political forms as well, and so far as landscape and climate are concerned, Australia is not one place. It might be time to forget likeness and look closely at the many varieties of difference we now exhibit, to let notions of what is typically Australian lapse for a time while we investigate the different sorts of landscape the country presents us with, the different styles, social, political, educational of the states, the different styles of our cities, and even of suburbs within cities, and for those of us who are concerned with literature, for example, to ask ourselves how many different sorts of Australian writing there may be and how much the differences between them may be determined by the particular social habits and physical features of place. Is there, to come back to the present occasion, a Brisbane way of experiencing things that we could isolate in the works of writers who, even if they have not spent their writing life in the city, grew up there, and were in their first experience of the world shaped by it? Is there something in the style of mind of these writers, even in their use of language, a restlessness, a delight in variety and colour and baroque effects, in what I called earlier 'drama' and 'shifting views' that we might trace back to the topography of the place and the physical conditions it imposes on the body, to ways of seeing it imposes on the eye, and at some less conscious level, to embodiments of mind and psyche that belong to the first experience, and first mapping, of a house?

1985/1997

The Only Speaker of His Tongue

He has already been pointed out to me: a flabby, thickset man of fifty-five or sixty, very black, working alongside the others and in no way different from them—or so it seems. When they work he swings his pick with the same rhythm. When they pause he squats and rolls a cigarette, running his tongue along the edge of the paper while his eyes, under the stained hat, observe the straight line of the horizon; then he sets it between his lips, cups flame, draws in, and blows out smoke like all the rest.

Wears moleskins looped low under his belly and a flannel vest. Sits at smoko on one heel and sips tea from an enamel mug. Spits, and his spit hisses on stone. Then rises, spits in his palm and takes up the pick. They are digging holes for fencing-posts at the edge of the plain. When called he answers immediately, 'Here, boss,' and then, when he has approached, 'Yes boss, you wanna see me?' I am presented and he seems amused, as if I were some queer northern bird he had heard about but never till now believed in, a sort of crane perhaps, with my grey frock-coat and legs too spindly in their yellow trousers; an odd, angular fellow with yellow-grey side-whiskers, half spectacles and a cold-sore on his lip. So we stand face to face.

He is, they tell me, the one surviving speaker of his tongue. Half a century back, when he was a boy, the last of his people were massacred. The language, one of hundreds (why make a fuss?) died with them. Only not quite. For all his lifetime this man has spoken it, if only to himself. The words, the great system of sound and silence (for all languages, even the simplest, are a great and complex system) are locked up now in his heavy skull, behind the folds of the black brow (hence my scholarly interest), in the mouth with its stained teeth and fat, rather pink tongue. It is alive still in the man's silence, a whole alternative universe, since the world as we know it is in the last resort the words through which we imagine and name it; and when he narrows his eyes, and grins and says 'Yes, boss, you wanna see me?', it is not breathed out.

I am (you may know my name) a lexicographer. I come to these shores from far off, out of curiosity, a mere tourist, but in my own land I too am the keeper of something: of the great book of words of my tongue. No, not mine, my people's, which they have made over centuries, up there in our part of the world, and in which, if you have an ear for these things and a nose for the particular fragrance of a landscape, you may glimpse forests, lakes, great snow-peaks that hang over our land like the wings of birds. It is all there in our mouths. In the odd names of our villages, in the pet-names we give to pigs or cows, and to our children too when they are young, Little Bean, Pretty Cowslip; in the nonsense rhymes in which so much simple wisdom is contained (not by accident, the language itself discovers these truths), or in the way, when two consonants catch up a repeated sound, a new thought goes flashing from one side to another of your head.

All this is mystery. It is a mystery of the deep past, but also of now. We recapture on our tongue, when we first grasp the sound and make it, the same word in the mouths of our long dead fathers, whose blood we move in and whose blood still moves in us. Language *is* that blood. It is the sun taken up where it shares out heat and light to the surface of each thing and made whole, hot, round again. *Solen*, we say, and the sun stamps once on the plain and pushes up in its great hot body, trailing streams of breath.

O holiest of all holy things!—it is a stooped blond crane that tells you this, with yellow side-whiskers and the grey frockcoat and trousers of his century—since we touch here on beginnings, go deep down under Now to the remotest dark, far back in each ordinary moment of our speaking, even in gossip and the rigmarole of love words and children's games, into the lives of our fathers, to share with them the single instant of all our seeing and making, all our long history of doing and being. When I think of my tongue being no longer alive in the mouths of men a chill goes over me that is deeper than my own death, since it is the gathered death of all my kind. It is black night descending once and forever on all that world of forests, lakes, snow peaks, great birds' wings; on little fishing sloops, on foxes nosing their way into a coop, on the piles of logs that make bonfires, and the heels of the young girls leaping over them, on sewing-needles, milk pails, axes, on gingerbread moulds made out of good birchwood, on fiddles, school slates, spinning-tops—my breath catches, my heart jumps. O the holy dread of it! Of having under your tongue the first and last words of all those generations down there in your blood, down there in the earth, for whom these syllables were the magic once for calling the whole of creation to come striding, swaying, singing towards them. I look at this old fellow and my heart stops, I do not know what to say to him.

I am curious, of course—what else does it mean to be a scholar but to be curious and to have a passion for the preserving of things? I would like to have him speak a word or two in his own tongue. But the desire is frivolous, I am ashamed to ask. And in what language would I do it? This foreign one? Which I speak out of politeness because I am a visitor here, and speak well because I have learned it, and he because it is the only one he can share now with his contemporaries, with those who fill the days with him—the language (he appears to know only a handful of words) of those who feed, clothe, employ him, and whose great energy, and a certain gift for changing and doing things, has set all this land under another tongue. For the land too is in another language now. All its capes and valleys have new names; so do its creatures—even the insects that make their own skirling, racketing sound under stones. The first landscape here is dead. It dies in this man's eyes as his tongue licks the edge of the horizon, before it has quite dried up in his mouth. There is a new one now that others are making.

So. It is because I am a famous visitor, a scholarly freak from another continent, that we have been brought together. We have nothing to say to one another. I come to the fire where he sits with the rest of the men and accept a mug of their sweet scalding tea. I squat with difficulty in my yellow trousers. We nod to one another. He regards me with curiosity, with a kind of shy amusement, and sees what? Not fir forests, surely, for which he can have neither picture nor word, or lakes, snow-peaks, a white bird's wing. The sun perhaps, our northern one, making a long path back into the dark, and the print of our feet, black tracks upon it.

Nothing is said. The men are constrained by the presence of a stranger, but also perhaps by the presence of the boss. They make only the most rudimentary attempts at talk: slow monosyllabic remarks, half-swallowed with the tea. The thread of community here is strung with a few shy words and expletives—grunts, caws, soft bursts of laughter that go back before syntax; the man no more talkative than the rest, but a presence just the same.

I feel his silence. He sits here, solid, black, sipping his tea and flicking away with his left hand at a fly that returns again and again to a spot beside his mouth; looks up so level, so much on the horizontal, under the brim of his hat.

Things centre themselves upon him—that is what I feel, it is eerie—as on the one and only repository of a name they will lose if he is no longer there to keep it in mind. He holds thus, on a loose thread, the whole circle of shabby-looking trees, the bushes with their hidden life, the infinitesimal coming and going among grassroots or on ant-trails between stones, the minds of small native creatures that come creeping to the edge of the scene and look in at us from their other lives. He gives no sign of being special. When their smoking time is up, he rises with the rest, stretches a little, spits in the palm of his hand, and goes silently to his work.

'Yes boss, you wanna see me'—neither a statement nor a question, the only words I have heard him speak . . .

I must confess it. He has given me a fright. Perhaps it is only that I am cut off here from the use of my own tongue (though I have never felt such a thing on previous travels, in France, Greece, Egypt), but I find it necessary, in the privacy of my little room with its marble-topped washbasin and commodious jug and basin, and the engraving of Naomi bidding farewell to Ruth—I find it necessary, as I pace up and down on the scrubbed boards in the heat of a long December night, to go over certain words as if it were only my voice naming them in the dark that kept the loved objects solid and touchable in the light up there, on the top side of the world. (Goodness knows what sort of spells my hostess thinks I am making, or the children, who see me already as a spook, a half-comic, half-sinister wizard of the north.)

So I say softly as I curl up with the sheet over my head, or walk up and down, or stand at the window a moment before this plain that burns even at midnight: *rogn, valnøtt, spiseskje, hakke, vinglass, lysestake, krabbe, kjegle* . . .

1985

7 Last Words of the Emperor Hadrian[1]

> *Animula vagula blandula*
> *hospes comesque corporis,*
> *quae hunc abibis in loca,*
> *pallida, rigida, nudula,*
> *nec, ut soles, dabis iocos?*   5

1

> Dear soul mate, little guest
> and companion, what
> shift will you make

---

1 Hadrian (AD 76–138), emperor of Rome (117–38). According to the *Historia Augusta*, Hadrian composed 'Animula vagula blandula' shortly before his death.

now, out there
in the cold?
If this is a joke,   5
it is old, old.

                        2

Soul, small wandering one,
my lifelong companion,
where will you go
—numb, pale, undefended—
now the joke we shared is ended?   5

                        3

Little lightfoot
spirit, house
mate, bedfellow, where are you off
to now? Cat got
your tongue? Lost your shirt, caught   5
your death? Well the last laugh
is on you. Is on us.

                        4

Sweet urchin, fly
-by-night, heart's guest, my
better half and solace,
you've really done it
this time. You've played one trick   5
too many. Fool, you've laughed us
both out of breath.

                        5

If this is one of your jokes,
my jack, my jack-in-the-box,
lay off. Where
have you got to?
It's cold out there.   5
And what will you do
without me, you sweet idiot. Go naked?
Homeless? Come back to bed.

6

What's this, old mouse, my secret
sharer? Gone
where? Did you think I'd let
you slip away without me after
a lifetime of happy scrapes? Who   5
warmed you, clothed you, fed you, paid with laughter
for your tricks, your japes? Is this the one
joke, poor jackanapes, dear bugaboo,
your emperor does not get?

7

So you're playing fast
and loose, are you? You've cut
the love knot. Well let's see how you get
on out there without me. Who's kidding
who? Without my body, its royal   5
breath and blood to warm you, my hands, my tongue
to prove to you what's real,
what's not, poor fool, you're nothing.
But O, without you, my sweet nothing,
I'm dust.   10

2007

RUBY LANGFORD GINIBI
b. 1934

Born at Box Ridge Mission, Coraki, NSW, Dr Ruby Langford Ginibi is an elder of the Bundjalung Nation. She grew up in Bonalbo and attended high school in Casino. At fifteen she moved to Sydney where she qualified as a clothing machinist. For many years she lived and camped in the bush around Coonabarabran, fencing, lopping and ringbarking trees, pegging kangaroo skins and working in clothing factories.

Following her first book, *Don't Take Your Love to Town*, published in 1988, she has produced many award-winning works of autobiography, and published poetry and critical pieces on Aboriginal writing and politics. Her books include *Real Deadly* (1992), *My Bundjalung People* (1994), *Haunted by the Past* (1999) and *All My Mob* (2007). Ginibi is also a respected lecturer and speaker, having taught Aboriginal history, culture and politics at universities and colleges.

Her tribal name, Ginibi ('black swan'), was given to her in 1990 by her aunt, Eileen Morgan, a tribal elder of Box Ridge Mission. The mother of nine children, with many grandchildren and great-grandchildren, Ginibi was NAIDOC National Female Aboriginal Elder of the Year in 2007. In 2005 she was awarded the NSW Premier's Literary Awards' Special Award and in 2006 won the Australia Council for the Arts Writers' Emeritus Award. *AH/PM*

From *Don't Take Your Love to Town*
Chapter 10: Corroboree/Phaedra

[…] When we first moved into Ann Street, Surry Hills, we survived on my endowment and any casual work Lance could get, but it only covered food. I took the kids to The Smith Family to get outfitted and with eight of them we took up two fitting rooms. They got to know us well and we'd go home loaded up with brown paper parcels and cardboard boxes of tinned food. One morning they approached me at home and asked if they could take photos of the kids for their Christmas appeal. Somewhere in their files is a picture of me with a beehive hairstyle sitting on the front step of Ann Street nursing Pauline, who was two, and Ellen (four) sitting beside us.

Lance was working on the Water Board and I got a job around the corner at Silknit House making trousers for Reuben F. Scarf. I asked my cousin and his wife to stay and they saw the kids off to Cleveland Street School each day. Things were looking up. We bought a Ford Mainline ute and went to Paddys each Saturday for food, then we took the kids swimming at Coogee.

Nerida and her new man Booker Trindle turned up. Booker was a mate of Lance's from the days after Lance's mother had died and he was on the road. They'd worked together in the bush. I remembered Booker from the Clifton one night where Lance had introduced him as his brother. I shook his hand. He was very handsome and dressed in a suit. I was taken in but they were only conning me up. Now Booker and Neddy were living in Redfern.

Our favourite Koori watering hole was the Rockers. Its real name was the Macquarie, it was down in Woolloomooloo on the docks. They had big jazz bands and we got dolled up and went down sometimes to listen to the bands and have a few beers.

Lance and Booker wouldn't let Neddy and me go down there by ourselves, that was where the sailors drank and they were frightened they might lose us two good-looking sorts. We decided to give them a piece of their own medicine.

We sneaked down there one night and we were having a great time when who should walk through the doors of the pub but Lance and his sidekick Booker. 'There you are, you two,' they said, and, 'We've been looking for you everywhere.' We said we'd only just gotten there, which was a lie, we'd been there for a couple of hours and we were having a great time, but they frogmarched us out and told us to get home.

We said, 'We'll get a taxi,' and they said, 'Start walkin'.' Big men, and they made us walk all the way to Surry Hills. Blokes were driving past and whistling at us, and they'd tell them to piss off, and say to us, 'Keep walkin'.' I thought we'd never make it and we were buggered when we did get home. Well we never did that again, I mean sneak away by ourselves, it was a lesson well-learned for Neddy and me.

Not that they could put anything over us two, we were too cunning. They'd have to wake up early to catch us out.

'Look here,' Neddy said one day, 'there's a photo of you and the kids in the paper.' She handed me a copy of the *Mirror* and there we were, smiling for the Smithos.

Booker came in late that night, hair and clothes everywhere, he must've been on a binge for a week. Lance grabbed him by the arm. 'What the hell are you doin'? Look at you, why don't you look after yourself,' he said. 'Use my razor, come on, get in here and have a bath, here's a clean shirt, come on Booker, straighten yourself up.' The times Booker came in and didn't take any notice of Lance, Lance thumped him. They were like that, like brothers.

The kids were going to Sunday School round the corner in Commonwealth Street. The place was run by Central City Mission and was also a soup kitchen for the needy. They gave the kids bread and pies and cakes to bring home when we had no food. The Brown Sisters came to our rescue, they were called Our Lady of the Poor and wore brown habits.

I'd heard about the Aboriginal Progressive Association and I decided to go to the meetings. Charlie Perkins was there, and the Bostocks, Eadie and Lester, also Bertie Groves, Charlie and Peggy Leon, Joyce Mercy, Ray Peckham, Helen Hambly, Allan Woods and Isobel McAllum whose father was Bill Ferguson, a member of the Aborigines' Protection Board. We elected Charlie Perkins spokesman—he was still at university—and we met at the Pan Hellenic Club rooms in Elizabeth Street. Charlie organised that because he played soccer for the club. I was elected editor for our newspaper *Churringa* (meaning message stick). Ever since school and the long stories I'd wanted to do some writing, so I was happy.

It was about 1964 when we formed our first Sydney APA. We heard some dancers were coming down from Mornington Island to perform a corroboree at the Elizabethan Theatre in Newtown. At the next meeting we decided to apply for concessions. I'd never seen a corroboree or been in a big theatre before. Our seats were upstairs overlooking the stage.

When the lights went out we could see the glow of a fire on centre stage, with bodies huddled around it, and we could hear a didgeridoo in the background and clapping sticks and then the chanting. In a while the whole stage was aglow with the light from the fire, and the corroboree began.

A narrator talked over a microphone, explaining the action as the dancers performed. After each performance we clapped and clapped. Something inside me understood everything that was going on. I had tears in my eyes and I could feel the others in the group were entranced like me.

One story in particular made me sad. It was about a tribal family—man, woman and child. It told how another man came and took the woman away, and left the baby to die. The father searched and hunted until he found the man and speared him. His wife threw herself over a cliff and died. The final scene showed the father burying his child, and it was the most moving part of the corroboree. It showed him digging the earth up with his hands and placing the bark-covered body into the ground, and, as he was covering it with earth he'd smite himself across the chest and wail for the loss of his child and cover more soil over the body then smite himself again and this went on until he had it completely covered. I was crying by then.

Afterwards, we asked permission to visit them backstage. It was strange because they were dressed in khaki overalls and they were so tall, big rangy warriors all over six feet. Only one of them could speak English, a bit pidgin and they were wary as they looked at us, until the one who could speak explained that we were part of them, and then they gave us big toothy grins and we were shaking hands all round. I can remember almost every detail from that night.

I went to a meeting of the APA on National Aborigines' Day in Martin Place. The Governor General and several other dignitaries (black and white) were going to speak. I wore a fur stole over my dress. I put my stilettos on and did my hair up. At Martin Place I met up with the others and found a seat. The Police Band sat behind us. A man on the dais was singing in the lingo and I listened closer. It was Bundjalung language, words and sounds I hadn't heard for a long time. It was an eerie feeling in amongst the skyscrapers.

I looked harder and I recognised the singer, it was Uncle Jim Morgan. When the singing stopped a hand tapped me on the shoulder and a voice said, 'Hello Mrs Campbell.' Someone from the time I was with Gordon, I thought, turning around. Coona. It was Max Gruggan, the policeman who used to pull Gordon out of the pub and send him home to Charlie Harvey's property. 'I didn't hardly recognise you, all done up,' he said. We swapped notes—he'd transferred to Penrith in the meantime. I couldn't concentrate much because I was thinking about Uncle Jim Morgan and the singing.

In a while I went and found Uncle Jim. I hadn't seen him since I was at school in Bonalbo and he was glad to see me too, like meeting someone from your own town in another country. He had to go soon after and so I put word out about him.

Some time later my cousin Margaret in Wollongong sent me two paper clippings—one about Grandfather Sam and one about Uncle Jim. JAMES MORGAN LIVED IN TWO WORLDS, it said. He had collapsed and died shortly before he was to address a large crowd in Casino for National Aborigines' Day. 'A full-blood Aborigine, Mr Morgan was known as "the last of the Dyrabba tribe".' Dyrabba? That was the name of our street in Bonalbo.

'He was born on the site of Casino racecourse ... He was a fluent speaker of Bunjalong [spelt that way] and had a working knowledge of the twelve dialects in the Bunjalong area which extends from Ipswich to Grafton ... He was also an expert on folklore of this area. He made many recordings for the Richmond River Historical Society ...'

This meant I could find out some more about my history. I decided to write to the RRHS for the tapes.

His funeral was to be held at the chapel at Box Ridge, he was to be buried at Coraki cemetery. Home ground.

1988

JILL KER CONWAY
b. 1934

As detailed in her popular memoir, *The Road from Coorain* (1989), Jill Ker Conway was born and grew up in outback NSW. After the death of her father, the family moved to Sydney, where Conway was educated. She left Australia in 1965 after being turned down (due to gender bias) for a trainee post with the Department of External Affairs. Conway attended Harvard University, where she received her PhD in 1969. After teaching at the University of Toronto, Canada, Conway became president of Smith College, Massachusetts, the largest women's college in the United States, from 1975 to 1985. *The Road from Coorain* was made into a television film in 2001. As well as her own memoirs, Conway has written extensively on autobiography (especially women's), education and women's studies. *DM*

From *The Road from Coorain*
Chapter 4: Drought

[. . .] After the June shearing of 1944, we knew that if it did not rain in the spring our gamble was lost. The sheep would not live through until another rainy season. There were so few to feed by September 1944 that our friends and helpers, Ron and Jack Kelly, left for another job. We on Coorain[1] waited for the rain which never came. The dust storms swept over us every two or three weeks, and there was no pretending about the state of the sheep when we travelled around the property. The smells of death and the carrion birds were everywhere. The starving animals which came to our feed troughs were now demented with hunger. When I ran off as decoy to spread out a thin trail of grain while the troughs were filled, they knocked me over and trampled me, desperate to tear the grain from the bag. Their skeletal bodies were pitiful. I found I could no longer bear to look into their eyes, because the usually tranquil ruminant animals looked half crazed.

---

1   The name of the family's property in NSW.

We lost our appetite for meat because the flesh of the starving animals already tasted putrid. I was never conscious of when the smell of rotting animals drowned out the perfumes from my mother's garden, but by early December, although it still bloomed, our nostrils registered only decaying flesh. By then the sand accumulating on the other side of the windbreak was beginning to bend the cane walls inward by its weight, and we knew it was only a matter of time before it too was engulfed.

My mother, as always, was unconquerable. 'It has to rain some day,' she told my father. 'Our children are healthy. We can grow our food. What does it matter if we lose everything else?' She did not understand that it mattered deeply to him. Other memories of loss from his childhood were overwhelming him. He could not set out in mid-life to be once more the orphan without patrimony. As he sank into deeper depression, they understood one another less. She, always able to rouse herself to action, could not understand how to deal with crippling depression, except by a brisk call to count one's blessings. This was just what my father was unable to do.

My brothers were summoned home two weeks early from school, though to help with what was not clear. There was pitifully little to do on Coorain. There were the same burlap troughs to mend, the same desperate animals to feed, but the size of the task was shrinking daily. The December heat set in, each day over 100 degrees. Now so much of our land was without vegetation that the slightest breeze set the soil blowing. Even without the dust storms, our daily life seemed lived in an inferno.

My mother's efforts to rouse my father were indefatigable. One Saturday in early December was to be a meeting of the Pastures Protection Board in Hillston. Early in the week before, she set about persuading him to drive the seventy-five miles with his close friend Angus Waugh. Reluctantly, he agreed. The Friday before, a minor dust storm set in, and he decided against the drive. It was fearfully hot, over 108 degrees, and we passed a fitful evening barricaded in against the blowing sand.

The next morning I awoke, conscious that it was very early, to find my father gazing intently at me. He bent down to embrace me and said good-bye. Half asleep, I bid him good-bye and saw his departing back. Suddenly, I snapped awake. *Why is he saying good-bye? He isn't going anywhere.* I leapt out of bed, flung on the first clothes to hand, and ran dry-mouthed after him. I was only seconds too late. I ran shouting after his car, 'I want to come. Take me with you.' I thought he saw me, but, the car gathering speed, he drove away.

Back in the house, my mother found me pacing about and asked why I was up so early in the morning. I said I'd wanted to go with my father, and wasn't sure where he went. He was worried about the heat and the adequacy of the water for the sheep in Brooklins (a distant paddock), she said, and had gone to check on it. It was a hot oppressive day, with the wind gaining strength by noon. I felt a leaden fear in my stomach, but was speechless. To speak of my fears seemed to admit that my father had lost his mental balance. It was something I could not say.

His journey should not have taken more than two hours, but then again he could have decided to visit other watering places on the property. When he was not home by two, my mother and Bob set out after him. Neither Barry nor I, left behind, was inclined to talk about what might have happened. Like a pair of automatons, we washed the dishes left from lunch and settled in to wait. When no one returned by four, the hour when my mother stoked the stove and began her preparations for dinner, we went through the motions of her routine. The potatoes were peeled, peas shelled, the roast prepared, the table laid.

Eventually, Bob arrived home alone. There had been an accident, he said. He must make some phone calls and hurry back. We neither of us believed him. We knew my father was dead. Finally, at six o'clock, the old grey utility my father drove hove into sight driven by my brother Bob; my mother's car followed, with several others in its wake. She took the time to thank us for preparing dinner before saying she had something to tell us alone. We went numbly to our parents' bedroom, the place of all confidential conversations. 'I want you to help me,' she said. 'Your father's dead. He was working on extending the piping into the Brooklins dam. We found him there in the water.' My eyes began to fill with tears. She looked at me accusingly. 'Your father wouldn't want you to cry,' she said.

We watched woodenly as my father's body was brought to rest in that same bedroom. We were dismissed while she prepared it for the funeral which would take place in two days. In the hot summer months, burials had to be speedy and there was no need for anyone to explain why to us children. We had been dealing with decaying bodies for years. Because of the wartime restrictions on travel and the need for haste, there was little time to summon family and friends. Telegrams were dispatched but only my mother's brother and sister-in-law, close to us in Sydney, were actually expected. Eventually, we sat down to dinner and choked over our food, trying desperately to make conversation with the kindly manager from a neighbouring station who had come to help. The meal seemed surreal. The food on the plate seemed unconnected to the unreal world without my father in it in which I now lived. I was haunted by the consciousness of his body lying close by in the bedroom, which my mother had sternly forbidden me to enter.

After we went sleeplessly to bed, we heard a sound never heard before, the sound of my mother weeping hopelessly and inconsolably. It was a terrible and unforgettable sound. To moderate the heat we slept on a screened veranda exposed to any southern breeze which might stir. My brother Barry's bed was next to mine. After listening to this terrible new sound, we both agreed that we wished we were older so that we could go to work and take care of her. We tossed until the sun rose and crept out of bed too shocked to do more than converse in whispers.

My mother soon appeared, tight-lipped and pale, somehow a ghost of herself. Dispensing with all possibility of discussion, she announced that Barry and I were to stay with friends for a few days. She did not want us to see our father buried, believing that this would be too distressing for us. Though we complied without questioning the plan, I felt betrayed that I would not see him to his last rest. She, for her part, wanted to preserve us from signs of the body's decay. As we set out, driven by the kindly Morison family, who had cared for me during my mother's illness, we passed the hearse making its way towards Coorain. Its black shape drove home what had happened.

How my father's death had actually come about we would never know. He was a poor swimmer, and had attempted to dive down in muddy water to connect a fresh length of pipe so that the pump for watering the sheep could draw from the lowered water level of the dam. It was a difficult exercise for a strong swimmer, and not one to undertake alone. Why he had chosen to do it alone when my two brothers, both excellent swimmers, were at home, we could not understand. I did not tell anyone of his early morning visit to me. I realized that we would never know the answer to the question it raised. [. . .]

1989

BOB RANDALL
b. 1934

Bob Randall is a singer, songwriter, teacher and activist. He is from the Yankunytjatjara people and is a traditional owner of the Uluru lands, NT. His mother, Tanguawa, worked as a housemaid at Angus Downs cattle station for Randall's father, station owner Bill Liddle. Randall and his mother lived away from the main house with their extended family and he had little contact with his Scottish father. Randall was taken from his mother at the age of seven. He spent time in an Alice Springs institution for children, Croker Island Reservation, and in Sydney.

Randall married, completed a welfare residential worker's course, moved to Darwin and began finding his family while establishing a career as an Aboriginal educator.

In 1970, Randall helped establish the Adelaide Community College for Aboriginal people and lectured at the college on Aboriginal cultures. Randall has also established Aboriginal and Torres Strait Islander centres at other universities. Many consider his song 'Brown Skin Baby' an anthem of the stolen generation. *AH/PM*

Brown Skin Baby

Yaaawee, yaahaawawee,
My brown skin baby they take 'im away.

As a young preacher I used to ride
my quiet pony round the countryside.
In a native camp I'll never forget   5
a young black mother her cheeks all wet.

Yaaawee, yaahaawawee,
My brown skin baby they take 'im away.

Between her sobs I heard her say,
'Police bin take-im my baby away.   10
From white man boss that baby I have,
why he let them take baby away?'

Yaaawee, yaahaawawee,
My brown skin baby they take 'im away.

To a children's home a baby came,   15
With new clothes on, and a new name.
Day and night he would always say,
'Mummy, Mummy, why they take me away?'

Yaaawee, yaahaawawee,
My brown skin baby they take 'im away.   20

The child grew up and had to go
From a mission home that he loved so.
To find his mother he tried in vain.
Upon this earth they never met again.

Yaaawee, yaahaawawee,   25
My brown skin baby they take 'im away.

INGA CLENDINNEN
b. 1934

Inga Clendinnen, who grew up in Geelong, is a historian, archaeologist and anthropologist. She was educated at the University of Melbourne, and after teaching there for some years she worked at La Trobe University. Illness led to her writing *Tiger's Eye* (2000), an innovative mix of childhood autobiography, Australian history, 'autopathography' and fiction. Clendinnen has also published works on Mayan and Aztec culture, the Holocaust (*Reading the Holocaust*, 1998, was a 1999 *New York Times* Best Book of the Year), and Australian Indigenous history. In 1999 she gave the Boyer lectures (published as *True Stories*, 2000). Her long essay *The History Question: Who owns the past* (2006) discusses the differences between history, fiction and myth. DM

From *Tiger's Eye*
Snakes and Ladders

[. . .] After more than a year of waiting, and mainly I assumed because of my mental deterioration, I had slithered sufficiently far down the slope of debility to warrant the ultimate gamble. I was accepted onto the waiting list for a liver transplant, or—an alternative, and, as it proved, ironical usage—I was 'activated'. Accepting the congratulations of friends, I repacked my hospital case, settled outstanding accounts. And began to wait.

Euphoria evaporated as I came to realise the constrictions of this limbo. I found I was implicated in a strange game between myself and fate, or the devil. The name you choose for your opponent does not matter. What you may not choose is the nature of the game: it is always Snakes and Ladders. But with a twist. The twist is that while there are lots of snakes of various sizes and degrees of viciousness, there is only one ladder: the transplant operation.

Most patients spend six months or more on the waiting list, and this when they are already miserably ill. They hang between the world in which well people plan, arrange to meet, have expectations of themselves and of others, and their own secret world of perfected solipsism. The snakes are there, unseen, but rearing in the path. You can see the ladder, too, though vaguely. And you know that it may be phantasmal: that the telephone may not ring, that you will land on that last long snake—and down you will go. Fantasies about independence, about effecting or affecting, have long since evaporated. You are not even competent to tend your own body. The clock runs slow and slower, a few memories flap and bang in the near-derelict premises of your mind.

And you wait. It is not possible to hope, because you know everything depends on chance: the savage chance of a brutal accident somewhere in some not too remote place; the chance that a fatally injured victim of that accident survives long enough to reach a hospital; that he or she had one day checked a box or filled out a card, or that a family in the midst of anguish will hear and agree to a barbarous request. That the blood grouping and fine matching will be right. That there is no-one in your particular category in greater need. That the surgical teams can be assembled, a theatre cleared. All that, before the telephone will ring. Truly, Tezcatlipoca[1] rules.

---

1   A central deity in Aztec religion.

People on the waiting list are always secretly, guiltily tense on public holidays. Road accidents happen on public holidays.

Late on such a day the telephone rang, and I was back in the turning world again. As I walked through Casualty for the preliminary X-rays and tests, medicos and technicians I thought scarcely knew me smiled and wished me luck. Everyone seemed to share my suppressed jubilation. The preparation, in a ward already familiar, was amiable and deceptively casual. With no more than the pre-medication I went happily to sleep.

What happened next I have tried to record as exactly as I was able.

CRISIS

First Day. I am back. I am in Intensive Care. Hard light, the whirrings and cluckings of invisible machines, the sighing of invisible doors. And whispering, lots of whispering. Someone keeps whispering to me: 'Now, Inga, I am going to . . .' Whisper whisper. On and on. Susurrating. I have never used that word before, never thought it but that is what this person, this woman, is doing. I am pleased to have the right word. I would like to say, 'Stop susurrating! Just do it!' but there is a tube in my nose and a mask over my mouth and anyway I am tired. And I can't see her; she's somewhere behind me, and there are too many tubes, I can't turn my head. I am weighed down like Gulliver.

Now she flicks into view. I can see her out of the corner of my eye. She is thin, pale; she lives inside this underground spaceship. She flicks past, flicks on clear plastic gloves, a little see-through apron, like a French sex farce. What is she going to do? Ridiculous. She flicks between the thick plastic flaps at the end of the cubicle. They are not see-through. They are solid, slabby, like cods' eyes. There is a big metal clock hanging at the end of my metal bed. Its face is blank: there are no numbers, though it has a lot of hands. Or is it that the numbers are there and I can't see them? I don't have my glasses. What have they done with my glasses? Why have they given me a clock?

More people, three or four, tugging at me, pulling at me, all of them talking, talking. Explaining. Shut up; just do it. There is a phone behind my head: the woman is susurrating into that. There is a noise, a vague ululation, deep in my right ear: music? Someone says, 'They're ready for her upstairs.' They start fiddling with a tuft of tubes growing out of my neck, just under that same ear. I wish they'd stop, I think I feel sick; I think I need to concentrate.

Now someone, not the first woman, a new one with hair like bright metal, is screwing spiky plastic things, red, yellow, blue, bright as kindergarten toys, into each of the tubes under my ear. There are a lot of them, they are heavy, they pull my head right over, one eye is looking at the ceiling. They are not toys, they are African earrings, but I am sure you are not meant to put them in all at once. You are meant to put them in one by one, over months, years, so your ears stretch to hold them all. But the woman does not want to wait, she is not going to wait, she is going to put them all in at once, THERE and THERE and THERE. She fans them out on the pillow. She is pleased with her work. She stands back. She says, 'Now you can take her up to the ward.'

Second Day. I know the ward; I have been here before. But this part is new, I have never seen this narrow corridor. They have to edge the trolley out of the corridor into a room. As it swings I see a bright yellow sign with black letters: 'Stop! Infection Control.' It is a small white room with a high narrow bed. Tall machines stand placidly around. They look like friendly elephants. One whole wall is glass. A grey pigeon is flying diagonally across it as they scoop me onto the bed. Hello pigeon!

I lie in my high white room. People come and go. They are all in a good mood, but they do not like my earrings: they click their tongues; they try to coil them up, over my ear so they won't drag so much. Someone is playing a radio somewhere. A choir, male, German, heavy, boom boom. Wagner. I hate that kind of music, but today I do not mind. I am calm as a spider hanging at the end of its silken thread. I do not know the thread is attenuating.

Then it breaks. And I fall.

Second Night. I am a naked worm, skinless, blind; I am a blind leech, I must find a body. I stretch and yearn towards every sound: who's there? Let there be someone. Control yourself. If I cannot see it is only because it is night. I am not blind, it is only that it is night. Please, let there be someone.

The air moves, goes still, turns solid: Carrie? Carrie is solid and calm as a tree. She smells of mint and cold water. She leans over me, her leaf hands brush me here, there. I like Carrie.

But it is Muna I love. She comes to me so quickly through the dark, I hear the pad-pad of her feet, her little snuffling breath as she comes. I snuffle up her smell: something bitter, a Chinese herb, the orange she ate at break. She tells me my name, 'Inga', putting a little feathery upward curl on the end. It sounds light, and happy. She makes me a body out of pillows: Inga, this is for your back, this is for your legs. And this, gently now, gently, this is for your front. O, thank you Muna, thank you. She talks to me, explains what she is doing. We are gardeners together, restoring a garden: this must be done and that must be done and when we have done all these things it will all be put to rights. I hear her talking to four-year-old Paulie in the next room in exactly the same way. Paulie, who screams and weeps through the night, is quiet for Muna.

I know why he screams. We have plastic bladders attached to our bodies, he and I. They slowly fill with fluid from somewhere inside. They are heavy when they are full, and they shift a little when you move. I hear him say, softly, 'The fish, the fish are biting me.' He thinks there are fish in the bladders. There are no fish. How do you tell a four-year-old there are no fish?

There is another person, a man, further down the corridor. You remember the word, the sound, that used to be written in the old comic books? 'Aaarrghh!' That was how they wrote it. 'Aaarrghh!' the balloon would say, when someone fell out a window. I had never heard it, I didn't think it was a real sound. Now I hear it often. He says it, the man down the corridor. First he says, 'Get away from me you bastards.' That is when they come into the room. Then he says, 'Get away, leave me alone, get away.' That is when they touch him. Then he makes that sound. 'Aaarrghh.'

I am falling again.

Third Day. My eyes are closed, but there is a film being run. It is being projected onto the inside of my eyelids. I think it is a film. I am looking at a clay-coloured surface, a pitted surface. Is it just my eyelid? No, it is a film, it is beginning, pay attention now. The surface is clay. It is very smooth; it looks as if it has been washed or smoothed with water. A cave? I can't see properly: the light is shuddering, the camera is jerking about. A bison, is that a bison, a black bison on the wall?

The camera lurches to a stop, pans back, waits. Yes, a bison. And over there, that red, an antelope. Stone Age paintings. Altamira? Lascaux? No time: the camera is moving again. Concentrate. The walls are sagging, collapsing into clay soup. Now the walls are gone, and we are skimming over a clay lake. The surface is sleek, still. Then it quivers. The camera swoops. A tiny split opens. There is a little eye in there. It looks out at me, winks. Then it vanishes. A face is making itself out of the clay, heaving, puffing, pulling itself out of the clay. It's out! It writhes into a grin, splits, plops back. Now faces are bubbling and plopping everywhere. They grin, laughing at me with their wet clay mouths. I am frightened of them; they want to do me harm. I look hard at one and it collapses, slides back into the soup, hides. Then it peeks out again. STOP IT.

The camera stops. It is thinking: what will I do to her next? Ah! It is off again, hold on! The clay has turned to sand, flying sand. We are pulsing over a desert; long smooth waves pulsing over long, smooth, pulsing waves of sand. I can't focus, everything is moving so fast. There is a hump or swelling ahead; it is coming up fast. The camera brakes, a showy skidding ski-stop, the wind whips away the veils of sand, presto! The corpse of a dog, a yellow dog, its feet in the air. It has dried to hair and bone and long black leather lips; the belly is gone, just the ribs and the haunch-bones left, and a few bleached tatters of hide. The long teeth are exposed, and the full depth of the jaws: a snarl, or pain? I can't tell. I don't care. The dog is dead. The camera waits. I say, forget it, you can't scare me with that, you can't scare me with old Simba whatever state she's in. You will have to do better than that.

There is a furious blur like a hive gone mad: the camera is angry. Then it squats down, eyes me. Pure malevolence. It begins to move, slowly. The ululation in my ear shapes itself into a vague melody: some men singing, far away and softly, the barest thread of sound unravelling in the breathing silence. I follow the thread. It wavers upwards, lifts, drops. Words form in my mind. 'Underneath the lamplight, by the barrack gate.' Lili Marlene. Now I see dim shapes. They are men, heavily burdened. Their heads are bent, they are moving very slowly. Mourners? They are coming up out of the ground, out of slits in the ground. Dead men, moving their slow dead limbs, climbing out of their graves? No, not graves. They are climbing out of trenches. Barbed wire loops and coils on the sand. The men begin to run towards the wire. They run with long, dream-like steps, their knees lifting. This is a slow-motion film. They fling their legs out, their pale eyes shine. They are looking at the sky.

They hit the wire. They rise higher, float for a moment. Then they fall. Now they are tumbling, rolling, until they are tight-wrapped in the wire, hooked on the barbs. Their mouths open into round black holes. I am meant to think they are screaming, Oh, Oh, Oh! Their eyes stretch round as their mouths, Oh, Oh! The camera is pleased, it says there, look at that.

I say, No! This is a useless film, it wouldn't fool anybody, no-one would believe it. The camera scowls. It shuffles sideways, glides into the air, and pulls into tight close-up. Panning slowly, it moons into every staring face. It slides closer. It peers into their mouths: open wide now. It grazes their eyeballs. It puts out its tongue, licks delicately, there is the taste of salt in my mouth. *Jesus.* Stop. Stop. Stop *now.* You can't scare me with your lousy film. It's stupid, anyway, you can't do trench warfare in a desert. For trenches you need mud.

I say it, and the mud comes, great sleek waves of it, engulfing everything. Now the men in the wire are floundering, drowning, basting themselves with mud, turning into mud. Their eyes and mouths are full of mud, their arms and legs move like eels under the smooth clay skin. The mud belches and heaves. Horses are screaming off camera, somewhere to the left. That's not fair, you shouldn't use horses, you shouldn't bring horses in. The camera sniggers.

A line of stretcher-bearers is trotting past. The stretchers are heavy, you can see from the men's hunched shoulders, their jerking heads. A pair jogs past me. Their stretcher is empty, the body has slipped off, I can see it, there, in the mud, but they do not know it is empty, that they are jog-jogging to no purpose, because they are blind. One of them lifts his head as he passes, the face swings towards me. His eye sockets are empty, but I know him. I know him. He is my father.

Fourth Day. My eyes are open. I can see the walls, the window. No pigeons. There are people in the corridor, Jenny, and a man, Frank I think.

The film has stopped, but the Germans are still singing deep in my ear, and full volume now. It's Wagner again, I don't know the phrase, but I know it's Wagner, one great straining phrase repeating itself, over and over, always the same, moaning and straining. I hate Wagner, with his stupid fat phoney climaxes. But now it is daylight, so why can I still hear the music? They must be real after all, they must be in the bathroom, there must be ten or more German soldiers singing in my bathroom. Are they really there? I was hallucinating in the night, but I shouldn't be now, not in daylight, not with people just outside in the corridor.

I can be sly too. I wait for the nurse. It's Carrie with her freshwater smell. I ask her is there a radio somewhere, the music is bothering me, could she please have them turn it down? She says there is no radio, but if the music is bothering me—does that mean she can hear it, too?—I should put on my headphones. She looks for them, finds them in the drawer, fits them on her head, smiles, and says, 'You're in luck. It's the Duke.' She lifts my earrings, carefully slips the headphones over my ears (they are warm from her ears) and it is. It is the Duke. Mood Indigo. Sweet Jesus, it is the Duke.

The Duke smiles and sways, weaving his casual magic. I can hear the Germans in the background: they are faltering, trying to regroup. The Duke tosses a long, curving necklace of notes, catches it, tosses it higher. He is winning, he is forcing them back, he is winning, he will win. I fumble for the tiny knob, find it, turn the volume HIGH.

I have realised something. I must get this clear before the dark comes again. That yellow dog. That was Simba. It is true that she trusted me, and I had her killed. But I am not guilty because she was dying, she was in pain. She wasn't frightened, old Simby; I was holding her when she died—sneezed, and died. The trenches, the stretcher-bearers. The mud, coming just when it did, when I said it should. I know too much about these scripts. They are doing this to me, but I am helping them; I am watching, but I am also behind the camera. I do not control it, I cannot control it, but I am there. Somewhere.

I must get control of the script. But how can I, when I am so tired? And how can I concentrate with this damned music going in my head?

Then I see the boy in the corner. He's young, only about seventeen, in uniform, with a rifle and a knapsack, and he is slumped in the corner under the window. He is German, and he is exhausted. His face is yellow. He could be bleeding, but I can't see any blood.

Our eyes lock. He looks at me with terrible collusive intimacy as if the skin of our eyes is pressed together: please, don't tell them, please, let me rest for a while. I can see the pale stubble on his chin, smell the wet woollen smell of his uniform. This is the worst vision of all, because he is slumped there, I can see him, I can smell him, but I think he is not real. Carrie did not see him.

Or did she see him, and say nothing?

I stare at the boy, he stares at me. Then the Germans shout, and he is gone. There is only the shining floor, the light from the window, the empty corner.

Fourth Night. The camera is back. I thought it had gone, but it was only resting. Waiting. It dances about, jumping at me, pretending to be glad to see me. Off again.

It is dark now, and windy. We are flying over a plain. There is a city, with walls around it. Medieval? Chinese? I can't tell, I can't recognise anything, what is this script? Concentrate. A big city: there are thoroughfares, arches, stone columns. But there are no people. The camera swivels, points: yes, I see, there are some people, over there; as we swoop towards them they scuttle like cockroaches, they vanish into cracks. There is a castle, or palace, with banners, red and gold. There are black signs on them, arabesques. Or dragons; they might be dragons.

We are descending now, hovering, at the entrance, over the forecourt. The great jade doors are levered apart, and in front, on the stairs, there is a pile of metal. It is not as rigid as metal. Flesh? They are men, men in iron; are they drunk, or dead? The camera prances over, sniffs at a rusted corselet. Not rust, blood. Dead. A pile of men in armour, dead.

We don't care; we float up the wide azure stairs, slide through the doors, drift through the reception rooms. The mother-of-pearl walls are hung with tapestries of every-colour silk; they throb in the wind of our passing. Statues stand at intervals. Their hands are empty. They should hold flowers, or torches. All the rooms are empty. No courtiers, no attendants—nobody.

At last, in the centre of a great octagonal room, there are bow-legged men in loincloths, squatting around a fire. They are roasting some small animal: there is a stench of scorching hair and flesh. They are burning the furniture: delicate wooden legs lie around like antelope bones.

The camera sniffs, picks up its skirts, and whirls into the private apartments. They are empty too. No-one has lived here for months. Dust is thick on the gilded mouldings, the great beds are stripped, the dragon bedposts guard nothing. We prowl, peering, sniffing. Nothing.

Down the staircase again, out to the working parts of the palace. No-one is working, but I can hear shouts, screams, from the kitchens and cellars, and the narrow space between the battlements and the walls is crammed with people. They are peacocking like gipsies in wraps and turbans and skirts of silk, torn from the tapestries on the walls, and they are all drunk. The palace has been looted by its own people.

Then I see him. They have forced him up onto the parapet and forgotten about him. He has no clothes, the emperor has no clothes at all. His wrinkled hide is bare, except for a few tatters of silk clinging to the shrunken buttocks. The wind is tugging at them; it will soon have them off him. He is shuffling from one bloodied, yellow foot to the other, turning slowly, revolving, gazing into the night sky. He is dancing for the moon. He is quite, quite mad.

More shouts from below, more wails, not all from women, and the clang of weapons: an attack? The camera leaps over the parapet, thrusts itself into the fray, come on! Men-at-arms are reeling, whacking at one another: huge, iron-clad, black-cloaked Darth Vaders, whacking and whacking like mechanical monsters. But no-one is falling: they lurch and whack, lurch and whack. At last a monstrous giant sags, is clubbed to the ground, whack, whack, whack. Blood dribbles through the metal casing; the clanking carcase is lugged away. And five huge warriors, identical, in identical dark armour, come lumbering out. To take his place. More shapes rise to meet them: whack, whack, whack.

This battle will never end. It is not intended that this battle should end. An ending is not in the script.

The camera is bored. It jiggles about, scratches itself. Then it wanders away, away from the thuds and the clangs. We are in the kitchen garden now, I can smell the rosemary and the lavender. From here the battle sounds like a Chinese opera, all cymbals and flutes and drums. The stars are out. The camera sits down beside me, nuzzles my hand. It is feeling friendly: it leans against me, shuts its eyes, goes to sleep. I sleep too.

A young colleague has sent me flowers: a tall construction of spiky proteas, topped by the azure and flame spears of strelitzias, bird of paradise flowers. When they brought me up from Intensive Care they were there, floating on a high shelf like an Aztec warrior's war crest.

As I drift in and out of consciousness, I see them, floating.

Now I remember the tiger. I invoke the tiger. I see his black-barred face, his golden eyes. Stiffen the sinew. Summon up the blood. Concentrate.

I am making these dream-stories. I do not choose them, they terrify me, I think they might kill me. Nevertheless, I am making them. This must be what they call paranoia, these visions. To stop them unspooling I must understand why I am making them, and what I am making them from.

The cave. I don't know. I have seen the caves at Altamira. I don't see why they should matter. The dog is Simba. The trenches. My father was in

France, he drove an ambulance, therefore the stretcher-bearers. I was angry with him because he would not say war was terrible, when I had read about it and knew that it was. But I had known that before, a long time before. I already knew it was terrible, and that was why I was angry. How did I know that it was terrible?

The other film, the war in the ruined palace. Is it my ruined body, its people rioting through the halls? Mother-of-pearl walls. The mindless, endless battle. The drugs? I don't know. I am tired now, tired of thinking. Concentrate. The bare-arsed old emperor on the parapet, who is he? My mind? My self?

No. I am not the emperor. If I am there at all, I am one of those shreds of silk, streaming, tearing in the wind.

I do not think the film will come back. Sleep now.

Fifth Day. Today the nurses arrange me in the chair, 'just for ten minutes'. They have taken away my African earrings: only one plug, the yellow one, is left, dangling at the end of its plastic. I fumble through my first shower, carefully lifting the other tubes sprouting from under my breasts to wash, careful not to look down, not to look in the mirror. Today I have my first non-family visitor. She is reassured. She says, 'How wonderful! You are yourself again.'

I am not. I am held together by shadow knitting.

Sixth Day, Seventh Day. Everyone is saying how well I am; that I will be able to go home soon. It is true I am better. All the tubes are gone except for one to the bile duct, and that will come home with me. I walk for kilometres around the corridors: my record is five kilometres in one morning. But I still seem to have no skin; I respond to everything. And so irritable. I scribble great lists, of what I must do, of what other people must do. And I talk. I listen to myself talking. I sound like a megalomaniac. I think I am out of control.

They say that all this time I have been on a high from the bolus of drugs they gave me during the operation. That is why I have been so frantic. They say it happens to everyone. Now I have crashed, and that happens to everyone too. In time, I will pick myself up. They say.

I have been thinking about the mud film, the 1914 war. My father's war. Before I knew about his war I knew about the other war, because of the Americans we adopted, the marines my mother adopted, when I was . . . seven? I could write by then, so about seven. Mickey Espejo and the others, members of the family, part of the household. 'They are only boys,' my mother would say, 'only babies.' Her pet Mickey looked like a baby, a soft brown smiling baby. The one I liked was Steve. Steve Wresser. I used to write to him when they were in the training camp at Ballarat, and he would write back. Then they went to a place called Guadalcanal. Three of them came home. One of them, Eightball, was blind, and Mickey didn't look like a baby any more. Steve Wresser, the one I used to write to and who always wrote back, was dead, killed there somehow. They had photographs of the place. It looked muddy. I have not thought of him for years, but I have never forgotten him. I can see him now, although he has been dead for half a century. Hello Steve. I named my first son Stephen, I thought for other reasons, but perhaps it was for you.

After you were dead, I could not bear to watch the soldiers marching along Noble Street, with the people waving and smiling. My mother would be there too. With her little flag, waving. She knew what they were going to do to you, to them, but she still waved her flag. My mother, my undemonstrative mother, who had looked at Mickey on the day he came back to her door, and took his face in her hands, and pulled his head against her breast, and held it there until he started to cry, held it there until he had stopped crying. Perhaps I have spent my life trying to understand that.

I go home tomorrow, just for a few hours, to get used to it. Then the next day, just for a few hours. Then for good. For good.

Fourteenth Day. There has been a setback. I have had a golden staph infection, but I will be home soon. Perhaps tomorrow.

Later. I must tell you something. On the day I was discharged from the hospital, the day I left the ward, I heard the man down the corridor say something in an ordinary voice. He had never done that before. There had only been shouts and screams. He said, quietly, perhaps to someone in his room, perhaps to nobody, 'Help me. I am being held here against my will.' The person, if there was one, asked him why he thought that, why was he being held? He answered softly, hopelessly, wearily, 'I don't know'.

As I write this he is still there, still lost in a place of terrors. Truly, Tezcatlipoca rules. [. . .]

2000

RANDOLPH STOW
b. 1935

Novelist and poet Randolph Stow was born in Geraldton, WA, and educated there and at the University of Western Australia. During the 1960s he tutored in English at the University of Adelaide and worked as an anthropologist's assistant in New Guinea, an experience that provided the setting for his novel *Visitants* (1979), which is set in Papua in 1959. He also taught and studied at Yale and at the University of Leeds; by the end of the 1960s he had settled permanently in England.

His first novel, *A Haunted Land*, was published in 1956 and the following year he published both his first collection of poems, *Act One*, and a second novel, *The Bystander*. It was his third novel, *To the Islands* (1958), a very early example of Australian anti-triumphalist historical fiction, that firmly established his reputation as a fiction writer and it is still one of his best-known works. It was followed in 1963 by *Tourmaline*.

Each of Stow's first three novels has a certain hyper-real quality and a preoccupation with spiritual progress or haunting; his fourth and most accessible novel and also his best-known in Australia, *The Merry-Go-Round in the Sea* (1965), is a more muted and realist semi-autobiographical work, a coming-of-age novel that also takes in the effects of the Second World War and explores different experiences of isolation and masculinity in characters of varying ages.

Midnite: The story of a wild colonial boy (1967) is a popular children's book based on stories of the WA bushranger Moondyne Joe; this was Stow's last book with an Australian setting. *The Girl Green as Elderflower* (1980), which Stow has said is his favourite among his novels, is set in Suffolk in the 1960s and makes use, as does much of Stow's earlier work, of mythological material. *The Suburbs of Hell* (1984) is a metafictional thriller set in an imaginary town with the sinister name of Tornwitch.

Stow has also written for the stage: *Midnite* was recast as a stage play in 1978, and he has also written two libretti for operas by English composer Peter Maxwell Davies, *Eight Songs for a Mad King* (1969) and *Miss Donnithorne's Maggot* (1974). KG

From *The Merry-Go-Round in the Sea*
Chapter 1

The merry-go-round had a centre post of cast iron, reddened a little by the salt air, and of a certain ornateness: not striking enough to attract a casual eye, but still, to an eye concentrated upon it (to the eye, say, of a lover of the merry-go-round, a child) intriguing in its transitions. The post began as a square pillar, formed rings, continued as a fluted column, suddenly bulged like a diseased tree with an excrescence of iron leaves, narrowed to a peak like the top of a pepperpot; and at last ended, very high in the sky, with an iron ball. In the bulge where the leaves were was an iron collar. From this collar eight iron stays hung down, supporting the narrow wooden octagonal seat of the merry-go-round, which circled the knees of the centre post rather after the style of a crinoline. The planks were polished by the bottoms of children, and on every one of the stays was a small unrusted section where the hands of adults had grasped and pulled to send the merry-go-round spinning.

When the merry-go-round was moving it grated under its collar. But now it was still, there were no children playing about it, only the one small boy who had climbed out of the car by the curb and stood studying the merry-go-round from a distance, his hands jammed down inside the waistband of his shorts.

Under his sandals, leaves and nuts fallen from the Moreton Bay figtrees crunched and popped. Beyond the merry-go-round was the sea. The colour of the sea should have astounded, but the boy was seldom astounded. It was simply the sea, dark and glowing blue, bisected by seagull-grey timbers of the rotting jetty, which dwindled away in the distance until it seemed to come to an end in the flat-topped hills to the north. He did not think about the sea, or about the purple bougainvillea that glowed against it, propped on a sagging shed. These existed only as the familiar backdrop of the merry-go-round. Nevertheless, the colours had entered into him, printing a brilliant memory.

He went, scuffing leaves, to the merry-go-round, and hanging his body over the narrow seat he began to run with it, lifting his legs from the ground as it gained momentum. But he could not achieve more than half a revolution by this means, and presently he stopped, feeling vaguely hard-used.

His mother was in the Library, getting books. He could see her now, coming out on to the veranda. The Library was a big place with an upstairs. It used to be the railway station in the Old Days, which made it very old indeed. In fact, everything about the merry-go-round was old, though he did not know it. Across the street the convict-built courthouse crumbled away, sunflowers sprouting from the cracked steps. The great stone barn at the next corner was Wainwright's store, where the early ships had landed supplies. That, too, was crumbling, like the jetty and the courthouse and the bougainvillea-torn shed, like the upturned boat on the foreshore with sunflowers blossoming through its ribs.

The boy was not aware of living in a young country. He knew that he lived in a very old town, full of empty shops with dirty windows and houses with falling fences. He knew that he lived in an old, haunted land, where big stone flour-mills and small stone farmhouses stood windowless and staring among twisted trees. The land had been young once, like the Sleeping Beauty, but it had been stricken, like the Sleeping Beauty, with a curse, called sometimes the Depression and sometimes the Duration, which would never end, which he would never wish to end, because what was was what should be, and safe.

He stood by the merry-go-round, watching his mother. She went to the car and opened the door, putting her books in. Then she looked up, anxious.

'Here I am,' he called.

'You're a naughty boy,' she said. 'I told you to stay in the car.'

'I want a ride,' he said, 'on the merry-go-round.'

'We haven't time,' said his mother. 'We're going to Grandma's to pick up Nan and then we're going to the beach.'

'I want a ride,' he said, setting his jaw.

She came towards him, giving in, but not meekly. 'Don't *scowl* at me, Rob,' she said. She had curly brown hair, and her eyes were almost as blue as the sea.

He stopped scowling, and looked blank. He had blue eyes like hers, and blond hair which was darkening as he grew older, but was now bleached with summer. Summer had also freckled his nose and taken some of the skin off it. When he squinted he could see shreds of skin on his nose where it was peeling.

'Lift me up,' he said.

His mother stooped and lifted him to the seat of the merry-go-round. 'Oof,' she said. 'You are getting heavy.'

'Aunt Kay lets me ride on her back,' he said, 'and she's old.'

'Aunt Kay is very naughty. You mustn't let her give you piggybacks.'

'You're not as strong as Aunt Kay,' he said.

'Do you *want* a ride ?' asked his mother, dangerously.

'Yes,' he said. 'Push me.'

So she heaved on the iron stay that she was holding, and the merry-go-round started to turn. It moved slowly. She hauled on the other stays as they passed, but still it moved slowly.

'Faster,' he shouted.

'Oh, Rob,' she said, 'it's too hot.'

'Why don't you run round with it,' he called, 'like Mavis does.'

'It's too hot,' said his mother, with dampness on her forehead.

The merry-go-round revolved. The world turned about him. The Library, the car, the old store, the courthouse. Sunflowers, Moreton Bay figtrees, the jetty, the sea. Purple bougainvillea against the sea.

'That's enough,' his mother said. 'We must go now.' The merry-go-round slowed, and then she stopped it. He was sullen as she lifted him down.

'Mavis made it go fast,' he said. 'She ran with it.'

'Mavis is a young girl,' said his mother.

'Why did Mavis go away?'

'To get married.'

'Why don't we have another maid?'

'People don't have maids now,' said his mother.

'Why don't people have maids?'

'Because of the war. People don't have maids in wartime.'

He was silent, thinking of that. The war was a curse, a mystery, an enchantment. Because of the war there were no more paper flowers. That was how he first knew that the curse had fallen. Once there had been little paper seeds that he had dropped into a bowl of water, and slowly they had opened out and become flowers floating in the water. The flowers had come from Japan. Now there was a war, and there would never be paper flowers again. The people in Japan were suddenly wicked, far wickeder than the Germans, though once they had only been funny, like Chinamen. For days and days he had heard the name Pearl Harbor, which was the name of a place where the people in Japan had done something very wicked. It must be a place like Geraldton. The sea he was looking at was called the Harbour.

At a place like Geraldton the people in Japan had done something very wicked, and nothing would ever be the same again.

His mother had almost reached the car. She turned and looked back. 'Come along,' she called, 'quick sticks.'

He followed, crunching the big dry leaves. He was thinking of time and change, of how, one morning when he must have been quite small, he had discovered time, lying in the grass with his eyes closed against the sun. He was counting to himself. He counted up to sixty, and thought: That is a minute. Then he thought: It will never be that minute again. It will never be today again. Never.

He would not, in all his life, make another discovery so shattering.

He thought now: I am six years and two weeks old. I will never be that old again.

He climbed into the car beside his mother. The car jerked and moved, turning down the street between the courthouse and the store. The street was sandy, barren. The houses looked old and poor. Only the vacant blocks offered splashes of colour, bright heads of sunflowers, the town's brilliant weed.

He thought, often, of himself, of who he was, and why. He would repeat to himself his name, Rob Coram, until the syllables meant nothing, and all names seemed absurd. He would think: I am Australian, and wonder why. Why was he not Japanese? There were millions of Japanese, and too few Australians. How had he come to be Rob Coram, living in this town?

The town was shabby, barren, built on shifting sandhills jutting out into the sea. To the north and south of the town the white dunes were never still, but were forever moving in the southerly, finding new outlines, windrippled, dazzling. If ever people were to leave the town the sand would come back to bury it. It would be at first like a town under snow. And then no town at all, only the woolwhite hills of Costa Branca.

To the north and south the dunes moved in the wind. Each winter the sea gnawed a little from the peninsula. Time was irredeemable. And far to the north was war.

Mrs Maplestead's house was an old station homestead sitting in a town. This was because to Mrs Maplestead, and to Miss Mackay MacRae, her sister, and to the late Charles Maplestead, her husband, a house meant a homestead and nothing less. The house was really two houses. At the front, there was a house for living in, a stone house of the convict era with massive walls and dark small rooms. At the back there was a wooden house composed of store rooms, some of which had highly specialized functions, among them an apple room, where big yellow-green Granny Smith apples lay about on tables, smelling sweetly. Joining the two houses was a covered cemented place, darkened by the rainwater tanks. And hung from the beams over the cement was a swing, which dated from the days when Rob had been the only grandchild.

As the years passed, Mrs Maplestead's homestead had become more townified. The underground tank was unroofed and filled now, and Miss MacRae grew chrysanthemums inside its round wall. The cowshed sometimes stabled a horse, but no longer a cow, since the last Maplestead cow had got drunk on bad grapes, and walked round and round the paddock in circles, and died. But the contents of the house had never changed. Anywhere in Mrs Maplestead's store-rooms one was likely to come across an odd stirrup, a bit, part of a shearing-piece, a lump of gold-bearing quartz. The late Charles Maplestead had thrown nothing away, and some of his leavings were inexplicable. No one could explain the two copper objects Rob had found in the wash-house, but everyone was agreed that there was only one thing they could be. They were false teeth for a horse.

He was satisfied with that. Sometimes when he asked what something was they would say: 'It's a triantiwontigong. It's a wigwam for a goose's bridle.' That made him furious.

Mrs Maplestead's house had a garden. At some time in the past load upon load of rich loam had come from one of Charles Maplestead's farms, pockets of red soil had been imbedded in the sand, and things grew. But the best thing in the garden had been there always. It was the giant Moreton Bay figtree that arched over the stone house, carpeting the ground with its crackling leaves and dropping its dried fruits, clatter clatter, on the iron roof.

Mrs Maplestead hated the tree. It choked up the gutters and buried the lawns. It pushed up the footpath in the street with its roots and tangled electric light wires in its branches. But the boy and his Aunt Kay loved it. At dawn and sunset the butcher-birds came, they warbled under the great dome of the tree, and their voices echoed as if they were singing in a huge empty rainwater tank, which was something that the boy himself liked to do.

Now the southerly had come in, the tough leaves of the tree were making a faint clapping. The boy followed his mother through the side gate in the plumbago hedge. The flowers of the white oleander beside the gate were withered and browned by the hot easterly that blew in the mornings, and in the heat the bigger flowers of the red oleander smelled overwhelmingly, sickeningly sweet. They walked the path beside the veranda, under swaying date-palms that were softly scraping the veranda roof. The dates were green, on stalks that were bright yellow. He reached out and pulled one off the tree and bit into it, and instantly his tongue dried up and shrivelled in his mouth and he stopped in the path and spat, and kept on spitting, spitting among the fallen jacaranda flowers, which were a colour he had no name for, neither blue nor purple, but more beautiful than any colour in the world. [. . .]

1965

THOMAS KENEALLY
b. 1935

Thomas Keneally, one of Australia's most prolific literary novelists, was born in Sydney and spent his early childhood in the coastal regions of northern NSW. In 1942 his family moved back to Sydney; his father joined the RAAF and served in the Middle East. In 1952 Keneally, educated by the Christian Brothers, entered St Patrick's Seminary in Manly. He left in 1960, shortly before he was to be ordained, suffering what he described as a nervous breakdown. He married in 1965.

His first novel was *The Place at Whitton* (1964), a murder mystery set in a seminary, followed in 1965 by *The Fear*. In 1967 he published *Bring Larks and Heroes*, part of a revived literary and historical interest in Australia's convict history during the 1960s; this accomplished novel examines the dilemmas of Catholic convicts and military in the face of a hostile administration during the earliest years of the penal colonies, and typifies much of Keneally's fiction in its dramatisation of the conflict between individuals and social and political structures. His next novel, *Three Cheers for the Paraclete*, was published the following year.

During this period Keneally supported himself by working as a clerk, builder's labourer and schoolteacher; from 1968 to 1970 he taught drama at the University of New England before leaving for London, where he spent the next two years. He returned to Australia in 1972 and during the 1970s published five novels, including *The Chant of Jimmie Blacksmith* (1972), which in 1978 was made into a feature film directed by Fred Schepisi, and *Blood Red, Sister Rose* (1974), which is about one of Keneally's enduring preoccupations, Joan of Arc.

In 1982 Keneally published *Schindler's Ark*—later republished as *Schindler's List* when the feature film of the same name, directed by Steven Spielberg, was released in 1994—for which he became the first Australian writer to win the Booker Prize. He has since written a number of novels, many of which have autobiographical underpinnings and all of which have a central engagement with some moral question or dilemma, often in the form of a historical or political event. He has also written screenplays, stage plays, and popular history and biography.

Keneally has been a prominent figure in Australian literary life for many years, not only as a writer but also serving as chair of the Australian Society of Authors (1987–90), a member of the Literature Board of the Australia Council for the Arts (1985–88) and president of the National Book Council (1985–89). He has also been active in a number of political causes, most notably as a committed advocate of an Australian republic and of Aboriginal rights. His interest in the plight of Eritrea is reflected in his novel *Towards Asmara* (1989), while *The Tyrant's Novel* (2003) critically addresses the treatment of asylum seekers by the Australian government. *KG*

From *Bring Larks and Heroes*
Chapter 1

At the world's worse end, it is Sunday afternoon in February. Through the edge of the forest a soldier moves without any idea that he's caught in a mesh of sunlight and shade. Corporal Halloran's this fellow's name. He's a lean boy taking long strides through the Sabbath heat. Visibly, he has the illusion of knowing where he's going. Let us say, without conceit, that if any of his ideas on this subject were *not* illusion, there would be no story.

He is not exactly a parade-ground soldier today. His hair isn't slicked into a queue, because the garrison he serves in has no pomade left, and some idle subaltern is trying to convert the goo into candles. Halloran's in his shirt, his forage jacket over his left arm. He wears gaiters over canvas shoes. Anyone who knew firearms would take great interest in the musket he's got in his right hand. It's a rare model that usually hangs in the company commander's office.

The afternoon is hot in this alien forest. The sunlight burrows like a worm in both eye-balls. His jacket looks pallid, the arms are rotted out of his yellowing shirt, and, under the gaiters, worn for the occasion, the canvas shoes are too light for this knobbly land. Yet, as already seen, he takes long strides, he moves with vigour. He's on his way to Mr Commissary Blythe's place, where his secret bride, Ann Rush, runs the kitchen and the house. When he arrives in the Blythes' futile vegetable garden, and comes mooning up to the kitchen door, he will, in fact, call Ann *my secret bride, my bride in Christ*. She *is* his secret bride. If Mrs Blythe knew, she would do her best to crucify him, though that he is a spouse in secret today comes largely as the result of a summons from Mrs Blythe six weeks ago.

One Sunday about New Year, Halloran came to the kitchen door. Ann rushed out to him, and pressed his shoulders with both hands. This economy of endearment was made very spontaneously; and so it's necessary to say that Ann is not always spontaneous with Corporal Halloran. She sometimes suspects his motives; more often, she suspects God's.

'Promise to wait here, Halloran,' she said, pointing at the threshold. She was whispering like a girl today, not like a conspirator; and she was openly exalted to see him. 'Mrs Blythe wants to talk to you. I was to tell her when you came.'

Hence the rapture, he thought. The front parlour is taking *cognizance* of us, as they say in court.

'What does she want?'

Ann squinted and made a gesture of tamping down his voice with both hands.

'I think she wants to make sure you're decent.'

'Decent!' he hissed. He wasn't angry in any honest sense. Anger was futile since Mrs Blythe had the sovereignty over Ann. 'Who's that old Babylonian whore of a heretic to worry whether I'm decent?'

Girlish for once, Ann rocked on her hips, and kept her laughter in with both hands. 'You make me feel I'm ungrateful,' she said.

'To her?' he asked. 'Ungrateful to *her*? I think she might have her eye on your boy Halloran.'

The girl's mouth went haughty at the very idea.

'She's a most sober woman. It's impossible.'

'She wouldn't be the first one who ever wanted to wriggle round the sofa with a well-bred boy like me, who's got no diseases and doesn't look too bad.'

'You make me laugh,' she said.

She bent with her forefingers of one hand in her mouth and laughed over the top of them. The laughter was supple and shivered with colour like a tree. As soon as Halloran was aware that it was beautiful in itself, instead of relishing it, he winced with pity. He winced, visibly or otherwise, any time that her defencelessness was revealed. The poets promised the young some sort of leisure of love, some easeful immunity. Forget the leisure of love! A long acrid pity for an Ann who would weep, bleed and perish in season, possessed him most of his days.

However, he covered up the fact that her mortality had stung him. He lowered his eyes and uttered a few worn-out vows, and she took his hesitancy for a sort of ardour, and hunched her shoulders with delight. Once again, poets and story-tellers had formulated what a courting male should say, had created the counterfeit coinage of love; and a man was stuck with it.

She told him to wait, and he prepared himself to face Mrs Blythe. He laboured into his jacket. One of his elbows caught in its hot sleeve, and he snorted. He flattened his canvas hat and stowed it in against his ribs. He forced the uppers of his shoes, which had come adrift from the bark-thin soles, into trim shape.

Ann was back.

'Be humble now, Phelim,' she whispered.

Humbly, his canvas feet scraped up the few blocks of sandstone that gave into the back parlour.

He followed Ann around the flanks of a pretentious mahogany table where Mr Blythe starved Mrs Blythe twice a day. The Blythes had shipped out such substantial furniture, because the Home Secretary had intended a volume of industry within the new colony that would make a Commissary a substantial figure, doing substantial work. But the industries had been all still-born; and all Blythe did now was to see that everyone was given two and a bit pounds of flour, two and a bit pounds of meat and a few sundries of other food each week. He restricted his own household to this bare ration.

Such moral heroism, rare amongst Commissary officials, had been gingerly praised by His Excellency when the new ration was announced to the garrison. One look into Blythe's household, however, gave a person an indication of Blythe's true motive: that he was trying to starve his wife, short of killing her, until her pious gut cracked. King in the food store, he could at will prise the lid off a barrel of cheeses and filch one from the top. The Portsmouth victuallers would be blamed for such casual losses as went to keep the Commissary robust.

Now Ann and Halloran had come into the hall. It was breathless and dark, seeming full of the grey ashes of that smouldering day.

'Be humble, love,' she repeated, and knocked on a properly-panelled door towards the front of the house.

'Ongtray!' called Mrs Blythe.

'She means go in,' Ann hissed at him.

'I know, I know.'

'Turn the handle!' called Mrs Blythe, as if a door with a turning handle were a specialty to him.

So Halloran turned the handle, and came into the room where Mrs Blythe used all the day on her devotions and her leg ulcers. She sat in a heavy, straight-backed Italianate chair. Her feet rested on a hassock, and there was a rug over her knees. On a table to her left stood all that was needed to rub, anoint, lance, probe, cauterize and dress her leg. A squat stone lamp, the spoons and needles and lancet, the rags and jars of stewing poultice were, all together, the staple of her life. For Mrs Blythe had been blessed with a putrid leg as other women are with children.

On her right, amongst a deal of impassive mahogany, a slender half-circle of walnut, meant to go against a wall but free to wander in view of Mrs Blythe's disorder, attended its mistress on foal's legs. Her books were heaped on it in two tiered pyramids. Halloran had a passion for the leather wholesomeness of books, and the aley smell of book-mould was for him the smell of matured wisdom. So much so that he thought Aquinas must have smelt like that, and Solomon in his chaster days. There was time to read two titles: *Primitive Christianity* by Bishop Cave, *Sermons for Several Occasions* by John Wesley. Then he had to turn to Mrs Blythe.

She had her square owl's face with its baggy jaws fixed on him. All her hair, not a wisp excepted, was swept up into a tight cap, so that eyes predominated and looked perilously alert. Halloran avoided taking her on eye to eye. He gazed at an empty space to the left of her head, and dominated it in a relevantly direct, respectful, staunch and soldierly manner.

'Corporal Halloran,' she muttered speculatively, as if it mightn't be such a bad name for a terrier or a horse.

'Yes, madam.'

'Errh . . .,' she said by way of a dainty parenthesis, and wriggled her afflicted leg about on the hassock. 'I've asked some of the officers who have visited my husband here, about what sort of young man you are.'

'Yes, Mrs Blythe.'

'I was able to ask Captain Allen also, your company commander, I think. He claims that you are a most temperate and reliable young man.'

'Thank you, madam.'

'No, don't thank me, young man. For this reason, that I find that a soldier's idea, any soldier's idea, of what is temperate and reliable to be very lacking.'

She leant on one buttock as pain diverted her for some seconds. Her narrow mouth opened to the spasm, not altogether humourlessly or ungratefully.

Shuddering, she asked him, 'Do you love Ann?'

Halloran's eyes, having been drawn by the lady's virtuoso agony, returned to the empty space with which he'd earlier chosen to deal. Whatever could the woman mean by the word, when she locked Ann up in the kitchen at night against her predatory husband, while she herself sat here morning and afternoon with pain licking up and down her limbs?

'Yes, Mrs Blythe,' Halloran decided, loath.

'I am not the type of lady who lets her servants go to hell in their free time, Corporal.'

'I'm sure, Mrs Blythe,' Halloran rumbled, out of the deeps of his blushing throat.

No one would go to hell in peace in her household. Not even old Blythe could damn himself at leisure. For Mrs Blythe had confided once to Ann, and Ann had ultimately reconfided to Halloran, the story of how her husband had *walked disorderly* with a domestic in Portsmouth. Even Ann had thought that, in view of what probably passed between Blythe and the girl, *walked disorderly* was a poor choice of terms. Mrs Blythe's father had obtained this expiatory post on the edge of the Southern Ocean for his son-in-law, and bullied him into it. The old man was an august Staffordshire potter, now clawing up the breakneck face of his eighty-sixth European winter; and mad Mrs Blythe wrote to him with ruinous frequency, begging him to exclude herself and indecent Mr Blythe from the inheritance.

'Since the day I had Ann assigned me on the *Castile*,' the lady was grinding on, 'she has been as close to me as a servant can be. I approve her industry, and her standards of behaviour are remarkable in this human sink in which we serve our King, Halloran.'

'Yes, madam.'

Madam took a large, manly handkerchief from her sleeve. She rubbed her neck which grew lividly out of her old lace fichu. Apart from the question of the potter's fortune, had that flawed skin and baggy throat once put furies into Blythe's loins?

'I will not speak indirectly, Halloran,' she said, chin up and the handkerchief rubbing. 'I know how men live in this small parish of hell. I ask you straight. Have you ever lived in concubinage?'

'No,' he said grudgingly. 'No.' Not, he thought, that there would be any concubinage on the earth if all women shared the complexion of Mrs Blythe's flesh and spirit. 'You're not the only one who fears hell, Madam.'

'I do not fear hell, young man. I have a Saviour. And answer me properly!'

'No, I haven't lived in concubinage, Mrs Blythe.' He swallowed. 'I live for Ann.'

'Why don't you marry Ann, then ? It is better to marry than to burn.'

As this random lump of St Paul hit him in the eye, he snorted, continuing in mental revolt. Could the woman believe that someone had once burnt for her, and that her dumpy flesh had quenched any fires?

Suffer it to be said that Halloran was doing better with Mrs Blythe than many an Irishman would have. After all, he knew what a large word like concubinage meant, although he claimed to have never practised it; and Mrs Blythe somehow expected, when she used the word, that Halloran would understand it. Although he comes from a tiny place along Wexford Bay, he studied for two years, until he was nineteen, in the Bishop's house in Wexford itself. It was planned that he would be going to the Sulpicians in Paris to be trained and priested. However, he was, there in Mrs Blythe's sitting-room, as he is here in the forest, a corporal of Marines in a different world. Nonetheless, he could remember that in Wexford he read some moral treatises that advocated marriage as a remedy for lust and a cure for the sin of Onan; and he thought, that Sunday when Mrs Blythe quoted scripture, that, in common with such moralists, she wouldn't have recognized love on a fine day, with the sun on its face. [. . .]

1967

From *Schindler's Ark*
Chapter 8

[. . .] Twenty-three year old Edith Liebgold was assigned a first-floor room to share with her mother and her baby. The fall of Cracow eighteen months back had put her husband into a mood verging on despair. He'd wandered away from home as if he wanted to look into the courses open to him. He had ideas about the forests, about finding a safe clearing. He had never returned.

From her end window Edith Liebgold could see the Vistula through the barbed-wire barricade, but her path to other parts of the ghetto, especially to the hospital in Wegierska Street, took her through Plac Zgody, the Place of Peace, the ghetto's only square. Here on the second day of her life inside the walls she missed by twenty seconds being hustled into an SS truck and taken to shovel coal or snow in the city. It was not just that work details often, according to rumour, returned to the ghetto with one or more fewer members than when they left. More than these sort of odds, Edith feared being forced into a truck when, half a minute earlier, you thought you were going to Pankiewicz's pharmacy, and your baby was due to be fed in twenty minutes.

Therefore she went with friends to the Jewish Employment Office. If she could get shiftwork, her mother would mind the baby at night.

The office in those first days was crowded. The Judenrat had its own police force now, the Ordnungdienst expanded and regularised to keep order in the ghetto, and a boy with a cap and an armband organised queues in front of the office.

Edith Liebgold's group were just inside the door, making lots of noise to pass the time, when a small middle-aged man wearing a brown suit and a tie approached her. They could tell that they'd attracted him with their racket, their brightness. At first they thought he intended to pick Edith up.

'Look,' he said, 'rather than wait, there is an enamel factory over in Zablocie.'

He let the address have its effect. Zablocie is outside the ghetto, he was telling them. You can barter with the Polish workers there. He needed ten healthy women for the night-shift.

The girls pulled faces, as if they could afford to choose work and might even turn him down. Not heavy, he assured them. And they'll teach you on the job. His name, he said, was Mr. Abraham Bankier. He was the manager. There was a German owner, of course. What sort of German? they asked. Bankier grinned as if he suddenly wanted to fulfil all their hopes. Not a bad sort, he told them.

That night Edith Liebgold met the other members of the enamel works nightshift and marched across the ghetto towards Zablocie under the guard of a Jewish OD, a policeman of the ghetto Order Service. In the column she asked questions about this Deutsche Email Fabrik. They serve a soup with plenty of body, she was told. Beatings? she asked. It's not that sort of place, they said. It's not like Beckmann's razor-blade factory, more like Madritsch's. Madritsch's is all right and Schindler's too.

At the entrance to the factory, the new nightshift workers were called out of the column by Bankier and taken upstairs and past vacant desks to a door marked *Herr Direktor*. Edith Liebgold heard a deep voice tell them all to come in. They found the Herr Direktor seated on the corner of his desk, smoking a cigarette. His hair, somewhere between blond and light brown, looked freshly brushed; he wore a double-breasted suit and a silk tie. He looked exactly like a man who had a dinner to go to but had waited especially to have a word with them. He was immense, he was still young. From such a Hitlerite dream, Edith expected a lecture on the war effort and production norms.

'I wanted to welcome you,' he told them in Polish. 'You're part of the expansion of these works.' He looked away, it was even possible he was thinking, Don't tell them that, they've got no stake in the place.

Then, without blinking, without any introduction, any qualifying lift of the shoulders, he told them, 'You'll be safe working here. If you work here, then you'll live through the war.' Then he said good night and left the office with them, allowing Bankier to hold them back at the head of the stairs so that the Herr Direktor could go down first and get behind the wheel of his car.

The promise had dazed them all. It was a godlike promise. How could a man make a promise like that? But Edith Liebgold found herself believing it instantly. Not so much because she wanted to, not because it was a sop, a reckless incentive. It was because in the second Herr Schindler uttered the promise it left no option but belief.

The new women of Deutsche Email Fabrik took their job instruction in a pleasant daze. It was as if some mad old gypsy with nothing to gain had told them they would marry a count. The promise had forever altered Edith Liebgold's expectation of life. If ever they did shoot her, she would probably stand there protesting, 'But the Herr Direktor said this couldn't happen.'

The work made no mental demands. Edith carried the enamel-dipped pots, hanging by hooks from a long stick, to the furnaces. And all the time she pondered Herr Schindler's promise. Only madmen made promises as absolute as that. Without blinking. Yet he wasn't mad. For he was a businessman with a dinner to go to. Therefore, he must *know*. But that meant some second sight, some profound contact with god or devil or the pattern of things. But again, his appearance, his hand with the gold signet ring, wasn't the hand of a visionary. It was a hand that reached for the wine, it was a hand in which you could somehow sense the latent caresses. And so she came back to the idea of his madness again, to drunkenness, to mystical explanations, to the technique by which the Herr Direktor had infected her with certainty.

Similar loops of reasoning would be traced this year and in years to come by all those to whom Oskar Schindler made his heady promises. Some would become aware of the unstated corollary. If the man was wrong, if he lightly used his powers of passing on conviction, then there was no God and no humanity, no bread, no succour. There were of course only odds, and the odds weren't good.

1982

RODNEY HALL
b. 1935

Poet and novelist Rodney Hall was born in Warwickshire to an English father and an Australian mother who had come to England to make a career as an opera singer. Hall's father died when he was a baby and his mother decided in the aftermath of the Second World War to return to Australia with her son. Hall was educated in Bath and then in

Brisbane, leaving school at sixteen but later gaining an arts degree from the University of Queensland.

Like David Malouf (qv), Hall began his writing career as a poet, publishing his first collection, *Penniless Till Doomsday*, in 1962. In the course of the 1960s and '70s he published ten volumes of verse and during the same period began to write fiction, beginning with *The Ship on the Coin* (1972). After the success of his third novel *Just Relations* (1982), which won a number of major awards, Hall concentrated increasingly on writing fiction.

Kisses of the Enemy (1987) is, like the more recent *The Last Love Story* (2004), a novel set in Australia's near future, but after its publication Hall then focused on the country's past, with the three novels that were subsequently published together as *The Yandilli Trilogy* (1994): *Captivity Captive* (1988), *The Second Bridegroom* (1991) and *The Grisly Wife* (1993). In these novels Hall, like many other Australian novelists of the 1980s and '90s, explores the country's colonial past and the gradual loosening of the ties to 'home'. *The Yandilli Trilogy* was followed by *The Island in the Mind* (1996) and *The Day We Had Hitler Home* (2000). In 2002 he published a major volume of verse, *The Owner of My Face: New and selected poems*.

As well as being a prolific writer, Hall has been an advocate of political causes and an influential presence in Australian literary and cultural politics and infrastructure. As a young poet in Brisbane he made the acquaintance of Vance and Nettie Palmer, Alan Marshall and Dymphna Cusack (qqv); he also met the poet Kath Walker, later Oodgeroo Noonuccal (qv), which was the beginning of his longstanding commitment to and advocacy of Aboriginal and Torres Strait Islander advancement. He has worked as a scriptwriter for television and radio, a film critic for the ABC, poetry editor of the *Australian*, and poetry adviser to publishers Angus & Robertson. In 1968 he co-edited with Thomas Shapcott (qv) the landmark anthology *New Impulses in Australian Poetry*, and also edited *The Collins Book of Australian Poetry* (1981). He was chair of the Australia Council from 1991 to 1994. KG

From *Just Relations*
Book 3, Part 2: The Violinist

[. . .] My aunt Annie is a remarkable woman, sensible and strong. Wake up Vivi, she said, you're coming to live with me and I shall love to have you. Let me tell you everything now so you'll hear it all at once and never again, your father's dead, he simply couldn't bear the pain, so he did what any sensible person would do, he put a stop to it. He just said, I won't stand for any more. She packed another pile of my things in the bag. The clothes looked so small. That is to say, Aunt Annie said, he swallowed a handful of the sleeping tablets he had for his pain. He left one tablet over. Now that's a mystery. As though he might need it later if things didn't work out.

I was too stunned to cry. My feeling, at the age of twelve, was recognition: I'd always known he could be dead like this. But it would be unpardonable if I did not cry, for Auntie's sake as my relative. So I burst into a loud hacking and moaning. She folded me against her, another thin rag of clothing to be packed, and she said, you're such a good girl Vivi, you don't have to cry in front of me. Then I really did cry because I didn't have to.

In his coffin my father looked exactly like himself but with one eye a bit crooked, and his cheeks a shade too pink. The thing that made me believe he was finally dead was the cottonwool he wore stuffed in his ears and nostrils. He was dressed in his suit, his splendid formality. As a child what preoccupied me was how had he done it: did he dress before he took the pills? Perhaps I might have been more shocked hadn't there been so many flowers in the room: Auntie's signature. I hardly dared imagine where they had come from. So I watched him sealed away and buried, exotic as a tropical bird.

My aunt, determined to console me at whatever price, promised me the most precious thing in her house to help me forget. I imagined the clock, the ornaments, some lump of furniture, her black cashbox. When she brought me the gift from upstairs, explaining that she kept it under her bed, I was surprised to see it was a simple wooden case which for one painful moment resembled a miniature coffin. Open it my dear, her voice trembled with excitement, I can't wait! Inside lay a violin. Now, said Auntie almost crossly, do what I say or you won't be any good at all.

She took up the instrument herself and tuned it. Imagine my astonishment. She was the last person on earth to have a violin. Then to watch her wooden fingers lifting and falling like mechanical hammers and her whole body trembling as she swept the bow its full length this way and that. I could have laughed because she handled everything as if she knew what she was doing. The violin gave out a simple spritely dance tune, stiff and rough but somehow filled with feelings that made a lump rise in my throat. Auntie, I gasped in admiration, you never told! When she finished the tune she put the instrument into my hands. Tuck it under your chin, she said grimly. Like this, now take the bow like this, no like this, no, thumb there duffer, no, knuckles in a straight line, no the two small fingers don't touch it, no, fingers together, no the horsehair at a slant, no the other way, no square to the strings, no wrist higher than that, wrist not elbow, elbow down wrist up knuckles up fingers relaxed, horsehairs on a tilt . . . now draw the bow gently down, down further, keep going. To my utter astonishment the bow produced a long clean note from the violin with only two hitches as I lost confidence. Suddenly Auntie smiled. It's yours now Vivi. She turned the smile away to a dim corner of the room. And if you don't use it right and practise I'll put you out on the street to beg.

Come on Aunt Annie, I cried, proud and delighted with the note I had made, Daddy already buried and forgotten, teach me, teach me to play. No, she replied and took the violin away, you're going to learn from someone who can really show you, you're going to be a famous violin player, before I die I want to buy a ticket and hear you play in a concert, you can sit me in the front row so I can catch your eye when you get it right. I wished then that the future would allow me to do something for Aunt Annie, something really spectacular to make her gasp.

What do you remember about the old days? I cajoled her because she was now a mystery. The old days? she answered vigorously. What old days? I don't remember a thing, what do the old days matter when there's today to live and tomorrow to think about? A little while later she added, relenting, I made one mistake in the old days and never forget that, I married a man who didn't love me and I refused a man who did. Can you think of anything—now my great-aunt was shouting at me—anything more criminal than that, to wreck two lives, to make a good man miserable all his days and make my husband miserable too, as well as myself into the bargain? I've got two pieces of advice for you my girl and you'd better take note: don't let other people try to live your life for you, and don't get married. So I asked her who was she going to get to teach me the violin then? I know who, she said, I've had my eyes peeled for some time and that's a fact.

Auntie found me a violin teacher. She dug up someone who had played with the BBC Symphony Orchestra, she prised him out of retirement, she carted me off to his cottage and sat me in the porch, she set him up in front of his music stand and called me into the room when she was ready. Now, she announced to Mr Rosenbloom, this is my grandniece who will become a violinist and this is her violin. He peered at me over the top of ridiculous half-moon spectacles like the most perfect absent-minded professor. Really, he said and held out his hand for the violin. I passed it to him. Good morning, he said to the violin. [. . .]

1982

Missing Person

My father died when I was six months old and people started right in
loudly praising what a natural gentleman he was and kept it up
for decades—showing off their privilege (my ignorance of who
I came from) as if they also might know secrets
I would have to fumble in myself for thirty years to find.   5

My father had some pact with light
no one ever got a proper photograph
always a flaw would blot his eyes or else some fog (the family
mystery on summer days) seeped through his image or
a ghost would flood the lens with milk   10

My father's dead toys haunted backs of drawers
and cupboard tops
        as collar studs and golf tees

an altimeter a pressure gauge to check the tyres (though since he
died we never had a car)   15
            a little silver case of calling cards.
Our mother told us we must not forget

We went to find him down behind the Odeon
where repetitious Hitlers raised their arms on clips of wasted newsreel
and my only uncle dropped dead of a secret though   20
the war was over and himself quite free of children (even our
Sydney cousins living with their mother's harsh regrets)

I dared to hope my father might be on a coil of film
even as a spy or traitor dug from bins of garbage at the gate
among unwanted miniatures of Alan Ladd—thwarted we popped   25
huge dead lamp globes up against the wall instead

A father was a luxury a father was a risk a father
was the chance of roast meat more than our wartime once a week
a father was a field of mushrooms found by chance or
meeting with a bull on guard   30
a father was big as that man helping pitchfork stooks of hay
though closer—he wouldn't be hard work to care for
            (no)
                                                                                          2002

THOMAS SHAPCOTT
b. 1935

Born in Ipswich, Queensland, Shapcott worked as an accountant until 1978. Immensely active in literary life, he was a foundation member (1973–76) and then director (1983–90) of the Literature Board of the Australia Council. As well as numerous poetry collections he has published anthologies, volumes of short stories, children's books, young adult fiction, libretti, a memoir, a history of the Literature Board, two studies of the artist Charles Blackman and eight novels. He was executive director of the National Book Council (1991–97) and held the inaugural Chair of Creative Writing at the University of Adelaide (1997–2005). He is married to the poet Judith Rodriguez.

Shapcott's own importance is sometimes obscured by his encouragement of the younger 'revolutionary' poets of the 1960s and '70s known as the Generation of '68 (a term probably coined by Shapcott). His anthology *Australian Poetry Now* (1970) is a key document in that group's evolution. Shapcott's own poetry, however, has ranged widely, from relatively conventional early work to the experimentation of the 1970s. His best collections, such as *Shabbytown Calendar* (1975) and *The City of Home* (1995), show the importance of place and autobiography. *DM*

The City of Home

The City of Home is reached only in dreams.
It has a town centre, a river with curved bridges

and the famous clocktower. There are always pigeons
which signify abundance not overpopulation.

There are no walls, no toll gates, no ribbon developments   5
full of hoardings, carpet Emporia or used car allotments.

The City of Home has retained only stone monuments and spires
and the shady maze of the Municipal Gardens

or perhaps secret childhood wildernesses of bramble
—the smell of lantana still clings to an old pullover.   10

You approach from the air; it is a plan, a totality.
It is worthy of all your best secrets and the secrets of others.

Like all great cities, the City of Home reaches back
into all the generations, all the inheritances

though you have your own special associations   15
and insist on the second seat outside for your coffee.

There is no other coffee, no taste in all the world
to compare with that coffee! Yes, you insist, the second chair

the one under the awning where you can glimpse the fountain
and the bronze angel. The City of Home is like no other city   20

not even the City of Remembering or the Cities of the Plain.
The City of Home has only one drawback, but that is terrible:

The City of Home is empty of people.
All its songs are the songs of exile.

                                                        1995

For Judith Wright

I

A physical presence of shade; the idea of shelter.
An encounter with moss and the coldness of water—
so cold that below the first inch your skin burned
like tumbling in ice, and this on hot days
that had melted the century.   5
I think of water-spiders like toy boats and of leeches
you learned the knack of pulling from your ankle.
I remember my first sense of wonder—no other term—
looking up through the line-tug of thin tree trunks
to some imagined escape up in the high air   10
and the very curtain of shadow at the forest edge.
I knew myself from the first to be a person of shadow
and the cool places. It is not surprising the rainforest
drew its leaves up on all sides towards me
even on days of impossible oppression   15
when humidity made water like claws
on the back of every leaf.
My first memories of the Queensland rainforest return me
        to the hills and gullies around Nambour.
I think of palm groves, lawyer-cane and cunjevoi leaves.   20
        I remember the tick that killed our dog.

After the beginning in those childhood years of rock-wallabies
        and birds scuffing or flicking off colour
I began to read. I was taken to the words
for all the things I had thought I had not thought   25
I was led by words to the thoughts beyond the leaf-mould
of my rememberings and the hidden waterfalls
where sound preceded words but was still waiting.
You showed me waiting.
You in becoming my guide placed the poems under my tongue   30
as if they were cool water pebbles. Your patience
had moulded those poems against aeons.
When I entered the rainforest again I followed the pebbles
and everything I had seen or touched or been stung by
        claimed me again, there was no holding, no holds,   35
        and from your words I discovered my own landmarks.
To get to the rainforest I had come the long way
it was as if I were returning there.

II

The day you took me down, yourself, into the Tamborine rainforest
to give your guided tour, each site known, each plant enumerated,
it was for both of us the language of ritual, words of the Service,
beads and genuflections
which is the way we inhabit discovery   5
to make it known if not understood.
Your own poems remained closer to the word like that pebble
still lodged under my tongue.
I sensed then, already, that you had gone from the rainforest
back to some more gaunt, open country   10
of whitened bones and terrible betrayals
to learn that other world, too,
with its quartz blades and its spearheads
—the land after the burning
    the land after the fifty thousand years of burning   15
    the land after the conquest of burning
    land for the first time staked and claimed
    and possessed
    if not owned.

1995

CHARLES PERKINS
1936–2000

Charles Nelson (Charlie) Perkins was born at the Alice Springs Telegraph Station Aboriginal Reserve, NT. His parents were Arrente and Kalkadoon people. At the age of ten he was removed from the reserve and sent to a home for boys in Adelaide, where he completed his schooling. He qualified as a fitter and turner in 1952. A talented soccer player, Perkins played as a professional with English club Everton, and on his return to Australia with Adelaide Croatian and Sydney Pan-Hellenic.

While studying at the University of Sydney, Perkins became active in the Indigenous rights struggle and co-founded the group Student Action for Aboriginals. Inspired by the American civil rights movement, he led the 1965 Freedom Ride to NSW country towns, where he and fellow students protested against racial discrimination. That year Perkins was the first Aboriginal person to graduate from university.

In 1969 he joined the Commonwealth Office of Aboriginal Affairs. In 1975 he published his autobiography, *A Bastard Like Me*. By 1984 he was deputy secretary of the Department of Aboriginal Affairs. A well-known and controversial national figure, Perkins resigned in 1988 after a clash with his Minister over allegations of financial mismanagement that were later dismissed.

In later years Perkins lived in Alice Springs. His lifelong love of sport led him to mentor several Aboriginal athletes. In 1993 he was elected to ATSIC, serving as deputy chairman (1994–95). He was honoured as one of the *Bulletin*'s '100 Most Influential Australians' in 2006. *AH/PM*

Letter to the Editor

I would like to enlighten E.J. Smith, who asked in a letter to *The Australian* on March 27 why part-Aboriginal people such as myself identify as Aboriginals.

Firstly we were usually born on Mission Stations, Government Reserves or shanty towns. We received aid only as far as it was convenient for the white people. We were therefore identifiable to ourselves as well as white people as 'the Aboriginals'.

Secondly we were related by kinship, blood and cultural ties to our full-blood parents or grandparents. This tie can never be broken merely because the degree of 'blood' may vary, or if white authority or individuals wish it so. An example of this is the Northern Territory where before 1956 an Aboriginal was any person with one drop of Aboriginal blood in his veins—the definition was reversed by law only some ten years ago. Very convenient for the law-makers, but imagine its effect on the Aboriginal family. Aboriginals are not like white people. They love their children, whatever shade. Generally, in the past, the white people never really wanted us. When they did it was usually on their terms for sexual, economic or paternal reasons.

Thirdly many thousands of our people were forced to carry passes—much like passports—if ever we wished to mix in the white community. This carried our photograph, plus character references. We were labelled as fit and proper Aboriginals to associate with white people. I was one of the few Aboriginals in Adelaide who refused to carry a pass or 'dog ticket' as we called it. All my life, before I graduated from the University of Sydney, I was categorised by law and socially as an Aboriginal. Now that I have graduated I am suddenly transformed by people such as Smith, into a non-Aboriginal.

This conveniently puts me into a situation where I must, according to official assimilation policy, forget my people, my background, my former obligations. I am now 'white'. I therefore am not supposed to voice an opinion on the scandalous situation Aboriginal people are in nor am I entitled to speak any longer as a 'legal Aboriginal'. All this because I have received my degree and am in a position to voice an opinion. Or could it be that I, and others like me, could influence the unacceptable social-racial status quo in Australia?

Fourthly there can be no real comparison between a nationality and race. A nationality is a mere political or geographic distinction between people. Race on the other hand goes much further into the biological (colour) and cultural (kinship, customs, attitudes) field.

The Aboriginal people in Australia today—full-blood and part blood—do not want the sympathy of white people with an attitude such as Smith's. We have had enough of this in the past.

What we want is good education, respect, pride in our ancestry, more job opportunities and understanding.

It seems people such as Smith carry a guilt complex of past mistreatment, and would want to now stop the truth from being revealed, and hence control Aboriginal advancement.

If Australians would delve into our social history in a truthful manner they would be horrified at the result of the investigation.

The story is not a nice one and Aboriginals have suffered as a consequence.

All our lives Aboriginals have lived in a secondary position to the white Australian.

I no longer wish for this situation. Therefore I, and approximately 250,000 others like me, claim our ancestry. We are Aboriginal Australians—proud of our country and our race.

1968

ERIC WILLMOT
b. 1936

Scholar, award-winning engineer, administrator and author, Eric Willmot was born on Cribb Island, near Brisbane. In boyhood he moved from school to school in Queensland and NT. After primary school he became a drover and horse breaker, completing his education after a rodeo accident at eighteen left him unable to ride. He graduated from the University of Newcastle in 1968 with a science degree, then taught mathematics before gaining a master's degree in educational planning.

Willmot has worked throughout the world as an educator and administrator. He has been Director-General of Education in South Australia, and head of AIATSIS. His advocacy for a national Aboriginal media network assisted in the creation of the Broadcasting for Remote Aboriginal Communities Scheme and satellite services for Aboriginal communities. He has published scholarly work and historical fiction, notably *Pemulwuy: The rainbow warrior* (1987). Willmot's inaugural David Unaipon lecture at the University of South Australia in 1988 was published as 'Dilemma of Mind' (1991). *AH/PM*

From *Pemulwuy*
Chapter 44: A War of Worlds

Pemulwuy followed Wilson's advice carefully. His forces spent the spring and early summer of 1800 terrorising the settlers—and more importantly their families. The Eora would wait patiently until all or at least some of the adult males were away from the homesteads, then attack it. These raids were aimed strictly at inspiring terror: spears through thatching and windows, firing sheds, stealing supplies, and all done with much noise and fuss. The attacks usually lasted less than an hour, and then the Eora were gone.

This was hardly what Pemulwuy would have called war, but it destroyed the cunning and dangerous wheat protection squads. They became too afraid to leave their families. Pemulwuy did not set fire to the wheat in 1800. He was poised for the summer of 1801, the year of Governor King.

Pemulwuy had Wilson write out for him a message to the new governor. It was written on a piece of canvas with charcoal and hung from a tree on the outskirts of Sydney. It read:

GOVERNOR KING
ALL ENGLISH GO BACK TO SYDNEY
PEMULWUY

The response to Pemulwuy's offer was very simple and quickly delivered. Pemulwuy must surrender himself to the authorities in Parramatta where King and the New South Wales judiciary would then consider his future with some leniency.

Pemulwuy's reply was equally swift. He set fire to virtually all of the country west of Toongabbie. This was again part of the strategy of terror. Pemulwuy had found that the threat of a bushfire sent the protection squads home. Burning wheat on its own brought them onto the offensive.

The skies above Sydney remained black and grey with the smoke from the burning of the New South Wales forests. The huge fuel burden from the last summer and winter now kindled a wall of fire that swept down on Parramatta. The Eora people had been warned well in advance. Not only did they move from the path of the fire; they placed themselves in suitable positions to hunt the fleeing fauna. The British settlers, on the other hand, had no way of dealing with these horrific fires. They seemed so well placed that all suspected they had been deliberately lit. When Pemulwuy's warriors started appearing from the flames and smoke, setting fire to everything that had not burned, they were sure.

The Eora rode the flames like surf, assisting them to jump the firebreaks, lighting them anew when they went out.

While Awabakal and Weuong burnt out Toongabbie and Castle Hill, Pemulwuy set fire to Prospect Hill. By April the whole Parramatta district was a black, bleak mess of charcoal. The wheat and maize crops were virtually a total loss. Looting and minor raids picked the bones of the corpse of this latest British adventure.

Late in April the fires started to move down the north side of the harbour towards Lane Cove, but they were stopped by rain. The summer offensive ended.

The British were in complete disarray. The grain crops had failed, and they were now burdened by refugee settlers. Their old enemy of eleven years had unleashed a weapon against which they had no defence. The dreams of these adventurers lay in the ashes of New South Wales.

A meeting in Sydney of senior officers of the New South Wales Corps had almost ended in a riot. Lieutenant Marshall had finally cracked, physically attacking Abbott and Macarthur and calling them rogues and scoundrels.

King stepped in.

'We have a colony facing its gravest threat and you fight among one another like unruly children!' he scolded.

He gave the Rum Corps an ultimatum:

'Drive the natives from the Parramatta region or abandon all the inland settlements.'

This did, indeed, send the Corps scurrying back to their posts. Not only had King threatened their own holdings, but he had now given them a direct order to take the land from the Eora. The age of the peacemakers, Phillip and Hunter, was finally over.

Under this new policy, the approach of the New South Wales Corps was simple: take a large force, attack all known Eora campsites, and kill everybody found there.

Wilson argued bitterly with Pemulwuy.

'They are using the same method against you,' he insisted. 'Your advantage is that your people are mobile. You must continue to attack their houses.'

Pemulwuy reluctantly agreed. He pursued a desperate war of attrition.

No-one will ever know how many people were killed in New South Wales in that winter of 1801. Both societies were devastated, and when the green grass grew in the blackened valleys of New South Wales in September, there were few British or Eora families to welcome it. If Pemulwuy had not been alive the Eora nation would have given up in that spring of 1801.

Pemulwuy's power among his people remained undiminished, but the Eora, like the Tharawal, had lost the heart to fight on. The spring brought with it an epidemic of influenza, which swept through the weakened Eora groups like Pemulwuy's summer fires. This particular epidemic also hit the settler families hard and weakened their resolve to return to their burnt and wasted farms. The pressure from British society to return was, however, very great. If one family failed to return, another would quickly step into their shoes. This fierce competitive spirit among the Europeans was something that the Eora could not even imagine, and certainly did not possess.

The bushrangers were in high spirits. They saw their ally Pemulwuy as achieving a brilliant victory over the British.

'One more summer,' Thrush said to Pemulwuy, 'and we will have them in the sea.' Pemulwuy smiled, but most of his face showed no emotion whatsoever. Pemulwuy was very concerned at the ability the Rum Corps and their police had shown in locating Eora camps that winter.

'I must leave for a while,' he said. 'Special business.'

In mid-September Pemulwuy left his group and walked to his secret place. A dreaming site of his father's.

The site was not very imposing. It lay on the side of a hill in a sandstone outcrop. This site had been continuously maintained by Pemulwuy's paternal line for thousands of years. Pemulwuy entered a small, shallow cave. Its walls had been marked by men so distant and mysterious in their antiquity that the question of what the marks were never crossed Pemulwuy's mind.

Pemulwuy touched the rock walls with his fingertips, closed his eyes and sang a soft, melodious chant. The cave slowly filled with the song, which deepened in timbre. The song floated down to the face of the rise and fulfilled its meaning and purpose.

Its meaning was the land: as it had always been. Its purpose was renewal: renewal of the spiritual communion of the Eora people and this land their source.

When he had done with the site Pemulwuy climbed to the hilltop and sat with his chin on his knees. He looked across this countryside as he had with his father. He could see nothing but the forest, but he had a vision of open space and farms. He struck his head to put the vision away, but it persisted. He cried out:

'What is it I must do?'

The voices of the land swept up the slope in answer; there was an urgency in them. They gave him warnings, but had no special form; no words on which to form action, only sadness.

1987

BURNUM BURNUM
1936–1997

Born at Wallaga Lake, NSW, Burnum Burnum was an activist, rugby player, actor, author, dreamer and respected Aboriginal elder. Removed from his parents at the age of three months and named Harry Penrith, he spent his early years in children's homes, where he was raised to believe he was white. In the 1960s, he searched for his Aboriginal identity, joined the struggle for Aboriginal rights, and took the name of his great-grandfather, meaning 'Great Warrior'. He attended the University of Tasmania and became an active member of the Aboriginal community, helping to organise the 1972 Aboriginal Tent Embassy in Canberra. On Australia Day 1988 he famously declared Aboriginal possession of England, raising the Aboriginal flag on the English coast at Dover. *AH/PM*

The Burnum Burnum Declaration

I, Burnum Burnum, being a nobleman of ancient Australia do hereby take possession of England on behalf of the Aboriginal People.

In claiming this colonial outpost, we wish no harm to you natives, but assure you that we are here to bring you good manners, refinement and an opportunity to make a Koompartoo—'a fresh start'.

Henceforth, an Aboriginal face shall appear on your coins and stamps to signify our sovereignty over this domain.

For the more advanced, we bring the complex language of the Pitjantjajara; we will teach you how to have a spiritual relationship with the Earth and show you how to get bush tucker.

We do not intend to souvenir, pickle and preserve the heads of 2000 of your people, nor to publicly display the skeletal remains of your Royal Highness, as was done to our Queen Truganinni for 80 years. Neither do we intend to poison your water holes, lace your flour with strychnine or introduce you to highly toxic drugs.

Based on our 50,000 year heritage, we acknowledge the need to preserve the Caucasian race as of interest to antiquity, although we may be inclined to conduct experiments by measuring the size of your skulls for levels of intelligence. We pledge not to sterilize your women, nor to separate your children from their families.

We give an absolute undertaking that you shall not be placed onto the mentality of government handouts for the next five generations but you will enjoy the full benefits of Aboriginal equality.

At the end of two hundred years, we will make a Treaty to validate occupation by peaceful means and not by conquest.

Finally, we solemnly promise not to make a quarry of England and export your valuable minerals back to the old country Australia, and we vow never to destroy three-quarters of your trees, but to encourage Earth Repair Action to unite people, communities, religions and nations in a common, productive, peaceful purpose.

1988

ALEX MILLER
b. 1936

Novelist Alex Miller was born and grew up in London, and migrated to Australia alone at seventeen. He worked as an itinerant stockman on Central Queensland and Gulf Country cattle stations before moving to Melbourne and studying for an arts degree. He has taught writing and worked as an art dealer, farmer and public servant.

Miller was active in the Melbourne theatre revival during the early 1980s as a co-founder of Anthill Theatre and the Melbourne Writers' Theatre, and has written two stage plays. His first novel, *Watching the Climbers on the Mountain*, was published in 1988; others include *Conditions of Faith* (2000), *Prochownik's Dream* (2005) and *Landscape of Farewell* (2007). His two best-known and most critically successful novels are *The Ancestor Game* (1992) and *Journey to the Stone Country* (2002), both of which won the Miles Franklin Literary Award. *KG*

From *The Ancestor Game*
Chapter 4: *The Winter Visitor*

[. . .] After absences lasting more than half a year he came to me each time as if from a strange apartment which communicated with the part of the house in which I lived by a hidden staircase or passage. When he was absent from us I spent many hours searching for the entrance to this secret way and often imagined I had found it. For a time after his departure I learnt to dull the sharpness of my grief with a resort to the fantastic, and in my daydreams I joined him in a land of pure imaginings which, for me, must lie beyond the hidden doorway. Together he and I, like the mythical *feng* and *huang* of the Chinese other-world, the heavenly emissary which appears when the land enjoys the gods' favour, journeyed side by side and danced our benevolent dance in perfect harmony upon the land which blessed our presence. Daily reality in Coppin Grove by comparison to this fanciful world seemed to me for some years during my childhood to be a meaningless folly pursued by persons of an unmitigated and grim practicality. A world of persons who did not deserve my compassion. No word from my mother or sisters, no matter how kind or well-intentioned, drew from me for years anything but disdain. Until, at the last, one by one, they had all reluctantly abandoned me to my folly, seeing in my presence among them not a daughter or a sister but a stranger in their midst.

On each subsequent visit he was always changed from the way he had been when I had seen him last. And so, I am certain, was I. We met on each occasion as new people, freshly burnished from our travels. The father with whom I dwelt for months at a time in my imaginary landscape was forced to retreat into the shadows of fiction whenever my real father arrived. He always came unexpectedly and unannounced.

On a bitterly cold day when I was eleven—it must have been the winter of 1889—I was practising Franz Schubert's Fantasia in C—how could I forget, for it is based on his beautiful song 'Der Wanderer'. I was lost to my surroundings, struggling to master the unfamiliar fingering, when I became aware that someone was near me. I ceased playing and swung around upon the stool. He stood in the doorway. We gazed at each other. In that moment I felt for him the purest, the most distilled, love. We did not embrace. We never embraced. But gazed upon each other's beloved countenance in wonderment. We dwelt in splendour. Schubert's chord loitered in the room as if it were the ghost of that great sadness which all humanity must bear.

'Please don't stop,' my father implored me gently.

'I have just finished, father,' I replied and I slipped quickly from the stool and hurried from the room by the door furthest from him.

He called to me, 'Stay a moment Victoria. I have a present for you.'

But I could not stay. I ran to my room and locked the door and stood dry-eyed before my mirror and solemnly announced to my faithful sister from the other-world, 'The Phoenix has returned to us.' I did not see him again until dinner. The formality of this occasion rendered our meeting easier for me. The ceremony, that is, which was required from each of us shielded me from emotions which I might otherwise have found it difficult to deal with. I believed he too, and that he alone of all those present, understood this exactly as I understood it. His gift to me was waiting in my place. They watched me while I opened it. For my eight sisters there were fine silks from Hangchou and for my mother a carpet from Tibet.

From its bed of silvery wild grass, a grass so soft it was like the fur of a young rabbit against my fingers—a grass so unlike the coarse grasses that grew beside the Yarra and in the paddocks around Hawthorn that it could only have come from the other-world—from this nest I drew forth an earthenware horse glazed with subtle green and orange glazes. It was a horse of fine proportions, realistically formed. It stood with its head slightly turned and its mouth open, alert to the will of its rider. It was caparisoned with a Persian saddle and rosettes of green frogs on the harness. This tall, noble steed I recognised as none other than the legendary *Tianma*, the heavenly horse of the West. I looked at my horse with pride. This supernatural beast would carry me safely and swiftly to the furthest lands which my father might ever visit. It was a horse perfectly fashioned to inhabit the unearthly shadows of my fiction. Carefully I replaced it in its nest of wild grass and put it to one side. I did not need to look at my father to share with him the meaning of this gift. I understood that henceforth I was to travel with him.

My mother did not resist suggesting, 'I am sure Victoria wishes to thank you.' It was her way of letting me know that she acknowledged on my behalf no special preferment with my father. I raised my eyes and looked at her with a contempt that the dead might well bear towards the living. How little you can know or understand of this, my look was intended to convey. I remember she blushed. She was a loving and sensitive wife and the kindest mother ever blessed with eight dutiful daughters, an abundance of worldly goods and a robust constitution. But she was also Irish and her anger could be sudden, implacable and violent in its expression. But I was not afraid of her. How should I be? For I had my secret. So I smiled and waited for her to tell me to leave the room and to go to bed without my dinner. I knew my father would not intervene. My mother was the empress of this world, the mistress of the house at Coppin Grove, her domain bounded by the road and the river and by the summerhouse, and by the edge of the native trees yonder. But not extending beyond these boundaries. Beyond her domain lay my freedom. And his. I did not care for this world at all, nor for its rewards. I laughed at them. When Katherine married the mayor and they moved to their great house in Brighton I felt sorry for her. I saw that she had been taken to a prison from which there could be no escape.

How many years was it from the gift of the horse to the terrible day I learned that not only the existence of my mother and sisters but my own existence as well had never been made known to my father's Chinese wife and son in Shanghai? That day I learned I had not existed for him in the Northern Hemisphere, with his number one family, as it became clear. Though I am not certain that in his youth he meant this to be so. I believe it was something deeper than himself which eroded our validity for him over the years. There are certain actions for which people should not be held personally accountable. There are ancient forces which make their way through us as rivers make their way through landscapes, reshaping features we had thought permanent, moving what we had thought to be stilled for ever, and wearing away resolves in us that are not touched even by our strangest imaginings. We are not only that person we think we are, but more. As my father I knew he loved me. But he was also a man from China.

This bright autumn day with the sun warm against my shoulders, the twenty-seventh of May 1908, he is dying. My half-brother from Shanghai, who is wholly Chinese, is with him. I can see my brother's shadow at the window. He stands behind my father's chair and waits to become the second Feng. He is a practical man. I believe Australia means nothing to him . . . I would like to cease writing and walk among the trees, among that remnant of bushland which lies yonder, between the riverbank and the road . . . The shadow of my brother has gone from the window. My father, the first Feng, is dead. I am alone, now, with my horse and my fiction. I am in my thirtieth year. I have been many years in preparation. Now even Shinjé, the Lord of Death herself, could not be better mounted for such a journey as I intend to make.

The light beside my bed was still on. The book lay on the covers near my hand. I picked it up and remembered I'd finished reading it before going to sleep. There were three hundred and two pages. I closed my eyes again and it was all still there. I watched her cantering away into her fiction on her orange and green horse through the patch of sunlit bush. I watched her setting out on her journey, riding bravely into the unknown landscape of her fiction, aware of her inevitable solitude. Her black hair streamed out behind her and the hooves of her supernatural horse threw a fine golden dust into the bright summer air, a dust which rose into the branches of the slim gumtrees and lingered there long after she had gone. Watching her I *was* her, the way one is the character within whose persona one transcends oneself; and strives with that person, as vulnerable as they to the dangers and difficulties which are encountered; hope and anxiety and fear dancing together in one's brain. Opposed to us on the journey was the dark sign with which she had announced her work: Beauty, truth and rarity, grace in all simplicity, here enclosed in cinders lie.

1992

HERB WHARTON
b. 1936

Born in Yumba, an Aboriginal camp in the south-western Queensland town of Cunnamulla, Wharton worked as a stockman, drover and labourer before taking up writing around the age of 50. His first novel, *Unbranded* (1992), is based on his experiences as a stockman in the Australian outback. Since then he has published several collections of prose and poetry, and a young adult novel. He is popular around the world for his storytelling. His works include *Yumba Days* (1991), *Where Ya' Been, Mate?* (1996), *Imba (Listen): Tell you a story* (2003) and *Kings with Empty Pockets* (2003). *AH/PM*

Boat People—Big Trial

From high up on the crumbling ochre-red ridge, the dark men looked down on the wet glistening mudflats of the mangrove swamps as the tidal waters receded. Farther along, a crocodile slithered and slid across the mud bank, disturbed by voices from a boat that drifted across the flats towards the watching men. The frantic hand waving and gesturing from the people in the boat looked comical to the Aborigines. It seemed as though the boat mob had only just realised they were stranded high and dry, miles inland, as the king tide rapidly receded into the now shallow tidal channel.

From the ridge, the dark men observed about ten people on the deck of the small boat, all talking excitedly as they waved. '*Bloody boat people*' the Aborigines thought. As they looked down they could not make out any of the words spoken by the boat mob—and in any case they would not have been able to understand their lingo. Looking up, the boat mob pointed towards the Aborigines, dark shapes against the reddish hill and cloudless blue sky.

One Aborigine standing at the edge of the rocky outcrop gave a small, regal wave as a friendly gesture. This brought renewed waving and louder talk from the boat. 'Looks like the silly bastards are stranded high and dry until the next king tide,' the Aborigine remarked.

'Bloody boat people,' muttered another Murri, one of the elders of the group. 'What shall we do with them? For hundreds of years they've been coming here. At first they used to come then sail away again. Now they come to stay. For over two hundred years they've come here, taken our land, killed our people and disrupted our laws.'

All the Aborigines knew the stories handed down from father to son—of murder, rape and mayhem and the theft of their tribal land.

Cursing all boat people once again, the old man was for leaving these new arrivals to their fate. But another Aborigine said: 'We can't judge these boat people by others of the past. That's like judging people by the colour of their skin.'

The old man repeated in powerful lingo what he thought of boat mobs, whatever the colour of their skins, but the younger man argued: 'We can't just walk away and leave them stranded.'

Soon the Aborigines were deep in an earnest discussion about what they should do, while the old man shook his head. 'Only bad omens come in boats,' he muttered.

By now, the boat people had begun to wade ashore, stumbling knee-deep in mud towards the hill top where the heated discussion still raged. Finally justice prevailed, and soon the Aborigines were heading down the ridge towards them.

The Murris had prepared themselves for hunting as their ancestors had done for tens of thousands of years. They carried spears and boomerangs and their bodies were marked in red and white. Only the headbands they wore—red, black and yellow, the colours of their national flag—belonged to the present day.

This was no ordinary Aboriginal mob straight out of the Dreamtime, even though this is how they would have appeared to the descendants of that first great wave of boat people who landed two centuries ago. As they headed towards the boat people, who were now stepping out of the soft slimy mud onto high ground, one Aborigine was heard to remark: 'At least these fellas aren't wearing leg irons.'

'No guns either,' said one of his companions. These boat people evidently belonged to some small peaceful tribe.

Amongst the Aboriginal 'savages' were two trained lawyers, as well as office workers and school teachers, besides the tribal elders, who knew and cared nothing about the laws and legends, history and religion of the White man, brought to their land a mere two hundred years ago. The lawyers, office workers and school teachers had gathered together to learn from the elders about their own culture and their own laws, which dated back one hundred thousand years or more. They were learning of other ways besides adaptation to ensure the survival of their tribe. Out here they had discovered the greatest school of all. For a week now they had been on pilgrimage through their tribal homeland, renewing their affinity with the land and the laws and legends of the Dreamtime.

Led by one who appeared to be their leader, the boat mob approached the now silent band of Blacks. Here was a mob of real wild Blacks, the leader thought to himself, just as they had so often been portrayed by White Australia. The leader of the boat mob could speak English, but he doubted whether these Black savages would understand him. And he was quite sure they would not understand his own lingo. So he began to speak in pidgin English, gesturing wildly with his arms all the time.

'We boat people,' he said. He pointed to himself, then to the boat, and gestured towards the distant horizon. 'We look for asylum—we refugees.'

His words came out like bullets from a machine-gun, thought one of the Aborigines, who had served in the Vietnam War. He and the rest of his tribe remained silent, their faces expressionless.

'We lost, we boat people seeking refuge,' the leader went on. But he thought that no matter what he said it would all be meaningless to these ignorant Stone-Age Blacks. 'We want to go see your big fella boss,' he said despairingly. Then he fell silent as the Aborigines gathered around in a circle and began talking in their own lingo. The boat people watched them fearfully. Maybe they would be speared and eaten, they thought. The Blacks talked on, with occasional bursts of laughter.

'These silly bastards want to find refuge—they want to know how to get to the nearest town and police station or government office,' said one of the Aboriginal school teachers. 'They also need fresh water and food—they've probably lived for months on that boat, escaping from their homeland.'

The old tribal elder who had spoken before said that he did not trust people who could leave the place where they had been born, to go to another country. For him, for all of them, their land was their mother, a sacred place. No matter what injustices they had suffered, nothing could ever break that tie with their own land and with the Dreamtime. Yet every one of this boat mob had left his own land.

At last one of the lawyers, who specialised in Aboriginal legal rights, addressed the leader of the boat mob in a cultured English accent. 'You are certainly lost, old chap. Miles from anywhere—two hundred kilometres from the nearest township and about a thousand from the nearest government Immigration office. But I can surely tell you exactly where you are right now.' Looking up at the sun, he recalled the exact place where the tidal stream appeared on the White man's map. 'You are twenty-eight degrees south of the twenty-second parallel. Furthermore, I must inform you that you are standing on the ancient tribal land of the Mungas—and you are trespassing.'

Taken aback, the boat leader gaped at the Aborigine for a moment. Then he began to talk again in his machine-gun voice, his arms still waving wildly as he repeated desperately, over and over: 'We refugee, refugee. Want asylum, big asylum …'

'Oh, I know where they want to go,' said one of the tribal elders who had once visited the city. 'I know that place where all them *womba* people been locked up.'

'Nah, nah, not that asylum,' said another Aborigine. 'They looking for a proper sit-down place. Might be they okay, this mob. No leg irons, no guns. Might be we getting a better class of boat people, old man. What you think?'

1996

DORIS PILKINGTON
b. 1937

Doris Pilkington (Nugi Garimara) was born on Balfour Downs Station in the East Pilbara, WA. At a young age she and her sister were removed by authorities from their home and were sent with their mother to Moore River Native Settlement. At eighteen, Pilkington left the mission system as the first of its members to qualify as a nursing aide at the Royal Perth Hospital. After marrying and raising a family, she studied journalism and worked in film and television production.

Her novel *Caprice: A stockman's daughter* (1991) won the David Unaipon Award in 1990. As well as adult fiction, she has written children's fiction, and autobiography, most notably *Follow the Rabbit-Proof Fence* (1996), which was adapted into the internationally acclaimed feature film, *Rabbit-Proof Fence* (2002), directed by Phillip Noyce. *Home to Mother* (2006) is a version of the story written for younger readers.

In 2002 she became co-patron of the state and federal Sorry Day Committee's Journey of Healing. *AH/PM*

From *Follow the Rabbit-Proof Fence*
Chapter 5: Jigalong, 1907–1931

[...] In July 1930, the rainy season was exceptionally good. For the Mardu people throughout the Western Desert this was the season for taking long walks in the bush, foraging for bush tucker and feasting on the day's catch. Every Mardu welcomes the glorious warm weather, when the azure skies are even bluer against the grey-green mulga trees and the red dusty earth; grass grows under the small shrubs and between the sandy patches around the rocky ledges and even the spinifex is fresh and green. Alas, like everything that is revived and resurrected by the winter rains their beauty and brilliance is shortlived. They seem to fade and die so quickly.

Molly and Gracie spent a lovely weekend with their families digging for kulgu yams and collecting bunches of yellow flowers from the desert oaks, which they brought home to share with those who stayed behind to take care of the old people and the dogs. They soaked bunches of flowers in a bucket of water to make a sweet, refreshing drink. The other bush foods, such as the girdi girdi, murrandus and bush turkeys, were shared amongst the community. After supper the weary girls curled up in their swags and in no time at all, they were fast asleep.

Early next morning, Molly's step-father Galli rose at dawn and lit the fire. He made a billy of tea and sat under the shade of a large river gum, drinking a mug of warm tea. He glanced over to the sleeping forms of his two wives, and called out, 'Come on, get up.' The women began to stir. Galli then cut a piece of plug tobacco and crushed it in his hand, mixed the pure white ashes of the leaves of the mulga tree into it then put it into his mouth and began to chew the gulja, spitting the juice occasionally. In the old days, the people would collect and chew the leaves of wild or bush tobacco that grew on the cliffs or on rock ledges.

The Mardus preferred the white man's tobacco, plug tobacco, because it was easily available and also it was stronger and lasted longer. They chewed it and spat out the juice, the same way that other races chewed betel leaves.

Maude was Galli's second wife. She and his other wife both belonged to the same group under the kinship system. Both were Garimaras, the spouse category for Galli. Between them they prepared breakfast for the whole family, which included three big dampers cooked in the hot ashes of the fire and the girdi girdi left over from the hunting trip in the bush. They all agreed that it had been a successful and enjoyable day.

Molly and Daisy finished their breakfast and decided to take all their dirty clothes and wash them in the soak further down the river. They returned to the camp looking clean and refreshed and joined the rest of the family in the shade for lunch of tinned corned beef, damper and tea. The family had just finished eating when all the camp dogs began barking, making a terrible din.

'Shut up,' yelled their owners, throwing stones at them. The dogs whinged and skulked away.

Then all eyes turned to the cause of the commotion. A tall, rugged white man stood on the bank above them. He could easily have been mistaken for a pastoralist or a grazier with his tanned complexion except that he was wearing khaki clothing. Fear and anxiety swept over them when they realised that the fateful day they had been dreading had come at last. They always knew that it would only be a matter of time before the government would track them down. When Constable Riggs, Protector of Aborigines, finally spoke his voice was full of authority and purpose. They knew without a doubt that he was the one who took their children in broad daylight—not like the evil spirits who came into their camps in the night.

'I've come to take Molly, Gracie and Daisy, the three half-caste girls, with me to go to school at the Moore River Native Settlement,' he informed the family.

The old man nodded to show that he understood what Riggs was saying. The rest of the family just hung their heads refusing to face the man who was taking their daughters away from them. Silent tears welled in their eyes and trickled down their cheeks.

'Come on, you girls,' he ordered. 'Don't worry about taking anything. We'll pick up what you need later.'

When the two girls stood up, he noticed that the third girl was missing. 'Where's the other one, Daisy?' he asked anxiously.

'She's with her mummy and daddy at Murra Munda Station,' the old man informed him.

'She's not at Murra Munda or at Jimbalbar goldfields. I called into those places before I came here,' said the Constable. 'Hurry up then, I want to get started. We've got a long way to go yet. You girls can ride this horse back to the depot,' he said, handing the reins over to Molly. Riggs was annoyed that he had to go miles out of his way to find these girls.

Molly and Gracie sat silently on the horse, tears streaming down their cheeks as Constable Riggs turned the big bay stallion and led the way back to the depot. A high pitched wail broke out. The cries of agonised mothers and the women, and the deep sobs of grandfathers, uncles and cousins filled the air. Molly and Gracie looked back just once before they disappeared through the river gums. Behind them, those remaining in the camp found strong sharp objects and gashed themselves and inflicted wounds to their heads and bodies as an expression of their sorrow.

The two frightened and miserable girls began to cry, silently at first, then uncontrollably; their grief made worse by the lamentations of their loved ones and the visions of them sitting on the ground in their camp letting their tears mix with the red blood that flowed from the cuts on their heads. This reaction to their children's abduction showed that the family were now in mourning. They were grieving for their abducted children and their relief would come only when the tears ceased to fall, and that will be a long time yet.

At the depot, Molly and Gracie slid down from the horse and followed Constable Riggs to the car.

Mr Hungerford, the Superintendent, stopped them and spoke to Riggs.

'While you are here, there's a native woman with a fractured thigh, in the other natives' camp, the one on the banks of the river. Can you take a look at her, Constable?'

'Yes, I'll examine her,' replied the Constable.

'I'll come with you,' said Hungerford. 'We'll borrow that native boy Tommy's horse and sulky,' he added. 'I'll fix him up with some rations later as payment.'

After Riggs had splinted the woman's leg, he told Hungerford that he would have to take her back with him to the Marble Bar Hospital. 'Lift her gently onto the sulky,' he asked her two brothers who were standing watch nearby.

As Hungerford seated himself beside Constable Riggs he said, 'And by the way, the other woman, Nellie arrived from Watchtower Station while you were collecting Molly and Gracie. You know the one suffering from VD. She needs to go to the hospital too.'

'Alright,' Riggs replied. 'But I still intend to speak to Frank Matthews, the station manager about her and remind him that he has no right to examine or treat any of the natives here. That should be left to us. We are the Protectors of Aborigines in this district.'

Constable Rigg was referring to the Protection Policy Regulation, number 106m:

Whenever a native falls ill, becomes diseased or sustains an accident and such illness, disease or accident appears to an employer to require medical attention or hospital treatment beyond that which can be efficiently or reasonably given at the place of employment, the employer shall as soon as reasonably possible, send the native to the nearest or most accessible hospital or to the nearest protector and thence to the nearest and most, accessible hospital at the protectors discretion.

The crippled woman, Mimi-Ali, was transferred from the sulky to the car with Molly and Gracie.

'Tommy,' yelled Constable Riggs. 'Take your horse and sulky to Walgun Station and wait for me there,' he ordered.

'Molly and Gracie, you had better sit in front with me, and you Nellie, can sit in the back with Mimi-Ali,' said Riggs as he cranked the car.

Half an hour later he was greeted by Matthews. 'You have a load this time, Constable Riggs,' he said as the officer got out of the car.

'Yes, I know. It can't be helped. I've got the two sick native women. Which reminds me, there is something I must speak to you about.'

The Constable explained the duties of the Protectors of Aborigines in the Nullagine district and cautioned Matthews that he should not take on those responsibilities himself.

'I'd better get moving,' said Constable Riggs. 'I have to search around for Daisy. I'll call in next time I'm on patrol in the district.'

The patrol officer drew up in front of the Walgun Homestead gate and was greeted by Mr and Mrs Cartwright, managers of the station.

'Hello,' said Don Cartwright as he shook hands with the visitor.

'Come inside and have a cuppa tea,' said his wife warmly, pointing towards the door.

'Thank you, but not just yet. I must find the half-caste girl, Daisy,' he said. 'She's somewhere between here and Murra Munda Station, near the soak. I already have the other two, Molly and Gracie in the car with

Mimi-Ali from Jigalong and Nellie, the cook from Watchtower Station who are in need of medical attention.'

'But where are you taking those half-caste girls?' asked Mrs Cartwright.

'They're going south to the Moore River Native Settlement, where we hope they will grow up with a better outlook on life than back at their camp,' he answered with great satisfaction.

'I'll leave the car here but first I'll drop the women off at the native workers' camp. I'll take Molly and Gracie with me, though,' he said. 'I don't want them to clear out.'

Constable Riggs drove slowly down to the camp, followed closely by Tommy with his horse and sulky. Soon, he and Tommy were heading across the flats, over the spinifex grass and through the mulga trees in search of Daisy, who was with her family at the camp. Finding her had proved more difficult than the Constable expected. He had searched the Jimbalbar and Murra Munda area on horseback covering 60 kilometres, and a further 30 kilometres in the dry, rough country between Murra Munda and Walgun stations before he finally found her. The search was so tiring that he decided to spend the night at Walgun Station. His passengers stayed at the camp with Gracie's mother Lilly, her grandmother, Frinda, and some other relatives.

At 3.30 in the morning, on 16 July, the Constable noticed that rain was threatening. The roads were bad enough as it was, but when wet they were even more hazardous so he decided to make a start.

'I don't want to be marooned on the road with these natives,' Constable Riggs explained to the Cartwrights.

'We understand,' said Mrs Cartwright, 'we'll see you when you're in the district. Have a safe trip home.'

'Thank you. I'd better get going,' he said. 'The women must have finished their breakfast by now, so I'll go down and pick them up. Thanks again for your hospitality.'

Gracie's mother, old Granny Frinda and other relations in the camp began to wail and cry.

'Worrah, Worrah! He take 'em way, my grannies [granddaughters],' wailed the old lady, as she bent down with great difficulty and picked up a billy can and brought it down heavily on her head. She and the rest of the women began to wail louder, their hearts now burdened with sadness of the girls' departure and the uncertainty of ever seeing them again. The girls were also weeping. The wailing grew louder as the vehicle that was taking them away headed towards the gate. Each girl felt the pain of being torn from their mothers' and grandmothers' arms.

As the car disappeared down the road, old Granny Frinda lay crumpled on the red dirt calling for her granddaughters and cursing the people responsible for their abduction. In their grief the women asked why their children should be taken from them. Their anguished cries echoed across the flats, carried by the wind. But no one listened to them, no one heard them.

A couple of hours after the three girls had been driven away, Gracie's mother, distraught and angry, was still sitting on the ground rocking back and forth. Maude and her brother-in-law had ridden over in a horse and cart to discuss the distressing news and stayed to comfort and support each other. Some time later, she calmed down enough to hurl a mouth full of abuse at Alf Fields, Gracie's white father, who was standing silently near the galvanised iron tank. She screamed at him in Aboriginal English and Mardu wangku, and beat his chest with her small fists.

'Why didn't you stop them?' she cried out in anger and frustration.

'I couldn't stop them taking my daughter—yes, she is my daughter too,' he said sadly. He was so proud of his beautiful black-haired daughter whom he had named after his idol, English singer Gracie Fields.

He tried to explain to her mother that the patrol officer was a government representative and an officer of the Crown. Had he interfered or tried to stop the man he would have been arrested and put in gaol and charged with obstructing the course of justice. Gracie's mother didn't listen.

'You are a white man too, they will listen to you. Go and talk to them,' she pleaded softly.

'I am sorry but I can't do anything to stop them taking our daughter away from us,' he said finally.

She couldn't accept his excuse or forgive him for just standing by and doing nothing to prevent their daughter from being taken away from them. She packed up and moved to Wiluna.

1996

LES MURRAY
b 1938

Recognised internationally as Australia's most successful poet, Les Murray grew up on his grandfather's small dairy farm in Bunyah, NSW, the loss of which caused much distress. After buying part of the property in 1975, Murray and his family returned to Bunyah permanently in 1985. The other most significant event of Murray's early life was the death of his mother (from an ectopic pregnancy) when he was twelve, recalled in 'Three Poems in Memory of My Mother, Miriam Murray née Arnall'. As discovered by his biographer, Peter F. Alexander, the local doctor would not send an ambulance without being told what was wrong with the patient. Murray's father refused to tell him, and the delay proved to be fatal.

Murray began, but did not complete, an arts degree at the University of Sydney. After travelling around Australia, Murray worked as a translator at the ANU, lived with his family in England and Europe, and worked briefly in Canberra as a public servant, before deciding in 1971 to become a freelance writer. Since that time he has published poetry, essays and reviews, and been the recipient of numerous literary fellowships and prizes. These include the T.S. Eliot Poetry Prize in 1996 and the Queen's Gold Medal for Poetry in 1999. He has been editor of *Poetry Australia* (1973–80), poetry editor for Angus & Robertson (1976–91) and, since 1989, literary editor of *Quadrant*. In 1996 he collapsed with a liver infection that almost killed him. One positive outcome of this, as Murray discussed in *Killing the Black Dog* (1997), was that the illness did away with the depression that he had been suffering for years.

Murray's poetry has received both great critical and popular acclaim. In his own poems and in his anthologies (such as *The New Oxford Book of Australian Verse*, 1986) Murray has sought the widest audience and scope for contemporary poetry. At his most ambitiously nationalistic, Murray also attempts to fuse the rural, urban and Aboriginal strands of Australian culture, a project seen in his earlier collections, such as *Ethnic Radio* (1977). But this unifying project has a concomitant concern with division, seen throughout Murray's career (especially in the scandalous collection, *Subhuman Redneck Poems*, 1996), which has often been marked by polemic, controversy and political interventions.

He is undoubtedly the most significant exponent of the pastoral mode in Australia, his poems figuring the bush as a source of renewal and social cohesion. The animal world is also a source of a quasi-visionary insight, as seen in the title sequence of *Translations from the Natural World* (1992). As this collection shows, Murray's poems are far from pastoral simplicity. His extraordinary erudition, linguistic facility, metaphorical inventiveness, love of punning and store of ideas are all vast. His body of work is extremely diverse, ranging in scale from epigrams to epic, the latter seen in his verse novel, *Fredy Neptune* (1998). Various editions of his *Collected Poems* have appeared over the last decade, most recently in 2006. His essays have been collected in various works, most notably *A Working Forest* (1997). DM

Rainwater Tank

Empty rings when tapped give tongue,
rings that are tense with water talk:
as he sounds them, ring by rung,
Joe Mitchell's reddened knuckles walk.

The cattledog's head sinks down a notch   5
and another notch, beside the tank,
and Mitchell's boy, with an old jack-plane,
lifts moustaches from a plank.

From the puddle that the tank has dripped
hens peck glimmerings and uptilt   10
their heads to shape the quickness down;
petunias live on what gets spilt.

The tankstand spider adds a spittle
thread to her portrait of her soul.
Pencil-grey and stacked like shillings   15
out of a banker's paper roll

stands the tank, roof-water drinker.
The downpipe stares drought into it.
Briefly the kitchen tap turns on
then off. But the tank says Debit, Debit.   20
                                                            1977

The Quality of Sprawl

Sprawl is the quality
of the man who cut down his Rolls-Royce
into a farm utility truck, and sprawl
is what the company lacked when it made repeated efforts
to buy the vehicle back and repair its image.   5

Sprawl is doing your farming by aeroplane, roughly,
or driving a hitchhiker that extra hundred miles home.
It is the rococo of being your own still centre.
It is never lighting cigars with ten-dollar notes:
that's idiot ostentation and murder of starving people.   10
Nor can it be bought with the ash of million-dollar deeds.

Sprawl lengthens the legs; it trains greyhounds on liver and beer.
Sprawl almost never says Why not? with palms comically raised
nor can it be dressed for, not even in running shoes worn
with mink and a nose ring. That is Society. That's Style.   15
Sprawl is more like the thirteenth banana in a dozen
or anyway the fourteenth.

Sprawl is Hank Stamper in *Never Give an Inch*[1]
bisecting an obstructive official's desk with a chainsaw.
Not harming the official. Sprawl is never brutal   20
though it's often intransigent. Sprawl is never Simon de Montfort
at a town-storming: Kill them all! God will know his own.[2]
Knowing the man's name this was said to might be sprawl.

Sprawl occurs in art. The fifteenth to twenty-first
lines in a sonnet, for example. And in certain paintings;   25
I have sprawl enough to have forgotten which paintings.

---

1   A 1971 film, also known as *Sometimes a Great Notion*. Hank Stamper was played by Paul Newman.
2   In 1209 during the 'Albigensian crusade' against Cathar heresy, the city of Béziers was besieged. When the city's walls were breached, Simon de Montfort (1160–1218), the commander of the crusade, pointed out that it was impossible to tell the difference between Catholics and heretics. A papal legate Arnaud Amalric (d. 1225) responded with the words 'Kill them all. God will know his own.'

Turner's glorious *Burning of the Houses of Parliament*
comes to mind, a doubling bannered triumph of sprawl—
except, he didn't fire them.

Sprawl gets up the nose of many kinds of people   30
(every kind that comes in kinds) whose futures don't include it.
Some decry it as criminal presumption, silken-robed Pope Alexander
dividing the new world between Spain and Portugal.
If he smiled *in petto*[1] afterwards, perhaps the thing did have sprawl.

Sprawl is really classless, though. It's John Christopher Frederick Murray   35
asleep in his neighbours' best bed in spurs and oilskins
but not having thrown up:
sprawl is never Calum who, drunk, along the hallways of our house,
reinvented the Festoon. Rather
it's Beatrice Miles[2] going twelve hundred ditto in a taxi,   40
No Lewd Advances, No Hitting Animals, No Speeding,
on the proceeds of her two-bob-a-sonnet Shakespeare readings.
An image of my country. And would that it were more so.

No, sprawl is full-gloss murals on a council-house wall.
Sprawl leans on things. It is loose-limbed in its mind.   45
Reprimanded and dismissed
it listens with a grin and one boot up on the rail
of possibility. It may have to leave the Earth.
Being roughly Christian, it scratches the other cheek
and thinks it unlikely. Though people have been shot for sprawl.   50
                                                                                                                    1983

Second Essay on Interest: The Emu

Weathered blond as a grass tree, a huge Beatles haircut
raises an alert periscope and stares out
over scrub. Her large olivine eggs click
oilily together; her lips of noble plastic
clamped in their expression, her head-fluff a stripe   5
worn mohawk style, she bubbles her pale-blue windpipe:
the emu, *Dromaius novaehollandiae*,
whose stand-in on most continents is an antelope,

1   Italian: 'in the heart'.
2   Bea Miles (1902–73), an Australian bohemian rebel. *Lilian's Story* (1985) by Kate Grenville (qv) is based on
       her life.

looks us in both eyes with her one eye
and her other eye, dignified courageous hump,   10
feather-swaying condensed camel, Swift Courser of New Holland.

Knees backward in toothed three-way boots, you stand,
Dinewan,[1] proud emu, common as the dust
in your sleeveless cloak, returning our interest.
Your shield of fashion's wobbly: You're Quaint, you're Native,   15
even somewhat Bygone. You may be let live—
but beware: the blank zones of Serious disdain
are often carte blanche to the darkly human.
Europe's boats on their first strange shore looked humble
but, Mass over, men started renaming the creatures.   20
Worship turned to interest and had new features.
Now only life survives, if it's made remarkable.

Heraldic bird,[2] our protection is a fable
made of space and neglect. We're remarkable and not;
we're the ordinary discovered on a strange planet.   25
Are you Early or Late, in the history of birds
which doesn't exist, and is deeply ancient?
My kinships, too, are immemorial and recent,
like my country, which abstracts yours in words.
This distillate of mountains is finely branched, this plain   30
expanse of dour delicate lives, where the rain,
shrouded slab on the west horizon, is a corrugated revenant
settling its long clay-tipped plumage in a hatching descent.

Rubberneck, stepped sister, I see your eye on our jeep's load.
I think your story is, when you were offered   35
the hand of evolution, you gulped it. Forefinger and thumb
project from your face, but the weighing palm is inside you
collecting the bottletops, nails, wet cement that you famously swallow,
your passing muffled show, your serially private museum.
Some truths are now called *trivial*, though. Only God approves them.   40
Some humans who disdain them make a kind of weather
which, when it grows overt and widespread, we call *war*.
There we make death trivial and awesome, by rapid turns about,
we conscript it to bless us, force-feed it to squeeze the drama out;

1   Dinewan the Emu appears in Dreamtime stories.
2   The emu appears with the kangaroo on the Australian Coat of Arms.

indeed we imprison and torture death—this part is called *peace*— 45
we offer it murder like mendicants, begging for significance.
You rustle dreams of pardon, not fleeing in your hovercraft style,
not gliding fast with zinc-flaked legs dangling, feet making high-tensile
seesawing impacts. Wasteland parent, barely edible dignitary,
the disinterested spotlight of the lords of interest 50
and gowned nobles of ennui is a torch of vivid arrest
and blinding after-darkness. But you hint it's a brigand sovereignty
after the steady extents of God's common immortality
whose image is daylight detail, aggregate, in process yet plumb
to the everywhere focus of one devoid of boredom. 55
1983

Bats' Ultrasound

Sleeping-bagged in a duplex wing
with fleas, in rock-cleft or building
radar bats are darkness in miniature,
their whole face one tufty crinkled ear
with weak eyes, fine teeth bared to sing. 5

Few are vampires. None flit through the mirror.
Where they flutter at evening's a queer
tonal hunting zone above highest C.
Insect prey at the peak of our hearing
drone re to their detailing tee: 10

ah, eyrie-ire, aero hour, eh?
O'er our ur-area (our era aye
ere your raw row) we air our array,
err, yaw, row wry—aura our orrery,
our eerie ü our ray, our arrow. 15

A rare ear, our aery Yahweh.
1986

Hearing Impairment

Hearing loss? Yes, loss is what we hear
who are starting to go deaf. Loss
trails a lot of weird puns in its wake, viz.
Dad's a real prism of the Left—
you'd like me to repeat that? 5

It's mind over mutter at work
guessing half what the munglers are saying
and society's worse. Punchlines elude to you
as Henry Lawson and other touchy drinkers
have claimed. Asides, too, go pasture.   10
It's particularly nasty with a wether.

First you crane at people, face them
while you can still face them. But grudgually
you give up dinnier parties; you begin
to think about Beethoven; you Hanover   15
next visit here on silly Narda Fearing—I SAY
YOU CAN HAVE AN EXQUISITE EAR
AND STILL BE HARD OF HEARING.

It seems to be mainly speech, at first,
that escapes you—and that can be a rest,   20
the poor man's escape itch from Babel.
You can still hear a duck way upriver,
a lorry miles off on the highway. You
can still say boo to a goose and
read its curt yellow-lipped reply.   25
You can shout SING UP to a magpie,

but one day soon you must feel
the silent stopwatch chill your ear
in the doctor's rooms, and be wired
back into a slightly thinned world   30
with a faint plastic undertone to it
and, if the rumours are true, snatches
of static, music, police transmissions:
it's a BARF minor Car Fourteen prospect.

But maybe hearing aids are now perfect   35
and maybe it's not all that soon.
Sweet nothings in your ear are still sweet;
you've heard the human range by your age
and can follow most talk from memory;
the peace of the graveyard's well up   40
on that of the grave. And the world would
enjoy peace and birdsong for more moments

if you were head of government, enquiring
of an aide Why, Simpkins, do you tell me
a warrior is a ready flirt?   45
I might argue—and flowers keep blooming
as he swallows his larynx to shriek
our common mind-overloading sentence:
I'M SORRY, SIR, IT'S A RED ALERT!

1987

Poetry and Religion

Religions are poems. They concert
our daylight and dreaming mind, our
emotions, instinct, breath and native gesture

into the only whole thinking: poetry.
Nothing's said till it's dreamed out in words   5
and nothing's true that figures in words only.

A poem, compared with an arrayed religion,
may be like a soldier's one short marriage night
to die and live by. But that is a small religion.

Full religion is the large poem in loving repetition;   10
like any poem, it must be inexhaustible and complete
with turns where we ask Now why did the poet do that?

You can't pray a lie, said Huckleberry Finn;
you can't poe one either. It is the same mirror:
mobile, glancing, we call it poetry,   15

fixed centrally, we call it a religion,
and God is the poetry caught in any religion,
caught, not imprisoned. Caught as in a mirror

that he attracted, being in the world as poetry
is in the poem, a law against its closure.   20
There'll always be religion around while there is poetry

or a lack of it. Both are given, and intermittent,
as the action of those birds—crested pigeon, rosella parrot—
who fly with wings shut, then beating, and again shut.

1987

The Tin Wash Dish

Lank poverty, dank poverty,
its pants wear through at fork and knee.
It warms its hands over burning shames,
refers to its fate as Them and He
and delights in things by their hard names: 5
rag and toejam, feed and paw—
don't guts that down, there ain't no more!
Dank poverty, rank poverty,
it hums with a grim fidelity
like wood-rot with a hint of orifice,   10
wet newspaper jammed in the gaps of artifice,
and disgusts us into fierce loyalty.
It's never the fault of those you love:
poverty comes down from above.
Let it dance chairs and smash the door,   15
it arises from all that went before
and every outsider's the enemy—
Jesus Christ turned this over with his stick
and knights and philosophers turned it back.
Rank poverty, lank poverty,   20
chafe in its crotch and sores in its hair,
still a window's clean if it's made of air,
not webby silver like a sleeve.
Watch out if this does well at school
and has to leave and longs to leave: 25
someone, sometime, will have to pay.
Shave with toilet soap, run to flesh,
astound the nation, rule the army,
still you wait for the day you'll be sent back
where books or toys on the floor are rubbish   30
and no one's allowed to come and play
because home calls itself a shack
and hot water crinkles in the tin wash dish.

     1990

The Last Hellos

Don't die, Dad—
but they die.

This last year he was wandery:
took off a new chainsaw blade

and cobbled a spare from bits.   5
Perhaps if I lay down
my head'll come better again.
His left shoulder kept rising
higher in his cardigan.

He could see death in a face.   10
Family used to call him in
to look at sick ones and say.
At his own time, he was told.

The knob found in his head
was duck-egg size. Never hurt.   15
Two to six months, Cecil.

I'll be right, he boomed
to his poor sister on the phone
I'll do that when I finish dyin.

★

Don't die, Cecil.   20
But they do.

Going for last drives
in the bush, odd massive
board-slotted stumps bony white
in whipstick second growth.   25
I could chop all day.

*I could always cash
a cheque, in Sydney or anywhere.
Any of the shops.*

Eating, still at the head   30
of the table, he now missed
food on his knife side.

*Sorry, Dad, but like
have you forgiven your enemies?
Your father and all of them?*   35
All his lifetime of hurt.

I must have (grin). *I don't*
think about that now.

★

People can't say goodbye
any more. They say last hellos.   40

Going fast, over Christmas,
he'd still stumble out
of his room, where his photos
hang over the other furniture,
and play host to his mourners.   45

The courage of his bluster
firm big voice of his confusion.

Two last days in the hospital:
his long forearms were still
red mahogany. His hands   50
gripped steel frame. *I'm dyin.*

On the second day:
You're bustin to talk but
I'm too busy dyin.

★

Grief ended when he died,   55
the widower like soldiers who
won't live life their mates missed.

Good boy Cecil! No more Bluey dog.
No more cowtime. No more stories.
We're still using your imagination,   60
it was stronger than all ours.

Your grave's got littler
somehow, in the three months.
More pointy as the clay's shrivelled,
like a stuck zip in a coat.   65

Your cricket boots are in
the State museum! Odd letters
still come. Two more's died since you:
Annie, and Stewart. Old Stewart.

On your day there was a good crowd,   70
family, and people from away.
But of course a lot had gone
to their own funerals first.

Snobs mind us off religion
nowadays, if they can.   75
Fuck thém. I wish you God.

         1996

The Instrument

Who reads poetry? Not our intellectuals;
they want to control it. Not lovers, not the combative,
not examinees. They too skim it for bouquets
and magic trump cards. Not poor schoolkids
furtively farting as they get immunized against it.   5

Poetry is read by the lovers of poetry
and heard by some more they coax to the cafe
or the district library for a bifocal reading.
Lovers of poetry may total a million people
on the whole planet. Fewer than the players of *skat*.   10

What gives them delight is a never-murderous skim
distilled, to verse mainly, and suspended in rapt
calm on the surface of paper. The rest of poetry
to which this was once integral still rules
the continents, as it always did. But on condition now   15

that its true name is never spoken: constructs, feral poetry,
the opposite but also the secret of the rational.
And who reads that? Ah, the lovers, the schoolkids,
debaters, generals, crime-lords, everybody reads it:
Porsche, lift-off, Gaia, Cool, patriarchy.   20

Among the feral stanzas are many that demand your flesh
to embody themselves. Only completed art

free of obedience to its time can pirouette you
through and athwart the larger poems you are in.
Being outside all poetry is an unreachable void.   25

Why write poetry? For the weird unemployment.
For the painless headaches, that must be tapped to strike
down along your writing arm at the accumulated moment.
For the adjustments after, aligning facets in a verb
before the trance leaves you. For working always beyond   30

your own intelligence. For not needing to rise
and betray the poor to do it. For a non-devouring fame.
Little in politics resembles it: perhaps
the Australian colonists' re-inventing of the snide
far-adopted secret ballot, in which deflation could hide   35

and, as a welfare bringer, shame the mass-grave Revolutions,
so axe-edged, so lictor-y.
Was that moral cowardice's one shining world victory?
Breathing in dream-rhythm when awake and far from bed
evinces the gift. Being tragic with a book on your head.   40
                                                                  1999

The Cool Green

Money just a means to our ends?
No. We are terms in its logic.
Money is an alien.

Millions eat garbage without it.
Money too can be starved   5
but we also die for it then,
so who is the servant?

Its weakest forms wear retro disguise:
subtly hued engraved portraits
of kings, achievers, women in the Liberty cap,   10
warlords who put new nations on the map—

but money is never seen nude.
Credit cards, bullion, bare numbers,
electronic, in columnar files

are only expressions of it,   15
and we are money's genitals.

The more invisible the money
the vaster and swifter its action,
exchanging us for shopping malls,
rewriting us as cities and style.   20

If I were king, how often
would I come up tails?
Only half the time
really? With all my severed heads?

Our waking dreams feature money everywhere   25
but in our sleeping dreams
it is strange and rare.

How did money capture life
away from poetry, ideology, religion?
It didn't want our souls.   30

2006

FRANK MOORHOUSE
b. 1938

Frank Moorhouse was born in Nowra on the south coast of NSW and was educated in Nowra, Wollongong and Sydney. He began his writing career as a cadet journalist on Sydney's *Daily Telegraph* and worked in the early 1960s on a variety of rural newspapers. From 1967 to 1969 he worked in Sydney with the ABC as a radio announcer and subeditor.

His first book, *Futility and Other Animals*, was published in 1969 but it was his second, *The Americans, Baby* (1972), that made him one of the foremost young Australian writers of the 1970s; with Peter Carey, Murray Bail (qqv) and Michael Wilding, Moorhouse was hailed as part of a new wave in Australian short fiction.

Moorhouse's prolific output—he published five collections of short fiction during the 1970s—has been achieved in tandem with the active participation in the various infrastructures of Australian literary culture that has marked his entire career. As a gesture of protest against the fact that it was impossible to get stories with sexually explicit content published anywhere but in 'girlie' magazines, Moorhouse and several other writers established the literary supplement *Tabloid Story*, which ran from 1972 to 1980.

During this period Moorhouse was working with poet Judith Wright (qv) on a campaign to make changes to copyright law that eventually resulted in the founding in 1988 of Copyright Agency Limited, of which he has served as director. He has worked as a union organiser for the Australian Journalists' Association, president of the Australian Society of Authors, and chair of the Australian Copyright Council. He also wrote several screenplays, including the feature film *Between Wars* (1974).

Moorhouse coined the phrase 'discontinuous narrative' to describe his collections of stories about the 'urban tribe', stories that could be read individually but were connected to each other by recurrent characters and settings as well as their common subject matter. He published seven such collections in the course of the 1970s and '80s. *Forty-Seventeen* (1988) also consists of individual stories, but they are sufficiently strongly linked by their common subject matter, themes and characters to form a single cohesive narrative.

He made a dramatic departure from this form in 1993 with the publication of *Grand Days*, a long, intricate novel about the founding of the League of Nations that reflected Moorhouse's lifelong interest in politics national and international, as well as his focus on characters who depart from the social and sexual norms of quiet and anonymous married life. His heroine, Edith Campbell Berry, is a young, intelligent Australian woman who negotiates her professional and sexual education with aplomb. The time-honoured literary conceit of the innocent abroad runs all through Moorhouse's work, not only in such collections of comic writing as *Room Service* (1985) and *Loose Living* (1995) but also in his fiction.

Moorhouse lived overseas for most of the 1990s, in Switzerland, France, the UK and the US; much of this time was spent in Geneva researching *Grand Days* and its companion novel, *Dark Palace* (2000). His status as a literary journalist and essayist was reconfirmed in 2006 by his influential and prize-winning essay 'The Writer in a Time of Terror'. *KG*

From *Forty-Seventeen*
From a Bush Log Book 2

He said on the telephone that he would be using a German solid-fuel stove in the bush.

'I'll put your father on,' his seventy-year-old mother said, and he pictured them passing the telephone between them, and he heard her say to his father in a very audible conspiratorial whisper, 'He says he is going to use a German solid-fuel stove.' His father came on and said the German solid-fuel stove or any-nationality-fuel stoves were banned.

What he didn't say to his father and mother was that he intended to have camp fires regardless of the fire bans. He was now forty and could damn well light a fire, legal or illegal, if he damn well wanted to. And they were disappointing him too with this fire panic. They were bush people who'd brought him up on bush codes of perseverance and on all the bush drills. Why else as a little boy had he crouched shivering and sodden at damp, smoking camp fires blowing his very soul into the fire to get it to flame. Or suffered fly-pestered pink-eye and heat headaches in the dust of summer scout camps, his ears ringing with the madness of cicadas in the hot eucalyptus air, doggedly going about his camp routines. He'd paid. And his family always lit correct fires that caught with the first match. His family knew that the bigger the fire the bigger the fool. He and his family had a pretty good relationship with fire.

On the way through to the bush he paid them a postponed Christmas visit. It was in fact his second trip to the Budawangs in two weeks. For

Christmas he'd gone to the Budawangs with Belle but now felt he needed to go there alone. He wanted now to apologise to the bush for having taken Belle there. Belle had been wrong. Belle belonged in the Intercontinental. That wasn't really it, he wasn't sure why he wanted to go back into the bush again alone. He'd apologised to Belle for having taken her into the bush where she didn't belong.

As he stopped in the driveway of the family home they came out from the sunroom where they'd been waiting for him. His father leaned in the car window and said, 'It's a ticking bomb out there.'

His mother wanted to organise another Christmas dinner, to repeat Christmas for him.

He begged off, 'I've done a lot of moving about this year—I had my report to do—I have to go back to Canberra to present it to a standing committee—I just need to for a few days—no people. It's for the good of my soul.'

His mother understood soul.

'We expected you for Christmas,' his father said, 'I can't see what could be more important than family Christmas.'

What had been more important than family Christmas had been trying to forget his work on the nuclear fuel cycle, and turning forty. He'd tried with Belle and it had worked except for the bush part. He was going to try the bush part again, alone.

'It's a very silly move from a number of points of view,' his father went on as they moved into the house.

He said he could smell rain about.

They didn't comment. His family didn't believe that you could 'smell' rain. He wasn't sure that he believed you could smell rain.

His mother wanted to freeze his steak he'd bought for the bush but he told her not to freeze it.

He asked her though to mend his jeans—as a way of giving her some part to play.

'You're old enough to know better,' his father said, punishing the newspaper with slaps of his hand.

His mother came back with her sewing basket. 'I'll mend it with especially strong cotton,' she said. 'My mother used this cotton.'

'Your mother used it—that same reel?'

'You don't use much of it,' she said to block his incredulity, 'so it never runs out.'

She mended his jeans by hand.

'You shouldn't go into the bush in old clothes,' she said, 'you don't want clothes falling apart in the bush.'

He'd not forgotten that dictum.

'I've put your steak in the freezer,' she said, biting the thread through with her teeth.

Later he excused himself from the room and removed the meat from the freezer.

After years of opposing frozen food his mother now preferred it. From pre-refrigeration days of her youth, his mother now obsessively feared 'things going bad' and in her old age froze everything.

Regardless of his wishes she put together a repeat of a family Christmas.

'What are you going to eat out there?' his nephew asked at the meal.

All questions from nephews and nieces were trick questions.

'Mainly tinned food,' he said, knowing this would lose him marks.

'You're not walking far then,' his nephew said with the smile of the experienced.

'I'm not walking far,' he said, an apology to the whole family for having included any tinned food for a camp. 'It's a lazy camp.'

They didn't know of such a thing.

'I've never carried a can of tinned food into the bush in my life,' his brother declared.

'If he can carry it he can take it,' his sister said, quoting an infrequently used family dictum; used only to excuse foolishness, eccentricity. It was like an appeal to the High Court on some nearly forgotten constitutional ground. He smiled thankfully at her.

'You won't be able to heat them,' his father said, seizing on this as a way of stopping him.

'With this heat they'll be hot enough to eat straight out of the can.'

His father grunted.

You could heat things by putting them under your hat all day, French peasants cooked little birds that way. He didn't say this. Or in your armpit. He didn't say this either.

'You'll need a hot meal in the evening,' his mother said, 'for strength.'

'I think, Mother, he's old enough to feed himself,' his sister said, again acting as his advocate.

'Run to the fire and out the other side,' his nephew said to his father, talking across him, 'isn't that the way you handle bush fire?' His nephew smirked, he now had him trapped in a bush fire.

'If it isn't burning on the other side,' his brother said, 'and if it doesn't have a second front.'

'And that's if you get through the first wave of fire,' his nephew said, with an estimating glance at him which indicated that he didn't think he was the sort of person who would make it through the fire.

'Wet the sleeping bag, unzip it, and pull it over your head,' he said to the nephew and brother. 'Isn't that how it's done?'

His brother said if there was enough water around to wet a sleeping bag and if the sleeping bag wasn't synthetic.

'Don't try to beat the fire uphill—you won't,' his nephew said.

'I wouldn't try,' he said to his nephew.

His nephew obviously thought he was the sort of person who would try. His nephew tossed a nut into the air and caught it in his mouth.

'I know the fastest way to be found if you're lost in the bush.'

'What's that?' His nephew was sceptical.

'You stay where you are, mix a dry martini and within minutes someone will turn up and tell you that you're mixing it wrong.'

The table looked at him unsatisfied, and he knew they hadn't got the joke, they weren't a martini family and they blamed him, he could tell, for making a joke outside the comfortable boundaries of their shared lore. He'd blundered again. He didn't handle being a member of a family very well.

'Why are you going?' his brother asked.

'Foolhardiness,' his father said.

He told them he was going to the upper reaches of the Clyde River which he hadn't done yet in his walking. He wanted to look at Webb's Crown, a remaining block of plateau around which the river had cut itself on both sides, leaving Webb's Crown like a giant cake in the middle of the river.

'It's nothing to look at,' his nephew said.

He couldn't very well say he was going into the bush to apologise to the bush for having taken the wrong person to that part of his metaphorical self. Or that he'd taken Belle, his great-grandmother whore reincarnated into the bush when he should've taken her to Las Vegas.

And when would he be able to go aimlessly into the bush, without plan?

His family always worked the plan.

As a kid he'd just 'gone into the bush' and one thing suggested another, invitations were issued by caves, clearings, high points, creeks—they all called you to them.

'I'd like to go into the bush without a plan,' he said, to see how they'd jump, 'to go into the bush idly.' The word 'idly' was strange to the dining room.

'Plan the work: work the plan,' his father said.

'If you didn't have a plan how would you know where to go next?' asked his nephew.

An existential question.

'It's the journey not the destination,' his ever-protective sister said.

He thought it was both. But he didn't want to have her offside too. 'I hated all that up-at-dawn, fifty-kilometre-day regimented walking we all went in for as kids,' she added.

As he was putting his things into the car the next day his mother gave him a two-litre plastic container of water and told him to put it in his pack.

It wouldn't fit in his pack but he told her he was going, anyhow, to the river.

He tried to ask casually, 'Which side of the family were bushwalkers—was grandmother a bushwalker?' he asked.

'Oh no,' she said, 'she was a city lass.'

'Great-grandmother?' He knew the standard answer.

'She's a bit of an unknown quantity,' she said, 'she lived in Katoomba and that's about all we know. She worked at the Caves.'

He wondered again if that was all she knew. He never got further than that answer.

His father wouldn't come out to say goodbye. His going into the bush was a direct refusal of an order.

His mother said she would pray for rain.

'Don't flood the river on me,' he said.

He drove as far as he could into the bush and then, hoisting his pack, left the car—going through the Act of Severance, the break with habitation and people, the solitary swimming out into the wilderness.

For him it always required a mustering of will and it always brought about a tight alertness. He'd taken 15 mg of Serepax on the drive up to the bush to counteract his family's sapping and to calm him for the bush.

He's taking drugs, he heard his nephew say.

But the tightness continued. Again, as always, the small cold warning spot of fear switched on as the connections with safety receded.

As he walked deeper into the bush his mind monitored his system, running over his body like a hand, a detector listening for fault.

The bush flies were thick but he'd seen them thicker and anyhow he'd made a détente with the flies. He said peace to the flies, peace.

He talks to the flies.

He came to the slab of rock and he laughed to himself about making love to Belle, holding her so the flies crawled over her face. There were three kinds of flies this time, he noticed, which he wasn't allowing to bother him.

Something about fucking a girl on the rock and flies. Choice.

As he stood on the slab and recalled the perfect Christmas dinner she'd cooked, he realised that his effort this time to somehow 'erase' the mistake of bringing Belle into the bush was not going to work. He had inscribed it deeper by doing it. And it didn't worry him now anyhow. She was maybe a reincarnation of his great-grandmother and that was that. Whatever that meant.

He's going on about the great-grandmother again.

He decided to go down into the gorge by way of a descending creek, barely running, which led him to a rainforest on the slope of the gorge. Vines, moss, a dense overhead canopy of branches and vines, silence. He liked the dank chambers of rainforest—they were like a nightclub in the daytime, broken sunlight, a smell of trapped staleness. He sat for a while in the dankness. The flies would not come there.

Maybe this is where Belle and he should have come for Christmas. Or maybe this was where he should lie down and never rise, there in the decay.

He wants to lie down in all the crap.

But he went on, down the remaining stretch of creek, blocked here and there with boulders, and then dropping steeply to the river. Reaching the river was a minor exultation. It was no great river at this point but it ran with enthusiasm and had a thin waterfall. He stood under the fall naked—waterfalls, however thin, always suggest that you watch them or stand under them.

He's standing there under the waterfall testing a waterproof notepad.

After two hours or so of more walking he began to lose alertness and decided to make camp.

He wasn't a follower of the Fung Shui approach to camp sites, the search for the most propitious site. He accepted 'good' camp sites when they came around the corner—the running creek, the camping cave, the grassy knoll. But most of all he liked making camp in unpromising situations. He liked to shape an unpromising site into shelter. Sometimes he was reluctant to leave those camps he'd won from rough conditions. He supposed this was 'very Western'. He used to say in restaurants back in Sydney and Vienna that he went into the bush to have a dialogue with Western Man but instead he invariably became a Man from a Western.

Ha, ha.

He took off his pack and declared 'this is it'. As the gypsies would say, anyone who now approaches this place would have to ask permission to sit by 'his' fire and should not walk between him and his fire, and should approach with sufficient noise so as not to be mistaken for a stalking enemy. But in all the years he had walked in the Australian bush he had never come across another person.

Something about gypsies, he's talking about gypsies.

There had been times when he'd fancied he heard someone 'out there' and sometimes he kept his loaded Luger pistol at hand to keep away the phantoms. There were also the times when he would have quite liked someone to come out of the bush to join him and drink bourbon at the camp fire. He heard voices at times, but knew them for what they were.

He packs iron. He packs iron!?

He built his fire in the almost dry river bed where a narrow stream of water still ran in a wide bed of sand. But when he came to light the fire he couldn't find the disposable lighter which he used in the bush. He remembered checking the equipment against the thirty-one-item equipment list before he started. He was, he thought, good at lists. His family were excellent at lists. Last year he'd bought a replica of a 1930 brass smokestone lighter from the United States for the look of it—from an Early Winters catalogue. But the fuel dried out of the smokestone lighter in the summer heat. He'd gone back to the cheap disposable lighters. But it was missing.

He went through the equipment. No lighter. From the moment you left the car behind you things began to go against you in the bush—something always got broken, something spilled, something was lost, something forgotten with his drill rarely forgotten. Everything began to degenerate—batteries, food. From the moment you left civilisation you had only so long to live.

He forgot his lighter.

His incompetence about the lighter appalled him. Fire was crucial. He went to the emergency kit where he had a box of waterproof matches. They were there. Go on, deduct points, he said to his nephew, take off ten points.

Fifty.

He lit the camp fire.

He grilled his steak on a green forked stick, baked two potatoes in the coals. He wondered if his mother had taken the lighter from his pack. Impossible.

He for-got his ligh-ter.

He for-got his ligh-ter.

He ate two marshmallow biscuits.

After dinner he killed the fire and went up beside the tent on the grass. It was a cool evening and he thought he could detect rain in the air, a fall in barometric pressure maybe.

He settled down with a flask of Jack Daniels bourbon, sipping it from his Guzzini goblet which he carried for sipping Jack Daniels in the bush.

He wished himself a good fortieth year.

He ate smokehouse almonds. He felt the bush to be benign for the first time on this trip. He had shed the pangs of isolation. After the second bourbon an emphatic peace fell about him. He finished the evening writing languid notes—a conversation with himself, it sure as hell beat a lot of conversations he'd had that last year.

He's sloshed.

In his tent, in his sleeping bag, his torch hanging from the ceiling, he read a few pages of *Buddenbrooks*. Having run away from his own bourgeois mercantile family he immersed himself in the fortunes of Mann's German bourgeois family of the nineteenth century.

> Herr Ralf von Maiboom, owner of the Poppenrade estate, had committed suicide by shooting himself with a revolver, in the study of the manor-house. Pecuniary difficulties seem to have been the cause of the act.
>
> 'With a revolver?' Thomas Buddenbrook asked, and then, after another pause, he said in a low voice, slowly, mockingly, 'That is the nobility for you.'

He says we're bourgeois.

During the night he was woken by rain and said to himself, 'Well done, Mother.' and drifted back to sleep with the pleasure of being in a wild environment but secured against it, he liked weathering out storms in a tent.

In the morning it was drizzling but he took out the German solid-fuel stove and set it up in a small pocket cave, the size of a fireplace, for the making of the morning coffee to begin a wet day in the bush.

Make a fuzz-stick. No need for the emergency stove just because of a little drizzle.

He didn't feel like fooling around with damp wood.

Strip dead wood from standing trees.

He *knew* how to make a fire in the wet. He just wasn't going to crouch and blow his soul into a damp fire.

Having set up the stove he couldn't find the matches.

He went into the tent and made a cramped search through his things again, taking everything out of the backpack, and emptying the food bag.

My God, now he's lost the matches.

Dismayed, disbelieving, he sat in the tent surrounded by his thirty-one items of gear and tried to think what could have happened to the matches.

Twenty-nine items of gear.

Yes, twenty-nine items of gear, yes.

He searched the route from the tent to the dinner fire, to the side of the river course where he'd washed, to the place where he'd sat sipping his bourbon. He went to where he'd had a piss.

He considered the possibility that an animal, a possum maybe, had taken them; but he would then have expected to find remains of chewed matches. Frankly, he'd never had a possum take anything, at any camp. Once a dingo pup had taken some food from a pot. What would an animal want with waterproof matches?

He thinks a possum took them.

He crawled back into the tent, the drizzle barely making a sound on the tent, and reported to his captain-self that he'd lost the matches—had failed to pack the lighter and then had lost the emergency matches.

He really has lost the matches.

He could perhaps do something fancy like using a magnifying glass from his monocular.

If there was sun.

Yes, if there was sun.

He hadn't mastered the bow and friction drill method. And he really didn't understand what tinder was.

Doesn't know what tinder is.

In the tent he ate all the marshmallow biscuits, dulled still with disbelief about the matches.

He eats marshmallow biscuits for breakfast. What?! He takes marshmallow biscuits into the bush!?

For godsake he was forty and he could damn well eat what he wanted for breakfast.

But they didn't make him feel good.

As he brooded, it came to him as a dim signal from a long way off that there was a conspiracy going on.

The parent within was hiding the means of making fire from the wilful child. It was such a pedantic case of the psychopathology of everyday life. It offended him and its realisation brought him no relief.

He's saying it all has to do with Freud.

He forced himself to get out of the tent. He put on his poncho again and stood in the drizzle, dispirited. He decided to take a walk downstream for a while, maybe to Webb's Crown. But after fifteen minutes of hard going, the drizzle, the lost matches and the marshmallow breakfast broke his resolve and he gave up and began to make his way back to the camp.

'I am a Marshmallow Bushman,' he said. 'We are the Marshmallow Men. We are the stuffed men.'

He began to break camp.

Eyre, Stuart, Sturt. The explorers would not have been defeated by their mothers' magical interference.

Did his great-grandmother have a part in this? Belle, the reincarnation of his great-grandmother. Wrong person to have brought into the bush. Painted fingernails. Painted toenails. Luxury life whore. There to apologise.

Something about the great-grandmother again.

He would go back to the city and hole up at the Intercontinental.

Ring Belle.

As he pulled down the tent he found the matches. They were under the eaves of the tent just where the fly of the tent came near to the ground. Somehow they'd fallen from his pocket the night before and bounced under the eave. They hadn't 'fallen', they'd been put there by the invisible hand of his mother.

The whole trip had been spooked. Too many relatives, living and dead, were meddling with his mind. The bush of the district was too strong a psychic field this Christmas.

He's thrown it in.

In the drizzle, he zigzagged his way up the steep, wooded slope of the gorge, hauling himself up the successive rock ledges which characterised that country.

He reached the plateau and the drizzle stopped and was replaced by a fog which came swirling in over the range. Visibility dropped to about two metres and he walked by compass.

'Stop it, Mother. You've prayed too hard. We've got fog.'

His compass brought him to the car and he congratulated himself on his navigation.

Not bad, not bad for someone who forgets the lighter and loses the matches.

He dumped his pack in the luggage compartment of the car and found the lighter lying there. He got out of his wet clothes into the dry city clothes. He combed his hair in the rear-vision mirror. He switched on the radio to music and swigged from the flask of bourbon, surrounded by white fog.

He felt safe from his mother's fog and rain for the time, and from his great-grandmother's disdain for the bush, if that was what he was copping, and from the mockery of his nephew. For the time. In the car. In the fog.

1988

MUDROOROO
b. 1938

Mudrooroo (born Colin Johnson) was born at East Cuballing, near Narrogin, WA. His grandfather was of African-American descent. From the ages of nine to sixteen he lived in a Christian Brothers' orphanage, and remained a ward of the state until he was eighteen. Mudrooroo's experiences of being a non-white, institutionalised child in a racist society had a profound influence. He spent a year in Fremantle Prison, and then lived for a time in the home of the writer Dame Mary Durack, who acted as his literary patron, writing the foreword to his semi-autobiographical novel, *Wild Cat Falling* (1965), which was acclaimed as the first novel by an Indigenous Australian.

In the 1960s Mudrooroo travelled extensively. He spent some years in India as a Buddhist monk, then returned to work at Monash University and study at the University of Melbourne. In 1988, the Bicentennial year, he changed his name to Mudrooroo Narogin, a name that evolved into Mudrooroo Nyoongah, and then simply Mudrooroo, meaning 'Paperbark'. Mudrooroo's novels, beginning with *Long Live Sandawara* (1979), have been notable for their experimental, ambitious nature. *Doctor Wooreddy's Prescription for Enduring the End of the World* (1983), widely recognised as the author's masterpiece, deals with the systematic attempt in the early nineteenth century to exterminate Indigenous Tasmanians. *Master of the Ghost Dreaming* (1991), which begins the four-novel series of that name, is also concerned with this period of colonial history.

Mudrooroo is also a poet and a critic. His *Writing from the Fringe: A study of modern Aboriginal literature in Australia* (1990), was an early, sometimes controversial, example of its kind. In the 1990s he held a number of academic positions, including head of Aboriginal Studies at Murdoch University, Perth. His prize-winning cultural study, *Us Mob: History, culture, struggle*, was published in 1995. In 1996 a controversy arose over Mudrooroo's identification as an Indigenous Australian. It was revealed that Mudrooroo's sister had conducted genealogical research and found no Aboriginal ancestry in the family. Extensive debate ensued about the issues of authenticity and what constitutes Aboriginal identity. After resigning from Murdoch University, and living for a time in Queensland, in 2001 Mudrooroo returned to India and pursued further studies in Buddhism. *DM*

From *Master of the Ghost Dreaming*
Chapter IV

Fada was not to be denied his little pleasures and Ludjee was to perform for him yet again. The excuse, for Fada was one for excuses, was to sketch a primitive scene for the chapter on food gathering in his definitive work. And so, with Ludjee behind him carrying a heavy armchair, he made his way towards the base of the rocky headland on the left side of the cove which served as a small port for the mission. When they reached the beach, he was not content with setting up his seat on the sand, but needed it on the headland from the end of which Ludjee would supposedly be diving for shellfish. He believed in being as near the scene as possible; but this meant that Ludjee had to lug the ungainly object directly over the rough boulders which made up the headland. It was hard going clambering over the broken surface. What made it worse was the heavy skirt dragging at her legs and threatening at every step to trip her up. It stopped her from stepping from boulder to boulder and she had to wade through the rock pools where the slippery bottom sent her sprawling on more than one occasion. Finally, soaked through and out of breath, she thudded the chair down on the flat surface of a rock with a sigh.

But her work was not yet done. Fada had her adjust his seat to the best possible advantage. He made such a fuss that she felt like flinging the chair and him after it into the sea, and all the time the drag of that heavy wet material was imprisoning her. It was enough to make a body cry, not in pain but in anger. At last Fada was satisfied. He sat enthroned, dry and comfortable, while the woman nearby was glad that it was a sunny day. She would have liked to take off her wet dress, but she knew that Fada would become upset. She stood there waiting and watching as he opened his sketchbook, and examined his charcoal stick to see that it was sharp; finally he looked up at Ludjee and ordered the woman to divest herself of her clothing.

Ludjee knew what his flushed face could mean, but after lugging the chair and becoming soaked to the bone, she didn't care. It was just another thing wrong with the ghosts and perhaps one day they would learn to accept the human body as it was, instead of hiding it under layers of thick cloth. She had never come close to understanding the urgency with which Fada ordered human beings to cover themselves up. They seemed to have a horror about humanity which might be put down to their once being human and dark. Why, she had never seen Mada once unclothed. She was always swathed in yard upon yard of material which seemed to weigh down her gaunt body. No wonder she had grown so wasted. She had so much to support, that her strength had given out, and now she spent most of the time lying down. It was really strange, even if she did not fully accept her husband's theory that their bodies were made of solidified fog and that if they went unclothed for any length of time, they would slowly begin to evaporate. This might make sense to Jangamuttuk, for he had never felt the heavy solidity of a ghost body. Ludjee on more than one occasion had felt the hardness of a ghost body, not only pressing on her, but penetrating her as well, and it had felt as solid as her own husband's. What was different however was their colour and smell. The colour was maggot white, the colour of fog as Jangamuttuk had declared. Their skin in fact was opaque like mist and underneath veins could be seen pulsing with blood. This at least showed that they had blood, as did their cuts and wounds which ran a rich red; but it was the smell that alarmed her when she had to endure the actual pressure of their bodies. It was a sort of musty smell, a reeking of decay. And even their taste was different; rancid and bad, but now even her own people tasted like that. The stale ghost food and clothing had altered their metabolism, had made them sick and smelling of corpses.

She thought this while she struggled out of the sodden cloth woven from the hair of that animal which was kept on another island close by. As the last shreds left her body, she breathed deeply and stretched happily. What did she care that Fada was running his eyes over her breasts and buttocks, or that the flush on his face had deepened.

Fada feasted on her body, his eyes misting with memories. The first time he had seen her she had been as slim as a boy; since then her body had thickened into the body of a mature woman. He gulped as she raised her arms. Her heavy breasts flattened out on her chest. A forbidden memory of his youth in the East End of London came to him. He remembered the illustrations that some of his mates passed around while they bragged of their conquests. He thought of Mada and one conquest too many. His desire left and thinking that he had conquered temptation just as much as those mates of his had conquered a slut or two, or nil, he huskily ordered the woman to go to the very edge of the point and pose there as if she were about to dive into the ocean.

'But Fada,' she exclaimed, 'ain't no shellfish here.'

'It does not matter. I want you to pose for me. I'll put you down on paper.'

'Capture my soul,' the woman whispered.

'But where is your net, where is your wooden chisel? It must be authentic. It must be as you once did.'

'Fada, we don't make them old things no more. All finished now same longa fish.'

'Ludjee, you know that I have a collection of artefacts in my house. Go there, take a net and wooden chisel and come right back. Quickly now, the tide's on the turn.'

Ludjee with rebellion in her heart ceased to pose and slumped. Why did he have to spoil everything? Why couldn't she enjoy this moment without his incessant commands destroying it? She began to make her way back to the beach. At least she was joyously naked and could feel the warm breeze on her skin. But he spoilt even this. Fada instantly ordered her back and gave her a lecture on wearing clothing at all times. She was about to retort that sometimes he liked her without it, but decided that there was little point in making it an issue. So she dragged on the sodden cloth and then struggled along to the beginning of the point and to the bungalow.

Fada stared after the graceless creature struggling along from rock to rock. He smiled as he saw her slip and tumble into a pool. Such a shabby figure, he thought; then dismissed the thought as being beneath him. It was absolutely necessary to train them into civilised behaviour. How could he have them going about naked, a snare and a trap for all the men on the island? Better to have their charms covered and concealed. At least in this matter he had to remain firm. He thrust the sight of her naked body away from his mind and set himself to enjoy the pleasant afternoon on the point. He smiled the smile of a man at peace with himself and his world. On days like this, he could believe that he was living in paradise. How the golden rays of the sun flooded the island turning it into a scene of primeval beauty.

Away towards the horizon, huge clouds sailed majestically by. He amused himself in finding the shapes of animals in them. There was a dragon humped up towards the west; above floated what looked like a lizard or an iguana; there a fish, and what did that look like but the fair body of a naked English beauty. He cast his eyes down to where the sea foamed off the small flat green islands which surrounded this larger one, on which he had set up his mission. One of the other islands he had begun using to pasture the mission's flock of sheep. Even there, there had been casualties, and he nodded his head in sadness, then cheered up, for the situation had improved enough for him to send the schooner out under the command of his son to butcher some of the animals for fresh meat. He scanned the horizon, for the vessel should be well into the return voyage, but there was no sign of it. Well, it was perfect weather for sailing and with the tide on the turn, his son should have no trouble in reaching the cove by evening.

He turned his attention inland. Behind the narrow coastal plain the central spine of the island loomed with more than a suggestion of menace about it. This he put down to the gloomy forests which dominated the steep slopes in mass confusion. Indeed, it was the trackless jungle of his worst dreams. On arriving on the island with a detachment of soldiers (they had been sent to guard the working party of convicts which cleared the forest and erected the mission buildings) he had once set out to conquer the peak. He thought that the view from the summit must be wonderful and a British flag flying there would mark the whole island with the promise of superior culture and civilisation. He had set out with high hopes of reaching the summit by early afternoon. Somehow he had lost his way and pushing his way through the almost impenetrable jungle had reached a clearing overgrown with tall grass. Exhausted, he had sat down to rest and had fallen asleep. He awoke in terror, his whole body covered with leeches. Only quick thinking had saved him from death. Fortunately, he had packed a large container of salt in his lunch and so he sprinkled some of it on the blood suckers. They curled up and dropped off. Free of most of them, he blundered back the way he had come. Thankfully, it was all downhill and he managed to stagger to the compound before collapsing from loss of blood.

The incident had put all ideas of climbing the mountain out of his mind for ever. Somehow Jangamuttuk must have known of Fada's aversion when the rogue had decided to camp high up on the slope. Fada examined the slope and eyed the massive boulder which clung to the hillside. It rested on what, at least from that distance, looked like two columns of rock. He should have brought his glass to make out the details, he thought, but no matter. A thin line of smoke rose from, or near, or under the boulder. That must be the camp of that old rascal, Jangamuttuk. He would clamber up there one day and order him down into the mission. Then, he felt the itching of the leech scars over his body and shuddered. Let the old rascal stay in his camp and be drained of blood. It would serve him right. [. . .]

1991

ROBERT HUGHES
b. 1938

As detailed in his memoir *Things I Didn't Know* (2006), Robert Hughes was educated by the Jesuits and attended the University of Sydney. He worked as an art critic for the Sydney *Observer* and the *Nation* before moving to England in 1964, where he worked for newspapers such as the *Times* and the *Observer*, and published works of art history, including *The Art of Australia: A critical survey* (1966). In 1970 he became the art critic for *Time*. He has since become an internationally renowned art critic, capable of offering scathing criticisms of established artists. *The Shock of the New* (1980) was a popular and critical success as both a BBC television series and book. Hughes has also made television documentaries on American art, Goya and Australia. His study of Australia's convict history, *The Fatal Shore* (1987), was an international bestseller, though Hughes was criticised over his use of sources. Hughes has also written works on Barcelona and fishing, and published a work of cultural polemic, *Culture of Complaint* (1993), written in the US. His essays appear in *Nothing if Not Critical* (1990). DM

From *Culture of Complaint*

[. . .] One of the more disagreeable moments of my education was having to stand up and speak extempore in Latin for four minutes, before other schoolboys and our Jesuit teacher, on Horace's famous tag, *Coelum non animam mutant qui trans mare currunt*—'Those who cross the sea change the sky above them, but not their souls.' I resented this, not only because my Latin was poor, but because the *idea* struck me as wrong—the utterance of a self-satisfied Roman, impervious to the rest of the world. Hegemonic Horace.

But most Australians were on his side. The motto of Sydney University expressed contentment with the colonial bind: *Sidere mens eadem mutato*, another version of Horace's imperial thought—'The same mind under changed skies.'

Our education would prepare us to be little Englishmen and Englishwomen, though with nasal accents. We would not be accepted as such by the English themselves: we were not up to that. No poem written by an Australian was going to make its way into the anthologies of English verse—our national fate was to read those anthologies, never to contribute to them. It seemed natural to us that our head of state, with constitutional power to depose any democratically elected Australian prime minister, should be a young Englishwoman who lived 14,000 miles away. What native-born Australian could possibly be as worth looking up to as this Queen? Our Prime Minister, Robert Menzies, last of the true Australian imperialists, said we were 'the Queen's men', 'British to the boot-heels'. When asked what his dream of felicity would be on leaving politics, he unhesitatingly replied, 'A book-lined cottage in Kent.'

In those days we had a small, 95 percent white, Anglo-Irish society, in whose public schools you could learn Latin but not Italian, ancient but not modern Greek. What we learned of the world in school came through the great tradition (and I use the word without irony) of English letters and English history. We were taught little Australian history. Of the world's great religions other than Christianity—Judaism, Buddhism, Hinduism, Islam— we were as perfectly ignorant as a row of cats looking at a TV set; or would have been, if Australia had had television in 1955, which, luckily, it did not. I didn't meet a Jew until I got to University, and you can imagine the line the Jesuits took on the Spanish Inquisition and the policies of Ferdinand and Isabella. I didn't even know what an *Episcopalian* was. Not until my late teens did I have a conversation with an Australian Aborigine, and it was short. There were no Aboriginal students, let alone teachers, at Sydney University. The original colonists of Australia—whose ancestors had walked and paddled there, across the string of islands that lay between 'our' continent and Asia, around 30,000 BC—were completely unknown to us city whites, and their history and culture fell into a box marked 'anthropology', meaning the study of exotics with whom one had nothing in common, and whose culture had nothing of value to contribute to ours. Thinking so was our subliminal way of warding-off the suspicion that ours had contributed nothing but misery and death to theirs.

My father, who was born in 1895, was like every other Australian of his generation when he spoke of Asia. He saw it as a threat—not surprisingly, since Australia had been at war with Japan from 1941 to 1945, and lost many young men in the Pacific islands, in New Guinea, on the Burma Road and in hellish concentration camps like Changi. Only by a hair's breadth and the force of American arms did we escape being forcibly co-opted into what Tojo[1] called the Greater East Asian Co-Prosperity Sphere.

Such national experiences, mixed with a long tradition of Sinophobia—for the racially exclusive White Australia Policy was a left-wing law, originally designed to keep cheap coolie labour out of Australia—did not predispose even intelligent Australians, like my father, towards an appreciation of Zen calligraphy or the finer points of tea. He kept a captured Japanese flag in a cupboard (not on the wall) and sometimes I would take out this rusty square of cotton with the brilliant red circle and the frayed rip in it, which I assumed to be a bullet-hole, and reflect that but for the grace of God it might now be flying over Royal Sydney Golf Club. (The Japanese, at the time, did not play golf.)

Who talks of 'Asia' or 'Asians' now—even as we utter our vague generalizations about 'European' culture? There are only Chinese, Japanese, Indonesians, Cambodians, and within even these national categories lie complexities of identity and heritage that are lost on the distant foreigner. But my father thought even more abstractly than this. He rarely mentioned Asia to me. He called it the Far East, meaning the Near North, and would not have considered going there. Far East of where? East of Eden: that is, east of England, a country in which, by his death, he had spent less than three of his fifty-six years, in between tours of duty flying a Sopwith Camel in France for his King and Empire in World War I. Today, if you asked a twelve-year-old Australian boy what he thought about 'the East', he might hesitate: what does the oldie mean? New Zealand is in the east; maybe he means that, or Peru, which is even farther East.

---

1   Hideki Tojo (1884–1948), Japanese prime minister during much of the Second World War.

So you might say that my upbringing was monocultural, in fact classically colonial, in the sense that it concentrated on the history, literature and values of Western Europe and, in particular, of England, and not much else. It had very little relationship to the themes of education in Australia today, which place a heavy stress on local history, the culture of minorities, and a compensatory non-Anglocentric approach to all social questions. 'Multiculturalism' has been a bureaucratic standard there for the best part of twenty years now, and its effects have been almost entirely good. It reflects a reality we have in common with the even more diverse, but culturally reluctant, USA—which, put in its simplest terms, is that the person on the bus next to you in Sydney is just as likely to be the descendant of a relatively recent arrival, a small trader from Skopelos, a mechanic from Palermo, a cook from Saigon, a lawyer from Hong Kong or a cobbler from some *stetl* in Lithuania as the great-great grandchild of an Englishman or Irishman, transported or free. The length of one's roots, as distinct from their tenacity, is no longer a big deal in my country, whatever passing pangs of regret this may induce in the minority of Australians whose families have been there for most of its (white) history. By the 1970s Australia had ceased to be a 'basically British' country anyway, and there was no feasible way of persuading the daughter of a Croatian migrant of the mystic bond she was supposed to feel with Prince Charles or his mother—or of the enduring usefulness, to her education, of the history of the Plantagenets. It is probable that young Australians, away down there in what so many Americans still persist in imagining as a sort of Texas conducted by other means at the bottom of the globe, have a far better picture of the rest of the world—Near North included—than their American equivalents have or are likely to get. They have been given it by education and, of late, by television: the Australian government sponsors not just a few programs but an entire network channel, SBS, broadcasting seven days a week, which presents news, documentaries, film and commentary from all over the world, in twenty languages from Arabic to Tagalog (with English subtitles). One can imagine the howls of outrage about 'cultural fragmentation' that would issue from the mandarins of American conservatism if Washington were to even think of spending taxpayers' money on such a scheme in the United States. Yet if SBS's programming has any effect on the Australian polity, it is probably to cement it through mutual tolerance and curiosity rather than to fragment it into zones of cultural self-interest. In Australia, no Utopia but a less truculent immigrant society than this one, intelligent multiculturalism works to everyone's social advantage, and the conservative crisis-talk about creating 'a cultural tower of Babel' and so forth is seen as obsolete alarmism of a fairly low order. [. . .]

1993

MARY ROSE LIVERANI
b. 1939

As recounted in her autobiography *The Winter Sparrows: Growing up in Scotland and Australia* (1975), Mary Rose Liverani arrived in Australia at the age of thirteen when her family migrated from Scotland and settled in Wollongong, NSW. Liverani has subsequently written arts journalism. *DM*

From *The Winter Sparrows*
Chapter 13: Dear Folks

I am waiting for Australia to enchant me. To distract me from the past. To become the hypnotic present.

Today I had my very first Australian cut. The first in the family. A sliver of raw steel was sticking out from the side supports of the gangway and it pricked me on the left calf as I put my right foot down on Terra Australis. Two gouts of blood blotched the concrete in tooth-edged circles before a path was found down my leg and into my sock. 'Take care,' my father warned, when I yelled 'Hey, look!' Cuts cannot be neglected here. The germs are ferocious in this water-sodden heat. I licked my finger and rubbed at the slit skin carelessly. What was the use of having a cut in Australia if it didn't develop its own unique characteristics? I would see how terrible the germs are.

Boys were punting a ball in a side street we passed on the way up from the ship. My father insisted they were ordinary kids like us, nothing special, and he wouldn't stop to stare. I wanted to see their faces close up and listen to their voices, but he loped away from us, bobbing up and down on what Mammy called his two left legs, opening and shutting them like scissors cutting up yard after yard of space. 'There's a train waiting,' he panted, when we grumbled in line behind him, straggling in and out like the tail of a kite.

He was wrong. The train had gone when we reached the station.

'Damnation. Two more hours.'

We consumed square pies with interest rather than hunger, prising open the lids and examining the gritty meat curiously.

'There's a lot o' empty space in here.'

'That's for people who're no' very hungry,' my father joked.

Bits of meat and gristle bloodied with red sauce began to dribble down best clothes.

'Christ, you eat like a pig. Here you, take him tae a bubbler and wipe that mess off his clothes.'

We couldn't find a bubbler in the Ladies' Waiting Room where eating food was strictly forbidden, but rows of wash basins with peeling taps and flaky porcelain were perched like cranes on single legs underneath dulled mirrors. Most extraordinary were the toilets with two bowls plonked side by side.

'This might be a toilet for twins,' Margaret suggested.

'Or best friends,' whispered hungry Susan who was always hiding at keyholes.

Margaret placed her two hands side by side between the bowls.

'Look at the wee space between them. Two fat women would be touching each other. Ugh.'

We looked at each other, horrified. Nae peace tae read a book, even.

Then, reluctantly, for we might need it again and would then have to pay another penny, we let the door slam and 'vacant' rushed round to shove 'engaged' into the lower half of the dial.

We wandered aimlessly over the station, stopping to read the headlines on the newspapers. The *Sydney Daily Telegraph*.

'Hey, look at that. You spell Sydney with a y not an i.'

Then we examined the yellow indicators above our heads, astonished at what we saw.

'They use other countries' names here: Newcastle, Hamilton, Toronto, Aberdeen, for goodness sake. Fancy using Scottish names.'

'Well, what about New South Wales?'

'Aye, and what if it had been called New West Scotland?'

Then we tried the Aboriginal names. 'What does "gatta" mean? This place is called Cool an gatta.'

'What's the opposite of Bulli?'

'Coweye, stupid.'

Robert, who was gazing around him, suddenly grabbed my father's arm.

'Hey, Da, there's an Aborigine!'

We all stared at the little dark man he was pointing to pushing an empty trolley. My father put down the paper he was reading (it was called the *Common Cause*) and glanced quickly at the little man.

'Don't go pointing at people like an ignoramus,' he snapped. 'And that man's no' an Aborigine. He's a Greek or an Italian. Jesus, did they no' teach ye anything at school, in geography?'

We played games in a frenzied squandering of time. Half an hour was spent, heedlessly running and taking wide stretched leaps over Susan's or Robert's bent back. But sometimes we ran, only to stop abruptly on the points of our shoes, pawing the air and holding in our stomachs to prevent a collision with a frozen-eyed man or woman whose sight was fixed on things inward.

My mother was fretful.

'Ye'll have tae stop playing leapfrog. Ye're getting in people's way and they're staring at us.'

And when we looked, so they were. Brown paper carrying bags lying on their ankles, or smallish suitcases with the corners pulled back and thick, ochre coloured cardboard exposed, clamped firmly between long, thin thighs and sharp chin. They were gaping at us. All along a red-brown seat. Sadie stuck her tongue out.

'Oh,' my mother said, affronted, and gave her a slap.

Waw—waw, and teeth grinding, ankles crossing and uncrossing, fingers beating restlessly and buttocks rotating on the hard wooden slats.

'Let's see who can spit the furthest.'

My mother jumped up from her seat and ran along the line, slap slapping, shake shaking.

'Ah've just about had you lot. Sit there and don't move a muscle or ah'll gie ye all a belting right here in front o' the world.'

Then only the eyes moved. Sliding sideways, crossing inwards, whirring round and round.

'Can you do it anti-clockwise?'

A sly look at my mother's tense face.

'Watch. Ah'm goin' tae pass mah hand over mah face and then ye'll see Dracula.'

'Och, that wasnae very scary. Ah can dae it better.'

My mother shut the *Readers' Digest* and glanced across at the waiting carrier bags and peeling suitcases.

'Christ, what are they doin' noo?' And she got up and hurried along to us.

'Dae ye have tae sit there making faces and makin' exhibitions o' yourselves? Look at these people watching ye.'

Susan sighed.

'Jings, ye cannae dae anything here except breathe.' Then she turned her head and looked across at the long seat opposite carefully rolling her eyes and sticking her two eye teeth into her bottom lip.

My mother didn't see her. But the others did, and felt they had been avenged.

'Here, there's only twenty minutes left,' my father announced standing up. 'The train'll be in. We can go and sit in it.'

It was leaving from platform 11. All stations to Gullawobblong.[1]

'It's a slow train,' my father said.

And we all tried to push through the barrier at once.

'Christ, ah'm goin' tae kill that lot,' my mother swore.

In the train, however, she beamed happily when she came to inspect and found all the younger ones asleep, lying across each other like kittens.

---

1   A fictional name for Wollongong.

'Thank God for that,' she said to Margaret and me. 'Ah can relax noo.'

And down the aisle she went to her own seat beside my father.

Though it was getting dark we could still see out of the window. Margaret had the window seat, so I watched from crab eyes the man sitting opposite us. He wore a cardigan and hat. The skin on his face looked rough and tough and he had thin, drained lips. He sat with his knees spread open and his hands hanging between them, the fingers tapping each other restlessly. A few minutes after the train left the station he tapped his fingers together with a last flourish, one after the other as if he were running them down piano keys, and leaning forward said:

'You kids mind if I smoke?'

Well, I nearly died. To ask us if we minded anything! The only time that was ever said to us was in the tone that meant quit it or I'll punch your nose. Do you *mind*, with a filthy look. Meaning, I blooming well mind what *you're* doing.

Margaret didn't hear him but I said:

'Good heavens, no.'

He dug around in the pocket of his cardigan and drew out a blue cellophane packet. I recognised it. It was a shag bag, and sure enough he opened it and took out a packet of cigarette papers. He tipped some shag along the fold of a smoothed-out paper, shaking it a bit to even it out, then he licked the edges of the paper and stuck them together. Some shag was hanging out both ends, so he nipped it off with his fingernails. They were black and long. Margaret had turned away from the window and was watching him the same as I was.

'Hey mister,' she said, embarrassing me and breaking the golden rule of silence with strangers, 'mah faither's got a wee machine for doin' that. It makes the cigarettes even all the way and they don't have wee bits hanging out the end.'

The man tugged at a few more threads of tobacco and lit the cigarette before he acknowledged the speech.

'Is that a fact?'

'My word.'

The man smiled with his eyes though the rest of his face was quite still.

'Well that sounds like a very fine machine. Very fine. But you see, I'm not all that keen on mass production. I like all my smokes to taste different, see. It's like having a cup of tea. Even with the same brand you can get a lot of different tastes. Depends on how you make it.'

We sat thinking. It made sense. Then the man spoke again. It was clear he felt comfortable with us now.

'Where are you kids going?'

'Gullawobblong.'

'Nice town. Lots of beaches. And steelworks for making money.' He flicked some ash on to the floor. Dirty thing. 'Poms, aren't you?'

What were Poms? Margaret never liked to show her ignorance.

'We're Protestants,' she said.

It was a useless attempt. I could see by the quick flicker of the man's lips that she'd said something stupid. He tried to cover it up.

'Then you're Protestant Poms.'

There was little point in going on with this game. It was like twenty questions. So I confessed that we weren't familiar with the word.

'Poms are short for Pommies. People from England.'

'From England or Britain?' I asked quickly.

He shrugged his shoulders and stared out of the window.

'What's it matter? They're all the same.'

Then he saw by my face I was annoyed and added:

'It's the English really. They're the Pommies.'

'Well,' I said, 'we're Scottish and there's a big difference, you know. But you haven't told us what Pommie means.'

He tapped his teeth with his long fingernail.

'I don't really know, kid. Something to do with their skins.'

'Is it good or bad?' I persisted.

He shook his head from left to right in a negative gesture.

'Bad. It means "I don't like you mate"!'

Then he changed the subject, wrenching it out of its ugly shape.

'What do you think of the bush?'

I felt anxious to please him somehow, so I looked along his wiggling fingers that pointed outside the window, and tried to single out particular leaves. It was impossible.

'Which one?'

'Which what?'

'Which bush?'

Oh dear. It was easier to talk broken English with Frank, the Italian fish shop owner. The man was exasperated. He made a queer sound in the back of his throat and withdrew into himself. His lids, drawing down over his eyes, said 'the end' and I folded my hands together on my lap, irritated because I didn't know what I'd done to be so annoying. From time to time I looked over at the man. A fine, dark glitter, sharp across his face, told me his eyes weren't perfectly shut. But he was sleeping, quietly soughing through his teeth. I nudged Margaret. She was dozing with her cheek on the hand that rested against the glass.

'That man,' I whispered, trying not to move my lips, 'that man is queer.'

She didn't answer.

We went into a tunnel that was longer than the others and fumes came rushing in through the open windows. I licked them off my mouth, trying not to breathe and then we were again in the cold dusk, high above the sea, on the top of a scarp that was curving round like the bend in an elbow. Down below, tucked into the curve, was a tiny village. The sea was its boundary, like the stroke of the letter d. The few houses looked private and secure, propped up against the strong back wall. Quiet and cosy.

Then I felt fingers tapping on my knee. It was the man. He was leaning over to get my attention.

'It's the lot,' he said.

'The lot of what?'

'The lot—' he swung his arm widely this time. 'The grass, the trees, the ferns.' He swung again like a drunk man. 'Everything's the bush.'

'Och, is that what ye mean?'

He nodded deeply, pleased that I understood at last.

'Yeah, well what do you think?'

This time I did the shrugging. Grass and stuff. What could you say? We were going through a gorge now because the tops of the trees below the window looked like huge dark cauliflowers, and as I followed the growth up the slopes ahead the trees became a furry animal crawling on its belly.

'Everything seems to be coming or going,' I said, finally.

He sat up straight, his face watchful, and I sensed he was preparing to do battle for his bush. He was listening, not with interest but with ammunition.

'What do you mean?'

I swung my arm the way he had.

'The trees and the little bushes. They're all young, just growing, or they're all twisted, just dying. There don't seem to be any tall straight trees that are in the middle. Look at those,' I said, pointing. 'That tree's like an old hand springing out of the earth without a wrist, even. It hasn't got a proper trunk in the middle.'

'Maybe it's not a proper tree,' he argued craftily. 'It may be just scrub. But we've got mighty trees, you know. How do you think we get our telegraph poles?' he cried, delighted with his inspiration. There was nothing I could say to that. 'The bush', he went on like a salesman, as if he wanted me to buy it, 'goes on forever so that it never seems to move at all. All together, it is always there. Nobody saw its beginning, and it'll likely see our end. So you're wrong, you see. Got no understanding of it at all.'

And he sat back, satisfied. This time his lids dropped heavily, curtaining off his mind. There were to be no more encores. He was still sleeping when the train really stopped at Gullawobblong. The other stops had only been pauses, but this was arrival.

Frowning, my mother swept the platform with her eyes. No one else had swept it, all day. Cold dry dust rushed up our noses making them twitch, jamming the narrow passages between our eyes. When you blew, nothing shifted and your head ached with the strain. Outside the station we huddled together eyeing the taxis, jealous of their warmth inside and hoping my father would see them. He wasn't looking at them.

'The Immigration Department said there'd be transport here,' he muttered, 'but it's probably gone, since we came on a later train.'

We were in a street shaped like a bottle opener, big and round at the station end with a narrow neck leading to another street which my father said was Gullawobblong. Some dark green buses were lined up behind a sign that said: Bus Stand Only. My father strode across to the front one, and called out to the driver who had a paper spread out across his steering wheel.

'Hey mac, do any of these buses go to Kershley Hostel?'

The bus driver just shook his head over the top of the paper.

'Shit,' said my mother. 'We'll have tae take a taxi. Here, Robert, go and ask how much it costs.'

The driver pushed his hat to the back of his head the way they do in F.B.I. pictures. The hat was an F.B.I. hat.

'Kershley Hostel, mate? That'll set you back about seventeen bob.'

My father scowled at him.

'That's a helluva lot, mate. It's in NSW, this hostel ah have in mind.'

The driver stared at my father without a word and then turned his head away.

'That's all ah've got,' my mother hissed under her breath. 'Have ye any money on ye?'

'A couple o' quid. The hostel'll feed ye till ah get paid next week.'

'Right, get in then,' my mother ordered us.

But the taxi driver had been watching us and he put his hand out arrestingly as I started to climb in, holding Anne.

'Sorry mate. You can't all fit in here.'

I ignored him and threw myself in, dropping Anne on the floor and falling on top of her.

'Aw come on Mister,' I said, trying to beg. 'They're mostly half sizes and we can sit them on our knees.'

We kept cramming in and cramming in. Sadie squeezed herself right under the driver's armpits and his arms were stretched up so that he had to rest them on the steering wheel. He was snorting and grumbling and then I heard the word the man had mentioned on the train.

'Bloody Pommies.'

I was proud of my new knowledge and I rapped him on the neck.

'We're Scottish, mister.'

So he would know we knew. But he didn't like us just the same. You could tell. He drove angrily, pulling and hauling at the things in his car, bumping us up and down so we kept falling against each other and my father, after bouncing his head against the ceiling, cried:

'Take it easy, mac. Ye'd think ye were driving through paddocks.'

And up we went again. All in silence.

When we arrived at some lighted buildings miles and miles out in the country, the taxi stopped and we all clambered out. My mother counted the money and handed it to the driver.

'Thanks, laughing boy,' she said, 'ye'd be an ornament in any company.'

The driver grumbled something and slammed the door and my mother, in a rage, yelled at him:

'Aw, go and get stuffed!'

It's probably not a very nice thing to say, really, though the stuffed fox Archie had among his unredeemed pledges looked very lifelike, but my father gets boiling mad when my mother says it. Personally, I don't think it sounds nearly as bad as eff and see. Or even shit. It's not even a swear word. As soon as she said it my father dumped the bag he was carrying on the ground. It went squelch, and I realised that we were walking in some kind of a bog. Stuff was oozing into my socks.

'Look,' he bellowed, quietly, a lot of force but not much loudness. My father hates attracting attention. 'Look, is it necessary tae say that tae every stranger ye meet on the byways? Jesus, it sounds awful. Stick tae shit, will ye in future!'

'It's shit that sticks,' my mother said primly, but I could feel she was laughing. 'Och,' she spluttered, getting angry again, 'people like that gie me the jaundice. Goin' aroon as if they need a purge.'

We waited, at my father's admonition, while he squelched quickly towards the little building with the light. In a few minutes, the light came splashing the ground near our feet and we were beckoned over. He was with the manager of the hostel. Glad to meet you. Welcome to Australia. Hope you'll be happy here. You must be hungry. Fish and chips in the kitchen. Twice cooked, twice as tasty, eh? Stores first. Sheets, blankets, cutlery. Here, catch. Big family. Biggest we've had. We've allocated you a whole hut. Keys. I'll take you down and then you can eat. Sorry I've had to put you in with the Italians. British are at the other end. Just pile up the dishes in the sink. Breakfast starts at six. Goodnight. Goodnight. Goodnight.

1975

CLIVE JAMES
b. 1939

Clive James was born and educated in Sydney. As described in the first volume of his autobiography, *Unreliable Memoirs* (1980), James's father, who had survived being a prisoner of war in the Second World War, died on the way home to Australia. In 1961 James moved to England, where he still lives, to study at the University of Cambridge, after which he worked as a freelance writer. From 1972 to 1982 he was the television critic for the *Observer*. James began a successful television career in 1983 with *The Late Clive James*. His television programs include the *Postcard* series of travel documentaries, and the documentary series *Fame in the Twentieth Century* (1993). James has also worked in radio, often broadcasting with the poet Peter Porter (qv).

James's first books were works of criticism. Since then he has published poetry, four novels, non-fiction and travel writing. His poems have been collected as *The Book of My Enemy* (2003), which includes the lyrics to the songs that James wrote with the singer Pete Atkins in the 1970s and the 2000s. James is probably best known for his work in the media and for his autobiographies. In 2001 the first three volumes were collected as *Always Unreliable: The memoirs*. A fourth volume, *North Face of Soho*, appeared in 2006. DM

From *Unreliable Memoirs*
Chapter 1: The Kid from Kogarah

I was born in 1939. The other big event of that year was the outbreak of the Second World War, but for the moment that did not affect me. Sydney in those days had all of its present attractions and few of the drawbacks. You can see it glittering in the background of the few photographs in which my father and I are together. Stocky was the word for me. Handsome was the word for him. Without firing a shot, the Japanese succeeded in extricating him from my clutches. Although a man of humble birth and restricted education, he was smart enough to see that there would be war in the Pacific. Believing that Australia should be ready, he joined up. That was how he came to be in Malaya at the crucial moment. He was at Parit Sulong bridge on the day when a lot of senior officers at last found out what their troops had guessed long before—that the Japanese army was better led and better equipped than anything we had to pit against it. After the battle my father walked all the way south to Singapore and arrived just in time for the surrender. If he had waited to be conscripted, he might have been sent to the Western Desert and spent a relatively happy few months fighting the kind of Germans whose essential decency was later to be portrayed on the screen by James Mason and Marlon Brando. As it was, he drew the short straw.

This isn't the place to tell the story of my mother and father—a story which was by no means over, even though they never saw one another again. I could get a lot of mileage out of describing how the good-looking young mechanic wooed and won the pretty girl who left school at fourteen and worked as an upholsterer at General Motors Holden. How the Depression kept them so poor that they had to wait years to get married and have me. How fate was cruel to both of them beyond measure. But it would be untrue to them. It was thirty years or more before I even began to consider what my parents must have meant to each other. Before that I hardly gave them a thought, except as vague occurrences on the outskirts of a solipsistic universe. I can't remember my father at all. I can remember my mother only through a child's eyes. I don't know which fact is the sadder.

Anyway, my mother let our little house in Kogarah and we went to stay with my Aunt Dot in Jannali, another half hour down the Illawarra line. The move was made on the advice of my father, who assumed that the centre of Sydney would be flattened by Japanese bombs about two hours after the whistle blew. The assumption proved to be ill-founded, but the side effects were beneficial, since Jannali was a perfect spot to grow up in. There were only a dozen or so streets in the whole area. Only one of them was paved. The railway line ran through a cutting somewhere in the middle. Everything else was bush.

The houses were made of either weatherboard or fibro. Ours was weatherboard. Like all the others, it was surrounded by an area of land which could be distinguished from the bush only because of its even more lavish concentrations of colour. Nasturtiums and honeysuckle proliferated, their strident perfumes locked in perpetual contention. Hydrangeas grew in reefs, like coral in a sea of warm air. At the bottom of the back yard lay an air-raid trench full of rainwater. I fell into it within minutes of arriving. Hearing a distant splash, Aunt Dot, who was no sylph, came through the back door like a train out of a tunnel and hit the lawn running. The door, a fly-screen frame with a return spring, made exactly the same sound as one of those punching-bags you try your strength on. Aunt Dot was attired in a pink corset but it didn't slow her down. She covered the ground like Marjorie Jackson, the girl who later became famous as the Lithgow Flash.[1] The earth shook. I was going down for the third time but I can distinctly remember the moment she launched herself into the air, describing a parabolic trajectory which involved, at one point, a total eclipse of the sun. She landed in the trench beside me. Suddenly we were sitting together in the mud. All the water was outside on the lawn.

Usually my mother was first to the rescue. This time she was second. She had to resuscitate both of us. She must have been in the front of the house looking after my grandfather. He needed a lot of looking after. Later on my mother told me that he had always been a selfish man. She and Aunt Dot had

---

1   Australian Olympic athlete (b. 1931) (later governor of South Australia).

given a good part of their lives to waiting on him. Mentally, he had never left England. I remember him as a tall, barely articulate source of smells. The principal smells were of mouldy cloth, mothballs, seaweed, powerful tobacco and the tars that collect in the stem of a very old pipe. When he was smoking he was invisible. When he wasn't smoking he was merely hard to pick out in the gloom. You could track him down by listening for his constant, low-pitched, incoherent mumble. From his carpet slippers to his moustache was twice as high as I could reach. The moustache was saffron with nicotine. Everywhere else he was either grey or tortoise-shell mottle. His teeth were both.

I remember he bared them at me one Christmas dinner. It was because he was choking on a coin in a mouthful of plum pudding. It was the usual Australian Christmas dinner, taking place in the middle of the day. Despite the temperature being 100°F in the shade, there had been the full panoply of ragingly hot food, topped off with a volcanic plum pudding smothered in scalding custard. My mother had naturally spiced the pudding with sixpences and threepenny bits, called zacs and trays respectively. Grandpa had collected one of these in the oesophagus. He gave a protracted, strangled gurgle which for a long time we all took to be the beginning of some anecdote. Then Aunt Dot bounded out of her chair and hit him in the back. By some miracle she did not snap his calcified spine. Coated with black crumbs and custard, the zac streaked out of his mouth like a dum-dum and ricocheted off a tureen.

Grandpa used to take me on his knee and read me stories, of which I could understand scarcely a word, not because the stories were over my head but because his speech by that stage consisted entirely of impediments. 'Once upon a mpf,' he would intone, 'there wah ngung mawg blf . . .' My mother got angry with me if I was not suitably grateful to Grandpa for telling me stories. I was supposed to dance up and down at the very prospect. To dodge this obligation, I would build cubby-holes. Collecting chairs, cushions, bread-boards and blankets from all over the house, I would assemble them into a pill-box and crawl in, plugging the hole behind me. Safe inside, I could fart discreetly while staring through various eye-slits to keep track of what was going on. From the outside I was just a pair of marsupial eyeballs in a heap of household junk, topped off with a rising pall of sulphuretted hydrogen. It was widely conjectured that I was hiding from ghosts. I was, too, but not as hard as I was hiding from Grandpa. When he shuffled off to bed, I would unplug my igloo and emerge. Since my own bed-time was not long after dark, I suppose he must have been going to bed in the late afternoon. Finally he went to bed altogether.

With Grandpa laid up, I was the man of the house, except when Uncle Vic or Ray came home on leave. Uncle Vic was Aunt Dot's husband and

Ray was her son, therefore my cousin. Uncle Vic was an infantry corporal stationed in New Guinea. Sometimes when he got leave he would bring his Owen gun home, minus the bolt. I was allowed to play with the gun. It was huge. I stumbled around pointing it at bull-ants' nests. The bull-ants, however, didn't bluff so easily. The only argument they understood was a few gallons of boiling water poured down their central stair-well. I once saw Uncle Vic administer this treatment, in revenge after half a dozen bull-ants stung me on the right foot. They were the big red kind with the black bag at the back. When that size bull-ant stings you, you stay stung. My foot came up like a loaf of bread. I just lay in the road and screamed. The same foot got into even worse trouble later on, as I shall relate.

While I staggered around blasting the nasturtiums, Uncle Vic did a lot of enigmatic smiling. One day I struggled all the way down to the railway cutting so that I could show the gun to some local children I hoped to impress. They hadn't waited. I could see them climbing the hill on the other side of the railway line. I shouted to them, holding the gun up as high as I could, which I suppose was no height at all. They couldn't hear me. I think it was the first big disappointment of my life. When I came back dragging the gun through the dirt, Uncle Vic did a bit more of his enigmatic smiling. Talking to him years later, I realised why he was so quiet at the time. It was because he wasn't too thrilled about what he had seen in New Guinea. Japanese scouts used to sneak up on our sentries through the thick white morning jungle mist and punch meat-skewers through their heads from ear to ear.

Ray was more forthcoming, until he got sick. He was a fitter with the RAAF somewhere up there but after his first leave he never went back. He just stayed around the house in his dressing-gown, getting thinner. He used to let me stand on his feet while he walked me around. The game was called Giant Steps. I loved it. Then the day came when he didn't want to play it any more. My mother told me he wasn't strong enough. I got into trouble at the dinner table when I asked him why he was holding his fork with both hands.

So really my mother was the only pillar of strength available. One parent is enough to spoil you but discipline takes two. I got too much of what I wanted and not enough of what I needed. I was a child who was picked up. The effects have stayed with me to this day, although in the last few years I have gradually learned to blame myself instead of circumstances. My mother had a strong will but she would have had to be Fabius Cunctator[1] to cope with my tantrums when I didn't feel like going to school. Every second day I played sick and stayed home. Her only alternative was to see how far

---

1   Quintus Fabius Maximus Verrucosus (c. 280–203 BC), Roman politician and general known as Cunctator ('the delayer') because of his tactics in troop deployment during the Second Punic War.

she could drag me. She would have had a better chance dragging a dead horse through soft sand. The school was a single-room wooden hut with twelve desks. Painted cream, it sat in half an acre of dirt playground about a mile from our house. Bushfires burned it down every couple of years but unfortunately it was easy to replace. The first year of school wasn't so bad. I liked Miss Dear. Usually I got more questions right than anybody else and was awarded first choice of blocks. I chose the set with the arches and the columns. I would go off on my own into a corner of the playground and build structures akin to the Alhambra or the Escorial,[1] throwing a fit if any other child tried to interfere.

Even the best set of school blocks wasn't as good as the set I had at home. Passed on to me by Grandpa, they were satin-smooth Victorian creations of inch-by-inch oak, every length from one to twelve inches, plus arches, Doric columns, metopes, triglyphs and sundry other bits and pieces. With them I could build a tower much taller than myself. The usual site was the middle of the lounge room. A length of cotton could be tied to one of the lower columns, so that I could retire into hiding and collapse the tower by remote control at the precise moment when Aunt Dot lumbered into range. It made a noise like Valhalla falling. She would have one of her turns—these needed plenty of space—and demand that I be sent to school next day.

Toys were scarce. A few crude lead soldiers were still produced so that children could go on poisoning themselves but otherwise there was almost nothing. It was a big event when my mother bought me a little painted red cow. Presumably it was English. I took it to school and lost it. Next day she came with me to school, wanting to find out what had happened to it. My carelessness with everything she bought me went on hurting her for years. She construed it, accurately, as ingratitude. From the sensitivity angle I was about as obtuse as a child can be. I was sensitive enough about myself, but that's a different thing.

School, passable for the first year, became unbearable in the second, when the kind Miss Dear was supplanted by a hard case called Miss Turnbull. Dark, cold and impatient, Miss Turnbull might have been the firm hand I needed, but already I was unable to cope with authority. I still can't today, tending to oscillate between nervous flippancy and overly solicitous respect. In those days, when I was about a third of my present height and a quarter of the weight, there was nothing to do except duck. I did everything to get out of facing up to Miss Turnbull. I had Mondayitis every day of the week. As my mother dragged me down the front path, I would clutch my stomach, cross my eyes, stick out my tongue, cough, choke, scream and vomit simultaneously.

---

1   A Moorish fortress and a Spanish monastery.

But there were some occasions when I ended up at school no matter what I did. It was then revealed that I had Dropped Behind the Class. Words I could not recognise would come up on the spelling wheel. The spelling wheel was a thick card with a window in it and a cardboard disc behind. As you turned the disc, words appeared one at a time in the window. I remember not being able to pronounce the word 'the'. I pronounced it 'ter-her'. The class had collective hysterics. They were rolling around on the floor with their knees up. I suppose one of the reasons why I grew up feeling the need to cause laughter was perpetual fear of being its unwitting object.

From the start of Miss Turnbull's reign until the day we left Jannali, every morning I would shout the house down. For my mother, the path leading from the front porch to the front gate became a Via Dolorosa. My act reached ever new heights of extravagance. Either it worked or it didn't. If it didn't I would sit in school praying for the bushfires to come early and incinerate the place. If it did I would either hang around the house or go and play with Ron, a truant of my own age who lived next to Hally the butcher down near the station. Ron was a grub. I was always being warned off him because he was so filthy. He and I used to squat under his house tweaking each other's ding, watching each other pee, and so on. I can't remember it all now. I suppose I have repressed it. If there was any sexual excitement, it took the form of intense curiosity, just as I was curious about my mother when we were in the bath together. I remember the shock of seeing Ray undressed. He looked as if he had a squirrel hanging there. I had an acorn.

Ron's wreck of a mother used to give us buttered bread with hundreds and thousands on it. It was like being handed a slice of powdered rainbow. They must have been a poor family but I remember my visits to them as luxuries. As well as the Technicolor bread and butter, there were vivid, viscid green drinks made from some kind of cordial. Ron's place would have been Beulah Land except for one drawback. They had a cattle dog called Bluey. A known psychopath, Bluey would attack himself if nothing else was available. He used to chase himself in circles trying to bite his own balls off. To avert instant death, I was supposed to call out from the front gate when I arrived and not open it until I was told that Bluey had been chained up. One day I opened it too early and Bluey met me on the front path. I don't know where he had come from—probably around the side of the house—but it was as if he had come up out of the ground on a lift. He was nasty enough when chained up but on the loose he was a bad dream. Barking from the stomach, he opened a mouth like a great, wet tropical flower. When he snapped it shut, my right foot was inside it.

If Bluey hadn't been as old as the hills, my foot would have come right off. Luckily his teeth were in ruins, but even so I was only a few tendons short of becoming an amputee. Since Bluey's spittle obviously contained every bacterium known to science, my frantic mother concluded that the local doctor would not be enough. I think I went to some kind of hospital in Sutherland. Needles were stuck into me while she had yet another case of heart failure. Bluey was taken away to be destroyed. Looking back on it, I can see that this was tough on Bluey, who had grown old in the belief that biting ankles was the thing to do. At the time I was traumatised. I loathed dogs from that day forward. They could sense my terror from miles away. Any dog could back me against a wall for hours. Eventually I learned not to show fear. The breakthrough came when I managed to walk away from a dog who had me bailed up against the door of a garage. Admittedly he was only a Pekinese about eight inches long, but it was still a triumph. That was more than a year ago.

1980

GERALD MURNANE
b. 1939

Born in Melbourne, Gerald Murnane became a school teacher in the 1960s, subsequently working for the Victorian Education Department (1969–73). From 1980 he taught creative writing at Prahran College of Advanced Education (later Victoria College and Deakin University), retiring in 1995. He was well known as an influential teacher. Also well known is Murnane's dislike of travel: he has never flown in a plane. Murnane's small but difficult body of work comprises novels and fictions that are widely divergent in subject and approach. Characteristic concerns, however, are to do with the relationship between language and reality, and the nature of creativity. Murnane's work is often solemnly humorous and ironic. His essays, many of which blur the line between 'story' and 'essay', are collected in *Invisible Yet Enduring Lilacs* (2005). DM

Why I Write What I Write

I write sentences. I write first one sentence, then another sentence. I write sentence after sentence.

I write a hundred or more sentences each week and a few thousand sentences a year.

After I've written each sentence I read it aloud. I listen to the sound of the sentence, and I don't begin to write the next sentence unless I'm absolutely satisfied with the sound of the sentence I'm listening to.

When I've written a paragraph I read it aloud to learn whether all the sentences that sounded well on their own still sound well together.

When I've written two or three pages I read them aloud. When I've written a whole story or a section that you might call a chapter, I read that aloud too. Every night before I start my writing I read aloud what I wrote the night before. I'm always reading aloud and listening to the sounds of sentences.

What am I listening for when I read aloud?

The answer is not simple. I might start with a phrase from the American critic Hugh Kenner . . . *the shape of meaning.* Writing about William Carlos Williams, Kenner suggested that some sentences have a shape that fits their meaning while other sentences do not.

Robert Frost once wrote: 'A sentence is a sound on which other sounds called words may be strung.'

Robert Frost also had a phrase, 'the sound of sense', to describe what he listened for in writing. Frost likened this sound to the pattern we hear when the sound of a conversation, but not the sounds of actual words, reaches us from a nearby room.

Robert Louis Stevenson had a different notion of what a sentence should do.

> Each sentence, by successive phrases, shall first come into a kind of knot, and then, after a moment of suspended meaning, solve and clear itself.

I don't say that I swear by any of these maxims that I've quoted. But each of them lights up a little part of the mystery of why some sentences sound right and some don't.

A word I haven't mentioned yet is *rhythm.* A lot of nonsense is talked about rhythm. Here's something that is far from nonsense.

> Rhythm is not an ideal form to which we fit our words. It is not a musical notation to which our words submit. Rhythm is born not with the words but with the thought. Good writing exactly reproduces what we should call the contour of our thought.

I found these words in a book published nearly sixty years ago: *English Prose Style,* by Herbert Read.

The *contour of our thought* is a magical phrase for me. It has helped me in times of trouble in the way that phrases from the Bible or from Karl Marx probably help other people.

You will not be surprised to know that Virginia Woolf had a deep insight into this matter of the rightness of sentences. Here is something she wrote about it.

> Style is a very simple matter, it is all rhythm. Once you get that, you can't use the wrong words . . . This is very profound, what rhythm is, and goes far deeper than words. A sight, an emotion, creates this wave in the mind, long before it makes words to fit it, and in writing one has to recapture this, and set this working (which has nothing apparently to

do with words) and then, as it breaks and tumbles in the mind, it makes words to fit in.

Something else I listen for when I read aloud . . . I listen to make sure that the voice I'm hearing is my own voice and not someone else's voice. I don't always succeed in this, of course. Sometimes when I read my writing of a few years ago I recognise that I've imitated in a few places the voices of others.

I listen for the sound of my own voice because I remember something the Irish poet Patrick Kavanagh once said: 'This is genius—a man being simply and sincerely himself.'

And still another thing I hope to hear in my sentences is the note of authority. John Gardner said authority is the sound of a writer who knows what he's doing. He cited as his favourite example of prose ringing with authority this opening passage from a famous novel.

Call me Ishmael. Some years ago—never mind how long precisely—having little or no money in my purse, and nothing particular to interest me on shore, I thought I would sail about a little and see the watery part of the world.[1]

I've said I write sentences, but you probably expect me to say what the sentences are about.

My sentences arise out of images and feelings that haunt me—not always painfully; sometimes quite pleasantly. These images and feelings haunt me until I find the sentences to bring them into this world.

Note that I didn't say 'to bring them to life'. The person who reads my sentences may think that he or she is looking at something newly alive. But the images and feelings behind my words have been alive for a long time beforehand.

This has been a very simple account of something that begins to make me dizzy if I think about it for too long. The only detail I can add is to say that as I write, the images and feelings haunting me become linked in ways that surprise and amaze me. Often if I write one sentence to put into a form of words a certain image or feeling, I find as soon as I've written the sentence that a new throng of images and feelings have gathered to form a pattern where I had not known a pattern existed.

Writing never explains anything for me—it only shows me how stupendously complicated everything is.

But why do I write what I write?

1   The opening of Herman Melville's *Moby-Dick* (1851).

Why do I write sentences? Why does anyone write sentences? What are sentences? What are subjects and predicates, verbs and nouns? What are words themselves?

I ask myself these questions often. I think about these matters every day in one way or another. For me these questions are as profound as the questions: why do we get ourselves born, why do we fall in love, why do we die?

If I pretended I could answer any of these questions, I'd be a fool.

1986/2005

BARBARA HANRAHAN
1939–1991

Barbara Hanrahan was born in Adelaide. Her father died when she was one and she was raised by her mother, grandmother and great-aunt. Her childhood was the focus of her first work, the memoir *The Scent of Eucalyptus* (1973), described by Geoffrey Dutton as 'the most evocative account of growing up in suburbia that exists in Australian literature'. Hanrahan trained to be an art teacher and sailed to London in 1963 to study printmaking at the Central School of Arts and Crafts, as described in her semi-autobiographical fictions, particularly *Michael and Me and the Sun* (1992). In 1965 she settled down with inventor and sculptor, Jo Steele. The intricacies of their enduring relationship are detailed in *The Diaries of Barbara Hanrahan* (1998, ed. Elaine Lindsay), published posthumously.

The death of her grandmother in 1968 prompted Hanrahan to record her childhood memories. Although she had previously dismissed the idea that she could be both an artist and a writer, she found the two forms of creativity to be complementary. In her wish to be 'original', she ignored Australian literary trends. Hanrahan and Steele divided their time between London and South Australia.

By 1984, when she was diagnosed with an aggressive sarcoma at the base of her spinal cord, she had had 21 one-woman exhibitions and published eight books. For the next seven years she concentrated on staying alive long enough to complete what she saw as her creative task of fulfilling the promise of her father's brief life and revealing God's goodness in the world.

Hanrahan's fifteen books of fiction and memoir and many artworks reveal her fascination with her suburban Adelaide childhood, the interplay of good and evil, and the lives of working-class men and women in the first half of the twentieth century. She insisted she wrote for ordinary people, not for academics. Her work is intensely personal and reflects her belief in the importance of recording otherwise unacknowledged lives. *EL*

Tottie Tippett

She used to dream she could fly like an angel, but she didn't know where she wanted to fly to. She just had to use her hands and go, but she always woke up before she left the ground (if you flew that'd be the end of you). Riding was the nearest thing to flying—the faster the pony went the happier she was; the harder she rode the better she liked it. Though once she had a nasty buster on Maud when she came back from the Ardrossan Post Office with the letters; and she rode Ruby, the cream pony, when she brought the cows in and stayed on her back when she opened the gates and once she fell off and skinned all her knees. When she rode the ponies on the cliffs they'd go down the steep path by Mallee Creek to the beach, and she'd really have to hang on. Riding, she never had any fear. Then she had confidence in herself and everything, she always had an idea that God was going to look after her. But she was frightened of the sea and couldn't swim. The seas round that part of the Peninsula were so rough that when you looked out from the front door of the house, one minute you could see the steamer from Port Adelaide making for the jetty, then the next it'd be hidden by the waves.

Her father had helped put the new piles in the jetty and the first thing she remembered was walking down there with his dinner on a plate, wrapped in a tea-towel to keep it warm. She was only four then, and when she was six Queen Victoria died, and the next year it was the earthquake and her mother knelt down in the front room and prayed they'd be saved. And that year, 1902, was when her father got smoker's cancer on his lip. He was a fine looking man, clean-shaven, who never hit her, but he'd sometimes tell her to get out of the road. Towards the end they had to syringe the food into him and he only had half a face. Her mother was changing the bed when he lay back on the pillow and died.

Because he'd been born in Germany their surname sounded like the dirty word. Her mother was that angry when the Aldridges said their name the bad way—but Mother couldn't write; it'd been Father who'd written all their names in the big German Bible that was kept in the front room cupboard. Her name was written in as Ernestina Louisa, but they called her Tottie, and sixteen brothers and sisters came before her. Her sisters were Emma, Lizzie, Elsie, Clara, Rosie, Winnie, Gertie, Hilda; two of her brothers had died as infants of convulsions, then there was Herb, Arthur, Dick, Jack, Bill and Tom.

Some of them had married and moved away years ago, so Tottie didn't know them. Arthur drove the coach from Ardrossan to South Hummocks before he went to live with Elsie, who'd married a fellow from Yongala where the cauliflowers weighed twelve pounds each and foxes bit out the lambs' tongues. Tom was the only one in the family who had a big nose and Bill had lovely curly hair. Jack worked at the butcher's in Ardrossan and his wife made a gallon of soup at a time and it was that thin you didn't know whether you were having soup or water. When Dick shifted to Adelaide his wife took to the drink and one day when he came home from work all the furniture was gone (she'd sold it for booze). Winnie and Gertie were the ones who'd nursed Father and then they went up to Maitland as housemaids, to work off the debt to the doctors. Hilda was very dainty and thought she was a bit above everybody else. Rosie got struck by lightning—Mother put her to bed but in the morning she was dead. Clara's husband was a fisherman at Port Wakefield, where there were picture shows and Japanese wrestling tournaments and a circus; after Clara died he still sent a box of fish over now and then, and it was always Tottie's job to clean them.

Over at Kadina a fellow had six or seven girls in the family way, and Mother was horrified at girls wandering. She whipped Hilda with a piece of rope tied to a stick when she sneaked down to the town one evening. 'Your body is your own,' she'd say. 'Don't let anybody interfere with it.' She'd married Father when she was fifteen; they'd come to Ardrossan when the country was all mallee scrub, tea-tree and kangaroo bush, and lived in a hole in the ground before they built the house. After he died, she took the steamer to Adelaide to see a Chinese doctor and then she married Andy Yates, the carrier. Andy had been bitten by a snake when he reached into a burrow to grab a rabbit (he killed it, then put his finger on a plough wheel and cut it off with a blunt tomahawk). He was a small man, gingerish, and Mother was boss. The ponies were always sweaty after Andy had been riding them (he had to keep riding all day to see the cows didn't get to the wild onion weed that went straight to their milk)—sometimes when Tottie rode Ruby to bring the cows in, she was so sweaty that the saddle slipped round and off she'd come. Tottie walked in her sleep. She'd fetch the milk-can, then put it down beside her mother and Andy's bed and get in with them.

As well as the cows they had pigs and sheep, hens and geese and a bit of wheat. When the geese were sitting, they pecked at Tottie and chased her. She stuck a big thick goose's quill through a cork in a bottle of milk to bottle-feed her pet lamb. She loved him but he grew fatter and fatter, and one day she came home from school to find that Andy had killed him—he was hanging in the meat house, cut up. Tottie hated Andy then, but she still ate the lamb chops for tea.

A sailor gave Jack a monkey. Monkeys were dirty little beggars and Mother made Tottie and Hilda stay inside when he sat on the underground tank stand and fiddled with himself. Monk was a curiosity in the district; he used to get up to some tricks. He walked along the telegraph wires and followed Tottie to school. Once he got down the chimney of old lady Aldridge's bakehouse and threw the dough that was rising over the walls. He kept going off to the rubbish dump but got tangled up in some wire and they found him there, dead.

There was no money to splash round, they couldn't even afford a headstone for Father's grave. But the front room had boards on the floor, not dirt like the other rooms, and at Christmas there were cherries to eat. Mother had a china ornament in the shape of a hen sitting on a china nest and she made wonderful dampers that tasted better than bread. Mother had nice skin, no pimples or anything; she dressed up in leg-of-mutton sleeves and a hat with a feather, and one Sunday she went to the Methodist Church, the next to the Church of England, but she had a bit of Catholic in her somewhere. Old Mrs Wundersitz visited Ardrossan twice a week from Maitland to meet the steamer and get her vegetables, and as soon as her one-horse van came into sight, the kettle would be put on. When the Afghan hawker came walking round with his big white bag on his back full of sheets and pillowslips, laces and ribbons, he always stayed in the wash-house overnight, and Mother would never have a word out of place said to him (he was a neat old man with a turban who cleaned his teeth with a stick off a gum tree and his teeth were as white as snow). She was kind to anybody who passed the house, swaggies and all.

Ardrossan was a little town famous for its cliffs and farm implement factory where Mr Smith had perfected his stump-jump plough, the Vixen. And Mr Cane was the butcher, Mr Polkinghorne the baker, Mrs Huckvale had the hotel; and Barton's, opposite the Institute and Post Office, sold groceries, ironmongery, furniture, drapery and clothing, boots and shoes, and patent medicines; and Tiddy's was another shop to sell all sorts, and the early settlers had carted water from Tiddy Widdy Wells. There was a Vigilance Committee, a brass band, and the football club's first uniforms were made out of sugar bags dyed blue and white. In summer, when the tide was out, boys dived off the ketches *Stormbird* and *Crest of the Wave* to have a swim; and every New-Year's Day, past inhabitants of the district came back to Ardrossan on the steamer and there was a picnic on the beach (the only thing that spoilt the beach was that the tide fretted the cliff away and they got dirty sand).

Mr Ryan was the schoolmaster and you were in awful trouble if you copied, but Tottie never needed to because she was a clever scholar; she liked arithmetic and reading and was a very good writer. She sat next to her best friend, Lily Slaughter, whose mother was half an Aborigine, but only one of the Slaughters had turned out really black—they called him Israel, he ran the hand-truck up and down the jetty to load goods on to the steamer. Annie Evans sat in the seat in front; she had a lot of hair and was one of the certain kind of people who bred lice. One day Tottie's head felt itchy so she got straight on to the fine-tooth comb and found a couple of big ones. She had a beautiful head of hair and was scared stiff; she rubbed kerosene into her scalp, just to be sure, and made it all red and itchy.

When Tottie left school at thirteen, she wanted to be a dressmaker and she dreamt of a dress of heliotrope cotton voile with a six-gored skirt, a blouse of Peking messaline, a coat with a suggestion of the Russian mode. But Mother wouldn't let her use the sewing-machine, so she had to watch for her chance—they were down with the cows and the needle went through her finger and she worked the machine till she got it out and never ever told a soul. When she learnt to sew she made dresses for her mother and she had a wonderful eye for measurement, but mostly she milked the cows and drove the dogcart into Ardrossan to sell milk from a five gallon container with a tap on it; and she sold eggs and did Mrs Tiddy's washing. Tottie's ambition was to always go on working.

The evangelist came to church and told about scarlet and crimson as indicating shades of guilt in the same kind of sin—murder would be a scarlet sin if committed by a worldly person, but hatred would be a crimson stain (a sin of deeper dye) if cherished by a child of God. Old Mr McGeoch, who was a bit cranky and often called out in church, shouted that all mankind had inherited sin-tainted blood from Father Adam; Tottie and Lily went forward with the others who believed in the new age of Messiah's Kingdom and vowed they'd never touch alcohol. A young man took Tottie home from church, but when they were crossing the paddocks he put the hard word on her and tried to have connections. Tottie yelled out and Andy Yates heard and the young man ran away. You wouldn't have thought he was a bad fellow, but they found out afterwards he had Frys' girl in the family way already. When Tottie had her monthlies, she soaked her towelling squares in disinfectant then boiled them clean, but she couldn't hang them out to dry where her brothers, or anyone passing on the road, might see (and you couldn't have anything on the line on a Good Friday).

The Peninsula resembled Italy in that it was shaped like a long boot. Ardrossan was on the east coast; to the north were the copper-mining towns of Moonta, Wallaroo and Kadina, where most of the people were Cornish. Gertie married a miner and lived at Wallaroo; Winnie married one, too, and lived at Kadina; Hilda put on more airs than ever when she married a fellow who was high up in the Post Office in Adelaide (he was something to do with Excise and got Hilda going on the wine—she took to it and never let it go). Tottie was the only one left at home and her mother bought her a spring mattress and her brothers and sisters were jealous because they'd never had such a luxury. But one of the Bowmans' girls who wore flimsy dresses to the dances in the Institute caught a chill and then died of consumption (all the dogs in the town were howling that night—they knew), and Tottie started coughing, though she didn't go dancing, and the doctor said it was the sea air so her mother sent her to live with Gertie.

Gertie and her husband knew a good-looking young miner who had a one-horse phantom buggy and when Tottie said she never went anywhere because she had no one to go with, he said he'd drive her down to Wallaroo Bay. Tottie took Gertie's little girl, Violet, with her because she didn't want him to start anything, but when they got to the wharf he wanted her to sit on his lap. He said if she wouldn't he'd throw the bloody kid in the sea—he didn't, but Tottie and Violet had to walk home.

A woman at Kadina wanted a girl for housework, so Tottie went to live where there was electric light. The woman had a hand-painted miniature on her hatpin, a gypsy table and a bamboo whatnot, but she was so mean that Tottie hardly ever got a decent meal—she ate what she could grab, she felt hungry all the time. The woman kept her children in the kitchen and one day she gave the baby a bone to suck, but it started to choke and Tottie had to stick her finger down its throat to hook it out. The children wiped their noses on their sleeves and she had to do the washing; she had to clean the fowl-house and afterwards she was lousy with lice. If she came in by the front door, not the back one, the woman had a shot at her and when Tottie gave in her notice, she said she couldn't understand her, she was such an independent sort of girl.

Tottie started doing housework for the DeLaines. Mr DeLaine was a family butcher who sold fritz and paloney and nice juicy joints and when he came home from the shop he'd throw his trousers over the back of a chair and all his money would fall out. Tottie said she wished he wouldn't do it but Mrs DeLaine said it didn't matter, she knew Tottie would never take anything that didn't belong to her.

Kadina was a town full of shops, nearer to the Wallaroo Mines than Wallaroo itself. Levy's Café had a real American crystal soda fountain; Miss Snodgrass taught the New Method of Music where your tuition fee was refunded if you couldn't play a tune in a week, and Miss Ruby Arscott was prepared to receive pupils for the typewriter. The Juvenile Druids sometimes marched the streets in torchlight procession, the Mendelssohn Choir sang in the Town Hall; on Sunday nights in summer, after church, the Federal Band gave a sacred concert in the rotunda. The Salvation Army were a happy mob and played every Saturday night as the miners and their families came in to do their marketing.

There were picture shows at Kadina and when Tottie went to see *Camille*, as played before Royalty in Europe, the grocer's boy said he'd walk her home. But while she was watching Sarah Bernhardt, a strange man next to her started talking and when *Camille* ended she went off with him, leaving the grocer's boy standing there. He was a miner named Joe Tippett and after he took Tottie home that was it—then they were going together.

Joe was a nice looking fellow, eleven years older than Tottie. He wasn't very boisterous but had a lovely voice and could sing 'Cupid is the Captain of the Army' and 'Baby's Prayer'. He lived out at Jericho, on the other side of the mines to Jerusalem, with his mother and father who'd been born in Cornwall. Mrs Tippett wasn't a bad old stick; she was short and stumpy and she'd once had a little shop at Jericho where she'd sold a bit of this and a bit of that, but she'd had to give it up when the horse kept bolting on her way back from market. Old Mr Tippett was doubled up with rheumatics and kept coughing because of miner's complaint. Cornish people said some peculiar words and liked their pasties and kept goats. If they had people come to tea they'd go out and call the goat in and milk it, and one dinner-time Mrs Tippett asked Tottie if she'd ever tasted kid pie. When Tottie said she wouldn't be able to eat it, Mrs Tippett said she just had. And it'd been such beautiful white meat.

Apart from her father and Andy Yates, Joe was the first man to kiss Tottie. He wasn't too pushy but she was frightened to get romantic, it was a funny feeling. But she must have liked him, she kept going with him. He took her to the pictures every Saturday night, and she helped Mrs Tippett make his flannel shirts for the mine, and she made calico chemises, combinations, petticoats and nightdresses trimmed with lace and ribbon and featherstitch braid for her glory box (she didn't trouble much about fiddly things like doilies). Tottie didn't know if she wanted to get married or not, but the War had started and people weren't nice to you if you had a German name (her brother Bill had changed his already), and when Joe asked her if she'd get engaged to him, she said Yes.

Tottie's engagement ring had three rubies and two diamonds and she dreamt of a fish-tail train, a horseshoe of orange-blossom, a shower bouquet of white sweet peas and silk streamers . . . and the bride was exquisitely dressed in cream, daintily veiled in embroidered ninon . . . plenty of confetti and rice . . . and the bride wore a smart travelling costume of golden brown, a cream hat with old gold mount, and black furs . . . Her wedding dress took a fair while to make. It was plain with a bow up the side and she had a short net veil and Mrs DeLaine lent Tottie her white satin shoes. Joe's sister, Nell, was the bridesmaid and they were married in the Church of Christ, then went to Mr and Mrs Tippett's for a sit-down meal. They didn't have a honeymoon but went straight to the house Joe had bought near his parents'. But their friends had played a trick and the doorway was blocked with mallee roots. Tottie and Joe had to move them away in their wedding clothes before they could get in.

Joe wasn't a fussy eater and he grew some beautiful lettuces but when there was a dust storm all the milk and cream in the Coolgardie safe was ruined. It was strange being married. When Joe was in bed, Tottie threw the quilt over the brass rail at the end, bobbed down, got undressed behind it, and put on her nightie. He never knew what she went through when he did it; in the morning she'd feel that sick and bad she'd cry down the bottom of the yard.

Tottie and Joe's place didn't have any fence round it, and one day after hanging out the washing, Tottie went to see Winnie and came home to find

Murphys' cows had eaten her best nightdress. Horrie May, who lived across the flat, used to go round pinching people's mallee roots, but somebody caught up with him when they put some dynamite in their woodpile.

They hadn't been able to afford a photo when they were married, so about ten months afterwards they put on their wedding clothes and had one taken and only Tottie knew she was going to have a baby. When it was time, Joe brought Mrs Carmody, the midwife, over in the spring dray and she massaged Tottie's back. It didn't take long; they named him after Lloyd George, the great statesman. Tottie and Joe used to wheel him in his pram from Jericho all the way into Kadina to watch the pictures every Saturday night.

While the War was on, more and more copper was wanted, but when it ended the price of copper fell sharply. The mines started putting people off and Joe lost his job. There was no work at Kadina or Wallaroo or Moonta and the only job he could find was up the river at Renmark, picking grapes. Tottie and Lloyd George went with him in the train to Adelaide and then there was another train to Morgan; then they drove in an open Ford car with mail tins and all sorts packed round their legs and the driver stopped where there were pools on the road and scooped up water in a jug and put it in the radiator. Tottie and Joe made plans all the way. Renmark was a fruit colony full of grape-vines and orange groves; lemon, peach, apricot and olive trees—perhaps one day they might even have a fruit block of their own. When they arrived, Mr Bruce, who had something to do with the meat business, had beef sandwiches made for them.

The cliffs of Ardrossan rise up, sandstone-red—so old, pitted with holes where the pigeons nest; each hole fringed with a white spatter of bird droppings. The pigeons hunch watchful in their holes, they moan and keen, the cliff rumbles with bird calls. Old cliffs that rise up so straight, like the walls of a red castle; they are streaked with cracks, and the bits of sandstone that have fallen off litter the beach; a creaking sound seems to come from the rock pools. Pigeon wings fan and flutter, make a papery clap . . . And in Tottie and Joe's house in Jericho, the mice got in and ate all the paper off the walls.

1987

GERMAINE GREER
b. 1939

Germaine Greer—academic, feminist, media star, provocateur—is one of Australia's most famous expatriates. She was born in Melbourne and educated at the universities of Melbourne, Sydney and Cambridge. Attracted to the intellectual movements of her time, she was involved in 'The Drift' in Melbourne, and the libertarian anarchism of 'The Push' in Sydney.

In 1968 she was awarded a PhD for her thesis on Shakespeare, and accepted a lectureship at Warwick University. In 1970 she published *The Female Eunuch*, one of the most famous works of feminist polemic in modern times, which made Greer an instant celebrity. After leaving her lectureship, Greer travelled the world. She was arrested in New Zealand in 1972 for swearing during a speech. Throughout her career, Greer worked in academia, most notably at Cambridge and Warwick, but she has remained a celebrity, especially in England where she lives (appearing, for instance, on *Celebrity Big Brother* in 2005), and in Australia, where her name continues to evoke strong feeling. Recent local controversies include her statement in 2000 that she would not return to Australia unless she received permission from 'the traditional owners of the land'; her proposal in 2001 for an Aboriginal treaty; and her comments after the death in 2006 of the celebrity wildlife expert Steve Irwin.

Greer's writings are profoundly varied, dealing in literary criticism (*Shakespeare: A very short introduction*, 1986, and *Slip-Shod Sibyls: Recognition, rejection and the Woman poet*, 1995), art history (*The Obstacle Race: The fortunes of women painters and their work*, 1979), politics (*Whitefella Jump Up: The shortest way to nationhood*, 2003), medicine (*Sex and Destiny: The politics of human fertility*, 1984) and autobiography (*Daddy, We Hardly Knew You*, 1989). In her writings on gender, Greer has critiqued Western patriarchy as oppressing women through the institution of the nuclear family and the medical establishment. At times Greer's positions on issues such as female circumcision have caused consternation among other feminists. *Daddy, We Hardly Knew You* is both a family memoir and an account of how Greer researched the stories of her family. DM

From *Daddy, We Hardly Knew You*
Queensland, December 1987

What shall I do here, blind and fatherless?
Everyone else can see, and has a father.
                    Marina Tsvetayeva, *The Poet*, 3

There was still one stone left unturned. When I asked my mother about the legend of my father's jackerooing, she came up with two incantations. 'Googie Bassingthwaighte,' she said, 'Thargomindah and Jackson.' Thargomindah is a town in south-western Queensland and the Bassingthwaightes are sheep-farmers in the Darling Downs. My mother didn't know why she remembered these names or what they could refer to, so I went to Australia again to find out.

Googie Bassingthwaighte, or Muir as he was christened, known to all as Googie for reasons that no one can remember, got to dreaming of being a cattle baron in the early twenties, and decided that he'd like to try for a big cattle lease up in the Warrego. 'You'd better find out what it's all about,' said his Dad and packed him off from the family sheep farm at Jinghi Jinghi where the native grasses grow feathery and tall, to the red dust country up near Longreach. Goog was small, 'born in a drought,' he says, 'never had much condition on me', but he was wiry and strong. He rode in the picnic races at nine stone seven and won more than his fair share of them. If you ask him what his best day was he has trouble remembering whether it was the day he rode six winners or the day he won three races on the same horse.

Nowadays he keeps no horses and he doesn't raise cattle in the west of Queensland, for he bought a farm near his father and his brothers when he got married and he called it after a long-submerged memory of the Bassingthwaightes in England, 'Marnhull'. The Bassingthwaightes are unlike the Greers. They are calm and steady and continuous. Googie looks through the long windows of his weatherboard house out under the galvanised iron verandah to where his nephew's sheep graze on his land because his nephew's pasture has gone dry, and his grandson's utility truck roars past on his way down to the gate. His nieces and grand-daughters drop in to leave treats in his refrigerator. But since Googie's wife died the grape-vines are slowly withering in the garden on the north side of the house and the flower beds have disappeared. Googie keeps no horses now. His brother is the secretary of the Racing Board and regularly tours all the country race tracks, but since drugs and big money took over Australian racing Googie has no interest. He keeps no dog, which might seem odd, but people who have worked with dogs, and loved the dogs they worked with, don't like lapdogs.

If you pet a drover's dog you'll get the rough side of his tongue. Petting will ruin a good dog, they say. An Australian kelpie, called after the first breeding bitch of the strain, will work until it drops, and it won't drop, they say, until both the drover and the mob have been dead a week. Drovers and musterers are attached to their dogs, I think, but they never pull their ears or pat them, or give them treats. Showing affection to a good dog ruins it, turns it into a flatterer and a fawner, a slobberer and a groveller, which is what most of the dogs you meet have become. A dog will rule you if you let it. If you die, of course, it's just as likely to stay by your corpse until it starves to death, when if it had any sense it would eat you and move on. Man and dog are supposed to have a wordless attachment. Perhaps my father thought of me as his kelpie. Maybe he believed a rough caress or a word of praise would have ruined me. I think it's no truer of a dog than a woman, actually.

The dogs got their revenge. They went bush and bred and now they run in packs throughout central Australia. The graziers who abandoned sheep-farming 'when the dogs got bad' blame the blacks who made no attempt to keep down their numbers on the central Australian reservations. They forgot the truth of the adage, 'Every dog will have its day.'

Nowadays Googie's a cat man. 'There's always a couple round the house,' he said and grinned. 'I shoot the kittens when there's too many.' I looked shocked. 'Just put the saucer of milk down, kitten puts his head in, I put the barrel up against his head. Never knows what hit him.' I thought of the terrified cats I had taken to the vet to be put down, that clung to my sweater as the vet tried to pull them off and take them behind the scenes.

I've begged the vets to kill them at home in my lap but either the vets won't come or when they come they prove to be clumsy with the lethal injection. If only I had the courage and the steady hand and the gun, to pour a saucer of milk and steady the barrel against an unsuspecting head. I liked Googie very much. He took himself totally unseriously, but he was game, funny, strong, uncomplaining and unexpectedly tender. He complimented me ironically on my bushcraft, when I didn't get lost driving through the fenceless properties on the Darling Downs. We both smiled bitterly at the joke, for bushcraft is now map references and sign reading.

I didn't ask him if he missed the horses, because I knew the answer. Every Australian who lives outside a city, not that there are many of them, misses the horses. The horse has gone from the Australian bush. There's not an old-timer that doesn't regret it bitterly. They'll buttonhole you in the bar and tell you, 'Two things ruined this country, the road train and the trail bike.'

The road trains are built for the wide highways and vast distances of the United States. European road-trains are dinky-toys by comparison. These have enormous tractor engines with huge staring eyes and vast wheels broader in circumference than my car was high. On the narrow metalled roads of rural Australia they blast along spewing empty stubbies out of their windows. Even when I drew as far over on to the soft shoulder as I could get, the side draught lifted my Holden off the road as if it had been made of paper. These enormous gleaming missiles mow down confused kangaroos, wallaroos, wallabies, emus, sheep, and occasionally the feral pigs that feed on the corpses of all of them, even buffaloes, without knocking the ash off the driver's cigarette.

From Roma to Cunnamulla I drove through an honour guard of dead animals, mostly kangaroos that lay like sleeping schoolgirls with their elegant heads pillowed on the edge of the tarmac and their small hands tucked under their chins. Others had been knocked head first into the ground and pushed along at high speed so that their heads had completely disappeared. Around them lay huge shiny stains like varnish where the blood had dried when the sun came up. There were some that were no more than jigsaws of whitening bones, others that were parchment, some that were blue and gleaming and wore a coronet of flies, others that had been slit open by the tusks of feral pigs, others that had been spread along the road like a carpet of fur. The distance from Roma to Cunnamulla is nearly six hundred kilometres and I reckon there was a dead kangaroo for every kilometre. Sometimes the stink crept into the car and once a sated blowfly came popping out of the air conditioning duct.

The graziers from Darby were not ruing the slaughter of marsupials and emus, by any means. As they said bitterly, 'Americans always ask us if it's true that the kangaroo is becoming extinct. It's the damn grazier that's a threatened species!' Presumably, if Darwin is right, the kangaroos that are fond of investigating the strange lights and noises on Australia's roads at night will be selected out and the species will become road shy. It is my habit to hit the road just before dawn and drive slowly to see the creatures on their way to bed. None of them seemed to realise how dangerous I was. The male kangaroos would pause and turn and come towards me as if to ask my business. Major Mitchell cockatoos, corellas, budgerigars, would stop feeding and wait politely till I had passed, raising their crests like incroyables flirting their fans. Lizards would stop crossing the road, and lift their heads to see me pull up beside them, then they would puff up or display their frills or push their tails up like spikes, imagining that their fierce display would make me vail my crest and vacate their territory. They could not understand that I was a human bullet rocketing through their ecosphere. An Australian bustard showed me why he was almost extinct, for he refused to run let alone fly, and stood by the road, a tall bird on short legs, examining me haughtily and shaking his swept-back head locks in disbelief. I pressed the button and my window slid down. 'Can't you understand how destructive I am?' I asked him softly. Again he shook his head. I discovered that if I talked softly to the animals they would pause and listen with their faces towards me. All except the emus that is. The emus would always whirl in a fantastic frou-frou of plumes and dash off, running full tilt through fence wires that parted with a noise like snapping fiddle-strings.

The road train ruined the cattle country because the road train replaced droving. The stock routes now are empty. Instead the cattle are moved east for fattening on truck beds, standing in two tiers, jammed together so they cannot fall, faint with fear and thirst. Petrol is cheap and manpower is expensive. Mostly the animals are on their way to be sold, either to a slaughtering company or to a farmer who has grass or feed lots to fatten them on. They say that when the feed is good you will still find men droving cattle down the old routes, but the people who say that have never seen it. They are the kinds of people who think one article in a Sunday supplement describes reality. 'Don't know how to do it any more,' the locals said to me at Thargomindah. 'Only a handful of dark boys still work with horses.' The aboriginal stockman is dying out along with his beloved horses.

The drover might be an extinct species but the jackeroo is not. These days he dashes round in a cloud of dust in a Japanese four-wheel-drive pick-up truck, usually yellow, with his Japanese trail bike stashed on the back. The pick-up is yellow so that it can be more easily seen from the air, for the annual muster these days is made by helicopter. The jackeroo rides his fences and checks his waterholes on his trail bike and he gets his orders by radio. That now you could imagine Reg Greer[1] doing more or less, but the notion of Reg Greer on a horse, or a bike for that matter, is laughable. Still, Reg Greer at thirty-five could well have been a different animal from Reg Greer at eighteen or twenty. Perhaps he tried the jackerooing and perhaps he failed. And perhaps the country people would remember a dark-haired skinny boy with a weak chest who kept coming off his horse. There was one thing that bore out his story, such as it was.

When he was describing his dreams to the forces' psychiatrist in 1943, Reg Greer told him that he had a recurrent nightmare about cattle running him down, 'the idea of cattle running him down,' the doctor said, and then quoted him with mildly satiric intent, 'Fierce-looking things, you know.' When I told them this at Jimbour, the assembled country-folk shouted at once, 'He's been jackerooing! He's been in a rush!'

I had simply thought it funny that a man who was frightened of cattle had been sent jackerooing. 'No,' they said, 'everybody's frightened of cattle.'

'You can be travelling with a mob, and for no reason they'll panic and wheel and rush right over you.'

Then I understood. 'Oh, a stampede,' I said stupidly.

'Yes,' they said but they would not use the fancy word. 'You can be sleeping out on the track and they'll rush right over your campsite. There's no precautions you can take, because it's completely unpredictable. The cattle can get spooked by a shadow or the weather. Or anything. And then they rush. No. Your Dad had been jackerooing all right. It was the doctor who didn't know his arse from a hole in the ground.' As usual.

'There was a drover called Jackson,' said Googie thoughtfully. 'And he used to work Cooper's Creek way and the channel country. Worked round there for years. He was one of the best. Your father'd remember if he jackerooed with him.' I reckon he would have and I reckon he'd have told us yarns about it, if he had ridden with Jackson.

Most Tasmanians who came up to central and western Queensland were not young toffs coming for the experience—according to legend one grazier used to charge jackeroos £500 a year—but shearers making the long trek up the wool track, for money. Thousands of Tasmanians crossed to the mainland and travelled north every year. The town of Longford supplied so many men (who stayed on the mainland for nine months out of the twelve) that it was known as the shearers' widow. The three Greig boys from Longford started travelling the wool track before the turn of the century, and their sons joined them when they left school. There was a Bill and a Bob in that first generation. Young Bill said, 'You could have as soon stopped me breathing as stopped me going shearing.' He was off with his father

---

1   Greer's father.

and his uncles when he was fourteen. There were six Greig boys shearers in that generation; perhaps there was a Reg among them. Shearers often worked under assumed names; some were 'wife-starvers', others were on the run from the law for one reason or another, others were avoiding creditors. The tradition of changing names came easily to the shearers, especially if they had been involved in industrial disputes and their name was out on the bush telegraph as that of a troublemaker.

It's not illegal to change your name in Australia. You can be known by any name you like and you are not obliged to register the change. You may marry, vote, take out credit cards, open bank accounts as Mickey Mouse or Albert Einstein, and thereby commit no offence, provided you are not marrying or voting for the second time. Some of the shearing confraternity used so many different names that they had difficulty remembering what name they gave the woolgrower. The publicans cashed their cheques without fuss for most of the money came back into their tills anyway; to their mates the men were known as Lofty, if they were short, or Bluey if they had red hair, or Curly if their hair was straight. Those were the names that counted; when the police came looking for a name the men on the track could honestly say that they'd never heard of him, and at the same time send a message on the bush telegraph that only the wanted man would understand.

I was doing something pretty un-Australian riding down my father's mysterious past. No names, no pack-drill is the Australian way. The 'Labor' government of Bob Hawke tried to introduce the 'Australia Card', so-called in a crass attempt to deny the fact that it was that most un-Australian thing, an identity card. In a most Australian way Hawke gave the dirty work of presenting this unpopular idea to the voting public to the only woman in his cabinet. It failed and her political career ended abruptly. The information is still stored on government computers, and the cards sit in the government store in Deakin,[1] waiting for the tide of reaction to release them on the world. Meanwhile the real rulers of the country, the media oligarchs, keep up the pressure for the destruction of the last liberty, the freedom to go bush, by reporting every case of working-class fraud, known to Australians as 'dole bludging'. I sat in my Holden, encumbered with credit cards, driving licence, car-hire agreement, passport, enough identification to satisfy the Kremlin. What if all of it was in a shonky name?

The Tasmanians, completely ID free, went by train to Adelaide and then caught the 'Ghan' to the end of the line. With them travelled their Cressy bicycles (made in Longford). Unbelievable as it sounds they rode to the sheep stations on their bikes, first up to Cordilla Downs and then south through some of the most inhospitable country in the world. The distances were huge.

1   A suburb of Canberra.

One man travelled three thousand miles on his bike in the year. And when they got home they won all the cycle races, as William Martin Greer did at the Caledonian Games in Launceston in 1910. When the tyres wore out or the tubes finally gave way after repeated punctures from the thousand million iron-hard burrs they rode across, they bound the wheel rims with greenhide. The Tasmanians were famous for their funny men. Tall stories are a tradition on the track; Ray Watley from Tasmania told Patsy Adam-Smith[1] that 'riding a bike from Bourke my tyre wore out so I killed a tiger snake and wrapped it round the rim, shoved its tail in his mouth and off I pedalled!' The only marking of the route were the pads left by the camel trains by which the Pathans brought essential supplies to the isolated stations. If there was a dust storm or a wind the pads blew away. If the shearers got lost, they died of thirst. The dust and the glare played merry hell with their eyes.

Nowadays Australians going bush travel in four-wheel-drive leisure vehicles, with winches and cables and spotlights, with water tanks and refrigerators, with dinghies tied to the roof and trail bikes lashed on the back. The outback is tourism now. I can remember laughing when some Americans took me for a trip down a bayou in Louisiana, and winched their aluminium boat into the water and unloaded portable refrigerators and air cushions and god knows what else besides. When I was growing up you didn't spend a couple of thousand dollars before taking off for the bush; you just shot through. When town life turned too hard, men went walking the track, with nothing but a swag, a blanket, flour, sugar, tea, tobacco and a water-bottle. The swagman is extinct, I think. I've driven thousands of miles on the unsealed tracks back of Bourke and Cobar and I've never seen a single man walking the track. Nowadays if you saw a man in a bowler hat riding a bike across the spinifex you'd know you were hallucinating.

When the shearers got cars they took off in them with the hoods down, sitting on the backs of the seats like young bloods going on a works picnic. I guess that's why I took my fancy Holden sedan with no bush extras down roads where leisure vehicles with four-wheel-drive and steel-belted radials fear to go. I didn't even have any boots with me. Perhaps I am the granddaughter of one of those hard-arsed cyclists of long ago. I'd have been embarrassed to do a trip like that in a land-cruiser with spare wheels and water-cans on the roof. The old Tasmanian shearers would have thought I took myself too seriously by half if I had.

And here's a funny thing. The mainlanders say you can always tell a Tasmanian because he 'loses his H's at Hamilton and picks them up at Ararat'. Daddy used to do that. 'I've hearned more money than you're hever likely to,' he used to say.

---

1 Patsy Adam-Smith (1924–2001), popular historian.

Googie's niece Mary Grant and her husband Jim made me welcome as only country people can. Mary thought the best way to spread the word that we were looking for a jackeroo from the twenties called Reg Greer was to activate the bush telegraph by having a party. People came from far and wide, bringing dishes for supper, along with good humour and kindly interest. They were good talkers, as the generation that grew up before mass media always is. The result was one of the best parties I've ever been to. Mary's daughter came home from the Dalby hospital, where she was nursing, to be in the fun, but really to visit the two horses that looked on from under the trees. She was wearing a thin dress of white lawn, but she made no move to change or even to put boots on before going out to the horses. When she appeared on the white horse's back in the doorway of the house she had not bothered to saddle him either. I understood then why there was a ramp up to the back door of the kitchen; the horses were in the habit of walking through the house to say hello. A half-grown golden pullet dozed on the window sill by the kitchen sink, opening one eye and cheeping if we splashed her when we were rinsing the glasses. Nothing more different than the cruel world of the road-trains could be imagined. When the beautiful girl rode her horse up to the door and looked in to greet the guests, the visitors crowded to speak to this human-animal hybrid. The horse nibbled their palms with his soft lips. [. . .]

1989

PETER STEELE
b. 1939

Peter Steele was born in Perth and became a Jesuit priest. From 1985–91 he was the provincial superior of the Society of Jesus. At his retirement in 2006 from the University of Melbourne, where he had worked since 1966, he held a personal chair. He has also been a visiting professor at a number of American universities, including Georgetown University in Washington, DC. As well as a poet, Steele is a stylish critic, having written studies on Jonathan Swift, autobiography, modern poetry and Peter Porter (qv). His poetry is equally essayistic and witty, and is open to both the pleasures of the quotidian and the difficulties of history. He has written two sumptuously illustrated volumes of poetry about visual art: *Plenty* (2003) and *The Whispering Gallery* (2006). *DM*

Ape

Watching the mind go out when a friend or brother
    is dying, it's as if a great
ape were given his freedom at last. No more
    need for the taking of clues from those
so like and so completely other; an end
    to being thought a harbinger

5

of ill for those who happen to dream about you;
    and silence, in place of the loud taxing
with lust, with sloth, with all the cavalcade
    of things resented because feared.   10

Instead, there's the immitigable forest,
    greening itself in vindication
of hope's archaic shoots. The deeper you move,
    the more your solitude is licensed,
displayed at last as a kind of radiant darkness   15
    where stalk, bewildered, memory,
adumbration, doubt, incomprehension,
    hatred's net and trident, and,
recalcitrant to saddles but receptive
    to innocence, the unicorn of love.   20
1999

J.S. HARRY
b. 1939

J.S. (Jan) Harry was born in Adelaide and has lived in Sydney since the 1960s. She has been poetry editor of *Ulitarra* and held a number of jobs, including that of educational bookseller. Her work is exact and exacting, commonly dealing with the play of language, while being attuned to the suffering and extremity found in the 'real' world. Harry's *Selected Poems* appeared in 1995. Since the 1990s she has written a discontinuous sequence of poems featuring 'Peter Henry Lepus', in which Beatrix Potter's Peter Rabbit travels the world discussing the nature of reality with various philosophers (including Wittgenstein, a long-time influence on Harry's poetry). These are collected in *Not Finding Wittgenstein* (2007). As 'Journeys West of "War"' illustrates, Harry's poetry is—despite its obliquity—powerfully political. *DM*

Journeys West of 'War'

1 'WIND ON FENCING WIRE'

Where is he? Peter Henry Lepus wonders.
He is squatting—well past sunset—
in one of the few
mapped
    depressions   5
in Iraq's Western Desert,
ears turned to one side,
listening to the 'Wind on Fencing Wire'.
Its whistly noises seem to come from somewhere near.

He's heard this CD played before   10
when he was chewing creek-side grass that grew
—hard, tough, & slightly sour—
near a roadworkers' camp at Oodnadatta.
He remembers a composer from Western Australia
who worked with 'natural sounds',   15
& a tape recorder.

Corning through strange cracklings
& noises of static
like those emitted
by Josh Smith's   20
radio
in Baghdad,
he hears an alien voice
speculate:
Maybe it's the wind   25
that played on the Rabbit-Proof Fence[1]
in 'Australia . . . del Espiritu Santo'?[2]

Who is listening?
Is it Professor Ayer, he thinks, or *could it*
be Joshua Smith?   30

He'd left Joshua Smith
walking the Baghdad streets, dodging car bombs,
looking for his wives,
& travelled, mostly at night,
                    eventually hitching a ride   35
with a scrawny desert-bound camel
                    —'strayed'—it'd said,

from one of the city's bazaars, where,
being long unsold, it had suspected,
its merchant was going to kill it.   40
Too skinny to fetch a good price I am,
it'd snorted noisily, then had harrumphed.
Thin camels get eaten in Baghdad.
Peter had not enjoyed the ride.

---

1   The State Barrier Fence of Western Australia, a pest-exclusion fence initially constructed between 1901 and 1907. Cf Doris Pilkington (qv).

2   'Australia . . . of the Holy Spirit': quote from Portuguese navigator Pedro Fernandes de Queirós (1563–1615).

Its back is not easy to sit on, he'd concluded.   45
Had been glad to leap off when the camel bent legs
& collapsed to rest on the riverbed at sunset.

Peter's looking for Professor Alfred Jules Ayer,
& a group of British
phenomenalist philosophers, who wish   50
to discuss
the professor's work,
                    & to experience
the desert's mirages.
Ayer is observing the behaviour   55
of wind, sun, & sand.
When Peter last saw him
Professor Ayer was on a camel heading east,
the pursuing philosophers
far behind him.   60
They seemed to march as a group, their faces
red, their knees, red, too.
A few, Peter saw, had blisters,
sun-dried, gummed with sand.
Some legs looked very white   65
where the socks had fallen down.
Peter's camel had not been impressed,
nor wanted to go any closer.
It'd harrumphed again, which Peter
had learnt, by this time, was a sign of   70
displeasure. He'd been disappointed.
He wants to gain answers to his questions
about the roles
the words
            'language'   75
                'truth'
                    & 'logic'
have played
in Professor Ayer's life.

Peter's found an abandoned philosophy notebook,   80
with some writings about 'Illusion'.
                Working his way round boulders
& up the bank, cautiously he stops,
ears lowered & flattened,

to observe, keeping as close as possible to the ground.　　　　85
There is someone sitting, knees crossed,
with a camera round his neck. The 'Wind on Fencing Wire''s
being twanged across the desert
from a radio beside a bed roll & a pack.
This person is talking　　　　90
perhaps to himself or into a little machine
with an aerial, positioned on a plastic sack,
beside a baby-carrots' can, which Peter, inching
towards, sees is empty.

The man, Max Strang, is testing a mobile phone,　　　　95
which he's just acquired, he says,
from one of the 'post-Saddam entrepreneurs'.

Yeah, there've been more bombs, one near the airport,
there's trouble getting round, street sniping
still going on—some Yanks got shot.　　　　100
The voice sounds like one Peter's heard before
on Sydney radio, talking from Iraq.
It's in mid-flow . . .
He's had no real scoops to send, before, or after, the war,
failed to get himself embedded, with the Coalition Forces　　　　105
or with the Yanks; the local TV
won't use him, his Arabic's not good—
besides, it's the wrong kind,
not Formal, literate, written . . .
but street speech　　　　110
he's picked up outside Iraq. He's come to the desert
to tape the nocturnal hyenas.
Thinks he might sell
some Iraqi 'natural sound'
to a friend who's a muso　　　　115
at Griffith, just moved from Woy Woy,
near where
Spike Milligan used to live. If that doesn't work,
he's heard a rumour about some gold . . .
& a man who's lost a lot of wives . . .　　　　120

He is talking to someone called 'Weasel' Smith,
who writes under the pseudonym 'Botany' Jones.
　　　　　　　　　　　　　　　　Peter,

who has uncomfortable memories
associated with the English rural weasel,   125
begins to twitch,
anticipating mention of
their custom of 'eating rabbit'. He watches
Max Strang's mouth & throat, trying
to forget weasels,   130
& their larger cousins, the stoats,
&, to remember,
he, Peter Henry Lepus, squats,
as a scribe,
in a different country,   135
having travelled
into another time, as well as text.

He thinks of his *Rabbit History of Philosophers*,
of where to begin it,
whether with Zarathustra, in Persia,   140
(six twenty-eight to five thirty-one B.C.) or with
the one called Thales, who's said
to have travelled to 'Babylon', which,
Peter's read, lies south of Baghdad,
& of what the Flowerbed Rabbit would say . . .   145
Wherever she is, he cannot reach her from here.
Dejectedly, he begins to listen to Max Strang
angrily informing Weasel Smith

about his failed feature story—on how
half a million Iraqi children under five   150
are estimated to have died
between nineteen hundred & ninety,
when the UN trade sanctions were imposed
& nineteen hundred & ninety-eight,

as a result of poor health of mothers,   155
the more general
collapse of health services,
& the lack of power
for the country's water supply
—an ongoing problem—. He castigates editors.   160
Weasel Smith cuts in, very loudly, *one dead Aussie now—with a*
good shot—taken alive & smiling, in Iraq—
that might make the news.

Max Strang begins to run his fingers
through his greasy hair & talk about   165
how long it is since he's been under a shower.
He's decided.
He doesn't want to *make the news* any more.

Over his shoulder, clinging to the strap of his camera,
Peter sees a tiny form emerge.   170
It has eight thin legs & looks like a baby Huntsman Spider.
I'm Clifta Webb, it says.
Do you know the way to Persia?
It is wearing tiny red cargo pants, over its four
lower legs, the 'waist' ending only part way up   175
a small, distended, glistening abdomen.
You could go down the Shatt al-Arab,
Peter says, thinking fast.
Why do you want to go to Persia?

Though, on the map, Iraq & Iran nestle together,   180
he does not think so tiny a creature as this junior spider
could travel, by land, so far, directly east,
walking on those short eight legs—
perhaps even through the dangers of Central Baghdad . . .

Perhaps you could drop yourself onto a boat;   185
you would need to travel down the Tigris
or the Euphrates, to get to the Shatt al-Arab,
then perhaps . . . do some floating . . . to reach Iran—
maybe jump onto one of the minesweepers . . .

His nose & forehead wrinkle.   190
She would have to get to a river with water, first.

Clifta is starting to spring about restlessly
on Max Strang's long black oily neck hairs
just above his open collar. Max is now talking to Weasel Smith's
girlfriend, calling her   195
darling, very softly, over & over.
He does not seem to notice Clifta.
I've seen boats with thatched tops—
Iraqis living on them—
on one of the rivers,   200

Peter begins slowly. He is thinking
such a thatched top
would make a good place
for a spider to hide in.
Clifta stares at Peter. His eyes are big & dark.   205
He does not look like a Huntsman Spider.
He does not look at all like a great huntsman . . .
She begins to recite:
. . . *They say the Lion and the Lizard*
    keep   210
The Courts where Jamsh´yd gloried
    and drank deep:
        And Bahrám, that great Huntsman—
            the Wild Ass
Stamps o'er his Head, and he lies fast   215
    asleep.[1]
Peter looks hard at Clifta. He can see her better
now Max Strang has turned his neck.
The light from Max Strang's torch
makes scarlet specks glitter on her cargo pants   220
as she moves around his hair.
She will have to take those cargo pants off, Peter thinks,
if she is to travel
less noticeably
on the pale   225
desert sand. He asks
Are 'Jamsh´yd' & 'Bahrám' philosophers?

&, with less interest, belatedly,
because, after some thought,
he still does not understand: 230
What does your poem . . . mean?

Clifta does not answer directly.
She heard it from her mother,
while roaming in a Sydney park
around her mother's hairy legs   235
amid hundreds of other week-old sibling spiders.
She thinks she might be related

---

1   A misquotation of lines 65–68 of Edward FitzGerald's translation (1859) of the *Rubáiyát of Omar Khayyám*
    ('Huntsman' should read 'Hunter').

to the great Huntsman of the *Rubáiyát*. Since the poem
has been translated from the Persian, she has stowed away,
on the person of the newsman, & in his camera case,   240
to go to Persia, to try to gather 'facts'
for the Huntsman's Family Tree.

2 WHAT IS 'THE WORLD'?

What is 'The World'?
Peter has read
in the Hindu Upanishads
that 'the world before creation
was water'. If you could find   5
'the world before creation', you could find
where water might have been
perhaps, & perhaps,
there might still be some there, he thinks.
He has been reading about the pre-   10
Socratic philosophers—east & west—
from some small books he found in English
in an empty house outside Baghdad,

& wondering, for the umpteenth time,
where his *Rabbit History of Philosophers*   15
should begin. Perhaps there was a primordial,
even famous, rabbit philosopher
from whom the Pre-Socratics
made their start?
When he talks of this to Clifta, she jumps sideways   20
& begins excitedly to talk.
She has an in-the-beginning story to tell.
Once was a female Huntsman Spider, from whose egg-sac
sprang earth, water, sky, & 'world', & from whom
the first lemon-scented gum trees grew, as well   25
as the angophoras, the acacias,
& the Sydney blue gums that were made
for Huntsman Spiders to live & hunt beneath.

Peter is reminded Clifta travelled to Iraq
under or around the collar of,   30
or perhaps, in the camera case that hung from,
Max Strang's hairy Sydney neck.
She is not an English spider.

He worries. If she is too small
to make a web, what does she eat?   35

They are travelling down the riverbed, looking
for the camel, in case it can be persuaded
to take Clifta, not to Baghdad, but to somewhere
lower down, where, on Peter's map, the Euphrates
has water, & there may be boats . . .   40
It's a city camel. Peter thinks it may not
have realised, initially, the north-western channels
have no water. Eventually, it, too, will need
to drink, it may, even now,
be travelling south & east . . .   45
Clifta is scuttling along, quite fast
but she seldom
goes in a straight line
down the riverbed, she inspects behind rocks
& large pebbles. Each time, he   50
has to stop, & wait for her to re-emerge.
He has no idea what she is looking for.

They've left Max Strang waiting for the desert hyenas
which he is hoping
to tape. They have seen no hyenas.   55
Max Strang was on his mobile again,
speaking softly to Weasel Smith's girlfriend,
trying to persuade her to give up on Weasel Smith
& come & join him, soon, in Iraq.
Peter's learnt Max has a ride   60
back to Baghdad, arranged with an Iraqi
who has camels, but who will not arrive
for about a week.
Max Strang is a patient man. He has
water & a tin pyramid of cans.   65
                                        For hyenas he is
prepared to wait.
            Clifta
had been impatient.
She'd wanted   70
to get off his neck.

It is not happy travelling. The sun moves slowly overhead.
Clifta's begun another recitation of the poem

Arachnid Fitzgerald translated from the Persian,
& although there have been intermissions, when she scuttled,   75
Peter, by now, is becoming pretty bored with it.
He is also itchy, gritty, & more than a little hungry.
A wind has arisen, on the desert above,
which blows more sand into his fur, even though
they are below the worst of it. Faintly he hears   80
English voices, above the wind,
& struggles
through slipping sand
up the bank. The last two stragglers from the hiking group
of phenomenalist philosophers   85
have caught the reluctant camel. One is attempting
to drag it by a rope, dodging
its snorts & attempts to bite.
The other, doing nothing, stands well behind.
They are headed back towards Baghdad. Their water cans &   90
backpacks have been secured to the camel's sides.
Peter can hear the camel harrumphing crossly:
they have not thought to give it any water. Baghdad
is exactly where it does not want to go.
Abruptly it sits down, refusing to move.   95
What kind of 'Phenomenology'
are they studying, Peter wonders. He has read—
a very little—about Husserl's
'Realist Phenomenology', & that
Husserl maintained 'the mind'   100
& nothing else in 'the world'
has 'a directedness' towards something
outside itself. He thinks about the camel
which seems to be directed, now,
towards gaining water, & of Clifta   105
who seems to be directed backwards in time
towards locating an ancient starting point
of Huntsman Spiders . . .

Peter has no idea how many books
it might take, to do   110
the Huntsman's Family Tree,
nor to trace Clifta's ancestors back
to the civilisation
of Ancient Persia.

He has seen spiders' webs glistening at night   115
the lines going out . . . perhaps . . . towards
the stars; he imagines, though her search
could not be infinite, it might seem so . . .
Husserl wrote: there always has to be a
'consciousness   120
          of something', & whether,
or not, there is a 'world of objects'
outside the objects of our consciousness,
can, quite simply, be bracketed out.

Clifta, Peter thinks, wants to find   125
something in 'the world
that is bracketed out'.
                    If she
finds 'Persia',
she can, perhaps,   130
gain sense-data
about her ancestor,
the Huntsman of the *Rubáiyát*,
& she won't need to prove,
Peter thinks, with effort,   135
that her 'facts'
'exist'
outside her consciousness . . .

From the channel of the Euphrates, he sees
her tiny indignant form emerge. *I want to go to Persia NOW,*   140
she says. The English philosophers
have given up,
have unloaded the camel, & abandoned it. They
have taken their desert-sand-coloured selves
in their pale sandals   145
away, quite fast. The camel staggers up.
There is water in the river
to the south-east, Peter says. *If you take me—&,* he points, to the
agitated tiny spider, *I think I can find*
the main channel of the Euphrates, where we can drink. If we   150
follow it down to the Delta, there'll be date palms, shelter
& plants to eat . . . He turns to face Clifta.
In the Delta, you will be closer to 'Persia'—
it is called 'Iran' now—&, in the Hawr al-Hammar,
there may be many boats . . .   155

                                                                            2007

GEOFF PAGE
b. 1940

Geoff Page was born in Grafton, NSW. He was educated in Armidale and attended the University of New England. He moved to Canberra to teach in 1964 and has remained there since. He was head of English at Narrabundah College from 1974 until his retirement in 2001. Page is the author of numerous collections of poetry, including *Smalltown Memorials* (1975) and *Collected Lives* (1986), which show his characteristic concern with people and places. Having written two prose novels, in recent years Page has written a number of verse novels, including *Freehold* (2005). Page has also written criticism and plays, and edited a number of anthologies. His anthological critical work *80 Great Poems from Chaucer to Now* appeared in 2006. *DM*

Smalltown Memorials

No matter how small
Every town has one;
Maybe just the obelisk,
A few names inlaid;
More often full-scale granite,   5
Marble digger (arms reversed),
Long descending lists of dead:
Sometimes not even a town,
A thickening of houses
Or a few unlikely trees   10
Glimpsed on a back-road
Will have one.

1919, 1920:
All over the country;
Maybe a band, slow march;   15
Mayors, shire councils;
Relatives for whom
Print was already
Only print; mates,
Come back, moving   20
Into unexpected days;
A ring of Fords and sulkies;
The toned-down bit
Of Billy Hughes[1] from an
Ex-recruiting sergeant.   25
Unveiled;

---

1   William Morris (Billy) Hughes (1862–1952), prime minister of Australia 1915–16 and 1916–23.

Then seen each day—
Noticed once a year;
And then not always,
Everywhere.   30
The next bequeathed us
Parks and pools

But something in that first
Demanded stone.

                                                   1975

ANDREW TAYLOR
b. 1940

Born in Warrnambool, Victoria, Andrew Taylor attended the University of Melbourne,
where his interest in poetry was encouraged by Vincent Buckley (qv). He travelled
overseas in the early 1960s, and taught at the University of Adelaide from 1971 to 1992,
when he became the foundation professor of English at Edith Cowan University, WA.
As well as numerous collections of poetry—brought together in his *Collected Poems*
(2004)—Taylor has written for children, edited works, written libretti, co-translated a
collection of German poetry, *Miracles of Disbelief* (1985), and written the first full-length
deconstructive study of Australian poetry, *Reading Australian Poetry* (1987). Innovative
and wide-ranging, Taylor's poems often reflect his travels, as well as a strong sense of
local place, such as in *Sandstone* (1995). Taylor frequently meditates on the relationship
between landscape and human experience. As 'The Dead Father' shows, Taylor can also
combine artfulness with emotional intensity. *DM*

The Dead Father

Rainy wind's banging the back gate
open to the street
where neighbours shelter behind verandas—
though a shadow of blue sky
claims this is only a shower   5
and will pass over like the day itself

Inside it's warm and the kitchen smells
toasty and full of 3YB[1] and coffee
my father's on holiday
we'll go for a picnic and light a fire for chops   10
and watch his spirit spiral toward heaven
through the dripping trees

---

1   A radio station in Warrnambool, Victoria.

My lemon tree
unburdened at last of its fruit
stretches and shakes ungovernably in the wind—   15
why after nine years should his death be here
in a moment of rain and my small garden
blown suddenly open to the street?

★

His method of relaxing
was to change from blue business suit   20
into brown—late in the forties
brown was relaxing, or was it
really that those brown suits hanging thriftily on
since the thirties were only good now
for gardening and our winter   25
picnics?
   I couldn't tell
who rebelled one summer in the relentless forties
and came to lunch late without a shirt
and was tolerated from then on   30
aged about eight

★

Considering our picnics were laboriously organised
sequences of semi-disasters—
rain, totally burnt chops, blow-outs
several almost-bushfires—   35
and I as the youngest whimperingly tired
aching in knees and armpits
boneless and sagged and asleep before home—
why did they bother?
The garden was almost as big as a farm—   40
I even lost my fourth birthday there
absorbed in my city in a sandpit

Is that why I like this now
my small all-at-a-glance yard
its intricate alleys and stalks   45
its endless ways of finding myself
in rain and mistily
face to face with him?

★

He was the gentlest person I've known—
hurting him was like hacking with a pick   50
in a claypan
        I'd do it over and over
until I'd hacked a big O of anguish
in his face and then I'd watch it
close over, swallowing the pain   55

It was much the same in hospital—
we'd watch the green flicker of his heart
stumble over the screen
while his hand closed on mine
obliterating it in his   60
just-endurable present

He said he didn't feel any pain
when he died
he'd taken it so far inside
it was only a little more of himself   65
he had to know and finally
bequeath to us

★

He comes back these winter days
as the time he went to Sydney and I stayed
two weeks with his mother, rain falling   70
like today. In an iron house
she taught me the sound of rain
who had grown up under tile.
I discovered I'd been sleeping deaf
to one of the world's replenishing noises   75

He's a weather mood
an adjunct of loneliness—
once I went into a dozen bars
'Hey, have you seen my Dad
the one who died ten days ago?'   80
'Have a drink, son' they'd say

'you might just catch him up
if you don't hurry.
So take it easy.'

1982

JIMMY PIKE
c. 1940–2002

Walmajarri man Jimmy Pike was born and grew up in the Great Sandy Desert, WA. He was a former stockman on Kimberley cattle stations who was imprisoned for murder in 1981. While in prison he took up painting and met the writer Pat Lowe. Born in England in 1941, Lowe migrated to Australia in 1972. In the late 1970s she worked as a clinical psychologist at Fremantle Prison. She moved to Broome in 1979. After Pike's release from prison in 1988, Pike and Lowe went to live at Kurlku, near Fitzroy Crossing. In the early 1990s they returned to Broome and Pike's career as an artist began to flourish. In 1999 he became the first Australian artist to have his work displayed in the China National Art Gallery, Beijing. Pike and Lowe collaborated on a number of children's books, including *Jilji: Life in the Great Sandy Desert* (1990), *Yinti: Desert child* (1992), *Desert Dog* (1997), *Jimmy and Pat Meet the Queen* (1997), *Desert Cowboy* (2000) and *Jimmy and Pat Go to China* (2006). Lowe is also the co-author of *Two Sisters: The story of Ngarta and Jukuna* (2004), a book about Pike's nieces. *AH/PM*

From *Yinti*
Ranyjipirra!

One early morning, Yinti had a drink of water, picked up his spear, and set off on his own. After walking for a while, he found the fresh tracks of a cat, and started to follow them. This was hot-weather time, and Yinti walked fast, while the morning was still cool enough. The tracks led him all the way to a foxhole.

Yinti looked in at the entrance to the hole, and he saw a cat, sleeping. He looked in the other entrance and there, to his surprise, was another cat. Both cats woke up suddenly, and they rushed out of the hole and took off running before Yinti had time to aim his spear.

Yinti started off after one of the two cats. It was a big male. He followed it for a long, long way. The sun was high now and the day was hot. Yinti's mouth was getting dry from lack of water.

After a long time the cat's tracks led Yinti right up to a bandicoot's hole. By the time he got there, the cat had already run down inside it. Now, a bandicoot digs a deep hole, with lots of twists and turns. That's what makes it such a difficult animal to catch. A hunter can spend half the day trying to dig it out, and all the time he is digging from the top, the bandicoot is busily digging itself deeper still.

Yinti knew he would not be able to dig the cat out of the bandicoot's hole. He was already tired and hot and very thirsty. All he could do was turn round and head back to the waterhole.

The journey back to camp took much longer than the journey out. Yinti set off walking, but before he got far he had to stop to rest. He lay down under a tree and closed his eyes, trying not to think about his dry throat. As soon as he closed his eyes, he could hear a strange noise: 'Toom, toom, toom, toom!' Ranyjipirra!

Yinti's eyes popped wide open. He looked round, but could see nothing. All he could hear was that fearful noise: 'Toom, toom, toom, toom!' He jumped up, and started off again across the hot sand.

Before long, Yinti had to have another rest. He lay down again, in the shade of a turtujarti tree, and started to go to sleep. But no sooner had he closed his eyes than the noise began again: 'Toom, toom, toom, toom!' The ranyjipirra was following him!

Yinti knew about ranyjipirra. His mother had often warned him to be careful when he went out alone, in case a ranyjipirra got him. And now here was one of them, coming up behind him. What if it jumped on him and grabbed him while he slept?

Really frightened now, Yinti jumped up and went on walking. Every time he stopped to rest, the same thing happened: 'Toom, toom, toom, toom!'

At long last, Yinti could see the sandhill where his family had their camp. He was so tired and thirsty he could hardly walk. He just managed to climb the last few steps up to the tree where his brother Kana and Mana his niece were already sitting. By their side was the big makura of water Yinti's mother had filled and left for them.

Yinti was perishing for a drink of water. He fell down on the sand, and put his mouth to the coolamon. He sucked up some water, and swilled it round his mouth, then spat it out again.

He drank and swallowed a few small mouthfuls. Thirsty as he was, Yinti knew that if he drank a lot of water all at once after hunting on a hot day, he would make himself sick. So he drank slowly, a little at a time. Then he lay down, eyes closed, in the shade of the tree, his arms flung out on the sand. His voice was so hoarse he couldn't speak.

Kana and Mana could see that Yinti was exhausted. Instead of asking him questions about his day's hunting, they sat quietly beside him. The two youngsters filled up their mouths with water, bent over Yinti, and sprayed the water over his body to cool him down. The sound of the ranyjipirra had gone, and Yinti fell into a deep sleep.

1992

J.M. COETZEE
b. 1940

John Maxwell Coetzee was born in Cape Town, South Africa, and grew up there and in Worcester, in Western Cape Province. He had a bilingual childhood, going from an Afrikaans-speaking background to English-speaking schools. He studied English and mathematics at university in Cape Town before moving in 1962 to England, where he worked as a computer programmer, and then to the US, where he gained a PhD in literature. He has since had a distinguished academic and literary career, teaching in universities in South Africa and the US. He moved to Adelaide in 2002 and became an Australian citizen in a special ceremony in 2006. He has said that in changing countries he did not so much leave South Africa as come to Australia.

With Nadine Gordimer, Coetzee has been one of the chief contemporary chroniclers and writerly consciences of his native country, with many English-speaking readers owing their knowledge of South Africa largely to his fiction. His first novel, *Dusklands*, was published in 1974 and gained immediate critical attention; with the publication of *Waiting for the Barbarians* in 1980, Coetzee gained a substantial international readership. His next novel, *Life and Times of Michael K* (1983) won the Booker Prize, which he won again with *Disgrace* (1999), thereby becoming the first writer to win the prize twice. He was awarded the Nobel Prize for Literature in 2003.

Coetzee is a profoundly intellectual writer, his fiction saturated in the history of literature and philosophy and engaging in particular with the Russian novelists of the nineteenth and twentieth centuries. He has also published several collections of essays, and in recent times the genres of fiction and essay have merged in his work, both generically and in terms of content. He has also written two volumes of 'fictionalised autobiography': *Boyhood: Scenes from provincial life* (1997) and *Youth: Scenes from provincial life II* (2002).

His fiction explores, in narratives of individual lives, the politics of imperialism and colonialism, the politics of race, and some classic issues in Western philosophy, particularly the mind/body problem, the problem of evil, and the situation of the outsider. His concern with cruelty in its diverse manifestations has emerged in recent years as a particular preoccupation with the way that human beings treat and think about animals. His most recent novels—*Elizabeth Costello* (2003), *Slow Man* (2005) and *Diary of a Bad Year* (2007)—have been set in Australia and have engaged in various direct ways with the country, its people and its politics. *KG*

From *Elizabeth Costello*
Lesson 8: At the Gate

[. . .] 'Elizabeth Costello, applicant, hearing number two,' intones the spokesman of today's board (the chief judge? the judge-in-chief?). 'You have a revised statement, we understand. Please proceed with it.'

She steps forward. 'What I believe,' she reads in a firm voice, like a child doing a recitation. 'I was born in the city of Melbourne, but spent part of my childhood in rural Victoria, in a region of climatic extremes: of scorching droughts followed by torrential rains that swelled the rivers with the carcases of drowned animals. That, anyhow, is how I remember it.

'When the waters subsided—I am speaking of the waters of one river in particular now, the Dulgannon—acres of mud were left behind. At night you would hear the belling of tens of thousands of little frogs rejoicing in the largesse of the heavens. The air would be as dense with their calls as it was at noon with the rasping of cicadas.

'Where do they suddenly arrive from, these thousands of frogs? The answer is, they are always there. In the dry season they go underground, burrowing further and further from the heat of the sun until each has created a little tomb for itself. And in those tombs they die, so to speak. Their heartbeat slows, their breathing stops, they turn the colour of mud. Once again the nights are silent.

'Silent until the next rains come, rapping, as it were, on thousands of tiny coffin lids. In those coffins hearts begin to beat, limbs begin to twitch that for months have been lifeless. The dead awake. As the caked mud softens, the frogs begin to dig their way out, and soon their voices resound again in joyous exultation beneath the vault of the heavens.

'Excuse my language. I am or have been a professional writer. Usually I take care to conceal the extravagances of the imagination. But today, for this occasion, I thought I would conceal nothing, bare all. The vivifying flood, the chorus of joyous belling, followed by the subsiding of the waters and the retreat to the grave, then drought seemingly without end, then fresh rains and the resurrection of the dead—it is a story I present transparently, without disguise.

'Why? Because today I am before you not as a writer but as an old woman who was once a child, telling you what I remember of the Dulgannon mudflats of my childhood and of the frogs who live there, some as small as the tip of my little finger, creatures so insignificant and so remote from your loftier concerns that you would not hear of them otherwise. In my account, for whose many failings I beg your pardon, the life cycle of the frog may sound allegorical, but to the frogs themselves it is no allegory, it is the thing itself, the only thing.

'What do I believe? I believe in those little frogs. Where I find myself today, in my old age and perhaps my older age, I am not sure. There are moments when it feels like Italy, but I could easily be mistaken, it could be a quite different place. Towns in Italy do not, as far as I know, have portals (I will not use the humble word *gate* in your presence) through which it is forbidden to pass. But the Australian continent, where I was born into the world, kicking and squalling, is real (if far away), the Dulgannon and its mudflats are real, the frogs are real. They exist whether or not I tell you about them, whether or not I believe in them.

'It is because of the indifference of those little frogs to my belief (all they want from life is a chance to gobble down mosquitoes and sing; and the males among them, the ones who do most of the singing, sing not to fill the night air with melody but as a form of courtship, for which they hope to be rewarded with orgasm, the frog variety of orgasm, again and again and again)—it is because of their indifference to me that I believe in them. And that is why, this afternoon, in this lamentably rushed and lamentably literary presentation for which I again apologize, but I thought I would offer myself to you without forethought, *toute nue* so to speak, and almost, as you can see for yourselves, without notes—that is why I speak to you of frogs. Of frogs and of my belief or beliefs and of the relation between the former and the latter. Because they exist.'

She comes to a stop. From behind her, the sound of gentle handclapping, from a single pair of hands, the cleaning woman's. The clapping dwindles, ceases. It was she, the cleaning woman, who put her up to it—this flood of words, this gabble, this confusion, this *passion*. Well, let us see what kind of response passion gets.

One of the judges, the man on the extreme right, leans forward. 'Dulgannon,' he says. 'That is a river?'

'Yes, a river. It exists. It is not negligible. You will find it on most maps.'

'And you spent your childhood there, on the Dulgannon?'

She is silent.

'Because it says nothing here, in your docket, about a childhood on the Dulgannon.'

She is silent.

'Is childhood on the Dulgannon another of your stories, Mrs Costello? Along with the frogs and the rain from heaven?'

'The river exists. The frogs exist. I exist. What more do you want?'

The woman among them, slim, with neat silver hair and silver-rimmed glasses, speaks. 'You believe in life?'

'I believe in what does not bother to believe in me.'

The judge makes a little gesture of impatience. 'A stone does not believe in you. A bush. But you choose to tell us not about stones or bushes but about frogs, to which you attribute a life story that is, as you concede, highly allegorical. These Australian frogs of yours embody the spirit of life, which is what you as a storyteller believe in.'

It is not a question, it is, in effect, a judgement. Should she accept it? *She believed in life*: will she take that as the last word on her, her epitaph? Her whole inclination is to protest: *Vapid!* she wants to cry. *I am worth better than that!* But she reins herself in. She is not here to win an argument, she is here to win a pass, a passage. Once she has passed, once she has said goodbye to this place, what she leaves behind of herself, even if it is to be an epitaph, will be of the utmost inconsequence.

'If you like,' she says guardedly.

The judge, her judge, looks away, purses her lips. A long silence falls. She listens for the buzzing of the fly that one is supposed to hear on such occasions, but there does not appear to be a fly in the courtroom.

Does she believe in life? But for this absurd tribunal and its demands, would she even believe in frogs? How does one know what one believes in?

She tries a test that seems to work when she is writing: to send out a word into the darkness and listen for what kind of sound comes back. Like a foundryman tapping a bell: is it cracked or healthy? The frogs: what tone do the frogs give off?

The answer: no tone at all. But she is too canny, knows the business too well, to be disappointed just yet. The mud frogs of the Dulgannon are a new departure for her. Give them time: they might yet be made to ring true. For there is something about them that obscurely engages her, something about their mud tombs and the fingers of their hands, fingers that end in little balls, soft, wet, mucous.

She thinks of the frog beneath the earth, spread out as if flying, as if parachuting through the darkness. She thinks of the mud eating away at the tips of those fingers, trying to absorb them, to dissolve the soft tissue till no one can tell any longer (certainly not the frog itself, lost as it is in its cold sleep of hibernation) what is earth, what is flesh. Yes, that she can believe in: the dissolution, the return to the elements; and the converse moment she can believe in too, when the first quiver of returning life runs through the body and the limbs contract, the hands flex. She can believe in that, if she concentrates closely enough, word by word. [. . .]

2003

GEOFFREY LEHMANN
b. 1940

Born in Sydney, Geoffrey Lehmann graduated in arts and law from the University of Sydney. He has practised as a solicitor, becoming a partner at the international accounting firm Price Waterhouse, lectured in law and taxation at the University of NSW, and co-authored a standard text on taxation law. Lehmann's first collection of poetry appeared in a joint volume with Les Murray (qv), *The Ilex Tree* (1965). Two of Lehmann's characteristic concerns are seen in this volume: family and historical characters. These two features receive their fullest expression in Lehmann's best-known works, *Ross' Poems* (1978) and *Nero's Poems* (1981). Lehmann has also published a novel and a study of Australian primitive painters, and edited a number of anthologies, including two with Robert Gray (qv). *DM*

Thirteen Long-Playing Haiku

I

A cigarette stuck to his lips,
at night the amateur broadcaster
washes his precious vinyl LPs
in warm soapy water,
and coughs himself to sleep.

5

Next day the needle
sticks in the grooves
and his voice is a croak on air.

II

Small silver discs whose binary code
is read by a ruby laser
obsess my days and nights,
colourful illustrations in their jewel cases,
and sleeve note stories   5
of Ravel walking along the beach
at Monte Carlo,
Brahms's hopeless love for Clara.

III

Our demographic:
aged over 50, male.
Some buy numerous versions of a single piece,
others—'completists'—want
a composer's every work.   5
Some study ratings in guides for hours,
want no repeats in their collection
and insist on original instruments.
Others go crazy at sales
and emerge from an orgasm of spending   10
loaded with CDs,
blinking in the sunlight.

IV

I replace Allegri *after* Alkan.
I'd forgotten
there was a double 'l' in Allegri.

V

Members of a masonic order
standing apart from wives and partners
we furtively exchange information
about bargains and rarities.
As our collections grow   5
we abandon the mainstream,
and develop bizarre tastes.

VI

Some of us file composers
in alphabetical order,
and have systems
for filing within a composer.
Alphabetists avoid compilations.   5
Do you file
the string quartets of Debussy and Ravel
under D or R?

VII

'Where's *Einstein on the Beach*?'[1]
the free-filers ask their overflowing
and continually circulating collections,
stacked under beds, in broom cupboards,
discs piled in drawers   5
and detached from their jewel cases.
For a week Philip Glass hides
between Louis Armstrong in Paris
and Monteverdi's *Orfeo*,
then moves on and finds new companions.   10

VIII

The older dealers understand their clients.
A woman is buying *Figaro* for her daughter:
'Isn't Mozart a bit light?'
'Madam,
is the ceiling of the Sistine Chapel "a bit light"?'   5
Wrapping my purchase,
he diagnoses me
through Henry Kissinger glasses:
'If you can't make up your mind what to play,
play your collection   10
in alphabetical order.'

IX

Arriving home at night
with my newspaper neatly
folded under my arm,

1   An opera by Philip Glass and Robert Wilson (1976).

I'm bailed up by my son
at the top of the stairs: 5
'Mum, he's hiding more CDs
in his *Financial Review.*'

X

Driving a carload of young women,
to a tax class I'm giving,
I turn the ignition key.
Will I switch off John Cage's
Sonatas and Interludes for Prepared Piano?   5
I let the CD play unannounced
and roll back the sunroof.
The car fills with sunlight and young women's
    conversation
punctuated by strange and luminous percussions.
Gulls and the grey arch of Sydney's Harbour Bridge
    pass over us.   10
They thank me as we park:
'That was very pleasant.'

XI

A second-hand music shop
leaves a message on my voicemail.
Within minutes I'm sorting through
thousands of baroque and early music CDs.
'A deceased estate,   5
he was a baroque man—'
they quote an amateur broadcaster's name.
'I'm a baroque man too,' I say.
But not like this,
every little byway explored,   10
volumes of duets for recorders,
lute music that would play for weeks,
lovingly assembled
by a narrow and exact mind.
Shaken, I buy just some Ockeghem and Handel.   15

At home I open a jewel case and smell ash—
the dead man's cigarettes.
'Dad,' the voices say,
'it'll happen to you—to your collection.'

XII

The collector writes his own valedictory:
'We approve
how you studiously play
almost every CD you buy.
We forgive the occasional omission,   5
one or two missed in a boxed set of Schubert lieder,
and those you never play, but love
as a memento
of the same performance on much played vinyl.
We admire your urge to know and experience   10
blues, minimalism, a capella masses,
Alkan to Zelenka—even Broadway musicals.
The collector's life is solitary and odd,
his assembly of objects
meaningful only to himself.'   15

XIII

I'm tipping CDs into the 10 stack
in the boot of my red car,
constructing my new identity:
Handel's *Saul,* Schnittke's concerto grosso,
some John Lee Hooker,   5
Lou Reed's *Transformer*—
some of the dead broadcaster's treasures,
his Buxtehude La Capricciosa variations.
I'm also removing my old self,
replacing the discs in their cases.   10
I have the jewel cases laid out
like a neurosurgeon's instruments,
as I withdraw and insert,
fingertips gingerly holding each disc by its edge,
checking each label is up.   15
Tonight I'm driving to a beach house
three hours of tunnels and freeways,
past dairy country,
through eucalypt forests
and along a moonlit peninsula,   20
the music and the road
a single line of thought.

2004

MURRAY BAIL
b. 1941

Novelist and short-story writer Murray Bail was born and grew up in Adelaide. He left Australia in 1968 and lived abroad for six years, first in India and then in England and Europe; while living in London he wrote for the *Transatlantic Review* and the *Times Literary Supplement*.

The year after his return to Australia he published his first book, *Contemporary Portraits* (republished in 1984 as *The Drover's Wife and Other Stories*), a collection of stories that led Bail to be associated with other young male writers of the 1970s—mainly Peter Carey and Frank Moorhouse (qqv)—who were working in the short-story genre in a non-realist mode that included fabulism, surrealism, literary self-reflexiveness and experiments in narrative voice and chronology.

His first novel, *Homesickness* (1980), identified Bail as one of the most original and accomplished writers in the country. Taking on the big theme of national identity and the equally big theme of art and representation, *Homesickness* is a substantial and polished tale of a group of Australians travelling abroad who trek through endless galleries and museums but understand only what they are already educationally or intellectually equipped to understand, and sometimes merely see themselves reflected.

Bail's monograph on the painter Ian Fairweather was published the following year and his second novel, *Holden's Performance*, in 1987; in this novel the Adelaide boy Holden Shadbolt grows up to represent Australian men of the 1950s and '60s in general, whom Bail represents as literal-minded and limited in imagination, naively believing everything they read or hear and 'performing' mechanically as if they were cars.

His third novel, *Eucalyptus* (1998), is another fable of Australia, a witty romance with an overt basis in the structures and motifs of folktale as well as indulging Bail's long preoccupation with the pleasures and absurdities of taxonomy and classification. A Prospero-like father figure called Holland, obsessed with the national tree to the extent that he has planted hundreds of different species of eucalypts on his land, sets a test for the suitors of his beautiful daughter Ellen: the successful suitor will be the one who can identify every tree.

Among many other things, this is a satire on the longstanding domination in Australian cultural debate of the importance of 'the rotten landscape', which Bail first directly addressed in his 1975 story 'The Drover's Wife'. Saturated with literary reference and allusion, *Eucalyptus* is also a gender-reversed echo of the story of Scheherazade, whose endless magical storytelling saves her life, and a rewriting of the classic George Eliot novel *Middlemarch*, in which the beautiful young heroine has two suitors, the dry-as-dust, sterile scholar and the luminous, mercurial young romantic.

Bail has also published two collections of autobiographical accounts of his writing practice and experience: *Longhand: A writer's notebook* (1989) and *Notebooks 1970–2003* (2005). *Camouflage* (2000) contained two new short stories and selected stories from his earlier work. *KG*

Life of the Party

Please picture a pink gum-tree in the corner of a backyard. This is a suburban gum sprouting more green in the lower regions than usual, and a tree-house hammered into the first fork. A stunted tree, but a noteworthy one in our suburb. I live with my wife Joy and two boys Geoffrey and Mark in a suburb of white fences, lawns and tennis courts. It has its disadvantages. On Sundays drivers persist in cruising past, to peer and comment as we tend our gardens. I wonder what their houses are like. Where do they live? Why do they drive around to see the work done by other citizens? Let me say I am concerned and curious about these things.

Last Sunday was a day of warm temperatures; pure pleasure, really. Tennis sounds filled my ears, and the whine of weekend lawnmowers. There was smoke from burning autumn leaves. I went down to the back of my yard, waited, looked around, and climbed to the tree-house.

I am forty-five years of age, in reasonable shape all round. On Sundays I wear brown shorts. Still, it was a climb which was tricky in spots, and then as I settled down the house itself wobbled and creaked under my weight. The binoculars I placed on one of Geoffrey's nails; I moved my weight carefully; I surveyed my backyard and the squares of neighbouring houses. Half an hour remained before the party began.

On my left was Hedley's, the only flat roof for miles. He was out the front raking leaves. The sight of rubbish smoke billowing from that tin drum of his made me wonder at lack of thought. We had no washing on the line but was Hedley's act typical of a non-conformist, the owner of a flat-roofed house? It was just a question. It reminded me of his car (a Fiat), his special brand of cigarettes, his hair which was slightly grey, and his wife, Zelda. Everything she did seemed to begin with Z. An odd game, but true. It was Zelda who owned the street's zaniest laugh, had zealous opinions on the best-sellers, and always said zero instead of the more normal nought or nothing.

In the next house I could see a tennis game. That accounted for the steady plok, plok and random shouts. I trained my glasses on the play without knowing the score. The antics of those people in slow distant motion was quite fantastic. To think that a wire box had been built to dart about in, to chase a small ball in, and shout. That was George Watkins. As director of a profitable girdle factory he has an inside story on human fitness. He's also a powerful surfer and when I see him walking he shouts to me, 'How you going, Sid?'

The first time I played a game with big Watkins he aced me and aced me in front of his friends and my wife. Invitations have been received since, but I miss the game to avoid additional embarrassment.

Across the street I could distinguish the drive and the side of Pollard's leafy yard. This is a Cape Cod type of house. As expected Pollard was there, walking up the drive, stopping at plants, hands in trousers, pausing, checking bricks, until he reached the footpath. There, he looked up and down, waiting for mail, visitors, his Prodigal Son, news of some description. He parades the width of his house, a balding figure with a jutting stare like the house.

To my right a widow lives with her daughter. The street was alarmed when Gil died—he seemed to be as healthy as any of us. A short time after, she had a swimming pool dug and tiled and can be heard splashing during days of hot temperature. From my position, as I waited, the waters were calm. Then I thought I saw a man there, lying beneath one of her pool trees, a solid hairy specimen, on one of those aluminium extension chairs. No? The glasses showed an image of some description. She is wearing slacks, and is blonde and nervous.

Finally, there was the house next door on my right. The binoculars were hardly needed: I was looking down into the weedy garden, and as usual not a soul could be seen. These neighbours are the J.S. Yamas. In three years I suppose I have seen them . . . a dozen times. We have not spoken yet. He has nodded, yes, and smiled, but not spoken. This indifference deeply offends my wife.

'It's wrong the way they don't mix in!'

'Why?'

'Everyone needs neighbours and friends. To talk to.'

'Why?'

'You can't live by yourself,' she says. 'What if something happens?'

That was her frustration as I remember it. Naturally enough, the Yamas' silence made them more and more discussed. The street kept its eyes open. Thinking about it: the Yamas have a private income; he could be a scholar of some sort; it could be, of course, that one of them is in shocking health, though I doubt it from what I sense of the place. He looks foreign, not Australian, and a fairly decent type.

At that time my yard was silent. Joy was at our beach-house with Geoffrey and Mark. I had said to them on Saturday night: 'Look, I have to duck up to town tomorrow.' Arriving, I arranged the place and made for the tree-house. I had raised the venetians and left the screen door open. We have lawn smoothing over most of our yard, and concrete blocks form a path. (I used to say that ours was a two-lawnmower house—one for the front and one for the back—until people took me seriously.) Halfway between the back door and the tree stands a permanent brick barbecue, tables and white chairs.

I had invited a dozen or so couples. On the tables I placed plenty of beer, glasses, knives and forks, serviettes, and under Joy's fly-proof net a stack of steaks, sausages and piles of bread rolls. Tell me a friend of yours who doesn't enjoy a barbecue on Sunday! From Geoffrey's tree-house I waited for the guests to arrive. Then a movement occurred on my left. A door slammed, a floral dress fluttered, down my drive came Norm Daniels and his wife. With the binoculars I caught their facial expressions. They began smiling. He adjusted his blue short-sleeved shirt as they neared the front door.

I waited. The Daniels now came around the house, puzzled by the no-answer at the front, seriously looking down the drive; certainly bewildered.

Had they arrived on the wrong day? Then, of course, they turned and sighted the barbecue all laid out, and their relief was visible.

Daniels was monk-bald to me as I stared down. He waited among the tables as his wife called through the back door, 'You-who!' She smiled at the fly-screen, then shook her head at the tables and chairs.

'Not there?' Daniels asked.

'They must have gone out for a sec.'

He looked at his watch, settled back, and began eating one of my rolls. 'Want one?' he asked. She shook her hair. Surrounded by someone else's fresh meat and utensils, she seemed uncomfortable.

Another car pulled up. Daniels went over to the drive. 'Down the back!' he called out.

It was Lennie Maunder. About fifty, he was as soft as pork, wore bermuda shorts, and had a bachelor's lopsided walk.

'No one's here,' Daniels explained. 'They must have gone out for a sec. I'm Norm Daniels. My wife, Joan. Pleased to meet yah. We might as well hang around till they get here.'

They sat down and I couldn't catch all their words. It was a distraction trying to listen to them and watch for the next arrival. The word 'insurance' floated up to my tree, so I knew Daniels had started on occupations. They were not drinking at this stage, and when Frank and elegant Georgina Lloyd came down they seemed embarrassed, caught as it were, and stood up stiffly, bumping chairs, to smile.

Two more couples arrived, the men with bottles.

'Well,' Andy Cheel said, 'we might as well have a beer!'

Laughter. The sun was beaming. They began drinking.

The women were seated together, and pecked at the air like birds. I heard Frank Lloyd extroverting into Sampson's ear. Tiny for his name, Sampson was in a bank somewhere, and accordingly grey. Nodding, he said, 'This is right. This is right. Yes, this is right.'

Lloyd was in advertising and already into his third glass. He blew froth from the top of it. 'Ahhh,' he said, and half-closed his eyes.

The chairs were comfortable, the voices grew louder. Latecomers arrived. Norm Daniels and Lloyd realized they were friends of Ed Canning.

'Come over here, you bastard,' they said to him. Lloyd shouted, 'Who's the old bag you've got with you?'

'Oh, you!' said Canning's wife. She was quite heavy, but pleased with Lloyd's compliment.

'Have a beer,' he said, 'Sid's not here yet.'

And Bill Smallacombe, who was climbing at Myers, arrived without his wife.

I had a brief mental picture of Joy. In bed one night she sat up and said: 'I saw Bill Smallacombe at lunch today with a young girl.' She fell back disappointed, full of indignant thoughts; a brown-haired concerned wife is my Joy. As I watched the party I imagined Joy submitting to the sun on the sand, breasts flattened, lying there keeping an eye on young Geoffrey and Mark. She must be satisfied with my career so far and is privately contented when I rush to town on business.

They were all there now, and the drinking had loosened muscles, floated the mouth muscles, wobbling the sincerities. The perils of Sunday afternoon drinking! Ed Canning and Frank Lloyd had taken off their shirts, Lloyd's wife loosened her blouse buttons, familiar backslapping occurred; laughter, so much laughter. I noticed the bachelor Maunder began stealing beer from someone else's glass. Bill Smallacombe drank heavily and kept going inside to use my lavatory. Clem Emery I could hear repeating the latest stock market prices, and Sampson was complaining that his new concrete path had been ruined overnight by a neighbour's dog.

'What say we get stuck into the grub?' yelled Andy Cheel.

They all crowded forward, chewed on their words, dropping sauce and bones on the lawn, and briefly my name.

'Clear those bottles off the table, Ed, before they fall off,' said Canning's wife. She was wearing tight blue slacks.

Carrying four to each hand he lifted the bottles over legs, lawn, to dump them behind the garage. Two were dropped on the last load, and broke with an evil loudness. Someone called out, 'He dropped his bundle!' and they laughed and laughed.

Later, Ed's wife said, 'You should see their lounge!'

'Those curtains I didn't like,' said Georgina Lloyd. 'I suppose Joy picked them.'

'I've been with her when she's bought stuff that really makes you wonder,' said Joan Daniels.

'Where do you think they got to, anyway?' she asked vaguely.

By about half-past four the party was noisy. This was emphasized when the Watkins' tennis game suddenly stopped. And from the corner of my eye I caught grey-haired Hedley next door creeping towards our fence. I waited. Hedley squatted down, peered between the planks at the goings-on. He hadn't shaved over the weekend, he twitched his nose, and at one stage scratched between his legs. For a good fifteen minutes Hedley spied before retreating. At his door he said something to his wife, and they went inside. Directly over the road, half-hidden by cars, George Pollard on the footpath faced the direction of our house. The other neighbours were either out or had decided to display no interest at all.

'Only a few bottles left,' Cheel announced loudly. 'Sid's got Scotch inside, but we'd better not.'

'Why not?' asked Lloyd.

There was laughter at that, and I had to smile.

Lloyd touched Canning's wife on her behind. 'You old bag,' he said. She allowed his arm to go around her neck as he lit a cigarette.

Lloyd later tried a hand-stand between two chairs, tricky at his middle age, and swung off balance, knocking chairs and breaking glasses. He landed on a pile of chop bones; he lay there sweating, his chest heaving.

'When are you getting your pool?' Georgina asked Clem Emery.

'Say seven weeks. We'll have a bit of a do one night.'

'Yes, yes, don't forget us,' others shouted.

Then Smallacombe came wandering down to the tree. He stopped right at the foot, kicked a tin, grunted, and loudly urinated. The others glanced vaguely. Sampson turned, but it did seem natural enough, relieving yourself against a gum-tree on a Sunday afternoon.

Frank Lloyd, trying to balance a bottle on the hairs of one arm, was pulled away by his wife. 'Come on, darl. We must be off.' She called to the rest, 'We'll be seeing you.'

'Gawd, it's twenty past six.'

The Daniels moved out with the Lloyds.

'What about this mess?'

'She'll be right.'

Smallacombe belched.

'Leave it.'

My tree was draughty. They had me bored. I wanted them to go, to leave my place. Why do they linger, sitting about?

Gradually they gathered sunglasses, car keys, their cardigans and handbags, and drifted up the drive in a sad fashion as if they were leaving a beach.

At the gate Ed Canning stopped and shouted, 'I've never been so drunk in all my life!' It was a voice of announcement, sincere, and clearly loud enough to reach my tree. My binoculars showed middle-aged, sun-glassed Canning rigid with seriousness after his statement. Canning, the manager saving for boat and beach-house; his wife had begun yoga classes.

Finally, there was the accelerating procession of shining sedans, saloons, station-wagons, stretching past my house. Most of them I noticed had tow bars fitted. Canning, Smallacombe, Cheel, Emery, Sampson, Maunder, etc. One of them sounded his horn three, four times in passing. Was it Smallacombe? He was one of my friends. A stillness occurred, a familiar hour was beginning, lights flickered. And sliding down the tree I had to think about: who would have sounded his horn at me?

1975

JENNIFER RANKIN
1941–1979

Jennifer Rankin was born in Sydney. She published three collections of poetry, including one, *Earth Hold* (1978), illustrated by John Olsen. Her posthumous *Collected Poems* (1990) was edited by Judith Rodriguez. Rankin also wrote plays for stage and radio. Her poems are compressed, intense and often deal with the complexities of familial relationships. *DM*

Cliffs

Where the cliff cleaves up
clean into the sky
I see my day cut through

and again another cliff

and again   5

cleaving up.

Then it is the faulting
the falling in folds
the going back into the sea.

And this day and again this day   10
and again days.

Birds fly in formation.
They jettison space
while at the cliff line
a twigged bush thinly etches away   15
the hard edge.

Cliffs heave in blue air

heaving and faulting
rising and falling
bird flight, twig etching,   20

cleaving up and folding back.

                                             1977/1990

Slow Wing

Morning cresting in on fine rain
heaping up old light
sky swollen with cloud

and I sit in this still house
where the thick oak door   5
thuds with its latch
when you leave.

Morning cresting in on fine rain
over the trees.

                                                 1978/1990

First Poem—Metamorphosis

Now is the time to go back.
In the stillness I too am changing,

she-wolf in the forest
dingo in the desert-cave

even my thighs take on again their haunching.   5
I feel the fur flatten along my limbs.

And I am at that table,
old soft-grained brown table,
I am standing eye-level with the surface
nose quivering at the edge.   10

Your firm hands are working material
twisting the silver wheel
stitching through the soft stuff
stitching together my memory

and that unwavering gaze out of my own eyes?   15
What world of tabletop does it encompass?

Everything was there you know,
a universe laid out on a vast flat surface
everything was ready for prophecy
and I, a small girl, blessed with a small girl's silence.   20

                                                 1990

BEVERLEY FARMER
b 1941

Beverley Farmer was born in Melbourne and educated at Mac.Robertson Girls' High School and the University of Melbourne. She taught French and English in Melbourne high schools during the 1960s and in 1965 married a Greek immigrant with whom, in 1969, she moved to Greece. The couple returned to Australia three years later and ran a restaurant on the Victorian coast before separating in 1976.

Farmer's first novel, *Alone*, was published in 1980 but it was not until 1983, with the publication of the short-story collection *Milk*, which drew extensively on her experiences in Greece and as part of a Greek family, that she gained widespread critical recognition and readership. *Milk* was followed by another collection of short fiction, *Home Time* (1985), and the novel *The Seal Woman* (1992).

Much of Farmer's writing is experimental. *A Body of Water* (1990) is a writer's journal combining autobiographical writing interspersed with finished short stories. She returned to fiction and to her earlier rich seam of Greece-related material with the luminous and elegiac novel *The House in the Light* (1995), and her *Collected Stories* was published the following year. She departed again to more experimental writing in *The Bone House* (2005), three long essays forming 'an extended meditation on the life of the body and the life of the mind'. She has become increasingly well known in recent years as an essayist and photographer. *KG*

Ismini

Behind its hooded verandah the house was deep in evening shadow. Ismini unlocked the front door, trudged through the green gloom to the kitchen and dumped her schoolbag on the plastic table cloth among long slabs of late sun. A fly nodded, stroking its hinged legs.

With a wince she unwrapped the two slimy speckled translucent squids and rinsed them under the tap. Their beaks and torn eyes had to be prised out, then the fretted glassy backbones, the inksacs. She cut up the ornate tentacles and the sheaths of their bodies. She made a salad glowing green and red, put it with the *retsina* and the blubbery squid in the refrigerator, poured a glass of milk and sat down to her homework.

One morning on a hot wooden jetty her father had hauled a squid out of the flashing sea. Dripping, its bright mantle fading, it had shuddered and wheezed at her feet, blind in the white sun, as it died.

Oh, what is it, Baba?

Kalamari.

Mummy, Baba's caught a kamalari!

Oh yes, look. A squid.

In English it was a different creature.

'Write a pen-portrait of a person you know well. The subject's appearance, attitudes, way of life, character, should be covered. 250–500 words.'

She scribbled notes. My Grk grandmother. Yiayia Sophia. Will Mrs Brown object if the subject is dead? She won't know. Red eggs for Easter, the lamb on the iron spit, the awful offal soup. The brain broiled in the charred skull. Mother cat, kittens buried alive. Bad luck to kill a cat. Perpetual mourning.

A hard marker, Mrs Brown had said that Ismini was clever and should have no trouble getting a studentship to Teachers' College, if that was what she wanted. Mrs Brown had said after class that she might need Ismini to baby-sit on Saturday if her live-in girl was still ill. Oh yes, I'd love to, Mrs Brown.

The deep sun was making Ismini's face burn like a brass gong in the window pane, like the mask of Agamemnon, long-eyed, long-lipped. Her breasts lay round and heavy under her uniform. She fingered her warm hair.

Doan be hard on your Yiayia, Ismini *mou*. She give up everythink to come out here, look after us.

We didn't need her, Baba, did we?

We need her, you know that. She been like a mother to you.

She's always picking on me.

She just frighten. She tell your Theia she see your mother in you.

Oh does she? Good!

Baba once said Ismini could cook squid better than Mummy could, even better than Yiayia. These squids were fresh ones from the market especially for his birthday. Out of her pocket money she had bought real Greek *feta* cheese and the *retsina* and a carton of the Greek cigarettes he loved, Assos Filtro, supplied by Poppy's sister, an air hostess. In Greece, Baba said, they didn't celebrate birthdays. Mummy loved birthdays. If Mummy had been Greek and not Australian, who knew if she would have left home like that? Theia Frosso said no Greek woman would. Today there was no letter, no birthday card, in the box. Yet they had been one flesh.

She had run into Mummy the other day by chance in the Mall. She had stopped to chat, her own mother, grinning and tapping her foot on the hot tramlines, lighting a quick cigarette and blowing out smoke. She was really sorry to have to rush off like this.

I saw Mummy in town today, Baba.

Doan talk to me about that bitch.

'Ismini?' Theia Frosso was shrilling from outside. Ismini sighed. Theia Frosso, not her real aunt but Baba's second cousin, lived next door and felt responsible. The doors slammed. She strutted in, kissed Ismini and sank on to her usual chair.

'Ach! All alone, you poor gel, why you doan come an watch television with the kids, eh?'

'I haven't even started my homework, Theia.'

Ismini poured her the daily, the ritual dose of sweet vermouth; caught a coil of her orange-peel preserve glowing and porous in the jar of heavy syrup and set it still in the spoon on a glass dish; poured iced water; mixed coffee for two in the red *briki*. It frothed and sputtered in the gas flame. She bit her lip.

'It boil out? Is nothing. *Yeia mas.*' Theia Frosso ate and drank and licked her lips. 'I tell you, your Baba, he a very lucky, he hev a daughter like you look after him. A good little Greek housewive.'

'I'm not really Greek.'

'What you tokkink about? You Greek.'

Theia Frosso lit a cigarette and turned the coffee cups upside-down to read the future in the grounds. Yet Theia Frosso was *moderna*: she encased her flab in pantsuits, she dyed her hair red, she smoked cigarettes.

The telephone rang.

'Hullo?'

Theia Frosso was intent.

'Ismini? Hullo, love, it's me. Look, somethink's come up, I be home late. Sorry, eh? You doan mind, do you, love?'

'Well, how late will you be?'

'Dunno for sure. Doan wait up.'

'You won't be home for dinner?'

'Doan worry, I grab a *souvlaki.*'

'Baba, I got *kalamaria!*'

'Tomorrow. We hev them tomorrow. Sorry, love, I gotta go, I double-parked. Make sure you lock up, all right?'

'All right. *Yeia sou.*'

'*Yeia.*'

She slammed the phone down. Happy birthday, Baba.

'He hev gel fren.' Theia Frosso giggled, inspecting the brown ripples in Ismini's cup. 'You hev to expect. A taxi-driver metink lotsa people. He still a quite yunk men, you know thet.'

'So what if he has?'

'He never tell you, *kale*, he be shame.'

'Why should he be?'

'Mama? Eh, Mama?' Theia Frosso's scrawny youngest was shrilling out over the grey fence. She rose sighing, her duty done at least, stubbed out her cigarette, planted more rubber kisses.

'Without me they can do nothink. Sorry, I betta go. You come an hev dinner, eh? Why you wanna stay here all alone? No good for you.'

'Too much to do, Theia.'

Ismini rinsed the dishes. The sun had left the window in a bronze haze. She switched the sallow bulb on and sat down under it to write.

MY GREEK GRANDMOTHER

My Greek grandmother, Yiayia Sophia, was swathed in her widow's mourning clothes and headscarf until she died. Her mouth was folded over her toothless gums, her skin yellow and creased, her grey hair worn in two long pigtails even in bed. A wick floating in oil on water kept a flame sputtering all night in front of the ikon in her room.

She knew all the prayers. All through Lent she fasted until she could hardly stand, her candle shaking, outside the church at the Easter midnight service. There were fireworks hanging and flaring, and we all cracked our red eggs and ate them and nursed our candle flames all the way home for luck. Then we had to eat her magieritsa.

I remember her hoarding our hens' eggs for days beforehand and hard-boiling them on Holy Thursday in red dye. We polished them, still warm, with cloths dipped in oil. She baked plaited tsoureki *loaves. She made the* magieritsa, *the traditional soup of lamb offal, flushing out the lungs and entrails with the garden hose, screeching at the avid hens, stirring it all in the pot with onions and herbs like a witch at her cauldron.*

The lamb itself my father had skinned and impaled on an iron rod. Its red eye-sockets, its grinning teeth with the spit thrust out like an iron tongue. All Easter Sunday morning it was twisted and basted over the trench of coals, speckled with charred herbs, while it turned dark brown and neighbours and relatives danced to the record player on the back lawn. When they split the skull for my grandmother, she offered me a forkful of the brains.

'Eat it, silly,' she cackled. 'God gave it to us.'

'Ugh, no! I don't want it.'

She shrugged, mumbling the grey jelly.

Our cat had kittens once. A lovely pure black cat, a witch-cat, she lay purring, slit-eyed, as they butted and squeaked at her pink teats. Our cat was necessary, as the hens attracted mice. Kittens weren't. One day the cat was crying and clawing at a damp patch of ground under the tomatoes. I dug up the corpses, their fur and tiny mouths and moonstone eyes all clogged with earth. I accused Yiayia.

'Don't be silly,' was all she said.

She is dead and buried herself now, in foreign earth. I saw her dying, her old mouth agape fighting for breath; and dead in her coffin at last, a yellow mask and folded lizard-claws. She was always too old to love me. I'm too old to hate her any more.

(430 words)

At the funeral Baba had sobbed on Theia Frosso's shoulder. Mummy hadn't been there. Ismini shuddered. In her old sepia wedding picture nailed up beside the ikon, Yiayia had Ismini's face: everyone said so. Ismini had wanted to burn all the photos, but Baba made her put them back up in the hollow room. There was one of Mummy in Greece, on a plump donkey with her legs sticking stiffly out; Baba was there, and Yiayia, swathed even then, and a crowd of solemn children with shaved heads. Mummy looked happy.

The phone rang. Ismini's lip curled. So he was sorry, was he? Well, better late than never.

'Yes.'

'Hullo? That's you, Ismini, is it? Oh good.'

'Oh! Mrs Brown!'

When she had just finished the essay!

'I was hoping you'll still be free to baby-sit for us this Saturday. Have I left it too late?'

'Oh yes, I'd love to!'

'Oh good. The thing is, though, we'll be very late home. Will your parents let you stay the night?'

The wood-fire whispering, Ismini thought, flaring over the crammed bookshelves and the sofa bed in the bow window.

'Oh, yes!'

If Baba says no this time, then I'll leave home.

'You're sure? Oh good. I'll pick you up at seven on Saturday, then. Can you hear the bub bawling his head off? I'd better go. 'Bye, Ismini.'

The first time she stood for ten minutes on their front verandah, too nervous to knock. When she asked Mrs Brown what to do if the baby cried, the eight-year-old scoffed, but the two-year-old patted her knee: I'll help you, Minnie, he said. He always stops for me.

They sat round the fire while she read them Little Golden Books; calling her Minnie Mouse, exploding with giggles, chanting Meany, Meany, when she said lights out at nine.

I'm eight. I don't have to go to sleep yet.

You do so. Mummy said. He does so have to, Minnie.

Shut up you.

It was a funny name though, a fancy classical name, a whim of her pompous old godfather's, when she should have been called Sophia after Yiayia. His wife had lapped Ismini in rosy withering flesh, pressing lips soft as a cocoon on her wincing cheeks. Once her parents split up, her godparents stopped visiting. Only her name was left of them.

If Baba said no, she couldn't stay the night, then she'd ring Mummy. No, don't be silly. The last time, a man had picked up the phone. Lyn, it's for you, he'd called.

Mummy, it's me. Can you come over just for a while? Baba's gone out. Can you, please?

Darling, no, sweet, you know I can't, I have to get up at five to go to work—

I want to talk to you!

Well go ahead, sweet, what's the matter?

Baba says I can't go to Poppy's birthday party.

Oh, lovey, I'm sorry. What a shame.

I'm sixteen! I'm not a child! The whole form's going. He won't let me go anywhere. Please, will you just ring and talk to him?

He wouldn't listen to me. You know that. God, I'm the last person—

I'm sorry. You're otherwise engaged, aren't you?

Ah, Ismini—

She'd cut Mummy off. Mummy hadn't tried to ring back. Baba had been right all along, of course: forget about your Mummy, Ismini *mou*, she doan want you. Sixteen, Ismini said aloud, is old enough to leave home legally. She wondered if Poppy would like to share a flat.

It was getting late. She trailed down the dark passage to her father's room. Its velvet curtains were the same, like sleek brown fur, and the painted-over fireplace in the wall, and in the wardrobe doors those long hazed mirrors that she and Mummy had always polished together. She had dressed up and posed in the dim mirrors. Baba slept alone now. When nightmares had woken her he had come and carried her in to sleep between their big warm bodies.

Mummy's old forgotten red nightdress lay hidden under sheets in the bottom drawer. Ismini undressed to slip it on: it fitted now. She stroked Red Ruby on her lips and cheeks, and rimmed her long eyes with kohl. She brushed out her hair. In the blurred gold of the mirror a dusty ghost looked back.

Once, black and faceless against a half-light from the passage, Mummy had stooped over her, dragged down her pants and crammed a suppository like an iron spit up her bottom. She had had to rush out to the toilet, her bowels surging and snorting. Poppy said sex hurt like that. Poppy was raped.

Room by room Ismini snapped on the lights and checked that all the doors and windows were locked. Yiayia's room of dead faces, the kitchen, laundry, bathroom, the musty sitting room, and her own room last.

She had been lying awake, trying to make sense of their jumbled shouts in the kitchen, when Mummy had come bursting in, sobbing and shuddering, and slammed the door. They clung together in the dark until at last Baba's yells and crashes petered out, daring only to whisper.

I'm leaving. This time I'm leaving.

What's happened?

He's insane. He's capable of anything. God, I hate that man!

But what about me?

I'll have to go into hiding. I'll find somewhere to live where he won't find me. Ring you at school.

I'm coming with you!

No, sweet, you can't. He won't let you go. He'd stop at nothing if I took you. He said so.

Mummy, don't go. Don't, please.

In the chill of daybreak they found him asleep with his head in his bloodstained arms on the kitchen table glittering with smashed glass. Mummy crept past with her suitcase. Ismini draped his jacket over his wet shoulders, switched off the light, and crawled back into bed.

Now Mummy got up before daybreak and stood waiting among furled glittering lamps and skeletons of trees for the first golden tram to trundle up wrapped in fog like a caterpillar in a cocoon.

If I fail HSC, Ismini had remarked the other day, you can get me a job at the hotel with you.

Oh, you'll pass. Still want to be a teacher?

I don't know what I want.

In the kitchen Ismini lit the stump of her Easter candle and switched off the light to watch the little flame flap and tower. She thought of opening the *retsina*. No. Well, why not? She prised the cap off and filled a glass with the acrid wine. Happy birthday, Baba. She drank it in gulps, and ate all the salad, since it wouldn't keep, dipping chunks of bread in the juice, sucking the olive pits. Lovely ripe plums for later.

By candlelight her arms shone, and her breasts too, only half hidden in crimson silk.

You're so beautiful, he would say, sitting opposite, and she would smile mockingly over the rim of her glass at this dark tall grave man, a man who had lived, who had known sorrow. His name? What did it matter? He would bend to heap hot kisses on her hands.

Ah! But you're too innocent, my darling.

I'm so tired of innocence. Slowly, significantly.

God! Don't tempt me! And overcome by a wave of passion, crushing her fiercely in his arms, he would carry her limp and golden to her bed.

Ismini took a long swig and held her glass against the swelling candleflame. Light swung rocking all over her, the kitchen walls, the window panes. The luminous crimson plums sat glowing there. She bit one through its skin and its juice spurted.

Darling, she murmured out loud across the table. Oh, my darling.

1983

ROGER McDONALD
b 1941

Roger McDonald was born in Young, NSW, and was educated at the University of Sydney. In the 1960s he worked as a school teacher, and later joined the ABC, directing programs and films for ABC Education in Hobart and Brisbane. From 1969 to 1976 he was poetry editor of the University of Queensland Press, during which time he published two collections of his own poetry. In 1976, McDonald moved to Canberra and became a full-time writer. His first novel, *1915* (1979), about Gallipoli, was adapted into a television series (1982). His other novels include *Mr Darwin's Shooter* (1998) and *The Ballad of Desmond Kale* (2005), winner of the Miles Franklin Literary Award. McDonald has also written scripts for television, non-fiction and the autobiographical works *Shearers' Motel* (1992), based on his time as a shearers' cook, and *The Tree in Changing Light* (2001). DM

From *Shearers' Motel*
Being a Sheep

It was not a happy time up there in the most desolate corner of the State. There were too many sheep on Wilga and they turned it into a desert in a good season. 'I could tell you tales, really, I was appalled, absolutely appalled,' said an English woman he met who had worked in the kitchen the previous year, but had shot through, going to work in the roadhouse fifty kilometres to the east. 'My observations were such that I felt, you know, this is crazy, this is absolutely crazy. The world has passed them by up here.

'Honestly, I prefer sheep to some people, the way they are.'

Sheep looked at him dolefully from the yards beside the Wilga shed, where they were brought in during the day for the next day's shearing. They were creatures with no reason to like him, or anyone else for that matter. Their mistrust was all-inclusive. They knew that at any moment the sky would fall in, and when it did, whose fault would it be? If they were human someone would ask what the problem was, but because they were sheep the problem was them.

Dust choked them and they sneezed and coughed and made more dust with their trotting hooves. It was a fine dust composed of dried crystals of urine and shredded sheepshit and sand. Mixed in was a variety of spilled chemicals, jetting mixes and dips, bituminous and milky substances from old bottles, from the nozzles of plastic knapsack dispensers, and from rusted, leaking containers dropped under floorboards.

All it took was a noseful of this pungent sheep-dust to rouse the feeling of dreary confrontation that characterised Wilga. It was the smell greeting new arrivals at the station gate, where sheep always gathered, mobbing up to an exit (as long as they weren't made to). Workers who'd been away for a while spat and wrenched the flimsy gate-hinges back: 'Fuckin' sheep again'.

Sheep packed into a corner and squashed each other. They stayed dead-still for a moment, then broke without warning, slamming against a far fence, bodies wedged hard, lungs straining, heads jammed up stiffly. Panic was in the air. Resentment. A crow-cry punctuated the moment.

It was all overstated. Melodramatic. It couldn't last. Sheep couldn't be convincing about one passion before replacing it with another. Some of them began staring at the ground as if it were grass. They made the watcher into an illusion too.

Then they went hard at it again, in their eternal scrum. They were locked into mob rule. Soon there would be an event involving mass numbers of sheep being inspired by other sheep to move farther and farther back until, at the last moment, when all seemed lost, a way of escape would miraculously appear. A mass exodus against the imprecations of men and dogs would occur. And it would be a phenomenon in their lives. It would be something new, something never before encountered: a way through, a release—a gate, a race, a ramp. Sheep lived in a hell of short-term memory loss. Tremendous relief would be expressed in a thundering and rattling of wooden planks, and they would pour upwards into the silvery light of the shed, possessed by heavenly thoughts—then *shit* but they knew this would happen, *piss* but their lives could have told them—and it would be the same thing all over again, mayhem and panic and slaughter in the shadows of the Wilga shed where men pointed and dogs harried.

Nothing would ever change in the patterns of sheep. It was all written, all enacted, all fatal. No wonder sheep lay down and wouldn't get up. They knew about death but were dumb in the face of it. They seemed always at screaming point, rolling their eyes, keeping their lips sealed. Their only wish was to be left alone to work something out. What had they done? What was their crime? Why was it always their day of atonement? Sheep led the life of abused innocents. They were all children.

A shearer named Oxley with a pigtail like a pirate told anyone who listened that if they wanted to give him an enjoyable weekend they could just hand him a rifle and let him loose on the mob. 'What cynic godhead made them?' asked an Australian poet. Move a mob one way it elected another—get them to jump a stream, and they'd run with the current, go over a cliff and drown. Banjo Paterson wrote: 'Merinos made our men sardonic or they would weep.'

The Wilga cocky hardly ever smiled, but he grinned at Oxley's rifle-toting plan. He was victimised by sheep. He must have thought, if only sheep grew something other than wool. If only their booms didn't make him buy in panicky haste; if only their busts didn't make him suicidal. There were times when he could have 'shore them and shot them and still made ten bucks a head'. Sheep dragged him out to drive through paddocks of dead ones. Their diseases and their doggedness bled his days of hours. In a boom year there was flystrike, barley grass, corkscrew grass blindness, no good workers on tap, just the dregs. Because of sheep his wife and children stayed in the city, living it up for as long as they could, or merely surviving. And so he went mad from want of society, with just the company of sheep. Look at these shearers here, these Kiwis and odd bods, never taking wool from the right places, leaving second cuts, ignoring the hocks, blind to the meaning of a man's life, that is, his sheep—pissing off with a snarl if a legitimate word of criticism was breathed in defence of a man's clip, which would fetch— what? Anyone know?

Every wasted moment in the shed saw wool prices falling. Men were walking around scratching their arses when they should have been shearing. Every slow-down in the shed meant backlog in the holding paddocks. 'It slows it all down and you've got less tucker for the following mobs to eat and then she sort of dominoes back,' raved the cocky. 'If that eats the paddock then all the rest have got nothing or it half-eats it out and the next mob half-eats it out . . .'

It drove him back up to the house and back into the bottle again. He pulled the blinds. What he felt about sheep he shifted on to men. 'Shearers are natural pigs. I know them. They look at the food and if there's just the right amount they think, "Oh, that's nice. I might want to come back for seconds", so they take extra, and everyone when they sit down eats everything on their plate or tries to. But if there's plenty they think, "Oh, well, I can always come back for seconds", so they leave it. And then they'll eat what's on their plate, they'll get talking to someone, forget they want more and therefore there's a heap to chuck out, whereas if just the right amount is cooked you run short; you'll never ever achieve the spot-on, everyone happy and there's nothing to throw out.'

He only wished he could din this into the heads of his sheep who ate through his dreams.

To get away from Wilga faster they shore on the weekend. Oxley said his Aussie mates might come over on Sunday afternoon and check them out. They were staunch unionists. He'd seen them in the pub on the way up there. They had a Maori girl shearer with them. They had a feeling there'd be shearing on Sunday and were dead against it. Oxley just said, fine, come on over, stay for tea.

'I've fought my way from one end of Australia to the other,' boasted Oxley. 'I'm not allowed in many pubs any more. You want to meet me, I'll say I'll meet you up at this pub, don't go to that one, that one or the other one because I'm barred from all them but I'm still all right in this one. We're a warlike race. That's why we're into fighting.'

Oxley's Aussie girlfriend said, 'Oh, yeah, you fight because you're a bunch of dorks. You want to fight. You're male, you're up for it.'

The cook was in the kitchen the whole day checking the window to see if any vehicles were coming down the track. He had his escape route planned into the scrub. Nobody came.

When a red-eyed wether escaped, knocking people over and kicking through smoko boxes, spilling tea everywhere, ruining the cakes, bucking like an oversized maggot, he joined the chase.

He went round a corner of the wool bins and the wether propped, skidded, and met plenty of opposition, slipping the grasp of oversized men whose life was spent shearing, fighting, and playing rugby. They laughed and swore. Then he was the one.

He wasn't strong. His last game of rugby was thirty-five years ago in the under-sixteen F's, when he lay on Rose Bay oval feigning injury, watching legs run away from him, an interesting perspective. Now when a head groined him, anger caught flame. It was enough. The weight of the sheep knocked him over, but he rolled with the force, face full of burrs, holding on somehow, tongue tasting lanolined shit, hearing the scrabble of hooves on greasy boards till a hand reached down and released him.

It was Oxley's hand. 'Good on ya, Cookie'—Oxley getting his sheep back, kneeling on it, kneeing it hard, punishing it for being a sheep, releasing a nasty oof from its lungs before he shore the rest of the wool off, with lots of careless cuts and the cocky glaring at him.

'Gerrouta my sight, ya blowfly,' Oxley muttered into the wool, swivelling himself around, aiming his arse at the cocky, sweat flying.

Cookie went outside to clean up. Washing his face and hands at the tankstand, cooling off, he told himself that full-on anger and ceaseless obsession were a warning, a caution. What was the point of it? He was angry when the sheep rammed him, but he couldn't stay angry. His hatred of sheep was team dislike, solidarity with Oxley, understanding of the owner.

Around the yards, sheep's baffled, philosophical eyes watched him as if in a dream of himself. Sheep weren't as separate as he thought.

He used his brain like a sheep would. Looked back the other way from the sheep-angle, easing his head around stiffly, not blinking, shivering in the dust and forty-degree heat, allowing his pulse-rate to quicken at shadows, to slow when a wagtail leapt on his head. He let himself doze while a green fly tickled folds of pink skin and laid an egg there. He moved from moment to moment without any feeling of consequence or memory. He saw sheep and people gliding together. He felt how a sheep feels, let through a gate, leaping and flying with brief freedom. He felt himself settle and fan across the earth, the most perfect of sheep moments, the mob spreading, the only sound a determined ripping of grass-stems. This was the life of the sheep! Then a sound, maybe just another sheep coughing, and all of us look up. We wait for movement at the corners of our eyes. One of our number starts to scamper, and it's as if a message is passed around, *This is it, the big moment. Go for it!* Galloping and thundering in the dust we go to hell.

It was no good. He could never go the whole way with sheep. There was no way through. Sheep were a closed circle.

There at Wilga yards dogs lay flat in the dust, eyes bright for the chance of relationship. A station hand came past, offering a friendly smoke. The cocky's sister-in-law, up for holidays to help with the shearing, smiled at him under the brim of her hat as she whipped past on her motorbike, long hair flying. Nice woman—the guys all watched her, looking for a chance, always hoping.

This wouldn't happen among sheep.

For sheep, love possibilities were no go. The ram moved through the mob serving a hundred ewes a night and still the ewes munched into the dawn unmoved. Separation from human responses was total. No deal, said sheep. We are as unlike you as you can imagine. Only you cannot imagine. Your betrayal is complete even as you hold us prisoner to your responses. Sheep—if they could say it—would prefer a redefinition of their role, right down to mutual non-existence. Go a-fucking-way from here, they would ask. If they could colonise another planet they would. Make it Mars—red dust, lack of water, ferocious winds. Just the ticket. Once, back in genetic history, sheep must have been going somewhere, must have had a master mystical plan. But something had happened, some hurt, some shock in the species' childhood.

Say it was when the first shepherd appeared.

Say it was the first shearer.

1992

GERRY BOSTOCK
b. 1942

Playwright, poet and film-maker Gerry Bostock was born in Grafton, NSW, of Bundjalung descent. A founder of the Aboriginal Black Theatre in the 1970s, he co-directed the documentary film *Lousy Little Sixpence* (1981), which examined the employment conditions of children forcibly removed by the Aborigines Protection Board. *Here Comes the Nigger* (1977) was first produced by the Black Theatre in 1976. *AH/PM*

From *Here Comes the Nigger*
Act I, Scene II

SAM *and* VERNA *can be heard coming up the stairs laughing and joking. The door opens.* VERNA *enters carrying the groceries. She crosses the room and puts the bag on the table and looks around the room.* SAM *enters, closes the door and takes a few paces and stops. He puts the suitcase down.*

SAM: [*smiling*] Well, don't just stand there. Go and put the tucker away, woman.

VERNA: [*She picks up the groceries and turns to him, smiling.*] Still the male chauvinist, hey, big brother?

SAM: Old Aboriginal custom.

VERNA: [*She crosses to the kitchen as* SAM *picks up the suitcase.*] You'll never change.

SAM: I hope not.

VERNA: So do I, big brother!

SAM: [*He crosses the room and places the suitcase down by the settee.*] Thanks kid. You made my day.

VERNA: [*from the kitchen*] Don't mention it. Do the same for a black-fella!

SAM: Oooh, you're all heart, kid. You're all heart.

VERNA: [*re-entering the room*] Well, how's my big-time brother, the poet?

SAM: [*grins*] Still struggling, sis. Still struggling. And how's my triple certificated nehse [nurse]?

VERNA: Oh, Sam … [*She crosses the room and hugs him.*] Gee, it's good to see you, Sam. It's really good to be back home.

SAM: It's good to have you back.

VERNA: Miss me …?

SAM: I sure did … we both did. We missed you a lot. [*He holds her at arm's length.*]

VERNA: I missed you too. [*She kisses him. He hesitates and they both seem embarrassed.*]

SAM: How … anyway, how'd you like to hear some good, black music?

VERNA: Yeah … yeah, I'd like that … [*She regains her composure.*] How about something to drink … you want the usual?

SAM: Plenty o' pips in the lemon juice, hey!

VERNA: Sure thing, big brother. [*She crosses to the kitchen.* SAM *goes to the stereo.*]

SAM: Ya hear anything of Bobby Randall in Adelaide?

VERNA: Yeah. He's lecturing at the Torrensville School of Advanced Education.

SAM: Oh …? What's he doing there? [*He feels the records, searching for the one he requires.*]

VERNA: The Black Studies Course. He's teaching black kids about culture and identity.

SAM: Well, that's something ya don't get in the average school.

VERNA: Yeah. Not even the white kids can get it.

SAM: I'm glad somebody's gettin' through to our own kids … and if anyone can do it, it'll be someone like Bobby Randall. He's a really great guy.

VERNA: He sure is. And he's a real black-fella, too; not like some o' them coconuts!

SAM: Coconuts …? What do you mean?

VERNA: Brown on the outside and white on the inside.

SAM: [*finds the record and puts it on the turn-table*] I got Bobby's latest record the other day … listen to this.

VERNA: [*Enters the room with two drinks. She places one on the bookshelf and approaches* SAM *with the other as he plays the record.*] Gettin' any lately, big brother? [*She takes his right hand and places the drink in it. He gives her a smile.*]

SAM: I know love's suppose t'be blind … but I ain't found anyone that blind enough, yet!

VERNA: [*giving him a sexy hug*] Nemmine. Ah still loves ya, honey! [*He gives her a playful slap on the backside.*]

SAM: [*smiles*] Garn, ya gin. I bet ya say that t'all us handsome black-fellas!

VERNA: [*She snaps her fingers and wriggles her hips.*] Whell … white might be right, but black is beautiful! Anyway, I'd rather be a slack black than an uptight white!

SAM: [*grins*] All-a-tarm, baby. All-a-tarm! [*They both laugh.*] Come on. Let's sit down.

VERNA: Wait'll I get my drink, hey. [*She gets her drink and tastes it.*] Mmmm. I needed this. [*They cross to the settee.*] I see Billy's put up some new posters.

SAM: Yeah. He likes to change them now and again.

VERNA: How's he been? [*They sit down.*]

SAM: [*grins*] Bloody unbearable. Ya wouldn't believe it … [*She turns to him and smiles.*]

VERNA: I know what's wrong with him. He's sex-starved, the bastard!

SAM: This could be true!

VERNA: Too bloody right, it's true! But then, so am I.

SAM: You gins are all the same, hey?

VERNA: I don't see any of you black-fellas knockin' us back. [*They laugh as they sip their drinks.*]

SAM: By the way, I got a letter from the Aboriginal Publications Foundation yesterday.

VERNA: Yeah?

SAM: I sent them a couple o' the poems ya wrote out for me before ya went to Adelaide.

VERNA: What'd they say?

SAM: Aaagh, not much. They just sent me a cheque for fifty dollars.

VERNA: [*She smiles, then squeezes his hand.*] Gee, that's great, big brother. Fame and fortune at last, hey?

SAM: They can shove the fame. All I want's the fortune.

VERNA: Ya startin' t'sound like one o'them Black Bureaucrats from Canberra, now.

SAM: [*smiles*] How about that.

VERNA: I got me doubts about you, Sam. [*They smile warmly at each other.*]

SAM: How was South Australia, anyway?

VERNA: Why d'ya think I came home!

SAM: It's like that, hey?

VERNA: Yeah. It gave me the shits. It really did!

SAM: Billy said you were working with some black-fellas on a reserve … what were they like?

VERNA: The blacks were good. The whites were shit-house.

SAM: [*holds her hand*] Ya want t'talk about it, sis? [*She looks at him in silence.*] Well, what about it, sis?

VERNA: Ya know, Sam, before I went to the Centre I use to think us Kuuris on the coast had it bad, but truly, you should see how some o' the country blacks have to live. It's really bad.

SAM: I thought you were suppose to be based in Adelaide?

VERNA: [*She regains her composure and sips her drink.*] I was there for a couple of weeks but then I went up to the Centre with a Medical team from Royal Adelaide.

SAM: [*smiles*] Learn a bit, did ya?

VERNA: You better believe it.

SAM: Yeah? What was it like?

VERNA: Bloody incredible! Jeeze, the whites out there reminded me of the Hitler Youth and the Pious Pioneer all rolled into one.

SAM: [*gives a short laugh*] Now that's laying it on a bit thick, isn't it?

VERNA: Oh, Sam. If only you could see, and could see just some of the kids I had to treat …

Ya know, big brother, I thought I was tough … I mean, really tough. I thought nothing, nothing at all could get under my skin until I saw our little Black babies out there.

Medical terminologies like trachoma, malnutrition, scurvy and scabies didn't mean a thing to me when I saw those kids out there. All I could think of when I saw them was that they were our future Black Nation; a Black Nation with pussed-up eyes, bloated bellies and bodies riddled with sores and bleeding scabs … if you could see something like that, Sam, you wouldn't forget it in a hurry.

SAM: But you're a trained nurse. You've seen worse things than that.

VERNA: Yes. And I tried to be cold-blooded about it at first, but seeing so many sick black babies in so many different areas just turned my gut. A person can only take so much …

SAM: What about the Department … what are they doing about it?

VERNA: Sweet F.A.! The bastards don't give a damn, and besides, the only way blacks can get anything out of the Department is to shack up with the mongrels who control the purse-strings.

SAM: But what about the blacks who work for the Department …?

VERNA: Them blacks in Canberra are all the same. They're nothing but Black Bureaucrats; Black puppets dancing to the white man's tune.

SAM: But surely some of them are at least trying to do something?

VERNA: Look brother, if by chance them Blacks in Canberra manage to get off their ahrse and go to an Aboriginal Reserve, they don't live with the grass-roots people and experience conditions for themselves; no, instead they go and stay in posh hotels where they can go to buffet luncheons and have room-service with hot and cold running women. Why should they worry about the Blacks? They've got it made.

SAM: [placing an arm around her] It's okay, sis. You're home now. [He sips his drink.] Mmmmm. You still fix a mean drop.

VERNA: [Recovering her composure, she lifts her head and kisses him on the cheek.] Thanks, Sam.

SAM: [He flips the lid of his watch and feels the dial for the time.] Well … Billy should be home soon.

VERNA: Mmmm. I might go and have a shower and get freshened up.

SAM: Good. When he comes in I'll get Billy to go up the pub and get something more to drink.

VERNA: [getting up and preparing to leave] Good thinking ninety-nine. And get him to pick up a flagon o' Red. [She goes toward the bathroom door and turns.] Ya know what they say about the Old Red Ned … puts lead in ya pencil!

SAM: S'no good having lead in your pencil if you got no bastard to write to … [They both laugh. A pause. Sam smiles.] Garn, peasant. Go and have ya shower.

VERNA: Okay bundji … I'm goin', I'm goin'.

[She enters the bathroom. SAM gets up and goes over to the lounge chair and feels for the guitar, finds it, picks it up and then sits down and begins to tune it. Sound FX of flushing toilet. VERNA comes out, picks up her suitcase and goes to the bedroom. SAM sings a song. VERNA enters the room with a towel wrapped around her and goes to the bathroom as the song ends. SAM again tunes the guitar. Sound FX of shower. The bathroom door is slightly ajar.]

VERNA: [*from bathroom*] How are your studies coming along? [SAM *is lightly strumming the guitar.*]

SAM: [*smiles*] Got meself a new tutor. [*He stops strumming.*]

VERNA: What happened to the last one ya had … that nice Mr Bates?

SAM: Yates!

VERNA: What?

SAM: [*He puts the guitar aside and raises his voice.*] My old tutor was Mr Yates; not Bates! He had to leave town for a while. [*He gets up and goes to the table and pours himself another drink.*]

VERNA: Who's ya new tutor?

SAM: It's a Miss Odette O'Brien. [*He sips his drink and smiles. Sound FX of shower turns off.*]

VERNA: Who did you say?

SAM: A Miss Odette O'Brien. She's comin' around t'morra afternoon. You can meet her then, if ya like? [*He goes back to the chair.*] Hope she's a good sort. But ya never know ya luck in a big city. [*He sips his drink and almost spills it at* VERNA's *next remark.*]

VERNA: Are you another one of these black-fellas who talk black and sleep white!

SAM: [*sitting down, and taking occasional sips*] What did ya say? A what?

VERNA: She a gubbah chic?

SAM: I dunno … yeah … I suppose she is … [*Sound FX of shower back on.* SAM *ponders.*] Billy asked me that too … but I wonder what makes Verna say something like that … [*Raising his voice*] Why did ya say that, Verna?

    [*Sound FX off. The bathroom door opens and* VERNA *pokes her head out. She has a towel draped around her body and a smaller one covering her wet hair. She has a worried expression on her face.*]

VERNA: I just don't want t'see ya get hurt, that's all. [*She goes back into the bathroom. Annoyed,* SAM *rolls a cigarette.*]

SAM: What are ya talking about? She's only going to tutor me; nothing else … anyway, what harm could a white girl do here … [*Looking hurt*] After all, I'm just a poor, helpless blind man.

VERNA: [*grinning, coming back to the door*] Helpless, my black foot! [*More tenderly*] Look, Sam. All whites want to do is to change you into a black version of themselves. They want to civilise the native, and when they've had their bit, when they've got what they wanted and ripped-off as much as they could, they'll piss you off. And what will you be then: just another screwed-up black-fella! [*She re-enters the bathroom.* SAM *is silent for a moment as he expresses disbelief at* VERNA's *comment. Sound FX back on.*]

SAM: [*chuckles*] What d'ya reckon she's gonna do? Come in here, get her gear off and say, 'Here I am, Darkie … let it all hang out!' [SAM *continues to chuckle.* VERNA *can be heard laughing in the shower.*]

VERNA: Hey, Sam! You better watch it, bud. You know what they say: 'If ya start mixing with white stuff too much it might rub off on ya!'

[SAM *is about to answer when* BILLY *bursts into the room. He looks excited as he glances about. Startled,* SAM *looks toward him.*]

BILLY: Hey, Sam! Where is she?

VERNA: In here … waiting! [BILLY *gives a joyful yell.*]

BILLY: You little beauty! [*He strips off his shirt as he moves to the bathroom.* SAM *follows his every movement and smiles humorously, if somewhat uncomfortably. With a contemptuous grin to* SAM, BILLY *throws his shirt to the floor and enters the bathroom.* VERNA *squeals with laughter as* BILLY *wrestles with her.*]

BILLY: Hey, Sam! Come an' look at this! [*Both* BILLY *and* VERNA *are laughing.*]

VERNA: Billy … cut that out!

BILLY: Sam! Come on in … COME ON!

VERNA: Billy! Bill … OOoooohhh … EEeeeee … Billlly … stop that ya mongrel!

[SAM *walks across the room, feels the shirt, picks it up, folds it and puts it on the settee. He then goes to the table and begins to clear it. The laughter still continues in the bathroom.*]

Fade out

1977/1990

HELEN GARNER
b. 1942

Born Helen Ford in Geelong, Victoria, Helen Garner went to school in Geelong and then majored in French and English at the University of Melbourne. She worked for some years as a teacher, in London and then in Melbourne, before she was sacked from the Victorian Education Department in 1972 for talking frankly to high school students about sex, after which she spent two years writing for the counterculture magazine *Digger*. She has been a full-time writer since the commercial and critical success of her first novel, *Monkey Grip* (1977).

Monkey Grip caused a sensation in Australian literary circles for its explicit treatment of sex, heroin addiction, the counterculture and the emotional lives of women. The responsive and innovative feminist publishers McPhee Gribble saw the importance of the kind of writing Garner was doing and their publication of this novel was the beginning of a long and productive author–publisher partnership. The novel is regarded as a key early text in the explosion of Australian women's writing and literary feminism in the late 1970s and throughout the '80s, in the wake of international second-wave feminism. Garner's third book of fiction, *The Children's Bach* (1984), was rapturously reviewed and is widely regarded as her masterpiece. It was followed in 1985 by the short-story collection *Postcards from Surfers*.

Between 1985 and 1995 Garner published essays, articles, screenplays, short stories and novellas, including the innovative *Cosmo Cosmolino* (1992). In the mid-1990s she became engulfed in controversy, after writing about an incident at Melbourne

University's Ormond College culminated in the Master of the College being charged with sexual assault. Garner's book *The First Stone* (1995), a personal account of the events and the aftermath, was a touchstone for tensions in the community about feminism and sexual assault, and was absorbed into the debates then being conducted about third-wave feminism.

Garner published two collections of essays, *True Stories* (1996) and *The Feel of Steel* (2001), before returning to full-length non-fiction with *Joe Cinque's Consolation* (2004), another personal account of a controversial Australian court case.

Throughout her literary career Garner has been an innovative writer in her uses of and experiments with genre. *Honour and Other People's Children* (1980) and *Cosmo Cosmolino* both consisted of long short stories or short novellas that were linked thematically or by common characters and settings, while Garner's non-fiction has been controversial largely because of debates about what actually constitutes non-fiction. In her essays and longer non-fiction works, her method has been to write from the openly autobiographical point of view that foregrounds the personal experience of an event, whether as an observer or as a participant. *KG*

From *The Children's Bach*

'You have to tell me a story,' said Poppy to her father. 'Before you go to work.'

'You're too old,' said Philip. 'Why don't you just read, or do some practice?'

'It's not the same. It's no fun on my own.'

'Don't make me feel guilty,' he said. 'Someone has to bring home the bacon.'

'Why can't you work in the daytime like everybody else?'

'I can't, and you know why. I don't know any stories any more.'

'Yes you do. Stories from your life. Just make something up, like you used to. It's easy. You go 'Once upon a time', and then say whatever comes into your head.'

She plumped up the doona and moved over to make room for him. He sat down on the edge of the bed. 'When you go to high school next year,' he said, 'are you going to tell your friends your father still tells you a story every night?'

'That depends,' said Poppy, 'on whether they're the right sort of person. Come on. I'm listening.'

'Once upon a time,' said Philip. 'There was a wonderful cafe. It opened very early in the morning. No. It stayed open twenty-four hours. It never closed. They never turned off the machine. That's why the coffee was perfect.'

It was easy. He slid into it.

'At night, because of the noise of people laughing, they turned up the treble on the jukebox. But in the early mornings, in the peaceful shift when customers on their way to work were reading the papers, you could clearly hear the trip and run of the bass lines. Some people came alone, with a library book, dressed in clean clothes of sober cut and colour. Others brought their children and taught them, with smiles and soft words, how to behave in a public place. The clever children read aloud to their parents from the Situations Vacant, the Houses to Let. The big windows of the cafe faced east. People sat with their backs to the sun, and the iron bars of night softened in their shoulders. On the other side of the road, which sparkled with passing cars, a deep garden overflowed its iron fence.'

He glanced at her to see if he was getting too fanciful. She was looking at the ceiling. 'Don't drone,' she said, 'You're starting to drone.'

'It was a place that waited,' said Philip. 'It was a place of reason and courtesy. On the jukebox they had Elvis Presley. They had Elisabeth Schwarzkopf. They had Les Paul and Mary Ford singing "How High the Moon".

'People danced there, in the daytime, in the middle of the morning, down the aisle between the two long rows of tables. The songs they favoured were South American ones with titles the Australians passed over in ignorance, thinking them Italian: the songs were more passionate, more driven, more intellectual than anything we know of here. They danced in each other's arms, with their elbows up high and no expression on their faces: it was all form and precision. They did the tango, the rhumba, the samba. They knew the steps. They never stumbled. Their arms and legs were long and sinewy. The dresses were a spray of light. The men's trousers hit the shoe just right.

'There were two waiters. Neither of them had ever forgotten an order in his life. Kon, a Greek, was as handsome as a statue, cheerful and young. He had a glossy folder of photos of himself and wanted to get into modelling. Marcello was a reformed gambler with slicked-back hair and an expression of weary, courtly bitterness. He stood behind the machine, he held a drawer open with his thigh and counted money. He had confidence with a wad. He pinched each note between thumb and forefinger. He had been in Australia twenty years but he could still hardly speak English.

'There was graffiti in the lavatories. Linda Lovelace's mother went down on the *Titanic*. Lisa is a slut. Renato is a spunk and you molls will never have him signed Lucy and Maria. People in the Paradise Bar read the daily graffiti as if it was the news of the world.'

'As if it were,' said Poppy.

'The Paradise Bar does not serve alcohol. It doesn't need to. Something happens, once you pass that heavy fly curtain . . . Are you listening?'

It was dark. The television was turned down low in the other room. Poppy was dropping off. She rallied.

'Yes. Keep going. Once you passed the . . .'

'The Gaggia hissed. Behind it on a shelf stood a row of triangular bottles, red and green and yellow.'

He paused. She was breathing steadily.

'Pop?'

No answer. He dropped his voice and began to speak more rapidly. 'At night it's different. The waiters are low-browed and covered in tattoos. They wear black jeans and tight T-shirts. They look more like crims or bouncers than waiters. When they set down a cup of coffee some of it slops into the saucer. The owner of the Paradise Bar seems uncertainly in control of his employees. Dope is bought and sold at the Paradise Bar. It is not the kind of place outside which you would like to see your daughter sitting, under the Cinzano umbrellas. On Saturday nights you cannot get a seat at any of its twenty tables. The marbled concrete floor is slippery with spilt liquid. Occasionally some girl, limp with excess, collapses into the arms of her shrieking friends. They hustle her outside, holding her by the shoulders and the ribcage. Her feet in their flat shoes drag behind her in ballet position. Hot Valiants cruise close to the kerb, gunning their motors. The games jingle their piercing tunes in the big back room, the air is thick with smoke, other things are going on upstairs. The Italian kids walk in and out with a lot of money on their backs. They walk in and out, shaking out their expensive haircuts, shaking their glossy Italian hair.'

She was fast asleep. He did not know whether she had done her homework. For dinner they had gulped a souvlaki, walking home through the park. He got off the bed. At the door he turned round and said in a whisper,

'And men fuck girls without loving them. Girls cry in the lavatories. Work, Poppy. Use your brains.'

1984

The Life of Art

My friend and I went walking the dog in the cemetery. It was a Melbourne autumn: mild breezes, soft air, gentle sun. The dog trotted in front of us between the graves. I had a pair of scissors in my pocket in case we came across a rose bush on a forgotten tomb.

'I don't like roses,' said my friend. 'I despise them for having thorns.'

The dog entered a patch of ivy and posed there. We pranced past the Elvis Presley memorial.

'What would you like to have written on your grave,' said my friend, 'as a tribute?'

I thought for a long time. Then I said, '*Owner of two hundred pairs of boots.*'

When we had recovered, my friend pointed out a headstone which said, *She lived only for others.* 'Poor thing,' said my friend. 'On *my* grave I want you to write, *She lived only for herself.*'

We went stumbling along the overgrown paths.

My friend and I had known each other for twenty years, but we had never lived in the same house. She came back from Europe at the perfect moment to take over a room in the house I rented. It became empty because the man—but that's another story.

My friend has certain beliefs which I have always secretly categorised as *batty*. Sometimes I have thought, 'My friend is what used to be called "a dizzy dame".' My friend believes in reincarnation: not that this in itself is unacceptable to me. Sometimes she would write me long letters from wherever she was in the world, letters in her lovely, graceful, sweeping hand, full of tales from one or other of her previous lives, tales to explain her psychological make-up and behaviour in her present incarnation. My eye would fly along the lines, sped by embarrassment.

My friend is a painter.

When I first met my friend she was engaged. She was wearing an antique sapphire ring and Italian boots. Next time I saw her, in Myers, her hand was bare. I never asked. We were students then. We went dancing in a club in South Yarra. The boys in the band were students too. We fancied them, but at twenty-two we felt ourselves to be older women, already fading, almost predatory. We read *The Roman Spring of Mrs Stone*. This was in 1965; before feminism.

My friend came off the plane with her suitcase. 'Have you ever noticed,' she said, 'how Australian men, even in their forties, dress like small boys? They wear shorts and thongs and little stripey T-shirts.'

A cat was asleep under a bush in our back yard each morning when we opened the door. We took him in. My friend and I fought over whose lap he would lie in while we watched TV.

My friend is tone deaf. But she once sang 'Blue Moon', verses and chorus, in a talking, tuneless voice in the back of a car going up the Punt Road hill and down again and over the river, travelling north; and she did not care.

My friend lived as a student in a house near the university. Her bed was right under the window in the front room downstairs. One afternoon her father came to visit. He tapped on the door. When no-one answered he looked through the window. What he saw caused him to stagger back into the fence. It was a kind of heart attack, my friend said.

My friend went walking in the afternoons near our house. She came out of lanes behind armfuls of greenery. She found vases in my dusty cupboards. The arrangements she made with the leaves were stylish and generous-handed.

Before either of us married, I went to my friend's house to help her paint the bathroom. The paint was orange, and so was the cotton dress I was wearing. She laughed because all she could see of me when I stood in the bathroom were my limbs and my head. Later, when it got dark, we sat at her kitchen table and she rolled a joint. It was the first dope I had ever seen or smoked. I was afraid that a detective might look through the kitchen window. I could not understand why my friend did not pull the curtain across. We walked up to Genevieve in the warm night and ate two bowls of spaghetti. It seemed to me that I could feel every strand.

My friend's father died when she was in a distant country.
'So now,' she said to me, 'I know what grief is.'
'What is it?' I said.
'Sometimes,' said my friend, 'it is what you expect. And sometimes it is nothing more than bad temper.'
When my friend's father died, his affairs were not in order and he had no money.

My friend was the first person I ever saw break the taboo against wearing striped and floral patterns together. She stood on the steps of the Shrine of Remembrance and held a black umbrella over her head. This was in the 1960s.

My friend came back from Europe and found a job. On the days when she was not painting theatre sets for money she went to her cold and dirty studio in the city and painted for the other thing, whatever that is. She wore cheap shoes and pinned her hair into a roll on her neck.

My friend babysat, as a student, for a well-known woman in her forties who worked at night.
'What is she like?' I said.
'She took me upstairs,' said my friend, 'and showed me her bedroom. It was full of flowers. We stood at the door looking in. She said, "Sex is not a problem for me." '

When the person . . . the man whose room my friend had taken came to dinner, my friend and he would talk for hours after everyone else had left the table about different modes of perception and understanding. My friend spoke slowly, in long, convoluted sentences and mixed metaphors, and often laughed. The man, a scientist, spoke in a light, rapid voice, but he sat still. They seemed to listen to each other.

'I don't mean a god in the Christian sense,' said my friend.

'It is egotism,' said the man, 'that makes people want their lives to have meaning beyond themselves.'

My friend and I worked one summer in the men's underwear department of a big store in Footscray. We wore our little cotton dresses, our blue sandals. We were happy there, selling, wrapping, running up and down the ladder, dinging the register, going to the park for lunch with the boys from the shop. *I* was happy. The youngest boy looked at us and sighed and said, 'I don't know which one of youse I love the most.' One day my friend was serving a thin-faced woman at the specials box. There was a cry. I looked up. My friend was dashing for the door. She was sobbing. We all stood still, in attitudes of drama. The woman spread her hands. She spoke to the frozen shop at large.

'I never said a thing,' she said. 'It's got nothing to do with *me*.'

I left my customer and ran after my friend. She was halfway down the street, looking in a shop window. She had stopped crying. She began to tell me about . . . but it doesn't matter now. This was in the 1960s; before feminism.

My friend came home from her studio some nights in a calm bliss. 'What we need,' she said, 'are those moments of abandon, when the real stuff runs down our arm without obstruction.'

My friend cut lemons into chunks and dropped them into the water jug when there was no money for wine.

My friend came out of the surgery. I ran to take her arm but she pushed past me and bent over the gutter. I gave her my hanky. Through the open sides of the tram the summer wind blew freely. We stood up and held on to the leather straps. 'I can't sit down,' said my friend. 'He put a great bolt of gauze up me.' This was in the 1960s; before feminism. The tram rolled past the deep gardens. My friend was smiling.

My friend and her husband came to visit me and my husband. We heard their car and looked out the upstairs window. We could hear his voice haranguing her, and hers raised in sobs and wails. I ran down to open the door. They were standing on the mat, looking ordinary. We went to Royal

Park and flew a kite that her husband had made. The nickname he had for her was one he had picked up from her father. They both loved her, of course. This was in the 1960s.

My friend was lonely.

My friend sold some of her paintings. I went to look at them in her studio before they were taken away. The smell of the oil paint was a shock to me: a smell I would have thought of as masculine. This was in the 1980s; after feminism. The paintings were big. I did not 'understand' them; but then again perhaps I did, for they made me feel like fainting, her weird plants and creatures streaming back towards a source of irresistible yellow light.

'When happiness comes,' said my friend, 'it's so thick and smooth and uneventful, it's like nothing at all.'

My friend picked up a fresh chicken at the market. 'Oh,' she said. 'Feel this.' I took it from her. Its flesh was pimpled and tender, and moved on its bones like the flesh of a very young baby.

I went into my friend's room while she was out. On the wall was stuck a sheet of paper on which she had written: 'Henry James to a friend in trouble: "throw yourself on the *alternative* life . . . which is what I mean by the life of art, and which religiously invoked and handsomely understood, je vous le garantis, never fails the sincere invoker—sees him through everything, and reveals to him the secrets of and for doing so." '

I was sick. My friend served me pretty snacks at sensitive intervals. I sat up on my pillows and strummed softly the five chords I had learnt on my ukulele. My friend sat on the edge of a chair, with her bony hands folded round a cup, and talked. She uttered great streams of words. Her gaze skimmed my shoulder and vanished into the clouds outside the window. She was like a machine made to talk on and on forever. She talked about how much money she would have to spend on paint and stretchers, about the lightness, the optimism, the femaleness of her work, about what she was going to paint next, about how much tougher and more violent her pictures would have to be in order to attract proper attention from critics, about what the men in her field were doing now, about how she must find this out before she began her next lot of pictures.

'Listen,' I said. 'You don't have to think about any of that. Your work is *terrific*.'

'My work is terrific,' said my friend on a high note, 'but *I'm not.*' Her mouth fell down her chin and opened. She began to sob. 'I'm forty,' said my friend, 'and I've got *no money.*'

I played the chords G, A and C.

'I'm lonely,' said my friend. Tears were running down her cheeks. Her mouth was too low in her face. 'I want a man.'

'You could have one,' I said.

'I don't want just any man,' said my friend. 'And I don't want a boy. I want a man who's not going to think my ideas are crazy. I want a man who'll see the part of me that no-one ever sees. I want a man who'll look after me and love me. I want a grown-up.'

I thought, If I could play better, I could turn what she has just said into a song.

'Women like us,' I said to my friend, 'don't have men like that. Why should *you* expect to find a man like that?'

'Why shouldn't I?' said my friend.

'Because men won't do those things for women like us. We've done something to ourselves so that men won't do it. Well—there are men who will. But we despise them.'

My friend stopped crying.

I played the ukulele. My friend drank from the cup.

1985

At the Morgue

In everyone's mental image of a city there is a dark, chilled, secret place called the City Morgue. We know these exist because we've seen them at the movies. If you had asked me where Melbourne's mortuary was, I wouldn't have had a clue. I might have gestured vaguely towards the murkier end of Flinders Street—but like most Melburnians I had no idea that half a mile from the leafiest stretch of St Kilda Road, in there behind the National Gallery and the Ballet School and the Arts Centre with its silly spire and its theatres and orchestras and choirs, stands a wide, low, new, clean, bright, nautical-looking structure, with a cluster of slender steel chimneys and a crisp little landscaped garden: the Coronial Services Centre, which was opened in 1988 and houses the Victorian Institute of Forensic Pathology. This is where I found the mortuary.

If you die in an accident, or unexpectedly, or by violence, or in police or state custody, or by suicide, or in a fire, or if no doctor is prepared to sign a certificate stating that you have died of natural causes, your death is called a reportable death. Your body is taken to the mortuary, where you enter the jurisdiction of the coroner. He, on behalf of the people of

Victoria, wants to know exactly why you died. And until the cause of your death has been established to his satisfaction, in most cases by means of an autopsy, your body will remain in his care. You have become what is known as a coroner's case—a coroner's body.

The first one I saw, from a raised and glassed-in viewing area, was lying naked on its back on a stainless-steel table in the infectious room of the mortuary. It was the body of a young man. Because he had been found with a syringe nearby, he'd already had a battery of tests. He was infected with hepatitis C, a virulent form of the disease for which there is no vaccination and which eighty percent of IV drug deaths are found to be carrying: thus, the lab technician was not only gowned up and gloved like a surgeon, but was wearing a hard clear perspex mask which covered his whole face and gave him the look of a welder. The other actor in this odourless mime-autopsy was also a man, a pathologist. He wore no mask but was otherwise dressed like the technician. Both of them moved around on the spotless tiles in big stiff white rubber boots.

Before I could get my bearings (and my notebook was already hanging by my side, forgotten) the technician stepped up to the corpse's head and sank a needle into its left eye. The first sample of fluid laid aside, he moved down to the dead man's hip, plunged another syringe into his abdomen just above his pubic hair and drew out a sample of his urine. Then he picked up a scalpel and walked around to the right side of the dead man's head.

I would be lying if I claimed to be able to give a blow-by-blow account of the first autopsy I witnessed. The shock of it made me forget the sequence. Time slid past me at breathless speed. The pathologist and the technician moved as swiftly and as lightly as dancers. My eyes were too slow: they kept getting left behind. If I concentrated on one thing, another procedure would suddenly be launched or completed elsewhere. So this is not official. It is not objective.

I saw that the scalp was slit and peeled forward over the face like a hairy cap, leaving the skull a shining, glossy white. The skull was opened by means of a little vibrating handsaw. The brain was lifted neatly out (so clean, perfect, intricately folded—so valuable-looking), but also, before I could contemplate it, the torso was slit from the base of the neck to the pubis in one firm, clean-running scalpel stroke, then someone seized a pair of long-handled, small-beaked shears and smoothly snipped away the arcs of ribs which protect the heart and lungs—and there it lay, open to view, the brilliantly, madly compressed landscape of the inner organs.

It can't be, but I thought that the two men paused here for a second, to give us time to admire.

Out come the organs now, neatly scalpelled away from their evolved positions. The technician, working blind in the hollow cave of the torso, lifts them out in glistening slippery handfuls. I recognise small and large intestines, liver, kidneys: but there is plenty more that I'm ignorant of, an undifferentiated collection of interior business. The technician lays it all out beautifully on the steel bench for the pathologist, who is separating, checking, feeling, slicing, sampling, peering, ascertaining. Each organ is put on the scales. Its weight is scribbled in blue marker onto a whiteboard on the wall. The contents of the dead man's thorax are heaved out: his lungs, his heart, his windpipe, even his tongue, the topmost muscle of this complex mass of equipment: to think he used once to talk—or sing! Now his neck looks hollow and flat.

His intestines, his organs, all his insides are examined and then placed between his legs on the steel table. I can't believe all this has happened so fast. But the technician is scouring out the hollow shell of the skull, using the same rounded, firm, deliberate movements of wrist and hand that my grandmother would use to scrub out a small saucepan. At this moment I think irresistibly of that action of hers, and her whole kitchen comes rushing back into my memory, detailed and entire. I have to shove it out of the way so I can concentrate.

The technician balls up several pages of the *Age* and stuffs the cleaned skull with them. He slots into its original position the section of the skull he removed earlier, and draws the peeled-down scalp up off the face and over the curve of bone where it used to grow; he pulls it firmly back into place. He takes a large needle and a length of surgical thread, and stitches the scalp together again. He stuffs the hollowed neck with paper, forming and shaping skilfully and with care.

He places the body's inner parts into a large plastic bag and inserts the bag into the emptied abdominal cavity; then he takes his needle again, threads it, and begins the process of sewing up the long slit in the body's soft front. The stitch he uses is one I have never seen in ordinary sewing: it is unusually complex and very firm. He tugs each stitch to make sure it is secure. The line of stitches he is creating is as neat and strong as a zip.

At some stage, without my noticing, the pathologist has left the room.

During the sewing, most of the watchers in the viewing suite drift out of the room. Only two of us are left behind the glass, standing in silence, keeping (I suppose) a kind of vigil: it would be disrespectful, having witnessed this much, to walk away while he is still half undone. The stitching takes up more time (or so I calculate, in my semi-stupor) than all the rest of the process put together. The meticulous precision of the job is almost moving: the technician is turning an opened, scientifically plundered coroner's body back into a simple dead one, presentable enough to be handed back to the funeral directors and to his family, if he still has one—his family who are presumably, at this very moment, somewhere out there in the oblivious city, howling or dumbly cradling their grief.

It's almost over now. Outwardly, he is whole again. The technician turns on a tap and hoses the body down. With wet hair the young man looks more life-like and more vulnerable, like someone at the hairdresser. But the water flows over his half-open eyes which do not close. Yes, he is dead: I had almost forgotten.

His fingertips and nails are black. As the technician raises the body slightly to hose under it, its right arm flips out and protrudes off the edge of the table in a gesture that makes him look more human, less like a shop dummy, less obedient. The technician replaces it alongside the torso, and once more the young man is docilely dead. The technician dries the young man's face with a small green cloth. This closes his eyes again. His mouth moves under the force of the cloth just as a child's will, passively, while you wipe off the Vegemite or the mud; his lower lip flaps and then returns to a closed position.

The technician removes from under the young man's shoulders a curved block of wood which, yoga-style, has been broadening out his chest and keeping his chin out of the action throughout the autopsy. His head, released, drops back onto the steel surface. The table is tilted to let the water and a small quantity of blood and tissue run down the plug-hole near the corpse's feet. His genitals are long and flaccid. His hands are scrawny. He is very thin. As the technician pulls the trolley out of the dissection bay and swings it round towards the door, the sudden turning movement displaces the young man's hand so that it flips over his genitals, covering them as if in modesty or anxiety.

Now, because of the danger of hepatitis C infection, the technician must manoeuvre the body feet first into a thick, white plastic bag. It's hard for someone working on his own. It's like trying to work a drunk into a sleeping-bag. It takes a lot of effort and muscle. At last he has the body and the head encased in plastic. He draws up the neck of the bag, grabs a bit of it in each hand, and ties it in a neat knot. He slaps a sticker onto the outside of the bag. It's big and I can see it from here. It reads: BIOLOGICAL HAZARD.

The technician opens the door of the infectious room and wheels the trolley out. The room is empty. I look at my watch. I have been standing here, completely absorbed, for forty minutes.

On my way home I would have liked to jabber to strangers about what I had seen in the mortuary, but at the same time I felt I should keep my mouth shut, probably forever. I stopped off at the Royal Women's Hospital to visit some close friends whose baby daughter had been born early that same morning. The labour had been long and hard, and they were all exhausted, but calm. The baby was still bruised-looking and rather purple. Her struggles to be born had left her head slightly lop-sided, an effect which the doctors said would soon correct itself. Somebody said, 'Her head is shaped like a teardrop.' We all laughed.

I didn't tell my friends where I had spent the morning. I stood beside the baby's cot and gazed down at her. Her eyes were closed. Her hands were clasped near her cheeks. Her mouth moved constantly, and small waves of what looked like expression kept passing over her wrinkled face. The baby and the corpse did not seem to be connected to each other in my mind. They inhabited separate compartments, and my thoughts skipped and slithered from one to the other and back again.

The people who work at the mortuary are not used to being interviewed. They know that the picture the general public has of them is a macabre cliche. But they are not the skulking ghouls of legend. Far from it: they are as ordinary as can be. And they are young. Except for the coroner himself, Hal Hallenstein, a sombre, chastening man in a dark suit, I am at all times the oldest living person in the room. The more time I spend with the manager, the scientists and the technicians, Rod, Jodie, Barry, Kevin and (although she is a Bachelor of Science) 'Little Alex', the more impressed I become.

Just as well. You need somebody trustworthy for a guide when you're taken into the big storage chamber called 'the fridge' and confronted with a long row of dead bodies, twelve or fifteen of them, laid out on steel trolleys.

I experience an atavistic urge to make a sign of reverence.

Only one of the bodies is covered: a very small baby, wrapped up, as firmly as if it were alive, in a pastel cotton blanket, and laid on a metal shelf at eye level.

A dead body, stripped of clothes, makes perfect sense of itself in no language but its own. It packs a tremendous wallop. In its utter stillness it seems preoccupied with some important matter that you are ignorant of. It has an authority, in its nakedness, which transcends whatever puny thoughts you, the stranger, may entertain about it. It has presence. And yet it is no longer a person.

But it takes me more than one visit to realise this. At first I keep pestering for each body's story. Oh, what happened to this poor man? Look at this lady—oh, poor thing—what have they done to her? To the technicians and the pathologists, these matters are of academic interest only. They are patient with me and, because I'm their guest, they oblige me by calling up the details of 'the circumstances', as they call them, on the computer. Fell off a truck, they say. Suspected heart failure. Looks like a suicide. MVA (motor vehicle accident).

But their tone is abstracted. They can't afford to dwell on the personal or the tragic. They get at least one suicide a day—'we've got bags and bags of ligatures out there', somebody tells me. They have to perform autopsies on dead babies and murder victims. Their detachment is very highly developed and they have to maintain it. It is precious to them. It is their only defence.

So after a while I control myself and try to copy them. Some of their composure begins to rub off on me. It's amazing how quickly you can get used to the company of the dead. Of course, I am in the privileged position of an observer. Later, Barry, a brilliant dissector who worked and studied his way up from being a porter at Charing Cross Hospital in London to his current position as senior technician, remarks to me, 'You never get completely detached. I've been in this work for eight and a half years. Every now and then I say to myself, "Well, now I've seen everything"—and then next day a case will come in that'll shock even me. You never get used to the homicides—what people will do to each other.'

'It's not such a different job as other people think it is,' says Jodie, who at twenty-five is senior scientist in the mortuary. 'Often I think our lab's just the same as any other, except that our specimens are bigger.' She is sitting in the manager's office in her blue surgical gown and her socks, having left her huge white boots behind at the mortuary door. Like all the technicians who spoke to me, she has a very direct gaze, and an air of unusual maturity and calm.

'I was the first woman here,' she says. 'The guys taught me everything. The first day I was here I went home all worked up, I'd had such an interesting and exciting day. Day two, it caught up with me. It was the smell, maybe, or the blood. They were doing eight post-mortems at once and everyone was busy; they were all gloved and gowned up, and someone looked at me and said, "Jodie, you're going pale." I walked into the change room and passed out.

'But the techs were fantastic. Someone said, "Come over here. I'll make you concentrate on one small area." I did, and then I was all right. But it took me a while till I could step over that red bench into the lab without thinking, "What am I doing here?"'

She laughs, sitting there quietly with her hands folded in her lap. She is not what you would call tough: she's got a rather sweet, open face, with intelligent eyes; but she has the firmness of someone who's had to work out a few important things earlier than your average Australian twenty-five-year-old. She commands respect without having to try.

'Staying detached,' she says, 'is hardest with the kids that come in. The cot-death babies, or kids that die in accidents or fires. It's terrible. With every grown-up case you can manage to convince yourself that there's a reason, but with kids—they're innocent. They haven't done anything. One day I was working with Barry, who's got young kids. We opened up the little coffin, and when we saw the baby in there, so young, wrapped up and holding a furry toy, we looked at each other and we both had tears in our eyes.' She shrugs, and drops her glance to her lap. 'We quickly started work. You can't afford to feel those things. You'd go crazy.'

'With the SIDS babies we take extra time. We wash and powder them. And during post-mortems we're really careful not to damage them. You feel they've been through enough. We rebuild and reconstruct them really carefully. Funny—when you're holding a dead baby in your arms, you know it's dead, but you still have the instinct to support the head, and not to let it drop back.'

'You've got death at the back of your mind all the time,' says Barry. 'Like when you're backing out of the drive, you're extra conscious. The child that gets crushed by a car in the drive is always after a toy that was under the car. It's always a toy.'

'You realise how easily death can happen,' says Jodie. 'And there's a certain case for each of us—something you see that you relate to in a way you don't . . . like. It might be a shoe on someone that's brought in, a shoe like ones you've got at home, or the sort that your brother wears. Only a small thing . . . but it can trigger something in you. You have to keep a split between your natural feelings and what you do.'

Everything the technicians say stresses their mutual respect and their sense of being a team. I ask why they appear to be doing all the cleaning of the mortuary, as well as their scientific work. 'There's a lot of weird people in the world,' says Jodie. 'People you wouldn't want to trust around dead bodies. And other people refuse to come in here. Sometimes we can't get tradesmen to do maintenance work. They won't come in unless we can guarantee they won't see anything upsetting. Still, our floors are shinier than the ones in the rest of the building—did you notice?—shinier than the ones the contract cleaners do.'

To spend hours in the eight-bay lab, standing at the elbow of Barry as he works in silent absorption, or beside David, a pathologist and assistant director of the institute, is to realise that it's a place of study, of teaching and learning, of the gathering and organising of information. David is a natural teacher. He chatters to me as he works on a body, wanting me to notice the creamy-yellow, waxen globules of subcutaneous fat, or the weak, exhausted-looking muscle of a damaged heart, or the perfect regularity and beauty of the striations of windpipe cartilage. 'Exactly like reinforced garden hose—look!'

The radio is on softly in the far corner of the room, spinning out a long, dated guitar solo. Someone in the corridor whistles along to it. Somebody else, going to the shop, calls out for lunch orders. It's not so different from the outside world after all.

'After I'd been working here for a while,' says Rod, 'I found I'd lost my fear of death. I don't know what the soul is—that spark—and no one knows what happens to it at death. But it's certainly gone before people reach here.'

'You have to realise,' says Jodie, 'that what we deal with here isn't really death. We see what's left behind after death has happened—after death has been and gone.'

For days after my visits to the mortuary my mind was full of dark images. At first I kept thinking I could smell blood, on and off, all day. Once I tore open a paper bag of pizza slices which had got squashed on the way home, and the dark red and black of their mashed surfaces reminded me of wounds. My bike helmet knocked lightly against the handlebar as I took it off, and the sound it made was the hollow *tock* of a skull being fitted back together after the brain has been removed. In the tram my eyes would settle on the wrinkled neck of an old woman: she'll soon be gone.

There is nothing so utterly dead as a dead body. The spirit that once made it a person has fled. But until I went to the mortuary I never had even the faintest inkling of what a living body is—what vitality hovers in its breath, what a precious, mysterious and awesome spark it carries, and how insecurely lodged that spirit is within the body's fragile structures.

1996

DAVID WILLIAMSON
b.1942

One of Australia's most productive and popular playwrights, David Williamson was born in Melbourne and grew up in the Victorian country town of Bairnsdale, returning to Melbourne to gain tertiary qualifications in mechanical engineering and social psychology. He had a brief academic career lecturing in both these subjects, during which his first full-length play, *The Coming of Stork*, was produced in 1970 and published in 1974. He resigned from Swinburne Institute of Technology in 1972 to become a full-time writer after the critical and commercial success of his plays *Don's Party* (1971/1973) and *The Removalists* (1971/1972), both of which were first performed in 1971 at Melbourne's Pram Factory and La Mama theatres respectively.

President of the Australian Writers' Guild for thirteen years, Williamson has had more than 25 plays produced and has also written extensively for the screen, including the original screenplay for Peter Weir's *Gallipoli* (1981) and the 1982 film adaptation of Christopher Koch's (qv) novel *The Year of Living Dangerously*.

Williamson has remained a prolific and successful playwright for 35 years, attributing his output not to workaholism but simply to pleasure: 'I enjoy my work,' he has said. 'I like to write, and if I'm not writing a play I need to be doing something else, like a screenplay.' He has sometimes fallen foul of critics who have regarded some of his work as excessively middlebrow, reflecting too benignly the sometimes trivial pre-occupations of his middle-class characters, but audiences—most of whom have much in common with Williamson's characters—have almost always flocked to his plays. *Emerald City* (1987/1987) was such a success commercially that it is said to have rescued the Sydney Theatre Company from crippling debt.

In an interview in 1979 Williamson quoted screenwriter Johnny Dingwall's description of the writer as 'storyteller to the tribe', saying that that was how he saw his own role as a playwright. His plays have accordingly reflected both the events and the preoccupations of Australian life, from the 1969 federal election (*Don's Party*) and the aftermath of the Vietnam War (*Jugglers Three*, 1972/1974) to football (*The Club*, 1977/1978) and feminism (*Dead White Males*, 1995/1995). In the same interview Williamson spoke of his preference for writing about characters in action and conflict, doing what he calls 'situational sparring', exercising 'their intellect, their power struggle, their emotional needs, their competitive instincts'.

His play *Influence* (2005/2005) is an ironic treatment of a recent phenomenon in Australian life, the rise of the 'shock jock' radio announcer and the disproportionate social and political influence such figures can wield. This play broke all Williamson's previous box office records, and he announced at the time of its production that it would be his last. *KG*

From *Emerald City*
Act 1, Scene 1

COLIN *stands by a window, gazing out. He is a handsome, engaging man in his late thirties whose natural disposition is warm and open, though when he feels uncertain or under attack, he's capable of an aloof, almost arrogant air and of sharp retaliation. He is watched by* ELAINE ROSS, *a shrewd capable woman in her fifties.*

COLIN: [*turning away from the window*] What other city in the world could offer a view like this?

ELAINE: Rio. But I'm prepared to believe it's the second most beautiful city in the world.

COLIN: I used to come here when I was a kid and go back with my head full of images of lushness. Green leaves spilling over sandstone walls, blue water lapping at the sides of ferries. Flame trees, jacaranda, heavy rain, bright sun.

ELAINE: [*drily*] Yes, there's no lack of colour.

COLIN: Everything in Melbourne is flat, grey, parched and angular. And everything is controlled and *moderate*. It never rains in buckets like it does here in Sydney, it drizzles. The wind never gusts, it creeps along the streets like a wizened old mugger and slips a blade into your kidneys. Sydney has always felt like a city of sub-tropical abundance.

ELAINE: Abundance. [*Nodding*] Yes. There's abundance. Sometimes I'm not sure of what.

COLIN: There's a hint of decadence too, but to someone from the puritan south, even that's appealing.

ELAINE: I didn't drag you up here, then?

COLIN: No, I would've come years ago, but I couldn't persuade Kate. She's convinced Sydney is full of con men, crooks and hustlers.

ELAINE: She's right.

COLIN: Melbourne has its quota of shysters.

ELAINE: Sydney is different. Money *is* more important here.

COLIN: Why more so than Melbourne?

ELAINE: To edge yourself closer to a view. In Melbourne all views are equally depressing, so there's no point.

COLIN: [*laughing*] I'm not convinced.

ELAINE: It's true. No one in Sydney ever wastes time debating the meaning of life—it's getting yourself a water frontage. People devote a lifetime to the quest. You've come to a city that knows what it's about, so be warned. The only ethic is that there are no ethics, loyalties rearrange themselves daily, treachery is called acumen and honest men are called fools.

COLIN: I thought you liked the place?

ELAINE: I do. It's my city and I accept it for what it is. Just don't behave as if you're still in Melbourne, because if you do you'll get done like a dinner.

[ELAINE *exits.* COLIN *moves thoughtfully to centre stage.* KATE *walks on. She's* COLIN's *wife. An attractive, vivacious and intelligent woman in her thirties. Her frowning earnestness often makes her funny when she's not trying to be.*]

COLIN: This is an amazing city.

KATE: [*bluntly*] I hate it.

COLIN: [*suddenly angry*] Christ, Kate! If you're going to be this negative right from the start, let's just cancel everything and go back south.

KATE: We can't. You insulted everybody as soon as you knew we were going.

COLIN: It's a stunning city, Kate. You should see the view that Elaine's got.

KATE: To judge a city by the views it offers is the height of superficiality. This city is *dreadful*. The afternoon paper had three words on the cover: 'Eel Gets Chop', and no matter how much I juggle that around in my mind I can't find a meaning that justifies the whole front page of a newspaper.

COLIN: To judge a city by *one* afternoon newspaper is also the height of superficiality.

KATE: *All* the media here is devoted to trivia. The places to be seen dining in, the clothes to be seen wearing, the films to be seen seeing—it's all glitter and image and style. New York without the intellect.

COLIN: What's Melbourne? Perth without the sunshine?

KATE: People in Melbourne care about more than the image they project.

COLIN: They seem just as eager for money and fame as anyone is.

KATE: My friends don't care about money and fame. Terri works her guts out in the Western suburbs helping kids fight their way out of intellectual and physical poverty. Sonia tries to repair the psyches of wives whose husbands beat the Christ out of them, and Steve uses his legal skills to try and stop the powerless being ripped off by the powerful—

COLIN: [*interrupting*] Have you ever seen any of them laugh? Wait, I'm wrong. I have. When one of Sonia's battered wives sliced off her husband's member. She had quite a chuckle over that one. And she didn't want the wife to go to prison because it was only a 'one off' act.

KATE: They might have tunnel vision in some areas—

COLIN: [*interrupting*] Some areas? That lot are so paranoid they blame the C.I.A. if the weather turns cloudy!

KATE: At least they don't live their lives totally for themselves.

COLIN: You know what I couldn't stand about them? Their smug self-righteousness. They were all earning salaries five times the size of any of the poor bastards they were supposed to be helping.

KATE: All right. You didn't like them. I did.

COLIN: I have heard Terri laugh too, come to think of it. When I fractured my elbow tripping over that clump of wheezing fur she claims is a cat.

KATE: They used to laugh a lot. Just not when you were around.

COLIN: What's that meant to mean?

KATE: You picked a fight with them every time they opened their mouths.

COLIN: Can you blame me? They made it quite clear they despised the films I'd written.

KATE: Colin, you're paranoid.

COLIN: They despised them. My scripts were about the lives of middle-class trendies. The truth was *they* were the biggest middle-class trendies of the lot. Steve managed to hate my films without ever *seeing* one.

KATE: [*laughing*] Colin, you're totally paranoid.

COLIN: [*agitated that she won't believe him, impassioned*] He told me with immense pride that he'd never seen an Australian film in his life, and that in the last ten years he'd never seen a film that didn't have subtitles. How trendy can you get? How many working-class Australians drink vintage wine every night of the week like that lot did? How many working-class Australians go to listen to Hungarian string quartets? How many working-class Australians find the neo-realist fabulism of the South American novel 'sadly passe'? Those friends of yours were right on the cutting edge of middle-class trendiness, yet they kept telling me—not directly and honestly like their beloved working-class would—but subtly and snidely, that if I was a *real* writer I'd be tackling the problems of the real people in our society. The poor, the maimed, the halt and the blind. I must never, never write about the lifestyles *they* themselves were leading. *Pricks!* Loathsome, do gooding, trendy pricks! Stuff them!

KATE: Perhaps they felt it was a little self-indulgent to concentrate on the the problems of the middle-class when the problems of the disadvantaged are so much more acute.

COLIN: I see. The middle-class have no *real* problems. So how is it they manage to pack so many traumas and breakdowns into their sunny middle-class lives? How is it that they unerringly turn every relationship they embark on into the storyline of a soap opera?

KATE: I don't think that comment's justified Colin. Teresa's been married for eighteen years.

COLIN: Yes, but has anyone ever *seen* Gavin in the last fifteen? I know he's supposed to be writing poetry upstairs, but my guess is that he's been in Katmandu since the early seventies.

KATE: [*finding his histrionics amusing*] Colin.

COLIN: I know the middle-class shouldn't have emotional problems—they're infinitely better off in a material sense than your average third world villager—but for some perverse reason they successfully screw up their lives with great flair, and I find that interesting, and I'm going to keep charting their perturbations and try and make some sense of it all, and those Chardonnay socialists of Melbourne aren't going to stop me!

KATE: [*to the audience*] If I hated Sydney that much, why did I agree to come? In hindsight I suspect that there was something in me that responded to that odd, pulsing, garish city to the north. A reckless streak, a habit of getting quickly bored—I think that deep down I felt something might *happen* up here. And until it did I was in the happy position of having Colin to blame for all the misfortunes that befell us.

COLIN: [*to the audience*] I shouldn't've been so bloody reckless. What kind of idiot uproots himself from a lifetime of connections for childhood memories of flame trees and jacarandas? Lunatic. But *was* it just that? Wasn't there a little grub in my soul hungry for the lionising and celebrity mania that grips the harbour city? [. . .]

1987

JOHN A. NEWFONG
1943–1999

John Archibald Newfong was born in Brisbane and spent his early years on Stradbroke Island, his mother's traditional country. The first Aboriginal journalist to be employed in the Australian print media, he trained at the *Sydney Morning Herald* and enjoyed a long career writing for Australian newspapers. Newfong was also a highly respected Aboriginal political leader. In 1961 he joined the Queensland Council for the Advancement of Aborigines and Torres Strait Islanders and by 1970 had been elected general secretary of FCAATSI. An organiser and 'ambassador' for the 1972 Aboriginal Tent Embassy and an executive founding member of the National Aboriginal Conference (1977–79), Newfong was twice editor of the Aboriginal magazine *Identity*. From the 1970s he used his considerable experience to direct public relations for Aboriginal organisations and authorities, and later lectured extensively in Australian universities, teaching journalism, media studies, Indigenous health and government relations. *AH/PM*

To Number One Fella Big White Boss

Since you become big fella number one white boss me bin thinkin'—before, when we bin goin' Canberra, we bin talkin' white fella way. Yous bin saying, when yous gettum gubberment, you come up our way and you gonna talk black fella way.

But you like all white cockies, when yous gotta pay our people big fella white man's wage, yous allas say we no work good. Then yous say our people not know 'bout da politics and dat none can work for you. Our people know 'bout politics 'cause dat's da only way we gonna live in dis white fella's world. Yous allas say you gonna help us do things black fella way but, in 1970 at da FCAATSI Conference, you bin turn aroun' an' vote against us like all da other white people. You reckon then dat we black fellas gotta lot to learn and now you still say we not learnin' fast enough to tell you what black fellas is all about. You gotta have white people and dese white people 'aven' bin near us 'cept now when day got big job with big white fella pay.

When you come up here we no get to talk to you. All you do is fly in aeroplane with all dem other white fellas and black fellas that we don' know. My people bin thinkin' 'bout dis other black fella down there that runnin' dis magazine all about us but you no bring 'im. 'Stead you bring all those white fellas. When we ask you 'bout dis black fella wid this magazine all about us, you say you got no room an' 'im gone walkabout. But you bring your sons and one of dem when 'im go back Melbourne, 'e laughs 'bout us black fellas' 'gripes and groans'. How you gonna change all those other white fellas down dere when you not able change own sons?

You say before you gett'm gubberment dat you gonna give us back da land. What you bin doin' since you gettum gubberment? All yous bin done is give da Gurindji what da last gubberment give dem. You no give us back da land you only tell us like those other white fellas in Parliament House before you dat we borrow the land.

You say you stop mining companies from takin' our land then why you no give it to us? Why you say we only borrow it? This mean when you want it back you come and take it. Then where we gonna go? You no better than all da others.

It because dem other Liberal–Country white fellas say we only borrow da land and not own it like we used to dat our fellas camp in front Parliament House in da first place. Now you say da same thing as those other fellas when they da boss so we think we gotta camp down your way again. You give some our people in Redfern in Sydney lot o' money for houses but they think dis only 'cause you want dem to forget 'bout us black fellas here in da bush. They think all dis money for houses still no good if we not gonna get back tribal land.

All you done since you bin made big fella boss number one is say we can have free lawyer, free dentist, and free pill. When we try to get lawyer they tells us dat we gotta ring you in Canberra but we got no money for dat. When we try to get dentist they tell us we not real Aboriginal. But when black woman gets sick they give her da pill whether she want it or not or they cut her with the knife so she no have any more black babies.

You bin talkin' 'bout dis for long time now you say black women havin' too many babies but you not bin doin' anything 'bout food for these babies—all you doin' is talkin'.

You tell us dat when you white fellas become boss dat we gonna be equal. You tell us dat some your tribe want to help us but some your tribe more equal than others. We bin tried to talk with these fellas for long time now but they not interested in us.

Before you fellas become boss of dis place last year you tell us Dr Cairns[1] him bin gonna make us equal like your other friends in the Labor Party but Dr Cairns never bin one to talk with us. You say yous all socialist and want us all equal but Dr Cairns just like all the rest of yous. Him still bullyman anyway.

Only few of you fellas bin showin' any interest in us. Dat Tom Uren[2] fellah him not bad bloke but dat Jimmy Keeffe[3]—him da fella. Dat Manfred Cross[4] fella 'im good bloke too. He pretty quiet but 'im don' go roun' talkin' 'bout what 'im bin doin' for us.

You not doin' anythin' yet. Anyone think you doin' us a favour when you talkin' 'bout us. You not doin' us any favours. When you start doin' somethin', you only payin' your rent.

1973

ROBERT ADAMSON
b. 1943

As described in his two autobiographical works, *Wards of the State: An autobiographical novella* (1992) and *Inside Out* (2004), Robert Adamson grew up in Sydney, but spent much time in the Hawkesbury River district, where he had family connections. After problems at school (and later when working as an apprentice pastry chef) Adamson spent time in institutions for juveniles and Maitland Prison, where he discovered poetry. After his release from prison, Adamson became editor of *Poetry Australia* in 1970, a significant publishing outlet for the New Australian Poetry. Adamson has been an important publisher, establishing Prism Books, Big Smoke Books (with Dorothy Hewett (qv)), and Paper Bark Press (with his wife Juno Gemes and Michael Wilding). *The Golden Bird: New and selected poems* (2008) is a thematic summary of Adamson's poetic career.

Since publishing his first poetry collection, *Canticles on the Skin* (1970), Adamson has received much critical acclaim and won numerous literary awards. His early poetry draws on his experiences in prison and on the Hawkesbury. While the latter remains important to his poetry, Adamson has demonstrated numerous styles and concerns. The eponymous poem in *The Rumour* (1971), a long self-reflexive sequence on the nature of poetry, is an early manifestation of Australian postmodernism. 'The Rumour' also set

---

1   Jim Cairns (1914–2003), left-wing activist and Labor politician during the 1960s and '70s.
2   Left-wing activist and Labor politician from the late 1950s until 1990 (b. 1921).
3   Queensland-based left-wing activist and Labor politician.
4   Labor member for the federal seat of Brisbane (1961–1975 and 1980–1990), member of FCAATSI and highly respected agitator for Aboriginal social justice.

the scene for a characteristic of Adamson's later works: the adumbration of homages and creative quarrels with his literary precedents, mentors and friends (which include Bob Dylan, the symbolists—especially Mallarmé—and the American poet Robert Duncan).

Adamson ranges from the ultra-Romanticism of *Cross the Border* (1977), to the minimalist realism of *Where I Come From* (1979), and the postmodernism of *Waving to Hart Crane* (1994). Romanticism, however, provides a kind of continuity. Despite the un-Romantic landscapes of *Where I Come From*, the emphases on place, origins and marginalised characters manifest a Romantic aesthetic. In *The Clean Dark* (1989) there is a post-Romantic emphasis on the relationship between subjectivity, creativity and sexuality. In *The Goldfinches of Baghdad* (2006) Adamson still haunts the Hawkesbury, employing myth and nature poetry to meditate on the links between art and suffering, poetry and the world. Along with J.S. Harry and Jennifer Maiden (qqv), he has found a way of talking about political problems (especially the so-called war on terror) that is both urgent and compellingly poetic. *DM*

Sonnets to be Written from Prison

For James Tulip

1

O to be 'in the news' again—now as fashion runs
everything would go for 'prison sonnets': I'd be on my own.
I could once more, go out with pale skin
from my veritable dank cell—the sufferer, poking fun
at myself in form, with a slightly twisted tone.   5
My stance, ironic—one-out, on the run.
Though how can I? I'm not locked up: imagine a typewriter
in solitary. I dream my police unable to surrender—
I'm bored with switching roles and playing
with my gender; the ironies seem incidental, growing thin.   10
Here's the world—maybe what's left of it—
held together by an almost experimental sonnet.
Surely there must be some way out of poetry other than
Mallarme's: still-life with bars and shitcan.

2

Once more, almost a joke—this most serious endeavour
is too intense: imagine a solitary typewriter? Somehow
fashion runs its course: I am not in pain—
So there's hardly need to play on abstract repetitions
to satisfy a predecessor, poet or lawbreaker: I won't be clever   5
all the clever crims are not inside the prisons.
Here's the world—maybe what's left of my pretences—
I dream of being carried off to court again:
a sufferer, where all my deities would speak in stern

almost sardonic voices. 'Your Honour, please—   10
bring me to my senses.' There, I love confessions—
imagine writing prison sonnets 4 years after my last release.
If only all my memories could be made taciturn
by inventing phrases like: imagine the solitary police.

3

Yes your Honour, I know this is ridiculous—although—
I'm 'in the news'. I couldn't bring myself to do
one of those *victimless crimes*: I must suffer in more ways
than one. My crime's prepense is not to overthrow
social order, or to protest—it's my plan   5
to bring poetry and lawbreaking into serious interplay.
Imagine newspapers in solitary. I would walk right through
the court taking down copy 'catch me if you can'—
Defendant in contempt. There has to be a fight,
I can't imagine anything, if I'm not up against a law.   10
Here's the world—our country's first stone institution—
where inmates still abase themselves each night.
If I was in solitary I could dream—a fashionable bore,
writing books on drugs, birds or revolution.

4

I dreamed I saw the morning editions settle on the court—
emblazoned with my name, my 'story' so glib it made
no sense. The judge said 'emotional' but I thought
of the notoriety. This was the outward world, and my sad tirade
was 'news'—Though if I'd been rhyming sonnets   5
in solitary, my suffering alone, could make them art.
Now, imagine an illiterate in prison—but I have no regrets
I enjoy my laggings. I feel sorry for the warders.
The discipline always pulls me through, and my counterpart,
the screw, is tougher with the easy boarders—   10
This experience might feel profound—though irony's never
broken laws—so I'm against everything
but practical intuitions. My 'solitary etc' is too clever
by half now—but then, who's suffering?

5

I brood in solitary, it's a way to flagellation: thinking
of my day of 'release'—I shuffle friends like dates
on my calendar, marking them off at random.

Here's the world—the stewed tea I'm drinking
cold—how I suffer. When I walk through the front gates   5
into the country, what will I become?
I'll throw away the sufferer's comforting mask,
and turn against my memories, leaving a trail of perdition
behind me. Children and women will fall to my simple
intuitive reactions—not even the New journalists will ask   10
questions, nothing will be capable of feeding on
my actions and survive. My prison sonnets will be drugs
relieving pain: I have remembered helpless men
knocking their bars for hours with aluminium mugs—

6

We will take it seriously as we open our morning paper.
Someone's broken loose, another child's been
wounded by pen-knives. A small fire down the bottom
of a suburban garden smells of flesh. Dark circles under
the mother's eyes appear on television, she's seen   5
her baby at the morgue. Our country moves closer to the world:
a negro's book is on the shelves. The criminal's become
mythologized. Though yesterday he curled
over and didn't make the news. So the myth continues, growing
fat and dangerous on a thousand impractical intuitions.   10
The bodies of old sharks hang on the butcher's hooks.
In broad day somewhere a prisoner is escaping.
The geriatrics are floating in their institutions.
The myth is torn apart and stashed away in books.
                                                        1974

My Granny

When my granny was dying
I'd go into her bedroom
and look at her

she'd tell me to get out of it
leave this foul river   5

it will wear you out too

she was very sick
and her red curly hair
was matted and smelt of gin

sometimes I sat there all day   10
listening to the races
and put bets on for her at the shop

and I sat there the afternoon
she died and heard her say her last words
I sat there not telling   15

maybe three hours
beside the first dead person I'd seen

I tried to drink some of her gin
it made me throw up on the bed
then I left her   20

she said the prawns will eat you
when you die on the Hawkesbury River

                                                                 1979

Songs for Juno

i

My lies are for you, take them utterly, along
with the truth we are explorers for.
An old skiff mutters, pushes up Hawkesbury mud—
the image comes in, drifts, sinks, disappears:
shape-changing gods, we dream in separate bodies;   5
a part of it, we want feathers for sails;
the rivers we dance stand upright in the sky,
distance between them—though at headlands
fork, touching mix, become ocean.

ii

Wind and the sails full in dreaming with you.
We talk of great deserts, old chalk cities,
ice language and its lava. Then imagination darts,
Tasmania appears filling our bedroom, sails
are wings of geese, homing ocean, white tricks   5
of the distance. How do we leave our tiny pasts?
My love, time fragments, blows into space—

we ride, fly, sail in every way we find there is
to now. Bring us a new language, to remake
these questions, into dream, the gale, I whisper   10
to you softly.

iii

How long in these secret places from childhood—
the old embers smoulder on, the lowlands
laced with fire-lines, long spokes turning
in sky—were we at play—or were the games more
half-remembered charms, songs? We inhabit,   5
are rocked by still those innocent passions.
Dressed up for the new ritual, we move
the circle more than dance it. Take the moment,
hold it to you, the new, my brave and frightened
lover is a sacramental kiss. Our dreams touch—   10
warm with light. Give me your nightmares too.

iv

Paint flaking from the belly of an old clinker.
The boys with their rods, prawns
and bloodworms rubbed through their hair,
tasting the westerly around Snake Island—
and you sleeping, curled around the stern.   5
The mountains everywhere, skirts of the mangroves,
then at Dangar's jetty, an octopus
sucking for its life at the end of a line.
Blue wrens hovering for invisible insects, a shag
hunched on a wing. The trim park   10
patched there amongst the scribbly gums,
houses, a wash-shed, and in a backyard
lemongrass drying in the sunlight.

v

The new list begins.

1989

The Greenshank

Miklós Radnóti,[1] marched from forced labour
in Yugoslavia back into Hungary, came to rest
near a bend in the Radca, at what his translator
describes as 'a strange lonely place' where

---

1   Miklós Radnóti (1909–44), a Hungarian poet killed in the Holocaust.

the tributary joins 'the great river', a marshland   5
watched over by willows and 'high circling birds'.
Condors perhaps—they appear in the notes and
poems he was writing—under a foamy sky.

Huddled in a trench with the body of a friend
who'd been shot in the neck, he wrote with a pencil   10
stub in his notebook: *patience flowers into death.*
His wife's face bloomed in his head.

Thinking of the petals of crushed flowers
floating in a wake of perfume, he wrote to caress her
neck. The fascists' bullets wiped out his patience.   15
His written petals survive.

Today, we listen to the news of war
here in a river sanctuary my wife's unbending
will has created—horizontal slats of cedar, verticals
of glass—a Mondrian chapel of light.   20

This afternoon just before dark the first
greenshank arrived from the Hebrides.
Ignorant of human borders, its migration
technology is simple: feathers

and fish-fuel, cryptic colour and homing   25
instinct. This elegant wader landed on a mooring,
got ruffled in the westerly, then took off again,
an acrobatic twister, and levelled down

onto a mudflat—a lone figure that dashed across
the shore, stood on one leg, then, conducting   30
its song with its bill, came forward
in a high-stepping dance.

                                                              2006

Thinking of Eurydice at Midnight

My Siamese cat's left a brown
snake, its back broken, on my desk.
The underground throbs outside my window.
The black highway of the river's crinkled by a light

westerly blowing down. I want to give praise   5
to the coming winter, but problems
of belief flare and buckle under
the lumpy syntax. The unelected
President's[1] on the radio again,
laying waste to the world.   10

Faith—that old lie. I drag up
impossible meanings and double divisions
of love and betrayal, light and dark.
Where on earth am I after all these years?
A possum eats crusts on the verandah,   15
standing up on its hind legs.
My weakness can't be measured.
My head contains thousands of images—
slimy mackerel splashing about in the murk.
My failures slip through fingers pointed   20
at the best night of my life. This one.

The cold mist falls, my head floats in a stream
of thinking. Eurydice. Did I fumble? Maybe
I was meant to be the moon's reflection
and sing darkness like the nightjar. Why   25
wouldn't I infest this place, where the
sun shines on settlers and their heirs
and these heirlooms I weave
from their blond silk?

2006

PETER CAREY
b 1943

Peter Carey was born in the Victorian town of Bacchus Marsh and educated at Geelong Grammar School. In 1961 he enrolled in a science degree at Monash University but after a serious car accident gave up study and went to work in an advertising agency. He left Australia in 1967 to travel in Europe.

He returned to Australia in 1970 and his first book, the short-story collection *The Fat Man in History*, was published in 1974. It was immediately apparent to critics that Carey was a major talent and that his work emphatically departed from the traditions of realism and rural focus that had dominated Australian short fiction until the 1960s. His

---

1 George W. Bush—'unelected' because in the 2000 election Bush received fewer popular votes than his rival, Al Gore. Bush won the election on electoral votes.

second collection of stories, *War Crimes*, was published in 1979; two years later his first novel, *Bliss* (1981), was a major commercial and critical success.

From the publication of his next novel *Illywhacker* in 1985 to *My Illegal Self* (2008), Carey published a major novel regularly every three years or so, with other, smaller projects in between. The lush and hallucinatory historical novel *Oscar and Lucinda* (1988) won Carey his second Miles Franklin Literary Award and his first Booker Prize. Films of *Bliss* (directed by Ray Lawrence) and *Oscar and Lucinda* (directed by Gillian Armstrong from a screenplay by Laura Jones) appeared in 1985 and 1997 respectively.

In 1989 Carey moved to New York, where he has lived ever since, teaching creative writing at several different universities. *Jack Maggs* (1997), a book in the 'empire writes back' mode, reimagines Dickens's *Great Expectations* from the point of view of the convict Magwitch, and features a character based on Dickens himself. In a speech at the University of Queensland when the novel was published, Carey said, 'Magwitch was my ancestor . . . I needed to write his story. I wanted to reinvent him.'

Like *Oscar and Lucinda*, Carey's *True History of the Kelly Gang* (2000) won both the Miles Franklin Literary Award—his fourth—and the Booker Prize, which he was only the second person, after J.M. Coetzee (qv), to win twice. *True History of the Kelly Gang* is an astonishing feat of ventriloquism, reimagining one of the great Australian icons, the bushranger Ned Kelly (qv).

My Life as a Fake (2003) takes another figure from Australian mythology, this time the apocryphal poet Ern Malley (qv) (a 1940s Australian literary hoax), as its subject and rewrites the story with Malley as a kind of Frankenstein's monster, an invented creature that takes on a life of its own and then turns on its creator. In this novel and its successor, *Theft: A love story* (2006), Carey has again reworked one of his favourite clusters of subject matter—the fraud, the hoax, the impersonation, the trick—and the relation of all these things to art.

Carey continues to write about, to reimagine and to reinvent his home country from the critical distance of New York. 'There is a basic thing which is just called home,' he said in a 2007 interview, 'which all of your musculature and everything in you feels when you get off an aeroplane and there's a certain sort of air, a certain sort of light.' *KG*

American Dreams

No one can, to this day, remember what it was we did to offend him. Dyer the butcher remembers a day when he gave him the wrong meat and another day when he served someone else first by mistake. Often when Dyer gets drunk he recalls this day and curses himself for his foolishness. But no one seriously believes that it was Dyer who offended him.

But one of us did something. We slighted him terribly in some way, this small meek man with the rimless glasses and neat suit who used to smile so nicely at us all. We thought, I suppose, he was a bit of a fool and sometimes he was so quiet and grey that we ignored him, forgetting he was there at all.

When I was a boy I often stole apples from the trees at his house up in Mason's Lane. He often saw me. No, that's not correct. Let me say I often sensed that he saw me. I sensed him peering out from behind the lace curtains of his house. And I was not the only one. Many of us came to take his apples, alone and in groups, and it is possible that he chose to exact payment for all these apples in his own peculiar way.

Yet I am sure it wasn't the apples.

What has happened is that we all, all eight hundred of us, have come to remember small transgressions against Mr Gleason who once lived amongst us.

My father, who has never borne malice against a single living creature, still believes that Gleason meant to do us well, that he loved the town more than any of us. My father says we have treated the town badly in our minds. We have used it, this little valley, as nothing more than a stopping place. Somewhere on the way to somewhere else. Even those of us who have been here many years have never taken the town seriously. Oh yes, the place is pretty. The hills are green and the woods thick. The stream is full of fish. But it is not where we would rather be.

For years we have watched the films at the Roxy and dreamed, if not of America, then at least of our capital city. For our own town, my father says, we have nothing but contempt. We have treated it badly, like a whore. We have cut down the giant shady trees in the main street to make doors for the school house and seats for the football pavilion. We have left big holes all over the countryside from which we have taken brown coal and given back nothing.

The commercial travellers who buy fish and chips at George the Greek's care for us more than we do, because we all have dreams of the big city, of wealth, of modern houses, of big motor cars: American Dreams, my father has called them.

Although my father ran a petrol station he was also an inventor. He sat in his office all day drawing strange pieces of equipment on the back of delivery dockets. Every spare piece of paper in the house was covered with these little drawings and my mother would always be very careful about throwing away any piece of paper no matter how small. She would look on both sides of any piece of paper very carefully and always preserved any that had so much as a pencil mark.

I think it was because of this that my father felt that he understood Gleason. He never said as much, but he inferred that he understood Gleason because he, too, was concerned with similar problems. My father was working on plans for a giant gravel crusher, but occasionally he would become distracted and become interested in something else.

There was, for instance, the time when Dyer the butcher bought a new bicycle with gears, and for a while my father talked of nothing else but the gears. Often I would see him across the road squatting down beside Dyer's bicycle as if he were talking to it.

We all rode bicycles because we didn't have the money for anything better. My father did have an old Chev truck, but he rarely used it and it occurs to me now that it might have had some mechanical problem that was impossible to solve, or perhaps it was just that he was saving it, not wishing to wear it out all at once. Normally, he went everywhere on his bicycle and, when I was younger, he carried me on the cross bar, both of us dismounting to trudge up the hills that led into and out of the main street. It was a common sight in our town to see people pushing bicycles. They were as much a burden as a means of transport.

Gleason also had his bicycle and every lunchtime he pushed and pedalled it home from the shire offices to his little weatherboard house out at Mason's Lane. It was a three-mile ride and people said that he went home for lunch because he was fussy and wouldn't eat either his wife's sandwiches or the hot meal available at Mrs Lessing's café.

But while Gleason pedalled and pushed his bicycle to and from the shire offices everything in our town proceeded as normal. It was only when he retired that things began to go wrong.

Because it was then that Mr Gleason started supervising the building of the wall around the two-acre plot up on Bald Hill. He paid too much for this land. He bought it from Johnny Weeks, who now, I am sure, believes the whole episode was his fault, firstly for cheating Gleason, secondly for selling him the land at all. But Gleason hired some Chinese and set to work to build his wall. It was then that we knew that we'd offended him. My father rode all the way out to Bald Hill and tried to talk Mr Gleason out of his wall. He said there was no need for us to build walls. That no one wished to spy on Mr Gleason or whatever he wished to do on Bald Hill. He said no one was in the least bit interested in Mr Gleason. Mr Gleason, neat in a new sportscoat, polished his glasses and smiled vaguely at his feet. Bicycling back, my father thought that he had gone too far. Of course we had an interest in Mr Gleason. He pedalled back and asked him to attend a dance that was to be held on the next Friday, but Mr Gleason said he didn't dance.

'Oh well,' my father said, 'any time, just drop over.'

Mr Gleason went back to supervising his family of Chinese labourers on his wall.

Bald Hill towered high above the town and from my father's small filling station you could sit and watch the wall going up. It was an interesting sight. I watched it for two years, while I waited for customers who rarely came. After school and on Saturdays I had all the time in the world to watch the agonizing progress of Mr Gleason's wall. It was as painful as a clock. Sometimes I could see the Chinese labourers running at a jog-trot carrying bricks on long wooden planks. The hill was bare, and on this bareness Mr Gleason was, for some reason, building a wall.

In the beginning people thought it peculiar that someone would build such a big wall on Bald Hill. The only thing to recommend Bald Hill was the view of the town, and Mr Gleason was building a wall that denied that view. The top soil was thin and bare clay showed through in places. Nothing would ever grow there. Everyone assumed that Gleason had simply gone mad and after the initial interest they accepted his madness as they accepted his wall and as they accepted Bald Hill itself.

Occasionally someone would pull in for petrol at my father's filling station and ask about the wall and my father would shrug and I would see, once more, the strangeness of it.

'A house?' the stranger would ask. 'Up on that hill?'

'No,' my father would say, 'chap named Gleason is building a wall.'

And the strangers would want to know why, and my father would shrug and look up at Bald Hill once more. 'Damned if I know,' he'd say.

Gleason still lived in his old house at Mason's Lane. It was a plain weatherboard house with a rose garden at the front, a vegetable garden down the side, and an orchard at the back.

At night we kids would sometimes ride out to Bald Hill on our bicycles. It was an agonizing, muscle-twitching ride, the worst part of which was a steep, unmade road up which we finally pushed our bikes, our lungs rasping in the night air. When we arrived we found nothing but walls. Once we broke down some of the brickwork and another time we threw stones at the tents where the Chinese labourers slept. Thus we expressed our frustration at this inexplicable thing.

The wall must have been finished on the day before my twelfth birthday. I remember going on a picnic birthday party up to Eleven Mile Creek and we lit a fire and cooked chops at a bend in the river from where it was possible to see the walls on Bald Hill. I remember standing with a hot chop in my hand and someone saying, 'Look, they're leaving!'

We stood on the creek bed and watched the Chinese labourers walking their bicycles slowly down the hill. Someone said they were going to build a chimney up at the mine at A1 and certainly there is a large brick chimney there now, so I suppose they built it.

When the word spread that the walls were finished most of the town went up to look. They walked around the four walls which were as interesting as any other brick walls. They stood in front of the big wooden gates and tried to peer through, but all they could see was a small blind wall that had obviously been constructed for this special purpose. The walls themselves were ten feet high and topped with broken glass and barbed wire. When it became obvious that we were not going to discover the contents of the enclosure, we all gave up and went home.

Mr Gleason had long since stopped coming into town. His wife came instead, wheeling a pram down from Mason's Lane to Main Street and filling it with groceries and meat (they never bought vegetables, they grew their own) and wheeling it back to Mason's Lane. Sometimes you would see her standing with the pram halfway up the Gell Street hill. Just standing there, catching her breath. No one asked her about the wall. They knew she wasn't responsible for the wall and they felt sorry for her, having to bear the burden of the pram and her husband's madness. Even when she began to visit Dixon's hardware and buy plaster of paris and tins of paint and water-proofing compound, no one asked her what these things were for. She had a way of averting her eyes that indicated her terror of questions. Old Dixon carried the plaster of paris and the tins of paint out to her pram for her and watched her push them away. 'Poor woman,' he said, 'poor bloody woman.'

From the filling station where I sat dreaming in the sun, or from the enclosed office where I gazed mournfully at the rain, I would see, occasionally, Gleason entering or leaving his walled compound, a tiny figure way up on Bald Hill. And I'd think 'Gleason', but not much more.

Occasionally strangers drove up there to see what was going on, often egged on by locals who told them it was a Chinese temple or some other silly thing. Once a group of Italians had a picnic outside the walls and took photographs of each other standing in front of the closed door. God knows what they thought it was.

But for five years between my twelfth and seventeenth birthdays there was nothing to interest me in Gleason's walls. Those years seem lost to me now and I can remember very little of them. I developed a crush on Susy Markin and followed her back from the swimming pool on my bicycle. I sat behind her in the pictures and wandered past her house. Then her parents moved to another town and I sat in the sun and waited for them to come back.

We became very keen on modernization. When coloured paints became available the whole town went berserk and brightly coloured houses blossomed overnight. But the paints were not of good quality and quickly faded and peeled, so that the town looked like a garden of dead flowers. Thinking of those years, the only real thing I recall is the soft hiss of bicycle tyres on the main street. When I think of it now it seems very peaceful, but I remember then that the sound induced in me a feeling of melancholy, a feeling somehow mixed with the early afternoons when the sun went down behind Bald Hill and the town felt as sad as an empty dance hall on a Sunday afternoon.

And then, during my seventeenth year, Mr Gleason died. We found out when we saw Mrs Gleason's pram parked out in front of Phonsey Joy's Funeral Parlour. It looked very sad, that pram, standing by itself in the windswept street. We came and looked at the pram and felt sad for Mrs Gleason. She hadn't had much of a life.

Phonsey Joy carried old Mr Gleason out to the cemetery by the Parwan Railway Station and Mrs Gleason rode behind in a taxi. People watched the old hearse go by and thought, 'Gleason', but not much else.

And then, less than a month after Gleason had been buried out at the lonely cemetery by the Parwan Railway Station, the Chinese labourers came back. We saw them push their bicycles up the hill. I stood with my father and Phonsey Joy and wondered what was going on.

And then I saw Mrs Gleason trudging up the hill. I nearly didn't recognize her, because she didn't have her pram. She carried a black umbrella and walked slowly up Bald Hill and it wasn't until she stopped for breath and leant forward that I recognized her.

'It's Mrs Gleason,' I said, 'with the Chinese.'

But it wasn't until the next morning that it became obvious what was happening. People lined the main street in the way they do for a big funeral but, instead of gazing towards the Grant Street corner, they all looked up at Bald Hill.

All that day and all the next people gathered to watch the destruction of the walls. They saw the Chinese labourers darting to and fro, but it wasn't until they knocked down a large section of the wall facing the town that we realized there really was something inside. It was impossible to see what it was, but there was something there. People stood and wondered and pointed out Mrs Gleason to each other as she went to and fro supervising the work.

And finally, in ones and twos, on bicycles and on foot, the whole town moved up to Bald Hill. Mr Dyer closed up his butcher shop and my father got out the old Chev truck and we finally arrived up at Bald Hill with twenty people on board. They crowded into the back tray and hung on to the running boards and my father grimly steered his way through the crowds of bicycles and parked just where the dirt track gets really steep. We trudged up this last steep track, never for a moment suspecting what we would find at the top.

It was very quiet up there. The Chinese labourers worked diligently, removing the third and fourth walls and cleaning the bricks which they stacked neatly in big piles. Mrs Gleason said nothing either. She stood in the only remaining corner of the walls and looked defiantly at the townspeople who stood open-mouthed where another corner had been.

And between us and Mrs Gleason was the most incredibly beautiful thing I had ever seen in my life. For one moment I didn't recognize it. I stood open-mouthed, and breathed the surprising beauty of it. And then I realized it was our town. The buildings were two feet high and they were a little rough but very correct. I saw Mr Dyer nudge my father and whisper that Gleason had got the faded 'U' in the BUTCHER sign of his shop.

I think at that moment everyone was overcome with a feeling of simple joy. I can't remember ever having felt so uplifted and happy. It was perhaps a childish emotion but I looked up at my father and saw a smile of such warmth spread across his face that I knew he felt just as I did. Later he told me that he thought Gleason had built the model of our town just for this moment, to let us see the beauty of our own town, to make us proud of ourselves and to stop the American Dreams we were so prone to. For the rest, my father said, was not Gleason's plan and he could not have foreseen the things that happened afterwards.

I have come to think that this view of my father's is a little sentimental and also, perhaps, insulting to Gleason. I personally believe that he knew everything that would happen. One day the proof of my theory may be discovered. Certainly there are in existence some personal papers, and I firmly believe that these papers will show that Gleason knew exactly what would happen.

We had been so overcome by the model of the town that we hadn't noticed what was the most remarkable thing of all. Not only had Gleason built the houses and the shops of our town, he had also peopled it. As we tip-toed into the town we suddenly found ourselves. 'Look,' I said to Mr Dyer, 'there you are.'

And there he was, standing in front of his shop in his apron. As I bent down to examine the tiny figure I was staggered by the look on its face. The modelling was crude, the paintwork was sloppy, and the face a little too white, but the expression was absolutely perfect: those pursed, quizzical lips and the eyebrows lifted high. It was Mr Dyer and no one else on earth.

And there beside Mr Dyer was my father, squatting on the footpath and gazing lovingly at Mr Dyer's bicycle's gears, his face marked with grease and hope.

And there was I, back at the filling station, leaning against a petrol pump in an American pose and talking to Brian Sparrow who was amusing me with his clownish antics.

Phonsey Joy standing beside his hearse. Mr Dixon sitting inside his hardware store. Everyone I knew was there in that tiny town. If they were not in the streets or in their backyards they were inside their houses, and it didn't take very long to discover that you could lift off the roofs and peer inside.

We tip-toed around the streets peeping into each other's windows, lifting off each other's roofs, admiring each other's gardens, and, while we did it, Mrs Gleason slipped, silently away down the hill towards Mason's Lane. She spoke to nobody and nobody spoke to her.

I confess that I was the one who took the roof from Cavanagh's house. So I was the one who found Mrs Cavanagh in bed with young Craigie Evans.

I stood there for a long time, hardly knowing what I was seeing. I stared at the pair of them for a long, long time. And when I finally knew what I was seeing I felt such an incredible mixture of jealousy and guilt and wonder that I didn't know what to do with the roof.

Eventually it was Phonsey Joy who took the roof from my hands and placed it carefully back on the house, much, I imagine, as he would have placed the lid on a coffin. By then other people had seen what I had seen and the word passed around very quickly.

And then we all stood around in little groups and regarded the model town with what could only have been fear. If Gleason knew about Mrs Cavanagh and Craigie Evans (and no one else had), what other things might he know? Those who hadn't seen themselves yet in the town began to look a little nervous and were unsure of whether to look for themselves or not. We gazed silently at the roofs and felt mistrustful and guilty.

We all walked down the hill then, very quietly, the way people walk away from a funeral, listening only to the crunch of the gravel under our feet while the women had trouble with their high-heeled shoes.

The next day a special meeting of the shire council passed a motion calling on Mrs Gleason to destroy the model town on the grounds that it contravened building regulations.

It is unfortunate that this order wasn't carried out before the city newspapers found out. Before another day had gone by the government had stepped in.

The model town and its model occupants were to be preserved. The minister for tourism came in a large black car and made a speech to us in the football pavilion. We sat on the high, tiered seats eating potato chips while he stood against the fence and talked to us. We couldn't hear him very well, but we heard enough. He called the model town a work of art and we stared at him grimly. He said it would be an invaluable tourist attraction. He said tourists would come from everywhere to see the model town. We would be famous. Our businesses would flourish. There would be work for guides and interpreters and caretakers and taxi drivers and people selling soft drinks and ice creams.

The Americans would come, he said. They would visit our town in buses and in cars and on the train. They would take photographs and bring wallets bulging with dollars. American dollars.

We looked at the minister mistrustfully, wondering if he knew about Mrs Cavanagh, and he must have seen the look because he said that certain controversial items would be removed, had already been removed. We shifted in our seats, like you do when a particularly tense part of a film has come to its climax, and then we relaxed and listened to what the minister had to say. And we all began, once more, to dream our American Dreams.

We saw our big smooth cars cruising through cities with bright lights. We entered expensive night clubs and danced till dawn. We made love to women like Kim Novak and men like Rock Hudson. We drank cocktails. We gazed lazily into refrigerators filled with food and prepared ourselves lavish midnight snacks which we ate while we watched huge television sets on which we would be able to see American movies free of charge and forever.

The minister, like someone from our American Dreams, re-entered his large black car and cruised slowly from our humble sportsground, and the newspaper men arrived and swarmed over the pavilion with their cameras and notebooks. They took photographs of us and photographs of the models up on Bald Hill. And the next day we were all over the newpapers. The photogaphs of the model people side by side with photographs of the real people. And our names and ages and what we did were all printed there in black and white.

They interviewed Mrs Gleason but she said nothing of interest. She said the model town had been her husband's hobby.

We all felt good now. It was very pleasant to have your photograph in the paper. And, once more, we changed our opinion of Gleason. The shire council held another meeting and named the dirt track up Bald Hill, 'Gleason Avenue'. Then we all went home and waited for the Americans we had been promised.

It didn't take long for them to come, although at the time it seemed an eternity, and we spent six long months doing nothing more with our lives than waiting for the Americans.

Well, they did come. And let me tell you how it has all worked out for us.

The Americans arrive every day in buses and cars and sometimes the younger ones come on the train. There is now a small airstrip out near the Parwan cemetery and they also arrive there, in small aeroplanes. Phonsey Joy drives them to the cemetery where they look at Gleason's grave and then up to Bald Hill and then down to the town. He is doing very well from it all. It is good to see someone doing well from it. Phonsey is becoming a big man in town and is on the shire council.

On Bald Hill there are half a dozen telescopes through which the Americans can spy on the town and reassure themselves that it is the same down there as it is on Bald Hill. Herb Gravney sells them ice creams and soft drinks and extra film for their cameras. He is another one who is doing well. He bought the whole model from Mrs Gleason and charges five American dollars admission. Herb is on the council now too. He's doing very well for himself. He sells them the film so they can take photographs of the houses and the model people and so they can come down to the town with their special maps and hunt out the real people.

To tell the truth most of us are pretty sick of the game. They come looking for my father and ask him to stare at the gears of Dyer's bicycle. I watch my father cross the street slowly, his head hung low. He doesn't greet the Americans any more. He doesn't ask them questions about colour television or Washington D.C. He kneels on the footpath in front of Dyer's bike. They stand around him. Often they remember the model incorrectly and try to get my father to pose in the wrong way. Originally he argued with them, but now he argues no more. He does what they ask. They push him this way and that and worry about the expression on his face which is no longer what it was.

Then I know they will come to find me. I am next on the map. I am very popular for some reason. They come in search of me and my petrol pump as they have done for four years now. I do not await them eagerly because I know, before they reach me, that they will be disappointed.

'But this is not the boy.'

'Yes,' says Phonsey, 'this is him alright.' And he gets me to show them my certificate.

They examine the certificate suspiciously, feeling the paper as if it might be a clever forgery. 'No,' they declare. (Americans are so confident.) 'No,' they shake their heads, 'this is not the real boy. The real boy is younger.'

'He's older now. He used to be younger.' Phonsey looks weary when he tells them. He can afford to look weary.

The Americans peer at my face closely. 'It's a different boy.'

But finally they get their cameras out. I stand sullenly and try to look amused as I did once. Gleason saw me looking amused but I can no longer remember how it felt. I was looking at Brian Sparrow. But Brian is also tired. He finds it difficult to do his clownish antics and to the Americans his little act isn't funny. They prefer the model. I watch him sadly, sorry that he must perform for such an unsympathetic audience.

The Americans pay one dollar for the right to take our photographs. Having paid the money they are worried about being cheated. They spend their time being disappointed and I spend my time feeling guilty that I have somehow let them down by growing older and sadder.

1974

From *True History of the Kelly Gang*
Parcel 1: His Life Until the Age of 12

I lost my own father at 12 yr. of age and know what it is to be raised on lies and silences my dear daughter you are presently too young to understand a word I write but this history is for you and will contain no single lie may I burn in Hell if I speak false.

God willing I shall live to see you read these words to witness your astonishment and see your dark eyes widen and your jaw drop when you finally comprehend the injustice we poor Irish suffered in this present age. How queer and foreign it must seem to you and all the coarse words and cruelty which I now relate are far away in ancient time.

Your grandfather were a quiet and secret man he had been ripped from his home in Tipperary and transported to the prisons of Van Diemen's Land I do not know what was done to him he never spoke of it. When they had finished with their tortures they set him free and he crossed the sea to the colony of Victoria. He were by this time 30 yr. of age red headed and freckled with his eyes always slitted against the sun. My da had sworn an oath to evermore avoid the attentions of the law so when he saw the streets of Melbourne was crawling with policemen worse than flies he walked 28 mi. to the township of Donnybrook and then or soon thereafter he seen my mother. Ellen Quinn were 18 yr. old she were dark haired and slender the prettiest figure on a horse he ever saw but your grandma was like a snare laid out by God for Red Kelly. She were a Quinn and the police would never leave the Quinns alone.

My 1st memory is of Mother breaking eggs into a bowl and crying that Jimmy Quinn my 15 yr. old uncle were arrested by the traps. I don't know where my daddy were that day nor my older sister Annie. I were 3 yr. old. While my mother cried I scraped the sweet yellow batter onto a spoon and ate it the roof were leaking above the camp oven each drop hissing as it hit.

My mother tipped the cake onto the muslin cloth and knotted it. Your Aunty Maggie were a baby so my mother wrapped her also then she carried both cake and baby out into the rain. I had no choice but follow up the hill how could I forget them puddles the colour of mustard the rain like needles in my eyes.

We arrived at the Beveridge Police Camp drenched to the bone and doubtless stank of poverty a strong odour about us like wet dogs and for this or other reasons we was excluded from the Sergeant's room. I remember sitting with my chilblained hands wedged beneath the door I could feel the lovely warmth of the fire on my fingertips. Yet when we was finally permitted entry all my attention were taken not by the blazing fire but by a huge red jowled creature the Englishman who sat behind the desk. I knew not his name only that he were the most powerful man I ever saw and he might destroy my mother if he so desired.

Approach says he as if he was an altar.

My mother approached and I hurried beside her. She told the Englishman she had baked a cake for his prisoner Quinn and would be most obliged to deliver it because her husband were absent and she had butter to churn and pigs to feed.

No cake shall go to the prisoner said the trap I could smell his foreign spicy smell he had a handlebar moustache and his scalp were shining through his hair.

Said he No cake shall go to the prisoner without me inspecting it 1st and he waved his big soft white hand thus indicating my mother should place her basket on his desk. He untied the muslin his fingernails so clean they looked like they was washed in lye and to this day I can see them livid instruments as they broke my mother's cake apart.

TIS NOT POVERTY I HATE THE MOST
NOR THE ETERNAL GROVELLING
BUT THE INSULTS WHICH GROW ON IT
WHICH NOT EVEN LEECHES CAN CURE

I will lay a quid that you have already been told the story of how your grandma won her case in court against Bill Frost and then led wild gallops up and down the main street of Benalla. You will know she were never a coward but on this occasion she understood she must hold her tongue and so she wrapped the warm crumbs in the cloth and walked out into the rain. I cried out to her but she did not hear so I followed her skirts across the muddy yard. At 1st I thought it an outhouse on whose door I found her hammering it come as a shock to realise my young uncle were locked inside. For the great offence of duffing a bullock with cancer of the eye he were interred in this earth floored slab hut which could not have measured more than 6 ft. × 6 ft. and here my mother were forced to kneel in the mud and push the broken cake under the door the gap v. narrow perhaps 2 in. not sufficient for the purpose.

She cried God help us Jimmy what did we ever do to them that they should torture us like this?

My mother never wept but weep she did and I rushed and clung to her and kissed her but still she could not feel that I were there. Tears poured down her handsome face as she forced the muddy mess of cake and muslin underneath the door.

She cried I would kill the b——ds if I were a man God help me. She used many rough expressions I will not write them here. It were eff this and ess that and she would blow their adjectival brains out.

These was frightening sentiments for a boy to hear his mamma speak but I did not know how set she were until 2 nights later when my father returned home and she said the exact same things again to him.

You don't know what you're talking about said he.

You are a coward she cried. I blocked my ears and buried my face into my floursack pillow but she would not give up and neither would my father turn against the law. I wish I had known my parents when they truly loved each other. [. . .]

2000

BARRY ANDREWS
1943–1987

Barry Andrews was a critic, scholar and co-founder of the Association for the Study of Australian Literature. At the time of his death he was senior lecturer in English at the Australian Defence Force Academy (ADFA). He edited, and wrote a study on, Price Warung (qv) and he co-edited (with William H. Wilde and Joy Hooton) *The Oxford Companion to Australian Literature* (1985/1994). The 'Barry Andrews Memorial Lecture' was inaugurated in 1988 at ADFA (later part of the University of NSW). 'Lap, Phar' comically parodies the style of the *ADB*, and other such works. *DM*

Lap, Phar

LAP, PHAR (1926–32), sporting personality, business associate of modest speculators and national hero, was born on 4 October, 1926, at Timaru, New Zealand, the second of eight children of Night Raid and his wife Entreaty, née Prayer Wheel. The family had military connections, including Carbine and Musket (qqv), although Raid himself had emigrated to Australia during the First World War.

A spindly, unattractive youth with chestnut hair, Lap was educated privately at Timaru until January, 1928, when he formed a liaison with the Sydney entertainment entrepreneur Harold Telford. With Telford, Lap moved to Sydney and established premises in the suburb of Randwick. A number of short term (distance) ventures were unsuccessful, although after James E. Pike (qv) commenced employment and Telford became a silent partner, the business flourished. A small, dapper man who dressed flamboyantly in multicoloured coats and hats, Pike's nervousness caused him to lose weight before each speculation with Lap; yet their affiliation lasted for over two years and proved beneficial to hundreds of Australian investors.

The most successful years were between 1930 and 1932, when the business expanded into Victoria, South Australia and Mexico. Pike and Lap received numerous awards for services to the entertainment industry, including an MC in 1930; they shared with Telford a gross taxable income of over 50,000 pounds. This income was substantially increased, however, by generous donations from several Sydney publishers, including Ken Ranger and Jack Waterhouse (qqv).

Early in 1930 Lap journeyed to North America to strengthen his interests there; Telford, who disliked travelling, and Pike, who had weighty problems to contend with, stayed behind. Tall and rangy, known affectionately as 'Bobby', 'The Red Terror' and occasionally as 'you mongrel', Lap died in mysterious circumstances in Atherton, California, on 5 April 1932, and was buried in California, Melbourne, Canberra and Wellington. A linguist as well as businessman, he popularised the phrase 'get stuffed!', although owing to an unfortunate accident in his youth he left no children.

I. Carter, *Phar Lap* (Melbourne, 1971), and for bibliog; information from J. O'Hara and T.H. Mouth; inspiration from anon. ADB contributors.

1977/2001

JOHN TRANTER
b. 1943

The poet John Tranter was born in Cooma, NSW. Since 1978 he has lived in Sydney, a locale which often inhabits his poems (as in 'Ode to Col Joye'). Tranter has travelled extensively, and lived in Singapore from 1971 to 1973, where he was the Asian editor for Angus & Robertson. He worked for ABC radio in the 1970s and '80s, and he has also been an editor, publisher and teacher of creative writing. He is married to the literary agent Lyn Tranter.

In addition to his own large body of innovative work, which has won numerous awards, Tranter was instrumental in defining the Generation of '68 poets in his anthology *The New Australian Poetry* (1979). In 1997 he established the free online journal of poetry and poetics, *Jacket*. Tranter's first collections are early expressions of Australian postmodernism in their move away from referentiality and the idea of the poet as a transcendent authority within the poems. *Red Movie* (1972), *Crying in Early Infancy* (1977) and *Dazed in the Ladies Lounge* (1979) use fragmentation, formalism and self-referentiality to brilliant stylistic effect. Tranter's recent work, found in *Studio Moon* (2003), shows that this earlier formalism is more broadly a profound interest in revisionism and intertextuality. Tranter's 'versions' (reworkings of poems too free to be called translations), 'terminals' (poems that use the terminal words of the lines of others' poems) and computer-generated poems produce startlingly original work using overtly revisionist techniques. 'After Hölderlin' (one of Tranter's versions) shows that such revisionism can produce strongly contemporary work. Despite the formal variety of Tranter's work, it illustrates a number of abiding concerns to do with childhood, nostalgia, popular culture, violence and memory. *DM*

At the Laundromat

FAMOUS POET JETS HOME TO USA!
How lucky to live in America, where
supermarkets stock up heavily on writers!
Thinking of the famous poets floating home
to that luxurious and splendid place   5
inhabited by living legends like an old movie
you blush with a sudden flush of Romanticism
and your false teeth chatter and shake loose!

How it spoils the magic! In America no writers
have false teeth, they are too beautiful!   10
Imagine meeting Duncan[1] in the laundromat—
in America it happens all the time—you say
Hi, Robert!—and your teeth fall out!
And you can't write a poem about that!

1977

Ode to Col Joye[2]

You open your eyes and realise
it's the morning of a summer's day in Sydney
and it's going to be—not a John Betjeman day,[3]
though you can hear church bells
    faintly across Annandale,   5
and not a John Forbes[4] day, though
the first thing you notice is your suntan lotion
on the dressing table beside a beach towel
decorated with a crude scene of coconut palms
    and a jet bomber   10
pencilling a faint vapour trail
    across the Malayan sky
          no,
not one of those days, and you think about
    the exact shape of your headache   15
and the taste of the first disprin of the day
and you wonder if it will be fine or cloudy
    and then
the hollow yet insistent sound of a Coke can
    rolling along the gutter   20
fills you in—
      it's a *Ken Bolton*[5] day!
          and,
as if to underline the accuracy of the hesitance
of your mental sketch of an approach   25
    to the definition of the day itself
a paperboy shouts something like
          New York!
    New York!

1   Robert Duncan (1919–88), American poet.
2   Col Joye (b. 1936), Australian popular singer and entrepreneur.
3   Popular English poet (1906–84) whose autobiography in verse is *Summoned by Bells* (1960).
4   John Forbes (qv).
5   Ken Bolton (qv).

(you're not sure . . . perhaps 'No Work?')   30
   and when you get up
wearing your shortie pyjamas
    you find a note on the kitchen table
      on a sheet of blue and white paper
to say that Bill and Kerry have gone to the beach,   35
   and after that
a lunch party at Anna's, hard-edge
   coloured cocktails!
to which *no one* will be invited! you
               gasp   40
as the water gushes
        cold out of the shower—
it's enough
    to be having a shower
        in the hot   45
blue summer morning in Sydney, an ambience
that no Melbourne poet will ever appreciate,
   and you almost
blame them for that! but 'blame' is very
   un-Sydney, so you   50
smile and finish your shower
having adjusted the warmth of the water
   thinking of Bondi Beach
and of the poets you know who will not be
    planning to go to Bondi today, after all,   55
     they never do, but
at least one of them will be planning to
   write a poem
about not going to Bondi!
       and it's perfect!   60
as perfect as a milkshake at the Bondi Pavilion
whipped at exactly the right degree of chill
   to get a froth up—a skill
that no Brisbane poet will ever
   comprehend—   65
     whoops!
       you slip in the shower
but regain your balance, and that too
   is a metaphor!
that no Canberra poet will ever endorse,   70
       and

in a leisurely and very Sydney way you write
with a soapy finger on the wall
   of the shower recess
an alternative version of Laurie Duggan's[1]   75
  'South Coast Haiku'
   a 'North Coast Haiku':

         The milk can
      falls off the back of the truck
    crushing the Bonsai Marijuana   80

   but you condemn it immediately
for being too
   political
     and the shower does the rest—
                 no,   85
it's not a Les Murray[2] day, though yesterday
Doug Anthony's[3] name was all over the news-stands
and you found a mysterious copy of *The Land*[4]
on your porch, bleached by sun and rain;
   and it's not a Bob Adamson[5] day,   90
    though last week a bank robber
ran amok and was shot to death just
five blocks away, under a windy Sydney sky
full of light and utterly lacking in remorse,
   as Melbourne skies are never   95
    lacking in remorse
and it's not a Poets' Union[6] day, though
last Sunday was full of bickering relatives and
   nothing much got done,
I guess that was a Poets' Union day,   100
   though it lacked a 'chair'
we have a 'chair' today and I'm
   sitting on it
     it's not
a Sandra Forbes[7] day, though the light is so   105

---

1   Laurie Duggan (qv).
2   Les Murray (qv).
3   John Douglas Anthony (b. 1929), a well-known politician of the conservative Country Party.
4   Australian rural newspaper, established 1911.
5   Robert Adamson (qv).
6   Formed in Melbourne in 1977.
7   Sydney-based arts administrator.

pretty as to be truly beautiful in a very 'Sydney'
        and 'cool' manner,
and yesterday I read a poem by Auden ending
        'I love America,
so friendly, and so rich!' and I thought   110
it must be a John Ashbery day, though 'John'
is hardly 'friendly', though perhaps
                                'rich'
and rather too 'American'
                        it's the kind of day   115
where I notice that my Renault—
        a beat-up Renault; how
                Sydney, and how French!—
has the name RENAULT on its side in chrome letters—
how metonymic   120
        that the name of the object is seen as
being part of the object to which it refers
it's a day for writing
        a self-referential line like this
and getting it done in time for a coffee   125
        and a Chesterfield filter cigarette
and watching the smoke-ring blur
        in front of the window
                like a circular argument
                        about Mannerist art   130
as confused as the smoke now
        dispersing from the window
revealing a view of—
                        yes, it's *Sydney*! and a
small figure in the lower left-hand corner   135
crudely sketched with a Faber 4-B pencil
        and labelled KEN BOLTON
is gazing through a window at the viewer—
        yes, *you*!
and from his sternly-thinking head issues a balloon   140
with the words
                it's a
                John Tranter day
not like last Monday, for example,
        which was serious and very   145
                Alan Gould,[1] or maybe Kevin Hart:[2]

1 Alan Gould (qv).
2 Kevin Hart (qv).

a stranger in the bus said severely
        'I ran into Wilson the other day
                in the Common Room,
and I gave him a piece of my mind!'   150
(in my pocket there's a postcard from Martin Duwell,[1]
a volcano rising from the sea near Reykjavik) 'I'm
        an Anglican,' the stranger says
and you notice the way the light gleams wetly
        from his glasses   155
'but I'm not your average gutless (. . .)
        (obscured by traffic noise)
'No!' he says loudly, 'I'm
                        committed!'
and his friend looks at him as though he were mad—   160
        the Anglican, not the friend, though
he looks a bit funny, too—maybe
        it was really a Don Chipp[2] day after all,
wherein morals, politics and literature
        commingle   165
like the ingredients of the hard-edge cocktail
that Ken is now drinking with an obviously
        'non-committal air', thinking
'Maybe it's a failed Rodney Hall[3] day,
        that the earnestness of the air   170
is inadequate to sustain . . .'
                        but it's not,
it's a day for writing something 'fresh'
        for *Surfers Paradise*[4]
and that makes it a Col Joye day; that,   175
        and the bright air
        glistening with poetry and the desire to please.

                                                                        1979

Country Veranda
(Dry Weather)

This country veranda's a box for storing the sky—
        slopes, acres of air
        bleached and adrift there.

---

1   Australian poetry critic, publisher and academic (b. 1948).
2   Don Chipp (1925–2006), Australian politician and inaugural leader of the Australian Democrats.
3   Rodney Hall (qv).
4   A small, very occasional literary magazine (edited by John Forbes (qv)) in which this poem first appeared.

From outside, a shade-filled stage, from inside
    a quiet cinema, empty   5
    but for the rustling view

where a parrot scribbles a crooked scrawl of crayon
    and off-stage a crow
    laments his loneliness

and six neat magpies, relaxed but quite soon   10
    off to a General Meeting
    stroll, chortle and yarn.

When the summer sun cracks the thermometer, laze
    there in a deck chair,
    shake out the paper   15

and relax with the local news: who won the cake
    in the Ambulance raffle;
    what the Council did

about the gravel concession down at the creek, who
    suffered a nasty fall   20
    but should be well in a week

(Rain)

From that open room where sheets hang out to dry—
    cool, wet pages
    whose verses evaporate—

you stare out at the trees semaphoring their sophistry: 25
    their tangled, pointless plots
    and obsessive paraphernalia,

drenched among the spacious palaces of vertical rain
    where no phone rings
    and neighbours are distant.   30

Behind that ridge of mist and blowing eucalypt tops
    the world waited once:
    exotic, inexhaustible.

You've been there now, and found that it's not much fun.
On the veranda, silence   35
fills the long afternoon.

1988

Having Completed My Fortieth Year[1]

Although art is, in the end, anonymous,
turning into history once it's left the body,
surely some gadget in the poet's head
    forces us to suffer

as we stumble through the psychology of it: 5
the accent betraying a class conflict
seen upside-down through a prism, the bad luck
    to be born in a lucky country—

yet in the end it is our fault, i.e. my fault
not to be born Frank O'Hara[2] and cursing   10
a whole culture for it—it's no excuse
    not to be run over at thirty,

to live on, turning out couplets
with the fecundity of a sausage machine
but without the cachet of the Imperial drawl,   15
    not even a cute lisp;

above all to miss out on drugs and Sodom
in the mindless mid-afternoon heat among
the nylon swimsuits and the beery surfers,
    a trial, not a vacation—   20

the girl around the corner gagging on whisky
in the schoolyard after dark, the boss
clocking off and weaving out the back door:
    'I'll be at the pub . . .'

well, at forty, the pieces lie about   25
waiting to be picked up and puzzled over
and fitted into a pattern, after a fashion,
    one I'm not fond of—

1   Cf Peter Porter's (qv) poem.
2   Frank O'Hara (1926–66), 'New York' school poet.

1064 | JOHN TRANTER

there are two sorts of people: those who say
with an owlish look 'There are two sorts of people',   30
and those who don't; then there are the writers
    who live on another planet,

their droppings bronzed like babies' booties
and we're glad to see things so transmogrified
though we suspect that life's not always rhymed   35
    quite as neatly as that,

and then there are those for whom every voyage
is an opportunity to lash the rowers,
the sun rising over something absolutely
    dreadful every day: 40

a people totally given to the cannibal virtues,
a set of laws designed to confuse and punish,
an art that shrinks experience into a box then
    hermetically seals the lid;

but squabbling over Modernism won't help,   45
England needs liberating but not by me,
she has concocted her own medications after all
    for marsh fever and the sinks,

so I'm stocking the fridge with Sydney Bitter,
checking the phone numbers of a few close friends   50
while the conservatives see to it that I conserve
    my sad and pallid art

and I'm hoping that the disk drive holds out
at least till the fag-end of the party
so my drunken guests may go on bopping till they   55
    drop into their mottoes

as I did some twenty years ago,
embarking on this yacht, this drudger's barge,
being 'absolutely modern' as my mentor taught[1]
    from the embers of his youth,   60

---

1   Arthur Rimbaud (1854–91), French poet, who wrote in his book of prose poems, *Une Saisin en Enfer
(A Season in Hell)* (1873), 'Il faut être absolument moderne'. (One must be absolutely modern.)

and hardly guessing then what would turn up:
these postcard views from a twinkling and distant
colony, of the twin cities: dying heart of Empire,
    sunset on the Empire State.

        1988

After Hölderlin[1]

a version of Hölderlin's 'When I Was a Boy'

When I was a young man, a drink
often rescued me from the factory floor
or the office routine. I dreamed
in the mottled shade in many a beer garden
among a kindness of bees and breezes,   5
my lunch hour lengthening.

As the flowers plucked and set in the little bottle
on the table still seem to hanker for the sun,
nodding in the slightest draft, so I
longed for a library loose with rare volumes   10
or a movie theatre's satisfying gloom
where a little moon followed the usherette
up and down the blue carpeted stairs.

You characters caught up in your emotions
on the screen, how I wish you could know   15
how much I loved you; how I longed
to comfort the distraught heroine
or share a beer with the lonely hero.

I knew your anxieties, trapped
in a story that wouldn't let you live;   20
I felt for you when you were thrown from the car
again and again; when the pilot
thought he was lost and alone,
I was speaking the language of the stars
above his tiny plane,   25

murmuring in the sleepy garden, growing up
among the complicated stories.
These dreams were my teachers

---

1   Friedrich Hölderlin (1770–1843), German poet.

and I learned the language of love
among the light and shadow   30
in the arms of the gods.

2003

BARRY HILL
b. 1943

Barry Hill was born in Melbourne and grew up in a politically active household in a working-class Melbourne suburb. He has worked as a teacher, journalist and psychologist.

Hill worked in London on the *Times Educational Supplement* before returning home to Melbourne in 1972 and becoming the founding education editor of the *Age*. He has been a full-time writer since 1975.

Already the author of a book on the Victorian education system called *The Schools* (1977), Hill published his first collection of short stories, *A Rim of Blue*, in 1978, followed by his first novel, *Near the Refinery* (1980), and a second collection of stories, *Headlocks and Other Stories*, in 1983. His literary output has been prodigious for several decades across a range of genres: he has won major awards for his fiction, poetry, radio drama, social history and local history. His epic, ground-breaking biography of anthropologist T.G.H. Strehlow, *Broken Song: T.G.H. Strehlow and Aboriginal possession* (2002), won five major national awards.

All of his work concerns itself, formally or informally, with politics and philosophy. There are recurrent themes of masculinity, sexuality, fatherhood, and the nature of the relationship between body and soul; his vision is at once internationalist and intensely localised. *KG*

Lizards

They were easy enough to find. You only had to lift a rock in the stone wall and there they were: or there was one at least—flat as a tack, an eye watching, legs in that dancing position, like a frog about to leap, except that lizards seldom leap, they dart, sliding off and out and under. You have to be really quick; I had no trouble catching half a dozen in a Saturday afternoon.

Most of the kids chucked them away before we got home; or they let them go on the spot, since catching lizards wasn't much compared to catching snakes, which we were also after, moving around the stone walls as far as the coal dump, then out behind it onto the swampy part of the flats. Our house, in those days, was on the edge of the flats. I kept lizards because I liked them; I was not that keen on the big ones that reminded you of goannas, their pale bellies pulsing and swollen as if they'd been drinking too much beer as they lay in the sun, but the slim quick ones as long as your finger, I tucked into my pocket, or carried home in a brown paper bag. They seemed quite happy travelling there, in the folds of things, and when I showed them to mum and dad I had that nice feeling which comes from being proprietorial and kind.

I especially liked taking them into our front room when people were there. On Saturdays dad was usually talking with his union mates and members of the party. They were big blokes mostly (or they seemed to be at the time)—boilermakers, blacksmiths, welders, filling up our armchairs. They could talk those men, and to listen to some of them there you might have thought they were standing on boxes in the back yard: but when I came in with the lizards they went quiet, and grinned, and asked if they could have a look.

I held up my favourite. The best way to hold a lizard is just below the skull, towards the back of its head rather than low down near the throat. When you're not squeezing its gizzard it can look at its audience quite comfortably.

Give it a run, someone said, as if he was unhappy with the idea of anything being held in captivity.

No, I'd say, it's not ready yet. What I meant was that it would run under his chair and try to get into the fringe of the mat. It would be hard to get out again, and mum would go crook.

Let's have a go, he said, reaching towards the lizard.

I backed off a bit. I don't want it to drop a tail, I explained.

Fair enough, mate.

They were all pretty pleased with this and went on talking. I could hear mum in the kitchen, coughing, and moving about getting the cups and saucers. I sat down on the floor, slipping the lizard up under my collar. I felt it wriggle to the back of my neck, and settle down to doze, apparently soothed by the growling tones of the conversation.

There was a war on, I knew that much. The newsagent was selling a beaut new comic called 'Marines', and one copy my dad had held up to his mates, saying, 'propaganda'. They had shaken their heads and the comic was passed back to me. I remember reading it in a fresh light then; I could see that the Yanks couldn't be as good as all that, even though the drawings were the best I'd seen. Yet each week the comic seemed to have more rather than less pages for the same price.

I listened to them talk about the war, and I heard them speculate on the possibilities of the General getting permission to drop the bomb. There were no comics, as yet, about the bomb; or, if it came to that, about the banning of the party. As I understood it, the Government wanted to lock up people like my dad and his mates, and if they didn't watch out it would happen soon, while no one else gave a damn.

Most people don't care, one way or the other, someone said. Capitalism has it in the bag.

Oh yes they do, it's a matter of people being brought into the picture, becoming part of the struggle.

Let's hope so, I heard my father say, as the tea was served.

As much as a boy of that age could, I worried too. A disciple, I entered into their disgruntlements, and the tension and determination that went into their conversation made me feel satisfied rather than unhappy; it gave me a sense of self-assurance, as if an important part of me could afford to stretch out and be comfortable against the body of their opinion. Even today, I think that I owe a good deal of myself to the strength and warmth that inhabited the room, though the odd thing was that there was an undercurrent to their conversation which made me think of crabs rather than lizards.

The crabs we used to hunt at the back beach. We tied cat's meat to a length of string and when the tide was out fished the crabs out from beneath the rock ledges. As soon as a claw took hold of the meat you pulled it up, flicking the crab onto the dry rock. Then with the knife you stabbed the crab through the back; there was an explosion of sea water and flesh, and the crab was grounded. Some of us had spears—bamboo with scrap metal as tips, which we used as well, crushing through the shells as near to dead centre as possible, swearing and screaming at the crab as we did.

It was interesting the way we carried on like that. I remember using words that I was not going to use freely again until I'd grown up, but somehow, leaping and dancing about the broken shells, it seemed the right thing to do, a way of making up for the creatures being so well defended, and otherwise so inaccessible. Since so much that worried my dad and his mates was invisible and intractable, I suppose I felt that some purpose might be served by yelling a lot, and tearing into things, though at the time, I was incapable of making this connection clear to myself, or to anybody else.

In any case I had come to prefer lizards. I liked their silkiness, their liquid movements and their apparent adaptability, and I had been pleased to leave the crabs rotting in the sun, despite the fact that if I'd brought them home alive dad would have cooked them in a pot and eaten them as a treat—as chicken was then a treat, and pork. Lamb was not a treat as we had it hot every Sunday and for the following two nights ate it cold with plenty of pickles. The point is, I didn't care for delicacies so much as keeping things that seemed to invite a secure alternative to what they had known, and which seemed able to survive in the conditions I was able to provide myself.

The box I built for the lizards was about three feet long with wire netting on top. Beneath the wire were rocks, weeds, sand, clay soil—an attractive and varied landscape, with a lake as its centre. This was the top of a jam jar filled with water from the gully trap. From the army of ants at the base of the gully trap it was a simple matter to ambush provisions for the lizards; flies were harder to get, but you could raid the cobwebs in the back of the tool shed. All food was placed into the nooks and crannies

of the lizard's garden, and for ages it puzzled me as to why they seemed to
have very little appetite.

At school, my lizard for the day was transferred from pocket or collar to
another box: the pencil case which sat on the edge of my desk. It seemed
happy enough in there. Occasionally, when we were not flat out putting our
hands up to answer questions, I gave it a run on top. It would make a dart
for the aisle and was checked with a ruler when it dipped its tongue into the
inkwell, I would, for its own good pull it back then before it got too frisky,
I put it back in the case—though never, never, before showing it to Mary,
the girl who sat right in front of me.

Mary had long blonde hair that hung down her back as far as my pencil
case, and when I chose to fiddle about in that area the tips of her hair
touched my knuckles.

Look, I'd say. She was the first girl I ever wanted to show anything to.

I can see, she replied. She was not frightened. I was not trying to scare
her as some kids would.

Does it have a name?

Nup.

It looks sick, she said.

It did too, now that she came to mention it. At recess time I let it run
along the wet bottom of the tap troughs. Afterwards I gave her another
look.

You're torturing it, she said. The comment hurt me deeply, and made
me realize, much later, how much I'd been in love with her. She had
given me my first experience of hopes dashed. At the time it struck me
that the word torture was vicious and unjust, entirely unsuited to my best
intentions, and I had as much trouble getting to grips with it as my dad
and his mates were having with terms like purge, and slave labour camp. It
was a word that I found impossible to accept, until, one by one, my lizards
began to die. I'd open the garden box, lift a stone, and there another would
be—dead, and wizened looking. I imported new batches but they went as
well. Then Stalin died too, and I could see that my dad was having to do
a lot of thinking about that. My box had become pungent and rank, as if
disappointment, or folly, had developed a special smell of its own. Mum
helped me clean the box out: in the end I gave lizards away, and threw myself
into that enterprising schoolground sport of marbles.

We give up one thing, we take up another, something is cleared away,
something else takes its place: life seems to be like that. In the years I was
going through school, from primary school into high school, moving past
the Merit Certificate that had been the stopping post for my father and his
mates, the stone walls out on the flats were being taken down, thistles cleared
away, the swamps drained and cranes and wild duck driven off. Lizards and

snakes moved west as the great paddocks were bought up and sold for factory allotments. One day a leaflet appeared in our letter box saying that the sky at night would take on an orange glow: we were not to be alarmed at this, the leaflet said, as the new cloud was harmless. A refinery was to be built, and a refinery had to burn off its waste.

The construction of the refinery was followed by a plant to produce carbon black: then another which turned out polyethylene and styrene; and another which extracted chemicals from the by-products of its neighbours. A petrochemical complex as big as any in the world had grown up, the affairs of which were directed from boardrooms as far as Kansas City and London, places I had read about in books. There was something remote and grand about the gleaming assembly of pipes and tanks that roared and hissed all day and all night, ejecting their flames, invisible heat, and unnameable gases into the sky.

The landscape was becoming, now I think of it, more political, but the strange thing was that in so many other ways our life was not. Over many weekends dad spent his time building a garage to house and protect our first car. We already had a refrigerator, and mum had enough money left out of housekeeping to layby a washing machine. In the old days, when I left my towel at the beach, I got into trouble: there were now plenty of towels to go round which meant that, my anxiety lowered, I seldom left a towel or anything else behind. In fact in most respects this was an orderly, forward-looking period, where talk about the days when people had to battle for a decent living, while it was interesting in a way (and was written up in some of our history books), was not the sort of information you needed to base a decision on. We were eating chicken once a week, I was getting on well at school and mum and dad were going to keep me there until I had gone as far as I could go—so while none of these things were planned, they kept happening, they evolved, enemy or no enemy.

Oh, there *was* an enemy all right, I still felt that. At school I spent a lot of time defending, or being seen to defend, moves to oust the agents provocateurs in Hungary, the liberation of Tibet from feudalism, and the assaults from all fronts upon our unions, the unions which some of dad's mates were now working for full time, having responded to suggestions that organization at levels other than the shop floor was necessary. The enemy was the mis-representer of the truths I had carried within me for so long, and I saw no reason why people should get away with mutilating them. I was an energetic protagonist, sometimes lying low and making quick, attacking runs on an argument; sometimes using crab hunting strategies. These habits I carried from school to university, through election campaigns and into the movement against the next war in Asia, the war that never ceased to remind me of the one dad and his mates had worried about when I was a boy. Now we—two or three generations—were in a united opposition, we had revived the old warmth and strength and there was no questioning the worth of any of us. The war carried on, as did we, opposing it, and the battle, from my point of view, was desperate and exhilarating. At the same time the experience was profoundly and unexpectedly tedious, as if I had found myself marching backwards, wearing someone else's heavy trousers.

Social being determines consciousness. But consciousness, I had also come to feel, is made by one's willingness to shed one's social being. I had become a teacher. I was already paid to stand and talk. Now I would go off to London, to live. There I found that I enjoyed the sound of people talking differently. I must say that at the time I thought much of this talk, in its fluency and ease, in its poise and assurance, in its gracious assumption that if an enemy was to be identified it was hardly worth mentioning, was in many ways preferable to my own, and that it was worth emulating. The feeling I had then was akin to one I'd had in the school playground, soon after becoming adept at marbles. Most of us remember the feeling surely? The kids have suggested that you join a team, play as a group, the better to knock the dickens out of the big kids. But you decline; you hold out—no you'll keep playing alone. You squat at the end of the ring with your taw at the ready. It's a hot day and the northerly scorches the back of your neck. You take a shot—a good one: you take another, which earns you the next. On you go, and before you know it you've cleaned up the ring, your pockets are full of glass eyes and though the others are watching, you can't help strutting: you just have to walk off and sit down in the shade and count the proceeds.

From London I wrote regularly to my parents. They were proud of my achievements: a post-graduate degree and then a research job with the BBC. Had I gone over to the other side? Hardly: my letters conveyed a radical critique of the circles I was moving in, mixed with acerbic remarks about the defensiveness of dad's union, and the lame political inheritance at home. Communiqués are neat cocktails, and I was becoming a pretty smooth operation. In the absence of—what, an alternative?—I was going as far as I could go. And the journey was unquestionably an achievement, a mark of my freedom, which in turn, was as concrete a measure of accomplishment as marbles filling your hip pocket, marbles that one could not help but take out one at a time to hold up against the light, inspecting each for flaws. For brief periods it is sometimes possible to fully possess things without being troubled by the hollowness of winning.

St Augustine refers somewhere to a *ventosa professio*, a puffed-up profession, and to *ventosa tempora*, a puffed-up existence, which indicates that Communism is not the only faith which is intolerant of egoisms. My melancholia was probably in search of a religious house to inhabit, but I had little time for a credo that made a sin of disobedience and knowing.

Nor did I like the idea that all worldliness was empty, as if the devil, or the self as the devil in thin disguise, had put a straw up my bum and blown me up like a frog. When I saw kids do that at school I ripped their straws into pieces, and pushed them about. Besides, I knew, deep down, that I had not really changed and was, for better or worse, the same person I'd been years before. I knew this most clearly late in the evenings at London dinner tables, when conversation turned to questions of class (which I liked to pronounce as in 'mass') and power. Then out of the dark, drunken vacuity of self, out of the rage that lusts for its own form, there was no more pretending, and the buggers had to sit back and listen. I made them suffer, they copped it, they were left sitting there, and hours later when I returned to my place, I discovered that I was in myself positively happy.

We come home in order to be real again, and when I decided to come back, after five years away, my mother was ill, and the nation on the eve of an election. For the first time in the history of my generation there might be a change of Government. There was: a Labor Government took office; there was a bubble of optimism and reform and then it burst—pricked by the tip of an enemy weapon. We caught a glimpse of the steel, then it had gone again. There were protests, but life gradually slipped back to normal. People drove about in their station wagons, pulling their trailers and boats; they pushed lawnmowers, hedge clippers, car washers: they buzzed at the end of hair dryers, fruit mixers, electric toothbrushes and dish washers, while his union, my father told me, was worrying the issue as to whether the order for their next fleet of cars should go to the established American firm or to the Japanese company about to open a new plant near our petro-chemical complex. I should have known from this perhaps, that my seeing his mates again was going to be as painful as anything I had known.

I met them one at a time, mostly, through the period my mother was convalescing from one of her lung infections. They had dropped in to see dad, and I was sometimes sitting on the end of mum's bed. Hi, hello Jack. Ah, they'd say, how are you going? Terrific thanks. We shook hands, letting go after the standard indications of strength. I asked about the union, the latest campaign. They inquired about my job, and whether I had further plans to travel. We swapped comment on recent Government bastardries. Then, that was it.

We had nothing more to say to each other. They went back into the front room to talk with dad, leaving me with mum. While trying to talk with her my mind ran back through the conversation: maybe I had been a bit sharp, a bit glib, rather brittle; there was still the overlay, perhaps, of the old London—'his master's'—voice. It occurred to me that it might serve a reconciling purpose to pick myself up and join them in the front room, claiming one of the chairs that they had occupied for so long. But I dismissed the idea as I did not wish to leave my mother alone, and in any case I realized that my presence would cramp their style: I'd read too many books, done too much, in going as far as I could, had gone too far. It would be stupid to say that they disliked me personally. But to most of them I was the lizard that had dropped its tail.

The idea of telling them about complex feelings at dinner tables was too silly for words: saying what brought me back would have been exhibitionist. Then of course there was an obvious fact; they were remembering me most clearly as a small boy, with my future before me, a future they would not have presumed, in our era of opportunity, to confine. In many ways then my need for some comradely recognition must surely be an expression of egoism. This is one truth I am trying to face, just as I'm trying to live with the steady decline of my mother.

She has been going down for a number of years. Her lungs, her heart, the circulation of her blood, are cracking up. Most of all her lungs are failing her, and it is all she can do, some days, to prepare a meal. The most ego-less person I know, self-denying to a fault, has difficulty walking from the oven to the kitchen table, and when she gets as far as the garden she inhales, as best she can, the air of our neighbourhood: with what she has working of the wretched sacks in her chest, she takes in the output from our petrochemical complex.

Her throat and neck have become swollen from the exertion of breathing. Her face is ruddy, blotched and puffy, and even describing her like this makes me wince on her behalf, for her despair at the disintegration of her looks. She would prefer to have no face at all. Already she has known degrees of self-loathing that would send most men to their graves in a month. Yet there is nothing direct, is there, that the men, my dad and his mates, I—can do? We live where we live. It must be conceded that the drugs which have helped wreck my mother's appearance have also given her great relief, and that no doubt many of them have their origins in some of the plants nearby. You have to retain a degree of rationality about such matters.

Going away, then coming back, makes any steady change, or no change, much more conspicuous, and the other thing I struggle to be rational about is the fact that I have seldom, as an adult, found it easy to talk with my mother. She remembers my lizards all right, but I have spent so much time, over the years, in a spoken or silent dialogue with my dad and his mates, a dialogue that she has removed herself from or was in other ways discouraged from joining, that I find it difficult to get a bearing on her being.

There are long silences between us: one of us seems always to be waiting for my father to come in. I fear that I lack generosity. As I sit with her I often think of Brecht's song about his mother. *Oh, why do we not say the important things, it would be so easy, and we are damned because we do not,* and at night when I leave to go home, I drive out and around the complex, circling and circling.

1983

PHILIP McLAREN
b. 1943

Philip McLaren's family comes from the Warrumbungle Mountains area, NSW, and he is a descendant of the Kamilaroi people. He has worked as a television producer, director, designer, illustrator, architect, sculptor, lifeguard and copywriter. He has been a creative director in television, advertising and film production companies, both in Australia and overseas. After this varied career, McLaren focused on writing and was one of the first Aboriginal authors to publish in the crime-writing genre. His books include *Sweet Water ... Stolen Land* (1993), *Scream Black Murder* (1995), *Lightning Mine* (1999) and *There'll Be New Dreams* (2001). *AH/PM*

From *Sweet Water ... Stolen Land*
Chapter 1

The raw, tumultuous outback lay open.

The horse sensed the storm ahead. His nostrils flared and he tossed his head as he sniffed the wind. There was a sudden drop in temperature—it had been a very warm day. Red dust was carried high on the wind as it swirled, gaining in velocity as it moved south across the open plains. Dark clouds rolled over the spectacular Warrumbungle Mountains towards Gudrun and Karl Maresch as they rounded a bend and headed directly into the strong wind. The rain came soon after. The wind drove the cool rain onto the faces of the newcomers. Huge icy raindrops that usually preceded hail fell in walls of water, soaking deep into the dry red loam.

Karl steered the horse and sulky off the wide stock trail to shelter behind an outcrop of sandstone boulders. He took an oilskin sheet from under the seat and pulled it over them both in a makeshift tent as they moved to sit on the floor of the buggy.

Lightning flashed all around. A mighty thunderclap directly overhead caused Gudrun to tense her grip on Karl's arm. He was of true stoic German character. He knew Gudrun feared electrical storms yet he could not find it in himself to comfort her.

They had been to Gunnedah. It was an unusual trip for them to make because the Coonabarabran township was much closer. But Karl had decided they should see Gunnedah in the summer. It was 1869, an exciting time in Australia. The newly settled land declared its challenge to the adventurous.

Coonabarabran, along with almost every plains community in Australia, had already planned its future based on agriculture: wool, wheat and cash crops for the tables of Europe. A certain Lewis Gordon first proposed a town plan survey for Coonabarabran in 1859 although the area had been opened up by a Government sponsored expedition in 1817.

'The storm's moving quickly,' Karl said quietly in German. 'It will blow over soon.' He was wrong; the lightning became more frequent, the rain heavier.

Gudrun was often bemused by the fact that she now lived in Australia. She had never seriously considered living abroad, although when she was in her early teens occasionally she thought it might be exciting to live in London for a time—she spoke English very well. Then she met Karl Maresch and was totally swept off her feet. He was so confident. He had strong, unwavering opinions about the world that he couched in well developed philosophical and theological argument. To a young woman growing up on a farm on the outskirts of Munich, he was every inch the intellectual. He had read the lesson frequently at her church and took charge of a Bible class that she attended during the week. She had always admired him, even when she was a little girl. Gudrun was nineteen and Karl thirty-five when they married four years ago. The simple ceremony was conducted by his father, also a Lutheran pastor, in the tiny church at Grafing, south of Munich.

Lightning flashed and thunder followed immediately. Now the storm's centre was directly overhead. In another bright flash Gudrun suddenly saw an Aboriginal family sitting opposite them. They were huddled together, sheltering under an overhanging rock about thirty yards away across a small clearing.

The Aboriginal family—a man, his wife and two children—were looking at the white-skinned Europeans under their makeshift shelter on the horse buggy.

Ginny and Wollumbuy were married under Aboriginal law. Both their families still followed the old ways. At first it was said they could not marry, but later a way was found so that they could conform to complicated kinship laws. Wollumbuy first saw Ginny when he came to visit her clan several summers ago at Gunnedah, where she was born and raised. His own large family had walked more than one hundred and fifty miles over the mountains from their camp on the coast near the newly-built town of Coffs Harbour. It was a very long walk of the kind families used to make. Wollumbuy sang Ginny his love songs and she heard them in her sleep. He danced a magic, erotic love dance for her around the campfire and she awoke feeling stirred and excited. Their two children came quickly, answering the hope and tradition of Kamilaroi marriages.

Now Ginny took her youngest to her breast. He needed comfort from the storm. The wind blew in on them and Wollumbuy grimaced as another thunderclap shattered the air. He grabbed at the stone talisman Ginny's mother had made for him as a wedding gift which he always had hanging from his belt. He held it firmly.

They had come from Gunnedah to set up camp at the foot of Old Belougerie, a massive sacred rock spire that rose vertically from the foot of the mountains, towering high above the well-treed peaks. His people knew that the good spirits protected all people living within sight of the rock so that they lived long and happy lives.

Ginny suspected that some day Wollumbuy would want to take her back to his father's country, to stay at his home at Moonee beach camp. She thought it would be exciting to live near Belougerie, even for a short while. Large Aboriginal camps were seen less now than ever before. The Kamilaroi people had been forced off their ancestral lands onto hastily established missions. The whites were building fences everywhere. They had no regard for wild life, no understanding or feeling for the land. All hunting would soon be ruined. They had already cleared far too many plants and trees. Her three favourite bunyah-bunyah nut trees were destroyed last year to make way for more grazing land for sheep and other animals whose cloven hooves destroyed the delicate topsoil and laid bare the earth.

White people actually wanted to *own* the land! She wondered secretly if some day they would claim ownership of the sky, the stars, the clouds, the rain, the rivers and the ocean. She suspected that if they could find a way to do it, they would.

'There, I think it's stopped,' Karl said, almost in a whisper. The rain had eased but it certainly had not stopped. As he pulled the oilskin back, small pools of water that had collected on it ran down his arms under the sleeves of his jacket. He cursed, wiped the water away and took up the reins. He called to the horse as he sat upright on the leather upholstered seat. They were on their way again. The Neuberg Lutheran mission was only a couple of hours away. It was thirty miles from Coonabarabran and fifty-five miles from Gunnedah, built at the foot of Baraba Mountain on the eastern side of the Warrumbungle Range. Lutherans made ideal missionaries. They were well received by almost all international governments because of their basic belief that the State ought to be above the church.

Ninety years ago, Australia was built by convict labour. The government of Mother England transported convicts to aid the colonisation of the large South Land. The number of convicts needed for the planned settlements seemed to override more important criteria for transportation, such as skills, age or marital status. Fleets of convict slaves sailed south. The wretched human cargo knew little about the colonies, except for terrifying rumours of black savages and strange animals that aided Satan's work in a new-fashioned hell.

The Australian Government was still benefitting from the gold rush of the previous decade, which brought with it a huge influx of free immigrants. Whole towns sprang up overnight as the plains west of Sydney offered up their riches. Now plans of bigger proportions were being hatched; anything seemed possible. But the problem that always caused delay was the scarcity of labour. Back in England, the idea that transportation was a beneficial and morally sound way to rehabilitate prisoners had nowadays to be demonstrated to the government.

The colony of South Australia was founded in 1834 by free settlers. They were wealthy Nonconformists dissatisfied with government rule in England; they banded together to form the South Australian Colonisation Committee. One of its members, George Fife Angas, emigrated to South Australia in 1848. He put forward his high-flown reasons for a new settlement:

My great object was in the first instance to provide a place of refuge for pious Dissenters of Great Britain who could in their new home discharge their consciences before God in civil and religious duties without any disabilities. Then to provide a place where the children of pious farmers might have farms in which to settle and provide bread for their families; and lastly that I may be the humble instrument of laying the foundation of a good system of education and religious instruction for the poorer settlers.

Angas advanced the princely sum of eight thousand pounds to entice persecuted Prussian Lutherans into establishing missions to 'enable Aborigines to come to where they might worship God and at the same time bind them to the missions as tenant farmers for a mandatory thirty years'. As well as destroying large segments of Aboriginal culture for ever, Angas had put in place his perfectly legal method of solving the rising costs of labour: the enslavement of Australia's Aboriginal people. Yet slavery was something he had publicly opposed forty years earlier in England. Obviously, when it came to his private business dealings a different set of principles applied.

Filled with righteousness and armed with faith, the Lutherans ventured to outback Australia to convert the Aboriginal people—to tell them, with absolute conviction, that forty thousand years of Aboriginal Dreaming was wrong. They passed on the word of the Lord and set about redeeming the heathen Australians through education, Christian principles and ethics, and tenant farming.

1993

WILLIAM YANG
b 1943

Born in North Queensland in 1943, William Young—whose grandparents had migrated from southern China to northern Australia in the 1880s—changed his name to William Yang in 1983. He studied architecture at the University of Queensland, then worked as a playwright from 1969 to 1974 before embarking on a career as a freelance photographer. *Sydney Diary* (1984) documents his photographic exhibition of the same name, frankly depicting the city's gay scene. As Yang began to explore his Chinese heritage he also integrated his skills as writer and visual artist, performing monologues with slide projection in the theatre. *Sadness*, first performed in 1992, was published in 1996 and then adapted for film by director Tony Ayres (1999). Like much of Yang's work, *Sadness* mourns loss—of cultural heritage through assimilation, of friends to AIDS—while celebrating life. *NJ*

From *Sadness*
Chapter 6: Family

Dimbulah, the town where I grew up, started as a railway junction between mining towns. There were minerals in the district, not gold, but tin and wolframite. Later it became a tobacco-growing district.

My father came to Dimbulah in the 1930s. He'd already met my mother in Cairns, he courted her for two years. He moved to Dimbulah and started the shop, then he proposed to my mother and they married.

My mother said, 'He wanted someone to help him with the shop.' But she also told me at another time that she was madly in love with him. So my mother was in two worlds here. In the pragmatic traditional Chinese world, marriage was merely an economic contract, but my mother had been born here and she allowed herself the indulgence of love and romance.

During the war things were tight and people owed them money. One of them gave my parents his farm in lieu of the debt and they became tobacco farmers.

We were all born in Dimbulah. We were brought up in the western way. None of us learned to speak Chinese. This was partly because my father, a Hukka, spoke Mandarin, whereas my mother, a See Yup, spoke Cantonese, and they spoke English at home. My mother could have taught us Cantonese but she never did—frankly she couldn't see the point.

One day, when I was about six years old, one of the kids at school called at me 'Ching Chong Chinaman, Born in jar, Christened in a teapot, Ha ha ha.' I had no idea what he meant although I knew from his expression that he was being horrible.

I went home to my mother and I said to her, 'Mum, I'm not Chinese, am I?' My mother looked at me very sternly and she said, 'Yes, you are.'

Her tone was hard and I knew in that moment that being Chinese was some terrible curse and I could not rely on my mother for help. Or my brother, who was four years older than me, and much more experienced in the world. He said, 'And you'd better get used to it.'

So for most of my life I've had negative feelings about being Chinese, which is rather ironic since now I seem to have made a career of it.

In the 1950s my parents built their dream home. They had Italian builders and I think it ended up looking a bit Italian.

When I saw it on my trip north, it was in a very bad state of repair and it was empty.

I want to jump eighteen months . . . to another time when, by some stroke of fate, my sister came out for a visit from America.

We all went up to North Queensland for a holiday, my mother, my brother, my sister and I.

I remembered so much more when I was with them. Someone would say something and it would spark off something in me. It was as though we had a collective memory.

My mother had a wonderful time seeing her old friends. But ten days after . . . she had returned home to Brisbane, my mother died suddenly.

She had a stroke on the Friday and she went into hospital in a paralysed condition. As she lay there I think my mother had a choice, be it subconscious. Either she could cling to life, come back crippled and maybe linger on a few more years, or she could let go.

I think that the trip to North Queensland gave her a bit of space. She had a chance to see all the places of the past, she had a chance to see old friends and relatives, she had a chance to say goodbye, she had her family around her, she was happy. I think this allowed my mother to slip gently into the next world.

When I was coming back from my first trip north, I stopped at the Innisfail Court House and I asked the woman behind the counter if she had anything on the trial of Peter Danelchenko. She went into an adjoining room, climbed up a ladder to a top shelf (I could see her from the counter) and brought down a dusty cardboard carton marked 1920 to 1930.

'Yes, there's something here. But it's not the transcript of the trial that you wanted, it's the deposition of the witnesses.'

In those days when there was a serious case like a murder, the magistrate had a preliminary hearing of the witnesses to see if there was enough evidence for a trial. They don't always do this nowadays. So these depositions, or sworn evidences, are from that preliminary hearing.

The testimonies of the simple Chinese labourers are vastly different from the testimonies of the policemen, one of whom gave a statement that is so biased it's almost absurd.

I think I can say that the police were out to get Fang Yuen or, rather, that they were trying to save the white man. In those days killing a Chinaman was not considered a serious crime. [. . .]

No one was right about the motive for the crime. It wasn't about a card game or a gambling debt, although it was about money, indirectly.

What the two men argued about was the weight of cane that went in railway trucks to the mill. I guess Fang Yuen accused Danelchenko of cooking the books, then they had a fight and Danelchenko shot him. [. . .]

My mother gave evidence at this hearing. She was asked about the diamond ring and she said she had never seen Fang Yuen take it off. So the diamond ring was a real object. It shocked me to see my mother's signature on that page because she never told me about it.

I think this event was a very traumatic experience for my mother. She was only sixteen at the time and her way of dealing with it was to put it out of her mind completely. She literally blotted it out. I feel the legacy of this murder came down to me in that my ethnicity was suppressed.

Although there wasn't a spear, as Aunty Kath had claimed, there was a knife and the body fell under the bed, so her story wasn't quite as far fetched as I had thought. The coroner found a bullet in the window mullion and he said for the bullet to enter at that angle, Danelchenko's account of the action was untrue. So, while David's story about the bullet ricocheting off the mullion was not accurate, there were elements of fact in it.

I didn't tell my mother I had these documents because I knew they would upset her. At another time I might have challenged her—'You never told me!'—but this time I let it go. It was one secret I let her take to the grave.

1996

ROBERTA SYKES
b. c. 1943

Roberta Sykes was born in Townsville to a white mother who did not tell Sykes the identity of her absent father who may have been an African-American serviceman. Her experiences as a person of colour suffering from profound violence and racism are described in her autobiographical trilogy *Snake Dreaming* (1997–2000). Active in Aboriginal politics since the late 1960s, she was the first executive secretary of the Aboriginal Tent Embassy in Canberra in 1972, and later established the group Black Women's Action. After working for government departments, Sykes attended Harvard University in the 1980s, where she received her master's and doctorate in education, being described at the time as the first Aboriginal Australian to graduate from an American university. On her return to Australia, Sykes continued to work in Aboriginal politics.

In addition to her autobiography, she has written two works on race relations, two collections of poetry—*Love Poems and Other Revolutionary Acts* (1979) and *Eclipse*

(1996)—and edited an anthology on prominent Australian women. She also assisted in the writing of Shirley Smith's *MumShirl: An autobiography* (1981). The publication of her first volume of autobiography, *Snake Cradle* (1997), raised questions (strikingly similar to those directed at Mudrooroo (qv)) about Sykes's status as Aboriginal. Supporters of Sykes point to the fact that she was treated as an Indigenous Australian during her childhood, that she strenuously supported Aboriginal rights and interests, and that she has described herself as 'black'. Critics (including Pat O'Shane, a NSW magistrate and member of the Yalanga people) claim that she showed an ignorance of Aboriginal culture and did not correct media reports that she was Indigenous. Sykes has responded to the controversy with silence. *DM*

From *Snake Cradle*
Chapter 2

[. . .] Within three blocks of our house was St Anne's Church of England school. We walked by it many times as we passed on our way to town. We couldn't see into the main schoolyard as it had a high fence and tall buildings, but tucked into one corner was a hall, and on some afternoons we'd see girls inside playing, exercising and vaulting, and occasionally singing.

The area consisted of hills and dales, and the hall stood on much lower ground than the footpath which ran alongside it. We'd squat down to peek in to see the girls through the tiny gaps between the open flaps. The hall didn't have windows, just flaps, common at the time, made of timber and propped open with sticks to allow in air and light when the building was in use.

One day Mum said the school was having an open day. Prospective kindergarteners were invited to spend half a day there, prior to starting at the beginning of the following year. She dressed me up and marched me down to the school but from the minute she left me there, I knew I wasn't going to be welcome.

As I wasn't an enrolled student, and this was only to be a 'test run', Mum hadn't gone to the expense of buying me a uniform. I was unaware that there was such a thing as a uniform until that day. Vicious little girls circled me, pulling at the pretty frock Mum had insisted I wear in order to impress the school with my worthiness, and taunting me. I was so taken by all the new things I was seeing, in the schoolyard, the playing courts and the classroom buildings, that I didn't take too much notice of their meanness.

Sometime that morning, we were brought into the hall, and I was excited at seeing it from the inside. The regular pupils knew what they were to do, and soon, under the teacher's eye, had built up a structure of steps and stairs made of forms and positioned themselves in rows. The teacher told us new girls to fit ourselves into the formation. The little white girls were quickly pulled up into the lines, and I was left walking up and down the rows, trying to find a space for myself anywhere, while the teacher moved her papers and song books around on her stand out the front.

I went to all the lines along one side, but could find no room. The girls were shuffling around to fill up the gaps and not let me in. The structure was close to the wall but not tight against it, so I decided I'd cross behind it and go along the lines on the other side. As I did so, two girls began kicking me around the head and shoulders. When I looked up I saw that they weren't looking down at me, their heads were facing straight in front so that the teacher wouldn't know what they were doing.

I put my arms up around my head to protect myself, and I noticed that the girls kicking out at me were holding onto other girls in order to keep their balance. I slid past them, but behind the lines it was dark and I felt hot, terribly hot, and my perspiration and tears were making the top of my dress wet. As I continued along a third girl struck her foot out at me and hissed, 'Get away.' The wooden forms they were standing on rocked when she moved so suddenly and viciously.

I could see daylight at the end of the formation and I stumbled on towards it. The girls tensed and I sensed the teacher coming towards the back. One girl said, 'Don't telltale, darkie.'

The teacher's voice came clearly. 'Who said that?'

There was no reply. The teacher reached the end of the row and peered towards me. She reached in and grabbed me by the arm, dragging me clear of the desks and the wall. Everyone had turned and was watching me.

I'd like to think the teacher just didn't know what was going on, that she was busy with her work and failed to notice the increasing skittishness of the group of girls as they realised that by shuffling around they could keep me out and torment me.

After a moment of excruciating embarrassment and agony, which stands out in my memory of this event, the teacher hoisted me up by the arm and toted me outside. She carried me at arm's length away from herself to a tap in the playground where she put my head under the cold running water several times, and between each dumping I was drawn up, spluttering and coughing all over myself.

Sufficiently wet to please her, she pulled the skirt of my pretty frock up to wipe my face dry with it. Another teacher came towards us and asked if anything was the matter. She was told that I was having a turn from the heat, and asked to look in on my teacher's class until she got me 'settled down'.

Eventually, I was left sitting alone on a low bench that was nailed around the bottom of the thick trunk of a tree, with my new little school port beside me, watching the dappled sunlight as it played between the leaves, making interesting patterns of light and shadow, keeping my mind blank and waiting for my mother. After a long wait, Mum appeared around the corner of a building across the schoolyard just as the girls were filing out of the hall. I picked up my port and walked towards her, ignoring the girls, and when I came up level with her I put my hand in hers to pull her out of there as fast as I could. The teacher ran over, calling, 'Mrs Patterson, Mrs Patterson,' and when Mum stopped, she was told, 'Your daughter had a turn from the heat.'

I already knew this was not the sort of thing I could tell my mother about. At other times, people had called me and my sisters names in the street when she was with us and Mum had just said, 'Don't take any notice of them,' and dismissed the incidents. On a much earlier occasion, after a similar occurrence, I had asked Mum, 'What's a "nigger"?' She was powdering her face and paused but didn't answer. So I pressed on. 'Well, what's a "black gin"?'

'Where did you hear that?' she reluctantly replied, her lips pursed tensely. I could sense that she had become angry because I hadn't backed off when she didn't answer my first question, so I ran away.

Later that day she told me, not for the first time and probably by way of explanation, 'When people say rude things to you, just remember you're as good as anyone else.' I recall thinking then that I'd seen some ugly people in town, drunks rolling around in the streets and the like, and it hurt me to hear her say I wasn't any better than these people—which was probably a very negative reaction to what she thought was good advice. 'As good as anyone else' was one of Mum's stock phrases in the peptalks she gave us about racism, and every time I heard it, it grated on me. It always seemed to me that she was putting me on the same level as racists themselves.

Although I didn't bother her with the details of what went on during my 'open day' at St Anne's, I let her know I would not be happy to go to there, even though it was the closest school. Mum tried to terrify me by telling me stories about what sort of things might happen to me if I went to the state school, but I already knew what sort of things happened at St Anne's. [. . .]

1997

ROBERT DREWE
b. 1943

As narrated in his memoir *The Shark Net* (2000), Robert Drewe was born in Melbourne and grew up in Perth. He began his journalistic career in 1961, working for the *West Australian*. He was the literary editor of the *Australian* (1971–74) and has held positions with the *Age* and the *Bulletin*. He has won a number of Walkley Awards. Beginning with *The Savage Crows* (1976), Drewe has published six critically acclaimed novels, including the historical novel *Our Sunshine* (1991), about the bushranger Ned Kelly (qv). His three collections of short stories include the immensely popular *Bodysurfers* (1983), which, like *The Shark Net*, was adapted into a television series. *Our Sunshine* was adapted into the feature film *Ned Kelly* (2002). Drewe's work has also been adapted for radio and stage.

Wide in imaginative scope, Drewe's work is often concerned with identity and Australian history, especially with regard to race relations (*The Savage Crows* concerns the genocide of Tasmanian Aborigines). He has been a major force in representing Australia as a coastal culture. In addition to his fiction he has edited *The Picador Book of the Beach* (1993) and *The Penguin Book of the City* (1997). *The Shark Net: Memories and murder* intertwines Drewe's memories of growing up in Perth in the 1950s and early '60s with an account of the notorious serial killer Eric Cooke. As is characteristic of Drewe's work generally, the memoir mixes bleak content with a comic tone. *DM*

From *The Shark Net*
People of the Dunes

We moved into a house in the dunes. Everyone lived in the dunes. From King's Park, on top of the highest dune, you could look down and see the whole city spread along the coastal dunes and around the sandy river flats, from the ocean to the ranges.

Something strange happened in the south in the late afternoon. When you looked south from King's Park the whole sand plain and the farthest suburban roofs and treetops joined the clouds in a dense purple mirage which imitated a European forest. It was a gloomy storybook place of tall, angry-looking trees and hills and castles. But in real life we were all living in bright sunlight and on flat, dry sand.

Some people lived in the loose white sand near the ocean. Even though everyone in Perth lived in the dunes I thought of them as the Sand People. Every afternoon the fierce sea wind, which they dismissed as The Breeze, blew their sand into the air and scalloped and corrugated their properties.

Sun and wind had rearranged the appearance of the Sand People, too— tanned, freckled, scabbed and bleached them. With their darker skins, red eyes, raw noses and permanent deep cracks in their bottom lips, they looked nothing like Melbourne people. Some were as eroded as the cliffs, their noses and ears worn and peeled away, so that grown men had the snubbed features of boys. Around their edges—noses, ear tips, cheeks, shoulders—they were pink and fraying. Shreds of skin poked up from their general outline and fluttered in the sea breeze. Boys bled if they smiled too fast.

From a distance most of the adults seemed stained a smooth reddish-brown—my paintbox burnt sienna—but close-up at the beach, walking behind them down the wooden ramp to the sand, you saw they were stippled like people in newspaper photographs, spotted with hundreds of jammed-together freckles and moles—brown and black on a pink background. There were women with chests and backs like leopards.

The men and boys all looked tough but relaxed, even sleepy. My mother said they were half-dazed from the sun. They were indeed slow smilers, but I could see it was because they were being careful of their split bottom lips.

I was impressed that all the males and some of the younger girls went bare-legged and barefoot most of the year. From my sandalled perspective it seemed clear that life in all of Western Australia, not just near the sea, revolved around bare feet. There was obviously something important going on with feet.

Foot knowhow seemed the key to belonging. Feet were an instant giveaway for a newcomer. Only mothers' boys and English kids—or Melbourne boys—wore sandals in summer. Or, worse, shoes and socks. So said Miss Langridge, my new second-grade teacher, when I relayed to her my mother's message that despite Miss Langridge's advice to the contrary she would be continuing to send me to school with 'covered feet'.

Miss Langridge attempted to mask the bitter plump redness of her face with overlapping layers of powder which subdued her colour to pink. She bent down and hissed at me, 'Does your mother think her little darling will get a cold in the tootsies?' The force of her words dislodged tiny clumps of powder from her cheeks and they floated in the air between us.

The heat was just part of the daily contest for feet. Boys merely wandering home along the road felt bound to compete at withstanding the searing sand, melting bitumen, rocky road verges, bottle shards and grass prickles with their bare soles. The darker the surface the hotter, but it hardly mattered; everything underfoot was either sizzling, prickly or sharp. Feet, generally, took a thrashing. Those grazed ankles and blackened toenails, the blood-blistered heels, the festering reef-cuts criss-crossing their soles, showed a boy's familiarity with reef, surf and cliff-face. Their feet were painted so boldly with Mercurochrome and flavine antiseptic they looked like they were wearing red and yellow socks.

Their brave bare toes gripping their verandas, the Sand People were forever squinting into the summer sun and wind, the winter rain and gales. Whenever we drove along the coast road I'd follow their gaze out to sea and wonder what they were looking at. There was nothing out there. They seemed so proud of their views but all I could see were straight lines of sand, water and sky, the speck of Rottnest Island on the horizon and the wind forever chopping the ocean.

They acted like they owned the weather and the coastline, too. But my father told me knowledgeably that their situation depended on limestone. 'They'd be lost without it.' They'd had to build high limestone foundations to stop their houses sliding down the sandhills, and they'd had to erect limestone battlements against the onslaughts of the wind—called the Fremantle Doctor because it brought relief to the sunstruck city. Even so, their houses rattled and whined and their clotheslines bent like trees in the wind. You could see their fly-away front yards streaming down the street.

The roads lay under drifts of sand as white and thick as snow. Everything outdoors was faded, pitted and smoothed by salt, sun and sand.

The coastline reminded me of ancient religious backdrops at Sunday School: the Dead Sea and places waiting for a miracle. It looked as old and bare as the moon. It was also like living in a geography lesson here where the land and sea met. The Indian Ocean was supposed to be constantly invading the shore and the land plants forever edging towards the sea. But apart from the wind nothing seemed too busy to me. The only flicker of activity was from blue-tongue lizards rustling in the pigface and a sand-coloured bush whose spidery tumbleweeds blew along the beach faster than I could run. On the sand cliffs above the shore the wind fizzed through a single clump of pine trees. The way the swings creaked and swung in the children's playground even when it was empty made me think little ghosts were playing there. Drowned kids perhaps.

After a while I worked out why the Sand People were always staring over the cliffs and out to sea. They were trying to see Africa. It was an exciting idea that Africa was the next continent, just over the horizon. In the atlas it was a straight line from us to Namibia in south-west Africa or, going the other way, Valparaiso, Chile. We were thirty-two degrees south. That sounded much colder than it was, until you found the places that were the same latitude north: Tijuana, Mexico, and Casablanca, Africa.

Casablanca sounded right to me. From the sea, the houses of the Sand People loomed like Foreign Legion forts. In the sun their quivery roofs melted into Sahara mirages. There was nothing in the straight white coastline to give your eyes a rest—no bays, few trees, to break the line and the glare and the shuddering mirages. Often on hot days the smell of something dead rose from the dunes and filled your head. Perhaps it was a blue-tongue stoned by boys. You became dizzy and got a headache if you looked towards Africa too long on a summer day.

My mother had been given bad information about Western Australia by a great-uncle who'd gone to Kalgoorlie looking for gold in 1902. He warned her of 'boiling brain'. Apparently it was an extreme form of sunstroke. It began with a severe headache. You turned feverish, her great-uncle said, and then delirious, and you saw spots like hundreds of red suns. If an ice-cold bath and a dark room didn't bring you round, you thrashed about and died.

Because she was an outdoor person herself her boiling-brain warnings rang true with me. She'd been a sportswoman: a swimmer, tennis player and horse rider. But Victoria's weather was colder. Her beach experience was in relatively sheltered Port Phillip Bay. At first she was suspicious of the surf and relentless sun. Now we were in a strange, hot, dry land, she was a mother, and she was taking no chances.

I imagined a boiling brain. It looked like a big jellyfish melting on the sand—just a circular outline of smeared and fading slime. For our first few summers, whenever Billy or I made a particular peculiar face on a hot day, or said something odd—and she was the judge of the strangeness of these grimaces or statements—she'd feel our foreheads and stare into our eyes to see if we were delirious. Just in case, she ran a mental check on us.

'Where do you live?' she'd snap. 'How old are you? Where does Dad work?'

'Goodyear,' I cracked once. That earned me a smile. It was lucky he wasn't there then. He would have thought I had boiling brain.

Eventually Billy and I turned the delirium tests into a farce. We cottoned on to the particular strange expression that panicked her: a sort of jaw-dropping, upward eye-rolling and stretching of the face, as if our skin was too tight. And after a day in the hot sun, it did feel ready to burst. We made this moronic stretching face all the time. The shouts of, 'Come quickly, Mum. He's got boiling brain!' palled for her much sooner than they did for us.

At the same time as my mother was testing us daily for boiling brain she scoffed at the local mothers' remedy for sunburn: a potion of brown vinegar, sliced tomato and cucumber. When my new red- and yellow-footed friends padded into our house with tomato skins sticking to their shoulders and cucumber seeds in their ears, she sniffed the spicy air and said, 'It's not only people who don't wear hats who've got boiling brains.'

My father's bald, pale head never went uncovered outdoors, but for reasons of vanity rather than health. According to him, the real beach terror lay in the undertow, the shark: the unruly sea itself. He preferred to keep his distance from the coastline.

For him the coast was under a cloud in any case. He'd just had a shock at work. Head office had suddenly recalled the State manager, Ern Kellam, and abruptly appointed Ken Scrutton, an older Dunlop man from South Australia, in Kellam's place. The Scruttons had moved into a big old house on the wind-buffeted hill above the ocean at Cottesloe. It was a bigger and better house than ours. For my father it was a symbol of head-office injustice. 'You wouldn't catch me living there in a fit,' he said. 'Blowing a gale all day long.'

As Kellam's deputy my father had presumed he'd get the job. But Kellam hadn't gone to bat for him. 'I was knifed, pure and simple.' For weeks this was the drift of my parents' after-dinner conversations. Night after night I heard my mother making soothing murmurs over their last cigarette and glass of beer. She pointed out yet again that he'd been assistant manager for less than a year. 'You're only thirty-five. There's plenty of time.'

But my father was in a hurry. He was on the ladder now. He was working harder and finding it increasingly difficult to relax outside work. When it was hot he sometimes took us to the ocean after work or at weekends, but it was under sufferance, and he regarded it warily. The ocean was such a mysterious, unknown quantity that he even put a veto on us using inflatable tubes and surfboards. We could only use them in the river. He thought a rip would suck us out to sea on our Dunlop products. The irony of Dunlop sweeping his children to destruction was too terrible to contemplate.

Every time we ventured to the ocean, he'd bravely test the waters first. While we squirmed and jumped impatiently on the shore, he'd gingerly dive in, immediately leap up, shake his head and go, '*Whoo!*' Then he'd brush the water back over the skin of his head, smooth back his hair at the sides, stretch out his arms to balance himself upright in the surf, blow his nose, and shake his head in wonderment at the extraordinary phenomenon of wave motion.

In control of events now, he'd frowningly survey the adjacent waters for seaweed. If a piece of kelp bobbed nearby he'd snatch it up and elaborately dispose of it, flinging it far from him, as if he mistrusted its sinister kelpish intentions. From his solemn manner you'd think he was rendering a valuable service to all swimmers. Of course they were all carelessly brown and horizontal, languidly stroking past or riding waves to shore, while he bobbed there, white, serious and vertical, clearing the waterways and gauging the tides. Finally he'd stamp towards us and brusquely motion us in. 'Be very careful,' he'd warn. 'There's an undertow today.'

All this was my parents' Melbourne viewpoint. I didn't find any of these things—waves, weather or the prospect of white pointers— unsatisfactory. I loved the whistling, windy Scrutton house with pine cones thudding on its roof. I wanted desperately to be like the salad-smelling Sand Children.

I envied their rakish red and yellow feet. I envied the vinegary confidence with which they peeled sheets of skin from their shoulders and passed them around for comparison at the Saturday afternoon pictures. The aim was to peel off a perfect unbroken strip of skin from shoulder to shoulder. I was filled with wonder that in this delicate parchment you could see every pore.

Most of all, I envied the superior foods they claimed to live on. Salad was for smearing on their burnt bodies—what they ate was fish and chips, chocolate-coated icecreams, spearmint milkshakes, Passiona drink and hamburgers, the aroma of whose frying grey mince patties and onions attracted both Sand People and outsiders after dark to a stark but oddly thrilling clifftop caravan named EATS.

Some boys also ate themselves. Their scabs, of course—even Melbourne boys ate those—but also nose-skin, cheek-skin, forehead-skin and especially shoulder-skin. By now I was impressed, but not at all surprised, by boys who ate their own flesh. The coast seemed generally strange and risky. In a place smelling of coconut oil, hot human skin, drying kelp and fried onions, I thought anything could happen. Where else but the white sand could there be such prospects for pleasure and danger?

2000

GERARD WINDSOR
b. 1944

Gerard Windsor was born in Sydney and educated by the Jesuits at St Ignatius' College, Riverview. In 1963 he entered Loyola College in Watsonia, Victoria, as a Jesuit novice. After five years there, as recalled in his memoir *Heaven Where the Bachelors Sit* (1996), he was sent by the Jesuits to the ANU to enrol for a Bachelor of Arts degree; he left the priesthood at the end of his first year there, completed his degree, and in 1972 moved back to Sydney to study further, later working for two years as a tutor at the University of NSW and then for four years as an editor at the multicultural public broadcaster SBS. He has been a full-time writer since 1986.

Windsor's first two books were collections of short stories—*The Harlots Enter First* (1982) and *Memories of the Assassination Attempt and Other Stories* (1985)—and the third a novella, *That Fierce Virgin* (1988). During the 1990s he published several volumes of writing that combined stories, memoirs, autobiography and essays, most of them about his Jesuit history, his family and his Irish background. In 2004 he returned to fiction writing with a dark and controversial tale of rape and incest, the novel *I Have Kissed Your Lips*. Windsor is a highly respected essayist and critic and in 2005 won the Pascall Prize for Critical Writing. *KG*

Addendum to the First Fleet Journals

There is no question of our superiority over the natives. Not morally nor even in point of civilisation. I am simply making a tactical assessment. No doubt they exist in large numbers, but they have no habit at all of congregation, and no experience of cooperation. Numerically greater than ourselves they may be, but their disposition to remain in family groups leaves them already fragmented.

Secondly, we have firearms.

I have just discovered we have a further advantage. The realisation was providential. We could have given away the advantage ignorant that we had ever owned it. It has been another useful lesson in the obscurantism of our own assumptions. Certainly, in this instance, it never occurred to me to inspect myself with the eyes of the natives.

By all the standards I have hitherto encountered, the natives are the abnormal ones—bearded, naked, unperfumed. We imagine they simply see in us the reverse image of all that. It never crossed my mind that the perception of such qualities as clean-shaven and clothed involved in turn other perceptions or problems. But I recall now that the Aztecs, seeing the Spaniards astride horses (creatures they had never encountered), presumed one single, terrifying being, part-animal, part-man. Not till one of the conquistadores fell from his mount, dislodged by their missiles, were the Aztecs' eyes opened.

In our own case I doubt that the natives' perception is so terrifying. But they are puzzled and maybe even awed. While we are conscious of the right attitude we should have towards them, they remain uncertain of their stance towards us. That situation could, with great advantage, be prolonged. I must puzzle out the requisite course of action.

Our complexions, wigs, clothes, clearly intrigue them. One feature in particular takes their fancy. They are making increasing ado about our fall-fronts; a great deal of quite disconcerting staring in that region, gestures, and bemusement alternated with much communal giggling. I took this to be merely the primitives' response to our notions of modesty. Today, however, an exploring party under my command encountered a group of natives, and my eyes were opened. With unabashed forwardness and immediacy one bold native approached one of the common seamen, and poked towards his fall-front with a club. The sailor leaped back, the watching natives hooted, but the man with the club held his ground. There were women in his own party, though at a slight distance. Talking loudly he pointed first at them, then at his own member, and finally at the seaman he had singled out. He repeated this procedure several times, but it was unnecessary, for I had firmly grasped his meaning. He wanted to know whether this object of his attentions, and indeed all of us I presume, were male or female. I was not the only person who understood. A private of marines tucked his musket under his arm, and dropped his hands to the buttons of his fall-front. Only my slightly faster perception had me ready to shout an effective prohibition. He blushed in a somewhat surly way and resumed his musket. Upon my command we all withdrew.

1. Our garb provides a complete disguise. This raises several considerations. Tens of centuries of progress in suiting the apparel to the specific personality of the male is nullified.

Even more strange, not one of our actions, apparently, has betrayed the male in us. We have hunted, shot, parleyed, given and taken commands, acted in military order. Yet none of this behaviour has impressed upon the natives what sex we are. It has not even suggested it to them.

2. Complete as this mystification is, it is sure to be dissipated soon. We have minimal time. It will take only one convict, sailor, marine, even officer, to loosen his fall-front, or lower his breeches within sight of one native, and the power will drop from us.

3. This power consists, oddly, in the natives being quite unaware of our potential. Most strikingly they do not know whether they should make love to us or not.

4. Unbuttoning, therefore, must have the effect of prohibiting advances of any intimacy.

5. But, alternatively, would unbuttoning mean that we are extending a sign of fraternity?

6. Conversely, as long as we keep our fall-fronts in place, does it mean that not only are we determined to retain our dominance, but that we are refusing to entertain any bond of fraternity?

7. But, on the other hand, since when has keeping the buttons on our fall-fronts deliberately in place been equivalent to the exercise of domination? It is unlacing that strip of cloth that is generally regarded as unleashing power.

8. But, in our case, exposure in any form can only mean loss of authority and power.

9. The question then, is how do we minimise that loss.

10. Some form of ritual unveiling suggests itself so that the occasion becomes a revelation rather than an exposure.

11. The obvious course is to take a large party of senior officers and men to a spot frequented by the natives. To call out, in precise military fashion, a predetermined fellow of the most impressively virile proportions, and to give him a brisk order to display himself.

12. A further detail is whether he should be entirely flaccid, not entirely, or altogether otherwise.

13. An even prior question is whether the actor should be an officer or an enlisted man, or even indeed a convict. Would the occasion be demeaned by the use of a felon? Is it so unequivocally dignified and noble a moment that only a gentleman is eligible? Is there any chance of the act becoming risible—so that only some common fellow should be compromised by the indignity of it?

14. The reaction of the natives is unpredictable. We do not know whether their god is perhaps, as it were, the god of a gentle breeze rather than the god of the howling wind. They might be more affected, in the desired way, by something that we might regard as more discreet and homely.

15. If the natives are unpredictable, so too perhaps are the men under my command. If they were to be officially combed for this ideal representative—presuming we could decide on what was ideal—I do not believe I could guarantee to control their response. My strong suspicion is that they would treat the matter with great jocularity. Commands, particularly those coming down from the highest authority, cannot be treated with jocularity without weakening the tight structure of discipline I need to maintain.

16. I strongly doubt whether most of my subordinate officers could appreciate my method of operation. They would have difficulty understanding the delicacy and stylishness of approach that I see as necessary.

17. Yet I cannot conduct the search by myself nor stage-manage the denouement on my own.

18. To throw away this fortuitous advantage would be a tragic pity, a stern question mark against the supposed superiority of the white man. Our ingenuity and inventiveness cast into great doubt.

19. I'll start again. The natives are unable to descry the male in us. So they treat us warily and with awe. We obtain dominance, and time.

20. Yet my men will betray themselves, and any flawless plan to ennoble that betrayal is beyond me. When the exposure is committed, it will, to my mind, be done crudely and humiliatingly.

But then it may not appear so to the natives. Further, the sight of one man may not tell them anything about the others. I have no notion how far inductive reasoning is natural to them. The man with the wig, the man with the beard, the man with the epaulettes may all be different sexes to them.

Mystery upon mystery. The waters are muddied endlessly. And for me too. Ambiguity and multiplicity piling one upon the other. I cannot exploit it. I can only extend it. What was the problem?

21. Tomorrow I will disembark the women. Let them go to it.

1985

ROBERT DESSAIX
b. 1944

As recounted in his memoir *A Mother's Disgrace* (1994), Robert Dessaix was born in Sydney and adopted at an early age. Being a talented linguist, Dessaix studied Russian literature in Moscow in the late 1960s and early '70s, and taught Russian language and literature at the University of NSW and the ANU for almost twenty years. Upon gaining his PhD, Dessaix changed his surname from 'Jones' (the name of his adoptive parents) to 'Dessaix' (the name of his biological parents). From 1985 to 1995 he produced and presented the ABC radio program 'Books and Writing'. As well as memoir, journalism and reviews, Dessaix has written fiction (including *Night Letters*, 1997, and *Corfu*, 2001), and creative non-fiction (such as *Twilight of Love: Travels with Turgenev*, 2004). He edited the Oxford University Press anthology *Australian Gay and Lesbian Writing* (1993), as well as a number of collections of essays. His own essays have been collected in *(And So Forth)* (1998). DM

From *A Mother's Disgrace*
Chapter 2: Motherlands

[...] Let me describe to you a city I know well, but you could not be expected to. The old town, where some of the zigzagging streets are still cobbled and the castle keep called Mokkó still stands intact and grey-black on the highest point, is on a promontory at the mouth of a small but swiftly flowing river. If we walk north from the keep, away from the sea (a choppy strait, with the mountains on the offshore island clearly visible to the south in good weather), we come to a more ordered, European part of the city—almost like Helsinki, really, with gracious Palladian buildings (mostly ochre and cream, but some duck-egg blue) enclosing thinly planted squares and lining well-planned streets. There are a few cafés and restaurants dotted about the streets here but if it were lunchtime and we wanted a more crowded, bohemian atmosphere we might head more east towards the escarpment above the river. This is the part of the city that was 'outside the walls' in an earlier century, so the streets are narrower and more crooked and the buildings quainter and pokier. There's the odd glimpse across the river below to pines and sand-dunes on the other bank. If you wanted something more up-to-date—shopping malls, glass and chrome delis, that sort of thing—you'd have to go northwest from the centre, out into the suburbs stretching between the sea and the mountains just a few kilometres inland. Down on the sea on the other side of the promontory from the river is a pleasant little bay—in fact, that's what it's called in the local language, The Little Bay—with a promenade and some expensive private houses with lush gardens on the hill behind. It's quite a high hill—well, it curves round to form the promontory—so if you're down on the promenade at the water's edge you can't see the mountains hemming in the city from the north or the magnificent monastery, almost a Potala, soaring up brown and white and sheer above the foothills. Idyllic, really, although the winters can be severe.

This city does exist, but not quite in the same way as, say, Vancouver or Wellington. I don't wish to sound mystical, but it's existed for me since I was a small boy of about six, pottering around in the backyard where the bush came up through the chook-yard to the edge of the back lawn. It was there in that backyard I started to imagine my own Pure Land. It wasn't just a fantasy or a game I played there with myself; it was and still is a parallel world.

Not long ago I stood looking at a Tibetan painting of Shambhala in the Royal Academy in Piccadilly. Shambhala is a word which changed over the years in English to become Shangri-la, which sounds more evocative to our ears, I suppose, but also more vulgar. At the centre of this painting is a round, white city, Shambhala, the Pure Land. To the eye it's Lhasa-like, clustered on a mountain like a flock of goats. There are no people in this round city, just houses and pavilions and a maze of alleys. Around this city, this Pure Land where perfection and non-being are somehow one, lies a ring of mountains, then a ring-shaped sea, then another ring of mountains and another sea—seven rings of mountains in all and seven seas. I stood immersed in this Tibetan painting for a very long time. It meshed quite miraculously with the pure lands I'd inhabited in my mind most of my life—like my secret island it's the embodiment of myth and at the same time 'real', lying just off the coast of India—and it also meshed with the sense I have of a more circular inner geometry.

I say that because, as a Westerner, I've been brought up to see life as linear, sequential and consequential, as heroic or tragic, modelled ideally, perhaps, on Jesus of Nazareth's or less loftily on any adventurer's. Yet deep down I know that a life can be pictured, construed, made sense of in terms of a completely different geometry altogether. With nothing at its core. I'm no mystic—there's a kind of Gallic rationalism in me so deep-seated I can't meditate for more than five minutes without tumbling into analysis and measurement and the prisonhouse of language—but this Tibetan painting seemed to me to map my life in a way more conventionally dramatic geometries did not.

Like the painting in the Royal Academy, my Shambhala too had streets and houses, rivers, lakes and mountain ranges and was an island. Already at six I could have drawn you a street map of the main city (severely rectilinear) and pinpointed it for you in my school atlas: it was (and is) just south of the Aleutians in the North Pacific. For tuppence in those days you could take home books from the musty one-roomed shop at the edge of the local shopping-centre we called the Library. I often borrowed books about the Arctic, especially Iceland and Greenland. There weren't many, so I took home the ones they had many times and I think the map of Iceland impressed itself on my consciousness early on and helped to shape my own Land. I hesitate to tell you what I call it—it's not that it's sacred or a secret, it's just that I want to keep it pure. And I fear your scorn.

Perhaps it's a case for psychiatric intervention, but over the four decades since I first drew a map for myself of the Righteous City—all right, call it K.—with its righteous rectangles, its parks and squares and public ponds, my Pure Land has not clouded over and disappeared from view as it ought to have done, but has grown denser and more economically and politically complex, and my map of the city has spread into a map of the island. And across the island snake railway lines (I used to know the timetables) and roads both paved and unpaved, there are airports, hospitals, castles, police academies, monasteries, prisons, cafés, theatres, bridges, mines, hotels, even benches in particularly sunny spots on certain promenades. I can tell you the rates at the health farm in the mountains near the Blue Lake or take you on a tour of the Buddhist monastery on a clifftop in the south. I can recommend certain cakes in a café in a town called V. (oddly enough, a mainly Russian Orthodox town and an important site of Orthodox pilgrimage) and run through the family history of the eighteenth-century rulers of the district of B. I live there, after all. Even as I write this, I realise I'm being careful not to tell you a single untruth.

A lively imagination in thrall to a single obsession, you're thinking to yourself, *The Magic Faraway Tree* gone pathological. Possibly so, but not a total waste of time. It took about twenty years for me to realise that through the matrix of this imagined Motherland, unaware of what I was doing, I was working out and articulating to myself all sorts of religious, philosophical, sexual, psychological and other problems. While studying one religion, for example, in my everyday life, I was actually elaborating and entertaining other religious philosophies which flourished in my land (more gnostic in tenor, although I didn't know the word). While eating meat I could debate radical vegetarianism as provincial government policy on an offshore island. As my distaste for Eastern European socialism strengthened, I could write articles defending it in my head for the Party daily newspaper in the north of my Land, where a Communist government had been in power since 1947. A fortified border cut the island (and my psyche) in two. It came down several years before the Germans demolished theirs, at about the time I settled down with P.

But it gets madder. When I was about eleven I started reading up on artificial languages—Esperanto, of course, but also Volapük, Pirro's Universal-Sprache, Interlingua and other concoctions. I was starting to learn Latin and Russian, already spoke a little French, and for £2/1/6 I bought myself a copy of Frederick Bodmer's *Loom of Language: A Guide to Foreign Languages for the Home Student*. So while other little boys were playing cricket in the street after school or going to Scouts or torturing small animals, I was comparing Greek script with the Cypriotic syllabary, musing on sound changes in medieval French and learning quite a lot about the differences between Swedish and Danish, not to mention Dutch, from the fascinating word lists in the Language Museum at the back of the book. All this must have been having some effect on the sort of teenager I was becoming.

One effect, apart from a complete lack of interest in cricket or indeed in playing any kinds of games with little boys, even cards, was the immediate need I felt to create a Pure Language for my Pure Land. I would set up my own loom and weave my own language. Now, many children make up private languages, I know—sisters talk with brothers in secret codes, only children compile private vocabularies, prepubescent fraternities have their ritualistic gobbledygook and so on. But starting from the age of about eleven I began to do something much more ambitious and, I suppose, eccentric: I began to construct an Indo-European language of enormous grammatical and morphological complexity, with a history going back to pre-Roman times in Asia Minor, sound shifts, three scripts (one syllabic, thanks to the Cypriots), two main dialects and several regional variations on those dialects. If I'm alone and in a compulsively Pure-Landish mood, I'll chat to myself in this language (the dialect depends on the persona I'm entering) and certainly all my dogs have heard a lot of it. As far as I know, no one else has ever heard or read a word of it. (Well, you've actually read one word, *mokkó* (n., neut. sing. nom.): 'a small keep' (from the root *mok*—'to close off').

This is madness sprouting madness, you must be thinking. I suppose it is in a way, but my rational self seems powerless to stop it. It just proliferates in my head like a vine. Part of me lives there and has done for over forty years. Although I do remember making resolutions on significant dates (my twenty-first birthday, for example, my thirtieth birthday, a New Year's Eve or two) to give it all up like masturbation, to put it away like some childish thing, it's not something I can just swear off.

English is filtered through it all the time. I make myself translate almost everything I hear—phrases from conversations, the titles of books and films, news items, advertisements. Obsessively, I force conjunctions to occur between language systems. Meaning only occurs in conjunctions, after all— words and things, words and words, words and memories (the universe and God, for that matter). If something just hangs in a vacuum (like a godless universe) it has no *meaning* as such at all. So I hear a phrase like 'right and wrong', for example, and think to myself: now, how would I say that in my language? And immediately I'm aware that 'right and wrong' are just English words with a history. They've been applied to different things at different times in different social contexts, of course, and whatever translation I choose can't be expected to come with the same baggage. The history of my Land is, after all, very different from England's, as are its mores, its value systems and its social structures. And so, as I try out this word and that (bearing in mind, let's say, that both the English 'wrong' and the French 'tort' have to do with twisting), groping for a way to express this phrase in my own tongue, I become intensely aware of how relative and personal concepts like right and wrong are, how socially determined, and how imprisoning knowing just one language can be. And over the years that's been true of many key words in my psychic development—obvious ones like 'good', 'evil', 'God' and 'love' over which I've battled with myself for decades, but also more peripheral ones like 'home', 'friend', 'intelligence'—yes and even 'mad'. This kind of awareness changes absolutely everything. It was having to say to myself in my own language 'I love him', 'he loves her', 'I love rhubarb', 'I love Mozart' and 'God loves me' that first made me ponder what love means. These are lengths mad Billy Liar[1] did not go to with his fantasies about the Republic of Ambrosia. But Billy Liar, unless I'm mistaken, was trying to escape from a dreary middle-class post-war England. I don't think I was trying to escape from anything.

In some ways all I was trying to do by spending part of my time in a parallel world was to belong somewhere, to give myself a history I had some control over. I'd known ever since I could know anything that I didn't come

---

1 The eponymous hero of a novel (1959) by the English writer Keith Waterhouse (b. 1929).

from where I was. Wisely or unwisely, Jean and Tom[1] had told me before memories begin that my mother and father had not been able to keep me and that they, Jean and Tom, had wanted to have me very much because they couldn't have their own children. So on the one hand I seemed to have landed on my feet while on the other, from a very early age, I was confronted with the fact that there are times when people must abandon those they love. As I grew older I seem to remember the story changed a little: my father had died in an air-crash and so my mother had married someone else. (Strangely close to the truth, as it turned out, but not something Jean and Tom could have known.) I was also told my mother's maiden name and that it was French. Once Jean even cut a photograph out of the social pages of the *Daily Telegraph* showing a group of smiling middle-class women one of whom was a Dessaix. She came from a nearby Sydney suburb. I remember feeling intrigued but not deeply moved.

On hot afternoons on the back verandah Tom, now sixty-odd, would sit learning French from phrase books and grammars in order to speak to me in French—and not just *passez-moi le beurre, s'il vous plaît*, either. Given that he'd left school at about twelve in 1901, the son of pub-owners in Port Augusta, this was no mean achievement. And it went further: he took out a subscription to *Le Courrier australien* and joined a society for French-speakers, something rather more demotic than the Alliance française—sailors from French ships used to appear at the get-togethers (*les amicales*, they were called), songs were sung and long rambling stories were told, just the sort of thing Tom revelled in. And when Jean went back to work we had a cleaning-lady from Noumea I used to talk to in French—a small-boned, waspish woman who pursed her lips so tightly I could hardly understand a thing she said.

None of this was affectation, it was generosity of spirit, it was an offering. Tom was a man with a big, soft heart and a kind of Irish love of words and the games you can play with them. *Satu, dua, tiga, empat, lima* . . . I see him again now, in his old Hawaiian shirt and shorts, sitting on the back verandah with the races switched off, teaching me to count to ten in Malay, which he'd picked up in the merchant navy forty years before, and then in Pushtu, which he'd learned from the Afghan camel-drivers passing through Port Augusta in the 1890s. He wasn't averse to telling my mother and me over dinner what 'thank you very much' was in Cantonese, either, or in Russian (he'd been to Vladivostok before the Revolution), a habit which seemed to nettle Jean. She took delight in mispronouncing his French phrases—*oh, mercy buckets*, she'd say, or *Quel horror! It's pleuting!* We weren't fazed.

---

1   Dessaix's adoptive parents.

It *was* moving to think that I had been abandoned by a beautiful French mother ('pretty and petite' was how Jean put it—I scarcely wondered how she knew) and by my brave and handsome father the pilot. He always remained nameless and mysterious—all I knew about him was that the almoner at the hospital where I was born had thought him 'very good-looking'. What was moving to me as a child was the story, not the facts. The idea of being reunited with my mother, strange as this may seem, did not much interest me. At least, not in real life. Of course, I used to fantasise that my father was King of Bessarabia and that my kingdom would be restored to me, that out there somewhere, perhaps on the next tram I caught or standing in line at the fish shop, were brothers and sisters who looked exactly like me (no one else seemed to, after all) and who would reclaim me right there on the tram or in the fish shop. And when for some years in the late 'fifties I worked in a large city bookshop during the Christmas school holidays, I used to dream that one day a woman would come up to me with a book and say: 'Charge it, please, to Yvonne Dessaix.' What on earth would I say? I was moved by the scene in my head, and went over and over it, but I don't know that I really wanted it to happen in real life, right there in Paperback Fiction. [. . .]

1994

PAUL KEATING
b.1944

Paul Keating was born in Sydney and left school at fifteen. In 1969 he was elected to the House of Representatives and in 1975 he became the youngest ever federal minister, as minister for Northern Australia in the Whitlam Cabinet. After serving in the Labor shadow ministry (1976–83), Keating became treasurer when the Australian Labor Party (ALP) was returned to government in 1983, a position he held until 1991 when he became prime minister. Having won what was considered an unwinnable election in 1993, Keating resigned from Parliament after the defeat of the ALP in the 1996 election. His period as prime minister was marked by a desire for further engagement with Asia, reconciliation with Australia's Indigenous peoples and making Australia a republic.

His speeches were published as *Advancing Australia* in 1995. He is the subject of numerous studies, including a prize-winning biography by his ex-speech writer, Don Watson, called *Recollections of a Bleeding Heart: A portrait of Paul Keating PM* (2002). He is also the subject of *Keating: The musical* (2005). DM

The Ghost of the Swagman

This is one to tell our grandchildren about: we were in the North Gregory Hotel when Australia celebrated the first performance of 'Waltzing Matilda' one hundred years before. And we were all in evening dress, which is something the swagman would have found amusing but maybe the squatter, the troopers and Banjo Paterson would have appreciated. All would have liked the irony in it.

I was in Bourke yesterday—another place in the romance of the swag, and another place suffering the drought. Yesterday in Bourke the town was gathered for an extraordinary event: an international marathon race from Bourke to Parramatta to raise money for the Fred Hollows Foundation. Fred Hollows is buried in Bourke, and they celebrate his memory as a man who loved the bush and the values of the people who live there. His work was, in many ways, an extension of the old idea of mateship, and through it he lifted all our spirits and raised our goals. Here in Winton, in an altogether different way, these celebrations are reminding us of the same things. They are reminding us of the spirit of the bush and commemorating a song which has lifted our spirits for one hundred years. There are no limits to the power of a good song.

I read on the way up here that ten thousand people would be in Winton this weekend. That has to be a very considerable boost to Winton as it struggles through the drought. Music has more than charms—it has profound economic effects. In times like this it is not as good as rain, but it may well be the next best thing.

'Waltzing Matilda' was born in a drought era, of course, and it is not hard to imagine that this might have had some effect on the melancholy theme of the song. And there is equally no doubt that in all the varieties of hard times 'Waltzing Matilda' has galvanised the spirit of countless Australians. If culture is that which defines a people, if it is the expression of their collective sentiment, 'Waltzing Matilda' sits at the centre of *our* culture—it's a wellspring of the national sentiment, a pool, a billabong.

I suspect there is no one here who has not at some time, somewhere in the world, heard or remembered the tune and felt deeply affected by it. I'm sure it has brought Australians home before they intended to, and given others the strength to stay away a bit longer. For a century it has caused Australian hearts to beat faster. I venture to say it has caused more smiles and tears, and more hairs to stand up on the backs of Australian necks, than any other thing of three minutes' duration in Australia's history.

It has long been our unofficial national song. Not our anthem—as I've said before, one can't sing too solemnly about a jumbuk. But 'Waltzing Matilda' is Australia's song, and it always will be. Think what it has withstood down the years: wave after wave of American and British popular music; the cultural cringe and all that post-colonial posturing; the urbanisation of Australia, which might have been expected to dilute the old bush sentiments; and mass immigration and multicultural Australia, which changed the face and the fabric of our society.

'Waltzing Matilda' has endured them all. It has endured through wars and depressions, good years and bad. It has endured some terrible renditions—by both local and overseas performers, including Tom Waits.

I don't think we should make it official and issue some kind of decree. But I think we all know that 'Waltzing Matilda' is as beloved as the anthem and probably more so; and, entirely without prejudice to the status of 'Advance Australia Fair', we might sing 'Waltzing Matilda' at a lot more public occasions than we presently do. I hope these celebrations serve as a bit of a trigger for this. It is to we Australians what 'Land of Hope and Glory' is to the British, or 'America the Beautiful' and 'God Bless America' are to the people of the United States. I see no reason why, at all but the most formal events, and state events, people should not choose freely between the two songs.

I have no doubt that all through these celebrations people will be talking about why 'Waltzing Matilda' endures. Why it means so much to us. I know some will also be asking who the swagman was and what, therefore, the song was meant to signify. I won't be buying into the historical debate, but I suppose every Australian is entitled to say—even *obliged* to say—what the song means to him or her. I don't think I was the only Australian kid who wondered, when he learned the words at school, what sort of swagman is this? Jolly one minute, drowning himself the next? Shouldn't it have been, 'Once a very serious swagman'? Or a solemn swagman? Even an unstable swagman? These questions about the psychology of the song were later replaced with social and political interpretations—even ideological interpretations. There is no question that it is easy to take from the lyrics an affirmation of the idea of the fair go which still strikes a powerful chord in Australians. And it may always do so.

Paterson's story describes a class struggle, and if ever there was a class struggle in Australia it was in the 1890s. His sympathy is with the battler in the struggle—the swagman against the squatter. So again we can see it as an egalitarian song. We can interpret 'Waltzing Matilda' as a celebration of our rebellious nature, as part of the tradition which began at Castle Hill and runs all the way through Frank the Poet, the Eureka Stockade and Ned Kelly. We can think of the swagman's jump into the billabong as an Australian statement of liberty or death.

But, the truth is, none of these things come into my mind when I hear it sung. They didn't come into my mind when the entire crowd gathered in Croke Park in Dublin sang it before the Gaelic football final when I was there two years ago. I don't know what came into my mind then—I think the experience emptied it of all rational thought. But afterwards I was aware of the extraordinary power of this song on an Australian's senses. All sorts of music can move us, but to hear 'Waltzing Matilda' sung so fervently and beautifully by the people of another country twelve thousand miles from home is to know that nothing can move us like our own song.

It is to know that a national song is not something to be interpreted intellectually. When you hear it, you don't think about a political position, or social and psychological issues. Nor do you think about the historical context of droughts and strikes a century ago. What 'Waltzing Matilda' tells us in an entirely uncomplicated way is that we are Australian. And it tells us in a way that I think is equally Australian in character—it tells us without beating drums or waving flags, or pounding our chests. It tells us with a simple melody and a story, and a highly ironic story at that.

There is no national song I know of quite like it in the world. I think what happened with Banjo Paterson and 'Waltzing Matilda' happened in the realm of the spirit. I think he wrote a story to a tune which quite mysteriously—in ways we'll never know—picked up the spirit of the place as it was then; and, like the ghost of the swagman, it never died. And it touches us as a ghost might, as the spirit of the bush might. When we were kids, that was the other line I think we used to wonder about: the one which says, 'His ghost may be heard as you pass by the billabong'. I confess to wondering what you would hear. What sort of noise would the old swagman make—what does it sound like when you stuff a jumbuk in a tucker bag?

It took me ages to realise that this was Banjo Paterson's whole trick—the *song* is the ghost of the swagman, and a hundred years later we are hearing it as loud as ever.

1995

DAVID FOSTER
b. 1944

Novelist, poet and essayist David Foster was born to radio-comedian parents in Katoomba, NSW. After establishing a distinguished academic record as a scientist in his twenties, he abandoned the academy in 1972 to direct his intellectual energies into his writing, supporting himself in a variety of jobs: pool foreman, truck driver, jazz drummer, postman, fisherman and removalist. He has a double black belt in tae kwon-do and is an avid reader of classical literature.

His first book, *North South West: Three novellas*, was published in 1973, and *The Pure Land*, published the following year, won Foster the first of his many literary awards. Two ferociously funny satirical novels, *Moonlite* (1981) and *Plumbum* (1983), were followed by the more gently humorous *Dog Rock: A postal pastoral* (1985), a tale narrated by a philosophical country postman called D'Arcy D'Oliveres. D'Arcy reappears in the sequel, *The Pale Blue Crochet Coathanger Cover* (1988), and again as the narrator of Foster's masterpiece, *The Glade Within the Grove* (1996), a huge, noisy, epic novel that, as critic Susan Lever says, 'demonstrates the full range of Foster's talents and obsessions'. Some of these obsessions include masculinity, spirituality, classical literature, trees, music, martial arts, and the place of Christianity and other religious systems and beliefs in the history of Western civilisation.

In 1999 he published *Studs and Nogs: Essays and polemics 1987–98*, a reminder of his gifts as an essayist and polemicist. His 1999 novel *In the New Country* is another venture into benignly comic mode on the theme of the Irish in Australia, part of Foster's longstanding preoccupation with the place of spirituality in contemporary Australia.

Foster is a formidably intellectual writer, a well-read and iconoclastic thinker with an astonishing literary range. His work includes, and often combines, a number of usually incompatible literary modes: satire with epic, parody with allegory, comedy with crime. He has published over twenty books—novels, novellas, short stories, poems and essays—and, with his wife Gerda, a book of practical gastronomical philosophy called *A Year of Slow Food* (2001); subtitled 'Four seasons of growing and making your own food in the Australian countryside', this book is a reminder (as are many of his essays and some of his fiction) of Foster's early training and experience as a scientist. *KG*

From *The Glade Within the Grove*
Chapter 54

[. . .] 'Oh my God!'

'Unreal.'

'Faarck.'

It is hard to believe there were trees this size up and down the whole East Coast, so thickly on the Hawkesbury River—today a bright green drain—the pioneer had to work with a torch in his non-axe-bearing hand. But then, there were sperm whales in Sydney Harbour, and they didn't long survive the advent of the outcast. Cedar getters were just whalers who didn't want to wet their feet. These river dolphins were blue whales, sperm whales, relics, up for grabs. Any convict wanting to turn over new leaf had them for minimal effort. What wouldn't they have been worth? Won't warp, cut easy, float, durable, branchless boles. Gone, within the century, but only the best parts of the best, and biggest, trees. What remained was left to rot, and crush the sapling growth.

'Att, these trees are *unreal*. Thank you so for bringing us.'

'Any camellias here, man?'

How to convey the UnReality? What a copse! Bastard rosewood, grazed low by cattle into shrub on the plateau, fifty feet here. Lilly pilly and sassafras, which, together with the roaming blackwood, constitute the canopy of the bastard brush on Bunoo Bunoo—where rainforest and wet sclerophyll contend with each other, and rabbits and cows—big trees, in the absence of the frosts and winds, that kill the first seasonal shoots. Sassafras, of the fragrant leaf, seen on the red hill as a wanderer, sprouting, trampled, from a dozen suckers, where Angus steers scratch ornery hides and rip off all the leaves in spite, just to spit them out again: here, although close to its recognised range, a hundred feet tall. Who would dare fell one of these boys for golden deal, to be milled as mousetraps? Lilly pilly, commonly coppiced by cows, two feet high on the headlands of Wilson's Promontory, fifty feet tall here, five feet broad.

How many staves for a beer barrel could you knock out of this blackwood? You'd need a pair of binoculars just to see the crown. And the same holds true of this pittosporum, one of our esteemed native daphnes, an ornamental hedge in the Southern Highlands, often seen by letterboxes. Keep the Ventolin handy, when this bloke buds up. And above the decomposing logs, the stinging nettles, the kangaroo apple, above the filmy fern; lianas, the diagnostic feature of the warm, as distinct from the cool, temperate rainforest. Anchor vines, and here, interloping from the sclerophyll, the running postman, dusky coral pea, wonga vines, thick as a man's tattooed arm. Caving ladders, or the skill of a Tarzan, needed to find the leaves. All you can see from the gloom of the ground is a mess of tangled rope, like a drunken deckie's effort to throw a springer over an A-frame. And we could go on, we could fill books. Huge man ferns, and you would call them man ferns here, in the Tasmanian mode; coachwoods, one of only two native timbers to meet specifications for aircraft construction; logged here, so smallish, and suitable only for shoe heels and sewing machine bobbins, but with black wattle and Christmas bush, gum vine, native crab apple—all found here, or hereabouts—comprising the Cunoniaceae family, confined exclusively to the East Coast. And what can we say of these leatherwoods, except they make the best honey in the world? How the television botanists, the sawyers of the softwood mills how the apiarists of Mole Creek, the backpackers from Stuttgart, how the organic chemists of Sydney Uni, the freelance photographers, how they would all like to get their mitts on this magnificent freak of Nature. But it can't happen, not while the local member is a mate of Horrie MacAnaspie's.

The Seven Sisters—for so they are yclept—grow touchingly close to each other. No lianas obscure them; no other species grow between. They grow straight up, and their canopy is a hundred and fifty feet above the Valley floor. The trunks measure twenty feet in circumference ten feet off the ground. The only comparable softwoods remaining on the island continent would be the bull kauri at Lake Barrine, on the Atherton Tableland in North Queensland, or maybe one of the twenty-three surviving adult Wollemi pine discovered by a canyoning abseiler in the Blue Mountains as recently as 1994. Check out the big bull kauri, multiply them by two, put them away, last of their kind, in some sacred, secret place; now you understand why the Family join hands and hug each other and weep and scratch deferentially the grey bark, to smell the red heartwood, sweet with ancient wisdom. Now they know why they came to this Valley, and are blown away that they came before they knew why they had come.

'Shoulda told us about these trees, Ginnsy.'

'I tried to, man, but words can only do so much.'

'Then ya shoulda written some music.'

'Come on! Is this a fit subject for a blues?'

'Beautiful, yaa, but it's all Maya.'

'Wake up to yourself, Balthazar.'

'How old would you say these trees are, Attis?'

'Bout a thousand years old.'

'Lie down and look up, Diane. Wow! Just lie down and look up at *that*. Great to see a trunk that size, swayin to and fro in a breeze. And listen to the creaking of the ship's timbers. It's like being on a ship.'

'It's more like a man and a woman making love.'

'Woohh! You got a leech here.'

'Wah! Get it off of me!'

Red cedar today abounds, but *diminuendo*. In the Kangaroo Valley, on the benches and gullies of the foothills of the Wollongong scarp, it may still be found a hundred feet tall, but never more than three feet wide. Can it, will it, grow again ever, as it grew in pre-European days? Until a thousand years, or more, have passed, non-scientists cannot tell. But the prospect of a fine cabinetwood maturing a millennium must be deemed remote in a world where the human population doubled over the past fifty years. World population, about 500 million in the time of Juvenal—David Suzuki says one billion, Paul Ehrlich about a third of that: I'd say they were guessing—was only one or two billion by the time of the Industrial Revolution. By 1990, it was five billion.

And yet in the 1790s, when the cedar getters were doing their ugly thing, it was found, back home, that coke could be used instead of charcoal, to smelt iron. Thus was preserved the pitiful remnant of England's native forest. You wouldn't have wagered on the future of English oak, in 1700.

Estimated to have covered a mere one per cent of the Australian landmass in 1788, and back to maybe a quarter of that by the time of which we speak, the rainforest in the absence of fire is advantaged by the Greenhouse effect. But if climatic instability precipitates as some think it may a new Ice Age . . .

The plant species of Australia survived well the last Ice Age. This was not the case in Britain, where more extensive glaciation caused many, if not most, plant species to become extinct.

But let's look on the bright side. See the tiny seedling that waits so patiently in the gloom of the forest floor for a gap in the canopy? [. . .]

1996

PETER SKRZYNECKI
b 1945

Peter Skrzynecki spent his early years in Poland before his parents migrated to Australia in 1949. After living for a time in the migrant camp outside Parkes, NSW, the family moved to Sydney, where Skrzynecki grew up. He has worked as a teacher. Migrant experience is a dominant theme of much of Skrzynecki's poetry, especially *Immigrant Chronicle* (1975), and of his memoir, *The Sparrow Garden* (2004). Skrzynecki has also written novels and collections of short stories. *Old/New World: New and selected poems* appeared in 2007. *DM*

Migrant Hostel

Parkes, 1949–51

No one kept count
Of all the comings and goings—
Arrivals of newcomers
In busloads from the station,
Sudden departures from adjoining blocks   5
That left us wondering
Who would be coming next.

Nationalities sought
Each other out instinctively—
Like a homing pigeon   10
Circling to get its bearings;
Years and place-names
Recognised by accents,
Partitioned off at night
By memories of hunger and hate.   15

For over two years
We lived like birds of passage—
Always sensing a change
In the weather:
Unaware of the season   20
Whose track we would follow.

A barrier at the main gate
Sealed off the highway
From our doorstep—
As it rose and fell like a finger   25

Pointed in reprimand or shame;
And daily we passed
Underneath or alongside it—
Needing its sanction
To pass in and out of lives   30
That had only begun
Or were dying.

1975

ANNE SUMMERS
b 1945

Born in Deniliquin, NSW, and educated at the universities of Adelaide and Sydney, Anne Summers has had a wide-ranging career as a writer, journalist and bureaucrat. She ran the Office of the Status of Women in the Prime Minister's Department (1983–86), was adviser to Prime Minister Paul Keating (qv) (1992) and has edited and written for numerous Australian and overseas newspapers and magazines. Summers was one of the founders of *Refractory Girl*, editor and joint owner of *Ms* and *Sassy*, political correspondent for the *Australian Financial Review*, and first woman president of the national press gallery (1982). Her best-known book is the polemical *Damned Whores and God's Police: The colonization of women in Australia* (1975), a feminist critique of Australian history and society. Summers has also co-written a bibliography of Australian women's writing, and written *Ducks on the Pond* (1999), an autobiography, and *The End of Equality: Work, babies and women's choices in 21st century Australia* (2003). DM

From *Damned Whores and God's Police*
Chapter 6: The Family of Woman

GOD'S POLICE

The God's Police stereotype describes and *prescribes* a set of functions which all Australian women are supposed to fulfil: the maintenance and reproduction of the basic authority relations of society. The prototype of these is found within 'the family' and it is here that women ideally perform their task, but the task of shoring up these authority relations requires extensive support systems, among them the education and social welfare network. The God's Police stereotype permits women to work within these areas, so long as they perform the prescribed functions and do not contradict any other fundamental tenets of the stereotype.

Women do not therefore necessarily have to be married in order to earn this label; the kind of work they do and their social/sexual lives will determine this. For instance, a single woman teacher or social worker would be seen as God's Police. So would nuns who teach or do other forms of charitable work. Single women who live with men without being married to them constitute an increasingly large group, and as their numbers increase so does the acceptability of their lifestyle. But at present we cannot say that their mode of living is totally accepted by society at large and so their status is uncertain. If it is counter-balanced by their working at one of the above-mentioned jobs then some sections of society are prepared to regard it benignly; for other groups this in itself is sufficient reason to condemn them and they argue about the undesirable moral influence such women could exert.

But the God's Police stereotype applies primarily to women within families and has as its *raison d'être* the perpetuation of the bourgeois family.

This stereotype describes a socially and politically conservative function: the policing and preservation of existing relations. That they need to be policed suggests that they are not very firmly implanted in Australian social practice, but while it is the case that they need to be transmitted to each generation, this policing notion is historically derived and arises from the peculiar conditions existing at the time of the formation of 'the family' in Australia. [. . .] The main task of God's Police is to instil in husbands, sons, daughters or pupils the necessity of submission to existing class, sex and race authority structures. So long as such submission is maintained these oppressive and exploitative relations persist. Women are thus called upon not merely to perform an authoritarian function within a society—and within institutions such as family, school etc.—where they have virtually no power, but also to police the perpetuation of the very authority structures which oppress them. Women are specially prepared for this task when, as young girls, they are taught to be submissive and passive, to conform and obey, to imbibe the morality of their generation and class and to impart its contents to the more recalcitrant of their peers.

Women are caught in a contradictory situation whereby they pass on and police a morality which they did not devise and which includes as one of its precepts the notion that women are inferior. They can only perform this schizophrenic role if they are unaware of the authority they possess and, having internalized their roles obediently and unquestioningly, they equate their tasks with what is 'natural' to their sex. Women are further duped by the superficial status which is accorded to conformers to the God's Police stereotype: they are rewarded with a degree of respect from the men whose consciences they are.

The other singular attribute of the God's Police stereotype is that it is asexual. This is why it can simultaneously accommodate married, single and widowed women so long as they perform the policing function. It is conveniently forgotten that married women must have sexual intercourse in order to reproduce: a general Australian puritanism has managed to convince itself that Mothers are not sexual creatures and female sexuality is either denied or else relegated entirely to the Damned Whore stereotype. (This curious attitude can be partly explained by the historical circumstances which led to the Damned Whore stereotype dominating white society in Australia for the first fifty years of its existence; the eventual revulsion against it as the bourgeois family and its concomitant God's Police notion of women gradually became dominant, led to a denial of women's sexuality even within marriage. [. . .]

The authority which women possess within families, schools and as social or welfare workers is not absolute. It is contingent authority which is why it does not carry any power. It can only be exercised while it is recognized and upon those who are prepared to recognize it. Women are incapable of enforcing it upon anyone, even their children, if their authority is disputed. And of course it often *is* disputed and then women are, once again, left hapless and helpless, stripped of the one means by which society allows them to gather status and respectability. A woman in this position will be described as being unable to control her children, as having committed some wrong so as to have lost her husband's respect (or why else would he spend each night in the pub?) and she will thus negate some of the meagre benefits which accrued to her upon marriage.

The God's Police stereotype by itself could barely win any woman's allegiance, even with its enticements of status and respectability. But the point of the polarized stereotypes is, as Eva Figes[1] pointed out, their rigidity: if you don't conform to one you are automatically cast into the other. The alternative stereotype often affords women substantially more personal freedom but it does not possess the comforting mantle of status and respectability. It is, rather, a punitive stereotype which entails relegating women classified by it to the *demi-mondaine*. The God's Police stereotype, on the other hand, is posited as the apotheosis of womanhood, as that to which all women strive. This idealization of women's vocation is peddled to unsuspecting women while the contradictory aspects of the role itself, as well as the unequal nature of the meeting of needs in the marriage union, are disguised by the accolades poured upon the stereotype and the superficial status afforded to women who try to conform to it.

DAMNED WHORES

The Damned Whore stereotype is a negative one; it is used to describe women who do not appear to be engaged in maintaining existing authority relations and is most often applied to women who are seen as actively contravening these relations—especially those governing women themselves. In practice it is often punitive as the very labelling of a

---

1   English writer and feminist (b. 1932).

woman as 'unrespectable' deprives her of any status and, as is shown below, often involves her losing many of the rights she is supposedly guaranteed as a citizen. The very fear of being castigated as Damned Whores keeps women in line; most women have no option but to conform to the God's Police stereotype in order to guarantee societal approbation and thus try to avoid these punitive measures. This stereotype is mainly applied to three groups of women: prostitutes, lesbians and women in prisons or detention homes. It is *assumed* that there is a necessary contradiction between being a prostitute or a lesbian and fulfilling the God's Police function; women in custody are actively *prevented* from doing so.

In contrast to God's Police, the Damned Whore stereotype is avowedly, although not exclusively, a sexual category. The prototype is the prostitute and, with her, any other women who trade on their bodies, such as strippers, as well as call girls, hostesses, massage parlour workers and the host of occupations which are euphemisms for selling some form of sexual service. But also included in this stereotype are any women who are sexually 'liberated', women who have extra-marital sexual relationships and especially those who bear children out of wedlock. There are obviously many, many women included in this stereotype but their numbers are partly disguised by further labels or descriptions which are used to categorize them, for example, gangsters' molls, bikies' girl-friends, groupies.

Many male groups like surfers or the men who congregate around a particular pub or a social or even political activity have names for the women who attach themselves to the group, proffering sex in return for some recognition and status as a group member. These names, like the ones mentioned above, are always denigratory and serve to differentiate *those* women from respectable women. The latter are the women these men would marry, and the labels they assign to the women who trail after them are designed to be constant reminders of the low esteem in which they are held. Other labels are used to identify women who are seen as 'fair game' to rapacious men. The purpose of such labels is always to single out sexually active or acquiescent women and to contrast them with the sisters, mothers or girl-friends of these men. In this way they both perpetuate the dual stereotypes and also tend to relegate the women so labelled to inconsequence. The latter tactic only works if the women accept the labels—but they often have little choice, especially if they are very young, very poor, come from certain suburbs or if they are black.

Women, too, have internalized the stereotypes and have accepted men's right to decide which one they belong to and it is only very strong women who can assert their right to be sexually active and not be treated purely as sex objects. The fear of being labelled a 'moll' or a prostitute deters many young women from using contraceptives: they argue that if they take 'the

Pill' they are admitting (to themselves) that they are promiscuous and that their boy-friends will think this of them. Their reasoning often leads to a pregnancy which, if they cannot marry to 'legitimize' the child, confers on them the very label they were trying to avoid.

1975

ROBERT GRAY
b. 1945

The poet Robert Gray grew up in Coffs Harbour, NSW. He became a cadet journalist for a country newspaper, but moved to Sydney where he worked in journalism, advertising and bookselling. He has, with the help of grants, supported himself by his writing. Among his collections of poetry are *Creekwater Journal* (1974), *The Skylight* (1984), and *Certain Things* (1993). His *New Selected Poems* (1998) is one of a number of such collections. Gray's poetry includes haiku, long sequences, prose poems and, increasingly, more traditional verse forms. His work is imagistic and precise, often attempting to represent actual places and events. 'Diptych' is one of a number of poems that deal with the poet's childhood. His memoir, *The Land I Came Through Last*, was published in 2008. Gray co-edited, with Geoffrey Lehmann (qv), the polemical poetry anthologies *The Younger Australian Poets* (1983) and *Australian Poetry in the Twentieth Century* (1991). He also co-edited, with Vivian Smith (qv), *Sydney's Poems* (1992). *DM*

Diptych

1

My mother told me of the way she often stayed awake
in those years, and of a certain night
at a wooden farmhouse,
on the end of the barred darkness and the dark leaf-mulch of the drive,
in which she waited on the steps with a mosquito-smoke,   5
listening for my father, once again, when the pubs had closed, knowing
    he'd have to walk
'miles, in his state', or would sleep in the weeds by the road,
if no one dropped him at our gate
(since long before this he had driven his own car off a mountain-side
and becoming legend had ridden   10
on the easily-felled banana palms
of a steep plantation, right to the foot and a kitchen door,
the car reared high, and slipping fast, on a vast
raft of sap-oozing fibre,
from which he'd climbed down, unharmed, his most soberly polite,   15
had raised his hat, to the terrified
young woman, with a child in arms—who must have appeared

slowly, like a photograph
developing in a dish—and had never driven again).
This other night my mother was reluctant   20
to set off on her search, poking underneath the lantana bushes, down
    every slope,
leaving us kids in the house asleep, our cough
trundling among us,
and fell asleep herself, clothed, on the unopened bed,
but leapt upright, sometime later, at the foulest taste—glimpsed   25
he was still not home—and rushed out, gagging,
to find that, asleep, she'd bitten off the tail
of a small lizard, dragged through her lips. That bitterness (I used to imagine),
running onto the verandah to spit,
and standing there, spat dry, seeing across the silent, frosty bush   30
the town had disappeared,
except for the frail water of a few street lights.

Yet my mother never ceased from what philosophers invoke,
from extending 'care',
although she had only read the *Women's Weekly*,   35
and although she could be 'damned impossible' through a few
    meal-times, of course.
That care for things, I see, was her one real companion in those years.
It was as if there were two of her,
a harassed person, and a calm, that saw what needed to be done, and
stepped through her, again.   40
Her care you could watch reappear like the edge of tidal water
in salt flats, about everything.
It was this made her drive out the neighbour's bull from our garden
    with a broom,
when she saw it trample her seedlings—
back, step by step, she forced it, through the broken fence,   45
it bellowing and hooking either side sharply at her all the way, and I
six years old on the back steps calling
'Let it have a few old bloody flowers, Mum.'
No. She locked the broom handle straight-armed across its nose, and
    was pushed right back herself
quickly across the yard. She   50
ducked behind the tomato stakes,
and beat with the handle, all over that deep hollowness of the muzzle,
poked with the straw at its eyes,
and had her way, drove it out bellowing;

and me, slapping into the steps, the rail, with an ironing cord,   55
or rushing down there, quelled also,
repelled to the bottom step, barracking. And all,
I saw, for those little flimsy leaves
she fell to at once, small as mouse prints, among the chopped-up loam.

2

Whereas, my father only seemed to care he would never appear a drunkard
while ever his shoes were clean.
A drunkard he defined as someone who had forgotten the mannerisms
of a gentleman. The gentleman, after all, is only known,
only exists, through manner. He himself had what seems to have been
       perfect form,   5
of a kind. I can imagine no one
with a manner more easily and coolly precise. With him,
manner had subsumed all of feeling. To brush and dent the hat
which one would doff, or to look about over each of us
then unfold a napkin   10
and allow the meal, in that town where probably all of the men
sat to eat of a hot evening without a shirt,
was his cold passion. After all, he was a university man
(although ungraduated), something more rare then. My father, I see, was
       hopelessly melancholic—
the position of those wary   15
small eyes, and thin lips, on the long-boned face
proclaimed the bitterness of every pleasure, except those of form.
He often drank alone
at the RSL club, and had been known to wear a carefully-considered tie
to get drunk in the sandhills, watching the sea.   20
When he was ill and was at home at night, I would look into his bedroom,
at the end of a gauzed verandah,
from around the door and a little behind him,
and see his frighteningly high-domed skull under the lamp-light,
       as he read
in a curdle of cigarette smoke.   25
Light shone through wire mesh onto the packed hydrangea-heads,
and on the great ragged mass of insects, like bees over a comb, that
       crawled tethered
and ignored right beside him. He seemed content, at these times,
as though he had done all that he could
to prove a case against himself, and had been forced, objectively, to
       give up.   30

He liked his bland ulcer-patient food
and the heap of library books I brought. (My instructions always were:
'Nothing whingeing. Nothing by New York Jews;
nothing by women, especially the French; nothing
translated from the Russian.')   35
and yet, the only time I actually heard him say that he had enjoyed anything
was when he spoke of the bush, once. 'Up in those hills,'
he advised me, pointing around, 'when the sun is coming out of the sea,
      standing among
that lifting timber, you can feel at peace.'
I was impressed. He asked me, another time, that when he died   40
I should take his ashes somewhere, and not put him with the locals, in the
      cemetery.
I went up to one of the places he had named
years earlier, at the time of day he had spoken of, when the half-risen sun
was as strongly-spiked as the one
on his Infantry badge,   45
and I scattered him there, utterly reduced at last, among the wet,
      breeze-woven grass.
For all his callousness to my mother, I had long accepted him,
who had shown me what I found was a recourse,
although not enough for him,
and had left me to myself. And I had come by then to see that all of us
      inhabit pathos.   50
Opening his plastic, brick-sized box, that morning,
my pocket-knife slid
sideways and pierced my hand—and so I dug with that one
into his ashes, which I found were like a mauvish-grey marble dust,
and felt that I needn't think of anything more to say.   55
                                                                     1984

MICHAEL LEUNIG
b. 1945

Leunig is Australia's most popular cartoonist. His immediately recognisable visual world is marked by humour and pathos, and populated by quizzical humans, dogs, ducks and cockatoos. While characteristically 'philosophical' and profoundly whimsical, Leunig's work can also be bitingly political. His cartoons often incorporate text, including poems. His work has inspired two stage productions, and in 2001 was adapted for television (using claymation). As well as cartoons, his published works include prayers, stories and poetry. In 1999 he was named an Australian National Living Treasure. *DM*

One of the Preambles[1]

We the people of Australia, being of indeterminate origin and inclination, not knowing who we are or what we believe in, and not much caring, yet squabbling and squabbling and squabbling—always bloody squabbling— hurried off our feet, cranky as hell, sick with worry, scared to death, up to our ears in debt, and being fairly illiterate, misled, caged, cooped, processed, drugged, dispirited, feckless, confused, hypnotised, conforming, crass—and pretending that we're *not* any of these things—do hereby declare that it's just one big stuff-up, they're all corrupt, what will be will be, and you're a long time dead. No worries, mate.

2004

The Life Cycle of the Supermarket Trolley

Supermarket trolleys come ashore under the full moon to lay their eggs in the sand. When the eggs hatch, the young trolleys make their way to the supermarket, where they assemble in the carpark. Now they begin their strange life engulfing and disgorging vast quantities of consumer items.

After several years, when they have reached maturity, the trolleys escape individually into the surrounding streets, and by various routes— drains, canals, rivers—they make their way back to the sea, where they mate in deep water and wait for the full moon to begin the cycle all over again.

2004

How Democracy Actually Works

After voting, the ballot papers are collected and taken to a furnace. There they are burned to fire a boiler which provides steam for a turbine, which drives a generator and produces electricity. The electricity is then conveyed to the parliament building by a special power line, where it is directed into a forty-watt lightbulb in the gents' lavatory. If you walk behind the building late at night, you can look up and see a dimly lit window and be reassured that your vote *does* matter.

2004

---

1   The Australian Constitution contains no preamble. Prime Minister John Howard proposed a preamble that was defeated in a referendum in 1999 (which included the more politically important question as to whether Australia should become a republic).

KEV CARMODY
b. 1946

Kev Carmody grew up on a cattle station in the Darling Downs area of south-eastern Queensland. When he was ten, he was taken from his parents and sent to a Christian school, which he has described as 'little more than an orphanage'. A travelling singer-songwriter based in southern Queensland, Carmody regularly tours Australian jails, where he plays to the Aboriginal inmates. His music employs a range of styles, including country, folk and rock'n'roll. He collaborated with singer-songwriter Paul Kelly (b. 1955) on the musical *One Night the Moon* (2001). Their song 'From Little Things Big Things Grow', about the Gurindji strike and Vincent Lingiari (qv), an Aboriginal rights activist who led the Wave Hill walk-off, has become an anthem for Indigenous rights and other grassroots movements for social change. *AH/PM*

From Little Things Big Things Grow

Gather round people, I'll tell you a story
An eight year long story of power and pride
British Lord Vestey[1] and Vincent Lingiari
Were opposite men on opposite sides

Vestey was fat with money and muscle   5
Beef was his business, broad was his door
Vincent was lean and spoke very little
He had no bank balance, hard dirt was his floor

From little things big things grow
From little things big things grow   10

Gurindji[2] were working for nothing but rations
Where once they had gathered the wealth of the land
Daily the pressure got tighter and tighter
Gurindji decided they must make a stand

They picked up their swags and started off walking   15
At Wattie Creek they sat themselves down
Now it don't sound like much but it sure got tongues talking
Back at the homestead and then in the town

From little things big things grow
From little things big things grow   20

---

1   Lord Vestey of the British Pastoral Company Vestey's, which owned Wave Hill Cattle Station.
2   Gurindji: the Aboriginal people in the Kalkaringi (Wave Hill) region.

Vestey man said 'I'll double your wages
Seven quid a week you'll have in your hand'
Vincent said 'Uh-uh we're not talking about wages
We're sitting right here 'til we get our land'
Then Vestey man roared and Vestey man thundered   25
'You don't stand the chance of a cinder in snow'
Vince said 'If we fall others are rising'

From little things big things grow
From little things big things grow

Then Vincent Lingiari boarded an aeroplane   30
Landed in Sydney, big city of lights
And daily he went round softly speaking his story
To all kinds of people from all walks of life

And Vincent sat down with big politicians
'This affair' they told him 'it's a matter of state   35
Let us sort it out, your people are hungry'
Vincent said 'No thanks, we know how to wait'

From little things big things grow
From little things big things grow

Then Vincent Lingiari returned in an aeroplane   40
Back to his country once more to sit down
And he told his people 'Let the stars keep on turning
We have friends in the south, in the cities and towns'

Eight years went by, eight long years of waiting
'Til one day a tall stranger appeared in the land   45
And he came with lawyers and he came with great ceremony
And through Vincent's fingers poured a handful of sand

From little things big things grow
From little things big things grow

That was the story of Vincent Lingiari   50
But this is the story of something much more
How power and privilege cannot move a people
Who know were they stand and stand in the law

From little things big things grow
From little things big things grow   55
                                                        1993

JOHN MUK MUK BURKE
b. 1946

Born in Narrandera, NSW, of a Wiradjuri mother and an Irish father, John Muk Muk Burke spent many years teaching music and art in schools in New Zealand, Darwin and outback NT. He has lectured at the Centre for Aboriginal Studies at Northern Territory (now Charles Darwin) University and worked with Aboriginal inmates at the Goulburn Correctional Centre. His novel, *Bridge of Triangles*, won the David Unaipon Award in 1993. He is also the author of *Night Song and Other Poems* (1999). *AH/PM*

A Poem for Gran

Flatwalk field of Suffolk—
Your insular chalk walls are crumbling.
The last of summer's apples
Are tumbling from your trees;
Your larders are fully laden   5
With earth-grown food—
A goodly preparation
For the cold and coming winter.

For your winter winds do whistle
Over flat fields, squat villages   10
And important towns.
And everywhere, sensible people are preparing.

The hay is gathered in
For the sheep's hard winter
And the hay is gathered in   15
For the street's hard sound
And the hay is gathered in
For the apples in the attic.

All over drifts the first smoke
Of winter's falling.   20
From a soft room of lavender
A little girl is calling.
Born at the ingathering
Of the good things of the earth.

And from overhead we see the red house   25
On the high street, the river turgid,

The tower Norman. Solid trees and lonely lanes.
And overhead the sky is grey and all around
Is England.

1999

DRUSILLA MODJESKA
b. 1946

Drusilla Modjeska was born in England and, after living in New Guinea in the 1960s, has lived in Australia since 1971. She was educated at the ANU and the University of NSW, where she wrote a PhD thesis that was subsequently published as *Exiles at Home: Australian women writers 1925–1945* (1981), a work that had a major influence on the feminist revision of Australian literary history. Modjeska has also had an impact on Australian life writing. *Poppy* (1990), her memoir of her mother, and *The Orchard* (1994) were innovative auto/biographical works. *Stravinsky's Lunch* (1999) was a double biography of the Australian artists Stella Bowen (1893–1947) and Grace Cossington Smith (1892–1984). Modjeska has also edited a number of works, including (with Marjorie Pizer) the poems of Lesbia Harford (qv). Her essays appear in *Timepieces* (2002). *DM*

From *Stravinsky's Lunch*
Chapter 1: Grace Cossington Smith

[…] It wasn't strange for a conservative family on the outskirts of a conservative city to produce an arty daughter; family attics and even the basements of our galleries and museums contain remnants of their efforts. Many a neglected daughter has dreamed of redemption as fine as Grace Cossington Smith's. What is extraordinary, and very wonderful, is that one such daughter, living an almost Edwardian existence, overcame the invisibility, the loneliness, the slights and the fantasies to produce images by which we have come to know ourselves as creatures of the twentieth century.

Who was the young woman who, as G.C. Smith, exhibited *The Sock Knitter* in Sydney in 1915, as the AIF dug in on the Gallipoli Peninsula? Who was she, this young woman who painted *Trees* with an eye that wouldn't be matched for twenty years? Who was this Miss Smith who could see human dilemma in a half-built bridge and show it to us as intensely as it has ever been seen? How did she come to make the moves, and view the world in such a way that these were the canvases she painted? What were her allegiances? How did she take her lunch?

It would be a great deal easier if she were a character of fiction, if I could show her to you as a young woman playing tennis in the first summer of the Great War, the ping of the ball as she lobbed it back across the net, or running with one of her sisters towards their mother watching from a chair on the verandah. Or if I could take you into her studio on the other side of the tennis court where the garden dipped into the gully. If the hand of imagination could turn the handle, open the door and turn up the lamps so that you could see her at her easel, her springy hair tied back in a loose knot.

Let's move along a bit, and say it's 1926 and she's working on *Trees*, giving form to movement, and also stillness, with those splashes of colour which bring the gum tree into the modern world. If she were a character of fiction, this young woman working out her oddly private aesthetic at the bottom of the garden, I could slip straight into an interior monologue, and tell her story from inside out. The first person could slide from me to her. *There is a path*, I'd say in her voice. *Look, you can see it. There, beneath the trees, beyond the tennis court. Step on that path and my heart lifts in wonder. Everything lifts. Tiredness lifts and is blown away with the wind. Listen, can you hear the birds? In that gum. There. Open the door, and you'll see. There. And the parrots in the firewheel tree, look—its scarlet flowers grow straight from the branch. One day I'll paint them. Just at this moment I'm busy with this tree. I have a strange sensation, as if I am the tree, as if I am the colour I squeeze from the tube.*

I am here, come in, let me open the door.

But she isn't a character. Thanks to Daniel Thomas,[1] *Trees* hangs in the Newcastle Gallery; you can go and see it for yourself. And perhaps you will see her there, and the difficulty of finding her, the presence behind the canvas, will be mine alone. The temptation of fiction rests, as it always does, on sleight of hand; two pieces of coloured scarf go into the conjuror's sleeve, and out comes a rabbit or a dove. The danger of turning real people into fiction is that fiction takes life from wherever it can find it, so the fictional being swells with well-nourished certainty while the original person, the person we want to understand with all the hesitations and awkwardnesses of real life, can be replaced in our imaginations as if she were indeed real; the necessary mystery is lost and, knowing too much, we forget how little we know.

There is another conundrum at the heart of Grace Cossington Smith's story. Her paintings swell with the superabundance of life, they are the wonder of her, they are absolutely her, or at any rate *hers*; but the actuality of her daily life, her daily being, slips away behind them. Grace Cossington Smith, once a sister, a daughter, *a sweet Christian lady*, and now a cultural icon, exists in an extreme state of contingency. I can't tell you how she walked, or laughed, or sneezed. I can't tell you what was in her head when she painted *Trees*. I can tell you that in the small snippet of tape that exists of her voice, she sounds terribly English, somewhere between the Queen and an elderly aunt; she has a light, fluttery, slightly trilling voice. When she says that people watching her as she sketched put her off, the word *off*

---

1 Curator (b. 1931), emeritus director of the Art Gallery of South Australia, Adelaide.

is pronounced *orf.* It is a way of speaking, precise and elongated, that is as distant as the sound track of a crackly film.

Other than that, she has left very little trace of herself. Her private, personal self. There are few interviews, few letters, few photos, no diaries. The work, the shining work, hides as much as it reveals. As I endeavour to find a coherent story, a pattern, a shape for the work, and for the woman who gave us these astonishing paintings, I am working all the time with bright patches of light in deep shade. As if, in a splash of sunlight, she is suddenly there, visible, at hand, understandable; but such appearances are brief, fluttering. Stella Bowen told her own story from inside out, and she alerted us to its essential drama. Grace painted the life around her and breathed herself into her work with such transforming and elusive power that she vanishes in the very act of giving us herself.

The sensation I get, trying to write about her, is rather like looking at her late interiors, those wonderful paintings, dense with yellow, in which a cupboard door swings open, and you have the feeling that if you just leaned a little more this way or that, or poked your neck through the picture plane, you'd be able to glimpse her. But she placed that mirror, she tilted it, and she cannot be seen. She is not there. The painting is redolent of her, every brush stroke was made by her, and yet where is she, this Grace Cossington Smith? Who was the inhabitant of this bedroom with its neat, narrow bed and its door open onto the verandah and the garden beyond?

I can tell Stella Bowen's story; it's a story I know, a story I understand. I am of a generation which has lived its own version of that story: sex and love and betrayal, babies and work (babies *or* work), Paris, cafés, a precarious independence. I am of a disposition that understands all too well the struggle between the desire to give in to the narrative of love and the almost automatic habit of keeping on, of somehow managing. I know the insistence of work and the support that comes from one's bruised and brilliant women friends. I even know Grace Crowley's[1] rather more genteel version of it. I know the desire to make something of an ambivalent femininity by creating an enigmatic link between the man one keeps secret in the background of life, and the work that takes us forward with something to argue for. All this I understand.

But Grace? No husbands. No babies. No affairs. No scandals. No cafés in Paris. By the time she was my age, the most exciting thing that happened in a year was when her sister Diddy bought a car and they could venture further afield. Diddy would put a deck chair in the boot so that she could read or snooze while Grace sketched. In the prejudices of our time,

---

1   An Australian artist (1890–1979).

Grace's story, viewed externally, would never make a book. In the prejudices of her time, she was, simply, a spinster.

This time the hand of imagination lifts the curtain to a tennis court no longer used unless the nieces, her brother Gordon's girls, come over on holiday weekends. A week interrupted by nothing more strenuous than a tea party for neighbouring ladies. Cakes, chairs of slatted cane, tea pots, comfortable cardigans. There are still odd train trips into town, over the bridge we know how to see because she painted it for us; best dresses for a concert or ballet; shopping at Farmers' or at David Jones, and a cup of tea in the lacquer room. Church every Sunday. The last two sisters alone in the house where once there'd been five—four girls and one brother. Running onto the lawn, it had been their racquets that had met the dull thwack of the ball and sent it back across the net. It had been Grace who had run ahead to their mother, to kiss her temple, her two young sisters dressed as Quaker girls grinning for her camera.

Who was she, this girl who comes to us in these slender glimpses? Who was this young woman who saw a kind of fundamental knowledge in a tangle of branches? Who opened the door to her studio and bowed before the colour—'it has to shine; light must be in it'—which she saw in the world around her, and squeezed from her tubes of paint? What did she know of the stiffening body which thirty years later would lift the deck chair and easel from the boot of the car? Did she already have a premonition, did she already know the shape of the woman who would open the cool, quiet house while her sister parked the car in the garage? When she pushed open the door of her studio to put down the easel, had her hope for the journey been replaced with resignation for the road?

It's all nonsense of course.

It's imagining that comes from the word spinster and not from the strange paradoxes of Grace herself. I can't even answer the most basic of questions: did she choose this way of living, or was it thrust upon her? Did she develop the life of the spinster into an art-form, virtue stitched from necessity, or did she use it as a ruse for a very different life? Was she released into her art by her distance from men? Was it easier for her, or harder? Was art given a free run, untrammelled by the vagaries and exigencies of love? How did she remain alive to the world around her without the charge and satisfactions that come to us when we plunge into love? How did she hold desire at bay? What went on under the spinsterly camouflage, if camouflage it was? What held her to her work? What did she mean when she said she painted what she saw? What, in any case, did she see?

Who was she, this sweet Christian lady? This great Australian artist?

How shall I tell her story?

1999

MARTIN JOHNSTON
1947–1990

Martin Johnston—the son of Charmian Clift and George Johnston (qqv)—was born in Sydney and raised partly in Greece, a place that informs much of his writing. He returned with his family to Australia in 1964. He discontinued his studies at the University of Sydney to pursue a career in journalism (though this did not eventuate). Johnston spent some years back in Greece, working on his poetry and an experimental novel, *Cicada Gambit* (1983). He began, but did not finish, a biography of his parents, was a subeditor and subtitler for SBS television and travelled in Europe before returning to Australia in 1989. Johnston published three volumes of poetry, including *The Sea-Cucumber* (1978) and *The Typewriter, Considered as a Bee-Trap* (1984). A selection of his poetry and prose, edited by John Tranter (qv), was published in 1993. Johnston's early death from alcoholism was shadowed, according to Tranter, by a sense of rootlessness, and the effects of his parents' lifestyle and their subsequent deaths. Johnston's poems are complex, erudite and, as *The Oxford Companion to Australian Literature* (1994) puts it, 'responsive to literary traditions different from those recognised by other Australian poets of his generation'. *DM*

The Sea-Cucumber

For Ray Crooke[1]

We'd all had a bit too much that night when you brought out your painting,
the new one, you remember, over Scotch in the panelled kitchen,
and my father talked about waiting. Well, he was doing that, we knew,
or it could have been the dust you'd painted, the way you'd floated
a sfumato background almost in front of the canvas   5
so your half-dozen squatting dark figures couldn't see it
that moved him in that moment softly, in damp stone, outside time.
He was as garrulous as ever, of course, but somehow,
in a time of his own, it seemed that he was pressing
every word-drop, like the wine of a harvest not quite adequate,   10
to trickle in brilliant iridules across the stained table:
what sorts of eucalypt to plant—so that they'd grow quickly—
art dealers, metaphysics, three old men he'd seen
at Lerici, playing pipes and a drum under an orange sky.
Memory finds a nexus, there in your image,   15
people just waiting, not even conscious of it,
or of ochre and sienna pinning them in an interstice of hours.
None of this, you see, will really go into writing,
it takes time to leech things into one's sac of words.
The bloated sea-cucumber, when touched, spews up its entrails   20

---

1   Ray Crooke (b. 1922), an Australian painter, won the Archibald Prize in 1969 for his portrait of George Johnston (qv), Martin Johnston's father.

as though that were a defence; my father's old friend
the gentle little poet Wen Yi-tuo,[1] who collected chess sets
and carved ivory seals in his filthy one-room hut,
is gutted one night and flung into the Yangtze.
The dark river runs through your dusty pigments.   25
Ferns, moss, tiger-coloured sun beat at the window with banners
but the dust ripples between trees, and among the waiting
glints of earth and metal are wiped from the fading hand.
These people of yours, Ray, they are that evening
when we first saw them, or the other one when my father   30
planted nineteen saplings in our backyard, or when you looked at them
later and said, They're coming on, and his fingers
drummed a long nervous question on the table, though he agreed.
And we were all waiting, though not in your style of art:
more of a pointillism in time, disconnected moments,   35
a flash of light over an empty glass, a half-finished volume of Borges,
the cabbage palm stooping at dusk into the chimneys,
certain paintings, Corelli, or a morning like the fuzz of a peach,
all bright and disparate. But I think, remembering that painting
of yours, that if one could step away, ten yards, or twenty, or years,   40
at an angle perhaps, a frame would harden into cedar
and through a haze of dust we would see all the brilliant dots
merge into a few figures, squatting, waiting.

                                                                    1978

'The typewriter, considered as a bee-trap'

For Roseanne

The typewriter, considered as a bee-trap,
is no doubt less than perfectly adapted
to its function, just as a bee-trap,
if there are such things, would hardly be the ideal contrivance
for the writing of semi-aleatory poems about   5
bee-traps and typewriters. Why, in any case,
you are entitled to ask, should I
want to trap bees at all? What do with them
if caught? But there are times, like today,
when bees hover about the typewriter   10
more frequently than poems, surely knowing best
what best attracts them. And certainly at such times,

---

1   Wen Yiduo (1899–1946), Chinese poet and scholar.

considered in terms of function and structure,
the contraption could be argued to be
anything but a typewriter,   15
the term 'anything' being considered
as including, among all else, bee-traps,
softly mutiplying in an ideal world.

1984

BRUCE PASCOE
b 1947

Bruce Pascoe, a member of the Wathaurong Aboriginal Co-operative of southern
Victoria, has combined writing fiction and non-fiction with a career as a successful
publisher. He has also worked as a farmer, fisherman, barman, lecturer, Aboriginal
language researcher and as a labourer on archaeological sites.

From 1982 to 1998 Pascoe edited and published *Australian Short Stories*, an
influential quarterly journal of short fiction by new and established writers. He has
edited educational texts on Wathaurong history and language, and is a highly regarded
speaker on Aboriginal culture and social justice. Pascoe has continued to edit and
publish anthologies and translations of Australian stories, and has authored detective
fiction, children's books and historical and autobiographical works, including *The Great
Australian Novel* (1984), *Night Animals* (1986), *Ruby-Eyed Coucal* (1996), *Shark* (1999),
Nightjar (2000), *Earth* (2001), *Ocean* (2002) and *Convincing Ground: Learning to fall in love
with your country* (2007). *AH/PM*

The Slaughters of the Bulumwaal Butcher

Bodies had always been found. Dogs, kangaroos, sometimes even cattle and
horses had been found, dreadfully mutilated, the heads torn completely from
the bodies.

This was Nargun country, and the Aborigines said that these slaughters
had been occurring far back in black memory and were attributed to the
Nargun, the stone beast which on some still, frosty nights roamed through
the hills looking for food.

The white population claimed that an escaped panther from a travelling
circus was the culprit; others thought that a Yowie was responsible. Old Clive
Glossop, the post splitter, reckoned he had seen a huge hairy beast massacre a
big kangaroo in his paddock. The pile of Ruby port bottles outside his shack
was enough evidence for most people to discredit this story.

It's true that old Mrs Muir disappeared without trace ten years ago,
leaving the kettle on the stove and the radio tuned to 'Evening Concert', and
it's also true that Murphy's huge Friesian cow gave birth to an extraordinarily
ugly hairy calf; but all of these things were classified by most people as
those mysterious affairs that occur, but which have perfectly simple scientific

explanations. Mrs Muir could have fallen down a mine shaft, and Murphy's cow probably just had a freak calf. And Glossop—well, everybody knew about Clive Glossop.

But this was a bit different. Since the start of winter over twenty sheep had been killed. Their heads were torn from their bodies, and the guts and feet found strewn in their clotted blood. The manner of the deaths was similar to the mutilations of the kangaroos and dogs. Perc Hopkins, the Aboriginal rouseabout from the saw mill, saw one of the sheep and began grumbling about Narguns and pointed up into the hills where a huge granite tor stood out in the open pasture. That was the Nargun, Perc claimed, and any night he might wake up and come looking for tucker.

Although Perc immediately took his first holiday in thirty years and went to visit his cousins on the Murray, the whites still talked about some logical explanation, like an escaped panther or a Tasmanian Tiger. Clive Glossop insisted on his Yowie story, but he was given two bottles of Ruby port and sent home.

The massacre of sheep continued during the winter, and over the Sunday roast Les Patterson told his wife it was about time something was done. Les, a shire councillor and football club president, went to the pub on the following night and there he met Clarrie Watson, Dan Murphy and Tom Mullins, sheep farmers all. Little Phonce Wallace-Pimble, the chemist and Bulumwaal councillor, was also there, and so a meeting was held, and they determined that they would find the sheep killer and put a stop to this nonsense about Yowies, panthers and Narguns. The council had always held the responsibility for quelling civic imagination.

A week later this same group of solid citizens stood around the latest scene of massacre and counted the heads and remains of eleven sheep. Les pointed out the tyre marks in the mud a hundred yards down the track. Ten days later they stood looking down at the remains of more sheep scattered in the frosty grass.

Phonce Wallace-Pimble was short of breath in the crispness of the morning, and his face was wreathed in vapour as he ventured that this carnage might be the work of wild dogs and dingoes.

Les Patterson looked down at the little chemist and smoke seemed to snort from his nostrils as he declared such talk to be nonsense. Later he told Tom Mullins that he couldn't expect anything more sensible from a town man who didn't have the good sense to wear decent boots when walking around in frosty paddocks.

Les didn't miss the tyre tracks in the soft soil near the paddock gate, and later that day stood behind Jack Slattery's truck and recognized the same tread. Les rubbed his chin and went to the hotel. He leant on the bar as the others spouted their theories over foaming pots. Narguns, panthers, and Yowies were favoured possibilities, but wild dogs were, as always, clear favourites. Some farmers would have blamed wombats, koalas and corellas if they hadn't been vegetarians.

As the slaughters continued, the more bizarre and frightening theories gained credence. Herb Nash, the local alcoholic and wit, was scared of nothing, but suggested it could be the work of Mrs Kestrel, the local school mistress and witch. This became a popular theory among children: bloody sheep feet began to appear on the teacher's table, and mysterious bleatings would issue from a class of students who appeared to be working harder than they ever had before.

The story of the ram being let loose in the school house seemed a great joke and, in the hotel that night, the story went through many stages of elaboration, including wild exaggerations of the various delights and frights experienced by either the ram or Mrs Kestrel. That the school mistress's bloomers had been rent by the ram's horns could not be doubted because Les Patterson had seen them himself when he went to retrieve his stud ram. As a councillor his word could not be doubted and when he said he would kill the kid who kidnapped his ram, that was not doubted either, and several kids immediately went down with apparently incurable cases of flu, dysentery and fits.

It didn't seem quite so funny the next morning when the cleaner found Mrs Kestrel hanging from the school bell with a note addressed to her sister propped on the desk where all her papers and books had been carefully packed away. She had chalked a 'No School Today' notice on the board and left enough spelling and maths to last two weeks. It was considered by many rather unfortunate in retrospect that the words 'you, yew and ewe' had been included. Among the books she had corrected the night before, police found that a student, beside the poem 'Baa baa, black sheep', had chosen to illustrate it with a picture of a witch and a huge cauldron of dismembered sheep. Mrs Kestrel had begun to write the usual good work legend but had apparently stopped on seeing the illustration accompanying the poem. Neighbours who had heard a desultory clanging of the bell had thought the wind was responsible and had continued to watch Brian Naylor's version of the news.

Les was worried by other things. The death of the schoolteacher was the result of an unfortunate town prank, although he had harboured suspicions about the school mistress since he himself had been a child at the school. Mrs Kestrel had kept him in on one occasion and blasted him with tongue and cane, and he never forgot her piercing eyes and wicked laugh and the way her neck and face flushed with excitement as she beat and harangued her victim.

But Les knew she had not been responsible for the sheep. He also knew Jack Slattery, and Jack was a close friend, a solid citizen and a fellow member of the Chamber of Commerce. Times were becoming hard for graziers, and the whole district was suffering a prolonged recession. The export of stud rams had made an impact on traditional markets for Australian lamb, and many farmers, including Les, were mortgaged several times over.

Les decided that a visit to Jack Slattery was vital. Jack was curious when Les ignored his wife, the good Edith Slattery, and asked for a private talk. Jack was a genial man and thought that Les had found an excuse for the two of them to share a few beers and discuss the latest intrigues in the process of syphoning money away from the pre-school and elderly citizens' funds in order to seal certain access roads to rural properties.

Jack hurried to get cans and chips so that they could get down to tintacks. Les looked uncomfortable and finally said, 'Ar, look, Jack, it's about these sheep.' Jack began pouring beer into glasses with manic concentration.

'What sheep?' he said, apparently uninterested.

'Now come on, Jack, we've been mates for a long time. You know bloody well what sheep.' Jack was short, tubby, red-faced, bristly about nose and ears, but glassily clean shaven elsewhere. Les, lean and weathered with pale grey, penetrating eyes, regarded his friend with impatient discomfort. He was used to the dumb predictability of sheep, dogs and councillors, and this sophistry was making it difficult for him to find a comfortable position in his chair.

'Look, Jack, don't play possum with me. There's been over thirty sheep killed recently, and I've seen your tyre treads at the scene of every—well, every—slaughter.' The word was hard for Les to say, and he took a deep draught of beer.

The local butcher looked carefully at his angular friend, and his mind tried to assess the possibility of subterfuge, but then he relaxed and smiled. He was as concerned as a rabbit when it is cornered by a kangaroo dog. Under such circumstances intelligence is of no use; it is a contest between the relative power of jaws and flesh. Les, Jack decided, definitely had the canines. It was time for whippet and rabbit to make a deal.

Jack explained the expense of bringing meat from Bairnsdale, the poor economic climate of the town, his own financial difficulties due to an unfortunate gamble in gold investment and how he had decided to procure cheap meat for his butchery.

'We've always been good mates, Les,' he said, and on a sudden inspiration his pouch of brains tossed up an idea. 'Now, look, we could organize this properly. You farmer blokes are getting nothing for your sheep at the markets, and I can't compete with the big butchers, so why don't we keep the old panther scare going. We could—' He searched for details. 'We could form a syndicate of farmers and butcher our own sheep, leave the heads in the paddock and make a decent profit for a change. All we'd have to do would be to keep it quiet.' Jack and Les looked at each other.

The following evening a small group of farmers—Tom Mullins, Dan Murphy, Les Patterson, Clarrie Watson, Jack Slattery the butcher, and inevitably, despite Les's distaste for the man, Phonce Wallace-Pimble the chemist—talked over the scheme at a quiet table in the pub. A darts competition kept the other patrons engaged, and as the barman called for blokes to get their last drinks and get out, the syndicate shook hands.

The slaughters continued. The financial prospects of a few farmers improved, the butcher flourished, and the syndicate muddied the waters by shredding their sheep dogs' winter coats and fixing tufts of dog hair into the barbed-wire fences wherever a slaughter had taken place.

The wild-dog theory gained immediate credence, and syndicate members pointed at various reprobate town dogs, which were at once put to death. Les, Jack and Phonce got the council to put up vermin notices calling for the death of wild dogs, the government was approached by the shire to begin trapping dingoes, and funds were poured in by the local farmer-elected politician. Most of the money went to finish road works out to the farms of syndicate members and to provide a new awning for the chemist and butcher shops.

The dog trapper visited his traps for a fortnight without trapping or even seeing a wild dog, but the Lands Department forgot they had sent him there, and the computer kept on paying him. It seemed like a fair thing to him so he stayed on, bought a house, married the baker's daughter, failed to catch dogs, but succeeded in supporting the bar of the hotel.

The slaughters went on. Disgruntled sheep dogs had tufts of fur torn from their bodies so that it could be applied to barbed wire but, in general, rural life continued. Even the fortunes of the local footy sides picked up, and the Bulumwaal Blues registered their first win in three seasons. The butcher supplied free lamb chops to celebrate their victory.

One morning Jack Slattery and Clarrie Watson were just loading the last carcasses into the butcher's van when they saw old Clive Glossop hurrying into the bush towards his hut in the hills. Jack and Clarrie were holding the warm carcass of one of Clarrie's wethers between them, and they looked at each other. Old Clive had certainly seen them, but would anyone believe him? They quickly covered up the evidence of the slaughter and didn't even knot dog fur into the barbed wire.

That night in the hotel the syndicate met and digested the news that Jack and Clarrie brought to the meeting. The bar was rowdy and still incoherently celebrating the one consecutive win of the local footy team. Clarrie and Les were selectors for the team, and it was assumed that they were planning an assault on the Tabberaberra Tigers.

The syndicate could reach no decision. Their scheme was financially rewarding at a time when farmers around the continent were leaving their farms. And yet, one word from Clive Glossop, despite his reputation as an alcoholic, could cause a scandal, especially among the farmers in more desperate financial plight who had not been invited to join the Bulumwaal butchers' syndicate.

It was tentatively decided to buy off Clive with a side of lamb each month, a case of Ruby port and a generous contract for fence posts. Some of the syndicate members felt that the very inclusion of such vast quantities of Ruby port would make Clive an untrustworthy member of the party. They decided to meet the next night to discuss the matter further and in the meantime slaughters would temporarily cease.

The next night the syndicate stood silently at the bar ready to begin their meeting after a couple of quick pots to clear the head. Les put his glass down and was just about to begin when Phonce Wallace-Pimble burst in through the doors, hair dishevelled, tie askew, and eyes wild. The dart spectators stared at the little chemist, who was covering his face with tiny pink hands. The pub fell silent. The darts player stood with dart poised to throw. The barman poured beer all over his hand. The syndicate members were frozen, some in the act of finishing off the last drops of beer. Jack had a hand in his pocket ready for his shout, and Les's hand was placed on the bar in the manner of a chairman impatient to begin. All looked towards Phonce.

'It's Clive,' the chemist said, and passed an arm across his eyes. 'He's dead, he's dead, the dogs must have got him! His—his head's been torn off, and his body's gone except for the legs—' The barman came around the bar and pressed a stiff brandy into the chemist's quivering hand. Phonce drank quickly and went on. 'He'd been sick for a few days, and I ordered some medicine from Melbourne, and when I took it out to him, there he was— with this.' Phonce held up a port bottle and only Les noticed the peculiar brownish stain on the under side of Phonce's sleeve.

The syndicate members looked from one to the other, searching for the eyes of the one who had found the solution to their problem. Les looked at Phonce, and Phonce looked back. Les moved to the chemist's side and took the bottle from him and carefully lowered Phonce's upraised arm.

'Well, it looks like the dogs, all right,' said Les, and immediately the bar was full of conjectures, predictions and proposals, and more local dogs came under the scrutiny of the bar-room investigations. 'I betcha it's the bookie's Pekinese,' said a rugged gambler. Other eyes cast about the bar for dogs. The publican's black labrador, which had slept in a corner of the pub every night for fifteen years, suddenly woke up and found thirty men staring at him; he yelped once, dashed for the door, and was never seen again.

The council redoubled its efforts to raise government funds to deal with the menace, the Lands Department discovered that it still had a dog trapper in the area and immediately gave him the sack. The computer continued to pay for him for five years.

Worst of all, the sheep slaughters were repeated regularly, and on these nights many people had seen the ghost of old Clive Glossop roaming the paddocks screaming in a voice that echoed far across the moonlit paddocks, 'Butchers! butchers, butchers!'

The menace that threatened the flocks by night became known as the Bulumwaal Butcher and speculation on the form of the dread beast was both varied and bizarre. The local council had no answer to the problem, and people learned to live with the ravages of local livestock. And besides, the footy team won another game and the chemist turned on a pie night. Not such a bad bloke after all—for a chemist.

1986

ERROL WEST
1947–2001

Born in Tasmania of the Pairrebeene clan, Errol West (Japanangka) is best known for his strong advocacy of Aboriginal education in national and international forums. West worked closely with Aboriginal communities and chaired numerous committees that funded Aboriginal education, teacher employment and policy development. He also made a significant contribution to Aboriginal scholarship through his work at various universities. *AH/PM*

'Sitting, wondering, do I have a place here?'

Sitting, wondering, do I have a place here?
The breast of Mother Earth bore me, yet long I host a shell of
emptiness, a human husk winnowed in the draught of history,
    my
essence ground on the mill of white determination.   5

I fight though mortally wounded, life blood and spirit ebbing away
in the backwater of despair, caused by long-winded politicians'
promises and administration's cumbersome gait;
another realisation of my hopelessness produces; another promise,
implementation of a band-aid gimmick, you had better hurry   10
    it's
getting late, red tape, budgets, strategies,
Rape!

Return me to my beloved land, let me be me, don't you understand?

All I want is a private dying in the arms of my Mother Earth,   15
she

too is suffering; as a mother must when her children are ripped
away from her love, and the safety of her arms, no more to be cradled,
tenderly caressed by her heavenly smoldering essence.

                                                                                    1988

DAVID MARR
b. 1947

David Marr was born and educated in Sydney. Although a qualified solicitor and barrister he has not practised law. Instead, he began a successful journalistic career in 1972, as a reporter for the *Bulletin*. Marr has since worked for the *Sydney Morning Herald*, edited the *National Times*, hosted the ABC television program *Media Watch*, presented ABC Radio National's 'Arts Today' program, and reported for ABC TV's *Four Corners*. 'Black Death', his award-winning *Four Corners* story, concerned Aboriginal deaths in custody in Western Australia. Marr's books include *Barwick* (1980), a biography of the then Chief Justice Sir Garfield Barwick, and *Patrick White: A life* (1991). A winner of many major literary awards, Marr's biography of White (qv) was also a bestseller. Marr went on to edit *Patrick White: Letters* (1994). A strident critic of the Howard government (1996–2007), Marr co-wrote (with Marian Wilkinson) *Dark Victory* (2003), an account of the politicisation of Australian border security, and *His Master's Voice: The corruption of public debate under Howard* (2007). DM

From *Patrick White*
Chapter 25: The Prize

[. . .] White would not come out. A few men in the late 1960s, taking their cue from the Gay Rights movement in America, had begun to declare their homosexuality in public in order to campaign for the reform of laws which nearly everywhere in Australia made sex between men a crime. The notion of coming out struck White as preposterous. He declined to add his name to those homosexuals, churchmen, anarchists, lawyers and politicians appealing for reform. The first demonstrations for homosexual rights began in Australia in 1971. White never marched. His advice to those who suggested he take part was to get off the streets and get on with their lives.

Homosexuality was lived not debated by him. At lunch one day in 1972 White remarked that a poison-pen letter had come in the morning post. 'Just the usual sort of thing,' he said, refusing to give details. Lascaris[1] cheerfully volunteered: 'It said: you are living with a man, presumably white' (laughter) 'in an uncertain sexual relationship . . .' They were all old acquaintances around the table, but this openness seemed to distress White. He sat looking

---

1   Emmanuel 'Manoly' Lascaris (1912–2003), White's life partner.

into his plate as Lascaris rattled off the letter. He did not share the joke. Lascaris finished and White said flatly, 'Yes, that was it.'

White was contemptuous of those who pretended not to be homosexual. He made no secret of it, nor did he make declarations. As he gossiped about everyone in the most precise detail, so he gossiped about homosexuals, but his own sexuality was not a topic for general discussion at Martin Road. His house was never a homosexual enclave and he scorned those who lived in a coterie of queens. Yet for all this he and Manoly Lascaris were the best-known homosexual couple in the country. Australians took it on the chin. For homosexuals this long marriage was an emblem—at least from a distance—of stability and happiness.

'Manoly fortunately seems well,' White wrote in one of his New Year letters to Ronald Waters.[1] 'I am so lucky to have found him, and that it has lasted twenty-six years in spite of me.' Lascaris survived this life like a reef in a difficult stretch of sea. Visitors saw terrible storms at Martin Road. White snarled and raged. Grim things were said. Drink exaggerated it all, and in fury and self-disgust White wondered how Lascaris could love him—and this, in turn, made the rages worse. He who sought to possess all he loved found this man was not to be possessed. So the storms continued, blowing up out of a calm sea and dying away again. Living together, White once explained, 'means endless sacrifices . . . endless disappointments and patching up. I imagine only vegetables live happily ever after, and then only in a vague, vegetable way.' White's recipe for staying together was this: 'Laughter, love and now and then a really blistering row to clear the air.' David Moore[2] watched one of these rows, familiar to him now after knowing them for so many years, and wrote in his diary: 'M. took off his glasses and his eyes seemed to show unbearable sadness.'

Yet White would say that the only good thing he had done in his life was to find Manoly; that his existence was inconceivable without him; that his only loyalty was to Manoly; that Manoly was the source of any virtue in his own life. He once gave Margery Williams[3] a list of the worst that could happen to him. It began, 'if Manoly should die' and continued, 'if I should lose all my money, suffer a stroke, go blind, dry up as a writer, experience a foreign occupation'. He defended Lascaris ferociously. One night Douglas Carnegie, a grazier married to a great art collector, turned to Lascaris and asked, 'And what do you do?' There was a volcanic eruption from White. When *Time* wrote that Patrick White lived in Sydney 'with several dogs and a male housekeeper', he drew the magazine's attention

---

1   English actor and friend of White's.
2   An Australian friend of White's who worked as an editor at Angus & Robertson.
3   An English friend.

to 'an incorrect, and I should have thought gratuitous, biographical detail. The distinguished, and universally respected man who has given me his friendship and moral support over a period of thirty-four years, has never been a housekeeper. *I* am that, and shall continue playing the role at least till I am paralysed: it keeps me in touch with reality . . .' *Time* did not publish the rest of the sentence:'often remote from those who dish up their superficial, slovenly pieces for *Time Magazine*'.

They were still lovers. People sometimes assumed in a muddled way that the two men had entered some elderly celibate phase of existence. White corrected them sharply. A couple of years before his sixtieth birthday, he was joking with Ronald Waters about some friend who only found happiness when he became impotent. 'I'm sure I never shall,' White wrote. 'So here's to unhappiness. Of course that is only deep down amongst the fantasies, whereas in actual fact I am happier than most people have been.'

So dry were the early months of 1973 that flocks of sulphur-crested cockatoos flew in from the bush to plunder city gardens. When they first appeared on the lawn outside his window White stopped typing, but soon they were so at ease that Ethel sat with them and they preened and squabbled around her on the grass. Six, then twelve, then fourteen birds flew down each day. 'Manoly puts out sunflower seed and I suppose word has got round that the food is good,' White told David Campbell.[1] 'I can't think where they've come from. The only time I've seen them in mobs was when I was at Bolaro and they used to pull down the oats as soon as we had stooked them up at harvest. A wave of white cockatoos is the most beautiful, clumsy sight.' Campbell replied with a poem,

> cornstalks
> Down for the Show,
> Boasting of nuts they've cracked,
> Crops they've wrecked;
>
> And passing the word:
> Good pickings at Martin Road

White was tidying up the stories he had written in the last six years, and correcting proofs of *The Eye of the Storm*. The two tasks proceeded together. He was oxywelding 'Sicilian Vespers' as he answered publishers' queries on the novel. Should the Princess de Lascabanes hear 'rust rubbing against rust' as she flies on Air France? Cape cautioned that airlines were particularly

1   David Campbell (qv).

sensitive after recent crashes. The words were dropped. Did ecologists and private helicopters exist in the 1950s? Yes. Would he substitute 'dark brown' for 'nigger' in the Viking edition? He was surprised. 'By all means if you feel unhappy about it. "Dark brown" sounds a bit feeble. I'd prefer "burnt umber".' Are princes so rare in France that he should explain the Lascabanes' title? No. 'Princes are, indeed, rare in France, and usually rather parvenu, being descended from the royalty created by Napoleon ... But I can't very well go into a dissertation, can I? in a novel, any more than I could have given the recipes from Greek dishes referred to in my Greek stories in *The Burnt Ones*, as was more or less suggested. Mrs Hunter, in a conversation with Dorothy, does refer to Hubert de Lascabanes as "that upstart prince". Perhaps if I substitute *"parvenu"* for "upstart" it will demonstrate more emphatically that he is not of the best.' More play should be made, he thought, of princes and knights in the publishers' blurb: 'I think it might help sales in Australia, where so many are social snobs at heart in spite of all the talk of democracy.'

For 'Sicilian Vespers' he needed to check some Catholic details, so he returned to mass a couple of times at Christ Church, St Laurence 'to get a bit of religious feeling into me. I found drag queens with sequins on their eyelids screaming their heads off.' Once the second version of the story was finished he started to rework 'A Woman's Hand'. Even in the stories already published he found a lot he wanted to alter: not the general drift but many 'words and meanings'. As he revised, a new story came 'fully fledged' to him and he broke off to get a first version down on paper. 'The latest story is called "The Cockatoos",' he told Maschler,[1] and that would be the title of the collection. 'I can see a beautiful jacket.' The day he finished the first draft, David Campbell's poem arrived. It was something to add to the book of coincidences he always meant to keep. 'My life is made up of them.' He quizzed the poet on Air Force jargon and the lethal possibilities of double-barrelled shot guns.

Swapping back and forth from late to early versions of the six stories was relaxing work, and the only minor irritation was a stuck 'm' on his Olivetti. In July the typescript of the book was finished and despatched to his agent with a dedication: 'To Ronald Waters for having survived forty-eight years of friendship.' Waters was surprised and flattered by this, though he discovered he liked *The Cockatoos* least of all White's books. 'So gloomy. Everyone in it died.'

A spirit of creative housekeeping hovered over White. *A Fringe of Leaves* had been lying ten years in his drawer for Mrs Fraser[2] to recover, he said, from the mauling of librettists and composers. Now it seemed time to go

---

1 Tom Maschler (b. 1933), White's London publisher.
2 Eliza Fraser (c. 1798–1858?), a Scottish woman shipwrecked on the coast of Queensland in 1836. She is the subject of *A Fringe of Leaves* (1976).

back to her. White was still uncertain, and wanted to see the Barrier Reef for the first time, and be 'immersed in the seascapes and light before embarking on the Mrs Fraser novel—if I do'. In August, once the stories were cleared from his desk, he and Lascaris flew north and joined a cruise ship that took them through the Whitsunday Islands. This was school holiday time, and the decks were so crowded they thought themselves lucky to get 'one buttock on the seat'.

From Happy Bay he wrote to Alice Halmagyi:[1] 'This is the place we have liked most for fortunately it doesn't seem to appeal to the average tourist—because it has simplicity. I'd like to go back some time and spend a couple of weeks. The real nightmare is Daydream Island which has everything vulgar, including mature Hungarian whores stretched on banana-lounges. (One of them was having her thighs kissed as we passed.) Over everything hangs a stench of sewage. Swarms of tourists everywhere.' But the light and scenery of the reef confirmed the decision to return to the novel. 'It is every bit as beautiful as the Aegean, though with no human life of any interest—none of those cubist villages and chapels and monasteries.'

After a week they flew south, planning to stop at Gladstone for a few days, but the airline refused to land for only two passengers. In Brisbane offers were made to fly them back but White said, Home! They came down the coast over ports blocked by boom-time shipping. Somewhere in a hold lay *The Eye of the Storm*. The book was launched in London a few days after they returned to Sydney in late August. White now waited impatiently until October for the book to clear the wharves and reach the shops in Australia as the storm he both feared and longed for broke over Martin Road.

They had gone to their beds early on the night of 18 October after a hard day's housework. About 9 pm a loud knocking began on the door. The message was clearer than words. Lascaris went down to investigate and found journalists on the path and television crews setting up on the lawn. They were demanding to see Patrick White at once. He'd won.[2]

1991

AMANDA LOHREY
b. 1947

Amanda Lohrey was born in Hobart, into a working-class Catholic family of waterfront workers. She was educated at the University of Tasmania and at Cambridge University. Her first novel, *The Morality of Gentlemen* (1984), was about waterfront politics. Her second, *The Reading Group* (1988), caused a controversy in the Australian literary and political worlds when a Tasmanian Labor senator threatened a defamation action; the book was eventually recalled and pulped.

1   White's doctor.
2   The Nobel Prize for Literature.

As with her earlier novels, though with less emphasis on formal politics, *Camille's Bread* (1995), Lohrey's third and best-known novel, and *The Philosopher's Doll* (2004) both explore the way in which ideologies are lived out in daily private life, especially in their gender dynamics, and examine some of the compromises and tensions between political philosophy and lived experience. Lohrey is also highly regarded for her essays and literary journalism. *KG*

From *Camille's Bread*
Prologue

In the kitchen of a small house in Leichhardt, a young woman is dancing with her eight-year-old daughter. It's winter, and dark outside. A dish of lentil burgers sits warming on the hotplate and the strains of some exotic Latin tango strum insistently from a large black tape deck that stands on top of the fridge. Mother is clasping daughter in a parody of adult coupledom, each awkward and jolting with laughter as they stride, with exaggerated poise, up and down the skillion kitchen, sweeping across the black and white chequerboard tiles, heads tilted back, arms outstretched stiffly in the arch and demonic thrust of the tango. Dum dum, da da! da-da-da-da dah, dum dum da da! The mother is chanting time, pouting with mock seriousness, her cropped black hair standing upright in silky spikes of dishevelment and impatience. In her arms, her slight, fey, fair-haired daughter, hair drawn back in a French plait, her thin legs in dark green stockings and black lace-up school shoes, alternately mimicking the fierce concentration of her mother and erupting into loud, raucous schoolgirl laughter. For a moment, she breaks away to perform a dizzy pirouette on her own. 'See this step,' she says. 'You go, one two three four . . . and then you go . . .'

The telephone rings.

'Don't answer it,' says her mother. 'I'm sick of the phone. It's no-one we want to talk to. People shouldn't ring at mealtime. Mealtimes are for dancing.' But on these last words she is drowned out by a loud droning thunder as a low-flying 747 roars directly over the kitchen roof, its blinking tail lights creating a flash of momentary illumination in the small courtyard outside. The windows shudder and rattle in their frames but the two figures go on dancing, breaking off now into an improvised jive before the mother falls, feigning exhaustion, into a chair.

'I'm puffed,' she says, looking at her watch, 'and besides, it's past six.'

'No, try this. Look. You go . . .' and the child persists, executing a balletic turn on one foot, all loose limbs and fine ankles. But this time mother is insistent. 'No,' she says, 'that's it. I'm famished.' She gets up out of the chair and moves purposefully across to the stove, raising one finger in the air and pronouncing with melodramatic irony: 'Enough dancing. Time to eat.' At the stove she pauses, and stares into the iron whorls of the hotplate, still a little heady. These are the most blissful moments of her day. Just the two of them, gambolling in a playful embrace, like lovers; the feminine principle triumphant, ecstatic, cut loose in its own dream.

1995

ALF TAYLOR
b 1947

Alf Taylor is a poet and short-story writer born in Perth. He spent his early years with his family then was taken with his brother, as part of the stolen generation, to the New Norcia Mission. As a young man he worked around Perth and Geraldton as a seasonal farm worker, then joined the armed forces. He and his wife had seven children, only two of whom survived. Taylor is the author of three collections of poetry, and a collection of short stories called *Long Time Now: Stories of the Dreamtime, the here and now* (2001). *AH/PM*

The Wool Pickers

When the warm months take effect on the dry land, after the crops have been taken and the grass has been singed by the hot summer sun, that's the reminder of the fully fleeced sheep that perished during the bitterly cold winter. That's when Barney and his nephew Bill go wool picking (with the farmer's permission of course).

'Well,' said Barney to his nephew, 'It's a good day for the wool pickin', unna.'

'Yeah, Unc,' said Bill, looking up at the early morning sun, 'It's gunna get hot later on.'

'What ya reckon, feel like comin' out?' asked Barney.

'Course, you know me Uncle, bugger all else to do, runnin' low on tucker, dole cheque next week. Hell, dunno how we gunna live 'til then,' responded Bill.

'Right,' said the old fella, 'I'll get the ute ready, an' tell Auntie Florrie you an' me goin' out. You tell your yorgah too.'

'Course Unc, gotta tell my yorgah, she growlin' cruel already . . .'

'Get off your black hole Bill an' do somethin' solid, not wanna muntj alla time,' said Bill mimicking his woman. The old Uncle laughed as he watched his nephew walk away. *When you an' your yorgah fight, even the good Lord ducks for cover*, he thought, laughing to himself, making off to tell his wife Florrie.

Barney and Florrie were in their late sixties, and fifty of those years were together. Through thick and thin, through the days of alcoholic stupor and nights of alcoholic amnesia—and they were still together. Their three children, two boys and a girl, were living in Perth. All had good jobs and most importantly, they had lives of their own.

Barney often cursed himself for not having a clear head when they were growing up. Thankfully they understood now, stating a lack of opportunities for the Nyungah community in a small wheat-belt town.

'Me an' Bill goin' out to see if we can get some wool,' said Barney to his wife Florrie.

'You might gotta go long way out. Nyungahs bin pickin' close here,' she said.

'Boyyah any?' he asked and in the same breath added, 'You know petrol.' Knowing his wife usually had some put away somewhere. Ever since they both gave up the grog, about fifteen years ago, she always had enough till next Pension Day.

'Ready Unc?' asked Bill carrying his waterbag. Seeing Aunty Florrie he added, 'How you bin Aunty Florrie?'

'I bin good since I chuck away that stinken gerbah,' she replied, shaking her head.

'Yeah, you two look solid now,' said Bill. *Since these two gave up the gerbah, they seem so full of life. They looked better than the younger ones still on the gerbah,* he thought.

'Boyyah wa or you gimme, unna?' Bill asked, searching his pockets.

'Take em here,' Florrie said, passing a ten dollar note to Barney.

'How many bags you got Unc?' asked Bill.

''Bout five empty wheat bags,' replied Barney.

'Let's bullyaka then,' suggested Bill.

'You gottem gun?' asked Florrie.

'Yeah, under seat, you make em big damper. Might get yonga,' he said as he and Bill prepared to leave. He started the ute and pulled away from the house, both waving to Florrie.

As they headed north, they could see that the hot summer's sun had already done its damage to the landscape. About five months ago, the land was covered by lush green crops of wheat and a thick carpet of glistening green grass. Seeing the land now, with its lack of rain, even had the sand restless. The sands seemed to move with the strong breeze, although the gentle winds slowly stirring in the summer, were very few and far between. The soil with its great patience, suffered the onslaught of the menacing sun.

Nothing was said between the uncle and nephew. Barney moved along at a steady pace. He didn't want to go too fast in this heat, he was afraid the radiator might boil.

Gotta get it fixed next Pension Day, he thought. *Come next Pension it'll still be the same.* When he was home travelling within his own Shire boundary, he never had to worry, but trips like this it always came to his attention. He cursed himself out aloud.

'Hey, wassa matter Unc?' asked Bill and wondering if his old Uncle had lost his marbles.

'Nothing … um orright, juss diss bloody radiator. Keep meanin' to get him fixed. I don't worry about him, till I go on trips like diss,' he growled.

'How far you reckon we come Unc?' asked Bill.

Keeping his eye on the temperature gauge, 'Might be twenty miles, might be more,' he replied.

'Let's try the first farm we come to Unc,' said Bill, not wanting to be stuck in the middle of nowhere on this hot day. Barney slowed the ute down; it was a left turn towards the farm house. He could see that the sheep were thin as they ran away from the oncoming vehicle. *Rain and feed obviously very scarce out this way too*, thought Barney.

'Reckon he got some dead ones here,' said Bill, noticing the condition of the sheep.

'By gee, that cold weather we had in the winter musta downed a few,' replied Barney.

'Wonder if any Nyungahs been this way?' asked Bill as he slowed the ute down in front of the house, only to be greeted by barking dogs that seemed to come from nowhere.

'Where in the hell these poxy dawgs come from?' called out Barney as he wound his window up. There were about five sheep dogs running around his ute, barking and pissing all over the tyres. One big bastard was standing on his hind legs, his front paws leaning against Barney's door, barking furiously at him.

'Bugger diss!' said Barney, counting the fangs on the mutt's jaw.

'Shoo! Gone! Get!' shouted Bill also winding his window up very quickly.

Barney looked at his nephew and with a smile on his face said, 'Gone, go up to the house an' knock on the front door.'

'You gotta be jokin' Uncle! I'd rather fight ten drunken Nyungahs than wrestle with these poxy dawgs.'

'Ni, Boss comin' now,' said Barney, pointing towards the house.

'Duss him orright,' replied Bill as he watched him come towards the ute.

'Go on, piss off you bastards!' shouted the Boss. The dogs slinked off on his command. Winding the window down Barney said, 'Thanks Boss, I was a bit frightened for awhile.'

'Don't have to worry about them,' said the Boss, 'More likely to lick you to death.'

Duss what you reckon, thought Barney. 'That big bastard lookin' me in the eye, would frighten the shit out of the devil himself. He got more teeth than a crocodile, an' more sharper.'

'Well, what can I do for you?' asked the Boss.

Good, thought Barney, *no Nyungahs been out here.* Getting out of the ute and looking to see if the coast was clear, he asked, 'Wondering if you got any dead wool around the place?'

'Dead wool?' asked the Boss confused.

'You know,' said Barney, 'any sheep died over the winter months.'

'Oh, I understand now,' replied the Boss. 'As a matter of fact I have. That cold snap we had at the end of May and the beginning of June, that really took its toll on the sheep,' as he pointed towards the west paddock. 'There were quite a few that didn't survive.'

'Be orright if we have a look?' asked Barney.

'I suppose it's okay. As long as you shut the gates behind you and try not to frighten the sheep. I hate to see my sheep running around on a day like this,' he said.

'Duss true Boss,' said Barney. 'We be careful orright.'

'Also beware of your exhaust pipe when you travel over the stubble,' said the Boss pointing to the back of the ute. Barney got out and both he and the Boss checked under the ute.

'Your exhaust looks safe. Okay then ... and don't forget the gates,' said the Boss.

'We won't,' said Barney.

'By the way,' said the Boss, walking away and laughing, 'I guess you blokes wouldn't have won that four million in last night's Lotto draw!'

What datt yortj talkin' 'bout, thought Barney, 'Four million dollars. I wouldn't be here pickin' your dead wool, would I?' Shaking his head and getting into the ute.

'Choo, you solid Unc,' said Bill with the dollar signs in his eyes.

'Yeah,' said Barney. 'As soon as he said, what can I do for you, I knew Nyungahs never been here.'

They had to go through three gates before hitting their jackpot. Barney drove carefully through the paddocks, keeping away from the high stubble. Barney himself also climbed out with Bill to shut the gates.

'Here, look Unc!' shouted Bill, pointing. There before their very eyes, dead sheep were everywhere. The winter had been cruel to these sheep, which had yet to be shorn. Barney and Bill quickly and happily ripped the wool from the dead carcasses. These dead sheep had been lying here for at least three months or more. Perished in the winter and dried by the summer. The stench and the blowflies didn't deter the eager hands that shook the fleece from the bones and brushed the blowflies away at the same time. Their work exposed the maggots to the deadly sun, from which they cringed in the onslaught. The crows cawed out joyfully, as the rotting flesh was to be their feast when left behind by the eager hands.

For the dead wool, when sold in all its stinking glory would put food on the table, petrol in the tank and smoke back into the lungs of the two men.

'Dass all Unc!' cried Bill, sweating profusely as he hoisted the last of the five fully packed bags into the back of the ute.

'Gawd, diss place stinks,' called out Barney, not realizing he had been right in the middle of the stench for the last two hours.

'Let's bullyaka then Unc,' said Bill with a satisfied smile on his face.

'Yeah, you have boyyah till your day now,' smiled Barney as he edged his way through the gates and past the farmhouse. He wanted to thank the farmer for giving him permission to pick his dead wool.

There was no life around except the dogs and he wanted to get away from them quickly as possible. The drive back was even slower than the drive coming out, for he and Bill did quite a job back there.

'How much we get for this lot?' asked Bill.

'Orrr, dunno. Might be hundred dollars, might be more,' said the old fella with a twinge of tiredness in his voice.

'Never mind Unc. Long as my yorgah get some money, she'll be happy,' said Bill.

'The first thing um gunna do, is have a shower an' tell Florrie to get some mutton flaps,' he said, feeling the hunger pangs starting to attack his stomach. He was also beginning to realize that the stench was quite powerful in the cab of the ute.

'I hope Aunty Florrie made that big damper. I wanna get some off youse,' said Bill feeling the same.

'Nearly home soon,' said Barney, not worrying about the radiator as he put his foot down on the pedal.

'Hey, Unc, what that watjella said back at his farm. Something 'bout four million dollars. I thought he said four million sheep was dead. I was happy cruel, look,' laughed Bill.

'Naw,' Barney said, laughing. 'Four million Lotto draw last night.'

'What if you had four million dollars Unc? What you do?' asked Bill.

'Well,' laughed Barney, 'first thing I do is give my kids a million each.'

'What you an' Aunty Florrie gunna do with your million?' asked Bill laughing.

'Um gunna take Auntie Florrie to dat French River place, somewhere. And next we be goin' to see that Nyungah bloke. You know he was locked up in jail for twenty years an' come out to run his own country. Wass his name?' asked Barney.

'Or yeah Unc, I know. Or … Nelson Mandela. Yeah Unc, dass him. Anyway Unc, what you wanna meet him for?' wondered Bill.

'Look young Bill, all I wanna do is shake his han' an' tell him he horse of a Nyungah orright. After bein' locked up alla time. Come out an' be boss of his own country. He moorditj orright.'

'But he not Nyungah Unc. He South African,' Bill explained to his old Uncle.

'He still moorditj anyway,' said Barney. They were now driving through town and slowly making their way to the Woolbuyers. As he pulled up outside Willie the Woolbuyer's shed, Bill said to his old Uncle, 'Never mind Unc, you sit here an' rest. I'll take em into Willie's.' Barney watched his young nephew unload and take the old wool into the woolshed. It wasn't all that long before Bill came out with a smile on his face. As he passed the cheque to Barney, Bill said, 'We got one hundred dollars for that lot, one dollar a kilo he gave. Dass orright, unna.'

Barney was pleased. He headed for the bank where they cashed it. He gave forty dollars to Bill, whilst he in turn, kept sixty—fuel for the car. He dropped Bill off, who didn't live all that far and then headed home for a shower.

'You get em newspaper?' asked Florrie as Barney stepped inside.

'What you wanna paper for?' he asked. 'Anyway um gonna have a shower. Here boyyah, cause you goin' down town. An' get me some flaps,' he said passing the money to her.

After he'd showered and got himself cleaned up, he sat and had a cup of tea. It was peaceful and quiet. He kept wondering why Florrie wanted that paper. Barney couldn't read or write and he often got Florrie to read for him. He knew she was a good reader. Even at the ripe age of seventy. *Moorditj Yorgah*, he thought. Florrie came in carrying the shopping and put it on the table.

'Gawd, still warm outside,' she said.

'You get em paper?' he grunted.

'Course,' she said, grabbing the newspaper and taking off into the bedroom. Barney watched as she stopped to pick up her reading glasses and then watched her back disappear into the other room. Within minutes, the warm peaceful and quiet humidity of the early evening was shattered by a piercing scream.

'Choo, aye wassa matta?' shouted Barney, jolting back to reality and running into the bedroom. He froze in his tracks as he saw his wife sprawled on her back across the bed, white as a ghost shouting, 'Gawd, gawd. Thank you Granny Maud!'

Barney was speechless. Granny Maud had died forty years ago. When he and Florrie first got together as pups. Granny Maud had always called them that, and she was eighty when she died. Their first child was two then.

'I think I win plenty of boyyah!' was Florrie's only response when she came to. She composed herself and told him about the other day. She was lying on the bed, having a cry and thinking of Barney—old as he was—always going out to pick dead wool to put food on the table. Then she looked up and saw the spirit of Granny Maud, clapping her hands and smiling at her, then she disappeared. After that Florrie walked down town and saw on a poster at the newsagent's in big bold letters 'FOUR MILLION DOLLARS' to be won that night. She went in and bought a ticket. She had just checked her numbers with the paper, and she had gotten six numbers correct.

Still trembling, he asked, 'What Granny Maud got to do with it?'

Florrie told him when she had the last two children, Grannie Maud's spirit was by the bed, smiling and clapping as she was giving birth.

'Look at our beautiful children now. Granny Maud only brought good luck to me,' she whispered. She was thinking of Barney and the kids. Especially Barney—to take 'im to see the black man, who was put in jail an' came out to be boss of his own country, before they both passed away.

Barney grabbed and hugged her. With tears in his eyes, he whispered in her ear, 'He not Nyungah, he South African!'

1996

MICHAEL DRANSFIELD
1948–1973

The poet Michael Dransfield was born in Sydney. He attended the University of Sydney for a brief period before dropping out to concentrate on writing poetry, working intermittently and travelling in Tasmania and Queensland. Dransfield embraced the counterculture of the time, using drugs and protesting against the Vietnam War (for which he was conscripted, but excused on health grounds). Thomas Shapcott (qv), in his anthology *Australian Poetry Now* (1970), described Dransfield as 'terrifyingly close to genius'. In 1970 Dransfield's first book, *Streets of the Long Voyage*, was published. He published two more books in his lifetime: *The Inspector of Tides* (1972) and *Drug Poems* (1972). Three posthumous collections appeared, two edited by Rodney Hall (qv), who also edited Dransfield's *Collected Poems* (1987). Dransfield is the focus of Livio Dobrez's *Parnassus Mad Ward* (1990), and the subject of a biography by Patricia Dobrez, *Michael Dransfield's Lives* (1999). Felicity Plunkett has described Dransfield's poetry as illustrating a 'tension between an almost primitivist romantic nostalgia, and a protest against the forces of conservatism' (*Who's Who in Twentieth-Century World Poetry*, 2000). DM

Pas de Deux for Lovers

Morning ought not
to be complex.
The sun is a seed

cast at dawn into the long
furrow of history.   5

To wake
and go
would be so simple.

Yet

how the   10
first light
makes gold her hair

upon my arm.
How then
shall I leave,   15
and where away to go. Day
is so deep already with involvement.
                                                          1970

Fix

It is waking in the night,
after the theatres and before the milkman,
alerted by some signal from the golden drug tapeworm
that eats your flesh and drinks your peace;
you reach for the needle and busy yourself   5
preparing the utopia substance in a blackened
spoon held in candle flame
by now your thumb and finger are leathery
being so often burned this way
it hurts much less than withdrawal and the hand   10
is needed for little else now anyway.
Then cordon off the arm with a belt,
probe for a vein, send the dream-transfusion out
on a voyage among your body machinery. Hits you like sleep—
sweet, illusory, fast, with a semblance of forever.   15
For a while the fires die down in you,
until you die down in the fires.
Once you have become a drug addict
you will never want to be anything else.
                                                          1970

Flying

i was flying over sydney
in a giant dog

things looked bad

1972

JOHN SCOTT
b. 1948

John Scott was born in England, moved with his family to Melbourne in 1959, and graduated from Monash University. He spent some years school teaching, writing for television and radio, and completing a doctorate in creative arts. His early books appeared under the name John A. Scott. These works of increasingly experimental (and interconnected) poetry blurred distinctions between genres, between lyric and narrative poetry, and between poetry and prose itself. Since the 1990s, Scott has concentrated on prose fiction. His novella *What I Have Written* (1993) has been filmed from his own screenplay (1995). His *Selected Poems* was published in 1995. He retired from a teaching position in the Faculty of Creative Arts at Wollongong University in 2005 and became an honorary associate professor of English at the University of Sydney. *DM*

Pride of Erin

The public telephone is a cage for the exhibition of Chrissie.
She comes from Science to the shop.
Saunters with her friends through a suburb of dogs, keeping ahead of
    evening, just beating it inside.
Smoke from the slow-combustion heaters.
A sun, low in the sky, giving lamplight and no warmth.   5
A dying star and the domino theory of barking, when light starts to fail.
She has trouble with the door; with instructions.
Is afraid of losing her coin; doesn't have another one on her right now.
Is afraid of *not at home. Might be round at Greg's.*
And outside, Sharon and Cheryl and Debbie are wearing duffel coats, in range. 10
She is a carrier of nomadic truth.
Wishes commitment.
Knows of energies deep within her, under pressure, that she squanders on
    choir or keeping things clean.
No-one guesses them.
They are efforts of will.   15
Soldiers win medals with them.
She watches the duffel coats picking at dusk.
Watches the way teenage girls jostle and shift; are non-committal, like baboons.

Can't stop herself being like this most times.
Finds herself doing it.   20
Wonders if noticing things is the essence of growing old; and that as we
    pass some mid-point it falls away again, eventually back to nothing.
With difficulty, she comes from the booth into what is left of today.
Makes her turn.
Watches her friends move on.
In the darkness they seem to float, like objects displacing their own weight
    in water.   25
                       1984

Plato's Dog

Thirty years ago, Marseille lay burning in the sun, one day.[1] That's Dickens.
Tonight when I go home, everything's going to be exactly where I left it,
this time. That's me. I'm good with words. For example, this bar reminds me
of someone eating with their mouth open.

Tonight's a bad night. Tonight I'm on milky drinks because I've seen
people drink them and the barmaid told me how some older blokes order
'koala and milk'[2]—and not joking either—because they've just heard it
wrong. When you swirl them round the glass they settle into these curves.
Like the rings of Saturn. I'm good with words. Though someone once told
me I 'possessed a humour incompatible with sexuality'. That is, I entertain,
but at the end of the night they go home with someone else.

Tonight's not a good night. At the table behind me there's an argument
about Human Nature. Someone brings up Plato's dog. And someone else
says 'who?' and the first bloke explains, except I know it's not *Plato's* dog, and
be blowed if I can think whose dog it should be. I stare at the ashtrays, all an
equal distance above sea-level. Like lane-markers in the pool of the bar.

The barmaid's reaching for bottles; lost in her unrequited dance. I
swirl the last of my milky drink and engage this couple across from me in
conversation.

—Excuse me, I say. Remember when you were a kid and listening to
the radio, and there'd be songs you'd sing all the way through, and years later
you'd hear the song again and realise you'd been singing the wrong words.

They look up and wait a bit.

—You know *She Loves You*, she says. There's a line in that that says 'Pride
can hurt you too' and for years I thought it was 'Invite her to your room'.

—And sometimes you never *knew* the words, I add. But you could
imitate the sounds. And you'd be singing along with all these nonsense words.

---

1   The opening sentence of Charles Dickens' *Little Dorrit* (1857).
2   Kahlua and milk.

That's how I figure life. You're either misunderstanding or not understanding at all.

We fall silent. The way you do after laughing a lot.

—I never knew if it was 'inside a zoo' or 'in Xanadu' in *Baby You're a Rich Man*, the man offers. But the moment's passed.

Maria would've been fixing me something to eat right now, so I'd have something to sit down to when I got in. A bowl of soup, say. And the idea of the soup almost makes me cry—the way I almost cried when I caught a glimpse of her standing on the front porch in that dreadful pink wrapper as I drove off. And the slippers she wore that looked like she was treading on two poodles.

You see, I can cope with the people, and the arguments. But the objects defeat me every time.

Outside it's drizzling again. But tonight's been OK. No-one asked me to leave. They just watched me—maybe listened to me. I was probably the centre of a dozen conversations back then, while I sat there, and while I walked out, one day.

1989

GALARRWUY YUNUPINGU
b. 1948

A member of the Gumatj clan of the Yolngu people, Galarrwuy Yunupingu was born at Melville Bay near Yirrkala, NT. He first attended the mission school at Yirrkala and for two years studied at the Methodist Bible College, Brisbane. In the early 1960s he joined his father Mungurrawuy, a Gumatj clan leader, in the struggle for Aboriginal land rights and the Yirrkala protest against bauxite mining, helping to create the Yirrkala Bark Petition in 1963 and bringing Aboriginal land rights to national attention. In 1975 he joined the Northern Land Council of which he was chairman from 1977 to 2004 and in 2001 was elected as co-chair of the Aboriginal Development Consultative Forum in Darwin. A senior ceremonial leader of his people, he was Australian of the Year in 1978 and named an Australian Living National Treasure in 1998. Barunga is located in the NT. Wenten Rubuntja, an artist and activist who died in 2005, was Chairperson of the Central Land Council when he co-presented the following petition to Prime Minister Bob Hawke. *AH/PM*

Barunga Statement

We the indigenous owners and occupiers of Australia call on the Australian Government and people to recognise our rights:

*   to self determination and self management including the freedom to pursue our own economic, social, religious and cultural development;

- to permanent control and enjoyment of our ancestral lands;
- to compensation for the loss of use of our lands, there having been no extinction of original title;
- to protection of and control of access to our sacred sites, sacred objects, artefacts, designs, knowledge and works of art;
- to the return of the remains of our ancestors for burial in accordance with our traditions;
- to respect for promotion of our Aboriginal identity, including the cultural, linguistic, religious and historical aspects, including the right to be educated in our own languages, and in our own culture and history;
- in accordance with the Universal Declaration of Human Rights, the International Covenant on Economic, Social and Cultural Rights, the International Covenant on Civil and Political Rights, and the International Convention on the Elimination of all forms of Racial Discrimination, rights to life, liberty, security of person, food, clothing, housing, medical care, education and employment opportunities, necessary social services and other basic rights.

We call on the Commonwealth to pass laws providing:

- a national elected Aboriginal and Islander organisation to oversee Aboriginal and Islander affairs;
- a national system of land rights;
- a police and justice system which recognises our customary laws and frees us from discrimination and any activity which may threaten our identity or security, interfere with our freedom of expression or association, or otherwise prevent our full enjoyment and exercise of universally-recognised human rights and fundamental freedoms.

We call on the Australian Government to support Aborigines in the development of an International Declaration of Principles for Indigenous Rights, leading to an International Covenant.

And we call on the Commonwealth Parliament to negotiate with us a Treaty or Compact recognising our prior ownership, continued occupation and sovereignty and affirming our human rights and freedoms.

1988

JOHN CLARKE
b. 1948

The comedian, actor, writer and satirist John Clarke was born in New Zealand and moved to Australia in 1977. Clarke has written for television (such as the satire *The Max Gillies Show*) and film (co-writing the screenplay for Paul Cox's *Lonely Hearts*), as well as writing and performing the satirical 'great interviews' series on television with Bryan Dawe. In 2000 Clarke appeared in, co-wrote and co-produced *The Games*, a satirical account of the 2000 Sydney Olympic Games. He has appeared in numerous films and stage plays, and is the author of a comic novel, *The Tournament* (2002). *The Complete Book of Australian Verse* (1989) parodies canonical poets as Australians. *DM*

Muse of Bauxite[1]

W.H. AUDING

Wisty Huge Auding published his first collection, Poems, *in 1928, followed by* A Whole Lot More *in 1932 and* When We Were Very Old *in 1960. He died in 1968, 1971, and again in 1973.*

About Telecom they were never wrong,
The Old Masters, how prescient they were
About existential services;
How well they knew the mundane brutality of increasing
    charges for items which don't exist,   5
How, while oafs deliberate, holding money
Up to the light, agreeing it should be described
Not as a profit but as an operating surplus,
There always must be, bleak-faced, random and frantic,
Victims, trying to make urgent calls on public phones   10
    dangling
From walls in a twisted piss-smelling tardis,
And in the distance a man sits on a park-bench,
Explaining to his grandchild the merits of competition.

In Nolan's *Ned Kelly* series, for instance, how everyone's face   15
Is either hidden or green; hidden, encased
In metal, in uniform, angled, straight and hard,
Or green, and how, when Scanlon is shot from his horse
And falls, he falls up,
Unsurprised, a bystander,   20
He's thinking 'Dearie me,
Another ballsup'.

        1989

---

1   A parody of 'Musée des Beaux Arts' by W.H. Auden (1907–73).

A Child's Christmas in Warrnambool[1]

DYLAN THOMPSON

Martyr to the turps, Dylan Thompson frequently woke in unfamiliar
circumstances and attempted to catch the speech rhythms of the sea.

One Christmas was so like another in those years around
the sea town corner now, that I can never remember
whether it was 106 degrees in 1953 or whether it was 103
degrees in 1956. All the Christmases roll into one down
the wave-roaring salt-squinting years of yesterboy.   5
My hand goes into the fridge of imperishable memory and out
come: salads and sunburn lotions, the brief exuberant hiss
of beer being opened and the laugh of wet-haired youths
around a Zepher 6, the smell of insect repellent and
eucalyptus and the distant constant slowly listless bang of   10
the fly-wire door. And resting on a formica altar, waiting
for Ron, the biggest Pav[2] in the world; a magic Pav,
a cut-and-come-again Pav for all the children in all the towns
across the wide brown bee-humming trout-fit sheep-rich
two-horse country.   15
And the Aunts. Always the Aunts. In the kitchen on the
black-and-white photographed beach of the past, playing
out the rope to a shared childhood, caught in the
undertow and drifting.
And some numerous Uncles, wondering sometimes why they   20
weren't each other, coming around the letterbox to an attacking
field in the Test match and being driven handsomely by
some middle-order nephew, skipping down the vowel-
flattening pitch and putting the ball into the tent-flaps on
the first bounce of puberty.   25
                                                                   1989

PATRICK DODSON
b. 1948

Born in Broome, WA, Patrick Dodson is of Yawuru descent. He and his younger
brother Mick (qv) were made wards of the state in 1960 after the death of their father.
They were sent to Monivale College in Hamilton, Victoria, on scholarships to finish
their education. Patrick became a seminarian and was ordained in 1975 as the first
Indigenous Catholic priest. In this challenging role he sought to balance and blend

1   A parody of 'A Child's Christmas in Wales' by Dylan Thomas (1914–53). Warrnambool is a Victorian
    country town.
2   Pavlova, a dessert originating from Australia and New Zealand.

Catholicism and Aboriginal spiritual belief. After many years of confrontation with the ecclesiastical hierarchy he left the priesthood in 1981.

Since then he has been an Aboriginal rights activist, and a civil member of a number of official commissions concerned with Aboriginal affairs. He is a former director of the Central Land Council and of the Kimberley Land Council. In 1989 Dodson was appointed a commissioner for Aboriginal Deaths in Custody and was chairman of the Council for Aboriginal Reconciliation (1991–97). *AH/PM*

Welcome Speech to Conference on the Position of Indigenous People in National Constitutions

[…] A century ago our Constitution was drafted in the spirit of *terra nullius.* Land was divided, power was shared, structures were established, on the illusion of vacant possession. When Aboriginal people showed up which they inevitably did they had to be subjugated, incarcerated or eradicated: to keep the myth of *terra nullius* alive.

The High Court decision on native title shatters this illusion and Aboriginal and Torres Strait Islander people have survived to make their contribution to the shape of the nation's political and legal future.

The nation has now woken from two centuries of sleep to become aware that Aboriginal and Torres Strait Islander people were owners of the land and were managers of the country long before the Union Jack was raised and rum drunk, here or elsewhere. While it may seem to be a new dawn for Australia's indigenous people, it has been a rude awakening for others. A moment of truth has arrived. The deeds of the past and present require those who have benefited most to take the steps towards those who have suffered most in the last 204 years. They must reconcile themselves with a new reality and then find the path of restitution that will lead to reconciliation.

No longer can Aboriginal property rights be ignored. No longer can indigenous customary laws and traditions be disregarded. The decision brings the wider Australian community closer to a true reconciliation on honest, negotiated terms with Aboriginal and Torres Strait Islander Australians.

A century after the original constitutional debate we have an opportunity to remake our Constitution to recognise and accommodate the prior ownership of the continent by Aboriginal and Torres Strait Islander people. But in this new debate there is a danger of history repeating itself. There is a danger of Aboriginal and Torres Strait Islander rights to land and cultural identity being ignored in the rush to establish a republic with minimal change to the Constitution. There is a danger of new arrangements to share power being developed without seeing and somehow meeting the Aboriginal and Torres Strait Islander peoples' yearning to escape the powerlessness of exclusion and dispossession. There is a danger of a new

Constitution being drafted that tries to capture the spirit of a modern Australia, but that denies the spirit of indigenous Australia.

Terra nullius may be gone but the old habits of constitutional drafters die hard. The silences and omissions of the past echo loudly in the present. [...]

1993

PAM BROWN
b. 1948

Pam Brown was born in Seymour, Victoria. She became involved in the anti-Vietnam War movement in the 1960s, and in the 1970s she was bass player in the feminist rock group, Clitoris Band. She has worked at university libraries and lectured in film and video. She worked for a time at the Experimental Art Foundation in Adelaide (with Ken Bolton (qv)) and later became associate editor of the online poetry journal, *Jacket*. She has published numerous works of prose, drama and poetry, including *Dear Deliria: New and selected poems* (2002) and *Text Thing* (2002). Her poems are often epigrammatic and enigmatic, charting the way of the self through a complex world of signs, memories and sensations. *DM*

At the Wall

I'd written myself into a wall
James Baldwin

our soft little lives
    are asleep

sarajevo srebrenica palestine
    rwanda kabul

a half-empty bottle   5
    of old formalities
thrown in the mud

'we are all of us in the gutter
    but some of us are looking
        at the stars'   10
        said o. wilde
not another twenty years
    of that, I hope

our feckless little aspirations
    require the lowest   15
        common denominator

so show me the book
    that shows me

rows of terrariums
   growing horrible viral cells   20
genetic cultures
    dropping enormous
       thick clots

the artists
     are affected   25
clumsy vision
     stuck with lumps

the artists
     could be
lost   as well   30

invited
    to a 'private viewing'—
an occasion
   usually called
     an 'opening'   35

you see
   backward lurchings
& hear vacuous flatteries
    & the S&M pose
     hit hurt   ooh ahh   40
looking like petals
  acting like engines
making minor contributions
   to the 'cutting edge'
(80s talk   90s clothing)   45

will anyone ever
    agitate
       again?

when will they occupy
    the privatised academies?   50

all talk & theory
older & older
less & less wise

statues are toppling
before they are built   55

so   at the bar,
my pal remembers
a quote
from Mark Twain or someone
'the means have become   60
more expedient
but the goals are lost'
I write it down
on the back
of a blank   65
TAB trifecta ticket

here,   in the country
without guilt,
when will the menacing,
the history,   70
begin?

1994

ROSIE SCOTT
b. 1948

Rosie Scott was born in New Zealand, and has lived in Australia since the mid-1980s. She has published poetry, a play, a collection of essays (*The Red Heart*, 1999), and novels. Scott has been an active member of the Australian Society of Authors, the Queensland Literary Board and International PEN Sydney Centre, serving as vice-president (2002–05). She founded and chaired PEN's Writers in Detention Committee in 2004 with Thomas Keneally (qv). *DM*

The Value of Writers

In every society and age there has always been a constant—our great need to hear stories that elucidate and celebrate our lives, stories that help us make sense of our experience. It is the very timelessness of the solitary act of creation of stories that makes reading one of the deepest, most satisfying experiences in some people's lives. In this sense the best storyteller has to be honest, imaginative, courageous, compassionate and wise enough to interpret and reflect the complexities of the world in a way that we both recognise and are disturbed by. Fiction is, as Kafka put it, 'the axe that breaks the frozen sea within us'.

I'm only talking about the very best writers here, for in the meantime of course there are writers of every kind. Bestselling fashionable ones who disappear by the end of the decade, writers who go in and out of vogue and then settle permanently on the cultural horizon, bestselling writers who *are* the best, writers who are so plain awful they know it in their bones, writers who write one perfect thing and never need to write again—and each of them contributes to the rich contemporary mix that hits you when you enter a bookshop. Each writer contributes to society, but in the end, time winnows most of us away. Some writers slip through the net, particularly women writers, but it is a salutary experience for any writer who might be getting things a little out of proportion to walk into one of those old lending libraries miraculously preserved in some secondhand bookshops. Row upon row of those dusty old hardbacks up to the ceiling by author upon author you have never heard of, books that haven't been read for years and never will be again.

V.S. Pritchett wrote: 'The best writers do something specific to their readers. They heighten and transfigure the world you see for ever: like the clot of a spirit level steadily carried.' This excellence, despite all the problems of evaluation and cultural relativism that the concept implies, is the ultimate arbiter, and time is the only true test of that excellence. And excellence is something writers themselves must gauge for themselves; only they can know how far they've pushed themselves—how honest their writing is. Writers, I believe, mostly know in their heart of hearts the truth of their work and, irrespective of critical reception or sales, they ignore this knowledge at their peril. This quote from Janet Frame's *Envoy from Mirror City* is definitive to me: 'A writer must stand on the rock of her own self and her judgement or be swept away by the tide or sink in the quaking earth.'

But writers have to learn a very complicated balancing act. On the one hand they must safeguard this private act of creation and ability to be their own most severe critic at all times; on the other they must develop a public persona, to carry out the necessary publicity with grace, as well as contributing to the literary community and society in general with courage. It is very easy to get lost in all this. Using the sort of gothic metaphor I love, American movie director Mike Nichols in a recent interview said that times are so dangerous now in terms of the publicity trap that he sees Medusa as the most useful myth. People who look back and see themselves as the public sees them, even for a minute, are immediately lost, he said; in looking the Medusa full in the face they are turned to stone.

This is wonderfully exaggerated of course and he is talking about American society, but the fact is that for a lot of writers, dealing with publicity is a major source of anxiety. It is about trying to earn a living without compromising too much. Using the media is, to use another full-blooded metaphor, rather like riding on the back of a tiger. Earning a living is one thing, being turned to stone or being eaten by a tiger is another. (Mixing metaphors is something else again!)

Which of course brings me to that most difficult and public part of a writer's life—how we earn our living. The issue of state funding for writers is a constant source of debate, fuelled by the cliché perpetuated in the media of superannuated, bitchy, irrelevant writers living on vast and unending amounts of taxpayers' money and writing their unread books. Countries such as Britain, the US and New Zealand, where market forces rule, have all scaled down state support for writers and, ironically, the argument has been advanced that Australia should do the same thing.

There are lots of people around who believe that if writers don't sell, they should assume they are not good enough and give up. There is nothing new of course in using the market as the final arbiter of the worth of a writer. Writers as worthless as Keats, Edgar Allan Poe and Kafka lived and died in poverty, struggling terribly all their lives to support themselves and keep their creativity alive. There is nothing new either in the concept of wealthy patrons bankrolling artists in recognition that their worth is not necessarily commensurate with their income. What *is* new is the idea that the state itself, without political interference, could subsidise writers. In the brave words of the Australian Literature Board charter, its goals (among others) are 'to support writers whose work contributes to the development, diversity and excellence of Australian writing'.

The Literature Board has been resoundingly successful, and, as Hilary McPhee[1] said recently in a speech at the Warana Festival, has worked well for writers for 20 years, helping to foster an internationally acclaimed literature that is also read and valued by Australians. If you need any proof of this, Australians spend something like $250 million a year on Australian books alone—a fact that should keep even economic rationalists happy! There are immense difficulties in the administration of such a brave and visionary scheme—how to know who to support, how to please everyone, how to be most efficient with the small amount of money available. There will always be jealousy, carping and the odd injustice, but the Literature Board's adherence to the principles of arm's-length funding, peer decision-making and excellence as the sole criterion have kept it, as 70 percent of writers in a recent survey agreed, an effective, well-run, efficient

1   Publisher (b. 1941), chair of the Australia Council for the Arts (1994–97).

institution. Like democracy it has to be constantly appraised and tinkered with, and remain open to those directly involved, and, like democracy, in spite of manifest flaws, there is no alternative that comes anywhere near it.

This brings me to another connected controversy: the perception among some people, who are usually on a salary, that we writers are on easy street, cosseted and insulated by fellowship after fellowship, unable to function on the good old free market. There *are* people who have received more fellowships than average, usually for very good reason. For instance, it is common knowledge that Les Murray[1] is one of those, but I have never heard a writer begrudging him this. Les Murray is incontestably one of Australia's finest poets, and if the fellowships helped him along, then the Literature Board is fulfilling its charter splendidly.

Poetry, even our very best, could never be described as a money-spinner. Speaking as a writer who has applied for two fellowships in six years and received one with great appreciation, who has made a reasonable, above-average income from mostly fiction writing, and who has worked, at last count, in 25 paying jobs in my life, I can say easy street is a few blocks away yet.

There are some complicated points at issue here. On the most basic level, writers, like everyone who works and contributes to society, deserve a living wage (although of course there are a few who would dispute even that). The question is who is to pay them using what criteria. At a time when such vital areas of the nation's infrastructure as health and education are being subjected to the bulldozer of economic rationalism, we can take nothing for granted. A writer's worth to society cannot always, nor should it be, evaluated in terms of dollars and cents. What worth, for instance, does society place on a great poet like Judith Wright[2] who writes like an angel and has also devoted her life to conservation and to justice for Aboriginal people? Assuming always that the first and only criterion for financial support for writers is literary excellence, do the economic rationalists who are now in the forefront of every bureaucracy also value such altruism? Altruism is not 'factored in', to use their language, because it is not a value they recognise, let alone cherish.

So what is the worth on the profit and loss sheet of writers who are not blown by the prevailing winds, who act as a conscience for society like Judith Wright? I know that it is mostly unfashionable to believe that great writers can be involved in social change, but just one glimpse into the files of Amnesty and PEN prove that fashion, as always, is not a very reliable guide. The evidence is overwhelming, for instance, that dictatorships seem to find writers very dangerous indeed. A tragic example was the execution

1   Les Murray (qv).
2   Judith Wright (qv).

of the Nigerian writer Ken Saro-Wiwa for his stand against the alliance of the dictatorship in his country with Shell Oil. Nearer to home, Pramoedya Anatatoer, described as Indonesia's greatest living writer, now 70 years old, has been in prison for 13 years because of his opposition to the government. As Ismail Kadare, Albania's leading novelist and exile wrote, 'Dictatorship and genuine literature know of only one way to cohabit—by devouring each other night and day.'

While Aboriginal writers like Oodgeroo Noonuccal[1] come closest to this edgy position by pointing out uncomfortable things in their fiction that many people would rather not know about, Australia also has a long and honourable tradition of writers, from Dorothy Hewett[2] to Henry Lawson,[3] who have in their work and lives been involved in social change. We are extremely privileged to live in Australia for so many reasons. In my travels to overseas festivals it is a matter of pride to me that most writers view Australia as head and shoulders above most other nations in its support of writers, a support untainted by political pressure. As readers and writers we can be thankful for this enlightened and civilised state of affairs, and the obvious benefits to us and to society that flow from it. The Literature Board could be dismantled or reduced in a matter of minutes by a politician's signature; it needs constant safeguarding against political opportunism and ignorance.

Writing remains the difficult, mysterious, complicated, addictive process it has always been. Writers will continue to write their own truth as they see it, however difficult the conditions are, as they did even in the bad old days when some of them had to live and die in poverty to do it. For, as Keri Hulme[4] said, 'Telling stories, playing with words is for me a way of reaching beyond my narrow life—it uncrowds my head, pacifies the ghosts and in a very small way, makes my life worth while.'

1999

ALAN WEARNE
b 1948

Alan Wearne was born and grew up in East Melbourne. He attended Monash University, where he was central to the vibrant poetry-reading scene there. Wearne has worked at various jobs, and since 1998 has lectured in creative writing at the University of Wollongong. A well-known member of the Generation of '68, Wearne is best known for his verse narratives: 'Out Here' (originally published in *New Devil, New Parish*, 1976, and republished separately in 1987), *The Nightmarkets* (1986) and the two-volume *The Lovemakers* (2001/2004). These latter two works (especially the 14,500-line

1   Oodgeroo Noonuccal (qv).
2   Dorothy Hewett (qv).
3   Henry Lawson (qv).
4   New Zealand author (b. 1947) of *The Bone People* (1984).

The Lovemakers) are notable for their scale. Each presents diffuse and interconnected narratives through numerous vernacular dramatic monologues. Wearne's use of verse forms shows an impressive skill in combining the formalist with the apparently realist. 'Out Here', like Wearne's subsequent works, also shows an interest in suburban realities, which Wearne presents using both satire and pathos. As Michael Heyward writes in the 1987 edition, this combination represents a 'compassionate critique'. The same could be said of many of the characterisations in *The Nightmarkets*, which is largely concerned with a generation of 1970s radicals coming to terms with changing times. *The Lovemakers*, which is even harder to characterise than *The Nightmarkets*, widens the milieu to include suburban characters, urban professionals and members of an urban criminal underclass. Wearne's ability to present the different jargons and languages of these characters shows a major thematic interest in the relationship between language, power and reality. As Christopher Pollnitz writes in *DLB* (2006), '*The Lovemakers* is at once ambitious, literary modernist fiction and antiliterary iconoclastic, postmodern poem—a verse novel engaged in brinkmanship with the unsolved contradictions of the genre.' His latest collection is *The Australian Popular Songbook* (2008). DM

From *The Lovemakers*
Lovelife (vi)

BARB AND NEIL (III)

Neil was in Melbourne attending a funeral,
he called up his old flame to check out her scene.
She was delighted and jumped at a meeting,
before he'd fly out from Tullamarine.[1]

Her heart was kickstarted, it wouldn't stop thumping   5
with part what had happened and part might've been.
Then she panicked: if Neil has a touch of the cold feet
won't he run off to Tullamarine?

His toes though were warm, for the past urged his ardour,
put it down to nostalgia/the odd wayward gene.   10
And as for their 'sex', all he did was imagine
a jet taking off from Tullamarine.

They met at Brunetti's. Recognition! Adjustment!
(They'd both put on weight i.e., neither was lean.)
So Barb broke the ice with 'Australia's best coffee!   15
There's sure nothing like *this* at Tullamarine!'

So, how was Roger? (Not that he knew Roger.)
Her shoulders were shrugging like *See what I mean?*

1   The site of Melbourne's international airport.

Their marriage still worked though, small-scale if functional,
more like Moorabbin than Tullamarine.   20

Still the family had grown with strapping twin daughters.
Her son was an adult now, long past a teen;
who'd dropped out of uni to work on an oil rig
(and she'd driven *him* out to Tullamarine!).

'Well I have a girlfriend,' Neil turned confessional,   25
'all decks should be cleared Barb, best to come clean.
We live in the country, where she runs a bush band;
and one place she'd loathe would be Tullamarine.'

And then there was Benny, Barb sure had liked Benny
(who may've been gay but was hardly a queen).   30
Well Neil had flown down with Benny-and-partner,
who'd gone home that morning via Tullamarine.

'Can you imagine the tricks they get up to?'
Barb interjected '. . . err, mighty obscene?
They must be a circus, though we wouldn't try them: 35
those Mardi Gras specials from Tullamarine.'

So both, as you've guessed, coincided in basics,
they still voted Labor, though tending to Green.
      But he looked at his watch, as time ticked, insistent,
onward and onward to Tullamarine.   40

Then, coffee over, a quick browse at Readings;
Carlton just glowed in its bright autumn sheen.
And Barb was determined she'd drive him to Tulla
(that's Melbourne, you're dead right, for Tullamarine).

Though this inner-Barb was advising her outer: 45
Love's still an addiction, might have to wean.
Here's not the first junkie going cold turkey
twitching and sweaty at Tullamarine.

Before they drove off then Neil watched his ex-lover
give a touch o' th' lippy to complete her smart preen;   50
Whilst out on the freeway thoughts turned generational
(through Essendon, Niddrie to Tullamarine):

'Back in the days of Cyril and Cecil,
Nancy and Stella, Gladys and Reen,
no-one on earth made their love quite as we would,   55
when cows grazed their full out at Tullamarine.

'Or think of my parents Elwyn and Ronald
(what is your mother's name? Noelene?):
retirees on super, scooting to Surfers,[1]
whose raunchy weekends start at Tullamarine.'   60

    . . . yes we still feel the same Neil noted amazed, and
no woman that I've met was less a machine.
It's great and it's ghastly we'll still love each other
long after I've boarded at Tullamarine.

All else is a bagatelle sent to distract us   65
(if within there's a battle near internecine).
    Then he noticed a signpost, it stopped his reverie:
MELBOURNE AIRPORT (TULLAMARINE).

So they took a deep breath for the final encounter
(one round remaining in their magazine).   70
Who cared if the airline were Ansett or Qantas,
two adults were kissing at Tullamarine.

    Then an idea occurred (though the thought gave her shivers)
which verged on the dodgy yet wouldn't demean
to publish a book, obscure in its self-help: 75
How to Farewell Your Ex from Tullamarine.

    Some women would chortle, some look abandoned,
a few might be blasé, still others would keen.
Barb took on all four modes as Neil taxied past her.
    Full throttle then lift-off from Tullamarine.   80
                                     2004

Come on Aussie

Know why we've stuffed our good and great because?
Let's palm this answer down like ruck to rover:
    It's babyboomer partytime in Oz.[2]

---

1   Surfers Paradise in Queensland.
2   Author's note: '"It's Babyboomer Partytime in Oz" is the title of a cassette album by Nigel T and the Oz
    Party People, a Perth-based nostalgia cover band.'

Ask Renee, ask Raelene, Rhonda, Roz
and each will turn to screeching like a plover: 5
'Know why we've stuffed our good and great because?

All day we've swatted blowie, cockroach, moz,
howling, as we flailed their endless hover,
It's babyboomer partytime in Oz!'

Yet more than has-beens this crowd never was.   10
Mere loose no balls thumped past extra cover.
Know why we've stuffed our good and great because?

Well work these out (nay, I prithee coz):
white fools in dreadlocks hollering 'Yo mother!
It's babyboomer partytime in Oz!'   15

Lusting legs, arse, tits, mouth, eyes and schnoz
(no other way folks, just that kind of lover!)
know why we've stuffed our good and great? Because,
baby, It's boomer partytime in Oz!

         2008

ALAN GOULD
b. 1949

The poet, novelist and critic Alan Gould was born in London of English-Icelandic parents. As the child of a British army serviceman, he lived with his family in England, Ireland, Iceland, Germany and Singapore before coming to Australia in 1966. As a student at the ANU, Gould was active in anti-Vietnam War protests. In addition to five novels, Gould has published numerous collections of poetry, a number of which—such as *Astral Sea* (1981) and *Mermaid* (1996)—show his abiding concern with maritime themes. Gould was the founding editor of *Canberra Poetry* and the Open Door Press. *The Past Completes Me: Selected poems 1973–2003* appeared in 2005. *DM*

Rain Governs the Small Hours

It starts as it might end,
a one-finger typist composing on your roof.
And then, like cause and effect,
the ovation of a vast convention.

But really the downpour is   5
an efficient administration,

invisible, but zoning the world
along a complex border of surfaces;

the Wet, the Dry. There are no infringements,
although it's your zone always   10
that is the one beleaguered
as sleep beleaguers life.

And like the unborn, you lie content
curled in the midst of water
as the red digits of the electric clock   15
flicker like a blood-vessel,

and a five a.m. kitchen light wavers
like the world at the end of a tunnel.
It ends, not quite as it began—
one finger tap-tapping a single key.   20
                                                1986

LAURIE DUGGAN
b. 1949

Born in Melbourne, Laurie Duggan attended Monash University, where he was involved in poetry readings. He has taught creative writing, been an art critic and a scriptwriter, and was poetry editor of *Meanjin* (1994–97). Duggan's poetry characteristically employs found text, bricolage and ironic juxtaposition. Such a technique finds its apotheosis in his prize-winning 'documentary poem', *The Ash Range* (1987), a bricolage history of Gippsland (in south-east Victoria) that uses newspaper reports, letters, diaries and histories. Epic in scale, it uses fragments and arresting images to emphasise the past's oddity and figures ignored by conventional history.

Stylistically heterogeneous and formally promiscuous, Duggan is a master parodist and translator. He is also one of Australia's funniest poets, as seen in his brilliant free translations of the first-century Roman poet Martial. As shown in *Memorials* (1996), his many autobiographical poems are documentary, rather than confessional, in nature. *New and Selected Poems 1971–1993* was published in 1996. In 2005 *Compared to What: Selected poems 1971–2003* was published in England, as was a new edition of *The Ash Range*. In 1999 Duggan was awarded his PhD in Fine Arts from the University of Melbourne, and his thesis was published as *Ghost Nation: Imagined space and Australian visual culture 1901–1939* (2001). Much of Duggan's poetic work shows an interest in the relationship between visual art and poetry. Popular music is another abiding concern. After some years living in Queensland (which coloured his 2003 collection *Mangroves*), Duggan moved to England in 2007. His diaries (from 1968) have been published in the Australian Poetry Resources Internet Library. *DM*

From *The Ash Range*
Chapter 11: JANUARY 1939

11.1

In the State of Victoria, the month of January of the year 1939 came towards the end of a long drought which had been aggravated by a severe hot, dry summer season. For more than twenty years the State had not seen its countryside and forests in such travail.

Creeks and springs ceased to run. Water storages were depleted.

The soft carpet of the forest floor was gone; the bone-dry litter crackled underfoot.

Fires had been burning for weeks. No one took the situation too seriously. A lot of the country was so steep and rugged that it would have been an almost impossible task to fight them with the equipment then available.

One fire took three or four weeks to come through the hills to where it claimed attention. In that time it travelled about forty miles. About Christmas another was seen, but once again it was not considered dangerous.

These fires were lit by the hand of man.

11.2

1/1/1939
Fire broke out near the back road between Woodend and Trentham and was noticed first at about 10.30 a.m. spreading with extraordinary speed through the dry undergrowth.

2/1/1939
Fires are burning in the bush lands on the west side of the Bonang Highway, in country between Orbost and Delegate, from Little Bill down towards Orbost, to practically Godbers at Martin's Creek.

BRIGHT, Monday—When the wind changed about 6 p.m. to-day from the north to the south the town became enveloped in a dense pall of smoke. Serious fires are raging near Wandiligong, at German Creek, Buckland Valley, Snake Valley and Porepunkah.

3/1/1939
WALWA, Tuesday—Fierce fires are burning at many points in the Alps. The average temperature over the last three days has been 104 degrees which is quite exceptional for the upper Murray.

WANGARATTA, Tuesday—The fire that has been burning in the Toombullup district since December 23 has assumed large proportions in the last two or three days.

RAIN PROSPECTS/LITTLE HOPE FOR FALLS

A heavy smoke haze, which extended across Bass Strait as far as Tasmania, caused a false alarm yesterday regarding the seriousness of bush fires in Victoria.

The *Ormonde*, on a voyage from Burnie to Sydney, ran into such dense smoke that she had to slow down and sound her fog siren. Two elderly women passengers nearly caused a panic when they woke to find their cabin full of smoke and ran on deck in their nightclothes after alarming others.

8/1/1939
BAIRNSDALE, Sunday—The sky was completely overcast with dense clouds of smoke swept up from fires in the mountain ranges by a northerly wind. A small party of men, including the sons of Mr Lind, Deputy Premier, were fighting a fire early this morning that broke out on an old road from Lindenow to Bulumwaal, via Mount Alfred. Fragments of burning leaves from this fire were falling in Bairnsdale, eight miles distant.

HEYFIELD, Sunday—So deep was the smoke from district bush fires to-day that it became necessary for light to be lit in houses during luncheon.

Word was received in the afternoon that a big fire was raging further north, in the hills of Licola.

11.4

10/1/1939
ALL HEAT RECORDS BROKEN / Max. Temperature, 113 / Only Slight Relief Forecast

Wild Birds Overcome Fear Of Man

Three Tons Of Dead Fish

Snowy River Never Lower

POWELLTOWN IS THREATENED / FATE OF FOUR MILLS UNCERTAIN / ERICA CIRCLED BY ROARING FLAMES / Dugouts With Oxygen, Safe Haven For Men / ATTEMPT TO SAVE £30,000 WORTH OF TIMBER / RUBICON ENDANGERED

BRIGHT, Tuesday—A serious fire is raging on the Bogong high plains and is threatening the safety of over 7000 cattle. The fire, fanned by a strong wind, has been advancing on a front of over 25 miles wide in the vicinity of The Twins, near Mt St Bernard, and a large party of cattlemen has left Harrietville under Messrs C. Wraith and J. Treasure, both experienced bushmen, to burn breaks in an attempt to check the blaze.

11/1/1939
19 BODIES OF BUSH FIRE VICTIMS RECOVERED / TWELVE IN RUBICON FOREST / SEVEN NEAR ACHERON WAY / MANY STILL MISSING IN DEVASTATED AREA

Several fires at Erica have linked up and the hills early this morning presented a bed of red embers ready to be awakened by the next northerly.

Fires are still burning fiercely in the Tolmie Ranges and the Bogong high plains, at one end of which is Omeo, where business men closed their shops yesterday to go out to try to check a tremendous fire.

Flights over the bush fire areas were being offered by aircraft operators at Essendon aerodrome yesterday. Visitors were met by ticket sellers with the invitation, 'Take a flight over the city or over the bush fires, sir?' Aeroplane trips to the burning forests were quoted at 30/-.

Telephone communication to St Bernard has been cut off as a result of the flames, and cars are unable to reach the Mount Bernard hospice. A tourist party was unable to get through to-day, and returned to Bright this evening.

12/1/1939
FIRES UNDER CONTROL / NEW PERIL LIKELY TO-DAY / THRILLING STORIES OF RESCUED MEN

The huge fire on the Dargo High Plains continues to burn fiercely. No communications have been received from the party under Messrs Wraith and Treasure. To-day Messrs E. Weston, R. Gay and R. Blair left Bright for the Bogong High Plains in an endeavour to save numerous cattlemen's huts and mustering paddocks.

The fire was raging furiously in the dense timber just beneath the snow-line.

TALLANGATTA—The historical village of Granite Flat, formerly known as Snowy Creek, was destroyed by fire yesterday. Fire-fighters at Cravensville did good work burning trails and saving property.

OMEO—The situation was satisfactory last night, but stronger winds may easily bring the flames near the town.

NEW ADELAIDE RECORD / Temperature, 117.7 Degrees

11.7

For some days before the big fire actually occurred, matches burned with a white flame.

A red glow in the west indicated that a wall of fire was advancing towards Cobungra. Gas formed from burning trees was swept ahead of the inferno and exploded in the sky. Cattlemen who came to Omeo on Saturday, stated that the flames from fires on the Bogongs were hundreds of feet above the mountain tops.

Workmen employed on the Hill Top Hotel construction went to Cobungra Station to assist in fighting the fire, but they were trapped when the wind caused fresh outbreaks. With refugees from the station, including several children, they plunged into the Victoria River, and remained there until rescued.

Jack Read had taken off for a big dam he knew was there and when he arrived there were three bulls in the dam, but he didn't care, he just went straight in. 'As soon as I got in there I found three kangaroos, two wallabies, four snakes, all in together.'

Les Watts had to get in the creek at Cobungra with the four tyres of his old Chev car blazing.

Even if the break had been five miles wide, it could not have controlled the fire on the thirteenth. It was jumping from five to ten miles at a time.

The body of a stockman was found at Cobungra Station.

Percy Kerr showed us photos, post card size, of cattle that blew up with the heat of the fire.

OMEO—The fire swept over the mount at 8.30 p.m. on Friday. The hospital, from which two man and three woman patients were removed to safety was destroyed. Because of the heat the car which removed them could not be started, and Matron Lee played a hose on the car. When fear of the fire was greatest the matron was preparing morphia for patients.

The Omeo Hospital was completely burnt out. Patients and staff were evacuated to the Hill Top Hotel, as yet without a roof.

The historic Golden Age Hotel, 22 homes and 11 shops were destroyed.

The third storey of the Golden Age got on fire just underneath the spouting on the top floor. Peter Ryan's schoolmaster had to get out the window. Washington was also in the Hotel, and he said he'd go below, so he went down in the cellar where all the grog was kept. Two fellows had to go down and get him out. Later even the cellar caught on fire, all the bottles and everything burst, it just left nothing . . .

At Sandy's store 5000 gallons of petrol, stored in drums, exploded. The firemen, working 30 yards away, remained at their post and saved Slater's Cafe.

The gale suddenly changed, and a strong north wind blew the inferno back. The fire that burnt out the Splitter's Mount area acted as a formidable break and the Tambo Valley suffered little damage.

It burnt nearly to Swift's Creek. Right down past Jack Condon's.

11.8

16/1/1939
FIRE DANGER PASSES / DEATHS NOW 68 / POLICE WARN LOOTERS

RAIN SUBDUES BUSH FIRES / ANOTHER DEATH REPORTED / VICTIM IDENTIFIED / MAN MISSING FROM MT HOTHAM

OMEO, Monday—In marked contrast to conditions which prevailed on Friday, when the temperature was 115 deg., rain which commenced early this morning, was falling throughout the district, and mist was driving across the high plains, where the temperature was below 55 deg. All fires in the locality are extinguished and all district residents are accounted for.

All but one or two homesteads between Mt Hotham and the Golden Age had been destroyed. Practically all stock in the area 40 miles west of Omeo perished.

CORRYONG—The dangers of bush fires spreading at Thougla, Biggara, and Cudgewa are remote.

17/1/1939
OMEO, Tuesday—No floods have occurred near Omeo. Reports that communication with the town had been severed were without foundation.

There has been no danger of pollution of the water by dead stock. Less than an inch of rain has fallen and it is still drizzling to-day.

About 400 refugees from the Omeo district and Cobungra are being cared for by the local bush fire relief committee. At least 72 families are homeless.

The road to Mt Hotham is blocked by fallen logs.

1987

From *The Epigrams of Martial*

I xxv

Give to the nation
    this book
   shaped and polished,
that may stand the rarefied wind
     that sweeps eagles   5
   over the Black Mountain
and the flickering light where scholars
    delve amid dust
  in basement stacks.
Admit your own fame   10
   with no hesitation;
  its reward for your care
that these passages, alive beyond you,
    flourish now;
  glory is lost   15
on an urn of ashes.

I xxxvii

You drink from crystal
   and you piss in brass;
it's the vessel between
    that lacks class.

III xviii

Your asthma has won
   the audience's sympathy;
don't lose it by reading
   your poems.

III li

He says:
'I like the way you wear your clothes.'
    He means:
'I'd like to get into your pants.'
    She says: 5
'Your tie's crooked.'
    She means
to settle on a bar stool.

IV lv

Let those of Carlton
chant of Carlton.
Let Alan Wearne[1] chant
    of Blackburn.
But let us, sprung from   5
    Eastern stock
be unashamed to recall
    Croajingalong,
excellent in marble;
    Mitta Mitta   10
in gold and tin;
the meanders of the Snowy;
the shallow beds of the Tambo;
the valleys of Wulgulmerang
    and W Tree . . .   15
Do you, reader, laugh
at these rustic names?
These are the names I prefer
    to Holmesglen.

V li

Shorthand writers
    crowd around the man
        with a cricket bat
who can barely read two words
    off an idiot card   5
        for a TV commercial.

---

1   Alan Wearne (qv).

VI xxiii

I can't guarantee you a stiff prick
But I'm always prepared to give you the finger.

VII iii

If you haven't been given
a free copy of my book
it's because I don't want
a free copy of yours.

VII iv

Those about to die young,
        the insane, the criminal,
they encourage them all
            to write poetry.

VII lxxvi

Because you are rushed to
        Government House,
invited to editors' conferences
        in distant capitals,
presented at college charades   5
where farmers' boys strain
        in tuxedos,
do not overestimate yourself:
you entertain the rich;
they do not love you.   10

VIII xx

Dransfield,[1] who wrote
        200 poems each day,
was wiser than his editor
        who printed them.

X iv

You, who set the texts,
        for whom 'the Walkman
drowns out the great liberal tradition',
        forget for a moment
            your alter egos;   5

1   Michael Dransfield (qv).

forget damp blankets, razors,
     rubber tubing;
forget the lull of Miltown, the rites
  of Lady Lazarus;[1] forget
    'The Auschwitz Poems';[2]   10

and don't waste your blood
    on a bathtub:
blush instead at these epigrams of mine
  as you read them, recognizing
    your own manners.   15

        XI xvii

Not all of this book is for late night reading;
some of it goes well with a hangover.

        XII xiii

For the rich, hatred
is cheaper than charity.

        XII lxxviii

I've written nothing against you, reader,
but since you don't believe me
maybe I will.

          1989

Drinking Socially

Shapes of smoke on the bar window:
a History of Unemployment in Parkville.[3]
The college chaps talk on
    —these nouveaux barflies—
as cars pass in the frosty air   5
and the trams head north to Coburg.
And with that cocky farmers'
    attempt at etiquette
the young gents ask the barmaid her name
    and fail to give their own.   10
          1990

1   'Lady Lazarus', a poem by Sylvia Plath (1932–63).
2   A collection (1986) by Lily Brett (b. 1946).
3   The suburb in which the main campus of the University of Melbourne is located.

Air Time

At the mercy
of what I'm given
to work with
radiant windows
dust hanging   5
in the atmosphere
morning radio
the city mythologies.
That streets will
eventually lead down   10
to the water
impossible to
reconfigure, days
marked by weather,
words, hills   15
hidden in cloud.
Surrounded by
moisture try
to make gleaming
surfaces, rust-free   20
amid ephemera,
eroded inscriptions,
a rock wall
roped figures climb.

2003

GLENYSE WARD
b. 1949

Born in Perth, at the age of one Glenyse Ward was removed from her parents by the Native Welfare Department and placed in the St John of God's orphanage, Rivervale, WA. She was later sent to St Francis Xavier Native Mission in Wandering Brook.

When her mission education ceased she was put to domestic work, first at the mission and in 1964 as a servant to a wealthy white family. A year later she left for Busselton, where she was employed as a domestic in the Busselton Hospital kitchen. In 1987 she began publishing autobiographical fiction, winning the Federation of Australian Writers' Patricia Weickhardt Award to an Aboriginal Writer in 1992. *AH/PM*

From *Wandering Girl*
Running Whenever She Needed Me

Just as I was about to be attacked by a mob of vicious turkeys, I awoke to the sound of high pitched ringing. Jolted out of my terrible nightmare, I reached out, grabbed the clock to turn the alarm off, then lit up the old burner. I pulled my towel off the edge of my bed, to wipe the sweat off my face. My heart was still beating fast and my legs felt as if they had been running all night!

I lay back to let my nerves settle down and to come back to reality with myself. I lay there thinking about what sort of a day I was going to have. I felt real happy that they were going out again. It would give me an opportunity to go down and have a yarn with old Bill. I'd get him to come up and have a cup of tea with me. I might even ask him to help me cut some wood, because the thought of all that chopping made me feel weak. I just wished I knew what time her sons were going out. As soon as they left, I'd head straight down to the orchard.

I thought I'd better hurry up and get started on my jobs. Suddenly, I remembered that she wanted breakfast early. Now that I had shaken that horrible nightmare out of my system, I got myself dressed. Thinking, 'It's too cold for a shower,' I decided I'd have one later when everyone had left the farm.

I could use her shower room. It was so much nicer and warmer, as her toilet and shower room were in her bedroom. I remembered her powder smelt lovely. I liked the lavender one. I'd put some of that on me after my shower.

As soon as I was dressed I went to my own wash-house and freshened up my face and combed my hair. Back at my room, I just chucked my toiletries on the bed and slammed the door. Then I grabbed the old burner and broom, intending to start down from the orchard and work my way up to the front, then finish off my chores at the shoe rack. I had to polish their shoes and make sure they were spotless before they left for town.

So I made my way down to the bottom end of the driveway and started sweeping up all the leaves and dust. The wind was blowing hard, and I began to get a bit frustrated. I was fighting a losing battle—the more leaves I swept together the more the wind would blow them all over the place.

I thought, 'I'll just sweep from side to side. Too bad if the wind blows the leaves back again.' So I hurried up and made a quick job of it. I put the lantern and broom back where they belonged, then went to the shoe rack to start polishing the shoes.

When I finally finished the shoes I didn't feel like going all the way down to the paddock to pick her oranges. So I went into my room and got two out of my fruit bowl, which I had picked from the orchard a week before. They were a bit soft, but she wouldn't know. At least, there'd be a lot of juice in them. In the kitchen, I took a glass from the cabinet and squeezed the week-old oranges.

Um they were juicy too! I poured the rich juice into the glass and filled it up. I had a taste to see if the juice was sweet. It tasted alright to me, so I tidied my mess up, put a clean doyley over the glass, then set about getting breakfast.

When I put the bacon and eggs on I didn't forget myself. If she told me off I'd just say that I was making some for her sons too, playing dumb to the fact that she had already explained to me about the boys—besides, I couldn't help the way I was, just a shadow in this mansion. I went into the dining room to set the table up and make sure everything was laid out correctly, then went back into the kitchen. I glanced at the clock. It was about ten minutes to seven. I put the kettle on.

She called out to me from the dining room that she and Mr Bigelow were ready for their breakfast, but as I was setting up the trolley, she came in to drink her orange juice. The perfume she had on her was very strong, a sickly sort of smell. I caught a good whiff of it as she passed me. Her rouge and makeup always fascinated me. She often looked like she was ready for the circus.

I was just about to take the trolley in when she sort of tugged at the sleeve of my dress and told me that she'd wheel it in. She moved me out of the way abruptly and told me to bring in the bacon, eggs and toast when she rang the bell. 'Don't worry about making coffee. Just put the boiling water in a jug and bring it in with you when I am ready for the main breakfast.'

She went into the dining room with the trolley and shut the door behind her, leaving me standing there empty-handed. I thought that I'd better have my cereal, so I got my old tin plate out, filled it up with weeties, poured milk and sugar over them, then began. She rang the bell.

I dropped the spoon, quickly hopped up, got the plates of bacon and eggs, took them into the dining room, placed them on their individual places, then stood back to see if there was anything else she wanted before I went back into the kitchen.

As I stood there I got a fit of the sniffles and took out my old rag, which I had tucked in my sleeve jumper, and blew into it in a most profound manner, making the most peculiar noise.

She stood up in a very angry mood and told me to leave the room at once. What I had done was very rude—to blow my nose in front of decent citizens like her and her husband. If I happened to do it again she was going to report me to the priest at the mission. This was one thing she would not tolerate, especially from her servant. I shook as I made my way out to the kitchen.

Every time she scolded me I felt like I was dirt; but as I explained before, I sort of overlooked the situation. I could see the funny side of things. I was a person that nothing could ever get down for long. I was a happy go lucky girl!

Sometimes when she scolded me, I thought she was quite comical, but I never dared laugh in front of her. It was always at the back of her, or when she was out of my sight.

Even when the nuns scolded me at the mission, I could always see the funny side, especially when my mates were around me. We used to think it was a big joke to be slapped and told off. I mean we wouldn't laugh straight away, but only afterwards when we caught up with one another in the dining room or kitchen. We'd look at one another, and that was it! We'd have a good old laugh.

How I wished my mates were with me. Next time I went to town, I'd get some writing paper and write some letters. It seemed ages since I'd heard from anyone. My only contact with the mission had been about two weeks previously, when she mentioned that the priest from the mission wrote to ask her how I was progressing. 'Great news,' I thought. I could imagine the reply back from her, probably a real thriller!

Suddenly, I heard her yoohooing out for me. I put my thoughts to one side, and ran into the dining room to see what she wanted.

Over the months that I had been here, through her manner of expectation and through fear of being scolded, I had developed a habit of running whenever she needed me. So I ran in to see what she wanted.

She just told me she was on her way out and my last instructions were not to touch the phone, and also her bedroom needed doing. She told me I was to cook tea for them and have everything ready for them when they pulled up. She told me where I would find a leg of silverside. I was to boil that up and they would have it with cauliflower, pumpkin and mashed potatoes.

So off she went with Mr Bigelow to her car. I waited back in the dining room till I saw the car go down the driveway and head in the direction of town. I thought to myself that I'd clear all the dishes away and make sure the dining room was tidy and clean for her sons.

I wished they would hurry up and have their breakfast and go, as I felt uncomfortable knowing that they were around. I couldn't relax. I wanted to eat my bacon and eggs in peace, have my shower and then escape down to the orchard.

1987

KEN BOLTON
b 1949

Ken Bolton is a poet, editor, publisher and art critic. Born in Sydney, he has lived in Adelaide since 1982, where he has worked for the Experimental Art Foundation, edited the literary journals *Otis Rush* and *Magic Sam*, and run a small press called Little Esther Books. He has written numerous collections of poetry, some of which are co-written with John Jenkins. *Selected Poems: 1975–1990* appeared in 1992. His poetry, often comic in tone, is characterised by an attention to the real and immediate. The title poem in *Untimely Meditations* (1997) is a rare instance of contemporary Australian poetry in the mode of literary and cultural criticism. *DM*

Paris to Pam Brown[1]

I have hardly seen the Eiffel tower—

                        even

from a distance

               living a week in Paris

With another week to go   5

               I think I will

hardly see it

            I walk our street in

the Bastille

         & sit & have coffee or a   10

Ricard or pastis

         or walk hours in

the Louvre

         attending   to the confident

stylish   15

       look of the French

                 their little

dogs

       their cars, their motor scooters,

                      zipping—   20

always zipping

        up on the footpaths

               the cars

effortfully manoeuvring

           around one another— 25

where they have parked at an angle

            across a corner

1 Pam Brown (qv).

across a drive
                 the large doleful phlegmatic man
& his timid little dog   30
                    (The dog stands under him
tiny & leonine, trembling
                       between the ornate curlicue
legs
        of the chair that supports *cet homme*   35
                               while
a larger dog passes
                  & a small Citroen   or Opel
attempts to park
             or attempts to leave   40
                       a sip of coffee
& the car is gone & another one replaces it
                        I guess it *was* going
or we'd be looking at the same car, right?
                     —in the rue vielle du   45
temple
       where I don't see any temple, either
                        tho I see
'something' large & impressive.
                  I think the temples   50
—read, I think, synagogues—in this former Jewish
Quarter
       were pulled down
                Slightly warmer coloured
& a Moroccan in a burnous   55
                & just one
striped awning   (orange & white)
                     it would look
Eastern enough
       —like a Prud'hon or Gerard[1] or other   60
orientalist painting
             or one of those watercolours Australian
artists did
       of the Middle East
               while employed by the   65
army
       to Record Our Exploits—late Streeton or

1   French painters Pierre Paul Prud'hon (1758–1823) and Baron François Gérard (1770–1837).

Roberts   or whoever else went (Dundas?)[1]
                                  the walls
of the buildings slope back slightly in some of the alleys   70
& in one this slope
                       is matched by an equivalent
lean
      from the other side   out over the alley
                           to meet   75
the shrinking, retreating wall opposite.
                          It looks
expressionist, or stagey
                those Australian paintings
were mostly empty   80
           as I recall
                 or empty*ish*
                      as
tho our tour of duty
              was rather boring or alien   85
or the artist got there first
              or too late, after
the soldiers had moved on
               I wonder what Paris
thinks of Pam   90
         —which scans so much better than
Pam thinks of Paris
             but I wonder what she did think?
Paris thinks nothing of us
              as I sit here sipping   95
or it thinks I sit badly
             or my suit is an odd cut
Tho it's glamorous enough
            or so *I* think
                  The Swiss poet   100
was lovely
       & loveable partly for the dagginess of his Swiss
appearance
        apparent to us
             —so apparent to Paris?   105
I know nothing
        including, it appears, not necessarily even

---

1   Australian artists Arthur Streeton (1867–1943), Tom Roberts (1856–1931) and Douglas Dundas (1900–81).

what 'scan' means

        (I meant only 'sounds')

             I wonder   110

what Pam did think.

        I don't mean as a question—

as a report on myself: that is what I do,

          I wonder.

Would *she* be as beautiful in Australia?   115

(of a young woman cycling by)

         How small *are*

they, these apartments, in which these dogs & people live?

Is that black guy happier here than he would be

in London?   120

        (it seems so) How old is that, that bit

of building there

          sticking out from behind that modern one

a pale ochre with tiles that are funny & deep red &

unusually spikey & stickle-backed?   125

          & isn't the gilding a

little extreme on that figure of *Mercury*

         off in the distance

atop his enormous pedestal?

        Gee, Guido Reni[1]   130

is a little overrated

      & Simon Vouet[2] definitely

             &

I wouldn't leave Paris   (for ages)   if I had the money

           1997

JENNIFER MARTINIELLO
b. 1949

A writer, artist and academic born in Adelaide of Arrernte, Chinese and Anglo-Celtic descent, Jennifer Martiniello has lectured in education at the Canberra Institute of Technology and the University of Canberra and worked with Indigenous communities in regional NSW and Victoria. In 2005 she was the public officer of the Indigenous Writers Support Group in Canberra and a member of the Publishing Advisory Committee of Aboriginal Studies Press at AIATSIS. She has edited a number of anthologies, including *Black Lives, Rainbow Visions: Indigenous sitings in the creative arts* (1999), *Writing Us Mob: New Indigenous voices* (2000) and *Talking Ink from Ochre* (2002), and is the author of a collection of poetry, *The Imprint of Infinity* (1999). *AH/PM*

---

1   Guido Reni (1575–1642), an Italian painter.
2   Simon Vouet (1590–1649), a French painter.

Uluru by Champagne

you
are a flame in the blue
dome of heaven
eternal
bubble of evanescent   5
earth, the mother rising
in the spirits of her children
the land your
magic
spun   10
between suns
horizon to horizon

you are
blue earth, red sky, deep shadow

the imprint   15
of infinity on my soul
                                                      1999

Emily Kngwarreye[1]

your face
is the grace a harsh life
bestows on its survivors, each crease
a bar whose notes, escaping their dirge,
run for the high octaves like a bird   5
to a joyous freedom once the doors
of the cage are broken

deep-coloured as the millennia
sediments that scar the cliff faces of sacred country
your face is as ancient a bed to flowing water   10
carving its agelessness into the land the way
wisdom enscripts its elusive dance upon
humanity

---

1 Emily Kngwarreye (c. 1910–96) was an internationally acclaimed Aboriginal artist from the Utopia Community in the NT.

and I watch you
slowly measuring out the journeylines with a finger   15
brushed with red earth and hear the dust
that others only see as a place to put their boots
open its voice and speak,
see your hand on the cave walls where they
have held the ochred spirit in the rock for all   20
eternity, and watch how the sun shifts
to accommodate your shadow, effortlessly,
day after day without tiring

I watch you bend
your face to greet the waterhole, see   25
how your laughter is caught up in the transient
ripples and released without possessive grasping
to share you with reed, tree,—how you
and it are the same manna
born in the same creation   30

I see ... beyond the verticals
and horizontals of skin the hundred boys who've
died in custody and whom you've mourned, the warp
and weft of sorrow in your face for all the young women
whose eyes do not know their country or their mothers   35
but whose children still belong to your body—how your skin
stretches to embrace their homecoming with every
carefully recorded story, mother, son, daughter,
place and time—the same way your smile
stretches other boundaries   40

sometimes beyond comprehension
and lesser visions restrained to the finite byte
of desert stopover, campfire talk, a desperate camera-clutch
at a surreal otherworld that fail to distinguish how you
rise from earth, become   45
ancestor, mother, daughter, grandmother, granddaughter,
terrain, sacred physicality—fail to see
how the one spirit makes you blood and rock, well
and water

your face wears the intaglio of embattled anguish,   50
betrayal, theft, deceit, massacre and grief survived—

and when I remember the zealot piety and passion
of ANZAC, two world wars, Korea, Vietnam,
I remember also that you witnessed all of them
for nine generations and more; and as I watch you   55
bend to trace creation in red earth with a finger
more purposeful than Michaelangelo's Sistine god's
I see a light more eternal kindle in those you teach,
see each one, mirror-like, reflect the tireless radiance
of an inevitable grace   60
2002

YAHIA AL-SAMAWY
b. 1949

Yahia Al-Samawy was born and educated in Iraq, where he worked in teaching and journalism. He was imprisoned and tortured under Saddam Hussein's regime. He fled Iraq and spent a number of years in exile in Saudi Arabia before migrating with his family to Australia in 1997. He has published several collections of poetry in Arabic and has received a number of major awards, including the Prize of the Arab Union for Poetic Creativity. *Two Banks with No Bridge*, a chapbook of poems translated from Arabic by Eva Sallis, was published in 2005. Sallis (b. 1964) is a novelist, translator and human rights advocate. Her novels include *Hiam* (1998) and *The Marsh Birds* (2005). In 2001 she co-founded Australians Against Racism. She is now known as Eva Hornung. *DM*

Your Voice is My Flute

Your voice is my flute
It tamed the viper of sadness in my garden
And my flowers bathed in perfume
Your voice, O my pure guide
Is a beam of light.   5
I spread over it
The shirt of my secrets . . .
And a luminary page
On which I wrote my most chaste poems
A grassy cloak . . .   10
That enveloped a heart
Once fearful of cold and tempest

Your voice became a part of me
I never heard it except
A mist emerged from a homely gleaming   15
Intoxicating me without sinfulness

The cloudless skies become drunk at my window
It grows a hymn for me in the field of my guitar

Your voice was the first in the funeral procession
For the desolation that had darkened my path   20
Your voice was the first to guide me
To the lands of sweet basil and bay
It made me pure

A bridge of affection was erected between the butterflies
And the wind and fire   25
Rain down your pure melodies in my hearing
To keep my heartstrings beating
Ten years—
And I am still at the door of your love, fasting
When will be the time to eat and drink?   30

Ten years
And I am still on the heap of my years, vigilant
Waiting for your crescent face that lights my thoughts
With water and fire

Ten years—   35
And no season of rain has passed over my plains

And here I am
I carve with a rib into the stone of yearning
Perhaps a stone will bring me
Glad tidings of upwelling water to my trees!   40

2005

JENNIFER MAIDEN
b. 1949

Jennifer Maiden was born in Penrith, NSW. After leaving school at the age of thirteen, she worked at a number of jobs before graduating from Macquarie University. She has subsequently been a professional writer, publishing poetry, fiction, writing for children, plays and radio scripts. Maiden has been at the forefront of reinvigorating political poetry in the last 30 years. Her poetry has moved from the elliptical politics of *The Problem of Evil* (1975) to the self-conscious allegory of *The Trust* (1988) and the self-reflexive, essayistic works of *Mines* (1999) and *Friendly Fire* (2005). In these later works Maiden combines the lyric mode with satire, verse essay, diary and occasional verse. Her 'parallel' poems illustrate hidden connections between apparently divergent topics. Her work can be urgently topical, especially in her interventions in the Iraq War. The key sequence of *Friendly Fire*, 'George Jeffreys', is an anatomy of George W. Bush's 'war on terror'. *DM*

Dracula on the Monaro

In humility, I should remember
that God did not give me
George Bush Junior of Texas, but
I'll admit before that an apathy
of sorts had descended on the bow-   5
of-burning-gold for a while, and arrows-
of-desire.   The Monaro[1]
is not dry with winter and no place
ever does clouds better. They do
unfold and are also   10
fat like knobby cherubs, layer
upon layer of plump cream, which must
have reminded the tribespeople
travelling to the feast at Mt Jagungal
of the most delicious Bogong moths: 15
a smoky trance, a feast. I
have needed to be on the Monaro
so much that it seemed impossible
to see these vast clouds, these poplars
silvergilt in wind again, but   20
now here I feel nothing: when you are
thirsty, the water has no taste,
though clouds are a fistful, mouthful.
On the horizon, a white parade
of arced ark animals. Even in the mountains,   25
in spring, these clouds remain clouds
grounded, circle the frozen wattle's
lemon sequins, blend with snow
crystal to drifting crystal, remind
me how once I thought most beauty   30
was indistinct at its edge, remind
me how before Barrett Reid[2] died
he wrote me 'warm wishes from this
winter garden' in a letter. I
think of the current fashion   35
to object to writers who write
about other writers, and of how

1   A highland region in the south of NSW and the ACT.
2   Barrett Reid (1926–95), editor of *Overland* (1988–93), art critic and poet.

Campbell[1] farmed this Monaro, and Les
Murray[2] rabbited for him. Maybe
Les was successful. I can't see any   40
Campbells or rabbits and the few
road-kill bodies are fox and kangaroo.
                              You know,
in this autumn we will know
warm wintergartens trellised red with snow,   45
and writers write of writers as earlier ones drew
living food or the spirits of lightning, as any
schoolboy or soldier who draws
nudes on his notebook or wall, not
thinking the art will achieve   50
a storm or full stomach, a girl. Any
writer is a private revolution, all
writing is desire, although such
axioms are vulnerable. The high
plains wind thins charcoal   55
cloud into string hearts. The Monaro
does darkness well. My father
told me of running wildly home
across a bridge here after
he read *Dracula* as a boy. Bram Stoker   60
would understand the Monaro, its
vulnerable desire, and Texas
is never empty, if the blood
like water does not taste when one is thirsty.

                                                                  2005

Old Europe Stared at Her Breakfast

*(US Defence Secretary Rumsfeld dismissed those European
countries which opposed the US attack on Iraq as only 'Old Europe')*

Old Europe stared at her breakfast,
buttered her croissant, sipped coffee
which tasted like a gun
and blinked her grey eyes to restore the sun.
Old Europe grasped at the old A. J. P. Taylor   5
line, 'but in politics the impossible

---

1   David Campbell (qv).
2   Les Murray (qv).

always happens' more and more, hoped
for example, that the fact that the 'plant'
for weapons in Northern Iraq was shown
on the BBC an empty ex–Media   10
Centre, and miles away a plain village,
hoping not to be bombed, because by
mistake young Colin,[1] who apparently
mistook often, used its name
at the UN as that of the 'plant',   15
would be accepted as a fact and then
protected, thought Old Europe
as her France loved to protect facts,
as her Germany to act, or her Belgium to be. But,
she reflected, in doubt and in debt,   20
the future is not an ally
over the sea which just needs to be
convinced but a masked soldier, dead
to Agincourt, Darmstadt, Verdun,
wanting oil and meat and not   25
understanding how a continental breakfast
keeps the blood in your head, your brain
not your gut. Old Europe set her spine
straight in the doorway sun. Her hand
crumbled bread as if it were old bone.   30
                                                          2005

KEVIN BROPHY
b. 1949

Born in Melbourne, Kevin Brophy was educated by the Jesuits and at the University
of Melbourne where he studied literature and psychology. He held numerous jobs,
including schoolteacher and disability worker, before becoming an academic, and later
associate professor in creative writing at the University of Melbourne. In 1980 he
began the literary journal *Going Down Swinging* with Myron Lysenko, which he co-
edited until 1994. Brophy has published novels, short fiction, poetry and two ground-
breaking critical works that theorise creativity, including *Creativity: Psychoanalysis,
surrealism and creative writing* (1998). Despite this variety, Brophy's work consistently
shows an attention to the everyday and its strangeness. Brophy's poetry, seen for
instance in *Portrait in Skin* (2002) and *Mr Wittgenstein's Lion* (2007), blends the lyrical
self with surrealist energy and formal experimentation. His innovative criticism often
employs narrative. *DM*

---

1   Colin Powell (b. 1937), United States Secretary of State, 2001–05.

Box

The universe is box shaped
and death will be box-shaped too.

Everything I own
I put into boxes
and send to a warehouse   5
constructed according to
the principles of the box:
six sides, rectangular
more often than square,
a series of clever folds   10
and a little glue.

In the glue
of cardboard boxes
there are traces
of melted-down horse,   15
a box shaped creature.
Beneath the feathers of birds
you will find they are box-shaped too
and the egg is a misshapen box
hopelessly inadequate for stacking.   20

Your head is a box
Every idea is a box
as is every philosophy
and any computer
you can think of.   25
A tree is a box or will be a box.

A box is the shape of a fact.
Every musical instrument is a box.
Like the wheel, we cannot survive without it.
It keeps for us what must be pressed down   30
in darkness
locked away and hidden from children.
On the sides of my boxes
prepared for the final boxing-up
are messages, as there should be: 35
'fresh produce packed by

Gayndah Packing Co-op'
Says one.
'Gaiety' says another
on all its sides   40
and another, 'Horizon'.

I have rented this box-shaped storage shed
and gathered these masterful boxes
for filling with my boxed-up life.
There will be a darkness   45
within darkness as night
(like a box)
comes over the warehouse.

                                                   2007

JOHN FORBES
1950–1998

The poet John Forbes was born in Melbourne and grew up in Sydney (with periods in New Guinea, Malaya and Townsville, where his father was posted as a meteorologist). Forbes was educated in Catholic schools and at the University of Sydney. His early poetic influences were, along with Gerard Manley Hopkins, contemporary American poets such as John Ashbery and Frank O'Hara. In the early 1970s he met Laurie Duggan, Alan Wearne and Martin Johnston (qqv), members (along with Forbes and others) of the Generation of '68, an anti-establishment group attracted to experimentation and radical politics.

Forbes's first book, *Tropical Skiing* (1976), is exuberant and abstract, and, like his later work, marked by surreal associations, philosophical scepticism and promiscuous cultural references. Such traits show Forbes to be an early postmodern Australian poet. His fascination with 'poetic election' and the condition of being a poet in Australia is expressed in the deeply ironic 'On the Beach: A Bicentennial poem' (which appeared in *The Stunned Mullet*, 1988).

In 1989 Forbes left Sydney to live in Melbourne, where he earned money from grants, literary journalism and teaching writing. In the 1990s he was also poetry editor of *Scripsi*; poetry reader for Fremantle Arts Centre Press; and poetry editor and consultant for Angus & Robertson. By the time of his last overseas trip in 1997 (to work at a regional English university), Forbes's health, damaged by drinking and drug use, was bad. His posthumous collection, *Damaged Glamour* (1998), while marked by a pathos associated with age and disillusion, retains the poet's formal and linguistic brilliance. His *Collected Poems* was published in 2001, and *Homage to John Forbes*, a tribute edited by Ken Bolton (qv), in 2002. *DM*

To the Bobbydazzlers

American poets!
you have saved
America from
its reputation

if not its fate   5
& you saved me
too, in 1970
when I first
breathed freely
in Ted Berrigan's   10
Sonnets, escaping
the talented earache of Modern
Poetry.
                    Sitting
on the beach I   15
look towards you
but the curve
of the Pacific
gets in the way
& I see stars   20
instead knocked
out by your poems
American poets,
the Great Dead
are smiling   25
in your faces.
I salute their
luminous hum!
                                                    1976

Stalin's Holidays

The quick brown fox jumps over the lazy dog.
Juniper berries bloom in the heat. My heart!
'Bottoms up, Comrade.' The nicotine-stained
fingers of our latest defector shake as they
reach for Sholokhov's *Lenin*—the veranda is   5
littered with copies—no, commies, the ones
in comics like 'Battle Action' or 'Sgt Fury
& His Howling Commandos'. Does form follow
function? Well, after lunch we hear a speech.
It's Stephen Fitzgerald back from 'Red' China.   10
Then, you hear a postie whistle. I hear without
understanding, two members of Wolverhampton
Wanderers pissed out of their brains, trying
to talk Russian. Try reading your telegram—

'mes vacances sont finies: Stalin'.[1] But we don't   15
speak French or play soccer in Australia, our
vocabulary and games are lazier by far. Back
in the USSR, we don't know how lucky we are.

                                                              1977

Ode/'Goodbye Memory'

Goodbye memory & you my distances
calling love me across the vast golf course
to the greens whose flags no wind will ever ruffle
              Goodbye memory & goodbye
to the sheets held against hot windows   5
on days when the morning's blue intensity so crushes me
I breathe with the gasps of a fat sprinter & only
a teenybopper's crystal sigh answers, so dumbly,
the immense chances the collision of deckchairs
from the briefcase full of words insomnia unpacks endlessly   10
              Goodbye memory,
                      Goodbye pyjamas
now summer's cool air will rustle forever against my balls
overpowering like a muscle dreams so rusty no art
is bad enough to do their boredom justice   15
              Goodbye memory
                      & the way the mind groans
over its trivia throwing the scrapbook into
the sunrise thinking look how I shine convinced
the day riots because I glance   20
the mind spoils even the hamburger, training words till
they're all reflex & cooing for torment like a lover
                      in love with feeling his love so pure
              So goodbye words
              & goodbye writing, more   25
ambivalent than a two-brained dinosaur & just as doomed!
                      & goodbye to you, poetry
ludicrous sex-aid greasing the statues of my mind
              Hello the yellow beach & the beauty
that closes a book. Hello the suntanned skin   30
              & underneath that skin, the body.
                      Goodbye Memory!

                                                              1980

---

1 'My holidays are finished: Stalin'.

Speed, a Pastoral

it's fun to take speed
& stay up all night
not writing those reams of poetry
just thinking about is bad for you
                    —instead your feelings   5
follow your career down the drain
& find they like it there
among an anthology of fine ideas, bound together
by a chemical in your blood
that lets you stare the TV in its vacant face   10
& cheer, consuming yourself like a mortgage
& when Keats comes to dine, or Flaubert,
you can answer their purities
with your own less negative ones—for example
you know Dransfield's[1] line, that once you become a junkie   15
you'll never want to be anything else?
            well, I think he died too soon,
as if he thought drugs were an old-fashioned teacher
& he was the teacher's pet, who just put up his hand
            & said quietly, 'Sir, sir'   20
            & heroin let him leave the room.
                                                        1988

Love Poem

Spent tracer flecks Baghdad's
bright video game sky

as I curl up with the war
in lieu of you, whose letter

lets me know my poems show   5
how unhappy I can be. Perhaps.

But what they don't show, until
now, is how at ease I can be

with military technology: e.g.
matching their *feu d'esprit* I classify   10

---

1   Michael Dransfield (qv).

the sounds of the Iraqi AA—the
thump of the 85 mil, the throaty

chatter of the quad ZSU 23.
Our precision guided weapons

make the horizon flash & glow   15
but nothing I can do makes you

want me. Instead I watch the west
do what the west does best

& know, obscurely, as I go to bed
all this is being staged for me.   20
                                         1992

Anzac Day

A certain cast to their features marked
the English going into battle, & then, that

glint in the Frenchman's eye meant 'Folks,
clear the room!' The Turks knew death

would take them to a paradise of sex   5
Islam reserves for its warrior dead

& the Scots had their music. The Germans
worshipped the State & Death, so for them

the Maximschlacht was almost a sacrament.
Recruiting posters made the Irish soldier   10

look like a saint on a holy card, soppy & pious,
the way the Yanks go on about their dead.

Not so the Australians, unamused, unimpressed
they went over the top like men clocking on,

in this first full-scale industrial war.   15
Which is why Anzac Day continues to move us,

& grow, despite attempts to make it
a media event (left to them we'd attend

'The Foxtel Dawn Service'). But The March is
proof we got at least one thing right, informal,   20

straggling & more cheerful than not, it's
like a huge works or 8 Hour Day picnic—

if we still had works, or unions, that is.

1998

KATE GRENVILLE
b.1950

Novelist Kate Grenville was born Catherine Gee in Sydney and grew up there. She
worked for several years in the Australian film industry before travelling to the UK and
Europe, spending three years in London before moving to the US to study in 1980,
and returning to Australia in 1983. Her first book of fiction, the short-story collection
Bearded Ladies, was published in 1984.

Lilian's Story (1985), based on the Sydney eccentric Bea Miles, a famous figure
in the streets of Sydney around the middle of the twentieth century, is a fictionalised
exploration of the forces that might have shaped a woman's life in that time and place.
The novel *Dreamhouse* (1986), like Grenville's first two books, is also grounded in and
animated by its feminist energies and strategies.

Grenville continued her overtly feminist project in *Joan Makes History* (1988), a novel
conceived as part of, and as a response to, Australia's 1988 Bicentennial celebrations;
using a technique that recalls Virginia Woolf's *Orlando*, Grenville takes Joan—a minor
character from *Lilian's Story*, now given centre stage—through several incarnations to
show the conditions of women's lives at different stages of Australia's history. Grenville
married Australian cartoonist Bruce Petty in 1986 and their two children were born in
1986 and 1990. Since 1990 Grenville has published three books on the craft of writing,
one co-written with fellow novelist Sue Woolfe.

In 1994 Grenville published *Dark Places*, a major novel that reprises the character
of Albion, the controlling father in *Lilian's Story*, and retells the story from his
point of view. *The Idea of Perfection* (1999) is a gentle 'middle-aged love story' about
two life-damaged characters who find each other in a small Australian town. This
novel won Grenville her first major international literary prize, the Orange Prize for
Fiction, in 2001.

Grenville's historical novel *The Secret River* (2005) won numerous awards, including
the Commonwealth Writers Prize. *The Secret River* uses material from the history of
Grenville's convict ancestors to dramatise and fictionalise the early settlement of NSW,
attempting to tell the story of the dispossession of Aboriginal people without demonising
the settlers, many of whom were transported convicts and therefore also at the mercy
of the British government and legal system. This novel won acclaim from readers and
critics, apart from those who found Grenville's position on race relations history either
too radical or too conservative, but she was engulfed in controversy when an off-the-cuff
remark on radio about the relationship between history and fiction sparked a national
debate on the subject. She has written about her experience researching material for this
novel in *Searching for the Secret River* (2006). *KG*

From *Lilian's Story*
Part 3: A Woman

HOW MANY BIRTHDAYS LEFT?

It was a race now between my death and my decay. Few people knew the exact date of my birth, and few cared, but I did, and I did not want either death or decay before I had done everything I could. *I want a birthday frock*, I told the woman in the St Vincent de Paul shop. *I want to look very pretty, a birthday girl.* The woman was full of aplomb and smiled a gold-toothed smile, fuller of Jewish charm than dowdy Catholic piety. *Certainly, Madame*, she said, and came out from behind the sad cartons of cracked boots, holding a tape measure like someone in a salon. It could have been that in her old country, where charm and gold teeth were more common than here, she had often held tape measures around large women, and done it with the same aplomb she did now. *And how old are you, if it is not indiscreet?* the woman asked as she embraced me with the tape, but I wanted to play ladies and keep my secret. *Oh, terribly old*, I said secretively. *And I am going to have a birthday in King Street.*

I had never worn blue nylon frills before and could not recognise myself in the small mirror. *Is this me?* I asked, watching squares of myself in blue nylon as the woman moved the mirror up and down for me. *Yes*, she smiled, so that her gold glittered, *it is you, and you are Lil Singer, I think*. I was always pleased to be recognised, and was feeling a little hysterical from the blue nylon. *My life is almost gone*, I told this sympathetic woman, who had the air of one who had been surprised too many times to be surprised ever again, *but I think it has been worthwhile*. I laughed at the cracked boots so that a woman in flowered cotton, who had peeked in at the door, left again quickly, and my laugh turned to crying because I would have liked another life, or even the same one over again.

There were many guests at my party, though most of them in their folly and simplicity of mind did not realise they were watching a celebration. King Street stood and stared as I paced slowly in front of a tram that rang and rang its bell like a birthday chorus. When the driver leaned out of his cabin and yelled, I waved at him like the Queen, feeling the blue frills shiver in the breeze, and called, *Thank you, thank you*, because I knew that under the words he was shouting, he was doing his best to wish me a happy birthday. At the top of King Street I stood aside and waved as the tram twirled around the corner into Macquarie Street, and I had to sit for a little while in the gutter to catch my breath. *It is the excitement of my birthday*, I explained to the policeman who appeared beside me. *When you are old you will know what I mean.* I nodded closely into his face, where the blood roared with youth beneath the skin. *It is tiring, being old*, I told him, *even though I have never cultivated the burden of memory.*

He left me at last, with backward glances, and although I did not want to walk any more, I levered myself up off the pavement at last and began to walk back towards the park. I longed for the cool grass beneath me and forced one foot after the other against a great weight pressing me backwards. But I fell in the middle of that crowded lunchtime pavement, and I felt my broad feet slide out from under me and the unfriendly clutch of gravity. Everyone stared but no one stopped. I must have been a frightening sight, and it was years since anyone but myself had seen my white thighs, and I saw the glare of them stun the strangers as they stared and stared from beyond the circle of shock that enclosed me. My hat had slipped over one eye, down over my nose, its elastic folding an ear over onto itself so the roar of the traffic, and a bus snarling up the hill beside me in the gutter, were sounds inside my own head, hurting, trying to get out. I laughed and laughed, feeling my fat shake, and could not stop laughing, because my legs, stuck out in front of me in a big foolish way, would not move to bear my weight again. I struggled, and sat on warm bitumen and settled my hat on my head again and again, and my laugh was louder as my fear was greater. I laughed until I heard it sound like a roar of fright, trying to pretend to everyone, and to myself, that it was just old Lil making a monkey of herself and having a fool around with her hat.

I seemed stuck for ever to this patch of grey footpath. *This is not the spot where I wish to die*, I thought, *not this bit of my native place*, and I wondered if I had shouted it, the way the dark suits were staring. Everything was staring eyes in a hopeless sweat of never being able to rise again, like a cow gone down finally, but this was no sweet pasture, and the hot grit was vile under my palms.

I began to realise that I had to ask for help, but did not know how, because I had not asked anyone for help for too long, and I was having a problem with my words. They were not organising themselves in my mouth as they had always done, but were coming out in a kind of mooing. The faces stared and moved on, someone tittered, and there was no young red-faced policeman now when I needed one, only faces that did their best not to see me, busy men striding so quickly they were on me before they saw, and had to sidestep with a skip so as not to lose the pace of their day. One could not step sideways in time, his life was moving so quickly, but had to step over my purple hand as it propped me up, and met my eyes and was frightened. I held up a hand, and could not stop the noises coming out of my face, and it was all the best I could do to ask for help, and I was trying through the thick blubber of my lips to say, *Just get me on my feet and I will be right as rain*. But the sounds coming out of my face were not words, and my hand continued to wave out towards those white faces and they moved away like lights at night, and others took their place, but no one could break the circle around me to touch my hand and bring me back to my body.

Until at last the woman in lilac shantung was kneeling beside me and her handbag of lizard skin was lying in the grit. The woman in lilac shantung took my hand and knelt so violently I heard stitches crack, and supported me with an arm around my shoulder, and I could smell her perfume. I watched very closely as the pearls gleamed against the skin of her neck, which was no younger than mine, but had not been exposed to so many cold nights on a beach. The woman in lilac shantung was wearing lilac gloves but as she knelt beside me becoming dirty she tore off those gloves and smoothed the hair back from my face with a soft pampered hand. *Lil, dear, you will be all right in a moment, rest for a moment.* I was not surprised that she knew who I was, but I was pleased, and lay back against her arm knowing again that fame of a kind must have come to me, for a stranger in lilac to be calling me so familiarly by name. But when she looked up, still kneeling beside me, and spoke appealingly to one of the suits, making her voice helpless and charming, so that the suit stopped, and promised, and moved off on his errand of mercy, I recognised that charm, that tilt of the ageing throat with the pearls slipping against the skin. I recognised that the woman in lilac shantung was Ursula, and I was silenced by surprise.

In the ambulance I could see her knees and was touched by the way the skin was grey with pavement dirt, and how each knee was capped by the large round hole in each stocking. On the skirt of the lilac shantung were marks and smudges now that looked permanent, like those on my own, humbler clothes. In the smell of starched sheets and antiseptic I was calmer now, and fingered the lilac shantung, and would have liked to smooth the skin of the knees, but did not dare. I whispered, and although the words did not quite come out the way they were intended, Ursula understood, and brushed at the marks, and wet a finger with spit to see if they would be removed that way. *No, it does not matter, Lil,* she said. *It is time I gave up pretending.* There were many questions we could have asked each other, because the girls we had been when we last saw each other had long been lost in the elderly women we had become, but Ursula had been watching me grow old and famous. She would have read about me in the papers, would have cut out the pieces, perhaps, to show Rick when he was still her husband and not the bride of Trotsky. And I was too weary now for any questions, and the movement of the ambulance through the streets of my city was making it too hard for me to shape words or even thoughts.

ALL MY SISTERS

I continued to resist and smile, and try to pretend I could return to my life in the park, until the Sisters smiled and took away my book bag. *We will keep it safe for you,* they said, and they were right, I had no need of books now, or anything else. All that I was to know, I knew. They were kind and pale-skinned, all those nuns, and I came to enjoy the fragrance of starched cotton and old incense.

In the beginning they all looked the same to me, their faces all smooth and dry, like the clean sole of a foot, under their veils. It surprised me, how weak I had become, and how it became less of a luxury and more of a necessity, to have one or other of those pale women brush my hair for me or button my clothes. *Here we go, Lil*, they murmured and smiled. In the beginning I said, *Thank you Sister, thank you Sister*, until I was sick of it, but when I learned their outlandish names I felt easier, and realised that Sister Annunciata could be made to giggle under her veil so her flat black front shook, that Sister Evangelina of Montefiore could answer me quote for quote from William no matter what I tried her on, and that Sister Frederica with the moustache was too pious, or sad, to be any fun, but spooned the porridge into the mouths of those who could not manage, and crossed herself instead of laughing.

Even nuns grow huge under their habits, and Sister Isola could have balanced my weight on the other end of a see-saw, and would have tried if there had been one handy, in spite of being a serious woman at times, with large brown eyes full of innocent intelligence, who took seriously her responsibility towards all these nuns and helpless old people.

Sometimes the kiddies visited us, and would be red in the face from their charitable deed. *Merry Christmas and God bless you*, some blonde innocent would say, and try to smile as she handed me a cube of bath salts or a bookmark. God was still nobody I knew, but I knew about kindness, and watched the heat in her cheeks as she did her best to provide me with *a few minutes' chat*, as they had all been told to. I decided that she needed a little of my wisdom, and told her, *Do not worry about getting old gracefully, girlie, be foolish and loud if you feel like it*. I saw her beginning to look alarmed, but I had more to say: *Dignity and respect are humbug, remember that, girlie*. This blonde girl was still smiling a fixed smile at me but she was inching away and her eyes were darting past me, enviously watching her classmates, who were happy shouting at deaf Bess, or looking at the hand-crocheted handkerchief that Doris's daughter had made for her. My poor red girl, who was so clean and scrubbed and optimistic she could only have been class captain, was at last rescued by Sister Isola. She brushed her off towards tremulous Annie who had missed out on a visitor, and roared in her big fat way, that I liked because it was the same big fat way that I roared, *Lil, do not bully the poor child with your wisdom*. She winked from her big brown eye, so that we both had to laugh our big fat laughs, and everyone stopped for a moment and stared, even deaf Bess and the girl who was becoming hoarse, trying to *have a little chat* with her.

You should be ashamed, Lil, Sister Isola said later, and I was, because I could remember being young and blushing, although I had never had the consolation of being class captain. But I could also remember how you remembered things, at that age, and hoped she might remember what I had said. *Everyone should be warned off humbug*, I told the room when Sister Isola had gone. *Humbug is bad for one's immortal soul.* Deaf Bess sitting by the window nodded and smiled at me, nodded and smiled, and Doris said loudly, *Three rows of triple chain and a scallop of interlocked filigree stitch*, and smoothed and smoothed the hankie, shredded with age and too many tears, on her knee.

VISITS

They told us carefully what would be happening. We had all been led or wheeled into the big dining room and Sister Isola had spoken with great clarity above the burblings and poppings, the crackling noises of old uncontrolled farts, the snores from the ones who were too far gone to be awake even for this, and above the occasional shouts of deaf Bess who thought she was whispering. Sister Isola explained very carefully about the saintly visitor we would be receiving, the great honour, the blessedness of being so close to someone so holy. *It is the Pope*, I thought, and felt a ticking pulse of the old excitement and devilry in my veins. *I will go down in the books as the one who made the Pope listen.* I was already preparing what I would like to tell him, and jigging from one buttock to the other on the hard seat, and rehearsing a few good phrases, because now that my time was nearly up I wanted more than ever to be remembered in the books.

It was a disappointment to realise at last that Sister Isola, solemn today in her fat, was talking simply about another holy woman, one who washed lepers in Calcutta and did not flinch from the starving. I was disappointed, but even in this, my old age and great weakness, I was able to accommodate myself to the vagaries of life, and began to prepare another kind of thing to say. I was not so sure, though, of being brave with someone who had seen suffering on a large scale. I would have been more sure of myself with a man who had spent his life in cloisters full of red robes.

Sister Isola understood me like myself. *Now, Lil*, she said, *I am fond of you, and do not wish you to be exposed to the temptation to sin.* She smiled her wicked nun's smile at me, which made her eyes disappear into her cheeks the same way mine did, and there was a wink so fleeting no one could have held her responsible for it. *We have planned something you will enjoy, Lil. You are a good girl, and will understand.*

When they dressed me in my woolies, and took me to the front door on the day of the visit, I did not object. They had been praying and cleaning mightily for weeks now, and deaf Bess had been given a new frock, because of so many breakfasts on the other, and quivering Annie had been propped up in the wicker chair with the cushions carefully arranged. While I was waiting, sitting on the doorstep watching the gate, I could hear the crowing and clucking as the nuns encouraged the evacuation of all the old bowels. The nuns had explained that the morning cup of tea would be brought *afterwards*, in case there should be any accidents, and Sister Annunciata was brushing the thin hair of all the bed cases, and trying to straighten their wobbly old necks on the pillow. There was such a mewing and murmuring, such a bustle of starch and bombazine, such unaccustomed flowers in vases and such a glare of polish and shine that I was pleased to be leaving, and stood up impatiently, and shouted, *Taxi! Taxi!* until it drew up at the gate.

Taxis had begun to smell differently since I had last been in one, and everyone seemed to drive much faster and more recklessly. For the first few miles I sat back against the plastic and panted, and prepared to stick my head out the window like a dog, and be sick. At last I remembered I was not a dog, and said in a loud though reedy voice, *Slower, driver, slower, or you will part me from my breakfast.* He drove more slowly after that, and I began to enjoy my day, and made him stop so I could join him on the front seat, and loved it all.

It is not everyone who has a chance for a last look, but I did. I saw the white castle by the water where Frank had offered solace when it was needed. I cried a little for Frank, who had gone in pain, probably, but quickly. This man who drove was not Frank, but was old enough to be sympathetic, and did not mind stopping for a while, and let me cry for Frank. *Call me George, Lil,* he said, and I was not sure I fancied his freedom with my name, but he was the guide for my last journey, so I shook his hand and called him George. *George,* I asked, *am I famous?* George laughed a phlegmy smoker's laugh and cried *By George I'll say you are, Lil, if that is the kind of fame you are after.* I did not know what kind of fame I was after, but I was pleased. *Any kind will do, George,* I said, and dried my last tear.

George took me past the station, where I had caught the trains and buses, when I had still travelled to the country, and he made a slow stately tour of the university. I would have liked to get out and weep a little over the quadrangles, the bell tower where F.J. Stroud had cried his slimy tears, and would have liked to make myself dizzy once more in that steep lecture hall. But my old swollen legs would not support me that far now. And I was intimidated by the young girls striding in their trousers, and boys with long hair and beads around their foreheads. None of these people copied their notes from one page to another, I could tell, and none wore pink sashes or had glory boxes, though I thought they probably schemed and sighed just as everyone always had.

And Duncan? I wondered, watching a serious pair of men in tweed— the men in tweed would never change, and would always take themselves seriously, but would be forgotten—where was Duncan, and what had become of Joan? I lay back against the sweating plastic seat, watching the men in tweed pretending they were the great minds of their generation, and could imagine Joan leathery, a famous horsewoman, out there with the men when it was time to muster, shouting with the best of them, red in the face and as foul of mouth as the rest. I could imagine Duncan on the other side of the dusty mob, proud of his leathery wife, could see them later in the kitchen with the corned beef between them. I could imagine them sitting there together belching, easy companions and mates after so many years.

But it was also easy to imagine Joan tired of the isolation, the absence of cheap Chow feeds and men to shock, and the Country Women's Association no fun to scandalise, but just dull the way they all left you alone and sneered at your scones. I could imagine the row with Duncan, the flight back to the city, to a life of alimony and gin perhaps, or great art in a smell of turps, or renunciation and good works. Joan was someone for whom it was easy to write many histories. Duncan was even easier. He would have grown drier and sandier with each year, would have lost his hair, would always have a face as brown as the earth, and a pale forehead from the felt hat he would wear year after year. It would be dark with old sweat around the band, and holes would eventually wear through on the folds, but it would have to go to his grave with him.

The story of all our lives is the story forward to death, although each of us might hope to be the exception. I have lived, and have seen more dawns than most people, and seen more different kinds of expressions on the faces of ordinary men and women in the street. I have seen much, but would not claim to have seen everything. I would not mind another century or two, to see some more. Perhaps in my second century I could choose to be lovely, slim, delectable as a peach, the jewel of some man's heart.

My life now is in its time of long shadows over the grass, the sad look of faraway hills slipping into dimness, a blue so melting as to be one with the sky. I fill myself now, and look with pity on those hollow men in their suits, those hollow women in their classic navy and white. They have not made themselves up from their presents and their pasts, but have let others do it for them, while I, large and plain, frightening to them and sometimes to myself, have taken the past and the present into myself. My flesh will become still one day soon, cold within a few hours, disgusting in a week, clean white bones eventually, or a handful of ash. But my name will live, in the different kinds of smiles on the faces of people remembering me, and that is enough immortality for me.

Death will come to us all, may come as we wash our hands before dinner, or walk fast to catch a bus to take us somewhere there was no need to go. There have been as many deaths in the world as there have been lives, and although on the slippery seat of the taxi I might shed some tears for Frank and Duncan and Ursula, and their private deaths, and for my own, fast approaching, all that is invisible in the eyes of history.

Drive on, I told George. He heard the tears in my voice and turned to stare, but I was impatient with the curiosity of the living now, and waved my hands at him until he looked away. *Drive on, George*, I cried at him. *I am ready for whatever comes next.*

1985

KENNY LAUGHTON
b. 1950

Kenny Laughton was born in Alice Springs and is of Arrernte descent. He is a Vietnam veteran who served two tours of duty as a combat engineer between 1969 and 1971. On his return to Australia and subsequent discharge from the armed services, Laughton went home to Alice Springs where he spent the next twenty years working for the Commonwealth, the NT public service and also in the private sector. He is is the editor of *The Aboriginal Ex-Servicemen of Central Australia* (1995), and the author of *Not Quite Men, No Longer Boys* (1999), an account of his military experiences in Vietnam, and a poet. *AH/PM*

The Tunnel Rats of Phuoc Tuy[1]
Ode to 1 Field Squadron

They sent us here to be tested in battle,
To uphold traditions, forged by Aussies before,
To a war with no boundaries, uniforms or direction,
The one they would call the 'unwinnable war'.

We sweated and fretted through rivers and thick jungle,   5
Through rubber, 'wait-a-while' and bamboo.
Not quite men but no longer boys,
But would they remember us, the 'Tunnel Rats of Phuoc Tuy'.

We walked with the foot soldier and rode with the tracks,
Through paddy-fields and villages, with our world in our packs.   10
We faced the Long Hais[2] and saw our mates die,
In death's bloody, unexpected, explosive roar.

---

1   Phuoc Tuy, a province in the south of Vietnam, was a prominent base for Australian soldiers during the Vietnam War.
2   A range of hills in Vietnam.

Through minefields and traps that clung to the hillside,
Like incurable, festering, cancerous sores.

We wept as we loaded our mates onto choppers,   15
For their last ride, through a South Asian sky.
We were choked with emotions, our feelings ran high,
What else could we say but 'mate, goodbye'.
Not quite men but no longer boys,
But would they remember us, the 'Tunnel Rats of Phuoc Tuy'.   20

We honed our skills on stealth and detection,
Through villages, bunkers and tunnels galore.
We soon became noticed for our strange affliction,
Of the many safety pins we wore.
But still we delivered through Monsoon or dry,   25
Splinter-teams and mini-teams at the ready,
'Where's the F.E.s?' we would hear someone cry.

Like rats we would crawl through chambers of tunnels,
In search of the cunning, elusive V.C.
But like D445 they would run and survive,   30
Like 'will-o-the-wisps' you see.
Not quite men but no longer boys,
But would they remember us, the 'Tunnel Rats of Phuoc Tuy'.

Now that it's over and much has been said,
On valour, courage and heroic deeds.   35
My mind still wanders to the old squadron lines,
Where many a tale could be told.
Of soldiers and sappers who all did their jobs,
And some paid the price for being so bold.
They gave of their lives in the field of battle,   40
And long may we honour our illustrious dead.

Through time's abyss, I still remember,
The sign in the troop lines that read
And I quote with pride and a lump in my throat,
'Through these gates pass the greatest F.E.s in the world' unquote.   45
Not quite men but no longer boys,
But will they remember us, the 'Tunnel Rats of Phuoc Tuy'.

1987/1999

PHILIP SALOM
b 1950

Philip Salom grew up in Western Australia. He began a degree in agricultural science, but abandoned his studies, travelled, and returned to complete a degree in creative writing at the Western Australian Institute of Technology (later Curtin University). He has published nine books of poetry, including *Sky Poems* (1987) and two novels, and has won numerous poetry awards, including twice winning the Commonwealth Poetry Prize. He moved to Melbourne in the mid-1990s and now teaches creative writing at the University of Melbourne. *New and Selected Poems* was published in 1998. In 2004 he was awarded the Christopher Brennan Prize, a lifetime award 'for poetry of sustained quality and distinction'. Conceptually sophisticated and wide-ranging, Salom's poetry is notable for its metaphorical richness. *DM*

Seeing Gallipoli from the Sky

To remember the veterans with my child-illusion:
war had turned their faces white
around the eyes, the skin had gone translucent.
Or consider the days of Anzac in the streets
not only those in suits come back on duty   5
but the ghosts among their ritual ranks
always in uniform. That or the shock in sepia
of platoons just hours before they left. The shock
that shifts across the brain from left to right
from the hemisphere of fact to dream,   10
like troopships that crossed the hemispheres
and left men wondering: was it fact or nightmare?
Without a template of history to hold on these images.
They got one, and nothing could shake it.
Like the enemy it was sudden and total   15
and like nothing else in the army
it fitted their bodies perfectly.
It would become a kind of hair shirt
that could be worn with bounce ...

You see them level and sealed in   20
or splayed like asteroids
among the dimmed star-shells
or their centres gone like a ring of keys
where they stalled on the slopes and were covered in.
The blown end of a Lee Enfield[1]   25

---

1   A service rifle used in the First World War.

makes the weapon seem a crossbow.
There the isolated spine is curved as a bow
the loose ribs are warped arrows
the earth has kept them close
in its grip and quiver, only sometimes   30
loosing an arrow in slow and gentle course
out into the daylight.

You begin to mend them. Firstly
you give them back their bodies.
You pick the rosette from a man's chest   35
pluck each petal of blood and let it drop into obscurity
(there is no copy of it back at home).
His was the famous rush towards machine-gun pits
but his medals were put too deep, and by the wrong side.
The stem cannot be seen, nor the bullet that gave seed   40
passing through sternum, heart, lodging against the vertebrae.
And the uprush of bloom into the khaki.

Bruises, those coloured moulds, lessen and are gone.
Ignore the condition of his arteries, whether the joints
gave trouble—they were too young. Your miracles   45
are for the body and now its dreams,
for these have lapped his gaunt face
like the midnight waves of evacuation.
But there's something arcane about the clay
when the fierce Turkish sunlight baked it round his body.   50
The particles became magnetic, but the magnet's
pulling wrongly: you've stripped his oppressors
from him but he sprawls down facing East
the light jostling his body, its energetic tearing song
calling him to fight—this is where he is intense   55
this harsher light must be Australia.

He sits up, slowly, exactly as machinery into place
or like a fold-out cardboard shape with savage detail
the machine-gun straightening up, locking its steel legs.
The sudden racket as the shots begin, chronic and nervous . . .   60
He will not return as one who went to die well,
coming home like a kind of migrant
strange and unaccustomed, to be made a boy again
—city boy to find his streets

or country boy finding the bright train back   65
as through the eye of a needle
unthreading his name from the obelisk not yet built.

To grind away Mondays at the office
or the callous-breaking afternoons on land
dreaming of food through the other war of Depression.   70
Beside the wireless, monument of the everyday,
strong again, voting conservative
as he mostly would, forgetting violence
until the next war, seeing that one through
or dying again.   75
Or being again returnee, to a time where the world view—
his slow meccano—would crumple, seem obsolete.

                                                             1987

LOUIS NOWRA
b 1950

Playwright Louis Nowra grew up in Melbourne in a household that he described as 'violently unhappy'. He changed his birth surname of Doyle, taking instead the name of a town in NSW where his car once broke down. He learned about theatre as a child in the company of an uncle who was a theatre director, and after early struggles at school he later gained academic success but left La Trobe University before finishing his degree.

Nowra was part of the explosion of productivity that took place in Australian theatre in the early 1970s. His first play, *Kiss the One-Eyed Priest* (unpublished), was produced at Melbourne's La Mama theatre in 1973 and he has been a prolific writer of plays, television and film scripts, novels and non-fiction ever since. Before he turned to writing full time he supported himself in a number of jobs, including as a truck driver, a ferry steward and as director of Gilbert and Sullivan's *Trial by Jury* in the Plenty Mental Hospital, an experience he enjoyed and used in the writing of *Cosi* (*1992*/1992).

With only a few breaks, Nowra has had at least one play in production somewhere in Australia almost every year since 1973; notably in 1995 four different Nowra plays were produced in three different cities. His best-known works include *Albert Names Edward* (*1976*/1983), *Inner Voices* (*1977*/1977), *The Precious Woman* (*1980*/1981), *Summer of the Aliens* (*1992*/1992) and *Miss Bosnia* (*1995*/unpublished), as well as *Cosi* and *Radiance* (*1993*/1993), both of which were later made into feature films. His stage adaptation of Xavier Herbert's (qv) novel *Capricornia* was first performed in 1988.

Nowra is a metaphorical thinker and a politically engaged dramatist with a particular commitment to and engagement with Aboriginal issues and rights. The symbolic and exotic settings of many of his plays have led certain literal-minded critics to accuse him of a lack of 'Australianness', a charge against which he was once publicly defended by Patrick White (qv). Since the late 1990s he has written a number of non-fiction books: an autobiography, *The Twelfth of Never* (1999); a book about legendary Australian cricketer Shane Warne called *Warne's World* (2002); a memoir, *Shooting the Moon* (2004); and a collection of essays entitled *Chihuahas, Women and Me* (2005). KG

From *Radiance*
Act 1, Scene 1

The large living room of a wooden house on stilts. It is late morning and harsh tropical light pours in through the slats in the many shutters. MAE *is wearing a dowdy black frock and is lost in thought as she stares at a chair.* MAE *touches the chair with her foot as if making sure that there is no one there. As she talks she strikes matches and throws them at the chair.*

MAE: Are you still there? You are, aren't you? I'll have to burn down this place to get rid of you. Ghosts burn, did you know that? And you'll burn. It'll all burn down, even ghosts can't live in a place that doesn't exist any more. I'll do it. I'll have the courage. Everything will burn. And then you'll be gone. The whole world will burn. I'll hold my hands out, like warming them before a fire.

> [MAE *looks at a piece of paper in her hand and then at the chair.*]

[*To chair*] He did the dirty on you. Did the dirty on us both. He'll see it burning, but he'll be too late. They'll see it burning from miles and miles around. Like cracker night. Everything up in flames.

> [NONA *enters wearing what can only be described as 'a little black dress'. She is also made up as if heading off to a party.* MAE, *surprised by* NONA's *sudden appearance, hides the piece of paper from* NONA.]

[*Shocked*] You can't wear that.

NONA: Why not?

MAE: Not to your mother's funeral.

NONA: I'm not fully dressed yet. I've still got to put on my knickers.

MAE: The dress. I meant the dress.

NONA: What's the matter with it?

MAE: You're almost naked.

NONA: If I was I wouldn't be wearing it. I can't get by without my little black dress. [*She goes to her open suitcase, its clothes are neatly stacked.*] You been at my suitcase?

MAE: Just tidying up.

NONA: [*scattering clothes*] It just makes things harder to find. You got any black knickers?

MAE: [*irritated*] We'll never get there!

> [MAE *goes into the other room,* NONA *holds up an even shorter dress, this time red, against her body.*]

NONA: [*calling out*] What about red? Or is that bad taste at your mum's funeral?

MAE: [*off*] Yes.

NONA: [*half to herself*] Is that yes, it's bad taste or yes, wear the red?

> [*She throws the dress back on the suitcase and takes out some black high heels.*]

[*Calling out*] I bought these shoes especially for today.

> [NONA *turns on the radio then lifts up her dress and with a pair of tweezers starts to pluck her pubic hair. On the radio is* DOYLE, *the local priest.*]

DOYLE: The world is full of temptation. As it should be. Because it is only by confronting temptation that we confront ourselves and become victorious over ourselves . . .

MAE: [*off*] No black, what about white?

NONA: [*to herself, incredulous at* MAE'*s bad taste*] White!

DOYLE: The Lord will forgive sin but he will not forgive evil and many people have evil in their hearts. They may not do evil unto others, but they think evil and to think evil is as great as committing an evil deed. There are people in this town, yes, in this very town, who work, shop, play sports; seemingly good, generous people, but in their hearts is evil, evil that festers, evil that thinks evil of others and those people are just as severe sinners as those who commit evil deeds . . .

> [MAE *enters with a black dress and stops stunned as she sees an unconcerned* NONA *pluck out her pubic hair.*]

MAE: What are you doing?

NONA: Making the perfect bikini line.

MAE: Why don't you just shave the whole lot off and be done with it?

NONA: It would only attract child molesters.

> [NONA'*s answer throws* MAE.]

[*Referring to the radio*] Who's the nutter?

MAE: Father Doyle.

NONA: The one who's doing the service?

> [MAE *nods.*]

I hope he doesn't go on like that at Mum's funeral.

> [NONA *turns the radio onto another station.*]

Hey, do they still have listings of what's on? Like sports day? Who's in hospital? Rodeos? I was kind of hoping there was a rodeo in town. My father could be in town. Maybe he heard about Mum's death.

MAE: [*abruptly turning off radio*] There's no rodeo in town. I want you to put this on.

NONA: [*taking it with distaste*] This? [*Putting it against her body*] I look like a frump.

MAE: It's respectful. You have to respect the dead.

NONA: Why? It wouldn't be me. Mum wouldn't recognise me in this.

MAE: [*irritated with her*] Just try it on.

NONA: I'll dip it in mud and go grunge. I'll do up this place grunge. Anything would be better.

MAE: You don't like the way I've done it up?

NONA: I'm pretty good at decoration. Now that it's ours—

MAE: Things still have to be sorted out.

NONA: What things?

[MAE *looks at the mess* NONA *has already created around her suitcase and gives an exasperated sigh.*]

MAE: Your place must be like a pigsty.

NONA: [*starting to undress*] I'm a pig.

[MAE *picks up the red dress and puts it against herself.*]

MAE: My God, it's like wearing a handkerchief. You don't wear this in public.

NONA: [*putting dress over her dress*] Where else would I wear it?

[NONA *gazes glumly at the dress. Indeed, it is frumpy looking.*]

Do you wear this one?

MAE: It's not mine. It's Mum's.

NONA: I can't wear a dead woman's clothes.

MAE: She didn't die in it.

NONA: What did she die in?

MAE: You serious?

NONA: Oh, yes. When I die I want to look a beautiful corpse. The sort that turns every man into a necrophiliac. What was she wearing?

[*Pause.* MAE *looks at* NONA *wondering if* NONA *is pulling her leg, but she seems serious.* NONA *sits in the chair to put on her high heels.*]

MAE: I can't remember . . . just a nightgown, with a dressing gown, I think.

NONA: Where did she die? Not where I slept last night? I'm not sleeping there tonight.

MAE: Here. That chair.

[NONA *jumps up.*]

NONA: Shit! You serious?

MAE: In that chair. Around this time. Late morning. I'd come back from shopping in town and there she was. Like she was sleeping. Purple lips. Dried saliva on her chin.

NONA: Did she look happy?

MAE: She looked empty. Hollow. Like if you tapped her, there would only be a hollow sound.

NONA: What were her last words?

MAE: I said I was shopping.

NONA: I mean the last words you heard.

MAE: Gurgle, gurgle . . .

[NONA *pretends she hasn't heard* MAE*'s sarcastic reply and walks in her high heels, testing them out.*]

NONA: I should have worn them in.

MAE: Don't wear them if they hurt.

NONA: No pain makes a girl plain. [*Indicating* MAE*'s dress*] You'll need the gumboots for your outfit. I hate this dress.

MAE: I want you to wear it for the funeral.

NONA: It's not me. I bet Cressy is going to wear something stylish. I bet you. And I'll look awful.

MAE: She's not coming.

NONA: What?

MAE: She said it was too far away.

NONA: Why didn't you tell me? You're always hiding things from me.

MAE: No, I'm not. I told you she was in London.

NONA: [looking at CD cover] She looks great. You've never seen her on stage, have you?

   [MAE shakes her head.]

I saw her in Madame Butterfly. In Adelaide. I didn't tell her I was coming. I dragged my boyfriend along. She was fantastic. You know, dying at the end, singing her heart out, killing her kid. So I ask to go backstage. I tell this creep on the door that she's my sister. Bouncers are such arseholes. And there she is. In her dressing-room. Like a florist shop. She's sitting in her chair, the mirror lights around her like some sort of halo. She's still got her make-up on—Jap eyes, white skin, like a mask. You know the only photo she had in her dressing-room? Me, when I was about five. Can you beat that? I tell her how much I liked Madame Butterfly and she goes 'Madama Butterfly'. Like, how was I to know? It was my first opera. My boyfriend was a bit out of place—he only liked Acid Jazz—so he went out to wait for me and Cressy says, 'Oh, he's so handsome, Nona, but thick as a brick.'

MAE: That's terrible.

NONA: He was just a bloke, right? Dead ordinary. I stayed with him longer than I would have just to prove her wrong, but she was right.

   [NONA laughs, MAE is bemused.]

MAE: Did you go out with her—

NONA: It was great. Japanese. I mean, like she was still in character, so we had to eat Japanese. On the floor. We had that horseradish stuff that burns your mouth.

   [Pause.]

Why did you buy it, you don't have a CD player?

MAE: [shrugging] Seeing she doesn't send us any, I thought I may as well. Didn't even get a discount because she's my sister. [A beat] Half price for a half sister.

NONA: It still makes her your sister. Two halves make a whole.

MAE: [gazing at cover of CD] She looks . . . different.

NONA: It's all make-up. I look really different when I'm photographed.

MAE: [pointing to the red dress] Is that how you like looking? Like a street walker?

   [NONA is so astonished by MAE's outburst, she almost laughs.]

   [Silence.]

NONA: [*pointing to chair*] Was it always there?

    [MAE *is puzzled.*]

Did she always sit there, in that spot?

MAE: Towards the end.

NONA: Because she wanted to watch the sea?

MAE: Who knows what was going on in her noggin?

NONA: I've never seen a dead person.

MAE: There's no art to dying. It's shitting, farting, crying, pissing yourself. That's how most people die, Nona.

NONA: You were born a nurse.

MAE: That's how people die.

NONA: I bet you she was looking at the island.

    [CRESSY *enters and stands there, smiling, expectant. She is dressed in a stylish and expensive black dress. Silence.* MAE *and* NONA *are surprised to see her.*]

CRESSY: You can tell a small town, everyone leaves their front doors unlocked.

    [*Silence.*]

NONA: [*pleased, praising her*] You look deadly.

CRESSY: Bit jet lagged.

MAE: [*incredulous*] Cressy . . .

    [MAE *doesn't know how to react to her sister's appearance.*]

CRESSY: [*smiling to* MAE] I'm no ghost.

    [*Awkward pause.* CRESSY *seems tense, uneasy to be back in the house.*]

It's so hot.

NONA: I'll get you a glass of water.

    [CRESSY *puts her travelling valise on the chair.*]

Don't!

CRESSY: Why?

NONA: Mum died there.

    [NONA *then rushes out. Puzzled,* CRESSY *picks up a burnt match, one of several on the chair.*]

MAE: I was trying to set fire to it.

CRESSY: I came through town from the airport. Not much has changed. Like the dirt road here. The six palms along the beach have gone.

MAE: Rotted, so they were cut down.

CRESSY: Taxi drivers always keep their windows open. I've got dust in my throat.

    [*A beat.*]

I'm heading back tomorrow.

MAE: Whatever you like.

CRESSY: I can stay in town.

    [NONA *enters and gives* CRESSY *a glass of water.*]

MAE: The motel on Johnston Street's got new air conditioning.

[*She exits.* CRESSY *looks to* NONA *as if she can give some reason for* MAE*'s abruptness.*]

NONA: She's a bit tense. The funeral, I guess.

[*Pause.*]

CRESSY: I forgot how hot it gets in the tropics. I'm dripping.

NONA: Late this afternoon it'll be the sea breeze. Mae said you weren't coming.

CRESSY: I told her. [*Pause*] We need the breeze, there's hardly any air.

NONA: I could get you a fan only it's broken.

CRESSY: [*not greatly liking the water*] Tap water. [*Looking around*] Not so down at heels, the house.

NONA: Mae did it up. Now it's ours we'll do it up properly.

CRESSY: Smaller. [*Opening valise*] What time's the funeral?

NONA: Soon. I think. Well, Mae's been fussing around, so I think it's soon.

[CRESSY *takes out a stylish black hat.*]

Chic.

CRESSY: We'll kill 'em at the gravesite.

[NONA *laughs.* CRESSY *stares at* NONA*, making her a little uncomfortable.*]

NONA: I've got pimples or something?

CRESSY: [*a nervous laugh*] No . . . I forgot how grown-up you are, that's all.

[MAE *enters with two hats.*]

MAE: I've got some hats.

CRESSY: I bought mine with me.

MAE: For me and Nona. [*She gives one to* NONA.]

NONA: I am not wearing this. It's ultra, ultra daggy, Mae.

[MAE *hands her the other one.*]

Mega daggy.

MAE: [*trying on one*] Suit yourself.

CRESSY: You've done the house up well. The shutters, the walls, everything.

MAE: Two years. I had time on my hands.

NONA: Who's going to be there?

[MAE *shrugs.* NONA *notices* CRESSY *pacing.*]

Sit down, Cressy.

CRESSY: Been cooped up in the aeroplane.

NONA: It's like you've taken some bad speed.

[CRESSY *goes to sit down.*]

MAE: [*to* CRESSY] No time to sit down, we have to make tracks.

[NONA *closes the shutters, running rapidly from one to the other, talking as she does so.*]

NONA: [*looking at* MAE] Do you really think you should wear that hat?

MAE: I like it.

[NONA *suddenly takes off the dress, revealing her 'little black dress' underneath.*]

NONA: I have to wear this; it's me.

MAE: You planning to pick up a mortuary assistant?

[NONA *starts to plough through her suitcase and takes out a vermilion wig and a strawberry blonde one.*]

NONA: Why should people look bad at a funeral? [*Holding up wigs*] Which one?

CRESSY: [*bemused*] Whatever makes you feel good.

NONA: [*putting on vermilion wig*] This one, then.

[CRESSY *and* MAE *exchange glances.* CRESSY *looks* NONA *up and down.*]

CRESSY: [*referring to* NONA*'s dress*] If brevity is the soul of wit then your dress will be worth a few laughs at the gravesite.

NONA: Better than waterworks.

MAE: Come on, we should be going. [. . .]

1993

MICK DODSON
b. 1950

Mick Dodson was born in Katherine, NT, and is the brother of Patrick Dodson (qv). He is a member of the Yawuru people of the southern Kimberley region, WA. A lawyer, academic and advocate, Dodson worked with the Victorian Aboriginal Legal Service (1976–81) and became a barrister in 1981. He joined the Northern Land Council as senior legal adviser in 1984 and became director of the Council in 1990. He is a member of the United Nations Permanent Forum on Indigenous Issues and was a founding director of the Australian Indigenous Leadership Centre, as well as a member and chairman of AIATSIS.

From 1988 to 1990 Dodson was Counsel assisting the Royal Commission into Aboriginal Deaths in Custody and he was Australia's first Aboriginal and Torres Strait Islander social justice commissioner with HREOC, serving from 1993 to 1998. In 2003 Dodson was appointed Inaugural Professor of Indigenous Studies at the Australian National University and convenor of its National Centre for Indigenous Studies. *AH/PM*

We All Bear the Cost if Apology is Not Paid

The Commonwealth Government has finally responded—in part—to the National Inquiry into the Separation of Aboriginal and Torres Strait Islander Children from their Families. While there are some laudable initiatives that will have tangible effects, there exists a matter of much greater significance, which the Government's response fails to grasp.

In its response, the Government fails to appreciate that the way forward for all Australians has as much, if not more, to do with spiritual repair as with material programs.

Australians cannot escape the uncomfortable truth that policies and practices of the past were inherently racist. 'Half-caste' children, and others, were taken from their families for no reason other than the colour of their skin.

Despite the best motivation of the individuals involved in administering these policies, or their belief that what they were doing was in the best interests of the children, the facts remain that the aim was the destruction of a group of people—the Aboriginal people. No amount of welfare or well-modulated phraseology can remove this reality.

The package announced by the Minister for Aboriginal Affairs, Senator John Herron, focuses principally on the welfare-related recommendations, insultingly dismissing as 'not applicable' the fundamental principle of self-determination. It excludes any indigenous organisation from participating, in any formal way, in the monitoring of government application of the recommendations.

The package omits any attention to fundamental issues of compensation and it excludes the recommendations on training and learning that would ensure schools' curricula include compulsory modules on the history and effects of forcible removal. This flies in the face of the minister's statement that 'we must learn from the past so that we do not allow such circumstances and policies to happen in our community again'. If we don't teach, how can we learn?

Indigenous people repeatedly told the inquiry that an apology would make an enormous difference to their ability to overcome the traumas they have suffered. Without an expression of real regret evidenced by a national parliamentary apology the package is fundamentally flawed.

The justifications for refusing to offer an apology are spurious straw-clutching. There is no legal impediment to stop such an initiative. Further, the Government's argument that a national apology is untenable, given the large proportion of Australians who have arrived in the past 20 years, is fallacious and does not reflect the views of many Australians.

Today's Australians are not being asked to accept individual guilt, but collective responsibility. Ethnic communities have offered their apologies to indigenous people. Their mood is captured in the remark of Mr Randolph Alwis, the chairman of the Federation of Ethnic Communities Councils of Australia, who recently said that 'we are part of the current society and society is a continuum. Anything we can do to help the reconciliation process, we will do.'

Above all, the Government's refusal to apologise stands in sharp contrast to the plethora of formal apologies from parliaments around Australia, churches, community groups, ethnic organisations, schools, local governments, unions, leading non-government organisations, and the thousands of individual

Australians who have signed petitions, written letters and declared their sorrow. Indeed, these groups, and many individual Australians, have felt compelled to make it clear that they directly endorse the Human Rights and Equal Opportunity Commission's recommendation that there be a national apology.

The Government also has reasserted its rejection of indigenous people's right to compensation. The Government made it clear in its initial submission to the inquiry that it did not consider compensation appropriate. The national inquiry considered this, along with a wealth of expert advice, and concluded that an essential component of reparation for past wrongs was monetary compensation.

It is regrettable that the Government's view has not changed. An absence of any statutory compensation fund is already resulting in recourse to the courts at significant legal cost to taxpayers and potentially significant compensation payments.

However, there are some positive initiatives. In targeting health, counselling services and family reunion, the Government shows that it appreciates the long-term impact of removing Aboriginal and Torres Strait Islander children from their families, on the wellbeing of those families and communities.

Programs to expand indigenous link-up programs will provide much needed practical support for the bringing together of families torn apart by past government policies. The provision of more than $39 million to enhance counselling and mental health services for people affected by separation also will help.

Aboriginal people know what it means to be poor—and know that material assistance is not irrelevant. But we also know it is not material wealth that makes a family. If there is a lesson to be learned from our families being broken apart, it is about love, understanding, and the seeking and giving of forgiveness.

These are values that could make an Australian family of all people within this country. Many know this. The Commonwealth Government's failure to understand has resulted in a failure at the heart of its response. As a consequence, we are all the poorer.

1997

ALEXIS WRIGHT
b. 1950

Alexis Wright is from the Waanyi people from the highlands of the southern Gulf of Carpentaria. She has worked in government departments and Aboriginal agencies across four states and territories as a manager, educator, researcher and writer. Wright coordinated the NT Aboriginal Constitutional Convention in 1993 and wrote

'Aboriginal Self-Government' for *Land Rights News*, later quoted in full in Henry Reynolds' *Aboriginal Sovereignty* (1996). Her involvement in Aboriginal organisations and campaigns has included work on mining, publications, fund raising and land rights both in Australia and overseas. As well as writing essays and short stories, Wright is the author of *Grog War* (1997), an examination of the alcohol restrictions in Tennant Creek, and two novels, *Plains of Promise* (1997) and the multi-award-winning *Carpentaria* (2006), the first work by an Indigenous author to win the Miles Franklin Award outright. She edited *Take Power Like This Old Man Here: An anthology of writings celebrating twenty years of land rights in Central Australia, 1977–1997* (1998). *AH/PM*

From *Plains of Promise*
Chapter 6: The Timekeeper's Shadow

[…] It was a dangerous time to travel alone over the land: it was waking-up season. Elliot's journey back through the Channel Country and along his Dreaming line, intermeshing between snake-rivers to the Great Lake was carried out in the Dry. It was at this time that whatever powerful essences lay submerged all around rose from the earth. You needed to take extra precautions to remain safe. He was careful to eat sparingly from a limited amount of available food, so that he would not create any noticeable odours which the spirits would notice. Suspicious of every movement around him, even a leaf fluttering in the breeze, he starved himself to avoid the risk. The pathway he followed was dimly visible in his mind as a narrow, hazy tunnel. Should he penetrate its walls, even though soundless to his ear, this would create disturbance amid the serene surroundings and awaken the restful state of the spiritual environment and bring forth its malignant powers.

The most perilous time of all came early in the evening, when the dying sun beamed its last light onto the sandhills and over the dead grassland. This was the time you needed to take cover, when the last screeches of the black cockatoos with their red tails died away and the land was quiet. It was best to sit it out for the night. Beyond his camp, Elliot watched the bush pigeons fossicking amongst dry twigs in the red, glowing grasses. Although he lay with some sense of security beneath a gidgee tree, his father's totem, he was brooding about how he could get rid of the pigeons. No point in being cautious on the one hand then gamble in your camp at night.

Over the passing of many nights he repeatedly whispered to the pigeons, urging them to take flight and seek the safety of cover. Sometimes the birds took a moment and made head-wobbling movements as if they took notice of his words and actions, but they did not fly off. Mainly they ignored him. At first he tended to dismiss their lack of intuition, but as days of travel grew into weeks and he sat swathed in his sweat under a tree where the breeze did not penetrate, he heard the echoes of the great spirits thundering in the distant hills and started to have second thoughts about the nature of birds. He changed his attitude towards their presence. He felt he was right to do so, for he was trained in religious knowledge of the land by the thoughts of the elders, through a straight line of law since time began and the land and everything in it had been created. It was his duty to do his utmost to maintain harmony in the world that owned him.

As each day passed on his long journey he began to lose sight of the reality of St Dominic's and his own place in the Mission. He tried in vain to recall people's faces, the inside of his father's dwelling … try as he might he could not do it. It was like lifting his weight in lead. He had become obsessed by the pigeons. Before dusk each day he tried every evasive angle he had been taught—movements which were now an instinctive part of his nature—to try to rid himself of the birds. He had always been able to outsmart anyone: at St Dominic's people knew this side of Elliot's nature well. Some bore scars as reminders of times they had tried to call his bluff.

Try as he might, he could not escape the pigeons. He never saw them during daylight. It was only at dusk, when he made his camp, that they appeared. Sometimes he hid from them in low bushes. At other times he buried himself in the deep sand of a dry river bed, hiding there for hours until it was dark. He arose from his makeshift grave only to find the pigeons looking at him from a short distance away. By now, the birds were cooing and scratching the dirt right next to the place where he slept. They would be gone in the morning, but Elliot never saw them leave.

The night is broken into stages in the Hot. Early on the ground retains the stored energy of the sun and radiates uncomfortable heat—it is impossible to lie on this hot ground and sleep. Hours later, it cools: the dry, brittle earth sighs and expands in vast yawns. This is the signal for creatures and men, big red stony devils, to lie stretched out asleep on their sleeping mother. It is the time of the creaks and moans of the great spirits awakening. Rocks, trees, hills and rivers—all are awake at this time. Released from their sedated daytime state, the spirits of the land travel from place to place. The air, the sky is alive with the ancestral spirits of the land. As Elliot endured another night of restless sleep, he knew it was best to sing their songs and urge them towards good feelings.

No one was able to look after the land any more, not all of the time, the way they used to in the olden days. Life was so different now that the white man had taken the lot. It was like a war, an undeclared war. A war with no name. And the Aboriginal man was put into their prison camps, like prisoners in the two world wars. But nobody called it a war: it was simply the situation, that's all. Protection. Assimilation … different words that amounted to annihilation. The white man wanted to pay alright for taking the lot. But they didn't want to pay for the blackman's culture, the way he thinks. Nor for the blackman's language dying away because it was no longer tied to his traditional country … now prosperous cattle station or mining project. The white people wanted everyone to become white, to think white. Skin and all. And they were willing to say they will pay out something for that, even though they believed what happened was not worth much. They could not actually see the value for their money—not like buying grain or livestock.

Yet no one could change the law—so Elliot muttered to himself as he crossed the whiteman's roads or stepped across tyre marks made by vehicles that had been bogged at river crossings. In spite of the foreign burrs and stinging nettles along the river banks—nothing foreign could change the essence of the land. No white man had that power.

Elliot visualised the hands of white people writhing with some kind of illogical intent to misuse and swallow up what was not on a map imprinted in the ancestry of their blood. Hands that hung limp when the land dried up. That buried dead children, set tables with no food to eat. Hands that tried to fight the fires that destroyed the crops and livestock they valued so much. The essence of their souls. He saw the same hands gesturing with self-centred righteousness, a backhand flick to explain hard times, without thought of the true explanations for disaster from the land itself. Good season, bad season! Their palms opened to beg for more government money to keep their stranger life afloat. Kill off whatever got in the way of it. Put it down to bad luck when things were bad. Put it down to good luck when things went right. A simplistic way of ignoring their own ignorance. Sit in one spot and eat it all away. A laconic race living on its wit's end in order to voice its demands and ordered others to fall into line.

The night might have been enjoyed once. He thought of the days when the spirits and the black people would have spoken to each other. But the blackman's enforced absence from his traditional land had inspired fear of it. They had to alter old, ongoing relationships with the spirits that had created man and once connected him to the earth.

As the weeks passed, Elliot the Traveller became convinced he would not live to be an old man. Cattle lay dead beside the mud-cracked waterholes of the dry riverbeds. Kangaroos and wallabies lay nearby. He had been sent at the wrong time. The restless spirits exchanged thunderous blows of anger, tying earth and sky into knots. *Wrong! Wrong! Wrong!* They raced up and down the sky in the pitch-black night. Giant arms struck out with a fearful force, felling giant ghost gums which nearly killed him as they crashed to the ground.

Why had the elders sent him in the first place? Yes, he was convinced they had hatched a plan to get rid of him. *'You won't get me,'* he repeated to himself a thousand times a day. He was no longer distracted by their attempts to cloud his thinking—for it must have been they who had taken away his memory of St Dominic's. Why did they want him dead? For the first time he imagined he saw deception in his own father's face. *This is a lot of trouble you have gone to*, he screamed. *Why? Why here and not there?* If the elders did have some sinister plan for him, Jipp the self-appointed augur would not have been any the wiser. Elliot traced and retraced every detail of his life for clues.

Perhaps it was his tendency towards violence. Surely not, when even the most demure of young women with babies in their tummies stomped through the village yelling at their husbands after they had quarrelled with them—'You wait! I'll be coming for you with a big knife! As soon as I get some money I am going to buy a knife for you.' While the husband, looking like a piece of well-kneaded dough, trotted along after her at a safe distance. Then she yelled again: 'to rip your guts out!' And you could believe it would happen. And alongside, her two-year-old, shaping up his little fists, kicked each leg back towards his father to demonstrate he was on his mother's side and he meant business, too.

No, it was not his violence. His magic then? Almost everyone in the community was wary of his knowledge of magic. When he was younger he would run and complete a somersault in mid-air, land on his feet and do it again up and down the road between the village and Mission. He made tobacco tins glow in the dark. Children begged him to show them. Watching, their mothers' eyes nearly popped out of their heads and they chased their kids away with sticks. He balanced stones on the tops of sticks and made them twirl around. The old men found interesting stones to challenge him. He beat them each time. He could sketch faces to the exact likeness, and left the portraits blowing around in the wind. That nearly frightened people half to death. Their fear was a source of amusement to him. They believed he was trying to steal their souls to serve himself. That he might be in secret collusion with the spirit world.

Elliot believed he could count on one hand the number of occasions when he had infringed the law during his thirty years of life. Trivial matters. Nothing to deserve this punishment. So what could it be? Perhaps some great danger threatened his people and his own life was considered inconsequential, a trivial matter in the greater scheme of things. Did the community fear of more suicides override one sacrifice? Had they agreed that he should provide that sacrifice? Who could know the true malevolence of Ivy Koopundi—or the combined force of her people, the guardians of the majestic spiritual being? Could their power, in some explicable way, stretch out to kill anyone, anywhere? Were they able to make those deaths appear as suicides? What pitiful chance did he have of confronting this power?

So, Elliot told himself, he was soon to become the sacrificial lamb for Ivy Koopundi. Why had not somebody simply murdered her in the middle of some moonless night? It would have been easy enough. He should have thought of it himself. He had no difficulty in recalling the way her sly face watched him everywhere he went. Jumping in front of him from right to left, left to right, the whole day, trying to send him crazy. Why had he not recognised the same sly look on the faces of Pilot and May Sugar and those other two old grannies? It was all as plain as day to him now.

Yes, it was her. He had been careful that she, above all, should have no knowledge of his travelling—yet there she stood in the dark shadows the morning he left. Further back, he recalled the day Old Maudie died, and the sidelong glance she had thrown him on her way through the village, a glance that chilled the base of his neck. She was a different kind. Not happy like his own people, who could joke about life, no matter what. They might be treated like dogs, but they could laugh just the same. They came from the spirits, and to the spirits they would return. That was the law. Always look above. Ivy played another role, and laughing at life was not part of it.

So be it. If this journey led to death then he must allow it to happen. But the pigeons … were they a warning to him, a contradiction of prediction?

1997

From *Carpentaria*
Chapter 1: From Time Immemorial

[…] The ancestral serpent, a creature larger than storm clouds, came down from the stars, laden with its own creative enormity. It moved graciously—if you had been watching with the eyes of a bird hovering in the sky far above the ground. Looking down at the serpent's wet body, glistening from the ancient sunlight, long before man was a creature who could contemplate the next moment in time. It came down those billions of years ago, to crawl on its heavy belly, all around the wet clay soils in the Gulf of Carpentaria.

Picture the creative serpent, scoring deep into—scouring down through—the slippery underground of the mudflats, leaving in its wake the thunder of tunnels collapsing to form deep sunken valleys. The sea water following in the serpent's wake, swarming in a frenzy of tidal waves, soon changed colour from ocean blue to the yellow of mud. The water filled the swirling tracks to form the mighty bending rivers spread across the vast plains of the Gulf country. The serpent travelled over the marine plains, over the salt flats, through the salt dunes, past the mangrove forests and crawled inland. Then it went back to the sea. And it came out at another spot along the coastline and crawled inland and back again. When it finished creating the many rivers in its wake, it created one last river, no larger or smaller than the others, a river which offers no apologies for its discontent with people who do not know it. This is where the giant serpent continues to live deep down under the ground in a vast network of limestone aquifers. They say its being is porous; it permeates everything. It is all around in the atmosphere and is attached to the lives of the river people like skin.

This tidal river snake of slowing mud takes in breaths of a size that is difficult to comprehend. Imagine the serpent's breathing rhythms as the tide flows inland, edging towards the spring waters nestled deeply in the gorges of an ancient limestone plateau covered with rattling grasses dried yellow from the prevailing winds. Then with the outward breath, the tide turns and the serpent flows back to its own circulating mass of shallow waters in the giant water basin in a crook of the mainland whose sides separate it from the open sea.

To catch this breath in the river you need the patience of one who can spend days doing nothing. If you wait under the rivergum where those up-to-no-good Mission-bred kids accidentally hanged Cry-baby Sally, the tip of the dead branch points to where you will see how the serpent's breath fights its way through in a tunnel of wind, creating ripples that shimmer silver, similar to the scales of a small, nocturnal serpent, thrashing in anger whenever the light hits its slippery translucent body, making it writhe and wrench to escape back into its natural environment of darkness.

The inside knowledge about this river and coastal region is the Aboriginal Law handed down through the ages since time began. Otherwise, how would one know where to look for the hidden underwater courses in the vast flooding mud plains, full of serpents and fish in the monsoon season? Can someone who did not grow up in a place that is sometimes under water, sometimes bone-dry, know when the trade winds blowing off the southern and northern hemispheres will merge in summer? Know the moment of climatic change better than they know themselves? Who fishes in the yellow-coloured monsoonal runoff from the drainages, with sheets of deep water pouring into the wide rivers swollen over their banks, filling vast plains with floodwaters? The cyclones linger and regroup, the rain never stops pouring, but the fat fish are abundant.

It takes a particular kind of knowledge to go with the river, whatever its mood. It is about there being no difference between you and the movement of water as it seasonally shifts its tracks according to its own mood. A river that spurns human endeavour in one dramatic gesture, jilting a lover who has never really been known, as it did to the frontier town built on its banks in the hectic heyday of colonial vigour. A town intended to serve as a port for the shipping trade for the hinterland of Northern Australia.

In one moment, during a Wet season early in the last century, the town lost its harbour waters when the river simply decided to change course, to bypass it by several kilometres. Just like that. Now the waterless port survives with more or less nothing to do. Its citizens continue to engage in a dialogue with themselves passed down the generations, on why the town should continue to exist. They stayed on to safeguard the northern coastline from invasion by the Yellow Peril. A dreadful vision, a long yellow streak marching behind an arrowhead pointing straight for the little town of Desperance. Eventually the heat subsided. When the Yellow Peril did not invade, everyone had a good look around and found a more contemporary reason for existence. It meant the town still had to be vigilant. Duty did not fall on one or two; duty was everybody's business. To keep a good eye out for whenever the moment presented itself, to give voice to a testimonial far beyond personal experience—to comment on the state of their blacks. To do so was regarded as an economic contribution to State rights, then, as an afterthought, to maintaining the decent society of the nation as a whole.

2006

BRIAN CASTRO
b. 1950

Novelist Brian Castro was born at sea between Macao and Hong Kong, an appropriate birthplace for someone whose richly heterogeneous cultural heritage has provided the subject matter for much of his writing and the central metaphor for almost all of it. Castro's father was the descendant of Spanish, Portuguese and English merchants who had settled in Shanghai at the turn of the century; his mother was born in Canton, the daughter of a Chinese farmer and an English missionary.

Castro came to Australia with his family in 1961 and was raised in a trilingual household where English, Portuguese and Cantonese were all spoken. His secondary and tertiary education took place in Sydney and he taught languages in schools for several years before becoming a full-time writer.

After his first novel, *Birds of Passage* (1983), the next work for which Castro gained favourable critical attention was *Double-Wolf* (1991), a complex, witty novel about literary and psychoanalytic theory. His seventh novel, *Shanghai Dancing* (2003), which he describes as 'fictional autobiography', won numerous literary awards. His densely intellectual, multi-layered and often playful fiction is primarily about language—writing, reading and speaking—and demands an attentive, intelligent reader.

Castro has also written a collection of essays entitled *Looking for Estrellita* (1999) and several radio plays and stage plays. He has worked in Australia, France and Hong Kong as a teacher and writer. *KG*

From *Shanghai Dancing*
The Life of Emotions

In which we learn a little of my mother.
Father plays the hero while on heroin.

My father complained that my mother embarrassed too much.

I still do not know if, using the Hispanglo intransitive, he really meant that Mother suffered often from embarrassment, or whether he used to *be* embarrassed by her. This question of embarrassment is a big issue. Perhaps it would not exist if the word had not existed. *Embarras.* Obstacle, obstruction, constraint. In that solid sense she was simply blocked by a lack of expression. But it is the sense in which the word slides into something else that is the problem. Perplexity, bashfulness, timidity. It is, of course, the condition of the pre-war Chinese middle-class woman. She was supposed to be shy and modest. Shyness and modesty covered an embarrassing lack. Of education, empowerment. She was easily embarrassed. This was charming; the blush, the retirement to a dark corner, the coquettish glance. She could easily embarrass. This was more serious. She could never be on parity with a Western man. A Western man's baggage of oriental delights included tumult in a woman's demeanour. In my mother's case, this tumult was the result of a memory of horror. In her embarrassment, it was necessary to forget, to hide, to cover up, before she started screaming; before she embraced her terror. She howled for no reason at all. She broke the nights into little pieces.

She did not like to touch anyone. I have never seen my mother dance. My first memory: I am in my crib. She is there, then she disappears. I add: nightclubs; the smell of men; tobacco; alcohol. Unfriendly laughter. I burst out crying. She returns. When I think of my mother dancing I can only think of my mother as missing. Memory: a man with only one arm. When I think of my mother dancing I think of a time of war. She once had to dance, my father told me when he was very drunk, with a Japanese colonel. Apparently for that, my half-sisters came home from a visit to an enemy battleship with bags of sugar, rice and coffee, dragging the bags upstairs and pulling each other's pigtails and cheerfully pouring the loot into their suitcases and hiding them behind the wardrobe until my mother began to beat both her daughters and her stepdaughters and struck them on the legs with a feather duster and locked all the food up in the kitchen cupboard. When my mother dances, she is missing. She wants to forget something and she repeats whatever it is over and over again to herself, her embarrassment forcing her to code each event, memory, smell, face, in a series of tortured phrases. Her half-English face turns half red. Clarity, she says, I only want clarity. Jasmine! she shouts. Out of the blue. It is her name. She often calls out her own name. And then, in moments when she thinks she is truly alone, she yells Sun Yat-sen! At the top of her voice.

A repression of the body is a repression of memory. My mother is embarrassed to touch, to kiss, to show any affection which betrays either the code of familiarity or the code of horror. Life exists for her as though it were behind glass; as though she were under glass like my grandmother in her coffin. I don't know whether much affection existed between them. The English woman and her half-Chinese daughter. The English woman of politics and religion with the Chinese husband who had withdrawn into the minutiae of arteries and jawbones. The Chinese girl who ran the streets in her pigtails with cherries hung on her earlobes and the dour father who isolated himself in his rooms near the hospital in Shanghai and who only spoke on weekends when he would laugh at the dog's antics or point out to her the honeycombed interiors of calcified marrow. They were all behind glass. They existed in their booths of bones and sorrow. I do not remember my mother touching me when I was a child. *Pour elle, embrasser, c'est aussi d'être embarrassée*, my father said, his eyes clouding over with memories of his first wife. All the wrong emotions. For your mother, to kiss had become embarrassing. For her, for him. He made us kiss his ring like a bishop's. *Bem-vindo papai!* My father kissed a lot of people. His lips were extremely agile and active. I remember my baby-amah's silken back, the long tresses of her oiled black hair. I remember saying to my mother over and over again, during moments of crisis: you must love me! You *must!* . . . in the way my baby-amah pleaded. I have inherited this embarrassment of riches from my mother and her side of the family . . . a combination of British stiff upper lip and Chinese self-effacement. I have hardly said the word *love* to anyone. When I do, I do not exist. I do not know if by it I mean what it is supposed to mean, nor do I know why it feels so sad. I do not know if it is a binding contract, but I know its shape: it is the obstruction, the impediment, against which all writing rises, a force of death that is not myself.

I am six and I watch my mother dress for the Governor's Ball. We are living in a two-storey house with gardens and garage and my father has rung from the office and has ordered the chauffeur to bring up the Mercedes. There are poinsettias on the balcony. The dog is sniffing at something in the flame-leaves and my half-sisters are fighting in their wing of the house. My mother wears a filmy cheongsam with an array of underclothes which disturbs me and makes me uncomfortable, as if she is too cold and transparent. Her collar is high and seems to be floating off on wings and she tries on her tiny sable coat. She puts on a record and closes her door. I watch through a crack between the hinges and the jamb. She is pretending to hold something in front of herself. She prances a few steps, then she sways. She watches herself in the mirror. She dances, seemingly invisibly, holding an invisible partner. Her high heels click and click on the marble floor. Jasmine! She says softly. She dances to forget. In the lounge room I can hear the phone ringing. It rings and rings and then stops. Perhaps someone has picked it up, but my mother knows nothing about it and continues dancing, enveloped by her non-existent partner. She stops. Clarity! I only want clarity, she says in Chinese. She drops her arms. [. . .]

2003

ANIA WALWICZ
b. 1951

Born in Poland, Ania Walwicz arrived in Australia in 1963. As well as a writer she is a visual artist, having graduated from the Victorian College of the Arts, Melbourne, a performance artist and a librettist. She has taught as a lecturer in the School of Creative Media, RMIT. Her writing, which can most easily be described as experimental prose poetry, uses a fractured style, employing various voices, often to subvert accepted notions of identity, gender and ethnicity. Her works include *Boat* (1989) and *Red Roses* (1992). *DM*

Australia

You big ugly. You too empty. You desert with your nothing nothing nothing. You scorched suntanned. Old too quickly. Acres of suburbs watching the telly. You bore me. Freckle silly children. You nothing much. With your big sea. Beach beach beach. I've seen enough already. You dumb dirty city with bar stools. You're ugly. You silly shoppingtown. You copy. You too far everywhere. You laugh at me. When I came this woman gave me a box of biscuits. You try to be friendly but you're not very friendly. You never ask me to your house. You insult me. You don't know how to be with me. Road road tree tree. I came from crowded and many. I came from rich. You have nothing to offer. You're poor and spread thin. You big. So what. I'm small. It's what's in. You silent on Sunday. Nobody on your streets. You dead at night. You go to sleep too early. You don't excite me. You scare me with your hopeless. Asleep when you walk. Too hot to think. You big awful. You don't match me. You burnt out. You too big sky. You make me a dot in the nowhere. You laugh with your big healthy. You want everyone to be the same. You're dumb. You do like anybody else. You engaged Doreen. You big cow. You average average. Cold day at school playing around at lunchtime. Running around for nothing. You never accept me. For your own. You always ask me where I'm from. You always ask me. You tell me I look strange. Different. You don't adopt me. You laugh at the way I speak. You think you're better than me. You don't like me. You don't have any interest in another country. Idiot centre of your own self. You think the rest of the world walks around without shoes or electric light. You don't go anywhere. You stay at home. You like one another. You go crazy on Saturday night. You get drunk. You don't like me and you don't like women. You put your arm around men in bars. You're rough. I can't speak to you. You burly burly. You're just silly to me. You big man. Poor with all your money. You ugly furniture. You ugly house. Relaxed in your summer stupor. All year. Never fully awake. Dull at school. Wait for other people to tell you what to do. Follow the leader. Can't imagine. Work horse. Thick legs. You go to work in the morning. You shiver on a tram.

1981

Little Red Riding Hood

I always had such a good time, good time, good time girl. Each and every day from morning to night. Each and every twenty-four hours I wanted to wake up, wake up. I was so lively, so livewire tense, such a highly pitched little. I was red, so red so red. I was a tomato. I was on the lookout for the wolf. Want some sweeties, mister? I bought a red dress myself. I bought the wolf. Want some sweeties, mister? I bought a red dress for myself. I bought a hood for myself. Get me a hood. I bought a knife.

1982

SALLY MORGAN
b. 1951

Sally Morgan's *My Place* (1987) is one of the most successful Australian autobiographies ever published. Morgan grew up in Perth and, after her father's death, she and her four siblings were raised by her mother and grandmother. Having been told that she had an Indian background, she discovered at the age of fifteen that she was of Aboriginal descent, from the Palku (or Bailgu) people of the Pilbara. This discovery culminated in the writing of *My Place*, which incorporates the life stories of her mother, grandmother, and her grandmother's brother. *My Place* was an immediate bestseller (it has sold more than half a million copies), receiving numerous awards and extensive critical attention, including some criticism for its depiction of Aboriginal identity. It was later adapted into a four-book collection for younger readers. Morgan subsequently gained an international reputation as an artist, and has written and illustrated children's books. Works include *Wanamurraganya: The story of Jack McPhee* (1989), *The Flying Emu and other Australian Stories* (1992) and *The Art of Sally Morgan* (1996).

In 1997 Morgan was appointed director of the University of Western Australia Centre for Indigenous Art and History. *AH/PM*

From *My Place*
Chapter 24: Where There's a Will

[…] A few days later, I rang Aunty Judy. I explained that I was writing a book about Nan and Arthur and I thought she might be able to help me. We agreed that I would come down for lunch and she said she could tell me who Nan's father was. I was surprised. I had expected to encounter opposition. Perhaps I wanted to encounter opposition, it fired my sense of injustice. I felt really excited after our talk on the telephone. Would I really discover who my great grandfather was? If I was lucky, I might even find out about my grandfather as well. I was so filled with optimism I leapt up and down three times and gave God the thumbs up sign.

My day for lunch at Aunty Judy's dawned, and was too beautiful a day for me to fail. Mum had agreed to drop me in Cottesloe where Judy was now living, and mind the children while we had our talk.

'Can't I come, Mum?' Amber wailed as we pulled up out the front of Judy's house.

'Sorry, Amber,' I replied, 'this is private.' I leapt from the car, all vim and vigour. 'Wish me luck, Mum.'

During lunch, we chatted about diet, health foods and the impurities in most brands of ice-cream, then Aunty Judy said, 'You know, I think I have some old photos of your mother you might be interested in. I'll have to dig them out.'

'Oh great! I'd really appreciate that.'

'I'll tell you what I know about the station, but it's not a lot. You know, a relative of ours published a book a while ago and they got all their facts wrong, so you better make sure you get yours right.'

'That's why I'm here. I don't want to print anything that's not true.'

After lunch, we retired to the more comfortable chairs in the lounge-room.

'Now, dear,' Aunty Judy said, 'what would you like to know?'

'Well, first of all, I'd like to know who Nan's father was and also a bit about what her life was like when she was at Ivanhoe.'

'Well, that's no problem. My mother told me that Nan's father was a mystery man. He was a chap they called Maltese Sam and he used to be cook on Corunna Downs. He was supposed to have come from a wealthy Maltese family, I think he could have been the younger son, a ne'er-do-well. My mother said that he always used to tell them that, one day, he was going back to Malta to claim his inheritance. The trouble was he was a drinker. He'd save money for the trip and then he'd go on a binge and have to start all over again. He used to talk to my father, Howden, a lot. He was proud Nanna was his little girl.'

'Did he ever come and visit Nan when she was at Ivanhoe?'

'Yes, I think he did, once. But he was drunk, apparently, and wanted to take Nanna away with him. Nan was frightened, she didn't want to go, so my mother said to him, you go back to Malta and put things right. When you've claimed your inheritance, you can have Daisy. We never saw him again. I don't know what happened to him. Nan didn't want to go with him, we were her family by then.'

'Did you meet Maltese Sam?'

'Oh, goodness, no. I was only a child. My mother told me the story.'

'How old was Nan when she came down to Perth?'

'About fifteen or sixteen.'

'And what were her duties at Ivanhoe.'

'She looked after us children.'

'Aunty Judy, do you know who Mum's father is?'

'Your mother knows who her father is.'

'No, she doesn't. She wants to know and Nan won't tell her.'

'I'm sure I told your mother at one time who her father was.'

'She doesn't know and she'd really like to. It's very important to her.'

'Well, I'm not sure I should tell you. You never know about these things.'

'Mum wanted me to ask you.'

Aunty Judy paused and looked at me silently for a few seconds. Then she said slowly, 'All right, everybody knows who her father was, it was Jack Grime. Everyone always said that Gladdie's the image of him.'

'Jack Grime? And Mum takes after him, does she?'

'Like two peas in a pod.'

'Who was Jack Grime?'

'He was an Englishman, an engineer, very, very clever. He lived with us at Ivanhoe, he was a friend of my father's. He was very fond of your mother. When she was working as a florist, he'd call in and see her. We could always tell when he'd been to see Gladdie, he'd have a certain look on his face. He'd say, "I've been to see Gladdie", and we'd just nod.'

'Did he ever marry and have other children?'

'No. He was a very handsome man, but he never married and, as far as I know, there were no other children. He spent the rest of his life living in Sydney, he was about eighty-six when he died.'

'Eighty-six? Well, that couldn't have been that long ago, then? If he was so fond of Mum, you'd think he'd have left her something in his will. Not necessarily money, just a token to say he owned her. After all, she was his only child.'

'No, there was nothing. He wasn't a wealthy man, there was no money to leave. You know Roberta?'

'Yes, Mum's been out to dinner with her a few times.'

'Well, she's the daughter of Jack's brother, Robert. She's Gladdie's first cousin.'

'Mum doesn't know that, does Roberta?'

'Yes, she knows. She asked me a year ago whether she should say something to your mother, but I said it'd be better to leave it.'

'Perhaps Mum could talk to her.'

'Yes, she could.'

'Can you tell me anything about Nan's mother?'

'Not a lot. Her name was Annie, she was a magnificent-looking woman. She was a good dressmaker, my father taught her how to sew. She could design anything.'

Our conversation continued for another half an hour or so. I kept thinking, had Mum lied? Did she really know who her father was? Was she really against me digging up the past, just like Nan? I had one last question.

'Aunty Judy, I was talking to Arthur, Nan's brother, the other day and he said that his father was the same as yours, Alfred Howden Drake-Brockman. Isn't it possible he could have been Nan's as well.'

'No. That's not what everyone said. I've told you what I know; who Nan's father is. I'm certain Arthur's father wasn't Howden, I don't know who his father was.'

'Arthur also told me about his half-brother Albert. He said Howden was his father, too.'

'Well, he went by the name of Brockman so I suppose it might be possible, but certainly not the other two.'

'Well, thanks a lot, Aunty Judy, I suppose I'd better be going, Mum will be here any minute. She's picking me up.'

'You know who you should talk to, don't you? Mum-mum. She's still alive and better than she's been for a long time.' Mum-mum was a pet name for Aunty Judy's mother, Alice.

'She must be in her nineties by now', I said. 'Do you think she'd mind talking to me?'

'No, I don't think so, but you'd have to go interstate, she's in a nursing home in Wollongong. You could probably stay with June.' June was Judy's younger sister, Nan had been her nursemaid, too.

'I'll think about it, Aunty Judy. Thanks a lot.'

'That's all right, dear.'

I walked out to the front gate and, just as I opened it, Mum pulled up in the car.

'How did you go?' she said eagerly.

'All right,' I replied. 'Mum, are you sure you don't know who your father is? You've lied about things before.' It was a stupid thing to say, Mum was immediately on the defensive.

'Of course I don't know who my father is, Sally. Didn't you find out, after all?' She was disappointed. I felt ashamed of myself for doubting her.

'No Mum, I found out. It was Jack Grime, and Roberta is your first cousin.'

'Oh God, I can't believe it!' She was stunned.

'Can you remember anything about him, Mum? You're supposed to look a lot like him.'

'No, I can't remember much, except he used to wear a big gold watch that chimed. I thought it was magical.'

'Judy said he used to visit you when you were working as a florist, can you recall any times when he did?'

'Well yes, he popped in now and then, but then a lot of people did. I was a friendly sort of girl. Sometimes, I would go and have lunch with him at Ivanhoe, that was after Nan had left there. To think I was lunching with my own father!'

An overwhelming sadness struck me. My mother was fifty-five years of age and she'd only just discovered who her father was. It didn't seem fair.

'Mum, are you going to say anything to Nan?'

'Not now, maybe later, after I've had time to think things over. Don't you say anything, will you?'

'No, I won't. Does she know I've been to see Judy?'

'Yes, she knew you were going. She's been in a bad mood all week. Did you find out anything else?'

'Judy says Nan's father was a bloke called Maltese Sam. That he came from a wealthy family and wanted to take Nan away with him.'

'Maltese Sam? What an unusual name. I've never heard anyone talk about him. Arthur's coming tomorrow night, I'll ask him what he thinks. Of course, you know who he says is Nan's father, don't you?'

'Yeah, I know. Judy doesn't agree with him.'

The following evening, Mum and I sat chatting to Arthur. After we'd finished tea, I said, 'I visited Judith Drake-Brockman the other day, Arthur.'

'What did you do that for?'

'Oh, I thought she might be able to tell me something about Corunna Downs and something about Nan.'

'You wanna know about Corunna, you come to me. I knew all the people there.'

'I know you did.' I paused. 'Can I ask you a question?'

'You ask what you like.'

'Judy told me Nan's father was a chap by the name of Maltese Sam, have you ever heard of him?'

'She said WHAT?'

Arthur was a bit hard of hearing sometimes, so I repeated my question.

'Don't you listen to her,' he said when I'd asked again. 'She never lived on the station, how would she know?'

'Well, she got the story from her mother, Alice, who got the story from her husband, Howden, who said that Annie had confided in him.'

Arthur threw back his head and laughed. Then he thumped his fist on the arm of his chair and said, 'Now you listen to me, Daisy's father is the same as mine. Daisy is my only full sister. Albert, he's our half-brother, his father was Howden, too, but by a different woman.'

'So you reckoned he fathered the both of you.'

'By jove he did! Are you gunna take the word of white people against your own flesh and blood? I got no papers to prove what I'm sayin'. Nobody cared how many blackfellas were born in those days, nor how many died.

I know because my mother, Annie, told me. She said Daisy and I belonged to one another. Don't you go takin' the word of white people against mine.'

Arthur had us both nearly completely convinced, except for one thing, he avoided our eyes. Mum and I knew it wasn't a good sign, there was something he wasn't telling us. So I said again, 'You're sure about this, Arthur?'

'Too right! Now, about this Maltese Sam, don't forget Alice was Howden's second wife and they had the Victorian way of thinking in those days. Before there were white women, our father owned us, we went by his name, but later, after he married his first wife, Nell, he changed our names. I'll tell you about that one day. He didn't want to own us no more. They were real fuddy-duddies in those days. No white man wants to have black kids runnin' round the place with his name. And Howden's mother and father, they were real religious types, I bet they didn't know about no black kids that belonged to them.'

We all laughed then. Arthur was like Mum, it wasn't often he failed to see the funny side of things.

When we'd all finally calmed down, he said, 'You know, if only you could get Daisy to talk. She could tell you so much. I know she's got her secrets, but there are things she could tell you without tellin' those.'

'She won't talk, Arthur,' I sighed. 'You know a lot about Nan, can't you tell us?'

He was silent for a moment, thoughtful. Then he said, 'I'd like to. I really would, but it'd be breakin' a trust. Some things 'bout her I can't tell. It wouldn't be right. She could tell you everything you want to know. You see, Howden was a lonely man. I know, one night at Ivanhoe, we both got drunk together and he told me all his troubles. He used to go down to Daisy's room at night and talk to her. I can't say no more. You'll have to ask her.'

'But Arthur, what if she won't tell us?'

'Then I can't, either. There's some things Daisy's got to tell herself, or not at all. I can't say no more.'

After he left, Mum and I sat analysing everything for ages. We were very confused, we knew that the small pieces of information we now possessed weren't the complete truth.

'Sally,' Mum said, breaking into my thoughts, 'do you remember when Arthur first started visiting us and he said Albert was his full brother?'

'Yeah, but that was before he knew us well.'

'Yes, but remember how he almost whispered when he told us the truth about Albert? He didn't want to hurt the feelings of any of Albert's family and he loved him so much I suppose he thought it didn't matter.'

'Yeah, I know. You think there might be more to Nan's parentage.'

'It's possible.'

'There's another possibility. Howden may have been her father, but there could be something else, some secret he wants to keep, that is somehow tied in with all of this. Perhaps that's why he didn't look us in the eye.'

'Yes, that's possible, too. And I can't see why he wouldn't tell us the truth, because he knows how much it means to us. I don't think we'll ever know the full story. I think we're going to have to be satisfied with guesses.'

'It makes me feel so sad to think no one wants to own our family.'

'I know, Mum, but look at it this way, just on a logical basis, it's possible he was her father. We know he was sleeping with Annie, and Arthur said that even after he married his first wife, he was still sleeping with Annie, so he could have sired her.'

'Yes, it's possible.'

'Well, that's all we can go on then, possibilities. Now Judy said Jack Grime was your father, but maybe he wasn't. He was living at Ivanhoe at the time you were born, but that doesn't necessarily mean he fathered you, does it?'

'Oh God, Sally,' Mum laughed, 'let's not get in any deeper. I've had enough for one night.'

1987

MARCIA LANGTON
b. 1951

A leading Aboriginal scholar and a descendant of the Yiman people, Marcia Langton grew up in Queensland and spent many years working as an activist with local and overseas social justice organisations. During the 1980s she trained in anthropology at ANU, and from the 1990s she has researched and taught in a range of disciplines, including gender and identity studies, Aboriginal land rights, resource management and Aboriginal creative expression. Langton's films include: *Jardiwampa: A Warlpiri fire* and *Blood Brothers*. She was professor of Aboriginal and Torres Strait Islander Studies at Charles Darwin University before being appointed Foundation Professor of Australian Indigenous Studies at the University of Melbourne. *AH/PM*

From 'Well, I Heard It on the Radio and I Saw It on the Television ...'[1]
Section 3: Decentering the 'Race' Issue

THE RETURN OF JEDDA

[Charles] Chauvel's *Jedda* (1955) expresses all those ambiguous emotions, fears and false theories which revolve in Western thought around the spectre of the 'primitive'. It rewrites Australian history so that the black rebel against white colonial rule is a rebel against the laws of his own society. Marbuk, a 'wild' Aboriginal man, is condemned to death, not by the white coloniser,

---

1   Refers to the Yothu Yindi song 'Treaty' (1991).

but by his own elders. It is Chauvel's inversion of truth on the black/white frontier, as if none of the brutality, murder and land clearances occurred.

The witchcraft or sorcery of Marbuk lures away Jedda, the young Aboriginal woman, from the civilising influence of the homestead couple who have adopted her and provided her with decent clothes, food and education (symbolised by Humphrey McQueen's piano[1]). As Jedda plays the piano, 'tribal chants' rise up and take control of her Aboriginal mind buried deep within her new, constructed, made over, civilised one. She follows Marbuk into the bush where he performs a magical rite, to which she has no resistance. She pays for her 'instinctive, native weakness' with her life when she is dragged over a cliff by Marbuk who is fleeing from Joe, the good 'half-caste boy'.

In *Night Cries, A Rural Tragedy* (1990), [Tracey] Moffatt brings Jedda (played by myself) back to life as if forty years have passed. Jedda is now caring for her adoptive mother who is ancient and waiting to die. None of the male characters have survived and the homestead is a ruin.

Moffatt's 'feminine gaze' reconstructs the relationship between Jedda and her adoptive mother as one between women as independent beings, but perhaps they are not whole. The characters are imagined beings, ghostlike, merely guides to what the audience might invent, just as Chauvel's *Jedda* was. *Night Cries* can be read as an autobiographical exploration of Moffatt's relationship with her own foster mother. The film asks questions about the role of 'mother' in adoptive mother/daughter relationships.

The lives and experiences of Jedda and her adoptive mother in Moffatt's reconstruction of them are not mediated by men, not by Jedda's adoptive white father nor by Marbuk, the handsome black outlaw/seducer, nor by Joe, the sensible, civilised half-caste ringer to whom Jedda should have been *attracted* and become married.

All the men are disappeared.

What Moffatt was trying to *correct* in the text of *Jedda* is the Western fascination with the 'primitive'.

Moffatt's inversion of colonial history is to play out the worst fantasies of those who took Aboriginal children from their natural parents to assimilate and 'civilise' them. Perhaps the worst nightmare of the adoptive parents is to end life with the black adoptive child as the only family, the only one who cares. Moffatt's construction of that nightmare is subversive because the style and materiality of the homestead set is so reminiscent of Aboriginal poverty.

Chauvel's once privileged homestead now resembles the inside of a humpy. Moffatt takes us from the homestead—an exhibition of the wealth

---

1   In a famous essay in *The New Britannia* (1970), historian Humphrey McQueen described the piano as 'the inevitable accompaniment of colonial hopes and despairs'.

extracted from the slave labour of the Aboriginal men and women on the Australian pastoral station—to the poverty represented in her sets. The middle-aged Aboriginal woman on the now deserted station feeds the dying white mother canned food, and all the excesses of the historical/economic moment of the Australian cattle station are collapsed.

But what about the black men disposed of by Moffatt? Their absence deserves some attention because of what they signify some forty years after the making of *Jedda*. Moffatt's inversion forces the audience to look not at the desire of Chauvel's *Jedda* but at death, and at the consequences of Western imagination of the 'primitive', as we wait in the deteriorating homestead with a middle-aged Aboriginal woman and her dying mother.

Today, *Jedda* is sickening and, at the same time, laughable in its racism. (Indeed, some people might have seen it then as racist.) It was a big, although not very successful feature movie, and has become since an icon of Australian film.

What response did the audience of the 1950s have to this film? Our speculations might begin with the possible colonial/gender reactions. There is the implicit impossibility of white men being threatened by Marbuk, precisely because he inevitably dies as a result of his breach of Aboriginal law. He is eliminated. So inexorably will his 'race' die out because of the asserted inherent Darwinian weakness of Aborigines, morally and genetically, according to Australian eugenicist theory.

Could there have been a secret identification with Jedda among the white women in the cinema audience? Might they have been captivated and fascinated by the story of Marbuk's sorcery and seduction (silently subverting in the heat of the dark cinema the repressive patriarchy which they had to endure); a seduction so much more exciting and dangerous than the Rock Hudson type of seduction in the Hollywood romance?

Tarzan of the Apes, also known as the Earl of Greystokes, may have had a similar attraction. But Marbuk is 'genuinely' 'wild' and so much more mysterious and *unknowable*. Chauvel really did exceed, however subtly for the times, the pinnacle of primitive sexual licentiousness as Tarzan represented it then [...]

Tarzan can go on for hundreds of episodes because he is the coloniser, if somewhat mystified in his pseudo-primitive costume. Indeed, Tarzan and Jane marry, presumably in a High Church of England ceremony, and social relations are normalised even if the monkeys are still living in the bedroom in the trees.

But Marbuk and his paramour, the poor seduced Jedda, must die. It is precisely because of Marbuk's lust that Chauvel destroys him. His is the lust of a 'real primitive'. He is an outlaw. He refuses to submit to civilisation.

As fictive male characters, Tarzan, Marbuk and Joe are imagined models of 'race' and gender. The difference between them as models of men is their place in colonial mythology and in the power relations which they represent. They have their equivalents in the anthropomorphised models of colonialism.

Tarzan's equivalent is Babar the Elephant orphaned by a white hunter. On finding civilisation after a short walk from the jungle, he is clothed in a delightful green suit and is educated in Paris, all at the expense of the rich old woman who finds him wandering the streets of the city.

Joe is the emasculated native and black buffoon of a thousand movies. Marbuk's equivalent is King Kong.

BLACK LIKE MI

Each representation of Aboriginal people is a reconstruction, an imagined experience, a tale told with signifiers, grammatical and morphological elements, mythologies.

The *Black Like Mi* series (1992) is a photographic essay by Destiny Deacon on representations of black women using images of black dolls and covers from books such as *Venus Half Caste*. It was shown at the Boomalli [Aboriginal Artists] Co-operative [Sydney]. Deacon, a tutor in English Literature at Melbourne University, identifies the resonances of early melodramatic representations of native women in films and literature of the 1940s and 1950s through the medium of photography. Previously, Moffatt had reinvented the half-caste siren in the photographic essay, *Something More* (1989).

Deacon explains to us in the two photographs, *Dark Times with Otis and Alias 1* and *2*, that the 'black velvet' perception of the lascivious white male gaze on Aboriginal woman is a mediated sexual experience. These two photographs in particular, but also the series as a whole, reverse the pornographic experience—the signification of the 'black velvet' image.

There is a song about 'black velvet' from the Australian pastoral frontier which expresses the colonial lust of drovers demanding a fuck after a hard day's work. The term has passed into 'redneckspeak', and the subliminal power of the concept also ricochets around most of the sexual images of Aboriginal women.

Deacon has a black female doll, dressed in red, black and yellow, who lies in bed next to a black male doll. She is reading to him from the novel, *Venus Half Caste*. In the next scene, she has rolled over on her side and is reading to herself from the book, doubtless having a little black doll fantasy about 'inter-racial sex'.

'Ha, ha ha, I wonder how little black dolls do it?' she forces us to ask. We black girls have a special experience with little black dolls because they are a very recent, modern artefact in Australia. When we were growing up there were only golliwogs. Then Black Americans demanded in the 1970s that the toy market produce beautiful, well-dressed black dolls, formed in plastic to appear life-like, just like the white dolls. So we came to them late in life.

I remember my first experience in my thirties, standing gazing at a black doll. Everywhere around were these white dolls, loaded with cultural meaning: Barbie, with her gorgeous wardrobe, an appendaged boyfriend, the ultimate toy boy, with a lot of style; Cindy, with a pretty pink gingham check dress and white shoes and socks, who walked and talked. But only little white girls could look into the eyes of these post-oedipal mirrors and find that wonderland of self-imagination.

Imagine the power we black girls derived from, at last, having that experience with a black doll. Deacon gazes through the mirror of the little black doll. Hers is also the feminine gaze. As she looks at the black dolls, boy and girl, in bed, she erases the possibility of white men seeing this sexual scene that she has created. She denies white male voyeurism. She denies the aural, sexual and colonialist conquest. At the same time, in a sideways glance, she places the white male within her view, the white male who imagined the 'black velvet' and who, as a subject/object of Deacon's representation, is denied a peep at the doll.

She makes impotent the white male fantasy of 'black velvet'.

1993

STEPHEN EDGAR
b. 1951

Stephen Edgar was born in Sydney. He moved to Tasmania and, after living in Hobart for over 30 years (where, among other things, he was sometime poetry editor of *Island*), returned to Sydney in 2006. Since 1985 he has published six volumes of poetry, including *Corrupted Treasures* (1995), *Lost in the Foreground* (2003) and *Other Summers* (2006). These have been praised (by, among others, Clive James (qv)) for their formal control, craft and lyricism. *DM*

All Will be Revealed

In the nudist camp identity is lost
Behind disguise.
See, over all the fashions of the self,
Whatever size,

They're slipping on identical pink suits   5
Of nakedness.
On either sex there stretches, nips or droops
Its single dress.

Where have they gone, the friends who brought me here?
Where are the strangers 10
Hiding? The eyes like bullets aimed against
Uncertain dangers

Ricochet from nudity's blank walls.
In such a place
One might devise a nightclub for dresstease 15
Where they could face,

To whistles, randy cries of 'Get it on!',
Themselves as lewd
Performers who would strut their bump and grind,
Beginning nude, 20

Discarding part by part their bare accord,
Till they finessed
The erotic climax of true self-display,
Completely dressed.
                                                1995

Sun Pictorial

How formal and polite,
How grave they look, burdened with earnest thoughts,
In all these set-up sepia stills,
Almost as if, embarrassed and contrite
To be caught practising their fatal skills, 5
They'd stepped aside from slaughter for these other shots.

The American Civil War,
The first war captured by the photograph
In real time. Even the dead
Seem somehow decorous, less to deplore 10
The sump of blood to which their duty bled
Than to apologize, humbly, in our behalf.

We know how otherwise
It was. They knew it then. The gauche onset
Of murderously clumsy troops, 15
Dismemberment by cannon, the blown cries
Through powder smoke, mayhem of scattered groups
In close engagement's pointblank aim and bayonet.

How far from then we've come.
The beauties of the Baghdad night still stun   20
Me: a blue screen where guns and jets
Unloose the lightnings of imperium—
Intense enough to challenge a minaret's
Aquamarine mosaic in the blinded sun

At noon—and smart bombs fall   25
Through walls to wipe the city street by street.
Morning, and in the camera's light
The formal corpses ripen. Who can recall
By day precisely what they watched last night?
Or find the unknown soldier in a field of wheat?   30

Being surplus, like the killed,
Millions of those old plates were simply dumped.
And in a modern version of 'swords
To ploughshares', many were reused to build
Greenhouses, ranged and set in place as wards   35
Above the rife tomatoes as they blushed and plumped,

While, through the daily sun's
Pictorial walls and roofs, the long, desired,
Leaf-fattening light fell down, to pore
Upon the portraits of these veterans   40
Until their ordered histories of the war
Were wiped to just clear glass and what the crops transpired.

2003

JILL JONES
b 1951

Born in Sydney, Jill Jones has worked in arts administration, publishing and journalism, and as an academic. As well as poetry she has written fiction, criticism and a blog. Her five books of poetry, including *Screens Jets Heaven: New and selected poems* (2002) and *Broken/Open* (2005), characteristically deal with the quotidian as both sensate and an effect of language and culture. Her urban settings are both lyrical and realistic. *DM*

The Night Before Your Return

The night is kind tonight,
the sky is purple,
clouds are orange,

and planes fly away
to the south.   5
I need no fan, a cricket sings.

And you are under heat in Brisbane.

The Turks do not sing,
one phone over the road softly rings,
and I have drunk pale green tea   10
from an old cup.
I have not done
what I ought to have done.
The window is open
as the mind at midnight,   15
cars fade away,
carriages rattle through timetables.

You are asleep and out of range.

Spiders work, their lines
arrange like poetry,   20
another train embraces
the lone traveller,
and there are always the dogs.
I am clean, naked and cool.

You are covered in distance   25
that you unwrap tomorrow,
driving down
over rivers, across valleys,
through hot towns, dry acres,
into the wet south of my dreams.   30
                                                             2002

PETER GOLDSWORTHY
b 1951

Peter Goldsworthy was born in the South Australian country town of Minlaton and grew up in a musical family. He graduated in medicine from the University of Adelaide in 1974 and continues to work part-time as a general practitioner while maintaining a prolific output as a writer across several genres.

His first collection of poems, *Readings From Ecclesiastes* (1982), won the Commonwealth Poetry Prize. He published several collections of poetry and short stories before the appearance of his first novel, *Maestro* (1989), a classic coming-of-age narrative featuring a gifted and slightly sinister music teacher whose story has dark roots in the Second World War. Since then he has published several novels, including *Three Dog Night* (2003).

Goldsworthy's excursion into speculative fiction, the darkly comic *Honk if You Are Jesus* (1992), was adapted as a stage play and performed to critical acclaim at the 2006 Adelaide Festival of Arts, and the 1999 novella *Jesus Wants Me for a Sunbeam* has been produced in a dramatised version on CD.

He published a collection of essays, *Navel Gazing*, in 1998, and is sought after and respected as a literary critic. He was chair of the Literature Board of the Australia Council for the Arts from 2001 to 2006.

His fiction often poses the question 'What if . . .?' and then follows that through to sometimes shocking conclusions. Much of his work reflects his calling as a doctor, exploring situations in which some bodily crisis must be resolved or played out to the end.

Music has been a strong influence throughout Goldsworthy's career and he has worked as a librettist in two highly successful collaborations with Australian composer Richard Mills, first on their adaptation of Ray Lawler's (qv) 1955 stage play *Summer of the Seventeenth Doll* (1996) and then on the original opera *Batavia* (2001). His poetry has been set to music by Australian composers Mills, Graeme Koehne and Matthew Hindson, and he is the father of concert pianist Anna Goldsworthy. *KG*

The Kiss

The thunder is closer now, almost seismic, as much inside the car as outside.

'Just made it,' Kenny says. He noses the dusty Mercedes in among the pillars that support the house, and switches off the ignition and lights. Utter darkness.

'Relax,' Tom says somewhere in that darkness. 'The car would have dried overnight.'

His voice, as disembodied as the thunder, seems to have Kenny surrounded.

'Yeah—streaked like a fucking zebra.'

'You worry too much. Live a little, for Christ's sake.'

His friend is right, Kenny knows. They could have joyridden the dusty back roads till dawn and still had time to clean the car; his parents are not due back till late the next day. 'It's my neck,' he says. 'Not yours.'

Tom isn't listening. 'Take the old zebra for another gallop,' he mutters somewhere, and chuckles again, pleased with himself. 'Take the old zebra back out on the savannah . . .'

'Just empty the fucking ashtray before you get out,' Kenny says.

There is no anger in his words; the obscenity comes as naturally as music, a necessary rhythm.

'Say please.'

'Just do it.'

He climbs from the car and walks out from beneath the house into the October light-and-sound show. The humid weight of the impending Wet presses down upon him, squeezing an answering wetness like a kind of juice from his skin, but he is beyond the discomforts of heat and sweat. The dark night air carries powerful scents: a cusp-mix of Wet season and Dry, dust and imminent rain. The thunder is constant, a rumbling sound horizon. Lightning flashbulbs the darkness, alternating night and day. The first rains are surely no more than hours away, although they have seemed no more than hours away for weeks. Tom's voice, at his shoulder, startles him. 'Drink?'

The sherry flagon is offered; Kenny waves it away. Tom takes a swig before speaking again.

'This is just a tease,' he says. 'Foreplay. The Wet is still a week away.'

'Bullshit. It's going to piss down any second.'

Mention of the various liquids—rain, sherry, piss—seems to increase the pressure in Kenny's bladder. He vaults the low back fence and walks to the edge of the small cliff above the beach. Lightning flickers with special intensity on the far side of the harbour—a distant fireworks, embedded in banked cloud. Perhaps the Dry has already ended over there. More lightning; the mudflats below are revealed, hidden, then revealed again, the low-tide line half a mile out. Tom materialises at his side; they unzip and send two long, steady arcs of urine over the edge of the cliff and down into the darkness of the mangroves. Years before, it would have been a simple contest—higher, further; contests mostly won by Tom. Now, sixteen years old, sweet-and-sour sixteen, Kenny is finding words more useful weapons. 'It's a lightning conductor,' he says.

'What is?'

'Piss, stupid.'

The idea strikes them as hilarious; they laugh convulsively, their streams becoming broken, scattering showers.

Tom leans back and aims his cock near-vertically. 'Way to go!'

The dare is unpunished by the heavens. Kenny vaults back over the fence, grabs the garden hose, twists on the tap and aims the gushing water at his friend.

'Mine is bigger than yours!'

'Longer, maybe.'

Tom, taller and stronger, soon wrests the nozzle from him; the spray is turned back into his own face, point-blank. The coldness of the water—a deep earth-cold—gives only temporary reprieve from the sticky heat. They lie in soaked clothes, on wet grass, sweating. The night is dead calm; no air movement cools their skins.

'Sure you don't want a drink?'

Tom's words remind Kenny there is work to be done, evidence to be disposed of. He pushes himself to his feet, walks back beneath the house and gropes inside the car between lightning flashes. The brandy bottle is still half full, to be watered down and replaced in the liquor cabinet. The moulded glass bottle of sparkling wine—Pineapple Pearl—is empty; its absence from his parents' fridge still seems a gamble worth taking. He checks the ashtray. Of course it has not been emptied; he empties it himself. The picnic rug on the back seat is briefly illuminated. He bundles it up, steps back onto the lawn, and shakes out the gritty beach sand over his wet friend.

'Do you mind?' Tom says.

'What are you complaining about? You've been rolling around in the sand with Debbie all night.'

'Jealousy's a curse, Kenny.'

Is he jealous, Kenny wonders? If so, jealous of whom? Of Tom for beating him to the pleasures of Debbie, or of Debbie for intruding on a boys' night out?

Tom rambles drunkenly on, beyond nuances. 'I thought you were never going to leave us. I thought you were going to hang around and watch.'

'Who needed to watch? I could hear everything half a mile up the beach.'

'What's that supposed to mean?'

'The noise she was making. What were you *doing* to her?'

'How could she make any noise? Her mouth was full.'

Kenny almost chokes himself with laughter; Tom can always make him laugh. He flings the rug into the air above his friend; it seems to hang there, a parachute canopy, momentarily suspended, floating on the viscid air, before settling.

'Fold that up. Please.' He strips off his wet shirt, slings it over the clothesline, then climbs the steps up into the house. The slatted metal louvres that form the outside walls of each room have been cranked wide open, but no breeze yet enters. He switches the big overhead fan to maximum notch, the heavy air begins to stir. He is searching the fridge when Tom appears in the door with a roughly bundled picnic rug under his arm.

'Anything cold?'

'Butter,' Kenny tells him. 'Eggs.'

'Very funny. Anything to drink?'

'Milk.'

Tom topples theatrically backwards onto the sofa, as if shot. 'What I need is a swim,' he announces.

The lightning flicker, on cue, might have been a warning sent from Kenny's parents. 'Swim in the bathtub,' he tells his friend. 'The car stays where it is.'

'We could break into the pool.'

'How do we get there? Transporter beam?'

Flopped on his back on the sofa, Tom takes another swig of sherry, thinking. 'The water tank? It's closer than the pool.'

'We'd still have to fucking drive there.'

Even as he speaks, the notion of a swim is growing on Kenny. Debbie has been dropped home not more than an hour past her curfew, the night is still young, its hours small and empty. The alcohol is leaching from his system, he is feeling restless again.

'We could ride,' he finally announces. 'If you can keep your bike upright.'

The task does not seem beyond them as they sit beneath the big, cooling fan. Tom rises and follows him unsteadily down the steps. The pushbikes are leaning against a pillar beneath the house; they set off immediately, riding abreast, bare-chested, weaving and wobbling a little. The lightning has eased but their sweating torsos glisten as they pass through the successive light-fields of the streetlamps. The night air is resistant to movement, hot and viscous, difficult to breathe. Tom, heavy with his own thick flesh, is soon struggling for air. The cooling breeze of their own motion fails to keep pace with the outpouring of sweat; soon Kenny, too, is up off his saddle, standing high on the pedals, pushing down as if riding uphill but getting nowhere fast, tethered to his starting point by invisible elastic.

At the top of the descent to the beach-flats they pause to take breath. Sporadic flashes of lightning illume the view. On the far side of the wide flats the road rises again to Bullocky Point. The huge tank and its reservoir of cooling water is still impossibly distant, perched high on the far point.

'Seemed like a good idea at the time,' Kenny says.

'Not one of your better ones.'

'It gets worse. We'll have to ride all the way back home afterwards.'

'So you don't want a swim?'

'Did I say that?'

A slow, drunken smile creases Tom's face. 'You're not fucking suggesting?'

Kenny answers by turning his bike back towards home. His friend hoots loudly. 'I don't believe my ears. Half an hour ago you were shitting yourself about the car.'

'I'm older now.'

'You grow up quick.'

They ride home at speed, forcing themselves through the muggy air, knowing the tank is much closer now, even if they are pedalling in the opposite direction.

'Bring the sherry!' Tom shouts upstairs as Kenny fetches the car keys, but Kenny already has the flagon in hand, feeling reckless and ready for anything, as if overcoming his guilt about taking the car is the first step in a more general unravelling. The night is beginning again for the two of them—the old boyhood team, no outsiders. He backs out of the drive at speed, crashes through the gear change, and accelerates away with a squeal of tyre rubber.

'Petrol's low,' Tom notices.

The news seems only mildly alarming. At the top of the beach road Ken switches off the engine, and coasts in neutral down the long incline, windows wound open, the air moving sweetly across his upper body. Many times the boys have freewheeled down this same slope on their pushbikes, the contest to glide as far as possible without pedalling, slowing gradually once the beach flats are reached. Tom benefits from his extra bulk; sometimes he can nurse his faltering bike as far as the gardens. The heavy metal mass of the car carries them even further before Kenny restarts the engine for the last ascent.

The big water tank looms out of the darkness on Bullocky Point, a squat, square concrete fortress, or gun emplacement. Kenny parks on the far side, hidden from the main road. Tom is first out of the car, stripping himself one-handed, sherry flagon clutched in the other. He kicks himself free of shorts and thongs and rapidly clambers up the rusted metal ladder fixed to the northern wall of the tank, still wearing his jocks. As Kenny joins him at the top, he is draining the last of the sherry. They gaze down from a high ledge into the dark interior. No water level can be seen; the inside ladder descends into blackness.

Kenny feels a flicker of apprehension. 'Maybe it's empty.'

'Better toss something in,' Tom says, and grapples playfully with his friend, jostling him towards the edge.

'Fuck off.'

Tom releases him, and with a flip of his wrist tosses the empty flagon far out into the void. The splash is invisible, but noisily resonant, amplified within the vast echo chamber.

'Last one in!'

'You don't know how deep it is!' Kenny shouts, but Tom has already launched himself out into nothingness.

This time the splash is visible, a brief silver explosion against a dark field, followed by the glimmer of spreading ripples catching and reflecting the weak light. Tom's voice follows, echoing loudly within the four walls. 'Chicken!'

Kenny leaps immediately from the ledge, freefalling, it seems, for far too long. The sudden cold smack of the water is half reassuring, half shocking, stopping his heart, paralysing his breathing muscles. He surfaces, unable to breathe for a long moment. The walls and corners of the tank are as black as ink, but as his eyes accommodate he begins to sense the pale moon of a face somewhere in the centre, lit only by the faint glimmer of starlight and the cloud-reflected lights of the town. 'So—what *did* you do with Debbie?' he asks the moon-face.

'A gentleman never tells,' the face says.

They might be shouting, their voices are so amplified, reverberant. Kenny lowers his. 'What's being a gentleman got to do with you?'

Tom laughs as loudly as ever. 'I thought you said you could hear everything.'

'It didn't leave a lot to the imagination.'

'It was weird, Kenny. She let me do everything—except kiss her. Said I was too pissed.'

'I'd have to be pissed *to* kiss her.'

Tom ignores him. 'She told me a good story. She was kissing some guy at a party last year and he suddenly stops, turns away to spew up over her shoulder, then goes right on kissing her.'

'Choice,' Kenny says, and kicks away, a few lazy backstrokes. When he turns back, his friend's face has vanished.

Ribbit, a frog croaks, a throaty basso in a dark corner. *Ribbit.*

Kenny's tone is scornful. 'Five out of ten.'

A human voice answers. 'It wasn't me, fuckwit.'

'You expect me to believe there are frogs in here?'

'Where would you spend the Dry if you were a frog?'

'How would I get in? Hop from rung to rung?'

Tom's face materialises, pale grey on black, and they float in silence on their backs, side by side, for a time.

'Where is the ladder?' Tom asks.

'Had enough?'

'I'm feeling a bit wonky. I might throw up.'

'Don't expect a goodnight kiss.' Kenny peers up at the high rim of the tank, an ill-defined margin between the total blackness of the interior and the star-pricked darkness of the night sky. A first, slight shiver: he, too, has no idea which side the ladder is on.

'I'll feel around the edge.' He kicks himself to the nearest corner of the tank, finding it by touch, then sets off, sidestroke, trailing one hand along the slimy wall. A faint premonition of tiredness enters the muscles of his upper arms, a slight heaviness, or resistance to movement; after the second corner he rolls onto his back and propels himself using his legs alone, long lazy frog-kicks.

'Where are you?' Tom's voice is some distance away, but loudly resonant, rebounding between walls.

'On the last wall. Can't find it.' As he floats, resting, the obvious strikes him. 'It's the end of the Dry. The water level is below the bottom rung.'

'So what do we fucking do? Wait for the monsoon to float us up?'

They tread water in silence, listening. The thunder is no more than a distant grumble, a faint tremor in the water. Or is the tremor internal, another shiver? Kenny earnt his Lifesaving Certificate years before, half rite-of-passage, half trial-by-ordeal. He feels at home in the water—but the weary ache in his upper arms is growing.

'I'm not feeling good about this,' Tom is saying somewhere.

'We'll be fine. Just float till daybreak.'

'Then what? No-one will find us.'

'We can yell.'

Silence, then Tom again: 'I am going to throw up.'

'Hold onto it, for Christ's sake.'

The noise of retching is close at hand.

'Choice,' Kenny mutters. 'Fucking choice.' Lying on his back, half sunk in the huge mattress of water, he scrutinises the tops of the walls. Shreds of cloud move slowly across the starry square of the night sky, as if on some darkened movie screen. 'You okay?'

Tom seems to spit his answer out, as if the words are the last vestige of vomit. 'Fucking wonderful.'

Kenny floats on, trying to keep calm, to think things through, but Tom won't leave him alone. 'How did we get into this fucking mess?'

'You jumped, remember?'

'You didn't fucking stop me!'

'So it's my fault?' Silence in the great vault, till a thought strikes Kenny. 'Which side is the ladder on?'

'The school side.'

He feels a stirring of anger towards his friend. 'I know that, dickhead. Which side? North?'

'North-west.'

'Then the ladder is on the far wall. Look at the clouds. The weather is coming from the north-west.'

'So?'

'Maybe I can give you a leg up. Try and grab it.'

'Grab something I can't even *see*?'

'You got any better ideas?' Kenny kicks across the tank to the northern wall, then sidestrokes slowly from one corner to the other, measuring the length of the wall in handspans, counting each aloud.

'What the fuck are you doing?'

'Shut up—now I have to start again.'

Tom keeps his mouth shut, compliant for the first time that night, perhaps for the first time in all their years of friendship. Reaching the end of the wall—a hundred and seventy-two spans—Kenny counts back half that number and scratches an invisible groove into the soft rind of slime above the water level.

'What if the ladder's off-centre?' Tom asks.

'Just get over here.'

Kenny treads water below the imagined ladder, willing it to be there. He clasps ten fingers together to form a foothold, Tom plants his right foot into this makeshift stirrup and heaves himself up. The weight submerges Kenny completely; he surfaces to find Tom a few feet out, breathing hard.

'Nothing there.'

'Two steps this time—one onto my hands, then up onto my shoulders.' The force of the recoil submerges him again, more deeply. After regaining his breath, they try again. 'We're doing this the wrong way around. I should be on top.'

He launches himself upwards from Tom's clasped hands, his own hands finding nothing in the darkness but the dry, crusted wall. Tom's panicky voice is echoing through the chamber as Kenny surfaces after the fifth or sixth such attempt. 'I've got a cramp.'

Kenny is hit in the face by a flailing arm.

'Kenny? Give us a hand. I need to hold onto something.'

'Lie on your back. All you have to do is float.'

Tom rolls onto his back, but almost immediately rolls over again. 'Jesus— now the other one is seizing up. All that fucking jumping.'

'Float on your back. I'll stretch your legs.'

But Tom is grasping at him again, frantic. 'Just let me hold on for a minute.'

The weight of his bigger friend submerges Kenny; he kicks free underwater, on the edge of panic himself. 'Where are you?' Tom is shouting as he breaks surface. 'Kenny? Where are you?'

'Keeping my distance unless you do what I fucking say.' This time the words sink in. Kenny supports Tom with one hand beneath the chin, keeping the mouth and nose just above the surface. He has to work harder himself, treading water at jogging pace, and knows he cannot continue indefinitely.

But Tom is in some pain. Breathing heavily his words come in gasps. 'Jesus, Kenny, what are we going to do?'

The question shocks Kenny; it seems too general, too open-ended. Far better to stick to particulars. 'Panic makes cramp worse. It'll ease if you stretch the legs.'

'It's not easing.'

'It will. Try to ignore it.' His mind gropes for solutions. He tries to remember the lifesaving lessons, three long years before. Half the battle is mental—is that what he had been taught? 'You know,' he says in Tom's ear, 'You still haven't told me.'

'About what?'

'What do you think? I've been trying to get it out of you all night.'

Tom needs a long moment to realise what he is talking about. 'One thing for sure,' he finally says, 'I'm not going to die a fucking virgin.'

'A *fucking* virgin?' Kenny says, and Tom manages a small laugh.

'It's easing,' he says. 'Oh, fuck, thank Christ. It's easing.' He laughs again, more loudly, a mixture of relief and embarrassment. His tone is forced and hearty, covering its recent tracks. 'We'll try again. You do the jumping.'

'I think we should save our energy.'

'Then crack another joke. It was the joke that did the trick.'

Laughter on demand proves impossible; all the jokes Kenny has ever heard seem to have done a moonlight flit from his mind, untraceably. 'I could sing a song,' he says.

'What song?'

'Any song. "Baa, Baa Black Sheep". "Twinkle, Twinkle Little Star".'

'The other leg's cramping.' Tom's voice is edgy with panic again. 'Jesus— think of something. You're the brains of this outfit.'

For the first time Kenny wonders if he might be close to cramp himself. He shoves the thought from his mind. Old voodoo habits: to think a fear is to make it real, to conjure it up. Then suddenly he is too busy for such thoughts; Tom has rolled onto his belly and is clawing at him again, pushing him under.

'We're going to drown. We're going to fucking drown!'

A stray finger pokes Kenny's eye; he insectively twists free and kicks away a metre.

'Where are you? Oh, Jesus—you giving up on me?'

'Just letting go for a few seconds. I need to piss.'

'Piss here. You've got to hold me.' Tom's plea is gurgled through a swallowed mouthful of water, but Kenny kicks further away into the darkness. A horror story from the paper some weeks before comes back to him: of a married couple who hit a reef somewhere out among the islands and took to the water in life-jackets. The woman had been injured in the collision; after a few hours in the water, sharks began to nibble at her torn legs. Reef sharks, not quite big enough to end it quickly, but big enough to tear off small mouthfuls: toes, fingers, chunks of calf and thigh.

Knowing she could not survive, the woman had told her husband to swim away. And he had swum away, into the night, his wife lost to him, being eaten alive, her cries chasing him through the darkness.

'Help me, Jesus, Kenny—*help* me!'

Kenny silently eases his head beneath the surface of the water, croc-fashion, and kicks further away from his friend. He surfaces some distance off, but senses that Tom might still locate him.

'Help me! Help! . . . Help me!' The gurgled cries carom between the high walls, amplified terribly. Even more terrible is the short silence that follows.

'I'll help if you don't fucking panic!' Kenny shouts. 'I'll help if you shut the fuck up!'

Tom breaks surface, swallowing water, choking as much as shouting. Hiding in the darkmost corner, the thought comes to Kenny that if he waits till the noise subsides, waits till Tom has nearly drowned, he might then resuscitate him, and hold him afloat, becalmed, in the Correct Lifesaving Position till dawn. He listens to his friend's frantic shouts and splashings, staying mum. He is acting only partly on instinct; he also knows exactly what he is doing. And knows that he knows, a realisation that fills him with shame. That shame is easily turned into anger against Tom. Dumb, drunk Tom. Scared, panicky Tom—who would have thought it? The noise of his begging fills the chamber: 'Somebody—help me! Please!' Tears fill Kenny's already wet eyes. He slips his head beneath the surface to wash away the heat of those tears, but the flail of Tom's struggles is only amplified by the medium of water. Kenny even fancies he can hear the voice calling to him underwater, gasping a last burble of syllables, a bubbling 'Kenny, Kenny.' Or is it—it might be—'Mummy, Mummy'?

He surfaces, and this time swims towards these desperate, choking sounds, unable to keep his distance. 'Tom?' he shouts. 'Tommy?'

Tom has vanished.

'You stupid bastard,' he shouts. 'You stupid fucking bastard! Where are you? If you're fucking hiding from me!'

He duckdives beneath the surface repeatedly, groping in the dark water with hands that grasp nothing. His legs and arms ache; exhausted, he turns onto his back to rest, but floating also becomes an ordeal. The great mass of fresh water seems no longer able to support him, or else he cannot relax. He chokes on a swallowed mouthful, but without panic; he is too weary for panic. He feels dulled, numbed, emptied now even of anger.

His unfeeling mind is nevertheless capable of thought. The hour must be . . . three a.m.? Four? An hour or two, at most, till daybreak, and someone spots the abandoned Mercedes. Will he have enough energy to shout? And if so, how often? Regularly, like the sweep of a lighthouse? Once every ten seconds? Once a minute? And what of cramp? The possibility has become unworrying, as if the capacity for fear has also drained from him, his reserves of adrenaline, the raw fuel of worry consumed by the ordeals of the night. The problem of cramp seems no more than that: a problem to solve, a kind of algebra, remote from real events and things.

A large object bumps gently, surprisingly, against him as he floats, and rebounds slowly from the collision, like an astronaut adrift in space.

'Tom?'

He reaches out a hand and grabs at an arm. Tom is floating face up—what does that mean? He remembers that drowned women float face up, but men, for some reason, face down. Might Tom still be alive, then? Still breathing? His earlier plan, or self-justification, seems plausible again: wait till drowning has calmed Tom, then resuscitate him. He tugs the floating body towards him, treading water. Lifesaving Certificate routines come back to him: he pinches the nostrils shut between the thumb and forefinger of his right hand; with his left he hooks down the chin to open the mouth. Leaning his elbow and shoulder on the half-submerged body, he presses his open mouth onto Tom's and breathes out, hard. The mouth is cold and wet and carries the faint taste of sour, regurgitated sherry, but Kenny is beyond squeamishness. The downward pressure of his mouth pushes Tom's head beneath the surface, but he senses a slight inflation of the chest against his elbow. He senses this, also: as the chest inflates, the body rides higher in the water, made more buoyant.

When he removes his mouth the chest relaxes, the drowned man exhales—a dead man breathing—and the body resubmerges perceptibly. A strange thing: the body is cold to touch, water-temperature, but its breath is warmish, released from a still warm interior.

He presses his mouth to the other mouth again, and again, but the effort of keeping his friend's head above water is exhausting. His heart pounds, his own breaths come in large gasps; he floats for a time, breathing slowly and deeply, trying to calm himself. Then realises he has released Tom without noticing; the body has drifted away into darkness—only a few feet away—and rolled face down. He thinks again of how the body rode higher in the water when its lungs were buoyed by air. *The* body? Its? He almost winces to find himself thinking this way—but shame now seems beyond his exhausted emotions. The words are surely necessary instruments of thinking, long-handled tongs, keeping emotion at a distance. Somehow he knows that survival might depend on such tongs. His mind grasps again at the thought: inflating the lungs buoys the body. Might he use it as a lifebuoy? He had refused to allow the drowning man to cling to him; might he now cling to the drowned?

He rolls the body over like a log, and by pressing his weight onto the torso levers the face above water. He turns the head to one side, hooks open the mouth with two fingers and drains out as much water as possible. As before, he breathes into the mouth, pinching the nostrils, and is gratified as the lungs fill and expand. A small gush of water escapes as he pulls his mouth away; he takes a quick deep breath and applies his mouth again. A sigh of air escapes after the second inflation. How many breaths can two waterlogged lungs hold? He breathes again, and again, forcefully, holding the mouth closed between breaths, until a blurt of air escaping under pressure between the squeezed lips tells him he has reached end-point. Keeping the nostrils and mouth pinched shut with his right hand, he floats now without effort, half supported by the inflated body, as if by an inner tube or life-preserver. Absurd images from a childhood spent in swimming pools clog his head: car tyres, rubber ducks, inflatable crocodiles, arm-floaties. Floatie. The child's word sounds grotesque; he feels a sudden urge to laugh, a desire to laugh, sensing also that by laughing he might be able to cry.

Neither proves possible.

After some minutes his clenched right hand begins to cramp. A better idea: clamping its nose and mouth shut with his left hand, he peels the jocks from the body with his right, flexing the knees, tugging them down, then finally pushing them from the feet with his own feet. After a top-up inflation, he stuffs the sodden garment into the mouth, wedging it with two fingers deeply inside the throat, blocking the escape of air from both nose and mouth.

Now he floats more comfortably, sprawled across the submerged torso, feet trailing. The coldness of the water strikes him for the first time since he leapt from the high ledge, hours before. He shivers slightly, but only briefly, for the air on his exposed arms and head is humidly warm. The body beneath him, its face a few inches from his, begins to resume a human identity, begins to reclaim its proper name: Tom, his friend. He log-rolls it again, face down, more to prevent the escape of air from the mouth, he tells himself, than to avoid the nearness of that face.

He remembers, suddenly, the sherry flagon. Might it still be bobbing on the surface, close at hand? Could Tom have used it as a life-support? Why hadn't they thought of it? Too drunk? Too panicked? Of course it must have filled with water and sunk. Other, more random thoughts begin to jump in and out of his head, of the kind that visit exhausted brains late at night: weird, disconnected patterns of recent events, of school, home, his parents' absence, Debbie and Tom on the beach, long ago now, years in the past. From this half-conscious delirium he might have drifted more deeply into sleep, but the noise of passing birds—the screech of black parrots—rouses him. He lifts his head. The square screen of sky above is fading from black to pale blue, the wispy shreds of cloud are reddening with the usual tropic abruptness. The inside walls of the great tank have already emerged from darkness, and with them the rusting ladder, bolted to the northern side, its lowest rung a good body-length above the water level.

No rain has fallen in the night, although somewhere thunder is grumbling again, and lightning is planting its stiletto heel upon the earth: a faint tremor in the air, an invisible ripple in the water. It seems to Kenny that now, at last, the Wet is no more than a few hours away: an idle thought, another day's conversation starter.

As he clings to the cold, buoyant body, he speaks the words aloud, finding comfort in their familiar social surface, beneath which trembles only the faintest anxiety, a sensation which he can't fully identify and is still too weary to bring into sharper focus, but which seems to settle at last on the memory of the dusty car outside: his father's precious Mercedes, unsheltered, windows wound down, soon to be rained on, and in.

2004

Australia

Our earthen dish is seven parts water,
one part china, and a tiny bit japanned.
Its spread of foods is well-presented:
ice sculptures at both poles, and licking-salt
elsewhere. Give me a lever large enough—   5
a cosmic fork or skewer—and I would take it
to a table: its sherbet fizz of surf,
the creamy ice-cones of its toothy alps,
the spice of islands dotted here and there
like cloves jammed in an onion. Turning   10
this common dish as slowly as a day, I'd taste
the sweet-and-sour river deltas, the swamps
about its world wide waist, all of which
smell fishy. As do many maps of Tasmania,
most of them in other places: forest fuzz   15
itchy with green pubic life. Lastly comes
our smaller plate, single and tectonic:
our turf, or lack of it, our baked and gritty
crust, lightly watered, sifter dusted,
and sarcastic with odd hints of eucalypt.   20
Its thousand mile creek tastes too salty,
its muddy waters barely moving, but still
moving enough to stir a homesick heart.

2004

SAM WATSON
b. 1952

Sam Watson is a poet, activist, lecturer, playwright and storyteller of the Birri-Gubba (from his grandfather) and Munaldjali (from his grandmother) nations and lives in Brisbane. His political activism began as a student in the 1960s over the White Australia policy. He went on to play support roles in the 1967 referendum campaign, the Gurindji land rights struggle and other campaigns for Indigenous equality and justice. He studied law and arts at the University of Queensland in the early 1970s. Watson pioneered programs in law, medicine and housing, focusing on Indigenous communities, and was a co-founder of the Brisbane chapter of the Black Panther Party of Australia. His novel *The Kadaitcha Sung* was published in 1990. Watson co-produced the film *Black Man Down* (1995), and made his playwriting debut in 2007 with *The Mack*, written in association with the Brisbane-based Kooemba Jdarra theatre company. Watson is the father of the poet Samuel Wagan Watson (qv). *AH/PM*

From *The Kadaitcha Sung*

When time was still young the gods created substance from the firmament. They made the land and the waters, and then they made life. The land and the waters would serve to reflect the void, and life would bow down and worship the gods, as the gods needed to be worshipped. They brought forth fowl for the air, fish for the oceans and beasts for the land. Men and women were created to have dominion over all; they would live upon the land. The men and women must worship the gods and keep the laws of the gods, and they must ensure that the natural order of all things was kept. One god, a greater being, made his camp on the rich veldts and in the lush valleys of the South Land. He was called Biamee and he loved all life. In time he came to love the tribes of man above all others, for they revered him and his laws. For many aeons the land and the people basked in Biamee's beneficence, and all was well. But there came the time when Biamee longed for his camp among the stars and he made plans to return there. But the tribes became fearful. The world was still a savage place.

So the great one made a veil of mists that hung upon the South Land and hid it from all. Then Biamee called an ancient clan of sorcerers from the heavens to stand in his place. They were known as the Kadaitcha and they were powerful. Then came the day that the tribes farewelled Biamee as he ascended from his most sacred altar, in the vast red rock that sat upon the heart of the land.

The tribes welcomed the Kadaitcha into their midst and the ancient ones took the shape of men, so that they could live within the camps and not cause fear. The chief of the Kadaitcha clan was called Kobbina. He made his camp beneath the red rock that held Biamee's altar and then he looked for a wife. A handmaiden at the court of the moon spirit was fair and she had no man, so she became Kobbina's woman. Her name was Meeyola and she gave the chief twin sons, named Koobara and Booka.

There came the time when Biamee and his fellow gods needed the wisdom of Kobbina in their council, so they called for the chief to join them for all eternity among the stars. Kobbina's heart swelled with pride, but then his spirit became heavy, for now he would have to choose which of his sons would follow him as the Turrwan, or high man. The law was such that only the oldest son could follow, but Meeyola loved them both and would not reveal which of the babies was first born. Kobbina must make the decision and he cast his eye upon the young men. Koobara was tall and fair, and even though he was only a novice his wisdom was great and his patience legend. On the other hand Booka was squat and ugly, possessed of a violence that was fearful to behold. But Biamee's patience grew thin and the chief had to decide, so Kobbina called to his hosts to gather at his camp at the next full moon.

At that sit-down Kobbina walked to his sons and laid his hand upon Koobara, but Booka's rage exploded into a terrible cataclysm of bloodletting. He smote his father and killed him; Booka's followers leaped to his side and fell upon Koobara and his sub-priests. Meeyola fell with a mortal wound and blood ran in a terrible flood. From on high Biamee saw all, and with a heavy heart he began to descend from the astral plane so he could take a direct hand in the dispute. The conflict raged until Koobara's forces sensed the coming of Biamee, which gave them new strength. The evil Booka left a rearguard and fled the battlefield; he had to stop Biamee.

Beneath the red rock was a vast cavern and within the bowels of that cavern was a stone platform that held the Rings of Bora, nine sacred circles of stones that were Biamee's only doorway into the world of men. Booka attacked the altar with a desperate fear, for unless he closed the Ring, Biamee would return and banish Booka to the eternal pits.

The altar was guarded by the four sisters of the winds, who were no match for the violence of Booka and his band. Booka secured the cavern and then he strode through the Rings of Bora and removed the key to the circle, the egg-shaped Kundri stone, the heart of the Rainbow Serpent. The Rings were locked and Biamee was denied his garden. From on high the god swore eternal vengeance, but he was powerless and Booka mocked him. The renegade then raped and blinded the four sisters, to signify his ultimate rejection of Biamee and his laws. By the time Koobara arrived, Booka was gone and the Kundri stone had been stolen. He tended to the four female spirits and then he tried to commune with Biamee, but it was useless. The mortal plane was now isolated and godless.

Booka waged a long and terrible campaign against his brother, and great was the devastation and loss of life. The evil one caused the mists to lift from the land and other mortals saw its wealth and abundance; they came in their hordes and they slaughtered the helpless tribes with a monstrous lust. These new tribes came from all corners of the outside world and from all the families of man, but they did not know Biamee and they did not know of his laws. The fair-skinned ones laid waste to the garden and the chosen people.

Denied his birthright by his own tribe, Booka joined with the new settlers so he would secure position within their order. The unholy alliance was awesome and the tribes were decimated; they lost their lands and they were herded into compounds like animals. Koobara and his sub-priests were overwhelmed until finally Biamee was able to re--establish a fragile link with them. The god told them of an ancient spell that would imprison Booka within a magic wall and would give them time to recover. Koobara sang the proper songs and danced the proper dances: he called to the proper gods and at the right time the spell was invoked. Booka was confined to a thin strip of coastal land that housed a new village called Brisbane, and there he stayed while Koobara regathered the tribes and strengthened their defences against the invaders.

As time passed the violence lessened and the tribes that survived began to rebuild. They started to adapt to life under the new masters and Koobara was pleased. He had secured most of the sacred sites, and now that the people were safe, he could make preparations to wrest the Kundri stone from Booka.

Booka raged within his gaol, but he could do nothing until, sensing that his brother had grown careless and vulnerable, he plotted for his death. From afar, he murdered Koobara and became the last of the Kadaitcha clan. Such had been the scale of the killings that none other remained to deny him.

But Koobara's son had been born of a white woman, and Biamee promised his people that the Kadaitcha child would deliver them.

1990

KEVIN HART
b. 1954

Kevin Hart was born in England and moved with his family to Brisbane in 1966. He was educated at the ANU and the University of Melbourne. His PhD thesis was published as *The Trespass of the Sign: Deconstruction, theology and philosophy* (1989). After working at Deakin University and Monash University, where he gained a personal chair, he left Australia in 2002 to take up a professorial position at Notre Dame University, USA. In 2007 he accepted a position at the University of Virginia. Hart has written scholarly works on Samuel Johnson and Maurice Blanchot.

Initially Hart was seen as one of the so-called Canberra School of poets, a group that included Alan Gould and Geoff Page (qqv). Hart's first book of poems, *The Departure* (1978), set the tone for much of what was to follow: meditative, spare lyrics, informed by Hart's philosophical reading and knowledge of non-Anglophone poetic traditions. Hart's poems—considered religious by many critics—are usually outwardly simple, often relying on a battery of images (such as clocks, heat and night). As Carrie Olivia Adams writes in *DLB*, Hart's poems 'are recognized for their union of linguistic lucidity and intellectual complexity'. Often preoccupied with death, Hart's poems (especially among his later books) are also concerned with the body and eroticism. *Flame Tree*, a selection of his poetry, was published in 2001. *DM*

Facing the Pacific at Night

Driving east, in the darkness between two stars
Or between two thoughts, you reach the greatest ocean,
That cold expanse the rain can never net,

And driving east, you are a child again—
The web of names is brushed aside from things.   5
The ocean's name is quietly washed away

Revealing the thing itself, an energy,
An elemental life flashing in starlight.
No word can shrink it down to fit the mind,

It is already there, between two thoughts,   10
The darkness in which you travel and arrive,
The nameless one, the surname of all things.

The ocean slowly rocks from side to side,
A child itself, asleep in its bed of rocks,
No parent there to wake it from a dream,   15

To draw the ancient gods between the stars.
You stand upon the cliff, no longer cold,
And you are weightless, back before the thrust

And rush of birth when beards of blood are grown;
Or outside time, as though you had just died   20
To birth and death, no name to hide behind,

No name to splay the world or burn it whole.
The ocean quietly moves within your ear
And flashes in your eyes: the silent place

Outside the world we know is here and now,   25
Between two thoughts, a child that does not grow,
A silence undressing words, a nameless love.

                                                        1991

The Calm

There is a cancer fiddling with its cell of blood
A butcher's knife that's frisking lamb for fat
And then there is the Calm.

All over the world numbers fall off the clocks
But still there is the Calm. There is a sound 5
Of a clock's hands

And then there is the Calm.

Now there are children playing on a beach
Out on the Marshall Islands
With fallout in their hair, a freak snowfall. 10
There is no Calm

But then there is the Calm.

All night I feel my old loves rotting in my heart
But morning brings the Calm

Or else the afternoon. 15

Some days I will say yes, and then odd days
It seems that things say yes to me.
And stranger still, there are those times
When I become a yes

(And they are moments of the Calm). 20

1995

DOROTHY PORTER
1954–2008

The poet and librettist Dorothy Porter was born in Sydney. She is best known for her five verse novels, beginning with *Akhenaten* (1992). The most successful of these, *The Monkey's Mask* (1994), was a bestseller, and has been adapted for audio book, stage play, and—most notably—a feature film in 1999. Relying on dramatic monologue, a narrative built up through lyric moments, intensity and striking imagery, *The Monkey's Mask* (like her other verse novels) is an original mix of genre fiction and poetic technique. As Rose Lucas writes in *DLB*, Porter 'can be seen as a feminist poet, concerned with the representation and exploration of female experience, female voices, and female—especially lesbian—sexuality'. The relationship between self and other, and the theme of risk, are constants across Porter's work. Porter has also written two young adult novels, the libretti for two operas by Jonathan Mills (including *The Eternity Man*, 2002, which was a joint winner of the London Genesis Inaugural Opera Prize in 2003), and the lyrics for a jazz song cycle performed by Katie Noonan and Paul Grabowsky, *Before Time Could Change Us* (2003/2005). *DM*

From *The Monkey's Mask*

TROUBLE

'Jill'
I challenge the mirror
'how much guts have you got?'

I like my courage
   physical   5
I like my courage
   with a dash of danger.

In between insurance jobs
I've been watching
   rock climbers   10
      like game little spiders
         on my local cliff

I've got no head for heights
   but plenty of stomach
      for trouble   15

trouble
   deep other-folks trouble
      to spark my engine
        and pay my mortgage

and private trouble   20
   oh, pretty trouble

to tidal-wave my bed

I'm waiting

I want you, trouble,
   on the rocks.   25

I'M FEMALE

I'm not tough,
   droll or stoical.

I droop
   after wine, sex
      or intense conversation.   5

The streets coil around me
    when they empty
I'm female
I get scared.

BLUE MOUNTAINS RECLUSE

I came for the quiet
I don't mind the cold

but thick mists
thick neighbours

and involuntary celibacy   5

are as inducive to hard drinking
as diesel fumes, high rent
and corrupt cops

I don't like bush walks
or Devonshire Teas   10

I can't remember what adrenalin
tastes like

I need Sydney
I need a new job.

MY CAR

My place is my car.

Peace. Action.
Business and pleasure.

The glove box
crammed with tapes   5

Patsy Cline twining round me
like a clove cigarette

my windows my work
I spy with my little eye

the cheating world.   10

THE NEW JOB

The phone's made of
foaming soap

I'm washing my hands

the phone's getting
smaller and smaller   5

but keeps ringing

ringing
it's the phone

christ, what's the time?
I wake up   10

too fast

the sun sharp
in the crack of the curtains

my feet freeze
as I pad to the phone   15

a woman's voice
pure North Shore[1]

her phone manners
taking forever

yes, I'm Jill Fitzpatrick   20
yes, I do Missing Persons

how nice a friend of your husband's
remembers me

from a little internal matter
with his solicitor   25

---

1   The well-to-do area of Sydney, on the northern side of the harbour.

cleared up nicely
client got his money back

father of six, Grand Mason Pooh-Bah
didn't go to gaol

yes, I remember   30
the hush money bonus

for a job discreetly done

and now the whole North Shore
loves me

so, Mrs Norris   35
you haven't seen your daughter

for how long?

                                                     1994

MICHAEL GOW
b. 1955

Playwright Michael Gow was born in Sydney and educated at the University of Sydney. His first play was *The Kid* (*1983*/1983); his second, *Away* (*1986*/1986), struck a chord with Australian theatregoers and educators and has been taught in schools and universities and regularly revived on stage. Set at the end of 1968, *Away* takes the ritual of an Australian 'Christmas away' by the beach, examining crises in the lives of three families and giving their intertwining stories the magical echoes and overtones of Shakespearean transformations and redemption.

Gow's plays *Europe* (*1987*/1987) and *1841* (*1988*/1988) examine Australia's relationship with the Old World; he joined many other Australian writers in choosing to examine Australian history in the Bicentennial year of 1988, for which *1841* had been commissioned by the Adelaide Festival of Arts. In recent years Gow has turned more to theatre directing and screenwriting, and has won major awards for both as well as for his stage plays. He adapted Henry Handel Richardson's (qv) classic Australian novel *The Fortunes of Richard Mahony* for the stage in 2002. *KG*

From *Away*
Act 4, Scene 1

The beach.
VIC, HARRY, JIM *and* GWEN.

VIC: The headland shelters the beach from the wind. You can sit round there under the rocks on the coolest day and be as hot as chips. There's a rockpool over there that's almost a perfect rectangle. You'd think it had been carved out by human hands. The bottom's covered in sand. Even I go in it and I'm terrified of what might be hiding in most rockpools. At the other end there's a cave that you can get into at low tide. It goes right in under that dairy on the hill, the one you drove past on the way in here. There's a track from the cave right up the cliff onto the headland. At night up there you can see the lights of the town, way, way over there and the lighthouse on the island. And past that headland there's a beach that must be, oh, five—?

HARRY: Five at least, seven—

VIC: Yes, seven miles long without a break. We walk around there for a picnic. You get halfway along and look back and there are just three lines of footprints trailing away into the distance. It's marvellous to sit in the middle of that beach, the three of us. Sometimes when it's really hot it's nice to slip your bathers off in the water and just swim about like a fish.

JIM: It is a lovely spot, isn't it?

[GWEN *nods unwillingly.*]

HARRY: And at the end of that beach there's a headland, a big rock platform. In the middle there's a carving in the rock. A man with a spear. And a big kangaroo. How old did that fellow say it was?

VIC: Five thousand years. At least.

HARRY: Five thousand years!

VIC: It is a wonderful place. And what a piece of luck you found it.

JIM: It was just chance, wasn't it?

[GWEN *nods again.*]

After that storm we salvaged what we could and dried it out. We thought we'd just go straight home. There didn't seem much point in carrying on after that washout. There doesn't seem to be a reason to carry on with your holiday when your van's a wreck, your boat's smashed on the rocks and all your clothes are soaked. But we tried to save something of the holiday and spent a few nights in this motel. It was a funny place. Run by this old cheese who wore thongs all the time. They were old thongs, very loose and you could hear her, flap, flap, flap, coming down the passageway. They'd stop for a second, then start again. I suppose she was listening at a door. I don't know what she thought people might be up to, the rooms were really tiny. We stuck it out for a couple of nights. But . . . we didn't enjoy it. It wasn't our sort of place. So we decided to head for home. We drove all day yesterday and we were getting pretty hot and tired and the girl suddenly pointed at a road sign and said we had to turn off the highway. She really wanted us to, kept insisting. So I turned the car around and drove back to the road sign and turned off down the dirt road. And when we came up over the last hill and saw the beach . . .

HARRY: Yes, you were very lucky.

VIC: And you got here in time for the campers' amateur night. It's how we end our holidays. It's a great night. You'll laugh till you're sick.

HARRY: It's a great way to end a holiday.

VIC: And it's been a wonderful holiday this year.

> [CORAL *enters in a flowing kaftan, dark glasses, a huge straw hat over a scarf.*]
> Look, there she is, the artist.
> [*She waves.* CORAL *goes out without seeing them.*]

Isn't she an interesting looking woman? She's been here a few days now. She just arrived one morning, all by herself. I think she might be an artist or something, so that's what I call her. She goes and sits on the rock ledge for hours and stares into the sea. She keeps to herself, right away from everyone. The world is full of interesting people.

GWEN: [*violently*] The world is full of mad people. Everywhere, mad people. Why do they have to live like that? Mad people, weird, sick, sordid people. How do they bear having no worthwhile aim? I'm tired of people who don't want to improve. I'm sick to death of people who are happy to just stay in the mud, in the swamp, just thrashing about, who don't try for a better life, to fight their way out with their bare hands. I hate them—they're happy in their filthy little holes like that motel—that was a nightmare!—I hate them. They're everywhere. Like ants, swarming everywhere, no direction, no ambition—

> [*She stifles herself. Silence.*]

VIC: I think we should go for a walk.

GWEN: No.

VIC: Us girls. Along the water.

GWEN: No.

VIC: Just a stroll. Come on.

JIM: Go on. Breathe some sea air.

> [*The women go. Silence for a while.*]

HARRY: Yes, you were lucky.

JIM: It was the girl's idea completely. She . . . my wife, gave up. She was very upset. But the girl kept on at me. She didn't let up until we were on that dirt road. She's a handful.

> [*Pause.*]

HARRY: This is a wonderful country. We're still not used to a hot Christmas.

JIM: My wife is not really an angry woman. She has high hopes.

HARRY: We have no regrets. We don't get homesick. Only once a year. We book a telephone call to our old street. In Nottingham. We get out the photo album. Remember for a while. But we have no regrets. This country . . . and often when we do think back, all we can think of is the cold, the tiny houses, the rationing, the rubble after the war. It was a rubbish dump. A lot wanted to stay and help to build again. But we didn't want to. We felt held back. We knew why the sailors had called it the Old World. It was like living with an elderly relative, tired, cranky, who doesn't want you to have any fun but just worry about their health all the time. Nagging you, criticising you, making you feel guilty for any enjoyment you might manage to find. No regrets. In a funny kind of way we're happy. Even while we're very, very sad. We have no regrets, but we have no hopes. Not any more. We might get some, but it's unlikely, I think. Our son is very sick. It's a cancer of the blood. He was very bad this year, we thought it was time to get ready. But he got through it. It's called 'in remission'. But it will come back. Every day we watch for bruises. Or to see if he's more tired than usual. We made it into another year at least. But we don't look forward. We haven't given up, no, no. That would be a mistake. We don't look back and we don't look forward. We have this boy and we won't have him for long. And whatever he does, that will have to be enough. The Chinese don't believe in being too upset when someone dies. That would mean you thought they'd died too soon and what they'd done up till then didn't amount to much. We will be sad, of course.

[*Silence.*]

JIM: I can't think of anything to say.

HARRY: Don't ever say anything about it. Ever. Give me your word.

JIM: I won't.

HARRY: He doesn't know. He won't know. We mustn't let him know. He must not be afraid. He must never suspect. He must look ahead even if we never do. Understand?

JIM: I promise.

HARRY: We don't tell most people. Very occasionally we run into someone who needs to know. But we don't tell very many. Did you manage to save your fishing gear?

JIM: A few reels. The rods were broken or washed away.

HARRY: What a pity.

[*The women come back. They have been crying and are supporting each other.*]

VIC: Here she is. I brought her back. The water's very warm today. We had a quick paddle.

[*Silence for a moment. They all look at each other.*]

HARRY: The boy wants some things in town for the show tonight. We'd better make tracks.

VIC: Come to the concert.

HARRY: Of course they will.

VIC: You'll have a wonderful night.

HARRY: They'll be there, won't you?

JIM: We'll be there.

[VIC *and* HARRY *go. Silence.*]

GWEN: If you want to ask me what I think or how I feel . . . I couldn't say.

JIM: I can guess.

GWEN: What do you think of me? You must hate me? Why do you still bother? I'm sorry . . . there are all these questions I want to ask. And not just you. Everybody.

JIM: Do you want to head off?

GWEN: Go home? No.

JIM: Do you feel all right?

GWEN: I feel . . . give me a drink.

[*He gets her one.*]

I feel . . . no, I can't say, I can't tell you. Those two people . . . what am I trying to say?

JIM: Here's your drink. Is your head aching?

GWEN: I'm not sure. What am I trying to say?

JIM: Don't worry yourself.

GWEN: I have to. I have to worry myself. What is it I'm trying to say?

JIM: You're over-tired.

GWEN: Don't protect me. Tell me what I'm feeling.

JIM: Shocked?

GWEN: Yes . . .

JIM: Amazed, sad?

GWEN: Not those things. They're so weak.

JIM: The girl would know. She'd hit the nail on the head.

[*She tries to take a Bex powder.*]

GWEN: I can't take this powder. I can't make it go in. I want to take it and it won't go in. I'm going to be sick.

JIM: Give it to me.

GWEN: There's a terrible taste in my mouth.

JIM: I'll get rid of it. Relax.

GWEN: I'm sorry.

JIM: You should lie down.

GWEN: No. Let's walk. Come on, down to the water. The water's so warm.

[*They go.*]

1986

GRAEME DIXON
b. 1955

Graeme Dixon, whose mother is Noongar from Katanning and whose father is an English migrant orphan, grew up at the now infamous Fairbridge Farm School in NSW. At the age of sixteen, Dixon was sent to Fremantle Prison where he spent most of the next nine years, and it was there that he began writing. His poetry collection *Holocaust Island* (1990) was the inaugural winner of the David Unaipon Award in 1989. He is also the author of *Holocaust Revisited: Killing time* (2003). *AH/PM*

Six Feet of Land Rights

If we never succeed in reclaiming our country
doomed to live life paying rent to the gentry
It would be a good thing if after our death day
for that six feet of earth we didn't have to pay
It would ease the pressure, on those of our kind 5
Poor, mourning, sad people, left living behind
It would make the last day easier to face
if that financial burden was lifted
from our poverty-ridden race
Then when the reaper comes 10
to switch off our lights
our souls may rest in peace, knowing
at last! Six feet of land rights.

1990

Holocaust Island

Nestled in the Indian Ocean
Like a jewel in her crown
The worshippers of Babel come
To relax and turn to brown
To recuperate from woe and toil 5
and leave their problems far behind
To practise ancient rituals
The habits of their kind

But what they refuse to realise
Is that in this little Isle 10
are skeletons in their cupboards
of deeds most foul and vile
Far beneath this Island's surface
In many an unmarked place
lie the remnants of forgotten ones 15
Kia, members of my race.

1990

ARCHIE ROACH
b 1955

The award-winning singer-songwriter Archie Roach was born at Mooroopna, south-west Victoria. In 1956 he and his family were moved to Framlingham Mission (near Warrnambool), after which Roach was removed from his family, placed in an orphanage and eventually fostered to a family that nurtured his interest in music. As a young man, Roach left his foster family and spent many years living on the streets as an alcoholic, attempting to find his family. Roach met up with Ruby Hunter, his lifelong partner, and together they have made a home for their children, continuing to make music. Based in Melbourne, their band The Altogethers was noticed by singer-songwriter Paul Kelly, who supported Roach's musical career and who co-produced his first album, *Charcoal Lane* (1990). Roach's 'Took the Children Away' became an iconic song of the stolen generation. Roach has released three further albums, and he features on the soundtrack to Rolf de Heer's film *The Tracker* (2002). In 2000 Roach filmed *Land of the Little Kings*, about the stolen generation, and worked with the Bangarra Dance Theatre on the production *Skin. AH/PM*

Took the Children Away

This story's right, this story's true
I would not tell lies to you
Like the promises they did not keep
And how they fenced us in like sheep
Said to us come take our hand   5
Sent us off to mission land
Taught us to read, to write and pray
Then they took the children away.

Took the children away
The children away   10
Snatched from their mother's breast
Said it was for the best
Took them away

The welfare and the policeman
Said you've got to understand   15
We'll give to them what you can't give
Teach them how to really live
Teach them how to live they said
Humiliated them instead
Taught them that and taught them this   20
And others taught them prejudice

You took the children away
The Children away
Breaking their mother's heart
Tearing us all apart   25
Took them away

One dark day on Framlingham
Came and didn't give a damn

My mother cried go get their dad
He came running fighting mad   30
Mother's tears were falling down
Dad shaped up, he stood his ground
He said you touch my kids and you fight me
And they took us from our family

Took us away   35
They took us away
Snatched from our mother's breast
Said this is for the best
Took us away

Told us what to do and say   40
Told us all the white man's ways
Then they split us up again
And gave us gifts to ease the pain
Sent us off to foster homes

As we grew up we felt alone   45
Cause we were acting white
Yet feeling black
One sweet day all the children came back
The children came back
The children came back   50
Back where their hearts grow strong
Back where they all belong
The children came back
Said the children came back
The children came back   55
Back where they understand
Back to their mother's land
The children came back

Back to their mother
Back to their father   60
Back to their sister
Back to their brother
Back to their people
Back to their land

All the children came back   65
The children came back
The children came back
Yes, I came back

                                        1990

GAIL JONES
b. 1955

Gail Jones was born in Harvey, WA, and was educated at the University of Western
Australia, where she became an associate professor, teaching literature, cinema and
cultural studies. Her first book was *The House of Breathing* (1992), a collection of short
stories, followed by another story collection, *Fetish Lives* (1997). Her first novel, *Black
Mirror*, appeared in 2002 and since then she has published three more novels: *Sixty Lights*
(2004), *Dreams of Speaking* (2006) and *Sorry* (2007). *Sixty Lights* won five major national
awards.

   Jones writes sophisticated fictions and metafictions whose subject matter is
often art and representation itself; her fiction frequently turns on questions of narrative,
language, history and modernity. She is also well known as a literary critic, essayist and
scholar. *KG*

Modernity
I

In the history of film there is this poignant tale. A young girl, visiting Moscow
from her home in Siberia, goes to the cinema to see her very first movie. She
is absolutely terror-stricken. Human beings are visually torn to pieces, the
heads thrown one way, the bodies another. Faces loom large or contract to
tiny circles. There are severed heads, multiple dismemberments, and horrible
discontinuities. The girl flees from the cinema, and as an incidental service
to the history of representation writes a letter to her father describing in
detail the shocking phenomenon she has witnessed.

The movie showing in that terror-causing Moscow cinema, in, let us say, the
bleak winter of 1920, was a comedy.

Imagine this girl. Imagine Siberia.

II

Integrity

In Siberia one knows one's body to be whole because the elements assail it
with a totalising force. The air is scintillatingly cold and algebraically precise;
there is a mathematical quality to its cutting of angles, its calculable degrees
of effect upon the skin, its common-denominative power, its below–zero
vital-statistics. In the Siberian cold one feels every extremity, is equated
instantaneously to the exactitude of each limb. Even in her favourite bearskin

hat, her sealskin coat and her fluffy muff of mink (a gift from the requisite doting Babushka who, in order to buy it, pawned an old grandfather clock from the time of the Tsars), the girl is still rudely recalled to her body. Decked in dead animals she remains feelingly human.

Space

She will push, this girl, through the virgin snow. She will push with her snowboots and her inadequate animal vestments through the all new hectares of still-astonishing white, hectares which, with the sun, will surely bedazzle. She will pass large larch trees hung ornamentally with serrations of ice. Wolf prints sprinkle a pocked track to somewhere. And, looking backwards, she confirms absolutely her own foot-printing pathway.

Space is the lack of conclusion to her horizons. It is the perspectival extensiveness of the trans-Siberian railway, metallically trailing. It is the ample dimensions of snow on snow, so emphatically brilliant that she must squint to discern her journey through every single step of its immaculate empire.

Time

She knows, as we think we all do, time's unamenable incessancy. The clock that used to stand in her grandmother's bedroom ticked in totalitarian and purposive circles. Its hands were definitive, its face as indisputable and blandly commanding as a uniformed apparatchik.

Her grandmother's voice is another aspect of time. Since the death of her mother (a premature extinction in an unromantic snowstorm), this voice is to the girl a regular and reliable instatement of order. Next summer, says Babushka. Last winter, says Babushka. When I was a child of six or seven . . . She manages the continuum. There is never any doubting the steady progress to next summer. The larch trees await. The very landscape is bound to perpetual and carefully demarcated mobility. And history itself—by government decree—will later submit to subsections of Five Year Plans.

Setting

Of her home nothing is left to the risks of fiction. It is completely actual and labelled everywhere. The town the girl lives in is called Turukhansk and it sits, in a smug and geographical certainty, at the fork of the Yenisey and Nizhnyaya rivers.

The girl knows this place as she knows her own body; that is to say, with coy particularity. There are parts of the town intimate as her hands, the cobbled alleyway to school, a handsome bowed bridge, the cavities of the market place; specifically a small bakery that, apart from the usual and all-too-familiar black bread, sells light and dainty pastries displayed with memorable panache in its gas-luminous window. There are also unmentionable places and habitations, but she knows these exist as surely as she knows of her own definite but impossibly unregardable heart.

Density

Solid, so solid, is the world of Turukhansk. Once, just once, the girl rode on a speeding troika right out of the town and to the furthest, ice-burdened limits of the world.

There were three snorting horses of massive rotundity—flanks, bellies, the head's bulbous cheeks—and they strove through snow that stirred up in wild eddies and stung incisively. She could feel the muscular energy and rhythm of their gallop; she could see the long heads bobbing and the rim of broad rumps shifting and moving in concert. The breath of the horses was powerfully visible, their odour profound. Bells were atinkle on leather harnesses.

And her father, who seemed himself suddenly newly substantial and corporeal, expanded, upholstered, assuming the impressiveness of horse-flesh, reached over and clasped her in an exhilarated embrace.

Narrative

Do not think that this girl from Siberia is uneducated. Each winter-starless night she follows Cyrillic intricacies stretching in long lines into the mythological soul-land of her Mother Russia. There is the omnipresent bible (Russian in tone), there are the national novels of great solemnity, and there are numerous folktales, all enchanting and instructive. Hers is a country both—contradictorily—filled up with stories and sensationally material. And from her Babushka comes the knowledge of other realms: that she is superintended by the unquiet ghost of her mother, by the never-ending story of family melodramas, by plots of kin.

Sometimes this girl will weep in the dark, not for the banal complications of adolescence, but for the burden of narratives she is compelled to bear, for inner insurgencies clashing with no less force than the Red Armies with the White.

Identity

You will have seen the wooden dolls for which Siberia is famous, dolls which sit, one inside the other, in a series of smaller and smaller otherwise identical versions. These dolls give the girl an image of self: she may be different with, say, Babushka and father, but these selves are all uniform, and neatly composed and contained. She has the conservative's assurance of inner conformity. She knows her self-sameness. Symmetries abound. In the mirror, unquestionably, is her exact adequation.

As she lies awake in the early morning, watching the crystals of snowflakes alight and dispose themselves dawn-lit and lace-wise upon the glass of her window, the girl thinks often of the dolls, one inside the other. She likes to imagine that her absent mother was also, in some way, a kind of replica of herself, that she is constant in image and form even through the passage of generations. By this means she staves off the fracturing power of grief.

Voices

Apart from the management of time and the deployment of story the girl loves the act of voice for its invisible tendernesses.

As Babushka rakes charcoal beneath the samovar she sings in sweet inflections so sonorous and pathetic that her granddaughter, enthralled, feels brimful of emotions. The songs seem to invade her; she swells at their presence. There are neatly rhymed couplets and poetic descriptions of perfect Romances and yearning Love. Language carries within it an irresistible tangibility.

Occasionally, by yellow candlelight, her father takes up a book and reads aloud from the works in translation of his favourite English poet. Once he read of a mad king caught foolishly in a storm and the girl realised, in a moment of vision, that the entire world was Russian, that its rhetorics and its extremity had somehow mysteriously extended to the four corners of the globe. From her father's voice came universality. From the movements of his tongue world-wide concordance.

Bodies

There is a man in Turukhansk so large in circumference that he is reputed to have cut a semi-circle in his mahogany dining table, simply to accommodate his ungainly girth. Babushka loves this story. She is interested in bodies and talks of them continuously. Illnesses. Births. Deaths. Copulations.

The girl touches her own shape with concupiscent affection. She enjoys her baby-fat and her enlargening breasts. She imagines kisses on the bowed bridge and embraces beneath the larch trees. And once every year, when she has a chance to partake of dainty pastries, she recalls the man so large that he must cut out the world in the pattern of his belly.

When the girl leaves to go outside her grandmother offers, customarily, an ancient folk saying: *Rug yourself well or the wind will enter your body and blow away your soul.* This is a disturbing thought. The girl steps into the cold, into its white-blue squalls, hugging her own garments as if they could provide an adhesive to hold her together. In the cold she knows her body better than anywhere else.

Faces

These are indubitable. She studies faces. To see them together you would say that the girl was in love with her father. She gazes up at his face as he reads the latest broadsheet on the trouble in the Stanovoy and Ozhugdzhur mountains. She regards with lover-propinquity his Semitic nose and his brown hooded eyes. She dwells on the crinkles of his balding hair, is captivated by the peaked configuration of his lips. The grandmother, nearby, is of distinctly unSemitic and peasantish visage, but as utterly intimate.

One can kiss these faces. These faces can be clasped between two cradling hands. These faces come with the ponderous and heavy-weighted import of presence.

III

In the especially harsh winter of 1920 our heroine visited for the first time her father's family in Moscow. She descended from the world-famous trans-Siberian railway and fell into the arms of a second, unknown and much wealthier Babushka, a woman who wore about the neck an entire flattened fox, depending sadly nose-downwards.

There was the speed of a slow car, unfathomable chatter, and then the girl realised, incontrovertibly, that she was surrounded by the city. It was a place in which a palpable post-revolutionary unease was contested, again palpably, by a more inveterate aura of historical stolidity. It was a place, that is, in which one might expect dissimilarities and dissimulations.

Faces blurred past. Tall buildings loomed. Red flags, in their hundreds, gestured and stirred.

The visit to the cinema came in the second week. This is what happened. The new grandmother unwisely sent her charge in alone. She equipped her with a handful of roubles and kopeks and left her there at the entrance, a mere babe, as it were, in technological woods.

The girl entered a little late and was perplexed by the darkness. There were straight rows of people—somewhat like those assembled for the pantomime at home—but ahead, inexplicably, was not the space for dramatic action but a rectangle of snowy screen. It stretched across the wall, pure and auspicious. The girl took her modest place among the rows of spectators, of whom she knew not one, and patiently waited. Somewhere to the left a man began slowly playing an inconspicuous piano. Then there was a soft whirring sound behind, like the wind in the eaves, or the wing beat of cabbage-moths, and a long cone of white light shot instantly above her head. This was a bright enlightenment, newfangled, stunning, a distillation of incandescence too shiningly imperious to appear in any way artificial. It might almost have been some kind of Divine Revelation, the trajectory, perhaps, of a passing angel, a signal through space, the pointing finger of God. The girl felt her girl's body tense up intolerably. There was a sensation in her chest of flight and flutter. And then, before another single second had a chance to pass by, there were Russian-letter titles (mysteriously writ), displayed broadly and boldly upon the screen. So that was it. A type of large book. A system of pages. Communal reading.

The piano player pounded a crass fortissimo.

What followed was devastating. The titles gave way to a regime at once human and strikingly inhuman. By some dreadful magic the players appeared to have been robbed of both colour and regularity. Their faces and clothes were crepuscular grey, and their sizes expanded and diminished with awful elasticity. Moreover they moved wholly within the frame of the rectangle; they did not seem to inhabit any ordinary space. It was some condition of suspension within which bodies were dangled upon the screen in a peculiar coalition of living-semblance and deathly, wraith-like abstraction. Thus transfixed these victims were rendered mute; they cavorted in dumbshow, mouthed words ineffectually, produced verbal nothings.

(And rising above the piano was the almost deafening sound of a battering heart-beat.)

It was at the point when the very first close-up occurred, presenting, in the blink of an eye, a gargantuan decapitation, that the girl suddenly comprehended what it was that she saw. It was her mother's death. As the cruel Siberian wind cuts and slices, so too this dissection of the human body. This was how, in her imaginings, she had figured the long-ago maternal dissolution; that a woman, snow-bleached and lacking in the gust-resisting weight of the living, lacking the heaviness of fat men who create the world in their own shape, lacking the cosy enclosure of animal garments, the density of horses, the authority of Babushka, the accessible face, had submitted to execution by the Tundra winds. Bits of her body had exploded into the tempest, dis-assembled, sundered. Bits of her body had become indivisible from the blurring snow; her inner warmth was ransacked and replaced by cold, her face obliterated, her cry silenced, her soul blown away. In the terrible pelting of the pitiless storm her houseless head was blasted, rendered hollow and windowed as the carcass of a doll. Wracked. Wrecked. Breathtakingly undone.

The girl from Siberia sitting, bolt upright, in the fourth row from the front was completely terror-stricken. There, caught uncannily on the unreal screen, with its distortions of scale and time, its slow dissolves, its clever montage, she had faced in chimerical vision her own perilous vulnerability.

She fled from the cinema, her screams piano-accompanied.

IV

This was a moment of modernity. All that had been solid melted into air. Not electricity or the revolution, not plane travel or radio, but the cinema had inaugurated a new order of perception. The girl of the story was not, as it happened, called Anna Akhmatova or Marina Tsvetaeva, but like the poets she had experienced the metaphysics of fragments. She ran screaming into the winter light of the city of Moscow carrying in her head an unprecedented multiplicity.

Yet when the girl returned home, when she arrived in the arms of her real Babushka—expecting at last to retell the dreadful vision, to collapse, to cry, to blubberingly divulge—it was not cinematic disintegration she described. She did not tell of the deranged and incoherent bodies of the players, nor of how these recalled to her a personal haunting. Instead she dwelled, in concentration, on single detail: there had been a cone of bright light, a white passageway of floating motes, delicate, enchanting, apparently transcendental, which might, after all, have somehow mystically signified the transit of angels.

1992

PETER ROSE
b. 1955

Peter Rose grew up in Wangaratta, Victoria. His father was Bob Rose, the famous player and coach of Collingwood Football Club. As described in his memoir *Rose Boys* (2001), Rose's brother Robert had his sporting career cut short after a car accident that left him a paraplegic. Peter Rose chose a literary career, beginning in bookselling, becoming a publisher for Oxford University Press (Melbourne) and, in 2001, the editor of *Australian Book Review*. Rose has written a novel, as well as four collections of poetry, including *Rattus Rattus: New and selected poems* (2005). Often complex, ironic and allusive, Rose's poetry can also be satirical, as seen in his discontinuous 'Catullan' sequence, which imitates the Roman poet Catullus in a contemporary mode. *DM*

Donatello in Wangaratta

It is a kind of speculative night,
the room so close and populous,
resonant with every rover in the town.
A butcher who is all Adam's apple
stammers for a joke. There's talk of
stratagems and cakewalks; some triumph
is intended or delayed. Dumb,
I wake from a terrible gulping sleep,

5

dreams of an antic pogrom,
the goanna we hacked that afternoon   10
and threw beheaded in a box.
How we gathered in the dream and in the life—
a posse of us, myself as scout,
surprising it dozing on a fence;
my father, too, awoken from untimely sleep,   15
singleted in the afternoon, but dutiful.
Then we all looked up and saw,
saw goanna flinching on a wall,
beautiful as the tattooed Icarus
with his methodical axe.   20
Then sleep, sleep for sleep's sake,
a chant of wasps around a bush
and something leaking in its blood.
Returned blinking to that room
I choose the bonhomie of women,   25
shades of Swan Street circling
in a sugary alliance. One
I recognize is bearing meringues,
spectacular in their dollopery,
hanging like perilous, illustrated towers.   30
It must be night, or something obscurer,
ill-defined, say five o'clock,
the light beginning to wane
and something toppling in the fire.
Whose bored hand on the pianola,   35
strumming not ivory but case?
Whose handsome wrist drawing me
to the isolating performance?
Impatient of music, the pedal of tactics,
childlike despite yourself,   40
despite your height, your dark evidence,
you finger my new red Caxton encyclopedia,
perplexed at such a gift (for I am six),
turn the page, a robe on enlightenment,
reveal David[1] gleaming, audacious,   45
uniting us in his slim mimicry.
And suddenly the room is alight,
fired with its own brazen iconography,

---

1   A bronze statue (c. 1440s) by the Italian artist Donatello (c. 1386–1466).

silencing and separating as it unites—
hieroglyphics of blood,   50
sprays of instinct on a wall—
reshaped in its own tense and furtive imagery.

1998

From *Rose Boys*
Chapter 1: Scrapbooks

AUGUST 22, 2000. In an upstairs study in Adelaide, the bells of the neighbouring cathedral blessedly still, strong coffee at the ready, I open my brother's old scrapbook. It is just one of several I have brought with me. Curious documents: these bibles of scrap, collages of self-delight. I have never kept one myself. That would be a thin volume anyway. Perhaps my diaries, stacked in a trunk, fill that need. I will draw on them, too, as I contemplate my brother.

I open his scrapbook at random. It parts at a front-page story drawn from the Melbourne *Herald* of 15 February 1974. The old gothic masthead is sallow with age but full of information. The newspaper, costing six cents, seven by air, comprises thirty-eight pages—quite puny, I think. There are no lifestyle or gourmet or computer sections to bolster it. After a long career in publishing, editing thumping dictionaries and reference books, I find thirty-eight pages innocent, pamphlet-like.

But there is nothing derisory about the circulation, proudly advertised to the right—'495 133 daily sales'. Quaintly, beneath the masthead, there is a telephone number, with six digits. I want to ring it. I want to speak to someone there. Perhaps I would get through to a night editor, lighting another cigarette, waiting for a disaster. The front page, neatly clipped and stuck in the scrapbook, is eclectic and prompts reflections about 1974. Patty Hearst had just been kidnapped. Brandt and Brezhnev, Heath and Franco, Trudeau and Tito—all those fascists and bourgeois reactionaries we vilified at school—were in power. Richard Nixon hung on grimly after Watergate. Billy Snedden, incredibly, was Australia's alternative prime minister.

The front page is dominated by a photograph of a white Volkswagen. It is a confronting image, for the car has been badly damaged, its front crushed. I don't recognise the pale weatherboard house in the background. I wonder how the Volkswagen got there, who moved it. The car's roof, like the numberplate, is missing. A caption tells me it was removed when they freed the driver. Both doors are open. I wonder if the radio is still playing, the horn wailing unstoppably. The lights are missing and the bumper bar lies buckled on the ground. It all reminds me of one of those expensive crumpled sculptures you see outside office towers.

The bonnet is stained with oil or paint from a passing truck. Bits of metal poke out dangerously. A man in short sleeves, posed by the anonymous photographer, stands by the passenger door. He peers into the car in a kind of stupor. Judging by his Brylcreemed hair, muscular arms and stern mien, he lives in the country. I wonder what he saw in the wreckage. I want to ask him what was left. Cigarette butts? The Ballarat racing guide? Myriad sporting pages? Crushed cans of soft drink, beer? A thin suede tie for formal occasions? A baby's dummy, spat out during some weekend outing? Pizza containers? Pizza, even?

My eyes, blank as the short-sleeved witness's, avoid the long accompanying report on the front page. I am not ready for that yet. But I note the weighting of the main headline and the awkward construction: 'ROSE PARALYSED IN CAR ROLL'. It sounds almost contradictory, like a pratfall. There are three other smaller headings—'Trapped for 90 minutes', 'At races', 'Sedation'—plus three photographs of the victim. In one, weedily moustached, he grins at the camera. In another, longer-haired, he cuts a cricket ball to the boundary. In the bottom one, taken during his schooldays, he kicks a football with an intensity that reminds me of a much earlier photograph. His young wife is there too, near my father, who looks away.

Next to this clipping is a front-page story from the *Australian* of the same day. This headline is blunt: 'CRICKET, FOOTBALL STAR IS PARALYSED'. Subheadings tell me that Dad was hastening to join him and that sympathisers had already sent money. There are two photographs of Robert. In one he defends his wicket with a characteristically straight bat. The top one, much larger, is arresting. A handsome young man with fair hair and a five o'clock shadow stares at the camera. Lips parted, eyes wide open, he seems shocked to find himself in this company. So profound is his surprise I almost expect his prominent Adam's apple to gulp.

But something is wrong—or should I say, more wrong? This is not the right face. It's not the paralysed cricket, football star we know. He is not, in short, my brother. In their haste the sub-editors chose an image from the wrong photo file.

Nevertheless, I knew our startled interloper, Dennis O'Callaghan. He played football for Collingwood while Dad was coach. A quiet young man, he never expected to end up on a front page, headlined and paralysed.

It was the first mistake.

Not that Dennis O'Callaghan wasn't accident-prone. I vividly remember one mishap at our house. This was after the 1970 grand final, in which Dennis played. I had often wondered how my parents' new spindly olive-green Scandinavian Fleur lounge suite would stand up to the weight of all those footballers. It seemed too fine, too chic. I fancied that we would find out that night, given the chaotic atmosphere.

My parents had arranged the party before the grand final. Everyone, even the knockers, expected it to be a celebration. Collingwood, coached by my father, had a superb team that year. After two narrow losses in recent grand finals, a premiership seemed inevitable. Carlton, under Ron Barassi, was no less talented, but Collingwood had beaten them three times that season, including the second semi-final.

Things went according to plan during the first half of the grand final. By half-time Collingwood led by almost eight goals. Peter McKenna already had five. But he had also collided with his bullish team-mate Des Tuddenham a few minutes before half-time. McKenna was seriously concussed and shouldn't have played on. Tuddenham wasn't untouched, either. Ron Barassi didn't know this, of course, but he did have an idea. It was called handball, handball, handball.

Many furphies surround that most famous of grand finals. One has it that Collingwood started opening the champagne during half-time. Dad denies this. He was too worried about the injuries to his stars. Play resumed. The second half was calamitous and horrible to watch. Carlton surged forward and overwhelmed Dennis O'Callaghan and the other defenders. Barassi's rejuvenated handballers snatched victory in the last few minutes. Collingwood, unbelievably, had lost.

After the game my mother and I fought our way through the despondent/ triumphant mob to get to the rooms. Our progress was slow, for it was a record crowd—121 696 people. My brother wasn't with us. A huge crowd had assembled outside the rooms. Later, George Harris, Carlton's provocative president, damned the club by saying that its supporters heckled the players as they emerged. I very much doubt this. Everyone was too busy crying. I myself was devastated by the result. Apparently I became so upset during the final quarter, as Carlton overhauled Collingwood, that my maths teacher, who was sitting with us, became worried about me. He rang up later that night to find out how I was. I'm surprised that we heard the telephone above the din.

The atmosphere at the party was shaky at first. Most of the guests were in bad shape. A kind of collective shock had stunned people. No one remembers when the party got under way. Dad thinks we called at the club en route to our house in Lemana Crescent, but he can't be sure. Peter McKenna doesn't even recall playing in the second half, let alone the aftermath. When Martin Flanagan interviewed 'Twiggy' Dunne for his book *1970*, Twiggy remembered playing billiards at my parents' house. We didn't own a billiard table.

Our small house was soon overflowing. I had never seen so many people seriously out of control. All of fifteen, I knew it was going to be a great party. The noise was impressive as people began to relax. They had dressed up. Several of the women were wearing lace-up hotpants with long leather boots. The players removed their official ties and blazers. A business acquaintance of my father chainsmoked in a corner, using our television's teak top as an ashtray. His wife, considerably younger and taller than he, wore a tight-fitting leopard-skin dress. She reminded me of Ava Gardner, of whom I had seen photographs in my movie magazines. She had long dark hair and a majestic throat. It takes a lot to turn footballers' heads, especially when they have just lost a grand final in bitter circumstances, but the leopard skin seemed to work.

Well after midnight, my mother went into the kitchen and began mopping the floor, which was under several inches of champagne. 'Christ, Elsie, you're fussy!' someone said. Meanwhile, a sophisticate in a little black dress sat on our matching teak gramophone and played Mum's EP of Sinatra's 'My Way' over and over again, as if it were the only record we owned. My brother, smoking and drinking on the balcony with his mates, must have been desperate to play Led Zeppelin, Jimi Hendrix or the incomparable Cream.

The party lasted all night. It was still going in the morning when Dad left to appear on *World of Sport*, a mandatory Sunday morning commitment for coaches. Dad hadn't slept at all. Nowadays, a tennis player, defeated so mortifyingly, would avoid such an interview, happily incurring a ten thousand dollar fine, but Dad felt he had to 'front up'.

Just as the interview began, Lou Richards and Jack Dyer, two of the programme's hosts, came up with an unsubtle mock-rendition of Collingwood's theme song. They were off-camera but quite audible. 'Good Old Collingwood for Never,' they sang merrily. The interview went ahead but when it was over Dad went looking for Lou, who had been his captain when Collingwood won the 1953 premiership. Dad, a former boxer, intended to confront his old team-mate. He went right through the television studio but couldn't find Lou, who had disappeared.

That afternoon, when it was all over, we cleaned up. While Dad, Robert and I surveyed the heap of empty bottles and Scandinavian kindling, Mum polished the kitchen floor and tried to disguise the burn marks on the teak television. Domestic order swiftly regained, Mum knew she had to get Dad away from the media, and from himself. They packed a few things and drove around Victoria for several days, stopping at a different motel each night. One evening they found themselves in Gippsland and had dinner in a small timber town. The waitress recognised Dad but couldn't think of his name. Perplexed, she kept asking him who he was. He didn't enlighten her. Meanwhile Robert and I stayed at home with the dog. Years later, during an interview, Robert recalled that the house was like a morgue for days.

We thought it couldn't get any worse than that. We thought it was one of those tragedies they write about so freely in the sporting pages. We wondered if Dad would recover from such a perverse loss.

But had he courted defeat? I remembered something he had said after the 1966 grand final, which Collingwood had lost by one point. Dad gave a press conference that night. During it he wondered aloud, in his self-deprecating way, if he was jinxed. He later regretted this speculation, for it stuck. By 1970, after three grand final defeats in bizarre circumstances, people were beginning to believe him.

Three decades later, studying Dennis O'Callaghan's amazed and likeable face in Robert's scrapbook, I can still picture him and a fellow backman crammed on the chic Fleur sofa with their girlfriends. And I can still remember the sound it made when it collapsed, sending the four of them toppling onto the floor. People laughed at them and joked about the Rose jinx. The end, as Frank Sinatra repeatedly sang, was near. Everyone agreed it was ironic. Dennis and his mate, the dispirited defenders, were the quietest people at the party.

And I wonder what Dennis O'Callaghan's mother thought that morning, four years later, when, alerted by some bewildered relative, she went out and bought the *Australian* and saw her son's photograph beneath the brutal headline.

2001

OUYANG YU
b. 1955

Ouyang Yu was born in China's Hubei province and educated at Wuhan University and East China Normal University before moving to Melbourne in 1991, where he completed a doctorate on representations of Chinese in Australian literature at LaTrobe University. Ouyang writes, translates and self-translates in English and Chinese. Best known as a poet, he has also published controversial fiction and criticism. His poetry adopts complex and experimental strategies to explore his experience as a writer who moves between cultures. Since 2005 he has spent part of each year at Wuhan University, where he is professor of Australian Literature. Collections include *Moon over Melbourne: Poems* (1995), *Songs of the Last Chinese Poet* (1997) and *New and Selected Poems* (2004). *NJ*

The Ungrateful Immigrant

If you are looking for one
Don't look further for he is here
Writing the poem about the hows and the whys and the nos

You expect me to be integrated into the mainstream
I don't care although I become a citizen   5
Not to strengthen your national identity as you like to think

But in order to travel more freely in the rest of the world
You expect me to speak English and write English
Which I can do but not so that you think I am English

But to do just what I am doing here   10
Writing poems that do not sit comfortably with your
Another day another dollar mentality and nationality

You think that because I came to and live in Australia
I should be grateful for the rest of my life
But you don't know that I already regret that I've made an irreversible
    mistake   15

And you have made a mistake, too, I think
Because years ago you promoted Australia in our country so aggressively
Why not be honest and say: We don't fucking want you Asians, PERIOD!

And you know what I think you should do to make me grateful?
Strip me of my citizenship and send me back to China in forced
    repatriation   20
Like you have done to so many of them

You think I am serious?
Of course I am not
What do you reckon?

                                                                       2004

Listening to the Chinese Woman Philosopher

In Campsie, Sydney, I met a non-stop Chinese
Woman philosopher who questioned me sharply if I knew anything
About philosophy and did not wait for me to finish pretending
When she said:

This mathematical shape is square   5
Containing many different numbers
When enlarged infinitely you can see that it largely remains square
Although inside it there is infinite change
One tiny detail turning into a myriad of forms
That's what I call can know and cannot know   10
You can never say you can know you can never say you cannot know
For a drop of water reflects seven colours of the sun
And the intricate lines on the palm of a hand

Tell about your previous life and after life
Just like your own identity is enshrined in your fingerprint   15
Just like your innermost secret is found in a swab of the inside of your mouth
Just like this doctor I know who can diagnose your hidden diseases in
     your eyeball
A kind of miniature map of Sydney

'and just like a fingertip, a toe or a blade of grass,' I offered
'that can offer us access to a world of infinite possibilities or secrets   20
if we can find a way to read it?'

'yes,' the Chinese woman philosopher said
as the night outside became suddenly loud
with raindrops, each luring me to explore its difference from the other
                                                                              2005

GIG RYAN
b 1956

Born in England, Gig Ryan grew up in Melbourne. Ryan has worked a number of casual jobs and been the recipient of several fellowships. A well-known poet, Ryan is also a singer-songwriter, and has been a member of the bands Disband and Driving Past. Since 1998 she has been the poetry editor of the *Age*. Ryan's books include *The Division of Anger* (1980), *Pure and Applied* (1998) and *Heroic Money* (2001). Her poetry is satirical, oblique and inhabited by scraps of discourse. Often employing the monologue, Ryan's verse can be characterised as angry and erudite, political and sensate. *DM*

If I Had a Gun

I'd shoot the man who pulled up slowly in his hot car this
                                 morning
I'd shoot the man who whistled from his balcony
I'd shoot the man with things dangling over his creepy chest
in the park when I was contemplating the universe   5
I'd shoot the man who can't look me in the eye
who stares at my boobs when we're talking
who rips me off in the milk-bar and smiles his wet purple smile
who comments on my clothes. I'm not a fucking painting
that needs to be told what it looks like.   10
who tells me where to put my hands, who wrenches me into
                                 position
like a meccano-set, who drags you round like a war
I'd shoot the man who couldn't live without me

I'd shoot the man who thinks it's his turn to be pretty   15
flashing his skin passively like something I've got
to step into, the man who says *John's a chemistry Phd*
and an ace cricketer, Jane's got rotten legs
who thinks I'm wearing perfume for him
who says *Baby you can really drive* like it's so complicated,   20
male, his fucking highway, who says *ah but you're like that*
and pats you on the head, who kisses you at the party because
everybody does it, who shoves it up like a nail
I'd shoot the man who can't look after himself
who comes to me for wisdom   25
who's witty with his mates about heavy things
that wouldn't interest you, who keeps a little time
to be human and tells me, female, his ridiculous
private thoughts. Who sits up in his moderate bed
and says *Was that good* like a menu   30
who hangs onto you sloppy and thick as a carpet
I'd shoot the man last night who said *Smile honey*
don't look so glum with money swearing from his jacket
and a 3-course meal he prods lazily
who tells me his problems: his girlfriend, his mother,   35
his wife, his daughter, his sister, his lover
because women will listen to that sort of rubbish
Women are full of compassion and have soft soggy hearts
you can throw up in and no-one'll notice
and they won't complain. I'd shoot the man   40
who thinks he can look like an excavation-site
but you can't, who thinks what you look like's for him
to appraise, to sit back, to talk his intelligent way.
I've got eyes in my fucking head. Who thinks if he's smart
he'll get it in. I'd shoot the man who said   45
Andrew's dedicated and works hard, Julia's ruthlessly ambitious
who says *I'll introduce you to the ones who know*
with their inert alcoholic eyes
that'll get by, sad, savage, and civilised
who say *you can* like there's a law against it   50
I'd shoot the man who goes stupid
in his puny abstract how-could-I-refuse-she-needed-me
taking her tatty head in his neutral arms like a pope
I'd shoot the man who pulled up at the lights
who rolled his face articulate as an asylum   55
and revved the engine, who says *you're paranoid*

with his educated born-to-it calm
who's standing there wasted as a rifle
and explains the world to me. I'd shoot the man who says
Relax honey come and kiss my valium-mouth blue.   60
                                                                    1980

Hay Fever

She packed a tizz
when the *Surprise* rang out
I'd rather be on my indoor trampoline
striving. I mean cancel the cake OK?
Friends mug around the door like a tent   5
and yeah I jammed into my jeans and pearls
but look around, a bunch of sores I don't,
exponentially, want. And then Trace came
with all his postponed options like some massive RDO[1]
I had to stat or impinge   10
I mean it's my party You can go coruscate
and braid your hair or lounge

The way he hasn't the faintest
and then out of nowhere gasps out of a shop
larger than life or near it   15
You always know the arid tarmac of return
where all your green drive dissipates
in jars of rent or slush
I thought it might amuse him but instead
mistaking valour for gravity he wept   20
Maroon trees brush nylon air
birds beseech and caw
                                                                    1998

Critique of Pure Reason

It's touché to the second form of boredom
your unpronounceable library
cascading errors and warbling trees
I write them back
and ask for the Portuguese dictionary   5
lost and empty in the hour of plight

---

1   Rostered Day Off.

Your name flaps outside the newsagent
Titanic books sink without a trace
Outside, beautiful purpose reigns
and sombre ducts excising air   10
As if you look into a clogged basin of horrible truth
lights tasselled through the CBD's thoroughfares
in the stripped-car street
introducing the documentary of itself
History slides off the television   15

2001

PAT TORRES
b. 1956

Born in Broome, WA, Pat Torres is a writer, artist, illustrator, community worker, health worker, educator and Aboriginal administrator. Since 1987 she has published autobiographical works, stories for children, poetry and critical writing, and is involved in recording Aboriginal oral history in the Kimberley. *AH/PM*

Gurrwayi Gurrwayi, The Rain Bird

Gurrwayi Gurrwayi
It's the Rain bird call,
Don't hurt him or kill him,
Or the rain will always fall.

Gurrwayi Gurrwayi
Gawinaman jina gambini bandalmada.
Malu minabilga gamba bandalmada.
Galiya yiljalgun wula widu jayida.

1987

Wangkaja, The Mangrove Crab

Wangkaja, the mangrove crab,
His meat is so good to eat.
Hiding under the muddy sand,
Look out it's under your feet.

Mabu warli wangkaja miliya.
Ingadin jimbin jabarlbarl burrgadja ingan niminy.
Niwalgun juyu wangkaja ingan
jabarlbarl ingan walabunda juyu.

1987

MANDAWUY YUNUPINGU
b. 1956

A Yolngu man of the Gumatj clan, Yunupingu was born at Yirrkala in Arnhem Land, NT. His father was a signatory to the 1963 Yirrkala Bark Petition, and he was raised in a politically active environment. He gained his teaching certificate in 1977, started teaching at the Yirrkala Community School, and was the first Yolngu person to earn a university degree, graduating with a Bachelor of Arts (Education) from Deakin University in 1988. He was assistant principal of the Yirrkala Community School from 1989 and its principal from 1990; he became a leader in the 'both-ways' curriculum, teaching both Yolngu and European cultures. While teaching, Yunupingu also wrote songs and in 1985 he co-founded the music band Yothu Yindi (Yolngu for 'child and mother') with his nephew Witiyana Marika. Yothu Yindi's second album *Tribal Voice* (1991) was extremely successful, its hit single 'Treaty' (co-written by the band with Paul Kelly and Midnight Oil's Peter Garrett) topping the charts as a focal point for popular awareness of Aboriginal social justice. On 26 January 1993, Yunupingu was named Australian of the Year by the National Australia Day Council. He continues to make music and is a significant contributor to Aboriginal cultural and political life. *AH/PM*

Treaty

Well I heard it on the radio
And I saw it on the television
Back in 1988, all those talking politicians
Words are easy, words are cheap
Much cheaper than our priceless land   5
But promises can disappear
Just like writing in the sand

Treaty yeah treaty now treaty yeah treaty now

Nhima djatpangarri nhima walangwalang
Nhe djatpayatpa nhima gaya' nhe marrtjini yakarray   10
Nhe djatpa nhe walang
Gumurr-djararrk Gutjuk

This land was never given up
This land was never bought and sold
The planting of the Union Jack   15
Never changed our law at all
Now two rivers run their course
Separated for so long
I'm dreaming of a brighter day
When the waters will be one   20

Treaty yeah treaty now treaty yeah treaty now

Nhima gayakaya nhe gaya' nhe
Nhe gaya' nhe marrtjini walangwalang nhe ya
Nhima djatpa nhe walang
Gumurr-djararrk yawirriny'   25

Nhe gaya' nhe marrtjini gaya' nhe marrtjini
Gayakaya nhe gaya' nhe marrtjini walangwalang
Nhima djatpa nhe walang
Gumurr-djararrk nhe yå

Promises disappear—priceless land—destiny   30
Well I heard it on the radio
And I saw it on the television

But promises can be broken
Just like writing in the sand

Treaty yeah treaty now treaty yeah treaty now   35
Treaty yeah treaty now treaty yeah treaty now
Treaty yeah treaty ma treaty yeah treaty ma
Treaty yeah treaty ma treaty yeah treaty ma

1991

JUDITH BEVERIDGE
b. 1956

Judith Beveridge was born in London and migrated with her family to Australia in 1960. She attended the University of Technology, Sydney, and has held a number of part-time jobs, allowing her to concentrate on her poetry. Her three collections—*The Domesticity of Giraffes* (1987), *Accidental Grace* (1996) and *Wolf Notes* (2003)—have received wide praise and numerous awards. She became poetry editor of *Meanjin* in 2005. Her poetry is marked by technical control, intense clarity and imagistic brilliance. Her sequence 'Between the Palace and the Bodhi Tree' (from *Wolf Notes*) powerfully recreates the time that Siddhartha spent wandering before achieving enlightenment and becoming the Buddha. *DM*

Yachts

They are the sound of teacups wheeled off,
of a woolly butt's littlest birds rattling
song-bottles in all its sun-tiered racks.

And if you can imagine brittle bells
fiddled with and shaken, if you can hear   5
a woman placing her earrings in a pearl

shell, if you can hear the chime from
a lacquered box at the gateway to a Palace,
if you can hear the feet of a bird on tin

shingles in the depth of an agate sky,   10
then you'll know too the sound of a latch
dropping shut, and you'll know the little

shovelfuls of laughter children scatter
on the grass. You'll know the call
of an oriole on a lakeside walk and how   15

rain drips from branch to branch in bushes
that have broken out in buds. And you
might even know, some evening when

the weather's calm, the sky still blue,
how a child drops a soupspoon in a dish.   20
Or you might hear the bird, the one that

calls to whoever sits on the porch on
a summer's night and listens to the tripping
of bells from a bay, having already

struggled up a precipitous pass   25
and dared difficult, sultry questions
with their face open to the sea.

Maybe you only hear yourself stumble
up a staircase and drop your keys. Maybe
you only hear the sharp strike-notes   30

of bell-ringers announcing the passing
of another life, or hear your name on
the lips of sailors who sit with spray

on their fingers as they pull in the weights
and chip and chisel into the night.   35
Perhaps you hear your life winched in

under a dying sun. Or perhaps you hear
a child count stars in the water off a rickety
pier—despite clouds moving in, despite

gulls in the wind just off the masts.   40
                                                     1996

How to Love Bats

Begin in a cave.
Listen to the floor boil with rodents, insects.
Weep for the pups that have fallen. Later,
you'll fly the narrow passages of those bones,
                              but for now—   5

open your mouth, out will fly names
like *Pipistrelle, Desmodus, Tadarida.*[1] Then,
listen for a frequency
lower than the seep of water, higher
than an ice planet hibernating   10
beyond a glacier of Time.

Visit op shops.[2] Hide in their closets.
Breathe in the scales and dust
of clothes left hanging. To the underwear
and to the crumpled black silks—well,   15
give them your imagination
and plenty of line, also a night of gentle wind.

By now your fingers should have
touched petals open. You should have been dreaming
each night of anthers and of giving   20
to their furred beauty
your nectar-loving tongue. But also,
your tongue should have been practising the cold
of a slippery, frog-filled pond.

Go down on your elbows and knees.   25
You'll need a speleologist's desire for rebirth
and a miner's paranoia of gases—

1 Genera of bats.
2 From 'opportunity shop', a charity shop selling secondhand goods.

but try to find within yourself
the scent of a bat-loving flower.

Read books on pogroms. Never trust an owl.   30
Its face is the biography of propaganda.
Never trust a hawk. See its solutions
in the fur and bones of regurgitated pellets.

And have you considered the smoke
yet from a moving train? You can start   35
half an hour before sunset,
but make sure the journey is long, uninterrupted
and that you never discover
the faces of those Trans-Siberian exiles.

Spend time in the folds of curtains.   40
Seek out boarding-school cloakrooms.
Practise the gymnastics of wet umbrellas.

                          Are you
floating yet, thought-light,
without a keel on your breastbone?   45
Then, meditate on your bones as piccolos,
on mastering the thermals
beyond the tremolo; reverberations
beyond the lexical.

                          Become adept   50
at describing the spectacles of the echo—
but don't watch dark clouds
passing across the moon. This may lead you
to fetishes and cults that worship false gods
by lapping up bowls of blood from a tomb.   55

Practise echo-locating aerodromes,
stamens. Send out rippling octaves
into the fossils of dank caves—
then edit these soundtracks
with a metronome of dripping rocks, heartbeats   60
and with a continuous, high-scaled wondering
about the evolution of your own mind.

But look, I must tell you—these instructions
are no manual. Months of practice
may still only win you appreciation   65
of the acoustical moth,
hatred of the hawk and owl. You may need

to observe further the floating black host
through the hills.

                                                            1996

The Saffron Picker

*To produce one kilogram of saffron, it
is necessary to pick 150,000 crocuses*

Soon, she'll crouch again above each crocus,
feel how the scales set by fate, by misfortune
are an awesome tonnage: a weight opposing

time. Soon, the sun will transpose its shadows
onto the faces of her children. She knows   5
equations: how many stigmas balance each

day with the next; how many days divvy up
the one meal; how many rounds of a lustrous
table the sun must go before enough yellow

makes a spoonful heavy. She spreads a cloth,   10
calls to the competing zeroes of her children's
mouths. An apronful becomes her standard—

and those purple fields of unfair equivalence.
Always that weight in her apron: the indivisible
hunger that never has the levity of flowers.   15
                                                      2003

KERRY REED-GILBERT
b. 1956

The daughter of Kevin Gilbert (qv), poet Kerry Reed-Gilbert is a Wiradjuri woman
from central NSW. She has worked as a consultant on Indigenous culture, history and
heritage, and as a human rights activist. Her photography has appeared in numerous
exhibitions across Australia. Reed-Gilbert first performed her poetry in 1993 at the Black
Women's Voices in the Park series at Harold Park, Sydney. She believes that through her
writing she is a 'messenger', the symbolic meaning of the White Cockatoo, her totem.

She has edited a number of anthologies of Indigenous writing, including *The Strength of Us As Women: Black women speak* (2000). Her books include *Black Woman, Black Life* (1996) and *Talkin' About Country* (2002). *AH/PM*

Let's Get Physical

Let's get physical
The man cried, five in the morning.
They lined up side by side. Row by row.

Let's get physical
The boss man cried as he started them off,   5
on their walk for miles.
In between rows they did walk.
Backs bent, too tired to talk.

Let's get physical
The white man cried as he watched them,   10
pick his cotton, make his money,
to put in his bank.

Let's get physical
The white man cried.
He'll never know,   15
the Koori pride,
that makes that man,
bend his back between his rows.

Koori pride is what it is,
that makes that Blackman bend his back,   20
to pick that cotton, to pay his rent,
to feed his kids.

Welfare cheques not for him.
A honest day's work says he'll win.
Kids' belly full that's all that matters.   25

Let's get physical
The white man cried, he doesn't look
to see the pride in the Blackman's eyes.

2002

HANNIE RAYSON
b. 1957

Playwright Hannie Rayson was born and educated in Melbourne. Her best-known play is *Hotel Sorrento* (*1990*/1990), which was dramatised as a feature film in 1995. Like fellow playwright David Williamson (qv), Rayson is known for her ability to put a finger on the pulse of contemporary Australian society and engage with its changing conditions, values and preoccupations from year to year.

Life After George (*2000*/2000) confirmed her reputation as one of Australia's leading contemporary playwrights, and established the dominant note of her plays: an examination of the way in which politics affects personal life and vice versa. *Life After George* is among other things a critique of the corporatisation of Australian universities. Since then Rayson's plays have become more overtly political, notably with *Two Brothers* (*2005*/2005), which closely recalls events and characters in recent Australian public life. She has also written for film and television. *KG*

From *Hotel Sorrento*
Act 2, Scene 1

The three sisters are sitting at the end of the jetty. Over to their right, EDWIN *is paddling in the shallows. The atmosphere is infused with a sense of melancholy.*

HILARY: Do you remember the Sorrento fair? [*Both* PIP *and* MEG *nod in recollection.*] Remember the year the fortune teller came?

MEG: He wasn't a fortune teller, was he?

HIL: What was he then?

PIP: He was a 'world renowned' palmist and clairvoyant. Punditt Maharaji.

MEG: That's right. It was written on the caravan. Punditt Maharaji.

HIL: What did he tell you? Do you remember?

MEG: Not really. Something like 'You are going to be rich and famous and travel vast distances across the sea.'

[*They smile.*]

HIL: What about you Pip?

PIP: Er . . . rich and famous and travel vast distances. Something highly personalised like that.

HIL: Do you know what he said to me? He said I was one of three.

PIP: That was a good guess.

MEG: What else?

HIL: That was it. The Rixon kids threw stones at the caravan and he went off after them.

PIP: I don't think you got your shilling's worth.

[*They muse over the memory. In the distance* PIP *sees* TROY *walking alone at the top of the cliff. He is looking out to sea.*]

PIP: There's Troy.

[*The other women look in that direction. They watch silently. There is a change in mood.*]

Still looking for Pop.

[*Silence*]

MEG: Poor kid. The sea will never give up its dead.

HIL: He's a different boy isn't he? He's just clammed up. He loved Dad so much. They had something very special those two. It's not fair is it?

[*Silence*]

People are always dying on him.

PIP: He's a survivor Hil. He is.

HIL: Yeah . . . but at what cost?

[*Pause.* MEG *looks at her penetratingly.* HIL *looks away.*]

PIP: What do you mean?

HIL: He feels responsible this time.

[*Silence*]

MEG: Yes. I know what that's like. [*They stare out to sea.* MEG *waits for a response. None is forthcoming.*] I think I'll go for a walk. [PIP *and* HILARY *say nothing.* MEG *makes her way over to* EDWIN.]

PIP: She can't concede can she, that anyone else could be hurting as much as she is? She's like a child.

[*Silence*]

You think I'm still an angry young thing, don't you? You may think this is bullshit, but I'm different when I'm away. I'm a different person. If you met any of my friends in New York and you said, 'Pippa's such a cot case isn't she?' they wouldn't know what you were talking about.

HILARY: I don't think you're a cot case.

PIPPA: Oh, I am. I know I am. But only when I'm here.

HILARY: Must be in the water.

PIPPA: I really did want people to see how much I'd changed. I was really looking forward to coming home you know. But people don't want to see that do they? They don't want to see what's new about you. They're suspicious of that. It's like you've reneged on who you are. And that's fixed. That's immutable. You are who you are and if you try and change, you must be faking. Bunging on an act. But over there people think differently. In fact, if you're not working to make positive changes in your life, they think you're in deep shit.

HIL: Yeah. So I hear.

PIP: You're cynical about that, aren't you?

HIL: No. I'm just not so sure that people actually *do* change.

PIP: Everybody has the potential. It's just whether we choose to take up on it or not.

HIL: Sounds like propaganda to me. I think I'd rather be saying, 'OK, this is who I am. Like it or lump it. May as well get used to it, and make the best of it'.

[PIPPA *makes no response. She looks out to sea.*]

Act 2, Scene 2

In the shallows.

EDWIN: What's up?

[MEG *sighs*]

MEG: 'We shall not cease from exploration.
And the end of all our exploring
will be to arrive at where we started
and know the place for the first time.'

EDWIN: T.S. Eliot.

MEG: Mm. I had hoped that I would know the place for the first time. But I'm not sure that I know it any better than when I left.

EDWIN: Things change in ten years Meg.

MEG: No. They haven't. That's just it. It's like there's this highly elasticised thread that's tied around us three and it stretches from Australia to Britain and to the States and all of a sudden it's just given out and thwack we're flung back together again. And we're just the same little girls, but this time in women's bodies. And we don't know any more than when we started out. [*Sighing*] I'm beginning to feel quite middle aged.

EDWIN: I'm not surprised. This town feels like everyone in it was born into middle age. D'you know, the only conversations I've had since we arrived, have been about children and compost.

MEG: People don't know what to say to us. Grief makes people realise how inadequate they are.

EDWIN: Yes.

[*Pause*]

Tell me, does anything ever happen here?

MEG: No. People live out quiet prosaic ineffectual lives and then they die. And the other people spend the rest of their lives utterly emotionally crippled by the experience. That seems to be the pattern.

[*Silence*]

EDWIN: I must say, Hilary is quite a remarkable woman isn't she?

MEG: Why do you say that?

EDWIN: The way she copes with things.

MEG: Oh, yes. Hilary copes. She 'copes' because she shuts down. That's the way she lives her life. She doesn't let herself feel. She doesn't think about things too deeply. It's like she made a decision a long time ago that she was done with crying. Nothing or nobody was ever going to hurt her again. So she 'copes' magnificently and people think she's so strong, so remarkable. I don't. I think she's a coward.

[*Silence*]

EDWIN: I think you're being very unfair. I can't imagine what it must be like for her. She's had to deal with three deaths. All of them tragic. I can't even begin to think how one would ever really deal with that.

MEG: No, perhaps you can't.

EDWIN: And I don't think you can either.

MEG: They were my parents too, Edwin . . .

EDWIN: I know.

MEG: And I was here, remember, when Gary died.

EDWIN: I know. But he wasn't your husband Meg.

MEG: No, he wasn't my husband. But I loved him. That's what you don't understand. I loved him too.

Act 2, Scene 3

HILARY *and* PIP *make their way up the path to the house. They stop for a breather and take in the view.*

HILARY: I dreamt last night that I married Edwin.

PIP: Whoa, that was nasty.

HILARY: I forgot to shave my legs.

PIP: Oh, Hil. That was an oversight.

HILARY: I know. I was wearing a short white dress and these terrible hairy legs. I just couldn't enjoy myself.

PIP: I can imagine. Did he wear pyjamas?

HILARY: No. He was wearing a purple suit.

[PIPPA *bursts out laughing.*]

PIP: I mean afterwards, you dill.

HIL: I didn't get that far. I woke up about half way through the reception.

PIP: That was lucky. You know I can't get my head around the possibility that anyone could actually lust after Eddie.

[HIL *laughs despite herself.*]

HIL: Oh, Pippa. You're dreadful. He's not that bad.

PIP: He is. He's ridiculous. Look at him down there. 'Paddling'. God help us. Anyway, I've always found Englishmen rather ridiculous. Well, can you imagine it. Grown men referring to their penises as their 'willies'. It's very off putting.

[*The two women walk up the path to the verandah.* TROY *comes out of the house.*]

HIL: Troy?

TROY: Yeah.

HIL: Who was that, driving off?

TROY: That guy Dick Bennett.

HIL: What did he want?

[TROY *holds up a single rose in a cellophane cylinder.*]

TROY: He left this.

HIL: He must be down for the weekend.

PIP: Who?

HIL: The guy who drove me to the beach . . . that day.

TROY: I think he's got the hots for you.

HIL: Don't be silly Troy. [HILARY *takes the rose and reads the card.*] What makes you say that?

TROY: He asked me if I wanted to go fishing.

PIP: Uh huh? That makes sense. A way to a woman's heart is a bucket of fresh flathead.

TROY: You'd be surprised the number of boring old farts that come round here with flowers asking me to go fishing.

HIL: Oh sure, Troy. They're bashing down the doors.

PIP: Maybe they've got the hots for you. Nice young boy like you. Anything's possible.

[TROY *gives her a 'don't be smart' look.*]

HIL: What did you say anyway?

TROY: 'No', of course. I don't want to go fishing with him.

[*He gets up to leave.*]

HIL: Why don't you go over and see one of your mates?

[TROY *shrugs and goes indoors.* HIL *and* PIP *exchange looks.* HILARY *sighs.*]

PIP: What's the card say?

HILARY: With deepest sympathy.

[PIP *nods*]

PIP: Do they really come round here asking him to go fishing.

HIL: What do you reckon?

[*Silence*]

PIP: You know what I reckon. I reckon you ought to pack up and leave.

[HIL *stops in her tracks.*]

You're marking time Hil. You've been marking time for years. Now's your chance.

Act 2, Scene 4

MEG *is wandering alone through the cemetery. A light rain is beginning to fall.* TROY *hovers some distance away, unseen by* MEG.

TROY: Meg? Aunt Meg?

[MEG *looks up and smiles wanly.* TROY *approaches gingerly. He hands her a coat.*]

Thought you might need this.

MEG: Thank you.

[*They stand together silently for a while.*]

I used to come here when I was a kid. Just wander around and read the tombstones. I still remember the names. Charlotte Grace Phelps and Frederic Earnest Phelps. See, September 12, 1890 and October 1, 1890. He died three weeks later. Lottie and Fred. D'you think he died of a broken heart? I used to imagine that he found life intolerable without her. Can you imagine loving someone so much that you just couldn't go on?

[*Pause*]

[TROY *shrugs*]

TROY: I just wanted to say that we read your book, Pop and me, but . . . we didn't finish it.

[MEG *nods*]

MEG: It's only a book.

TROY: He asked me to read it to him. We used to read it on the verandah when Mum was at work. We only had two chapters to go. [*He sighs*] I tried to read them last night . . . but . . . [*He shakes his head.*]

[*Pause*]

D'you know the part I liked best?

MEG: No?

TROY: When Helen and Grace meet in Italy.

MEG: That's the thing you have to be careful about with fiction. It leads us to believe that reconciliations are possible.

TROY: What d'you mean?

[TROY *looks at her intently, obviously wanting a response.*]

MEG: People coming together . . . reconciling their differences. It doesn't always happen.

TROY: It doesn't happen in real life, you mean?

MEG: Not always. No.

TROY: Well, why did you write it then?

[MEG *makes no reply.*]

1990

NICK CAVE
b. 1957

Nick Cave grew up in rural Victoria. He is best known for his work with the band Nick Cave and the Bad Seeds. Ranging across various styles (including blues, gospel and rock), Cave's songs are occupied by violent and archetypal themes and imagery. Cave has also written fiction, plays and the screenplay for the film *The Proposition* (2005), for which he also co-wrote the soundtrack. His novel, *And the Ass Saw the Angel* was published in 1989. He wrote the introduction to *The Gospel*

According to Mark for the Canon Pocket Bible Series. He is a musician of considerable influence. In 2007 he was inducted into the ARIA Hall of Fame and the subject of a major exhibition at the Melbourne Arts Centre. *DM*

Opium Tea

Here I sleep the morning through
Until the call to prayer awakes me
And there is nothing to do but rise
And follow the day wherever it takes me
I stand at the window and look at the sea   5
Then I make me a pot of opium tea

Down at the port I watch the boats come in
Watching boats come in can do something to you
And the kids gather round with outstretched hand
And I toss them a diram[1] or two   10
And I wonder if my children are thinking of me
For I am what I am and what will be will be
I wonder if my kids are thinking of me
And I smile and I sip my opium tea

At night the sea lashes the rust red ramparts   15
And the shapes of hooded men move past me
And the mad moaning wind, it laughs and it laughs
At the strange lot that fate has cast me
And the cats on the rampart sing merrily
That I am what I am and what will be will be   20
The cats on the rampart sing merrily
And I sit and I drink my opium tea

I'm a prisoner here, I can never go home
There is nothing here to win or to lose
There are no choices needing to be made at all   25
Not even the choice of having to choose
I am a prisoner, yes, but I am also free
'Cause I am what I am and what will be will be
I'm a prisoner here, yes, but I'm also free
And I smile and I sip my opium tea   30

1997

---

1   *Dirham* or *dirhem*: a unit of currency in several Arab countries.

KIM SCOTT
b. 1957

Kim Scott has written novels, a biography and a children's picture book, as well as poetry, stories and criticism. He was born in Perth, and is a descendant of the Noongar people. Scott graduated from Murdoch University. After teaching English for some time in urban, rural and remote secondary schools, including at an Aboriginal community in the north of WA, Scott began researching his family history. This led to his first novel, *True Country* (1993), which, along with *Benang: From the heart* (1999), explores the problem of self-identity faced by light-skinned Aboriginal people and examines assimilationist policies during the first decades of the twentieth century. In 2000, Scott was the first Indigenous writer to win the Miles Franklin Award, for *Benang*, sharing the prize with Thea Astley. *Kayang and Me*, a collaborative autobiography with senior Aboriginal woman Kayang Hazel Brown, was published in 2005. *AH/PM*

From *Benang*
We Move ...

I had a new game. I had never been one for games, but I was unusually thrilled, I was giggling like a child with the pleasure it gave me to share this one with Uncle Will. I could see, even within the composure and dignity he liked to feign, that it startled and excited him.

At the same time—and this helped his appearance of composure—he was I think stunned, and in awe of such freedom.

Previously I had performed it solely for the pleasure of seeing the terror, and—later—the *indignation* it aroused in Ern.

I simply indulged in my propensity to drift. In the mornings I would attach strong fishing line to a reel on my belt, anchor one end of it to the house and, stepping out the door, simply let the land breeze take me. I rose and fell on currents of air like a balloon, like a wind-borne seed. The horizon moved away so that the islands no longer rested on its line, but stood within the sea, and it seemed that the pulsing white at the island's tip was not a mere transformation induced by collision, but was a blossoming and wilting at some fissure where sea met land.

It was indeed a very long time after this—but it may have begun here— that I realised that I had come back from the dead, was one of those few. I may well be djanak, or djangha—so much so that I stumble at what is the correct dialect, let alone how I should spell it—but even then I had not completely forgotten who I am. I floated among the clouds, and even with a bleached skin, and an addled memory I nevertheless saw the imprint of the wind upon the turquoise ocean. I remembered the call of quails in the dune grasses, and thought of curlews crying from moonlit chalky paths, and the footprint such a bird would leave.

It was as if sunlight told me of the sameness of granite and sand, and—in the evenings—flickering firelight fed the fire of my life, of my breathing.

But I was telling of when Uncle Will and Uncle Jack had returned for me, and of when I was accustoming myself to this experience of drifting. I studied the pathways and tracks which ran along the coastal dunes, and saw the white beach as the sandy, solidified froth of small waves touching the coast. I noted how rocks and reef and weed lurked beneath the water's surface, and saw the tiny town of Wirlup Haven and how Grandad's historic homestead—as if shunned—clung to a road which was sealed and heading inland.

So it was not purely mindless, this floating on the breeze. It required a certain concentration, and I chose it not just for the fun, but also because I wanted to view those islands resting in the sea, and to get that aerial perspective. I couldn't have said why.

The wind ruffled my hair as I rode its currents toward the islands. At first I worried when I saw boats or any sign of human life marking land or sea, but such sightings were rare along that isolated stretch of coastline and, after a time, I realised that I could not be seen at all, except by my family.

Grandad used to stare in shock. It scared him. I loved that.

Uncle Will said he envied my unburdened existence. More pragmatically, he suggested I take another line, and try fishing as I drifted across the ocean.

I liked it best when the breezes were soft, and I watched whales, dolphins, the schools of salmon moving below me. Late in the day the breeze blew me back to the house.

The very first time he found me so tiny and out of earshot in the sky, Uncle Jack hauled me in like some sort of airborne fish. A sharp tug upended me, and then I was bent double, my limbs flapping with the force of such a retrieval into the land breeze.

'Shit, you made a mess of the line,' I said.

He snorted. 'You fuckin' silly little shit. What? You kartwarra, that it? You're something special, you know.' He was insistent and angry. 'I tell you you gotta go right back, you got something special there coming out. I can see where you come from all right. You oughta give away that reading and all those papers for a while.'

He wanted to take *all* of us?

Uncle Jack wanted to take us all driving. He wanted to show me some places. We could drive, and camp. We'd take Ern with us.

'Will?'

Uncle Will nodded.

Uncle Jack reckoned that the main roads more or less followed traditional runs; along the coast to where his Aunty Harriette had been born. The roads went inland from there, up to Norseton, and back to here. It's the waterholes, see. They used to follow the waterholes.

Rain still falls, water still gathers.

'Bring your papers with you if you like,' he said. 'Do all that. You can even fly yourself high as a kite, if you like, if you still wanna. No matter.'

'The main roads follow a traditional run,' he had said. 'And, you know, we showed all those white blokes.' He looked at Uncle Will. 'Your father, he was shown by your mother, and her mother. And there you were wanting to be a pioneer.'

It disturbs my clumsy narrative even more, of course, this sudden and contemporary journey. It disturbed me at the time also. I was scared, but seeing the reluctance in Ern's face convinced me it was the thing to do.

We drove for the afternoon, humming along the sealed road. A 'run', I kept thinking; we once walked where now we skim? The wind roared outside our small and stuffy capsule.

I remembered the little Uncle Will had written—it was not much more than notes scattered among Ern's well-organised papers. It was all about his father, as, perhaps, is my own.

Uncle Will had begun a little history of this region, and of his family. His motivation was the publication of a little booklet, a feeble local history, to which he had taken exception. He had written:

> We may see how greatly facts are distorted and these people are most misleading in their trying to put the arrival of their parents in the new field before many others, for the sake of being known as descendants of the first pioneers.

It was incomprehensible to me: Uncle Will, who had been refused 'Susso' in the Depression and told, instead, to go to the Aborigines Department for rations; Uncle Will, who had barely escaped being sent to a Mission or Native Settlement. Uncle Will desperately wanted to name his father as among the very first to 'settle' at Gebalup, and he scarcely wrote of his mother. Yet it was she who gave him his rights to be here.

He was of 'the first'.

I thought of how Uncle Will walked. Proudly, cautiously; like one provisionally uplifted, whose toes barely gripped the earth.

Grandad had written very little, yet he had organised and collected an array of material. Uncle Will had written a few pages from memory, and that was all he had. But I saw the evasion, the desire to compete and to say he was as good as anyone and that this seemed the only way possible. In his rather formal, affected language, there was this hint of an alternative:

Can you understand, dear people, why I'm rather diffident about discussing the early history of Gebalup as I knew it as a boy? The descendants have given their forebears images which they wish to see and present to the public in their most favourable light. It would be a continual source of acrimony were I to join in their discussions. So I think it much better for me to write all my thoughts down for the perusal and study of my younger relatives.

But then he'd faltered, and after a few hundred words had stopped.

My father had written nothing, and had just begun to speak to me when I killed him. Uncle Will was family, my father had said. Even your grandfather. That's all you've got, your family. Even if, sometimes, it hurts to have them.

Of course, this was not in any of the material I had read to my grandfather, the so-close-to-smug-in-his-victory Ernest Solomon Scat.

We camped close to Uncle Will's birthplace on our first night away. It was among ancient sea dunes, and nearby, behind a fence, there was a dam which, Uncle Will informed us, collected fresh water from a small spring.

The four of us sat around the campfire, sipping beer. It was a cold night and I was clumsy with the vast bulk of my clothing. I had wrapped a long scarf several times around both myself and a log, partly for the warmth, but also because, as Uncle Jack reminded me, drinking grog inevitably set me drifting off 'something cruel'.

'Somewhere here, eh? I was born somewhere around here,' said Uncle Will, suddenly.

'It was a hot day,' he said. We allowed him the authority to tell us of his birth. We assumed the story had been handed to him and not that he was possessed of a most remarkable memory.

When Uncle Will was born the sides of the tent had been lifted and tied to catch any movement of the air.

Fanny and old Sandy One arrived at the camp, and then Sandy One went to find the other men and left the three women to attend to the birth.

What other men? *Three* women?

Uncle Will and Uncle Jack had to explain to me who all these people were. Be patient, have patience, their sighs said.

Harriette and Daniel? I knew about them, Will's parents. Daniel Coolman of the missing lip and great bulk who was sown in a mine. Harriette, a shadowy but already powerful figure in my little history.

Dinah and Pat? I didn't know them. Uncle Pat, they told me, was Daniel's twin brother. Dinah was Harriette's sister. Aunty Dinah was the other daughter of Fanny and Sandy One Mason.

I worried, as any reader must also do, at this late and sudden introduction of characters. Except that for me it was not characters, but family.

'Yeah, well, there's lots all of us don't know,' said one of the old men.

And then it was definitely Uncle Jack who spoke. 'It's hard to know where to begin—except with each place we come to, really. Where we are right now.'

It was hot, back then, by the tiny pool, here; the heat snapped twigs from the trees, and they bounced off the heavy canvas roof of the tent. Fanny and Dinah murmured to Harriette.

Deep and rasping breaths. The soak's water is still. Campfire smoke grows straight to the sky. The women's breath is very warm, and there is so much moisture, all this liquid pooling beneath the trees.

The place's spirit continued to billow. Fanny felt so grateful.

As the wet child took its first breath they heard the leaves above them clacking and rustling. Will was rolled in white sand.

'This sand is so fine,' Uncle Will said, looking into our faces and letting it run through his fingers, 'it's like talcum powder.'

When Daniel took the child in his arms the women could not help but smile, he so thick and burnt and gnarled and the baby just a bundled heartbeat, mewing and clutching.

Daniel was happy. 'Now, this is the first white man born here. No doubt about that.'

Uncle Jack was smiling at Uncle Will, teasing him.

So where was Uncle Jack born?

He said he'd tell me that later. When we got back to the other side of Wirlup Haven. He hadn't been lucky enough to know his parents like Will had.

Harriette, Daniel, Dinah and Pat had come across from Dubitj Creek way (as you can imagine, I spent a lot of time consulting a map as we drove), where they had been carting goods to the goldfields. There's water all through there, the old men told me, and it was true that my map showed many small and temporary waterholes to which the main road clung. But a new railway line from the capital city had depleted the need for teamsters, and there was various troubles to get away from.

They tried roo shooting which—in those days—gave them enough cash for what they needed.

The truth is, the Coolman twins were happy. It was a decent life. Moving slow; hunting, drinking. There was always the chance of gold. They had wives who knew the country; who found water, food, a place to camp. The women could do everything. They could work like men, feed off the land, embrace their men and make them strong. And Sandy One Mason, their father-in-law, that enigmatic fellow they laughed at between themselves, was known by people all around this way; pastoralists, old miners, carriers, all of which could prove helpful when and if they needed to get work again.

There was no fear of attack, as was prevalent with some travellers. When the Premier Man John Forrest had come this way less than thirty years before, he and his party had kept a rostered watch each night. A publication of 1900, *In Darkest Western Australia*, devotes several pages to the threat of attack by the *blacks*. But when Daniel and Pat met any who were not like themselves they stood close behind the women. It was what Sandy One had advised them. Their faces would echo the expressions of those speaking this peculiar language, as they half-listened and tried to understand.

They gathered kangaroo skins. Or rather, the women gathered them. A trip back to Kylie Bay every few months meant they were making money. Do you wish to hear how they suffered; of their endurance, hardship, deprivation? In fact it was almost too easy a life. It was practically a relief to run out of grog and so they purposely deprived themselves, brought less of it with them—and even that they sipped with their wives.

They moved between the coast and the goldfields; between the old and the new telegraph lines; between the railway to the north and the ocean to the south. Finding where they could take a heavy cart. And, always, there might be gold.

Drinking. Fucking. They wandered, following gossip and getting Harriette and her sister Dinah to take them as far as the goldfields, where they thought they saw their women's people slumped in the dust, rotting from the inside out. The women brought them back, always, to no further than a day or two from the ocean.

No gold. Then suddenly you needed a licence to sell roo skins. They found themselves 'Gebalup' way, near the outer limit of the women's country, and fell in with the Mustle and Done families. The *landed gentry* of this story.

The four of us sat around the fire until late in the night. Perhaps it was the beer, but I felt very heavy, as if burdened. Old people surrounded me.

'Listen to the voices in the trees,' said Uncle Jack.

In the firelight the three men looked exceptionally old, ancient beyond their years. Grandad's face glistened with the tears which now so often came to him. Uncle Jack and Uncle Will's arrival had given him some protection from me, and I had not harmed him for months.

The intervals between Grandad toppling, and being propped up again, grew longer. The eyes of my uncles reflected the fire. I remember noticing my own hands, and being frightened at how old they looked in that light.

1999

MICHELLE DE KRETSER
b 1957

Michelle de Kretser was born in Colombo, Sri Lanka, and migrated to Australia with part of her family when she was fourteen. After a successful early academic career, including gaining her master's degree in Paris, she returned to Australia and worked for some years as an editor for Lonely Planet Publications. She was also a founding editor of *Australian Women's Book Review*.

Her first novel, *The Rose Grower* (1999), was critically well received and her second, *The Hamilton Case* (2003), won a number of major awards, including two prestigious international literary prizes. Her third novel, *The Lost Dog*, was published in 2007.

De Kretser is a sophisticated thinker and witty stylist whose novels reflect her own international background, speculating and meditating on the nature of exile, dislocation and postcolonialism and their effects on different people in different places. *KG*

From *The Hamilton Case*
Part III

[. . .] For Maud, each day discharged an identical freight of loneliness, monotony and long, voracious mosquitoes. Hardest to bear was the heat. When she lay in bed, the air was so heavy she felt its weight upon her. Her skin grew damp beneath its touch.

The house was dwarfed by its backdrop of trees, so that it appeared to crouch low on its haunches. In fact it had ceilings eighteen feet high, designed for coolness. Its walls were inset with lattice, its verandahs screened with rattan tats that could be lowered against the sun and sprayed with water. These were stratagems that presupposed currents of air, since an island race is fated to take its bearings from the sea. But the breeze that ruffled the coast was strangled by leafy ropes as soon as it ventured into the hinterland. The air was not air at all, thought Maud, felled on the verandah at ten in the morning, but a woven yellow haze. Spiders and green-veined orchids lived suspended in its honeyed weft.

She began to unpack a trunk and reached a layer of photographs in pokerwork frames. Ritzy failing to look sinister with a cutlass between his teeth. Herself at the same costume party, a slave girl whose gauzy attire displayed tantalising traceries of flesh. Claudia unsmiling on her wedding-day, Sam authoritative in a morning suit. Was it chance, wondered Maud, that preserved her children in images so much more formal than their parents? She picked up the photograph of Sam and studied his face. Why didn't she hate him? Wouldn't loathing be more natural than the massive indifference he triggered in her? He was her first born, the only child left to her, and a door within her slammed shut in his presence.

It had been the state of affairs between them for as long as she could remember. Once, coming away from a prize-giving at Neddy's, her husband had said, 'I say, old thing, you should try harder with Sam.' 'Should I?' said Maud, as startled by the fact of the reproach as by the point it delivered. 'Yes.' After a minute, 'Do you think he minds?' she had asked. 'I should say so.' Maud whistled—a vulgar habit she was cultivating. She had tried to concentrate on her son, to see him whole. It was useless. In her mind, she was always inspecting him from a height. The air between them was at once clear and impenetrable. Diamond-bright, diamond-hard: it characterised her manner with the boy. Among a set that valued astringency in human relations, her style passed as good form.

In those first months at Lokugama her dreams were of landscapes where the boundary between earth and water was blurred. She began each day charged with the promise of mutability. At night she walked beside waves or was carried on slow river currents to a boat that lifted and fell and leant to meet her. How could she not long for deliverance?

Yet a terrible jauntiness informed the notes she soon began composing. These were directed to friends who lived abroad: the Venetians, an Argentine industrialist, a stockbroker from Surrey, a Basque poet, a cluster of faded English civil servants. Within weeks she was writing compulsively, five or six bright, cloying letters a day. Colourful detail was her forte. She described *a troop of monkeys with sorrowful faces, speeding through the treetops.* She called up *manes of saffron-hued lantana.* Pride dictated that loneliness and despair, the companions on whom she closed her eyes every night, could never be cited. Instead, a blocked and stinking lavatory became *our preposterous plumbing.*

By the end of the third month it was plain her allowance wouldn't run to the postage. She borrowed two rupees from the bungalow-keeper and went on writing. *I wish you could see this marvellous old place. My father-in-law had latticed ducts set in the floor to blow air up the skirts of dancing ladies.* Or: *I have been gorging myself on rambutans. Such fruit! Spiked scarlet globes the size of a hen's egg, split open with a thumbnail to yield segments of delectable white flesh.*

All routine offers consolation. The truism extends also to cliché, to the comfort found in worn patterns of words. If Maud wrote of bougainvillea it was unfailingly *rampant.* The jungle *teemed with life.* The scent of temple flowers *flooded the evening air.* Language was a net, ready knotted, in which to capture the formless insistence of the world around her: to hold it still and render it legible.

Rain fell. When it stopped, thousands of wings filled the house. The insects flew into Maud's nostrils and beat in her ears. They drowned in a sauceboat. They seethed on her plate, shedding wings. They clotted every surface with their corpses. Half an hour later she seized a pen and wrote: *Never imagine that it is dull here. A continuous wave of squirrels, bats, hens, lizards, frogs, ants, wasps, beetles and crickets washes through this house. This morning brought the novel diversion of a swarm of winged termites.*

It was not her intention to deceive. There is an old instinct, at work in bordellos and the relations of East and West, to convert the unbearable into the picturesque. It enables a sordid existence to be endured, on one side, and witnessed, on the other, with something like equanimity. A visitor to Lokugama would have seen plaster that peeled like diseased skin, sagging rattan, the mildewy bloom of wood unpolished for decades. A horn at the gate would send Maud scuttling from the verandah, hissing for the bungalow-keeper. That same evening she could sit at the dining-table, its scratched varnish sticky along her bare arms, and evoke *the intoxicating scent of jasmine* or *the emerald flash of a parrot's wing.* The prose that thousands before her had applied like antiseptic to the island gushed from her nib. Rats thundered in the rafters. *Did you know,* she found herself writing, *that according to legend this was the Garden of Eden?*

In the weeks leading to the monsoon heat stacked up like yellow bricks. By afternoon all life was walled in. The sun was a ripe fruit, oozing towards collapse. Insects vanished, swallowed by the cracked earth. There were no birds.

Prickly heat, an affliction Maud thought she had discarded with the tedium of childhood, returned in angry lumps in the folds of her knees and elbows. Her nails left ribbons of skin in their wake. One morning dhobi-itch had stamped its rosettes along the line of a collar-bone. Sweat passing over the inflamed skin stung so painfully that she wept. This sweat was a further indignity: it poured down her flanks, broke out on her forehead, gathered in the intimate creases of her flesh. She would wake in the night to find a soaking sheet twisted about her hips.

From one day to the next her body became repellent to her. She became grateful for isolation, certain that she stank. Between breakfast and tiffin she had doused a dozen handkerchiefs in eau-de-Cologne and wiped herself down. She squandered a whole phial of orangewater, upending it over her bath. The monsoon arrived and the weather cooled by three perceptible degrees, and still the clothes she put on when she rose were musky with sweat by eleven.

At last she sent Sirisena into town with a chit for the doctor. When he came, he heard out her symptoms and asked two questions. Then he fingered his tie, with his gaze averted, and named her condition. Maud was dumbfounded: it was so simple and so absolute. Accustomed to regard herself as singular, she was unprepared for this last proof of commonality with her sex.

The oak-framed cheval glass that had occupied a corner of her bedroom when she came to Lokugama as a bride had long since given way to an oblong of pocked mirror. Maud braced herself and let her house-coat fall. Then she took inventory: twin purses of skin each with its warty stud, a little round loaf, a fistful of graying lichen. Below and above she had not the fortitude to venture. [. . .]

2003

ANTHONY LAWRENCE
b. 1957

Born in Tamworth, NSW, Anthony Lawrence left school at sixteen and became a jackeroo in the Riverina. After travelling, he spent time in Wagga Wagga where he worked as a schoolteacher and co-organised a writers' group. Lawrence then went to WA, where he worked as a fisherman and wrote. Later he moved to Tasmania. The poetry of his first books shows the effects of his earlier experiences, often dealing with the violence of life on the land. His poetry mixes narrative and lyrical impulses, as seen in the sequence 'Blood Oath', which deals with a real-life incident in which two young jackeroos died in outback WA. Lawrence's poetry is also often concerned with animals. *Skinned by Light: Poems 1989–2002* was published in 2002, and *Strategies for Confronting Fear: New and selected poems* in 2006. As shown in *The Sleep of a Learning Man* (2003), Lawrence's later poetry has an elegiac quality, while retaining the author's earlier thematic interests in the sea. He has written a novel, *In the Half Light* (2000). DM

The Language of Bleak Averages

1

After a four hour workout under my father's skull,
the young neurosurgeon's hands are white.

His eyes are Concentration Red. Caffeine-numb,
on a grid of hospital floors, I walk, seeing

the shaved scalp cut, peeled back and clamped, stagehands   5
in a spotlight trimming a blood-curtain's advancing folds,

then a plate of fretworked bone, lifted clear to expose
the source of my father's unbalanced body and moods—

a tumour, like the dark, cystitic head of a swamp flower
grafted to a host of nerveless coils.   10

After *Recovery*, that post-operative word for half an hour
of being watched and questioned back into the world,

a man I barely recognise sits up, stares through me,
and tries to claw the bindings from his head.

His corner of Intensive Care is lit with a gleaming life-   15
support machine and metal stand. A slow drip feeds

the line that feeds his vein. Beside his bed, flower-prints
on linoleum fast become a swirl of congealing blood.

A frozen splinter of tumour is with Pathology.
The test results are two days off, though the surgeon   20

tells me, in the language of bleak averages, that even
weeks of radiation will simply stall

the way this kind of cancer blooms again. I think
of a mangrove tree's air-drinking tapers, like a cluster

of slime-nourished, black asparagus. I think of how   25
the unfiltered shadows of grief return for years

beyond a life or love. As I rise to go, moonlight flares
into the ward, turning hospital gowns into folds

of alabaster, wired to fluids and electricity.
Somewhere near, a woman laughs from the depths   30

of sleep or delirium. As if in response, my father raises
his upturned palms and says *She's right, it's a joke*,

giving voice to uncertainty and pain—the stable currencies
of his faith. Then he coughs—a wet, bright sound—

nothing like *a trickle of small change being poured*   35
from hand to hand, which is what I thought

before poetry fell apart, and I was with a man
who lowered his palms, coughed again, and bled.

2

With the staples gone, the scar gleams like an inverted,
upper-case letter C through the most radical haircut

my father's ever had. The cortisone has reduced
the swelling in his brain, giving him a freedom of speech

and body he's never known. He is openly flirtatious,   5
asking the entire nursing station to join him

for dinner when he's better. They all said yes.
It's an invitation none will have to honour.

3

My father was assisted by a driver to his death—
a measured, battery-powered pack beside the bed
that eased a clear cocktail into his blood.
Euthanasia is illegal in Australia only on paper.

Hours before he died, emerging from his coma,   5
he sat up and clawed the air, saying *I am a mear cat.*

Then he went under. Holding his hand, his body
shutting down visibly, I remembered stories of light-

bulbs dimming, of wind bending glass when people died.
The light held on. The window glass moved   10

with a copy of my face when I looked at it.
His last breath was long, the exhalation silent.

When they came for him, he might have been someone
still expecting company—his open hands and mouth,

the comb-lines in his hair. He left the room on a false shelf   15
under a trolley laid out with towels, the woman steering him

pretending that this was nothing more
than laundry being taken down in the lift.

2003

A Profile of the Dead

The old men cough in their sleep like water-
fouled inboard motors, their dreams current lines
where no fish glide, in dangerous weather.

Awake, breathing evenly, with laughter
lighting their mouths, young men become, in time,   5
old men coughing in their sleep like water.

Many die here on the stones: a daughter
who fell, a son the groundswell claimed. They shine
where no fish glide, in dangerous weather.

Wybung Head, in fog, can be sinister—   10
a profile of the dead, a telling sign:
the old men cough in their sleep like water.

Tonight, to end her longing, waves caught her
side-on. Her seagoing body reclines
where no fish glide, in dangerous weather.   15

The full moon, rising, blows its aorta.
A gannet expires on a reef of slime.
The old men cough in their sleep like water
where no fish glide, in dangerous weather.

2003

LIONEL FOGARTY
b. 1958

Lionel George Fogarty is a respected poet and political activist, born on Wakka Wakka land at Barambah Mission, now known as Cherbourg Aboriginal Reserve, Queensland. He is of the Yoogum and Kudjela tribes and also has relations from the Goomba tribe. Educated to ninth grade at Murgon High School, he took various casual jobs, went ringbarking, worked on a railway gang and at sixteen moved to Brisbane.

In the early 1970s, Fogarty became increasingly aware of the injustices he had experienced on the reserve. Inspired by the growing Black Power movement, he combined writing poetry with a commitment to Aboriginal political struggles. He led protests against Aboriginal deaths in police custody. Fogarty has travelled in Australia and overseas as an ambassador for his Murri culture and Aboriginal causes; in 1976 he addressed the American Indian Movement of the Second International Indian Treaty Council in South Dakota, USA, deepening his commitment to the international fight for racial justice.

Fogarty's poetry powerfully challenges literary and political conventions by creating new possibilities for radical poetic expression. His poems demonstrate a commitment to Aboriginal social justice, his belief in land rights as the basis for an Aboriginal future without oppression, and convey his Murri beliefs, knowledge and experiences. His books include *Yoogum, Yoogum* (1982), *Kudjela* (1983), *Ngutji* (1984), *Jagera* (1990), *New and Selected Poems: Munaldjali, Mutuerjaraera* (1995) and *Minyung Woolah Binnung—What Saying Says* (2004).

As Fogarty's writing has become better known, he has continued to support local Aboriginal writing, and has passed on his stories in books for children, such as *Booyooburra* (1993), a traditional Wakka Wakka narrative published with the approval of his elders. *AH/PM*

Shields Strong, Nulla Nullas Alive

Morning dawning stems that core
won't adore poor poor songs
potentially people quit easy
rarely having arts
personal solos move.   5
Stunning outrageous woomeras
flew spears that side cornered
Arnhem Lands
Clapsticks local long maybe
normal entrance   10
finger nail giving painting
sane once again.
Carvings came flying through didgeridoos
over Kimberley roots.
Timber prides   15
simple ornament like mulga wood crafted
Maningrida distinct types.
Finely grained boomerangs
miniatures proved adults
shaped and thrown in the desert life.   20
Weaving fabrics
entirely rich relaxed music
designs your ochre coiled of unique colours.
Landscapes
lovers relate   25
snakes, wild dingo, emus, birds, animals
just like fruit salad.
Traditional authentic coolamons
Yes makers earlier include all.
Fantastic lush property   30

pumped to a gallon of manure
could you believe that this we were told
was better than
what we had.
An intact society based on quality of life.   35
How sad for you.
Or shields are strong
Nulla nullas alive.

1982

Decorative Rasp, Weaved Roots

If I am not a race
Then what am I
If we are not Aboriginals
Then what persons
I am.   5
If indigenous pictures relate descent
then we are facts
If citizens are short sighted
simplified and unrealistic
then similar aspirations will define us.   10
No overemphasised Killorans
Goona reviews assessments
when we know city and urban convenience you live.
Misconception false beliefs
democratically elected   15
self appointed you are
you are

pulling back his chin
cheekily nice grin
hygiene inspectors appeared   20
self importance glares
but she smiled obvious
hurrying chewing gum while being exploited
black employee, award rate soon embarassed your hate.

The bloody paper goggly eyed me   25
loud mouth white bastard
fuzzy fuzzy sly-groggers
we strip distress.

Yell, suddenly
amused that it's Anzac Day   30
buggered people dumbfounded
realised the stupid idiots would shift the mongrels who
informed.
Ridiculous but fucken mouth dropped
the chilling bay stinks   35
laughs in disgust
refilling with conversation
immediate headache croaked
sailing with oil lamp
to get the flagon we need.   40

Plenty flour, plenty beef
Big hassle
Cause instinctively we know we lucky lucky
exaggerated the worry
pinched death   45
dripping dust
lifted the damage halfway around
dragged tossed ripped
lost balance on the rocks
flew through the air.   50
The roadway crowd gathered
bringing sunlight
moaning
nourished crazy
as our belly smuggled the argument   55
poured the ingredients down
one time.

Journeyed away the 'troublemaker'
naturally
headbands of forums spitfired alternatives   60
listening
influenced swayed under the weather friends
primitive slips
they broke the filthy camera crew
whose landing fields were suspicious   65
asked and told questions
we whistled
knowing who cared anyhow ...

Couples contemplating
followed another bunch 70
of friggen portable rubbish public
jumped up propaganda
goddamned watching paradise
fair dinkum mates
think them sick scratched pissed patients 75
inmates of time.
Unloading a barrage of bitterness.
Tolerant 'old cobber' printed frame
printed til he got some great shots
not an entire obscene one. 80

Premier naming dams
excellent resort
signatures began to sign
interviews filmed the common kind.
Jail agents even. 85
The predicament now is bushwalking
with tears
is rumbling across waters
is the deepest de-camped poets
vained twisted and breathtaking 90
goodbye.
Happiness sundances Australian crawl.
That's what suicide say
that's what hate gave
that's what humans live 95
but index 1984
we are at the door
at the door
at the door.
Arise deep spirits. 100
1982

Ecology

I am a frill necked lizard
    roaming, providing
I am refuge by king brown taipan
    highly delightful sea bird
        catches the flint of my star skin colour. 5
I.

Am we pelicans of woodland brolga
    traditional yamming
yes roots, nuts
    differ to geese, hawks, quails   10
        that number plentiful.

Still I am dugong,
    kangaroo, cockatoo and grasshopper too.
Yes I am a termite, better still
    butterflies are my beetles, wasps friends   15
You are natures crocodile
    even pythons are not inadequate, nor geckoes.
We are goannas
    after salt water got grounded.

I am death   20
    harmless.
You are tropic cycles
    swamps got bad affinity
        says who.

Now a dingo arrives   25
    that diet attractive a woof woof
later bush tucker
    need a barramundi.

Later I am digging sticks
    then I am seeds winnowed for damper   30
I am club, woomera,
    an agile well-balanced bandicoot
flying fox and an ABORIGINAL
    our systems woven from an eco-system
so don't send us to pollution   35
    we are just trying to picture
        this life without frustration.

        1982

For I Come—Death in Custody

    I
    in a jail.
    Even a murri wouldn't know
    if him free.

The land is not free. 5
Dreamtime is not free.
No money needed.
See that scarred hand at work
that's cutting away
to freedom 10
Freedom.
Jail not for me
but a lot of my people in jail
White jail are cruel
Set up the family, stay away 15
come to see your murri
look big and grown
in learning, of our gods teaching.
What they give you in here?
Away from the corroboree 20
In the fuckin' jails
Murri get out, so we can fight
like the red man has done
Lord them a come.
My brother die there 25
in white custody
And I hate the way the screws patch up
and cover up.
He died at white hands
it was there, in their stinkin' jails 30
up you might blacks
Him not free
For when white man came
it's been like a jail
with a wife and a family 35
black man can stay in jail
like it's home.
Fuck, they hung us all.

For Brother D.L.

1990

Kath Walker

We are coming, even going
I was born in 1957
the year after I became a realist

I am a full blooded black Aussie
we want racialism   5
you got ostracism
black ascendance
Charter of Rights, she said
Hey, now they got dependents
exploitation is being done here   10
Self-reliance, not compliance
most will say, resign
circumscribe the enemy, not befriend
they will give oversight and
human segregationary rights.   15
No choice. No colour conscious.
Give us bigots who are not biased
Give us prevention, not ambition
Status, not condescension.
Give us Lord Christ and confidence   20
all we do is fellowship bureaucratic protection.
Give me settlements, camped in missions
Prohibition
from old, young time.
Thank you. Education makes us equals   25
Opportunities are disheartening
we defend white over-lordship
rebuff the independence
my laws ain't no cold choice.
Native, old salvation seller   30
we are the conquerors to take over
not Christ
So our land in law
must rank out aliens
in our banished race   35
though you baptised by
Just black …
                                                          1990

'Dulpai—Ila Ngari Kim Mo-Man'

Moppy, Aborigine, Gumbal Gumbal was he
Aborigines King Billy was him; lived
loved him people
around Tampa lands.

Lowood ancient copper blacks   5
never alive in them town camps.
Nature shared our environments
with physical effects
men, black was aware of that bush secret.
Then interwoven, fictional settlers   10
came upon their homes.
Tents went up. Gunga. Mia-mia.
Burned away. Torn, blown
Taken tribal implements, damaged.
Warlike colonies half-hearted   15
a magnificent death
on honest young Aborigines.
Race at Kilcoy, a bloody massacre.
Peace to a flower
gave more feeding to fires   20
of our escaping leaders.
High-pitched wails echoed
among a reddish-brown caraboo
named the great 'MOPPY'
Low voice, yet spoken aloud.   25
Ten clans, sounds confident
to your old fight
for even 1995 in future, lied Moy
boy and man will laugh mockingly.
Surprise them at morning rise   30
make useful every member of our tribe

Moppy,
Our ceremonies made sure that the children's
tribal nation, would and will
grow to prosper.   35
Dared, afraid, trembled.
Mr Moy Moy thought to make you
their prey after dark.
Moppy went to his people
gleaming eyes ready   40
to cold ray an evil whispered violent
flickering sign.
Moppy declared defiantly:
Elders we noisily here a startled voice
crashing solidly through this   45

civilised families drifted apart.
These were and are wrong, almost impossible
furious revenge came over the muttering.
Moppy 'savage', claimed a white woman.
Well about this forgetting time   50
meeting sat at ground level
and Aborigines talked
how to avoid directly these horse, cattle people
who stay:

Moppy stood on a rock   55
and finished his speaking in front of
over 600 Murri blackies.
Kind Billy Tampa, let his axes be taken
and they antagonise him
visible, plain, quickly people of this day   60
and age, are guilty
cos them hold opposite direction
in-out our history.
Angry Moppy must and still du du in safety
confided in all Murri here   65
So we stood, walked, corroboreed, war
painted in honour
to divert awful living at present '90.

Moppy, my Aborigines sang happy
and gladly   70
at Moppy's swift actions.
Lead us … lead us …
Even with your magical spells.
We all strict to your commandments.
Except, except the empty stomachs.   75
of the boasted, with the loud voices
and waka, no support.
Previous fighter Moppy.
I'm yours,
young, even old, to follow: 80

Over previous 500 years we might turn back
our times, forward times.
Moppy, Moppy … poets wise we am?
Don't balk balk the hero. Inda
Youdu, you you build our cultures.   85

Looking up at Moppy's reflection, father.
Moppy thundered myself to repeat a clearer respect
irrespective ...
The great strengthened Pemolroy pride
longer Murri calls, in feelings our same   90
'no shame'.
He show our world he cared
He's ancient, dilli blames the pain
Seize our brothers lame
Gross injustices, victimised miss the richer   95
and in waiting together
he futures a good education
pleasant for us Aborigines.
Tell it like it is
It's us who's on south laws   100
them are shadows to lifeless burries:

Up here blatant accidents
are made
to hand out lost wealth.
Now Mr Pemolroy   105
Australians scared us to death
not to fight.
Now control forefathers washed fears
We have no fear
we are clean   110
are we to inflame our truth:
My people over Australia ...
Perth, Darwin, Cairns, Bamaga, Broken Bay Cove
and Port Phillip Bay
over Murray Bridge and into Oodnadatta ...   115
Your Aborigines are not forbidden to think quickly
of your citizens.
Since trade arrival, they herded us
natives in thought, movements
so we think as them   120
and listen like systems of
controversy:

Well Moppy, Yagan, had respect.
Has private spiritual properties
If had learn a school option   125

Aborigines will find many Aussies
are 'dogs' within a potential 'dobbers' class
Governed like it was right
in your own neighbourhood.
Australia tribespeople are messengers   130
to arrange the visits
once on exchange
Our battle of sick men intruding
on small children's sounds, are mentally
wanderous   135
to hurt their camp feast.

Between Aborigines borders your ordeal
in screaming, robbing, discussing difficult
worked by a frenzy barrage of angry killing
of our beliefs.   140
When will eager poor fights erupt
our lightning bolts to the nam, Moppy
Furtively buried greeting threats:

Why waste the clenching fists
wild, sisters, flare a white insult   145
at last tempers striving companions
desperate clouds dust wattle
over and around those combatants
choking, fought insults
Moppy, Johnny Campbell …   150
Kagariu.
Clash of waddies or spears are helpless
to obscure,
this gashed groaning lost male.
Who have the half-dazed blacks roaming bush.   155
Now Aborigines only commence assault
cos those evil white or half whites
scratch and lash their minds
unbelieving
belief relaxing in homes: 160

Disobeyed.
The gods are what picked faith
will not hideaway.
In the next few moons

carried by our happiest challenge   165
love, are we willing to toughen coolamen.
Then a blurted shudder one gita morning.
Said Dundalli, attack
all through that long summer
so stagger their skilled mistakes.   170
So here are those instinctive moves
in migrant picking on an Aboriginal family.
And instead meat by mighty hunter
full-grown tricks me, your people
have to face: 175

    Unusually they crawled near their rich houses
asking beard or smoke—waterfire strangely
was curiously given.
That's true. When any black man goes to their fence
openly, wanting to speak face to face   180
to indifference that's been dropped …
them hide
their doubters sweetest decisions
just so they won't give up stolen love.
And our leaders will sing out   185
them is frightened of humans
one full to hear out.
This is the protest, not rested even
not honest, given of friendship
these days and nights   190
Oh great fighters in our region
to reach, jump on them from behind, cos trouble
are always overseas.
Forces sneak ageless, called careless
are what gubba man caution.   195
Wanta beware, for guns we can use
Not just whispered words:

    And some may chuckle
But we blackfella recognise them
at probably aroused times   200
timid, taught to live assailants.
Fire-blackened Lionel
I regained my senses
to secret the Murri world.

Submissively them shout terrible injustice   205
Where's the justice?

Duramula came to change
unbeliever to Aborigines present life.
Duramula is the voice bringer
Rhythm sticks we may hit   210
Rhythming a wavering power
won't give death
to those who have betrayed our leaders:

Changer of life
Punjel can change, boy into man   215
girl into woman
Boomed out an answer
now old women, louder and deeper
in the reality world.
Call them from their homes   220
And when they hear my voice
they must obey ... Ngunda ...
Me ... Nulli ... me ...
Sender, bring him back to life
as they must return to camp   225
Singer you are now living.
Emerging my tribe once more
Clinging to my brother-mate
at homeland, Jagera
Moppy ...   230
Wintu ...
Gifted I am from Punjel, Duramula
While there is a sun married to the moon
We are to give a raised initiation
Tell Moppy and Lionel, poet Fo   235
Are them sell-out to express emotions unveiled
Punjel, mina lo run Da
Biamie.
For everything that You have given to me
I in return give back to you   240
Moppy.

1990

Alcheringa

We learnt to love you in that
historical jail
and think of your glorious bravery
where intimate sunshine came
over the transparency mountain   5
we saw your black face smile
with whispers in the winter
we hear your black revolutionary
words (kill miggloo, kill darkie)
We are remaining at the fruits   10
of your vines.
Your firm liberating mind
sicks in our spirits
like a lengthening shadow
over all day light falls   15
Your jailed dance is freed
in our bodies and souls
We are breezing a wind of
continuous international
struggles.   20
We are receiving your high
delivered message
our duty is to free your
suppression. Our duty is
to strike the hatred on a hot   25
even cold night
Your love comes out under the land and up to our
hearts 'you swear, your violence'
But we feel your happier laughs
and rejoys at your release   30
You revolt in thunder
we resolute your pain
The flag we hold is on the
walls held in historical jails
We learnt now black man   35
you are not the jail
Cos we felt the death of many
people in history's goals
The historical future jail are
to be given liberation   40
                                                        2004

SARAH DAY
b 1958

Born in England, Sarah Day arrived in Australia in 1964. She is the author of four collections of poetry, as well as *New and Selected Poems* (2002), published in England. Her poems have been set to music by the British composer Anthony Gilbert. She has been poetry editor of *Island* and has taught English and creative writing. She lives in Tasmania. *DM*

Quickening

Your quickening has been a murmuring
in the next room that I have approached step by step
uncertain if at first that sound was human;
this nudging could have been a consonant
that slow wave rolling through me towards sleep—   5
a vowel.
As I inch towards the door
murmur shapes itself into a human voice,
a voice in the next room.
Soon I will make out your words   10
and listen to what you have to tell me.

                                                              1997

Take Heart

At night, two spoons in a drawer
your curve in my cave
I push my hand through the space
between your ribs and the inside of your arm
and I hold your heart in the palm of my hand   5
like a nervous fluttering boneless bat.
This worried mouse creature
in the cage of your chest
this animal
is what keeps you blood urgent   10
alive in fear and love
your solar centre
delicate flickering creature
alive in my hand while you sleep.

                                                       1997

PHILIP HODGINS
1959–1995

Philip Hodgins spent his childhood on his parents' dairy farm near Shepparton, Victoria. He was educated in Geelong, worked as a sales representative for Macmillan Publishers, and attended the University of Melbourne. In 1983 Hodgins was diagnosed with myeloid leukaemia, a fact dealt with in a number of poems in Hodgins's first book of poetry, *Blood and Bone* (1986), as well in later poems. Hodgins's poems often also dealt with Australian pastoral life in a fiercely unsentimental manner, as seen in *Animal Warmth* (1990) and *Up on All Fours* (1993). His verse novel, *Dispossessed: A tale of modern rural Australia* (1994), concerns a poor rural family about to be evicted from their farm. Hodgins co-founded the Mildura Writers' Festival, where the Philip Hodgins Memorial Medal for Literary Excellence is awarded each year in his memory. Hodgins died of leukaemia. In 1997 his *Selected Poems* appeared, and a revised edition appeared in 2000. Hodgins's poems have been praised for their formal control, understatement and sense of place. *DM*

A Palinode[1]

My second childhood has begun
but the rhythms and the rhymes aren't quite right.
The way my cells increase
is not unlike the vague, unbitten child
reaching up to childhood's end.   5
But with one difference.
My half a bucketful of blood
is filled with rumours of an early death
and I am alone in a room
full of dying flowers.   10
I think it is the body's palinode
and as far as I can see there is no God.

                                                              1986

Shooting the Dogs

There wasn't much else we could do
that final day on the farm.
We couldn't take them with us into town,
no-one round the district needed them
and the new people had their own.   5
It was one of those things.

You sometimes hear of dogs
who know they're about to be put down

---

1   A poem or song retracting an earlier statement by the poet.

and who look up along the barrel of the rifle
into responsible eyes that never forget   10
that look and so on,
but our dogs didn't seem to have a clue.

They only stopped for a short while
to look at the Bedford stacked with furniture
not hay   15
and then cleared off towards the swamp,
plunging through the thick paspalum
noses up, like speedboats.

They weren't without their faults.
The young one liked to terrorize the chooks   20
and eat the eggs.
Whenever he started doing this
we'd let him have an egg full of chilli paste
and then the chooks would get some peace.

The old one's weakness was rolling in dead sheep.   25
Sometimes after this he'd sit outside
the kitchen window at dinner time.
The stink would hit us all at once
and we'd grimace like the young dog
discovering what was in the egg.   30

But basically they were pretty good.
They worked well and added life to the place.
I called them back enthusiastically
and got the old one as he bounded up
and then the young one as he shot off   35
for his life.

I buried them behind the tool shed.
It was one of the last things I did before
we left.
Each time the gravel slid off the shovel   40
it sounded like something
trying to hang on by its nails.

1988/1997

Strathbogie Ranges 1965

We left the car just off the track
and wandered up towards the view.
It would have been about three o'clock.
The sky was Nunawading Blue.

A little way before the end   5
we stopped. Stretched right across the track
like something out of Disneyland
was this enormous carpet snake.

He was flicking his tongue at us
as if he couldn't keep it still.   10
We couldn't help but notice—
the tongue was something else's tail.

1988/1997

Cytotoxic Rigor

A chemical spill in the body. You're still alive,
though the vein they ran it through won't survive.

You stiffen and shake. You give yourself emphasis.
There are tears in your eyes. There's blood in your piss.

The drugs they've added to tone down the shock   5
are as useless as the words from a prayer book.

A creature expands in your guts, in your being.
It squirms and it grabs. It has no meaning.

You vomit through surges of nausea and pain.
And when there's nothing left to vomit you vomit again.   10

1995

VENERO ARMANNO
b. 1959

Venero Armanno was born in Brisbane of Sicilian parents who had migrated to Australia in 1949. His first book of fiction was a collection of short stories, *Jumping at the Moon* (1992). Since then he has published a number of novels, including the award-winning *The Volcano* (2001). He is also a scriptwriter and has written stage plays and screenplays.

His fiction reflects his Sicilian heritage and several of his novels and stories chronicle the history and development of Brisbane. He lectures in creative writing at the University of Queensland. *KG*

From *The Volcano*
Part 4: Sicilian Bandits

[. . .] From Mrs Wilson's boarding house they walked downhill along quiet suburban streets into the city, where they were meeting the others. The closer they came to the wider city streets, the more the traffic increased, rolling freely, the four of them listening to the hammering wheels of trams and the clanging of their bells. Men and women in their finest were heading into Saturday night. Emilio and Desideria watched while Antonio Calì and Santino Alessandro were always a little ahead, calling out to girls who stopped at shop windows to look at the latest buys, or the ones who hurried across intersections, long skirts swirling around bare ankles or stockinged calves.

With the morning's troubles now a little forgotten, to Emilio it was as if these hot, hilly, night-time thoroughfares and avenues held the real gifts he'd earned by coming to this country. A people in constant forward motion; a population ready to propel itself into the next available party, not to mention their all-too-plausible good future. The sight of his wife's new dress billowing against a sign that read *'EAT while you SLIM, Don't Starve to Reduce: BioChemic Laboratories (Aust), COMPLETE TREATMENT ONLY 47/6'* lifted his spirits. Here you could worry about how fat you were getting, not how emaciated because of starvation, so why worry about the future?

It was the beginnings of the Christmas holiday season. The further they went, the more Antonio and Santino—shiny black leather shoes, baggy trousers with sharp creases, white shirts and thin black ties, double-breasted jackets despite the heat, slicked-back hair, short side-levers, scrubbed faces softened by close cutthroat razor shaving and perfumed with men's cologne—seemed to increase in stature and confidence. Emilio saw how the one was no longer a lowly kitchen-hand and the other no longer a back-room pastry chef. They were instead all male qualities mixed up into two well-dressed boys. They were arrogant, respectful, strong, sharp, violent, gracious, good-hearted if they liked you, black-spirited if they didn't, lean, hungry, hopeful and immoderately vital—but most of all they were the quintessential foreign male youths, aching to find available and beautiful women in these streets somewhere, in these well-lit buildings somewhere, in these gathering places somewhere, and earn the right to prove themselves young practitioners of the physical art of loving the opposite sex. With Desideria's hand in his Emilio felt luckier, wiser, more worldly by half—and, he laughed inwardly, this was only the first time he was going 'onnadatown'.

In the heart of the city they stopped to admire the way the city shops had built strange little Christmas displays right in their main windows. Meanwhile, Antonio and Santino fidgeted, tapped their feet, lit cigarettes and flicked away matches, rolled their shoulders under the padding of their jackets and shot flinty glances at sweet passers-by. The streets were hung with lights and the lights hung with tinsel. Instead of the icy winds they would have been experiencing back home, here the Holy Season was heavy and hot and still. Sultry December air made the boys' cotton shirts want to wilt, their woollen jackets to sag, their oiled hair to flop limp and dead. It was as if sheer youthful exuberance was the only force that could negate such Saturday-night catastrophes. Antonio, Santino, and Emilio too—despite a climate that made you want to droop—looked sharp. And most of the young women who were stared at by the boys stared back, not at them but at Desideria. She was a cool breeze inside a hot one, impervious. Men and women alike looked at her twice, wondering, Who the Hell is that girl?

They went to look at more intricate *Santa Natale* displays in the shop windows, with moving pieces and music playing, now passing an enormous two-storey, decorated Christmas tree that was bursting with colour and glitter. Children who had written letters to a Heaven they believed existed on Earth (where a man with even more weight than Neapolitan Joe Turisi didn't swelter from the summer—and *merda*, how you sweltered in this country's season of the birth of *Gesù*!) pressed their faces to thick store-front glass in order to get a better look at the Magi and glowing baby, the scrappily-furred camels, the shining Star of Bethlehem, the wrapped and stacked gifts and treats that might soon open by themselves to reveal unimaginable wonders.

Antonio and Santino ran out of patience for these festive displays even though whole families were gathered in front of Woolworths and Allan and Starks stores, and Bing Crosby's mellow voice crooning 'White Christmas' ('A white Christmas? How about a broiling-in-your-own-blood Christmas, Mr Crosby?') invited you closer. Emilio and Desideria tried to stop again but the boys took each of them by the arm and dragged them past the line of neighbouring big stores until they were all the way down the main road of Queen, where car traffic jockeyed for position with the always victorious electric trams.

Then finally they were at Conny's café and its swinging doors. [. . .]

2001

TIM WINTON
b. 1960

Timothy John Winton was born in Perth and grew up in the beachside suburb of Scarborough and the coastal WA town of Albany, with holidays in his great-uncle's Greenough River beach house. As he once said at a writers' festival: 'All my lore is seaward.'

Winton studied creative writing at the WA Institute of Technology (now Curtin University), where he was taught by Elizabeth Jolley (qv), and became a professional writer and a household name at 21 when the manuscript of his novel *An Open Swimmer* (1982) shared first prize in the *Australian*/Vogel Literary Award. He has since published numerous novels, short stories and children's books.

He married the year his first book was published, and by the time he left Australia with his family to spend two years in Europe, where they lived for periods of about six months each in France, Ireland and Greece, he had published three novels and two collections of short stories. His best-known novel, *Cloudstreet* (1991), was adapted by playwrights Nick Enright and Justin Monjo as a highly successful stage play in 1998, a five-hour epic that opened in Sydney and toured internationally.

During the 1990s he wrote a number of children's books, notably his 'Lockie Leonard' series, the text for several picture books and travel books, and *Land's Edge* (1993), 'an autobiographical celebration of life by the sea'. His next two major novels, *The Riders* (1994) and *Dirt Music* (2001), were both shortlisted for the Booker Prize and with *Dirt Music* Winton won, in 2002, his third Miles Franklin Literary Award. His third collection of short stories, *The Turning*, was published in 2004.

Winton's fiction appeals to a wide range of readers, and he is one of a handful of Australian writers who combine high sales figures with frequent literary prizes. Part of his appeal comes from the particular clarity and focus both of his material and his world view; Winton is a Christian with a strong sense of the numinous and of the spiritual dimension of landscape as well as of human affairs, but these matters are implicit in his writing rather than spelt out. 'All my books are about people trying to make sense of things,' he has said, 'about the search for meaning . . . about people who are possessed by a vision.'

His passion for the beach and the sea reveals itself in almost all of his fiction, most of which is set by—if not in—the ocean, usually the coastal regions of WA that he has known from childhood. He has said that all of his writing has its foundation in the setting and landscape, and that his characters grow out of that source: 'If I get a grip on the geography, I can get a grip on the people.' KG

My Father's Axe

1

Just now I discover the axe gone. I look everywhere inside and outside the house, front and back, but it is gone. It has been on my front verandah since the new truckload of wood arrived and was dumped so intelligently over my front lawn. Jamie says he doesn't know where the axe is and I believe him; he won't chop wood any more. Elaine hasn't seen it; it's men's business, she says. No, it's not anywhere. But who would steal an axe in this neighbourhood, this street where I grew up and have lived much of my life? No one steals on this street. Not an axe.

It is my father's axe.

I used to watch him chop with it when we drove the old Morris and the trailer outside the town limits to gather wood. He would tie a thick, short bar of wood to the end of forty feet of rope and swing it about his head like a lasso and the sound it made was the whoop! of the headmaster's cane you heard when you walked past his office. My father sent the piece of wood high into the crown of a dead sheoak and when it snarled in the stark, grey limbs he would wrap the rope around his waist and then around his big freckled arms, and he would pass me his grey hat with bound hands and tell me to stand right back near the Morris with my mother who poured tea from a Thermos flask. And he pulled. I heard his body grunt and saw his red arms whiten, and the tree's crown quivered and rocked and he added to the motion, tugging, jerking, gasping until the whole bush cracked open and birds burst from all the trees around and the dead, grey crown of the sheoak teetered and toppled to the earth, chased by a shower of twigs and bark. My mother and I cheered and my father ambled over, arms glistening, to drink the tea that tasted faintly of coffee and the rubber seal of the Thermos. Rested, he would then dismember the brittle tree with graceful swings of his axe and later I would saw with him on the bowman saw and have my knees showered with white, pulpy dust.

He could swing an axe, my father.

And that axe is gone.

He taught me how to split wood though I could never do it like him, those long, rhythmic, semi-circular movements like a ballet dancer's warm-up; I'm a left-hander, a mollydooker he called me, and I chop in short, jabby strokes which do the job but are somehow less graceful.

When my father began to leave us for long periods for his work—he sold things—he left me with the responsibility of fuelling the home. It gave me pride to know that our hot water, my mother's cooking, the livingroom fire depended upon me, and my mother called me the man of the house, which frightened me a little. Short, winter afternoons I spent up the back splitting pine for kindling, long, fragrant spines with neat grain, and I opened up the heads of mill-ends and sawn blocks of sheoak my father brought home. Sometimes in the trance of movement and exertion I imagined the blocks of wood as teachers' heads. It was pleasurable work when the wood was dry and the grain good and when I kept the old Kelly axe sharp. I learnt to swing single-handed, to fit wedges into stubborn grain, to negotiate knots with resolve, and the chopping warmed me as I stripped to my singlet and worked until I was ankle-deep in split, open wood and my breath steamed out in front of me with each righteous grunt.

Once, a mouse half caught itself in a trap in the laundry beneath the big stone trough and my mother asked me to kill it, to put it out of its misery, she said. Obediently, I carried the threshing mouse in the trap at arm's length right up to the back of the yard. How to kill a mouse? Wring its neck? Too small. Drown it? In what? I put it on the burred block and hit it with the flat of the axe. It made no noise but it left a speck of red on my knee.

Another time my father, leaving again for a long trip, began softly to weep on our front step. My mother did not see because she was inside finding him some fruit. I saw my father ball his handkerchief up and bite on it to muffle his sobs and I left him there and ran through the house and up to the woodpile where I shattered great blocks of sheoak until it was dark and my arms gave out. In the dark I stacked wood into the buckled shed and listened to my mother calling.

I broke the handle of that axe once, on a camping trip; it was good hickory and I was afraid to tell him. I always broke my father's tools, blunted his chisels, bent his nails. I have never been a handyman like my father. He made things and repaired things and I watched but did not see the need to learn because I knew my father would always be. If I needed something built, something done, there was my father and he protected me.

When I was eight or nine he took my mother and me to a beach shack at a rivermouth up north. The shack was infested with rats and I lay awake nights listening to them until dawn when my father came and roused me and we went down to haul the craypots. The onshore reefs at low tide were bare, clicking and bubbling in the early sun, and octopuses gangled across exposed rocks, lolloping from hole to hole. We caught them for bait; my father caught them and I carried them in the bucket with the tight lid and looked at my face in the still tidal pools that bristled with kelp. But it was not so peaceful at high tide when the swells burst on the upper lip of the reef and cascaded walls of foam that rushed in upon us and rocked us with their force. The water reached my waist though it was only knee-deep for my father. He taught me to brace myself side-on to the waves and find footholds in the reef and I hugged his leg and felt his immovable stance and moulded myself to him. At the edge of the reef I coiled the rope that he hauled up and held the hessian bag as he opened the heavy, timber-slatted pots; he dropped the crays in and I heard their tweaking cries and felt them grovelling against my legs.

During the day my mother read *They're a Weird Mob* and ate raisins and cold crayfish dipped in red vinegar. We played Scrabble and it did not bother me that my father lost.

Lost his axe. Who could have stolen such a worthless thing? The handle is split and taped and the head bears the scars of years; why even look at it?

One night on that holiday a rat set off a trap on the rafter above my bed. My father used to tie the traps to the rafters to prevent the rats from carrying them off. It went off in the middle of the night with a snap like a small fire cracker and in the dark I sensed something moving above me and something warm touched my forehead. I lay still and did not scream because I knew my father would come. Perhaps I did scream in the end, I don't know. But he came, and he lit the Tilley lamp and chuckled and, yes, that was when

I screamed. The rat, suspended by six feet of cord, swung in an arc across my bed with the long, hairy whip of tail trailing a foot above my nose. The body still flexed and struggled. My father took it down and went outside with its silhouette in the lamplight in front of him. My mother screamed; there was a drop of blood on my forehead. It was just like *The Pit and the Pendulum*, I said. We had recently seen the film and she had found the book in the library and read it to me for a week at bedtime. Yes, she said with a grim smile, wiping my forehead, and I had nightmares about that long, hairy blade above my throat and saw it snatched away by my father's red arms. In the morning I saw outside that the axe head was dull with blood. After that I often had dreams in which my father rescued me. One was a dream about a burning house—our house, the one I still live in with Elaine and Jamie—and I was trapped inside, hair and bedclothes afire and my father splintered the door with an axe blow and fought his way in and carried me out in those red arms.

My father. He said little. He never won at Scrabble, so it seems he never even stored words up for himself. We never spoke much. It was my mother and I who carried on the long conversations; she knew odd facts, quiz shows on television were her texts. I told her my problems. But with my father I just stood, and we watched each other. Sometimes he looked at me with disappointment, and other times I looked at him the same way. He hammered big nails in straight and kissed me goodnight and goodbye and hello until I was fourteen and learnt to be ashamed of it and evade it.

When his back stiffened with age he chopped wood less and I wielded the axe more. He sat by the woodpile and sometimes stacked, though mostly he just sat with a thoughtful look on his face. As I grew older my time contracted around me like a shrinking shirt and I chopped wood hurriedly, often finishing before the old man had a chance to come out and sit down.

Then I met Elaine and we married and I left home. For years I went back once a week to chop wood for the old man while Elaine and my mother sat at the Laminex table in the kitchen listening to the tick of the stove. I tried to get my parents interested in electric heating and cooking like most people in the city, but my father did not care for it. He was stubborn and so I continued to split wood for him once a week while he became a frail, old man and his arms lost their ruddiness and went pasty and the flesh lost its grip upon the bones of his forearms. He looked at me in disappointment every week like an old man will, but I came over on Sundays, even when we had Jamie to look after, so he didn't have cause to be that way.

Jamie got old enough to use an axe and I taught him how. He was keen at first, though careless, and he blunted the edge quite often which angered me. I got him to chop wood for his grandfather and dropped him there on Sunday afternoons. I had a telephone installed in their house, though they complained about the colour, and I spoke to my mother sometimes on the phone, just to please her. My father never spoke on the phone. Still doesn't.

Then my mother had her stroke and Jamie began demanding to be paid for woodchopping and Elaine went twice a week to cook and clean for them and I decided on the Home. My mother and father moved out and we moved in and sold our own house. I thought about getting the place converted to electricity but the Home was expensive and Elaine came to enjoy cooking on the old combustion stove and it was worth paying Jamie a little to chop wood. Until recently. Now he won't even do it for money. He is lazier than me.

Still, it was only an old axe.

2

Elaine sleeps softly beside me, her big wide buttocks warm against my legs. The house is quiet; it was always quiet, even when my parents and I lived here. No one ever raised their voice at me in this house, except now my wife and son.

It is hard to sleep, hard, so difficult. Black moves about me and in me and is on me, so black. Fresh, bittersweet, the smell of split wood: hard, splintery jarrah, clean, moist sheoak, hard, fibrous white gum, the shick! of sundering pine. All my muscles sing, a chorus of effort, as I chop quickly, throwing chunks aside, wiping flecks and chips from my chin. Sweat sheets across my eyes and I chop harder, opening big round sawn blocks of sheoak like pies in neat wedged sections. Harder. And my feet begin to lift as I swing the axe high over my shoulder. I strike it home and regain equilibrium. As I swing again my feet lift further and I feel as though I might float up, borne away by the axe above my head, as though it is a helium balloon. No, I don't want to lift up! I drag on the hickory handle, downwards, and I win and drag harder and it gains momentum and begins a slow-motion arc of descent towards the porous surface of the wood and then, halfway down, the axe-head shears off the end of the handle so slowly, so painfully slow that I could take a hold of it four or five times to stop it. In a slow, tumbling trajectory it sails across the woodheap and unseats my father's head from his shoulders and travels on out of sight as my father's head rolls onto the heap, eyes towards me, transfixed at the moment of scission in a squint of disappointment.

I feel a warm dob on my forehead; I do not scream, have never needed to.

The sheets are wet and the light is on and Elaine has me by the shoulder and her left breast points down at my glistening chest.

'What's the matter?' she says, wiping my brow with the back of her hand. 'You were yelling.'

'A dream,' I croak.

3

Morning sun slants across the pickets at me as I fossick about in the long grass beside the shed finding the skeleton of a wren but nothing else. I shuffle around the shed, picking through the chips and splinters and slivers of wood around the chopping block, see the deep welts in the block where the axe has been, but no axe. In the front yard, as neighbours pass, I scrabble in the pile of new wood, digging into its heart, tossing pieces aside until there is nothing but yellowing grass and a few impassive slaters. Out in the backyard again I amble about shaking my head and putting my hands in my pockets and taking them out again. Elaine is at work. Jamie at school. I have rung the office and told them I won't be in. All morning I mope in the yard, waiting for something to happen, absurdly, expecting the axe to show like a prodigal son. Nothing.

Going inside at noon I notice a deep trench in the verandah post by the back door; it is deep and wide as a heavy axe-blow and I feel the inside of it with my fingers—only for a moment—before I hurry inside trying to recall its being there before. Surely.

I sit by the cold stove in the kitchen in the afternoon, quaking. Is someone trying to kill me? My God.

4

Again Elaine has turned her sumptuous buttocks against me and gone to sleep dissatisfied and I lie awake with my shame and the dark around me.

Some nights as a child I crept into my parents' room and wormed my way into the bed between them and slept soundly, protected from the dark by their warm contact.

Now, I press myself against Elaine's sleeping form and cannot sleep with the knowledge that my back is exposed.

After an hour I get up and prowl about the house, investigating each room with quick flicks of light switches and satisfied grunts when everything seems to be in order. Here, the room where my mother read, here, Jamie's room where I slept as a boy, here, where my father drank his hot, milkless tea in the mornings.

I can think of nothing I've done to offend the neighbours—I'm not a dog baiter or anything—though some of them grumbled about my putting my parents into the Home, as though it was any of their business.

I keep thinking of axe murders, things I've read in the papers, horrible things.

In the livingroom I take out the old Scrabble box and sit with it on my knee for a while. Perhaps I'll play a game with myself . . .

5

This morning when I woke in the big chair in the living room I saw the floor littered with Scrabble tiles like broken, yellowing teeth. Straightening my stiff back I recalled the dream. I dreamt that I saw my body dissected, raggedly sectioned up and battered and crusted black with blood. The axe, the old axe with the taped hickory handle, was embedded in the trunk where once my legs had joined, right through the pelvis. My severed limbs lay about, pink, black, distorted, like stockings full of sand. My head, to one side, faced the black ceiling, teeth bared, eyes firmly shut. Horrible, but even so, peaceful enough, like a photograph. And then a boy came out of the black—it was Jamie—and picked up my head and held it like a bowling ball. Then there was light and my son opened the door and went outside into the searing suddenness of light. He walked out into the backyard and up to the chopping block in which an axe—*the* axe—was poised. I felt nothing when he split my head in two. It was a poor stroke, but effective enough. Then with half in either hand—by the hair—he slowly walked around the front of the house and then out to the road verge and began skidding the half-orbs into the paths of oncoming cars. I used to do that as a boy; skidding half pig-melons under car wheels until nothing was left but a greenish, wet pulp. Pieces of my head ricocheted from chassis to bitumen, tyre to tyre, until there was only pulp and an angry sounding of car horns.

That does it; I'm going down to the local hardware store to buy another axe. It's high time. I have thought of going to the police but it's too ludicrous; I have nothing to tell: someone has stolen my axe that used to be my father's. A new axe is what I need.

It takes a long time in the Saturday morning rush at the hardware and the axes are so expensive and many are shoddy and the sales boy who pretends to be a professional axeman tires me with his patter. Eventually I buy a Kelly; it costs me forty dollars and it bears a resemblance to my father's. Carrying it home I have the feeling that I'm holding a stage property, not a tool; there are no signs of work on it and the head is so clean and smooth and shiny it doesn't seem intended for chopping.

As I open the front gate, axe over my shoulder, my wife is waiting on the verandah with tears on her face.

'The Home called,' she says. 'It's your father . . .'

6

The day after the funeral I am sitting out on the front verandah in the faint yellow sun. My mother will die soon; her life's work is over and she has no reason to continue in her sluggish, crippled frame. It will not be long before her funeral, I think to myself, not long. A tall sunflower sheds its hard, black seeds near me, shaken by the weight of a bird I can't see but sense. The gate squeals on its hinges and at the end of the path stand a man and a boy.

'Yes?' I ask.

The man prompts the boy forward and I see the lad has something in a hessian bag in his arms that he is offering me. Stepping off the verandah I take it, not heeding the man's apologies and the stutterings of his son. I open the bag and see the hickory handle with its gummy black tape and nicks and burrs and I groan aloud.

'He's sorry he took it,' the man says, 'aren't you, Alan? He—'

'Wait,' I say, turning, bounding back up the verandah, through the house, out onto the back verandah where Elaine and Jamie sit talking. They look startled but I have no time to explain. I grab the shiny, new axe which is yet to be used, and race back through the house with it. Elaine calls out to me, fright in her voice.

In the front yard, the father and son still wait uneasily and they look at me with apprehension as I run towards them with the axe.

'What—' The man tries to shield his son whose mouth begins to open as I come closer.

I hold the axe out before me, my body tingling, and I hold it horizontal with the handle against the boy's heaving chest.

'Here,' I say. 'This is yours.'

1985

ADAM AITKEN
b. 1960

The son of a Thai mother and an Australian father, Adam Aitken was born in London and spent his early years in Thailand and Malaysia. He was educated in Sydney. As well as poetry, he has written criticism and creative non-fiction. He has travelled widely, and much of his poetry is a sophisticated engagement with Asia and the intercultural links between Asia and Australia. In the words of the critic Martin Duwell, Aitken emphasises 'the personal as the place where the obsessions with place, empire, language, history and signs cohere'. Aitken's books include *Letter to Marco Polo* (1985), *In One House* (1996) and *Romeo and Juliet in Subtitles* (2000). *DM*

Post-colonial

They grew up—quicker, and rougher round the edges
than she'd planned, her children
hounding the North Shore's lower end,
losing laundry bags,
rationing snooker money.   5
They took their losses, spent their gains

with pin-point precision
back spin, double off the side cushion,
chalked up cues
passing back and forth, back and forth.   10

She was beautiful then, glamorous at a distance
illusion plus and licensed
forklift driver, Samuel Taylor Aerosols.
Suzy Wong they called her, Suzy Wong
with a Noel Coward accent   15
lamenting a lost chauffeur, her husband.
She should've been saving
for a new appliance
at Big Bear Shopping Mall.

Remember Louis the Fly[1]   20
spreading disease with the greatest of ease.
Remember Menzies,[2]
remember the CPA,[3] and all the mates
she cooked a hundred suppers for
when she'd read   25
a union intercedes. Why invoke
discrimination's house?
Vietnam consumed
truckloads of flagons, teenage poets
and the best efforts   30
of Dad's advertising
agency.
The phone was tapped for years.

I hope they wiped those tapes
of weeping and recrimination   35
but mostly
inarticulate
silence between shifts,
quiet lunch breaks,
a word with the manager,   40
prescriptions through a side window,
scribbled sick notes for the teacher.

---

1   Louie the Fly, cartoon character for a series of insecticide advertisements.
2   Robert Menzies (qv), known for his anti-union and anti-communist stance.
3   Communist Party of Australia.

They grew up—
quicker, and a little rougher round the edges
than she'd planned.   45
                                                                  1996

Changi[1]

Real orchid forest in Terminal 2
where gypsies rest, fazed
by taped bird-song. Unpack, repack
those dreams that don't need sleep.
On my Nintendo   5
Super Mario up to his tricks again
bouncing over cities, stretching
bandwidth, island-hopping the crevasse
of urban decay.
Programmed for 'invincible'.   10
On the X-ray my collection
of South East Asian coins,
more useless by the hour.
A metal detector singing jingles.
I leave a message   15
via credit card phone, my own
     message-machine voice
feeding back like hydroponics.
Visit my own web-site
at the Internet village,   20
terminalled to coffee and cyberspace,
jacked in to Borneo.
Two teenage attendants flirting
dressed in New Raffles White,
the colour for angels at a funeral   25
for nurses or lab attendants.
White noise, nothing's as it was,
as it seems, except—my email:
'I promise to come home, darling
please believe me.'   30
Midnight in Singapore.
The perfect transit lounge
unpacks, repacks, I find myself

---

1   An area at the eastern end of Singapore, site of a Japanese Prisoner of War Camp during the Second World
     War, now the site of Singapore's Changi Airport.

craving some obsolete science,
  archeology perhaps: 35
a litter bin overflowing with poems,
alive, odourless as these orchids,
close and colourful as your face on a VDU.
The birds, extinct, full throated, unseen
imagine themselves a forest 40
  circled by jets.
Their song glorious, their makers dead.

2000

LISA BELLEAR
1961–2006

Lisa Bellear was a Goenpul woman of the Noonuccal people of Minjerriba (Stradbroke Island), Queensland. A notably political poet, she was also a visual artist, academic and social commentator, being involved in Aboriginal affairs nationally. She was an executive member of the Black Women's Action in Education Foundation and a volunteer broadcaster on 3CR community radio for eleven years on the 'Not Another Koori Show'.

Her collection of poetry *Dreaming in Urban Areas* was published in 1996. Bellear also conceived and co-wrote the promenade-style theatrical work, *The Dirty Mile: A history of Indigenous Fitzroy* (2006). She performed her work nationally and internationally, and was widely published in journals, newspapers and anthologies. An avid photographer, Bellear took thousands of photographs over the many years she spent engaged with Indigenous affairs, both politically and socially. *AH/PM*

Women's Liberation

Talk to me about the feminist movement,
the gubba middle class
hetero sexual revolution
way back in the seventies
when men wore tweed jackets with 5
leather elbows, and the women, well
I don't remember or maybe I just don't care
or can't relate.
Now what were those white women on about?
What type of neurosis was fashionable back then? 10
So maybe I was only a school kid; and kids, like women,
have got one thing that joins their schemata,
like we're not worth listening to,
and who wants to liberate women and children
what will happen in an egalitarian society 15

if the women and the kids start becoming complacent
in that they believe they should have rights
and economic independence,
and what would these middle class kids and white women do
with liberation, with freedom, with choices of   20
do I stay with my man, do I fall in love with other
white middle class women, and it wouldn't matter if
my new woman had kids or maybe even kids and dogs
Yes I'm for the women's movement
I want to be free and wear dunlop tennis shoes.   25
And indigenous women, well surely, the liberation
of white women includes all women regardless …
It doesn't, well that's not for me to deal with
I mean how could I, a white middle class woman,
who is deciding how can I budget when my man won't   30
pay the school fees and the diner's card club simply
won't extend credit.
I don't even know if I'm capable
of understanding
Aborigines, in Victoria?   35
Aboriginal women, here, I've never seen one,
and if I did, what would I say,
damned if I'm going to feel guilty, for wanting something
better for me, for women in general, not just white
middle class volvo driving, part time women's studies students   40
Maybe I didn't think, maybe I thought women in general
meant, Aboriginal women, the Koori women in Victoria
Should I apologise
should I feel guilty
Maybe the solution is to sponsor   45
a child through world vision.
Yes that's probably best,
I feel like I could cope with that.
Look, I'd like to do something for our Aborigines
but I haven't even met one,   50
and if I did I would say
all this business about land rights, maybe I'm a bit
scared, what's it mean, that some day I'll wake up
and there will be this flag, what is it, you know
red, black and that yellow circle, staked out front   55
and then what, Okay I'm sorry, I feel guilt
is that what I should be shouting

from the top of the rialto building
The women's movement saved me
maybe the 90s will be different.   60
I'm not sure what I mean, but I know that although
it's not just a women's liberation that will free us
it's a beginning

                                                     1996

Woman of the Dreaming

My sweet woman of the Dreaming
Where is your soul,
I need to surround your body
With my spirit, the spirit
Of the embodiment of love   5
     anger
     pain
     disparate neutrality

My sister, lover, friend,
Let your soul and my soul   10
Fall in love

But love is so remote,
The gum trees are whispering
The Yarra Yarra is polluted
Koalas on Phillip Island are   15
So stressed that they too will
Be another victim of the
Invasion

1990, the beginning of the
Haul towards the new century   20
Where do you fit in my sister
No one but you know you
No one but me knows the love
I have for the world but ...
More apt the love I have   25
For you
     Sweet
     Strong
     Determined
     Misunderstood   30

Woman of the dreaming
Find your soul,
And peace and love and
Eternal fire and spirit will
Connect with our ancestors   35
And our land
Will begin to smile, again.

                                                         1996

Urbanised Reebocks

In a creek bed at Baroota
I lose myself amongst
the spirit of life of
times where people
that is Blak folk   5
our mob—sang and laughed
and danced—paint-em
up big, red ochre
was precious … go on
remember-hear the   10
sounds of flattened
ground and broken gum
leaves—

My feet slip out of their
urbanised reebocks/   15
of sadness, which
hides its loneliness
behind broken reebans[1]

Uncloaked feet hit
the earth …   20
And it's okay
to cry

                                                         1996

---

1   Author's note: 'I coined this word reeban—it comes from combining the words reebocks and raybans. I love wearing these types of shoes and sunglasses.'

Taxi

For Joan Kirner

splashed by a passing cab,
and another and another
there's rules you see;
don't. stop. for.
black women, accelerate   5
past black men
and pensioners on pension day
can't trust,
trash
got no cash   10
we're all *nuisances*
reminders of an unjust
world, where the poor,
people of colour
are at the mercy   15
of even taxi drivers.

        1996

RICHARD FLANAGAN
b. 1961

Richard Flanagan's concern for his home state of Tasmania is the source of much of his fiction and non-fiction and also of his political and environmental activism. He grew up on Tasmania's west coast, in the mining town of Rosebery and was educated at the University of Tasmania and Oxford University, as a Rhodes Scholar. *A Terrible Beauty: History of the Gordon River country* appeared in 1985. His first novel, *Death of a River Guide* (1994), draws imaginatively on his first-hand experience of the wild Franklin River. The cross-generational story in his best-selling second novel, *The Sound of One Hand Clapping* (1997), begins in a construction camp for a hydroelectric dam in the Central Highlands of Tasmania where postwar migrants, often refugees or 'displaced persons', work in harsh and alienating conditions. The novel explores the shadows of the past in the present. Flanagan wrote and directed the film version. *Gould's Book of Fish* (2001), a fiction that engages in baroque postcolonial style with the notorious history of Tasmania—then Van Diemen's Land—as a penal colony, won the 2002 Commonwealth Writers Prize. In *The Unknown Terrorist* (2006), Flanagan moves to contemporary Sydney in a novel that is disturbed by Australian responses to the 'war on terror'. *NJ*

From *The Sound of One Hand Clapping*
Chapter 11: 1989

[. . .] Sonja looked across from Bojan's room at the mirror-image of the single men's quarters in which she stood: another long skinny single-storey barracks clad in corrugated iron, doors running down its length, verandah above, washing hanging out the front upon pieces of nylon cord stretched from post to post, fraying singlets, khaki denim work trousers faded to the beautiful colour of eroded sandstone, coarse woollen jumpers in all colours, and t-shirts inscribed with the messages of a world that had no place for those who stretched into them, shift after shift after week after month after year. Men came and went from this battery-hen cage, and Sonja watched how at the far end of the single men's quarters opposite, a rolling fist of listless men folded and unfolded, tensed and untensed, as if forever unsure that their physical strength was not some cruel disability, talking in short sentences followed by long awkward laughs.

Behind each door was a miserable cell of a room, identical to the one in which she stood, the one which Bojan forever refused to call home, but in which he had lived for decades now, in various reincarnations at various hydro dam construction camps, each new cell sufficiently the same as the last for him to be confirmed in his belief that no single one could ever be special. It came with a steel bed and nothing else, because anything else the authorities rightly figured would be stolen. There was, in any case, scant space to contain much, but in spite of this some of the inhabitants would attempt to reform the cells as suburban lounge rooms, ludicrous and compressed dreams of stillborn domestic ambition. Others treated their room only as a bivouac, which they would soon be leaving forever as they headed out to meet their destiny somewhere else, anywhere else other than Tullah.

Bojan's room belonged, as did Bojan, nowhere. It was empty of aspirations, of delusions, of dreams. It was neat enough, sparkling in its austere emptiness on that day that Sonja visited, and she knew that her father would always keep it that way. He had always hated dirt, mess, evidence of what had been. In addition to his steel bed Bojan had a small TV. An old transistor in a leather case that she remembered from her childhood. A chest of drawers. A kitchen chair, steel tubed and orange vinyled. A small fridge. A small wooden wardrobe he had decorated himself, painting on each of its two doors a white flower with pointed petals. It was a quirk of his which she had forgotten, this painting of flowers on things, even on his construction helmet and her first hockey stick.

By day Bojan's room was lit, as each room was, by the dusty light that tumbled from the one small window set high up in the wall opposite the door. Sometimes he sat there, a silhouette of a man skewered into this world only by the shafts of light down which motes unrolled like illuminated letters in a mediaeval manuscript, and imagined himself a monk in some distant Balkan monastery. A man who had renounced everything and scourged his flesh daily in the hope, forever unrealised and unrealisable, of purging his soul of its terrible demons. He punished his innocent body terribly with drink and with labour, felt his flesh gnarl and wither, felt his guts bloat like a dead man's, felt his head throb with the dull agony of it all, but within him something sharp still cut, something undeniable, and as long as he felt that pain he knew there still remained within him a soul, and he would have done anything to be rid of it, would have renounced it, traded it, thrown it like rubbish on the road and walked on.

But it was not possible. [. . .]

1997

JORDIE ALBISTON
b 1961

Jordie Albiston lives in Melbourne. Her first book of poems, *Nervous Arcs* (1995), won the Mary Gilmore Award. Two of her collections, *Botany Bay Document* (1996) and *The Hanging of Jean Lee* (1998), are 'documentary poems', revising periods in Australian history to uncover women's experiences. Her other two collections—*The Fall* (2003) and *Vertigo: A cantata* (2007)—deeply connect emotion and form (especially repetitive and 'chain' forms). *DM*

The Fall

People will gasp. They'll point at you in disbelief, but before they can absorb the reality of what they're witnessing, the miracle will be over.
Paul Auster

She takes a tall building as hers is to be a very long fall.
She was always going to fall, whether she got to the top
Or not. Depression is holy. You have to be called.
She hears the children cheering inside: there is no hope.

She was always going to fall, whether she got to the top   5
And jumped, or was pushed. It says so in the contract.
She remembers the small print: *There will be no hope;*
However, cleanse your heart with prayer before combat.

She will jump. Or she will be pushed. See contract.
From this height, West 33rd Street has a silent mystique.   10
Her heart is clean out of prayer: nothing will extract
The dread, the black-dog knowledge it is all a mistake.

From the eighty-sixth floor, West 33rd Street is silent.
There is no consolation for those who cling to the railing

Only dread. She believes this is what the prophet meant.   15
With her body in her throat, she lets go, and is falling.

There is no consolation for those who cling to the rails.
I don't think I'm lost, but I don't know where I am.
She has let go, hesitated in the air. She has yet to exhale.
Her body hangs over a matrix of chaos and desolation.   20

She is not lost, but falling like Eve into the Big Apple.
Each year takes a minute, each week a singing second:
Her body hangs over a matrix of chaos, as she topples
Downwards, too fast for those below to comprehend.

In the air, a moment can take on the time centuries span.   25
She falls through former selves above a thousand heads.
No one looks up. No one looks towards the bright sedan:
Within a handful of time, it will be her crumpled bed.

She falls, self by self, over a crowd of a thousand heads.
Failing always at physics, this falling is her punishment: 30
In seconds, her crumpled body will lie in its metal bed
Where she shall sleep, no matter what the prophet meant.

Physics having failed her, she falls at the speed of night.
She is spinning through childhood on a taut yo-yo string
Aching for God, and some sleep. She is alone alright: 35
The playground, the pool. She is the one with no wings.

She spins through a childhood and the cool New York
Night, clutching an orchid in her white-gloved hand.
Wingless, she is tumbling through twenty-three years
Of astonishing despair. She is the Angel of Manhattan.   40

Clutching an orchid, she flies through the rhyme We All
Fall Down and cannot get up (the pool, the playground).
She is often astonished at the depth of despair in her soul:
Still she tries to find God, endeavours to never look down.

She is falling down, and cannot get up. It is the rhyme.   45
Her descent through adolescence with its paintbox of blood
Is final. She leaves her life and her longing for God behind.
If not this flight, then what in heaven can make her good?

She descends through adolescence, obsessed with its paints
And its blood. It feels always like falling (she never flew).   50
Nothing on earth can make her good, for she is tainted.
See, a stocking is down, she has already lost both her shoes.

Moments are made to be flown through: you climb, and
If you have the courage, leap. She knows this much is true.
Shoes gone, stocking down, orchid clutched in left hand   55
She hisses by on a seam of light only darkness could pursue.

If you have the courage, leap, the prophet may have said.
Clinging to life like a leaf in the suburbs, she never took
The plunge. But now, how she sings on that hissing thread!
How bright and thin the sound of her whistling rebuke!   60

She clings like a leaf to the life she never took to, falls
Towards womanhood where things start to look black.
The whistle of her descent becomes a God-awful squall:
In these final few feet, she knows there is no going back.

It is during womanhood that blacknesses start to appear.   65
Lay your hands upon me: can you feel my broken heart?
There is no going anywhere in these final falling years
No rehearsal, no second chance. This is the lonely part.

A broken heart can make a woman climb, and catapult.
(She flashes on being caught in her father's open arms.)   70
There is no rehearsal, no second chance, no way to halt
This lunge. She was always going to come to harm.

She falls into her father's arms from various heights:
This was the light that held her darknesses from her.
Now, as she plunges, she invites the harm of night.   75
Into the smog and the New York noise she is hurled.

Out of the darkness, she blurs into light for a moment.
No one has time to point or scream at the miraculous
Sight. The streetlights and smog receive an angel sent
From the Empire Deck. Those above are still oblivious.   80

And then the car. No one has time to point or scream:
The word Forgive is already forming on thickening lips

As she curls into metal, perfectly. The Empire is a dream
She always had. She was contracted to climb to the tip.

Her lipsticked mouth is locked around a word, Forgive.   85
Yes, depression is holy. (Another soul has just been called.)
The orchid is a contract she clutches in one hand: To live
You must climb to the very top, for it is a very long fall.

    2003

EMMA LEW
b. 1962

Emma Lew completed an arts degree at the University of Melbourne. She is the author of two prize-winning collections of poetry: *The Wild Reply* (1997) and *Anything the Landlord Touches* (2002). Her poetry is strongly attracted to the uncanny. *DM*

Marshes

They speak of stridency and of nothingness
and wrap up their shoulders in grey light.
I want to walk again in this miry place.
I want the fever and fret beneath, though
it's something I forget, like pain.   5

Sky a tent immaculately pitched and noon's
ghosts are creeping across paddocks.
Low, lame winds grow in the rushes—
the smoky pool mad in its sleep. I have
found earth still adhering. I wait for storms   10
to crack the glamour open.

I don't know the language of this country.
It begins in mists, sombre wild bees.
Moss sophistry while I lie listening. Dark
snake rumours grave in my ear.   15

Butterflies edged with wonder. Sly harrier,
cool stealing the day. A wraith's day—
slow and gentle and ravaged. This whole
calm world's sweet venom. My puritan
soul half in a sea, clawing deep in the peace   20
of mud.

    2002

Nettle Song

Why glimmer? Seize fire!
What has sunk? The sweet hour,
all havens, the corners—
gloom's in the folds!

The rose has broken,   5
I am in fever.
Lead me to hyacinths,
let me run to seed.

What's in your heart?
Glaciers, glaciers,   10
a strange, cruel starvation,
the smallest storm.

What are your riches?
Puddles and thistles,
Burst fruit, such ashes,   15
wild as I wish.

2002

LUKE DAVIES
b. 1962

Luke Davies, who was born in Sydney, is a novelist and poet. His first novel, *Candy* (1997), is both a love story and a tale of heroin addiction. Davies wrote the script of the film version of *Candy* (2006), which starred Heath Ledger and Abbie Cornish, and was directed by Neil Armfield. Davies's poetry is intense and intellectually adventurous. 'Totem Poem' (2004) is one of the most exuberant, indeed visionary, poems about love in Australian literature. Davies has also worked as a teacher, truck driver, journalist and script editor. *DM*

Totem Poem

In the yellow time of pollen, in the blue time of lilacs,
in the green that would balance on the wide green world,
air filled with flux, world-in-a-belly
in the blue lilac weather, she had written a letter:
You came into my life really fast and I liked it.   5

When we let go the basket of the good-luck birds
the sky erupted open in the hail of its libation;

there was a gap and we entered it gladly. Indeed the birds
may have broken the sky and we, soaked, squelched
in the mud of our joy, braided with wet-thighed surrender.   10

In the yellow time of pollen near the blue time of lilacs
there was a gap in things. And here we are.
The sparrows flew away so fast a camera could not catch them.
The monkey swung between our arms and said *I am, hooray,*
the monkey of all events, the great gibbon of convergences.   15

We were falling towards each other already
and the utter abandon to orbits was delicious.
The falcon rested on the little man's arm and falconry
was the High Path of the World. Whole minutes passed.
We were falling and the jungle fell with us.   20

She said *I came, I came to my senses really fast*
and you liked it. I was surrounded by the fluttering
of wings, nothing but a whirring in my ears,
and the whole earth tilted and I lost my reason.
For a time falconry was the high path of the world.   25

At night the sky was filled with animals.
Ganesh loomed large among those points of light.
He said *Change!* and we said *Lord we are ready*
to bend. Thou art the high exalted most flexible.
He said *Then I will enter into your very dreams.*   30

And the yellow-tailed black cockatoo, ablaze
in his own musculature, soared all night above the sunlit
fields of whisky grass that stretched inside me
to a river's edge. The great bird cawed its majesty,
a sonic boom; and even I was barely welcome there.   35

There was a gap in things; and all the lilacs bloomed.
Words split in our grasp. We were licking the cream
from the universal ice. Words foundered and cracked.
How the bonnet was warm on your bottom! And the metal
continued tick-ticking though the engine was off.   40

And the evening shuddered, since everything is connected.
I was licking the cream from the universal saucer.

I was all of Cheshire and points between.
You saw the great sky turn blacker, you saw the spray of stars
and your hair got tangled in the windscreen wiper.   45

At the hot ponds we stripped as night closed in.
I secretly admired your underwear, your long
elusive legs. In the spring where we lay side by side
we held hands. Up above the steam the sky. I said
That one is called Sirius or Dog Star, but only here on Earth.   50

And when since the stories foretold it we parted,
those birds were all released again. Such buoyancy.
They go on forever like that. How else to say thank you
in a foreign place? We are ever in the arms of our exile,
forever going one way and the other   55

though sometimes of course on a sphere that is not so bad.
I will meet you on the nape of your neck one day,
on the surface of intention, word becoming act.
We will breathe into each other the high mountain tales,
where the snows come from, where the waters begin.   60

In the yellow time of pollen when the fields were ablaze
we were very near bewildered by beauty.
The sky was a god-bee that hummed. All the air boomed
with that thunder. It was both for the prick
and the nectar we drank that we gave ourselves over.   65

And if every step taken is a step well-lived but a foot
towards death, every pilgrimage a circle, every flight-path
the tracing of a sphere: I will give myself over and over.
I have migrated through Carpathians of sorrow
to myself heaped happy in the corner there.   70

Nothing seemed strange in the world, you'll understand—
nothing ever more would. Monkey Boy came to me saying
Look—the moon of the moon. The little one circled the big one.
He crouched in the palm of my hand, tiny, sincere,
pointing at the sky. There was something sad about him.   75

The python was nothing, nothing at all, nothing
but strength shed to suppleness, nothing but will

encased in itself. The python was a muscle of thought.
Coiled and mute, in a place where nothing but rain fell,
the python thought: this is the beginning or end of the world.   80

The python was everywhere, everywhere at once, aware
only too much of that ageless agony: its existence.
I am tired, it said; and the stream burbled by.
I am waiting for the recoil, the uncoil, coil of night,
coil of stars, coil of the coldness of the water.   85

The python said *Who are these people?*
The whole city sweated, moved like a limb. The air
fitted like a glove two sizes too small and too many
singers sang the banal. The bars roared all night.
The kite hawks grew ashamed. All nature squirmed.   90

In the yellow time of pollen there's a certain slant of light
that devours the afternoon, and you would wait forever
at the Gare de l'Est, if time stood still, if she would come.
She is the leopard then, its silvery speed; where will you
wrestle her, and in what shadows, and on what crumpled sheets?   95

And all those sheets were pampas and savannas, the soft expanses
of all that would be absent forever, all that was
past, and future, and not here. And in a white rose
there were not to be found any secrets, since in its unfolding
there was no centre, nor in its decay. Only the random petals fallen.   100

In the yellow time of poppies when the fields were ablaze
those invisible pollens rained around us.
The days held us lightlocked in golden surrender
and all night long the night shot stars.
When my chest unconstricted at last, did yours?   105

The real issue, of course, was this: atomically, energetically,
everything was wave function. And a wave continues forever into space,
the wavelength never alters, only the intensity lessens, so
in the worst cosmic way everything is connected by vibrations.
And this, as even a dog would know, is no consolation.   110

Ah but the dogs will save us all in the end & even the planet.
Not the superdogs but the household friendlies, always

eager to please, hysterically fond, incessant, carrying in the very
wagging of their tales an unbounded love not even
therapists could imagine; their forgiveness unhinges us.   115

We were reduced to this: this day and night,
primary gold and indigo, the binary profusion
of distances guessed at, heat and cold, colours
logged in the retina and lodged in the spine;
we were dogs who knew the infinite is now,   120

that celandine was buttercup, that buttercup was marigold.
The dog star marked the dog days and the wild rose
was dog rose. The crow's-foot was wild hyacinth.
By day the correspondences were clear.
I walked across the whin land. Speedwell bluer than sky.   125

A practised ear could hear, between two breaths,
deep space wherein the mind collects itself.
Words foundered and cracked. *Nearly*
never bulled the cow. A shining isomorphousness
rang out. The roussignol sang all night.   130

All colours were shuffled endlessly but never lost.
A practised ear could hear, between two breaths,
the secret blackness of the snow
come flooding in. On summer's lawns
the ice-melt sprayed its figure-eights from sprinklers.   135

And everything stopped working, second time around,
as if it had never happened before. Fans
moved the corpses of fireflies through the rooms,
supplicant, pathetic, pleading in brittle postures.
Everything was magnified by their bug-eyed deaths.   140

We became solemn in that profusion
of dying. Cane toads fattened the asphalt
in the mist and the rain; our headlights caught them
tensed as if listening: they were waiting,
mute, for the imbecility of eternity.   145

The clocks merely pulsed, or rather the days.
Like shotgun spray on the weatherboard, sleep

scattered itself through the blurred heat
and secreted itself in the nooks of delirium.
Sometimes the magpies would wake us, or the phone,   150

mid-afternoon. And we needed nothing, not even hope,
being no different from the dragonflies,
or the cows in their despair. It appeared we lived
on sunlight and chocolate bars. You blossomed
so from not ever reading the newspapers.   155

Things came and went—the years and all the airports.
I was a shade scattering my shade seed
liberally to the winds and weathervanes.
There was not enough absence to go round.
I heard voices, *stabat mater*,[1] in the whine of jets   160

and in air vents and headphones a stream
trilling over rocks. On tarmacs and in transit
I saw your lips, your nakedness, the trees,
that dappled light. I dreamt of orchards.
The preciseness of the world came flooding in.   165

For every blossom there could be no turning back,
one path only to cup and fig, beyond
the belly of the heart's content, each precipice
a flood of salt and jewels. Tang
of the overwhelming, flooding in.   170

I saw a kestrel quiver but not move
high in the air as if a sculptor left it
unattended, incomplete, just waiting for
a sign, just give me an excuse. I heard
the bush rat squeal. For there is nothing   175

lost may not be found if sought.
The minotaur in the corral
who called himself Asterion
tramples me softly with his song and, frustrated,
head-butts the posts. I can but admire him.   180

---

1 A medieval Roman Catholic hymn beginning 'Stabat mater dolorosa' ('The sorrowful mother was standing').

In the yellow time of pollen when the air was weighed down
there were bees plump with syrup. There were figs
fit to burst at the seams. I understood
how language had emerged: in the Flesh of the Fruit.
I spoke my tongues against your breathlessness.   185

Down there nothing but eternity and praise.
To be alive I had to praise, to praise I had to
learn to speak. Speak loudly though to drown
the blood about to burst, to drown eternity
whose howl floods every canyon into nothingness.   190

In the blue time of lilacs the last colour standing
was the mauve that jacarandas leak when all else
has gone grey: last glow before night,
the brightest that earth ever gave. Far across
the estuary the mangroves rippled in the rain.   195

Pelicans plumped on the tide-posts, world-in-a-belly.
There was mud for the taking. The orb spiders
clung during storms to the high-tensile webs.
Much later the fruit bats, insane with greed, tore into the fig trees
and gnashed at the edges of dreams.   200

Time was merely the measure of motion
with respect to before and after. Meanwhile
the universe expands. The pine trees creaked.
The pine cones cracked. On a windless day there was time
to dream of you. The pine cones snapped open the silence.   205

All the fields and force fields stretched away to snow caps.
Gravitational, magnetic—there were even fields undreamt of;
and the green one where we lay, where we organised to meet,
where the wildflowers parted and the gorse looked like light,
was hidden in the cleft our kisses made.   210

Light stretches as it moves away. The peaks and contours
we explored had taught us time was malleable. All things
have mass except ideas. A hammock was therefore a metaphor like

breathe. A diamond meant nothing but *carbon-later-on.*
The flight paths of the pelicans smelled . . . like *luck.*   215

We were falling and the jungle fell with us.
It rained all through the pass; at every plateau praise.
World-in-a-belly. From the photon's point of view
the universe contracted to one point
and even as it left it had arrived.   220

To us the photon spread through space
in studious propagation. In an ocean the waves
had water to ride on, and sound waves fought their way
through air. But light was the medium itself.
Thousands of birds, the tiniest birds, adorned your hair.   225

In the driest season I drew my love from geometry.
I cried to learn a circle was a curve
of perfect equidistance from a point. In summer
wild sage grew in tufts on the slopes
where in spring the sun would melt the snows to scree.   230

All the while I was asking myself what was the
howling outside the hut I was mistaken I couldn't
recognise my own voice it was so loud I was having
trouble with inside and outside. You came to me
from God-knows-where in wider arcs than birds can make.   235

You made me calm. I said to God *God
how often do I thank you God?* I had had
so many years of beauty intruding on all I did I did
not think it might intrude on others. Others
showed no signs of it. But you said laughing *Taste it Taste it.*   240

And a wet front smothered the whole south coast &
our hazard lights flashed in the cloud of unknowing &
the semis overtook us and blinded us with spray.
I said to God *God I am speechless I am
contented I am very tired and I am rather in love.*   245

[. . .]

2004

CRAIG SHERBORNE
b. 1962

As recounted in his memoir *Hoi Polloi* (2005), Craig Sherborne, born in Sydney, spent some years in New Zealand before returning to Australia with his parents. He attended drama school in London, and has worked as a journalist for *Stock & Land* and the Melbourne *Herald Sun*. Sherborne's early works were dramatic (plays for stage and radio). His poetry has appeared in the collections *Bullion* (1995) and *Necessary Evil* (2006). *Hoi Polloi*, along with its sequel *Muck* (2007), have received much praise. 'Ash Saturday' is an elegy for the poet's father. *DM*

Ash Saturday

There is no God, I was made in *this* man's image:
those slate-dark eyes of his are mine,
the dented bridge of our his-my nose.
I laugh with his rasping cackle in me.
I walk with his stooping, trudging gait,   5
swearing his 'Jesus bloody Christ'
in a sudden fist-curl of temper.
My right ear points like a flesh-antenna as his does,
and being my father I bear his name.
Haphazardries of kin passed on from birth   10
that to see him wizened on his cancer bed,
his insides turned to water,
is to view my own death, my own Dorian Gray
smiling, weeping in the drug-bliss of sleeping
or counting out life on his fingers: 15
'I've got more money than I thought,' he says.
'And I can't even wipe my arse.'
I soak a flannel and do it for him,
the first time I've touched his privates.
The doctor says he could go on for hours,   20
but no he won't, the nurse assures me.
She gives him a last injection.
'If there's something unsaid, best say it now.
He won't wake up from this one.'

Now I scatter him in the surf.   25
This is what a man burns down to:
bone's grey grit like broken pebbles.
Not ash but grit and blood-brown dust

from the coffin they called 'Mahogany'.
The same salt 'n' pepper as his shaven stubble   30
that whiskered the sink-white from his razor,
the Brylcreemed hair he palmed skin-smooth
after combing with his tongue poked forward.
Some of him sticks to my swimming hands—
I shudder and dunk to wash him from me,   35
splash myself like an accidental ritual,
but it's too late, the symbol remains:
He always stood between me and death,
but now I'm next in line, I inherit his future,
a law bequeathed that's impossible to alter,   40
a murder-chain sanctioned as natural.

I've already moved into his death:
I've tried on his clothes for a decent fit
and sorted the rest for the Salvos.[1]
I used his screwdriver to jemmy the plug   45
from this beige plastic tube he came in.
It exhaled a false puff of breath.
In a minute I'll escort my mother from the beach,
her taking my arm like a younger he,
casting his funeral flowers to the shallows.   50
'Looks cold that water,' she'll worry with a shiver.
'You don't think we should have buried him?'
She'll complain how the pins-and-needles sand
is stinging her legs like mosquitoes.

She'll hope out loud there's nothing funny with his will   55
and expects her sister to be over for a hand-out.
Then we'll turn for one more chance to watch
where his slick dissolved in the buckled swell,
stretched into invisibility.
I'll blink and utter 'Goodness' with her   60
as if death really was a mystery after all
and dwells out there in all that sea and twilight.
But death's no mystery, not to me, not now.
I am its DNA.

2006

1   The Salvation Army.

RICHARD FRANKLAND
b 1963

Richard Frankland is a singer-songwriter, playwright and film-maker of Gunditjmara/ Kilkurt Gilga descent. He has written poetry, young adult fiction and musical theatre. Born on the coast of south-west Victoria, Frankland worked as a field officer during the Royal Commission into Aboriginal Deaths in Custody, which led to his appearance as a presenter in the award-winning Australian documentary *Who Killed Malcolm Smith?* (1992), which he also co-authored. His other film credits include writer/director for *Harry's War* (1999). Some of his songs have been recorded by Archie Roach (qv). His novel *Digger J. Jones* was published in 2007. *AH/PM*

Two World One

I'm a two world one
I live in two worlds
One time I must have lived in one

But tears fell and a baby taken
Under some law they said   5
A law from one world but not the other

I'm a two world one
I walk down two roads
One time I must have only walked down one

But surely a mother's heart was broken   10
At a birthing tree or birthing room
When I was taken

I'm a two family one
I live with two families
One is black one is white   15

But surely heritage is no barrier to love
Even though the papers scream
About the two hundred years of hurt and shame

I'm a two world one
I can see inside two worlds   20
But one day I'll only have to see in one

2001

JOHN KINSELLA
b. 1963

John Kinsella was born in Perth, and WA (especially the south-west) is a region that continues to feature largely in his poetry. Kinsella is a prolific writer and significant force in Australian and international poetry. As well as numerous collections of poetry he has published verse plays, a novel, a collection of short stories, criticism, two volumes of memoir and a libretto (an adaptation of Wagner's *Götterdämmerung*). He has also edited a number of works, including selections of Michael Dransfield's and Rodney Hall's (qqv) poetry, as well as many special journal issues and *The Penguin Anthology of Australian Poetry* (2009). He was founding editor of *Salt* magazine, and founder of Folio Press. He began the 'poetryetc' email discussion list, as well as an electronic resource of Western Australian writing. He also helped found the international publisher, Salt Publishing. In 1997 he was made a fellow of Churchill College, Cambridge. He is also a Professional Research Fellow at the University of Western Australia, and Adjunct Professor to Edith Cowan University, WA.

Kinsella describes himself as a 'vegan anarchist pacifist' and is a vocal supporter of environmental issues and Indigenous rights. He is married to the poet Tracy Ryan (qv), with whom he has collaborated. (Kinsella has also collaborated with many other writers, including Dorothy Hewett (qv)). Kinsella's memoir *Fast, Loose Beginnings* (2006) attracted some controversy. *Peripheral Light: Selected and new poems* (2003) was selected and introduced by the American critic Harold Bloom. Kinsella's experimental poetry has been collected as *Doppler Effect* (2004). As seen in collections such as *The Hierarchy of Sheep* (2001) and *The New Arcadia* (2005), his poetry is often anti-pastoral in nature, illustrating the hidden violence (and violent histories) of the pastoral scene. But as 'The Vital Waters' also shows, Kinsella evokes a plethora of regions, interests and cultural references in his wide-ranging poetry. As Ann Vickery writes in *DLB*, Kinsella illustrates 'a kind of rhizomatic belonging, identity constellating and diffused tangentially across the globe' (2006). *DM*

The Vital Waters

For Chris Hamilton-Emery, Robin Holloway, Tim, Alison, Tracy,
Stephen, Rod, John, Adam, Drew and Jeremy

About the asteroid belt of apples
fallen in the orchard,
leaves stacked up against the weight of micro-climates
and passers-by, the wind
untethers our lacunae,   5
touch-sensitive recollections
we get stuck in, where pleasure
is without extras,
and the swirl of components
makes anniversaries.   10

It looks benign, the Cam,[1]
even in violent weather, it rides

---

1 The river that runs through Cambridge in England.

only so high against the college stone,
threatens the bridge of sighs, the mathematical bridge
only so much; downriver, down below the lock,   15
residents of houseboats would say
it's rougher, the painted doors, thin bellies,
thrust against the backs, walking past,
you might imagine their overly sexual doings,
the smell of incense, the kaleidoscope of batik,   20
tough attitude to water rats; moving up to the Granta[1]
the punts shovel indolence and suppressed excitement,
not quite strong enough poler hanging over the water,
an entire family rugged up against the cold;
the mud below pasture, cloister manuscript articled   25
anecdote; it all being alike there's no allegory,
only simile, which is not what you'd be led to think
drinking against Hobson, being surrounded by gas-tower
youth in the Grafton Centre; the resident population
left at taxi ranks while Trinity students   30
own the straight line and either side of it
from the Blue Boar[2] home; only similes
as like to all the stones cobbled
in Saint John's where I often duck in for a piss
cutting through from Churchill to the Heffers bookshop,   35
or the Cambridge Health Food Shop, or even Sainsbury's
where recently in the absurdity of a metaphor, an employee
and a security guard held a patron hard to the floor,
his protesting 'Fuck off, I've done nothing wrong!'
walked around by those who don't want to know,   40
their *Guardians* tucked under arm, maybe a bottle of wine,
certainly Sainsbury's own brand hidden in double-layered
plastic bags; Erasmus hated the damp, Wittgenstein
had himself buried just behind Churchill, perpendicular
to the observatory where the actions of the sun   45
are noted by a famed astronomer and reported at High Table:
I like him crossing the Cam at Magdalene Bridge,
caught in the expanding gases of the sun,
a spot in time being a spot in the sun,
solar activity a field guide to form;   50
the Cam, sourced in Byron's Pool,

1   A pub on the Cam.
2   A pub near Trinity College.

infiltrated by chemicals and the by-products
of Monsanto's genetic modification; did you know
there's a nuclear reactor in the middle of town?
Did you know they dismantle animals bit by bit,   55
glass windows to the hearts: it's the ultimate
house of pain—and the students generally speak
politely and marry the like-minded, attending
the odd poetry reading; in the bike throng, a pedestrian
hits the ground, come off the grass! By the grace of the senate   60
you wander in your gown, the university locked in a sense
of competitive fun with the *other* university, red brick
starting blocks a touch of Milton or those decadent
pre-Raphaelites; the DNA smorgasbord, the swans
served up in Benedictus benedicat, a touch of the gong,   65
and drinks in the senior combination room—that's where
I met Said[1] and Vendler,[2] Wilson Harris[3] and a bunch of Nobel
Prize winners—Syd Barrett[4] lives in his mother's old home;
son of a doctor, he wandered the banks of the Cam,
tripped in the Gog Magogs,[5] grew intoxicated   70
in Wandlebury Wood—beetroot carrot aquaplane, hydrographer
tin cup, astronaut, and a theatre company loosening
the strings of a stratocaster, star fighter,
thin gypsum walls through which the utterances
of the Black Mountain School are heard; Syd Barrett's   75
history of art, preyed upon by video artists, village
idiots—them, not him—looking astonishingly
like Les Murray.[6] Cambridge dishes out the kudos,
coughing up the loot; there are at least half a dozen
toilet blocks that make entries out of exits,   80
libraries that make scholars out of poets,
Australian Rules following faculty and students,
drunk on XXXX or Fosters, or cascading
through episodes of *Neighbours*,
a refutation that cultural studies   85
is yet to make its mark where the Pearl shines
out of the dead clasp; in the old court

1   Edward Said (1935–2003), literary theorist, critic and political activist, a founding figure of postcolonial
    theory.
2   Helen Vendler (b. 1933), American poetry critic.
3   Wilson Harris (b. 1921), Guyanese writer.
4   Syd Barrett (1946–2006), a founding member of Pink Floyd.
5   Hills south-east of Cambridge.
6   Les Murray (qv).

a light shines out of *Macbeth*, a French horn
resonates through the stone, ivy turns
like a birthmark—spreading, yet fixed.   90

The growth of ancient stone at twilight
is sensed by one whose sight
is honed by the pulse of the river,
science of bridges, microcosm of pasture.

The riverlight feeds the roots of willows,   95
nettle spawn floats indolently on the vacation air:
the seasons are mixed here, and pheasants rise up out
of test crops, the pollen count low, heavy as shot;
Kipling makes Empire in the library
of Wimpole Hall, and throwing a whistleblower   100
a pound you damn history, fail to recall
that by agreement the ancient universities
survived the European war; runner-up to the VC's
medal for poetry back in the early nineteenth
century Wentworth's[1] Australia was simulacrum,   105
really, in the non-jargon use of the word; our
Australian daughter became Cambridge at Park Street
Anglican-assisted school—she likes hymns in the morning.

Castle Hill[2] remains indifferent to the breadth
of summer as back garden aviaries   110
burst with enthusiasm and small cars
parade themselves like a serenade;
the Gog Magog hills recline with sunset
and the child is able to say where she's
been and where she might go, mapping   115
from high ground as if all time has been taken.
Somewhere around here death broke
Hobson's girth, and this is what the drunk
reminds himself heading back home
after a riotous day in the Town & Gown,   120
and somewhere somebody refuses to age,
as the day condenses into an adage.

1   William Charles Wentworth (1790–1872), Australian explorer and politician, author of the poem
    'Australasia' (1823), which called for 'a new Britannia in another world!'.
2   An ancient site on the left bank of the Cam.

From Churchill, I most often cut through the orchard
of Saint Edmund's. The gardener there is a friend
by wave or single word, year after year, we trail   125
the seasons; he gave me the names of plants on
one occasion—our verbal moment; pigeons
and robins and squirrels work as a single
species below the hooded apple trees;
the windfalls before the ice comes   130
define the loss and presence,
the year gone but mid-year for some,
I cut through and past the fence lines,
past the barber's, up through Honey Hill,[1]
past Euclid's indecision, the plimsoll line   135
of the university; the sanitary religious
vocation, theology against the minuscule
enclosed park where the Saturday craft market
titillates the tourists come by the gay pub
I cherish, though I don't drink, come by to sample   140
what was once the Jewish ghetto, and staring below
the reflective surface of the Cam, figure
this is where I'll come, so tempted by conversion
in this city-village-town based on primary numbers,
port and sherry, piss-ups and hashish in the gardens,   145
bears and college cats, cars forbidden during term,
forbidden to every Dr Faustus made in the cellars,
made in the dining halls, in rooms of the more modern
colleges where the heating vacillates, in lecture theatres
with pitted writing boards; in blue and brown books,   150
in oval windows and choirs sonorously out of control,
pretending restraint, pretending committees
keep the place together, that the Thatcher papers[2]
are pivotal to the intestinal fortitude of the twentieth century.

The growth of ancient stone at twilight   155
is sensed by one whose sight
is honed by the pulse of the river,
science of bridges, microcosm of pasture.

Lion's Yard. Flashers. Sent Down.
Mould and watermarks, not far from the river.   160

1   An area of Cambridge.
2   The papers of Margaret Thatcher (British prime minister 1979–90) are held by Churchill College.

Out to lunch. Iambic pentecostal.
Saints and serifs. Marxist extroverts
and infiltrators, anamarxist overlords,
cricketers and all shades of blue.
In the theatres they—we—watch art   165
dressed up as porn. Trinity
funds the poorer colleges.
At King's, revolutions are funded
only in part; the horse sculpture
has bolted from Jesus College; the Cam   170
is also a place for ducks, insects,
bank-dwelling rodents.

The growth of ancient stone at twilight
is sensed by one whose sight
is honed by the pulse of the river,   175
science of bridges, microcosm of pasture.

A splice of Milton's mulberry tree[1]
grafts the bones of the Lindsays,[2]
or the bones of Queenie[3]
and her sharp conversationalism.   180
For eight years there were no anniversaries,
there weren't eight years and the anniversary
was a constant, hexes and nettles, bikes two abreast
down raceways, vivisectors who smile in passageways,
libraries that don't want books; their atheists   185
partially in the chapels, and light is the collation of factors,
as the silver oaks slice high winds, brighter than the moon
and its promise of choral interludes,
so brash in the dining rooms
when the rugby team has scraped home,   190
so obsessed with the retrievals of potlatch
and who has gone before—I deny prescience,
stolen spirits, dogs swimming the length
and breadth of Byron's pool—anything

---

1   A tree growing in the Fellows' Garden at Christ's College, Cambridge, planted in the year of John Milton's birth (1608) and named in his honour as a former student of the college. It is said that he composed 'Lycidas' while sitting under the tree.
2   A reference to Ian Gordon Lindsay (1906–66), Scottish architect, and his sister Ailsa Margaret Lindsay.
3   Q.D. (Queenie Dorothy) Leavis (1906–81), English literary critic, who often wrote collaboratively with her husband, the critic F.R. Leavis (1895–1978), who taught at Downing College, Cambridge.

can be re-created here, even the scorched   195
post-harvest Western Australian wheatbelt,
even the excesses of Silicon Valley.
Helen Vendler is said not to like Australian poetry—
generally, as a broader category—she is pleasant
to have a cool drink with in the refectory,   200
it's in the geology or geography but not necessarily
the genealogy; Empson's little desiring machines[1]
have fortunately kept little out, though
it has its ways at interviews, class
wins out, and oh, in some places   205
nice arse—bottoms, as in summers we watch
in groups and classes *A Midsummer Night's Dream*
in the gardens—the folk from Heffers bookshop
on a rug of their own, downing champers—hi, Adam,
fellow Syd aficionado, who has heard the notorious   210
bootlegs, the copies of sessions few have ever heard—
sketches of a Cambridge childhood, tripping
on snippets of Shakespeare and the gibbet
on the crossroads; on Midsummer Common
the people against cruelty, the hemp foodists,   215
the vegan straight-edges: Strawberry Fair,
Cambridge—Pagan Festival . . .?

On cowpat, grazing ground, long-haired overturf,
trance dance and hemp shirts, chai/tea tents
and guitar slayers, rude boys and Brisbane Hell's Angels,   220
'travellers', solstice-gazers and academics
strolling in circuits, dogs, imitators, WASPs, the occasional
Catholic, dope-cloud makers and casual inhalers,
vicarious participants, ecstasy and acid purveyors,
potage with grudges, legitimate cases, dogs   225
with thick collars. Fight! Fight! News later,
a chest-stabber, victim rehabilitates
on the bouncy castle in kids' corner,
hooked drummers and Korg[2] drivers, sorcerers
and preternatural shouters knowing self-worth,   230

---

1 William Empson (1906–84), influential English literary critic. He was expelled from Magdalene College
(and, indeed, the city of Cambridge itself) after prophylactics were found in his room. 'Desiring machines'
is a term invented by the theorists Deleuze and Guattari referring to an organised system of production
that controls flows.
2 A manufacturer of keyboards and digital musical equipment.

self-love, empire food, dogs. Sky broods
though mud in abeyance, this year low
on wallow: a light shower, a sunset
to dampen prospect, just slightly, dogs
with bristling collars. Opening blue   235
twilight, trance dance centres. Loop,
scratch, boom box. Shout. The country
of vegans like the fifth voyage of Gulliver
and Stephen Rodefer[1] collecting visuals
and gossip. Ankh and beads, beyond ecstatic,   240
flaps of cloth strung out by woofers,
O sonic boom box. Collect dance,
kids with collars, toes in the damp.
Hawk the cans. Bottles. Small pots
of amyl. Reggae tribes cross over   245
with ska-makers, vendors, hair-binders,
hot in the tent, pulsed and beaten,
whipped up slowly into bob and jump,
throwing ropes, flailing gunja-thick air.
Henna artists contract. Jar. Donor. Prayer,   250
Rodefer says: 'Only England can still get
truly medieval . . .' Sadistic piercers
and inscribers. Nervous handstanders
on guarana. Sex dance, trance dance, buzz.
Mumble, vibrating fingers, smoking implements   255
and lager, circus. Charms and spells
in blue and brown books, dogs, proofs
and magnets charged in the slam dance.

The growth of ancient stone at twilight
is sensed by one whose sight   260
is honed by the pulse of the river,
science of bridges, microcosm of pasture.

And Ted Hughes with the Addenbrookes nurse,[2]
so crucify me to the breast-milk-drinking master
bilingual in the oak closets,   265
oh Monsanto, Monsanto you're on the way out,

1   An American poet (b. 1940), one of the founders of the Language Poetry movement.
2   A reference to Carol Orchard, who married the English poet Ted Hughes in 1970. Addenbrookes is a large
    teaching hospital in Cambridge.

crux of life empire-builders coring shires
and asset stripping nation, hedgehog light,
infused summer evening, French knickers
and jock straps in Lion's Yard,[1] someone   270
throws up at a poetry reading; they closed
down the shelter run by ex-addicts
closed in and closed down—
under the bridge the rough sleepers
drop dead—all the time, dapper young men   275
and sharp young ladies (in Cambridge they
remain as such, no matter the linguistic
innovation), write smart articles
for *Varsity*, centring the culture.
Holy holy holy they worship   280
beside the off-licence, round church
Norman fetishes, rubbings
to pass the time where time is measured
subatomically—gangs of thieves work
the colleges, capricious around surveillance.   285
At Grantchester[2] some of us listen
to Bikini Kill,[3] in our heads,
beyond the reach of Monsanto.
Fuck you, Monsanto, fuck you.
Feed the poor, feed the earth?   290
Deniers, Monsanto, deniers.
Fuck it up. Good riddance,
and you're not the only player
in the anti-thinking school of Cambridge:
profit over ideas, and call it the new ethics,   295
where are the Leavisites when we don't
need them? Fin de fuck up.

The growth of ancient stone at twilight
is sensed by one whose sight
is honed by the pulse of the river,   300
science of bridges, microcosm of pasture.

The guitarist from Blur
made a Syd Barrett-inspired sculpture—

1 An area of Cambridge.
2 A village on the Cam outside Cambridge.
3 A punk rock group of the 'riot grrrl' movement (1990–98).

in the spirit of Cambridge—maybe—
he donated it to charity. 305
My head is lodged there.
It is a home. A cyclotron of language
that won't let up for a minute.
Part of me is in the infectious ward—
adult chickenpox—of Addenbrookes, 310
treated by the son of poet
Nathaniel Tarn[1]—international ritualism
of Cambridge—hey, I owe you one,
good bloke that you seem to be
in the ward of sweat and peyote. 315
The Wellcome trust spreads its wings—
there's an early Black Sabbath cult there.
Mice that grow ears—human ears,
and dogs that bark backwards.
See how words demean context. 320
Blood on the floor, protest.
It is summer, and yet so cold
at night we huddle under the blankets.
'You Australians are always
on about the weather . . .' 325

The growth of ancient stone at twilight
is sensed by one whose sight
is honed by the pulse of the river,
science of bridges, microcosm of pasture.
2004

Map: Land Subjected to Inundation

So that's salt, *the* salt, wonderland wanderlust
comeuppance, coo-ee refractor, TV static-inducer,
sullen receptor when crystals dampen
and melt, form a suggestion, this land
on the York map, Avon District, South-west Land Division, 5
South-west Mineral Field, fed by stream intermittent,
as high winds are ossified into not-that-far-off
contours and cliffs, trigonometrical station
on the infinitesimally

---

1   A British-American poet (b. 1928).

small reserve crowning Needling Hills, which the now—'owners'   10
won't let us climb:
          so how does that feel?
                  Uncle Jack's
old homestead 'Avonside' is listed, a square peg in a round hole
transmuted by grid convergence against the sheet centre,   15
                      interferon
fighting intrusion of recollection,
               that road we cut-up
on the Kwaka 100, small cc'd trail-bike that was big to us
and raced twenty-eight parrots in their lifts and dips   20
drawn out:
        they really *do* drag you off.
                Contour lines
show a gradual falling away—not that dramatic.
                 Wallaby Hills   25
at 59.2300 ha is only a semi-reasonable patch
set aside
      for the conservation of flora and fauna,
                  and we know
the fence is down on the Melbong Creek side and sheep   30
wander through into a place where their dead brethren are dumped,
grazing diminishing species of plants.
             This isn't for the sake
of the sheep, but the farmer extending the realm of grazing
to bulk them out, add a dimension to the quality of wool.   35
The landloss, water-tones sourced in the telephone paddock,
house dam paddock, running down through salt
as a drawcard, like an osmotic filter, sheep skin
a catalyst to seepage, and salt clustering
all about—   40
        it's the shape,
           the string in solution,
wide-eyed and close to formations,
              avatars and hucksters,
deeply serious holders of the 'Bolya',   45
           whom you respect
and fear:
      in subjugating and making his *Vocabulary*
of the Dialects of South Western Australia, Captain Grey[1]

---

1   Sir George Grey (1812–98), explorer, governor and politician, published his *Vocabulary of the Dialects spoken*
   by the Aboriginal Races of South-Western Australia in 1839.

noted of the Boyla-ya-gaduk, that flight and dispersal   50
in air are a pleasure, had at will, or a pleasure to transport
in such a fashion, as invisible they'll force entry as a shattering
of quartz and consume flesh,
                    these chips of white and apricot quartz
littering the waste of the place now labelled as 'land   55
                                        subjected
to inundation', that we call The Salt.
                        This creek or system of creeks
came out of the homeplace, fed by any poisons applied
to enhance the crops, fuel the generator that pushed out   60
little over thirty volts,
                    creek system that fed and feeds Pitt Brook
that feeds the Mackie River that feeds the Avon, contributing
to the salinity of the valley, this salt mine, this source
vicariously 'ours',   65
                    left behind, enriching
the nation's coffers, comeuppance, a sullen receptor
where crystals dampen and melt.

                                                      2005

TRACY RYAN
b 1964

Tracy Ryan grew up in Perth, where she attended university. With her husband, the poet John Kinsella (qv), she has lived in the United States and Cambridge, England. She has taught at universities, worked in libraries, and as a bookseller, tutor and editor. She is a poet and fiction writer. As well as books of poetry—which include *Killing Delilah* (1994), *Hothouse* (2002) and *Scar Revision* (2008)—she has written novels and co-written (with Kinsella) a book of short stories. Her work is attuned to the violence and mythic resonance of everyday life, and the vulnerability of the human subject. *DM*

Wungong[1]

I always dream he is down here
where he waved one hand and sank
in the still pool. I forget the real
dank fistful of dirt and agapanthus
we threw on him, I forget   5
red clods that adhered to
our soles and dust smeared

---

1   A dam reserve in Perth, WA.

on damp cheeks, the unjust softness
of kangaroo paws. I forget HE IS RISEN
clamped over the earth-mouth.   10
In dreams I come back for him
to the one dam you have never
written of.

                                                       1999

Eclipse, Kenwick,[1] 1974

It descended one schoolday
when we were children,
this darkness, the one condition
that enabled seeing
the element we turned in   5
yet allowed only partial vision:
bright ring, emblem of burning
bush and stark completion
slow-motion moon imposing
'O-gape of complete despair'   10
which is there, which is always
there; how we cherished
our little images,
pin-hole and television—
ersatz knowledges—   15
unaware you'd swallow year after
year after year and the one of us
who said, 'I am not afraid
to die because then I will see
the stars as I've always wanted.'   20
I have never forgotten
how still it was,
how the animals took on oddly
the same way they did
one summer, the day he died;   25
uneasy calm before that dry
and silent storm.
How we ate, drank and were merry
instead of lessons, and the teachers
told stories and pulled down the blinds.   30
                                                       1999

---

1   A suburb of Perth, WA.

CHRISTOS TSIOLKAS
b. 1965

Christos Tsiolkas was born in Melbourne to immigrant Greek parents. He graduated in arts from the University of Melbourne in 1987 and his first novel, *Loaded* (1995), gained immediate critical notice and some notoriety for its graphic and extreme representations of a certain kind of homosexual experience and identity politics. The novel was later made into a successful feature film, *Head On* (1998).

Tsiolkas's second novel, *The Jesus Man*, appeared in 1999 and his third, the award-winning *Dead Europe* (2005), caused even more controversy than *Loaded* had done ten years before, with its nightmare vision, its complex but uncompromising politics, and, again, its graphic representations of sex and violence. Tsiolkas is also a screenwriter and playwright, and has won awards for collaborative playscripts, including *Who's Afraid of the Working Class?* (1998) and *Non Parlo de Salo* (2005). *KG*

From *Dead Europe*
The Solid Earth Beneath My Feet

[. . .] I walked the town that day. This place, this small town high in the mountains, was where I came from. It was to this town that my mother had come down from the village for celebration and for dances; this is where she had first tasted ice-cream and bananas and oranges. They were so rare, she once told me. I was a child, lying next to her in bed, and she was in a silky heroin daze. I was wearing blue and white checked pyjamas and I was asking her about Greece. On drugs, she would answer. Fruit was so rare. But I remember my father took me to Karpenissi one morning, we had walked since dawn, and I saw an old man with a stick of bananas over his shoulder. I didn't ask for one, I knew they were expensive, but my Dad saw my hunger and he bought me one. He let me eat it all myself, did not even take a bite. Recalling her father, her face had become sad and old. She kissed me goodnight, grumbled that I did not know how lucky I was to be in a place where everyone ate bananas and peaches, apricots and oranges.

I held my camera tight in my hands and willed myself to see Greece, her home, through her eyes.

I took photographs of shopfronts, bakeries and butcher shops. I took photos of the old wooden walls of the town, of the new concrete apartments. I took photographs of the surrounding peaks and of young children playing soccer in side streets. I took photographs of a drunk old man, his teeth all gone, his eyes bruised. I took as many photographs as I could, switching film after film, so when I returned home I could ask my mother, Do you remember this? Does it still look the same?

Even as I pressed my finger on the shutter I was aware that the places I was framing through my viewfinder had changed unceasingly since my mother was born. I knew as I heard the click of the camera that my mother's hazy memories of this place she left when she was still a girl could not compete with the crisp colours and matt tones of the photographs I was now taking. I didn't care. I wanted her to have something more solid of memory than words. I took photograph after photograph. As this was a foreign light, as I did not know this intense but delicate Mediterranean light, so different from the harsh and boundless sun of my own country, I took shot after shot of the same scene, altering the exposure to ensure that the film would capture the houses, the fields, the narrow lanes, the faces, as I wished to preserve them. I altered the aperture and attempted to capture the soul of the town.

The old men of Karpenissi stared suspiciously at my camera. The old women I did not see, they kept indoors. I took seven rolls of film and I was exhausted by the time I walked back to the bus station. The chain-smoking man behind the counter was rude and unsympathetic to my requests. It seemed that buses to my mother's village only left on Wednesdays and Mondays and when I persisted in my pathetic Greek to discover an alternate route, he told me that the village was a clump of Devil's earth and why the fuck did I want to go there when Karpenissi had everything I needed as a tourist. I realised, when he made a disparaging aside to a bus driver, that he thought of me as a complete stranger, that my accent and manner had obscured all evidence of Greekness. I gave up my efforts and decided to hitch. I paid my bill at the hotel and I rang Giulia in Athens.

—*Gamouto, epitelos.* About fucking time.

It had been twelve years since I had heard her voice but I recognised it immediately, recognised the accent of her stilted English. It sounded like the way Slavic women in Australia tried to fix their lips around the hard Australian accent. Twelve years ago, my father's family had not been kind to me. They had taken me in, they had shown me the tourist sights of Thessaloniki, they had politely paid for my meals and my drinks, but they had not protested when I declared my intentions to travel on my own and they had been relieved to close the door after me. It had been an uncomfortable two nights I'd spent with my uncles and my aunts, my cousins—they doing their duty, I doing mine—sitting on sofas, listening to them gossip and laugh about people I did not know. It was uncomfortable because we could not talk about the one thing we had in common: my dead junkie father. Even his presence had been erased from their houses. His youthful image did not stare down from any of the old photographs that adorned their immaculate bourgeois homes and apartments.

Giulia, younger than I by a month, had sat across from me on a sofa and her penetrating dark eyes had unnerved me. She had interrogated me. Who did I vote for? Were there Greek members of Cabinet in Australia?

What was my perspective on the civil war? Was I a supporter of the Velvet Revolution? Did I agree that Scorsese owed his biggest debt to Rossellini? What was my favourite Dylan, my favourite Tsitsanis? Her sharp slanted eyes had scrutinised me, and I thought I had been a disappointment to her, clumsily answering her questions and making it obvious that Australians were ignorant and naive compared to the hunger of a Europe suddenly churning through the vast ramifications of the fall of the Soviet Bloc. But she had laughed when I told her my favourite Dylan was 'I Want You', and had started singing it, and she clapped her hands and squeezed my knees when I defended *Voyage to Italy* over *The Bicycle Thieves*. My aunt had cooked a large dinner and then I was off to the station to take the train to Belgrade. Giulia had jumped up and offered to drive me. I had said my goodbyes, received my stilted kisses, and thrown my black backpack into her car. She was driving silently, smoking a cigarette, and I remember feeling melancholy and alone. But we never arrived at the station. Instead, she stopped outside a cold grey Balkan apartment block and told me to grab my bag.

—Where are we?

—My friend Elena has an apartment here. She is in Rhodes for the summer. I have the key. You are staying here, she announced.

I laughed.

—Giulia, I have a train to catch.

—Forget it, your travels can wait. Here's my cousin from Australia, damned faraway Australia, and he's not leaving until we have a chance to talk.

We entered the apartment block, took the tiny creaking lift to the third floor and entered a cramped space filled with the fragile soothing smells of women with a balcony looking over the Port of Thessaloniki. I smoked a cigarette, breathing in the sea air and the summer wind, while Giulia fixed us drinks.

—Anyway, you can't leave yet, you've hardly seen anything of this city. She was standing in the doorway and sipping from a gin and tonic. Then, taking a seat beside me, looking out at the sea, she asked me very simply, Tell me, how did my uncle die? [. . .]

2005

ANDREW McGAHAN
b. 1966

Novelist Andrew McGahan was born in Dalby, Queensland, the ninth of ten children growing up on a wheat farm. After dropping out of university he lived an 'urban slacker' life in Brisbane until the commercial and critical success of his *Australian*/Vogel award-winning first novel, *Praise* (1992).

Praise was the first in a wave of Australian grunge novels in the 1990s; McGahan's second novel, *1988* (1995), a prequel to *Praise* again featuring its main character Gordon, looked back on the Australian Bicentennial celebrations, ironically contrasting the officially celebratory mood with the aimless incoherence of a certain kind of Australian masculinity. McGahan then turned to the well-marked conventions of the crime fiction genre to write *Last Drinks* (2000), a political crime novel about corruption in Queensland.

His fourth novel, *The White Earth* (2004), makes use of McGahan's own rural background and, again, of traditional literary genres—in this case the family saga and a particularly Australian form of Gothic—to investigate the history of Australian race relations and competing passions for the land, against the background of the *Native Title Act* 1993.

McGahan's overtly political and satirical dystopia *Underground*, a blackly funny and savage critique of the conservative Howard government, was published in 2006. He has also written stage plays and screenplays, including the adaptation of his own novel for the 1999 film of *Praise. KG*

From *1988*
Chapter 5

[. . .] 'Can I drive?' said Wayne.

I gave him the keys. He started up and we moved out of town. A few hundred yards along we pulled over. I watched while Wayne dug through his gear in the back seat. He came up with a large bag of marijuana.

'Did you bring any of this?' he asked.

'No.'

'It's okay. I've got three of these bags.'

He rolled a joint, lit it. We started up again. I stashed the bag in the back seat, then took drags when the joint came my way. I coughed a lot of it out again. I always coughed. Virgin lungs.

Wayne eased the Kingswood up to speed. It was getting towards mid-afternoon. I consulted the map. Mitchell was the next town, and after that some small place called Morven, where we'd turn and start heading north-west. I put the map down, stared out the window. The country was all reds and dull greens, scrub and ant-mounds. There wasn't much traffic. The odd car, a few semitrailers. Farm houses baked under the sky.

I remembered that we'd bought batteries for Wayne's stereo at the roadhouse in Roma. I dug around on the back seat, found the batteries, the stereo, and a box of cassettes. I inserted the batteries, then inspected the tapes. They were all outside their cases, most of them battered and spotted with thumb prints in various colours of paint.

'I don't recognise anything here except for Neil Young,' I said.

'Put the Big Black tape on.'

I found it, slipped it in, pressed play. It was loud and harsh and full of bass. It seemed appropriate. I leaned back. The joint moved in, mixed with the alcohol. Time drifted by.

I thought about things, forgot them. I stared at the blur out the window. It was strange. The trees seemed to move in close, then swerve away. I blinked, sat up. It was Wayne. He was swinging the car back and forth across the road.

I watched. He was crouched over the wheel, leaning with it as he turned. I decided he was ugly, almost hideously so. The angled elbows and knees, the sunburn, the tangled clumps of blond hair. He was *disgusting*.

Something flashed on the dashboard. It was the alternator light, blinking on and off. Then I saw the temperature gauge. It had swung right over to the red. I considered what that meant for a moment.

'Wayne,' I said, pointing.

He started, looked down. 'Oh.'

The car didn't slow. A few seconds passed.

I said, 'Don't you think you'd better stop.'

'Oh. Okay.'

He slowed, stopped, switched off the engine. I turned down the stereo. We listened to the hiss and splutter of the radiator boiling over.

'I have to admit,' I said, looking around, 'I did think we'd make it further than this.'

Wayne popped the hood and we climbed out to examine things. Water and steam were gushing out from under the radiator cap. The fanbelt was broken.

'Lucky we've got a spare one,' Wayne observed.

I found myself annoyed.

'Don't you ever look at the dashboard?'

'Sorry.'

'You didn't notice that the alternator light was on and that the temperature gauge was in the red?'

'How was I to know your car overheats.'

'It doesn't. How fast were you going anyway?'

'Not fast. I could barely even get up to a hundred. It drives very heavy.'

I thought, Heavy?

I said, 'What gear were you in?'

'It's an automatic.'

I went round to the driver's seat and looked in. Wayne hadn't put the shift in Park when he pulled up. It was still in the same gear he'd been driving in. It wasn't Drive or even Second. It was in Low.

'Have you *driven* an automatic before?'

He thought. 'I'm not sure. I drive my mother's car a lot, but it's a manual. Why?'

'You were going a hundred in first gear. Revving the absolute shit out of the engine. You're lucky it didn't explode.'

'No kidding.'

'Why didn't you notice?'

'Why didn't *you*. You're the machinery man.'

Why indeed?

'Well anyway,' I said, 'I bet that's why the fanbelt broke.'

'Is it hard to put on a new one?'

'Not if you've got a spanner.'

We went to the boot, unloaded everything, and searched in the recesses. We found the spare fanbelt, and a spanner. We tried the spanner on the tension bolt. It was too small. The bolt wouldn't move. We tried stretching the fanbelt over the wheels anyway. It was too tight.

'That's one thing your father didn't think of,' said Wayne. I threw the spanner away. 'I guess he assumed that even an *artist* would know how to drive.'

'What now?'

'What d'you think? We flag someone down.'

We waited. Wayne sat in the car, the stereo on again. Big Black didn't seem so impressive anymore. I sat on the hood, staring up and down the road. It was twenty minutes or so before a semitrailer appeared, coming towards us. A petrol tanker. I stood on the road and waved. It slowed and stopped, air brakes hissing. A thin face looked down from the cab.

'What's your problem?'

'Fanbelt. We need a spanner to put on the new one.'

He nodded. 'Got a set here somewhere.' He climbed down. He was small and wiry, dressed in shorts and a large black hat. Wayne and I stood there and watched while he changed the fanbelt. It was a two minute operation. No one spoke. When he was finished he repacked his spanners. 'There you go,' he said. He looked us over, Wayne mostly.

'You boys from Brisbane?'

'That's right.'

'Where you headed?'

'We're exploring the outback,' said Wayne.

Another long look. 'Hope you get there.' He headed back towards his truck.

'Thanks,' I said, after him.

Then he was in the cab, and pulling away.

'I don't think he liked us,' said Wayne.

'I don't think he cared.'

'Well isn't this the outback?'

'No.'

'Where the hell is it then?'

'I think I'll drive from here.'

'Fine.'

We refilled the radiator and climbed in. Wayne dialled up the stereo. I put the car firmly in Drive, and we moved on. [. . .]

1995

DELIA FALCONER
b. 1966

Delia Falconer was born in Sydney and has a PhD in English literature and cultural studies from the University of Melbourne. Her name became well known in Australian literature circles when she won a national essay prize and a national short-story prize in the same year, 1994, with two extraordinarily original and accomplished pieces of writing. By the time her first novel, *The Service of Clouds*, was published in 1997 she was well known as an essayist and critic and has continued to work in those fields, publishing articles, reviews and essays nationally and internationally. Her second novel, *The Lost Thoughts of Soldiers*, was published to critical acclaim in 2005.

Falconer's take on the world is so profoundly word-oriented that to some extent her style is intrinsic to her vision; in any genre, her writing demonstrates intellectual sophistication and a profoundly metaphorical habit of thought. Her fiction is stylistically rich and dense, frequently described as 'poetic'; her critical writing is lucid and incisive, and her stories and essays have been widely anthologised. *KG*

Republic of Love

I, Mary the Larrikin, tart of Jerilderie, have loved for roast beef and I have loved for the feather on a well-trimmed hat. In my room above the hotel bar I have felt a squatter's spurs and sucked once on a bishop's fingers. The perfumes of my thighs have greased many a stockman's saddle and kept him company through the lonely nights. Men can nose out my room from thirty miles away, their saddlebags tight and heavy with desire. But of all the men I have ever loved, Ned Kelly, dead three years before they put him in the ground, stole my heart away.

It is hard work loving a dead man: your pillow a gravestone: your arms a confessional. Dead men crawl into your bed at night and evaporate like steam with the rising of the sun. I never saw Kelly in the even light of day. Instead I saw the shadows of candle smoke drift across the smoothness of his hips. I dug my fingertips into the silver squares of window cast upon the muscles of his arms. But I saw enough and felt the rest with my famous mouth and hands. I can tell you that the insides of his thighs had been smoothed by the saddle. He was covered with scars paler than moonlight. He had a foreskin as soft as a horse's inner lip.

Mostly we fucked like greedy children trying to hold on to an Indian summer. Our love had ripened out of season and each full moon hung heavy on the frailest stem of night. But sometimes, in the quiet hour, when his beard rested on my breasts, Kelly told me about the Republic of Love.

In the Republic of Love, said Kelly, there will be no police to eavesdrop on our sleep. We will dream no more in timid whispers but laugh as loud as kookaburras in the dark. Our desires will dive through the hills like flocks of night birds. The dawn will echo with the yapping of our hopes.

In the springtime, when the snows melted, the ground was so damp it rotted beneath a horse's feet. In the morning clouds clung to the roads like sullen cobwebs. By midday they peeled off the mountainsides and stacked themselves like sodden hay in tiered bales that reached towards a hidden sun. It was a time for wet and stumbling love.

I am an indoor girl myself, but I could read Kelly's body like a map and feel what it was like gullying and ungullying through the deep-scored seams that marked those brilliant hills. After three days' ride his stirrups had stained the backs of his heels with orange. His wideawake was filled with melted hail up to the edges of its brim. When he hung his trousers by the fireplace the clouds which had caught in his pockets unfurled and rose up to the corners of the room. His whiskers had been brushed backwards by the stormy winds and stood out from his face. Scratch my beard for me, Mary my love, he said, it is crawling with lightning. I felt blue sparks crackle beneath my fingertips.

I stood naked before him. He wrapped his cool green sash around my waist and came in close to tie the bow. He said he held all the softness of Ireland wrapped up as a Christmas gift. When we lay on his jacket before the fire to make our clumsy love I felt mud slide across the surface of my skin. For weeks it bore the purple scent of Salvation Jane.

In the Republic of Love, Kelly said, we will soak beds thick with emerald sheets and curtains. There will be so much bread to go around that we will scoop out the hearts of loaves and use them for our babies' cradles. They will nestle in the warmth of the fresh-baked centres and rock sideways on the curving crusts.

Shortly before we met, Kelly had begun to rustle horses. He would come to me from the hills at night, his belly full of parrot. I knew without asking when he had shot and eaten lorikeet. His lips were as soft as feathers. He sweated rainbows. He played with thoughts on the tip of his tongue and mused with the subtlety of a philosopher between my legs.

Each theft, he said, avenged the times the squatters had impounded the Kellys' cattle for straying onto their glutted pastures. They are slick-lipped, swamp-hearted, rough-bellied toads, said Kelly, who begrudge us even the flies that circle round our heads. They would brand the water in the rain-clouds if they could.

I grasped him firmly in my hand and began the movements which would comfort him. He laughed and said the law had squeezed him harder there before. He told me of the arrest when the policeman Lonigan had cupped his fist around his balls and tried to wrench them off, his breathing fast, his face more crimson than a mangel-wurzel. From my work in this room I understood that impulse well. It is police and magistrates, I said, who fall on you like a cattle crush and make each act of love a punishment. They grind you against the mattress until your breath is thinner than a paper-knife. They lust to press you, dry and brittle, between the pages of the police gazette. They threaten to arrest you if you tell.

In the Republic of Love, Kelly told me, you can take any shape your loving chooses. You can fuck like a centaur at midnight and squeal like a poddy calf at noon.

There is one thing I can tell you with certainty. That day at Glenrowan may have been the first time Kelly wore an iron helmet but it was not the first landscape he had seen as if he was looking up from the bottom of his grave. Before we met he had spent ten years in prison where he had known the world only as a narrow strip of daylight.

He was born in the shadow of Mount Disappointment. Like the other Irish convicts' sons, he grew thin as a weed from the dusty cracks between the squatters' properties. His mouth set into a hard straight line. He had seen his father's body swell with dropsy before his death. He said it was as if Red Kelly's ankles at last had cracked the phantom shackles which had made them ache since those cold years in Van Diemen's Land. He had watched his mother stumble to unlatch the door with a baby on her hip when the police tried to make the Kellys soft by breaking their nights into tiny pieces. He had felt the slab walls quiver as the policeman Flood pinned his sister Annie with his belly, discharging the seed which was to stretch her taut until she died, weakened by the fleshy issue in her womb.

When he was five Kelly's mother explained to him that there were no days or seasons on the wrong side of the law. There were only lucky hours, she said, and nights of swift riding when you could slide in and out of the chilly pockets of the moon.

Later he gave up shearing because the sound of the metal reminded him of a warden's scissors clipping his hair down to its roots. He had stopped sawing wood in the Gippsland forests when the milky sun filtering through the treetops made him think of prison bars.

Before I was eighteen, Kelly said, my arse was polished by the courtrooms' wooden benches. My spine grew straight as a prison bunk. I have nine notches in my forehead made by the butt of a policeman's rifle. I think the granite I broke at Beechworth has passed into my blood for my veins feel as rough as sandpaper.

In Pentridge, in solitary confinement, Kelly spent six weeks with his head covered by a hood. Two slits were cut in the canvas for his eyes. That was when he began to see the landscape inside an angry frame with no soft tomorrows beyond its edges. It gave him ideas. He would turn ploughshares into armour, soldering and riveting the grimness of his gaze.

I stroked his chest and kissed his ear. I knew how it is to feel your body bruise and bend beneath a greater power. To this day my buttocks bear the impressions of floorboards and mattress buttons. I can still read the angry marks made by a grazier's signet ring upon my breasts. I loved Kelly the more for this. I asked him about the Republic of Love.

In the Republic of Love, Kelly replied, the prisons will be emptied and converted into breweries. Their quarries will be thick with waving heads of barley. The husks will drift across the lintels and gateways and wear away their English coats of arms. In the courtyards the smell of hops bubbling will lift away the stench of sweat. Barmaids will trail the scents of their soft perfumes along the dim, grey passages. In the banks, lovers will rut on crackling banknotes. They will roll in the safes until their backs are stained with mortgage inks. Sixpences will stick to them until they shine more silver than a blue-tongue lizard's belly.

The day the Proclamation of Outlawry was passed Kelly began to notice clods of grave dirt weighing down his trouser hems. He lost his boxer's gait and began to move as if he wore Red Kelly's irons. He said he could feel his soul trailing like a muddy shadow in his horse's wake, catching and tearing on each roughened patch of bark. When he stood in my room he squinted hard and nodded as we talked. He could not see my breasts and face at once.

That Act had closed even those narrow gaps, thinner than horizons, in which he had once moved. Since they had been ambushed at Stringybark the Kelly gang no longer held the rights of citizens. The Act put into words what they already knew: that they were unwelcome in this land which wore a crown. Any man offended by the sight of them could shoot them in the back. Ellen Kelly would soon be put in jail for giving birth to a bushranger. In his Sunday sermon at Mansfield the Anglican Bishop declared them dead already and damned to hell.

Odd to find yourself, said Kelly, staring through a dead man's face. Some days the landscapes he rode through looked as drab and frail as photographs which might lift at any moment from their edges. He had sepia nightmares in which he could not find his way from one image to the next, wandering forever in the soft jigsaw clefts of the Puzzle Ranges. On other days he found the dark blue curves and creases of the hills too beautiful. He lay in the darkness of a cave and saw Aaron Sherritt at the entrance, watching over Joe Byrne while he slept. He could hear Sherritt thinking clearly that the golden hairs on Joe's forearms made them look like angels' wings, while his lips smiled but never opened. Each night more disappointed ghosts joined Red Kelly in the darkness which had begun to press upon the edges of his vision. When he passed a house at dawn the smell of baking bread would nearly break his heart.

He said he thought of going to America, that free land, where he would race steam locomotives on a piebald horse across the plains.

This was the last time Kelly came to me. His eyes focused beyond my head. He mouthed me like a hungry phantom. He felt every part of me to prove that I existed. His fingers were as cool as apples. He took his green sash from my drawer and placed it on his folded clothes.

When he spoke about the Republic of Love his head was as heavy as a tombstone on my shoulder.

In the Republic of Love, said Kelly, there will be no fences. People will find new uses for ordinary things. They will cook toast on the rusting faces of branding irons. They will float down creeks on the discarded doors of shops. The telegraph wires will carry only lovesongs, tapped out in Morse like the rapid beatings of a heart.

Kelly did not see the betrayal in the face of the limping schoolteacher with chess-player's fingers who left the Glenrowan Hotel and waved his handkerchief like a salesman's wife at a train full of troopers. In the dock he stared past the crimson face of Judge Redmond Barry, mottling and shaking like a turkey's wattle. I want to believe that he did not flinch as the frail trap of the gallows shivered beneath his feet.

That night the soft head I had felt between my thighs was cut off and shaved bare before the mask-maker's steady hands shaped warm wax around its jaw. The firm muscles around Kelly's lips were torn away and discarded. His heart was stolen by the surgeon as a souvenir. His skull with the five smooth mounds that curved around its base was stroked by an idle policeman's fingers as it weighed down the papers on his desk.

Back in Jerilderie I continued with my whoring, staring beyond the publican's shoulder.

I looked towards the same place as Kelly.

That day neither of us blinked. If we concentrated hard enough we could sense each other breathing: feel the wet cages of our ribs pressing into one another: hear the spines of law books splitting beneath our backs: rolling, beyond our senses, into the Republic of Love.

1996

MELISSA LUCASHENKO
b 1967

Melissa Lucashenko is of European and Indigenous Yugambeh/Bundjalung heritage. Born and educated in Brisbane, Lucashenko studied at Griffith University, graduating with an honours degree in public policy. She worked for a short time in Canberra for the Department of the Prime Minister and Cabinet before moving to Darwin and then returning to Brisbane. At Griffith University she began PhD studies on the experiences of Aboriginal women at work. She left her studies to take up full-time writing, and has since written two adult novels, *Steam Pigs* (1997) and *Hard Yards* (1999), two young adult novels, *Killing Darcy* (1998) and *Too Flash* (2002), essays, stories, and a political study, *Policy and Politics in the Indigenous Sphere* (1996). *AH/PM*

From *Steam Pigs*
Chapter 6: Revolution

[…] There's a few kids hanging around outside the brick community centre, including one of Shane's friends in a landrights T-shirt eyeing Kerry's bike. Sensible girl, she's got a bloody great lock on the front wheel, but still, a kid can dream. Sue smiles hello at him, but he looks at her blankly, not recognising her and stoned off his head anyway. Jesus, you're a bit young for it aren't you mate, she thinks, and what'd Maureen say if she knew ya weren't at school? Inside she peers around the corner into the hall, then knocks on Kerry's door.

'Hang on, I'll be out in a sec. Who is it?'

'Um, Sue. From karate, you probably don't remember me … did you know there's kids outside looking over yer bike?' The door opens to reveal Kerry pulling her bike boots on.

'Oh, Sue! Yeah, I remember, how are ya? And I know the Centre kids are there, they're waiting to be picked up.'

'Pretty good. I s'pose. Did you go to Nepal?'

'Nah, ended up in Indonesia instead. Bit different, I know, but the money ran out quicker than I expected, and Bali's closer. Come in and sit down, do you want a coffee?'

'Yes please, white no sugar. Were you going somewhere?' still diffident about approaching the woman she didn't know at all well, and wondering about the merits of Bali versus Nepal. If all the blokes looked like Made, built like brick shithouses, she'd take Bali anyday.

'I told young George that I'd take him for a ride on Harriet if he went to school every day last week, and he did, amazingly enough, so I owe him a run into Beenleigh. But he can wait a minute.' Kerry sees Sue puzzled. '… oh, Harriet's the bike; Harriet the Harley,' she explains.

A cup of coffee in hand, Sue sinks into Kerry's armchair in the little room. Blond, tattooed Kerry has an openness and friendliness that puts her at ease, and they chat comfortably for ten minutes about bikes, Eagleby and the course Kerry's about to run. The unlikely social worker lights a cigarette and peers at Sue more closely for a moment.

'Hey, I've got a brilliant idea. Why don't you give us a hand with the conflict resolution?'

'Me? I was hoping for some tips from *you*.'

Sue didn't mention the fight her and Rog had the other night, when he'd thrown her up against the wall of the lounge, screaming abuse square in her face. She couldn't work it out at all, it was like another person. Not like Rog at all and anyway he was sorry after, bought her flowers and everything.

'Well, we're going to be doing stuff about self-esteem and body image, and part of the body image is about using your body to *do* stuff, not just to look at. I've got a Chinese friend coming down to teach some acrobatics one night, that sort of thing. So you could teach the women some basic karate moves, hey, what about it?'

Sue becomes enthusiastic with a little prompting. Karate is one thing she does feel confident about in front of strangers, and she's been helping Lou with the kids' class a bit lately too, so she knows what it's like to teach. Every Tuesday night for six weeks, it means shuffling her training around, but sounds like fun. She might meet some people she can relate to, as well.

'But where's it gonna be? There's karate here on Tuesday nights.'

'Oh, I'll hold it at my place, I reckon. I moved down here, you know. I've got an old Queenslander in Beenleigh.'

'Yeah, alright then. Sounds like fun. Maybe Roger'd like to come and help too.'

'Oh, my house is women's space, mate. Sorry. No men allowed, unless it's special circumstances, and especially not for stuff like this.'

'Oh … how does that work, though?' Sue asks sceptically. 'What if some bloke tried to come in, what would ya do?' Kerry looks faintly amused, but takes Sue's question seriously nonetheless.

'Well, it depends. Step one is, you explain the reasons women sometimes need to be on our own, away from men. And if that doesn't persuade him Inter-lech-ally, usually if you use the right tack, and defuse the situation by listening you can convince people to do just about anything. And if not,' she cracks her knuckles over her head melodramatically, 'then we kick the living shit out of em from here to Hobart, until they abjectly apologise on their knees, cravenly begging our forgiveness. Which of course we give them.' Kerry laughs at the girl's face. Sue is a bit stunned by the idea of women telling men they weren't allowed to go somewhere; if anyone but Kerry had suggested it she would have been unconvinced. Somehow though, coming from her it sounded almost reasonable. *Wild.* Most of the men she'd grown up with would give you a flogging for less. Wow. But should she tell Rog? And what would he say about her hanging around with this skinny feminist with the weird tats?

They swap phone numbers, then Kerry heaves her boots off the desk. 'Look, I better take George for this run before he slits his wrists. Why don't you come in again tomorrow and we can make some plans. Oh, hang on, tomorrow's no good, I'm going up the bush. Come in on Monday, why don't ya?'

Sue explains about her new job.

'Alright, well, I'll give you a ring over the weekend then, and we can start talking about the course, OK?'

'Yeah, sure.'

And with that, Kerry and Sue walk outside to the growing bunch of envious early teens who are waiting to see George's moment of glory. Kerry fires the bike up and the adolescent boys all just about cum at the sound, thinks Sue contemptuously. The kid hangs on to Kerry's leather jacket and they burn off up the road past the cemetery into town, leaving Sue to wander back home, thinking about her new job, and whether she could afford a bike herself. Have to be japcrap of course, but still— Brrrrrrrrrrrmmmmmmmmmmmmmm, burn the ute off, that'd really give Rog the shits! Pictures of bikes roaring in her head, Sue traipses back across the road, thinking about what Kerry's said, oblivious to the newly-sown seeds of revolution.

1997

SONYA HARTNETT
b. 1968

Sonya Hartnett was born and educated in Melbourne. She has been an enigmatic figure in Australian literature, eluding and defying attempts to classify her as a writer, ever since her first book, *Trouble All the Way* (1984), was published when she was still a teenager. Hartnett was for a number of years a prolific and prize-winning writer of children's and young adult fiction. Her novel *Sleeping Dogs* (1995) is a tale of extreme family isolation and sibling incest; not surprisingly, it generated considerable controversy both in Australia and internationally.

A major and recurrent theme in Hartnett's work is the cruelty, whether deliberate or merely unthinking, of adults to children and animals. Since the late 1990s her work has been less and less easy to classify in terms of the age of its readership, and two of her most recent novels, *Of a Boy* (2002) and *Surrender* (2005), are both about children but are unambiguously written for an adult sensibility. Hartnett was already well known and highly regarded nationally and internationally as a writer of young adult fiction, but these two novels brought her a new degree of attention from Australia's mainstream literary culture. She won the Astrid Lindgren Memorial Award in 2008. *KG*

From *Of a Boy*
Chapter 2

[. . .] The Metford children have been missing since Sunday afternoon—for more than twenty-four hours. The police are requesting that anyone with any information contact them—they put up a number that can be rung. When the report is finished and the newsreader comes back on the screen, his lips are pressed together by the seriousness of the thing.

The clink of the spoon against the rim of the bowl makes Beattie glance at her grandson. Adrian is in his pyjamas, his feet swaddled in fuzzy bedsocks. A fastidious child, he hasn't spilled a drop of the liquefied ice-cream, nor has a spot of it gone astray on his chin. He looks very pale against the darkness of the leather, and he has stopped eating the dessert. He can be fretful, easily put off his food. It is one of the things that annoy her about him.

Adrian worries about all sorts of things. Many of his fears he keeps private, sensing that there's something a touch ludicrous about them, but that does not lessen their power. He is afraid of quicksand—scared that one day he'll be walking along the street and find that the footpath is gobbling him down. He's heard about quicksand on TV and read about it in his grandfather's collection of *National Geographic*, the magazines a source of untold marvels and menace. In the streets he never sees any signs alerting pedestrians to the presence of the treacherous glug and he worries that he won't discover for himself what it looks like until it is way too late.

Naturally he dislikes seeing his cupboard door ajar, especially at night, especially when he knows that when he last saw it, the door was closed.

Spontaneous combustion worries him. He knows enough to know there's nothing one can do to avoid it—it's pointless, for instance, seeking the shade on a hot day, or keeping some distance from the gas stove, in the hope that this will ward off the smoking fate. If one is programmed to self-combust, it's going to happen eventually, regardless. It's like being born with six fingers, a curse.

Tidal waves are another thing. Adrian doesn't spend much time at the beach, but the concern is there. He envisages himself sucked far out to sea by the retreat of a great wave, bobbing helplessly among umbrellas and bottles of sunscreen. He thinks of the water not yet risen into the wave, swirling, scheming, passing the time, in the pits of the ocean, restive as blood.

And now there are sea-monsters, of course.

Others of his fears are more personal, they touch his heart like a needle through his skin. If he is in a shopping centre with Beattie and the alarm rings for closing time, he is almost frantic to drag her out the door. The idea of being locked inside a shopping centre fills him with absolute horror. He dreads and distrusts crowds, and amid them his one aim is to prevent himself

getting lost. To be lost in a crowd would, he thinks, be like being buried alive. His father had once taken him to a carnival that was dazzling with colour and fumes and bustle and noise, he'd been given a ball of fairyfloss and patted a Clydesdale's satin hide, but Adrian's strongest recollection is of the sweat that slicked his father's fingers as he clutched the man's hand in his own.

He worries that one day his grandmother will forget to pick him up from school. He thinks he could walk home if he had to, though the walk would take a long time, but when he tries to travel the route in his head, the streets twine and mingle like spaghetti in a can, disorienting him in his chair. Each time the school bell signals the end of another day, he feels a chill down his spine: maybe today is the day. To be lost or forgotten or abandoned and alone are, to Adrian, terrors more carnivorous than any midnight monster lurking underneath a bed.

And now there is this new fear, one that settles so comfortably among its myriad kin that it seems familiar, as if it's skulked there, scarcely noticed, all along. He does not know those Metford children, but they are children just like him, just like the children he sees every day at school. On the TV, in the Metford yard, he had glimpsed a black and white striped basketball exactly the same as his own. He does not recognise their street, though it's only twenty minutes' drive away, but he feels as though he has seen it before. The trees, the fences, the rooftops, the clotheslines—that is middle-class suburbia, and Adrian is a suburban boy. He has been to the birthday parties of his classmates and he knows that most things everywhere are more or less the same. A cat that strolls along the fence, a clock that ticks on the kitchen wall, fingerpaintings magneted to the fridge, sidetables marked with coffee-mug rings.

It has never occurred to him—and he blushes faintly, for being so stupid—to think that children can vanish. The Metfords have not been lost or abandoned—they have been made to disappear. They have not run away—they have been lifted up and carried. They've been taken somewhere as distant as Jupiter. Adrian has never thought that an ordinary child, a kid like himself or Clinton or that freckle-nosed girl, might be of interest to anyone excepting family and friends, that an ordinary child could be worth taking or wanting, a desirable thing. [. . .]

2002

ROMAINE MORETON
b 1969

A writer, film-maker and performance poet, Romaine Moreton is from the Goenpul people of Stradbroke Island, Queensland, and the Bundjalung people of northern NSW. Her family worked as seasonal farming labourers, later settling in the country town of Bodalla, NSW. In August 2002 Moreton toured Australia with African-American acapella band, Sweet Honey in the Rock, performing her signature spoken words before a sell-out crowd at the Sydney Opera House. Moreton's work responds to the environment and explores issues of identity. Two of her short films were shown at the Cannes Film Festival in 1999 and she appeared in an ABC documentary about her work, *A Walk With Words*, in 2001. She has published *The Callused Stick of Wanting* (1996) and *Post Me to the Prime Minister* (2004). *AH/PM*

Genocide is Never Justified

And the past was open to gross misinterpretation.

Why do the sons and daughters of the raped and murdered
deserve any more or any less than those who have prospered
from the atrocities of heritage?
And why do the sons and daughters refuse to reap   5
what was sown
from bloodied soils?
And why does history ignore their existence?

This land, *terra nullius* was never barren and
unoccupied!   10

This land was never void of human life!

Instead
thriving with the knowledge of tens of thousands of years.

Everywhere I look!
Ghosts!   15

Vacant, colourless faces stare back

Sans culture
sans the belief of deserving of equality,

Who was here first is not the question
anymore   20

It is what you have done since you arrived,
the actions you refuse to admit to,
the genocide you say you never committed!

Then why are my people so few
when they were once so many?   25
Why is the skin so fair when once as black as the land?

Colonised Rape.
Why are you so rich, by secular standards
and we now so poor, by secular standards
The remnants of a culture though,   30
still

                        Rich
                        In
                        Spirit
                        and   35
                        Soul
                                                               1995

SAMUEL WAGAN WATSON
b. 1972

Samuel Wagan Watson has Irish, German and Aboriginal (Bundjalung and Birri Gubba) ancestry. He is the son of Sam Watson (qv). Wagan Watson has won state and national awards for his poetry and prose, and prior to being a full-time writer was a salesman, public relations officer, fraud investigator, graphic artist, labourer, law clerk, film industry technician and actor.

In between writing and working on community projects, including poetry in the built environment (his poetry adorns the Eleanor Schonell Bridge in St Lucia, Queensland), Wagan Watson acts as a guest speaker, workshop facilitator and mentor in the creative arts. *Of Muse, Meandering and Midnight* (2000) won the 1999 David Unaipon Award. A later collection of poetry, *Smoke Encrypted Whispers* (2004), won the Book of the Year Award in the NSW Premier's Literary Awards for 2005. *AH/PM*

White Stucco Dreaming

sprinkled in the happy dark of my mind
is early childhood and black humour
white stucco dreaming
and a black labrador
an orange and black panel–van   5
called the 'black banana'
with twenty blackfellas hanging out the back
blasting through the white stucco umbilical
of a working class tribe
front yards studded with old black tyres   10

that became mutant swans overnight
attacked with a cane knife and a bad white paint job

white stucco dreaming
and snakes that morphed into nylon hoses at the terror
of Mum's scorn   15
snakes whose cool venom we sprayed onto the white stucco,
temporarily blushing it pink
amid an atmosphere of Saturday morning grass cuttings
and flirtatious melodies of ice-cream trucks
that echoed through little black minds   20
and sent the labrador insane

chocolate hand prints like dreamtime fraud
laid across white stucco
and mud cakes on the camp stove
that just made Dad see black   25
no tree safe from treehouse sprawl
and the police cars that crawled up and down the back streets,
peering into our white stucco cocoon
wishing they were with us

                                                                                              2004

For the Wake and Skeleton Dance

the dreamtime Dostoyevskys murmur of a recession in the spirit world
they say,
the night creatures are feeling the pinch
of growing disbelief and western rationality
that the apparitions of black dingos stalk the city night, hungry   5
their ectoplasm on the sidewalk in a cocktail of vomit and swill
waiting outside the drinking holes of the living
preying on the dwindling souls fenced in by assimilation

the dreamtime Dostoyevskys ponder
as dark riders in the sky signal a movement   10
for the wake and skeleton dance
it's payback time for the bureaucrats in black skins
and the fratricide troopers before them
with no room to move on a dead man's bed

is it all worth holding onto these memories   15
amidst the blood-drenched sands?
better to forget?

the dreamtime Dostoyevskys feel the early winter
chilled footsteps walk across their backs in the dark hours,
the white man didn't bring all the evil   20
some of it was here already
gestating
laughing
intoxicated
untapped   25
harassing the living
welcoming the tallship leviathans of two centuries ago
that crossed the line drawn in the sand by the Serpent
spilling dark horses from their bowels
and something called the Covenant,   30
infecting the dreamtime with the ghosts of a million lost entities
merely faces in the crowd at the festival of the dead,
the wake is over
and to the skeleton dance the bonemen smile
open season on chaos theory   35
and retirement eternal for the dreamtime Dostoyevsky
                                                                          2004

Cheap White-goods at the Dreamtime Sale

if only the alloy-winged angels could perform better
and lift Uluru; a site with grandeur
the neolithic additive missing from that seventh wonder of the world expo,
under the arms of a neon goddess, under the hammer in London,
murderers turning trustees   5
a possession from a death estate
maybe flogged off to the sweet seduction of yen
to sit in the halls of a Swiss bank
or be paraded around Paris' Left Bank
where the natives believe   10
that art breathed for the first time;
culture, bohemian and bare and maybe brutal
and how the critics neglect the Rubenesque roundness of a bora-ring
unfolded to an academia of art
yes, that pure soil in front of you   15
the dealers in Manhattan lay back and vomit
they're the genius behind dot paintings and ochre hand prints
rattling studios from the East Side to the Village
and across the ass of designer jeans

porcelain dolls from Soho wanting a part in it so bad   20
as the same scene discards their shells upon the catwalks
like in the land of the original Dreaming
comatose totems litter the landscape
bargains and half-truths simmer over authenticity
copyright and copious character assassination on the menu   25
sacred dances available out of the yellow pages
and
cheap white-goods at the Dreamtime sale!

2004

CHI VU
b. 1973

Chi Vu escaped from Vietnam by boat with her family at the age of five. After a year in a refugee camp on Pulau Bidong, Malaysia, they reached Australia and settled in Melbourne. After studying at the University of Melbourne, she became a short-story writer and scriptwriter. In 1996 Vu joined Melbourne's Footscray Theatre group as an actor and writer. Her first play, *A Story of Soil* (2000/2001) was in Vietnamese and English, exploring the situation of Vietnamese-born Australians and their generational struggles with their parents. *Vietnam: A psychic guide*, another bilingual play, was produced in 2003. *NJ*

From *Vietnam: A psychic guide*

Dear all,

I am in the splendour of Halong bay, the rocky outcrops the spine of a dragon floating in a sea of jade. A small boat speeds up alongside our ferry. The boy, with his mother and younger brother, holds up fresh fish and prawns in bamboo baskets; he holds up green shapely coral. He looks about 11 to me. I ask him how old he is. He is 16. I ask him if he and his mother catch these fish and prawns, and dive to the bottom of the China sea for the coral. He says that they do not, and tells me where they get them.

'They buy it from the market and resell it here,' I translate for my fellow traveller.

'Oh,' she says disappointed, 'Thanks for spoiling the illusion for me.'

Some travellers go to exotic places to pretend that people do not suffer deeply from their poverty and that they do not at times cheat and lie to try to escape it. Some people travel to let go of understanding what's happening around them, to be as nude and deluded as children. It is easy to watch them walk with an air of stupidity about them, smiling at everything.

There are those who travel to exotic places to feel sorry for the natives. 'They do not have any colouring pencils or crayons for the children to be creative,' they cry. They don't see the inventiveness of games created out of tin cans, rubber thongs, and bits of metal from the machines of war.

Love, Michelle.

Dear Kim,

I spotted a xe-om driver and negotiated a price with him. 'How much?'
    'One US Dollar.'
    'Too much. Local price is 40 cents.'
    'You are not local.'
    'My family came from here,' I smile.
    'Alright.' He smiles.
    I hopped on and he started his motorbike. He said, 'Vietnam is very poor. There is much suffering here. Is there suffering in your country?'
    We were speeding through the city, jumping the open gutters and the cracks of the city streets. I thought of old people dying alone in nursing homes in my foreign country. I thought of people chasing status down endless aisles in a giant shopping mall. 'Suffering. To be human is to suffer.' I looked at him carefully to see if he was satisfied with this answer. I wondered if he would get angry at me. He lowered his head for a moment and thought. Then he nodded to himself, and weaved through the traffic with renewed energy and speed. As I sat on the back-seat, I knew what I said was both true and untrue.

Hugs, Michelle.

CITY OF FACE

In the deep east beyond the river of honey, and the jungle of variegated jade, there is the city of Face.
    Once you arrive there, large sculptures of white clay with rounded mouths and Buddha cheeks are placed around the circumference of the city, and at regular points along the radii of the 'spokes' that reach in towards the centre. Each had been beautifully hand chiselled by an artist and two assistants, one of whom is solely there to sweep away the beautiful alabaster chips of hardened clay and burn them on small fires near to the sculpture.

It's face, after face, after face, as you walk towards the centre of the city. One who speaks and forgets to mention the white sculptures will have the polite inhabitants of Hanoi turn away, blush and look downwards, fall into silence or even vacate the premises without a further word.

If the traveller follows the radius of the white clay faces to its very heart, there is a small circle of these sculptures. One hears the voice of a beautiful, long-haired woman weeping in the middle of the night next to a small fire.

Dear K,

It is night and I am on a train heading to the mountains. I have mastered the art of disappearing. They looked but they didn't know where to find me. In being very still and small I have managed to vanish. I am in a cabin with the local people. Next door the foreigners have paid 3 times the price for the same journey. They are rowdy and sing. I am in a soft sleeper, and we sit in silence. There are 7 of us, in this 6-person cabin.

Suddenly the train conductor races in, followed by a young official. The official pulls down an empty, new Korean-made suitcase from the top bunk. The conductor puts his leathery hand on the suitcase. They struggle wordlessly for a few moments. Then the conductor says politely, containing the great strain in his body, 'Please, leave this suitcase here.' The official is angrier and younger. He says, 'I am taking it.' They continue to struggle silently. Everyone else in the cabin is watching, and not watching. No one bothers to say anything with their throats.

So this is what it feels like to disappear, I thought. I lie there and pretend that my invisibility has made me mute and blind as well. And heartless. But I do have a heart and so do the other people in this cabin.

Love, M.

CITY OF WORDS

I am building a city of words to replicate the city of things around me—of dust, of polyester shirts and trousers, of teeming humanity. Every day I pace the space of the city in my long walks in order to measure out the dimensions for my replica city of scribble.

Except my city of words is built with the square, angular exact bricks of your language, while the inhabitants of the city itself build theirs with the slippery, rounded, sing-song stone marbles of the Hanoian language. These round stones create their architecture not by their shape, but by their placement. I had failed before I had begun.

Dear Kim,

There are four words to a war. *Cach Mang* is the word northern soldiers used for themselves; *Bo Doi* is the word used in the south. The southern word for one of their own is *Linh Cong Hoa*. The northern word for the same soldier is *Nguy*.

'Did your parents not teach you the words of a war?' the taxi driver in *Da Nang* said to me.

'No,' I said, 'We talked of school, getting high grades, and buying a house so that no one can look down on us.'

His red eyes looked ahead, expressionless. 'It is not anyone's fault which side of a war they fight on. Where you live is who you fight for,' he said, erasing the eight years of hiding in the mountains for fighting for the losing side.

I entered the museum of sadness today.

Yours, Mich.

Dear Hai,

All my photos came out shit. I could hardly take photos of strangers as though their features, dress, or ways of living are completely foreign to me. That would be like me going to Sydney and taking photos of strangers there. Vietnamese photos are only for taking photos of relatives/friends, and certainly not lumps of rock by themselves. No, you have to get a relative or friend to stand in front of a piece of important rock or monument, in a stiff but friendly pose. For a Westerner you want a piece of untouched landscape, objective, silent, uninterrupted, lonely. Have you seen the traffic in Vietnam?

I could not take photos because I didn't know who the person pressing the button was.

—Michelle

Dear all,

I am sitting in the café of Babel. There is a pretty girl sitting on my right reading swirls and squiggles. I ask her which language it is. She tells me, smiling, that it is Hebrew. An older couple argue with each other by talking too loudly at their Vietnamese tour guide. They take turns being extra nice to him—entreating him to drink some beer with them, asking him whether he likes western coffee or not. They are scared out of their wits in this strange environment, and are to boot, unhappily married.

The layers of languages in this café is wonderful and scary. Perhaps the snake that is Hanoi is swimming along a river flowing out to sea. My uncle told me that in such a river there is a region of several kilometres where the sweet water of the river mixes with the saltwater of the sea. In this zone a special type of fish thrives. This is the meeting of east and west. It is the mixing of two mediums. It is where the other fish die.

The tour guide is bored, but attempting to be surprised by the old couple's questions about 'Vietnamese culture'. His eyes dart around the café. He looks at the girl reading the Jewish text for a while. He looks at an older Caucasian man with his hair combed over his bald patch learning Vietnamese poetry from a young tutor.

The tutor is pleased with the progress of this mature-aged student, and leans closer into the table. Just where the Caucasian man thinks he's going to use *'gap em o Chua Huong'* I don't know.[1] They are both drinking Tigers. It is a hot day. It is only 10 am and the sunlight is already golden pink, filtering through the doorway of the café in *Pho Co*.

Yours, Mich.

THE PRISM HEART

If you take a sharp knife to dissect my heart for the grit and sludge of hatred and prejudice, you will find it there. If you carve my heart in search of the red blood and scented flesh of compassion, forgiveness and courage, you will see that too. I am a prism of possibilities. And as you move, and as my breath moves me, the colours of the refraction are shifting, shimmering, shifting.

I have written these words by the many lakes of the city. During days of fear and paranoia, my handwriting shrivelled up into little black dots and swirls, barely readable by my own eyes or by any unwelcomed readers. My spine too, curled up like that of a circular insect. Sometimes I thought twice before writing down a thought or not. Maybe one can conceal conscious thoughts, even to oneself. But one cannot suppress feelings. And so my hand would betray me, and draw the thought anyway. Perhaps this is why there are so many artists in the city.

I have captured, in scribble, the various reflections in the water. To tell you a lie, to tell you a truth.

2003

---

1   Author's note: From an epic poem about two young lovers gazing at each other for the first time. Translation: 'I met her at the temple gate'.

GLOSSARY

All reasonable endeavours have been made by the editors to ensure appropriate translations of words from Aboriginal languages. In the instance where the author of an entry had not identified the language group their words were from (or had not provided their own glossary), the editors have taken the liberty of suggesting it was from the country in which that author was born (if that was stated by the author). Unfortunately, language translations could not be obtained for all words published in this anthology.

Alcheringa (Arrernte): term for the Dreamtime or creation period; also Altjeringa

applewood: any of several trees thought to resemble the apple, especially of the genera *Eucalyptus* and *Angophora*

Assimilation: the view that Aboriginal people should be removed from their own cultures and absorbed completely into Anglo-Australian culture, often reflected in government policies during the twentieth century

belar: any of several trees or large shrubs of the Casurina family with slender jointed branches and woody cones

Biamee: a creator spirit in south-eastern NSW; also Biami

bilby-heap: a bilby is a rabbit-eared bandicoot, a small burrowing marsupial once plentiful in inland Australia

billabong: a waterhole by a river or creek

blackfella: slang used by Aboriginal people for their own people

boob: a small jail cell

boomerang: wooden instrument used for hunting, and also used as a percussion instrument when two are hit together

bora rings: an initiation or ceremonial site; also rings of bora

boyyah (Noongar): money

brolga: a large grey crane

bullroarer: a wooden instrument whirled around the head, often for ceremonies restricted to initiated men

bullyaka (Noongar): take off

bundji: brother- or sister-in-law

bungarra: goanna

bunyip: a mythical spirit, often referred to as evil, which dwells in creeks, swamps and billabongs

chubel (Noongar): spear

churinga stone: sacred stone

clapstick: common name for wooden sticks struck together during ceremonial songs

cocky: farmer

coconut: Aboriginal slang term used for those people who are dark skinned but are considered by some to think or feel like white people

cooee: to shout out, usually to find someone or to locate the caller (thought to be from the Dharug nation of Sydney)

coolamon: wooden carrying dish; also coolamen, cooliman

corroboree: ceremonial gathering with song and dance

damper: traditional bread made from wheat and cooked on coals or in the ground

deadly: 'cool', good

didgeridoo/Yidaki (Yolngu): a large wind instrument made from hollowed-out hardwood trees and originally used in northern Australia (the Top End) by men

digger: from mid-nineteenth century, a person working on the Australian goldfields. During the First World War the term was applied to Australian soldiers and later used as a general term of address

dijwun: this one

dinkum: originally a British dialect term for 'work' but used in Australia from the early twentieth century to mean something or someone genuine, honest and reliable

doak (Noongar): throwing stick

doona: duvet or continental quilt

Dreamtime: the time of creation for Aboriginal people; also the Dreaming

dubakieny (Noongar): steadily, slowly

duco: originally the trade name of an automotive lacquer, still used in Australia as a colloquialism for any automotive paint

Duramula: Father/Creator

fella: Aboriginal slang for a person of either gender

fringe-dweller: person living on the fringe of a town or city

full-blood: term used by colonial cultures and authorities to differentiate between perceived degrees of Aboriginality

gerbah (Noongar): alcohol

gin: derogatory term used historically for an Aboriginal woman

girdi girdi (Mardujara language): hill kangaroo

gubba: usually derogatory generic slang term for a white man used by Aboriginal people in NSW and Victoria

gubberment: Aboriginal slang for government

gudeeah (Noongar): white person

gulja (Mardujara language): a mixture of tobacco and ashes

gunyah (Dharug): a shelter made from bushes and bark

half-caste: term used by colonial cultures and authorities to differentiate between perceived degrees of Aboriginality

inji stick (Noongar): decorated stick used in ceremonies

Integration: the view that Aboriginal people and their cultures should be allowed to live alongside Anglo-Australian culture, often reflected in government policies during the later twentieth century

jackaroo: young man, often from England or the city, working on a large sheep or cattle station in order to gain practical experience before running or managing a station himself

Jindyworobak: glossed as 'to annex, to join' in James Devaney's *The Vanishing Tribes* (1929). The name was adopted for a nationalist literary movement of the 1930s and '40s that looked to the Australian environment and Aboriginal culture for inspiration

jumbuck: a sheep

kaal (Noongar): fire

kadaitcha: term used widely among Central Australian groups to refer to a form of secret killing and other related rituals; also an Arrernte expression meaning 'evil person walking about'

kartwarra: mad, bad in the head

kia: yes

kienya (Noongar): shame

Koori: generic term used by Aboriginal people for themselves in much of NSW; also Koorie (in Victoria) and Goori (parts of northern NSW)

koort (Noongar): weak

kuliyah (Noongar): yes

lubra: derogatory term used historically for an Aboriginal woman or girl

Mabo: Eddie Koiki Mabo (1932–92)

Mabo judgment: A highly significant judgment of the High Court of Australia in 1992 (*Mabo v Queensland [No. 2]* (1992)), recognising claims by Eddie Mabo and others for common law ownership of their traditional lands at Mer Island, and more generally recognising the fiction of *terra nullius* in the acquisition of Australian territory by Britain

message-stick: wooden stick with a message carved into it, passed between clans and nations to transmit information or a message

miggloo: generic term used in Queensland for a white person

minditj (Noongar): stick

mission: pocket of land controlled by various religious factions to contain Aboriginal people under the policies of Protection and Assimilation; similar areas run by government agencies were called reserves

mob: an Aboriginal clan, nation, language group or community

moorditj (Noongar): deadly, in the sense of cool, good

mulga: acacia woodland or scrub

muntj: have sex

murrandu (Mardujara): goanna

Murri: generic term for Aboriginal people in Queensland

myall: derogatory term used to describe an Aboriginal person who is simple

narangy: a salaried worker on a rural station, as opposed to a stockman or others on a weekly wage

Native Title: concept in Australian law which recognises the ownership of land by Aboriginal peoples, first enacted in Parliament in the *Commonwealth Native Title Act 1993* following the Mabo judgment of 1992

Nebalee: great man of the heavens; also Neboolea

needlewood: any of several shrubs or small trees chiefly of the genus *Hakea* having rigid, needle-like leaves

New Woman: distinguished from the late Victorian or Edwardian New Woman, the new woman of the decades after the First World War was a modern figure in the UK and US as well as Australia, and represented a challenge to conventional roles for women

Ngarrindjeri: Aboriginal people (and their language) from the lower Murray River and Western Fleurieu Peninsula, SA; also Narrinjeri

nietjuk (Noongar): who

Noongar: Aboriginal people (and their language) from south-western WA; also Nyoongah, Nyungah

octoroon: term used by colonial cultures and authorities to differentiate between perceived degrees of Aboriginality

porcupine (grass): spinifex

Protection Act/s: acts of state and territory governments legislating state authority over Aboriginal cultures and communities, generally in force from the late nineteenth century to the mid-twentieth century

Protection Boards: government boards created to administer Aboriginal people and communities under the terms of the Protection Acts

Protector: officer of the Protection Board authorised to implement Board policies within state districts; the Chief Protector was the head of the Protection Board

quadroon: term used by colonial cultures and authorities to differentiate between perceived degrees of Aboriginality

quarter-caste: term used by colonial cultures and authorities to differentiate between degrees of perceived Aboriginality

Rainbow Serpent: a creation spirit

reserve: government-run compound used to hold Aboriginal people separate from the rest of the community and free up land for grants to new settlers; similar areas run by church groups were called missions

right skin: different spiritual and kin groups that determine the relationship of one Aboriginal person to another, and therefore who they can marry

rockboat: a stevedoring term

self-determination: Aboriginal self-governance without external influence

stolen generation/s: term used to describe the Aboriginal and Torres Strait Islander peoples forcibly removed from, and denied further access to, their families and communities under government policies between 1869 and 1969

supple-jack: any of several climbing or twining shrubs

swagman: someone who travels through the countryside looking for work, carrying his possessions in a rolled-up blanket

terra nullius: a Latin expression derived from Roman law meaning 'nobody's land'

tucker-bag: bag for carrying food

Uluru: one of Australia's most significant sacred sites and the world's largest monolith (formerly known as Ayers Rock); situated on the lands of the Anangu people in Uluru–Kata Tjuta National Park, NT

vox nullius: see *terra nullius*; 'nobody's voice', a coinage to suggest that, like Aboriginal rights to land, Aboriginal languages and voices did not warrant attention

waddy: hunting stick or war club

walkabout: travel embarked upon by Aboriginal people for the purpose of death and funeral ceremonies, cultural ceremonies, bartering, food, water and so on

watjella (Noongar): white person; also whitefella, wetjala

White Australia policy: unofficial name for government policies restricting immigration into Australia to Anglo-Celtic people, particularly during the late nineteenth to mid-twentieth centuries

wilgi (Noongar): specially prepared paint for ceremonies

womba: mad

woomera: spear thrower

wurlies: shelters made of branches or leaves

yabby: small freshwater crayfish found in south-eastern Australia

yongah (Noongar): kangaroo; also yonga

yorgah (Noongar): woman; also yorga

yortj (Noongar): penis

yumbah (Noongar): children

yowie: a large ape-like human, believed to roam in some parts of Australia, especially southern NSW; also yuwi

SELECTED READING

Michael Ackland, *That Shining Band: A study of Australian colonial verse tradition* (1994)
—— (ed.), *The Penguin Book of 19th Century Australian Literature* (1993)
Debra Adelaide (ed.), *A Bright and Fiery Troop: Australian women writers of the nineteenth century* (1988)
Ien Ang, Sharon Chalmers, Lisa Law and Mandy Thomas (eds), *Alter/Asians: Asian-Australian identities in art, media and popular culture* (2000)
Bain Attwood and Fiona Magowan (eds), *Telling Stories: Indigenous history and memory in Australia and New Zealand* (2001)
Bain Attwood and Andrew Markus (eds), *The Struggle for Aboriginal Rights: A documentary history* (1999)
Candida Baker, *Yacker: Australian writers talk about their work* (1986)
——, *Yacker 2: Australian writers talk about their work* (1987)
——, *Yacker 3: Australian writers talk about their work* (1989)
Faith Bandler, *Turning the Tide: A personal history of the Federal Council for the Advancement of Aborigines and Torres Strait Islanders* (1989)
Bruce Bennett, *Australian Short Fiction: A history* (2002)
Bruce Bennett and Jennifer Strauss (eds), *The Oxford Literary History of Australia* (1998)
Roger Bennett (ed.), *Voices from the Heart: Contemporary Aboriginal poetry from Central Australia* (1995)
Delys Bird, Robert Dixon and Christopher Lee (eds), *Authority and Influence: Australian literary criticism* 1950–2000 (2001)
Nicholas Birns and Rebecca McNeer (eds), *A Companion to Australian Literature Since 1900* (2007)
Michael Brennan and Peter Minter (eds), *Calyx: 30 Contemporary Australian Poets* (2000)
Anne Brewster, Angeline O'Neill and Rosemary van den Berg (eds), *Those Who Remain Will Always Remember: An anthology of Aboriginal writing* (2000)
David Brooks and Brenda Walker (eds), *Poetry and Gender: Statements and essays in Australian women's poetry and poetics* (1989)
Alexander Brown and Brian Geytenbeek, *Ngarla Songs* (2003)
Philip Butterss and Elizabeth Webby (eds), *The Penguin Book of Australian Ballads* (1993)

Fiona Capp, *Writers Defiled: Security surveillance of Australian authors and intellectuals 1920–1960* (1993)

Dennis Carroll, *Australian Contemporary Drama* (1995)

David Carter, 'Public Intellectuals, Book Culture and Civil Society', *Australian Humanities Review* 24 (2001/2002), www.australianhumanitiesreview.org/archive/Issue-November-2001/carter2.html

David Carter and Anne Galligan (eds), *Making Books: Contemporary Australian publishing* (2007)

Maryrose Casey, *Creating Frames: Contemporary Indigenous theatre, 1967–1990* (2004)

Patricia Clarke, *Pen Portraits: Women writers and journalists in nineteenth century Australia* (1988)

Patricia Clarke and Dale Spender (eds), *Life Lines: Australian women's letters and diaries, 1788–1840* (1992)

John Colmer, *Australian Autobiography: The personal quest* (1989)

John Colmer and Dorothy Colmer (eds), *The Penguin Book of Australian Autobiography* (1987)

Commonwealth of Australia, *Bringing Them Home: Report of the National Inquiry into the separation of Aboriginal and Torres Strait Islander children from their families* (1997)

Ann Curthoys, *Freedom Ride: A freedom rider remembers* (2002)

Rosamund Dalziell, *Shameful Autobiographies: Shame in contemporary Australian autobiographies and culture* (1999)

——(ed.), *Selves Crossing Cultures: Autobiography and globalisation* (2002)

Tanya Dalziell, *Settler Romances and the Australian Girl* (2004)

Helen Daniel, *Liars: Australian new novelists* (1988)

Jim Davidson, *Sideways from the Page: The* Meanjin *interviews* (1983)

Jack Davis and Bob Hodge (eds), *Aboriginal Writing Today: Papers from the first national conference of Aboriginal writers* (1985)

Jack Davis, Mudrooroo, Stephen Muecke and Adam Shoemaker (eds), *Paperbark: A collection of black Australian writings* (1990)

Robert Dessaix, *Australian Gay and Lesbian Writing: An anthology* (1993)

Robert Dixon, *Prosthetic Gods: Travel, representation and colonial governance* (2001)

——, *Writing the Colonial Adventure: Race, gender and nation in Anglo-Australian popular fiction 1875–1914* (1995)

Livio Dobrez, *Parnassus Mad Ward: Michael Dransfield and the new Australian poetry* (1990)

John Docker, *Australian Cultural Elites: Intellectual traditions in Sydney and Melbourne* (1974)

Josie Douglas (ed.), *Untreated: Poems by black writers* (2001)

Geoffrey Dutton (ed.), *The Literature of Australia* (1976)

Martin Duwell, *A Possible Contemporary Poetry* (1982)

Kay Ferres (ed.), *The Time to Write: Australian women writers 1890–1930* (1993)

Carole Ferrier (ed.), *As Good as a Yarn with You: Letters between Miles Franklin, Katharine Susannah Prichard, Jean Devanny, Marjorie Barnard, Flora Eldershaw and Eleanor Dark* (1996)

——(ed.), *Gender, Politics and Fiction: Twentieth century Australian women's novels* (1992)

Peter Fitzpatrick, *After 'The Doll': Australian drama since 1955* (1979)

Richard Freadman, *This Crazy Thing a Life: Australian Jewish autobiography* (2007)

Ken Gelder (ed.), *The Oxford Book of Australian Ghost Stories* (1994)

Ken Gelder and Paul Salzman, *The New Diversity: Australian fiction 1970–88* (1989)

Helen Gilbert, *Sightlines: Race, gender and nation in contemporary Australian theatre* (1998)

Kevin Gilbert (ed.), *Inside Black Australia: An anthology of Aboriginal poetry* (1988)

Terry Goldie, *Fear and Temptation: The image of the indigene in Canadian, Australian and New Zealand literatures* (1989)

Kerryn Goldsworthy (ed.), *Australian Love Stories* (1996)

——(ed.), *Australian Short Stories* (1983)

——(ed.), *Australian Women's Stories* (1999)

Heather Goodall, *Invasion to Embassy: Land in Aboriginal politics in New South Wales, 1770–1972* (1996)

Ken Goodwin, *A History of Australian Literature* (1986)

Robert Gray and Geoffrey Lehmann (eds), *Australian Poetry in the Twentieth Century* (1991)

——, *The Younger Australian Poets* (1983)

Michele Grossman et al., *Blacklines: Contemporary critical writing by Indigenous Australians* (2003)

Rodney Hall and Thomas W. Shapcott (eds), *New Impulses in Australian Poetry* (1968)

Susan Hampton and Kate Llewellyn (eds), *The Penguin Book of Australian Women Poets* (1986)

Martin Harrison, *Who Wants to Create Australia? Essays on poetry and ideas in contemporary Australia* (2004)

Kevin Hart (ed.), *The Oxford Book of Australian Religious Verse* (1994)

Anita Heiss, *Dhuuluu Yala (Talk Straight): Publishing Indigenous literature* (2003)

Anita Heiss and Penny van Toorn (eds), *Southerly: Stories without end*, vol. 62, no. 2 (2002)

Laurie Hergenhan (gen. ed.), *The Penguin New Literary History of Australia* (1988)

——, *Unnatural Lives: Studies in Australian fiction about the convicts, from James Tucker to Patrick White* (1983)

Barry Hill, *Broken Song: T.G.H. Strehlow and Aboriginal possession* (2002)

Bob Hodge and Vijay Mishra, *Dark Side of the Dream: Australian literature and the postcolonial mind* (1991)

Joy Hooton, *Stories of Herself When Young: Autobiographies of childhood by Australian women* (1990)

——(ed.), *Australian Lives: An Oxford anthology* (1998)

Jack Horner, *Seeking Racial Justice: An insider's memoir of the movement for Aboriginal advancement 1938–1978* (2004)

Kate Jennings (ed.), *Mother, I'm Rooted: An anthology of Australian women poets* (1975)

Ann-Mari Jordens, *The Stenhouse Circle: Literary life in mid-nineteenth century Sydney* (1979)

Nicholas Jose, 'Cultural Identity: "I think I'm something else",' in 'Australia: Terra Incognita?', *Daedalus*, vol. 114, no. 1 (1985)

Paul Kane, *Australian Poetry: Romanticism and negativity* (1996)

Robert Kenny and Colin Maxwell Talbot (eds), *Applestealers: Is a collection of the new poetry in Australia, including notes, statements, histories on La Mama* (1974)

Joan Kirkby (ed.), *The American Model: Influence and independence in Australian poetry* (1982)

Sylvia Kleinert, Margo Neale and Robyne Bancroft (eds), *The Oxford Companion to Aboriginal Art and Culture* (2000)

Leonie Kramer (ed.), *The Oxford History of Australian Literature* (1981)

Stella Lees and Pam Macintyre (eds), *The Oxford Companion to Australian Children's Literature* (1993)

John Leonard (ed.), *Australian Verse: An Oxford anthology* (1998)

——(ed.), *New Music: An anthology of contemporary Australian poetry* (2001)

Susan Lever, *Real Relations: The feminist politics of form in Australian fiction* (2000)

——(ed.), *The Oxford Book of Australian Women's Verse* (1995)

Martyn Lyons and John Arnold (eds), *A History of the Book in Australia, 1891–1945: A national culture in a colonised market* (2001)

James McAuley, *A Map of Australian Verse* (1975)

David McCooey, *Artful Histories: Modern Australian autobiography* (1996)

Lyn McCredden and Rose Lucas, *Bridgings: Readings in Australian women's poetry* (1996)

Lyn McCredden and Stephanie Trigg (eds), *The Space of Poetry: Australian essays on contemporary poetics* (1996)

Brian McFarlane, *Words and Images: Australian novels into films* (1983)

Susan McKernan, *A Question of Commitment: Australian literature in the twenty years after the war* (1989)

John McLaren, *Writing in Hope and Fear: Literature as politics in postwar Australia* (1996)

——, *Australian Literature: An historical introduction* (1989)

Humphrey McQueen, *The Black Swan of Trespass: The emergence of modernist painting in Australia to 1944* (1979)

Igor Maver (ed.), *Readings in Contemporary Australian Poetry* (1997)

John Maynard, *Fight for Liberty and Freedom: The origins of Australian Aboriginal activism* (2007)

Philip Mead, *Networked Language: Culture and history in Australian poetry* (2008)

Peter Minter (ed.), Blak Times: Indigenous Australia special issue, *Meanjin*, vol. 65, no. 1 (2006)

Drusilla Modjeska, *Exiles at Home: Australian women writers 1925–1945* (1981)

Aileen Moreton-Robinson (ed.), *Whitening Race: Essays in social and cultural criticism* (2004)

Howard Morphy, *Aboriginal Art* (1998)

Philip Morrissey, 'Stalking Aboriginal Culture: The Wanda Koolmatrie affair', *Australian Feminist Studies*, vol. 18, no. 42 (2003)

Mudrooroo, *The Indigenous Literature of Australia: Milli Milli Wangka* (1997)

——, *Writing from the Fringe: A study of modern Aboriginal literature* (1990)

Craig Munro and Robyn Sheahan-Bright (eds), *Paper Empires: A history of the book in Australia 1946–2005* (2006)

Martin Nakata, *Disciplining the Savages: Savaging the disciplines* (2007)

Brenda Niall and John Thompson (eds), *The Oxford Book of Australian Letters* (1998)

Richard Nile, *The Making of the Australian Literary Imagination* (2002)

Maggie Nolan and Carrie Dawson (eds), *Who's Who? Hoaxes, imposture and identity crises in Australian literature* (2004)

Marilla North (ed.), *Yarn Spinners: A story in letters—Dymphna Cusack, Florence James, Miles Franklin* (2001)

Geoff Page, *A Reader's Guide to Contemporary Australian Poetry* (1995)

Philip Parsons (gen. ed.), *Companion to Theatre in Australia* (1995)

Bruce Pascoe, *Convincing Ground: Learning to fall in love with your country* (2007)

Hetti Perkins, *One Sun One Moon: Aboriginal art in Australia* (2007)

Peter Porter (ed.), *The Oxford Book of Modern Australian Verse* (1996)

Alice Pung (ed.), *Growing Up Asian in Australia* (2008)

John Ramsland, *Remembering Aboriginal Heroes: Struggle, identity and the media* (2006)

Leslie Rees, *The Making of Australian Drama: A historical and critical survey from the 1830s to the 1970s* (1973)

Henry Reynolds, *The Law of the Land* (1987)

——, *The Other Side of the Frontier: Aboriginal resistance to the European invasion of Australia* (2006)

Michael Rose (ed.), *For the Record: 160 years of Aboriginal print journalism* (1996)

Jennifer Rutherford, *The Gauche Intruder: Freud, Lacan and the white Australian fantasy* (2000)

Judith Ryan and Chris Wallace-Crabbe (eds), *Imagining Australia: Literature and culture in the new New World* (2004)

Jennifer Sabbiono, Kay Schaffer and Sidonie Smith (eds), *Indigenous Australian Voices: A reader* (1998)

Selina Samuels (ed.), *The Dictionary of Literary Biography*, vols 230 (2001), 260 (2002), 289 (2004) and 325 (2006)

Kay Schaffer, *Women and the Bush: Forces of desire in the Australian cultural tradition* (1988)

Thomas Shapcott (ed.), *Australian Poetry Now* (1970)

——, *Contemporary American and Australian Poetry* (1976)

Shen Yuanfang, *Dragon Seed in the Antipodes: Chinese-Australian autobiographies* (2001)

Susan Sheridan, *Along the Faultlines: Sex, race and nation in Australian women's writing, 1880s–1930s* (1995)

Adam Shoemaker, *Black Words, White Page: Aboriginal literature 1929–1988* (1989)

Ken Stewart (ed.), *The 1890s: Australian literature and literary culture* (1996)

Andrew Taylor, *Reading Australian Poetry* (1987)

John Tranter (ed.), *The New Australian Poetry* (1979)

John Tranter and Philip Mead (eds), *The Penguin Book of Modern Australian Poetry* (1991)

Graeme Turner, *National Fictions: Literature, film and the construction of Australian narrative* (1986)

Penny van Toorn, *Writing Never Arrives Naked: Early Aboriginal cultures of writing in Australia* (2006)

Ann Vickery, *Stressing the Modern: Cultural politics in Australian women's poetry* (2007)

Elizabeth Webby, *Colonial Voices: Letters, diaries, journalism and other accounts of nineteenth-century Australia* (1989)

—— (ed.), *The Cambridge Companion to Australian Literature* (2000)

Richard White, *Inventing Australia* (1981)

Gillian Whitlock (ed.), *Autographs: Contemporary Australian autobiography* (1996)

——, *Soft Weapons: Autobiography in transit* (2007)

William H. Wilde, Joy Hooton and Barry Andrews (eds), *The Oxford Companion to Australian Literature*, 2nd edn (1994)

Sue Woolfe and Kate Grenville, *Making Stories: How ten Australian novels were written* (1993)

Alexis Wright (ed.), *Take Power Like This Old Man Here: An anthology of writings celebrating twenty years of land rights in Central Australia, 1977–1997* (1998)
Judith Wright, *Preoccupations in Australian Poetry* (1965)

Mena Abdullah and Ray Mathew: Thomas Shapcott (ed.), *Tense Little Lives: Uncollected prose of Ray Mathew* (2007)

Robert Adamson: *Swamp Riddles* (1974), *Mulberry Leaves: New and selected poems 1970–2001* (2001). Martin Duwell, *DLB* (2006)

Adam Aitken: Nicholas Jose, *DLB* (2006)

Jessica Anderson: Elaine Barry, *Fabricating the Self* (1996); Jenna Mead, *DLB* (2006)

Venero Armanno: *My Beautiful Friend* (1995), *Firehead* (1999)

Thea Astley: *Hunting the Wild Pineapple* (1979), *Beachmasters* (1985), *Reaching Tin River* (1990). Susan Lever, *DLB* (2004)

Louisa Atkinson: Patricia Clarke, *Pioneer Writer: The life of Louisa Atkinson—Novelist, journalist, naturalist* (1990)

Murray Bail: *The Pages* (2008). Michael Ackland, *DLB* (2006)

E.J. Banfield: Michael Noonan, *A Different Drummer: The story of E.J. Banfield, the 'Beachcomber' of Dunk Island* (1983)

Marjorie Barnard: *The Ivory Gate* (1920), *Macquarie's World* (1941), *Australian Outline* (1943), *The Sydney Book* (1947), *Sydney: The story of a city* (1956), *Australia's First Architect: Francis Greenway* (1961), *A History of Australia* (1962), *Lachlan Macquarie* (1964), *Miles Franklin* (1967)

M. Barnard Eldershaw: *Green Memory* (1931), *The Glasshouse* (1936), *Plaque with Laurel* (1937), *Essays in Australian Fiction* (1938), *Phillip of Australia: An account of the settlement of Sydney Cove 1788–92* (1938), *The Life and Times of Captain John Piper* (1939), *My Australia* (1939). Louise Rorabacher, *Marjorie Barnard and M. Barnard Eldershaw* (1973)

Barbara Baynton: Penne Hackforth-Jones, *Barbara Baynton: Between two worlds, a biography* (1989)

C.E.W. Bean: K. Fewster (ed.), *Bean's Gallipoli* (2007); K.S. Inglis, *C.E.W. Bean, Australian historian* (1970); D. Winter, *The War Writings of C.E.W. Bean* (1992)

Bruce Beaver: *The Hot Summer* (1963), *The Hot Men* (1965), *The Hot Spring* (1965), *You Can't Come Back* (1966), *Open at Random* (1967), *Lauds and Plaints* (1974), *Selected Poems* (1979), *New and Selected Poems: 1960–1990* (1991). Felicity Plunkett, *DLB* (2004)

Judith Beveridge: Margaret Bradstock, *DLB* (2006); Martin Duwell, 'Intricate Knots and Vast Cosmologies: The poetry of Judith Beveridge', *Australian Literary Studies*, vol. 19, no. 3 (2000)

Fred Biggs and Roland Robinson: Roland Robinson, *The Drift of Things* (1973), *The Shift of Sands* (1976), *A Letter to Joan* (1978). Brian Elliott, *The Jindyworobaks* (1979); Rex Ingamells et al. (ed.), *Jindyworobak Review* (1938–1948)

Geoffrey Blainey: *Triumph of the Nomads* (1975), *A Land Half Won* (1980), *A Shorter History of Australia* (1994), *A Short History of the World* (2000), *A Short History of the 20th Century* (2005)

Rolf Boldrewood: Paul de Serville, *Rolf Boldrewood: A life* (2000); Paul Eggert and Elizabeth Webby (eds), *Robbery Under Arms: A critical edition* (2006)

Ken Bolton: *At the Flash and at the Baci* (2006)

Martin Boyd: Kathleen Fitzpatrick, *Martin Boyd* (1963); Susan Lever, *DLB* (2002)

Christopher Brennan: Katherine Barnes, *The Higher Self in Christopher Brennan's 'Poems': Esotericism, romanticism, symbolism* (2006); Axel Clark, *Christopher Brennan: A critical biography* (1980)

John Le Gay Brereton: *Writings on Elizabethan Drama* (collected by R.G. Howarth, 1948). H.P. Heseltine, *John Le Gay Brereton* (1965)

Kevin Brophy: *Getting Away with It* (1982), *Visions* (1989), *The Hole Through the Centre of the World* (1991), *Replies to the Questionnaire on Love* (1992), *Seeing Things* (1997), *Explorations in Creative Writing* (2003), *What Men and Women Do* (2006)

Pam Brown: *This World / This Place* (1994)

Vincent Buckley: *Poetry and the Sacred* (1968), *Selected Poems* (1981). Chris Wallace-Crabbe, *DLB* (2004)

Ada Cambridge: Margaret Bradstock and Louise Wakeling, *Rattling the Orthodoxies: A life of Ada Cambridge* (1991); Audrey Tate, *Ada Cambridge: Her life and work 1844–1926* (1991)

David Campbell: *Devil's Rock and Other Poems* (1974), *Selected Poems* (1978). Vincent Buckley, *Essays in Poetry, Mainly Australian* (1957); Harry Heseltine (ed.), *A Tribute to David Campbell: A collection of essays* (1987); Leonie J. Kramer (ed.), *Poetry Australia: David Campbell* (1981)

Peter Carey: *The Tax Inspector* (1991), *The Unusual Life of Tristan Smith* (1994), *Theft: A love story* (2006), *His Illegal Self* (2008). Andreas Gaile (ed.), *Fabulating Beauty: Perspectives on the fiction of Peter Carey* (2005); Anthony J. Hassall, *Dancing on Hot Macadam: Peter Carey's fiction* (3rd edn, 1998), *DLB* (2004); Graham Huggan, *Peter Carey* (1996); Karen Lamb, *Peter Carey: The genesis of fame* (1992); Bruce Woodcock, *Peter Carey* (1996)

Brian Castro: *After China* (1992), *Drift* (1994), *Stepper* (1997), *The Garden Book* (2005). Bernadette Brennan, *DLB* (2006)

Nick Cave: *King Ink* (1988), *And the Ass Saw the Angel* (1989), *The Complete Lyrics 1978–2007* (2007). Amy Hanson, *Kicking Against the Pricks: An armchair guide to Nick Cave* (2005)

George Chanson: Hugh Anderson, *George Loyau: The man who wrote bush ballads* (1991)

Manning Clark: *In Search of Henry Lawson* (1978), *The Quest for Grace* (1990). Carl Bridge (ed.), *Manning Clark: Essays on his place in history* (1994); Stephen Holt, *Manning Clark and Australian History 1915–1963* (1982), *A Short History of Manning Clark* (1999); Brian Matthews, *Manning Clark: A life* (2008)

Marcus Clarke: Brian Elliott, *Marcus Clarke* (1969); Andrew McCann, *Marcus Clarke's Bohemia: Literature and modernity in colonial Melbourne* (2004); Lurline Stuart (ed.), *His Natural Life: A critical edition* (2001)

Inga Clendinnen: *Aztecs: An interpretation* (1991), *Dancing with Strangers: Europeans and Australians at first contact* (2004)

Charmian Clift: *The World of Charmian Clift* (1970), *Selected Essays* (2001)

J.M. Coetzee: *In the Heart of the Country* (1977), *Foe* (1986), *Age of Iron* (1990), *The Master of Petersburg* (1994), *Giving Offense: Essays on censorship* (1996). Teresa Dovey, *The Novels of J.M. Coetzee: Lacanian allegories* (1988); Graham Huggan and Stephen Watson (eds), *Critical Perspectives on J.M. Coetzee* (1996); Sue Kossew (ed.), *Critical Essays on J.M. Coetzee* (1998); Michael Marais, *DLB* (2000); Susan Van Zanten Gallagher, *A Story of South Africa: J.M. Coetzee's fiction in context* (1991)

Jill Ker Conway: *True North: A memoir* (1995), *When Memory Speaks: Reflections on autobiography* (1998)

Dymphna Cusack and Florence James: Marilla North (ed.), *Yarn Spinners: A story in letters—Dymphna Cusack, Florence James, Miles Franklin,* (2001); Marilla North, *DLB* (2002) (on Cusack)

Victor Daley: Frank Molloy, *Victor J. Daley: A life* (2004)

Eleanor Dark: *Slow Dawning* (1932), *Return to Coolami* (1936), *Storm of Time* (1948), *No Barrier* (1953), *Lantana Lane* (1959). Barbara Brooks and Judith Clark, *Eleanor Dark: A writer's life* (1998); Carole Ferrier (ed.), Eleanor Dark special issue, *Hecate*, vol. 27, no. 1 (2001)

Luke Davies: *Running with Light: Poems* (1999), *Isabelle the Navigator* (2000), *Totem* (2004), *God of Speed* (2008)

Jack Davis: Keith Chesson, *Jack Davis: A life story* (1988); Gerry Turcotte, *Jack Davis: The maker of history* (1994)

Bruce Dawe: *An Eye for a Tooth* (1968), *Beyond the Subdivisions* (1969), *Condolences of the Season* (1971). Dennis Haskell, *Attuned to Alien Moonlight: The poetry of Bruce Dawe* (2002); Peter Kuch, *Bruce Dawe* (1995)

Sarah Day: *The Ship* (2004)

D.H. Deniehy: Cyril Pearl, *Brilliant Dan Deniehy: A forgotten genius* (1972)

C.J. Dennis: *Backblock Ballads and Other Stories* (1913), *Doreen and the Sentimental Bloke* (1916), *The Glugs of Gosh* (1917), *A Book for Kids* (1921), *Rose of Spadgers* (1924), *The Singing Garden* (1935). Philip Butterss, *DLB* (2002); Alec H. Chisholm, *The Making of a Sentimental Bloke: A sketch of the remarkable career of C.J. Dennis* (1946); Ian F. McLaren, *C.J. Dennis: A comprehensive bibliography based on the collection of the compiler* (1979)

Jean Devanny: *Lenore Divine* (1926), *Old Savage and Other Stories* (1927), *Dawn Beloved* (1928), *Riven* (1929), *Bushman Burke* (1930), *Devil Made Saint* (1930), *Poor Swine* (1932), *Out of Such Fires* (1934), *The Ghost Wife* (1935), *The Virtuous Courtesan* (1935), *Paradise Flow* (1938), *The Killing of Jacqueline Love* (1942), *By Tropic Sea and Jungle* (1944), *Bird of Paradise*

(1945), *Roll Back the Night* (1945), *Cindie* (1949), *Travels in North Queensland* (1951), *Point of Departure* (1985). Carole Ferrier, *Jean Devanny: Romantic Revolutionary* (1999); Nicole Moore (ed.), *Sugar Heaven* (2002)

Rosemary Dobson: *Cock Crow* (1965), *Selected Poems* (1973). Marie-Louise Ayres, *DLB* (2002); Noel Rowe, *Modern Australian Poets* (1994), *Rosemary Dobson: A celebration* (2000)

Mick Dodson: 'The End in the Beginning: Re(de)fining Aboriginality' in Michele Grossman (ed.), *Blacklines: Contemporary critical writing by Indigenous Australians* (2003)

Patrick Dodson: Kevin Keefe, *Paddy's Road: Life stories of Patrick Dodson* (2003)

Michael Dransfield: Livio Dobrez, *Parnassus Mad Ward: Michael Dransfield and the New Australian Poetry* (1990); Patricia Dobrez, *Michael Dransfield's Lives* (1999); John Kinsella (ed.), *Michael Dransfield: A retrospective* (2002)

Robert Drewe: *A Cry in the Jungle Bar* (1979), *Fortune* (1986), *The Bay of Contented Men* (1989), *The Drowner* (1996), *Grace* (2005), *The Rip* (2008). Michael Ackland, *DLB* (2006)

Laurie Duggan: *Blue Notes* (1990), *The Passenger* (2006)

Louis Esson: Peter Fitzpatrick, *Pioneer Players: The lives of Louis and Hilda Esson* (1995)

Beverley Farmer: Lyn Jacobs, *Against the Grain: Beverley Farmer's writing* (2001), *DLB* (2006)

Robert D. FitzGerald: Julian Croft, *ADB* (2002)

Richard Flanagan: 'Out of Control: The tragedy of Australia's forests', *The Monthly*, no. 23, May (2007), *Wanting* (2008)

Matthew Flinders: Miriam Estensen, *The Life of Matthew Flinders* (2002)

John Forbes: *Stalin's Holidays* (1981), *New and Selected Poems* (1992). David McCooey, *DLB* (2006)

David Foster: *The Adventures of Christian Rosy Cross* (1985), *Testostero* (1987), *Mates of Mars* (1991). Susan Lever, *DLB* (2004), *David Foster: The Satirist of Australia* (2008)

Frank the Poet: John Meredith and Rex Whalan, *The Life and Works of Francis MacNamara* (1979)

Richard Frankland: 'Conversations with the Dead' in *Blak Inside: 6 Indigenous plays from Victoria* (2002)

Miles Franklin: Miles Franklin special issue, *Australian Literary Studies*, vol. 20, no. 4 (2002); Marjorie Barnard, *Miles Franklin: The story of a famous Australian* (1967); Paul Brunton (ed.), *The Diaries of Miles Franklin* (2004); Verna Coleman, *Miles Franklin in America: Her (unknown) brilliant career* (1981); Library Council of NSW, *Guide to the papers and books of Miles Franklin* (1980); Colin Roderick, *Miles Franklin: Her brilliant career* (1982); Jill Roe (ed.), *My Congenials: Stella Miles Franklin and friends in letters 1879–1954*, 2 vols (1993), *Stella Miles Franklin: A biography* (2008); Jill Roe and Margaret Bettison, *A Gregarious Culture: Topical writings of Miles Franklin* (2001)

Mary E. Fullerton: Sylvia Martin, *Passionate Friends: Mary Fullerton, Mabel Singleton and Miles Franklin* (2001); Jill Roe (ed.), *My Congenials: Miles Franklin and friends in letters 1879–1954*, 2 vols (1993)

Joseph Furphy: *The Annotated Such is Life: Being certain extracts from the diary of Tom Collins*, with an introduction and notes by Frances Devlin-Glass et al. (1991). John Barnes, *The Order of Things: A life of Joseph Furphy* (1990); John Barnes and Lois Hoffmann (eds), *Bushman and Bookworm: Letters of Joseph Furphy, 'Tom Collins'* (1995); Julian Croft, *The Life and Opinions of Tom Collins: A study of the works of Joseph Furphy* (1991); Miles Franklin, with Kate Baker, *Joseph Furphy: The legend of a man and his book* (1944); James Wieland, 'Australian Literature and the Question of Historical Method', *Journal of Commonwealth Literature*, vol. 20, no. 1 (1985)

Helen Garner: *My Hard Heart: Selected fictions* (1998), *The Spare Room* (2008). Kerryn Goldsworthy, *Helen Garner* (1996); Susan Lever, *DLB* (2006)

Kevin Gilbert: Pauline McMillan, 'Kevin Gilbert and "Living Black"', *Journal of Australian Studies*, no. 45, June (1995)

Ernest Giles: Ray Ericksen, *Ernest Giles: Explorer and traveller 1835–1897* (1978)

Mary Gilmore: *The Passionate Heart* (1918), *Under the Wilgas* (1932), *Fourteen Men: Verses by Mary Gilmore* (1954). Sylvia Lawson, *Mary Gilmore* (1966); Anne Whitehead, *Paradise Mislaid: In search of the Australian tribe of Paraguay* (1997); W.H. Wilde, *Courage a Grace: A biography of Dame Mary Gilmore* (1988); W.H. Wilde and T. Inglis Moore (eds), *Letters of Mary Gilmore* (1980)

Peter Goldsworthy: *Little Deaths* (1993), *New Selected Poems* (2001), *The List of All Answers* (2004), *Everything I Knew* (2008). Richard Hillman, *DLB* (2006); Andrew Riemer, *The Ironic Eye: The poetry and prose of Peter Goldsworthy* (1994)

Adam Lindsay Gordon: Geoffrey Hutton, *Adam Lindsay Gordon: The man and the myth* (1978); W.H. Wilde, *Adam Lindsay Gordon* (1972)

Alan Gould: *The Twofold Place* (1986)

Michael Gow: Luke Simon, *Michael Gow's Plays: A thematic approach* (1991)

Robert Gray: *The Skylight* (1984). Leon Cantrell, *DLB* (2006)

Germaine Greer: *The Madwoman's Underclothes: Essays and occasional writings 1968– 1985* (1986), *The Change: Women, ageing and the menopause* (1991), *The Whole Woman* (1999), *The Boy* (2003). Ian Britain, *Once an Australian: Journeys with Barry Humphries, Clive James, Germaine Greer and Robert Hughes* (1997); Christine Wallace, *Germaine Greer: Untamed shrew* (1997)

Kate Grenville: *The Lieutenant* (2008). Michael Ackland, *DLB* (2006)

Rodney Hall: Veronica Brady, *DLB* (2004)

Barbara Hanrahan: *Sea Green* (1974), *The Albatross Muff* (1977), *Where the Queens All Strayed* (1978), *The Peach Groves* (1979), *The Frangipani Gardens* (1980), *Dove* (1982), *Kewpie Doll* (1984), *Annie Magdalene* (1985), *A Chelsea Girl* (1988), *Flawless Jade* (1989), *Good Night, Mr Moon* (1992). Alison Carroll, *Barbara Hanrahan, Printmaker* (1986); Elaine

Lindsay, *DLB* (2004); Annette Stewart, *Woman and Herself: A critical study of the works of Barbara Hanrahan* (1998)

J.M. Harcourt: 'The Banning of *Upsurge*', *Overland*, no. 46 (Summer 1970–71). Richard Nile, Introduction in J.M. Harcourt, *Upsurge* (1986)

Lesbia Harford: Jeff Sparrow, '"Signed up in a rebel band": Lesbia Harford Re-Viewed', *Hecate*, vol. 32, no. 1 (2006)

Charles Harpur: J. Normington-Rawling, *Charles Harpur: An Australian* (1962)

J.S. Harry: *The Life on the Water and the Life Beneath* (1995). Fleur Diamond, *DLB* (2006)

Kevin Hart: *The Lines of the Hand* (1981), *Your Shadow* (1984), *Peniel* (1991), *New and Selected Poems* (1995), *Wicked Heat* (1999), *Young Rain* (2008). Carrie Olivia Adams, *DLB* (2006)

P.J. Hartigan: Frank Mecham, *'John O'Brien' and the Boree Log* (1981)

Gwen Harwood: *Selected Poems* (1975), *The Lion's Bride* (1981), *Bone Scan* (1988), *Night Thoughts* (1992), *The Present Tense* (1995). Cassandra Atherton, *'Flashing Eyes and Floating Hair': A reading of Gwen Harwood's pseudonymous poetry* (2006); Alison Hoddinott (ed.), *Blessed City: The letters of Gwen Harwood to Thomas Riddell, January to September 1943* (1990), *Gwen Harwood: The Real and the Imagined World* (1991); Elizabeth Lawson, *The Poetry of Gwen Harwood* (1991); Jennifer Strauss, *Boundary Conditions: The Poetry of Gwen Harwood* (1992); Stephanie Trigg, *Gwen Harwood* (1994)

Shirley Hazzard: Brigitta Olubas, *DLB* (2004)

Xavier Herbert: Laurie Clancy, *Xavier Herbert* (1981); Frances de Groen, *Xavier Herbert: A Biography* (1998); Frances de Groen and Laurie Hergenhan (eds), *Xavier Herbert: Letters* (2002); Harry Heseltine, *Xavier Herbert* (1973); Sean Monahan, *A Long and Winding Road: Xavier Herbert's Literary Journey* (2003)

Dorothy Hewett: *Collected Plays Volume 1* (1992), *Wheatlands*, with John Kinsella (2000), *Nowhere* (2001). Bruce Bennett (ed.), *Dorothy Hewett: Selected critical essays* (1995); Margaret Williams, *Dorothy Hewett: The feminine as subversion* (1992)

Barry Hill: *The Best Picture* (1988), *Raft: Poems 1983–1990* (1990), *Sitting In* (1991), *Ghosting William Buckley* (1993), *The Rock* (1994), *The Inland Sea* (2001), *The Enduring Rip* (2004), *Necessity: Poems 1996–2006* (2007)

Philip Hodgins: *Things Happen* (1995)

A.D. Hope: *Poems* (1960), *A Midsummer Eve's Dream: Variations on a theme by William Dunbar* (1970), *Judith Wright* (1975), *A Late Picking* (1975), *The Pack of Autolycus* (1978), *A.D. Hope: Selected Poetry and Prose*, David Brooks (ed.) (2000). David Brooks (ed.), *The Double Looking Glass: New and classic essays on the poetry of A.D. Hope* (2000); Robert Darling, *A.D. Hope* (1997); Kevin Hart, *A.D. Hope* (1992); Joy W. Hooton, *A.D. Hope* (bibliography) (1979); Leonie Kramer, *A.D. Hope* (1979); Ann McCulloch, *DLB* (2004)

Donald Horne: *Confessions of a New Boy* (1985), *Portrait of an Optimist* (1988)

Robert Hughes: *Donald Friend* (1965), *Heaven and Hell in Western Art* (1968), *Barcelona* (1992), *American Visions: The epic history of art in America* (1998), *A Jerk on One End: Reflections of a mediocre fisherman* (1999), *Goya* (2003). Ian Britain, *Once an Australian: Journeys with Barry Humphries, Clive James, Germaine Greer and Robert Hughes* (1997); A.P. Riemer, *Hughes* (2001)

Barry Humphries: *My Life as Me* (2002). Ian Britain, *Once an Australian: Journeys with Barry Humphries, Clive James, Germaine Greer and Robert Hughes* (1997); Peter Coleman, *The Real Barry Humphries* (1991); John Lahr, *Dame Edna Everage and the Rise of Western Civilization: Backstage with Barry Humphries* (1991); Paul Matthew St Pierre, *A Portrait of the Artist as Australian: L'oeuvre bizarre de Barry Humphries* (2004)

K.S. Inglis: *The Stuart Case* (1961), *The Australian Colonists* (1974), *This is the ABC: The Australian Broadcasting Commission, 1932–1983* (1983), *Whose ABC? The Australian Broadcasting Corporation 1983–2006* (2006)

Clive James: *Falling Towards England* (1985), *May Week Was in June* (1990), *Cultural Amnesia: Necessary memories from history and the arts* (2007). Ian Britain, *Once an Australian: Journeys with Barry Humphries, Clive James, Germaine Greer and Robert Hughes* (1997)

George Johnston: Max Brown, *Charmian and George* (2004); Josephine Jill Kinnane, *DLB* (2002)

Elizabeth Jolley: *The Travelling Entertainer* (1979), *The Newspaper of Claremont Street* (1981), *Woman in a Lampshade* (1983), *Foxybaby* (1985), *Central Mischief* (1992). Delys Bird, *DLB* (2006); Delys Bird and Brenda Walker (eds), *Elizabeth Jolley: New critical essays* (1991); Brian Dibble, *Doing Life: A biography of Elizabeth Jolley* (2008); Caroline Lurie (ed.), *Learning to Dance: Elizabeth Jolley—Her life and work* (2006); Paul Salzman, *'Helplessly Tangled in Female Arms and Legs': Elizabeth Jolley's fictions* (1993)

Jill Jones: *The Book of Possibilities* (1997)

Henry Kendall: Michael Ackland, *Henry Kendall: The man and the myths* (1995)

Thomas Keneally: *A Dutiful Daughter* (1971), *Gossip from the Forest* (1975), *Confederates* (1979), *A Family Madness* (1985), *The Playmaker* (1987), *Flying Hero Class* (1991), *An Angel in Australia* (2002), *Searching for Schindler* (2007). Peter Pierce, *Australian Melodramas: Thomas Keneally's fiction* (1995), *DLB* (2004); Peter Quartermaine, *Thomas Keneally* (1991)

John Kinsella: *Genre* (1997), *Poems: 1980–1994* (1997), *Grappling Eros* (1998), *Visitants* (1999), *Auto* (2001). Rod Mengham and Glen Phillips (eds), *Fairly Obsessive: Essays on the works of John Kinsella* (2000); Ann Vickery, *DLB* (2006)

Christopher Koch: *The Memory Room* (2007). C.A. Cranston, *DLB* (2004); Noel Henricksen, *Island and Otherland: Christopher Koch and his books* (2003)

Eve Langley: Lucy Frost, Introduction and Afterword in *Wilde Eve: Eve Langley's story* (1999); Aorewa McLeod, 'The New Zealand Novels of Eve Langley', *Southerly*, vol. 55, no. 2 (1995), 'Alternative Eves', *Hecate*, vol. 25, no. 2 (1999); Joy L. Thwaite, *The Importance of Being Eve Langley* (1989)

Ray Lawler: Peter Fitzpatrick, *DLB* (2004)

Henry Lawson: Manning Clark, *In Search of Henry Lawson* (1978); Christopher Lee, *City Bushman: Henry Lawson and the Australian imagination* (2004); Brian Matthews, *The Receding Wave: Henry Lawson's prose* (1972); Denton Prout, *Henry Lawson: The grey dreamer* (1963); Colin Roderick, *Henry Lawson: A life* (1991)

Louisa Lawson: Brian Matthews, *Louisa* (1987)

Geoffrey Lehmann: *Spring Forest* (1992), *Collected Poems* (1997)

Michael Leunig: *The Penguin Leunig* (1974), *Ramming the Shears* (1985), *A Common Prayer* (1990), *Poems 1972–2002* (2003), *Wild Figments* (2004). Pamela Bone, *Up We Grew: Stories of Australian childhoods* (2004); David Matthews and Murray Bramwell, *Wanted for Questioning: Interviews with Australian comic artists* (1992)

Norman Lindsay: *A Curate in Bohemia* (1913), *The Pen Drawings of Norman Lindsay* (1918), *Pen Drawings* (1924), *The Etchings of Norman Lindsay* (1927), *Watercolours and Etchings* (1930), *Mr Gresham and Olympus* (1932), *Pan in the Parlour* (1933), *Saturdee* (1933), *The Flyaway Highway* (1936), *Age of Consent* (1938), *The Cousin from Fiji* (1945), *Paintings in Oil* (1945), *Halfway to Anywhere* (1947), *Dust or Polish* (1950), *Bohemians of the Bulletin* (1965), *The Scribblings of an Idle Mind* (1966), *Rooms and Houses: An autobiographical novel* (1968). John Docker, *Australian Cultural Elites* (1974); John Hetherington, *Norman Lindsay: The embattled Olympian* (1973); R.G. Howarth and A.W. Barker (eds), *The Letters of Norman Lindsay* (1979); Joanna Mendelssohn, *Letters and Liars: Norman Lindsay and the Lindsay family* (1996); Douglas Stewart, *Norman Lindsay: A Personal Memoir* (1975)

Vincent Lingiari: Alexis Wright (ed.), *Take Power Like This Old Man Here: An anthology of writings celebrating twenty years of land rights in Central Australia 1977–1997* (1998)

Amanda Lohrey: *Vertigo* (2008). Jenna Mead, *DLB* (2006)

Lennie Lower: Barry Dickins, *Lennie Lower* (1982); Bill Hornidge, *Lennie Lower* (1993)

Elizabeth Macarthur: Lennard Bickel, *Australia's First Lady: The story of Elizabeth Macarthur* (1991)

James McAuley: *C.J. Brennan* (1963), *Captain Quiros* (1964), *A Primer of English Versification* (1966), *Surprises of the Sun* (1969), *The Personal Element in Australian Poetry* (1970), *The Grammar of the Real: Selected prose 1959–1974* (1975), *The Rhetoric of Australian Poetry* (1978), *James McAuley: Poetry, essays and personal commentary*, Leonie Kramer (ed.) (1988), *Collected Poems* (1993). Michael Ackland, *Damaged Men: The precarious lives of James McAuley and Harold Stewart* (2001); Peter Coleman, *The Heart of James McAuley: Life and work of the Australian poet* (1980); Michael Heyward, *The Ern Malley Affair* (1993); Lyn McCredden, *James McAuley* (1992); Cassandra Pybus, *The Devil and James McAuley* (1999)

Roger McDonald: *Water Man* (1993)

Andrew McGahan: Louise D'Arcens, *DLB* (2006)

Dorothea Mackellar: Adrienne Howley, *My Heart, My Country: The story of Dorothea Mackellar* (1989)

Jennifer Maiden: *Play with Knives* (1990), *Selected Poems* (1990)

Ern Malley: Max Harris, Introduction, *The Darkening Ecliptic* (1961); Michael Heyward, *The Ern Malley Affair* (1993); James McAuley and Harold Stewart, 'Ern Malley, Poet of Debunk: Full story from the two authors', *Fact*, 25 June (1944); Philip Mead, *Networked Language: Culture and history in Australian poetry* (2008); Maggie Nolan and Carrie Dawson (eds), *Who's Who? Hoaxes, imposture, and identity crises in Australian literature*, special issue, *Australian Literary Studies* (2004); K.K. Ruthven, *Faking Literature* (2001)

David Malouf: *First Things Last* (1980). Ivor Indyk (ed.), *David Malouf: A celebration* (2001); Philip Neilsen, *Imagined Lives: A study of David Malouf* (1990); Amanda Nettelbeck (ed.), *Provisional Maps: Critical essays on David Malouf* (1994), *Reading David Malouf* (1995); Brigid Rooney, *DLB* (2004)

J.S. Manifold: Rodney Hall, *J.S. Manifold: An introduction to the man and his work* (1978); William Hatherell, 'Some Versions of Manifold: Brisbane and the "myth" of John Manifold', *Australian Literary Studies*, vol. 21, no. 2 (2003)

Frederic Manning: Simon Caterson, 'The Fortunes of Private 19022' in *The Middle Parts of Fortune: Somme and Ancre, 1916* (2000); Verna Coleman, *The Last Exquisite: A portrait of Frederic Manning* (1990); Jonathon Marwil, *Frederic Manning: An unfinished life* (1988); Nettie Palmer, 'Frederic Manning: A philosopher as soldier', *Argus*, 20 May 1933, p. 9; J.H. Willis Jnr, 'The Censored Language of War: Richard Aldington's *Death of a Hero* and three other war novels of 1929', *Twentieth Century Literature*, vol. 45, no. 4 (1999)

David Marr: *The Ivanov Trial* (1983), *The High Price of Heaven* (1999)

Alan Marshall: *These Are My People* (1944), *Tell Us About the Turkey, Jo* (1946), *How Beautiful Are Thy Feet* (1949), *The Complete Stories of Alan Marshall* (1977). Jack Lindsay, 'A Triumph Over Adversity: Comments on Alan Marshall's writing', *Meanjin*, vol. 28, no. 3 (1969); Joanne McPherson, *DLB* (2002)

Olga Masters: Deirdre Coleman (ed.), *Olga Masters Reporting Home: Her writings as a journalist* (1990); Dorothy Jones, *DLB* (2006); William McGaw and Paul Sharrad (eds), *Olga Masters, An Autumn Crocus: Proceedings of the Olga Masters Memorial Conference, 8–10 July, 1988* (1990)

Robert Menzies: *The Forgotten People and Other Studies in Democracy* (1943), *The Measure of the Years* (1970). Judith Brett, *Robert Menzies' Forgotten People* (1992); A.W. Martin, *Robert Menzies: A life*, 2 vols (1993, 1999); Tim Rowse, *Australian Liberalism and National Character* (1978)

Louisa Anne Meredith: Vivienne Rae Ellis, *Louisa Anne Meredith: A tigress in exile* (1979)

Drusilla Modjeska: *Secrets*, with Amanda Lohrey and Robert Dessaix (1997)

Frank Moorhouse: *The Electrical Experience: A discontinuous narrative* (1974), *Conference-Ville* (1976), *Tales of Mystery and Romance* (1977), *The Everlasting Secret Family and Other Secrets* (1980), *Lateshows* (1990), *The Inspector-General of Misconception: The ultimate compendium to sorting things out* (2002), *Martini: A memoir* (2005). Alan Lawson, *DLB* (2004)

Sally Morgan: *Arthur Corunna's Story* (1990), *Mother and Daughter: The story of Daisy and Gladys Corunna* (1990), *Sally's Story* (1990). Delys Bird and Dennis Haskell (eds), *Whose Place? A study of Sally Morgan's 'My Place'* (1992); Julieanne Lamond, *DLB* (2006)

John Morrison: John McLaren, 'The British Tradition in John Morrison's Radical Nationalism', *Australian Literary Studies*, vol. 20, no. 3 (2002)

Mudrooroo: *The Song Cycle of Jacky* (1986), *The Garden of Gethsemane: Poems from the lost decade* (1991), *Wildcat Screaming* (1992), *The Undying* (1998), *Underground* (1999), *The Promised Land* (2000). Maureen Clark, *DLB* (2006); Adam Shoemaker, *Mudrooroo: A critical study* (1993)

Gerald Murnane: *Tamarisk Row* (1974), *The Plains* (1982), *Landscape with Landscape* (1985), *Emerald Blue* (1995). Imre Salusinszky, *Gerald Murnane* (1993), *DLB* (2004); 'A Tribute to Gerald Murnane', special issue, *Southerly*, vol. 55, no. 3 (1995)

Les Murray: *The Boys Who Stole the Funeral* (1979), *The People's Otherworld* (1983), *The Daylight Moon* (1987), *Dog Fox Field* (1990), *Conscious and Verbal* (1999), *The Biplane Houses* (2006). Peter F. Alexander, *Les Murray: A life in progress* (2000); Laurence Bourke, *A Vivid Steady State: Les Murray and Australian poetry* (1992); Bruce Clunies Ross (ed.), *Poetry of Les Murray: Critical essays* (2002); Carmel Gaffney (ed.), *Counterbalancing Light: Essays on the poetry of Les Murray* (1997); Steven Matthews, *Les Murray* (2002)

Narritjin Maymuru: Howard Morphy, Pip Deveson and Katie Hayne, 'The Art of Narritjin Maymuru', CD-ROM, ANU Centre for Cross-Cultural Research (2005)

John Shaw Neilson: *Collected Poems* (1934), *Poems* (1964), *Witnesses of Spring: Unpublished poems by Shaw Neilson* (1970). H. Anderson and L. Blake (eds), *John Shaw Neilson* (1972); C. Hanna, *The Folly of Spring* (1990), *Jock* (1999); Helen Hewson, *John Shaw Neilson: A life in letters* (2001); J.J. Phillips, *Poet of the Colours* (1988)

Doug Nicholls: Mavis Thorpe Clark, *Pastor Doug: The story of an Aboriginal leader* (1965), *The Boy from Cumeroogunga* (1979)

Louis Nowra: *The Misery of Beauty* (1976), *Visions* (1978), *Lulu* (1981), *The Golden Age* (1985), *Palu* (1987), *Deceit* (1996), *The Marvellous Boy* (2005). Veronica Kelly, *The Theatre of Louis Nowra* (1998); Gerry Turcotte, *DLB* (2006)

Bernard O'Dowd: Hugh Anderson, *The Poet Militant* (1969); Humphrey McQueen, *A New Britannia* (1983); A.A. Phillips, 'The Democratic Tradition', *Overland*, no. 5, (Spring 1955)

Oodgeroo Noonuccal: Anne Brewster, *DLB* (2004); Kathleen J. Cochrane and Ron Hurley (illustrator), *Oodgeroo* (1994); Adam Shoemaker (ed.), *Oodgeroo: A tribute* (1994)

Geoff Page: *Selected Poems* (1991), *A Reader's Guide to Contemporary Australian Poetry* (1995)

Nettie Palmer: *Henry Bournes Higgins: A memoir* (1931), *Australians in Spain*, with Len Fox (1937), *Henry Handel Richardson: A study* (1950). Vivian Smith (ed.), *Letters of Vance and Nettie Palmer 1915–1963* (1977)

Banjo Paterson: Colin Roderick, *Banjo Paterson: Poet by accident* (1993)

Charles Perkins: Peter Read, *Charles Perkins: A biography* (1990)

A.A. Phillips: *Responses: Selected writings* (1979)

Doris Pilkington: *Under the Wintamarra Tree* (2002)

Dorothy Porter: *The Night Parrot* (1984), *What a Piece of Work* (1999), *Wild Surmise* (2002), *El Dorado* (2007). Rose Lucas, *DLB* (2006)

Hal Porter: *Selected Stories* (1991). Mary Lord, *Hal Porter: Man of many parts* (1993); David McCooey, *DLB* (2002)

Peter Porter: *Poems Ancient and Modern* (1964), *The Last of England* (1970), *Preaching to the Converted* (1972), *English Subtitles* (1981), *Collected Poems*, 2 vols (1999), *Max is Missing* (2001). Bruce Bennett, *Spirit in Exile: Peter Porter and his poetry* (1991), *DLB* (2004); Peter Steele, *Peter Porter* (1992)

Katharine Susannah Prichard: *Black Opal* (1921), *Brumby Innes* (1927), *Moon of Desire* (1941), *The Roaring Nineties* (1946), *Golden Miles* (1948), *Winged Seeds* (1950), *Child of the Hurricane: An autobiography* (1963), *Subtle Flame* (1967). Jack Beasley, *Rage for Life: The work of Katharine Susannah Prichard* (1964); Delys Bird, *Katharine Susannah Prichard: Stories, journalism and essays* (2000); Ric Throssell, *Wild Weeds and Wind Flowers: The life and letters of Katharine Susannah Prichard* (1975)

Bob Randall: *Songman: The story of an Aboriginal elder of Uluru* (2003), *Tracker Tjugingji* (2003)

Kerry Reed-Gilbert: (ed.) *Message Stick: Contemporary Aboriginal writing* (1997)

Henry Handel Richardson: *The Young Cosima* (1939), *Myself When Young* (1948), *The End of a Childhood: The complete stories of Henry Handel Richardson* (1992). Michael Ackland, *Henry Handel Richardson* (1996); Axel Clark, *Henry Handel Richardson: Fiction in the making* (1990); Carol Franklin, 'H.H. Richardson's "Two Hanged Women": Our own true selves and compulsory heterosexuality', *Kunapipi*, vol. 14, no. 1 (1992); Dorothy Green, *Ulysses Bound: Henry Handel Richardson and her fiction* (1973); Catherine Pratt, *Resisting Fictions: The novels of Henry Handel Richardson* (1999); Clive Probyn and Bruce Steele (eds), *Maurice Guest: A critical edition* (1998), *The Fortunes of Richard Mahony: A critical edition* (2007)

Ricketty Kate: *Rhymes and Whimsies* (1938), *Out of the Dust* (1939). Colleen Burke, 'Expanding the Horizons: Researching neglected Australian women poets and writers', in Kerry Leves and Ellyn Lewis (eds), *The Book of Poets on the Heath* (1993)

Eric Rolls: Les Murray, 'Eric Rolls and the Golden Disobedience' in *Persistence in Folly* (1984)

Peter Rose: *Donatello in Wangaratta* (1998)

Steele Rudd: Richard Fotheringham, *In Search of Steele Rudd* (1995)

Gig Ryan: *Manners of an Astronaut* (1984), *Excavations: Arguments and monologues* (1990). Felicity Plunkett, *DLB* (2006)

Tracy Ryan: *Vamp* (1994), *Bluebeard in Drag* (1996), *The Willing Eye* (1999), *Jazz Tango* (2002), *Conspiracies*, with John Kinsella (2003)

John Scott: *The Quarrel with Ourselves and Confession* (1984), *St Clair: Three narratives* (1986), *Singles: Shorter works 1981–1986* (1989), *Before I Wake* (1996). Christopher Pollnitz, *DLB* (2006)

Kim Scott: *The Dregersaurus* (2001)

Thomas Shapcott: *Selected Poems 1956–1988* (1989), *Chekhov's Mongoose* (2000), *The City of Empty Rooms* (2006). Deborah Jordan, *DLB* (2004)

R.A. Simpson: *Poems from Murrumbeena* (1976), *The Midday Clock: Selected poems and drawings* (1999)

Kenneth Slessor: Graham Burns, *Kenneth Slessor* (1975); Adrian Caesar, *Kenneth Slessor* (1995); Geoffrey Dutton, *Kenneth Slessor: A biography* (1991); Brian Kiernan, *Considerations: New essays on Kenneth Slessor, Judith Wright and Douglas Stewart* (1977); Peter Kirkpatrick, *The Sea Coast of Bohemia: Literary life in Sydney's roaring twenties* (1992); Philip Mead (ed.), *Kenneth Slessor: Critical readings* (1997), *Networked Language: Culture and History in Australian poetry* (2008); Clement Semmler, *Kenneth Slessor* (1966), Douglas Stewart, *A Man of Sydney: An appreciation of Kenneth Slessor* (1970)

Vivian Smith: (ed.), *Letters of Vance and Nettie Palmer 1915–1963* (1977), *Familiar Places* (1978), *Effects of Light: The poetry of Tasmania*, with Margaret Scott (1985), *Nettie Palmer* (1988), *New Selected Poems* (1995). Noel Rowe, *DLB* (2006); Vivian Smith special issue, *Southerly*, vol. 56, no. 2 (1996)

Catherine Helen Spence: Susan Magarey, *Unbridling the Tongues of Women: A biography of Catherine Helen Spence* (1985)

Christina Stead: *A Little Tea, A Little Chat* (1948), *The People with the Dogs* (1952), *Dark Places of the Heart* or *Cotter's England* (1966), *The Little Hotel* (1973), *Miss Herbert (The Suburban Wife)* (1976), R.G. Geering (ed.), *Ocean of Story: The uncollected stories of Christina Stead* (1985), *Christina Stead: Selected fiction and nonfiction* (1994). Ann Blake, *Christina Stead's Politics of Place* (1999); Diana Brydon, *Christina Stead* (1987); R.G. Geering, *Christina Stead* (1969); Jennifer Gribble, *Christina Stead* (1994); Margaret Harris (ed.), Christina Stead Centenary Essays, special issue, *Journal of the Association for the Study of Australian Literature* (2003), *Dearest Munx: The Letters of Christina Stead and William J. Blake* (2005); Judith Kegan Gardiner, *Rhys, Stead, Lessing and the Politics of Empathy* (1989); Joan Lidoff, *Christina Stead* (1982); Kate Lilley (ed.), Christina Stead, special issue, *Southerly* (2003); Anne Pender, *Christina Stead: Satirist* (2002); Teresa Petersen, *The Enigmatic Christina Stead: A provocative rereading* (2001); Hazel Rowley, *Christina Stead: A biography* (1993); Susan Sheridan, *Christina Stead* (1988); Chris Williams, *Christina Stead: A life of letters* (1989)

Douglas Stewart: Nancy Keesing, *Douglas Stewart* (1969); David McCooey, *DLB* (2002); Clement Semmler, *Douglas Stewart: A critical study* (1974)

Louis Stone: Norman Lindsay, *Bohemians of the Bulletin* (1965); H.J. Oliver, *Louis Stone* (1968)

Randolph Stow: *Outrider: Poems 1956–1962* (1962), *A Counterfeit Silence: Selected poems* (1969). Anthony J. Hassall, *Strange Country: A study of Randolph Stow* (1986), (ed.), *Randolph Stow: Visitants, episodes from other novels, poems, stories, interviews and essays* (1990), *DLB* (2002)

Jennifer Strauss: *Family Ties: Australian poems of the family* (1998). Felicity Plunkett, *DLB* (2006)

Taam Sze Pui: Cathie R. May, *Topsawyers: The Chinese in Cairns, 1870–1920* (1984)

Tasma: Patricia Clarke, *Tasma: The life of Jessie Couvreur* (1994)

Alf Taylor: *Winds* (1994), *Rimfire* (2002)

Andrew Taylor: *Selected Poems: 1960–1980* (1982)

Kylie Tennant: *Australia: Her story* (1953), *Tether a Dragon* (1953), *Speak You So Gently* (1959), *Ma Jones and the Little White Cannibals* (1967), *The Man on the Headland* (1971). Jack Beasley, *Socialism and the Novel: A study of Australian literature* (1957); Margaret Dick, *The Novels of Kylie Tennant* (1966); Jane Grant, *Kylie Tennant: A life* (2006); Sharyn Pearce, 'Changing Places: Working-class women in the fiction of the Depression', *Westerly*, vol. 31, no. 4 (1986)

Colin Thiele: *Labourers in the Vineyard* (1970), *Selected Verse* (1970), *The Little Desert* (1975), *The Bight* (1976). Alison Halliday, *DLB* (2004)

Pat Torres: *The Story of Crow: A Nyul Nyul story* (1987)

John Tranter: *Parallax* (1970), *The Alphabet Murders* (1976), *Selected Poems* (1982), *Under Berlin* (1988), *The Floor of Heaven* (1992), *At the Florida* (1993), *Ultra* (2001), *Borrowed Voices* (2002), *Urban Myths: 210 poems* (2006). Martin Duwell, *DLB* (2004); Rod Mengham (ed.), *The Salt Companion to John Tranter* (2006); Noel Rowe, *Modern Australian Poets* (1994)

Christos Tsiolkas: *The Slap* (2008), 'Tolerance,' in *Tolerance, Prejudice and Fear* (2008)

Ethel Turner: Brenda Niall, *Seven Little Billabongs: The world of Ethel Turner and Mary Grant Bruce* (1979); A.T. Yarwood, *From a Chair in the Sun: The life of Ethel Turner* (1994)

David Unaipon: Mary-Anne Gale, 'Giving Credit Where Credit is Due: The writings of David Unaipon' in Gus Worby and Lester Irabinna Rigney (eds), *Sharing Spaces: Indigenous and non-Indigenous responses to story, country and rights* (2006); Sue Hosking, 'David Unaipon: His story' in Philip Butterss (ed.), *Southwords: Essays on South Australian writing* (1995)

Samuel Wagan Watson: *Hotel Bone* (2001), *Itinerant Blues* (2002), *Three Legged Dogs and Other Poems* (2005)

Chris Wallace-Crabbe: *In Light and Darkness* (1963), *I'm Deadly Serious* (1988), *Falling Into Language* (1990), *Whirling* (1998), *By and Large* (2001). David McCooey, *DLB* (2004)

Ania Walwicz: *Writing* (1982). Elizabeth Parsons, *DLB* (2006)

Glenyse Ward: *Unna You Fellas* (1991)

Price Warung: Barry Andrews, *Price Warung (William Astley)* (1976)

Judah Waten: David Carter, *DLB* (2004)

Francis Webb: *Leichhardt in Theatre* (1952), *Birthday* (1953), *Socrates and Other Poems* (1961). Bill Ashcroft, *The Gimbals of Unease: The poetry of Francis Webb* (1996); Michael J. Griffith, *God's Fool: The life and poetry of Francis Webb* (1991); Peter and Leonie Meere (eds), *Francis Webb, Poet and Brother: Some of his letters and poetry* (2001)

Patrick White: *The Cockatoos: Shorter novels and stories* (1975), *Big Toys* (1978), *The Night the Prowler* (1978), *Netherwood* (1983), *Signal Driver* (1983), *Collected Plays* (1985), *Three*

Uneasy Pieces (1987), *Patrick White Speaks* (1989). Michael Ackland, *DLB* (2002); May-Brit Akerholt, *Patrick White* (1988); Carolyn Bliss, *Patrick White's Fiction: The paradox of the Fortunate Fall* (1986); Simon During, *Patrick White* (1996); Martin Gray (ed.), *Patrick White: Life and writings—Five essays* (1996); Brian Kiernan, *Patrick White* (1980); Alan Lawson (ed.), *Patrick White: Selected writings* (1994); David Marr (ed.), *Patrick White: Letters* (1994); David J. Tacey, *Patrick White: Fiction and the unconscious* (1988); G. A. Wilkes (ed.), *Ten Essays on Patrick White: Selections from Southerly* (1970); Mark Williams, *Patrick White* (1993); Peter Wolf (ed.), *Critical Essays on Patrick White* (1990)

Anna Wickham: R.D. Smith (ed.), *The Writings of Anna Wickham: Free woman and poet* (1984); Jennifer Vaughan Jones, *Anna Wickham: A poet's daring life* (2003)

David Williamson: *What If You Died Tomorrow?* (1973), *The Department* (1974), *A Handful of Friends* (1976), *Travelling North* (1979), *Sons of Cain* (1985), *Money and Friends* (1991), *Brilliant Lies* (1993), *After the Ball* (1997). Katherine Brisbane (ed.), *David Williamson: A celebration* (2003); Peter Fitzpatrick, *Williamson* (1987); Brian Kiernan, *David Williamson: A writer's career* (1996), *DLB* (2004)

Eric Willmot: *Australia: The last experiment* (1987), *Below the Line* (1991). Lyn Jacobs, 'Mapping Shared Spaces: Willmot and Astley' in Gus Worby and Lester Irabinna Rigney (eds), *Sharing Spaces: Indigenous and non-Indigenous responses to story, country and rights* (2006)

Gerard Windsor: *Heaven Where the Bachelors Sit* (1996), *I Asked Cathleen to Dance* (1999), *I'll Just Tell You This* (1999), *The Mansions of Bedlam: Stories and essays* (2000). Peter Alexander, *DLB* (2006)

Tim Winton: *Shallows* (1984), *Scission* (1985), *That Eye, the Sky* (1986), *Minimum of Two* (1987), *In the Winter Dark* (1988), *Breath* (2008). Michael McGirr, *Tim Winton: The writer and his work* (1999); Hilary McPhee (ed.), *Tim Winton: A celebration* (1999); Richard Rossiter, *DLB* (2006); Richard Rossiter and Lyn Jacobs (eds), *Reading Tim Winton* (1993)

Alexis Wright: 'On Writing *Carpentaria*', *Heat*, no. 13, new series (2007), 'Fear', in *Tolerance, Prejudice and Fear* (2008)

Judith Wright: *The Gateway* (1953), *The Generations of Men* (1959), *Charles Harpur* (1963), *Preoccupations in Australian Poetry* (1965), *The Other Half* (1966), *Conservation as an Emerging Concept* (1970), *The Cry for the Dead* (1981), *Phantom Dwelling* (1985), *We Call for a Treaty* (1985), *A Human Pattern: Selected poems* (1990), *Born of the Conquerors: Selected essays* (1991), *Collected Poems: 1942–1985* (1994), *Half a Lifetime* (1999). Veronica Brady, *South of My Days: A biography of Judith Wright* (1998); Patricia Clarke and Meredith McKinney (eds), *With Love and Fury: Judith Wright's letters* (2006); Bryony Cosgrove (ed.), *Portrait of a Friendship: The letters of Barbara Blackman and Judith Wright* (2007); A.D. Hope, *Judith Wright* (1975); Jennifer Strauss, *Judith Wright* (1995); Shirley Walker, *Flame and Shadow: The poetry of Judith Wright* (1996)

Fay Zwicky: *Ask Me* (1990). Marcelle Freiman, *DLB* (2006)

SOURCES AND PERMISSIONS

The following works of reference have been used, and are acknowledged here instead of in individual biographies:

Reference works

William Arthur and Frances Morphy (eds), *Macquarie Atlas of Indigenous Australia* (2005)

Bain Attwood and Andrew Markus (eds), *The Struggle for Aboriginal Rights: A documentary history* (1999)

Bruce Bennett and Jennifer Strauss (eds), *The Oxford Literary History of Australia* (1998)

D. Horton (ed.), *Encyclopaedia of Aboriginal Australia* (1994)

Sylvia Kleinert, Margo Neale and Robyne Bancroft (eds), *The Oxford Companion to Aboriginal Art and Culture* (2000)

Philip Parsons (gen. ed.), *Companion to Theatre in Australia* (1995)

W. S. Ransom (ed.), *The Australian National Dictionary* (1988)

Selina Samuels (ed.), *The Dictionary of Literary Biography*, vols 230 (2001), 260 (2002), 289 (2004) and 325 (2006)

Elizabeth Webby (ed.), *The Cambridge Companion to Australian Literature* (2000)

William H. Wilde, Joy Hooton and Barry Andrews (eds), *The Oxford Companion to Australian Literature*, 2nd edn (1994)

Who's Who in Australia (present and past editions)

Websites

AustLit: The Resource for Australian Literature: www.austlit.edu.au

Australian Dictionary of Biography online edition: www.adb.online.anu.edu.au

Barani: www.cityofsydney.nsw.gov.au/barani/

Black Words, Aboriginal and Torres Strait Islander Writers and Storytellers subset of AustLit: www.austlit.edu.au/specialistDatasets/BlackWords

Kev Carmody: www.kevcarmody.com.au/biography.html

Gary Foley's Koori History website: www.kooriweb.org/foley/indexb.html

HREOC: www.hreoc.gov.au

Magabala Books: www.magabala.com
National Archives of Australia: www.naa.gov.au/fsheets/fs225.html

Mena Abdullah and Ray Mathew: *The Time of the Peacock* (Angus & Robertson, 1965). Reprint by ETT Imprint, 1992. Reproduced by permission of ETT Imprint.

Robert Adamson: 'Sonnets to be Written from Prison' from *Robert Adamson: Selected poems, 1970–1989* (UQP, 1989) (text reproduced from *Mulberry Leaves* (2001)). 'The Greenshank' and 'Thinking of Eurydice at Midnight' from *The Goldfinches of Baghdad* (Flood Editions, 2006). 'Songs for Juno' and 'My Granny' from *The Golden Bird: New and selected poems* (Black Inc, 2008). Permission granted by Golvan Arts Management on behalf of Robert Adamson.

Adam Aitken: 'Post-Colonial' from *In One House* (Angus & Robertson in association with Paper Bark Press, 1996). Reprinted by permission of Adam Aitken. 'Changi' from *Romeo and Juliet in Subtitles* (Brandl & Schlesinger, 2000). Reprinted by permission of Brandl & Schlesinger.

Yahia Al-Samawy: *Two Banks with No Bridge*, tr. Eva Sallis (Picaro Press, 2005). Copyright © Yahia al Samawy, translation Eva Sallis. Reprinted by arrangement, c/– Jenny Darling & Associates.

Jordie Albiston: *The Fall* (White Crane Press, 2003). Reprinted by permission of Jordie Albiston.

Jessica Anderson: *Tirra Lirra by the River* (Macmillan Australia Ltd, 1978). © Jessica Anderson 1978. Reprinted by permission of Pan Macmillan Australia Pty Ltd.

Barry Andrews: *The Australian Historical Association Bulletin*, no. 12, October 1977. Reprinted by permission of R.G. Pitchford.

Anonymous: 'A Swan River Eclogue' from *Tasmanian*, 26 March 1830.

Anonymous: 'The Eumerella Shore' from *Launceston Examiner*, 7 March 1861.

Anonymous: 'Jim Jones at Botany Bay' from Charles MacAlistar, *Old Pioneering Days in the Sunny South* (Chas. MacAlistar Book Publication Committee, 1907).

Anonymous: 'Moreton Bay' from Jack Bradshaw, *The Quirindi Bank Robbery* (T. Dimmock, c. 1899).

Anonymous: 'The Native's Lament' from *Colonial Times*, 5 May 1826.

Anonymous: 'The Wild Colonial Boy' from *The Colonial Songster*, 1881.

Venero Armanno: *The Volcano* (Knopf/Random House, 2001). Reproduced by permission of Random House Australia and by arrangement with Venero Armanno, c/– Curtis Brown (Aust.) Pty Ltd.

Mary Ann Arthur: General Correspondence CSO11/26 file 378, Archives Office of Tasmania, 10 June 1846.

Walter George Arthur: General Correspondence CSO11/26 file 378, Archives Office of Tasmania, 15 July 1846.

Thea Astley: *It's Raining in Mango* (Penguin Books, 1987). Reprinted by arrangement with the licensor, the Estate of Thea Astley c/– Curtis Brown (Aust.) Pty Ltd.

Louisa Atkinson: *Sydney Mail*, 12 January 1861.

Murray Bail: *Contemporary Portraits* (UQP, 1975). Reprinted by permission of Murray Bail.

E.J. Banfield: *The Confessions of a Beachcomber* (London: T. Fisher Unwin, 1908).

William Barak: *Argus*, 29 August 1882.

Marjorie Barnard: 'Australian Literature' ABC Radio (Broadcast Hobart, 25 September 1941). *The Persimmon Tree and Other Stories* (1985). Reprinted by arrangement with the licensor, the Estate of Marjorie Barnard, c/– Curtis Brown (Aust.) Pty Ltd.

M. Barnard Eldershaw: *Tomorrow and Tomorrow and Tomorrow* (London: Virago, 1983). Reprinted by arrangement with the licensor, Barnard Eldershaw, c/– Curtis Brown (Aust.) Pty Ltd.

Barbara Baynton: *Bush Studies* (London: Duckworth, 1902).

C.E.W. Bean: *On the Wool Track* (Cornstalk, 1925). Reprinted by permission of E.B. Le Couteur and Anne Carroll.

Bruce Beaver: *Bruce Beaver: New and selected poems, 1960–1990* (UQP, 1990). Reprinted by permission of the University of Queensland Press.

Lisa Bellear: *Dreaming in Urban Areas* (UQP, 1996). Copyright © The Estate of Lisa Bellear. Reprinted by permission of the University of Queensland Press.

Bennelong: Letter to Mister Philips, Sydney Cove, New South Wales, 1796. Original lost, copy held at National Library of Australia. NK4048, MS 4005.

Judith Beveridge: 'How to Love Bats' and 'Yachts' from *Accidental Grace* (UQP, 1996). Reprinted by permission of the University of Queensland Press. 'The Saffron Picker' from *Wolf Notes* (Giramondo, 2003). Reprinted by Permission of Giramondo Publishing Company.

Fred Biggs and Roland Robinson: 'The Star Tribes' from Roland Robinson, *Selected Poems* (Sydney: Angus & Robertson, 1989). Reproduced by permission of Harper Collins Publishers Australia.

Geoffrey Blainey: *The Rush that Never Ended* (Melbourne University Press, 1963, reprint 2003). Reprinted by permission of Melbourne University Publishing.

Barcroft Boake: *Where the Dead Men Lie and Other Poems* (Sydney: Angus & Robertson, 1897).

Rolf Boldrewood: *Robbery Under Arms* (London & New York: Macmillan, rev. ed. 1889)

Ken Bolton: *Untimely Meditations* (Wakefield Press, 1997). Reprinted by permission of Ken Bolton.

Gerry Bostock: *Meanjin*, vol. 36, no. 4 (1977). Copyright © Gerry Bostock. Reproduced by permission of Gerry Bostock.

A.J. Boyd: *Old Colonials* (London: Gordon & Gotch, 1882).

Martin Boyd: *Outbreak of Love* (John Murray, 1957). Reprinted by arrangement with the licensor of the Estate of Martin Boyd, c/- Curtis Brown (Aust.) Pty Ltd.

Kitty Brangy: National Archives of Australia, NAA: series B313/1, item 42.

Christopher Brennan: *Poems [1913]* (Sydney: G.B. Philip, 1914).

John Le Gay Brereton: *The Burning Marl* (Melbourne: Fellowship, 1919).

Kevin Brophy: *Mr Wittgenstein's Lion* (Five Islands Press, 2007). Reprinted by permission of Kevin Brophy.

Eliza Brown: Letter of 1847 from Peter Cowan (ed.), *A Faithful Picture: The letters of Thomas and Eliza Brown at York in the Swan River Colony, 1841–1852* (Fremantle: Fremantle Arts Centre Press, 1977). Reprinted by permission of The Fremantle Press.

Pam Brown: *Dear Deliria: New and selected poems* (Salt, 2002). Reprinted by permission of Pam Brown.

Thomas Brune: *Flinders Island Chronicle.* Papers of George Augustus Robinson. MLA 7073, vol. 52, Mitchell Library, Sydney.

Vincent Buckley: *Golden Builders and Other Poems* (Angus & Robertson, 1976). Reprinted by permission of the Estate of Vincent Buckley.

John Muk Muk Burke: *Night Song and Other Poems* (NTU Press, 1999). Copyright © John Muk Muk Burke. Reprinted by permission of John Muk Muk Burke.

Burnum Burnum: from Marlene J. Norst, *Burnum Burnum: A warrior for peace* (Kangaroo Press, 1999). Copyright © Marelle Burnum Burnum. Reprinted by permission of Marelle Burnum Burnum, widow of the late B. Burnum.

Ada Cambridge: 'Seeking' and 'An Answer' from *Unspoken Thoughts* (London: Kegan Paul, Trench, 1887). 'The Wind of Destiny' from *At Midnight and Other Stories* (London: Ward, Lock & Co., 1897)

Bessie Cameron: *Argus*, 5 April 1886.

David Campbell: *Collected Poems* (Angus & Robertson, 1989). Reprinted by arrangement with the licensor, the Estate of David Campbell, c/- Curtis Brown (Aust.) Pty Ltd.

Peter Carey: *Exotic Pleasures* (UQP, 1980). Copyright © 2001 Peter Carey. Reproduced by permission of the author c/- Rogers, Coleridge & White Ltd., 20 Powis Mews, London W11 1JN. *True History of the Kelly Gang* (UQP, 2000). Copyright © 2000 Peter Carey. Reproduced by permission of the author c/- Rogers, Coleridge & White Ltd., 20 Powis Mews, London W11 1JN, Faber & Faber Ltd and Random House Canada.

Caroline Carleton: *South Australian Lyrics* (Adelaide: J.H. Lewis & Co., 1860).

Kev Carmody: from Paul Kelly, *Don't Start Me Talking: Lyrics 1984–2004* (Allen & Unwin, 2004). © Paul Kelly and Kev Carmody. Reprinted by permission of Allen & Unwin Pty Ltd.

Brian Castro: *Shanghai Dancing* (Giramondo, 2003). Reprinted by permission of Giramondo Publishing Company.

Nick Cave: *The Complete Lyrics* (Penguin Books, 1997). Written by Cave and Savage (Mute Song/Mushroom Music), reprinted with kind permission.

George Chanson: *Colonial Lyrics* (Sydney: Beard and Holmes, 1872).

Ellen Clacy: *A Lady's Visit to the Gold Diggings of Australia in 1852–1853* (London: Hurst and Blackett, 1853)

Monica Clare: *Karobran: Story of an Aboriginal girl* (Hale & Iremonger, 1978). Copyright © Les Clare 1978, 1983, 1985. Reprinted by permission of Hale & Iremonger Pty Ltd.

Manning Clark: *A History of Australia*, vol. 1 (Melbourne University Press, 1978). Reprinted by permission of Melbourne University Publishing.

John Clarke: *The Even More Complete Book of Australian Verse* (Allen & Unwin, 1994). Reprinted in *A Dagg at My Table* (Text, 1998). Reproduced with permission from the Text Publishing Co. Pty Ltd.

Marcus Clarke: *His Natural Life* (Melbourne: George Robertson, 1874). 'Nasturtium Villas' from *Weekly Times*, 14 February 1874. Preface to Adam Lindsay Gordon, *Sea Spray and Smoke Drift* (Melbourne: Clarson, Massina & Co., 1876).

Inga Clendinnen: *Tiger's Eye: A memoir* (Text, 2000). Reproduced with permission from the Text Publishing Co. Pty Ltd.

Charmian Clift: *Images in Aspic* (Horwitz Publications, 1965). Copyright © Charmian Clift. Reprinted by arrangement with the Estate of Charmian Clift, c/– Barbara Mobbs.

J.M. Coetzee: *Elizabeth Costello* (Knopf/Random House, 2003). Copyright © J.M. Coetzee 2003. Reprinted by permission of David Higham Associates Ltd and Peter Lampack Agency, Inc.

Jill Ker Conway: *The Road from Coorain* (Heinemann, 1989). Copyright © 1989 by Jill Ker Conway. Reprinted by permission of Random House (UK) and Alfred A. Knopf, a division of Random House, Inc.

William Cooper: Melbourne *Herald*, 15 September 1933.

Dymphna Cusack and Florence James: *Come in Spinner* (William Heinemann Ltd, 1951). Reprinted by arrangement with the licensor, the Estate of Dymphna Cusack and the Estate of Florence James c/– Curtis Brown (Aust.) Pty Ltd.

Victor Daley: *Bulletin*, 11 June 1898.

Robin Dalton: *Aunts up the Cross* (Anthony Blond, 1965). Reprinted by Penguin (Aust.), 1997. Reprinted by permission of Robin Dalton.

Eleanor Dark: *The Timeless Land* (Sydney: Halstead Press, 1941). Reprinted by arrangement with the licensor, the Estate of Eleanor Dark, c/- Curtis Brown (Aust.) Pty Ltd.

Luke Davies: *Totem: Totem poem plus 40 love poems* (Allen & Unwin, 2004). Reprinted by permission of Allen & Unwin Pty Ltd.

Jack Davis: 'The First-born', 'The Black Tracker', 'Warru', 'Integration' from *The First-born and Other Poems* (Angus & Robertson, 1970). 'Walker' from *Jagardoo: Poems from Aboriginal Australia* (Methuen, 1978). Copyright © The Estate of Jack Davis. Reprinted by arrangement with the licensor, the Estate of Jack Davis, c/- Curtis Brown (Aust.) Pty Ltd.

Bruce Dawe: *Sometimes Gladness: Collected poems, 1954–1997* (Longman Cheshire, 1997). Reproduced by permission of Pearson Education Australia.

Sarah Day: *Quickening* (Penguin, 1997). Reprinted by permission of Sarah Day.

Michelle de Kretser: *The Hamilton Case* (Knopf/Random House, 2003). Reproduced by permission of Random House Australia and Michelle de Kretser.

D.H. Deniehy: Speech delivered on 15 August 1853, from *The Life and Speeches of Daniel Henry Deniehy* (Melbourne: George Robertson, 1884).

C.J. Dennis: *The Songs of a Sentimental Bloke* (Sydney: Angus & Robertson, 1957).

Robert Dessaix: *A Mother's Disgrace* (Angus & Robertson, 1994). Reprinted by permission of Australian Literary Management.

Jean Devanny: *Sugar Heaven* (Sydney: Modern Publishers, 1936). Reprinted by permission of Deborah Hurd.

Graeme Dixon: *Holocaust Island* (UQP, 1990). Copyright © Graeme Dixon 1990. Reprinted by permission of the University of Queensland Press.

Rosemary Dobson: 'Child With a Cockatoo', 'Over the Frontier' and 'The Almond-tree in the King James Version' from *Collected Poems* (Angus & Robertson, 1991). 'Who?' and 'Reading Aloud' from *Untold Lives and Later Poems* (Brandl & Schlesinger, 2000). Reprinted by arrangement with the licensor, Rosemary Dobson, c/- Curtis Brown (Aust.) Pty Ltd.

Mick Dodson: *Age*, 18 December 1997. Copyright © Michael Dodson. Reprinted by permission of Michael Dodson.

Patrick Dodson: Welcome Speech delivered on 4 June 1993. Copyright © Patrick Dodson. Reprinted by permission of Patrick Dodson.

Michael Dransfield: *Collected Poems* (UQP, 1987). Reprinted by permission of the University of Queensland Press.

Robert Drewe: *The Shark Net: Memories and murder* (Viking, 2000). Reproduced by permission of Penguin Group (Australia).

Laurie Duggan: *The Ash Range* (Pan 1987, reprint Shearsman, 2005). Reproduced by permission of Shearsman Books. *The Epigrams of Martial* (Scripsi, 1989). 'Drinking Socially' from *New and Selected Poems, 1971–1993* (UQP, 1996). 'Air Time' from *Mangroves* (UQP, 2003). Reprinted by permission of the University of Queensland Press.

Eliza Dunlop: *Australian*, 13 December 1838.

Stephen Edgar: 'All Will be Revealed' from *Corrupted Treasures* (Heinemann, 1995). 'Sun Pictorial' from *Lost in the Foreground* (Duffy & Snellgrove, 2003). Reprinted by permission of Stephen Edgar.

T.S. Eliot: Lines from 'Little Gidding' used in *Hotel Sorrento* are from *Collected Poems 1909–1962*. Reprinted by permission of Faber & Faber Ltd.

Louis Esson: *The Time is Not Yet Ripe* (Sydney: Currency Press, 1973).

A.B. Facey: *A Fortunate Life* (Fremantle Arts Centre Press, 1981). Reproduced by permission of Penguin Group (Australia).

Delia Falconer: From Kerryn Goldsworthy (ed.), *Australian Love Stories* (Oxford University Press, 1996). Also appears in *The Lost Thoughts of Soldiers and Selected Stories* (Pan Macmillan Australia, 2006). © Delia Falconer 2006. Reprinted by permission of Pan Macmillan Australia Pty Ltd.

Beverley Farmer: *Milk* (Penguin, 1983). Reprinted in *Collected Stories* (UQP, 1996). Reprinted by permission of the University of Queensland Press and Beverley Farmer.

William Ferguson and John Patten: from Jack Horner, *Vote Ferguson for Aboriginal Freedom* (Australian and New Zealand Book Co., 1974). Reprinted by permission of Phyllis Patten.

Barron Field: *First Fruits of Australian Poetry* (Sydney: George Howe, 1819).

Robert D. FitzGerald: *Forty Years' Poems* (Angus & Robertson, 1965). Reprinted by permission of Harper Collins Publishers Australia.

Richard Flanagan: *The Sound of One Hand Clapping* (Pan Macmillan Australia, 1997). © Richard Flanagan 1997. Reprinted by permission of Pan Macmillan Australia Pty Ltd.

Matthew Flinders: *A Voyage to Terra Australis* (London: G. & W. Nichol, 1814).

Lionel Fogarty: 'Decorative Rasp, Weaved Roots', 'Ecology' and 'Shields Strong, Nulla Nullas Alive' from *Yoogum Yoogum* (Penguin, 1982). Copyright © Lionel Fogarty. Reprinted by permission of Lionel Fogarty. 'For I Come—Death in Custody', 'Kath Walker', '"Dulpai Ila Ngari Kim Mo-Man"' from *New and Selected Poems: Munaldjali, Mutuerjaraera* (Hyland House, 1995). Copyright © Lionel Fogarty. Reprinted by permission of Lionel Fogarty and Hyland House. 'Alcheringa' from *Minyung Woolah Binnung: What saying says* (Keeaira Press, 2004). Copyright © Lionel Fogarty. Reprinted by permission of Keeaira Press.

Mary Hannay Foott: *Where the Pelican Builds and Other Poems* (Brisbane: Gordon & Gotch, 1885).

John Forbes: *Collected Poems, 1970–1998* (Brandl & Schlesinger, 2001). Reprinted by permission of Brandl & Schlesinger.

David Foster: *The Glade Within the Grove* (Random House, 1996). Reproduced by permission of Random House Australia and by arrangement c/- Cameron's Management.

Frank the Poet: Manuscript poem c. 1839, Mitchell Library, ML MSS C967, from Philip Butterss and Elizabeth Webby (eds), *The Penguin Book of Australian Ballads* (Melbourne: Penguin, 1993).

Richard Frankland: from Josie Douglas (ed.), *Untreated: Poems by Black writers* (Jukurrpa, 2001). © Richard Frankland. Reprinted by permission of Richard Frankland.

Miles Franklin: *My Brilliant Career* (Edinburgh: William Blackwood & Sons, 1901). Letter to Katharine Susannah Prichard, 20 November 1947, from Carole Ferrier (ed.), *As Good as a Yarn with You* (Melbourne: Cambridge University Press, 1992). Reprinted by permission of Mitchell Library, State Library of New South Wales. Original held at Mitchell Library, State Library of New South Wales, ML MSS 364.

Donald Friend: *The Diaries of Donald Friend*, vols 3 and 4 (National Library of Australia, 2005 and 2006). Reprinted by permission of the National Library of Australia. National Library of Australian Manuscripts Collection MS5959.

Mary E. Fullerton: *The Breaking Furrow* (Melbourne: Sydney J. Endacott, 1921).

Joseph Furphy: *Such is Life: Being certain extracts from the diary of Tom Collins* (Sydney: Bulletin, 1903).

Helen Garner: *The Children's Bach* (McPhee Gribble, 1984). *Postcards from Surfers* (McPhee Gribble, 1985). Reproduced by permission of Penguin Group (Aust.). *True Stories: Selected non-fiction* (Text, 1996). Copyright © Helen Garner. Reproduced by permission, c/- Barbara Mobbs.

Pearl Gibbs: Radio Broadcast, 2GB Sydney and 2WL Wollongong, 8 June 1941. © The Estate of Pearl Gibbs. Reprinted by permission of Anny Druett.

Kevin Gilbert: 'People *Are* Legends', 'Redfern', 'Me and Jackomari Talkin' About Land Rights' and 'Tree' from *The Blackside: People* Are *Legends and other poems* (Hyland House, 1990). 'Song of Dreamtime' from *Black from the Edge* (Hyland House, 1994). © The Estate of Kevin Gilbert. Reprinted by permission of Hyland House. *The Cherry Pickers* (Burrambinga Books, 1988) and Speech at the Aboriginal Tent Embassy, Canberra, 27 May 1992. © The Estate of Kevin Gilbert. Reprinted by permission of Eleanor Gilbert.

Ernest Giles: *Australia Twice Traversed* (London: Low, Marston, Searle & Rivington, 1889).

Mary Gilmore: Jennifer Strauss (ed.), *The Collected Verse of Mary Gilmore*, vols 1 and 2 (St Lucia: University of Queensland Press, 2004–2007). Reproduced by permission, courtesy of ETT Imprint.

Ruby Langford Ginibi: *Don't Take Your Love to Town* (Penguin, 1988). © Dr Ruby Langford Ginibi, 1988. Elder of Bundjalung Nation, Female Elder of National NAIDOC Week, Darwin 2007 (50 Years, Lookin' Forward and Lookin' Black). Reprinted by permission of the University of Queensland Press.

Peter Goldsworthy: 'Australia' from *The Best Australian Poetry 2005* (Black Inc., 2005). 'The Kiss' from *The List of All Answers* (Viking, 2004). Reproduced by arrangement with the licensor, Peter Goldsworthy c/– Curtis Brown (Aust.) Pty Ltd.

Adam Lindsay Gordon: *Bush Ballads and Galloping Rhymes* (Melbourne: Clarson, Massina & Co., 1870).

Alan Gould: *The Past Completes Me: Selected poems, 1973–2003* (UQP, 2005). Reprinted by permission of the University of Queensland Press.

Michael Gow: *Away* (Currency Press, 1986). Reprinted by permission of Currency Press.

Robert Gray: *New and Selected Poems* (William Heinemann Australia, 1995). Revised version (2008), reprinted by permission of Robert Gray.

Germaine Greer: *Daddy, We Hardly Knew You* (Penguin, 1989). Reprinted with permission by arrangement c/– Aitken, Alexander & Associates Ltd.

Kate Grenville: *Lilian's Story* (Allen & Unwin, 1985). Reprinted by permission of Allen & Unwin Pty Ltd.

Rodney Hall: *Just Relations* (Penguin, 1982). *The Owner of My Face: New and selected poems* (Paper Bark Press, 2002). Reproduced by permission of Rodney Hall.

Barbara Hanrahan: *Dream People* (Collins, 1987). Reprinted by arrangement with the licensor, the Estate of Barbara Hanrahan c/– Curtis Brown (Aust.) Pty Ltd.

J.M. Harcourt: *Upsurge* (Nedlands: University of Western Australia Press, 1986). Reprinted by permission of Diana Harcourt.

Lesbia Harford: 'In the Public Library' and 'My Heart is a Pomegranate' from Drusilla Modjeska and Marjorie Pizer (eds), *The Poems of Lesbia Harford* (Sydney: Angus & Robertson, 1985). 'Machinist's Song' from Marjorie Pizer (ed.), *Freedom on the Wallaby* (The Pinchgut Press, 1953). 'Grotesque' from Edward Kynaston (ed.), *Australian Voices* (Penguin, 1974).

Charles Harpur: Elizabeth Perkins (ed.), *Charles Harpur: Complete poems* (Sydney: Angus & Robertson, 1984).

Norman Harris: Public Records Office of Western Australia, AN 1/7, Acc.993, file A/94/1928. © The Estate of Norman Harris. Reprinted by permission of Myrtle Mullaley.

J.S. Harry: *Not Finding Wittgenstein* (Giramondo, 2007). Reprinted by permission of Giramondo Publishing Company.

Kevin Hart: *Flame Tree: Selected poems* (Paper Bark Press, 2002). Permission granted by Golvan Arts Management on behalf of Kevin Hart.

P.J. Hartigan: *Around the Boree Log and Other Verses* (Sydney: Angus & Robertson, 1921).

Sonya Hartnett: *Of a Boy* (Viking/Penguin, 2002). Reproduced with permission of Penguin Group (Aust.).

Gwen Harwood: 'Barn Owl', 'Matinee', 'Carnal Knowledge II', 'Andante', 'Dialogue', 'Mother Who Gave Me Life' and 'Bone Scan' from Gregory Kratzmann (ed.), *Gwen Harwood: Selected poems* (Penguin, 2001). Reproduced with permission of Penguin Group (Aust.). 'The Sick Philosopher' from Alison Hoddinott and Gregory Kratzmann (eds), *Gwen Harwood: Collected poems, 1943–1995* (UQP, 2003). Reprinted by permission of the Estate of Gwen Harwood. Letter to Tony Riddell from Gregory Kratzmann (ed.), *A Steady Stream of Correspondence: Selected letters of Gwen Harwood* (UQP, 2001). Reprinted by permission of the University of Queensland Press.

Shirley Hazzard: *People in Glass Houses* (Macmillan, 1967). Copyright © 1967 by Shirley Hazzard. Reprinted by permission of Farrar, Straus and Giroux, LLC and Virago, an imprint of Little, Brown Book Group UK.

Xavier Herbert: *Capricornia* (Sydney: Angus & Robertson, 1990). Reproduced by arrangement with the licensor, the Estate of Xavier Herbert, c/- Curtis Brown (Aust.) Pty Ltd.

Dorothy Hewett: 'Clancy and Dooley and Don McLeod', 'Grave Fairytale' and 'Living Dangerously' from *Dorothy Hewett: Collected poems* (Fremantle: Fremantle Arts Centre Press, 1995). Reprinted by permission of The Fremantle Press. *Wild Card* (Melbourne: McPhee Gribble, 1990). Reproduced with permission of Penguin Group (Aust.) and by arrangement with the Estate of Dorothy Hewett, c/- Hilary Linstead & Associates. *The Man from Mukinupin* (Sydney and Fremantle: Currency Press and Fremantle Arts Centre Press, 1979). Reproduced by permission of Currency Press Pty Ltd.

Barry Hill: *Headlocks and Other Stories* (Melbourne: McPhee Gribble, 1983). Reprinted by permission of Barry Hill.

Philip Hodgins: *Selected Poems* (Sydney: Angus & Robertson, 1997). Reprinted by permission of Janet Shaw.

A.D. Hope: 'Inscription for a War' from Shirley Cass, Ros Cheney, David Malouf and Michael Wilding (eds), *We Took Their Orders and Are Dead* (Ure Smith, 1971). 'Australia', 'Ascent Into Hell', 'Crossing the Frontier' and 'Death of the Bird' from *Collected Poems, 1930–1970* (Sydney: Angus & Robertson, 1972). 'Mayan Books' from *Orpheus* (Sydney: Angus & Robertson, 1991). Reprinted by arrangement with the licensor, the Estate of A.D. Hope, c/- Curtis Brown (Aust.) Pty Ltd.

Donald Horne: *The Education of Young Donald* (Sun Books, 1967), sourced from revised edition (Penguin, 1988). Copyright © Myfanwy Horne. Reprinted by permission of Myfanwy Horne.

Rita Huggins and Jackie Huggins: *Auntie Rita* (Aboriginal Studies Press, 1994). © Jackie Huggins. Reprinted by permission of Aboriginal Studies Press.

Robert Hughes: *Culture of Complaint* (Oxford University Press, 1993). Reprinted by permission of Oxford University Press.

Barry Humphries: 'Maroan' and 'Edna's Hymn' from *Neglected Creatures and Other Poems* (Angus & Robertson, 1990). *More Please* (Penguin, 1992). Letter to Richard Allen from Brenda Niall and John Thompson (eds), *The Oxford Book of Australian Letters* (Oxford, 1998). Reprinted by permission of David Higham Associates.

K.S. Inglis: *Sacred Places: War memorials in the Australian landscape* (Melbourne University Press, 2nd edn, 2005), assisted by Jan Brazier. Reprinted by permission of Melbourne University Publishing.

Clive James: *Unreliable Memoirs* (Jonathan Cape, 1980). Reprinted by permission of United Agents on behalf of Clive James.

George Johnston: *My Brother Jack* (William Collins & Sons, 1964). © George Johnston. Reproduced by arrangement with the Estate of George Johnston, c/- Barbara Mobbs.

Martin Johnston: *The Sea-Cucumber* (UQP, 1978). *The Typewriter Considered as a Bee-Trap* (Hale & Iremonger, 1984). Copyright © Rosanne Bonney. Reproduced by permission of Rosanne Bonney.

Elizabeth Jolley: 'Night Runner' from *Meanjin*, vol. 42, no. 4 (1983). Copyright © Elizabeth Jolley. Reproduced by arrangement c/- Jenny Darling & Associates.

Gail Jones: *The House of Breathing* (Fremantle Arts Centre Press, 1992). Reprinted by permission of The Fremantle Press.

Jill Jones: *Screens Jets Heaven: New and selected poems* (Salt, 2002). Reprinted by permission of The Fremantle Press.

Paul Keating: Mark Ryan (ed.), *Advancing Australia: The speeches of Paul Keating, Prime Minister* (Big Picture Publications, 1995). Reproduced with permission of the Hon. P.J. Keating.

Ned Kelly: Letter of February 1879, State Library of Victoria, MS 13361, from *The Jerilderie Letter* (Melbourne: Text Publishing, 2001).

Henry Kendall: T.T. Reed (ed.), *The Poetical Works of Henry Kendall* (Adelaide: Libraries Board of South Australia, 1966).

Thomas Keneally: *Bring Larks and Heroes* (Sun Books, 1967). *Schindler's Ark* (Hodder & Stoughton, 1982). Reproduced by arrangement with the licensor, Thomas Keneally c/- Curtis Brown (Aust.) Pty Ltd.

John Kinsella: 'The Vital Waters' from *The Best Australian Poetry 2005* (Black Inc., 2005). Reproduced by permission of John Kinsella. 'Map: Land Subjected to Inundation' from *The New Arcadia* (Fremantle Press, 2005). Reprinted by permission of The Fremantle Press.

Christopher Koch: *The Year of Living Dangerously* (Thomas Nelson Australia, 1978). Reprinted by Random House Australia, 1998. Reprinted by arrangement c/- Margaret Connolly & Associates.

Eve Langley: 'Native Born' from *Bulletin*, vol. 61.3129, 31 January 1940. Reproduced by permission of Karl Marx Clark, Rhaviley Langley-Clark and Arilev Bisi Clark. *The Pea Pickers* (Sydney: Angus & Robertson, 1942). Reproduced by permission of Harper Collins Publishers Australia.

Marcia Langton: '*Well I Heard it on the Radio and I Saw it on the Television…*': *An essay for the Australian Film Commission on the politics and aesthetics of filmmaking by and about*

Aboriginal people and things (Sydney, Australian Film Commission, 1993). © Australian Film Commission 1993. Reprinted by permission of the Australian Film Commission.

Kenny Laughton: *Not Quite Men, No Longer Boys* (Jukurrpa, 1999). © K.C. Laughton 1987. Reprinted by permission of Jukurrpa Books, an imprint of IAD Press.

Ray Lawler: *Summer of the Seventeenth Doll* (Angus & Robertson, 1957). Reprinted by Currency Press, 1978. Reproduced by permission of Currency Press Pty Ltd.

Anthony Lawrence: *The Sleep of a Learning Man* (Giramondo, 2003). Reprinted by permission of Giramondo Publishing Company.

Henry Lawson: 'The Union Buries Its Dead', 'The Drover's Wife' and 'In a Dry Season' from *While the Billy Boils* (Sydney: Angus & Robertson, 1896). 'Faces in the Street' from *In the Days When the World was Wide* (Sydney and London: Angus & Robertson and Young J. Pentland, 1896).

Louisa Lawson: *Dawn*, 5 June 1890.

Geoffrey Lehmann: from *The Best Australian Poetry 2005* (Black Inc, 2005). Reproduced by arrangement with the licensor, Geoffrey Lehmann c/- Curtis Brown (Aust.) Pty Ltd.

Jessie Lennon: *And I Always Been Moving! The Early Life of Jessie Lennon* (1995). © The Lennon Family. Permission given by Emily Betts (née Lennon) on behalf of the Lennon Family.

Michael Leunig: *Wild Figments* (Penguin, 2004). Reproduced by permission of Michael Leunig.

Emma Lew: *Anything the Landlord Touches* (Giramondo, 2002). Reprinted by permission of Emma Lew.

Norman Lindsay: *The Magic Pudding* (Sydney: Angus & Robertson, 1948). Reproduced by permission of Harper Collins Publishers Australia.

Vincent Lingiari: Petition, 19 April 1967. Reprinted by permission of Sharyn Jerry, Marie D. Jaban, Sabrina Jerry, Sarah Jerry, Jock Vincent, Ronnie Wavehill, Bernard 'Peanut' Pontiari and Ida Malinkya.

Mary Rose Liverani: *The Winter Sparrows* (Nelson, 1975). Reprinted by permission of Mary Rose Liverani.

Amanda Lohrey: *Camille's Bread* (Harper Collins, 1995). Reproduced by permission of Harper Collins Publishers Australia.

Lennie Lower: *The Best of Lennie Lower*, Cyril Pearl and WEP [*sic*] (eds) (Melbourne, Lansdowne Press, 1963).

Melissa Lucashenko: *Steam Pigs* (St Lucia: University of Queensland Press, 1997). © Melissa Lucashenko 1997. Reprinted by permission of the University of Queensland Press.

Elizabeth Macarthur: Letter of 1 September 1798, Macarthur Papers, Mitchell Library, State Library of New South Wales, from Joy N. Hughes, *The Journal and Letters of Elizabeth Macarthur 1789–1798* (Glebe: Historic Houses Trust of New South Wales, 1984).

James McAuley: *Collected Poems, 1936–1970* (Angus & Robertson, 1991). Reproduced by arrangement with the licensor, the Estate of James McAuley c/- Curtis Brown (Aust.) Pty Ltd.

Roger McDonald: *Shearer's Motel* (Picador, 1992). Reprint Random House, 2001. Reproduced by permission of Random House Australia and Roger McDonald.

Andrew McGahan: *1988* (Allen & Unwin, 1995). Reproduced by permission of Allen & Unwin Pty Ltd.

Dorothea Mackellar: *The Closed Door and Other Verses* (Melbourne: Australian Authors' Agency, 1911). Reproduced by arrangement with the licensor, the Estate of Dorothea Mackellar c/- Curtis Brown (Aust.) Pty Ltd.

Philip McLaren: *Sweet Water … Stolen Land* (Magabala, 1993). © Philip McLaren 1993 and 2001. Reprinted by permission of Magabala Books.

Jennifer Maiden: *Friendly Fire* (Giramondo, 2005). Reprinted by permission of Giramondo Publishing Company.

Frank Malkorda: From R.M.W. Dixon and Martin Duwell (eds), *The Honey-Ant Men's Love Song and Other Aboriginal Poems* (UQP, 1990). c/- Bawinanga Aboriginal Corporation. Translation permission from Margaret Clunies-Ross.

Ern Malley: *Angry Penguins*, no. 6 (Autumn 1944). Reprinted by arrangement, no. 6, (Autumn 1944) with the licensor, the Estate of James McAuley c/- Curtis Brown (Aust.) Pty Ltd and Lee Riley on behalf of the Harold Stewart Literary Estate.

David Malouf: '7 Last Words of the Emperor Hadrian' from *Southerly*, vol. 63, no. 1 (2003). 'Poem' and 'The Year of the Foxes' from *Selected Poems* (Angus & Robertson, 1991). 'The Only Speaker of His Tongue' from *Antipodes* (Chatto & Windus, 1985). 'A First Place', *Southerly*, vol. 45, no. 1, (1985). All works copyright © David Malouf. Reproduced by permission of the author c/- Rogers, Coleridge & White Ltd, 20 Powis Mews, London W11 1JN.

J.S. Manifold: *Selected Verse* (New York: John Bay, 1946). Reprinted by permission of Miranda Manifold.

Frederic Manning: *The Middle Parts of Fortune: Somme and Ancre 1916* (New York: St Martin's Press, 1977).

David Marr: *Patrick White* (Random House, 1991). Reprinted by permission of Random House Australia and Australian Literary Management.

Alan Marshall: *Tell Us About the Turkey, Jo* (Sydney: Angus & Robertson, 1946). Reproduced by arrangement with the licensor, The Estate of Alan Marshall c/- Curtis Brown (Aust.) Pty Ltd.

Jennifer Martiniello: 'Uluru by Champagne' from *Imprint of Infinity* (Tidbinbilla Press, 1999). 'Emily Kngwarreye' Jennifer Martiniello (ed.), *Talking Ink from Ochre* (2002) © Jennifer Avriel Martiniello. Reprinted by permission of Jennifer Martiniello.

Olga Masters: *A Long Time Dying* (UQP, 1985). Reproduced by permission of the University of Queensland Press.

Robert Menzies: 'The Forgotten People', ABC Radio (Broadcast Sydney, Melbourne and the regions, 22 May 1942); from M. Fullilove (ed.), *'Men and Women of Australia!'* (Sydney: Random House, 2005). Reproduced by permission of Heather Henderson.

Louisa Anne Meredith: *Notes and Sketches of New South Wales* (London: John Murray, 1844).

Alex Miller: *The Ancestor Game* (Penguin, 1992). Reproduced by permission of Allen & Unwin Pty Ltd.

Maggie Mobourne: National Archives of Australia. From facsimile copy of Maggie Mobourne to D.N. McLeod, 27 February 1900. NAA: series B337, item 507.

Drusilla Modjeska: *Stravinsky's Lunch* (Macmillan, 1999). Copyright © 1999 by Drusilla Modjeska. Reprinted by permission of Pan Macmillan Australia Pty Ltd and Farrar Straus and Giroux, LLC.

Frank Moorhouse: *Forty-Seventeen* (Viking/Penguin, 1988). Reprinted by Random House Australia, 2007. Reprinted by permission of Frank Moorhouse and Random House Australia.

Romaine Moreton: 'Genocide is Never Justified' from 'The Callused Stick of Wanting' in *Rimfire* (Magabala, 2000). © Romaine Moreton 1995. Reprinted by permission of Magabala Books.

Anna Morgan: *Labor Call*, 20 September 1934.

Sally Morgan: *My Place* (Fremantle Arts Centre Press, 1987). © Sally Jane Morgan, 1987. Reprinted by permission of The Fremantle Press.

John Morrison: *Australian New Writing*, no. 2, March 1944 (Sydney: Current Book Publishers). Reproduced by permission of the Estate of John Morrison.

Mudrooroo: *Master of the Ghost Dreaming* (Angus & Robertson, 1991). Reprinted by permission courtesy of the publisher, ETT Imprint.

Gerald Murnane: *Invisible Yet Enduring Lilacs* (Giramondo, 2005). Reproduced by permission of Giramondo Publishing Company.

Les Murray: 'Rainwater Tank', 'The Quality of Sprawl', 'Second Essay on Interest: The Emu', 'Bats' Ultrasound', 'Hearing Impairment', 'Poetry and Religion', 'The Time Wash Dish', 'The Last Hellos', and 'The Instrument' from *Collected Poems* (Duffy & Snellgrove, 2002) and *The Rabbiter's Bounty* (FSG, 1991). 'The Cool Green' from *The Biplane Houses* (Black Inc. and Carcanet, 2006). Reprinted by permission of Carcanet, Farrar Straus and Giroux, LLC and by arrangement c/- Margaret Connolly & Associates.

Narritjin Maymuru: © The Estate of Narritjin Maymuru. Reprinted by permission of Galuma Maymuru. Methodist Overseas Mission Papers, Mitchell Library, State Library of NSW, MSS MOM 465.

Bill Neidjie: from Keith Taylor (ed.), *Story About Feeling* (Magabala, 1989). © 1989 Bill Neidjie and Keith Taylor. Reprinted by permission of Magabala Books.

John Shaw Neilson: *The Collected Verse: A variorum edition*, Margaret Roberts (ed.), 2 vols (Canberra: Australian Scholarly Editions Centre, 2003).

John A. Newfong: *Identity*, vol. 1, no. 7 (July 1973).

Doug Nicholls: *Age*, 27 May 1963. © The Estate of Sir Douglas Nicholls. Reproduced by permission of Pastor Sir Douglas and Lady Gladys Nicholls Family.

Louis Nowra: *Radiance* (Currency Press, 1993). Reproduced by permission of Currency Press Pty Ltd.

Bernard O'Dowd: *Bulletin*, vol. 21.1056, 12 May 1900.

Oodgeroo Noonuccal: 'Aboriginal Charter of Rights', 'The Dispossessed', 'We Are Going', 'Assimilation—No!', 'Integration—Yes!', 'The Dawn is at Hand', 'No More Boomerang' and 'Ballad of the Totems' from *My People*, 4th edn (2008). Reproduced by permission of John Wiley and Sons Australia. Speech Launching the Petition of the Federal Council for Aboriginal Advancement, 6 October 1962. © The Estate of Oodgeroo Noonuccal. Reproduced by permission of Dennis Walker.

Ouyang Yu: 'The Ungrateful Immigrant' from *New and Selected Poems* (Salt Publishing, 2004. 'Listening to the Chinese Woman Philosopher' from *Space: New writing 2* (2005). Reproduced by permission of Ouyang Yu.

Geoff Page: *Smalltown Memorials* (UQP, 1975). Reproduced by permission of Geoff Page.

Nettie Palmer: Vivian Smith (ed.), *Fourteen Years: Extracts from a private journal 1925–1939* from *Nettie Palmer* (St Lucia: University of Queensland Press, 1988). Reproduced by permission of Equity Trustees Limited.

Bruce Pascoe: *Night Animals* (Penguin, 1986). © Bruce Pascoe. Reprinted by permission of Penguin Group (Aust.).

Banjo Paterson: *The Collected Verse of A.B. Paterson* (Sydney: Angus & Robertson, 1921).

Charles Perkins: *Australian*, 8 April 1968. © The Charlie Perkins Children's Trust. Reprinted by permission of Hetti Perkins, Trustee for the Charlie Perkins Children's Trust.

Constance Campbell Petrie: *Tom Petrie's Reminiscences of Early Queensland, Dating from 1837, Recorded by His Daughter* (Brisbane: Watson, Ferguson & Co., 1904).

A.A. Phillips: *Meanjin*, vol. 9, no. 4 (1950).

Jimmy Pike: *Yinti* (Magabala, 1992). © Pat Lowe and Jimmy Pike 1992. Reprinted by permission of Magabala Books.

Doris Pilkington: *Follow the Rabbit-Proof Fence* (UQP, 1996). © Doris Pilkington—Nugi Garimara 1996. Reprinted by permission of the University of Queensland Press.

Dorothy Porter: *The Monkey's Mask* (Hyland House, 1994). Copyright © The Estate of Dorothy Porter. Reproduced by arrangement c/- Jenny Darling & Associates.

Hal Porter: *The Watcher on the Cast-Iron Balcony* (Faber & Faber, 1963). Reproduced by permission of the Estate of Hal Porter.

Peter Porter: *Collected Poems* (Oxford University Press, 1983). Reproduced by permission of Oxford University Press.

Katharine Susannah Prichard: 'Marlene' from *Bulletin*, vol. 59.3027, 16 February 1938. Letter to Miles Franklin from Carole Ferrier (ed.), *As Good as a Yarn with You* (CUP, 1992). Original held at Mitchell Library, State Library of New South Wales, ML MSS 364. Reproduced by arrangement with the licensor, the Estate of Katharine Susannah Prichard c/- Curtis Brown (Aust.) Pty Ltd.

Bob Randall: from Jack Davis, Stephen Muecke, Mudrooroo Narogin and Adam Shoemaker (eds), *Paperbark: A collection of Black Australian writings* (UQP, 1990). © Bob Randall. Reprinted by permission of Bob Randall.

W.H.L. Ranken: *The Dominion of Australia* (London: Chapman & Hall, 1874).

Jennifer Rankin: from Judith Rodriguez (ed.), *Collected Poems* (UQP, 1990). Reproduced by permission of the University of Queensland Press.

Hannie Rayson: *Hotel Sorrento* (Currency Press, 1990). Reproduced by permission of Currency Press Pty Ltd.

Kerry Reed–Gilbert: *Talkin' About Country* (Kuracca Communications, 2002). © Kerry Reed-Gilbert. Reprinted by permission of Kerry Reed-Gilbert.

Annie Rich: Letter of 5 April 1882 from Dawn A. Lee, *Daughter of Two Worlds* (Aboriginal Affairs Victoria, 2002) with the assistance of Tess De Araugo. © Dawn Lee. Reprinted by permission of Dawn Lee. National Archives of Australia. NAA: series B313/1, item 42.

Henry Handel Richardson: *The Fortunes of Richard Mahony* (Melbourne: Heinemann, 1954).

Ricketty Kate: *Jindyworobak Anthology 1942* (Adelaide: F.W. Preece, 1942). Reproduced by permission of Lenore Bassan.

Archie Roach: *You Have the Power* (1994). © Archie Roach. Reproduced with kind permission of Mushroom Music and Archie Roach.

Eric Rolls: *A Million Wild Acres: 200 years of man and an Australian forest* (Thomas Nelson, 1981). Reproduced by permission of Penguin Group (Aust.) and Karen van Kempen, Executor of the Literary Estate of Eric Rolls c/- Cameron Creswell.

Peter Rose: 'Donatello in Wangaratta' from *Rattus Rattus: New and selected poems* (Salt, 2005). *Rose Boys* (Allen & Unwin, 2001). Copyright © Peter Rose. Reproduced by arrangement c/- Jenny Darling & Associates.

Jacob G. Rosenberg: *East of Time* (Brandl & Schlesinger, 2005). Reproduced by permission of Brandl & Schlesinger.

Steele Rudd: *On Our Selection!* (Sydney: Bulletin, 1899).

Gig Ryan: 'If I Had a Gun' from *The Division of Anger* (Transit Press, 1981). 'Hay Fever' from *Pure and Applied* (Paper Bark Press, 1998). Reproduced by permission of Gig Ryan. 'Critique of Pure Reason' from *Heroic Money* (Brandl & Schlesinger, 2001). Reproduced by permission of Brandl & Schlesinger.

Tracy Ryan: *The Willing Eye* (Fremantle Arts Centre Press, 1999). Reproduced by permission of The Fremantle Press.

Philip Salom: *New and Selected Poems* (Fremantle Arts Centre Press, 1998). Reproduced by permission of The Fremantle Press.

Henry Savery: *The Hermit in Van Diemen's Land* (Hobart: Andrew Bent, 1829).

John Scott: *Selected Poems* (UQP, 1995). Reproduced by permission of the University of Queensland Press.

Kim Scott: *Benang* (Fremantle Arts Centre Press, 1999). © Kim Scott 1999. Reproduced by permission of The Fremantle Press.

Rosie Scott: *The Red Heart* (Random House, 1999). Reprinted by permission of Random House Australia and by arrangement with Rosie Scott, c/- Curtis Brown (Aust.) Pty Ltd.

Alan Seymour: *The One Day of the Year* (Angus & Robertson, 1962). Reproduced by permission of Harper Collins Publishers Australia.

Thomas Shapcott: *The City of Home* (UQP, 1995). Reproduced by permission of the University of Queensland Press.

Craig Sherborne: *Necessary Evil* (Black Inc., 2006). Reproduced by permission of Black Inc. Publishing.

R.A. Simpson: *The Midday Clock* (Macmillan, 1999). Reproduced by permission of Pam Simpson.

Peter Skrzynecki: *Immigrant Chronicle* (UQP, 1975). Reproduced by permission of the University of Queensland Press.

Kenneth Slessor: 'Up in Mabel's Room' from *Darlinghurst Nights* (Angus & Robertson, 1981) and 'Backless Betty From Bondi' from *Backless Betty from Bondi* (Angus & Robertson, 1983). Reproduced by permission courtesy, ETT Imprint. 'Five Bells', 'Last Trams', 'South Country' and 'Beach Burial' from *Collected Poems* (Sydney: Angus & Robertson, 1994). Reproduced by permission of Harper Collins Publishers Australia.

Vivian Smith: *Along the Line* (Salt, 2006). Reproduced by permission of Vivian Smith.

Catherine Helen Spence: *Clara Morison* (London: John W. Parker, 1854).

Christina Stead: *For Love Alone* (Sydney: Angus & Robertson, 1966). 'Uncle Morgan at the Nats' from *Ocean of Story* (Melbourne: Penguin, 1986). Reproduced by permission of the Trustee for the Estate of the late C.E. Blake (Christina Stead).

Peter Steele: *Invisible Riders* (Paper Bark, 1999). Reproduced by permission of Peter Steele.

A.G. Stephens: *Bulletin*, 24 October 1896.

Douglas Stewart: 'The Fierce Country', 'Maree', 'Afghan', 'Place Names' and 'Sombrero' from *The Birdsville Track* (Sydney: Angus & Robertson, 1955). 'The Green Centipede' from *Selected Poems* (Sydney: Angus & Robertson, 1973). Reproduced by arrangement with the licensor, the Estate of Douglas Stewart c/- Curtis Brown (Aust.) Pty Ltd.

Louis Stone: *Jonah* (Sydney: Angus & Robertson, 1981).

Randolph Stow: *The Merry-Go-Round in the Sea* (MacDonald & Co., 1965). Copyright © Randolph Stow 1965. Reproduced by permission of Shiel Land Associates.

Jennifer Strauss: *Tierra del Fuego: New and selected poems* (Pariah Press, 1997). Reproduced by permission of Jennifer Strauss.

Charles Sturt: *Two Expeditions into the Interior of Southern Australia* (London: Smith, Elder, 1833).

Anne Summers: *Damned Whores and God's Police* (second revised edition, Penguin Books, 2002). Reproduced by permission of Anne Summers.

Roberta Sykes: *Snake Cradle* (Allen & Unwin, 1997). Reproduced by permission of Allen & Unwin Pty Ltd.

Taam Sze Pui: *My Life and Work* (private press, Innisfail, 1925).

Tasma: *A Sydney Sovereign and Other Tales* (London: Trubner and Co., 1890).

Alf Taylor: *Overland*, no. 144 (Spring 1996). Also appears in *Long Time Now: Stories of the Dreamtime, the here and now* (Magabala, 2001). © Alf Taylor. Reprinted by permission of Magabala Books.

Andrew Taylor: *Collected Poems* (Salt, 2004). Reproduced by permission of Andrew Taylor.

Watkin Tench: *A Complete Account of the Settlement at Port Jackson* (London: G. Nichol, 1793).

Kylie Tennant: *Ride on Stranger* (Sydney: Angus & Robertson, 1990). Reproduced by arrangement with the licensor, the Estate of Kylie Tennant c/- Curtis Brown (Aust.) Pty Ltd.

Audrey Tennyson: Letter of 26 July 1899, from Alexandra Hasluck (ed.), *Audrey Tennyson's Vice-Regal Days* (National Library of Australia, 1978). Originals held at National Library of Australia, Manuscripts Collection MS 479. Reproduced with permission of the National Library of Australia.

Colin Thiele: *Sun on the Stubble* (Rigby Ltd, 1961). Reprinted by permission of New Holland Publishers Australia.

Joe Timbery: *Churinga*, vol. 1, no. 10 (December 1968–March 1969). © The Estate of Joe Timbery. Reprinted by permission of Jeanette Timbery, Lynette Timbery and Joseph Timbery.

Pat Torres: *Jalygurr: Aussie animal rhymes* (Magabala, 1987). © Pat Torres 1987. Reprinted by permission of Magabala Books.

John Tranter: *Urban Myths: 210 poems* (UQP, 2006). Reproduced by permission of the University of Queensland Press.

Ida West: *Pride Against Prejudice: Reminiscences of a Tasmanian Aborigine* (revised edition, Montpelier Press, Hobart, 2004). © Ida West 1984, 1987, 2004. Reprinted by permission of Montpelier Press.

Herb Wharton: *Where Ya' Been Mate?* (UQP, 1996). © Herb Wharton 1996. Reprinted by permission of Herb Wharton.

Patrick White: *Voss* (Eyre & Spottiswoode, 1957). 'Miss Slattery and Her Demon Lover' from *The Burnt Ones* (Eyre & Spottiswoode, 1964). 'The Prodigal Son' from Imre Salusinszky (ed.), *The Oxford Book of Australian Essays* (Oxford University Press, 1997). Reproduced with permission by arrangement c/- Barbara Mobbs.

Anna Wickham: *Richards' Shilling Selections from Edwardian Poems* (London: Richards Press, 1936).

David Williamson: *Emerald City* (Currency Press, 1987). Reproduced by permission of Currency Press Pty Ltd.

Eric Willmot: *Pemulwuy* (Weldon's Pty Ltd, 1987). © Eric Willmot. Reprinted by permission of New Holland Publishers Australia.

Gerard Windsor: *Memories of the Assassination Attempt and Other Stories* (Penguin Books, 1985). Reproduced by permission of Gerard Windsor.

Tim Winton: *Scission* (McPhee Gribble, 1985). Copyright © Tim Winton. Reproduced by permission of Penguin Group (Aust.) and by arrangement c/- Jenny Darling & Associates.

George Worgan: Letter of 12–18 June 1788, from *Journal of a First Fleet Surgeon* (Sydney: Library Council of New South Wales in association with the Library of Australian History, 1978). Reproduced with permission from the Library Council of New South Wales. Original held in the Mitchell Library, State Library of New South Wales.

Alexis Wright: *Plains of Promise* (UQP, 1997). © Alexis Wright 1997. Reprinted by permission of the University of Queensland Press and Alexis Wright. *Carpentaria* (Giramondo, 2006). © Alexis Wright, 2006. Reprinted by permission of Giramondo Publishing Company.

Judith Wright: 'Skins' and 'Memory' from *Collected Poems, 1942–1985* (Sydney: Angus & Robertson, 1994). Reproduced by permission of Harper Collins Publishing Australia. 'At Cooloolah', 'Eroded Hills', 'Eve to Her Daughters', Nigger's Leap: New England', 'South of My Days', 'The Surfer', 'The Two Fires' and 'Woman to Man' from *A Human Pattern: Selected poems* (Sydney: ETT Imprint, 1996). Reproduced by permission, courtesy ETT Imprint.

William Yang: *Sadness* (Allen & Unwin, 1996). Reproduced by permission of William Yang.

Yirrkala People: Yirrkala Petition to the House of Representatives, August 1963. Reprinted by permission of Andrew Blake (Manager of the Buku-Larrnggay Mulka Centre, Yirrkala) on behalf of the Yirrkala Community. National Archives of Australia. NAA: series A6180.

Galarrwuy Yunupingu: Statement, presented to R.J. Hawke, Prime Minister, at the Barunga Festival, 12 June 1988. Reprinted by permission of Galarrwuy Yunupingu.

Mandawuy Yunupingu: 'Treaty' (Mushroom Music Publishing). Reproduced with kind permission of Mushroom Music and Allen & Unwin Pty Ltd.

Fay Zwicky: 'Tiananmen Square June 4, 1989' from *Poems, 1970–1992* (UQP, 1992). Reproduced by permission of the University of Queensland Press. 'Makassar, 1956' from *Picnic* (Giramondo, 2006). Reproduced by permission of Giramondo Publishing Company.

INDEX

*The editors would like to thank the following organizations
for their financial support of this project:*

MACQUARIE
UNIVERSITY
SYDNEY ~ AUSTRALIA

s y d n e y
PEN

Australian Government

Australian Research Council

Australian Government

SIDNEY MYER FUND

Australia Council
for the Arts

This project has been assisted by the
Australian Government through the
Australia Council, its arts funding and
advisory body

THE UNIVERSITY
OF ADELAIDE
AUSTRALIA

N M F

NELSON MEERS
FOUNDATION

Koori Centre,
The University of Sydney

DEAKIN
UNIVERSITY

AUSTLIT

AIATSIS
Australian Institute of Aboriginal
and Torres Strait Islander Studies